AN AMERICAN READER

An American Reader

A CENTENNIAL COLLECTION OF AMERICAN WRITINGS

PUBLISHED SINCE 1838 OF UNIQUE VALUE AS ENTER-

TAINMENT, AS A REFLECTION OF THEIR TIMES, AS HIS-

TORY, AND AS INTEGRAL PARTS OF THE NATIONAL

PAST. SELECTED FROM THE PUBLICATIONS OF

THE HOUSE OF PUTNAM

1838 - 1938

EDITED, WITH AN INTRODUCTION, BY BURTON RASCOE

NEW YORK: G. P. PUTNAM'S SONS

Copyright, 1938, by G. P. Putnam's Sons

All rights reserved. This book, or parts thereof, must not be reproduced in any form without permission.

MANUFACTURED IN THE UNITED STATES OF AMERICA
Designed by Robert Josephy

CONTENTS

Introduction—BURTON RASCOE: Publishing in America   xi

HISTORY

THOMAS PAINE: Of the Origin and Design of Government in General (*from "Common Sense"*)   9

THOMAS JEFFERSON: The Drawing-up of the Declaration of Independence (*from "The Autobiography of Thomas Jefferson"*)   15

JAMES MADISON: Examination of the Constitution (*from "The Federalist"*)   39

JAMES MADISON: Formation of the Constitution (*from "The Federalist"*)   47

JAMES MADISON: The Republican Principle (*from "The Federalist"*)   55

ALEXANDER HAMILTON or JAMES MADISON: On a Just Partition of Power (*from "The Federalist"*)   61

WILLIAM CABELL BRUCE: Benjamin Franklin (*from "Benjamin Franklin Self-Revealed"*)   66

THEODORE ROOSEVELT: The Purchase of Louisiana; and Burr's Conspiracy (*from "The Winning of the West"*)   74

MEADE MINNIGERODE: Tippecanoe, and Tyler Too! (*from "The Fabulous Forties"*)   103

LUCY BAKEWELL AUDUBON: Audubon in Kentucky (*from "The Life of John James Audubon"*)   117

FRANCIS PARKMAN: Scenes at Fort Laramie (*from "The California and Oregon Trail"*)   126

JAMES FENIMORE COOPER: Old Ironsides (*from Putnam's Magazine, May and June, 1853*)   137

ROBERT ALLERTON PARKER: Colonies and Communities (*from "A Yankee Saint"*)   191

ARTHUR CHAPMAN: Riders All (*from "The Pony Express"*)   206

FREDERICK LAW OLMSTED: A South Carolina Rice Plantation in the Fifties (*from "A Journey in the Seaboard Slave States"*)   213

vi CONTENTS

GERALD W. JOHNSON: The Background of the Civil War (*from "The Secession of the Southern States"*) 232

GEORGE HAVEN PUTNAM: Life in Libby Prison (*from "A Prisoner of War in Virginia"*) 245

RUTH PUTNAM: The Purchase of New York (*from Putnam's Monthly, October, 1909*) 256

THOMAS SPENCER JEROME: Ancient Rome and Modern America (*from "Aspects of the Study of Roman History"*) 259

CHARLES A. LINDBERGH: The Flight to Paris (*from "We"*) 268

PERIOD PIECES

WASHINGTON IRVING: The People of Connecticut (*from "A History of New York" by "Diedrich Knickerbocker"*) 277

GEORGE PALMER PUTNAM: Literature in America (*from "American Facts"*) 284

GEORGE PALMER PUTNAM: American Culture (*from "American Facts"*) 293

GEORGE WILLIAM CURTIS: "Our Best Society" (*from "The Potiphar Papers"*) 300

GEORGE WILLIAM CURTIS: A Meditation by Paul Potiphar, Esq. (*from "The Potiphar Papers"*) 317

JAMES RUSSELL LOWELL: A Fable for Critics 332

CHARLES F. BRIGGS ("Harry Franko"): Uncle Tomitudes (*from Putnam's Magazine, January, 1853*) 383

SUSAN WARNER ("Elizabeth Wetherell"): Christmas with the Chaunceys (*from "The Wide, Wide World"*) 392

FREDERICK S. COZZENS: Living in the Country (*from Putnam's Magazine, August, 1855*) 403

MYRTLE REED: The Roses and the Song (*from "The White Shield"*) 410

ELLIOTT FLOWER: A Stranger in New York (*from Putnam's Monthly, March, 1909*) 414

"THE LOUNGER": Notes from "The Lounger" (*from Putnam's Monthly, 1906-1910*) 420

GEORGE S. CHAPPELL: The Fatu-Liva Bird (*from "The Cruise of the Kawa" by "Walter E. Traprock"*) 431

RALPH BARTON: Science in Rhyme without Reason 436

LEE STROUT WHITE: Farewell to Model T 439

CONTENTS

ESSAYS

HENRY DAVID THOREAU: An Excursion to Canada (*from Putnam's Magazine, January, February, March, 1853*)   451

PAUL ELMER MORE: A Hermit's Notes on Thoreau (*from "Shelburne Essays"*)   486

MOSES COIT TYLER: The Literary Strivings of Mr. Joel Barlow (*from "Three Men of Letters"*)   498

FREDERICK BEECHER PERKINS: Connecticut Georgics (*from Putnam's Magazine, April, 1854*)   522

ELBERT HUBBARD: Walt Whitman (*from "Little Journeys"*)   538

JAMES McNEILL WHISTLER: The Ruskin Affair (*from "The Gentle Art of Making Enemies"*)   549
    Altercation with Oscar   562
    Oscar Again   564

THEODORE ROOSEVELT: The Man with the Muck-Rake (*from Putnam's Monthly, October, 1909*)   571

JOSIAH ROYCE: Provincialism (*from Putnam's Monthly, October, 1909*)   581

JOHN DEWEY: Man and Art (*from "Art as Experience"*)   585

THOMAS SPENCER JEROME: The Credibility of Testimony (*from "Aspects of the Study of Roman History"*)   600

EARNEST ALBERT HOOTON: Apology for Man (*from "Apes, Men, and Morons"*)   616

LOUIS KRONENBERGER: The Eighteenth Century Attitude (*from "An Eighteenth Century Miscellany"*)   638

DONALD CULROSS PEATTIE: Aries (*from "An Almanac for Moderns"*)   654

POEMS

EDGAR ALLAN POE: The Raven (*from "The Raven and Other Poems"*)   675
    Lenore   678
    Israfel   679

HENRY WADSWORTH LONGFELLOW: The Two Angels (*from Putnam's Magazine, April, 1855*)   681
    My Lost Youth (*from Putnam's Magazine, August, 1855*)   682

JAMES RUSSELL LOWELL: Without and Within (*from Putnam's Magazine, April, 1854*)   685

CONTENTS

GEORGE WILLIAM CURTIS: Spring or Summer? (*from Putnam's Magazine, January, 1853*) — 686
Gondola Songs — 687

WILLIAM CULLEN BRYANT: Robert of Lincoln (*from Putnam's Magazine, June, 1855*) — 688

WILLIAM HENRY HURLBERT: Sehnsucht (*from Putnam's Magazine, April, 1854*) — 691

WALT WHITMAN: Song of the Open Road (*from "Leaves of Grass"*) — 692

EDMUND CLARENCE STEDMAN: Amavi (*from Putnam's Magazine, October, 1854*) — 702

RICHARD HENRY STODDARD: Threnody (*from Putnam's Monthly, October, 1906*) — 703

RICHARD WATSON GILDER: Milton (*from Putnam's Monthly, February, 1909*) — 704

WILLIAM WINTER: The Rubicon (*from Putnam's Monthly, October, 1908*) — 705

RICHARD HOVEY: His Submission (*from Putnam's Monthly, September, 1907*) — 706

ROBERT LOVEMAN: Rose Song (*from Putnam's Monthly, August, 1908*) — 707

MADISON CAWEIN: My Romance (*from "Days and Dreams"*) — 707
A Niello (*from "Red Leaves and Roses"*) — 708
The Idyl of The Standing-Stone — 711

GUY WETMORE CARRYL: When the Great Gray Ships Come in (*from "The Garden of Years and Other Poems"*) — 712
"The Winds and the Sea Obey Him" — 713
The Débutante — 714
The Fog — 715

JAMES OPPENHEIM: At Twilight (*from Putnam's Monthly, January, 1908*) — 717

SARA TEASDALE: Song (*from "Helen of Troy and Other Poems"*) — 717
Less Than the Cloud to the Wind — 718
The Wayfarer — 718
The Song for Colin — 718

DON MARQUIS: October (*from Putnam's Monthly, October, 1906*) — 719

THEODOSIA GARRISON: At the Road's End (*from "As the Larks Rise"*) — 721
The House in Trouble — 721
Cophetua's Queen — 722

CONTENTS

CALE YOUNG RICE: The Winter Is Long (*from "High Perils"*)   722
    On Farms   723
    Katharsis   723

CAROLYN CROSBY WILSON: Mid Winter (*from "Fir Trees and Fireflies"*)   724
    Roads   724
    One Lack I Have   724
    On the Arrogance of Lovers   725

DAVID MORTON: Wooden Ships (*from "Ships in Harbour"*)   726
    Revelation   726
    Moonflowers   727
    Noon of Summer (*from "Spell against Time"*)   727
    Prescience   728

MARGARET EMERSON BAILEY: Close to the Earth (*from "White Christmas"*)   728
    Requiem   729
    Encounter   730
    White Christmas   730

JAKE FALSTAFF: Beautiful Sunday (*from "The Bulls of Spring"*)   731
    The Elfin Wife   733
    Valedictory   733

FICTION

HERMAN MELVILLE: Benito Cereno (*from Putnam's Magazine, October, November, December, 1855*)   741

EDGAR ALLAN POE: William Wilson (*from "Poe's Tales"*)   814

NATHANIEL HAWTHORNE: Young Goodman Brown (*from "Mosses from an Old Manse"*)   832

NATHANIEL HAWTHORNE: The Celestial Railroad (*from "Mosses from an Old Manse"*)   844

WASHINGTON IRVING: Guests from Gibbet Island (*from "Wolfert's Roost"*)   859

AMBROSE BIERCE: Chickamauga (*from "In the Midst of Life"*)   869

MELVILLE DAVISSON POST: The Men of the Jimmy (*from "The Strange Schemes of Randolph Mason"*)   875

EMILY JAMES PUTNAM: Helen in Egypt (*from "Candaules' Wife and Other Old Stories"*)   888

HENRY JAMES: The Bench of Desolation (*from Putnam's Monthly, 1909-10*)   904

ADVENTURE

BELMORE BROWNE: The Climbing of Mount McKinley (*from "The Conquest of Mount McKinley"*)   949

WILLIAM BEEBE: April Twenty-sixth, Nineteen Hundred and Twenty-three (*from "Galapagos: World's End"*)   970

ROY CHAPMAN ANDREWS: Finding the Baluchitherium (*from "On the Trail of Ancient Man"*)   983

ROCKWELL KENT: "Roll On" (*from "Voyaging: Southward from the Strait of Magellan"*)   993

RICHARD E. BYRD: Flight to the South Pole (*from "Little America"*)   1001

Bibliographical Notes   1015

INTRODUCTION

BURTON RASCOE

Publishing in America

ON THE *John o' London* bound for Boston out of Plymouth in the summer of 1638, one Rev. Jesse Glover suddenly booked passage for himself, his wife, five children and a locksmith. He also had listed on the ship's cargo manifest a chest of books, a font of type and a printing press. The clergyman had just learned that a John Harvard had died and had bequeathed to Newtown College in Massachusetts £780 and a library of three hundred books. The locksmith's name was Stephen Daye; he was brought along by the Rev. Glover because the clergyman was in a hurry and Daye was the only man he could locate who happened to know a little about printing and running a handpress. Glover had kept in touch with the affairs of the Massachusetts Bay Colony and, while waiting for the time to be ripe, he had collected enough money from his non-conformist parishioners to buy a press and some type to take to the New World and there further God's cause—as the non-conformists saw it—among the heathen. He planned to set up a bookselling and printing business in Newtown (later renamed Cambridge) and the college (later renamed Harvard) because he figured this academic place would certainly become a center of divine exegesis, and therefore a flourishing business ought to develop for him in the printing of sermons, refutations, pamphlets, proclamations and psalm books.

It is unpleasant to record that the Rev. Glover died en route. But his good wife had full instructions in case of his demise, which were that she should carry out his plans and manage the press and the bookselling business herself. Unfortunately these plans also went slightly awry. She presented herself and her project to the Rev. Henry Dunster, first president of the new college, by then called Harvard. That good and godly man immediately was smitten with the tender passion for the printing press and Mrs. Glover and presently married her—five children, locksmith and all. Times had been tough for President Dunster. He had often had difficulty in collecting his miserable salary from the General Court of the Massachusetts Bay Colony; his forty students usually paid him in farm produce, when they paid him at all, and the surplus of this produce over his needs he would have to chase around trying to sell or barter, in addition to his work as president, professor of divinity, manager and birchman, and treasurer of Harvard.

More plans went awry. President Dunster occasionally got a job-printing order for some pamphlets and sermons; but, although the locksmith, Daye, could set type slowly, he couldn't develop any real knack for running the press; he was slow and he botched the work; so the printer-president lost orders; in the space of twenty years Dunster was able to sell to his fellow scholars and divines only £25.10.0 worth of books out of the widow Glover's dowry. Worst of all, Mrs. Dunster died after bearing the president five children in addition to the five stepchildren he had to support; and one stepchild, John Glover, having come of age after his mother's death, promptly sued his stepfather for the press and for the restitution of sundry other properties and the monies received from the sale of the books, profits from the press, etc.—and *won*.

But whatever the mishaps that attended this Glover (sometimes called the Cambridge) press, it was the first printing press set up in America. On it was printed the first book published in America, "The Whole Booke of Psalmes."[1] An erroneous tradition credits Stephen Daye with various early American publications, all of which were books issued after Daye had given up printing, and had gone back to his old trade of locksmith. He was never a publisher.

---

[1] "The divines of the Massachusetts Colony wanted something untainted by imagination or beauty of form," writes Henry Walcott Boynton in "Annals of American Bookselling," 1932. "Within half a dozen years after the colony was founded they had collaborated on a psaltery sufficiently hand-hewn for their grim taste. Richard Mather, founder of the Mather tribe, and good John Eliot were among the authors."

Then years later, on June 15, 1648, the Rev. Sam Hough of Reading, Mass., made a notation in his diary. A witch had that day been hanged after trial in his town, the first in New England. Richard Mather's grandson, Cotton Mather, was graduated from Harvard, of which he said later that the teaching there was such that few of the students were "capable of edification from them." He ought to know. By 1692 the witchcraft mania had spread to Boston, and Cotton was right in the midst of it, writing in that year, in support of the hangings, the first New England book of vast popularity and importance, "Memorable Providences Relating to Witchcraft and Possessions."

INTRODUCTION

The first real publishing center in America, in fact, was neither Cambridge, nor Boston, nor New York. It was Philadelphia. And the first publisher in the modern sense of the word was a Philadelphian, Matthew Carey, among whose authors perhaps the most famous one was Parson (Mason Locke) Weems, author of the famous "Life of Washington" and inventor of the cherry-tree myth. Parson Weems was one of the first, if not the first, American author to have his books accepted by a publisher on the modern royalty or profit-sharing basis. Under this system, which Carey inaugurated, the publisher bets on his judgment of the salability of a book from manuscript he has read and accepted or upon a book he has engaged an author to do. He takes all the risk of printing, manufacturing, and distributing the book and agrees to pay the author a royalty out of the sales the book enjoys. If the book doesn't sell at all, or sells less than it costs the publisher to bring it out, the publisher loses.

But it is precisely this publishing gamble, initiated by Carey, that revolutionized the "publishing" business in America, made fortunes for publishers and authors and facilitated the spread of bookselling and book reading, thereby increasing literacy and knowledge to the enormous proportions to which they have now grown. Before Carey, so-called publishers were not publishers at all; they were job-printers who sometimes and even usually combined their trade with that of bookseller. If you were an author with a manuscript, seeking immortality or the illusion of immortality that the appearance of printed words within the covers of a book seems to convey, you took your manuscript not to a publisher but to a bookseller or "stationer." He might read your manuscript and agree to sponsor it, *i.e.,* display it for sale in his bookshop after it had been printed and published at your expense. He would permit the printer to say at the foot of the title page, "Printed for John Johnson, Bookseller & Stationer, 11 Regent St., Phila." You would give your printing and binding order to the printer for the number of copies Mr. Johnson thought he might be able to sell; you paid the printer's bill; Mr. Johnson stocked your book and merely acted as your agent in the sale of the book. Or if the bookseller was also a printer like Benjamin Franklin the process would be the same except that at the foot of the title page one would read: "Printed and Sold by B. Franklin, at the New Printing-Office near the Market." Then you paid B. Franklin for printing the book and also paid him a commission to sell it. You took all the risk; the "publisher" none. (This practice is not extinct; in certain circumstances, such as with memorial volumes where an expensively made book is not without merit but not likely to sell to more than a few customers other than members of the family or friends of the deceased, the reputable publisher may justifiably undertake to publish a book at the author's expense; but there are also "contract publishers" who are in business only to prey upon the vanity of very bad writers, solicit their manuscripts, charge them an excessive price for printing and publishing and agree to share the profits on a book they know will not, in the proper sense, sell.) ... It is astonishing that, under that earlier system, so many good books managed to get printed. But it also accounts for the fact that so many American books up until the beginning of the nineteenth century were either religious books or hymn books or political books or novels which nobody then or now could possibly read. The printing costs of the religious books were underwritten by the preacher's parishioners; the costs of the hymnals were underwritten by a whole denomination such as the Methodists or Baptists—which, incidentally, explains the "popularity" of such books which has dumbfounded and misled many historians and commentators; the "popularity" of such books among the purchasers was just the "popularity" of a textbook on commercial geography which a state school board has adopted as the official one the high-school kid must buy; and the costs of the unreadable novels were borne by the writers themselves, all of whom on investigation turn out to have been men of ample means, leisure and *coecthes scribendi*.... In a still earlier time, of course, there was the poet's patron, usually a man of the nobility, who paid for the publication of the poor poet's book of sonnets and, in return, got a dedication. Or the "stationer," *i.e.,* bookseller, might get hold of prompter's copies of an exceptionally popular playwright such as Shakespeare and pay for the printing and retain all the proceeds, giving the author or his heirs or assigns nothing. Still, book-buying or even an ability to read was not widespread in Elizabethan times; it is estimated that of both the first and second folios less than 500 copies were printed and sold altogether.

Almanacs, mostly plagiarisms then as now, were turned out in New England before 1700; but it was not until 1685 that book publishing got under way in the middle colonies with the publication of the "Kalendarium Pennsilvaniense; or, America's Messenger, Being an Almanack for the Year of Grace 1686." The author was Samuel Atkins, who described himself as "Student in the Mathematicks and Astrology." The title page bore the information that this compendium of knowledge was "Printed and Sold by William Bradford at Philadelphia in Pennsylvania."

In October, 1723, Benjamin Franklin arrived in Philadelphia with a loaf of bread in his pocket and a lot of original ideas in his head. One of these, when he had saved enough money out of his trade as a printer to buy his own press and bring out the first of his cherished projects, "Poor Richard's Almanack" (1733), was to print on the first copies that came off the press the words, "Third Impression," to create the assumption that it was selling like hot-cakes, which, indeed, it presently was. Soon he had a steady annual income of $15,000 from his almanack; his weekly *Pennsylvania Gazette* began to prosper; he had leisure to study and to indulge his bent, which was for civic service and improvement, and also for scientific experiment and invention. He followed his own Poor Richard precepts and prospered, until, when the time came for him to die at the age of eighty-four, he was one of the most useful and most honored men of his century.

The Matthew Carey mentioned above was also a faithful adherent to the precepts of Poor Richard, early to bed and early to rise, and all the rest. He was a Dubliner born who began his career as a pamphleteer, one of his pamphlets being designed to incite the Irish to revolt against England, as a result of which he had to flee to France. There he got a job in the American Embassy under Franklin. In time he returned to Ireland, published another seditious pamphlet, got thrown into prison whence he was released under the promise he leave the country forever. When he arrived penniless in Philadelphia, the Marquis de Lafayette, there at the time, had already heard of him through Franklin and Didot, the famous French printer. He gave Carey $400 with which to start a newspaper called *The Pennsylvania Herald*, in which Carey started banging heads right and left, with the result that he was laid up for sixteen months for being the slow shot in a duel.

When Carey got into the publishing business, he got into the publishing business. With a vim. He not only inaugurated the royalty system but inaugurated the first system in America of selling books by mail order advertising. He published and sold books not only at his store but bought a horse and rode about the country, getting subscriptions to his paper and advertising books he had for sale which he proposed to send and did send by mail or by private parcels delivery.

The rector of Mount Vernon Parish in Virginia was a colorful, energetic and fantastic fellow who combined preaching with barnstorming eloquence of various sorts and newspaper writing. When he had a book published, he sold that from the platform, too. His name was Mason L. Weems, but in his writings he called himself simply Parson Weems. His stuff became enormously popular; so Carey, first in so many practices of the publishing game, was the first to do a bit of author-swiping, snaring him away from a Baltimore publisher by the simple trick of offering to pay Weems for the privilege of publishing his work and paying him a royalty on each book sold instead of asking Weems to advance the money for the printing costs first. In January, 1800, there came to Carey's desk a letter from Weems reading:

"Washington you know is gone! Millions are gaping to read something about him. I am very nearly prime and cocked for 'em. 6 months ago I got myself to collect anecdotes of him. You know I live conveniently for that work. My plan! I give his history sufficiently minute—I accompany him from his start, thro the French & Indian & British or Revolutionary wars, to the President's chair, to the throne in the hearts of 5,000,000 people. I then go on to show that his unparalleled rise and elevation were owing to his Great Virtues. Thus I hold up his Virtues to the imitation of Our Youth. All this I have lined and enlivened with Anecdotes apropos interesting and Entertaining."

That is the sort of author publishers dream of having. Here was an author with a spot-news "natural," *about ready for delivery.*

Well, Weems' "The Life of George Washington with Curious Anecdotes, Equally Honorable to Himself, and Exemplary to His Young Countrymen" sold like wildfire, edition after edition having to be reprinted for years. Thirty years later, a learning-hungry, six-foot-four inch lad, learned that a neighbor had a copy of this famous book. He borrowed it, lay on the floor before the log fire of a log-cabin at nights to read it. One night he struck it between the chinks of the logs; a heavy rainstorm came up while he was asleep and almost ruined the book. The lad offered to shuck corn for thirty days to keep the book, and did. The lad, of course, was Abraham Lincoln.

The bookseller who got the exclusive agency for the sale of the Weems' book was J. B. Lippincott, later founder of the famous publishing firm of J. B. Lippincott & Co.

The bookseller who got the exclusive agency for the sale of the Weems' book in New York and environs was Charles Wiley, who had a bright son named John, of whom more presently.

works of Dickens, Kinglake's "Eothen," Goethe's Autobiography, and Carlyle's "Heroes and Hero-Worship" and "Sartor Resartus." The American publications included Poe's Tales and "The Raven," and Melville's "Typee."

Soon after Putnam's return from London the two partners, in friendly fashion, decided to go their separate ways, and in 1848 the firm of George P. Putnam came into being. He took with him most of the purely literary books except Ruskin, and John Wiley concentrated thereafter on scientific and technical works.

The first list of "G. P. Putnam, Broadway" contained a galaxy of names: Washington Irving (with whom he had contracted to take over all previous books and to publish all new ones), Poe, James Russell Lowell, Bayard Taylor, and George Borrow. Others followed in rapid succession: William Cullen Bryant and James Fenimore Cooper in the following year; Parkman's "The California and Oregon Trail" in 1850; in 1851 Hawthorne's "Mosses from an Old Manse" and the first book of Fredrika Bremer, the popular Swedish novelist. In 1852 came one of the great best-sellers of all time, "The Wide, Wide World," by "Elizabeth Wetherell" (Susan Warner), whose books were destined to reach nearly every American home. It was in this year also that *Putnam's Monthly Magazine* came into being, though the idea had germinated some time before. Among its early contributors were Lowell, Hawthorne, Holmes, Longfellow, Agassiz, Whittier, Parkman, Edward Everett Hale, Julia Ward Howe, Bayard Taylor, John P. Kennedy, Melville, Bryant, and Frederick S. Cozzens. The magazine ended a short but brilliant career during the panic of 1857 and was resumed for a short time in 1868.

After the Civil War, Major George Haven Putnam joined his father, and the firm name became G. P. Putnam & Son, to be changed to the plural form when two more brothers, John Bishop and Irving, were admitted to the firm. When the elder Putnam died in 1872 the three sons continued the business under its present name of G. P. Putnam's Sons. The firm thus came under the far-seeing and vigorous leadership of George Haven Putnam which lasted for nearly sixty years. He took, as the business developed, the principal responsibility for the publishing end. His brother Bishop, until his death in 1917, was the authority on manufacturing, and it was his initiative and enterprise that were chiefly responsible for the development of the separate manufacturing concern organized as The Knickerbocker Press. Irving Putnam devoted himself largely to the management of The Putnam Bookstore, which, under his management, became one of the landmarks of New York; he was active until his death in 1931.

The young firm weathered another serious panic in 1873 and went on from strength to strength. One helpfully successful book was brought in by its nineteenth-year-old author in 1880. Her father accompanied her, carrying a huge package of manuscript—200,000 words of it written in pencil on yellow paper. The father assured Major Putnam that the work would attract widespread attention. He was right, for the book was "The Leavenworth Case." The author, Anna Katharine Green, went on to write many more novels and live to a ripe old age. She had the perhaps unique experience of living to see her first book, which is still in print, go "out of copyright." (American copyright, with renewals, last for fifty-six years.)

Most of the publishing undertakings that had been started by the father were continued by the Putnam sons. The "Library of Choice Reading" furnished much of the material for a later collection of the classics; both Irving's and Cooper's works were eventually gathered together into complete library editions. The years the father had spent in London provided many valuable connections for Major Putnam, who often made two London trips a year. From England came distinguished biographies and histories to swell the growing list, and among the English novelists whose early work was sponsored by Putnam are such men as Galsworthy, Conrad, Hudson, E. M. Forster, and Walter de la Mare.

Major Putnam followed his father in writing books himself. Among them are a life of Lincoln, two volumes of reminiscences, a life of his father, several books on the history of bookmaking, and an authoritative work, "The Question of Copyright." Major Putnam continued until his dying day the fight George Palmer Putnam had begun for adequate copyright laws.

In 1884, an exuberant young New Yorker fresh from Harvard and a session of ranching in the West came to Putnam's offices in West 23rd Street and made known his desire to be a publisher. He became a special partner and showered the firm with publishing suggestions, usually not very practicable ones, except for his own excellent book, "The Naval War of 1812." Politics and public service wooed Theodore Roosevelt away from publishing, but he went on to write for Putnams within the next few years a series of books that included "The Winning of the West." ...

Throughout its history the House of Putnam has clung to its international character. The English connection has been steadily maintained, and the London house is perhaps the only one of American origin that has established itself as an independent and successful English publishing firm....

In reviewing the productions of a century, one is struck by the evidences of changing taste yet of an enduring national character. The House of Putnam concludes its first hundred years with pride in its contribution to the thought and culture of America; with confidence in the American future; and with hope that it may play a comparable role in the second century on which it now embarks.

To which I can add only this picture of George Haven Putnam on the evening of January 31, 1924. I was at a banquet. I was invited because I was a literary critic and editor of the *New York Tribune*. I had a department in the Sunday book section, entitled "A Bookman's Daybook," in which this entry was published on Sunday, February 14th:

The very best after-dinner speech I ever heard—and I have heard hundreds of them—was made by Major George Haven Putnam at a dinner given at the Aldine Club to-night for Melville Minton and Earle H. Balch on the eve of their going into the book publishing business for themselves under the firm name of Minton, Balch & Company. Minton has been with Charles Scribner's Sons for twenty years and Balch with G. P. Putnam's Sons since the war. The dinner was arranged by their associates in both firms and covers were laid for forty men.

Major Putnam is a well built, twinkling, active little man over eighty years of age. They tell me that he is at his desk every morning and that he displays in the editorial rooms the same elfish humor and urbane wit which distinguished his talk tonight. I talked with him for a few minutes before going in to dinner and he told me something of the history of the publishing business in New York. The firm of G. P. Putnam's Sons, founded by his grandfather, he said, is now the oldest house in continuity of family ownership. "One by one," he said, "houses which had been prosperous got inexplicably into difficulties and passed into other hands. Whether this was due to the changing points of view of the reading public or the uncertainty of foretelling what sort of books the public will buy I don't know."

When he got up to speak he reminded the fledgling publishers that one of the earliest of their line, Aldus Manutius, had been both idealistic and foresighted, combining high aims with shrewdness; he persuaded the Duchess of Padua it would be a great service in the furtherance of knowledge if he could publish Aristotle; and the Duchess sold her necklace to endow the enterprise, thereby giving "The Politics" and "The Poets" to Europe. "I can hardly hope that you will discover another Aristotle," he said, "but I do hope you get a Duchess. My next advice is that you immediately surround yourself with nephews, who later on will tell you that times have changed and that the books that sold yesterday are not the kind that sell today." Here he jested amiably at his nephews' expense and at his own, relating that among the difficulties that confronted him in the selection of books for publication was the insistence of his nephews that care must be taken to consider their "movie" possibilities. One of the great books he would like to revive, he said, was "Administrative Law," but he doubted whether it would do well as a "movie."

"The next thing," he said, "is to develop a race of appreciative authors. There is so much talk of the vast sums of money the highly successful authors make that now every author expects to reap a harvest of royalties on the first novel. Authors ask for big advances and are dissatisfied with royalty statements. I hit upon the idea of showing one lady through the storeroom of unsold books. I started with the inventory, which showed that of one large edition there on the shelves we had sold only twenty copies; then I went on until I came to the stacks of her own book, which showed a sale of three hundred copies, and I assured her that we had expectations of selling more, whereupon she went away a more appreciative author. Among my father's papers I found two I O U's signed by Edgar Allan Poe. They were both for $7, which was the amount he had to pay for board and lodging. The first was a simple I O U. The next one bore the words, 'in consideration of $7 received and hereby acknowledged, I do solemnly promise not to ask for further advances against the royalties on my book "Eureka."—E. A. Poe.' If authors nowadays were as modest as that in their demands we publishers would be spared much anxiety." He talked about best sellers of former years, Mark Twain's disastrous attempt at publishing and the establishment of the international copyright act; and all he said was graced with charm and wit and displaying a rich cultural background.

I was reminded of the delightful forthrightness and delicious humor of Major Putnam's friend and brother publisher, Henry Holt, who explains in his "Garrulities of an Octogenarian Editor" that he had been hampered until well along in middle life in expressing himself by the fear of saying the wrong thing until it occurred to him that whatever he said wouldn't matter a hundred years hence. Then he began to say anything he pleased. And I wondered if age had not brought this same self-assurance to Major Putnam. For I observed that most of those who talked after him, all being younger, were cramped and hesitant in their speech, as though they were letting their thoughts out at the rate of one in five.

Perhaps it was the inspiration of that valiant old gentleman's address at a banquet to do them honor that set things working vaguely in the minds of Messrs. Minton and Balch some day to take up the reins of G. P. Putnam's Sons, after the old gentleman had gone to his rest, and drive on for him and his tradition, still under the fine old firm name of G. P. Putnam's Sons.

HISTORY

THE SELECTIONS *for this anthology are made entirely from the books and magazines issued by one American publishing house, G. P. Putnam's Sons, during the one hundred years of its existence, and, of these, from only the work of Americans. The total number of books published since 1838 by this firm probably could not be ascertained even by protracted research; but these books have represented every variety and nationality, from standard works of reference such as the Cambridge History of American Literature to novels by Nobel and Pulitzer prize winners, from Ellen Key's revolutionary works on feminism to Dr. Marie C. Stopes' revolutionary works on marriage. On the Putnam lists have been masterpieces by Galsworthy, Conrad, Merejkowski, Hudson, Forster, Ferrero, Fogazzaro and Quiller-Couch.*

Obviously here was too bewildering a mass of world literature from which to attempt a selection.

The plan I finally decided upon was one which struck me forcibly after studying the trade catalogues that have been issued by this house through the years. It was clear to me that here was an opportunity to choose a selection of American writings which would not only be works of permanent and popular appeal but an anthology which would reflect implicitly the growth and development of American ideas, the growth and development of our indigenous native culture, with all the facets and the sidelights which reflect the changes in manners and customs, reading habits, interests, in the slow emancipation of American ideas and American literature from domination by the parent English language.

Our first break with England was primarily a political and economic one. As Lincoln was later to say, "there was brought forth upon this continent a new nation dedicated to the proposition that all men are created free and equal." It was a violent break; a revolution. But old habits are not easily broken, and old traditions, even the most hampering ones, do not readily die. So, long after the military and political severance had been effected in a successful war, the revolution for American ideals, for independence of mind and spirit, was fought for a very long time.

It is historically significant, it seems to me, that the young bookman from Maine, George Palmer Putnam, should have issued early in his career a book

("American Facts") which was primarily intended to establish this American independence of mind and spirit by challenging the false and contemptuous picture of American culture and the American scene which British travelers (and British who had never been to America) were forever propagating to the delight and complacency of the very insular English.

The new spirit which was born in this country was first expressed in the realm of political and social ideas by Paine, Madison, Jay, Hamilton, John Adams, Samuel Adams, Patrick Henry and Benjamin Franklin. But the beginnings of the new idiom that was to be peculiarly American and to reflect a new spirit in literature was first employed by Benjamin Franklin in the homely philosophy of "Poor Richard's Almanack" and the Autobiography. As surely as Franklin's wearing a coon-skin cap when he was Ambassador to France was an innovation and a protest against affectation, pomp and pretense, so was Franklin's use of a vigorous, concise, unornamented, direct style of writing the first steps in an American language, an innovation against the eighteenth century Latinity and ornamentation which had become the hallmarks of English prose. Franklin was as surely a progenitor of Artemus Ward, Mark Twain, Finley Peter Dunne, George Ade, O. Henry, Ring Lardner, Sherwood Anderson, Will Rogers, Don Marquis, the newspaper sports writers and columnists, and cartoonists like McCutcheon, Briggs, H. T. Webster and J. R. Williams, as Montaigne was the progenitor of Voltaire, Renan and Anatole France.

Following the essay from William Cabell Bruce's "Benjamin Franklin Self-Revealed" the selections give interesting and important stages in the expansion of the country. First there was the agricultural and pioneering era when the borders of the country began to move west.

An important incident in this period is graphically related by Theodore Roosevelt in "The Purchase of Louisiana and Burr's Conspiracy" from his monumental history of "The Winning of the West."...

One of the most fascinating and most colorful accounts of the Western migration was written by a young Harvard law graduate named Francis Parkman, who set out by boat from St. Louis with a party of land-hunters and gold-seekers on their way to the Northwest, moved by boat up the Missouri and the Platte, thence overland to Fort Laramie in Wyoming on the Oregon Trail. This adventure included hunting wild buffalo, encounters with hostile Indians, and hardships which permanently injured his health; but Parkman recounted the story of his trip to Fort Laramie and return so *dramatically and so vividly, with character sketches so humorously and realistically drawn that "The Oregon Trail" has become a classic of American literature. From this book I have taken the chapter describing Fort Laramie, the military outpost maintained by the government in Wyoming to protect the immigrant trains and settlers against massacres by the Indians....*

Close upon the heels of teams of horses, mules and oxen drawing covered wagons in the movement west, came the horsemen riding the fast and sturdy Indian ponies stationed at intervals along the trails to California by the original Wells-Fargo company whose founders saw the need and the commercial advantage of more rapid communication between the East and West coast before the coming of the trans continental railroads. The history of this fast mail service in the West is told by Arthur Chapman in "The Pony Express," from which I have selected a chapter telling about the gallant and hardy personnel....

Frederick Law Omsted's career is so astounding that I'll sketch it briefly, touching only the high spots, in order that you may wonder (as I did) why this singularly gifted and useful citizen is not better known. He was born in Hartford, Conn., in 1822, son of a prosperous merchant; graduated from grammar school and went to Andover, where he studied engineering. Couldn't find any engineering work to do on graduation, so worked two years in a dry-goods importing house in New York City. Attended law lectures at Yale for a year; sailed before the mast to Canton aboard the barque Ronaldson; *on return he studied farming for two years on his uncle's farm in Cheshire, Conn., and also learned the nursery business. In 1852 he began a tour of the Southern States on horseback and contributed letters to the* New York Times *giving his impressions of "A Journey in the Seaboard Slave States," which was published as a book in 1856. Journeyed to Mexico and California, came back as far as New Orleans and set out on a trip by horseback to Richmond and wrote of his observations under the title, "A Journey in the Back Country." Went into the publishing business with George William Curtis and was an editor of* Putnam's Magazine *at the same time. He went abroad in 1856 and on his return was appointed Superintendent of Central Park, later architect-in-chief of Central Park. With Dr. Bellows and Wolcott Gibbs he founded the Union League Club "to perpetuate the ideals of the United States Sanitary Commission"! (I'll bet that is news to a lot of present members of the Union League Club.) With Charles Eliot Norton he founded* The Nation. *He was appointed Commissmissioner of Yosemite and Mariposa Big Tree Grove. He planned the site and building arrangements of Johns Hopkins University. And of the Capitol building in Washington! He helped to design Stanford University. The man was a modern Leonardo da Vinci. His "A Journey in the Seaboard Slave States" from which the extract presented in this book is taken, has long been out of print and is known to only a few but those few cherish it as an indubitable classic....*

With the expansion of the country, the North rapidly yielded to the new industrialization whereas the South remained agricultural and committed to the economic as well as the moral disadvantage of slave labor. Gerald W. Johnson ably presents the causes which led up to the Civil War in "The Secession of the Southern States."...

George Haven Putnam, son of the founder of G. P. Putnam's Sons, was a writer and a fighter as well as a publisher and although his fight for the International Copyright Act was long and tenacious, his career as a soldier was brief and horrible. However, he wrote of his experiences in "A Prisoner of War in Virginia" with a vividness and detachment that must have excited the admiration of one of his most gifted writers of short stories, Ambrose Bierce....

One of the books I hold in most cherished admiration and one of those I most frequently re-read is "Aspects of the Study of Roman History" by Thomas Spencer Jerome. I have personally encountered no one who has read it or even heard of it, except the publishers, who tell me sadly that the sale of the book was practically nil, and the other (but this is only a suspicion, about which I'll tell you later). Yet to my mind Thomas Spencer Jerome was the most careful, the most exact, the most thorough, scholar in the field of Roman history and Latin literature that ever lived and, what is more, the most gracious stylist who ever wrote on those subjects, Gibbon included. "Aspects of the Study of Roman History" is a posthumous work, a compilation of Jerome's manuscripts by John G. Winter of the University of Michigan. These manuscripts, which he left when he died suddenly of a gastric hemorrhage on the Island of Capri on Easter Sunday, 1914, were the mere Prolegomena of a vast work on Roman Morals which had engaged his attention for many years.

Jerome was born in Saginaw, Michigan, January 24, 1864. His father was Governor of Michigan from 1881 to 1883. After getting an A.B. degree at the University of Michigan, he studied law and later went to Harvard where he emerged with the degree of Master of Arts and settled down in Detroit

to practice law. In this he was eminently successful, but his real interest was history.

During the Spanish-American War he went to Cuba, under appointment by the Secretary of War, where he acted as counsel to the Division of Transportation. His health appears to have been permanently undermined by this service in the yellow fever district. For one year he acted as Consular Agent at Sorrento and in 1901 he went to live in the Villa Castello as Consular Agent at Capri. There, in constant pain for thirteen years, he pursued his minute and enlightened (enlightened, *because he was no mere academic historian content to reiterate what others before him had concluded, but carefully examined every bit of evidence himself*) research into Roman history.

For this anthology I have chosen two selections from Jerome's posthumous (and only) book. I wish there were room to include the entire work. One of them I have chosen for the History section because of the parallel he drew between the origin and development of Rome and Modern America. The other I have chosen simply as an essay of the very highest type—informative, informed, serious in matter but urbane in mood, depth and brilliance combined to drive a lesson home to dogmatic and superficial muttonheads.

I said a moment ago that I suspected one man (whom I happen to know in person, slightly, and whose work I admire greatly) of having read "Aspects of the Study of Roman History" or at least of knowing Jerome in Capri. I invite your attention to "Cosmopolitans" by W. Somerset Maugham and to the story therein called "Mayhew." Listen to this: "I have never met a more interesting man than Mayhew. He was a lawyer in Detroit. He was an able and successful one. By the time he was thirty-five he had a large and lucrative practice, he had amassed a competence, and he stood on the threshold of a distinguished career. He had an acute brain, an attractive personality and uprightness." ... (There follows a passage about how Mayhew came to Capri, a description of the island; a description of Mayhew when he first arrived and of how he grew thin and frail; a description of Mayhew's vast library and of his masses of notes on Tiberius, etc.) ... "He sat down to write. He died.... That vast accumulation of knowledge is lost forever. Vain was that ambition, surely not an ignoble one, to set his name beside those of Gibbon and Mommsen. His memory is treasured in the hearts of a few friends, fewer, alas, as the years pass on, and to the world he is unknown in death as he was in life...."

Well, maybe not, Mr. Maugham, if you are talking about Jerome. What is more, Jerome probably had no ambition, vain or achieved, to set his name *beside those of Gibbon and Mommsen; for, in his essay on Tiberius alone, he makes credulous and superficial suckers out of both Gibbon and Mommsen. (And, by the way, my vast admiration for Mr. Maugham as a story-teller begins to weaken when he draws moral conclusions as he does in the sketch, "Mayhew.") ...*

The wiseheimers who so repeatedly shake their heads in print and say that Charles A. Lindbergh accomplished nothing aeronautically by his long flight to Paris. Maybe they know what they mean. I don't. Maybe he accomplished nothing "aeronautically" but he accomplished everything there was to accomplish at the time for aeronautics. He elevated the spirit of the world; he dramatized aeronautics in a way to capture the minds and imaginations of people; he lifted the aeroplane, from a mechanical gadget people thought was impractical and were afraid of, off the ground and up into the air where they could see it and picture themselves flying in one instead of being afraid of flying (for people don't make heroes without being able to identify themselves with them; and Lindbergh was, and is, a hero to more people than any man of his time).... Part of the hero worship came from the immense emotional stimulus readers derived from Col. Lindbergh's simple, unadorned, unemotional log of the flight. Contrary to irresponsible rumor, "We" was not ghost-written. Every line of it was written out in long-hand with a pencil by Lindbergh himself.

THOMAS PAINE

Of the Origin and Design of Government in General, With Concise Remarks on the English Constitution

[*Practically all of the political and social ideas which found expression in The Declaration of Independence and in the Constitution of the United States had their origin in the brain of Thomas Paine, who articulated them in a pamphlet called "Common Sense" which appeared in Philadelphia on January 1, 1776. "Common Sense" was an argument for the complete independence of the American Colonies from England. The most cogent and the most eloquent section of the pamphlet bore the subtitle, "On the Origin and Design of Government in General," wherein Paine's thesis was that kingships were outmoded and that a new age of reason had dawned which recognized the principle that every man born on this earth should have the privilege of competing on equal terms with any other man, with none of the handicaps of class and caste. It was an argument not only against the hereditary tenure of kings and nobles but against all the corollaries the aristocratic principle implies. The opening challenge of the Declaration of Independence is but a paraphrase of Paine's theories concerning freedom and equality.*

Paine was born in England in 1737 but went to America to live in 1774. After the revolution he was given a confiscated royalist farm near New Rochelle, New York, by a grateful Congress for his work toward the success of the War of American Independence. A vigorous and brilliant controversialist, he returned to England and issued a sensational reply to Thomas Burke's pro-royalist "Reflections upon the French Revolution" under the title "The Rights of Man". The treasonable nature of this pamphlet involved the publisher and distributors in severe difficulties after a million and a half copies had been sold, but Paine escaped to France to aid the revolutionary movement there, only to be thrown into prison by Robespierre for eleven months on account of certain portions of another broadside, "The Age of Reason," Part II of which also offended Washington. Paine turned his huge battery of invective upon the First President and became his bitterest and most relentless enemy but an ardent supporter of Thomas Jefferson, who sent an American naval vessel to bring him back.]

SOME WRITERS have so confounded society with government, as to leave little or no distinction between them; whereas they are not only different, but have different origins. Society is produced by our wants, and government by our wickedness; the former promotes our happiness *positively,* by uniting our affections; the latter *negatively,* by restraining our vices. The one encourages intercourse, the other creates distinctions. The first is a patron, the last a punisher.

Society in every state is a blessing, but government, even in its best state, is but a necessary evil; in its worst state, an intolerable one; for when we suffer, or are exposed to the same miseries *by a government,* which we might expect in a country *without government,* our calamity is heightened by reflecting that we furnish the means by which we suffer.

Government, like dress, is the badge of lost innocence: the palaces of kings are built on the ruins of the bowers of paradise. For, were the impulses of conscience clear, uniform, and irresistibly obeyed, man would need no other lawgiver; but that not being the case, he finds it necessary to surrender up a part of his property to furnish means for the protection of the rest; and this he is induced to do by the same prudence which in every other case, advises him out of two evils to choose the least.

Wherefore, security being the true design and end of government, it unanswerably follows, that whatever *form* thereof appears most likely to ensure it to us with the least expense and greatest benefit, is preferable to all others.

In order to give a clear and just idea of the design and end of government, let us suppose a small number of persons settled in some sequestered part of the earth, unconnected with the rest; they will then represent the first peopling of any country, or of the world. In this state of natural liberty, society will be their first thought. A thousand motives will excite them thereto; the strength of one man is so unequal to his wants, and his mind so unfitted for perpetual solitude, that he is soon obliged to seek assistance and relief of another, who in his turn requires the same.

Four or five united would be able to raise a tolerable dwelling in the midst of a wilderness; but *one* man might labor out the common period of life without accomplishing anything: when he had felled his timber he could not remove it, nor erect it after it was removed; hunger in the meantime would urge him from his work, and every different want call him a different way. Disease, nay, even misfortune, would be death; for though neither might be mortal, yet either would disable him from living, and reduce him to a state in which he might rather be said to perish than to die.

Thus necessity, like a gravitating power, would soon form our newly-arrived emigrants into society, the reciprocal blessings of which would supersede and render the obligations of law and government unnecessary while they remained perfect just to each other: but as nothing but heaven is impregnable to vice, it will unavoidably happen, that in proportion as they surmount the first difficulties of emigration, which bound them together in a common cause, they will begin to relax in their duty and attachment to each other; and this remissness will point out the necessity of establishing some form of government to supply the defect of moral virtue.

Some convenient tree will afford them a state-house, under the branches of which the whole colony may assemble to deliberate on public matters. It is more than probable that their first laws will have the title only of *Regulations,* and be enforced by no other penalty than public disesteem. In this first parliament every man, by natural right, will have a seat.

But as the colony increases, the public concerns will increase likewise, and the distance at which the members may be separated will render it too inconvenient for all of them to meet on every occasion as at first, when their number was small, their habitations near, and the public concerns few and trifling. This will point out the convenience of their consenting to leave the legislative part to be managed by a select number chosen from the whole body, who are supposed to have the same concerns at stake which those have who appointed them, and who will act in the same manner as the whole body would were they present.

If the colony continue increasing, it will become necessary to augment the number of representatives, and that the interest of every part of the colony may be attended to, it will be found best to divide the whole into convenient parts, each part sending its proper number; and that the *elected* might never form to themselves an interest separate from the *electors,* prudence will point out the propriety of having elections often; because as the *elected* might by that means return and mix again with the general body of the *electors* in a few months, their fidelity to the public will be secured by the prudent reflection of not making a rod for themselves. And as this frequent interchange will establish a common interest with every part of the community, they will mutually and naturally support each other, and on this (not on the unmeaning name of king) depends the *strength of government and the happiness of the governed.*

Here, then, is the origin and rise of government; namely, a mode rendered necessary by the inability of moral virtue to govern the world; here, too, is the design and end of government, viz., freedom and security. And however our eyes may be dazzled with show, or our ears deceived by sound; however prejudice may warp our wills, or interest darken our understanding; the simple voice of nature and reason will say, it is right.

I draw my idea of the form of government from a principle in nature, which no art can overturn, viz., that the more simple anything is, the less liable it is to be disordered, and the easier repaired when disordered; and with this maxim in view, I offer a few remarks on the so much boasted Constitution of England. That it was noble for the dark and slavish times in which it was erected, is granted. When the world was overrun with tyranny, the least remove therefrom was a glorious rescue. But that it is imperfect, subject to convulsions, and incapable of producing what it seems to promise, is easily demonstrated.

Absolute governments (though the disgrace of human nature) have this advantage with them, that they are simple; if the people suffer, they know the head from which their suffering springs; they know likewise the remedy, and are not bewildered by a variety of causes and cures. But the Constitution of England is so exceedingly complex, that the nation may suffer for years together without being able to discover in which part the fault lies; some will say in one and some in another, and every political physician will advise a different medicine.

I know it is difficult to get over local or long-standing prejudices, yet if we will suffer ourselves to examine the component parts of the English Constitution, we shall find them to be the base remains of two ancient tyrannies, compounded with some new republican materials.

First—The remains of monarchical tyranny in the person of the King.

Secondly—The remains of aristocratical tyranny in the persons of the Peers.

Thirdly—The new republican materials in the persons of the Commons, on whose virtue depends the freedom of England.

The two first, by being hereditary, are independent of the people; wherefore in a *constitutional sense* they contribute nothing toward the freedom of the state.

To say that the Constitution of England is a *union* of three powers, reciprocally *checking* each other, is farcical; either the words have no meaning, or they are flat contradictions.

To say that the Commons is a check upon the King, presupposes two things:

First—That the King is not to be trusted without being looked after, or in other words, that a thirst for absolute power is the natural disease of monarchy.

Secondly—That the Commons, by being appointed for that purpose, are either wiser or more worthy of confidence than the Crown.

But as the same Constitution which gives the Commons a power to check the King by withholding the supplies, gives afterwards the King a power to check the Commons by empowering him to reject their other bills, it again supposes that the King is wiser than those whom it has already supposed to be wiser than him. A mere absurdity!

There is something exceedingly ridiculous in the composition of monarchy; it first excludes a man from the means of information, yet empowers him to act in cases where the highest judgment is required. The state of a king shuts him from the world, yet the business of a king requires him to know it thoroughly; wherefore the different parts, by unnaturally opposing and destroying each other, prove the whole character to be absurd and useless.

Some writers have explained the English Constitution thus: The King, say they, is one, the people another; the Peers are a house in behalf of the King, the Commons in behalf of the people.

But this hath all the distinctions of a house divided against itself; and though the expressions be pleasantly arranged, yet when examined, they appear idle and ambiguous; and it will always happen, that the nicest construction that words are capable of, when applied to the description of something which either cannot exist or is too incomprehensible to be within the compass of description, will be words of sound only, and though they may amuse the ear, they cannot inform the mind, for this explanation includes a previous question, viz.: *How came the King by a power which the people are afraid to trust, and always obliged to check?*

Such a power could not be the gift of a wise people, neither can any power, *which needs checking,* be from God; yet the provision, which the Constitution makes, supposes such a power to exist.

But the provision is unequal to the task; the means either cannot or will not accomplish the end, and the whole affair is a *felo de se;* for as the greater weight will always carry up the less, and as all the wheels of a machine are put in motion by one, it only remains to know which power in the Constitution has the most weight, for that will govern; and though the others, or a part of them, may clog, or, as the phrase is, check the rapidity of its motion, yet so long as they cannot stop it, their endeavors will be ineffectual; the first moving power will at last have its way, and what it wants in speed, is supplied by time.

That the Crown is this overbearing part in the English Constitution, needs not be mentioned, and that it derives its whole consequence merely from being the giver of places and pensions, is self-evident; wherefore, though we have been wise enough to shut and lock a door against absolute monarchy, we at the same time have been foolish enough to put the Crown in possession of the key.

The prejudice of Englishmen in favor of their own government by kings, lords and commons, arises as much or more from national pride than reason. Individuals are undoubtedly safer in England than in some other countries, but the *will* of a king is as much the *law* of the land in Britain as in France, with this difference, that instead of proceeding directly from his mouth, it is handed to the people under the more formidable shape of an act of Parliament. For the fate of Charles I hath only made kings more subtle—not more just.

Wherefore, laying aside all national pride and prejudice in favor of modes and forms, the plain truth is, that *it is wholly owing to the constitution of the people, and not to the constitution of the government,* that the Crown is not as oppressive in England as in Turkey.

An inquiry into the *constitutional errors* in the English form of government is at this time highly necessary; for as we are never in a proper condition of doing justice to others, while we continue under the influence of some leading partiality, so neither are we capable of doing it to ourselves while we remain fettered by any obstinate prejudice. And as a man who is attached to a prostitute is unfitted to choose or judge of a wife, so any prepossession in favor of a rotten constitution of government will disable us from discerning a good one.

THOMAS JEFFERSON

The Drawing-Up of the Declaration of Independence

[*Next to Abraham Lincoln's Gettysburg Address, the preamble of the Declaration of Independence is probably the noblest prose writing produced in the Western Hemisphere. Like the Gettysburg Address, the preamble to the Declaration of Independence asserts to be true things which are not demonstrably true but are mystically true. Truth is an abstraction, and an abstraction cannot be demonstrated. It is poetry. And poetry is the spirit of Man, and the poetry of the preamble of the Declaration of Independence and of the Gettysburg Address is the spirit of the people of America.*

> *"Beauty is truth, truth beauty, that is all*
> *Ye know on earth, and all ye need to know."*

Thus spake Keats. And all that Americans on earth have known or needed to know is the beauty and the truth of the assertion that "all men are created free and equal."

Thomas Jefferson drafted the Declaration of Independence. He had the eloquence of the fiery Thomas Paine to draw upon, but there were politicians then as now and there were many matters to be considered. It was not an easy job. Jefferson has left for us an account of the happenings leading up to the signing of the Declaration of Independence. It is slightly at odds with John Adams's account, which is presented here as a footnote; but there is a thrilling eloquence to good Americans in every sentence of Jefferson's account and a beauty even in the abbreviations and strange spellings, which are preserved herewith.]

WHEN the famous Resolutions of 1765, against the Stamp-act, were proposed, I was yet a student of law in Wmsbg. I attended the debate however at the door of the lobby of the H. of Burgesses, & heard the splendid display of Mr. Henry's talents as a popular orator. They were great indeed; such as I have never heard from any other man. He appeared to me to speak as Homer wrote. Mr. Johnson, a lawyer & member from the Northern Neck, seconded the resolns, & by him the learning & the logic of the case were chiefly maintained. My recollections of these transactions may be seen pa. 60, Wirt's life of P. H.,[1] to whom I furnished them.

In May,[2] 1769, a meeting of the General Assembly was called by the Govr., Ld. Botetourt. I had then become a member; and to that meeting became known the joint resolutions & address of the Lords & Commons of 1768-9, on the proceedings in Massachusetts. Counter-resolutions, & an address to the King, by the H. of Burgesses were agreed to with little opposition, & a spirit manifestly displayed of considering the cause of Massachusetts as a common one. The Governor dissolved us [3]: but we met the next day in the Apollo [4] of the Raleigh tavern, formed ourselves into a voluntary convention, drew up articles of association against the use of any merchandise imported from Gr. Britain, signed and recommended them to the people, repaired to our several counties, & were re elected without any other exception than of the very few who had declined assent to our proceedings.

Nothing of particular excitement occurring for a considerable time our countrymen seemed to fall into a state of insensibility to our situation. The duty on tea not yet repealed & the Declaratory act of a right in the British parl to bind us by their laws in all cases whatsoever, still suspended over us. But a court of inquiry held in R. Island in 1762, with a power to send persons to England to be tried for offences committed here [5] was considered at our session of the spring of 1773. as demanding attention. Not thinking our old & leading members up to the point of forwardness & zeal which the times required, Mr. Henry, R. H. Lee, Francis L. Lee, Mr. Carr & myself agreed to meet in the evening in a private room of the Raleigh to consult on the state of things. There may have been a member or two more whom I do not recollect. We were all sensible that the most urgent of all measures was that of coming to an understanding with all the other colonies to consider the British claims as a common cause to all, & to produce an unity of action: and for this purpose that a commee of correspondce in each colony would be the best instrument for intercommunication: and that their first measure would probably be to propose a meeting of deputies from every colony at some central place, who should be charged with the direction of the measures which should be taken by all. We therefore drew up the resolutions which may be seen in Wirt pa 87. The consulting members proposed

[1] Patrick Henry. *Cf. post,* sketch of Patrick Henry, under 1814.
[2] May 8th.   [3] May 16th.
[4] A public room sometimes called the "long room" in the tavern. There is a picture of it in *The Century Magazine* for November, 1875.
[5] This was the famous "Gaspee" inquiry, the date being a slip for 1772.

to me to move them, but I urged that it should be done by Mr. Carr,[6] my friend & brother in law, then a new member to whom I wished an opportunity should be given of making known to the house his great worth & talents. It was so agreed; he moved them, they were agreed to nem. con. and a commee of correspondence appointed of whom Peyton Randolph, the Speaker, was chairman. The Govr. (then Ld. Dunmore) dissolved us, but the commee met the next day, prepared a circular letter to the Speakers of the other colonies, inclosing to each a copy of the resolns and left it in charge with their chairman to forward them by expresses.

The origination of these commees of correspondence between the colonies has been since claimed for Massachusetts, and Marshall II. 151, has given into this error, altho' the very note of his appendix to which he refers, shows that their establmt was confined to their own towns. This matter will be seen clearly stated in a letter of Samuel Adams Wells to me of Apr. 2, 1819, and my answer of May 12. I was corrected by the letter of Mr. Wells in the information I had given Mr. Wirt, as stated in his note, pa. 87, that the messengers of Massach. & Virga crossed each other on the way bearing similar propositions, for Mr. Wells shows that Mass. did not adopt the measure but on the receipt of our proposn delivered at their next session. Their message therefore which passed ours, must have related to something else, for I well remember P. Randolph's informing me of the crossing of our messengers.

The next event which excited our sympathies for Massachusets was the Boston port bill, by which that port was to be shut up on the 1st of June, 1774. This arrived while we were in session in the spring of that year. The lead in the house on these subjects being no longer left to the old members, Mr. Henry, R. H. Lee, Fr. L. Lee, 3. or 4. other members, whom I do not recollect, and myself, agreeing that we must boldly take an unequivocal stand in the line with Massachusetts, determined to meet and consult on the proper measures in the council chamber, for the benefit of the library in that room. We were under conviction of the necessity of arousing our people from the lethargy into which they had fallen as to passing events; and thought that the appointment of a day of general fasting & prayer would be most likely to call up & alarm their attention.[7] No example of such a solemnity had existed

[6] Dabney Carr. He married Martha Jefferson.

[7] "Mr. Jefferson and Charles Lee may be said to have originated a fast to electrify the people from the pulpit.... Those gentlemen, knowing that Robert Carter Nicholas, the chairman of the committee of religion, was no less zealous than themselves against the attempt to starve thousands of American people into a subservience to the ministry, easily persuaded him to put

since the days of our distresses in the war of 55. since which a new generation had grown up. With the help therefore of Rushworth, whom we rummaged over for the revolutionary precedents & forms of the Puritans of that day, preserved by him, we cooked up a resolution, somewhat modernizing their phrases, for appointing the 1st day of June, on which the Port bill was to commence, for a day of fasting, humiliation & prayer, to implore heaven to avert from us the evils of civil war, to inspire us with firmness in support of our rights, and to turn the hearts of the King & parliament to moderation & justice.[8] To give greater emphasis to our proposition, we agreed to wait the next morning on Mr. Nicholas,[9] whose grave & religious character was more in unison with the tone of our resolution and to solicit him to move it. We accordingly went to him in the morning. He moved it the same day; the 1st of June was proposed and it passed without opposition.[10] The Governor dissolved us as usual. We retired to the Apollo as before, agreed to an association,[11] and instructed the commee of correspdce to propose to the corresponding commees of the other colonies to appoint deputies to meet in Congress at such place, *annually,* as should be convenient to direct, from time to time, the measures required by the general interest: and we declared that an attack on any one colony should be considered as an attack on the whole. This was in May.[12] We further recommended to the several counties to elect deputies to meet at Wmsbg the 1st of Aug ensuing, to consider the state of the colony, & particularly to appoint delegates to a general Congress, should that measure be acceded to by the commees of correspdce generally.[13] It was acceded to, Philadelphia was appointed for the place, and the 5th of Sep. for the time of meeting. We returned home, and in our several counties

forth the strength of his character, on an occasion which he thought to be pious, and move a fast, to be observed on the first day of June."—Edmund Randolph's (MS.) *History of Virginia,* p. 24.

[8] Printed in Force's *Archives,* 4th, 1, 350.

[9] Robert Carter Nicholas.

[10] "It (the fast) was spoke of by some as a Schem calculated to *inflame* and excite an *enthusiastic* zeal in the Minds of the People under a Cloak of Religion, than which nothing could be more *calumnious and unjust....* The Resolution was not *Smuggled,* but proposed in a very *full* House, not above one Dissentient appearing amongst near an hundred members."— R. C. Nicholas' *Considerations on the Present State of Virginia Examined,* p. 40.

[11] Printed in Rind's *Virginia Gazette* for May 26, 1774. It was signed by eighty-nine members.

[12] May 27, 1774.

[13] This was in a separate resolution, adopted May 30th, by "all the members that were then in town." It was not to "elect deputies" but merely a reference of the consideration of important papers to such "late members of the House of Burgesses" who should then gather.

invited the clergy to meet assemblies of the people on the 1st of June,[14] to perform the ceremonies of the day, & to address to them discourses suited to the occasion. The people met generally, with anxiety & alarm in their countenances, and the effect of the day thro' the whole colony was like a shock of electricity, arousing every man & placing him erect & solidly on his centre. They chose universally delegates for the convention. Being elected one for my own county I prepared a draught of instructions to be given to the delegates whom we should send to the Congress, and which I meant to propose at our meeting. In this I took the ground which, from the beginning I had thought the only one orthodox or tenable, which was that the relation between Gr. Br. and these colonies was exactly the same as that of England & Scotland after the accession of James & until the Union, and the same as her present relations with Hanover, having the same Executive chief but no other necessary political connection; and that our emigration from England to this country gave her no more rights over us, than the emigrations of the Danes and Saxons gave to the present authorities of the mother country over England. In this doctrine however I had never been able to get any one to agree with me but Mr. Wythe. He concurred in it from the first dawn of the question What was the political relation between us & England? Our other patriots Randolph, the Lees, Nicholas, Pendleton stopped at the halfway house of John Dickinson who admitted that England had a right to regulate our commerce, and to lay duties on it for the purposes of regulation, but not of raising revenue. But for this ground there was no foundation in compact, in any acknowledged principles of colonization, nor in reason: expatriation being a natural right, and acted on as such, by all nations, in all ages. I set out for Wmsbg some days before that appointed for our meeting, but was taken ill of a dysentery on the road, & unable to proceed. I sent on therefore to Wmsbg two copies of my draught, the one under cover to Peyton Randolph, who I knew would be in the chair of the convention, the other to Patrick Henry. Whether Mr. Henry disapproved the ground taken, or was too lazy to read it (for he was the laziest man in reading I ever knew) I never learned: but he communicated it to nobody. Peyton Randolph informed the convention he had received such a paper from a member prevented by sickness from offering it in his place, and he laid it on the table for perusal. It was read generally by the members, approved by many, but thought too bold for the present state of things; but they printed it in

---

[14] By the original invitation, printed herein under June, 1774, it will be seen that the call was for June 23d, instead of the 1st.

pamphlet form under the title of *A Summary view of the rights of British America*. It found its way to England, was taken up by the opposition, interpolated a little by Mr. Burke so as to make it answer opposition purposes, and in that form ran rapidly thro' several editions.[15] This information I had from Parson Hurt,[16] who happened at the time to be in London, whither he had gone to receive clerical orders. And I was informed afterwards by Peyton Randolph that it had procured me the honor of having my name inserted in a long list of proscriptions enrolled in a bill of attainder commenced in one of the houses of parliament, but suppressed in embryo by the hasty step of events which warned them to be a little cautious.[17] Montague, agent of the H. of Burgesses in England made extracts from the bill, copied the names, and sent them to Peyton Randolph. The names I think were about 20 which he repeated to me, but I recollect those only of Hancock, the two Adamses, Peyton Randolph himself, Patrick Henry, & myself.[18] The convention met on the 1st of Aug, renewed their association, appointed delegates to the Congress, gave them instructions very temperately & properly expressed, both as to style & matter; and they repaired to Philadelphia at the time appointed. The splendid proceedings of that Congress at their 1st session belong to general history, are known to every one, and need not therefore be noted here. They terminated their session on the 26th of Octob, to meet again on the 10th May ensuing. The convention at their ensuing session of Mar, '75,[19] approved of the proceedings of Congress, thanked their delegates and reappointed the same persons to represent the colony at the meeting to be held in May: and foreseeing the probability that Peyton Randolph their president and Speaker also of the H. of B. might be called off, they added me, in that event to the delegation.

Mr. Randolph was according to expectation obliged to leave the chair of Congress to attend the Gen. Assembly summoned by Ld. Dunmore to meet on the 1st day of June 1775. Ld. North's conciliatory propositions, as they were called, had been received by the Governor and furnished the subject for which this assembly was convened. Mr. Randolph accordingly attended, and

[15] There are several errors in this statement, which are treated in the note on the pamphlet. See *post*, 1774.
[16] Rev. John Hurt.
[17] It is hardly necessary to state that this so-called bill was a myth, which had no basis in fact. But at the time when these leaders were risking such a proscription, it was the current belief, both in England and America, that steps would be taken against them, and it is not strange that, in the absence of the proof to the contrary which we now possess, it was believed in.
[18] See Girardin's *History of Virginia*, Appendix No. 12, note.—T. J.
[19] March 27, 1775. See Force's *Archives*, 4th, 11, 172.

the tenor of these propositions being generally known, as having been addressed to all the governors, he was anxious that the answer of our assembly, likely to be the first,[20] should harmonize with what he knew to be the sentiments and wishes of the body he had recently left. He feared that Mr. Nicholas, whose mind was not yet up to the mark of the times, would undertake the answer, & therefore pressed me to prepare an answer. I did so, and with his aid carried it through the house with long and doubtful scruples from Mr. Nicholas and James Mercer, and a dash of cold water on it here & there, enfeebling it somewhat, but finally with unanimity or a vote approaching it.[21] This being passed, I repaired immediately to Philadelphia, and conveyed to Congress the first notice they had of it. It was entirely approved there. I took my seat with them on the 21st of June. On the 24th, a commee which had been appointed to prepare a declaration of the causes of taking up arms, brought in their report (drawn I believe by J. Rutledge) which not being liked they recommitted it on the 26th, and added Mr. Dickinson and myself to the committee. On the rising of the house, the commee having not yet met, I happened to find myself near Govr W. Livingston, and proposed to him to draw the paper. He excused himself and proposed that I should draw it. On my pressing him with urgency, "we are as yet but new acquaintances, sir, said he, why are you so earnest for my doing it?" "Because, said I, I have been informed that you drew the Address to the people of Gr. Britain, a production certainly of the finest pen in America." "On that, says he, perhaps sir you may not have been correctly informed." I had received the information in Virginia from Colo Harrison on his return from that Congress. Lee, Livingston & Jay had been the commee for that draught. The first, prepared by Lee, had been disapproved & recommitted. The second was drawn by Jay, but being presented by Govr Livingston, had led Colo Harrison into the error. The next morning, walking in the hall of Congress, many members being assembled but the house not yet formed, I observed Mr. Jay, speaking to R. H. Lee, and leading him by the button of his coat, to me. "I understand, sir, said he to me, that this gentleman informed you that Govr Livingston drew the Address to the people of Gr Britain." I assured him at once that I had not received that information from Mr. Lee & that not a word had ever passed on the subject between Mr. Lee & myself; and after some explanations the subject was dropt. These gentlemen had had some sparrings in debate before, and continued ever very hostile to each other.

[20] It had already been referred to the Congress by New Jersey, May 20th, 1775.
[21] See *post*, under June 12, 1775.

I prepared a draught of the Declaration committed to us.[22] It was too strong for Mr. Dickinson. He still retained the hope of reconciliation with the mother country, and was unwilling it should be lessened by offensive statements. He was so honest a man, & so able a one that he was greatly indulged even by those who could not feel his scruples. We therefore requested him to take the paper, and put it into a form he could approve. He did so, preparing an entire new statement, and preserving of the former only the last 4. paragraphs & half of the preceding one. We approved & reported it to Congress, who accepted it. Congress gave a signal proof of their indulgence to Mr. Dickinson, and of their great desire not to go too fast for any respectable part of our body, in permitting him to draw their second petition to the king according to his own ideas,[23] and passing it with scarcely any amendment. The disgust against this humility was general; and Mr. Dickinson's delight at its passage was the only circumstance which reconciled them to it. The vote being passed, altho' further observn on it was out of order, he could not refrain from rising and expressing his satisfaction and concluded by saying "there is but one word, Mr. President, in the paper which I disapprove, & that is the word *Congress,*" on which Ben Harrison rose and said "there is but one word in the paper, Mr. President, of which I approve, and that is the word *Congress.*"

On the 22d of July Dr. Franklin, Mr. Adams, R. H. Lee, & myself, were appointed a commee to consider and report on Ld. North's conciliatory resolution. The answer of the Virginia assembly on that subject having been approved I was requested by the commee to prepare this report, which will account for the similarity of feature in the two instruments.[24]

On the 15th of May, 1776, the convention of Virginia instructed their delegates in Congress to propose to that body to declare the colonies independent of G. Britain, and appointed a commee to prepare a declaration of rights and plan of government.[25]

[26] In Congress, Friday June 7. 1776. The delegates from Virginia moved [27]

[22] *Cf.* note on Jefferson's draft, *post,* under July 6, 1775.
[23] "Scarcely I believe altering one" struck out in MS. by author.
[24] See *post,* under July 31, 1775.
[25] Printed in Force's *Archives,* 5th, VI, 461.
[26] Here, in the original manuscript, commence the "two preceding sheets" referred to by Mr. Jefferson, as containing "notes" taken by him "whilst these things were going on." They are easily distinguished from the body of the MS. in which they were inserted by him, being of a paper very different in size, quality, and color from that on which the latter is written.
[27] Introduced by Richard Henry Lee. His autograph resolution is reproduced in Etting's *Memorials of 1776,* p. 4.

in obedience to instructions from their constituents that the Congress should declare that these United colonies are & of right ought to be free & independent states, that they are absolved from all allegiance to the British crown, and that all political connection between them & the state of Great Britain is & ought to be, totally dissolved; that measures should be immediately taken for procuring the assistance of foreign powers, and a Confederation be formed to bind the colonies more closely together.[28]

The house being obliged to attend at that time to some other business, the proposition was referred to the next day, when the members were ordered to attend punctually at ten o'clock.

Saturday June 8. They proceeded to take it into consideration and referred it to a committee of the whole, into which they immediately resolved themselves, and passed that day & Monday the 10th in debating on the subject.

It was argued by Wilson, Robert R. Livingston, E. Rutledge, Dickinson and others

That tho' they were friends to the measures themselves, and saw the impossibility that we should ever again be united with Gr. Britain, yet they were against adopting them at this time:

That the conduct we had formerly observed was wise & proper now, of deferring to take any capital step till the voice of the people drove us into it:

That they were our power, & without them our declarations could not be carried into effect;

That the people of the middle colonies (Maryland, Delaware, Pennsylva, the Jerseys & N. York) were not yet ripe for bidding adieu to British connection, but that they were fast ripening & in a short time would join in the general voice of America:

---

[28] "The Congress sat till 7 o'clock this evening in consequence of a motion of R. H. Lee's rendering ourselves free and independent States. The sensible part of the House opposed the Motion—they had no objection to forming a Scheme of a Treaty which they would send to France by proper Persons & uniting this Continent by a Confederacy; they saw no wisdom in a Declaration of Independence, nor any other Purpose to be enforced by it, but placing ourselves in the power of those with whom we mean to treat, giving our Enemy Notice of our Intentions before we had taken any steps to execute them. The event, however, was that the Question was postponed; it is to be renewed on Monday when I mean to move that it should be postponed for 3 Weeks or Months. In the mean Time the plan of Confederation & the Scheme of Treaty may go on. I don't know whether I shall succeed in this Motion; I think not, it is at least doubtful. However I must do what is right in my own Eyes, & Consequences must take Care of themselves. I wish you had been here—the whole Argument was sustained on one side by R. Livingston, Wilson, Dickenson, & myself, & by the Power of all N. England, Virginia & Georgia at the other."—*E. Rutledge to John Jay, June 8, 1776.*

That the resolution entered into by this house on the 15th of May [29] for suppressing the exercise of all powers derived from the crown, had shown, by the ferment into which it had thrown these middle colonies, that they had not yet accommodated their minds to a separation from the mother country:

That some of them had expressly forbidden their delegates to consent to such a declaration, and others had given no instructions, & consequently no powers to give such consent:

That if the delegates of any particular colony had no power to declare such colony independant, certain they were the others could not declare it for them; the colonies being as yet perfectly independant of each other:

That the assembly of Pennsylvania was now sitting above stairs, their convention would sit within a few days, the convention of New York was now sitting, & those of the Jerseys & Delaware counties would meet on the Monday following, & it was probable these bodies would take up the question of Independence & would declare to their delegates the voice of their state:

That if such a declaration should now be agreed to, these delegates must retire & possibly their colonies might secede from the Union:

That such a secession would weaken us more than could be compensated by any foreign alliance:

That in the event of such a division, foreign powers would either refuse to join themselves to our fortunes, or, having us so much in their power as that desperate declaration would place us, they would insist on terms proportionably more hard and prejudicial:

That we had little reason to expect an alliance with those to whom alone as yet we had cast our eyes:

That France & Spain had reason to be jealous of that rising power which would one day certainly strip them of all their American possessions:

That it was more likely they should form a connection with the British court, who, if they should find themselves unable otherwise to extricate themselves from their difficulties, would agree to a partition of our territories, restoring Canada to France, & the Floridas to Spain, to accomplish for themselves a recovery of these colonies:

That it would not be long before we should receive certain information of

---

[29] That "every kind of authority under the said crown should be totally suppressed" and "to adopt such government as shall ... best conduce to the happiness and safety of their constituents."—*Journal of Congress*, II, 166, 174. Duane, in a letter to Jay, dated May 16th, states that "it has occasioned a great alarm here [Philadelphia], and the cautious folks are very fearful of its being attended with many ill consequences."

the disposition of the French court, from the agent whom we had sent to Paris for that purpose:

That if this disposition should be favorable, by waiting the event of the present campaign, which we all hoped would be successful, we should have reason to expect an alliance on better terms:

That this would in fact work no delay of any effectual aid from such ally, as, from the advance of the season & distance of our situation, it was impossible we could receive any assistance during this campaign:

That it was prudent to fix among ourselves the terms on which we should form alliance, before we declared we would form one at all events:

And that if these were agreed on, & our Declaration of Independence ready by the time our Ambassador should be prepared to sail, it would be as well as to go into that Declaration at this day.

On the other side it was urged by J. Adams, Lee, Wythe, and others

That no gentleman had argued against the policy or the right of separation from Britain, nor had supposed it possible we should ever renew our connection; that they had only opposed its being now declared:

That the question was not whether, by a declaration of independence, we should make ourselves what we are not; but whether we should declare a fact which already exists:

That as to the people or parliament of England, we had alwais been independent of them, their restraints on our trade deriving efficacy from our acquiescence only, & not from any rights they possessed of imposing them, & that so far our connection had been federal only & was now dissolved by the commencement of hostilities:

That as to the King, we had been bound to him by allegiance, but that this bond was now dissolved by his assent to the late act of parliament, by which he declares us out of his protection, and by his levying war on us, a fact which had long ago proved us out of his protection; it being a certain position in law that allegiance & protection are reciprocal, the one ceasing when the other is withdrawn:

That James the IId. never declared the people of England out of his protection yet his actions proved it & the parliament declared it:

No delegates then can be denied, or ever want, a power of declaring an existing truth:

That the delegates from the Delaware counties having declared their constituents ready to join, there are only two colonies Pennsylvania & Maryland whose delegates are absolutely tied up, and that these had by their instructions only reserved a right of confirming or rejecting the measure:

That the instructions from Pennsylvania might be accounted for from the times in which they were drawn near a twelvemonth ago, since which the face of affairs has totally changed:

That within that time it had become apparent that Britain was determined to accept nothing less than a carte-blanche, and that the King's answer to the Lord Mayor Aldermen & common council of London, which had come to hand four days ago, must have satisfied every one of this point:

That the people wait for us to lead the way:

That *they* are in favour of the measure, tho' the instructions given by some of their *representatives* are not:

That the voice of the representatives is not always consonant with the voice of the people, and that this is remarkably the case in these middle colonies:

That the effect of the resolution of the 15th of May has proved this, which, raising the murmurs of some in the colonies of Pennsylvania & Maryland, called forth the opposing voice of the freer part of the people, & proved them to be the majority, even in these colonies:

That the backwardness of these two colonies might be ascribed partly to the influence of proprietary power & connections, & partly to their having not yet been attacked by the enemy:

That these causes were not likely to be soon removed, as there seemed no probability that the enemy would make either of these the seat of this summer's war:

That it would be vain to wait either weeks or months for perfect unanimity, since it was impossible that all men should ever become of one sentiment on any question:

That the conduct of some colonies from the beginning of this contest, had given reason to suspect it was their settled policy to keep in the rear of the confederacy, that their particular prospect might be better, even in the worst event:

That therefore it was necessary for those colonies who had thrown themselves forward & hazarded all from the beginning, to come forward now also, and put all again to their own hazard:

That the history of the Dutch revolution, of whom three states only confederated at first proved that a secession of some colonies would not be so dangerous as some apprehended:

That a declaration of Independence alone could render it consistent with European delicacy for European powers to treat with us, or even to receive an Ambassador from us:

That till this they would not receive our vessels into their ports, nor acknowledge the adjudications of our courts of admiralty to be legitimate, in cases of capture of British vessels:

That though France & Spain may be jealous of our rising power, they must think it will be much more formidable with the addition of Great Britain; and will therefore see it their interest to prevent a coalition; but should they refuse, we shall be but where we are; whereas without trying we shall never know whether they will aid us or not:

That the present campaign may be unsuccessful, & therefore we had better propose an alliance while our affairs wear a hopeful aspect.

That to await the event of this campaign will certainly work delay, because during this summer France may assist us effectually by cutting off those supplies of provisions from England & Ireland on which the enemy's armies here are to depend; or by setting in motion the great power they have collected in the West Indies, & calling our enemy to the defence of the possessions they have there:

That it would be idle to lose time in settling the terms of alliance, till we had first determined we would enter into alliance:

That it is necessary to lose no time in opening a trade for our people, who will want clothes, and will want money too for the paiment of taxes:

And that the only misfortune is that we did not enter into alliance with France six months sooner, as besides opening their ports for the vent of our last year's produce, they might have marched an army into Germany and prevented the petty princes there from selling their unhappy subjects to subdue us.

It appearing in the course of these debates that the colonies of N. York, New Jersey, Pennsylvania, Delaware, Maryland, and South Carolina [30] were not yet matured for falling from the parent stem, but that they were fast advancing to that state, it was thought most prudent to wait a while for them, and to postpone the final decision to July 1. but that this might occasion as little delay as possible a committee was appointed [31] to prepare a declaration of independence. The commee were J. Adams, Dr. Franklin, Roger Sherman, Robert R. Livingston & myself. Committees were also appointed at the same time to prepare a plan of confederation for the colonies, and to state the terms proper to be proposed for foreign alliance. The committee for drawing the declaration of Independence desired me to do it. It

---

[30] "Had not yet advanced to" struck out in MS. by author.
[31] June 10, 1776.

was accordingly done, and being approved by them, I reported it to the house on Friday the 28th of June when it was read and ordered to lie on the table.[32] On Monday, the 1st of July the house resolved itself into a commee

[32] A different account is given of this by John Adams, as follows:

"The committee had several meetings, in which were proposed the articles of which the declaration was to consist, and minutes made of them. The committee then appointed Mr. Jefferson and me to draw them up in form, and clothe them in a proper dress. The sub-committee met, and considered the minutes, making such observations on them as then occurred, when Mr. Jefferson desired me to take them to my lodgings, and make the draught. This I declined, and gave several reasons for declining. 1. That he was a Virginian, and I a Massachusettensian. 2. That he was a southern man, and I a northern one. 3. That I had been so obnoxious for my early and constant zeal in promoting the measure, that any draught of mine would undergo a more severe scrutiny and criticism in Congress, than one of his composition. 4. And lastly, and that would be reason enough if there were no other, I had a great opinion of the elegance of his pen, and none at all of my own. I therefore insisted that no hesitation should be made on his part. He accordingly took the minutes, and in a day or two produced to me his draught. Whether I made or suggested any correction, I remember not. The report was made to the committee of five, by them examined, but, whether altered or corrected in any thing, I cannot recollect. But, in substance at least, it was reported to Congress, where, after a severe criticism, and striking out several of the most oratorical paragraphs, it was adopted on the fourth of July, 1776, and published to the world."—*Autobiography of John Adams.*

"You inquire why so young a man as Mr. Jefferson was placed at the head of the Committee for preparing a Declaration of Independence? I answer: it was the Frankfort advice, to place Virginia at the head of every thing. Mr. Richard Henry Lee might be gone to Virginia, to his sick family, for aught I know, but that was not the reason of Mr. Jefferson's appointment. There were three committees appointed at the same time. One for the Declaration of Independence, another for preparing the articles of Confederation, another for preparing a treaty to be proposed to France. Mr. Lee was chosen for the committee of Confederation, and it was not thought convenient that the same person should be upon both. Mr. Jefferson came into Congress, in June, 1775, and brought with him a reputation for literature, science, and a happy talent of composition. Writings of his were handed about, remarkable for the peculiar felicity of expression. Though a silent member in Congress, he was so prompt, frank, explicit, and decisive upon committees and in conversation, not even Samuel Adams was more so, that he soon seized upon my heart and upon this occasion I gave him my vote, and did all in my power to procure the votes of others. I think he had one more vote than any other, and that placed him at the head of the committee. I had the next highest number, and that placed me the second. The committee met, discussed the subject, and then appointed Mr. Jefferson and me to make the draft, I suppose because we were the two first on the list.

"The sub-committee met. Jefferson proposed to me to make the draft. I said: 'I will not.' 'You should do it.' 'Oh! no.' 'Why will you not? You ought to do it.' 'I will not.' 'Why?' 'Reasons enough.' 'What can be your reasons?' 'Reason first—You are a Virginian, and a Virginian ought to appear at the head of this business. Reason second—I am obnoxious, suspected, and unpopular. You are very much otherwise. Reason third—You can write ten times better that I can.' 'Well,' said Jefferson, 'If you are decided, I will do as well as I can.' 'Very well. When you have drawn it up, we will have a meeting.'

"A meeting we accordingly had, and conned the paper over. I was delighted with its high tone and the flights of oratory with which it abounded, especially that concerning negro slavery, which, though I knew his Southern brethren would never suffer to pass in Congress, I cerof the whole & resumed the consideration of the original motion made by the delegates of Virginia, which being again debated through the day, was tainly never would oppose. There were other expressions which I would not have inserted, if I had drawn it up, particularly that which called the King tyrant. I thought this too personal; for I never believed George to be a tyrant in disposition and in nature; I always believed him to be deceived by his courtiers on both sides of the Atlantic, and in his official capacity only, cruel. I thought the expression too passionate, and too much like scolding, for so grave and solemn a document; but as Franklin and Sherman were to inspect it afterwards, I thought it would not become me to strike it out. I consented to report it, and do not now remember that I made or suggested a single alteration.

"We reported it to the committee of five. It was read, and I do not remember that Franklin or Sherman criticised any thing. We were all in haste. Congress was impatient, and the instrument was reported, as I believe, in Jefferson's handwriting, as he first drew it. Congress cut off about a quarter of it, as I expected they would; but they obliterated some of the best of it, and left all that was exceptionable, if anything in it was. I have long wondered that the original draught has not been published. I suppose the reason is, the vehement philippic against negro slavery."—*John Adams to Timothy Pickering, Aug. 22, 1822.*

To this Jefferson replied:

"You have doubtless seen Timothy Pickering's fourth of July observations on the Declaration of Independence. If his principles and prejudices, personal and political, gave us no reason to doubt whether he had truly quoted the information he alleges to have received from Mr. Adams, I should then say, that in some of the particulars, Mr. Adams' memory has led him into unquestionable error. At the age of eighty-eight, and forty-seven years after the transactions of Independence, this is not wonderful. Nor should I, at the age of eighty, on the small advantage of that difference only, venture to oppose my memory to his, were it not supported by written notes, taken by myself at the moment and on the spot. He says 'the committee of five, to wit, Doctor Franklin, Sherman, Livingston and ourselves, met, discussed the subject, and then appointed him and myself to make the draught; that we, as a sub-committee, met, and after the urgencies of each on the other, I consented to undertake the task, that the draught being made, we, the sub-committee, met, and conned the paper over, and he does not remember that he made or suggested a single alteration.' Now these details are quite incorrect. The committee of five met; no such thing as a sub-committee was proposed, but they unanimously pressed on myself alone to undertake the draught. I consented; I drew it; but before I reported it to the committee, I communicated it *separately* to Doctor Franklin and Mr. Adams, requesting their corrections because they were the two members of whose judgments and amendments I wished most to have the benefit, before presenting it to the committee: and you have seen the original paper now in my hands, with the corrections of Doctor Franklin and Mr. Adams interlined in their own handwritings. Their alterations were two or three only, and merely verbal. I then wrote a fair copy, reported it to the committee, and from them unaltered, to Congress. This personal communication and consultation with Mr. Adams, he has misremembered into the actings of a sub-committee. Pickering's observations, and Mr. Adams' in addition, 'that it contained no new ideas, that it is a common place compilation, its sentiments hacknied in Congress for two years before, and its essence contained in Otis' pamphlet,' may all be true. Of that I am not to be the judge. Richard Henry Lee charged it as copied from Locke's treatise on government. Otis' pamphlet I never saw, and whether I had gathered my ideas from reading or reflection I do not know. I know only that I turned to neither book nor pamphlet while writing it. I did not consider it as any part of my charge to invent new ideas altogether, and to offer no sentiment which had ever been expressed before."—*Letter to J. Madison, Aug. 30, 1823.*

carried in the affirmative by the votes of N. Hampshire, Connecticut, Massachusetts, Rhode Island, N. Jersey, Maryland, Virginia, N. Carolina, & Georgia. S. Carolina and Pennsylvania voted against it. Delaware having but two members present, they were divided.[33] The delegates for New York declared they were for it themselves & were assured their constituents were for it, but that their instructions having been drawn near a twelvemonth before, when reconciliation was still the general object, they were enjoined by them to do nothing which should impede that object. They therefore thought themselves not justifiable in voting on either side, and asked leave to withdraw from the question, which was given them. The commee rose & reported their resolution to the house. Mr. Edward Rutledge of S. Carolina then requested the determination might be put off to the next day, as he believed his colleagues, tho' they disapproved of the resolution, would then join in it for the sake of unanimity. The ultimate question whether the house would agree to the resolution of the committee was accordingly postponed to the next day, when it was again moved and S. Carolina concurred in voting for it. In the meantime a third member had come post from the Delaware counties [34] and turned the vote of that colony in favour of the resolution. Members [35] of a different sentiment attending that morning from Pennsylvania also, their vote was changed, so that the whole 12 colonies who were authorized to vote at all, gave their voices for it; and within a few days,[36] the convention of N. York approved of it and thus supplied the void occasioned by the withdrawing of her delegates from the vote.

Congress proceeded the same day [37] to consider the declaration of Independance which had been reported & lain on the table the Friday preceding, and on Monday referred to a commee of the whole. The pusillanimous idea that we had friends in England worth keeping terms with, still haunted the minds of many. For this reason those passages which conveyed censures on the people of England were struck out, lest they should give them offence. The clause too, reprobating the enslaving the inhabitants of Africa, was struck out in complaisance to South Carolina and Georgia, who had never attempted to restrain the importation of slaves, and who on the contrary still wished to continue it. Our northern brethren also I believe felt a little

---

[33] George Read (opposing) and Thomas McKean.

[34] Cæsar Rodney.

[35] Dickinson and Robert Morris did not attend, Wilson changed his vote, and with Franklin and Morton, outvoted Willing and Humphreys.

[36] July 9th.

[37] Monday, July 1st. No sitting was held on Saturday.

tender under those censures; for tho' their people have very few slaves themselves yet they had been pretty considerable carriers of them to others. The debates having taken up the greater parts of the 2d 3d & 4th days of July were,[38] in the evening of the last, closed the declaration was reported by the commee, agreed to by the house and signed by every member present except Mr. Dickinson.[39] As the sentiments of men are known not only by what they receive, but what they reject also, I will state the form of the declaration as originally reported. The parts struck out by Congress shall be distinguished by a black line drawn under them; & those inserted by them shall be placed in the margin or in a concurrent column.[40]

[38] The "Resolution" for independence was under discussion on the 1st of July. The declaration on July 2d, 3d, and 4th.

[39] The question whether the declaration was signed on the 4th of July, as well as on the 2d of August, has been a much vexed one, but a careful study of it must make almost certain that it was not. The MS *Journal of Congress* (that printed by order of Congress being fabricated and altered) merely required its "authentication," which we know from other cases was by the signatures of the president and secretary; who accordingly signed it "by order and in behalf of the Congress," and the printed copies at once sent out had only these signatures. It is also certain that several of the members then in Congress would have refused to sign it on that day, and that the Congress therefore had good cause to postpone the signing till certain of the delegations should receive new instructions, or be changed; and also till its first effect on the people might be seen. For these reasons the declaration was not even entered in the journal, though a blank was left for it, and when it was inserted at a later period, the list of signers was taken from the engrossed copy, though had there been one signed on the 4th of July it would certainly have been the one printed from, as including the men who were in Congress on that day and who voted on the question, instead of one signed by a number of men who were neither present nor members when the declaration was adopted. Moreover, though the printed journal afterwards led John Adams to believe and state that the declaration was signed on the 4th, we have his contemporary statement, on July 9th, that "as soon as an American seal is prepared, I conjecture the Declaration will be subscribed by all the members." And we have the positive denial of McKean that "no person signed it on that day," and this statement is substantiated by the later action of Congress in specially permitting him to sign what he certainly would have already done on the 4th, had there been the opportunity. Opposed to these direct statements and probabilities, we have Jefferson's positive statement, three times repeated, that such a signing took place, but as he follows his nearly contemporary one with the statements that it was "signed by every member present except Mr. Dickinson," when we have proof positive that all the New York delegates refused to even vote, much less sign, and that Dickinson was not even present in Congress on that day, it is evident that this narrative is not wholly trustworthy.

[40] "I expected you had in the Preamble to our form of Government, exhausted the subject of complaint agt Geo. 3d & was at a loss to discover what Congress would do for one to their Declaration of Independence without copying, but find you have acquitted your selves very well on that score."—*E. Pendleton to Jefferson, July 22.*

"I am also obliged by ye Original Declaration of Independence, which I find your brethren have treated as they did ye Manifesto last summer—altered it much for the worse; their hopes of a Reconciliation might restrain them from plain truths then, but what could cramp them now?"—*E. Pendleton to Jefferson, Aug. 10, 1776.*

A DECLARATION BY THE REPRESENTATIVES OF THE UNITED STATES OF AMERICA, IN GENERAL CONGRESS ASSEMBLED

When in the course of human events it becomes necessary for one people to dissolve the political bands which have connected them with another, and to assume among the powers of the earth the separate & equal station to which the laws of nature and of nature's God entitle them, a decent respect to the opinions of mankind requires that they should declare the causes which impel them to the separation.

We hold these truths to be self-evident: that all men are created equal that they are endowed by their creator with <u>inherent and</u> inalienable rights; that among these are life, liberty, & the pursuit of happiness: that to secure these rights, governments are instituted among men, deriving their just powers from the consent of the governed; that whenever any form of government becomes destructive of these ends, it is the right of the people to alter or abolish it, & to institute new government, laying it's foundation on such principles, & organizing it's powers in such form, as to them shall seem most likely to effect their safety & happiness. Prudence indeed will dictate that governments long established should not be changed for light & transient causes; and accordingly all experience hath shown that mankind are more disposed to suffer while evils are sufferable, than to right themselves by abolishing the forms to which they are accustomed. But when a long train of abuses & usurpations <u>begun at a distinguished period and</u> pursuing invariably the same object, evinces a design to reduce them under absolute despotism, it is their right, it is their duty

certain

to throw off such government, & to provide new guards for their future security. Such has been the patient sufferance of these colonies; & such is now the necessity which constrains them to expunge their former systems of government. The history of the present king of Great Britain is a history of unremitting injuries & usurpations, among which appears no solitary fact to condradict the uniform tenor of the rest but all have in direct object the establishment of an absolute tyranny over these states. To prove this let facts be submitted to a candid world for the truth of which we pledge a faith yet unsullied by falsehood.

alter

repeated

all having

He has refused his assent to laws the most wholesome & necessary for the public good.

He has forbidden his governors to pass laws of immediate & pressing importance, unless suspended in their operation till his assent should be obtained; & when so suspended, he has utterly neglected to attend to them.

He has refused to pass other laws for the accommodation of large districts of people, unless those people would relinquish the right of representation in the legislature, a right inestimable to them, & formidable to tyrants only.

He has called together legislative bodies at places unusual, uncomfortable, and distant from the depository of their public records, for the sole purpose of fatiguing them into compliance with his measures.

He has dissolved representative houses repeatedly & continually for opposing with manly firmness his invasions on the rights of the people.

He has refused for a long time after such dissolutions to cause others to be elected, whereby the legislative powers, incapable of annihilation, have returned to the people at large for their exercise, the state remaining in the meantime exposed to all the dangers of invasion from without & convulsions within.

He has endeavored to prevent the population of these states; for that purpose obstructing the laws for naturalization of foreigners, refusing to pass others to encourage their migrations hither, & raising the conditions of new appropriations of lands.

obstructed by

He has <u>suffered</u> the administration of justice <u>totally to cease in</u> some of these states refusing his assent to laws for establishing judiciary powers.

He has made <u>our</u> judges dependant on his will alone, for the tenure of their offices, & the amount & paiment of their salaries.

He has erected a multitude of new offices <u>by a self assumed power</u> and sent hither swarms of new officers to harass our people and eat out their substance.

He has kept among us in times of peace standing armies <u>and ships</u> of war without the consent of our legislatures.

He has affected to render the military independant of, & superior to the civil power.

He has combined with others to subject us to a jurisdiction foreign to our constitutions & unacknowledged by our laws, giving his assent to their acts of pretended legislation for quartering large bodies of armed troops among us; for protecting them by a mock-trial from punishment for any murders which they should commit on the inhabitants of these states; for cutting off our trade with all parts of the world; for imposing taxes on us

in many cases

without our consent; for depriving us [ ] of the benefits of trial by jury; for transporting us beyond seas to be tried for pretended offences; for abolishing the free system of English laws in a neighboring province, establishing therein an arbitrary government, and enlarging its boundaries, so as to render it at once an example and fit instrument for introducing the same absolute rule into these states; *colonies* for taking away our charters, abolishing our most valuable laws, and altering fundamentally the forms of our governments; for suspending our own legislatures, & declaring themselves invested with power to legislate for us in all cases whatsoever.

He has abdicated government here withdrawing his governors, and declaring us out of his allegiance & protection. *by declaring us out of his protection, and waging war against us.*

He has plundered our seas, ravaged our coasts, burnt our towns, & destroyed the lives of our people.

He is at this time transporting large armies of foreign mercenaries to compleat the works of death, desolation & tyranny already begun with circumstances of cruelty and perfidy [ ] unworthy the head of a civilized nation. *scarcely paralleled in the most barbarous ages, totally*

He has constrained our fellow citizens taken captive on the high seas to bear arms against their country, to become the executioners of their friends & brethren, or to fall themselves by their hands.

He has [ ] endeavored to bring on the inhabitants of our frontiers the merciless Indian savages, whose known rule of warefare is an undistinguished destruction of all ages, sexes, & conditions of existence. *excited domestic insurrection among us, & has*

He has incited treasonable insurrections of our fellow-citizens, with the allurements of forfeiture & confiscation of our property.

He has waged cruel war against human nature itself, violating it's most sacred rights of life and liberty in the persons of a distant people who never offended him, captivating & carrying them into slavery in another hemisphere, or to incur miserable death in their transportation thither. This piratical warfare, the opprobrium of INFIDEL powers, is the warfare of the CHRISTIAN king of Great Brit ain. Determined to keep open a market where MEN should be bought & sold, he has prostituted his negative for suppressing every legislative attempt to prohibit or to restrain this execrable commerce. And that this assemblage of horrors might want no fact of distinguished die, he is now exciting those very people to rise in arms among us, and to purchase that liberty of which he has deprived them, by murdering the people on whom he also obtruded them: thus paying off former crimes committed against the LIBERTIES of one people, with crimes which he urges them to commit against the LIVES of another.

In every stage of these oppressions we have petitioned for redress in the most humble terms: our repeated petitions have been answered only by repeated injuries.

A prince whose character is thus marked by every act which may define a tyrant is unfit to be the ruler of a [ ] people who mean to be free. Future ages will scarcely believe that the hardiness of one man adventured, within the short compass of twelve years only, to lay a foundation so broad & so undisguised for tyranny over a people fostered & fixed in principles of freedom.

free

Nor have we been wanting in attention to our British brethren. We have warned them from time to time of attempts by their legislature to extend a jurisdiction over these our states. We have reminded them of the circumstances of our emigration & settlement here, no one of which could warrant so strange a pretension: that these were effected at the expense of our own blood & treasure, unassisted by the wealth or the strength of Great Britain: that in constituting indeed our several forms of government, we had adopted one common king, thereby laying a foundation for perpetual league & amity with them: but that

an unwarrantable
us

submission to their parliament was no part of our constitution, nor ever in idea, if history may be credited: and, we [ ] appealed to their native justice and magnanimity as well as to the ties of our common kindred to disavow these usurpations which were likely to interrupt our connection and correspondence. They too have been deaf to the voice of justice & of consanguinity, and when occasions have been given them, by the regular course of their laws, of removing from their councils the disturbers of our harmony, they have, by their free election, re-established them in power. At this very time too they are permitting their chief magistrate to send over not only soldiers of our common blood, but Scotch & foreign mercenaries to invade & destroy us. These facts have given the last stab to agonizing affection, and manly spirit bids us to renounce forever these unfeeling brethren. We must endeavor to forget our former love for them, and hold them as we hold the rest of mankind, enemies in war, in peace friends. We might have been a free and a great people together; but a communication of grandeur & of freedom it seems is below their dignity. Be it so, since they will have it. The road to happiness & to glory is open to us too. We will tread it apart from them, and acquiesce in the necessity which denounces our eternal separation [ ]!

have
and we have conjured them by
would inevitably

We must therefore
and hold them as we hold the rest of mankind, enemies in war, in peace, friends.

We therefore the representatives of the United States of America in General Congress assembled do in the name & by authority of the good people of these states reject & renounce all allegiance & subjection to the kings of Great Britain & all others who may hereafter claim by, through or under them: we utterly dissolve	We therefore the representatives of the United States of America in General Congress assembled, appealing to the supreme judge of the world for the rectitude of our intentions, do in the name, & by the authority of the good people of these colonies, solemnly publish and declare that these united colonies are & of right ought

all political connection which may heretofore have subsisted between us & the people or parliament of Great Britain: & finally we do assert & declare these colonies to be free & independent states, & that as free & independent states, they have full power to levy war, conclude peace, contract alliances, establish commerce, & to do all other acts & things which independent states may of right do.	to be free & independent states; that they are absolved from all allegiance to the British crown, and that all political connection between them & the state of Great Britain is, & ought to be, totally dissolved; & that as free & independent states they have full power to levy war, conclude peace, contract alliances, establish commerce & to do all other acts & things which independent states may of right do.
And for the support of this declaration we mutually pledge to each other our lives, our fortunes, & our sacred honor.	And for the support of this declaration, with a firm reliance on the protection of divine providence we mutually pledge to each other our lives, our fortunes, & our sacred honor.[41]

The Declaration thus signed on the 4th, on paper was engrossed on parchment, & signed again on the 2d. of August.[42]

[41] This is printed just as Jefferson prepared it for the press. By comparing it with the text as printed *post*, under July 4, 1776, it will be seen that he took the liberty of somewhat changing and even expunging portions.

[42] This is an interlineation made at a later period—apparently after the question as to the signing of the declaration was raised. Jefferson has also written the following on a slip and pasted it on the sheet:

"Some erroneous statements of the proceedings on the declaration of independence having got before the public in latter times, Mr. Samuel A. Wells asked explanations of me, which are given in my letter to him of May 12. 19. before and now again referred to. I took notes in my place while these things were going on, and at their close wrote them out in form and with correctness and from 1 to 7 of the two preceding sheets are the originals then written; as the two following are of the earlier debates on the Confederation, which I took in like manner."

JAMES MADISON

Examination of the Constitution

[*The Constitution of the United States of America had to be "sold" to the states and to the people, even after it was drawn up at the Constitutional Convention which assembled in Philadelphia on May 14, 1787, and the men to whom fell this difficult task were Alexander Hamilton, James Madison and John Jay. It was a difficult task, because here was a unique instrument in the holding together of a nation and in the governance of its peoples; the War of the Revolution, although it ended in victory for the confederation of states that had been British colonies in America, ended also in economic disaster; a depression seized upon the country; the new nation's finances were in collapse and its revolutionary paper currency worthless. The war had been fought largely on the question of taxation; so all proposals to raise money to support a central government were met with hostility and even open revolt. Ratification of the Constitution by nine of the thirteen states was necessary before the nation as a unit could exist.*

In October, 1787, there began to appear in the newspapers of New York the first of a series of eighty-five articles, signed "Publius", written in exposition and in defense of the new Constitution which was to take the place of the anarchical Articles of Confederation. These newspaper exhortations turned out to be the joint work of three young men, Hamilton (thirty), Madison (thirty-six) and Jay (forty-two), each animated by slightly different economic and political convictions but all united upon the imperative necessity of ratification before the union fell apart into a jealous and warring group of separate states. The principal political philosophy at issue was as to whether the new government was to be one with a strong central government to which the will of the separate states would be subordinate or whether it would be a representative government in which each state would enjoy a certain autonomy but in which the whole would be the strength of the sum of its parts. Hamilton was dubious about the democratic principle and, having little faith in the political sense of the common man, favored a limitation of state's rights and a concentration of power into the hands of a relative few; but his tendency to betray the political interests of the nation into the hands of the rich was tempered by the superior philosophy of Madison, who has been justly called "The Father of the Constitution."

The "Publius" letters appeared in book form in the spring of 1788 under the title "The Federalist," when the separate and joint authorships were identified. The papers constitute the most valuable analysis of, and commentary upon, the Constitution we have ever had, and they are the most elaborate and enlightening statement of the ideas of the "Founding Fathers". The Supreme Court has always gone to the Federalist papers, which are models of the expository style, in threshing out difficult points regarding the meaning of the Constitution.

The first definitive edition of "The Federalist" was prepared by Henry Cabot Lodge and published by G. P. Putnam's Sons in 1888. An edition prepared from this text and including The Call for the Federal Constitution, The Articles of Confederation, Resolutions Transmitting the Constitution to Congress, Washington's letter of Transmittal and The Constitution of the United States, was published in one volume in 1937 by the National Home Library Association of Washington, D.C., with an able introduction by Edward Mead Earle, professor of history at Princeton.]

TO THE PEOPLE OF THE STATE OF NEW YORK:

In reviewing the defects of the existing Confederation, and showing that they cannot be supplied by a government of less energy than that before the public, several of the most important principles of the latter fell of course under consideration. But as the ultimate object of these papers is to determine clearly and fully the merits of this Constitution, and the expediency of adopting it, our plan cannot be complete without taking a more critical and thorough survey of the work of the convention, without examining it on all its sides, comparing it in all its parts, and calculating its probable effects.

That this remaining task may be executed under impressions conducive to a just and fair result, some reflections must in this place be indulged, which candor previously suggests.

It is a misfortune, inseparable from human affairs, that public measures are rarely investigated with that spirit of moderation which is essential to a just estimate of their real tendency to advance or obstruct the public good; and that this spirit is more apt to be diminished than promoted, by those occasions which require an unusual exercise of it. To those who have been led by experience to attend to this consideration, it could not appear surprising, that the act of the convention, which recommends so many important changes and innovations, which may be viewed in so many lights and relations, and which touches the springs of so many passions and interests, should find or excite dispositions unfriendly, both on one side and on the other, to a fair discussion and accurate judgment of its merits. In some, it has been too evident from their own publications, that they have scanned the proposed Constitution, not only with a predisposition to censure, but with a predetermination to condemn; as the language held by others betrays an opposite predetermination or bias, which must render their opinions also of little moment in the question. In placing, however, these different characters on a level, with respect to the weight of their opinions, I wish not to insinuate that there may not be a material difference in the purity of their intentions. It is but just to remark in favor of the latter description, that as our situation is universally admitted to be peculiarly critical, and to require indispensably that something should be done for our relief, the predetermined patron of what has been actually done may have taken his bias from the weight of these considerations, as well as from considerations of a sinister nature. The predetermined adversary, on the other hand, can have been governed by no venial motive whatever. The intentions of the first may be upright, as they may on the contrary be culpable. The views of the last cannot be upright, and must be culpable. But the truth is, that these papers are not addressed to persons falling under either of these characters. They solicit the attention of those only, who add to a sincere zeal for the happiness of their country, a temper favorable to a just estimate of the means of promoting it.

Persons of this character will proceed to an examination of the plan submitted by the convention, not only without a disposition to find or to magnify faults; but will see the propriety of reflecting, that a faultless plan was not to be expected. Nor will they barely make allowances for the errors which may be chargeable on the fallibility to which the convention, as a body of men, were liable; but will keep in mind that they themselves also are but men, and ought not to assume an infallibility in rejudging the fallible opinions of others.

With equal readiness will it be perceived, that besides these inducements to candor, many allowances ought to be made for the difficulties inherent in the very nature of the undertaking referred to the convention.

The novelty of the undertaking immediately strikes us. It has been shown in the course of these papers, that the existing Confederation is founded on principles which are fallacious; that we must consequently change this first foundation, and with it the superstructure resting upon it. It has been shown, that the other confederacies which could be consulted as precedents have been vitiated by the same erroneous principles, and can therefore furnish no other light than that of beacons, which give warning of the course to be shunned, without pointing out that which ought to be pursued. The most that the convention could do in such a situation, was to avoid the errors suggested by the past experience of other countries, as well as of our own; and to provide a convenient mode of rectifying their own errors, as future experience may unfold them.

Among the difficulties encountered by the convention, a very important one must have lain in combining the requisite stability and energy in government, with the inviolable attention due to liberty and to the republican form. Without substantially accomplishing this part of their undertaking, they would have very imperfectly fulfilled the object of their appointment, or the expectation of the public; yet that it could not be easily accomplished, will be denied by no one who is unwilling to betray his ignorance of the subject. Energy in government is essential to that security against external and internal danger, and to that prompt and salutary execution of the laws which enter into the very definition of good government. Stability in government is essential to national character and to the advantages annexed to it, as well as to that repose and confidence in the minds of the people, which are among the chief blessings of civil society. An irregular and mutable legislation is not more an evil in itself than it is odious to the people; and it may be pronounced with assurance that the people of this country, enlightened as they are with regard to the nature, and interested, as the great body of them are, in the effects of good government, will never be satisfied till some remedy be applied to the vicissitudes and uncertainties which characterize the State administrations. On comparing, however, these valuable ingredients with the vital principles of liberty, we must perceive at once the difficulty of mingling them together in their due proportions. The genius of republican liberty seems to demand on one side, not only that all power should be derived from the people, but that those intrusted with it should be kept in dependence on the people, by a short duration of their appointments; and that even during this short period the trust should be placed not in a few, but a number of hands. Stability, on the contrary, requires that the hands in which power is lodged should continue for a length of time the same. A frequent change of men will result from a frequent return of elections; and a frequent change of measures from a frequent change of men: whilst energy in government requires not only a certain duration of power, but the execution of it by a single hand.

How far the convention may have succeeded in this part of their work, will better appear on a more accurate view of it. From the cursory view here taken, it must clearly appear to have been an arduous part.

Not less arduous must have been the task of marking the proper line of partition between the authority of the general and that of the State governments. Every man will be sensible of this difficulty, in proportion as he has been accustomed to contemplate and discriminate objects extensive and complicated in their nature. The faculties of the mind itself have never yet been distinguished and defined, with satisfactory precision, by all the efforts of the most acute and metaphysical philosophers. Sense, perception, judgment, desire, volition, memory, imagination, are found to be separated by such delicate shades and minute gradations that their boundaries have eluded the most subtle investigations, and remain a pregnant source of ingenious disquisition and controversy. The boundaries between the great kingdom of nature, and, still more, between the various provinces, and lesser portions, into which they are subdivided, afford another illustration of the same important truth. The most sagacious and laborious naturalists have never yet succeeded in tracing with certainty the line which separates the district of vegetable life from the neighboring region of unorganized matter, or which marks the termination of the former and the commencement of the animal empire. A still greater obscurity lies in the distinctive characters by which the objects in each of these great departments of nature have been arranged and assorted.

When we pass from the works of nature, in which all the delineations are perfectly accurate, and appear to be otherwise only from the imperfection of the eye which surveys them, to the institutions of man, in which the obscurity arises as well from the object itself as from the organ by which it is contemplated, we must perceive the necessity of moderating still further our expectations and hopes from the efforts of human sagacity. Experience has instructed us that no skill in the science of government has yet been able to discriminate and define, with sufficient certainty, its three great provinces —the legislative, executive, and judiciary; or even the privileges and powers of the different legislative branches. Questions daily occur in the course of practice, which prove the obscurity which reigns in these subjects, and which puzzle the greatest adepts in political science.

The experience of ages, with the continued and combined labors of the most enlightened legislators and jurists, has been equally unsuccessful in delineating the several objects and limits of different codes of laws and different tribunals of justice. The precise extent of the common law, and the statute law, the maritime law, the ecclesiastical law, the law of corporations, and other local laws and customs, remains still to be clearly and finally established in Great Britain, where accuracy in such subjects has been more industriously pursued than in any other part of the world. The jurisdiction of her several courts, general and local, of law, of equity, of admiralty, etc., is not less a source of frequent and intricate discussions, sufficiently denoting the indeterminate limits by which they are respectively circumscribed. All new laws, though penned with the greatest technical skill, and passed on the fullest and most mature deliberation, are considered as more or less obscure and equivocal, until their meaning be liquidated and ascertained by a series of particular discussions and adjudications. Besides the obscurity arising from the complexity of objects, and the imperfection of the human faculties, the medium through which the conceptions of men are conveyed to each other adds a fresh embarrassment. The use of words is to express ideas. Perspicuity, therefore, requires not only that the ideas should be distinctly formed, but that they should be expressed by words distinctly and exclusively appropriate to them. But no language is so copious as to supply words and phrases for every complex idea, or so correct as not to include many equivocally denoting different ideas. Hence it must happen that however accurately objects may be discriminated in themselves, and however accurately the discrimination may be considered, the definition of them may be rendered inaccurate by the inaccuracy of the terms in which it is delivered. And this unavoidable inaccuracy must be greater or less, according to the complexity and novelty of the objects defined. When the Almighty himself condescends to address mankind in their own language, his meaning, luminous as it must be, is rendered dim and doubtful by the cloudy medium through which it is communicated.

Here, then, are three sources of vague and incorrect definitions: indistinctness of the object, imperfection of the organ of conception, inadequateness of the vehicle of ideas. Any one of these must produce a certain degree of obscurity. The convention, in delineating the boundary between the federal and State jurisdictions, must have experienced the full effect of them all.

To the difficulties already mentioned may be added the interfering pretensions of the larger and smaller States. We cannot err in supposing that the former would contend for a participation in the government, fully proportioned to their superior wealth and importance; and that the latter would not be less tenacious of the equality at present enjoyed by them. We may well suppose that neither side would entirely yield to the other, and consequently that the struggle could be terminated only by compromise. It is extremely probable, also, that after the ratio of representation had been adjusted, this very compromise must have produced a fresh struggle between the same parties, to give such a turn to the organization of the government, and to the distribution of its powers, as would increase the importance of the branches, in forming which they had respectively obtained the greatest share of influence. There are features in the Constitution which warrant each of these suppositions; and as far as either of them is well founded, it shows that the convention must have been compelled to sacrifice theoretical propriety to the force of extraneous considerations.

Nor could it have been the large and small States only, which would marshal themselves in opposition to each other on various points. Other combinations, resulting from a difference of local position and policy, must have created additional difficulties. As every State may be divided into different districts, and its citizens into different classes, which give birth to contending interests and local jealousies, so the different parts of the United States are distinguished from each other by a variety of circumstances, which produce a like effect on a larger scale. And although this variety of interests, for reasons sufficiently explained in a former paper, may have a salutary influence on the administration of the government when formed, yet every one must be sensible of the contrary influence, which must have been experienced in the task of forming it.

Would it be wonderful if, under the pressure of all these difficulties, the convention should have been forced into some deviations from that artificial structure and regular symmetry which an abstract view of the subject might lead an ingenious theorist to bestow on a Constitution planned in his closet or in his imagination? The real wonder is that so many difficulties should have been surmounted, and surmounted with a unanimity almost as unprecedented as it must have been unexpected. It is impossible for any man of candor to reflect on this circumstance without partaking of the astonishment. It is impossible for the man of pious reflection not to perceive in it a finger of that Almighty hand which has been so frequently and signally extended to our relief in the critical stages of the revolution.

We had occasion, in a former paper, to take notice of the repeated trials which have been unsuccessfully made in the United Netherlands for reforming the baneful and notorious vices of their constitution. The history of almost all the great councils and consultations held among mankind for reconciling their discordant opinions, assuaging their mutual jealousies, and adjusting their respective interests, is a history of factions, contentions, and disappointments, and may be classed among the most dark and degraded pictures which display the infirmities and depravities of the human character. If, in a few scattered instances, a brighter aspect is presented, they serve only as exceptions to admonish us of the general truth; and by their lustre to darken the gloom of the adverse prospect to which they are contrasted. In revolving the causes from which these exceptions result, and applying them to the particular instances before us, we are necessarily led to two important conclusions. The first is, that the convention must have enjoyed, in a very singular degree, an exemption from the pestilential influence of party animosities—the disease most incident to deliberative bodies, and most apt to contaminate their proceedings. The second conclusion is that all the deputations composing the convention were satisfactorily accommodated by the final act, or were induced to accede to it by a deep conviction of the necessity of sacrificing private opinions and partial interests to the public good, and by a despair of seeing this necessity diminished by delays or by new experiments.

JAMES MADISON

Formation of the Constitution

TO THE PEOPLE OF THE STATE OF NEW YORK:

It is not a little remarkable that in every case reported by ancient history, in which government has been established with deliberation and consent, the task of framing it has not been committed to an assembly of men, but has been performed by some individual citizen of pre-eminent wisdom and approved integrity.

Minos, we learn, was the primitive founder of the government of Crete, as Zaleucus was of that of the Locrians. Theseus first, and after him Draco and Solon, instituted the government of Athens. Lycurgus was the lawgiver of Sparta. The foundation of the original government of Rome was laid by Romulus, and the work completed by two of his elective successors, Numa and Tullius Hostilius. On the abolition of royalty the consular administration was substituted by Brutus, who stepped forward with a project for such a reform, which, he alleged, had been prepared by Tullius Hostilius, and to which his address obtained the assent and ratification of the senate and people. This remark is applicable to confederate governments also. Amphictyon, we are told, was the author of that which bore his name. The Achæan league received its first birth from Achæus, and its second from Aratus.

What degree of agency these reputed lawgivers might have in their respective establishments, or how far they might be clothed with the legitimate authority of the people, cannot in every instance be ascertained. In some, however, the proceeding was strictly regular. Draco appears to have been intrusted by the people of Athens with indefinite powers to reform its government and laws. And Solon, according to Plutarch, was in a manner compelled, by the universal suffrage of his fellow-citizens, to take upon him the sole and absolute power of new-modelling the constitution. The proceedings under Lycurgus were less regular; but as far as the advocates for a regular reform could prevail, they all turned their eyes towards the single efforts of that celebrated patriot and sage, instead of seeking to bring about a revolution by the intervention of a deliberative body of citizens.

Whence could it have proceeded that a people, jealous as the Greeks were of their liberty, should so far abandon the rules of caution as to place their destiny in the hands of a single citizen? Whence could it have proceeded, that the Athenians, a people who would not suffer an army to be commanded by fewer than ten generals, and who required no other proof of danger to their liberties than the illustrious merit of a fellow-citizen, should consider one illustrious citizen as a more eligible depositary of the fortunes of themselves and their posterity, than a select body of citizens, from whose common deliberations more wisdom, as well as more safety, might have been expected? These questions cannot be fully answered, without supposing that the fears of discord and disunion among a number of counsellors exceeded the apprehension of treachery or incapacity in a single individual. History informs us, likewise, of the difficulties with which these celebrated reformers had to contend, as well as the expedients which they were obliged to employ in order to carry their reforms into effect. Solon, who seems to have indulged a more temporizing policy, confessed that he had not given to his countrymen the government best suited to their happiness, but most tolerable to their prejudices. And Lycurgus, more true to his object, was under the necessity of mixing a portion of violence with the authority of superstition, and of securing his final success by a voluntary renunciation, first of his country, and then of his life. If these lessons teach us, on one hand, to admire the improvement made by America on the ancient mode of preparing and establishing regular plans of government, they serve not less, on the other, to admonish us of the hazards and difficulties incident to such experiments, and of the great imprudence of unnecessarily multiplying them.

Is it an unreasonable conjecture, that the errors which may be contained in the plan of the convention are such as have resulted rather from the defect of antecedent experience on this complicated and difficult subject, than from a want of accuracy or care in the investigation of it; and, consequently, such as will not be ascertained until an actual trial shall have pointed them out? This conjecture is rendered probable, not only by many considerations of a general nature, but by the particular case of the Articles of Confederation. It is observable that among the numerous objections and amendments suggested by the several States, when these articles were submitted for their ratification, not one is found which alludes to the great and radical error which on actual trial has discovered itself. And if we except the observations which New Jersey was led to make, rather by her local situation, than by her peculiar foresight, it may be questioned whether a single suggestion was of sufficient moment to justify a revision of the system. There is abundant reason, nevertheless, to suppose that immaterial as these objections were, they would have been adhered to with a very dangerous inflexibility, in some States, had not a zeal for their opinions and supposed interests been stifled by the more powerful sentiment of self-preservation. One State, we may remember, persisted for several years in refusing her concurrence, although the enemy remained the whole period at our gates, or rather in the very bowels of our country. Nor was her pliancy in the end effected by a less motive, than the fear of being chargeable with protracting the public calamities, and endangering the event of the contest. Every candid reader will make the proper reflections on these important facts.

A patient who finds his disorder daily growing worse, and that an efficacious remedy can no longer be delayed without extreme danger, after coolly revolving his situation, and the characters of different physicians, selects and calls in such of them as he judges most capable of administering relief, and best entitled to his confidence. The physicians attend; the case of the patient is carefully examined, a consultation is held; they are unanimously agreed that the symptoms are critical, but that the case, with proper and timely relief, so far from being desperate, that it may be made to issue in an improvement of his constitution. They are equally unanimous in prescribing the remedy, by which this happy effect is to be produced. The prescription is no sooner made known, however, than a number of persons interpose, and, without denying the reality or danger of the disorder, assure the patient that the prescription will be poison to his constitution, and forbid him, under pain of certain death, to make use of it. Might not the patient reasonably demand, before he ventured to follow this advice, that the authors of it should at least agree among themselves on some other remedy to be substituted? And if he found them differing as much from one another as from his first counsellors, would he not act prudently in trying the experiment unanimously recommended by the latter, rather than be hearkening to those who could neither deny the necessity of a speedy remedy, nor agree in proposing one?

Such a patient and in such a situation is America at this moment. She has been sensible of her malady. She has obtained a regular and unanimous advice from men of her own deliberate choice. And she is warned by others against following this advice under pain of the most fatal consequences. Do the monitors deny the reality of her danger? No. Do they deny the necessity of some speedy and powerful remedy? No. Are they agreed, are any two of them agreed, in their objections to the remedy proposed, or in the proper one to be substituted? Let them speak for themselves. This one tells us that the proposed Constitution ought to be rejected, because it is not a confederation of the States, but a government over individuals. Another admits that it ought to be a government over individuals to a certain extent, but by no means to the extent proposed. A third does not object to the government over individuals, or to the extent proposed, but to the want of a bill of rights. A fourth concurs in the absolute necessity of a bill of rights, but contends that it ought to be declaratory, not of the personal rights of individuals, but of the rights reserved to the States in their political capacity. A fifth is of opinion that a bill of rights of any sort would be superflous and misplaced, and that the plan would be unexceptionable but for the fatal power of regulating the times and places of election. An objector in a large State exclaims loudly against the unreasonable equality of representation in the Senate. An objector in a small State is equally loud against the dangerous inequality in the House of Representatives. From this quarter, we are alarmed with the amazing expense, from the number of persons who are to administer the new government. From another quarter, and sometimes from the same quarter, on another occasion, the cry is that the Congress will be but a shadow of a representation, and that the government would be far less objectionable if the number and the expense were doubled. A patriot in a State that does not import or export, discerns insuperable objections against the power of direct taxation. The patriotic adversary in a State of great exports and imports, is not less dissatisfied that the whole burden of taxes may be thrown on consumption. This politician discovers in the Constitution a direct and irresistible tendency to monarchy; that is equally sure it will end in aristocracy. Another is puzzled to say which of these shapes it will ultimately assume, but sees clearly it must be one or other of them; whilst a fourth is not wanting, who with no less confidence affirms that the Constitution is so far from having a bias towards either of these dangers, that the weight on that side will not be sufficient to keep it upright and firm against its opposite propensities. With another class of adversaries to the Constitution the language is that the legislative, executive, and judiciary departments are intermixed in such a manner as to contradict all the ideas of regular government and all the requisite precautions in favor of liberty. Whilst this objection circulates in vague and general expressions, there are but a few who lend their sanction to it. Let each one come forward with his particular explanation, and scarce any two are exactly agreed upon the subject. In the eyes of one the junction of the Senate with the President in the responsible function of appointing to offices, instead of vesting this executive power in the Executive alone, is the vicious part of the organization. To another, the exclusion of the House of Representatives, whose numbers alone could be a due security against corruption and partiality in the exercise of such a power, is equally obnoxious. With another, the admission of the President into any share of a power which must ever be a dangerous engine in the hands of the executive magistrate, is an unpardonable violation of the maxims of republican jealousy. No part of the arrangement, according to some, is more inadmissible than the trial of impeachments by the Senate, which is alternately a member both of the legislative and executive departments, when this power so evidently belonged to the judiciary department. "We concur fully," reply others, "in the objection to this part of the plan, but we can never agree that a reference of impeachments to the judiciary authority would be an amendment of the error. Our principal dislike to the organization arises from the extensive powers already lodged in that department." Even among the zealous patrons of a council of state the most irreconcilable variance is discovered concerning the mode in which it ought to be constituted. The demand of one gentleman is, that the council should consist of a small number to be appointed by the most numerous branch of the legislature. Another would prefer a larger number, and considers it as a fundamental condition that the appointment should be made by the President himself.

As it can give no umbrage to the writers against the plan of the federal Constitution, let us suppose, that as they are the most zealous, so they are also the most sagacious, of those who think the late convention were unequal to the task assigned them, and that a wiser and better plan might and ought to be substituted. Let us further suppose that their country should concur, both in this favorable opinion of their merits, and in their unfavorable opinion of the convention; and should accordingly proceed to form them into a second convention, with full powers, and for the express purpose of revising and remoulding the work of the first. Were the experiment to be seriously made, though it required some effort to view it seriously even in fiction, I leave it to be decided by the sample of opinions just exhibited, whether, with all their enmity to their predecessors, they would, in any one point, depart so widely from their example, as in the discord and ferment that would mark their own deliberations; and whether the Constitution, now before the public, would not stand as fair a chance for immortality, as Lycurgus gave to that of Sparta, by making its change to depend on his own return from exile and death, if it were to be immediately adopted, and were to continue in force, not until a BETTER, but until ANOTHER should be agreed upon by this new assembly of lawgivers.

It is a matter both of wonder and regret, that those who raise so many objections against the new Constitution should never call to mind the defects of that which is to be exchanged for it. It is not necessary that the former should be perfect: it is sufficient that the latter is more imperfect. No man would refuse to give brass for silver or gold, because the latter had some alloy in it. No man would refuse to quit a shattered and tottering habitation for a firm and commodious building, because the latter had not a porch to it, or because some of the rooms might be a little larger or smaller, or the ceiling a little higher or lower than his fancy would have planned them. But waiving illustrations of this sort, is it not manifest that most of the capital objections urged against the new system lie with tenfold weight against the existing Confederation? Is an indefinite power to raise money dangerous in the hands of the federal government? The present Congress can make requisitions to any amount they please, and the States are constitutionally bound to furnish them; they can emit bills of credit as long as they will pay for the paper; they can borrow, both abroad and at home, as long as a shilling will be lent. Is an indefinite power to raise troops dangerous? The Confederation gives to Congress that power also; and they have already begun to make use of it. Is it improper and unsafe to intermix the different powers of government in the same body of men? Congress, a single body of men, are the sole depositary of all the federal powers. Is it particularly dangerous to give the keys of the treasury, and the command of the army, into the same hands? The Confederation places them both in the hands of Congress. Is a bill of rights essential to liberty? The Confederation has no bill of rights. Is it an objection against the new Constitution, that it empowers the Senate, with the concurrence of the Executive, to make treaties which are to be the laws of the land? The existing Congress, without any such control, can make treaties which they themselves have declared, and most of the States have recognized, to be the supreme law of the land. Is the importation of slaves permitted by the new Constitution for twenty years? By the old it is permitted forever.

I shall be told, that however dangerous this mixture of powers may be in theory, it is rendered harmless by the dependence of Congress on the States for the means of carrying them into practice; that however large the mass of powers may be, it is in fact a lifeless mass. Then, say I, in the first place, that the Confederation is chargeable with the still greater folly of declaring certain powers in the federal government to be absolutely necessary, and at the same time rendering them absolutely nugatory; and, in the next place, that if the Union is to continue, and no better government be substituted, effective powers must either be granted to, or assumed by, the existing Congress; in either of which events, the contrast just stated will hold good. But this is not all. Out of this lifeless mass has already grown an excrescent power, which tends to realize all the dangers that can be apprehended from a defective construction of the supreme government of the Union. It is now no longer a point of speculation and hope, that the Western territory is a mine of vast wealth to the United States; and although it is not of such a nature as to extricate them from their present distresses, or, for some time to come, to yield any regular supplies for the public expenses, yet must it hereafter be able, under proper management, both to effect a gradual discharge of the domestic debt, and to furnish, for a certain period, liberal tributes to the federal treasury. A very large proportion of this fund has been already surrendered by individual States; and it may with reason be expected that the remaining States will not persist in withholding similar proofs of their equity and generosity. We may calculate, therefore, that a rich and fertile country, of an area equal to the inhabited extent of the United States, will soon become a national stock. Congress have assumed the administration of this stock. They have begun to render it productive. Congress have undertaken to do more: they have proceeded to form new States, to erect temporary governments, to appoint officers for them, and to prescribe the conditions on which such States shall be admitted into the Confederacy. All this has been done; and done without the least color of constitutional authority. Yet no blame has been whispered; no alarm has been sounded. A GREAT and INDEPENDENT fund of revenue is passing into the hands of a SINGLE BODY of men, who can RAISE TROOPS to an INDEFINITE NUMBER, and appropriate money to their support for an INDEFINITE PERIOD OF TIME. And yet there are men, who have not only been silent spectators of this prospect, but who are advocates for the system which exhibits it; and, at the same time, urge against the new system the objections which we have heard. Would they not act with more consistency, in urging the establishment of the latter, as no less necessary to guard the Union against the future powers and resources of a body constructed like the existing Congress, than to save it from the dangers threatened by the present impotency of that Assembly?

I mean not, by any thing here said, to throw censure on the measures which have been pursued by Congress. I am sensible they could not have done otherwise. The public interest, the necessity of the case, imposed upon them the task of overleaping their constitutional limits. But is not the fact an alarming proof of the danger resulting from a government which does not possess regular powers commensurate to its objects? A dissolution or usurpation is the dreadful dilemma to which it is continually exposed.

JAMES MADISON

The Republican Principle

TO THE PEOPLE OF THE STATE OF NEW YORK.
The last paper having concluded the observations which were meant to introduce a candid survey of the plan of government reported by the convention, we now proceed to the execution of that part of our undertaking.

The first question that offers itself is, whether the general form and aspect of the government be strictly republican. It is evident that no other form would be reconcilable with the genius of the people of America; with the fundamental principles of the Revolution; or with that honorable determination which animates every votary of freedom, to rest all our political experiments on the capacity of mankind for self-government. If the plan of the convention, therefore, be found to depart from the republican character, its advocates must abandon it as no longer defensible.

What, then, are the distinctive characters of the republican form? Were an answer to this question to be sought, not by recurring to principles, but in the application of the term by political writers, to the constitutions of different States, no satisfactory one would ever be found. Holland, in which no particle of the supreme authority is derived from the people, has passed almost universally under the denomination of a republic. The same title has been bestowed on Venice, where absolute power over the great body of the people is exercised, in the most absolute manner, by a small body of hereditary nobles. Poland, which is a mixture of aristocracy and of monarchy in their worst forms, has been dignified with the same appellation. The government of England, which has one republican branch only, combined with an hereditary aristocracy and monarchy, has, with equal impropriety, been frequently placed on the list of republics. These examples, which are nearly as dissimilar to each other as to a genuine republic, show the extreme inaccuracy with which the term has been used in political disquisitions.

If we resort for a criterion to the different principles on which different forms of government are established, we may define a republic to be, or at least may bestow that name on, a government which derives all its powers directly or indirectly from the great body of the people, and is administered by persons holding their offices during pleasure, for a limited period, or during good behavior. It is *essential* to such a government that it be derived from the great body of the society, not from an inconsiderable proportion, or a favored class of it; otherwise a handful of tyrannical nobles, exercising their oppressions by a delegation of their powers, might aspire to the rank of republicans, and claim for their government the honorable title of republic. It is *sufficient* for such a government that the persons administering it be appointed, either directly or indirectly, by the people; and that they hold their appointments by either of the tenures just specified; otherwise every government in the United States, as well as every other popular government that has been or can be well organized or well executed, would be degraded from the republican character. According to the constitution of every State in the Union, some or other of the officers of government are appointed indirectly only by the people. According to most of them, the chief magistrate himself is so appointed. And according to one, this mode of appointment is extended to one of the coördinate branches of the legislature. According to all the constitutions, also, the tenure of the highest offices is extended to a definite period, and in many instances, both within the legislative and executive departments, to a period of years. According to the provisions of most of the constitutions, again, as well as according to the most respectable and received opinions on the subject, the members of the judiciary department are to retain their offices by the firm tenure of good behavior.

On comparing the Constitution planned by the convention with the standard here fixed, we perceive at once that it is, in the most rigid sense, conformable to it. The House of Representatives, like that of one branch at least of all the State legislatures, is elected immediately by the great body of the people. The Senate, like the present Congress, and the Senate of Maryland, derives its appointment indirectly from the people. The President is indirectly derived from the choice of the people, according to the example in most of the States. Even the judges, with all other officers of the Union, will, as in the several States, be the choice, though a remote choice, of the people themselves. The duration of the appointments is equally conformable to the republican standard, and to the model of State constitutions. The

House of Representatives is periodically elective, as in all the States; and for the period of two years, as in the State of South Carolina. The Senate is elective, for the period of six years; which is but one year more than the period of the Senate of Maryland, and but two more than that of the Senates of New York and Virginia. The President is to continue in office for the period of four years; as in New York and Delaware the chief magistrate is elected for three years, and in South Carolina for two years. In the other States the election is annual. In several of the States, however, no constitutional provision is made for the impeachment of the chief magistrate. And in Delaware and Virginia he is not impeachable till out of office. The President of the United States is impeachable at any time during his continuance in office. The tenure by which the judges are to hold their places, is, as it unquestionably ought to be, that of good behavior. The tenure of the ministerial offices generally, will be a subject of legal regulation, conformably to the reason of the case and the example of the State constitutions.

Could any further proof be required of the republican complexion of this system, the most decisive one might be found in its absolute prohibition of titles of nobility, both under the federal and the State governments; and in its express guaranty of the republican form to each of the latter.

"But it was not sufficient," say the adversaries of the proposed Constitution, "for the convention to adhere to the republican form. They ought, with equal care, to have preserved the *federal* form, which regards the Union as a *Confederacy* of sovereign states; instead of which, they have framed a *national* government, which regards the Union as a *consolidation* of the States." And it is asked by what authority this bold and radical innovation was undertaken? The handle which has been made of this objection requires that it should be examined with some precision.

Without inquiring into the accuracy of the distinction on which the objection is founded, it will be necessary to a just estimate of its force, first, to ascertain the real character of the government in question; secondly, to inquire how far the convention were authorized to propose such a government; and thirdly, how far the duty they owed to their country could supply any defect of regular authority.

First.—In order to ascertain the real character of the government, it may be considered in relation to the foundation on which it is to be established; to the sources from which its ordinary powers are to be drawn; to the operation of those powers; to the extent of them; and to the authority by which future changes in the government are to be introduced.

On examining the first relation, it appears, on one hand, that the Constitution is to be founded on the assent and ratification of the people of America, given by deputies elected for the special purpose; but, on the other, that this assent and ratification is to be given by the people, not as individuals composing one entire nation, but as composing the distinct and independent States to which they respectively belong. It is to be the assent and ratification of the several States, derived from the supreme authority in each State,— the authority of the people themselves. The act, therefore, establishing the Constitution, will not be a *national,* but a *federal* act.

That it will be a federal and not a national act, as these terms are understood by the objectors; the act of the people, as forming so many independent States, not as forming one aggregate nation, is obvious from this single consideration, that it is to result neither from the decision of a *majority* of the people of the Union, nor from that of a *majority* of the States. It must result from the *unanimous* assent of the several States that are parties to it, differing no otherwise from their ordinary assent than in its being expressed, not by the legislative authority, but by that of the people themselves. Were the people regarded in this transaction as forming one nation, the will of the majority of the whole people of the United States would bind the minority, in the same manner as the majority in each State must bind the minority; and the will of the majority must be determined either by a comparison of the individual votes, or by considering the will of the majority of the States as evidence of the will of a majority of the people of the United States. Neither of these rules has been adopted. Each State, in ratifying the Constitution, is considered as a sovereign body, independent of all others, and only to be bound by its own voluntary act. In this relation, then, the new Constitution will, if established, be a *federal,* and not a *national* constitution.

The next relation is, to the sources from which the ordinary powers of government are to be derived. The House of Representatives will derive its powers from the people of America; and the people will be represented in the same proportion, and on the same principle, as they are in the legislature of a particular State. So far the government is *national,* not *federal.* The Senate, on the other hand, will derive its powers from the States, as political and coequal societies; and these will be represented on the principle of equality in the Senate, as they now are in the existing Congress. So far the government is *federal,* not *national.* The executive power will be derived from a very compound source. The immediate election of the President is to be made by the States in their political characters. The votes allotted to them are in a compound ratio, which considers them partly as distinct and coequal societies, partly as unequal members of the same society. The eventual election, again, is to be made by that branch of the legislature which consists of the national representatives; but in this particular act they are to be thrown into the form of individual delegations, from so many distinct and coequal bodies politic. From this aspect of the government, it appears to be of a mixed character, presenting at least as many *federal* as *national* features.

The difference between a federal and national government, as it relates to the *operation of the government,* is supposed to consist in this, that in the former the powers operate on the political bodies composing the Confederacy, in their political capacities; in the latter, on the individual citizens composing the nation, in their individual capacities. On trying the Constitution by this criterion, it falls under the *national* not the *federal* character; though perhaps not so completely as has been understood. In several cases, and particularly in the trial of controversies to which States may be parties, they must be viewed and proceeded against in their collective and political capacities only. So far the national countenance of the government on this side seems to be disfigured by a few federal features. But this blemish is perhaps unavoidable in any plan; and the operation of the government on the people, in their individual capacities, in its ordinary and most essential proceedings, may, on the whole, designate it, in this relation, a *national* government.

But if the government be national with regard to the *operation* of its powers, it changes its aspect again when we contemplate it in relation to the *extent* of its powers. The idea of a national government involves in it, not only an authority over the individual citizens, but an indefinite supremacy over all persons and things, so far as they are objects of lawful government. Among a people consolidated into one nation, this supremacy is completely vested in the national legislature. Among communities united for particular purposes, it is vested partly in the general and partly in the municipal legislatures. In the former case, all local authorities are subordinate to the supreme; and may be controlled, directed, or abolished by it at pleasure. In the latter, the local or municipal authorities form distinct and independent portions of the supremacy, no more subject, within their respective spheres, to the general authority, than the general authority is subject to them, within its own sphere. In this relation, then, the proposed government cannot be deemed a *national* one; since its jurisdiction extends to certain enumerated objects only, and leaves to the several States a residuary and inviolable sovereignty over all other objects. It is true that in controversies relating to the boundary between the two jurisdictions, the tribunal which is ultimately to decide, is to be established under the general government. But this does not change the principle of the case. The decision is to be impartially made, according to the rules of the Constitution; and all the usual and most effectual precautions are taken to secure this impartiality. Some such tribunal is clearly essential to prevent an appeal to the sword and a dissolution of the compact; and that it ought to be established under the general rather than under the local governments, or, to speak more properly, that it could be safely established under the first alone, is a position not likely to be combated.

If we try the Constitution by its last relation to the authority by which amendments are to be made, we find it neither wholly *national* nor wholly *federal*. Were it wholly national, the supreme and ultimate authority would reside in the *majority* of the people of the Union; and this authority would be competent at all times, like that of a majority of every national society, to alter or abolish its established government. Were it wholly federal, on the other hand, the concurrence of each State in the Union would be essential to every alteration that would be binding on all. The mode provided by the plan of the convention is not founded on either of these principles. In requiring more than a majority, and particularly in computing the proportion by *States*, not by *citizens*, it departs from the *national* and advances towards the *federal* character; in rendering the concurrence of less than the whole number of States sufficient, it loses again the *federal* and partakes of the *national* character.

The proposed Constitution, therefore, is, in strictness, neither a national nor a federal Constitution, but a composition of both. In its foundation it is federal, not national; in the sources from which the ordinary powers of the government are drawn, it is partly federal and partly national; in the operation of these powers, it is national, not federal; in the extent of them, again, it is federal, not national; and, finally, in the authoritative mode of introducing amendments, it is neither wholly federal nor wholly national.

ALEXANDER HAMILTON OR JAMES MADISON

On a Just Partition of Power

TO THE PEOPLE OF THE STATE OF NEW YORK:

To what expedient shall we finally resort, for maintaining in practice the necessary partition of power among the several departments, as laid down in the Constitution? The only answer that can be given is, that as all these exterior provisions are found to be inadequate, the defect must be supplied, by so contriving the interior structure of the government as that its several constituent parts may, by their mutual relations, be the means of keeping each other in their proper places. Without presuming to undertake a full development of this important idea, I will hazard a few general observations, which may perhaps place it in a clearer light, and enable us to form a more correct judgment of the principles and structure of the government planned by the convention.

In order to lay a due foundation for that separate and distinct exercise of the different powers of government, which to a certain extent is admitted on all hands to be essential to the preservation of liberty, it is evident that each department should have a will of its own; and consequently should be so constituted that the members of each should have as little agency as possible in the appointment of the members of the others. Were this principle rigorously adhered to, it would require that all the appointments for the supreme executive, legislative, and judiciary magistracies should be drawn from the same fountain of authority, the people, through channels having no communication whatever with one another. Perhaps such a plan of constructing the several departments would be less difficult in practice than it may in contemplation appear. Some difficulties, however, and some additional expense would attend the execution of it. Some deviations, therefore, from the principle must be admitted. In the constitution of the judiciary department in particular, it might be inexpedient to insist rigorously on the principle: first, because peculiar qualifications being essential in the members, the primary consideration ought to be to select that mode of choice which best secures these qualifications; secondly, because the permanent tenure by which the appointments are held in that department, must soon destroy all sense of dependence on the authority conferring them.

It is equally evident, that the members of each department should be as little dependent as possible on those of the others, for the emoluments annexed to their offices. Were the executive magistrate, or the judges, not independent of the legislature in this particular, their independence in every other would be merely nominal.

But the great security against a gradual concentration of the several powers in the same department, consists in giving to those who administer each department the necessary constitutional means and personal motives to resist encroachments of the others. The provision for defence must in this, as in all other cases, be made commensurate to the danger of attack. Ambition must be made to counteract ambition. The interest of the man must be connected with the constitutional rights of the place. It may be a reflection on human nature, that such devices should be necessary to control the abuses of government. But what is government itself, but the greatest of all reflections on human nature? If men were angels, no government would be necessary. If angels were to govern men, neither external nor internal controls on government would be necessary. In framing a government which is to be administered by men over men, the great difficulty lies in this: you must first enable the government to control the governed; and in the next place oblige it to control itself. A dependence on the people is, no doubt, the primary control on the government; but experience has taught mankind the necessity of auxiliary precautions.

This policy of supplying, by opposite and rival interests, the defect of better motives, might be traced through the whole system of human affairs, private as well as public. We see it particularly displayed in all the subordinate distributions of power, where the constant aim is to divide and arrange the several offices in such a manner as that each may be a check on the other—that the private interest of every individual may be a sentinel over the public rights. These inventions of prudence cannot be less requisite in the distribution of the supreme powers of the State.

But it is not possible to give to each department an equal power of self-defence. In republican government, the legislative authority necessarily predominates. The remedy for this inconveniency is to divide the legislature into different branches; and to render them, by different modes of election and different principles of action, as little connected with each other as the nature of their common functions and their common dependence on the society will admit. It may even be necessary to guard against dangerous encroachments by still further precautions. As the weight of the legislative authority requires that it should be thus divided, the weakness of the executive may require, on the other hand, that it should be fortified. An absolute negative on the legislature appears, at first view, to be the natural defence with which the executive magistrate should be armed. But perhaps it would be neither altogether safe nor alone sufficient. On ordinary occasions it might not be exerted with the requisite firmness, and on extraordinary occasions it might be perfidiously abused. May not this defect of an absolute negative be supplied by some qualified connection between this weaker department and the weaker branch of the stronger department, by which the latter may be led to support the constitutional rights of the former, without being too much detached from the rights of its own department?

If the principles on which these observations are founded be just, as I persuade myself they are, and they be applied as a criterion to the several State constitutions, and to the federal Constitution, it will be found that if the latter does not prefectly correspond with them, the former are infinitely less able to bear such a test.

There are, moreover, two considerations particularly applicable to the federal system of America, which place that system in a very interesting point of view.

First. In a single republic, all the power surrendered by the people is submitted to the administration of a single government; and the usurpations are guarded against by a division of the government into distinct and separate departments. In the compound republic of America, the power surrendered by the people is first divided between two distinct governments, and then the portion allotted to each subdivided among distinct and separate departments. Hence a double security arises to the rights of the people. The different governments will control each other, at the same time that each will be controlled by itself.

Second. It is of great importance in a republic not only to guard the society against the oppression of its rulers, but to guard one part of the society against the injustice of the other part. Different interests necessarily exist in different classes of citizens. If a majority be united by a common interest, the rights of the minority will be insecure. There are but two methods of providing against this evil: the one by creating a will in the community independent of the majority—that is, of the society itself; the other, by comprehending in the society so many separate descriptions of citizens as will render an unjust combination of a majority of the whole very improbable, if not impracticable. The first method prevails in all governments possessing an hereditary or self-appointed authority. This, at best, is but a precarious security; because a power independent of the society may as well espouse the unjust views of the major, as the rightful interests of the minor party, and may possibly be turned against both parties. The second method will be exemplified in the federal republic of the United States. Whilst all authority in it will be derived from and dependent on the society, the society itself will be broken into so many parts, interests, and classes of citizens, that the rights of individuals, or of the minority, will be in little danger from interested combinations of the majority. In a free government the security for civil rights must be the same as that for religious rights. It consists in the one case in the multiplicity of interests, and in the other in the multiplicity of sects. The degree of security in both cases will depend on the number of interests and sects; and this may be presumed to depend on the extent of country and number of people comprehended under the same government. This view of the subject must particularly recommend a proper federal system to all the sincere and considerate friends of republican government, since it shows that in exact proportion as the territory of the Union may be formed into more circumscribed Confederacies, or States, oppressive combinations of a majority will be facilitated; the best security, under the republican forms, for the rights of every class of citizens, will be diminished; and consequently the stability and independence of some member of the government, the only other security, must be proportionally increased. Justice is the end of government. It is the end of civil society. It ever has been and ever will be pursued until it be obtained, or until liberty be lost in the pursuit. In a society under the forms of which the stronger faction can readily unite and oppress the weaker, anarchy may as truly be said to reign as in a state of nature, where the weaker individual is not secured against the violence of the stronger; and as, in the latter state, even the stronger individuals are prompted, by the uncertainty of their condition, to submit to a government which may protect the weak as well as themselves; so, in the former state, will the more powerful factions or parties be gradually induced, by a like motive, to wish for a government which will protect all parties, the weaker as well as the more powerful. It can be little doubted that if the State of Rhode Island was separated from the Confederacy and left to itself, the insecurity of rights under the popular form of government within such narrow limits would be displayed by such reiterated oppressions of factious majorities that some power altogether independent of the people would soon be called for by the voice of the very factions whose misrule had proved the necessity of it. In the extended republic of the United States, and among the great variety of interests, parties, and sects which it embraces, a coalition of a majority of the whole society could seldom take place on any other principles than those of justice and the general good; whilst there being thus less danger to a minor from the will of a major party, there must be less pretext, also, to provide for the security of the former, by introducing into the government a will not dependent on the latter, or, in other words, a will independent of the society itself. It is no less certain than it is important, notwithstanding the contrary opinions which have been entertained, that the larger the society, provided it lie within a practical sphere, the more duly capable it will be of self-government. And happily for the *republican cause,* the practicable sphere may be carried to a very great extent, by a judicious modification and mixture of the *federal principle.*

WILLIAM CABELL BRUCE

Benjamin Franklin

IN READING the life of Benjamin Franklin, the most lasting impressions left upon the mind are those of versatility and abundance. His varied genius lent itself without effort to the minutest details of such commonplace things as the heating and ventilation of rooms, the correction of smoky chimneys and naval architecture and economy. His severely practical turn of mind was disclosed even in the devices with which he is pictured in his old age as relieving the tedium of physical effort—the rolling press with which he copied his letters, the fan which he worked with his foot in warm weather as he sat reading, the artificial hand with which he reached the books on the upper shelves of his library. But, sober as Franklin's genius on this side was, it proved itself equal to some of the most exacting demands of physical science; and above all to the sublime task, which created such a world-wide stir, of reducing the wild and mysterious lightning of the heavens to captivity, and bringing it down in fluttering helplessness to the earth. It was a rare mind indeed which could give happy expression to homely maxims of plodding thrift, and yet entertain noble visions of universal philanthropy. The stretch between Franklin's weighty observations on Population, for instance, and the bright, graceful bagatelles, with which his pen occasionally trifled, was not a short one; but it was compassed by his intellect without the slightest evidence of halting facility. It is no exaggeration to say that this intellect was an organ lacking in no element of power except that which can be supplied by a profound spiritual insight and a kindling imagination alone. *The Many-Sided Franklin,* the title of the essay by Paul Leicester Ford, is a felicitous touch of description. The life, the mind, the character of the man were all manifold, composite, marked by spacious breadth and freedom. It is astonishing into how many different provinces his career can be divided. Franklin, the Man of Business, Franklin, the Philosopher, Franklin, the Writer, Franklin, the Statesman, Franklin, the Diplomatist, have all been the subjects of separate literary treatment. As a man of business, he achieved enough, when the limitations of his time and environment are considered, to make him a notable precursor of the strong race of self-created men, bred by the later material expansion of America. As a scientist, his brilliant electrical discoveries gave him for a while, as contemporary literature so strikingly evinces, a position of extraordinary pre-eminence. As a writer, he can claim the distinction of having composed two productions, *The Autobiography* and *The Way to Wealth,* which are read the world over. Of his reputation as a statesman it is enough to remark that his signature is attached to the Declaration of Independence, the Treaty of Alliance between the United States and France, the Treaty of Peace between Great Britain and the United States, and the Federal Constitution. Of his labors as a diplomatist it may be said that, if it is true that, without the continuous assistance of France, our independence would not have been secured, it is perhaps equally true that, without his wisdom, tact and European prestige, we should never have retained this assistance, so often imperilled by the jealousy and vanity of his colleagues as well as by the usual accidents of international intercourse. His life was like a full five-act play—prophetic prologue and stately epilogue, and swelling scene imposed upon swelling scene, until the tallow chandler's son, rising from the humblest levels of human fortune to the highest by uninterrupted gradations of invincible success, finally becomes the recipient of such a degree of impressive homage as has rarely been paid to anyone by the admiration and curiosity of mankind.

To such a diversified career as this the element of mere longevity was, of course, indispensable. Renown so solid and enduring as that of Franklin and acquired in so many different fields was not a thing to be achieved by a few fortunate strokes. He did not awake one morning, as did Byron, to find himself famous; though his fame in the province of electrical science travelled fast when it once got under way. Such a full-orbed renown could be produced only by the long gestation of many years of physical vigor and untiring activity. With the meagre opportunities afforded by colonial conditions for the accumulation of wealth, there had to be an extended period of unflagging attention to Poor Richard's saying: "Many a little makes a mickle." To this period belonged some things that the self-revelation of the *Autobiography,* unselfish as it is, cannot dignify, or even redeem from moral squalor, and other things which even the frankness itself of the *Autobiography* is not frank enough to disclose. Then there is the unique story, imprinted upon the face of Philadelphia to this day, of his fruitful exertions as Town Oracle and City Builder. Then there is the episode of scientific inquiry, all too brief, when the prosperous printer and tradesman, appraising wealth at its true value, turns away from his printing press and stock of merchandise to give himself up with enthusiastic ardor to the study of electrical phenomena. Then there is the long term of public employment, beginning with the Clerkship of the Pennsylvania Assembly and not ending until, after many years of illustrious public service as legislator, administrator, diplomatic agent and foreign minister, Franklin complains in a letter to Dr. and Mrs. John Bard that the public, not content with eating his flesh, seems resolved to pick his bones.

The amount of work that he did, the mass of results that he accomplished, during the long tract of time covered by his life, is simply prodigious. Primarily, Franklin was a man of action. The reputation that he coveted most was, as he declared, in a letter to Samuel Mather, that of a doer of good. Utility was the standard set by him for all his activities, and even his system of ethics did not escape the hard griping pressure of this standard. What he aimed at from first to last, whether in the domain of science, literature or government, was practical results, and men, as they are known to experienced and shrewd, though kindly, observers of men, were the agencies with which he sought to accomplish such results. He never lost sight of the sound working principle, which the mere academician or closet philosopher is so prone to forget, that the game cannot be played except with the chess-men upon the board. But happily for the world few men of action have ever bequeathed to posterity such abundant written records of their lives. When Franklin desired to promote any project or to carry any point, he invariably, or all but invariably, invoked the aid of his pen to attain his end. To write for money, or for the mere pleasure of writing, or even for literary fame was totally alien to the purposes for which he wrote. A pen was to him merely another practical instrument for forwarding some private aim of his or some definite public or political object, to which his sympathies and powers were committed, or else but an aid to social amusement. As the result of this secondary kind of literary activity, he left behind him a body of writings of one kind or another which enables us to measure far more accurately than we should otherwise have been able to do the amount of thought and performance crowded into those eventful years of lusty and prolific existence. In the Library of Congress, in the Library of the American Philosophical Society, in the Library of the University of Pennsylvania, in numerous other collections in both hemispheres are found the outflowings of a brain to which exuberance of production was as natural as rank vegetation to a fat soil. Nor should it be forgotten that many of his papers have perished, which, if still extant, would furnish additional proofs of the fertility of his genius and swell the sum of pleasure and instruction which we derive from his works. With the sigh that we breathe over the lost productions of antiquity might well be mingled another over the papers and letters which were confided by Franklin, on the eve of his mission to France, to the care of Joseph Galloway, only to fall a prey to ruthless spoliation and dispersion. To look forward to a long winter evening enlivened by the missing letters that he wrote to his close friends, Jonathan Shipley, Bishop of St. Asaph's, "the good Bishop," as he called him, Sir Edward Newenham, of the Irish Parliament, and Jan Ingenhousz, physician to Maria Theresa, would alone, to one familiar with his correspondence, be as inviting a prospect as could be held out to any reader with a relish for the intimate letters of a wise, witty and humorous letter-writer.

The length of time during which the subtle and powerful mind of Franklin was at work is, we repeat, a fact that must be duly taken into account in exploring the foundations of his celebrity. "By living twelve years beyond David's period," he said in one of his letters to George Whatley, "I seem to have intruded myself into the company of posterity, when I ought to have been abed and asleep." He was born in Boston, Massachusetts, on January 6 (old style), 1706, and died in the City of Philadelphia on April 17, 1790. At the time of his birth, Anne was in the fourth year of her reign as Queen of England, and Louis XIV, was King of France. Only eighty-five years had elapsed since the landing at Plymouth. More than three years were to elapse before the battle of Malplaquet, more than five years before the publication of the first *Spectator,* twenty years before the publication of *Gulliver's Travels.* Franklin's name was an honored one not only in his native land but beyond seas before any of the other great men who signed the Declaration of Independence had emerged from provincial obscurity. His birth preceded that of Washington by twenty-six years, that of John Adams by thirty years, that of Jefferson by thirty-seven years. Coming into the world only fifteen years after the outbreak of the witchcraft delusion at Salem, he lived to be a member of the Federal Convention and to pass down to us as modern in spirit and purpose as the American House of Representatives or the American Patent Office. He, at least, is a standing refutation of the claim that all the energetic tasks of human life are performed by young men. He was seventy years of age when he arrived in France to enter upon the laborious diplomatic career which so signally increased the lustre of his fame and so gloriously prospered our national fortunes; and he was seventy-nine years of age when his mission ended. But even then, weighed down though he was by the strong hand of time and vexed by diseases which left him little peace, there was no danger that he would be classed by anyone with the old townsmen of whom Lord Bacon speaks "that will be still sitting at their Street doore though thereby they offer Age to Scorne." After his return from France, he lived long enough to be thrice elected President of the State of Pennsylvania and to be a useful member of the Convention that framed the Federal Constitution; and only twenty-four days before his death he wrote the speech of Sidi Mehemet Ibrahim on the petition of the Erika, or Purists for the abolition of piracy and slavery which is one of the happiest effusions of his satirical genius.

Multos da annos is a prayer, we may readily believe, that is often granted by the Gods with a scornful smile. In the case of Franklin, even without such a protracted term of life as was his portion, he would still have enjoyed a distinguished place in the memory of men, but not that broad, branching, full-crowned fame which makes him one of the most conspicuous landmarks of the eighteenth century.

And fully in keeping with the extent of this fame was the extent of his relationship to the social and intellectual world of his time. The main background of his life, of course, was American—Lake Champlain, the St. Lawrence, the Charles, the Connecticut, the Hudson, the Delaware and the Ohio rivers; the long western reaches of the Atlantic; the dark curtain of firs and hemlocks and primeval masses of rock which separated the two powers that ceaselessly struggled for the mastery of the continent, and rarely lifted except to reveal some appalling tragedy, chargeable to the French and their dread ally, the Red Indian; Boston, New York, Philadelphia, Fort Duquesne —all the internal features and surroundings in a word of the long, narrow strip of English territory between Boston and Philadelphia with which he was so familiar, and over which his influence was asserted in so many ways. With the exception of his brief sojourn in London in his youth, his whole life was passed in the Colonies until he was fifty-one years of age. Before he sailed for England in 1757, upon his first foreign mission, the circumstances of his career had been such as to make him generally known to the people of the Colonies. His *Almanac,* his *Gazette,* his pithy sayings, his humorous stories, his visits to Boston, attended by the formation of so many wayside friendships, his postal expeditions, the printing presses set up by him at many different points, his private fortune, his public services, his electrical experiments were all breath for the trump of his fame. He knew Colonial America as few Colonial Americans knew it. He was born and reared in Boston, and, after his removal to Philadelphia, he revisited his native city at regular intervals. "The Boston manner, turn of phrase, and even tone of voice, and accent in pronunciation, all please, and seem to refresh and revive me," he said in his old age in a letter to the Rev. John Lathrop. Philadelphia, the most populous and opulent of the colonial towns, was his lifelong place of residence. In the *Autobiography* he refers to it as "A city I love, having lived many years in it very happily." He appears to have been quite frequently in New York. His postal duties took him as far south as Williamsburg, and the Albany Congress drew him as far north of New York as Albany. He was in the camp of Braddock at Frederick, Maryland, just before that rash and ill-starred general set out upon his long, dolorous march through the wilderness where disaster and death awaited him. Facts like these signify but little now when transit from one distant point to another in the United States is effected with such amazing rapidity, but they signified much under the crude conditions of colonial life. Once at least did Franklin have his shoulder dislocated by an accident on the atrocious roads of Colonial New England. Once he was thrown into the water from an upset canoe near Staten Island. His masterly answers, when examined before the House of Commons, showed how searchingly conversant he was with everything that related to America. For some of our most penetrating glances into colonial life we are indebted to his writings; particularly instructive being his observations upon population in the Colonies, the economic condition and political temper of their people and the characteristics and habits of the Indians. It was a broad experience which touched at one extreme the giddy and artificial life of Paris, on the eve of the French Revolution, and at the other the drunken Indian orgies at the conclusion of the treaty at Carlisle which Franklin has depicted in the *Autobiography* with a brush worthy of Rembrandt in these words: "Their dark-colour'd bodies, half naked, seen only by the gloomy light of the bonfire, running after and beating one another with firebrands, accompanied by their horrid yellings, form'd a scene the most resembling our ideas of hell that could well be imagin'd."

But the peculiar distinction of Franklin is that his life stands out vividly upon an European as well as an American background. It is interesting to contrast the scene at Carlisle with the opera in honor of the Comte du Nord, at which he was present, during the French mission. "The House," he says in his *Journal of the Negotiation for Peace with Great Britain,* "being richly finish'd with abundance of Carving and Gilding, well Illuminated with Wax Tapers, and the Company all superbly drest, many of the Men in Cloth of Tissue, and the Ladies sparking with Diamonds, form'd altogether the most splendid Spectacle my Eyes ever beheld." Until the august figure of Washington filled the eye of mankind, Franklin was the only American who had ever won a solid and splendid European reputation. The opportunity had not yet arisen for the lively French imagination to declare that he had snatched the sceptre from tyrants, but the first half of Turgot's tremendous epigram had been realized; for the lightning he had snatched, or rather filched, from the sky. It may well be doubted whether any one private individual with such limited pecuniary resources ever did as much for the moral and intellectual welfare of any one community as Franklin did for pre-revolutionary Philadelphia; but it was impossible that such aspirations and powers as his should be confined within the pale of colonial provincialism. His widespread fame, his tolerant disposition, his early residence in England, his later residence there for long periods, his excursions into Scotland and Ireland and Continental countries, the society of men of the world in London and other great cities combined to endow him with a character truly cosmopolitan which was to be still further liberalized by French influence. During his life, he crossed the Atlantic no less than eight times. After 1757 the greater part of his life was spent abroad. Of the eighty-four years, of which his existence was made up, some twenty-six were passed in England and France. He was as much at home on The Strand as on Market Street in Philadelphia. The friendships that he formed in England and France were almost as close as those that he had formed in Pennsylvania with his cronies, Hugh Roberts and John Bartram. He became so thoroughly domesticated in England during his periods of sojourn in that country that he thought of remaining there for the rest of his life, and yet, if the Brillons had only been willing to confer the hand of their daughter upon his grandson, William Temple Franklin, he would contentedly have died in France. If there ever was an American, if there ever was a citizen of the world, if there ever was a true child of the eighteenth century, it was he. His humanitarian sympathies, his catholic temper, his generous, unobstructed outlook enabled him without difficulty to adjust himself with ease to the genius of every people with whom he was brought into familiar contact. In America he was such a thorough American in every respect that Carlyle is said to have termed him on one occasion, "The Father of all the Yankees." In England he was English enough to feel the full glow of her greatness and to see her true interests far more clearly than she saw them herself. He had too many Anglo-Saxon traits to become wholly a Frenchman when he lived in France, but he became French enough truly to love France and her people and to be truly beloved by them. In the opinions of Sainte-Beuve he is the most French of all Americans.

THEODORE ROOSEVELT

The Purchase of Louisiana; and Burr's Conspiracy

A GREAT and growing race may acquire vast stretches of scantily peopled territory in any one of several ways. Often the statesman, no less than the soldier, plays an all-important part in winning the new land; nevertheless, it is usually true that the diplomatists who, by treaty, ratify the acquisition, usurp a prominence in history to which they are in no way entitled by the real worth of their labors.

The territory may be gained by the armed forces of the nation, and retained by treaty. It was in this way that England won the Cape of Good Hope from Holland; it was in this way that the United States won New Mexico. Such a conquest is due, not to the individual action of members of the winning race, but to the nation as a whole, acting through her soldiers and statesmen. It was the English navy which conquered the Cape of Good Hope for England; it was the English diplomats that secured its retention. So it was the American army which added New Mexico to the United States; and its retention was due to the will of the politicians who had set that army in motion. In neither case was there any previous settlement of moment by the conquerors in the conquered territory. In neither case was there much direct pressure by the people of the conquering races upon the soil which was won for them by their soldiers and statesmen. The acquisition of the territory must be set down to the credit of these soldiers and statesmen, representing the nation in its collective capacity; though in the case of New Mexico there would of course ultimately have been a direct pressure of rifle-bearing settlers upon the people of the ranches and the mud-walled towns.

In such cases it is the government itself, rather than any individual or aggregate of individuals, which wins the new land for the race. When it is won without appeal to arms, the credit, which would otherwise be divided between soldiers and statesmen, of course accrues solely to the latter. Alaska, for instance, was acquired by mere diplomacy. No American settlers were thronging into Alaska. The desire to acquire it among the people at large was vague, and was fanned into sluggish activity only by the genius of the far-seeing statesmen who purchased it. The credit of such an acquisition really does belong to the men who secured the adoption of the treaty by which it was acquired. The honor of adding Alaska to the national domain belongs to the statesmen who at the time controlled the Washington government. They were not figureheads in the transaction. They were the vital, moving forces.

Just the contrary is true of cases like that of the conquest of Texas. The government of the United States had nothing to do with winning Texas for the English-speaking people of North America. The American frontiersmen won Texas for themselves, unaided either by the statesmen who controlled the politics of the Republic or by the soldiers who took their orders from Washington.

In yet other cases the action is more mixed. Statesmen and diplomats have some share in shaping the conditions under which a country is finally taken; in the eye of history they often usurp much more than their proper share; but in reality they are able to bring matters to a conclusion only because adventurous settlers, in defiance or disregard of governmental action, have pressed forward into the longed-for land. In such cases the function of the diplomats is one of some importance, because they lay down the conditions under which the land is taken; but the vital question as to whether the land shall be taken at all, upon no matter what terms, is answered not by the diplomats, but by the people themselves.

It was in this way that the Northwest was won from the British, and the boundaries of the Southwest established by treaty with the Spaniards. Adams, Jay, and Pinckney deserve much credit for the way they conducted their several negotiations; but there would have been nothing for them to negotiate about had not the settlers already thronged into the disputed territories or strenuously pressed forward against their boundaries.

So it was with the acquisition of Louisiana. Jefferson, Livingston, and their fellow statesmen and diplomats concluded the treaty which determined the manner in which it came into our possession; but they did not really have much to do with fixing the terms even of this treaty; and the part which they played in the acquisition of Louisiana in no way resembles, even remotely, the part which was played by Seward, for instance, in acquiring Alaska. If it had not been for Seward, and the political leaders who thought as he did, Alaska might never have been acquired at all; but the Americans would have won Louisiana in any event, even if the treaty of Livingston and Monroe had not been signed. The real history of the acquisition must tell of the great westward movement begun in 1769, and not merely of the feeble diplomacy of Jefferson's administration. In 1802 American settlers were already clustered here and there on the eastern fringe of the vast region which then went by the name of Louisiana. All the stalwart freemen who had made their rude clearings, and built their rude towns, on the hither side of the mighty Mississippi, were straining with eager desire against the forces which withheld them from seizing with strong hand the coveted province. They did not themselves know, and far less did the public men of the day realize, the full import and meaning of the conquest upon which they were about to enter. For the moment the navigation of the mouth of the Mississippi seemed to them of the first importance. Even the frontiersmen themselves put second to this the right to people the vast continent which lay between the Pacific and the Mississippi. The statesmen at Washington viewed this last proposition with positive alarm, and cared only to acquire New Orleans. The winning of Louisiana was due to no one man, and least of all to any statesman or set of statesmen. It followed inevitably upon the great westward thrust of the settler-folk—a thrust which was delivered blindly, but which no rival race could parry until it was stopped by the ocean itself.

Louisiana was added to the United States because the hardy backwoods settlers had swarmed into the valleys of the Tennessee, the Cumberland, and the Ohio by hundreds of thousands; and had hardly begun to build their raw hamlets on the banks of the Mississippi, and to cover its waters with their flat-bottomed craft. Restless, adventurous, hardy, they looked eagerly across the Mississippi to the fertile solitudes where the Spaniard was the nominal, and the Indian the real, master; and with a more immediate longing they fiercely coveted the creole province at the mouth of the river.

The Mississippi formed no barrier whatsoever to the march of the backwoodsmen. It could be crossed at any point; and the same rapid current which made it a matter of extreme difficulty for any power at the mouth of the stream to send reinforcements up against the current would have greatly facilitated the movements of the Ohio, Kentucky, and Tennessee levies downstream to attack the Spanish provinces. In the days of sails and oars a great river with rapid current might vitally affect military operations if these depended upon sending flotillas up or down stream. But such a river has never proved a serious barrier against a vigorous and aggressive race, where it lies between two peoples, so that the aggressors have merely to cross it. It offers no such shield as is afforded by a high mountain range. The Mississippi served as a convenient line of demarcation between the Americans and the Spaniards; but it offered no protection whatever to the Spaniards against the Americans.

Therefore the frontiersmen found nothing serious to bar their farther march westward; the diminutive Spanish garrisons in the little creole towns near the Missouri were far less capable of effective resistance than were most of the Indian tribes whom the Americans were brushing out of their path. Toward the south the situation was different. The Floridas were shielded by the great Indian confederacies of the Creeks and Choctaws, whose strength was as yet unbroken. What was much more important, the mouth of the Mississippi was commanded by the important seaport of New Orleans, which was accessible to fleets, which could readily be garrisoned by water, and which was the capital of a region that, by backwoods standards, passed for well settled. New Orleans, by its position, was absolute master of the foreign trade of the Mississippi valley; and any power in command of the seas could easily keep it strongly garrisoned. The vast region that was then known as upper Louisiana—the territory stretching from the Mississippi to the Pacific— was owned by the Spaniards, but only in shadowy fashion, and could not have been held by any European power against the sturdy westward pressure of the rifle-bearing settlers. But New Orleans and its neighborhood were held even by the Spaniards in good earnest; while a stronger power, once in possession, could with difficulty have been dislodged.

It naturally followed that for the moment the attention of the backwoodsmen was directed much more to New Orleans than to the trans-Mississippi territory. A few wilderness lovers, like Boone, a few reckless adventurers of the type of Philip Nolan, were settling around and beyond the creole towns of the North, or were endeavoring to found small buccaneering colonies in dangerous proximity to the Spanish commanderies in the Southwest. But the bulk of the Western settlers as yet found all the vacant territory they wished east of the Mississippi. What they needed at the moment was, not more wild land, but an outlet for the products yielded by the land they already possessed. The vital importance to the Westerners of the free navigation of the Mississippi has already been shown. Suffice it to say that the control of the mouth of the great Fathers of Waters was of direct personal consequence to almost every tree-feller, every backwoods farmer, every landowner, every townsman, who dwelt beyond the Alleghanies. These men did not worry much over the fact that the country on the farther bank of the Mississippi was still under the Spanish flag. For the moment they did not need it, and when they did, they knew they could take it without the smallest difficulty. But the ownership of the mouth of the Mississippi was a matter of immediate importance; and though none of the settlers doubted that it would ultimately be theirs, it was yet a matter of much consequence to them to get possession of it as quickly as possible, and with as little trouble as possible, rather than to see it held, perhaps for years, by a powerful hostile nation and then to see it acquired only at the cost of bloody and, perchance, checkered warfare.

This was the attitude of the backwoods people as with sinewy, strenuous shoulder they pressed against the Spanish boundaries. The Spanish attitude, on the other hand, was one of apprehension so intense that it overcame even anger against the American nation. For mere diplomacy, the Spaniards cared little or nothing; but they feared the Westerners. Their surrender of Louisiana was due primarily to the steady pushing and crowding of the frontiersmen, and the continuous growth of the Western commonwealths. In spite of Pinckney's treaty the Spaniards did not leave Natchez until fairly drowned out by the American settlers and soldiers. They now felt the same pressure upon them in New Orleans; it was growing steadily and was fast becoming intolerable. Year by year, almost month by month, they saw the numbers of their foes increase, and saw them settle more and more thickly in places from which it would be easy to strike New Orleans. Year by year the offensive power of the Americans increased in more than arithmetical ratio as against Louisiana.

The more reckless and lawless adventurers from time to time pushed southwest, even toward the borders of Texas and New Mexico, and strove to form little settlements, keeping the Spanish governors and intendants in a constant fume of anxiety. One of these settlements was founded by Philip Nolan, a man whom rumor had connected with Wilkinson's intrigues, and who, like many another lawless trader of the day, was always dreaming of empires to be carved from, or wealth to be won in, the golden Spanish realms. In the fall of 1800, he pushed beyond the Mississippi, with a score or so of companions, and settled on the Brazos. The party built pens or corrals, and began to catch wild horses, for the neighborhood swarmed not only with game, but with immense droves of mustangs. The handsomest animals they kept and trained, letting the others loose again. The following March these tamers of wild horses were suddenly set upon by a body of Spaniards, three hundred strong, with one field-piece. The assailants made their attack at daybreak, slew Nolan, and captured his comrades, who for many years afterward lived as prisoners in the Mexican towns.[1] The menace of such buccaneering movements kept the Spaniards alive to the imminent danger of the general American attack which they heralded.

Spain watched her boundaries with the most jealous care. Her colonial system was evil in its suspicious exclusiveness toward strangers; and her religious system was marked by an intolerance still almost as fierce as in the days of Torquemada. The Holy Inquisition was a recognized feature of Spanish political life; and the rulers of the Spanish-American colonies put the stranger and the heretic under a common ban. The reports of the Spanish ecclesiastics of Louisiana dwelt continually upon the dangers with which the oncoming of the backwoodsmen threatened the Church no less than the State.[2] All the men in power, civil, military, and religious alike, showed toward strangers, and especially toward American strangers, a spirit which was doubly unwise; for by their jealousy they created the impression that the lands they so carefully guarded must hold treasures of great price; and by their severity they created an anger which, when fully aroused, they could not well quell. The frontiersmen, as they tried to peer into the Spanish dominions, were lured on by the attraction they felt for what was hidden and forbidden; and there was enough danger in the path to madden them, while there was no exhibition of a strength sufficient to cow them.

The Spanish rulers realized fully that they were too weak effectively to cope with the Americans, and as the pressure upon them grew ever heavier and more menacing, they began to fear not only for Louisiana, but also for Mexico. They clung tenaciously to all their possessions; but they were willing to sacrifice a part, if by so doing they could erect a barrier for the defense of the remainder. Such a chance was now seemingly offered them by France.

At the beginning of the century Napoleon was First Consul; and the France over which he ruled was already the mightiest nation in Europe, and yet had not reached the zenith of her power. It was at this time that the French influence over Spain was most complete. Both the Spanish king and the Spanish people were dazzled and awed by the splendor of Napoleon's victories. Napoleon's magnificent and wayward genius was always striving after more than merely European empire. As throne after throne went down before him he planned conquests which should include the interminable wastes of snowy Russia and the seagirt fields of England; and he always

---

[1] Pike's letter, July 22, 1807, in Natchez *Herald*; in Colonel Durrett's collection; see Coues's edition of Pike's "Expedition," LII; also Gayarré, III, 447.

[2] Report of Bishop Peñalvert, November 1, 1795, Gayarré.

dreamed of yet vaster, more shadowy triumphs, won in the realms lying eastward of the Mediterranean, or among the islands and along the coasts of the Spanish Main. In 1800, his dream of Eastern conquest was over, but his lofty ambition was planning for France the re-establishment in America of that colonial empire which a generation before had been wrested from her by England.

The need of the Spaniards seemed to Napoleon his opportunity. By the bribe of a petty Italian principality he persuaded the Bourbon King of Spain to cede Louisiana to the French, at the treaty of San Ildefonso, concluded in October, 1800. The cession was agreed to by the Spaniards on the express pledge that the territory should not be transferred to any other power; and chiefly for the purpose of erecting a barrier which might stay the American advance, and protect the rest of the Spanish possessions.

Every effort was made to keep the cession from being made public, and owing to various political complications it was not consummated for a couple of years; but meanwhile it was impossible to prevent rumors from going abroad, and the mere hint of such a project was enough to throw the West into a fever of excitement. Moreover, at this moment, before the treaty between France and Spain had been consummated, Morales, the intendant of New Orleans, deliberately threw down the gage of battle to the Westerners.[3] On October 16, 1802, he proclaimed that the Americans had forfeited their right of deposit in New Orleans. By Pinckney's treaty this right had been granted for three years, with the stipulation that it should then be extended for a longer period, and that if the Spaniards chose to revoke the permit so far as New Orleans was concerned, they should make some other spot on the river a port of free entry. The Americans had taken for granted that the privilege, when once conferred, would never be withdrawn; but Morales, under pretense that the Americans had slept on their rights by failing to discover some other spot as a treaty port, declared that the right of deposit had lapsed, and would not be renewed. The governor, Salcedo—who had succeeded Gayoso when the latter died of yellow fever, complicated by a drinking-bout with Wilkinson—was not in sympathy with the movement; but this mattered little. Under the cumbrous Spanish colonial system, the governor, though he disapproved of the actions of the intendant, could not reverse them, and Morales paid no heed to the angry protests of the Spanish minister at Washington, who saw that the Americans were certain in the end to fight rather than to lose the only outlet for the commerce

[3] Gayarré, III, 456.

of the West.[4] It seems probable that the intendant's action was due to the fact that he deemed the days of Spanish dominion numbered, and, in his jealousy of the Americans, wished to place the new French authorities in the strongest possible position; but the act was not done with the knowledge of France.

Of this, however, the Westerners were ignorant. They felt sure that any alteration in policy so fatal to their interests must be merely a foreshadowing of the course the French intended thereafter to follow. They believed that their worst fears were justified. Kentucky and Tennessee clamored for instant action, and Claiborne offered to raise in the Mississippi Territory alone a force of volunteer riflemen sufficient to seize New Orleans before its transfer into French hands could be effected.

Jefferson was President, and Madison secretary of state. Both were men of high and fine qualities who rendered, at one time or another, real and great service to the country. Jefferson in particular played in our political life a part of immense importance. But the country has never had two statesmen less capable of upholding the honor and dignity of the nation, or even of preserving its material well-being when menaced by foreign foes. They were peaceful men, quite unfitted to grapple with an enemy who expressed himself through deeds rather than words. When stunned by the din of arms they showed themselves utterly inefficient rulers.

It was these two timid, well-meaning statesmen who now found themselves pitted against Napoleon and Napoleon's minister, Talleyrand—against the greatest warrior and lawgiver and against one of the greatest diplomats of modern times; against two men, moreover, whose sodden lack of conscience was but heightened by the contrast with their brilliant genius and lofty force of character—two men who were unable to so much as appreciate that there was shame in the practice of venality, dishonesty, mendacity, cruelty, and treachery.

Jefferson was the least warlike of presidents, and he loved the French with a servile devotion. But his party was strongest in precisely those parts of the country where the mouth of the Mississippi was held to be of right the property of the United States; and the pressure of public opinion was too strong for Jefferson to think of resisting it. The South and the West were a unit in demanding that France should not be allowed to establish

---

[4] Gayarré, III, 576. The King of Spain, at the instigation of Godoy, disapproved the order of Morales, but so late that the news of the disapproval reached Louisiana only as the French were about to take possession. However, the reversal of the order rendered the course of the further negotiations easier.

herself on the lower Mississippi. Jefferson was forced to tell his French friends that if their nation persisted in its purpose, America would be obliged to marry itself to the navy and army of England. Even he could see that for the French to take Louisiana meant war with the United States sooner or later; and as above all things else he wished peace, he made every effort to secure the coveted territory by purchase.

Chancellor Robert R. Livingston, of New York, represented American interests in Paris; but at the very close of the negotiation he was succeeded by Monroe, whom Jefferson sent over as a special envoy. The course of the negotiations was at first most baffling to the Americans.[5] Talleyrand lied with such unmoved calm that it was impossible to put the least weight upon anything he said; moreover, the Americans soon found that Napoleon was the sole and absolute master, so that it was of no use attempting to influence any of his subordinates, save in so far as these subordinates might, in their turn, influence him. For some time it appeared that Napoleon was bent upon occupying Louisiana in force and using it as a basis for the rebuilding of the French colonial power. The time seemed ripe for such a project. After a decade of war with all the rest of Europe, France in 1802 concluded the Peace of Amiens, which left her absolutely free to do as she liked in the New World. Napoleon thoroughly despised a republic, and especially a republic without an army or navy. After the Peace of Amiens he began to treat the Americans with contemptuous disregard, and he planned to throw into Louisiana one of his generals with a force of veteran troops sufficient to hold the country against any attack.

His hopes were in reality chimerical. At the moment, France was at peace with her European foes, and could send her ships of war and her transports across the ocean without fear of the British navy. It would, therefore, have been possible for Napoleon without molestation to throw a large body of French soldiers into New Orleans for some years against American attack, and might even have captured one or two of the American posts on the Mississippi, such as Natchez; but the instant it had landed in New Orleans the entire American people would have accepted France as their deadliest enemy, and all American foreign policy would have been determined by the one consideration of ousting the French from the mouth of the Mississippi.

[5] In Henry Adams's "History of the United States," the account of the diplomatic negotiations at this period between France, Spain, and the United States is the most brilliant piece of diplomatic history, so far as the doings of the diplomats themselves are concerned, that can be put to the credit of any American writer.

To the United States, France was by no means as formidable as Great Britain, because of her inferiority as a naval power. Even if unsupported by an outside alliance, the Americans would doubtless in the end have driven a French army from New Orleans, though very probably at the cost of one or two preliminary rebuffs. The West was stanch in support of Jefferson and Madison; but in time of stress it was sure to develop leaders of more congenial temper, exactly as it actually did develop Andrew Jackson a few years later. At this very time the French failed to conquer the negro republic which Toussaint l'Ouverture had founded in Hayti. What they thus failed to accomplish in one island, against insurgent negroes, it was folly to think they could accomplish on the American continent, against the power of the American people. This struggle with the revolutionary slaves in Hayti hindered Napoleon from immediately throwing an army into Louisiana; but it did more, for it helped to teach him the folly of trying to carry out such a plan at all.

A very able and faithful French agent in the meanwhile sent a report to Napoleon, plainly pointing out the impossibility of permanently holding Louisiana against the Americans. He showed that on the Western waters alone it would be possible to gather armies amounting in the aggregate to twenty or thirty thousand men, all of them inflamed with the eager desire to take New Orleans.[6] The Mississippi ran so as to facilitate the movement of any expedition against New Orleans, while it offered formidable obstacles to counter-expeditions from New Orleans against the American commonwealths lying farther upstream. An expeditionary force sent from the mouth of the Mississippi, whether to assail the towns and settlements along the Ohio, or to defend the creole villages near the Missouri, could at the utmost hope for only transient success, while its ultimate failure was certain. On the other hand a backwoods army could move downstream with comparative ease; and even though such an expedition were defeated, it was certain that the attempt would be repeated again and again, until, by degrees, the mob of hardy riflemen changed into a veteran army, and brought forth some general like "Old Hickory," able to lead to victory.

The most intelligent French agents on the ground saw this. Some of Napoleon's ministers were equally far-sighted. One of them, Barbé Marbois, represented to him in the strongest terms the hopelessness of the under-

[6] Pontalba's "Memoir." He hoped that Louisiana might, in certain contingencies, be preserved for the French, but he insisted that it could only be by keeping peace with the American settlers, and by bringing about an immense increase of population in the province.

taking on which he proposed to embark. He pointed out that the United States was sure to go to war with France if France took New Orleans, and that in the end such a war could only result in victory for the Americans.

We can now readily see that this victory was certain to come even had the Americans been left without allies. France could never have defended the vast region known as upper Louisiana, and sooner or later New Orleans itself would have fallen, though it may well be only after humiliating defeats for the Americans and much expenditure of life and treasure. But as things actually were, the Americans would have had plenty of powerful allies. The Peace of Amiens lasted but a couple of years before England again went to war. Napoleon knew, and the American statesmen knew, that the British intended to attack New Orleans upon the outbreak of hostilities if it were in French hands. In such event Louisiana would have soon fallen; for any French force stationed there would have found its reinforcements cut off by the English navy, and would have dwindled away until unable to offer resistance.

Nevertheless, European wars, and the schemes and fancies of European statesmen, could determine merely the conditions under which the catastrophe was to take place, but not the catastrophe itself. The fate of Louisiana was already fixed. It was not the diplomats who decided its destiny, but the settlers of the Western States. The growth of the teeming folk who had crossed the Alleghanies and were building their rude, vigorous commonwealths in the northeastern portion of the Mississippi basin, decided the destiny of all the lands that were drained by that mighty river. The steady westward movement of the Americans was the all-important factor in determining the ultimate ownership of New Orleans. Livingston, the American minister, saw plainly the inevitable outcome of the struggle. He expressed his wonder that other Americans should be uneasy in the matter, saying that for his part it seemed as clear as day that no matter what trouble might temporarily be caused, in the end Louisiana was certain to fall into the grasp of the United States.[7]

There were many Americans and many Frenchmen of note who were less clear-sighted. Livingston encountered rebuff after rebuff, and delay after delay. Talleyrand met him with his usual front of impenetrable duplicity. He calmly denied everything connected with the cession of Louisiana until

[7] Livingston to Madison, September 1, 1802. Later, Livingston himself became uneasy, fearing lest Napoleon's wilfulness might plunge him into an undertaking which, though certain to end disastrously to the French, might meanwhile cause great trouble to the Americans.

even the details became public property, and then admitted them with unblushing equanimity. His delays were so tantalizing that they might well have revived unpleasant memories of the famous X Y Z negotiations, in which he tried in vain to extort bribe-money from the American negotiators;[8] but Livingston, and those he represented, soon realized that it was Napoleon himself who alone deserved serious consideration. Through Napoleon's character, and helping to make it great, there ran an imaginative vein which at times bordered on the fantastic; and this joined with his imperious self-will, brutality, and energy to make him eager to embark on a scheme which, when he had thought it over in cold blood, he was equally eager to abandon. For some time he seemed obstinately bent on taking possession of Louisiana, heedless of the attitude which this might cause the Americans to assume. He designated as commander of his army of occupation, Victor, a general as capable and brave as he was insolent, who took no pains to conceal from the American representatives his intention to treat their people with a high hand.

Jefferson took various means, official and unofficial, of impressing upon Napoleon the strength of the feeling in the United States over the matter; and his utterances came as near menace as his pacific nature would permit. To the great French conqueror, however, accustomed to violence and to the strife of giants, Jefferson's somewhat vacillating attitude did not seem impressive; and the one course which would have impressed Napoleon was not followed by the American President. Jefferson refused to countenance any proposal to take prompt possession of Louisiana by force or to assemble an army which could act with immediate vigor in time of need; and as he was the idol of the southwesterners, who were bitterly anti Federalist in sympathy, he was able to prevent any violent action on their part until events rendered this violence unnecessary. At the same time, Jefferson himself never for a moment ceased to feel the strong pressure of Southern and Western public sentiment; and so he continued resolute in his purpose to obtain Louisiana.

It was no argument of Jefferson's or of the American diplomats, but the inevitable trend of events, that finally brought about a change in Napoleon's mind. The army he sent to Hayti wasted away by disease and in combat with

[8] Jefferson was guilty of much weak and undignified conduct during these negotiations, but of nothing weaker and more petty than his attempt to flatter Talleyrand by pretending that the Americans disbelieved his admitted venality, and were indignant with those who had exposed it. See Adams.

the blacks, and thereby not only diminished the forces he intended to throw into Louisiana, but also gave him a terrible object-lesson as to what the fate of these forces was certain ultimately to be. The attitude of England and Austria grew steadily more hostile, and his most trustworthy advisers impressed on Napoleon's mind the steady growth of the Western-American communities, and the implacable hostility with which they were certain to regard any power that seized or attempted to hold New Orleans. Napoleon could not afford to hamper himself with the difficult defense of a distant province, and to incur the hostility of a new foe, at the very moment when he was entering on another struggle with his old European enemies. Moreover, he needed money in order to carry on the struggle. To be sure, he had promised Spain not to turn over Louisiana to another power; but he was quite as incapable as any Spanish statesman, or as Talleyrand himself, of so much as considering the question of breach of faith or loss of honor if he could gain any advantage by sacrificing either. Livingston was astonished to find that Napoleon had suddenly changed front, and that there was every prospect of gaining what for months had seemed impossible. For some time there was haggling over the terms. Napoleon at first demanded an exorbitant sum; but having once made up his mind to part with Louisiana his impatient disposition made him anxious to conclude the bargain. He rapidly abated his demands, and the cession was finally made for fifteen millions of dollars.

The treaty was signed in May, 1803. The definition of the exact boundaries of the ceded territory was purposely left very loose by Napoleon. On the east, the Spanish Government of the Floridas still kept possession of what are now several parishes in the State of Louisiana. In the far West the boundary-lines which divided upper Louisiana from the possessions of Britain on the north and of Spain on the south led through a wilderness where no white man had ever trod, and they were of course unmapped, and only vaguely guessed at.

There was one singular feature of this bargain, which showed, as nothing else could have shown, how little American diplomacy had to do with obtaining Louisiana, and how impossible it was for any European power, even the greatest, to hold the territory in the face of the steady westward growth of the American people. Napoleon forced Livingston and Monroe to become the reluctant purchasers, not merely of New Orleans, but of all the immense territory which stretched vaguely northwestward to the Pacific. Jefferson, at moments, felt a desire to get all this Western territory; but he was too timid and too vacillating to insist strenuously upon anything which he feared Napoleon would not grant. Madison felt a strong disinclination to see the national domain extend west of the Mississippi; and he so instructed Monroe and Livingston. In their turn, the American envoys, with solemn fatuity, believed it might impress Napoleon favorably if they made much show of moderation, and they spent no small part of their time in explaining that they only wished a little bit of Louisiana, including New Orleans and the east bank of the lower Mississippi. Livingston indeed went so far as to express a very positive disinclination to take the territory west of the Mississippi at any price, stating that he should much prefer to see it remain in the hands of France or Spain, and suggesting, by way of apology for its acquisition, that it might be resold to some European power! But Napoleon saw clearly that if the French ceded New Orleans it was a simple physical impossibility for them to hold the rest of the Louisiana Territory. If his fierce and irritable vanity had been touched he might, through mere wayward anger, have dared the Americans to a contest which, however disastrous to them, would ultimately have been more so to him; but he was a great statesman, and a still greater soldier, and he did not need to be told that it would be worse than folly to try to keep a country when he had given up the key-position.

The region west of the Mississippi could become the heritage of no other people save that which had planted its populous communities along the eastern bank of the river. It was quite possible for a powerful European nation to hold New Orleans for some time, even though all upper Louisiana fell into the hands of the Americans; but it was entirely impossible for any European nation to hold upper Louisiana if New Orleans became a city of the United States. The Westerners, wiser than their rulers, but no wiser than Napoleon at the last, felt this, and were not in the least disturbed over the fate of Louisiana, provided they were given the control of the mouth of the Mississippi. As a matter of fact, it is improbable that the fate of the great territory lying west of the upper Mississippi would even have been seriously delayed had it been nominally under the control of France or Spain. With the mouth of the Mississippi once in American hands it was a physical impossibility in any way to retard the westward movement of the men who were settling Ohio, Kentucky, and Tennessee.

The ratification of the treaty brought on sharp debates in Congress. Jefferson had led his party into power as the special champion of States' rights and the special opponent of National Sovereignty. He and they rendered a very great service to the nation by acquiring Louisiana; but it was at the cost of violating every precept which they had professed to hold dear, and of showing that their warfare on the Federalists had been waged on behalf of principles which they were obliged to confess were shams the moment they were put up to the test. But the Federalists of the Northeast, both in the Middle States and in New England, at this juncture behaved far worse than the Jeffersonian Republicans. These Jeffersonian Republicans did indeed by their performance give the lie to their past promise, and thereby emphasize the unworthiness of their conduct in years gone by; nevertheless, at this juncture they were right, which was far more important than being logical or consistent. But the northeastern Federalists, though with many exceptions, did as a whole stand as the opponents of national growth. They had very properly, though vainly, urged Jefferson to take prompt and effective steps to sustain the national honor, when it seemed probable that the country could be won from France only at the cost of war; but when the time actually came to incorporate Louisiana into the national domain, they showed that jealous fear of Western growth, which was the most marked defect in northeastern public sentiment until past the middle of the present century. It proved that the Federalists were rightly distrusted by the West; and it proved that at this crisis, the Jeffersonian Republicans, in spite of their follies, weaknesses, and crimes, were the safest guardians of the country because they believed in its future and strove to make it greater.

The Jeremiads of the Federalist leaders in Congress were the same in kind as those in which many cultivated men of the East always indulged whenever we enlarged our territory, and in which many persons like them would now indulge were we at the present day to make a similar extension. The people of the United States were warned that they were incorporating into their number men who were wholly alien in every respect, and who could never be assimilated. They were warned that when they thus added to their empire, they merely rendered it unwieldy and assured its being split into two or more confederacies at no distant day. Some of the extremists, under the lead of Quincy, went so far as to threaten dissolution of the Union, because of what was done, insisting that the Northeast ought by rights to secede because of the injury done it by adding strength to the South and West. Fortunately, however, talk of this kind did not affect the majority; the treaty was ratified and Louisiana became part of the United States.

Meanwhile, the creoles themselves accepted their very rapidly changing fates with something much like apathy. In March, 1803, the French Prefect Laussat arrived to make preparations to take possession of the country. He had no idea that Napoleon intended to cede it to the United States. On the contrary, he showed that he regarded the French as the heirs, not only to the Spanish territory, but of the Spanish hostility to the Americans. He openly regretted that the Spanish Government had reversed Morales's act in taking away from the Americans the right of deposit; and he made all his preparations as if on the theory that New Orleans was to become the centre of an aggressive military government.

His dislikes, however, were broad, and included the Spaniards as well as the Americans. There was much friction between him and the Spanish officials; he complained bitterly to the home government of the insolence and intrigues of the Spanish party. He also portrayed in scathing terms the gross corruption of the Spanish authorities. As to this corruption, he was borne out by the American observers. Almost every high Spanish official was guilty of peculation at the expense of the government, and of bribe-taking at the expense of the citizens.

Nevertheless, the creoles were far from ill-satisfied with Spanish rule. They were not accustomed to self-government, and did not demand it; and they cared very little for the fact that their superiors made money improperly. If they paid due deference to their lay and clerical rulers they were little interfered with; and they were in full accord with the governing classes concerning most questions, both of principle or lack of principle, and of prejudice. The creoles felt that they were protected, rather than oppressed, by people who shared their tastes, and who did not interfere with the things they held dear. On the whole, they showed only a tepid joy at the prospect of again becoming French Citizens.

Laussat soon discovered that they were to remain French citizens for a very short time indeed; and he prepared faithfully to carry out his instructions, and to turn the country over to the Americans. The change in the French attitude greatly increased the friction with the Spaniards. The Spanish home government was furious with indignation at Napoleon for having violated his word, and only the weakness of Spain prevented war between it and France. The Spanish party in New Orleans muttered its discontent so loud that Laussat grew alarmed. He feared some outbreak on the part of the Spanish sympathizers, and, to prevent such a mischance, he not only embodied the comparatively small portion of the creole militia whom he could trust, but also a number of American volunteers, concerning whose fidelity in such a crisis as that he anticipated there could be no question. It was not until December 1, 1803, that he took final possession of the province. Twenty days afterward he turned it over to the American authorities.

Wilkinson, now commander of the American army—the most disgraceful head it has ever had—was intrusted with the governorship of all of upper Louisiana. Claiborne was made governor of lower Louisiana, officially styled the Territory of Orleans. He was an honest man, loyal to the Union, but had no special qualifications for getting on well with the creoles. He could not speak French, and he regarded the people whom he governed with a kindly contempt, which they bitterly resented. The Americans, pushing and masterful, were inclined to look down on their neighbors, and to treat them overbearingly; while the creoles in their turn disliked the Americans as rude and uncultivated barbarians. For some time they felt much discontent with the United States; nor was this discontent allayed when, in 1804, the Territory of Orleans was reorganized with a government much less liberal than that enjoyed by Indiana or Mississippi; nor even when in 1805 an ordinary territorial government was provided. A number of years were to pass before Louisiana felt itself, in fact no less than in name, part of the Union.

Naturally, there was a fertile field for seditious agitation in New Orleans, a city of mixed population, where the numerically predominant race felt a puzzled distrust for the nation of which it suddenly found itself an integral part, and from past experience firmly believed in the evanescent nature of any political connection it might have whether with Spain, France, or the United States. The creoles murmured because they were not given the same privileges as American citizens in the old States, and yet showed themselves indifferent to such privileges as they were given. They were indignant because the National Government prohibited the importation of slaves into Louisiana, and for the moment even the transfer thither of slaves from the old States—a circumstance, by the way, which curiously illustrated the dislike and disapproval of slavery then felt, even by an administration under Southern control. The creoles further complained of Claiborne's indifference to their wishes; and as he possessed little tact he also became embroiled with the American inhabitants, who were men of adventurous and often lawless temper, impatient of restraint. Representatives of the French and Spanish governments still remained in Louisiana, and by their presence and their words tended to keep alive a disaffection for the United States Government. It followed from these various causes that among all classes there was a willingness to talk freely of their wrongs and to hint at righting them by methods outlined with such looseness as to make it uncertain whether they did or did not comport with entire loyalty to the United States Government.

Furthermore, there already existed in New Orleans a very peculiar class, representatives of which are still to be found in almost every Gulf city of importance. There were in the city a number of men ready at any time to enter into any plot for armed conquest of one of the Spanish-American countries.[9] Spanish America was feeling the stir of unrest that preceded the revolutionary outbreak against Spain. Already insurrectionary leaders like Miranda were seeking assistance from the Americans. There were in New Orleans a number of exiled Mexicans who were very anxious to raise some force with which to invade Mexico, and there erect the banner of an independent sovereignty. The bolder spirits among the creoles found much that was attractive in such a prospect; and reckless American adventurers by the score and the hundred were anxious to join in any filibustering expedition of the kind. They did not care in the least what form the expedition took. They were willing to join the Mexican exiles in an effort to rouse Mexico to throw off the yoke of Spain, or to aid any province of Mexico to revolt from the rest, or to help the leaders of any defeated faction who wished to try an appeal to arms, in which they should receive aid from the sword of the stranger. Incidentally, they were even more willing to attempt the conquest on their own account; but they did not find it necessary to dwell on this aspect of the case when nominally supporting some faction which chose to make use of such watchwords as liberty and independence.

Under such conditions, New Orleans, even more than the rest of the West, seemed to offer an inviting field for adventurers whose aim was both revolutionary and piratical. A particularly spectacular adventurer of this type now appeared in the person of Aaron Burr. Burr's conspiracy attracted an amount of attention, both at home and in the pages of history, altogether disproportioned to its real consequence. His career had been striking. He had been Vice-President of the United States. He had lacked but one vote of being made President, when the election of 1800 was thrown into the House of Representatives. As friend or as enemy he had been thrown intimately and on equal terms with the greatest political leaders of the day. He had supplied almost the only feeling which Jefferson, the chief of the Democratic party, and Hamilton, the greatest Federalist, ever possessed in common; for bitterly though Hamilton and Jefferson had hated each other, there was one man whom each of them had hated more, and that was Aaron Burr. There was not a man in the country who did not know about

[9] Wilkinson's "Memoirs," II, 284.

the brilliant and unscrupulous party leader who had killed Hamilton in the most famous duel that ever took place on American soil, and who, by a nearly successful intrigue, had come within one vote of supplanting Jefferson in the presidency.

In New York, Aaron Burr had led a political career as stormy and checkered as the careers of New York politicians have generally been. He had shown himself as adroit as he was unscrupulous in the use of all the arts of the machine manager. The fitful and gusty breath of popular favor made him at one time the most prominent and successful politician in the State, and one of the two or three most prominent and successful in the nation. In the State, he was the leader of the Democratic party, which, under his lead, crushed the Federalists; and as a reward he was given the second highest office in the nation. Then his open enemies and secret rivals all combined against him. The other Democratic leaders in New York and in the nation as well, turned upon the man whose brilliant abilities made them afraid, and whose utter untrustworthiness forbade their entering into alliance with him. Shifty and fertile in expedients, Burr made an obstinate fight to hold his own. Without hesitation, he turned for support to his old enemies, the Federalists; but he was hopelessly beaten. Both his fortune and his local political prestige were ruined; he realized that his chance for a career in New York was over.

He was no mere New York politician, however. He was a statesman of national reputation; and he turned his restless eyes toward the West, which for a score of years had seethed in a turmoil, out of which it seemed that a bold spirit might make its own profit. He had already been obscurely connected with separatist intrigues in the Northeast; and he determined to embark in similar intrigues on an infinitely grander scale in the West and Southwest. He was a cultivated man, of polished manners and pleasing address, and of great audacity and physical courage; and he had shown himself skilled in all the baser arts of political management.

It is small wonder that the conspiracy of which such a man was head should make a noise out of all proportion to its real weight. The conditions were such that if Burr journeyed West he was certain to attract universal attention, and to be received with marked enthusiasm. No man of his prominence in national affairs had ever travelled through the wild new commonwealths on the Mississippi. The men who were founding states and building towns on the wreck of the conquered wilderness were sure to be flattered by the appearance of so notable a man among them, and to be impressed not only by his reputation, but by his charm of manner and brilliancy of intellect. Moreover, they were quite ready to talk vaguely of all kinds of dubious plans for increasing the importance of the West. Very many, perhaps most, of them had dabbled at one time or another in the various separatist schemes of the preceding two decades; and they felt strongly that much of the Spanish domain would and should ultimately fall into their hands—and the sooner the better.

There was thus every chance that Burr would be favorably received by the West, and would find plenty of men of high standing who would profess friendship for him and would show a cordial interest in his plans so long as he refrained from making them too definite; but there was in reality no chance whatever for anything more than this to happen. In spite of Burr's personal courage he lacked entirely the great military qualities necessary to successful revolutionary leadership of the kind to which he aspired. Though in some ways the most practical of politicians, he had a strong element of the visionary in his character; it was perhaps this, joined to his striking moral defects, which brought about and made complete his downfall in New York. Great political and revolutionary leaders may, and often must, have in them something of the visionary; but it must never cause them to get out of touch with the practical. Burr was capable of conceiving revolutionary plans on so vast a scale as to be fairly appalling, not only from their daring, but from their magnitude. But when he tried to put his plans into practice, it at once became evident that they were even more unsubstantial than they were audacious. His wild schemes had in them too strong an element of the unreal and the grotesque to be in very fact dangerous.

Besides, the time for separatist movements in the West had passed, while the time for arousing the West to the conquest of part of Spanish America had hardly yet come. A man of Burr's character might perhaps have accomplished something mischievous in Kentucky when Wilkinson was in the first flush of his Spanish intrigues; or when the political societies were raving over Jay's treaty; or when the Kentucky legislature was passing its nullification resolutions. But the West had grown loyal as the nineteenth century came in. The Westerners were hearty supporters of the Jeffersonian Democratic-Republican party; Jefferson was their idol; they were strongly attached to the Washington administration, and strongly opposed to the chief opponents of that administration, the northeastern Federalists. With the purchase of Louisiana all deep-lying causes of Western discontent had vanished.

The West was prosperous, and was attached to the National Government. Its leaders might still enjoy a discussion with Burr or among themselves concerning separatist principles in the abstract, but such a discussion was at this time purely academic. Nobody of any weight in the community would allow such plans as those of Burr to be put into effect. There was, it is true, a strong buccaneering spirit, and there were plenty of men ready to enlist in an invasion of the Spanish dominions under no matter what pretext; but even those men of note who were willing to lead such a movement were not willing to enter into it if it was complicated with open disloyalty to the United States.

Burr began his treasonable scheming before he ceased to be Vice-President. He was an old friend and crony of Wilkinson; and he knew much about the disloyal agitations which had convulsed the West during the previous two decades. These agitations always took one or the other of two forms that at first sight wuld seem diametrically opposed. Their end was always either to bring about a secession of the West from the East by the aid of Spain or some other foreign power; or else a conquest of the Spanish dominions by the West, in defiance of the wishes of the East and of the Central Government. Burr proposed to carry out both of these plans.

The exact shape which his proposals took would be difficult to tell. Seemingly, they remained nebulous even in his own mind. They certainly so remained in the minds of those to whom he confided them. At any rate his schemes, though in reality less dangerous than those of his predecessors in Western treason, were in theory much more comprehensive. He planned the seizure of Washington, the kidnapping of the President, and the corruption of the United States navy. He also endeavored to enlist foreign powers on his side. His first advances were made to the British. He proposed to put the new empire, no matter what shape it might assume, under British protection in return for the assistance of the British fleet in taking New Orleans. He gave to the British ministers full—and false—accounts of the intended uprising, and besought the aid of the British Government on the ground that the secession of the West would so cripple the Union as to make it no longer a formidable enemy of Great Britain. Burr's audacity and plausibility were such that he quite dazzled the British minister, who detailed the plans at length to his home government, putting them in as favorable a light as he could. The statesmen at London, however, although at this time almost inconceivably stupid in their dealings with America, were not sunk in such abject folly as to think Burr's schemes practicable, and they refused to have anything to do with them.

In April, 1805, Burr started on his tour to the West. One of his first stoppages was at an island on the Ohio, near Parkersburg, where an Irish gentleman named Blennerhassett had built what was, for the West, an unusually fine house. Only Mrs. Blennerhassett was at home at the time; but Blennerhassett later became a mainstay of the "conspiracy." He was a warm-hearted man, with no judgment and a natural tendency toward sedition, who speedily fell under Burr's influence, and entered into his plans with eager zeal. With him Burr did not have to be on his guard, and to him he confided freely of his plans; but elsewhere, and in dealing with less emotional people, he had to be more guarded.

It is always difficult to find out exactly what a conspirator of Burr's type really intended, and exactly how guilty his various temporary friends and allies were. Part of the conspirator's business is to dissemble the truth, and in after-time it is nearly impossible to differentiate it from the false, even by the most elaborate sifting of the various untruths he has uttered. Burr told every kind of story, at one time or another, and to different classes of auditors. It would be unsafe to deny his having told a particular falsehood in any given case or to any given man. On the other hand, when once the plot was unmasked, those persons to whom he had confided his plans were certain to insist that he had really kept them in ignorance of his true intention. In consequence, it is quite impossible to say exactly how much guilty knowledge his various companions possessed. When it comes to treating of his relationship with Wilkinson all that can be said is that no single statement ever made by either man, whether during the conspiracy or after it, whether to the other or to an outsider, can be considered as either presumptively true or presumptively false.

It is, therefore, impossible to say exactly how far the Westerners with whom Burr was intimate were privy to his plans. It is certain that the great mass of the Westerners never seriously considered entering into any seditious movement under him. It is equally certain that a number of their leaders were more or less compromised by their associations with him. It seems probable that to each of these leaders he revealed what he thought would most attract him in the scheme; but that to very few did he reveal an outright proposition to break up the Union. Many of them were very willing to hear the distinguished Easterner make vague proposals for increasing the power of the West by means which were hinted at with sinister elusiveness; and many others were delighted to go into any movement which promised an attack upon the Spanish territory; but it seems likely that there were only a few men—Wilkinson, for instance, and Adair of Kentucky—who were willing to discuss a proposition to commit downright treason.

Burr stopped at Cincinnati, in Ohio, and at one or two places in Kentucky. In both States many prominent politicians, even United States senators, received him with enthusiasm. He then visited Nashville, where he became the guest of Andrew Jackson. Jackson was now major-general of the Tennessee militia; and the possibility of war, especially of war with the Spaniards, roused his hot nature to uncontrollable eagerness.[10] Burr probably saw through Jackson's character at once, and realized that with him it was important to dwell solely upon that part of the plan which contemplated an attack upon the Spaniards.

The United States was at this time on the verge of war with Spain. The Spanish governor and intendant remained in New Orleans after the cession, and by their conduct gave such offense that it finally became necessary to order them to leave, Jefferson claimed, as part of Louisiana, portions of both West Florida and Texas. The Spaniards refused to admit the justice of the claim and gathered in the disputed territories armies which, though small, outnumbered the few regular troops that Wilkinson had at his disposal. More than once a collision seemed imminent. The Westerners clamored for war, desiring above all things to drive the Spaniards by force from the debatable lands. For some time Jefferson showed symptoms of yielding to their wishes; but he was too timid and irresolute to play a high part, and in the end he simply did nothing. However, though he declined to make actual war on the Spaniards, he also refused to recognize their claims as just, and his peculiar, hesitating course tended to inflame the Westerners, and to make them believe that their government would not call them to account for acts of aggression. To Jackson, doubtless, Burr's proposals seemed quite in keeping with what he hoped from the United States Government. He readily fell in with views so like his own, and began to make preparations for an expedition against the Spanish dominions—an expedition which in fact would not have differed essentially from the expeditions he actually did make into the Spanish Floridas six or eight years afterward, or from the movement which still later his fellow Tennesseean, Houston, headed in Texas.

[10] Adams, III, 221.

From Nashville, Burr drifted down the Cumberland, and at Fort Massac, on the Ohio, he met Wilkinson, a kindred spirit, who possessed neither honor nor conscience, and could not be shocked by any proposal. Moreover, Wilkinson much enjoyed the early stages of a seditious agitation, when the risk to himself seemed slight; and as he was at this time both the highest military officer of the United States, and also secretly in the pay of Spain, the chance to commit a double treachery gave an added zest to his action. He entered cordially into Burr's plans, and as soon as he returned to his headquarters, at St. Louis, he set about trying to corrupt his subordinates, and seduce them from their allegiance.

Meanwhile, Burr passed down the Mississippi to New Orleans where he found himself in the society of persons who seemed more willing than any others he had encountered to fall in with his plans. Even here he did not clearly specify his purposes, but he did say enough to show that they bordered on the treasonable; and he was much gratified at the acquiescence of his listeners. His gratification, however, was overhasty. The creoles, and some of the Americans, were delighted to talk of their wrongs and to threaten any course of action which they thought might yield vengeance, but they had little intention of proceeding from words to deeds. Claiborne, a straightforward and honest man, set his face like a flint against all of Burr's doings.

From New Orleans Burr retraced his steps and visited Wilkinson at St. Louis. But Wilkinson was no longer in the same frame of mind as at Fort Massac. He had tested his officers, to see if they could be drawn into any disloyal movement, and had found that they were honorable men, firm in their attachment to the Union; and he was beginning to perceive that the people generally were quite unmoved by Burr's intrigues. Accordingly, when Burr reached him he threw cold water on his plans, and though he did not denounce or oppose them, he refrained from taking further active part in the seditious propaganda.

After visiting Harrison, the governor of the Indiana Territory, Burr returned to Washington. If he had possessed the type of character which would have made him really dangerous as a revolutionist, he would have seen how slight was his hope of stirring up revolt in the West; but he would not face facts, and he still believed he could bring about an uprising against the Union in the Mississippi valley. His immediate need was money. This he hoped to obtain from some foreign government. He found that nothing could be done with Great Britain; and then, incredible though it may seem, he turned to Spain, and sought to obtain from the Spaniards themselves the funds with which to conquer their own territories.

This was the last touch necessary to complete the grotesque fantasy which his brain has evolved. He approached the Spanish minister first through one of his fellow conspirators, and then in his own person. At one time he made his request on the pretense that he wished to desert the other filibusters, and save Spain by committing a double treachery, and betraying the treasonable movement into which he had entered; and again he asked funds on the ground that all he wished to do was to establish a separate government in the West, and thus destroy the power of the United States to molest Spain. However, his efforts came to naught, and he was obliged to try what he could do unaided in the West.

In August, 1806, he again crossed the Alleghanies. His first stop of importance was at Blennerhassett's. Blennerhasset was the one person of any importance who took his schemes so seriously as to be willing to stake his fortune on their success. Burr took with him to Blennerhassett's his daughter, Theodosia, a charming woman, the wife of a South Carolinian, Allston. The attractions of the daughter, and Burr's own address and magnetism, completely overcame both Blennerhassett and his wife. They gave the adventurer all the money they could raise, with the understanding that they would receive it back a hundredfold as the result of a land speculation which was to go hand in hand with the expected revolution. Then Blennerhassett began, in a very noisy and ineffective way, to make what preparations were possible in the way of rousing the Ohio settlers, and of gathering a body of armed men to serve under Burr when the time came. It was all done in a way that savored of farce rather than of treason.

There was much less comedy, however, in what went on in Kentucky and Tennessee, where Burr next went. At Nashville he was received with open arms by Jackson and Jackson's friends. This was not much to Jackson's credit; for by this time he should have known Burr's character; but the temptation of an attack on the Spaniards proved irresistible. As majorgeneral, he called out the militia of West Tennessee, and began to make ready in good earnest to invade Florida or Mexico. At public dinners he and his friends and Burr made speeches in which they threatened immediate war against Spain, with which country the United States was at peace; but they did not threaten any attack on the Union, and indeed Jackson exacted from Burr a guarantee of his loyalty to the Union.

From Nashville the restless conspirator returned to Kentucky to see if he could persuade the most powerful of the Western States to take some decided step in his favor. Senator John Adair, former companion-in-arms of Wilkinson in the wars against the northwestern Indians, enlisted in support of Burr with heart and soul. Kentucky society generally received him with enthusiasm. But there was in the State a remnant of the old Federalist party, which, although not formidable in numbers, possessed weight because of the vigor and ability of its leaders. The chief among them were Humphrey Marshall, former United States senator, and Joseph H. Daveiss, who was still district attorney, not having, as yet, been turned out by Jefferson.[11] These men saw—what Eastern policitians could not see— the connection between Burr's conspiracy and the former Spanish intrigues of men like Wilkinson, Sebastian, and Innes. They were loyal to the Union; and they felt a bitter factional hatred for their victorious foes, in whose ranks were to be found all the old-time offenders; so they attacked the new conspiracy with a double zest. They not only began a violent newspaper war upon Burr and all the former conspirators, but also proceeded to invoke the aid of the courts and the legislature against them. Their exposure of the former Spanish intrigues, as well as of Burr's plots, attracted wide-spread attention in the West, even at New Orleans;[12] But the Kentuckians, though angry and ashamed, were at first reluctant to be convinced. Twice Daveiss presented Burr for treason before the grand jury; twice the grand jury declared in his favor; and the leaders of the Kentucky Democracy gave him their countenance, while Henry Clay acted as his counsel. Daveiss, by a constant succession of letters, kept Jefferson fully informed of all that was done. Though his attacks on Burr for the moment seemed failures, they really accomplished their object. They created such uneasiness that the prominent Kentuckians made haste to clear themselves of all possible connection with any treasonable scheme. Henry Clay demanded and received from Burr a formal pledge that his plans were in nowise hostile to the Union; and the other people upon whom Burr counted most, both in Ohio and Kentucky, hastily followed this example. This immediate defection showed how hopeless Burr's plans were. The moment he attempted to put them into execution, their utter futility was certain to be exposed.

Meanwhile Jefferson's policy with the Spaniards, which neither secured peace nor made ready for war, kept up constant irritation on the border.

[11] For the Kentucky episode, see Marshall and Green. Gayarré is the authority for what occurred in New Orleans. For the whole conspiracy, see Adams.
[12] Gayarré, IV, 180.

Both the Spanish Governor Folch, in West Florida, and the Spanish General Herrera, in Texas, menaced the Americans.[13] Wilkinson hurried with his little army toward Herrera, until the two stood face to face, each asserting that the other was on ground that belonged to his own nation. Just at this time Burr's envoys, containing his final propositions, reached Wilkinson. But Wilkinson now saw as clearly as any one that Burr's scheme was foredoomed to fail; and he at once determined to make use of the only weapon in which he was skilled—treachery. At this very time he, the commander of the United States army, was in the pay of Spain, and was in secret negotiation with the Spanish officials against whom he was supposed to be acting; he had striven to corrupt his own army and had failed; he had found out that the people of the West were not disloyal. He saw that there was no hope of success for the conspirators; and he resolved to play the part of defender of the nation, and to act with vigor against Burr. Having warned Jefferson, in language of violent alarm, about Burr's plans, he prepared to prevent their execution. He first made a truce with Herrera in accordance with which each was to retire to his former position, and then he started for the Mississippi.

When Burr found that he could do nothing in Kentucky and Tennessee, he prepared to go to New Orleans. The few boats that Blennerhassett had been able to gather were sent hurriedly downstream lest they should be interfered with by the Ohio authorities. Burr had made another visit to Nashville. Slipping down the Cumberland, he joined his little flotilla, passed Fort Massac, and began the descent of the Mississippi.

The plot was probably most dangerous at New Orleans, if it could be said to be dangerous anywhere. Claiborne grew very much alarmed about it, chiefly because of the elusive mystery in which it was shrouded. But when the pinch came it proved as unsubstantial there as elsewhere. The leaders who had talked most loosely about revolutionary proceedings grew alarmed, as the crisis approached, lest they might be called on to make good their words; and they hastened to repudiate all connection with Burr, and to avow themselves loyal to the Union. Even the creole militia—a body which Claiborne regarded with just suspicion—volunteered to come to the defense of the government when it was thought that Burr might actually attack the city.

But Burr's career was already ruined. Jefferson, goaded into action, had issued a proclamation for his arrest; and even before this proclamation was issued, the fabric of the conspiracy had crumbled into shifting dust. The

[13] *Ibid.*, IV, 137, 151, etc.

Ohio legislature had passed resolutions, demanding prompt action against the conspirators; and the other Western communities followed suit. There was no real support for Burr anywhere. All his plot had been but a dream; at the last he could not do anything which justified, in even the smallest degree, the alarm and curiosity he had excited. The men of keenest insight and best judgment feared his unmasked efforts less than they feared Wilkinson's dark and tortuous treachery.[14] As he drifted down the Mississippi with his little flotilla, he was overtaken by Jefferson's proclamation, which was sent from one to another of the small Federal garrisons. Near Natchez, in January, 1807, he surrendered his flotilla, without resistance, to the acting governor of Mississippi Territory. He himself escaped into the land of the Choctaws and Creeks, disguised as a Mississippi boatman; but a month later he was arrested near the Spanish border, and sent back to Washington.

Thus ended ingloriously the wildest, most spectacular, and least dangerous, of all the intrigues for Western disunion. It never contained within itself the least hope of success. It was never a serious menace to the National Government. It was not by any means even a good example of Western particularistic feeling. It was simply a sporadic illustration of the looseness of national sentiment, here and there, throughout the country; but of no great significance, because it was in no sense a popular movement, and had its origin in the fantastic imagination of a single man.

It left scarcely a ripple in the West. When the danger was over Wilkinson appeared in New Orleans, where he strutted to the front for a little while, playing the part of a fussy dictator and arresting, among others, Adair, of Kentucky. As the panic subsided, they were released. No Louisianian suffered in person or property from any retaliatory action of the government; but lasting good was done by the abject failure of the plot and by the exhibition of unused strength by the American people. The creoles ceased to mutter discontent, and all thought of sedition died away in the province.

The chief sufferers, aside from Blennerhassett, were Sebastian and Innes, of Kentucky. The former resigned from the bench, and the latter lost a prestige he never regained. A few of their intimate friends also suffered. But their opponents did not fare much better. Daveiss and Marshall were the only men in the West whose action toward Burr had been thoroughly creditable, showing alike vigor, intelligence, and loyalty. To both of them the country was under an obligation. Jefferson showed his sense of this obligation in a not uncharacteristic way by removing Daveiss from office;

[14] E. G. Cowles Meade; see *Gayarré*, IV, 169.

Marshall was already in private life, and all that could be done was to neglect him.

As for Burr, he was put on trial for high treason with Wilkinson as State's evidence. Jefferson made himself the especial champion of Wilkinson. Nevertheless, the general cut a contemptible figure at the trial, for no explanation could make his course square with honorable dealing. Burr was acquitted on a technicality. Wilkinson, the double traitor, the bribe-taker, the corrupt servant of a foreign government, remained at the head of the American army.

MEADE MINNIGERODE

Tippecanoe, and Tyler Too!

i

Heaven, and historians, alone know, now, what it was all about. There had recently been a panic—two panics in fact, one in 1837 and another in 1839. Commercial houses on all sides were failing; banks were suspending; the States were rushing into bankruptcy; rent riots were occurring in New York; there was something deplorably wrong with the currency of the republic; the country was quite obviously going to the dogs. It was, at the time, all enormously alarming and vital. That no one, today, gives two pins about it is cause, perhaps, for optimism when present time problems boil over onto the national carpet.

Writing in his diary on January 1, 1840, Mr. Philip Hone found nothing better to say than that another year had passed, and that it would be well if black lines could be drawn around 1839 in the calendar. The year had been marked, it seemed to him, by individual and national distress in an unprecedented degree, "the effect of improvidence and a want of sound moral and political principles on the part of the mass of the people, and bad government and a crushing down of everything good and great to subserve party objects on the part of the rulers."

To make matters worse, the Democratic President—Mr. Martin Van Buren—sat calmly, it seems, in his gilded palace in Washington throughout these calamities, eating expensive soup from a silver tureen with a gold spoon, and driving haughtily in between times through the streets of the capital in his maroon coach with outriders. Yes sir. And not only that, but, would you believe it, there were Royal Wilton carpets on the floor, and chairs costing $600 a set, and gilded mirrors the size of barn doors in his Blue Elliptical Saloon.

Congressman Ogle, of Pennsylvania, knew all about it. On April 14, 1840, in a speech which reads like a house decorator's catalog, he put it to the free citizens of this country to say whether they were disposed to maintain for the President's private accommodation A Royal Establishment at the cost of the nation. Would they—when it came to voting on the Appropriation Bill in a presidential year—longer feel inclined to support their chief servant in a Palace as splendid as that of the Cæsars and as richly adorned as the proudest asiatic mansion? Would they? The Whigs thought it highly improbable, and Congressman Ogle took out his notes.

"Let us," he suggested to the Democratic congressmen who had not thought of doing so before, and showed very little inclination to do so then,

"let us survey its spacious courts, its gorgeous banqueting halls, its sumptuous drawing rooms, its glittering and dazzling salons, with all their magnificent and sumptuous array of gold and silver, crimson and orange, blue and violet, screens of Ionic columns, marble mantels ... gilt eagle cornices, rich cut glass and gilt chandeliers ... French bronze gilt lamps, gilt framed mirrors of prodigious size ... mahogany gilt mounted and rosewood pianofortes ... mahogany gilt bronze mounted secretaries, damask, satin and double silk window curtains"—Mr. Ogle had hardly begun—"Royal Wilton, and Imperial Brussels, and Saxon carpets, gilt and satin settees, sofas, bergeras, divans, tabourets and French comfortables, elegant mahogany gilt eagle mounted French bedsteads, gilt plateaus, gaudy artificial flowers, rich blue and gold bonbons, tambours, compotiers, ice cream vases, splendid French china vases, olive boats, octagonal bowls, silver tureens, boats and baskets of every rich work, golden goblets, table spoons, knives and forks...."

Mr. Ogle talked for several hours, in a manner highly diverting to the Whigs and increasingly depressing to the Democrats, although at the moment probably neither group realised the effect which his oration was to have on the presidential contest then already under way. He had set out to make a party speech, he ended by issuing the one great Whig document of the campaign. In the meantime, "how do you relish," he appealed to his delighted colleagues, "the notion of voting away the hard cash of your constituents for silk tassels, galloon, gimp and satin medallion to beautify and adorn the Blue Elliptical Saloon?"

Before the day was over, and long before the speech was over, Mr. Ogle had put the Blue Ellipitical Saloon irrevocably into national politics. He concluded on a note of high congressional oratory with the statement that if Mr. Van Buren chose to lay out hundreds of dollars in supplying his toilet with Double Extract of Queen Victoria, Corinthian Oil of Cream, Concentrated Persian Essence and Extract of Eglantine, it could constitute no valid reason for charging the farmers, laborers and mechanics of the country with bills for hemming his dish rags, for his larding needles, liquor stands and foreign cut wine coolers.

Mr. Ogle went home, feeling a trifle hoarse, no doubt, and Mr. Van Buren went to bed with the realisation that he had been made to appear somewhat ridiculous. Everybody laughed for a week. Double Extract of Queen Victoria!

Such a condition of affairs, even before Mr. Ogle had revealed it in all its sumptuous effrontery, had been intolerable. Down with the aristocratic, Anglomaniac Locofocos—so named from the time of their famous meeting when, the Whig landlord having turned off the gas, they were obliged to write their resolutions by the light of Locofoco friction matches. And down, particularly, with the despot Van Buren. In that clatterwhacking presidential campaign of 1840 the bulk of the nation was determined to vote for anybody —except Mr. Van Buren. The state of mind has been manifest more than once in American politics.

The anybody in 1840 turned out to be General William Henry Harrison —the defeated candidate of 1836—a gentleman from Ohio who had once won a battle. The Whigs, for their part, were determined to unite all factions—all the anti-renters, anti-slavers, abolitionists, conservatives, Webster-Whigs, Clay-Whigs, and all the other varieties of Whigs—and to win the election with a candidate who would satisfy all the groups, or at least antagonise as few of them as possible. Mr. Clay, the party favorite, the logical choice of Whiggery, had all the abolitionists and conservatives against him. Mr. Webster never had a chance, and knew it. After a round or two of complimentary ballots for Mr. Clay, the great Whig convention at Harrisburg nominated General Harrison and Mr. Tyler, and then listened to a portfolio full of speeches from the Clay men in which they explained at great length why they were in favor of Mr. Clay but had decided not to vote for him. It was a splendid moral victory for Mr. Clay, but the hero of Tippecanoe, and Tyler too, became the candidates of the Whig party.

2

The only thing which the Whig convention had neglected to do was to formulate a platform. In the midst of the general speech-making there had been no time for, and, apparently, not the slightest preoccupation over, so insignificant a feature of the campaign. The deficiency was almost immediately supplied, however, by the Locofoco press itself, much to its subsequent dismay and mortification. The, as it turned out, fatal blunder was committed by a Baltimore paper which, having had its attention drawn to a remark concerning General Harrison made by a friend of Mr. Clay, decided that it would be the best joke in the world to publish the entertaining statement. Unfortunately the joke, while an excellent one, was on the Democratic party.

What Mr. Clay's friend had said, on hearing of the nomination, was that if General Harrison were given a pension of $2000 a year and a barrel of hard cider he would be perfectly content to spend the rest of his days in his log cabin, studying moral philosophy.

This appraisal of the Whig candidate, enlarged upon and sneeringly reproduced by the Democratic press, elected him. What the blue elliptical saloon might not have achieved, the log cabin accomplished. The inevitable interpretation attached to the Locofoco guffaws over this personal item was that General Harrison, because he was a plain man, and a poor man, and a plebeian, was not fitted to be President of the United States. All of the plain, poor, plebeians in America immediately became extremely indignant. As in the case of the "Rum, Romanism and Rebellion" episode, the damage was done. In vain the Democrats pointed out that the statement had emanated, not from them, but from the most select Whig circles. In vain they protested that, far from sneering at the General, or at any quality which he might represent, they had merely repeated his own party's estimate of him. The country would have none of their belated excuses.

What? Sneer at the General because he was willing to live in a log cabin; because he was satisfied to partake of simple fare, as symbolised by hard cider in contrast to Mr. Van Buren's imported wines; because he was man enough to toil on his farm with his own hands; because he was a poor but honest citizen and not one of the "fawning minions of power"—well, the country guessed not! As well sneer at the Liberty Bell or the Pilgrim Fathers. A log cabin—and why not? Hundreds of Americans lived in log cabins, thousands of Americans had been born in log cabins, millions of Americans who had done neither had no trouble whatever in becoming patriotically sentimental over log cabins. Log Cabins—Home Sweet Home—The Old Oaken Bucket—these things were sacred. The nation was mortally offended. The Democrats had trodden on America's most cherished corn, attacked

America's most precious illusion, namely, that one man is as good as another.

In vain, once more, the Democrats pointed out that General Harrison was not a poor man, that he seldom if ever drank hard cider, that he had no occasion to toil on a farm, that not by any stretch of the imagination could he be said to live in a log cabin, since, quite evidently to anyone who cared to look, he lived in a fine residence surrounded by a two thousand acre estate—

"Fiddlededee!" the country replied to the Democrats, and believed all these things of its hero all the more firmly.

The Whig Log Cabin, Hard Cider campaign was under way, with a makeshift ticket, a fortuitous issue, and no platform whatever—but a contagious slogan was spreading throughout the land, and when America falls ill of a slogan nothing else matters.

3

The uproar began in the West. There were, of course, more log cabins in the West. At all events the West began to parade, and rally, and convene. In Columbus, Ohio, some twenty thousand people assembled from all over the State and marched eight abreast in a procession two miles long, carrying banners and transparencies—The Hero of Tippecanoe—The Farmer's President. Many of them had come in canoes and log cabins, mounted on wheels, and drawn by three and four pairs of horses. While the cabins trundled along the roads their escorts sat on the roof and drank hard cider. It must all have been extremely convivial and slightly befuddled. In Dayton, one hundred thousand came rolling in, and, after the cider had all been consumed, went rolling out again, looking for the next convention.

The contagion soon spread to the East. Rallies were held everywhere, attracting thousands of citizens who might better have been attending to their own affairs. Sixty thousand paraded in Boston, sixty thousand more in Syracuse. The nearer the date of election approached the greater the rallies became, the more people abandoned their work entirely in order to take part in these perambulating demonstrations of Whig enthusiasm. In New York the call went out for a:

"Great Moral Meeting in the Park this afternoon. A mighty, multitudinous, moral meeting will be held in the Park this evening of all the people in this city who are in favor of political morality in the use of the ballot box at elections. It will probably be the greatest meeting ever held in New York. All the virtuous, moral, honest friends of General Harrison ought to attend, and join in sentiment with every party in preserving the purity of the electoral franchise sacred from the atrocious demoralisation of Wall Street. Meet—meet—meet, friends of the old honest hero of Tippecanoe, and declare that you are not implicated, nor will defend the horrible morals of the Wall Street cliques. Come forth—come forth."

Wall Street, Wall Street—horrible morals, atrocious demoralisation—what a familiar sound, away back there already in 1840!

In Baltimore, delegates from every State in the Union came together at the Young Men's Whig Convention, and paraded themselves dizzy, dragging log cabins through the streets and pushing "Harrison balls" before them. One of these was eventually rolled to Philadelphia, where, most unfortunately for those concerned, it collapsed ignominiously in the midst of the procession, to the huge delight of onlooking Locofocos. Other Harrison balls were not so ill fated, however, and were rolled along the roads from town to town with a success presumably commensurate with the labor involved.

The feature of all these parades, of course, was the canoes and log cabins on wheels, but principally the log cabins. Tremendous affairs, some of them, with smoke issuing from a real chimney, and a coon-skin on the wall, and a barrel of cider beside the door, and always the latchstring hanging out. Aside from these traveling cabins, these itinerant emblems on wheels, every town, every village, had its Log Cabin headquarters for its Tippecanoe Club, in which loyal Whigs wearing wide awake hats and Tippecanoe badges and handkerchiefs convened to sing Tippecanoe songs and peruse Tippecanoe literature—the Tippecanoe Text Book, the Log Cabin Song Book, the Harrison Eagle, and in particular a certain Mr. Horace Greeley's Log Cabin newspaper. In some of the city cabins, they also convened for the purpose of imbibing large quantities of Tippecanoe "cider," so that the Whig party found it necessary to remind its followers that Log Cabin Clubs must not be converted into "rum holes."

Throughout the country the cry was "Tippecanoe, and Tyler too!" and "Harrison, two dollars a day, and roast beef!"—a sequence of somewhat heterogeneous wishes showing the simplicity of human desires in the Forties. Cider was the chosen beverage, the log cabin the cherished emblem, Tippecanoe the favorite name. Children screeched it over back fences and were christened with it, men swallowed it with their afternoon meal, women scrubbed it into their washing, darned it into their hose, rocked their cradles to its rhythm. Church bells chimed it, the wind rustled it in the leaves, birds sang it at sunrise. Out in the fields farmers cried "Go it Tip, Go it Ty" to their horses.

> "Tippecanoe—Tippecanoe—
> Tippecanoe, and Tyler too,
> Tippecanoe, and Tyler too,
> And with them we'll beat little Van, little Van,
> And with them we'll beat little Van..."

Who could resist such a battle cry! Even in New York Mr. Philip Hone—watching the Whig processions parade the streets at night with music, and banners and torches, and commenting on the manner in which his party, "with more adroitness than they usually display," had appropriated to its own use the famous Locofoco taunt—remarks that on all the transparencies the Temple of Liberty is transformed into a hovel of unhewn logs, and the military garb of the General into the frock coat and shirtsleeves of a gentleman farmer.

"The American eagle has taken his flight which is supplied by a cider barrel, and the long established emblem of the ship has given place to the plough. Hurrah for Tippecanoe is heard more frequently than Hurrah for the Constitution, and, whatever may be the result of the election, the Hurrah is heard and felt in every part of the United States."

4

The Locofocos, for their part, did not parade, or only very seldom and then in a supremely dignified, silk hatted manner. As one would expect from aristocrats who rode in maroon coaches and ate *pâté de foie gras* off gold plates—the fawning minions! It would obviously have been ill advised of them to cart replicas of Mr. Van Buren's gilded palace around the country, or brandish champagne bottles before the proletariat. And other guerdons had they none. What amusement they may have derived from the affair was obtained in solemn conclaves, in which earnest speeches were made about pressing affairs of state, to the accompaniment of Whig brass bands outside. Perhaps they passed resolutions calling for the hide of that Baltimore editor.

There is something immeasurably pathetic about those long faced, whiskered Democrats of 1840. They were ready to compete at the old stand, with issues, and platforms, and everything, while all their opponents thought of was to ride on top of log cabins and throw empty cider barrels around. They issued controversial propaganda, but their rivals merely set up theatrical props. They insisted on conducting a political campaign, when what the country was doing was following a traveling circus. Throughout the year, the zeal of the Democrats burned while Whiggery fiddled.

"Look here!" the Democrats cried, "the Whig candidate is a clodpoll, a dunderpate, and a ninnyhammer—he ought to be called General Mum—he sits all day like a squash—he hasn't any platform—he doesn't know B from a bull's foot!"

"What do we care!" the Whigs replied. "Tippecanoe, and Tyler too—

> "The people are coming from plain and from mountain,
> To join the brave band of the honest and free,
> Which grows as the stream from the leaf sheltered fountain,
> Spreads broad and more broad till it reaches the sea.
> No strength can restrain it, no force can retain it,
> Whate'er may resist, it breaks gallantly through,
> And borne by its motion, as a ship on the ocean,
> Speeds on in his glory
> Old Tippecanoe!
> The iron armed soldier, the true hearted soldier,
> The gallant old soldier of Tippecanoe!"

"Very well—what are you going to do about the currency?" the Democrats kept roaring. "What are you going to do about the national bank? What are you going to do about the panic?"

"Do?" the Whigs retorted. "PARADE—Tippecanoe, and Tyler too—

> "Oh know ye the farmer of Tippecanoe?
> The gallant old farmer of Tippecanoe?
> With an arm that is strong and a heat that is true,
> The man of the people is Tippecanoe...."

"But, but—hey, come back here a minute—he isn't a farmer at all!" the breathless Democrats pointed out.

"Do tell!" the Whigs exclaimed, and were off again with the left foot—

"Let Van from his coolers of silver drink wine,
And lounge on his cushioned settee,
Our man on his buckeye bench can recline,
Content with hard cider is he.
Then a shout for each freeman, a shout for each State,
To the plain, honest husbandman true,
And this be our motto, the motto of fate,
Hurrah for old Tippecanoe!"

The Democrats tried a new tack.

"Keep it before the people," they thundered, "that General Harrison was a Federalist—that he approved of selling white men into slavery—"

"What's that to us?" the Whigs hardly paused to enquire, before intoning:

"What though the Hero's hard, 'huge paws'
Were wont to plow and sow?
Does that disgrace our sacred cause?
Does that degrade him? NO!
Whig farmers are our nation's nerve,
Its bone, its very spine,
They'll never swerve, they did not swerve,
In days of old lang syne.

"No ruffled shirt, no silken hose,
No airs does Tip display;
But like 'the pith of worth' he goes
In homespun 'hoddin-gray.'
Upon his board there ne'er appeared
The costly sparkling wine,
But plain hard cider such as cheered,
In days of old lang syne."

"Keep it before the people," the Democrats had to shout to make themselves heard above the racket, "that General Harrison is an abolitionist—keep it before the people that as a soldier he was a coward—"

"Bah!" the Whigs countered. "Keep it before the people that Mr. Van Buren lives in a blue elliptical saloon surrounded by flunkies—keep it before the people that he perfumes himself with Double Extract of Queen Victoria

—keep it before the people that he has French tabourets in his parlor—step aside now and—

> "Make way for old Tip, turn out, turn out,
> Make way for old Tip, turn out!
> 'Tis the people's decree,
> Their choice he shall be,
> So Martin Van Buren turn out, turn out,
> So Martin Van Buren turn out!"

It was not a presidential campaign, it was a contest between two modes of dress, two varieties of beverage, two styles of architecture. It was lost by an inch or two of type in a newspaper, won by miles of parades. It was a jubilee of popular prejudice on wheels, set to the music of atrocious ballads. It was preposterous, and it was glorious sport. It was the Forties.

5

Mr. Van Buren only carried seven States.

The bewildered, and bitterly indignant, Democratic press wailed its loud misgivings over all this hornswogglery in gloomy, and not altogether unjustified, terms. The only hope was that the political buffoonery of 1840 would ever stand, solitary and alone, on the page of history, a damning stain on the brow of Federalism. No more might the world see coons, cabins and cider usurp the place of principles, nor doggerel verse elicit a shout while reason was passed by with a sneer.

"We have been sung down, lied down, drunk down!" So, dismally, they summed it up.

The Whig press, on the other hand, gave utterance to triumphantly sanctimonious outcries, the burden of which was that the people were free once more, that the election was a victory of principle over power, of liberty over despotism, of right and justice over wrong and oppression, of prosperity and happiness over widespread ruin and desolation. In short, that, to put it mildly—

"A great people have placed their seal of condemnation upon a band of the most desperate, aspiring, and unprincipled demagogues that ever graced the annals of despotism, a band of bold and reckless innovators calling themselves the democracy of the land, at whose head was Martin Van Buren, a monarchist in principle, a tyrant and a despot in practice."

They had such a pleasant polemic style in the Forties!

In the midst of the commotion the Philadelphia *Public Ledger,* for its part, sourly observed that:

"millions of dollars will now change hands on election bets, millions of days have been taken from useful labor to listen to stump orators, and millions more to build log cabins, erect hickory poles, and march in ridiculous, degrading, mob creating processions; millions of dollars have been wasted in soul and body destroying intemperance, in paying demagogues for preaching treason and bribing knaves to commit perjury and cast fraudulent votes. However high the hopes inspired by the election of General Harrison, they will prove to be delusive."

And so they did, but not precisely in the manner anticipated. The new president was inaugurated on March 4, 1841, during the course of which ceremony he made a long speech—but not as long as it had been before Mr. Clay ran his blue pencil through it—full of allusions to Rome, to Greece, to the Swiss Republic even, and with never a reference to any of the issues of the day. One month later he was dead.

6

New York solemnised the event in characteristic fashion. It held a mighty, multitudinous, moral parade. They had been parading for a year, those citizens of 1841, and the habit was strong upon them. And when, in the Forties, they set out to hold a parade, they did so earnestly and with considerable conviction. This one required three hours to swing into motion at the starting point in City Hall Park, "in one grand torrent of humanity forming a scene such as was never before witnessed on this continent"; it stretched unbroken from Chatham Square, through East Broadway, Grand Street and the Bowery, to Fourteenth Street and Broadway, "making a compact mass of four miles in length, flanked through its whole length by a mass of spectators of at least three times its numbers"; the head of the procession took some five hours to complete the circuit; over twenty thousand persons tramped patiently in its wake. And all in the midst of a miserable, bedraggling sleet storm.

One could not hope to improve on the New York *Herald's* account of this "Solemnisation of the Funeral Obsequies to the memory of Gen. Wm. Henry Harrison, Late President of the United States, by the People of the City of New York." It is the apotheosis of contemporary journalism. One can only regret the impossibility of reproducing it in its mournful entirety, diagrams, Funeral Urn, black borders and all.

"Saturday, the tenth of April, 1841," one learns, "was a solemn, a heart rending—a gloomy—and yet a happy day to the people of New York. Never was there such an occasion in her history as the one now passing before us. The solemnisation of the death of a pure, benevolent, brave, patriotic Chief Magistrate has united all parties in one broad and deep mass of honest patriotism and love of country. While the people mourn they also rejoice—rejoice that when a patriot dies, all party opposition dies with him, and his virtues, like his soul, rise, purified, to heaven...

"With these general reflections we shall now proceed to the particulars of the day. The Heavens were hung in black—gloom seemed to pervade the face of nature. Masses of clouds scudded mournfully across the lowering sky, and the smoke hung heavily above the city. At sunrise the flags of all the vessels were at half mast, as well as those of the Hotels, Theatres and all public places, and throughout the whole city men were seen busily engaged in hanging out crape, and other dark cloths, in festoons, while mournful emblems of grief and mortality met the eye in every direction." Broadway had "put on the weeds of woe," and the Bowery was "clad in the habiliments of profound grief."

By ten o'clock "the Societies, Trades Unions, Lodges of Odd Fellows, Fire and Military Companies with badges, ensigns and banners in mourning, were forming at their several rendez-vous and marching in a solemn procession towards the Park, around which the multitude was now collecting in dense masses, the whole forming at this early hour a grand and imposing spectacle, to see which every balcony in the vicinity was crowded.

"At twelve o'clock the procession began to form on the east side of the City Hall. At this time the crowd had become immense; from the lower end of the Park to the head of Chatham Square there was one dense mass of human beings of every age and sex. Every window was full, every balcony crowded, the roofs of the loftiest buildings covered, and the sidewalks, streets and squares densely filled with spectators. At one glance the eye took in a view of over ten thousand exclusive of those forming the procession."

They were always extremely responsive to numbers in the Forties.

At the City Hall "the scene was of a most exciting character." The edifice was crowded with city officials, veterans of 1812, sailors who had served on the *Constitution* and under Perry, Congressmen, foreign Consuls, distinguished guests, and representatives from Brooklyn. One wonders how they all got in and, when the time came, how they all got out again. Mr. Van Buren, Mr. Butler, and one or two more, however, while present, "were too aristocratic to mix with the others and make themselves common; they therefore kept themselves in a private room." They were lucky to find one, but they might at least have shared it with the representatives from Brooklyn. But Mr. Van Buren does not ever seem to have displayed any of those genial little insincerities which democracies require of their public characters.

7

The parade was headed by the military. Five thousand of them, with three key buglers playing *Oft in the Stilly Night* and eight bands, one of them "in straggling order" and another "shabbily dressed but playing very well." German Rifles, Tompkins Blues, Hibernian Greens, Pulaski Cadets, Montgomery Guards, Washington Greys, Mohegan Guards—companies in blue with red and white feathers, companies in green with red and white feathers, companies in blue with blue and white feathers, companies in blue with white belts, companies in red with no belts at all, companies in beaver caps, companies in green jackets, companies in light blue pants, companies in dark blue pants, companies in bright red pants. All very cold and wet.

"The Second Division, less regular, was, if possible, still more imposing. The Clergy, so numerous," seventy-two of them, "the United States Marines —whose officers looked noble—with their excellent band and exact discipline; the Golden Urn, protected by an Eagle and covered with crape, and inscribed with the names of the mighty dead," Washington, Hamilton, Lafayette and Harrison, "borne by the defenders of our noblest man of war; the horse, led riderless," by the General's negro valet; "the venerable pall bearers," in thirteen carriages; "the Ex-President," in a carriage with Mr. Butler and his child; "the official dignitaries of New York and Brooklyn— formed a scene of no common interest.

"In the Third Division, in solemn dignity," holding on to their top hats, "moved the higher dignitaries of the State and Nation and those whom the people have delighted to honor in times past, soldiers of the Revolution, members of the Society of Cincinnati, etc. The effect of all this, the banners shrouded, the staves of office with their golden heads covered with crape; and of so many of the eminent, the revered, the honored, and the brave, joining in the funeral of the departed, without any regard to party, was sublime."

"After the civil officers and the magistrates had passed—a most miserable looking set, particularly the magistrates—came the long and splendid line of New York Firemen; there must have been in all about three thousand firemen, it was a splendid sight."

A mile of firemen.

There followed twenty-one other divisions—including the Masons and Odd Fellows in full regalia; the entire enrollment, apparently, of Columbia College, "who did not look like very wise men although some were very handsome"; the children of the Public Schools, who were "very noisy, wrestled, and cried out Hurrah for Tippecanoe," which was scarcely the thing to do, perhaps; the members of the Tammany Society or Columbian Order; all the Tippecanoe Clubs and Harrison Associations; the citizens of Brooklyn; the Benevolent Societies and the Irish Societies; the Typographical Society, whose members were "the most intelligent looking body of men in the procession"; the Butchers and Cartmen, followed by the Library Association and the Society of Letters; the Journeymen Tailors, preceding the American Academy of Fine Arts; the Paul Jones Parading Club, whose title is not without a certain significant charm; and the Captains of the Watch, the Watchmen themselves, and the Lamplighters.

So this splendid Pageant of National Mourning, becraped, beplumed and bedrenched, passed before the eyes of admiring thousands, under a canopy of umbrellas. Perhaps some of them died of pneumonia afterwards.

One old lady, ninety years of age, followed the procession on foot the entire distance. She had been General Harrison's nurse.

LUCY BAKEWELL AUDUBON

Audubon in Kentucky

During his residence in Kentucky, Audubon spent all his leisure time in rambles through the wilds in search of natural history specimens. A variety of amusing incidents occurred in these travels, and the wanderer has given several of these in a full and connected form. His ready gun supplied abundant fare to his homely table. Wild turkeys, deer, and bears supplied constant wants, after a fashion that suited the hunter well. While resident there, a flat-boat reached the shore, containing ten or twelve stout fellows with their wives, and declaring themselves to be "Yankees," asked for work as wood cutters. Audubon, thinking that the boat contained wheat, held parley with the occupants, and finding that they were "likely" fellows, proposed to engage them to cut down a government lot of one thousand two hundred acres of fine timber he had purchased. The wood cutters made fast their craft to the bank, started a camp on shore, and, with their wives, managed to cook their meals out of the game supplied by the forest. Audubon and his miller visited the camp in the morning, was rather pleased with the appearance of the fellows, and engaged the gang. Commencing work, they soon showed their excellent training, felling the trees after the fashion of experienced woodmen. The daily and weekly allowance of wood contracted for was safely delivered, and Audubon had reason to feel much contentment with his servants. The miller was satisfied; and the master, to prove his appreciation of the valuable services, sent various presents of game and provisions to the strangers. Finding they had neglected to forward their usual supply one day, Audubon went off to their camp, found that the "Yankees" had gone off bodily, had taken his draught oxen with them, and had harried the place of all that could be lifted. He and his miller hunted down the river for the fugitives, but they had got a start and were not to be caught. Finding an escape into the Mississippi, the runaways voyaged out of reach of their victim, and a rare accident alone placed one of them within Audubon's power. While on board a Mississippi steamer, Audubon saw a hunter leave the shore in a canoe and reach the steamer. No sooner had the passenger reached the deck, than he recognized in him one of his plunderers; but the wood cutter, fearing an arrest, leaped into the stream and swam towards the shore. Entering a canebrake, he was lost to sight, and the naturalist was never gratified by either hearing of, or seeing any one of the fellows again.

In referring to Kentuckian sports, Audubon remarks that that State was a sort of promised land for all sorts of wandering adventurers from the Eastern states. Families cast loose from their homesteads beyond the mountains, wandered westward with their wagons, servants, cattle, and household gods. Bivouacking by some spring, in a glade of the primeval forest, near some well known "salt lick," where game would be plentiful, these Western representatives of the patriarchs moved on towards new resting-places, from which the red man, not without serious danger, had been driven. When a voyage by water was meditated as the easiest means of transporting the family and the baggage, a group of emigrants would build an ark on some creek of the upper waters of the Ohio, and in a craft forty or fifty feet long drift down the stream, carrying upon the roof the bodies of carts and wagons, upon the sides the wheels of the same.

Within these floating mansions the wayfarers lived, not without fear of impending dangers. To show a light through the loopholes within range of a redskin's rifle was certain death to the inmate; and night and day, while these arks drifted under umbrageous forests, their occupants were busy considering how their lives might be most dearly sold. Audubon notices curious practices connected with testing the skill of marksmen, not uncommon in his own time in Virginia. "At stated times, those desiring a trial of skill would be assembled," writes the naturalist, "and betting a trifling sum, put up a target, in the centre of which a common-sized nail is hammered for about two-thirds of its length. The marksmen make choice of what they consider a proper distance, which may be forty paces. Each man cleans the interior of his barrel, which is called *wiping* it, places a ball in the palm of his hand, pouring as much powder from his horn upon it as will cover it. This quantity is supposed to be sufficient for any distance within a hundred yards. A shot which comes very close to the nail is considered that of an indifferent marksman; the bending of the nail is, of course, somewhat better; but nothing less than hitting it right on the head is satisfactory. One out of three shots generally hits the nail, and should the shooters amount to half-a-dozen, two nails are frequently needed before each can have a shot. Those who drive the nail have a further trial amongst themselves, and the two best shots out of these generally settle the affair; when all the sportsmen adjourn to some house, and spend an hour or two in friendly intercourse, appointing, before they part, a day for another trial."

While at the town of Frankfort, Audubon had an opportunity of seeing the celebrated Daniel Boone "barking squirrels," or, in less technical phrase, driving them out of their hiding-places by firing into the bark of the tree immediately beside the position they crouch into. Audubon went out with Boone to see the sport, and writes:—

"We walked out together, and followed the rocky margins of the Kentucky river until we reached a piece of flat land thickly covered with black walnuts, oaks, and hickories. As the mast was a good one that year, squirrels were seen gamboling on every tree around us. My companion, a stout, hale, and athletic man, dressed in a homespun hunting shirt, bare-legged and moccasined, carried a long and heavy rifle, which, as he was loading it, he said had proved efficient in all his former undertakings, and which he hoped would not fail on this occasion, as he felt proud to show me his skill. The gun was wiped, the powder measured, the ball patched with six-hundred thread linen, and the charge sent home with a hickory rod. We moved not a step from the place, for the squirrels were so numerous that it was unnecessary to go after them. Boone pointed to one of these animals which had observed us, and was crouched on a branch about fifty paces distant, and bade me mark well the spot where the ball should hit. He raised his piece gradually, until the bead (that being the name given by the Kentuckians to the sight) of the barrel was brought to a line with the spot which he intended to hit, and fired.

"I was astounded to find that the ball had hit the piece of the bark immediately beneath the squirrel, and shivered it to splinters; the concussion produced by which had killed the animal, and sent it whirling through the air, as if it had been blown up.

"The snuffing of a candle with a ball I first had an opportunity of seeing near the banks of Green River, not far from a large pigeon roost, to which I had previously made a visit. I heard many reports of guns during the early part of a dark night, and knowing them to be those of rifles, I went towards the spot to ascertain the cause. On reaching the place, I was welcomed by a dozen of tall, stout men, who told me they were exercising for the purpose of enabling them to shoot under night at the reflected light from the eye of a deer or wolf by torchlight.

"At a distance of fifty paces stood a lighted candle, barely distinguishable in the darkness. One man was placed within a few yards of it, to watch the effects of the shots, as well as to light the candle, should it chance to go out, or to repair it, should the shot cut it across. Each marksman shot in his turn. Some never hit either the snuff or the candle. One of them, who was particularly expert, was very fortunate, and snuffed the candle three times out of seven, whilst all the other shots either put out the candle, or cut it immediately under the light."

During his residence in Kentucky, Audubon had frequent opportunities of joining in the great American festival of the 4th July. The particular occasion he describes as a "Kentucky Barbecue," and instances a very delightful jubilee held on the Beargrass Creek, at which all the settlers, with their wives and families, assisted. The festival was held in a forest glade by the river's side: the company arrived in their wagons, bringing provisions of every kind, such fruits as the country afforded, wine, and "Old Monongahela" whiskey. When the company had assembled, an immense cannon, built of wood hooped with iron, and lighted by a train, was fired, after which orations were made by various oracles. The good things provided were then largely enjoyed, after which dancing was indulged in with an enthusiasm suitable to such an occasion. Music was provided by various amateurs, and the fun was only closed by a ride home in the starlight.

"A maple sugar camp" was always a pleasant refuge to Audubon while wandering in the woods. He describes the wild appearance these camps presented when suddenly reached in the darkness, afar in the woodland solitudes, and only heralded by the snarling of curs and the howling of the sugar-makers.

Huge log fires, over which the sugar caldrons were boiled, gave the appearance of a witch incantation to a spectacle in which picturesquely-dressed Indians, rough backwoodsmen, and their strangely-dressed wives and children took part. Raised on a few stones placed around the fires, the sugar kettles were constantly tended by the women, while the men "bled" the sugar maple trees, stuck into the wounds they made, cane pipes, which drained the juice, and collected the maple sap into vessels made by splitting up a "yellow poplar" into juice troughs. Ten gallons of sap are required to make one pound of fine-grained sugar, which in some instances is equal to the finest make of candy. Such sugar sold in Kentucky, in the time of Audubon, for as much as a dozen cents in scarce seasons.

Racoon hunting was a pastime much enjoyed by Audubon, and he has left plentiful records of his enjoyment of the sport. He describes the hunter's visit to a homestead, and the preparations for a racoon hunt. The cost of ammunition was so considerable in the west, while the naturalist roved about, that the axe was reckoned a cheaper implement than the rifle to secure the prey. From the naturalist's journal the following description is given, inspired by the writer's own peculiar enthusiasm. The cabin is made comfortable by a huge pile of logs, laid across the fire; the sweet potatoes are roasted in the ashes; and when all is ready the hunters begin their work.

"The hunter has taken an axe from the wood pile, and returning, assures us that the night is clear, and that we shall have rare sport. He blows through his rifle, to ascertain that it is clear, examines his flint, and thrusts a feather into the touchhole. To a leathern bag swung at his side is attached a powder-horn; his sheathed knife is there also; below hangs a narrow strip of homespun linen. He takes from his bag a bullet, pulls with his teeth the wooden stopper from his powder-horn, lays the ball on one hand, and with the other pours the powder upon it, until it is just overtopped. Raising the horn to his mouth, he again closes it with the stopper, and restores it to its place. He introduces the powder into the tube, springs the box of his gun, greases the 'patch' over some melted tallow, or damps it, then places it on the honeycombed muzzle of his piece. The bullet is placed on the patch over the bore, and pressed with the handle of the knife, which now trims the edges of the linen. The elastic hickory rod, held with both hands, smoothly pushes the ball to its bed; once, twice, thrice has it rebounded. The rifle leaps as it were into the hunter's arms, the feather is drawn from the touchhole, the powder fills the pan, which is closed. 'Now I am ready,' cries the woodsman. A servant lights a torch, and off we march to the woods. 'Follow me close, for the ground is covered with logs, and the grape-vines hang everywhere across. Toby, hold up the light, man, or we'll never see the gullies. Trail your gun, sir, as General Clark used to say—not so, but this way—that's it. Now then, no danger you see; no fear of snakes, poor things! They are stiff enough, I'll be bound. The dogs have treed one. Toby, you old fool, why don't you turn to the right?—not so much. There, go ahead and give us a light. What's that? who's there? Ah! you young rascals! you've played us a trick, have you? It's all well enough, but now, just keep behind or I'll——' In fact, the boys with eyes good enough to see in the dark, although not quite so well as an owl, had cut directly across to the dogs, which had surprised a racoon on the ground, and bayed it, until the lads knocked it on the head. 'Seek him, boys!' cries the hunter. The dogs, putting their noses to the ground, pushed off at a good rate. 'Master, they're making for the creek,' says old Toby. On towards it therefore we push. What woods, to be sure! We are now in a low flat covered with beech trees.

"The racoon was discovered swimming in a pool. The glare of the lighted torch was doubtless distressing to him; his coat was ruffled, and his rounded tail seemed thrice its ordinary size; his eyes shone like emeralds; with foaming jaws he watched the dogs, ready to seize each by the snout if it came within reach. They kept him busy for some minutes; the water became thick with mud; his coat now hung dripping, and his draggled tail lay floating on the surface. His guttural growlings, in place of intimidating his assailants, excited them the more, and they very unceremoniously closed upon him. One seized him by the rump and tugged, but was soon forced to let go; another stuck to his side, but soon taking a better-directed bite of his muzzle, the coon's fate was sealed. He was knocked on the head, and Toby remarks, 'That's another half dollar's worth,' as he handles the thick fur of the prey. The dogs are again found looking up into a tree and barking furiously. The hunters employ their axes, and send the chips about.

"The tree began to crack, and slowly leaning to one side, the heavy mass swung rustling through the air, and fell to the earth with a crash. It was not one coon that was surprised here, but three, one of which, more crafty than the rest, leaped from the top while the tree was staggering. The other two stuck to the hollow of a branch, from which they were soon driven by one of the dogs. Tyke and Lion having nosed the cunning old one, scampered after him. He is brought to bay, and a rifle bullet is sent through his head. The other two are secured after a desperate conflict, and the hunters with their bags full, return to the cabin."

While resident in Kentucky, Audubon was visited by the eccentric naturalist, Rafinesque, whose manner of life, dress, and oddities of conduct appear to have greatly amused even one so little attentive to formalities as the ornithologist. The stranger reached the banks of the Ohio in a boat, and carrying on his back a bundle of plants which resembled dried clover. He accidentally addressed Audubon, and asked where the naturalist lived. Audubon, introduced himself, and was handed a letter of introduction by the stranger, in which the writer begged to recommend "an odd fish" which might not have been described in published treatises. Audubon innocently asked where the odd fish was, which led to a pleasant explanation and a complete understanding between the two naturalists.

"I presented my learned guest to my family," writes Audubon, "and was ordering a servant to go to the boat for my friend's luggage, when he told me he had none but what he brought on his back. He then loosened the pack of weeds which had first drawn my attention. The naturalist pulled off his shoes, and while engaged in drawing his stockings down to hide the holes in his heels, he explained that his apparel had suffered from his journey."

This eccentric's habits were neither tidy nor cleanly. He would hardly perform needful ablutions, and refused a change of clean clothing, suggested as being more comfortable. "His attire," remarks Audubon, "struck me as exceedingly remarkable. A long loose coat of yellow nankeen, much the worse for the many rubs it had got in its time, and stained all over with the juice of plants, hung loosely about him like a sack. A waistcoat of the same, with enormous pockets, and buttoned up to the chin, reached below over a pair of tight pantaloons, the lower part of which were buttoned down to the ankles. His beard was as long as I have known my own to be during some of my peregrinations, and his lank black hair hung loosely over his shoulders. His forehead was so broad and prominent that any tyro in phrenology would instantly have pronounced it the residence of a mind of strong powers. His words impressed an assurance of rigid truth, and as he directed the conversation to the study of the natural sciences, I listened to him with great delight. He requested to see my drawings, anxious to see the plants I had introduced besides the birds I had drawn. Finding a strange plant among my drawings, he denied its authenticity; but on my assuring him that it grew in the neighborhood, he insisted on going off instantly to see it.

"When I pointed it out the naturalist lost all command over his feelings, and behaved like a maniac in expressing his delight. He plucked the plants one after another, danced, hugged me in his arms, and exultingly told me he had got, not merely a new species, but a new genus.

"He immediately took notes of all the needful particulars of the plant in a note-book, which he carried wrapt in a waterproof covering. After a day's pursuit of natural history studies, the stranger was accommodated with a bed-room. We had all retired to rest; every person I imagined was in deep slumber save myself, when of a sudden I heard a great uproar in the naturalist's room. I got up, reached the place in a few moments, and opened the door; when, to my astonishment, I saw my guest running naked, holding the handle of my favorite violin, the body of which he had battered to pieces against the walls in attempting to kill the bats which had entered by the open window, probably attracted by the insects flying around his candle. I stood amazed, but he continued jumping and running round and round, until he was fairly exhausted, when he begged me to procure one of the animals for him, as he felt convinced they belonged to a 'new species.' Although I was convinced of the contrary, I took up the bow of my demolished Cremona, and administering a smart tap to each of the bats as it came up, soon got specimens enough. The war ended, I again bade him good-night, but could not help observing the state of the room. It was strewed with plants, which had been previously arranged with care.

"He saw my regret for the havoc that had been created, but added that he would soon put his plants to rights—after he had secured his new specimens of bats.

"Rafinesque had great anxiety to be shown a cane-brake, plenty of which were to be found in the neighborhood. The cane-brake is composed of a dense growth of canes, measuring twenty or thirty feet in height, and packed so closely that a man's body requires to be forced between the shafts of the canes. An undergrowth of plants and trailing climbers further prevents progression, which has to be accelerated by pushing the back between the canes. Game of all sorts frequent the cane-brakes, in which travelling is rendered disagreeably exciting by the presence of bears, panthers, snakes, and serpents. The cane-brakes are sometimes set fire to, and the water collected in the separate joints explodes like a shell. The constant fusilade occasioned by such explosions in the midst of a conflagration has occasioned the flight of parties not conversant with the cause, and who believed that the Indians were advancing with volleys of musketry. I had determined that my companion should view a cane-brake in all its perfection, and leading him several miles in a direct course, came upon as fine a sample as existed in that part of the country. We entered, and for some time proceeded without much difficulty, as I led the way, and cut down the canes which were most likely to incommode him. The difficulties gradually increased, so that we were presently obliged to turn our backs and push our way through. After a while we chanced to come upon the top of a fallen tree, which so obstructed our passage, that we were on the eve of going round, instead of thrusting ourselves through amongst the branches; when from its bed, in the centre of the tangled mass, forth rushed a bear with such force, that my friend became terror struck, and in his haste to escape made a desperate attempt to run, but fell amongst the canes in such a way that he was completely jammed. I could not refrain from laughing at the ridiculous exhibition he made, but my gaiety however was not very pleasing to the discomfited naturalist. A thunder-storm with a deluge of rain completed our experience of the canebrake, and my friend begged to be taken out. This could only be accomplished by crawling in a serpentine manner out of the jungle, from which the eccentric naturalist was delighted to escape, perfectly overcome with fatigue and fear. The eccentric was more than gratified with the exploit, and soon after left my abode without explanation or farewell. A letter of thanks, however, showed that he had enjoyed the hospitality, and was not wanting in gratitude."

In his Kentucky rambles Audubon had more than one opportunity of seeing and hunting with the famous Colonel Boone, the Kentucky hunter, and hero of a multitude of desperate adventures. On a particular occasion Boone spent a night under Audubon's roof, and related some of his adventures, among others, the following. On a hunting expedition in which Boone was engaged, the wanderer was afraid of Indians, and he consequently damped out his fire before falling asleep. He had not lain long before strong hands were laid upon him, and he was dragged off to the Indian camp. Avoiding every semblance of fear, Boone neither spoke nor resisted. The Indians ransacked his pockets, found his whiskey flask, and commenced to drink from it. While so engaged a shot was fired, and the male savages went off in pursuit, while the squaws were left to watch the prisoner. Rolling himself towards the fire, Boone burnt the fastenings which bound him, sprang to his feet, and after hacking three notches in an ash tree, afterwards known as "Boone's Ash," fled from the neighborhood. In years after, an engineer in Kentucky made the ash a point for a survey. A lawsuit arose out of a boundary question, and the only chance of closing it was by identifying "Boone's Ash." The hunter was sent for, and after some searching he pointed out the tree, in which the notches were detected after the bark had been peeled away. Boone's extraordinary stature and colossal strength struck Audubon as remarkable among a remarkable race; and the dreaded foe of the red man was notable for an honesty and courage that could not be questioned.

FRANCIS PARKMAN

Scenes at Fort Laramie

Looking back, after the expiration of a year, upon Fort Laramie and its inmates, they seem less like a reality than like some fanciful picture of the olden time; so different was the scene from any which this tamer side of the world can present. Tall Indians, enveloped in their white buffalo-robes, were striding across the area or reclining at full length on the low roofs of the buildings which enclosed it. Numerous squaws, gayly bedizened, sat grouped in front of the rooms they occupied; their mongrel offspring, restless and vociferous, rambled in every direction through the fort; and the trappers, traders, and *engagés* of the establishment were busy at their labor or their amusements.

We were met at the gate, but by no means cordially welcomed. Indeed we seemed objects of some distrust and suspicion, until Henry Chatillon explained that we were not traders, and we, in confirmation, handed to the *bourgeois* a letter of introduction from his principals. He took it, turned it upside down, and tried hard to read it; but his literary attainments not being adequate to the task, he applied for relief to the clerk, a sleek, smiling Frenchman, named Monthalon. The letter read, Bordeaux (the *bourgeois*) seemed gradually to awaken to a sense of what was expected of him. Though not deficient in hospitable intentions, he was wholly unaccustomed to act as master of ceremonies. Discarding all formalities of reception, he did not honor us with a single word, but walked swiftly across the area, while we followed in some admiration to a railing and a flight of steps opposite the entrance. He signed to us that we had better fasten our horses to the railing; then he walked up the steps, tramped along a rude balcony, and, kicking open a door, displayed a large room, rather more elaborately furnished than a barn. For furniture it had a rough bedstead, but no bed, two chairs, a chest of drawers, a tin pail to hold water, and a board to cut tobacco upon. A brass crucifix hung on the wall, and close at hand a recent scalp, with hair full a yard long, was suspended from a nail. I shall again have occasion to mention this dismal trophy, its history being connected with that of our subsequent proceedings.

This apartment, the best in Fort Laramie, was that usually occupied by the legitimate *bourgeois,* Papin, in whose absence the command devolved upon Bordeaux. The latter, a stout, bluff little fellow, much inflated by a sense of his new authority, began to roar for buffalo-robes. These being brought and spread upon the floor formed our beds,—much better ones than we had of late been accustomed to. Our arrangements made, we stepped out to the balcony to take a more leisurely survey of the long looked-for haven at which we had arrived at last. Beneath us was the square area surrounded by little rooms, or rather cells, which opened upon it. These were devoted to various purposes, but served chiefly for the accommodation of the men employed at the fort, or of the equally numerous squaws whom they were allowed to maintain in it. Opposite to us rose the blockhouse above the gateway; it was adorned with the figure of a horse at full speed, daubed upon the boards with red paint, and exhibiting a degree of skill which might rival that displayed by the Indians in executing similar designs upon their robes and lodges. A busy scene was enacting in the area. The wagons of Vaskiss, an old trader, were about to set out for a remote post in the mountains, and the Canadians were going through their preparations with all possible bustle, while here and there an Indian stood looking on with imperturbable gravity.

Fort Laramie is one of the posts established by the "American Fur Company," which well-nigh monopolizes the Indian trade of this region. Here its officials rule with an absolute sway; the arm of the United States has little force; for when we were there, the extreme outposts of her troops were about seven hundred miles to the eastward. The little fort is built of bricks dried in the sun, and externally is of an oblong form, with bastions of clay, in the form of ordinary blockhouses, at two of the corners. The walls are about fifteen feet high, and surmounted by a slender palisade. The roofs of the apartments within, which are built close against the walls, serve the purpose of a banquette. Within, the fort is divided by a partition: on one side is the square area, surrounded by the store-rooms, offices, and apartments of the inmates; on the other is the *corral,* a narrow place, encompassed by the high clay walls, where at night, or in the presence of dangerous Indians, the horses and mules of the fort are crowded for safe keeping. The main entrance has two gates, with an arched passage intervening. A little square window, high above the ground, opens laterally from an adjoining chamber into this passage; so that when the inner gate is closed and barred, a person without may still hold communication with those within, through this narrow aperture. This obviates the necessity of admitting suspicious Indians, for purposes of trading, into the body of the fort; for when danger is apprehended, the inner gate is shut fast, and all traffic is carried on by means of the window. This precaution, though necessary at some of the Company's posts, is seldom resorted to at Fort Laramie; where, though men are frequently killed in the neighborhood, no apprehensions are felt of any general designs of hostility from the Indians.

We did not long enjoy our new quarters undisturbed. The door was silently pushed open, and two eyeballs and a visage as black as night looked in upon us; then a red arm and shoulder intruded themselves, and a tall Indian, gliding in, shook us by the hand, grunted his salutation, and sat down on the floor. Others followed, with faces of the natural hue, and letting fall their heavy robes from their shoulders, took their seats, quite at ease, in a semi-circle before us. The pipe was now to be lighted and passed from one to another; and this was the only entertainment that at present they expected from us. These visitors were fathers, brothers, or other relatives of the squaws in the fort, where they were permitted to remain, loitering about in perfect idleness. All those who smoked with us were men of standing and repute. Two or three others dropped in also; young fellows who neither by their years nor their exploits were entitled to rank with the old men and warriors, and who, abashed in the presence of their superiors, stood aloof, never withdrawing their eyes from us. Their cheeks were adorned with vermilion, their ears with pendants of shell, and their necks with beads. Never yet having signalized themselves as hunters, or performed the honorable exploit of killing a man, they were held in slight esteem, and were diffident and bashful in proportion. Certain formidable inconveniences attended this influx of visitors. They were bent on inspecting everything in the room; our equipments and our dress alike underwent their scrutiny, for though the contrary has been asserted, few beings have more curiosity than Indians in regard to subjects within their ordinary range of thought. As to other matters, indeed, they seem utterly indifferent. They will not trouble themselves to inquire into what they cannot comprehend, but are quite contented to place their hands over their mouths in token of wonder, and exclaim that it is "great medicine." With this comprehensive solution, an Indian never is at loss. He never launches into speculation and conjecture;

his reason moves in its beaten track. His soul is dormant; and no exertions of the missionaries, Jesuit or Puritan, of the old world or of the new, have as yet availed to arouse it.

As we were looking, at sunset, from the wall, upon the desolate plains that surround the fort, we observed a cluster of strange objects like scaffolds, rising in the distance against the red western sky. They bore aloft some singular-looking burdens; and at their foot glimmered something white, like bones. This was the place of sepulture of some Dakota chiefs, whose remains their people are fond of placing in the vicinity of the fort, in the hope that they may thus be protected from violation at the hands of their enemies. Yet it has happened more than once, and quite recently, that war parties of the Crow Indians, ranging through the country, have thrown the bodies from the scaffolds, and broken them to pieces, amid the yells of the Dakota, who remained pent up in the fort, too few to defend the honored relics from insult. The white objects upon the ground were buffalo skulls, arranged in the mystic circle commonly seen at Indian places of sepulture upon the prairie.

We soon discovered, in the twilight, a band of fifty or sixty horses approaching the fort. These were the animals belonging to the establishment; who, having been sent out to feed, under the care of armed guards, in the meadows below, were now being driven into the *corral* for the night. A gate opened into this inclosure; by the side of it stood one of the guards, an old Canadian, with gray bushy eyebrows, and a dragoon pistol stuck into his belt; while his comrade, mounted on horseback, his rifle laid across the saddle in front, and his long hair blowing before his swarthy face, rode at the rear of the disorderly troop, urging them up the ascent. In a moment the narrow *corral* was thronged with the half-wild horses, kicking, biting, and crowding restlessly together.

The discordant jingling of a bell, rung by a Canadian in the area, summoned us to supper. The repast was served on a rough table in one of the lower apartments of the fort, and consisted of cakes of bread and dried buffalo meat, an excellent thing for strengthening the teeth. At this meal were seated the *bourgeois* and superior dignitaries of the establishment, among whom Henry Chatillon was worthily included. No sooner was it finished than the table was spread a second time (the luxury of bread being now, however, omitted), for the benefit of certain hunters and trappers of an inferior standing; while the ordinary Canadian *engagés* were regaled on dried meat in one of their lodging rooms. By way of illustrating the domestic economy of Fort Laramie, it may not be amiss to introduce in this place a story current among the men when we were there.

There was an old man named Pierre, whose duty it was to bring the meat from the store-room for the men. Old Pierre, in the kindness of his heart, used to select the fattest and the best pieces for his companions. This did not long escape the keen-eyed *bourgeois,* who was greatly disturbed at such improvidence, and cast about for some means to stop it. At last he hit on a plan that exactly suited him. At the side of the meat-room, and separated from it by a clay partition, was another apartment, used for the storage of furs. It had no communication with the fort, except through a square hole in the partition; and of course it was perfectly dark. One evening the *bourgeois,* watching for a moment when no one observed him, dodged into the meat-room, clambered through the hole, and ensconced himself among the furs and buffalo-robes. Soon after, old Pierre came in with his lantern, and muttering to himself, began to pull over the bales of meat and select the best pieces, as usual. But suddenly a hollow and sepulchral voice proceeded from the inner room: "Pierre, Pierre! Let that fat meat alone. Take nothing but lean." Pierre dropped his lantern, and bolted out into the fort, screaming, in an agony of terror, that the devil was in the store-room; but tripping on the threshold, he pitched over upon the gravel, and lay senseless, stunned by the fall. The Canadians ran out to the rescue. Some lifted the unlucky Pierre; and others, making an extempore crucifix of two sticks, were proceeding to attack the devil in his stronghold, when the *bourgeois,* with a crestfallen countenance, appeared at the door. To add to his mortification, he was obliged to explain the whole stratagem to Pierre, in order to bring him to his senses.

We were sitting, on the following morning, in the passage-way between the gates, conversing with the traders Vaskiss and May. These two men, together with our sleek friend, the clerk Monthalon, were, I believe, the only persons then in the fort who could read and write. May was telling a curious story about the traveller Catlin, when an ugly, diminutive Indian, wretchedly mounted, came up at a gallop, and rode by us into the fort. On being questioned, he said that Smoke's village was close at hand. Accordingly only a few minutes elapsed before the hills beyond the river were covered with a disorderly swarm of savages, on horseback and on foot. May finished his story; and by that time the whole array had descended to Laramie Creek, and begun to cross it in a mass. I walked down to the bank. The stream is wide, and was then between three and four feet deep, with a swift current. For several rods the water was alive with dogs, horses, and Indians. The long poles used in pitching the lodges are carried by the horses, fastened by the heavier end, two or three on each side, to a rude sort of pack-saddle, while the other end drags on the ground. About a foot behind the horse, a kind of large basket or pannier is suspended between the poles, and firmly lashed in its place. On the back of the horse are piled various articles of luggage; the basket also is well filled with domestic utensils, or, quite as often, with a litter of puppies, a brood of small children, or a superannuated old man. Numbers of these curious vehicles, *traineaux,* or, as the Canadians called them, *travois,* were now splashing together through the stream. Among them swam countless dogs, often burdened with miniature *traineaux;* and dashing forward on horseback through the throng came the warriors, the slender figure of some lynx-eyed boy clinging fast behind them. The women sat perched on the packsaddles, adding not a little to the load of the already overburdened horses. The confusion was prodigious. The dogs yelled and howled in chorus; the puppies in the *travois* set up a dismal whine as the water invaded their comfortable retreat; the little black-eyed children, from one year of age upward, clung fast with both hands to the edge of their basket, and looked over in alarm at the water rushing so near them, sputtering and making wry mouths as it splashed against their faces. Some of the dogs, encumbered by their load, were carried down by the current, yelping piteously; and the old squaws would rush into the water, seize their favorites by the neck, and drag them out. As each horse gained the bank, he scrambled up as he could. Stray horses and colts came among the rest, often breaking away at full speed through the crowd, followed by the old hags, screaming after their fashion on all occasions of excitement. Buxom young squaws, blooming in all the charms of vermilion, stood here and there on the bank, holding aloft their master's lance, as a signal to collect the scattered portions of his household. In a few moments the crowd melted away; each family with its horses and equipage, filing off to the plain at the rear of the fort; and here, in the space of half an hour, arose sixty or seventy of their tapering lodges. Their horses were feeding by hundreds over the surrounding prairie, and their dogs were roaming everywhere. The fort was full of warriors, and the children were whooping and yelling incessantly under the walls.

These new-comers were scarcely arrived, when Bordeaux ran across the fort, shouting to his squaw to bring him his spy-glass. The obedient Marie, the very model of a squaw, produced the instrument, and Bordeaux hurried with it to the wall. Pointing it eastward, he exclaimed, with an oath, that the families were coming. But a few moments elapsed before the heavy caravan of the emigrant wagons could be seen, steadily advancing from the hills. They gained the river, and, without turning or pausing, plunged in, passed through, and slowly ascending the opposing bank, kept directly on their way by the fort and the Indian village, until, gaining a spot a quarter of a mile distant, they wheeled into a circle. For some time our tranquillity was undisturbed. The emigrants were preparing their encampment; but no sooner was this accomplished than Fort Laramie was taken by storm. A crowd of broad-brimmed hats, thin visages, and staring eyes, appeared suddenly at the gate. Tall, awkward men, in brown homespun, women, with cadaverous faces and long lank figures, came thronging in together, and, as if inspired by the very demon of curiosity, ransacked every nook and corner of the fort. Dismayed at this invasion we withdrew in all speed to our chamber, vainly hoping that it might prove a sanctuary. The emigrants prosecuted their investigations with untiring vigor. They penetrated the rooms, or rather dens, inhabited by the astonished squaws. Resolved to search every mystery to the bottom, they explored the apartments of the men, and even that of Marie and the *bourgeois*. At last a numerous deputation appeared at our door, but found no encouragement to remain.

Having at length satisfied their curiosity, they next proceeded to business. The men occupied themselves in procuring supplies for their onward journey,—either buying them, or giving in exchange superfluous articles of their own. The emigrants felt a violent prejudice against the French Indians, as they called the trappers and traders. They thought, and with some reason, that these men bore them no good-will. Many of them were firmly persuaded that the French were instigating the Indians to attack and cut them off. On visiting the encampment we were at once struck with the extraordinary perplexity and indecision that prevailed among them. They seemed like men totally out of their element,—bewildered and amazed, like a troop of schoolboys lost in the woods. It was impossible to be long among them without being conscious of the bold spirit with which most of them were animated. But the *forest* is the home of the backwoodsman. On the remote prairie he is totally at a loss. He differs as much from the genuine "mountain-man" as a Canadian voyageur, paddling his canoe on the rapids of the Ottawa, differs from an American sailor among the storms of Cape Horn. Still my companion and I were somewhat at a loss to account for this perturbed state of mind. It could not be cowardice; these men were of the same stock with the volunteers of Monterey and Buena Vista. Yet, for the most part, they were the rudest and most ignorant of the frontier population; they knew absolutely nothing of the country and its inhabitants; they had already experienced much misfortune, and apprehended more; they had seen nothing of mankind, and had never put their own resources to the test.

A full share of suspicion fell upon us. Being strangers, we were looked upon as enemies. Having occasion for a supply of lead and a few other necessary articles, we used to go over to the emigrant camps to obtain them. After some hesitation, some dubious glances, and fumbling of the hands in the pockets, the terms would be agreed upon, the price tendered, and the emigrant would go off to bring the article in question. After waiting until our patience gave out, we would go in search of him, and find him seated on the tongue of his wagon.

"Well, stranger," he would observe, as he saw us approach, "I reckon I won't trade."

Some friend of his had followed him from the scene of the bargain, and whispered in his ear that clearly we meant to cheat him, and he had better have nothing to do with us.

This timorous mood of the emigrants was doubly unfortunate, as it exposed them to real danger. Assume, in the presence of Indians, a bold bearing, self-confident yet vigilant, and you will find them tolerably safe neighbors. But your safety depends on the respect and fear you are able to inspire. If you betray timidity or indecision, you convert them from that moment into insidious and dangerous enemies. The Dakota saw clearly enough the perturbation of the emigrants, and instantly availed themselves of it. They became extremely insolent and exacting in their demands. It has become an established custom with them to go to the camp of every party, as it arrives in succession at the fort, and demand a feast. Smoke's village had come with this express design, having made several days' journey with no other object than that of enjoying a cup of coffee and two or three biscuit. So the "feast" was demanded, and the emigrants dared not refuse it.

One evening about sunset the village was deserted. We met old men, warriors, squaws, and children in gay attire, trooping off to the encampment with faces of anticipation; and, arriving here, they seated themselves in a semi-circle. Smoke occupied the centre, with his warriors on either hand; the young men and boys came next, and the squaws and children formed the horns of the crescent. The biscuit and coffee were promptly despatched, the emigrants staring open-mouthed at their savage guests. With each emigrant party that arrived at Fort Laramie this scene was renewed; and every day the Indians grew more rapacious ond presumptuous. One evening they broke in pieces, out of mere wantonness, the cups from which they had been feasted; and this so exasperated the emigrants that many of them seized their rifles and could scarcely be restrained from firing on the insolent mob of Indians. Before we left the country this dangerous spirit on the part of the Dakota had mounted to a yet higher pitch. They began openly to threaten the emigrants with destruction, and actually fired upon one or two parties of them. A military force and military law are urgently called for in that perilous region; and unless troops are speedily stationed at Fort Laramie, or elsewhere in the neighborhood, both emigrants and other travellers will be exposed to most imminent risks.

The Ogillallah, the Brulé, and the other western bands of the Dakota or Sioux, are thorough savages, unchanged by any contact with civilization. Not one of them can speak a European tongue, or has ever visited an American settlement. Until within a year or two, when the emigrants began to pass through their country on the way to Oregon, they had seen no whites, except the few employed about the Fur Company's posts. They thought them a wise people, inferior only to themselves, living in leather lodges, like their own, and subsisting on buffalo. But when the swarm of *Meneaska,* with their oxen and wagons, began to invade them, their astonishment was unbounded. They could scarcely believe that the earth contained such a multitude of white men. Their wonder is now giving way to indignation; and the result, unless vigilantly guarded against, may be lamentable in the extreme.

But to glance at the interior of a lodge. Shaw and I used often to visit them. Indeed we spent most of our evenings in the Indian village, Shaw's assumption of the medical character giving us a fair pretext. As a sample of the rest I will describe one of these visits. The sun had just set, and the horses were driven into the *corral.* The Prairie Cock, a noted beau, came in at the gate with a bevy of young girls, with whom he began a dance in the area, leading them round and round in a circle, while he jerked up from his chest a succession of monotonous sounds, to which they kept time in a rueful chant. Outside the gate boys and young men were idly frolicking; and close by, looking grimly upon them, stood a warrior in his robe, with his face painted jet-black, in token that he had lately taken a Pawnee scalp. Passing these, the tall dark lodges rose between us and the red western sky. We repaired at once to the lodge of Old Smoke himself. It was by no means better than the others; indeed, it was rather shabby; for in this democratic community the chief never assumes superior state. Smoke sat crosslegged on a buffalo-robe, and his grunt of salutation as we entered was unusually cordial, out of respect, no doubt, to Shaw's medical character. Seated around the lodge were several squaws, and an abundance of children. The complaint of Shaw's patients was, for the most part, a severe inflammation of the eyes, occasioned by exposure to the sun, a species of disorder which he treated with some success. He had brought with him a homœopathic medicine-chest, and was, I presume, the first who introduced that harmless system of treatment among the Ogillallah. No sooner had a robe been spread at the head of the lodge for our accommodation, and we had seated ourselves upon it, than a patient made her appearance,—the chief's daughter herself, who, to do her justice, was the best-looking girl in the village. Being on excellent terms with the physician, she placed herself readily under his hands, and submitted with a good grace to his applications, laughing in his face during the whole process, for a squaw hardly knows how to smile. This case despatched, another of a different kind succeeded. A hideous, emaciated old woman sat in the darkest corner of the lodge, rocking to and fro with pain, and hiding her eyes from the light by pressing the palms of both hands against her face. At Smoke's command she came forward, very unwillingly, and exhibited a pair of eyes that had nearly disappeared from excess of inflammation. No sooner had the doctor fastened his grip upon her, than she set up a dismal moaning, and writhed so in his grasp that he lost all patience; but being resolved to carry his point, he succeeded at last in applying his favorite remedies.

"It is strange," he said when the operation was finished, "that I forgot to bring any Spanish flies with me; we must have something here to answer for a counter-irritant."

So, in the absence of better, he seized upon a red-hot brand from the fire, and clapped it against the temple of the old squaw, who set up an unearthly howl, at which the rest of the family broke into a laugh.

During these medical operations Smoke's eldest squaw entered the lodge, with a mallet in her hand, the stone head of which, precisely like those sometimes ploughed up in the fields of New England, was made fast to the handle by a covering of raw hide. I had observed some time before a litter of well-grown black puppies, comfortably nestled among some buffalo-robes at one side; but this new-comer speedily disturbed their enjoyment; for seizing one of them by the hind paw, she dragged him out and carrying him to the entrance of the lodge, hammered him on the head till she killed him. Aware to what this preparation tended, I looked through a hole in the back of the lodge to see the next steps of the process. The squaw, holding the puppy by the legs, was swinging him to and fro through the blaze of a fire, until the hair was singed off. This done, she unsheathed her knife and cut him into small pieces, which she dropped into a kettle to boil. In a few moments a large wooden dish was set before us filled with this delicate preparation. A dog-feast is the greatest compliment a Dakota can offer to his guest; and, knowing that to refuse eating would be an affront, we attacked the little dog, and devoured him before the eyes of his unconscious parent. Smoke in the mean time was preparing his great pipe. It was lighted when we had finished our repast, and we passed it from one to another till the bowl was empty. This done, we took our leave without further ceremony, knocked at the gate of the fort, and after making ourselves known, were admitted.

JAMES FENIMORE COOPER

Old Ironsides

IN THE course of the events connected with the naval history and the naval glory of the country, this ship has become so renowned by her services and her success as to be entitled to have her biography written, as well as those who have gained distinction on her deck. Half a century has endeared her to the nation, and her career may be said to be coexistent, as well as coequal in fame, with that of the service to which she belongs. It is seldom, indeed, that men have ever come to love and respect a mere machine as this vessel is loved and respected among the Americans, and we hope the day may be far distant when this noble frigate will cease to occupy her place on the list of the marine of the republic. It is getting to be an honor, of itself, to have commanded her, and a long catalogue of names belonging to gallant and skilful seamen, has already been gathered into the records of the past, that claim this enviable distinction. Among them we find those of Talbot, Nicholson, Preble, Decatur, Rogers, Hull, Bainbridge, and others, sea captains renowned for their courage, enterprise, and devotion to the flag. Neither disaster nor disgrace ever befell any man who filled this honorable station, though the keel of this bold craft has ploughed nearly every sea, and her pennant has been seen abroad in its pride, in the hostile presence equally of the Briton, the Frenchman, and the Turk.

The celebrated craft, of which we are now about to furnish a historical sketch was built under a law that was approved by Washington himself, as President, March 27th, 1794. This law, which authorized the construction of six frigates, the commencement of an entirely new marine, that of the Revolution having been altogether laid aside, was a consequence of the depredations of the Dey of Algiers upon the commerce of the nation. The keel of one of the four largest of these frigates was laid down at Boston, and was named The Constitution. Her rate was that of a forty-four, though she was to be what is called a single-decked ship, or to possess but one gun deck, in addition to her forecastle and quarter deck. In the last century, it was not unusual to construct vessels of this rate, which carried batteries on two gun decks in addition to those which were mounted on their quarter decks and forecastles; but, in this instance, it was intended to introduce a new style of frigate-built ship, that should be more than equal to cope with the old-fashioned ships of the same rate, besides possessing the advantage of sailing faster on a wind and of stowing much more freely. The gun deck batteries of these four ships were intended to be composed of thirty long twenty-four pound guns, while it was then very unusual for a frigate to carry metal heavier than an eighteen. This plan was carried out in three of the six new vessels; but, owing to some mistake in getting out the frame, that laid down at Norfolk, which was also intended for a forty-four, was, in the end, the smallest of the thirty-sixes. This was the ill-fated Chesapeake, a ship of which the career in the navy was almost as disastrous as that of the subject of our present memoir has been glorious and successful. The unfortunate Chesapeake would seem to have been commenced in error, and to have terminated her course much as it was begun.

The credit of presenting the plans for the three twenty-four pounder frigates that were built under the law of 1794, belongs of right to Mr. Joshua Humphreys, ship-builder, of Philadelphia, and the father of the gentleman of the same name, who is now the chief naval constructor. We are not certain, however, that the idea of placing such heavy metal in frigate-built ships is due to him, for the *Indien,* a ship built by order of Congress, at Amsterdam, during the war of the Revolution, had Swedish thirty-sixes in her, though she was not so long a vessel as either of those now built at home. As Mr. Humphreys was a builder of eminence at that time, however, it is possible his suggestions may have been attended to, even in that early day. The English certainly began to construct twenty-four pounder frigates at the close of the last, and near the commencement of the present centuries, as is seen in the Cambrian, Acasta, Endymion, &c. Let these facts be as they may, there is no question that the plans of Mr. Humphreys produced three as fine single-decked ships as were ever put into the water, and it would be difficult to say which was the preferable vessel of the whole number. Two of them, after a lapse of half a century, still remain in service, and both are favorite cruisers with those who like fast, comfortable, and efficient ships. The new frigates are all heavier, but this is almost the only superior quality of which they can properly boast.

The builder who had charge of the Constitution, while on the stocks, was

Mr. Cleghorn; but the foreman and the person who was supposed to be the efficient mechanic, was Mr. Hartly, the father of the present naval constructor, and the builder of the Argus brig, one of the finest vessels of her class that ever sailed under the American ensign.

Captains were appointed to each of the six frigates, as soon as their keels were laid, as indeed were several other subordinate officers. We may as well mention here, that the following rule for regulating the rank of the inferior officers was adopted. The captains having ranks assigned them by the dates or numbers of their commissions, in the usual way, it was ordered that the senior lieutenant of the ship to which the senior captain was attached should rank all the other first lieutenants, and the others should follow in the same order, down to the junior lieutenant of them all. The officer to whom the original command of the Constitution was confided was Capt. Samuel Nicholson, a gentleman who had served with credit throughout the war of the Revolution and once had worn a broad pennant. This gentleman, however, is not to be confounded with his elder brother, Capt. James Nicholson, who was at the head of the list of captains in the old navy, after Com. Hopkins was laid aside. Capt. Samuel Nicholson was the second in rank among the six captains appointed by the law of 1794, and all the Constitution's officers subsequently obtained similar rank in consequence. Barry alone ranked Nicholson, and the United States may be said to have ranked the Constitution.

The keel of the Constitution was laid in Boston, and some progress had been made in her construction, when a treaty of peace was signed with the Dey of Algiers without firing a shot. Of course this reconciliation was purchased by tribute. Congress now directed that the work on three of the six new frigates should be stopped, while the remainder were to be slowly completed. The three it was determined to complete were The States, Old Ironsides, and The Constellation. These three ships happened to be the most advanced, and the loss would be the heaviest by arresting the work on them.

Owing to these circumstances the Constitution was more than two years on the stocks, though commenced in haste—a delay that probably had its influence in making her a better ship than she might otherwise have been. Nevertheless the work on her was more advanced than on either ship, and, but for an accident, she would have added the distinction of being the very first vessel of the new and permanent navy that was got into water, to her other claims for renown. She stuck on the ways, and the States and Constellation were both launched before her. As it was, she was launched Sept. 20th, 1797.

In the course of the session of Congress that succeeded, the relations of the country with France became so seriously complicated that it was determined to repel the maritime aggressions of the sister republic by force. The sudden armament of 1795 was the consequence, and vessels of war were equipped and sent to sea as fast as circumstances would allow. Although one law was passed July 1st, 1797, "to man and employ the three frigates," and another was passed March 27th, 1798, appropriating a considerable sum with a similar object, neither was the first vessel got to sea, though the Constellation was one of the first, and the States was not far behind her. This occurred in June and July, 1798. In the latter month, and on the 20th of the month, Old Ironsides was first moved under her canvas. She did not go to sea, however, until the succeeding month, the orders of Captain Nicholson to that effect having been dated Aug. 13th.

On this, her first cruise, the officers attached to the ship appear to have been as follows, viz.:—The celebrated Preble, since the proudest name in American naval annals, was ordered to the ship as her original first lieutenant, but he got relieved from the duty, in consequence of some dislike of her commander, and never sailed in her until he did so with his broad pennant flying on board her. The complement of the frigate was composed of the following persons, and classes of persons, viz.:—

Captain,	1	Quarter Gunners,	11
Lieutenants,	4	Coxswain,	1
Do. Marines,	2	Sailmaker,	1
Sailing Master,	1	Cooper,	1
Master's Mates,	2	Steward,	1
Midshipmen,	8	Armorer,	1
Purser,	1	Master at Arms,	1
Surgeon,	1	Cook,	1
Do. Mates,	2	Chaplain,	1
Clerk,	1	Able Seamen,	120
Carpenter,	1	Do. Ordinary,	150
Do. Mates,	2	Boys,	30
Boatswain,	1	Marines,	50
Do. Mates,	2		
Gunner,	1		400

At that time a captain of such a ship as the Constitution received but $100 per month, pay, and eight rations, or $2, per diem; a lieutenant received $40 a month and three rations; midshipmen, $19 and one ration; able seamen, $17 a month and ordinaries, $12.[1]

It may be well to state here, that in the reports of government, the Constitution was paid for as being 1576, carpenter's measurement, and her cost is stated at $275,000. Considered in reference to ordinary measurement, the first is more than a hundred tons too much; and considered in reference to a complete equipment, the last materially too small. The first cost of such a ship as the Constitution must have exceeded $300,000.

Nicholson sailed in August, 1798, carrying Old Ironsides into blue water for the first time. His cruising ground was on the coast extending from Cape Henry to Florida, with orders to look out for Frenchmen. But the French, who were then at war with England, sent no heavy ships into the American waters, and it was soon found useless to keep a vessel of the Constitution's weight so near home. We find the ship, still under Nicholson, on the West India station at the close of the year, when she formed one of Barry's squadron. If her captain had originally worn a broad pennant in her, which we much doubt, although he appears to have had several small craft under his orders, it was now struck, Barry being the only commodore of the windward squadron, while Truxton, Nicholson's junior by four, having the leeward. Little connected with the Constitution occurred during this cruise, or indeed throughout that war, of an importance to be noted. The luck of the ship had not commenced, nor was there much chance of any thing being done of *éclat* by a vessel of her force, under all the circumstances. The English were every where, while the French had lost so many ships already, that it was of rare occurrence to fall in with one of their frigates. By a singular fortune, the only two frigate actions that took place in the whole of the quasi war with France fell to the share of one and the same ship, the Constellation, which took the Insurgente and beat off La Vengeance. The Constitution returned to Boston .... and her command was transferred to Talbot, who hoisted a broad pennant in her, as commodore of

---

[1] The writer of this sketch was once asked by a French admiral, "how much America paid her seamen?" The answer was, "$12, $10 and $8 according to class." "You never can have a large marine, then, on account of the cost." "That is not so clear. What does France pay for the support of the kingly office?" "About $8,000,000," said Lafayette, who was present, "and America pays $25,000 to her king or $100,000, if you will, including all expenses." "I think, Admiral, the difference would man a good many ships."

what was called the St. Domingo station. On this cruise Hull sailed as first lieutenant.

The second cruise of Old Ironsides commenced in August, 1799. Her orders were to go off Cayenne, in the first place, where she was to remain until near the close of September, when she was to proceed viâ Guadaloupe to Cape François, at which point, Talbot was to assume the command of all the vessels he found on the station. In the course of the season, this squadron grew to six sail, three frigates and as many sloops, or brigs.

Two incidents occurred to Old Ironsides, while on the St. Domingo station, that are worthy of being noticed, the first being of an amicable, and the second of a particularly hostile character.

While cruising to windward the island, a strange sail was made, which, on closing proved to be the English frigate, the ———.

The commander of this ship and Com. Talbot were acquaintances, and the Englishman had the curiosity to take a full survey of the new Yankee craft. He praised her, as no unprejudiced seaman could fail to do, but insisted that his own ship could beat her on a wind. After some pleasantry on the subject, the English captain made the following proposition; he had touched at Madeira on his way out, and taken on board a few casks of wine for his own use. This wine stood him in so much a cask—now, he was going into port to refit, and clean his bottom, which was a little foul; but, if he could depend on finding the Constitution on that station, a few weeks later, he would join her, when there should be a trial of speed between the two ships, the loser to pay a cask of the wine, or its price to the winner. The bet was made, and the vessels parted.

At the appointed time, the ——— reappeared; her rigging overhauled, new sails bent, her sides painted, her bottom cleaned, and, as Jack expressed it, looking like a new fiddle. The two frigates closed, and their commanders dined together, arranging the terms of the cartel for the next day's proceedings. That night, the vessels kept near each other, on the same line of sailing, and under short canvas.

The following morning, as the day dawned, the Constitution and the ——— each turned up their hands, in readiness for what was to follow. Just as the lower limb of the sun rose clear of the waves, each fired a gun, and made sail on a bow-line. Throughout the whole of that day, did these two gallant ships continue turning to windward, on tacks of a few leagues in length, and endeavoring to avail themselves of every advantage which skill could confer on seamen. Hull sailed the Constitution on this interesting occasion, and the admirable manner in which he did it, was long the subject of eulogy. All hands were kept on deck all day, and there were tacks on which the people were made to place themselves to windward, in order to keep the vessel as near upright as possible, so as to hold a better wind.

Just as the sun dipped, in the evening, the Constitution fired a gun, as did her competitor. At that moment the English frigate was precisely hull down dead to leeward; so much having Old Ironsides, or young Ironsides, as she was then, gained in the race, which lasted about eleven hours! The manner in which the Constitution eat her competitor out of the wind, was not the least striking feature of this trial, and it must in a great degree be ascribed to Hull, whose dexterity in handling a craft under her canvas, was ever remarkable. In this particular, he was perhaps one of the most skilful seamen of his time, as he was also for coolness in moments of hazard. When the evening gun was fired and acknowledged, the Constitution put up her helm, and squared away to join her friend. The vessels joined a little after dark, the Englishman as the leeward ship, first rounding to. The Constitution passed under her lee, and threw her main-topsail to the mast. There was a boat out from the ———, which soon came alongside, and in it was the English Captain and his cask of wine; the former being just as prompt to "pay" as to "play."

The other occurrence was the cutting out of the Sandwich, a French letter of marque, which was lying in Port Platte, a small harbor on the Spanish side of St. Domingo. While cruising along the coast, the Constitution had seized an American sloop called the Sally, which had been selling supplies to the enemy. Hearing that the Sandwich, formerly an English packet, but which had fallen into the hands of the French, was filling up with coffee, and was nearly full, Talbot determined to send Hull in, with the Sally, in order to cut her out. The sloop had not long before come out of that very haven, with an avowed intention to return, and offered every desirable facility to the success of the enterprise. The great and insuperable objection to its ultimate advantage, was the material circumstance that the Frenchman was lying in a neutral port, as respects ourselves, though watchful of the English who were swarming in those seas.

The Constitution manned the Sally at sea, near sunset, on the tenth of May, 1800, a considerable distance from Port Platte, and the vessels separated, Hull so timing his movements, as to reach his point of destination about mid-day of a Sunday, when it was rightly enough supposed many of the French, officers as well as men, would be ashore keeping holiday. Short sail was carried that night on board the Sally, and while she was quietly jogging along, thinking no harm, a gun was suddenly heard, and a shot came whistling over the sloop. On looking around, a large ship was seen in chase, and so near, as to render escape impossible. The Sally rounded to, and presently, an English frigate ranged alongside. The boarding officer was astonished when he found himself among ninety armed men, with officers in naval uniform at their head. On demanding an explanation, Hull told him his business, when the English lieutenant expressed his disappointment, candidly acknowledging that his own ship was waiting on the coast to let the Sandwich fill up, and get her sails bent, in order to send a party in, also, in order to cut her out! It was too late, however, as the Sally could not be, and would not be detained, and Hull proceeded.

There have been many more brilliant exploits than this of the Constitution, in sending in a party against the Sandwich, but very few that were more neatly executed, or ingeniously planned. The Sally arrived off the port, at the appointed hour, and stood directly in, showing the customary number of hands on deck, until coming near the letter of marque, she ran her aboard forward, and the Constitution's clambered in over the Sandwich's bows, led by Hull in person. In two minutes the Americans had possession of their prize, a smart brig, armed with four sixes and two nines, with a pretty strong crew, without the loss of a man. A party of marines, led by Capt. Cormick, landed, drove the Spaniards from a battery that commanded the anchorage, and spiked the guns. All this was against law and right, but it was very ingeniously arranged, and as gallantly executed. The most serious part of the affair remained to be achieved. The Sandwich was stripped to a girt line, and the wind blew directly into the harbor. As it was unsafe for the marines to remain in the battery any time, it was necessarily abandoned, leaving to the people of the place every opportunity of annoying their invaders by all the means they possessed. The battery was reoccupied, and the guns cleared of the spikes as well and as fast as they could be, while the Americans set about swaying up topmasts and yards and bending sails. After some smart exertion, the brig got royal yards across, and, at sunset, after remaining several hours in front of the town, Hull scaled his guns, by way of letting it be known they could be used, weighed, and began to beat out of the harbor. The Spaniards fired a few shot after him, but with no effect.

Although this was one of the best executed enterprises of the sort on record, and did infinite credit to the coolness and spirit of all concerned, it was not quite an illustration of international law or of justice in general.

This was the first victory of Old Ironsides in a certain sense, but all men must regret it was ever achieved, since it was a wrong act, committed with an exaggerated, if not an altogether mistaken notion of duty. America was not even at war with France, in the more formal meaning of the term, nor were all the legal consequences of war connected with the peculiar hostilities that certainly did exist; but with Spain she had no quarrel whatever, and the Sandwich was entitled to receive all the protection and immunities that of right belonged to her, as a French vessel, anchored in the neutral harbor of Port-au-Platte. In the end not only was the condemnation of the Sandwich resisted successfully, but all the other prize-money made by Old Ironsides in the cruise went to pay damages. The reason why the exploit itself never received the public commendation to which, as a mere military achievement, it was so justly entitled, was connected with the illegality and recklessness of the enterprise in its inception. It follows that this, which may be termed the Constitution's earliest victory, was obtained in the face of law and right. Fortunately the old craft has lived long enough to atone for this error of her youth by many a noble deed achieved in defence of principles and rights that the most fastidious will not hesitate to defend.

The Constitution returned to Boston in Aug. 1800, her cruise being up, not only on account of her orders, but on account of the short period for which men were then enlisted in the navy, which was one year. On the 18th Nov., however, she was ordered to sail again for the old station, still wearing the broad pennant of Talbot. Nothing occurred of interest in the course of this cruise; and, early in the spring, orders were sent to recall all the cruisers from the West Indies, in consequence of an arrangement of the difficulties with France.

It is certain that the good fortune of Old Ironsides did not appear in the course of this, her original service. While Nicholson had her, she does not seem to have captured any thing; and in Goldsborough's list of armed French vessels taken during the year 1798-9, and 1801, a period of near three years, during quite two years of which the ship must have been actively on her cruising grounds, he gives but four to the Constitution. These four vessels—La Tullie and L'Esther, two small privateers, the Sandwich and the Sally—the last of which, by the way, was an American, seized for illegal intercourse with the enemy.

By the peace establishment law, approved March 3d, 1801, all the frigates regularly constructed for the service were permanently retained in the navy. Old Ironsides enjoyed an excellent character among them, and was kept, of course, there being no other use for such a craft, indeed, in the country, than those connected with a military marine. Our frigate, however, was paid off and dismantled at Boston, where she remained unemployed from the spring of 1801 until the summer of 1803, rather more than two years, when Preble was ordered to her, with a broad pennant, in order to repair to the Mediterranean. As this was the commencement of the brilliant portion of Old Ironsides' career, it may be well to give a list of the officers who were now attached to, and who actually sailed in, her. It was the following:—

Commodore

Edward Preble

Lieutenants

Thomas Robinson	Jos. Tarbell
W. C. Jenckes	Sam. Elbert

Master

Nathaniel Haraden

This gentleman was known in the service by the sobriquet of "Jumping Billy."

Midshipmen

D. S. Dexter	W. Burrows
J. M. Haswell	D. Deacon
Ralph Izard	Heathcote Reed
Charles Morris	T. Baldwin
John Roe	Leonard Hunnewell
A. Laws	Jos. Nicholson
F. C. Hall	John Thompson, act'g.
I. Davis	

Of all these gentlemen, the present Commodore Morris and Mr. Hall, who is at present in the Marine corps, are now in the navy, and very few of the others still survive. They were not selected from the part of the country where the ship happened to lie, for by this time the navy had assumed so much of a fixed character that the officers were regarded as being at home in any portion of the republic. At Gibraltar, however, some important changes were made. Lt. Jenckes left the ship, and Lts. Dent and Gordon joined her, the former doing duty as acting captain. Midshipman Baldwin resigned, and Midshipmen Wadsworth, Alexis, Gadsden, Lewis, Israel, Ridgley, Carey, Robert Henly, and McDonough joined. With these alterations and additions the ship had five lieutenants and no less than twenty-three midshipmen. But changes soon occurred, which will be noticed in their places, the results of promotions and other causes.[2]

The Constitution sailed from Boston, on this new service, August 14th, 1803, and anchored at Gibraltar, Sept. 12th succeeding, making her passage in twenty-nine days. This was the first time our craft had ever shown herself in the European waters, her previous cruisings being confined to the West Indies and our own coast. It may as well be said here, that wherever she went, her mould and the fine order in which she was kept attracted general admiration.

The first service in which the gallant ship was employed in the other hemisphere, was to go off Tangiers, in a squadron composed of the Constitution 44, New York 36, John Adams 28, and Nautilus 12, in order to make a new treaty with the Emperor of Morocco. This important service successfully effected, Preble remained in and about the Straits, until the middle of November, employed in duties connected with his command. On the 23d October the ship sailed from Gibraltar for Cadiz, the Enterprise in company, and returned in a few days. While on this service, and when near

[2] Mr. Robinson is still living, having resigned a commander; Mr. Jenckes left the service; Tarbell died a captain, and Elbert a commander; Haswell resigned a lieutenant, and is dead; Dexter died a commander; Morris is now a commodore; Davis is out of service, and believed to be dead; Izard resigned a lieutenant, and is dead; Burrows was killed in battle, a lt. com.; Deacon died a captain; Laws resigned; Reed died a lieutenant; Rowe died, having been a lieutenant; Hall is now in the marine corps; Hunnewell out of service; Nicholson died a lieutenant. Of those who joined at Gibraltar or shortly after, Dent died a captain; Gordon died a captain; Wadsworth was blown up, a lieutenant; Gadsden died a lt. com.; Lewis was lost at sea a commander; Israel was blown up, a lieutenant; Ridgley is the present commodore; Henly died a captain; McDonough died at sea a commodore. The fortune of Alexis has been singular; he was born of a French noble family, and was sent, when quite young, to this country, to save his life, during the excesses of the French revolution. His real name was Louis Alexis de Courmont. As Lewis Alexis he rose to be a commander in the navy; but, at the restoration of the Bourbons, he was summoned to rejoin his family in France. He continued in the service notwithstanding, until about the year 1827 or 1828, as Capt. Alexis, when he was compelled to quit his family or resign. He preferred the latter, and is believed to be still living, as Mons. de Courmont. He was amiable, and much liked in the navy, and served gallantly at the defence of New Orleans.

McDonough had been left, by Bainbridge, as a prize-master, at Gibraltar, and thus escaped capture in the Philadelphia. He was early transferred to the Enterprise, Lt.-Com. Decatur, and was with that officer in all his battles off Tripoli. Morris, Ridgley, Wadsworth, Israel, Reed, Dexter, Haswell, and Izard, were all promoted in 1804.

the Straits, a large strange sail was made in the night, when the Constitution cleared, went to quarters and ran alongside of her. Preble hailed, and got no answer, but a hail in return. After some sharp hailing on both sides, Preble took a trumpet himself and gave the name of his ship, asking that of the stranger, with an intimation that he would give him a shot unless he replied. "If you give me a shot, I'll give you a broadside," returned the stranger in English. Preble now jumped into the mizzen-rigging, and called out distinctly, "This is the United States frigate Constitution, a 44, Edward Preble, commodore; I am now about to hail you for the last time—what ship is that?—Blow your matches, boys." "This is His Britannic Majesty's ship, Donnegal, a razee of 60 guns," was the answer. Preble told the stranger, in pretty plain terms, he doubted his statement, and that he should lie by him, until daylight, in order to ascertain his true character. Before things could be carried any further, however, a boat arrived from the stranger, who, as it now appeared, was the Maidstone 36, Captain Burdett. The delay in answering arose from a wish to gain time to clear for action, and get to quarters, Old Ironsides having got alongside so quietly that she had been taken by surprise.

After passing the time mentioned, in the vicinity of the Straits, the Constitution sailed in quest of declared enemies. She left Gibraltar on the 13th November, 1813, and proceeded first to Algiers, where she landed Colonel Lear, who had come out as Consul General. On the 20th she left Algiers, and on the 24th, while standing up the Mediterranean, on her way to Malta, she spoke an English frigate, which communicated a rumor, that the Philadelphia had run ashore, off Tripoli, and had fallen into the hands of the enemy. On reaching Malta, the 27th, while lying off the port, the unpleasant rumor was confirmed. The ship stood on without anchoring, and arrived at Syracuse next day.

Here, then, was Old Ironsides, for the first time, in the centre of the Mediterranean, and with something serious to do; more, indeed, than could easily be accomplished in a single ship. Her commander was as active a seaman as ever undertook an enterprise, and the career of the good ship, for the next seven months, though she did not fire a shot in anger during the whole time, was probably as remarkable as that of any vessel which ever floated, and which encountered neither enemies, shipwreck, nor accident of any sort.

The Constitution lay until the 17th December at Syracuse, when she sailed for Tripoli to look at her enemy, and to communicate with the unfortunate commander of the Philadelphia. On the 23d the Enterprise, Lieutenant Decatur, which was in company, captured a Tripolitan ketch, called the Mastico or Mistico, with seventy Turks of one sort and another on board her, the prize being sent in. While lying off Tripoli, on the 26th, it came on to blow fiercely, and the stout ship had need of all her excellent qualities to claw off shore. Her escape was somewhat narrow, but she went clear, and returned to Syracuse.

February 3d, 1804, Preble sent the Mastico, now named the Intrepid, to Tripoli on the well-known expedition to cut out the Philadelphia. All the connection our ship had with this successful and brilliant exploit, arose from the fact that her commander ordered it, and four of her midshipmen were of the party. These young gentlemen were Messrs. Izard, Morris, Laws, and Davis, all of whom returned safely, after their victory, to the steerage of Old Ironsides. Mr. Morris was shortly after promoted for being the first man on the Philadelphia's decks, as was Mr. Izard, for other good and sufficient claims. The last of these officers resigned about six years later, when first lieutenant of the old craft, and we shall have occasion hereafter to speak of Morris's service on board her, in the same character.

Having effected this important preliminary step, Preble set the ship in motion, in good earnest. On the 2d of March she sailed for Malta, arrived on the 3d, and returned on the 17th. On the 20th she sailed again for Tripoli, where she arrived in time to send in a flag on the 27th; a day or two later she sailed for Tunis, encountering a heavy gale on the passage, and anchored in the bay on the 4th of April. She left Tunis on the 7th, it blowing a gale from the northwest at the time, and reached Malta on the 12th; sailed for Syracuse on the 14th, and arrived on the 15th. All these movements were made necessary, in order to keep Tunis quiet, ascertain the state of things at Tripoli and obtain supplies at Malta. Business detained the ship at Syracuse until the 20th, when she was again off. On the 29th the busy craft again touched at Malta, having scoured along the enemy's coast, and on the 2d of May, less than a month from her appearance, the Bey of Tunis had the equivocal gratification of again seeing her in his harbor. War had been menaced, but peace succeeded this demonstration, and next day the ship was off for Naples, where she arrived on the 9th. The slow movements of the Neapolitans kept the active vessel ten days in that magnificent gulf, when away she went for Messina, with an order to get some of the king's gun-boats on board her. On the 25th she was at Messina and on the 30th she left that place, going round to Syracuse, where she anchored next day.

On the 4th of June, the Constitution was away once more for Malta, where she anchored on the 6th, and on the 9th she went to take another look at Tripoli. A flag was sent in on the 13th to know the Bashaw's ultimatum, but that dignitary refusing to accede to the terms offered, the Constitution got her anchor next day, and went to Tunis the third and last time, accompanied by two of the small vessels, as a hint to the Bey to remain quiet. The demonstration succeeded, and having reached Tunis on the 19th, the ship left it on the 22d for Syracuse, touched at Malta on the 24th, and reached her post on the 25th. On the 29th, away the frigate went again for Messina, arriving the 1st July, and sailing again on the 9th for Syracuse and getting in the same day.

Here was an activity almost without a parallel. Nor did it end here. On the 14th the good old craft lifted her anchor and went to sea; was in Malta on the 16th; left Malta on the 21st, and appeared off Tripoli, in company with all the force that had by this time been collected, in readiness to commence the war in earnest. We know very well that Preble's extraordinary energy was at the bottom of all these ceaseless movements; but the good old ship must come in for all that share of the credit, which properly belongs to a most admirably constructed machine. If the reader will recur to our dates he will find what was really done. Between the 2d March and the 25th July, there are 145 days, or less than five months. Between these dates, Old Ironsides left port eighteen times, without counting visits to different places where she did not anchor. The distances run were necessarily short, in some instances quite so, but the Mediterranean Sea was actually crossed in its entire breadth twice, and several of the passages were hundreds of miles in length. The ship that is in and out of port three times a month—and four times would be nearer the true proportion of the Constitution's movements—cannot be called idle; and our good craft, on all occasions, did her part of the duty admirably well.

It was not favorable weather for anchoring until the 28th, when Preble fetched up with all his squadron, which now consisted of fifteen sail, of one sort and another of fighting craft, with Old Ironsides at their head. The good frigate lay about a league from Tripoli, and the parties had now a good opportunity of looking at each other. The same day, however, a gale came on, and sent every thing out into the offing again; and it was August 3d before Preble brought his force in again.

The 3d August, 1804, will ever be memorable in American naval annals. It was the day on which Preble first attacked the batteries of Tripoli, and on which Decatur made his celebrated hand-to-hand assault on the gunboats, that had ventured to take up an anchorage outside the rocks. It does not come within the scope of our plan to give the particulars of the whole of this desperate engagement, and we shall confine ourselves principally to the part that was borne in it by the subject of our sketch. The battle itself began at three-quarters past two P.M., but it was a little later before Old Ironsides took a part in the fray. It ought to be mentioned here, that this ship had taken on board six long twenty-sixes at Syracuse, which had been mounted in her waist, and which were now manned by the marines, under Captain Hall; musketry being of no account in the service she was on. These six additional guns must have increased her entire armament to —— guns in broadside, and all along; viz., —— thirty twenty-fours below, —— twelves on the quarter-deck and forecastle, and the six twenty-sixes just mentioned.

The manner in which the Constitution went into action that day has often been the theme of praise. As she stood down to range along the rocks and batteries, and a harbor filled with armed craft, her people were aloft rolling up the light canvas as coolly as if about to come to in peaceable times, nor was a gun fired until as near the rocks as was deemed prudent, when she let the Turks have her larboard broadside, sending the shot home as far as the Bashaw's Castle. That was the first shotted broadside that Old Ironsides ever discharged at an enemy. As she was launched Sept. 20th, 1797, it follows that the good craft was just six years, ten months, and fourteen days old, ere she fired what may be called a shot in anger. No occasion had occurred on her previous service to bring the vessel herself alongside of an enemy, and here she was now commencing the brilliant part of her career, on the coast of Barbary, the very service for which she had been originally designed, though against a different prince. The ship kept ranging along the rocks, mole and batteries, often as near as within two cables' length of the first, and three of the last, silencing every thing that she could get fairly under her guns, so long as she lay opposed to it. The flotilla within the rocks, in particular, was the object of her attentions, and she made great havoc among its people by means of grape. It was when tacking or wearing, that the Constitution was most exposed, having no vessel of any size to cover her. It will be remembered that Tripoli mounted one hundred and fifteen pieces of heavy ordnance, behind stone walls, in addition to a large number of guns she had afloat, many of which were of as heavy calibre as any possessed by the Americans. At half-past four, the smaller vessels began to retire, covered by a blazing fire from the Constitution; and a quarter of an hour later, the frigate herself hauled off the land, and went out of action. In this, which may be termed her *début* in active warfare, our favorite ship escaped singularly well, considering the odds with which she had to contend, and the circumstances under which she fought. In all that service before Tripoli, she fought at great disadvantage, being held at precisely the distance that batteries wish to keep ships, by the rocks, within which it would have been madness for a single frigate to enter.

Although Old Ironsides was two full hours under fire, on the 3d August, time enough to have cut her into splinters, at the distance at which she was fought, and the number of guns that were brought to bear on her, had the Turkish gunnery been better than it was, she suffered very little, and not at all in her hull. One twenty-four pound shot passed through the centre of her mainmast, thirty feet above the deck; her main-royal-yard was shot away altogether; two lower shrouds and two back-stays were also shot away; and the running rigging, and sails generally, were a good deal cut. One heavy shot, supposed to have been a thirty-two, entered a stern port as the ship was wearing, and when she was most exposed, passed quite near to Preble, some accounts say actually beneath his leg, as he stood with it raised on the port sill, struck the breech of one of the quarter-deck twelves, which it damaged materially, and broke into fragments, that flew forward into the waist, along a deck crowded with men, of whom only one was injured. Here was the old ship's luck!—a good fortune or a providential care, as men may choose to regard the spirit of providential interferences, that has more or less attended the craft in all her subsequent battles and adventures. The man who was first wounded in battle, on the deck of Old Ironsides, deserves to have his name recorded. It was Charles Young, a marine, who had his elbow shattered by one of the fragments of the shot just mentioned. On this occasion, both Mr. Dent and Mr. Robinson were out of the ship. The former had been transferred to the Scourge, but commanded one of the bomb-ketches in the attacks; while the other, who had succeeded, as acting-captain of the frigate, commanded the other. Charles Gordon was now the first lieutenant, and did duty as such in the action, while Jumping Billy handled Old Ironsides under fire as he would have handled her in an American port.

The Constitution herself had no particular agency in the affairs which occurred between the 3d and the 28th August, though many of her officers and people were engaged. On the 7th, she lifted her anchor and stood in with an intention to mingle in the combat, but the wind coming out from the northward, it was thought imprudent to carry her as near the rocks as would be necessary to render her fire efficient, since the loss of a mast might have thrown her ashore. The 7th was the day on which Caldwell was blown up. Although the ship herself did not fire a shot that day, many of her people were in the thickest of the fight. The gun-boats and ketches received crews from the other vessels whenever they went into action, and that day, besides having her boats out in numbers, the Constitution put Mr. Wadsworth in No. 6, Trippe's boat, as her commander. The lateen yard of this boat was shot away in the action. Although the frigate did not engage, she kept so close in, directly to windward, as to overawe the Tripolitan flotilla, and keep them within the rocks. On the evening of the 7th, Chauncy joined from America, in the John Adams, armed *en flute*. The 28th was intended to be a day of special attack. All the boats of the squadron were manned and armed and sent to remain by the small vessels, in case the flotilla, which had shown some signs of a determination of coming to close quarters again, should put the intention in execution. To supply the places of those who left the ship, Chauncy joined her with several officers and about seventy seamen of the John Adams, and did duty as Preble's captain. Lieut.-Com. Dent also came on board—the ketches not engaging—and took charge of the quarterdeck. Izard, too, then a lieutenant on board the Scourge, which was not engaged, came on board his old ship. Wadsworth continued in No. 6, and Gordon took charge of No. 2, for the occasion. These changes made, the vessel was ready to engage.

The 28th was the day, when the attack commenced early in the morning; before it was light, indeed. For this purpose the American flotilla went quite close to the rocks, and began their fire through the openings. The brigs and schooners kept under way, near at hand, to cover them against any assaults from the enemy's boats, galleys, &c. All the Constitution's boats went in with the gun-boats, and were under fire from the first. As the day dawned, Old Ironsides weighed anchor, and stood in towards the town. Her approach was in the most admirable style, and Fort English, the Bashaw's Castle, the Crown, and Mole Batteries, all opened upon her, as soon as she came within range. The signal was now made for the gun-boats to withdraw, and for the brigs and schooners to take them in tow. Old Ironsides then took the game into her own hands, to cover the retreat, and may be said to have fought Tripoli single-handed. She ranged along within two cables' length of the rocks, and opened with round and grape on thirteen of the Turkish galleys and gun-boats, which had just been pretty closely engaged with the American.

For a few minutes the good old craft was a perfect blaze of fire, and she soon sunk one boat, drove two more ashore to keep from sinking, and scattered all the rest. Not satisfied with this, on went the frigate, until she got off the Mole, and within musket shot, when she hove to and sent ten broadsides into the different works. Three hundred round shot alone were fired, to say nothing of large quantities of grape and canister. After having been warmly engaged for near an hour, the flotilla being by this time out of danger, the gallant frigate herself filled and hauled proudly off the land, disdaining to fire any longer than she chose to engage.

Such work as this ought not to have been done by any single ship that ever floated, without her being cut to pieces. Nevertheless Old Ironsides was not really hulled; or if hulled at all, it was in a way so slight and peculiar as to induce Preble to report her as not having been hulled. Not a man on board her was injured, though grape was sticking in her side, and had passed through her sails in considerable quantities. Three lower shrouds, two springstays, two topmast back-stays, and the trusses, chains and lifts of the mainyard were all shot away, the running rigging suffered materially, and several round shot went through the canvas, but not a man was hurt. An anchor stock was shot away, and the larboard bower cable was cut. We think it probable that this last shot was the one which hit her figure-head. As Preble reports she was not hulled, meaning doubtless struck fairly in her main body by a round shot, and both an anchor stock and a cable were hit, it follows that the shot or shots which did this mischief must have passed ahead. Owing to the manner in which the ship lay exposed to guns at different points, nothing was more likely to occur than this. At all events it is known that Old Ironsides then carried an image of Hercules, with his club, as her figure-head, and that the head of this figure was knocked away, or materially injured before Tripoli. A canvas covering was put on to conceal the blemish, and continued there for some months. Chauncy did good service that day, and has thus left his name connected with the history of the gallant ship. At 11 in the forenoon, after such a morning's work, the Constitution anchored safely about five miles from the town, with all the squadron around her, when all hands went to work to repair damages.

On the 2d September, Preble got the whole squadron under way at 4 P.M., and kept it so all night. A little before midnight, the Constitution made a general signal to clear for action. At half past two next day, another signal was made to the gun-boats, then in tow of different vessels, to cast off, advance upon the enemy and commence an attack, which was done, in the direction of Fort English, or well to windward, while the ketches went nearer the town, and further to the westward, and opened with their mortars. All the brigs and schooners were pressing the enemy, at the harbor's mouth, or cannonading Fort English, while the Bashaw's Castle, the Crown, Mole and other batteries kept up a heavy fire on the ketches, which were in great danger; that commanded by Lieut.-Com. Robinson, being with difficulty kept from sinking. In order to cover these vessels, Old Ironsides now ran down inside of them and brought to, within range of grape as before, where she let fly eleven broadsides into the works. The berth of the good frigate was a warm one, as no less than seventy guns, or more than double her own number in broadside, bore on her at the same time, and they, too, all mounted behind stone walls. At half past 4, the wind had commenced hauling to the northward, when Preble made a signal for every thing to get away the land, and he hauled off into offing with his own ship. On this occasion the Turks threw a good many shells, besides round and grape, at Old Ironsides. One of these shells hit the back of the main-topsail, and nearly tore the sail in two. It was got into the top, however, and the sailmakers went to work on it, in the midst of the fray. Another shell went through the fore-topsail, and a third through the jib; making big holes, but doing no more harm. All the sails were much cut up, as was the running rigging, by round shot. The mainsheet, foretack, lifts, braces and bowlines were all hit, but nothing larger than grape touched the hull. As on the 7th, not a man was hurt!

When grape shot nearly bury themselves in the bends of such a ship as the Constitution, and she is fairly within the range of batteries, it is almost marvellous to think, that a vessel could be thus exposed, on three several occasions, and have but one man hurt. This was the last action in which the frigate was engaged in that war, however, and it is certain that in her three engagements with the batteries, and fighting not only against such odds, but under such disadvantages, she had but the single marine already named, Charles Young, injured on her decks.

The attempt with the Infernal came next, and in her went Wadsworth and Israel, with six of the Constitution's crew, to man the cutter. Somers had the Nautilus' boat, and four of his own men. All were lost of course, which made the total loss of the frigate out of her proper crew, while engaged before Tripoli, only two lieutenants and six men killed, and one marine wounded. The whole of the important service, indeed, effected by Preble, in his memorable forty days of active operations before the town, cost the country but thirty killed, and twenty-four wounded. Among those who fell, were one commander, four lieutenants, and one midshipman; and among the wounded, one captain (Decatur), and one lieutenant.

On the 10th, Com. Barron arrived with the President and Constellation, to relieve Preble. On the 12th, the squadron captured two Greek ships, loaded with wheat, that were trying to force the blockade, and Barron sent the frigate to Malta, with her prizes, where she arrived December 17th. Soon after reaching Malta, the command of Old Ironsides was transferred to Decatur, Preble returning home in the John Adams.

The active service of the war, so far as the larger vessels were concerned, had now terminated, though the blockade was maintained by different vessels. Decatur's command of the Constitution was of short continuance, Rodgers claiming her, on account of rank, and exchanging her for his old ship, the Congress. The transfer was made at Syracuse on the 6th November.

By this time Old Ironsides had used up, transferred, or lost, one way with another, about eighty of her original crew, and Barron ordered her to Lisbon, to pick up others there, if possible, assigning important duties to her near the Straits. The ship left Syracuse, November 27th, and having touched at Gibraltar and Tangiers, anchored before the town of Lisbon, December 28th. It was February 5th, before the men were picked up, when the ship sailed from Lisbon, and remaining off Tangiers, and about the Straits, for a few days, she proceeded aloft, again, and joined the squadron at Malta, on the 25th of the same month. Soon after she went off Tripoli, her old scene of glory, but returned by orders within the month. By this time the health of Barron was so bad, as to render Rodgers the efficient commander of the squadron, and the ship went off Tripoli, once more, coming in sight of the place, April 5th, 1805. The President, under Commander Cox, soon afterwards joined her, and on the 24th, Old Ironsides took an armed xebeck, and two Neapolitans her prizes, that were endeavoring to enter the port. Not long after, the ship went to Malta.

On the 22d May, Commodore Barron formally transferred the command of the squadron to Rodgers, who hoisted a pennant once more on board Old Ironsides. Commodore Rodgers had now the choice between the sister vessels, the President and Constitution, but he chose to keep the one he was in.

As the active season was at hand, it became necessary now to treat, or to prepare for another series of offensive operations. Col. Lear had been sent for by the Essex, and the Constitution going off Tripoli, the negotiations commenced which terminated in the desired peace, the end of all war. Nations go to war because they are at peace, and they make peace because they are at war! The negotiations that terminated the war with Tripoli, took place in the cabin of Old Ironsides. She had come late into the conflict, but had done more to bring it to a conclusion, than all the frigates that had preceded her, and was fated to see the end. It is said that this was the first treaty ever concluded with one of the States of Barbary, on shipboard. It was certainly a striking event for a hostile vessel to be thus employed, and proved the impressions which recent occurrences had made on the usually haughty Turk. The treaty was signed on shore by the Bashaw, however, and June 3d a copy was brought by the Danish Consul, Nissen, on board the Constitution, and delivered to Col. Lear and Rodgers. Old Ironsides now exchanged salutes with the town, and thus ended the war with Tripoli, after more than four years' continuance.

The occupation of the good craft did not cease, however, with the arrangement with the Bashaw, nor was she destined to return to this hemisphere for some time longer. The Bey of Tunis had manifested a warlike disposition for a long time, and a strong force being now in the Mediterranean, Rodgers saw that the present was a good occasion to bring that difficulty to a conclusion also. He had collected most of his vessels at Syracuse, where the Constitution arrived about the middle of June. At a later day the squadron passed over to Malta, and July 23d, 1805, Old Ironsides sailed from Malta, leading a squadron, composed of three other frigates, a brig, two schooners, a sloop, and several large American-built gun-boats, that had actually crossed the ocean that summer. The Congress and Vixen were already off the port, making, when every thing was collected, a force of five frigates, two brigs, two schooners, a sloop and four gun-boats. The Constitution led this respectable armament into Tunis Bay, July 30th, where it anchored on the 1st of August.

This demonstration had the desired result, and an arrangement of all the difficulties was happily effected by the middle of the month. The squadron lay in the bay thirty-two days, in order to make all sure, when it separated; some going one way, and some another, most returning home. Old Ironsides, nevertheless, was too much of a favorite to be easily given up. Rodgers continued in her until the succeeding year, when he gave her up, with the command of the squadron, to Campbell, who remained out for a considerable period longer, almost alone. It would be of little interest to turn over log-books, in order to record how often the ship went in and out of the different ports of the Mediterranean, but nothing of consequence occurred until near the close of 1807, when the ship had been from home quite four years.

By this time the relations between this country and England became much embroiled, and in the midst of all the other difficulties, occurred the attack on the Chesapeake, by the Leopard. The Chesapeake had been intended for the relief ship on the Mediterranean station, and she sailed near the close of June, on that duty. After the attack her cruise was abandoned, and in expectation of hostilities which threatened to be of early occurrence, this station itself was broken up. There were but two ships on it, the Constitution and the Hornet, and the times of many of the people of the former had long been up. There were a good many of the original crew of Old Ironsides still on board her, and these men had now been out four years, when they had shipped for only three. It is true, new engagements had been made with many of the men, but others had declined making any. In this state of things, Campbell brought the ship down to Malaga, and waited anxiously for the appearance of his relief. She did not come, but, in her stead arrived the report of what had occurred to her. It now became necessary for some one to go aloft, and Campbell determined to move the good ship, once more, in that direction. All hands were called to get the anchors, when the men refused to man the bars unless the ship sailed for home. There was a moment when things looked very serious, but Campbell was nobly sustained by his officers, with Ludlow at their head, and after a crisis, in which force was used in seizing individuals, and the marines were paraded, and found to be true, the insubordinate spirit was quelled. No one was ever punished for this attempt at mutiny, for it was felt that, on principle, the men had a great deal of right on their side. A law has since been passed to prevent the possibility of setting up a claim for discharges, until a ship is properly relieved.

At length the station was abandoned, and Old Ironsides sailed for her native place, Boston. On her arrival in that port, it was found necessary, however, to send her to New-York, in order to be paid off. She reached the last port in November 1807, and was dismantled for repairs.

Thus terminated the fourth of the Constitution's cruises, which had been twice as long as the three others put together, and a hundred times more momentous. She had now seen enemies, had fought them again and again, had witnessed the signing of treaties under her pennant, besides their dictation. In a word the good craft had been *magna pars* in many an important event. She was in some measure entitled to the character of a statesman, as well as that of a warrior.

The Constitution was now more than ten years old, and some serious repairs had become necessary. America did not then possess a single dry-dock, and preparations were made for heaving her out. This was done, at Brooklyn Yard, in the spring of 1808, when her copper was examined and repaired. All this time the ship was not properly out of commission; many officers were attached to her; and as soon as she was righted, and got her spars aloft, Rodgers, who commanded on the station afloat, as Chauncy did the yard, showed his broad pennant in her again. For a time, Lawrence acted as her first lieutenant, as did Izard, his successor, when Lawrence was transferred to the command of a brig. Nevertheless, the ship lay near, if not quite, a twelvemonth at the yard, before she received a full crew, and began to cruise.

This was a period when all the active naval force of the country was kept on the coast. The Mediterranean had been the only foreign station, after the peace with France, and that was broken up. Two home squadrons were maintained—one to the northward, under Rodgers, and one to the southward, under a different commander. The broad pennant of the commander-in-chief afloat, was flying on board Old Ironsides. This gave the old craft an opportunity of showing herself, and making acquaintances, in various of the home ports. Until Campbell brought her round to New-York, in 1807, to be paid off, it is believed she had never entered any American harbor but that of Boston, except Hampton Roads. Yankee born, and Yankee bred, she had had Yankee commanders, until Decatur got her; and in that day there was more of provincial feeling among us than there is at present. This was probably the reason that the Constitution was so often taken to Boston; out of which port she has sailed, owing to peculiar circumstances, on every one of her most successful cruises.

When Nicholson went on the southern coast, there was no port except Hampton Roads, in that quarter, into which he would be likely to go with so heavy a ship; and unless he did, we do not see when Old Ironsides could have been in any haven of the country, except Boston, until the close of the year 1807. This visit to New-York, however, broke the charm, and since that, nearly every important port of the coast, that has sufficient water to receive her, has had a visit. Rodgers kept Old Ironsides, until 18 , when he shifted his pennant to the President, under the impression that the last was the faster ship. Some persons fancied the good craft had lost her sailing.

* * * * * *

Deaths and resignations had made Rodgers the oldest officer afloat, and he did very much as he chose in these matters. Off the wind, the President was unquestionably one of the fastest ships that ever floated, but *on* a wind, the Constitution was her match, any day, especially if the vessels were brought to double-reefed topsails. The President was a more roomy ship, perhaps, tumbling home the least, but Old Ironsides was confessedly of the stoutest frame, and the best ribbed.

The sailing of many of the vessels fell off about this time, and we think an intelligent inquiry would show that it was owing to a cause common to them all. The commanders were anxious to make their vessels as efficient as possible, by loading them with guns, and filling them with men. The spars, too, were somewhat increased in weight, which produced an increase in ballast. The guns and spars were not of so much moment, but the additional men required additional provisions and water, and this sunk the hull deeper in the water, and demanded a greater moving power. When Barry first took the States out to the West Indies, she was one of the fastest frigates that ever floated, though the Constitution was thought to be her equal. About the year 1810, nevertheless, the States had got so bad a name for sailing, that she went by the *soubriquet* of the Old Waggon, and was held quite cheap by all who were in a hurry. The Macedonian, her prize, certainly beat her under a jury mizzenmast; but some one took the trouble to overhaul the hold of the States one day, and to lighten her, and now she defies the world!

Rodgers had a good and a deserved reputation for fitting out a ship; but he was fond of men, and usually filled his vessels too full of one thing and another. Owing to this, or some other reason, he lost his first love for Old Ironsides, and deserted her for the President.

It is a great mistake to try to give a puissant battery to a vessel that was never meant to carry one. One cannot make a frigate of a sloop-of-war, by any expedient; and the uses of an active sloop may be injured by an abortive attempt so to do. This is particularly true of very small, sharp vessels, which lose their trim by slight variations, and which, at the best, can be nothing but *small,* sharp vessels, and if properly stowed, of great efficiency, on account of their speed; if not, of very little, on account of an unavoidable want of force.

Hull succeeded Rodgers in the command of the Constitution, and the good ship was compelled to strike her broad pennant. As for Hull, he knew his ship well—having been a lieutenant in her, and her first lieutenant besides. Morris, too, who had sailed in her as a midshipman, under Preble, and who had been promoted *out* of her into the Argus, Hull's old brig, before Tripoli, now joined her, as her new first lieutenant. The transfer was made at

Hampton Roads, in the summer of 1810. During the remainder of the season, the ship cruised on the coast, and she wintered at New London.

Nothing worthy of being recorded occurred under this new state of things, until the Constitution was ordered to Europe, in the course of the year 1811, with Mr. Barlow on board, and with money to pay the interest on the Dutch debt. In that day, it was a common thing to send vessels of war across the Atlantic, on the errands of the public, though this was the first time, since 1800, that a ship as heavy as the Constitution was thus employed. Under Hull, while thus employed, the Constitution's lieutenants appear to have included Messrs. Morris, Page and Read. Of these officers, Messrs. Morris and Read are still living, and have carried broad pennants.

The ship sailed for Cherbourg direct. Off that port she found a strong British squadron, under the late Sir Pultney Malcolm, who was in the Royal Oak seventy-four. Old Ironsides, on this occasion, was nearly surrounded by Englishmen, all of whom came up on her quarters, one, a frigate, speaking her, first telling her own name, as is usual between vessels of war, and then asking hers. When the last was given, permission was asked to send a boat on board, which was readily granted. The English commodore now sent a request to see Captain Hull, on board the Royal Oak, if it were his intention to go into Cherbourg. The answer was, it was contrary to usage for an American captain to leave his vessel at sea, unless to wait on his own immediate superior. A second request followed, that he would not go in until a certain hour next morning. To this Hull replied, that he was bound into Cherbourg, with a minister on board, and he felt it to be his duty to enter the port the moment circumstances permitted. These were ticklish times—the affair of the Chesapeake, and the generally high pretensions of the English marine, placing every American commander strictly on the alert. No further communications passed, however, and the ship went into her port, as soon as circumstances would allow.

Having landed Mr. Barlow, the Constitution sailed for the Downs, where she obtained a pilot, and proceeded to the Texel. Here she sent ashore about $200,000 in specie, and returned to the Downs, whence she stood on to Portsmouth, anchoring at Spithead, among a force of between thirty and forty English cruisers. Hull now went up to London, leaving Morris in command. After lying at Spithead near a fortnight, an incident occurred that is well worthy of being mentioned. Nearly in a line with Old Ironsides, following the course of the tides, lay the Havannah, 36, one of the frigates then in port. One night, near the close of the first watch, Mr. Read having the deck, a man of the name of Holland contrived to get out of the ship, and to swim down to the Havannah, where he caught hold of something, and held on until he could make himself heard, when he was picked up greatly exhausted. The first lieutenant of the Havannah, knowing that Holland was a deserter from the Constitution, under his first professional impulse, sent the boat alongside of the American ship to report the occurrence, adding that the man was too much exhausted to be moved then, but that he should be sent back in the morning. Mr. Morris waited until ten o'clock, when he sent a boat alongside of the Havannah to procure the deserter. The first lieutenant of that ship, however, had seen the propriety of reporting the whole affair to the admiral (Sir Roger Curtis), who had ordered him to send the man on board his flag ship, the Royal William. Thither, then, it was necessary to proceed, and Mr. Read was despatched to that vessel with a renewal of the demand. This officer met with a very polite reception from the captain of the Royal William, who acquainted him with the fact, that no British officer could give up a man who claimed protection as a British subject. Holland was an Irishman, and had put in his claim to the protection of the British flag. To this Mr. Read replied, it might be true that the man was born in Ireland, but he had entered voluntarily into the American service, and was bound to adhere to his bargain, until the term of his enlistment had expired. The English officer could only regret that the respective duties of the two services seemed to conflict, and adhered to his first decision. Mr. Read then remarked that since the Constitution had lain at Spithead several letters had been received on board her from men professing to be Americans, who stated that they had been impressed into the English service, and should any of these men run and get on board the Constitution, that her commanding officer might feel himself bound to protect them. The captain of the Royal William hoped nothing of the kind would occur, and here the conversation ended.

 That night a man was heard in the water alongside of the Constitution, and a boat was immediately lowered to bring him on board. It was a seaman of the Havannah, who had fastened some shells of blocks beneath his arms, lowered himself into the water, and floated with the tide down to the American frigate, which he hailed. A boat was lowered and he was taken on board. A few minutes later a boat came from the Havannah to claim him. "You cannot have the man," said Morris; "he says he is an American, and claims our protection." "Can I see him?" asked the English lieutenant. "No sir."

"We will have him, as you will find out," said the young man, as he descended the ship's side and got into his own boat.

There was a good deal of negotiation, and some correspondence the next day. Morris had visited the admiral himself, and Hull arrived in the course of the day. The last approved of all that had been done. The deserter from the Havannah, whose name was Byrne, or Burns, had insisted that he was a native of New-York, and had been impressed, and it is not unlikely his story may have been true, as an English subject would hardly have ventured on the experiment he had tried. But true or not, the principle was the same, and Hull was determined not to give him up unless Holland was sent back. In each case the assertion of the man himself was all the testimony as to nationality, while Hull could show his deserter had shipped voluntarily, whereas Burns had been impressed.

The occurrence of such a transaction, in the roads of Spithead, in the height of a war, and among forty English cruisers, could not but produce a great excitement at Portsmouth. Every boat that came off to the Constitution brought rumors of a hostile character from the shore. "It was impossible," these rumors said, "that a foreign man-of-war could be permitted to quit the roads under such circumstances, carrying off an English deserter in her." Hull meant to do it, nevertheless, and Old Ironsides manifested every disposition to do her duty. A frigate anchored near her, and Hull took his ship outside of the fleet, where he was followed by the heaviest frigate in the roads. "This will do well enough," said Hull, to one of his lieutenants; "if they don't send any more I think I can manage that chap, and 'twill be a pretty fair fight." The Constitution went to quarters and lighted up her batteries, exercising guns for a quarter of an hour. The frigate came close to her, but no hostilities were offered, and the Constitution carried off her man unmolested.

Off Cherbourg the Constitution again fell in with the English blockading force. After communicating with one of the vessels she began to beat in towards the harbor. It was raining a little, and the day was clouded, though clear enough for all the purposes of war. The English vessels formed in a line ahead, and beat up a short distance to leeward of the American frigate, tacking as she tacked, while one of their light cruisers kept close under her lee. Hull, on quitting Cherbourg, had agreed on a signal, by which his ship might be known on her return; but some peculiar circumstances prevented the signal being shown just at that moment, and the batteries mistaking her for an enemy, began to fire. This was a most critical situation for Old Ironsides, as she was now near enough to be torn to pieces if she bore up, and the French commenced in earnest on her. As it was, every, or nearly every shot fired, hit her. Hull was standing in one of her gangways with Read near him, just as a gun was fired. Read was looking towards the battery that was firing, and Hull was looking inboard at that moment. As soon as the shot was clear of the smoke Read saw it, and he spoke to his captain requesting him to move. Hull did not move, however, or even look round, and the shot passed through the hammocks, within two or three feet of the place where he stood, knocked the stern of the launch into pieces, and damaged another boat that was towed alongside her. Another shot struck in the bend, just below the gangway, but did not pass through. Notwithstanding all this, Old Ironsides stood steadily on, and the signal was soon after shown, though not from the part of the ship agreed on. It was the nerve manifested on board that caused the French to cease firing, and the ship shortly after passed inside. This was the only occasion on which our gallant frigate ever received a French shot in her ribs, although she had been used in a French war.

After lying some time at Cherbourg, the Constitution sailed for home, reaching Hampton Roads late in the winter of 1812, or early in the spring. The ship was soon after carried up to Washington, and most of her people were discharged. Morris and Page left her, but some of her lieutenants continued attached to her—it being intended to fit her out again. Hull also continued his command. He told the Secretary of the bad sailing of the ship, and advised that she should be hove out that her copper might be examined. Harraden, her old master, under Preble, was then master of the Washington Yard, and he offered to put the ship in sailing trim, if Hull would give her up to him for that purpose. The arrangement was made, and Jumping Billy [3] went to work, like a true seaman as he was. After repairing the ship's copper, she was restowed with about two-thirds of her former ballast, and the effect was magical. Her old officers, when they came to try her, scarce knew the ship, she proved to be so much lighter and livelier than before. There is little question that Jumping Billy's precaution served Old Ironsides in the arduous trial she was now so soon to undergo.

Rumors of an approaching war began to circulate freely before the Constitution got fully equipped, and she soon dropped down as low as Alexandria.

[3] This soubriquet came from the name of a purchase that is called a "Jumping Billy," and which was a great favorite with this officer. Harraden passed with many persons as an Englishman; but, in truth, he was a native of Massachusetts, who had been impressed, and had served a long time in the English Navy.

This was about the beginning of June, 1812. At this time the ship had about two hundred and fifty men on board her, that had been collecting for a few weeks previously, and some of her late officers rejoined her. She was still off Alexandria when the news came down that war was actually declared against Great Britain. Read was the oldest lieutenant then on board, and he had all hands called and made them a speech. When he had ended, the men asked permission to cheer; a request that was granted of course, and nine hearty cheers succeeded. This demonstration of feeling, however, was scarcely over, when several of the crew came forward, and stated that they were English deserters, and they were afraid to serve against their native country. The case was stated to Hull, who ordered them all discharged. This done, the remainder of the people were perfectly ready to engage. About this time Beekman Verplanck Hoffman joined as one of the lieutenants.

The frigate gradually dropped down lower, receiving stores, and was joined again by Morris and Wadsworth, the former as her first, and the latter as her second lieutenant. Shortly after she went up the bay to Annapolis, where the equipment of the vessel was completed. Here John Shubrick and Aylwin, a new master, joined, and a draft of men came on also. This nearly filled up the complement; and Hull, who had joined in the river, was ordered to carry the vessel round to New-York. On the 5th of July the anchor was weighed, and Old Ironsides proceeded down the bay and to sea on the 13th to cruise in the third and last of her wars.

At this time the principal officers of this well-known frigate were Isaac Hull, Esq., captain; Messrs. Charles Morris, Alexander Wadsworth, George Campbell Read, Beekman Verplanck Hoffman, John Templer Shubrick, and Charles W. Morgan,[4] (acting) lieutenants; Messrs. Bush and Contee, lieutenants of marines; Wm. C. Aylwin, master; T. J. Chew, purser; and Amos A. Evans, surgeon. Among the midshipmen were Messrs. Gilliam, Beatty, Madison, Salter (now a captain), German, Gordon, Field, Baury (lost in the Wasp), Cross, Belcher, W. Taylor, Eskridge, Delany, Greenleaf, Griffin, and Tayloe. Morris, Read, and Wadsworth[5] are still living, as commodores; but Shubrick and Hoffman are both dead.

The Constitution got under way, from her moorings off Annapolis, July 5th, 1812, or sixteen days after the declaration of war. The intermediate time had passed in completing the crew and the equipments of the ship. A draft of men having arrived only the previous evening, Morris was occupied in station-

---

[4] Morgan died, a captain, Jan. 5th, 1853.
[5] Wadsworth died, a captain, April 5th, 1851, since the above was written.

ing them, as the vessel was leaving the bay. Many of the guns even had been taken on board low down in the Potomac, and a vast deal of necessary work had been done between the time when the ship left the Potomac and her day of going to sea. Much also remained to be done. The berth of a first lieutenant was no sinecure then.

Friday, July the 17th, the ship was out of sight of land, though at no great distance from the coast, with a light breeze from the N. E., and under easy canvas. At one, she sounded in twenty-two fathoms; and about an hour afterwards, four sail were made in the northern board, heading to the westward. At three, the Constitution made sail, and tacked in eighteen and a half fathoms. At four, she discovered a fifth sail to the northward and eastward, which had the appearance of a vessel of war. This ship subsequently proved to be the Guerriere, thirty-eight, Capt. Dacres. By this time, the other four sail were made out to be three ships and a brig; they bore N.N.W., and were all on the starboard tack, apparently in company. The wind now became very light, and the Constitution hauled up her mainsail. The ship in the eastern board, however, had so far altered her position by six, as to bear E.N.E., the wind having hitherto been fair for her to close. But at a quarter past six, the wind came out light at the southward, bringing the American ship to windward. The Constitution now wore round with her head to the eastward, set her light studding-sails and staysails, and at half-past seven beat to quarters, and cleared for action, with the intention of speaking the nearest vessel.

The wind continued very light at the southward, and the two vessels were slowly closing until eight. At ten, the Constitution shortened sail, and immediately after she showed the private signal of the day. After keeping the lights aloft near an hour, and getting no answer from the Guerriere, the Constitution, at a quarter past eleven, lowered the signal, and made sail again, hauling aboard her starboard tacks. During the whole of the middle watch the wind was very light, from the southward and westward. Just as the morning watch was called, the Guerriere tacked, then wore entirely round, threw a rocket, and fired two guns. As the day opened, three sail were discovered on the starboard quarter of the Constitution, and three more astern. At five A. M., a fourth vessel was seen astern.

This was the squadron of Com. Broke, which had been gradually closing with the American frigate during the night, and was now just out of gunshot. As the ships slowly varied their positions, when the mists were entirely cleared away, the Constitution had two frigates on her lee quarter, and a ship of the line, two frigates, a brig, and a schooner astern. The names of the enemy's ships have already been given; but the brig was the Nautilus, and the schooner another prize. All the strangers had English colors flying.

It now fell quite calm, and the Constitution hoisted out her boats, and sent them ahead to tow, with a view to keep the ship out of the reach of the enemy's shot. At the same time she whipt up one of the gun-deck guns to the spar-deck, and run it out aft as a stern chaser, getting a long eighteen off the forecastle also, for a similar purpose. Two more of the twenty-fours below were run out at the cabin windows, with the same object, though it was found necessary to cut away some of the wood-work of the stern frame, in order to make room.

By six o'clock the wind, which continued very light and baffling, came out from the northward of west, when the ship's head was got round to the southward, and all the light canvas that would draw was set. Soon after, the nearest frigate, the Shannon, opened with her bow guns, and continued firing for about ten minutes; but perceiving she could not reach the Constitution, she ceased. At half past six, Captain Hull sounded in twenty-six fathoms, when, finding that the enemy was likely to close, as he was enabled to put the boats of two ships on one, and was also favored by a little more air than the Constitution, all the spare rope that could be found, and which was fit for the purpose, was payed down into the cutters, bent on, and a kedge was run out near half a mile ahead, and let go. At a signal given, the crew clapped on, and walked away with the ship, overrunning and tripping the kedge as she came up with the end of the line. While this was doing, fresh lines and another kedge was carried ahead, and, though out of sight of land, the frigate had glided away from her pursuers before they discovered the manner in which it was done. It was not long, however, before the enemy resorted to the same expedient. At half past seven, the Constitution had a little air, when she set her ensign, and fired a shot at the Shannon, the nearest ship astern. At eight, it fell calm again, and further recourse was had to the boats and the kedges, the enemy's vessels having a light air and drawing ahead, towing, sweeping, and kedging. By nine, the nearest frigate, the Shannon, on which the English had put most of their boats, was closing fast, and there was every prospect, notwithstanding the steadiness and activity of the Constitution's people, that the frigate just mentioned would get near enough to cripple her, when her capture by the rest of the squadron would be inevitable. At this trying moment the best spirit prevailed in the ship. Every thing was stoppered, and Capt. Hull was not without hopes, even should he be forced into action, of throwing the Shannon astern by his fire, and of maintaining his distance from the other vessels. It was known that the enemy could not tow very near, as it would have been easy to sink his boats with the stern guns of the Constitution, and not a man in the latter vessel showed a disposition to despondency. Officers and men relieved each other regularly at the duty, and while the former threw themselves down on deck to catch short naps, the people slept at their guns.

This was one of the most critical moments of the chase. The Shannon was fast closing, as has been just stated, while the Guerriere was almost as near on the larboard quarter. An hour promised to bring the struggle to an issue, when, suddenly, at nine minutes past nine, a light air from the southward struck the ship, bringing her to windward. The beautiful manner in which this advantage was improved, excited admiration even in the enemy. As the breeze was seen coming, the ship's sails were trimmed, and as soon as she was under command, she was brought close up to the wind, on the larboard tack; the boats were all dropped in alongside; those that belonged to the davits were run up, while the others were just lifted clear of the water, by purchases on the spare outboard spars, where they were in readiness to be used again at a moment's notice. As the ship came by the wind, she brought the Guerriere nearly on her lee beam, when that frigate opened a fire from her broadside. While the shot of this vessel was just falling short of them, the people of the Constitution were hoisting up their boats with as much steadiness as if the duty was performing in a friendly port. In about an hour, however, it fell nearly calm again, when Capt. Hull ordered a quantity of the water started to lighten the ship. More than two thousand gallons were pumped out, and the boats were sent ahead again to tow. The enemy now put nearly all his boats on the Shannon, the nearest ship astern; and a few hours of prodigious exertion followed, the people of the Constitution being compelled to supply the place of numbers by their activity and zeal. The ships were close by the wind, and every thing that would draw was set, and the Shannon was slowly, but steadily, forging ahead. About noon of this day, there was a little relaxation from labor, owing to the occasional occurrence of cat's-paws, by watching which, closely, the ship was urged through the water. But at a quarter past twelve, the boats were again sent ahead, and the toilsome work of towing and kedging was renewed.

At one o'clock a strange sail was discovered nearly to leeward. At this moment the four frigates of the enemy were about one point on the lee quarter of the Constitution, at long gun-shot, the Africa and the two prizes being on the lee-beam. As the wind was constantly baffling, any moment might have brought a change, and placed the enemy to windward. At seven minutes before two, the Belvidera, then the nearest ship, began to fire with her bow-guns, and the Constitution opened with her stern chasers. On board the latter ship, however, it was soon found to be dangerous to use the main-deck guns, the transoms having so much rake, the windows being so high, and the guns so short, that every explosion lifted the upper deck, and threatened to blow out the stern frame. Perceiving, moreover, that his shot did little or no execution, Capt. Hull ordered the firing to cease at half past two.

For several hours the enemy's frigates were now within gun-shot, sometimes towing and kedging, and at others endeavoring to close with the puffs of air that occasionally passed. At seven in the evening the boats of the Constitution were again ahead, the ship steering S.W.½W., with an air so light as to be almost imperceptible. At half past seven she sounded in twenty-four fathoms. For hours the same toilsome duty was going on, until a little before eleven, when a light air from the southward struck the ship. The boats instantly dropped alongside, hooked on, and were all run up, with the exception of the first cutter. The topgallant studding-sails and staysails were set as soon as possible, and for about an hour the people caught a little rest.

But at midnight it fell nearly calm again, though neither the pursuers nor the pursued had recourse to the boats, probably from an unwillingness to disturb their crews. At two A. M., it was observed on board the Constitution, that the Guerriere had forged ahead, and was again off their lee beam. At this time, the topgallant studding-sails were taken in.

In this manner passed the night, and on the morning of the next day, it was found that three of the enemy's frigates were within long gun-shot, on the lee quarter, and the other at about the same distance on the lee beam. The Africa and the prizes were much further to leeward.

A little after daylight, the Guerriere, having drawn ahead sufficiently to be forward of the Constitution's beam, tacked, when the latter ship did the same, in order to preserve her position to windward. An hour later the Æolus passed on the contrary tack, so near that it was thought by some who observed the movement, that she ought to have opened her fire; but, as that vessel was merely a twelve-pounder frigate, and she was still at a considerable distance, it is quite probable her commander acted judiciously. By this time, there was sufficient wind to cause Hull to hoist in his first cutter.

The scene on the morning of this day was very beautiful, and of great interest to the lovers of nautical exhibitions. The weather was mild and lovely, the sea smooth as a pond, and there was quite wind enough to remove the necessity of any of the extraordinary means of getting ahead, that had been so freely used during the previous eight-and-forty hours. All the English vessels had got on the same tack with the Constitution again, and the five frigates were clouds of canvas, from their trucks to the water. Including the American ship, eleven sail were in sight, and shortly after a twelfth appeared to windward, that was soon ascertained to be an American merchantman. But the enemy were too intent on the Constitution to regard any thing else, and though it would have been easy to capture the ships to leeward, no attention appears to have been paid to them. With a view, however, to deceive the ship to windward, they hoisted American colors, when the Constitution set an English ensign, by way of warning the stranger to keep aloof.

Until ten o'clock the Constitution was making every preparation for carrying sail hard, should it become necessary, and she sounded in twenty-five fathoms. At noon the wind fell again, though it was found, that while the breeze lasted, she had gained on all the enemy's ships; more, however, on some than on others. The nearest vessel was the Belvidera, which was exactly in the wake of the Constitution, distant about two and a half miles, bearing W.N.W. The nearest frigate to leeward bore N. by W. ½ W. distant three or three and a half miles; the two other frigates were on the lee quarter, distant about five miles, and the Africa was hull down to leeward, on the opposite tack.

This was a vast improvement on the state of things that had existed the day previous, and it allowed the officers and men to catch a little rest, though no one left the decks. The latitude by observation this day, was 38°, 47 N., and the longitude by dead reckoning 73°, 57 W.

At meridian the wind began to blow a pleasant breeze, and the sound of the rippling under the bows of the vessel was again heard. From this moment the noble old ship slowly drew ahead of all her pursuers, the sails being watched and tended in the best manner that consummate seamanship could dictate, until four P. M., when the Belvidera was more than four miles astern, and the other vessels were thrown behind in the same proportion, though the wind had again got to be very light.

In this manner both parties kept pressing ahead, and to windward, as fast as circumstances would allow, profiting by every change, and resorting to all the means of forcing vessels through the water, that are known to seamen. At a little before seven, however, there was every appearance of a heavy squall, accompanied by rain; when the Constitution prepared to meet it with the coolness and discretion she had displayed throughout the whole affair.

The people were stationed, and every thing was kept fast to the last moment, when, just before the squall struck the ship, the order was given to clew up and clew down. All the light canvas was furled, a second reef was taken in the mizzen-topsail, and the ship was brought under short sail, in an incredibly little time. The English vessels, observing this, began to let go and haul down without waiting for the wind, and when they were shut in by the rain, they were steering in different directions to avoid the force of the expected squall. The Constitution, on the other hand, no sooner got its weight, than she sheeted home and hoisted her fore and main-top-gallant sails, and while the enemy most probably believed her to be borne down by the pressure of the wind, steering free, she was flying away from them, on an easy bowline, at the rate of eleven knots.

In a little less than an hour after the squall had struck the ship, it had entirely passed to leeward, and a sight was again obtained by the enemy. The Belvidera, the nearest vessel, had altered her bearings, in that short period, two points more to leeward, and she was a long way astern. The next nearest vessel was still further to leeward, and more distant, while the two remaining frigates were fairly hull down. The Africa was barely visible in the horizon!

All apprehensions of the enemy now ceased, though sail was carried to increase the distance, and to preserve the weather gauge. At half-past ten, the wind backed further to the southward, when the Constitution, which had been steering free for some time, took in her lower studding-sails. At 11, the enemy fired two guns, and the nearest ship could just be discovered. As the wind baffled and continued light, the enemy still persevered in the chase, but at daylight the nearest vessel was hull down astern and to leeward. Under the circumstances it was deemed prudent to use every exertion to lose sight of the English frigates; and the wind falling light, the Constitution's sails were wet down from the skysails to the courses. The good effects of this care were soon visible, as at six A. M. the topsails of the enemy's nearest vessels were beginning to dip. At a quarter past eight, the English ships all hauled to the northward and eastward, fully satisfied, by a trial that had lasted nearly three days and as many nights, under all the circumstances that can attend naval manœuvres, from reefed topsails to kedging, that they had no hope of overtaking their enemy.

The chase off New-York brought the Constitution largely before the public mind. It is true that this exploit was not one of a character to excite the same feeling as a successful combat; but men saw that the ships and crews that could achieve such an escape from a British squadron, must both of them have the right stuff for a glorious marine. Among the other amiable political misrepresentations of that day, it had been boldly asserted in the opposition prints, that the ship had gone to sea without the necessary supply of powder; and the assertion had been so audaciously and perseveringly made, as is most apt to be the case, with this class of moralists, who usually make up the deficiencies in their facts by the vigor of their assertions, that the public had been more than half disposed to anticipate some early disaster to this particular vessel, when the news arrived of her successful struggle with the only collected force the enemy then possessed in the American seas.

It was the good fortune of Old Ironsides to destroy two of the illusions of that portion of the people of this country, which had faith in English superiority in all things, then a numerous and devout class of believers, by first demonstrating that a Yankee man-of-war could get away from her enemy when there was occasion for the attempt, and that she could deal roughly with him, when the motive for avoiding an action did not exist.

It is worthy of remark that the English abandoned the chase of the Constitution, at eight in the morning, and that at half past eight the busy old craft seeing a stranger on her starboard bow, made sail in chase, to ascertain her character. The vessel proved to be an American brig. At ten, another vessel was chased and brought to, which also proved to be an American. At noon of the same day, having no further use for it, the boarding cutter was hoisted up, and the ship stood to the eastward, going into Boston a few days later, or near the close of the month.

Hull remained a very short time at Boston. It was the intention of the department to remove him from his ship, in order to give him the Constellation, in exchange with Bainbridge, the latter ranking him; and it has been sometimes imagined, that he was resolved to get another cruise out of his old craft, ere he was compelled to give her up. It is now known that Capt. Hull's orders had gone to New-York, to which place he had been ordered, and that he did not get them before he sailed a second time. The order to relinquish the ship to Bainbridge must have been issued at Washington, just after Hull reached Boston, and the receipt of his report of the chase was dated the very next day. This last letter was dated July 29th, and closed with these words—"Remain at Boston until further orders." Luckily, Hull did not get this letter until he returned from his second cruise, sailing again on the 2d August.

The Constitution now stood along the coast to the eastward, as far as the Bay of Fundy, and thence off Cape Sable and Halifax, meeting with nothing.

Passing near the Isle of Sables, she next went to the mouth of the St. Lawrence, where she made two captures of little value. On the 15th she chased a sloop of war with four merchant-men in company. The chases separated, one of them, a prize, being abandoned and set fire to. The sloop of war being to windward, the Constitution followed a ship, which proved to be an Englishman, with an American privateer prize-crew on board, that the sloop of war had brought to but had not taken possession of, in consequence of the appearance of the frigate. Another of the vessels was overhauled and recaptured, being an American, with an English prize-crew on board her. Mr. Madison [6] was put in charge of this vessel. After this little success, the Constitution stood to the southward and eastward, seeing nothing of any moment, until the 19th, when she made a suspicious sail from the mast-head, a long way to leeward. This was on the 19th, the frigate then being in N. Lat. 41°, 41', and W. Long. 55°, 48', or less than 700 miles nearly east of Cape Cod. Having looked for his enemy in the vicinity of Halifax, without success, Hull was now on his way to go off Bermuda, with a similar purpose, when he fell in with this vessel. The strange sail was first seen at two P. M., and at three she was made out to be a ship, under short canvas, and close hauled, apparently waiting for the Constitution to come down to her. At half past three, the stranger was distinctly made out to be a frigate, and little doubt was entertained of his being an enemy.

The Constitution continued to run down, until near enough to take a good look at the strange sail, when she came by the wind, and began to clear for action. While lying in this situation, the enemy having his main-topsail aback, gallantly waiting for his adversary, Hull reconnoitered, and made up his mind that he had a first-class English frigate to deal with. The top-gallant sails were furled, and her flying jib and all of her light staysails stowed. A second reef was taken in all the topsails, the courses were hauled up, and the royal yards sent down. By this time the ship was clear and the drum beat to quarters, when the crew responded with three hearty cheers. After this the helm was put up, and the ship bore directly down upon the enemy. The Constitution had about a league to run, before she could get alongside of the stranger. At five P. M., being then at long gun-shot, the Englishman showed three ensigns, in different parts of his vessels, and commenced firing at very long shot. After discharging the guns of one side, he would wear and fire those of the other. These manœuvres induced the Americans to yaw, to prevent being raked, though they fired but three or four guns in approaching.

[6] This gentleman was subsequently lost, in command of the Lynx.

These evolutions, and the short sail carried, retarded the approach of the Constitution essentially, and she was near an hour getting within a short range of her enemy. At six P. M. however, the Englishman bore up, and ran off with the wind on his larboard quarter, under his topsails and jib. The Constitution then set her main-topgallant-sail, to close. A few minutes later, the forward guns of the American ship, and the after guns of the English bore, when each party commenced his fire, the two frigates being within a hundred yards of each other. As the Constitution had the most way on her, she drew gradually ahead, until she came fairly abeam. Just as the two ships were square with each other, the mizzen-mast of the stranger came down, over the starboard quarter. This, of course, caused the American frigate to draw ahead still faster, and in about fifteen minutes after she had begun to fire, she was so far forward, as to induce Hull to luff short round his enemy's bows, to rake him. After having fired three raking broadsides, the Constitution attempted to wear and resume her former course, parallel to that of the Guerriere, but owing to the loss of braces and other running-rigging, the Constitution wore so slowly that the bow-sprit of the Guerriere passed diagonally over the quarter-deck of the Constitution, and finally dropped astern with her starboard bow against the Constitution's larboard or lee quarter gallery. This was an awkward position, and might have led to serious consequences, had not the enemy been pretty effectually threshed before it occurred. As it was, two or three of the Englishman's forward guns were discharged with effect into the stern and quarter of Old Ironsides, so close as to set fire to the cabin. Hoffman, who was in command there, behaved admirably, extinguishing the fire and protecting his men with great spirit and coolness.

While this scene was in the course of being acted below, one still more serious occurred on the quarter-deck. Both parties called away boarders, as the ships came foul. All the English boarders and marines collected forward, while the Americans rushed aft. Morris, Aylwin, and Bush (lieutenant of marines), were foremost among the Constitution's people. On the other hand, many of the English exhibited equal gallantry, and for a few moments the musketry did great execution. Lieutenant Morris was in the act of lashing some of the head-gear of the English frigate to the Constitution, when he was hit by a bullet in the body. Mr. Bush fell dead by a ball received in the forehead, and Mr. Aylwin was shot through the shoulder. Missiles were thrown by hand from ship to ship, but boarding was out of the question, on account of the sea, the distance between the bulwarks of the two frigates, and the force collected on the deck of each to repel such an attempt. However, several lives were lost and many brave men wounded, by the close and murderous fire of the musketry. The Constitution drew ahead and parted from her adversary, moving off on the same tack. As the two ships separated, the Englishman's fore and main mast both came by the board, leaving him wallowing in the sea and encumbered with wreck. Of course, this decided the affair, leaving Old Ironsides effectually the victor, and affording her time to look to the security of her own spars, which were of the last moment to her, in a sea that would certainly be soon swarming with enemies.

Having hauled off a short distance, and rove new rigging, besides looking to the stoppers and other securities for the masts. Hull was ready to run down on his enemy, who still kept a jack flying on the stump of his mizzen-mast. The Constitution accordingly wore ship, and coming close in on the enemy's weather bow, in a position to rake him, the jack came down, and the first English frigate that had done such a thing since the war of the Revolution, struck to an American. The prize proved to be the Guerriere, 38, a French-built ship, that had been taken by the English in the year ——, by the ——, Captain ——, and now commanded by Captain Dacres. The Guerriere was a fine vessel of her class, mounting on her gun-deck thirty eighteens, and nineteen carronades and chase guns on her quarter-deck and forecastle; or twenty-five guns in broadside. She is said, however, to have been pierced for twenty-seven guns in broadside, which was just the number now carried by the Constitution. Some explanation, nevertheless, becomes necessary, in order not to convey to the reader a false idea of the respective forces of these two ships. The gun-deck battery of the Constitution consisted then, as now, of thirty guns of the *bore* of twenty-four pounders. The shot, notwithstanding, owing to defective casting, often weighed less than twenty-two pounds. Now, a shot of the *size* of a twenty-four pound shot, that weighs less than ought to have been its weight in solid metal, is less efficient than one, even, that has the accurate proportions between its weight and its diameter. The elements of the momentum, the principle that controls the efficiency of a shot, are the same in both cases, though the momentum itself differs, on account of the greater resistance of the atmosphere to a large, than to a small shot. In the case of the guns of the Constitution, the influence of the diameter may not have amounted to much, especially in an action fought at such close quarters; though two pounds in the weight of a shot is a matter of some moment, in naval warfare. The carronades of both ships were thirty-twos, alike. As the defective castings pertained to nearly, if not to quite all the American shot used at that time, the difference applied to the carronade shot, as well as to those of the long guns, making the quarter-deck and forecastle batteries of the Guerriere, gun for gun, actually heavier than those of the Constitution.

Nevertheless, the Constitution was a vessel decidedly superior to her prize, in all and each of the elements of force. She was of more tonnage, had heavier spars, carried heavier metal, and had a larger crew. The inferiority of the Guerriere was most apparent, indeed, in the number of her crew, she having less than three hundred men at quarters, while our own ship had considerably more than four hundred. There is not much doubt, however, that three hundred men in the Constitution ought to have been able to contend with four hundred in the Guerriere, though, in that case, the conflict would have been nearer on an equality. It is no more than fair to mention, also, that while it would seem to be certain, that the Guerriere actually carried thirty guns on her gun-deck, her regular armament would have been only twenty-eight. She was somewhat longer than was usual for vessels of her class, and it has been asserted that two guns were mounted in her bridle-ports, to bring her by the head. These two guns, it will be remembered, on the other hand, were of particular service to her, on account of the peculiar manner in which the battle was fought, the Constitution being so much on the bows of her adversary. Here, then, had Old Ironsides fairly beaten an English frigate in a yard-arm fight, leaving her opponent without an upright stick in her, except the stumps of masts, while she still carried every essential spar of her own in its place!

As Morris was wounded, Wadsworth had to attend to the duty of the ship, and George Campbell Read was sent to take possession of the prize. Dacres was wounded, but not so seriously that he could not walk, and he was transferred to the vessel of his captor, a boat having been sent to apprise Hull of the name of his prize, and the state of his prisoner. Hull was a man of few words, and totally without flourish, but kind-hearted and direct. As Dacres went up the side of the Constitution, Hull appeared in the gangway, extended an arm, and said, as if addressing an old friend—"Dacres, give me your hand —I know you are hurt." This was not Decatur's or Truxtun's mode of receiving a captive.

Not long after the Guerriere was taken possession of, a strange sail was seen, and the Constitution cleared for another action, precisely as she had begun to chase on a former occasion, as soon as her enemies ceased chasing her. On this occasion, the stranger hauled off on perceiving the Constitution, he being most probably a merchantman. That night and next day, the prisoners were removed from the prize, and orders were given to set her on fire.

Hoffman was the officer employed on this duty, and he left the Guerriere in the last boat, about 3 o'clock in the succeeding afternoon. Shortly after, the ship blew up. Captain Dacres reported his loss in the action, at fifteen killed and sixty-three wounded; or a total of seventy-eight casualties. The Americans added one to this account. Captain Hull reported his loss at seven killed and seven wounded; or a total of fourteen casualties. Among the slain of the Guerriere, was her second lieutenant, and among her wounded, her captain, first lieutenant, master, etc. The Constitution lost her lieutenant of marines, the gallant Bush, and Morris was wounded, together with one other officer. Encumbered with so many prisoners, Hull now deemed it necessary to go into port. The ship had not received any material damage, but it was every way desirable to return home, for a short time at least. On reaching Boston, Hull gave up the ship, Bainbridge having had some time in his possession his orders to join her. It was September 15th, however, before the latter officer hoisted his broad pennant on board Old Ironsides.

The Constitution had been made a favorite ship under Preble, but this brilliant success added immensely to her favor with the nation. From this moment she became dear to every American, and it would have caused great pain to the entire Republic, had she fallen into the hands of the enemy. Still, there was no intention to keep her out of harm's way, in order to nurse her up as a thing merely to boast of. On the contrary, to sea she was immediately ordered again, and to sea she went, as soon as she could be got ready.

Bainbridge was to have a squadron, consisting of his own ship, the Constitution 44, the Essex 32, Capt. Porter, and the Hornet 18, Capt. Lawrence. The first and last of these vessels were at Boston, while the Essex was in the Delaware. Giving the last two places of rendezvous at different ports, the Commodore sailed, with the Hornet in company, October 26th, 1812. On this cruise there was necessarily some change of officers, in addition to that of the commanders. Morris having been promoted, George Parker, of Virginia, was ordered to the ship as her first lieutenant. Aylwin had been promoted to a lieutenant, and was junior of the ship. G. Campbell Read was transferred to the United States, and Wadsworth to the Adams, as her first lieutenant. This made the list of lieutenants read as follows, viz.: Parker, Hoffman, Shubrick, Morgan, and Aylwin. Of these, all but the senior-lieutenant had been in the ship since the commencement of the war.

The two ships were off St. Salvador, December 13th, having looked in vain for the Essex, at the appointed place of rendezvous. An English ship of war was lying in St. Salvador, and, in the expectation that she might be induced to come out, and engage the Hornet, Bainbridge left the latter ship alone, off the harbor, and stood along the coast to the southward, on the 26th of the month. Three days later, when in lat. 13° 6′ S. and long. 31° W., the Constitution saw two strange sail, in shore, and to windward. The smallest of these vessels continued to stand in for the land, which was then distant from the Constitution rather more than thirty miles; while the other, much the larger vessel of the two, edged away to take a nearer look at Old Ironsides. The wind was far from fresh, at E. N. E.

By 11 A. M., the Constitution's officers were satisfied that the ship to windward was an enemy's frigate, and being now nearer to the land than was desirable, in the event of a chase, the ship was taken to the southward and eastward, to draw the stranger off shore. At the same time, the royals were set, and the main-tack boarded, the stranger sailing the best, in the light wind that prevailed. At meridian each vessel showed her ensign; signals were also made on board each ship, but they proved to be mutually unintelligible. Some time after 1 P. M., the Constitution hauled up her mainsail, and furled her royals.

The action commenced about two. The English ship, which was afterwards ascertained to be the Java, was about a mile to windward of the Constitution, both vessels now heading to the southward and eastward, the Java being well on her antagonist's quarter. In this state of things, the Englishman had hauled down his ensign, though he kept a jack flying, and Old Ironsides threw a shot ahead of him, to induce him to show his colors. By some mistake, the order to fire this gun brought on a discharge of the Constitution's broadside, which was immediately returned. The Java going much the faster in the light wind which prevailed, she was soon so far ahead as to be able to attempt crossing the Constitution's bow. This induced Bainbridge to keep off and to wear, the Java coming round at the same time. Both vessels now headed to the westward. These changes brought the two ships much closer together, and within pistol-shot. The Java repeated the attempt to cross the Constitution's bow, but was again foiled by the latter ship's wearing. Both vessels came round at the same time, with their heads again to the eastward. The Java forereached as usual, and with a view to keep her weatherly position, she attempted to tack, but missed stays. At the same time, the Constitution wore, having lost her wheel early in the action. Old Ironsides coming round the soonest, got an effective raking fire into her enemy.

Both ships now ran off free, wearing again, the English still to windward, though greatly injured. At fifty-five minutes past two, finding his berth too hot, the Englishman attempted to run Old Ironsides aboard, actually getting his jib-boom into her mizzen-rigging. In this situation the good old craft punished her bold assailant very severely, nor did she let him get clear until the head of his bowsprit was shot away. Soon after, his foremast came down, and, in passing ahead, the two vessels ran so close together that the stump of the Englishman's bowsprit actually scraped over the Constitution's taffrail. In a moment the Constitution wore, and passing her enemy to leeward, wore again. The Java keeping off, the two ships once more ranged fairly alongside of each other, during which time the Englishman's mizzen-mast came down, leaving nothing standing on board him but his main-mast, and of that, the yard was shot away in the slings.

By this time the Java's fire had ceased, and Bainbridge, supposing her to have submitted, boarded his main-tack, and passed out of the combat, luffing directly athwart his adversary's bows. Standing on, a short distance to windward, the Constitution came to the wind, and passed an hour in securing her masts, and reeving new running-rigging. At the end of that time, an ensign was seen flying on board the Java, when Bainbridge wore short round, and ran down directly across his enemy's forefoot. This evolution was sufficient, and before a gun was fired the English flag was lowered, for the second time, to Old Ironsides!

The prize was the Java, 38, Capt. Lambert, with a large number of supernumeraries in her, bound to the East Indies. Her commander was mortally wounded, but her first lieuteuant reported her loss twenty-two killed, and one hundred and two wounded. This was a very severe loss, though Bainbridge thinks it was considerably greater. He says her loss was certainly sixty killed, and one hundred and one wounded. It is probable that more were killed, or died early of their wounds, than were reported by the English, and that fewer were killed than Bainbridge supposed. The English say that the ship's company and supernumeraries amounted to three hundred and seventy-seven souls, while the Americans affirm that they found a muster-roll in the ship, that was made out several days after she had sailed, and which had on it considerably more than four hundred names. All this is of little moment, as three hundred and seventy-seven men were quite enough for such a ship, no one who understands vessels ever supposing that the Java was equal in force to the Constitution.

It was the manner in which Old Ironsides invariably did her work, that excited the admiration of the knowing. On this occasion she had shot out of her adversary every spar she had (the mainmast coming down before she struck), while she herself could carry royals!

In her action with the Java, the good ship suffered more than she did in her previous engagements. She had nine killed and twenty-five wounded. Among the latter was Bainbridge himself, and Aylwin, the junior lieutenant, the same officer who was wounded in the combat with the Guerriere, died of hurts received in this battle. The ship, herself, was not much injured. Some of her spars were wounded, and a few shots struck her hull; but the great cause of surprise to the Americans was to know where all the enemy's shot had gone.

In consequence of the water's being so smooth, the Java was not much injured below the water-line. She might very well have been taken into port, but the experiment would have been hazardous on many accounts. She was without spars, far from America, the sea was covered with English cruisers, and the nearest countries were much under the control of English influence. Keeping all the circumstances in view Bainbridge removed all his prisoners, and two or three days after the action, he ordered Hoffman to blow up this prize, too, and return to St. Salvador. Here he landed his prisoners, among whom were Lt. Gen. Hyslop, with his staff, and several supernumerary sea officers.

As Old Ironsides rejoined her consort, the Hornet, the utmost anxiety prevailed on board the latter vessel, on the subject of the result of the action. The vessel in company with the Java previously to the battle, was an American prize, which had stood on toward St. Salvador, and fallen into the hands of the Hornet, off the port. Her prize-crew, of course, related the fact, that the Java had left her to engage an American frigate, but could say nothing of the result. Lawrence had great confidence in Old Ironsides, but as he approached her, he kept every thing ready for flight should it be necessary. It could be seen that stoppers were on the standing rigging, and that the ship had been in a warm combat; but where was the prize? It was possible, that the English had got hold of the good old craft, and had sent her in, to decoy the Hornet under her guns. The signals read well, but the prize-crew of the ship retaken, gave marvellous accounts of the Java, and of her all-powerful, double-jointed crew, and so many men might have been thrown on board our ship, as to have swept her out of our grasp! This feeling prevailed on board the Hornet, until the vessels were near enough to distinguish countenances, when the number of well-known faces that appeared above the Constitution's hammock-cloths settled the matter. Hearty cheers soon proclaimed that it was a

Lisbon, a large ship was run alongside of, in the night, and after some hailing, two or three shot were fired into her, to compel answers, when it was ascertained she was a Portuguese.

Defeated in his hopes of finding any thing where he was, and quite aware of the imprudence of staying long in any one place, Feb. 20th, Stewart up helm and stood off to the southward and westward, for twenty or thirty leagues. At 1 P. M. of that very day, a stranger was made on the larboard bow, and to leeward. The Constitution hauled up a little and made sail in chase. It was not long before another vessel was seen to leeward of the first, which, at 2 P. M., was made out to be a ship. All three vessels were now standing on the same tack, on bowlines, gradually nearing each other. At 4 P. M., the nearest of the strangers up helm and ran down to speak his consort, which was the commanding vessel, as it appeared in the end. Seeing this, Old Ironsides squared away in chase, setting every thing that would draw, alow and aloft. For an hour or more the two weathermost ships were thus running off, nearly dead before the wind, while the most leewardly vessel was luffing to close.

It may render the relation more clear if we at once say, that the two strangers proved to be the Cyane, 20, and Levant, 18, British vessels of war; the former mounting 34, and the latter 22 guns. The Cyane was commanded by Capt. Falcon, and the Levant by the Hon. Capt. Douglas, a son of Lord Douglas, who was the child that gave rise to the celebrated "Douglas cause," at the close of the last century.

Stewart could see that the nearest vessel was frigate-built, and had reason to suppose that both were enemy's ships of war. They had made signals to each other, and the ship to leeward soon ran off before the wind also, but under short canvas, to allow her consort to close. It is now understood that the ship to windward had signalled to the commanding vessel, an American frigate which was "superior to one, but inferior to us both," and that Capt. Douglas kept away under the impression that a night action might enable him to get some advantage in manœuvering. Stewart, who could not know this, supposed their object was to escape, and he crowded on his old craft until her main-royal mast came down. The chase gained after this accident.

At half-past five the two English ships were so near together that it was impossible to prevent a junction, and Old Ironsides, then rather more than a league distant from them, began to strip and clear for battle. A few minutes later, the Englishmen passed within hail of each other; soon after which they both hauled by the wind, with their heads to the northward, and shortened sail. It was evident they were clearing ship and intended to fight. As Old Ironsides was travelling towards them all this time, they soon fancied themselves in a state to weather on her, and both, at the same instant, set their main courses, and made all other sail in a taut-bowline. But it would not do; the good old craft was too much in earnest to be out-manœuvered in this wise, but came down so fast that in a few minutes they hauled up their courses again, and formed in line, the commanding ship, or the Levant, leading. At 6 P. M., Stewart let the enemy see the stars and stripes for the first time. On this hint the English set their own ensigns, and, five minutes later, Ironsides ranged up abeam of the Cyane, distant about a cable's length, passing ahead with her sails lifting, until the three vessels lay about equi-distant from each other. In this masterly position the Constitution let fly her first broadside, receiving those of her enemies.

For about a quarter of an hour the firing was very warm and unremitted, but at the end of that time, the enemy grew less active in his cannonading. Stewart now ordered his people to stand fast and let the smoke rise from the surface of the water, in order to get a better view of the state of things to the leeward. In a very few minutes this was obtained, and it was found that the Levant lay directly under the frigate's lee, while the Cyane was luffing to cross her wake, if possible. Old Ironsides now let the ship abeam have all her guns, and then backed astern, as if plying in a tides-way, and compelled the Cyane to keep off to avoid being raked. As it was, she got it abeam. The Levant was not idle, but, in her turn, she now luffed and tried to tack, in order to cross the frigate's forefoot, but the busy old craft was too nimble for her. Filling every thing, Stewart shot ahead, forced the sloop of war to wear, under a raking broadside, in order to keep clear of him, and to run off to leeward to get out of the range of his shot. The Cyane, perceiving the state of things, wore ship, when the Constitution came round too, and so quick as to rake this adversary, as she came by the wind. The Englishman came up as high as he could and fired his broadside, but, finding Old Ironsides closing on his weather quarter, he hauled down his ensign. Hoffman immediately took possession of him. As soon as this was done, Stewart went to look for the Levant.

In running to leeward, Capt. Douglas had no intention of abandoning his consort. He had found his berth too warm, and very wisely got out of it, as fast as he could; but having repaired his most material damages, as well as he was able, he had hauled up to look for her.

He met the Constitution about nine, there having been an intermission in the combat, of some duration, in consequence of this separation. The Levant knew nothing of the fate of the Cyane, and her commander probably thought the Yankee was running away from her, when he thus met him. Each vessel brought the wind abeam, and they crossed each other, on opposite tacks, firing in passing. The Levant was satisfied this would never do, but up helm and tried to escape. Old Ironsides followed, firing her chase guns with great deliberation and effect. Captain Douglas soon saw that every shot struck him and raked him, and he came by the wind, and fired a gun to leeward, in token that he gave it up. Shubrick was sent to take possession.

This combat was remarkable for its brilliant manœuvering. It is seldom that one vessel can fight two, at the same time, without being raked. This Stewart did, however, not only escaping from all the attempts of the enemy to get this advantage over him, but actually raking both of his adversaries, each in his turn. Taking the evolutions all together, it would not be easy to find an action in which a ship was better handled. Nor did the enemy neglect his duty. Old Ironsides was several times hulled, and her loss was three killed and twelve wounded. The English loss is uncertain, no English report of the action having been made, and there being supernumeraries in each ship. Forty-two wounded were found in the two ships, and the slain have been variously computed at, from thirty-five, down to ten or twelve. No officer was hurt on board the Constitution. This action, it will be remembered, was fought in the night, though there was a moon for a part of the time. The light of the moon proved of great service to one poor fellow. In the heat of the combat, a man at one of the forecastle guns fell, at the precise moment when a shot entered near him. He was reported dead, and an order was given to pass the body across the deck, and to throw it overboard. A midshipman and two men were thus employed, but were baffled in endeavouring to pass the shoulders through a port. The midshipman sprang over into the fore-chains to assist, when he saw some muscles of the supposed dead man's face twitching, and he ordered the body drawn back, and passed below to the surgeons. Before the Levant struck, the man was back at his gun, fighting as well as the rest of them. He was subject to fits and had fallen in one, but recovered in time to return to his quarters. The story should be told, as a warning against haste in such cases. Thousands are buried alive, on shore, and living men are sometimes committed to the deep in the hurry of sea-fights.

Stewart went to Port Praya, with his prizes, arriving there on 10th March.

In the mean time Ballard had been put in the Levant as prize-master, as due to his rank, and Shubrick went back to the frigate, acting as her first lieutenant. This change was not made, however, until the last came near losing his life on board the prize. It had been found necessary to get a new mizzen-top-mast aloft, the night possession was taken, and the spar came down in consequence of the mast-ropes parting. In descending, the head of the top-mast struck Mr. Shubrick on the head, and left him senseless for hours. Nothing saved his life but the fact that he wore the boarding cap, with which he had left his quarters, to take charge of the prize.

A vessel was chartered at Port Praya, for a cartel, and about a hundred of the English prisoners were sent to fit her for sea. In this state of things, and the very day after the arrival of Old Ironsides at Port Praya, occurred one of the narrowest escapes from her enemies it was ever the good fortune of this lucky ship to run.

The weather was thick, more particularly near the water, where lay a bank of mist, that could not be penetrated by the eye at any distance. A boat had just left the ship, with orders to tow the cartel off, and the duty of the vessel was in some measure at a stand. Shubrick, on whom the discharge of the executive duties of the vessel had fallen, in his new character of first lieutenant, was walking the quarter-deck, deeply ruminating on the business before him, when he heard an exclamation from one of the English midshipmen, who was aft on the taffrail. The lad had spoken to Capt. Falcon, late of the Cyane, his words being, "Oh! Capt. Falcon, look at the large ship in the offing!" So intent was Shubrick on his own ruminations, that these words might have passed unheeded for the moment but for the answer. "Hold your tongue, you little rascal," answered Capt. Falcon, in a low voice. This completely aroused the lieutenant, who, walking aft, saw, over the bank of mist, the upper sails of a large ship, that was apparently beating up to gain the harbor. After taking a good look at the stranger, Shubrick went below and reported the fact to the Captain. Stewart was shaving at the time, and without discontinuing the operation, he answered coolly, "Very well, sir. It is an Indiaman, or it may be a frigate—call all hands and heave short, and we'll go out and see what she is made of." Shubrick ordered "all hands up anchor," called, and then wet on deck to take another look at the stranger, while the men were tumbling up, and manning the bars. He now saw the upper sails of two more large ships in the mist, above the bank, all three beating up for the roads. Capt. Stewart was immediately informed of this, and without a moment's hesitation he gave the order to "cut." It is probable that this prompt command saved the ship. A signal was made for the prizes to follow, and the duty went on in the most beautiful and cool manner. In fourteen minutes after the first ship was seen, and in ten after the order to cut was given, Old Ironsides was walking out of the roads under her topsails. Preparations of all sorts were made rapidly, and away all three of the ships went together, just clearing the shore, and passing at gun-shot to windward of the strangers; now known to be heavy vessels of war, though no one, as yet, had seen their hulls. They were thought to be two ships of the line and a large frigate. As the Constitution cleared the land, she crossed topgallant yard, boarded her tacks, and set her staysails. No sooner were the Americans abeam of their enemies, than the latter tacked, and all six of the ships stood to the southward and eastward, carrying every thing that would draw, with about ten knot-way on them.

As Ironsides drew into the offing, she cut adrift two boats that were towing astern. As yet no one had seen the hulls of the enemy, though there could be no mistake as to their character. The mist seemed to settle, however, in the offing, lying nearer to the water, and the air become a little clearer aloft. The vessel that was taken for a frigate, weathered on every thing, her own consorts, as well as on the American vessels. The English officers, prisoners in the Constitution, could not conceal their delight, and confidently predicted the capture of Old Ironsides, and the recapture of their own vessels. They announced the chasing ships to be the Leander 50, Sir George Collier; Newcastle 50, Lord George Stuart, and Acasta 40, Capt. Kerr. The first two vessels were new ships on one deck, built expressly to overmatch the American 44's. The English prisoners were particularly confident "Kerr in the Acasta" would overtake the Constitution, which vessel they fancied could not sail, from seeing her jog along at an easy rate, in company with her prizes. Stewart kept her travelling on the present occasion, and it was not quite so easy a thing to come up with her, as hope had induced the prisoners to believe. One of the English captains was so sanguine as to get into the quarter-gallery, and make signs to the weatherly frigate, inviting her to come on, and exclaiming in the presence of American officers, "Capt. Kerr, I envy you your glory this day." With Stewart, himself, these gentlemen did not maintain much reserve, pretty plainly intimating that Old Ironsides had not the speed necessary to get clear of the "British Phœnix," as they termed "Kerr, in the Acasta."

Whatever may have been the fact, as regards our own honest old craft, it is certain the prizes were in a bad way. The Cyane was a short ship, mounting twenty-two guns on one deck and twelve above, and of course was not very weatherly. Stewart saw that the frigate, or supposed frigate—for no one had yet seen the hull of an Englishman—was weathering on her fast, and he made a signal for her to tack. Hoffman went round immediately, and passed his most dangerous adversary a short gun-shot to windward, on contrary tacks. Not a ship of the enemy went about. The "British Phœnix" stood gallantly on, endeavoring to get into the wake of the Constitution, and the Cyane was soon lost sight of in the haze. Hoffman was a practical, plain sailor, and knew perfectly well what he was about. Instead of running into port again, no sooner had the mist shut in the enemy, than he went about again, and continued making short tacks to windward for twenty-four hours, when, giving the islands a good berth, he squared away for America, bringing his ship successfully into New-York. She was taken into the service, and her namesake is now in the navy.

At half-past two, one of the English vessels was pretty well up, on the lee quarter of Ironsides. By this time the fog had packed on the water so low, that her officers could be seen standing on the hammock-cloths, though her ports were not yet visible. She fired, by division, and conjectures could be made concerning the extent of her batteries, by the flashes of her guns, as seen through the fog. The shot fell within a hundred yards of the Constitution, but did not rise again. After trying this experiment unsuccessfully, the firing ceased.

The Levant all this time was falling in astern, nearer and nearer to the weatherly frigate, or was getting into the very danger from which the Cyane had been relieved an hour or two before. Stewart made her signal to tack. Ballard went round immediately, but could not work off to windward as Hoffman had just done; for seven minutes after he had got about, all three of the Englishmen tacked, by signal, and were on his heels. This compelled him to run back into the roads and anchor. The enemy paid no attention to the neutrality of the island, but stood in after the Levant, and opened a heavy fire on that ship. The prisoners ashore joined them, and added the guns of the battery to the attack. Of course Ballard submitted, but he had some relief for his mortification in losing his ship, in what passed with the boarding officer. "I presume I have the honor to receive the sword of Captain Biddle, of the U.S. ship Hornet," said that gentleman, when Ballard offered his sword. "You receive the sword of Lieut. Ballard of the Constitution, prize master of His Britannic Majesty's late ship Levant," was the caustic reply. The enemy supposed the three ships they had chased to be the President, Com. Rodgers; Congress, Capt. Smith; and Hornet, Capt. Biddle. Had such been the case, they would have been much too strong to fight; but the truth rendered their little success bitter, rather than otherwise!"

As for Old Ironsides, she went steadily on her way, and was soon out of sight of her pursuers. Deep was the mortification of the English officers on board her, when they saw their three ships tack together, abandoning such a frigate as the Constitution, and following a prize into a neutral port! The "British Phœnix" was now changed into an Indiaman, and it never could be the squadron they had supposed. It was, however, and Sir Geo. Collier was much condemned for his course. In the end that officer committed suicide, though whether it was the consequence of morbid feelings in connection with this affair, or from some other cause, we do not know. He was in the Leander, the vessel farthest astern, and to leeward, and was not in as good a situation to make his observations, as he would have been on board the Newcastle, which was the vessel on the Constitution's lee quarter, and which fired at her. It is also said, that the Newcastle made a signal, that she had sprung her mainyard, a circumstance that may have contributed to Sir Geo. Collier's decision. Nevertheless, one cannot easily see why the Acasta, or the Leander, might not have been left to follow Old Ironsides alone, a course which would have been very apt to have brought on an engagement. The Acasta was a twenty-four pounder frigate, rating 40, besides being the "British Phœnix," and both the Leander and the Newcastle were thirty-two pounder vessels.

Whatever we may think of the manœuvering of the enemy, off Port Praya, we can have but one opinion of Old Ironsides, and her cool, judicious commander. Stewart deserves a great deal for the orders he gave, and the signals he made. Had the "British Phœnix" come up singly, it is highly probable she would have met with such a reception, as would soon have satisfied her that she was not engaged in child's play.

Stewart crossed the ocean to Maranham, where he landed his prisoners, on parole, and shaped his course for home, going into Boston in the month of May. Peace was actually made when he took the Cyane and Levant, though the captures were legal, in the latitude and longitude in which they were made, under the provision of the treaty.

Thus terminated the services of Old Ironsides, in the third of the wars she has seen. In each she was a useful and important vessel, but, in this last, her exploits surpassed those of any other vessel in the navy. In the short period of two years and nine months, she had fought three battles successfully, had captured five vessels of war, two of which were frigates, and one was frigate-built, and had been three times hard pressed in chases, by squadrons of greatly superior force. One of these chases was a naval incident of remarkable features, and was worth a victory any day, while another was of a character to reflect credit, in an almost equal degree, on the good old barky herself, and on the officer who commanded her. The names of Preble, Hull, Bainbridge and Stewart, were now inseparably associated with that of the ship, as indeed might it almost be said was that of Hoffman, who served in her throughout the war of 1812, with the exception of the short time he was in command of the Cyane, one of her prizes.

The remainder of the career of the Constitution, down to the present time, is not without its interest, though necessarily less brilliant than her services in a time of war. As she arrived so late in the season, she was not employed in the squadron that went against the Algerines, but was put out of commission. The good old ship, indeed, was now in want of a thorough repair. Her upper works had proved so rotten of late, that it was remarked when a shot went through them, it did not make splinters, an advantage in one respect certainly, but a very serious defect in all others.

From May 1815, until —— 1821, Old Ironsides lay at her native place, Boston, during which time she was thoroughly overhauled, and prepared for sea. Jacob Jones then hoisted a broad pennant in her, and took her to her old cruising ground, the Mediterranean. Nothing occurred worth recording on this occasion, with the exception of one somewhat painful event. One dark night, while she was in or near the Gut of Gibraltar, her officers below heard something brushing against her side, thumping along from gun to gun, as if she touched something in the line of her ports. Running on deck, it was ascertained that the old craft had rubbed somewhat hard against a small brig, which had not been seen until it was too late to avoid her. The brig was English, and, as it turned out, sunk almost immediately, her crew being saved by a vessel astern. This is almost the only serious accident that ever happened to the honest old craft, and this was serious to another, and not to herself.

ROBERT ALLERTON PARKER

Colonies and Communities

> ...*Not a scheme in agitation*
> *For the world's amelioration*
> *Has a grain of common sense in it*
> —*Except my own.*
> > —THOMAS LOVE PEACOCK.

I

THE ERA was one of disintegration. Portents of disaster, even of destruction for the nation, abounded. Many believed that the Union could not endure. Kabylism—the impulse to split up and to disperse into tribes—was a prevalent symptom of the early decades of the nineteenth century. The Mormons, under the leadership of Brigham Young, had just successfully completed their epic migration into the western desert, following in the footsteps of the Donner Party, which encountered so shocking a tragedy in the snows of the Sierras. Only a few years had elapsed since the Millerites had awaited in vain for the end of the world—had indeed set the very day in 1843; and had won such a following that all worldly affairs were settled by tremulous thousands. This day came, in 1843; came and passed, and yet survival by no means destroyed the faith of Miller's followers. Scattered like weeds over the continent, all sorts of theories proclaimed the immediate regeneration of society, the advent of a New Jerusalem. Josiah Warren's much-discussed doctrine of individual sovereignty, a sort of thorny anarchism, exercised a strong appeal to "rugged individualists." Fourierism was putting forth its ephemeral blossoms, known by the grandiose name of "phalanxes."

Catastrophism was in the air. The Abolitionist movement, headed by William Lloyd Garrison, was looked upon as a menace to the Union—as indeed it was. Every Utopian obsession somehow found a soil in which to strike root and flourish. No theory of social organization seemed so fantastic that it could not attract a little band of fanatical adherents. The very expanse of the North American continent, across which, even at the middle of the nineteenth century, the white race had as yet but faintly penciled in a vague outline of its civilization, invited social experimentation. When not to be had for the asking, land was almost dirt cheap. Natural resources seemed inexhaustible. To the dissatisfied, the gullible, the maladjusted and the adventurous, excursion rates to Utopia were offered by reformers, fanatics, or mere madmen gifted with the power of persuasion.

As early as 1824, Robert Owen had stirred the life of the nation with his appeals to kings and congresses, and soon afterward inaugurated his vast experiments at New Harmony, Indiana.[1] At the age of fifty-four this prophet of a new social order succeeded in gathering, on a farm of no less than thirty thousand acres, a family of nine hundred members. The world thrilled at his grandiloquent promise. Owen's influence assumed the proportions of a religious revival. No less than ten smaller communities of the Owenite type were organized in various states. New Harmony lasted about three years; the others dispersed at the end of three months. Through lectures, newspaper publicity, and the organization of local societies, Owen, his son Robert Dale Owen, and that indefatigable prophetess, Frances Wright, disseminated this new Utopian seed, until some elements of the plan were even injected into the platform of the Democratic party.

In studying these unprecedented manifestations of social reform, young John Noyes had been sharply struck with the similarity between the unquenched craving for social reconstruction and the revival wildfire that had swept over the country nearly twenty years before. Each had two great leaders, each two eruptions of enthusiasm. Nettleton and Finney led the religious revivals; Owen and Fourier (by proxy) injected the virus of Utopianism into the imagination of all who hungered for escape from harsh realities. Between 1831 and 1833 Charles Finney swept the nation like a tempest. The religious movement and the social movement, as Noyes surveyed them, seemed to alternate. Neither seemed able to rivet the attention of the public at one and the same time. Between 1831 and 1834, the American people seemed on the point of surrendering all earthly ties for the Kingdom of Heaven. A decade later (1842-43), Fourier, with his enticing picture of an earthly paradise, awakened new hopes. Hypnotized by the siren song of

---

[1] "The shrewd, gullible, high-minded, illustrious and preposterous father of Socialism and Coöperation"—so Lytton Strachey characterized Robert Owen. "Queen Victoria," p. 11.

Fourier's apostle, Albert Brisbane, the credulous felt that they stood at the threshold of a new Age of Harmony.

John Noyes was early convinced that salvation of soul and body could not be separately attained. Revolution must begin within. A man's deepest experiences, he insisted, were those of religion and love. These must be brought into the open—and were these not precisely the experiences about which men habitually remained silent? Noyes claimed that the great revivals and these laboratory experiments in socialism were among the most significant phases in American history. But both religion and social experiment had failed to bring heaven to earth, because they despised each other; because they could not coördinate their two great animating energies. Noyes saw that the salvation of the soul, for which the revivalists had cried in the wilderness, could never be attained under the *status quo* of social chaos. Equally impossible was social revolution—"for want of regeneration of the heart."

Delving into various experiments in communal life on the North American continent, Noyes discovered that Robert Owen was not the pioneer in this field of social reconstruction. At the beginning of the nineteenth century, George Rapp had led away from persecution in Europe a little band of German burghers and peasants who thrilled with the anticipation of the imminent advent of Christ and the coming of the millennium. In 1803 Rapp sought refuge in America. He bought five thousand acres of land in Butler County, Pennsylvania. Six hundred disciples followed in 1804. In 1805 they organized their community on the model of the Pentecostal Church. Though their fare was hard, they lived down calumny and suspicion, and under their patient toil, the acres yielded rich harvests. In 1807, the community adopted celibacy; but in other respects they were not ascetics. They indulged in music, painting, even sculpture. To the envy of surrounding neighbors, they cultivated their gardens. Yet, homesick perhaps, for a gentler climate which might remind them of their native Württemberg, they sold all, and migrated to Indiana. On the banks of the Wabash they built up a new village—which once again they named Harmony. Their numbers increased to nearly a thousand; but soon these Rappites were on the march again, driven perhaps, by some strange herdlike or atavistic instinct. They found themselves back in Pennsylvania, in Beaver County, near Pittsburgh. There, at last, in a village which they named Economy, they settled permanently, boring oil-wells, accumulating wealth. Close union protected this sect from persecution, from pestilence, from false brethren. But in the end they succumbed to the virus of accumulated wealth.

These Rappites taught Robert Owen his first practical lesson in communism. From them he purchased the cultivated tract in Indiana. This Montgomeryshire "infidel" found, ready-made, the village those children of faith had spent ten years in building up. When the migratory impulse had come upon them, the Rappites had sent as envoy Richard Flower, an Englishman, to interview Owen at New Lanark, and try to kindle his interest. Owen came, saw, and was conquered by this Utopia waiting only for the new social order to move in! Of the thirty thousand acres of land, three thousand were already under cultivation. There were nineteen detached farms; six hundred acres of improved land occupied by tenants; and a substantially planned and built village. He bought it all. Adherents flocked to this "New Harmony." The "industrious and well disposed of all nations" were invited—how soon was Owen to regret this promiscuous invitation! Within six weeks eight hundred men and women had accepted and that motley company was soon to grow to nine hundred. Inevitably, rapidly, black sheep crept into the fold. To the sputtering candle of Owen's idealism the needy, the defective, the discontented fluttered as moths to the flame. Indiscriminately, Robert Owen welcomed them all. Disconcerting incidents were excused on the ground that the change from an irrational to a rational society could not be accomplished overnight. Leaving all vexatious details of "transition" to his second-in-command, Robert Owen departed for Europe. When he sped back in January, 1826, Mr. Owen found all sorts of amusements flourishing. In the old Rappite Church a brass band blared; balls and concerts took up most of the evenings; five military companies did duty from time to time on the public square, and all at the expense of the founder. Differences of opinion soon led to the establishment of a second community, now also settled on the New Harmony estate.

In this lush, Utopian soil, the ignoble traits of human nature flourished like weeds. Though Robert Owen deluded himself into the belief that the community idea was making marked progress, it soon became imperative to abolish all offices and officers, and finally to appoint three worthies as a triumvirate. Dissatisfied adherents began to drift away. By December, 1826, an order decreeing the abolition of ardent spirits was prominently posted. With its nine hundred passengers, but with no captain or organized crew, Owen's ship was floundering helplessly to disaster. In consternation, Owen began to sell property to individuals. New Harmony was cut up into separate lots. Painted signboards began to appear on deserted buildings. On June

18, 1827, Robert Owen met his disillusioned followers to bid them a bitter farewell.

Owen had based this venture upon an ingenuous assumption of common honesty among his adherents; he was repaid with dishonesty. He had hoped for temperance, and was rewarded with drunkenness. Instead of industry, habits of idleness were all too evident. Dirt instead of cleanliness; waste instead of thrift; apathy instead of an appetite for knowledge—these were the successive steps to his complete disillusion. If the thousand persons who gathered at New Harmony had possessed all those sterling qualities of character which Owen naïvely assumed, there would have been small possibilities of attracting them to the community. Owen had never thought of that. Certain die-hards remained after the catastrophe. Among these survivors Socialism became an almost forbidden name. They were nauseated by their protracted diet of idealistic theories, appetizing to the inexperienced palate, but wormwood and gall to those who witnessed and lived through the recession of the new harmony into ancient discord.

Poor Robert Owen! This metaphysician of the old school, his idealism suckled, without doubt, on Jean Jacques Rousseau, endowed with an innate talent for fault-finding and intellectual negation—this cautious, thrifty son of a saddler, long habituated to the servility of cotton-mill hands, or to his New Lanark disciples, possessed no technique to defend himself against the "rugged American individualism" of that migratory era, against rogues who unerringly sniffed out his weaknesses. While he professed his conversion to socialism, Owen still held title to those thirty thousand acres he had bought from the equally canny Rappites; but his armor of idealism proved to be no protection against scoundrels who insinuated themselves into his confidence, exploited his vanity, swindled him, and deceived him in a manner worthy of the mad extravagance of a Ben Jonson comedy. Taylor and Fauntleroy, for instance, became Owen's associates and counselors. When Taylor's rascality became evident even to Owen's deluded eyes, Owen managed to rid himself of this rascal only by granting him a large tract of land. Taylor promptly announced that he would form a community of his own. An agreement was signed that he should have the land and all upon it. But previous to the signing of this document, this precursor of the modern racketeer made sure that a large quantity of farming implements, as well as livestock, had been transferred to his section of the land. And then, instead of founding the community he had planned, he began to operate a distillery. To add to the troubles of New Harmony, Taylor was soon dispensing whiskey. To his dismay, Owen discovered that he was not dealing here with any starved, servile peasantry. These Yankees retailed whiskey under his very nose. Taylor's distillery only hastened the catastrophe—and it twisted the knife in the wounded spirit. A few years later this disillusioned Socialist sought refuge in the spectral comforts of nineteenth-century spiritualism. This mild opiate helped him to forget Taylor and his rascality and all the rest of the Utopian saturnalia at New Harmony. The fault, Owen reassured himself, was never in his own theories, but in the ineradicable depravity of human nature.

2

In 1842 young Albert Brisbane returned to his native land, bearing aloft the banner of the incomparable Fourier, celebrated inventor of a panacea for all social disorder. In Paris, this wealthy young American had studied the ideas of all the great French reformers and reconstructors—the Saint-Simons, the Comtes, the Considérants, the Cousins. Theories of socialism were boiling merrily in the French *pot-au-feu* of the late thirties. Young Brisbane traveled far—to Greece, to Turkey. He had left his Buffalo home, a typical young American of the upper class, carrying with him all the conventional, dogmatic assumptions of his caste. Lacking nothing himself, he believed the world as it was could hardly be bettered. Greece awakened in young Mr. Brisbane the certainty that a woeful deterioration of man's estate had occurred since Pericles ruled Athens. By the time he had retraced his increasingly indignant steps to Paris, Brisbane's mind was awake and receptive for the message of social reconstruction. With burning interest he listened to the belligerent Saint-Simoneans, to the whole army of grandiloquent theorists and Utopians. Most impressive of all, to this susceptible young man from Buffalo, was the rosy vision of Charles Fourier.

When at last Albert Brisbane was ready to return to his native land, he had made the gospel of Fourier his very own. He was bent upon the establishment of "phalanxes" in all the states. To propagate this idea, Albert Brisbane made an arrangement with Horace Greeley for the outright purchase of a column in the New York *Tribune*. Albert Brisbane may be described as the original "columnist" of the American press. The widely-syndicated column of Arthur Brisbane, son of Albert, may be considered a direct heritage of this early venture in personal journalism. He put all conventional ideas of the typical American of the forties out of his head. He postponed marriage and the duty of raising a family. More important work confronted him. Albert Brisbane had already published "The Social Destiny of Man"—a little book which excited the Transcendentalists and laid foundations for an epidemic of social experiments.

Brisbane's articles at first appeared only twice a week; but in a few months they were appearing thrice a week, and then, due to growing interest, every day. A powerful rival, the New York *Herald,* twitted Horace Greeley as "our Fourierite contemporary." Albert Brisbane's agreement with Greeley gave him unrestrained freedom in publishing the ideas of his master. Before the growing public of the *Tribune* Brisbane presented his case with zest and eloquence. He enticed the well-to-do, encouraged the poverty-pinched, enchanted the moth-eaten gentility, tossed a word of encouragement to the working classes, annihilated caste prejudices, answered objections, silenced scoffers, visualized the imposing façade of Fourier's new temple of humanity, and triumphantly announced that "we have obtained a large hall seventy-seven feet deep by twenty-five feet wide, in Broadway, for the purposes of holding meetings and delivering lectures."

How persuasive it all seemed to young America of those innocent forties! How attractive, how plausible, how convincing this new Utopia emerged from the persuasive lips of gentlemanly young Mr. Brisbane! He beat the drum in his *Tribune* column for about a year; but that was sufficient to create a rush into his Utopian projects. In October, 1843, Mr. Brisbane brought out the first number of his own independent paper, entitled *The Phalanx*. This was a monthly, and recorded the establishment of "associations," organized according to the gospel of Fourier. Along about 1844, Brisbane even converted Brook Farm to Fourierism. Thus the literary responsibilities of his movement were transferred to the Brook Farmers. The Brook Farm *Phalanx* was succeeded by *The Harbinger*. A number of brilliant writers, in the prime of youth, with the zeal of young converts, were soon pleading the cause of Socialism of the Fourier brand.

Fundamentally, the basic ideas of Robert Owen and Charles Fourier were almost identical. Both aimed to reconstruct society by gathering large numbers into unitary dwellings. Owen visualized the communal residence as a great hollow square, not unlike a city block; the Frenchman pictured a great central palace with two lateral wings—like the palace of Versailles. Both discoursed eloquently upon the beauties of coöperative industry. Both had visions of great communal hives of humans. Owen favored communistic ownership; Fourier the joint-stock principle. The actual realization of Fourier's tantalizing mirage of a new society, its transference to the planes of reality, failed no less spectacularly than Owen's venture at New Harmony. Fourier was a poor man and a worker; Brisbane was a capitalist. From these differences we might conjecture that Fourier would not have succeeded so well as Brisbane did, in whipping up a vast, swift excitement, but would have conducted his operations to a safer end. Naturally, it was unfair to judge the French theory by Albert Brisbane's American experiments. But that movement revealed to John Noyes the futility of wasting genius on the development of social theories, if experimentation and execution must be left to second-rate men. "One would think that the example of their first Napoleon might have taught them that the place of the supreme genius is at the head of the army of execution and in the front of the battle with facts."

Noyes did not censure Albert Brisbane for mobilizing his rabble of ineffectual volunteers. In the last analysis, Noyes realized, it was Fourier who was primarily to blame for projecting the rosy mirage—poor, underfed Charles Fourier, with his compensatory vision of vast domains (none less than three miles square), his Watteau-like pictures of fruit-raising, his Horatian agriculture, his impractical rusticities, his assignment of twelve groups of amateur gardeners for developing separate and distinct varieties of the Bergamot pear! Yet how plausible, it all sounded to thousands who, from the Atlantic to the Mississippi, listened attentively to the disciple of this new saint! From remotest Wisconsin and deepest Louisiana reëchoed responsive amens. Hopefully men and women gathered in those obscure phalanxes, and struggled against appalling odds and vermin. Least of all could they be induced to relinquish their daily bickering over religious differences.

These sheep-like followers of the young idealist devised ways of intensifying ordinary aversions, multiplying their bitterness a hundred-fold. Departing from the tame bigotries of the orthodox, they created fresh intolerances of their own. Tattling, backbiting, slander afflicted them worse than "chills and fever." Epidemics of minor and major maladies overtook them.

Back to selfish and beggerly principles of strife and competition these pioneers usually beat a disorderly retreat—often helping themselves to all movable property, and decamping in the dead of night. So Albert Brisbane's dream that two or three thousand individuals—rogues, rascals and misfits—could be saved by the Fourier faith, was dissolved by contact with the acid reality of unregenerated human nature.

3

We must not ignore the fact that American "socialism" of the mid-nineteenth century contained none of the concept of class warfare so skillfully dramatized later by Karl Marx. Fundamentally, this early American socialism meant nothing more than a union of homes and of labor. The failure of the Owen experiment at New Harmony, the collapse of the phalanxes, resulted in a reaction toward extreme individualism—toward an ideal of civil rebellion. Just as in the troubled realm of religion the Antinomians swung to a pole opposite the legalists, so in the realm of social theory, Josiah Warren promulgated the doctrine of "individual sovereignty." Warren had been a member of the Owen Community at New Harmony, and out of disillusion at that celebrated fiasco, developed his gospel of the unqualified supremacy of the individual—thus winning himself a place as one of the pioneer philosophers of anarchism. Elaborated to the smallest detail, his theories included detailed plans for "equitable commerce" and "labor exchange." After the failure of New Harmony, Josiah Warren appeared in Cincinnati. There he opened a "Time Store," and operated it long enough to demonstrate, so he claimed, the truth of his basic principles. He divided off a portion of this shop by a lattice-work containing many racks and shelves, upon which was a variety of small articles. In the center of this lattice an opening was left, through which the store-keeper handed out goods and took pay. On the wall, back of the store-keeper and facing the customer, like a presiding deity, hung a great open-faced clock, and underneath it a dial. Molasses, corn, buckets, dry-goods and other commodities cluttered up the store. On the wall, conspicuous enough for all to see, hung a board on which were placed bills that had been paid to wholesale merchants for all the articles in the store; also orders of individuals for various things. Walking up to the wicket, the customer might request the store-keeper to serve him with some glue. He was immediately asked if he had a "Labor note." If he replied in the negative, he was told that he must get some one's note. His object in going there might have been to find out if Mr. Warren would exchange labor with him; but the abrupt reception had a disconcerting quality and many departed hastily. Those who were not thus discouraged procured a written labor note, promising so many hours labor at so much per hour. Entering the Time Store with note and cash, such customers informed the keeper of their needs—a jug of molasses, a few yards of Kentucky jean, or a bag of corn. As soon as the clerk began conversation or business, he set the dial under the clock, and marked the *time*. He then attended to his client, handed out the articles asked for, and in return took cash to equal the wholesale price of the article, and time out of the customer's "Labor note" to equal the time spent in making the sale. Five per cent was added to the cash cost, to pay rent and to cover incidental expenses. The apostle of individual sovereignty characterized himself as a "peaceful revolutionist" and published a paper of that name at a village he endowed with the modest name of Utopia. Apparently, if we may trust his editorial entitled "A Peep into Utopia," Warren was an adept in negation. "No organization, no delegated power, no laws or by-laws, rules or regulations, but such as each individual makes for himself and his own business; no officers, no priests nor prophets have been resorted to; nothing of this kind has been in demand.... We build on individuality; any difference between us confirms our position. Differences, therefore, like the admissible discords in music, are a valuable part of our harmony." Noyes characterized this type of revolt as *Porcupinism*.

In this discordant, inchoate social scene, Noyes saw no dearth of malcontents. Our country seems perpetually to replenish its caste of dissenters—of those, colloquially, "ag'in" the *status quo*. Compared to some of them, Mr. Thoreau seemed a timid conformist. There was, for example, John Collins of Boston. An agent of the Massachusetts Anti-Slavery Society, Mr. Collins had become more and more radical in his dislike of the government. In a series of "articles of belief and disbelief," to advertise the community he proposed to start on his farm near Skaneateles. Collins proclaimed his disbelief in the rightful existence of all governments based upon physical force, declaring them all organized *banditti* whose authority was to be challenged. "We will not vote under such governments, or petition to them, but demand them to disband; do no military duty; pay no personal or property taxes; sit upon no juries; refuse to testify in courts of so-called justice; and never appeal to the law for a redress of grievances, but use all peaceful and moral means to secure their complete destruction."

With these no-government and non-resistance principles, John Collins set out sanguinely to found "the most radical and reformatory" colony yet attempted in North America. But by May, 1846, he was forced to confess that his venture had been premature, owing chiefly to the moral defects of those who had with alacrity accepted his invitation to become members. Like the disillusioned Robert Owen, John Collins abandoned his cherished schemes of philanthropy and social improvement, and soon was seeking refuge in "the decencies and respectabilities of orthodox Whiggery."

Brook Farm, too, crashed to an ignominious finale. On March 3, 1846, a great fire swept through that well-publicized phalanstery and extinguished its energies and hopes. Thus closed dramatically the final phase in the six years of Brook Farm's existence. Through *The Dial* and later *The Harbinger,* the little band in Putney had watched with the closest attention every step of its progress—its inauguration under the banner of Fourier, its conversion to Swedenborgianism. Yet John Noyes had an instinctive distrust of Ralph Waldo Emerson and Margaret Fuller.

4

There was, however, one group of colonies, those of the Shakers, which possessed the power of survival. These were like monasteries for both sexes, and had been founded by the followers of Mother Ann Lee. Their earliest communal home had been established in 1776, at Neskeyuna, New York. Toward the close of the eighteenth century, these monastic farms were established in other townships in New York, thence throughout New England and even as far west as Kentucky, Indiana and Ohio.

Mrs. Ann Lee, founder of the sect had, in her early years, passed through an inferno of sexual experience, during her marriage to an incurable drunkard. She had suffered the agonies of torture and martyrdom in several childbirths, and all her babies had died in infancy. After the birth of the last infant, extracted by forceps, Ann Lee lay for several hours at the very edge of death. As she fought her way back to life, step by painful step, she then and there decided that she would never again indulge in carnal intercourse. By revelation, she avowed, she had received knowledge that this indulgence was the root of all evil. Soon thereafter, she began her impassioned testimony against sexual intercourse and against marriage.

Of great physical strength and endurance, Ann Lee set an example of hard work and rigid discipline. Her celibate followers developed into extraordinary designers and builders. An unimpaired, undiverted intensity of spirit animates the furniture they built for their community homes, as well as the building themselves—enduring records of the sublimation of their impulses.

Noyes had long admired the achievements of the Shakers, though their ideas concerning sexual love were diametrically opposed to his own. Not long after his marriage to Harriet Holton, finding himself near Harvard, Massachusetts, where a Shaker colony existed, he paid it a visit. He was courteously received by an elderly Shaker sister and engaged her in a sort of Socratic dialogue on the problems of earthly and Heavenly intercourse.

"The Lord commands husbands to love their wives," proclaimed Noyes. "We must be obedient to this; we must have the armor of righteousness on the right hand and on the left."

"Yea, that is all right," answered the Shaker sister. "But the world is not now as it was when Paul wrote: he had to deal with heathen that were in the worst state, and they had more than one woman; and Paul told them to love their wives so as to keep them from going to other women. This ceremony of marriage—the being 'published' and going before a minister—is nothing!"

"I agree with you that the ceremonies and ordinances of men are of little or no value," admitted Noyes. "But the connection of the sexes is altogether another thing. This is in accordance with the desires and organization of our nature as it was created, and is therefore an ordinance of God. If I understand your books, you yourselves allow that sexual intercourse was originally appointed by the Creator, under certain restrictions as to times and seasons."

The Shaker sister shook her head gravely and finally, without embarrassment, replied: "I guess not. We don't know what God did appoint: man did not wait to see. You will see; you are in the right way, but you have not traveled through. I have been where you are, and I have gone on. I have been looking at this matter a long time."

"I have been looking at it, too, a long time. I have been where you are, that is, I have taken the common and literal view of the text 'They that are accounted worthy,' but I have gone on and taken another lesson."

"You have backslidden, and will have to go over the ground again," the old woman retorted gravely. "If you are traveling any place and stop and go back, you will never get there. You turned back because you were thinking of getting married."

This outspoken reference to his own life brought a quick reply. "Not so!" exclaimed the young man from Putney. "I made up my mind about the matter before I had any idea of being married, and when I never intended or expected to be married according to the custom of this world."

"Well, be that as it may, I know that you are in an error. I have been where you are." Perhaps the good sister wished to bring this futile interview to a close. But she did not know John Noyes.

"And I say again, I have been where you are! As you say of me, so I say of you, you have traveled part way toward the truth, and have stopped. Now if you travel on you will find, as I have, that the Shaker doctrine is a great error."

The Shaker sister was not offended—not even shocked. "Do you think that we have not any light?"

A disarming innocence seemed to lie behind this question.

"No, I don't judge you, because I am not sufficiently acquainted with you," Noyes replied courteously. "I came here to reason with you. If you have had so much more experience than I and think me in error, you must convince me by argument.... In Christ all are one, and each owns all and all own each, and all are married to all. Of course, the supposed difficulty of determining whose wife the woman should be could not exist there (in heaven). We must remember that the exclusive and artificial marriage of this world is one thing, and natural sexual intercourse another; and Christ's answer only determines that such marriage as would make the difficulty proposed does not exist in heaven, while he leaves entirely untouched the question whether sexual intercourse exists there."

The Shaker sister gazed at the young heretic in silence. Finally she answered: "I should really think that one who has so much understanding of Scripture as you have would see the true meaning of that text. It says they are like angels; we must be like angels in this world."

"Well, how are the angels?" he demanded quickly. "Christ says, 'Except ye be converted and become as little children, ye shall not enter into the kingdom of heaven.' If we would be like angels then we must be like little children."

"We Shakers are like little children; we are all brothers and sisters," she answered, hoping for an escape from this argumentative visitor.

"Little children do not think evil of any part of their bodies or separate the sexes on account of it," he retorted. "Are you in this respect like little children?"

She became confused; she had no training in the finer points. But he could not leave without delivering his message: "You are not and never expect to be like little children. The truth is, little children are no more like Shakers than they are like the world. Little children represent the purity and innocence which belong to the kingdom of heaven; and so long as Shakers regard any passion or department of human nature as necessarily impure and carnal they cannot be in the child state, and so are not in the kingdom-of-heaven state."

"I wish some of the brethren who know how to handle these things were here. I am but a poor old woman!" the Shaker sister exclaimed.

Young Noyes found the Shaker brethren well able to defend their point of view in argument, unexpectedly penetrating in their analysis of the sexual customs of worldly society, yet with an intuitive comprehension of his point of view. Some mysterious attraction of opposites drew him to them.

Despite their limitations and apparent eccentricities, they demonstrated, for the shepherd of the Putney flock, that a communal life could be successfully lived within the framework of the nation.

Now, facing a new problem, and surveying all the various ventures in colonization that had been undertaken for almost a century, Noyes realized the almost insurmountable obstacles that might defeat the successful development of a Perfectionist Community. Yet, for reassurance, there stood the long record of success that had rewarded the patient efforts of the Shakers. Their colonies had, by some miracle, perpetuated themselves—though their members had not! Modestly yet eloquently their example testified to what might be accomplished.

Noyes was convinced that the success of the Shaker communities had encouraged the successive emigrations and experiments of the Rappites, the Zoarites, and the Ebenezers. These subsequent experiments in communal living were mere echoes of Shaker initiative—echoes which grew fainter and fainter, as the initial impulse toward a new form lost its *élan*.

When in England, Robert Owen had undertaken to convert his world to communism, consciously or unconsciously he was following the paths hewn out by the American Shakers. Was not Owen a distant follower of the Rappites? Noyes even went so far as to claim that Frenchmen like St. Simon and Fourier had been influenced by the Shakers. Tracing the genealogy of the movement for communal living (at a later date), he declared: "it is no more than bare justice to say that we are indebted to the Shakers more than to any or all other social architects of modern times. Their success has been the 'specie basis' that has upheld all the paper theories, and counteracted the failures, of the French and English schools. It is very doubtful whether Owenism or Fourierism would have ever existed, or if they had, whether they would have ever moved the practical American nation, if the facts of Shakerism had not existed before them and gone along with them. But to do complete justice we must go a step further. While we say that the Rappites, the Zoarites, the Ebenezers, the Owenites and even the Fourierists are all echoes of the Shakers, we must also say that that the Shakers are the far-off echoes of the Primitive Christian Church."

So Noyes sought to find inspiration in the example set by the followers of Mother Ann Lee.

Surely the territory of the United States was vast enough, extensive enough, free enough in tolerance of spirit to permit the fulfillment of another experiment. The country at large was far more open-minded than Putney.

But, confronted on all sides by the collapse of other colonies and communities, the outlook was far from encouraging to one who now found himself a fugitive from Vermont justice, accused of adultery and fornication; whose community had been dispersed, and who was reduced to the ignominy of sitting in exile, in the front parlor of a modest New York house—wondering how he could reassemble his scattered flock, how move forward in establishing the Kingdom of God.

ARTHUR CHAPMAN

Riders All

I

GREAT exploits in horsemanship became almost commonplace in the Pony Express service. Records for speed and endurance were made, which, if established under different circumstances, would have aroused nationwide interest. But most of such records were made as part of the day's work, with no time-keepers other than station men with an eye to the schedule, and with no glory to be won, other than the consciousness of a duty well performed.

The strain upon the riders increased proportionately after the service was made semi-weekly, instead of weekly, and relay stations were established from ten to twelve miles apart, instead of twenty-five miles. Perhaps the best evidence of the harsh demands made by the "Pony" upon its riders is to be found in the frequent changes of personnel. Among the eighty riders who started in the first interchange of mail between St. Joseph and Sacramento, few remained so much as a year. After the first twelve months of the service there were withdrawals due to two causes—enlistments on one side or the other in the Civil War, and the pushing of the transcontinental telegraph, which foreshadowed the doom of the courier service. In the main, withdrawals were for the reason that men could not stand the physical strain. It is probable that a complete roster of Overland Pony Express riders would total more than two hundred. Some of the men rode for a few weeks and others for a few days. Station keepers, stock tenders and even stage drivers were frequently required to substitute for saddlemen who were unable to go on. The riders who withstood the grind, month in and month out, were supermen of the saddle, whose extraordinary deeds have for the most part been lost, unfortunately, in the chaos of the frontier.

Riders were often called upon to "double" in the saddle—that is, to ride to the next "home" station, due to the non-arrival of the courier from the opposite direction. This meant from eight to twelve hours more in the saddle, and "taking the top off" at least six more of the fresh and speedy horses which were held in waiting at the relay stations.

Twenty-five or thirty extra miles meant nothing to a Pony Express courier, though it would be a fair day's ride in itself to anyone not inured to saddle fatigue. It is related of Johnny Frey that, when he had trimmed a few minutes from his incoming schedule, he would rein his foaming horse in front of the old Troy House, the first hotel in the settlement of Troy, Kansas, and ask:

"Is breakfast ready?"

On being answered in the negative, the rider would reply:

"Well, put something on the fire, and I'll go on to St. Joe and will be back here to eat!"

St. Joseph was from fourteen to sixteen miles from Troy, depending on the condition of the bottom lands along the Missouri and which one of several trails the "Pony" riders were taking to the Elwood ferry. Yet, in an incredibly short time, Frey would be back in Troy for the breakfast he had ordered!

"Johnny always sounded a special blast on his horn when he neared the Dave Hardy place near Cold Springs, where the widow Hargis lived with four grown daughters," said an old-timer who remembered the Pony Express days in that part of Kansas. "Johnny was always hitting a good clip, coming or going, when he reached Cold Springs, but he never failed to hold up for a second or two, so he could get the doughnuts or pie the girls brought out to him.

"At that time Miss Betty Hobbs, who was from New York State, was teaching the little school near Syracuse, the next station," went on my informant. "Clocks were scarce in those days, and you couldn't always tell whether they were running right or not. Well, no matter what the school clock said, Miss Betty always waited for the rider to go past on 'Pony day.' Those boys were so punctual, in and out of St. Joe, that you could set a clock by 'em."

Jack Keetley, a Marysville boy, was known as the "joyous jockey of the Pony Express." Keetley had the unusual experience of riding on more than one division—in fact he had ridden every mile of the trail from St. Joseph to Fort Laramie, though generally riding east of Marysville. Keetley, to settle a wager, once rode from Rock Creek to St. Joe and return, and then back to Seneca, a total distance of three hundred and forty miles. He was in the saddle thirty-one hours, without sleep or rest. Inasmuch as "Pony" riders frequently left the main trail in order to avoid bad road conditions, A. E. Lewis, then division superintendent at St. Joseph, went over Keetley's route with a "roadometer" which he possessed, to verify the distance that had been covered.

Alex Carlyle, who rode out of St. Joseph during the first two months of the "Pony," was a dashing, fearless rider, but had to retire on account of illness which developed into consumption and soon caused his death. Carlyle was once shot at, by an Indian in ambush. The Indian's aim was so good that the bullet knocked Carlyle's cap from his head. Thereafter Carlyle never would wear any kind of head covering, while riding.

Charley and Gus Cliff were riders who helped keep the "Pony" mail moving along the eastern division during the closing months of the service. They were appointed in the summer of 1861. Frey and several other riders had resigned to go into the army.

"Pony Express riding was not only hard work, but it was the lonesomest kind of a job," said Charley Cliff, recalling his days as a courier. "The only other rider I ever really knew was George Town, who took the mail from me at Seneca, when I had pounded out my eighty or eighty-five miles from St. Joe. My schedule called for eight hours on this run, but I could generally cut that time down considerably if I had to."

Jim Beatley was a notable figure along the route between St. Joseph and Rock Creek station. Beatley, like Frey, was noted for the wild horses he chose for his rides. In fact, any one of the Pony Express riders would have won popularity in the days of the Wild West show and the rodeo.

"It was common to find that you had drawn a bucking horse when you started out of a station," said Gus Cliff. "That was one reason why we gave them the spurs right from the start and kept them going. A good many of the horses we had were half broke—some of the best of them, in fact. A few days on the trail cured most of them of bucking, but some never quit, especially right after they had been saddled."

Henry Avis, whose run was from Mud Springs, through Fort Laramie to Horseshoe Creek, made a remarkable ride through "hostile" country at a time when the Indians were threatening. In the spring of 1861 the Sioux were unusually defiant. Before he left Mud Springs, Avis heard that raiding parties had been sighted farther along the trail. At Horseshoe the rumors grew more definite. An incoming stage driver reported a war party, evidently out for trouble, in the vicinity of Deer Creek. He was going to have a party of soldiers sent out from Fort Laramie, as he was convinced there was trouble in store.

There was no incoming rider at Horseshoe to relieve Avis. Getting a fresh mount, Avis started on with the mail, despite predictions that he would lose his scalp.

Avis, before entering the Pony Express service, had been with Major Dripps, the fur trader and explorer, and knew the ways of Indians. He was convinced that his horse could outrun any Indian pony, but he knew that speed would be of no avail if he ran into an ambush.

The country through which Avis was traveling was rolling prairie. When he approached the crest of a hill, the Pony Express rider would dismount and lead his horse. In this way he was able to make a survey from each hill-top, without emerging into full view of any Indians who might be coming toward him. At one or two bad turns in the trail, where there were wooded creek bottoms favorable to an ambushing party, Avis "cut across" through the sagebrush.

In this way he succeeded in getting to the Deer Creek station with the mail, to find that the predictions of the stage driver had come true. The Indians had made a raid on the station, but had contented themselves with driving off all the livestock. The courier who was due to depart for the west decided to wait for the arrival of the soldiers, but Avis, with no remount available, returned to Mud Springs. He was sixteen hours in the saddle and on foot, covering the one hundred and ten miles to Deer Creek. For this exhibition of nerve, under trying circumstances, Avis received a monetary reward from the company.

"Seth Ward was the station keeper at Fort Laramie," said Avis. "When he heard that I was headed right for an Indian raid, he thought it was the last time I'd ever wake him up to sign a waybill."

"Pony Bob" Haslam established a remarkable record for courage and endurance while the Pah-Ute war was on in Nevada. Haslam's run was from Friday's station to Buckland's (afterward Fort Churchill) a distance of seventy-five miles. At the outbreak of the Indian war, Haslam found, on arriving at the relay station west of Buckland's, that the Pah-Utes had driven off all the stock. Pushing on to Buckland's, he found that there was no rider to relieve him. Going on through the sink of the Carson to Sand Springs, sixty-five miles, Haslam got a change of horses. He traveled to Smith's creek, a total of one hundred and ninety miles from his starting place, and there exchanged mail with Jay G. Kelley, who had come on from the east.

On his return trip, nine hours later, Haslam found that the Cold Springs station had been raided. The station had been burned and the station keeper killed. On reaching Sand Springs he advised the keeper to come with him to the sink of the Carson. If the keeper had not heeded Haslam's advice, no doubt he would have been killed when the Sand Springs station was raided the next day.

Indians had been seen at the sink of the Carson, but, after a short rest, Haslam went on, arriving at Buckland's with the mail only three and one-half hours behind schedule time. After he had completed his run to Friday's station, he had covered three hundred and eighty miles, being thirty-six hours in the saddle and traveling through a hostile country, with danger threatening him in every canyon and at every turn of the trail.

2

The Pony Express was launched at a time when news events of great importance were "breaking" regularly. Extra demands were made upon men and horses when anything of unusual interest was scheduled. No comparison can be made so far as the resulting records are concerned, for the reason that weather and trail conditions were always different.

The first "flash" announcing the election of President Lincoln was sent by telegraph from St. Louis to St. Joseph, on November 7, 1860. It was carried by special Pony Express to the telegraph station at Fort Churchill, Nev., in a few hours less than eight days, the San Francisco newspapers issuing extras on November 14. The courier who carried the news from Julesburg to the *Rocky Mountain News* at Denver is said to have covered the last five miles at the rate of nineteen miles an hour.

President Buchanan's farewell message to Congress was sent by telegraph to Fort Kearney on December 6, 1860, and arrived at Fort Churchill on the evening of December 18, or twelve days *en route* by "Pony."

The greatest struggle against the odds imposed by bad weather conditions occurred when the Pony Express was called upon to carry through President Lincoln's inaugural message of March 4, 1861, in the quickest possible time.

Along the Pony Express line, division superintendents had been notified that the message must be put through, regardless of horseflesh. The superintendents had in turn notified station keepers to have the speediest horses in readiness. The riders themselves picked out the horses they were to be given at the relay stations, and the stock tenders had given these animals every care.

At the same time it was realized that the "Pony" was under its severest handicap. March is the worst time of year, as a rule, in the Rocky Mountains and the Sierras. On the plains it is generally a month of heavy snows.

The telegraph line had been completed to Fort Kearney on the east and Fort Churchill, Nevada, on the west, shortening the actual run of the Pony Express, so far as important messages were concerned, by approximately four hundred miles. But there were sixteen hundred miles to go, from one telegraph key to another, along the worst part of the route.

The Pacific Coast was all expectancy—witnessed by the following editorial in the San Francisco *Bulletin* of March 14:

> The next Pony will bring us news of the inauguration of President Lincoln, and possibly his inaugural address. The arrival of that Express may be expected at any hour, as it is probable that the riders on the route will exert themselves to make fast time.

Exert themselves! No men ever strove harder, nor was more ever demanded of gallant horses. Men and animals floundered through snowdrifts in the mountains and faced cutting winds and heavy snowfalls on the plains. Years afterward I talked with W. A. (Bill) Cates, who rode with the Lincoln message through seventy-five miles of windswept, snow-covered hills in Wyoming.

"It was tough going," said Cates. "The message got a good start out of Kearney, but the closer it got to the mountains, the worse the conditions got. We had the best horses available—several of them were killed—and, considering what we had to fight, the record was the most wonderful ever made by the Pony Express."

When Salt Lake City received the message, it was March 12—seven days consumed by the plucky riders in struggling through from Fort Kearney. The *Deseret News* reported upon the arrival as follows in its issue of March 13:

> The Pony Express, with Eastern advices, up to the fifth of March, arrived here yesterday morning at ten o'clock, bringing the anxiously looked-for inaugural message of Mr. Lincoln, but no account of the ceremonies. The telegraph operator at Kearney leads us to expect full and more comprehensive details by next Pony.

Fort Churchill, on March 17, reported to the Sacramento and San Francisco papers the arrival of the Pony Express at that station, at 8:30 o'clock that morning. The San Francisco *Bulletin* of March 18 printed the address in full.

So tense was the political situation at the time, and so eager were people to read what the new President had to say, that the newspapers made no comment on the struggle of men and horses to get the message across the desert and mountains in the quickest possible time. One can only read between the lines of the *Bulletin's* explanatory "bank" under its stock heading, "By Magnetic Telegraph":

"Per telegraph to St. Louis; thence by telegraph to Fort Kearney; thence by Pony Express to Sacramento; thence by telegraph to San Francisco."

In this is packed a lot of romance of early-day journalism. Twelve days to get news through from Fort Kearney to Sacramento, with couriers fighting blizzards and snowdrifts on the way! Twelve days of urging staggering horses along trails suddenly made white and unfamiliar. Twelve days of changing an icy *mochila,* with its all-important message, from one saddle to another! Editors, compositors and pressmen waiting in Pacific Coast newspaper offices—waiting for the "big news" which might be delayed by any one of a hundred happenings—a pony's misstep in the dark, a rider shot from ambush by Indians, a snowslide in the mountains, or a prairie trail lost by a half-frozen courier.

Many writers had mistakenly said that the Lincoln inaugural message went through *from St. Joseph to Sacramento* in seven days and seventeen hours. The newspaper records of the day, showing that the message was telegraphed from St. Louis to Fort Kearney, and that it took twelve days to reach Fort Churchill, Nevada, are in themselves sufficient refutation of this misstatement.

The winter schedule of the "Pony" varied from eleven days to seventeen days between Kearney and Churchill. It is to be assumed, from the bad weather conditions along the route early in March, 1861, that, had not extraordinary efforts been made, the seventeen-day limit would have been reached. The fact that the couriers who carried the Lincoln inaugural message cut *five days* from the time which they would have taken ordinarily, speaks eloquently enough of the struggle which men and horses waged against the elements.

FREDERICK LAW OLMSTED

A South Carolina Rice Plantation in the Fifties

A T THE HEAD of the settlement, in a garden looking down the street, was an overseer's house, and here the road divided, running each way at right angles; on one side to barns and a landing on the river, on the other toward the mansion of the proprietor. A negro boy opened the gate of the latter, and I entered.

On either side, at fifty feet distant, were rows of old live oak trees, their branches and twigs slightly hung with a delicate fringe of gray moss, and their dark, shining, green foliage, meeting and intermingling naturally but densely overhead. The sunlight streamed through, and played aslant the lustrous leaves, and fluttering pendulous moss; the arch was low and broad; the trunks were huge and gnarled, and there was a heavy groining of strong, rough, knotty branches. I stopped my horse and held my breath; I thought of old Kit North's rhapsody on trees; and it was no rhapsody—it was all here, and real: "Light, shade, shelter, coolness, freshness, music, dew and dreams dropping through their umbrageous twilight—dropping direct, soft, sweet, soothing, and restorative from heaven."

Alas! no angels; only little black babies, toddling about with an older child or two to watch them, occupied the aisle. At the upper end was the owner's mansion, with a circular court-yard around it, and an irregular plantation of great trees; one of the oaks, as I afterwards learned, seven feet in diameter of trunk, and covering with its branches a circle of one hundred and twenty feet in diameter. As I approached it, a smart servant came out to take my horse. I obtained from him a direction to the residence of the gentleman I was searching for, and rode away, glad that I had stumbled into so charming a place.

After riding a few miles further I reached my destination.

Mr. X. has two plantations on the river, besides a large tract of poor pine forest land, extending some miles back upon the upland, and reaching above the malarious region. In the upper part of this pine land is a house, occupied by his overseer during the malarious season, when it is dangerous for any but negroes to remain during the night in the vicinity of the swamps or rice-fields. Even those few who have been born in the region, and have grown up subject to the malaria, are said to be generally weakly and short-lived. The negroes do not enjoy as good health on rice plantations as elsewhere; and the greater difficulty with which their lives are preserved, through infancy especially, shows that the subtle poison of the miasma is not innocuous to them; but Mr. X. boasts a steady increase of his negro stock, of five per cent. per annum, which is better than is averaged on the plantations of the interior.

The plantation which contains Mr. X.'s winter residence has but a small extent of rice land, the greater part of it being reclaimed upland swamp soil, suitable for the culture of Sea Island cotton. The other plantation contains over five hundred acres of rice-land, fitted for irrigation; the remainder is unusually fertile reclaimed upland swamp, and some hundred acres of it are cultivated for maize and Sea Island cotton.

There is a "negro settlement" on each; but both plantations, although a mile or two apart, are worked together as one, under one overseer—the hands being drafted from one to another as their labour is required. Somewhat over seven hundred acres are at the present time under the plough in the two plantations: the whole number of negroes is two hundred, and they are reckoned to be equal to about one hundred prime hands—an unusual strength for that number of all classes. The overseer lives, in winter, near the settlement of the larger plantation, Mr. X. near that of the smaller.

It is an old family estate, inherited by Mr. X.'s wife, who, with her children, were born and brought up upon it in close intimacy with the negroes, a large proportion of whom were also included in her inheritance, or have been since born upon the estate. Mr. X. himself is a New England farmer's son, and has been a successful merchant and manufacturer.

The patriarchal institution should be seen here under its most favourable aspects; not only from the ties of long family association, common traditions, common memories, and, if ever, common interests, between the slaves and their rulers, but, also, from the practical talent for organization and administration, gained among the rugged fields, the complicated looms, and the exact and comprehensive counting-houses of New England, which directs the labour.

The house-servants are more intelligent, understand and perform their duties better, and are more appropriately dressed, than any I have seen before. The labour required of them is light, and they are treated with much more consideration for their health and comfort than is usually given to that of free domestics. They live in brick cabins, adjoining the house and stables, and one of these, into which I have looked, is neatly and comfortably furnished. Several of the house-servants, as is usual, are mulattoes, and good-looking. The mulattoes are generally preferred for in-door occupations. Slaves brought up to house-work dread to be employed at field-labour; and those accustomed to the comparatively unconstrained life of the negro-settlement, detest the close control and careful movements required of the house-servants. It is a punishment for a lazy field-hand, to employ him in menial duties at the house, as it is to set a sneaking sailor to do the work of a cabin-servant; and it is equally a punishment to a neglectful house-servant, to banish him to the field-gangs. All the household economy is, of course, carried on in a style appropriate to a wealthy gentleman's residence—not more so, nor less so, that I observe, than in an establishment of similar grade at the North.

It is a custom with Mr. X., when on the estate, to look each day at all the work going on, inspect the buildings, boats, embankments, and sluice-ways, and examine the sick. Yesterday I accompanied him in one of these daily rounds.

After a ride of several miles through the woods, in the rear of the plantations we came to his largest negro-settlement. There was a street, or common, two hundred feet wide, on which the cabins of the negroes fronted. Each cabin was a framed building, the walls boarded and whitewashed on the outside, lathed and plastered within, the roof shingled; forty-two feet long, twenty-one feet wide, divided into two family tenements, each twenty-one by twenty-one; each tenement divided into three rooms—one, the common household apartment, twenty-one by ten; each of the others (bedrooms), ten by ten. There was a brick fire-place in the middle of the long side of each living room, the chimneys rising in one, in the middle of the roof. Besides these rooms, each tenement had a cock-loft, entered by steps from the household room. Each tenement is occupied, on an average, by five persons. There were in them closets, with locks and keys, and a varying quantity of rude furniture. Each cabin stood two hundred feet from the next, and the street in front of them being two hundred feet wide, they were just that distance apart each way. The people were nearly all absent at work, and had locked their outer doors, taking the keys with them. Each cabin has a front and back door, and each room a window, closed by a wooden shutter, swinging outward, on hinges. Between each tenement and the next house, is a small piece of ground, inclosed with palings, in which are coops of fowl with chickens, hovels for nests, and for sows with pig. There were a great many fowls in the street. The negroes' swine are allowed to run in the woods, each owner having his own distinguished by a peculiar mark. In the rear of the yards were gardens—a half-acre to each family. Internally the cabins appeared dirty and disordered, which was rather a pleasant indication that their home-life was not much interfered with, though I found certain police regulations were enforced.

The cabin nearest the overseer's house was used as a nursery. Having driven up to this, Mr. X. inquired first of an old nurse how the children were; whether there had been any births since his last visit; spoke to two convalescent young mothers, who were lounging on the floor of the portico, with the children, and then asked if there were any sick people.

"Nobody, oney dat boy, Sam, sar."

"What Sam is that?"

"Dat little Sam, sar; Tom's Sue's Sam, sar."

"What's the matter with him?"

"Don' 'spec dere's noting much de matter wid him now, sar. He came in Sa'dy, complainin' he had de stomach-ache, an' I gin him some ile, sar; 'spec he mus' be well, dis time, but he din go out dis mornin'."

"Well, I'll see to him."

Mr. X. went to Tom's Sue's cabin, looked at the boy, and, concluding that he was well, though he lay abed, and pretended to cry with pain, ordered him to go out to work. Then, meeting the overseer, who was just riding away, on some business of the plantation, he remained some time in conversation with him, while I occupied myself in making a sketch of the nursery and street of the settlement in my note-book. On the verandah and the steps of the nursery, there were twenty-seven children, most of them infants, that had been left there by their mothers, while they were working their tasks in the fields. They probably make a visit to them once or twice during the day, to nurse them, and receive them to take to their cabins, or where they like, when they have finished their tasks—generally in the middle of the afternoon. The older children were fed with porridge, by the general nurse. A number of girls, eight or ten years old, were occupied in holding and tending the youngest infants. Those a little older—the crawlers—were in the pen, and those big enough to toddle were playing on the steps, or before the house. Some of these, with two or three bigger ones, were singing and dancing about a fire that they had made on the ground. They were not at all disturbed or interrupted in their amusement by the presence of their owner and myself. At twelve years of age, the children are first put to regular field-work; until then no labour is required of them, except, perhaps, occasionally they are charged with some light kind of duty, such as frightening birds from corn. When first sent to the field, one quarter of an able-bodied hand's day's work is ordinarily allotted to them, as their task.

From the settlement, we drove to the "mill"—not a flouring mill, though I believe there is a run of stones in it—but a monster barn, with more extensive and better machinery for threshing and storing rice, driven by a steam-engine, than I have ever seen used for grain before. Adjoining the mill-house were shops and sheds, in which blacksmiths, carpenters, and other mechanics—all slaves, belonging to Mr. X.—were at work. He called my attention to the excellence of their workmanship, and said that they exercised as much ingenuity and skill as the ordinary mechanics that he was used to employ in New England. He pointed out to me some carpenter's work, a part of which had been executed by a New England mechanic, and a part by one of his own hands, which indicated that the latter was much the better workman.

I was gratified by this, for I had been so often told, in Virginia, by gentlemen anxious to convince me that the negro was incapable of being educated or improved to a condition in which it would be safe to trust him with himself—that no negro-mechanic could ever be taught, or induced to work carefully or nicely—that I had begun to believe it might be so.

We were attended through the mill-house by a respectable-looking, orderly, and quiet-mannered mulatto, who was called, by his master, "the watchman." His duties, however, as they were described to me, were those of a steward, or intendant. He carried, by a strap at his waist, a very large number of keys, and had charge of all the stores of provisions, tools, and materials of the plantations, as well as of all their produce, before it was shipped to market. He weighed and measured out all the rations of the slaves and the cattle; superintended the mechanics, and made and repaired, as was necessary, all the machinery, including the steam-engine.

In all these departments, his authority was superior to that of the overseer. The overseer received his private allowance of family provisions from him, as did also the head-servant at the mansion, who was his brother. His responsibility was much greater than that of the overseer; and Mr. X. said he would trust him with much more than he would any overseer he had ever known.

Anxious to learn how this trustworthiness and intelligence, so unusual in a slave, had been developed or ascertained, I inquired of his history, which was briefly as follows.

Being the son of a favourite house-servant, he had been, as a child, associated with the white family, and received by chance something of the early education of the white children. When old enough, he had been employed, for some years, as a waiter; but, at his own request, was eventually allowed to learn the blacksmith's trade, in the plantation shop. Showing ingenuity and talent, he was afterwards employed to make and repair the plantation cotton-gins. Finally, his owner took him to a steam-engine builder, and paid $500 to have him instructed as a machinist. After he had become a skilful workman, he obtained employment as an engineer; and for some years continued in this occupation, and was allowed to spend his wages for himself. Finding, however, that he was acquiring dissipated habits, and wasting his earnings, Mr. X. eventually brought him, much against his inclinations, back to the plantations. Being allowed peculiar privileges, and given duties wholly flattering to his self-respect, he soon became contented; and, of course, was able to be extremely valuable to his owner.

I have seen another slave-engineer. The gentleman who employed him told me that he was a man of talent, and of great worth of character. He had desired to make him free, but his owner, who was a member of the Board of Brokers, and of Dr. ———'s Church, in New York, believed that Providence designed the negro race for slavery, and refused to sell him for that purpose. He thought it better that he (his owner) should continue to receive two hundred dollars a year for his services, while he continued able to work, because then, as he said, he should feel responsible that he did not starve, or come upon the public for a support, in his old age. The man himself, having light and agreeable duties, well provided for, furnished with plenty of spending money by his employer, patronized and flattered by the white people, honoured and looked up to by those of his own colour, was rather indifferent in the matter; or even, perhaps, preferred to remain a slave, to being transported for life to Africa.

The watchman was a fine-looking fellow: as we were returning from church, on Sunday, he had passed us, well dressed and well mounted, and as he raised his hat, to salute us, there was nothing in his manner or appearance, except his colour, to distinguish him from a gentleman of good breeding and fortune.

When we were leaving the house, to go to church, on Sunday, after all the white family had entered their carriages, or mounted their horses, the head house-servant also mounted a horse—as he did so, slipping a coin into the hands of the boy who had been holding him. Afterwards, we passed a family of negroes, in a light waggon, the oldest among them driving the horse. On my inquiring if the slaves were allowed to take horses to drive to church, I was informed that in each of these three cases, the horses belonged to the negroes who were driving or riding them. The old man was infirm, and Mr. X. had given him a horse, to enable him to move about. He was probably employed to look after the cattle at pasture, or at something in which it was necessary, for his usefulness, that he should have a horse: I say this, because I afterwards found, in similar cases on other plantations, that it was so. But the watchman and the house servant had bought their horses with money. The watchman was believed to own three horses; and, to account for his wealth, Mr. X.'s son told me that his father considered him a very valuable servant, and frequently encouraged his good behaviour with handsome gratuities. He receives, probably, considerably higher wages, in fact (in the form of presents), than the white overseer. He knew his father gave him two hundred dollars at once, a short time ago. The watchman has a private house, and, no doubt, lives in considerable luxury.

Will it be said, "therefore, Slavery is neither necessarily degrading nor inhumane?" On the other hand, so far as it is not, there is no apology for it. It is possible, though not probable, that this fine fellow, if he had been born a free man, would be no better employed than he is here; but, in that case, where is the advantage? Certainly not in the economy of the arrangement. And if he were self-dependent, if, especially, he had to provide for the present and future of those he loved, and was able to do so, would he not necessarily live a happier, stronger, better, and more respectable man?

After passing through toll-rooms, corn-rooms, mule-stables, store-rooms, and a large garden, in which vegetables to be distributed among the negroes, as well as for the family, are grown, we walked to the rice-land. It is divided by embankments into fields of about twenty acres each, but varying somewhat in size, according to the course of the river. The arrangements are such that each field may be flooded independently of the rest, and they are subdivided by open ditches into rectangular plats of a quarter acre each. We first proceeded to where twenty or thirty women and girls were engaged in raking together, in heaps and winrows, the stubble and rubbish left on the field after the last crop, and burning it. The main object of this operation is to kill all the seeds of weeds, or of rice, on the ground. Ordinarily it is done by tasks—a certain number of the small divisions of the field being given to each hand to burn in a day; but owing to a more than usual amount of rain having fallen lately, and some other causes, making the work harder in some places than others, the women were now working by the day, under the direction of a "driver," a negro man, who walked about among them, taking care that they left nothing unburned. Mr. X. inspected the ground they had gone over, to see whether the driver had done his duty. It had been sufficiently well burned, but not more than a quarter as much ground had been gone over, he said, as was usually burned in task-work,—and he thought they had been very lazy, and reprimanded them. The driver made some little apology, but the women offered no reply, keeping steadily and, it seemed, sullenly, on at their work.

In the next field, twenty men, or boys, for none of them looked as if they were full-grown, were ploughing, each with a single mule, and a light, New-York-made plough. The soil was friable, the ploughing easy, and the mules proceeded at a smart pace; the furrows were straight, regular, and well turned. Their task was nominally an acre and a quarter a day; somewhat less actually, as the measure includes the space occupied by the ditches, which are two to three feet wide, running around each quarter of an acre. The ploughing gang was superintended by a driver, who was provided with a watch; and while we were looking at them he called out that it was twelve o'clock. The mules were immediately taken from the ploughs, and the plough-boys mounting them, leapt the ditches, and cantered off to the stables, to feed them. One or two were ordered to take their ploughs to the blacksmith, for repairs.

The ploughmen got their dinner at this time: those not using horses do not usually dine till they have finished their tasks; but this, I believe, is optional with them. They commence work, I was told, at sunrise, and at about eight o'clock have breakfast brought to them in the field, each hand having left a bucket with the cook for that purpose. All who are working in connection, leave their work together, and gather about a fire, where they generally spend about half an hour. The provisions furnished, consist mainly of meal, rice, and vegetables, with salt and molasses, and occasionally bacon, fish, and coffee. The allowance is a peck of meal, or an equivalent quantity of rice per week, to each working hand, old or young, besides small stores. Mr. X. says that he has lately given a less amount of meat than is now usual on plantations, having observed that the general health of the negroes is not as good as formerly, when no meat at all was customarily given them. (The general impression among planters is, that the negroes work much better for being supplied with three or four pounds of bacon a week.)

Leaving the rice-land, we went next to some of the upland fields, where we found several other gangs of negroes at work; one entirely of men engaged in ditching; another of women, and another of boys and girls, "listing" an old corn-field with hoes. All of them were working by tasks, and were overlooked by negro drivers. They all laboured with greater rapidity and cheerfulness than any slaves I have before seen; and the women struck their hoes as if they were strong, and well able to engage in muscular labour. The expression of their faces was generally repulsive, and their *ensemble* anything but agreeable. The dress of most was uncouth and cumbrous, dirty and ragged; reefed up, as I have once before described, at the hips, so as to show their heavy legs, wrapped round with a piece of old blanket, in lieu of leggings or stockings. Most of them worked with bare arms, but wore strong shoes on their feet, and handkerchiefs on their heads; some of them were smoking, and each gang had a fire burning on the ground, near where they were at work, by which to light their pipes and warm their breakfast. Mr. X. said this was always their custom, even in summer. To each gang a boy or girl was also attached, whose business it was to bring water for them to drink, and to go for anything required by the driver. The drivers would frequently call back a hand to go over again some piece of his or her task that had not been worked to his satisfaction, and were constantly calling to one or another, with a harsh and peremptory voice, to strike harder, or hoe deeper, and otherwise taking care that the work was well done. Mr. X. asked if Little Sam ("Tom's Sue's Sam") worked yet with the "three-quarter" hands, and learning that he did, ordered him to be put with the full hands, observing that though rather short, he was strong and stout, and, being twenty years old, well able to do a man's work.

The field-hands are all divided into four classes, according to their physical capacities. The children beginning as "quarter-hands," advancing to "half-hands," and then to "three-quarter hands;" and, finally, when mature, and able-bodied, healthy, and strong, to "full hands." As they decline in strength, from age, sickness, or other cause, they retrograde in the scale, and proportionately less labour is required of them. Many, of naturally weak frame, never are put among the full hands. Finally, the aged are left out at the annual classification, and no more regular field-work is required of them, although they are generally provided with some light, sedentary occupation. I saw one old woman picking "tailings" of rice out of a heap of chaff, an occupation at which she was probably not earning her salt. Mr. X. told me she was a native African, having been brought when a girl from the Guinea coast. She spoke almost unintelligibly; but after some other conversation, in which I had not been able to understand a word she said, he jokingly proposed to send her back to Africa. She expressed her preference to remain where she was, very emphatically. "Why?" She did not answer readily, but being pressed, threw up her palsied hands, and said furiously, "I lubs 'ou, mas'r, oh, I lubs 'ou. I don't want go 'way from 'ou."

The field-hands are nearly always worked in gangs, the strength of a gang varying according to the work that engages it; usually it numbers twenty or more, and is directed by a driver. As on most large plantations, whether of rice or cotton, in Eastern Georgia and South Carolina, nearly all ordinary and regular work is performed *by tasks:* that is to say, each hand has his labour for the day marked out before him, and can take his own time to do it in. For instance, in making drains in light, clean meadow land, each man or woman of the full hands is required to dig one thousand cubic feet; in swamp-land that is being prepared for rice culture, where there are not many stumps, the task for a ditcher is five hundred feet: while in a very strong cypress swamp, only two hundred feet is required; in hoeing rice, a certain number of rows, equal to one half or two thirds of an acre, according to the condition of the land; in sowing rice (strewing in drills), two acres; in reaping rice (if it stands well), three-quarters of an acre; or, sometimes a gang will be required to reap, tie in sheaves, and carry to the stack-yard the produce of a certain area, commonly equal to one fourth the number of acres that there are hands working together. Hoeing cotton, corn, or potatoes; one half to one acre. Threshing; five to six hundred sheaves. In ploughing rice-land (light, clean, mellow soil) with a yoke of oxen, one acre a day, including the ground lost in and near the drains—the oxen being changed at noon. A cooper, also, for instance, is required to make barrels at the rate of eighteen a week. Drawing staves, 500 a day. Hoop poles, 120. Squaring timber, 100 ft. Laying worm-fence, 50 panels per hand. Post and rail do., posts set 2½ to 3 ft. deep, 9 ft. apart, nine or ten panels per hand. In getting fuel from the woods, (pine, to be cut and split,) one cord is the task for a day. In "mauling rails," the taskman selecting the trees (pine) that he judges will split easiest, one hundred a day, ends not sharpened.

These are the tasks for first-class able-bodied men; they are lessened by one quarter for three quarter hands, and proportionately for the lighter classes. In allotting the tasks, the drivers are expected to put the weaker hands where (if there is any choice in the appearance of the ground, as where certains rows in hoeing corn would be less weedy than others,) they will be favoured.

These tasks certainly would not be considered excessively hard, by a Northern labourer; and, in point of fact, the more industrious and active hands finish them often by two o'clock. I saw one or two leaving the field soon after one o'clock, several about two; and between three and four, I met a dozen women and several men coming home to their cabins, having finished their day's work.

Under this "Organization of Labour," most of the slaves work rapidly and well. In nearly all ordinary work, custom has settled the extent of the task, and it is difficult to increase it. The driver who marks it out, has to remain on the ground until it is finished, and has no interest in over-measuring it; and if it should be systematically increased very much, there is danger of a general stampede to the "swamp"—a danger the slave can always hold before his master's cupidity. In fact, it is looked upon *in this region* as a proscriptive right of the negroes to have this incitement to diligence offered them; and the man who denied it, or who attempted to lessen it, would, it is said, suffer in his reputation, as well as experience much annoyance from the obstinate "rascality" of his negroes. Notwithstanding this, I have heard a man assert, boastingly, that he made his negroes habitually perform double the customary tasks. Thus we get a glimpse again of the black side. If he is allowed the power to do this, what may not a man do?

It is the driver's duty to make the tasked hands do their work well. If, in their haste to finish it, they neglect to do it properly, he "sets them back," so that carelessness will hinder more than it will hasten the completion of their tasks.

In the selection of drivers, regard seems to be had to size and strength—at least, nearly all the drivers I have seen are tall and strong men—but a great deal of judgment, requiring greater capacity of mind than the ordinary slave is often supposed to be possessed of, is certainly needed in them. A good driver is very valuable and usually holds office for life. His authority is not limited to the direction of labour in the field, but extends to the general deportment of the negroes. He is made to do the duties of policeman, and even of police magistrate. It is his duty, for instance, on Mr. X.'s estate, to keep order in the settlement; and, if two persons, men or women, are fighting, it is his duty to immediately separate them, and then to "whip them both."

Before any field of work is entered upon by a gang, the driver who is to superintend them has to measure and stake off the tasks. To do this at all accurately, in irregular-shaped fields, must require considerable powers of calculation. A driver, with a boy to set the stakes, I was told, would accurately lay out forty acres a day, in half-acre tasks. The only instrument used is a five-foot measuring rod. When the gang comes to the field, he points out to each person his or her duty for the day, and then walks about among them, looking out that each proceeds properly. If, after a hard day's labour, he sees that the gang has been overtasked, owing to a miscalculation of the difficulty of the work, he may excuse the completion of the tasks; but he is not allowed to extend them. In the case of uncompleted tasks, the body of the gang begin new tasks the next day, and only a sufficient number are detailed from it to complete, during the day, the unfinished tasks of the day before. The relation of the driver to the working hands seems to be similar to that of the boatswain to the seamen in the navy, or of the sergeant to the privates in the army.

Having generally had long experience on the plantation, the advice of the drivers is commonly taken in nearly all the administration, and frequently they are, *de facto,* the managers. Orders on important points of the plantation economy, I have heard given by the proprietor directly to them, without the overseer's being consulted or informed of them; and it is often left with them to decide when and how long to flow the rice-grounds—the proprietor and overseer deferring to their more experienced judgment. Where the drivers are discreet, experienced, and trusty, the overseer is frequently employed merely as a matter of form, to comply with the laws requiring the superintendence or presence of a white man among every body of slaves; and his duty is rather to inspect and report than to govern. Mr. X. considers his overseer an uncommonly efficient and faithful one, but he would not employ him, even during the summer, when he is absent for several months, if the law did not require it. He has sometimes left his plantation in care of one of the drivers for a considerable length of time, after having discharged an overseer; and he thinks it has then been quite as well conducted as ever. His overseer consults the drivers on all important points, and is governed by their advice.

Mr. X said, that though overseers sometimes punished the negroes severely, and otherwise ill-treated them, it is their more common fault to indulge them foolishly in their disposition to idleness, or in other ways to curry favour with them, so they may not inform the proprietor of their own misconduct or neglect. He has his overseer bound to certain rules, by written contract; and it is stipulated that he can discharge him at any moment, without remuneration for his loss of time and inconvenience, if he should at any time be dissatisfied with him. One of the rules is, that he shall never punish a negro with his own hands, and that corporeal punishment, when necessary, shall be inflicted by the drivers. The advantage of this is, that it secures time for deliberation, and prevents punishment being made in sudden passion. His drivers are not allowed to carry their whips with them in the field; so that if the overseer wishes a hand punished, it is necessary to call a driver; and the driver has then to go to his cabin, which is, perhaps, a mile or two distant, to get his whip, before it can be applied.

I asked how often the necessity of punishment occurred?

"Sometimes, perhaps, not once for two or three weeks; then it will seem as if the devil had got into them all, and there is a good deal of it."

As the negroes finish the labour required of them by Mr. X., at three or four o'clock in the afternoon, they can employ the remainder of the day in labouring for themselves, if they choose. Each family has a half-acre of land allotted to it, for a garden; besides which, there is a large vegetable garden, cultivated by a gardener for the plantation, from which they are supplied, to a greater or less extent. They are at liberty to sell whatever they choose from the products of their own garden, and to make what they can by keeping swine and fowls. Mr. X.'s family have no other supply of poultry and eggs than what is obtained by purchase from his own negroes; they frequently, also, purchase game from them. The only restriction upon their traffic is a "liquor law." They are not allowed to buy or sell ardent spirits. This prohibition, like liquor laws elsewhere, unfortunately, cannot be enforced; and, of late years, grog shops, at which stolen goods are bought from the slaves, and poisonous liquors—chiefly the worst whisky, much watered and made stupefying by an infusion of tobacco—are clandestinely sold to them, have become an established evil, and the planters find themselves almost powerless to cope with it. They have, here, lately organized an association for this purpose, and have brought several offenders to trial; but, as it is a penitentiary offence, the culprit spares no pains or expense to avoid conviction—and it is almost impossible, in a community of which so large a proportion is poor and degraded, to have a jury sufficiently honest and intelligent to permit the law to be executed.

A remarkable illustration of this evil has lately occurred. A planter, discovering that a considerable quantity of cotton had been stolen from him, informed the patrol of the neighbouring planters of it. A stratagem was made use of, to detect the thief, and, what was of much more importance—there being no question but that this was a slave—to discover for whom the thief worked. A lot of cotton was prepared, by mixing hair with it, and put in a tempting place. A negro was seen to take it, and was followed by scouts to a grog-shop, several miles distant, where he sold it—its real value being nearly ten dollars—for ten cents, taking his pay in liquor. The man was arrested, and, the theft being made to appear, by the hair, before a justice, obtained bail in $2,000, to answer at the higher court. Some of the best legal counsel of the State has been engaged, to obtain, if possible, his conviction.

This difficulty in the management of slaves is a great and very rapidly increasing one. Everywhere that I have been, I have found the planters provoked and angry about it. A swarm of Jews, within the last ten years, has settled in nearly every Southern town, many of them men of no character, opening cheap clothing and trinket shops; ruining, or driving out of business, many of the old retailers, and engaging in an unlawful trade with the simple negroes, which is found very profitable.[1]

The law which prevents the reception of the evidence of a negro in courts, here strikes back, with a most annoying force, upon the dominant power itself. In the mischief thus arising, we see a striking illustration of the danger

[1] *From the Charleston Standard, Nov. 23rd,* 1854.—"This abominable practice of trading with slaves is not only taking our produce from us, but injuring our slave property. It is true the owner of slaves may lock, watch, and whip, as much as he pleases—the negroes will steal and trade as long as white persons hold out to them temptations to steal and bring to them. Three-fourths of the persons who are guilty, you can get no fine from; and, if they have some property, all they have to do is to confess a judgment to a friend, go to jail, and swear out. It is no uncommon thing for a man to be convicted of offences against the State, and against the persons and property of individuals, and pay the fines, costs, and damages, by swearing out of jail, and then go and commit similar offences. The State, or the party injured, has the cost of all these prosecutions and suits to pay, besides the trouble of attending Court; the guilty is convicted, the injured prosecutor punished."

which stands before the South, whenever its prosperity shall invite extensive immigration, and lead what would otherwise be a healthy competition to flow through its channels of industry.

This injury to slave property, from grog-shops, furnishes the grand argument for the Maine Law at the South.[2]

Mr. X. remarks that his arrangements allow his servants no excuse for dealing with these fellows. He has a rule to purchase everything they desire to sell, and to give them a high price for it himself. Eggs constitute a circulating medium on the plantation. Their par value is considered to be twelve for a dime, at which they may always be exchanged for cash, or left on deposit, without interest, at his kitchen.

Whatever he takes of them that he cannot use in his own family, or has not occasion to give to others of his servants, is sent to town to be resold. The negroes do not commonly take money for the articles he has of them, but the value of them is put to their credit, and a regular account kept with

[2] *From an Address to the people of Georgia, by a Committee of the State Temperance Society, prior to the election of 1855.*—"We propose to turn the 2,200 *foreign* grog-shop keepers, in Georgia, out of office, and ask them to help us. They (the Know-Nothings) reply, 'We have no time for that now—we are trying to turn *foreigners* out of office;' and when we call upon the Democratic party for aid, they excuse themselves, upon the ground that they have work enough to do in keeping these foreigners in office."

From the Penfield (Ga.) Temperance Banner, Sept. 29th, 1855.
"OUR SLAVE POPULATION.

"We take the following from the *Savannah Journal and Courier*, and would ask every candid reader if the evils referred to ought not to be corrected. How shall it be done?

"'By reference to the recent homicide of a negro, in another column, some facts will be seen suggestive of a state of things, in this part of our population, which should not exist, and which cannot endure without danger, both to them and to us. The collision, which terminated thus fatally, occurred at an hour past midnight—at a time when none but the evil-disposed are stirring, unless driven by necessity; and yet, at that hour, those negroes and others, as many as chose, were passing about the country, with ample opportunity to commit any act which might happen to enter their heads. In fact, they did engage, in the public highway, in a broil terminating in homicide. It is not difficult to imagine that their evil passions might have taken a very different direction, with as little danger of meeting control or obstacle.

"'But it is shown, too, that to the impunity thus given them by the darkness of midnight, was added the incitement to crime drawn from the abuse of liquor. They had just left one of those resorts where the negro is supplied with the most villainously-poisonous compounds, fit only to excite him to deeds of blood and violence. The part that this had in the slaughter of Saturday night, we are enabled only to imagine; but experience would teach us that its share was by no means small. Indeed, we have the declaration of the slayers, that the blow, by which he was exasperated so as to return it by the fatal stab, was inflicted by a bottle of brandy! In this fact, we fear, is a clue to the whole history of the transaction.'

"Here, evidently, are considerations deserving the grave notice of, not only those who own negroes, but of all others who live in a society where they are held."

them. He has a store, usually well supplied with articles that they most want, which are purchased in large quantities, and sold to them at wholesale prices; thus giving them a great advantage in dealing with him rather than with the grog-shops. His slaves are sometimes his creditors to large amounts; at the present time he says he owes them about five hundred dollars. A woman has charge of the store, and when there is anything called for that she cannot supply, it is usually ordered, by the next conveyance, of his factors in town.

The ascertained practicability of thus dealing with slaves, together with the obvious advantages of the method of working them by tasks, which I have described, seem to me to indicate that it is not so impracticable as is generally supposed, if only it was desired by those having the power, to rapidly extinguish Slavery, and while doing so, to educate the negro for taking care of himself, in freedom. Let, for instance, any slave be provided with all things he will demand, as far as practicable, and charge him for them at certain prices—honest, market prices for his necessities, higher prices for harmless luxuries, and excessive, but not absolutely prohibitory prices for everything likely to do him harm. Credit him, at a fixed price, for every day's work he does, and for all above a certain easily accomplished task in a day, at an increased price, so that his reward will be an increasing ratio to his perseverance. Let the prices of provisions be so proportioned to the price of task-work, that it will be about as easy as it is now for him to obtain a bare subsistence. When he has no food and shelter due to him, let him be confined in solitude, or otherwise punished, until he asks for opportunity to earn exemption from punishment by labour.

When he desires to marry, and can persuade any woman to marry him, let the two be dealt with as in partnership. Thus, a young man or young woman will be attractive somewhat in proportion to his or her reputation for industry and providence. Thus industry and providence will become fashionable. Oblige them to purchase food for their children, and let them have the benefit of their children's labour, and they will be careful to teach their children to avoid waste, and to honour labour. Let those who have not gained credit while hale and young, sufficient to support themselves in comfort when prevented by age or infirmity from further labour, be supported by a tax upon all the negroes of the plantation, or of a community. Improvidence, and pretence of inability to labour, will then be disgraceful.

When any man has a balance to his credit equal to his value as a slave, let that constitute him a free man. It will be optional with him and his employer whether he shall continue longer in the relation of servant. If desirable for both that he should, it is probable that he will; for unless he is honest, prudent, industrious, and discreet, he will not have acquired the means of purchasing his freedom.

If he is so, he will remain where he is, unless he is more wanted elsewhere; a fact that will be established by his being called away by higher wages, or the prospect of greater ease and comfort elsewhere. If he is so drawn off, it is better for all parties concerned that he should go. Better for his old master; for he would not refuse him sufficient wages to induce him to stay, unless he could get the work he wanted him to do done cheaper than he would justly do it. Poor wages would certainly, in the long run, buy but poor work; fair wages, fair work.

Of course there will be exceptional cases, but they will always operate as cautions for the future, not only to the parties suffering, but to all who observe them. And be sure they will not be suffered, among ignorant people, to be lost. This is the beneficent function of gossip, with which wise and broad-working minds have nothing to do, such not being benefitted by the iteration of the lessons of life.

Married persons, of course, can only become free together. In the appraisement of their value, let that of their young children be included, so that they cannot be parted from them; but with regard to children old enough to earn something more than their living, let it be optional what they do for them.

Such a system would simply combine the commendable elements of the emancipation law of Cuba,[3] and those of the reformatory punishment system, now in successful operation in some of the British penal colonies, with a few practical modifications. Further modifications would, doubtless, be needed, which any man who has had much practical experience in dealing with slaves might readily suggest. Much might be learned from the experience of the system pursued in the penal colonies, some account of which may be seen in the report of the Prisoners' Aid Society of New York, for 1854, or in a previous little work of my own. I have here only desired to suggest, apropos to my friend's experience, the practicability of providing the negroes

[3] In Cuba every slave has the privilege of emancipating himself, by paying a price which does not depend upon the selfish exactions of the masters; but it is either a fixed price, or else is fixed, in each case, by disinterested appraisers. The consequence is, that emancipations are constantly going on, and the free people of colour are becoming enlightened, cultivated, and wealthy. In no part of the United States do they occupy the high social position which they enjoy in Cuba.

an education in essential social morality, while they are drawing towards personal freedom; a desideratum with those who do not consider Slavery a purely and eternally desirable thing for both slave and slave-master, which the present system is calulated, as far as possible, in every direction to oppose.

Education in theology and letters could be easily combined with such a plan as I have hinted at; or, if a State should wish to encourage the improvement of its negro constituent—as, in the progress of enlightenment and Christianity, may be hoped to eventually occur—a simple provision of the law, making a certain standard of proficiency the condition of political freedom, would probably create a natural demand for education, which commerce, under its inexorable higher-laws, would be obliged to satisfy.

I do not think, after all I have heard to favour it, that there is any good reason to consider the negro, naturally and essentially, the moral inferior of the white; or, that if he is so, it is in those elements of character which should for ever prevent us from trusting him with equal social munities with ourselves.

So far as I have observed, slaves show themselves worthy of trust most, where their masters are most considerate and liberal towards them. Far more so, for instance, on the small farms of North Carolina than on the plantations of Virginia and South Carolina. Mr. X.'s slaves are permitted to purchase fire-arms and ammunition, and to keep them in their cabins; and his wife and daughters reside with him, among them, the doors of the house never locked, or windows closed, perfectly defenceless, and miles distant from any other white family.

Another evidence that negroes, even in slavery, when trusted, may prove wonderfully reliable, I will subjoin, in a letter written by Mr. Alexander Smets, of Savannah, to a friend in New York, in 1853. It is hardly necessary to say, that the "servants" spoken of were negroes, and the "supicious characters," providentially removed, were whites. The letter was not written for publication:—

"The epidemic which spread destruction and desolation through our city, and many other places in most of the Southern States was, with the exception of that of 1820, the most deadly that was ever known here. Its appearance being sudden, the inhabitants were seized with a panic, which caused an immediate *sauve qui peut* seldom witnessed before. I left, or rather fled, for the sake of my daughters, to Sparta, Hancock county. They were dreadfully frightened.

"Of a population of fifteen thousand, six thousand, who could not get away, remained, nearly all of whom were more or less seized with the prevailing disease. The negroes, with very few exceptions, escaped.

"Amidst the desolation and gloom pervading the deserted streets, there was a feature that showed our slaves in a favourable light. There were entire blocks of houses, which were either entirely deserted—the owners in many instances having, in their flight, forgotten to lock them up—or left in charge of the servants. A finer opportunity for plunder could not be desired by thieves; and yet the city was remarkable, during the time, for order and quietness. There were scarcely any robberies committed, and as regards fires, so common in the winter, none! Every householder, whose premises had escaped the fury of the late terrific storm, found them in the same condition he had left them. Had not the yellow fever scared away or killed those suspicious characters, whose existence is a problem, and who prowl about every city, I fear that our city might have been laid waste. Of the whole board of directors of five banks, three or four remained, and these at one time were sick. Several of the clerks were left, each in the possession of a single one. For several weeks it was difficult to get anything to eat; the bakers were either sick or dead. The markets closed, no countryman dared venture himself into the city with the usual supplies for the table, and the packets had discontinued their trips. I shall stop, otherwise I could fill a volume with the occurrences and incidents of the dismal period of the epidemic."

GERALD W. JOHNSON

The Background of the Civil War

A MAN named William Jackson moved about a littered and deserted room, carefully gathering up every scrap of paper that bore any writing. William Jackson was a conscientious soul. He had been told to deliver to the president of the convention for which he had acted as secretary certain of his records and to destroy all the rest; and on this afternoon of September 17, 1787, he carried out his instructions to the letter.

It may be argued with a certain plausibility that William, as he diligently cleared the desks and tables, emptied waste paper receptacles and retrieved crumpled sheets from the floor, was making the first move toward Secession; for his thoroughness in destroying the records assisted in keeping the country in ignorance of the process by which the Constitution was framed, and so contributed to that misconception of its nature which resulted in the outbreak of war in 1861. Not until fifty years later were the records kept by one of the delegates, James Madison by name, brought to light. Fortunately for posterity, "the great little Madison" was not so painfully conscientious as William Jackson. He, too, had kept fairly full notes of the proceedings and he did not destroy his records or turn them over to the Secretary of the Constitutional Convention; but in deference to the rule of secrecy imposed on all members, he kept them hidden for many years.

Before they were published, and before there was any general understanding of the compromises and concessions by which it was created, the Constitution had become a sort of fetish. Men's thinking stopped at the document itself, rarely penetrating to the spirit that informed it and gave it life. If they had been able to read in Major William's notes what the men who made the Constitution thought of it, would they have regarded it differently? Thirty years later Jackson told John Quincy Adams that General Washington had made him promise that the notes should not be published while Jackson lived, adding the somewhat wistful comment that he supposed the promise had cost him thousands of dollars. Certainly if the country had been well informed as to the way in which the framers of the Constitution regarded their work, its erection into a sort of untouchable Ark of the Covenant would have been more difficult. Perhaps the suppression of those notes cost America infinitely more than it cost William Jackson.

The fact is that when the Constitutional Convention completed its work and adjourned, the delegates who scattered to their homes were a badly scared group. What they had done appalled them. Half of them were almost persuaded that they had delivered their countrymen to a tyranny worse than the one the colonists had waded through seven years of blood and fire to shake off. The other half were almost sure they had enthroned the spirit of anarchy and doomed the young republic to early and irretrievable ruin. Franklin, who was, like Jefferson, almost pathologically optimistic, was probably the most confident among the leaders of that Convention; and in "the speech that gave us the Constitution" the best he could say was, "I consent to this Constitution because I expect no better, and because I am not sure it is not the best."

It is a far cry from saying "I am not sure it is not the best" to calling the Constitution the greatest single work ever struck off by the mind of man at one time; and if any member of the Convention had heard the prophecy that it would one day be so described by a Prime Minister of England, it is likely that his only reply would have been a rueful laugh.

Some of them were not disappointed, because they had expected nothing from the beginning. Hamilton, for instance, "had very little faith in federal government, or even in republican government, which it seemed to him impracticable to establish over so extensive a country as the United States." Fourteen of the fifty-five delegates refused to sign the thing after it had been completed; and even Jefferson read it in France with grave misgivings. His insistence upon the inclusion of a Bill of Rights is well remembered, but not the fact that at first glance he was appalled by the thought of a lower House chosen by direct vote of the people. Such a House, he thought, "will be very far inferior to the present Congress, will be very illy qualified to legislate for the Union, for foreign countries, etc.," but he was willing to accept this dubious method in consideration of the fact that it preserved the principle that the people should not be taxed except by representatives of their own direct choice. Not a few critics, observing the modern House of Representatives, are inclined to believe that this utterance entitles Jefferson to rank among the major prophets.

The Convention itself certainly did not regard its work as complete and perfect. The letter in which it transmitted the document to the Congress is almost apologetic in tone: "The Constitution which we now present is the result of a spirit of amity, and of that mutual deference and concession which the peculiarity of our political situation rendered indispensable." This is no thunder from Sinai. It is, rather, a confession that the thing was, at best, a patchwork compromise which owed whatever validity it might possess to the spirit of reasonableness and willingness to give and to take.

Evidence to this same effect might be piled up endlessly, but it is needless to labor the point. It is plain that the men of 1787 were under no illusions about their work. They regarded the Constitution as a makeshift arrangement, full of flaws and weaknesses, which could be expected to work only as long as the people of the United States maintained a spirit of tolerance and a desire to make the thing work. But they did believe that, given a spirit of tolerance on the part of the people, the organic law they had framed would answer the purpose very well. History has proved them right on both points. The country prospered amazingly under the new dispensation. But the time came when men forgot that the Constitution was merely a *modus vivendi* and insisted upon construing it by the doctrine of verbal inspiration. The outcome of that forgetfulness included, among other things, 549,543 corpses, ruin that required forty years to repair, and the creation of a host of ugly problems that are not yet solved.

From September 17, 1787, to December 20, 1860, was a period of seventy-three years. Every man who sat in the Constitutional Convention had long been dead. What was worse, their wisdom, too, had become mummified into tradition. It was no longer a living, supple, human thing. It had been transformed into a series of desiccated Articles of Faith. Men seized upon sayings of Jefferson, Washington, Madison and the rest and studied them avidly, but not to find out what they really meant. They studied to find means by which the words of the Founding Fathers might be employed to buttress their own ideas and to confound the arguments of their opponents.

As a matter of fact, the wisdom of the Fathers was not in the Constitution, not in the Declaration of Independence, not in any of the many formidable collections of their letters and documents which the men of the sixties raked for arguments. The most important part of their wisdom, as the Fathers themselves realized keenly and stated again and again, lay in their sharp appreciation of what Burke called "the mischief of not having large and liberal ideas in the management of great affairs." Therefore all the searching of the Scriptures that seemed so tremendously important in the decade between 1850 and 1860, resulted as such searches usually result when men search, not for truth, but for arguments. They found arguments in plenty —arguments on both sides in about equal numbers. But they missed completely the wisdom of the older generation, and simply proved once more that "the Devil can cite Scripture for his purpose."

This was the beginning, the cause, the real foundation underlying Secession. Negro slavery was involved, but as a contributing influence, not as the main factor. The tariff was involved, and in the minds of many Secessionists contributed much more directly to the break than did slavery. Industrialism was involved, and this was not only a contributing cause but proved in the end to be the deciding factor; for "electricity and steam," according to Charles Francis Adams, "decided the issue." But all these constituted merely the materials out of which Secession was built. The architect and builder was a statesmanship which had lost contact with the realities of the world; and this sort of statesmanship was about equally distributed on both sides.

Obviously, it is impossible to fix a date as the beginning of a spiritual change in the life of a nation. The narrative of Secession must, perforce, start with the first overt act. This occurred on December 20, 1860, when the State of South Carolina adopted an Ordinance of Secession, declaring that the bonds which had connected it with the United States were dissolved and it stood henceforth among independent nations.

Madness it indubitably was, as the event proved, but it was no sudden or unexpected outbreak. Nobody was startled, or very much shocked. A good many of the Abolitionists, indeed, were highly pleased. Secession had been talked, ever since the beginning of the republic, by men of the highest standing, North and South. As early as 1811 Josiah Quincy, of Massachusetts, had made a speech in the House of Representatives at Washington, declaring it his deliberate opinion that the admission of Louisiana as a state had dissolved the bands that bound the Union, and prophesying that the time would come when some of the States must secede. Three years later the Hartford Convention, including many of the most respectable persons in New England, all but fulfilled the prophecy—and that at a moment when the country was being unmercifully beaten by a foreign enemy.

Nor had the Secessionists failed to give the country fair and ample warning of what they proposed to do. Witness a reference, made by one of the most fanatical among them in a public letter as far back as 1857 to "that noble band of Southern Rights men who believe in secession, and have ever been ready to exercise it—upon whom the South can alone rely in her greatest need—who though not, perhaps, a majority, yet by their earnest action—by their intellectual ascendancy—their known political probity—the fairness and intensity of their faith have, since 1851, succeeded in giving direction and control to public opinion at the South."

The situation, in brief, was this: the old Democratic party that had ruled the country, with brief interruptions, since Thomas Jefferson in the election of 1800 not merely defeated, but obliterated, the Federalists, had at last been rent asunder. The tariff and slavery were the immediate issues, but the division went far deeper, of course. The party had been contending successfully with both the tariff and slavery from the beginning. There was no more reason why it should split on those issues in 1860 than there had been at any previous election—no reason, that is to say, other than the compelling and all-sufficient reason that on this occasion it lacked a Jefferson, or an Andrew Jackson, or even a Martin Van Buren to hold it together. It had not an opponent powerful enough to frighten it into cohesion. Henry Clay was dead. Daniel Webster was in the grave. It had sunk to the level at which the egregious James Buchanan could hold the titular leadership without being shriveled by the lightning of a first-rate intellect in the opposition. The Democracy had grown feeble and feckless. Its leaders were no longer statesmen, but merely politicians. Its policies were shaped by precedents and pull, no longer by intelligence.

This condition, as a matter of fact, was nothing new. Ever since 1840, when Van Buren had been thrown overboard, the Democracy had lacked a leader who really knew what he was about. Martin the Red Fox was not, Heaven knows, an intellectual mammoth, but he had at least some inkling of the trend the world was taking. He realized that Negro slavery was an anachronism and a nuisance. He was not particularly emotional over it, and he was the last man ever to have done anything violent about it; but he was against it, and he had the honesty and courage to say so.

But, unfortunately, two men had already impinged violently upon the public consciousness. These were Nat Turner, a Negro slave, and William Lloyd Garrison, a white abolitionist. Once they had got in their deadly work, reason and common sense were banished from the discussion and emotion, frequently lunatic emotion, ruled supreme. We shall return to Turner and Garrison later to give them the detailed consideration they deserve; suffice it to say, for the moment, that by 1840 even the Red Fox's relatively mild questioning of the value of the "peculiar institution"—the cant term for chattel slavery—was enough to cost him his political head.

However, in 1840 the economic tension between the two sections of the country was not yet great. For twenty years it continued to increase, and politicians, rather than statesmen, continued to occupy the White House. But by 1860, it was immense—so great that not even "the cohesive power of public plunder" could avail to maintain the Democracy as a single party representative of both sections. The South remained agricultural, while the North swiftly became industrialized. A glance at the statistics representative of the two sections is enough to convince any one even superficially acquainted with economics that, in the absence of bold and skillful leadership, a rupture was inevitable, as far as party politics was concerned, even if there had been no slavery question.

It came in 1860, when two Democrats were nominated by two factions of the party, and the result was that a wild man from nowhere was elected President of the United States, although he had received only a minority of the votes cast. The South knew little of this man, and that little it could hardly be expected to like. Abraham Lincoln was known to the South only as a backwoods lawyer whose professional ethics looked remarkably like those of a shyster, whose formal schooling had been negligible, and whose contacts with the world during his adult life had not been of a sort likely to confer much knowledge of the affairs of men. He had served for a short time in Congress, but without distinction. He was a shrewd campaigner, and his methods of attaining the nomination had been vigorously effective, if not overscrupulous. He had intrusted his campaign to exceedingly "practical" politicians, and there was no evidence that he disapproved in the least of their conduct. There was in the public record, in 1860, nothing whatever to prove that he was a great man, and there was much to indicate that he was a highly dubious politician, equipped with low cunning, but not burdened with either character or intelligence.

The sour humor of the situation lies in the fact that here was the man who could have saved the country. He had the humor, the insight, the adaptability and the freedom from servitude to ancient precedents that were needed. He was, in fact, a great leader; but Fate brought him on the stage in the guise of a clown, and nobody recognized him for what he was shortly to become.

But before he arrived in Washington, the die was already cast. Following South Carolina, Mississippi seceded on January 9, 1861, Florida the next day, Alabama the day after that, Georgia January 19, Louisiana January 26 and Texas February 1. Buchanan, the hold-over President, with the opportunity to do what Jackson did in 1832, did nothing but sit and stare while the Union crumbled under his eyes.

It is not unfair to assert that Buchanan had something like Jackson's opportunity, for in December, 1860, the South was far indeed from being united behind South Carolina. On the contrary, many of her ablest leaders deplored the adoption of the Ordinance of Secession. In November Breckinridge, recognized as the slavery candidate, had been repudiated at the polls in six of the Southern states. Jefferson Davis and Alexander Stephens, later to become President and Vice-President, respectively, of the Confederacy, were both outspoken against secession; and on December 19, the day before South Carolina plunged, Senator Andrew Johnson, of Tennessee, delivered a terrific blast against disunion. Virginia, North Carolina and Tennessee were strongly Unionist. They loved the Union, but they feared the North, and with good reason. Only a third of their people were slave-owners, only a tiny minority owned more than five Negroes; but they were all farmers or dependent upon agriculture, and the protective tariff demanded by the industrial North and promised by the new, victorious Republican party, obviously would crush them into ruin. Moreover, that part of the North which was most highly vocal was promising them more and worse than economic ruin. The North, even to conservative Southerners, was not Lincoln. They didn't know Lincoln. The North was the icy devil, Sumner, the whirling dervish, Garrison, the homicidal maniac, John Brown. What people would not have shivered at the idea of being delivered to the tender mercies of such as these? For they were promising, not merely bankruptcy, but a bath of blood and fire, an orgy of massacre, rapine and devastation.

A President who could have spoken "not as the scribes and Pharisees, but as one having authority," a President who could have spoken as Andrew Jackson spoke in 1832, would have received enthusiastic and immense support in the South. In December, 1860, the upper South would have liked nothing better than to rally behind a President of the United States who was known to be both honest and bold. All they desired was a man who would be fair, a man who would dare kick both South Carolina and the Abolitionists, a man who would put the country ahead of any section or any faction or any party in it—in short, a manful man. And all they had was James Buchanan.

The cream of the jest is the fact that just such woeful party hacks as this

Buchanan are the men most likely to be elected to the Presidency, as an examination of the list of men who have held that office will show. One excited commentator has declared, "Whenever there shall be written a complete and authoritative anatomy of ineptitude, its central chapter will concern itself with the life and public services of James Buchanan." Nonsense! So far from being *sui generis,* Buchanan was a pretty fair specimen of the type that has held the office more than half the time. He was merely a politician; and he seems the quintessence of absurdity only because the times happened to demand a man instead of a politician. Buchanan was not distinguished in anything, not even in futility. He was at least as good a President as Franklin Pierce, or Millard Fillmore, or John Tyler. If the times had been as calm and prosperous as they were between 1923 and 1929 this man "with the wry neck and the dubious eye" might have been as successful as Calvin Coolidge. It is perfectly obvious now that he was no good for his own time; but our study of his time will be fruitless if we assume that his residence in the White House was due to some inexplicable malignancy of fate. His presence there was due to the fact that he was precisely the sort of President that politicians like; and an indolent democracy usually permits the politicians to choose its President.

After the seventh State, Texas, went out, February 1, 1861, there was a long pause.

There were a few madmen on both sides who apparently were determined to precipitate bloodshed. Such Southerns as Rhett and Yancey, such Northerners as Garrison and Phillips, had perhaps worked themselves into a state of mind for which slaughter was the only catharsis. But the more responsible leaders were, to a man, appalled by the abyss opening at their feet. Jefferson Davis thought war could be prevented, and labored mightily to that end. So did Senator Seward, in spite of the fact that a few months previously he had been talking about the "irrepressible conflict" and by that phrase heaping fuel on the flames.

After February 1, even the blindest could see the grim reality of war, standing before their eyes; but that was still the only reality most of them could see.

The fact that men of all political persuasions rushed to Lincoln demanding that he do something to lay this devil, which their own incantations had conjured up out of the vasty deep, is evidence of their failure to grasp any reality other than that they were in a desperate situation. For Lincoln was the last man in the country to call on. He was President-elect, but he had won the election by a fluke, as every one knew. In the first place, his party had made a political deal by which it had sold its economic principles for Whig support in the East; and in the second place, the opposition had been split three ways, with the result that three-fifths of the voters had voted against the man who was to take the Presidency.

It is quite true, as various observers have pointed out, that even if the votes of Douglas, Breckinridge and Bell had all been given to any one of the three, Lincoln nevertheless would have carried the electoral college. But every one understood how the Republican party had secured those votes in such States as New York and Pennsylvania. They were the votes of former Whigs, and were given to the Republican party because that party had made a deal in 1860 whereby it threw overboard the Jeffersonian doctrine on which it was founded and on which it had fought the campaign of 1856, and had substituted therefor the Hamiltonian doctrine, particularly the protectionism, of the party of Webster and Clay. It was slick politics, and successful politics, but it was not the sort of thing calculated to inspire confidence in the stern, unbending integrity of the party that did it.

The inevitable result was that while men gave their confidence to some strange beings in 1861, while some people believed utterly in this mountebank, and others believed in that one, nobody believed in Lincoln. Least of all did Lincoln believe in Lincoln. He believed in the Union, he believed in the American people, apparently he believed in God, although he never bellowed about that. But right down to the most tragic moment in American history, that night when the victor lost the war in Ford's theater, Lincoln seems never to have put much faith in the theory that the Emancipator was a great man. This profound humility no doubt is one reason why he was so immeasurably great, but it was of no help to him in the spring of 1861.

For he knew he was President by luck and by politics, not by the will of the American people. Furthermore, his political position was exceedingly ticklish. He had the Presidency, but he had not yet a party; and a President without a party is the unluckiest of men. The Republicans, at this moment, were merely a loose alliance of highly discordant elements; and almost any sort of vigorous action on the part of their titular leader would have rent them into fragments.

It would be absurd, however, to suppose that this consideration was the decisive factor in preventing Lincoln from taking control of the situation when seven States were already out of the Union and at least seven others trembling on the verge of Secession. The Secessionists hoped to carry with them, in addition to the seven already out, North Carolina, Virginia, Tennessee, Arkansas, Missouri, Kentucky and Maryland. But all seven had balked. North Carolina, indeed, had actually voted down the proposal to hold a Secession convention. Andrew Johnson, in the flesh, was raving through Tennessee, and the spirit of Old Bullion Benton through Missouri. Revolutionary memories were reviving in Virginia, and the Old Dominion was considering the fact that, on the whole, she hadn't done badly in the Union. Kentucky, the mother of both Lincoln and Jefferson Davis, Maryland, and Delaware were seeing less and less to be gained by starting a new experiment in Government.

It is impossible to escape the conviction that as late as March 4, 1861, when Lincoln assumed the Presidency, one bold and resolute leader, having the confidence of the people, could have shattered the Secession movement. Nor is it possible to believe that Lincoln, being the man he was, would have hesitated to destroy his party utterly, if thereby he could have saved the Union. He was bold enough, and resolute enough; but he lacked the third element—he did not have the confidence of the people, especially of those in the critical border States.

And how was it possible for him to have had it? He was not merely a newcomer in politics, he was a new type in politics—new, that is to say, to the generation in control when he arrived on the scene. For twenty years the White House had been occupied by a succession of political hacks, and in so long a time the people had become habituated to their presence there. Politics, in spite of all the bawling about fundamental principles, had degenerated into a process of trickery and chicane; and the average voter, busy with his own affairs, was content to leave it at that. The Constitution had been delivered to the lawyers, and had become what any document becomes in the hands of lawyers, namely, an instrument to be construed exclusively by the letter which killeth, not by the spirit which maketh alive.

Lincoln, as it happened, was not a political hack, but a very potent and vigorous leader. This alone was enough to make him seem strange and therefore suspect. But in addition to that, he believed in the spirit of the Constitution, and he was practically the only man in public life who did. And this was enough to make him seem a heretic.

The man's comprehension of what the fathers had in mind when they spoke of "a spirit of amity and that mutual deference and concession which the peculiarity of our political situation rendered indispensable," is evident in every act and utterance of his in these trying days. His inaugural address is amazing in its tolerance. All he asked of the South was to be excused from committing political suicide by repudiating every promise he had made to his supporters. Such an offer, known to be made in good faith, could have been rejected by no group of rational men.

The ghastly humor of the thing is the fact that the South did not for a moment believe that the offer was made in good faith. The South had been listening too long to politicians to take their utterances at face value. This man seemed to the South to be a typical politician. Southerners had no strong reason to believe otherwise—he had come out of the West, breeder of many of the worst types of politicians, his campaign had been marked by numerous instances of "practical" politics, that is to say, by trickery, deception and highly questionable bargaining, and his success was due to the peculiar political set-up of the electoral college. So the South listened to his inaugural address, made the usual—and reasonable—discount of fifty per cent for a politician's lying, and struck a balance. The remainder was not enough. Lincoln did not get the situation in hand.

During the previous twenty years the South, and the rest of the country too, had listened to some of the most fantastic prevaricators the country has produced and had believed implicitly every word they said. But now when, in the face of a fearful crisis, she was presented with a man who spoke truth, she had not the faintest doubt that he was lying. And so she turned toward ruin.

Still, nothing happened. The seven seceded States met in convention in Montgomery, Alabama, February 4 and formed a government, dubbing it the Confederate States of America. They adopted a Constitution modeled on that of the United States, but modified in the direction of a weakening of Federal control. They elected Jefferson Davis, of Mississippi, and Alexander H. Stephens, of Georgia, President and Vice-President, respectively. And then they returned to the business of forcing the hands of the border States.

But these refused to be budged. North Carolina dourly, Virginia debonairly, Tennessee confusedly, clung to the Union. Without them the Confederacy was hopeless, as both Davis and Lincoln well understood. But they were all likely to turn against the side that fired the first shot, and this consideration held both sides motionless.

So time wore away until April 12, 1861. At the mouth of the harbor of Charleston, South Carolina, was Fort Sumter, held for the United States by a certain Major Anderson. On the mainland to right and left of the fort, the Confederate forces had erected earthworks from which the guns of many batteries commanded Sumter. Here Major Anderson was strangely besieged. When the Federal government attempted to send in provisions, the steamer bringing them was fired on and forced to go back; but the citizens of Charleston gladly sent to the fort barges laden with fruit, wines and all sorts of delicacies for the gallant Major and his beleaguered men. Every approach to the fort was commanded by shotted guns, and not so much as a rowboat could have reached it without being blown out of the water; but if the officers of the garrison wished to go to the city to attend a dinner party, or a ball, that was different; they were courteously permitted to pass the batteries and they were welcomed and royally entertained in Charleston. It was one of the politest sieges in the history of warfare.

But something had to be done. It was evident by now that North Carolina, Virginia and Tennessee, not to mention Kentucky, Missouri and Maryland, were definitely anti-Secessionist and had no intention of leaving the Union unless, and until, they were forced out. It was equally plain that Lincoln had no intention of forcing them out, if he could avoid it. The Secessionists thereupon decided that the only way of forcing them out was to force Lincoln to call on them to take up arms against the other Southern States.

Still Davis would not assume the responsibility of firing the first shot, and eventually the matter was taken out of his hands. Command of the Confederate forces at Charleston had been taken over by a strutting cock-sparrow of a man—but a first-rate soldier—named Pierre Gustave Toutant Beauregard, citizen of New Orleans, hero of the Mexican war, and late commandant of the United States Military Academy at West Point. Beauregard had been negotiating with Anderson for the peaceful evacuation of Sumter. The negotiations proceeded warily, but they proceeded until April 12. Anderson the day before had sent in a reply to certain demands. The reply should have been transmitted to President Davis for his decision, but Beauregard—or, perhaps, his aids—saw fit to omit this precaution and to issue an ultimatum. When it was refused, they turned loose their batteries on the fort and promptly blew Anderson out.

This cast the die. With all his desire for peace, Lincoln could not have people shooting at the United States flag without doing something about it. With all their dislike of Secession, the States of the upper South could not join in an invasion of the lower South. Lincoln called for 75,000 volunteers to bring South Carolina to terms, and Virginia went out, April 17, 1861.

Arkansas followed, May 6. North Carolina, still stubborn, hung on until May 20. And Tennessee, still confused, went out June 8. But that was the end. Missouri, Kentucky and Maryland, although torn by internal strife, never seceded, and some counties of Virginia broke away from the old State and came back into the Union as West Virginia.

Thus they went to battle—eleven States against twenty-two, in the beginning; twenty-three when West Virginia was admitted, twenty-four when Kansas came in; six million white people against twenty-two million; a rural agrarian population against a highly industrialized population; a cumbrous and obsolescent social system against the most modern, vigorous and aggressive social system of the time. It was worse than hopeless, it was grotesque. The miracle is that the doomed South sustained the struggle for four long years.

But that is another story. Incidentally, it is a story of dignity and truth, a story written by officers who were masters of their trade and troops whose courage and devotion have never been surpassed since armed men first drew up in order of battle. This much, at least, is to be said for the Civil War—at the first touch of the flame of that fiery furnace, the clowns, charlatans and frauds, the men of paper and the men of paste, North and South, shriveled and vanished, and the men who marched through and came out on the other side were the iron men.

GEORGE HAVEN PUTNAM

Life in Libby Prison

My experience as a prisoner in Virginia began on the 19th of October, 1864, a day made famous by Sheridan's decisive victory at Cedar Creek. At the time of the battle, my regiment, which belonged to Grover's division of the 19th Army Corps, occupied a position on the extreme left of the line that had been assigned to the corps. On our left, the field sloped down to the Shenandoah Pike, while on the farther side of the pike, a rising ground extending to the flank of Massanutten Mountain was occupied by the 8th Corps. The line of the entire army faced southward, the only direction from which an attack seemed to be possible.

It was difficult in any case to believe that an attack was to be anticipated even from so persistent and plucky an opponent as General Early. Within the preceding thirty days, Early's army had been sent whirling through Winchester, and had been driven back from its works on Fisher's Hill, with a serious loss of men and of guns. It seemed certainly very unlikely that these beaten, tired, and hungry troops could venture an attack upon Sheridan's lines.

The battle of Cedar Creek has been often described, and the main events are, of course, familiar to all of my readers who were present or who have kept themselves interested in the record of the decisive events of the war. My individual relation to it was but small, as I was "taken possession of" during the early hours of that strenuous morning. We were aroused in the foggy darkness by the sound of firing across the pike on our left. We realised that something was wrong with our friends in the 8th Corps, but it was impossible to see across the road, and during the first hour our understanding of what was happening was very confused. In falling into line on the alarm, we faced, as said, to the south, but when round shot came rolling along our trench from across the pike, it was evident that the attack to be repelled was to come from the east or from the southeast. Our brigade was wheeled to the left so as to face, or nearly to face, the pike, and before long the rest of the division wheeled in like manner, forming an extension of our line. A field-battery of four or six guns had been placed a little in advance of the position of my regiment. The first shots across the road had disabled some of the horses, and the men had dragged in behind our infantry line all of the guns but one. A brigade-commander (I think it was Colonel Dan. Macauley of the 11th Indiana) called from his horse (and it is my memory that at that hour but very few of the officers had ventured to mount their horses) for men to go out and drag in the last gun. A group of us started across the field, but just as we went forward, Macauley received a shot through his chest. The men in the line, finding that the "Butternuts" were working across the pike to the north, fell back, if I understand rightly not under any orders but with the instinct of veterans to keep themselves from being outflanked. When I reached the gun, I found that there were not enough men with me to make it possible to move the piece across the rough ground, and we were almost immediately cut off by an intervening line of the enemy. The slope was an uncomfortable resting-place, as for a brief time it was receiving a scattering fire from both sides. We lay down flat on the rough turf, and while I was not even at that time a large man, I remember having the uncomfortable feeling, as the zip, zip of the balls went over our heads, that I was swelling upward as big as an elephant. We had, however, but few minutes to be troubled with this phase of the situation, as the second line of the enemy soon came sweeping across the road and promptly took possession of our little group. I was the only officer in the lot and I think there may have been with me eight or nine men. As I saw the advance of the rebel line, I had hidden my sword in a cleft of the rock. It was a presentation sword bearing, in addition to my own name, those of the company officers of my regiment, and I have been hoping since the war that some impecunious Southerner would be interested, for a proper consideration, in looking up the owner; but I have had no tidings of it. I had in my belt a small Remington revolver and without thinking the matter out, I had, in place of disposing of the pistol, taken out and thrown away the cylinder. The first "Butternut" with whom I came in contact was a little excited; I think he must have gotten hold of a drop of 8th Corps whiskey. He took the pistol from my belt, and as long as he held it up straight in front of him, he was quite pleased with his acquisition. When on turning it, however, he discovered the absence of the cylinder, he was a very mad "reb" indeed. He brought up his Enfield with an imprecation and ordered the "damned little Yank" to find that cylinder. I was naturally not very much interested in meeting his wishes excepting for the purpose of getting rid of the threatening Enfield, and I had given the cylinder a miscellaneous chuck and should not have known where to look. Fortunately one of his officers was with reach and, knocking down his piece, sent him to the front, while myself and the men with me were taken across the creek to be placed with the prisoners that had been gathered in a little earlier from the camp of the 8th Corps.

In the course of an hour or so, these prisoners, aggregating, I think, ten or eleven hundred, were stood up in line, and certain non-commissioned officers, delegated for the purpose, "went through" each individual of the line with a thoroughness and precision that indicated previous practice. They took possession of overcoats, blankets, and the contents of our pockets—money as far as we had any, watches and knives; they also took what under the circumstances was the most serious loss for men who had a long march before them, our shoes. I was pretty well down on the left of the line and some time before my turn was reached I was able to note what were the articles that were being appropriated. I realised that a considerable march had to be made and I was not at all happy at the idea of being obliged to do my tramping without shoes or with the fragmentary apologies for shoes that the "rebs" were chucking back to the Yankees in exchange. I took my knife and made some considerable slashes in the uppers of my shoes. The result was that they were not considered worth appropriating and they fortunately held together during the march and for some time thereafter. The only other man in the line, as far as I noticed, who saved his shoes was a young staff-officer of the 6th Corps, Lieutenant VanderWeyde. I had observed the youngster before because he had small feet and wore patent leathers with which he seemed to be well satisfied. I remembered hearing some of our boys throwing out jeers at "pretty little patent leathers" as, a day or two earlier he had ridden through our camp. The smallness of his feet saved for him his pretty boots. These were taken off two or three times by the examiners but no one was able to put them on, and with a half-indignant good nature, the last examiner threw back the articles with the words, "Here Yank, you can keep your damned pretty little boots." As far as I can remember, VanderWeyde had the only decent looking boots to be seen that winter in my division of the prison.

We remained under guard in a field to the south of the Cedar Creek bridge until two in the afternoon. We were out of sight of the lines on which the fighting was being conducted, but we realised that our men must have been driven back and that Early's force was in close pursuit, because the sound of the firing had gone off far to the northward. Between twelve and two, there had been a lull or else the firing was so far distant that it no longer reached our ears. A little after two, there was a revival of the sound of musketry and we thought it was coming our way. The impression that there might be some change in the condition of affairs was strengthened by our being hurried into a column of march and started along the pike southward. Our hosts had forgotten to give us any mid-day meal and most of us had not had time for any breakfast before getting into fighting line in the early morning, so that we were rather faint for a hurried tramp. During one of the short rests that had to be allowed to tired-out men in the course of the afternoon, our brigade dog who had, very unwisely for himself, followed the line of march, was taken possession of by some hungry men and a little later on one of my own group was good enough to give me a hurriedly toasted chunk. I do not know how I should have been able to hold up for the afternoon if it had not been for my share of the dog.

While, on the ground of our being hurried southward, we were somewhat encouraged about the final outcome of the battle, it was not easy to believe that what had seemed in the early morning to be so thorough a defeat could have been changed into a victory. In fact, it was weeks, before, through the leakage of news into the prison, we got knowledge of the actual outcome of the day. In the course of the evening, our guards remembered to scatter among us a little hardtack taken from one of our own commissary waggons, but the ration was very small for the amount of marching that had to be done with it. Sometime before midnight, in company with VanderWeyde with whom I had fallen into "chumming" relations, I made a break for liberty. We remembered the region through which we had marched not long before as "ruthless invaders," and it was our idea to strike for a dry ditch which was on the farther side of a field adjoining the road. We bolted just behind the nearest guard and took him so far by surprise that his shot and that of the guard next in line did not come near enough to be dangerous, and we succeeded in tumbling into the ditch which we found unfortunately to be no longer dry. There was, in fact, an inch or two of water in the bottom. There was nothing to do but to lie quiet and wait until the column of prisoners and guards had passed. We were disappointed, however, to find that the sound of the marching continued for an indefinite period; and in fact pretty soon there were added to the tramp of feet sounds from a long series of wheels. It was evident that the trains, or such of the waggons as remained of the trains, were being moved southward. Then there came a rumble which seemed like that of fieldguns. While we were puzzling in our minds as to whether the whole army could really be on the retreat, the question was answered in a most unsatisfactory fashion. Not only were Early's troops marching southward but they were going with such urgency that the road was not sufficient for their purpose. They were straggling into the fields on both sides, and a group of two or three, too tired and too sleepy to watch their steps, tumbled into our ditch on top of us. They said things and so did we. Our state of mind was in fact like that of South Carolina three years earlier; we only wanted to be let alone. But that privilege was not granted to us. We were hustled out of the ditch, chilled and out of temper at our failure and at what seemed to us the unnecessarily rough treatment of our new captors. We were, so to speak, butted back into the road and hustled along from group to group until in the early hours of the morning we found ourselves again in the column of prisoners. I understood later that our cavalry had pursued that column through a large part of the night and we must have done pretty lively marching to keep ahead of them, but the horses doubtless were tired on their part.

It is my memory that the tramp to Staunton took the better part of three days. I recall our arrival in early morning in the main street of the little town, at breakfast time or at what seemed to us ought to be breakfast time. The prisoners were huddled into a little square in front of the inn and we were near enough to hear the sound of the rebel officers at breakfast. I think we could take in the pleasant smell of the ham and eggs. After what seemed to us a very long wait, the commissary came out on the little balcony of the hotel with some assistants bearing a few boxes of hardtack. These boxes were thrown over from the balcony into the square in such fashion that they broke as they fell and the officers on the balcony enjoyed the spectacle of the prisoners scrambling for their breakfast. Later in the day, we were put into box cars and started on the journey for Richmond. There was but a single track and our train was switched frequently to allow of the passing of passenger trains and supply trains, so that our progress to Richmond was slow. The officers were marched across the town to Libby Prison where the captain of our guard secured a receipt for us from Sergeant Turner, while the men were taken over to Belle Isle.

The first of the prison functions was the stripping of every man to the skin for the purpose of a further appropriation of any valuables that he might have succeeded in concealing. In this fresh search, 1 lost $150, that I had sewn into the inside of my shirt. The moneys that had been saved by a few of the officers after the first search were with hardly an exception, taken possession of at the second examination.

We were interested to see the adjutant of the prison noting down in a little memorandum book the sums taken from each man. "It will be all right, gentlemen," he said reassuringly, "these moneys will of course be returned to you." This ceremony completed, we were shown into the general living room on the top floor of the Libby building. It is my memory that at this time, October, 1864, the prison was full, but not crowded. Floor space was made for us under the supervision of one of our own officers who took upon himself the responsibilities of what might be called quartermaster's duties. At our request, VanderWeyde and myself were given floor space together, and we then took an account of our joint property. I had picked up en route (I do not recall where) a small piece of blanket and I had also succeeded in retaining a broken pocket-knife. My chum had a tin cup and a pocket-comb. These things were held in common. As personal appurtenances we had been fortunate enough to save our toothbrushes which the examining sergeant had not considered worth appropriating, and my chum, who was a clever artist, had also been able to retain possession of a pocket sketch-book and a pencil. These tooth-brushes later became noteworthy. It is my memory that there were not more than a dozen or so among about 350 officers. The possessors placed their tooth-brushes through the buttonholes of their blouses; partly because there was no other safe or convenient storage place, and partly perhaps to emphasise a sense of aristocratic opulence. We became known as the "tooth-brush brigade." My chum, with some protest from me against the using up of my knife, did some artistic carving on the handle of his brush, producing with no little skill a death's-head and a skeleton. Late in the winter, when we had been moved to Danville, one of the officers of the guard offered me for my brush $300, of course in Confederate currency. I expressed a little surprise that the article, no longer new, should have such selling value, and he began to reply, "Well, but you see now we cannot get any more," and then checked himself. The word "now" emphasised itself in my ear, and connecting this with certain rumours that had already leaked into the prison, I realised that Wilmington must have fallen and that no more tooth-brushes or other supplies from England could be secured. But this is, of course, advancing in my narrative.

In Libby, as later in Danville, the prisoners, comprising as said, only commissioned officers, maintained an organisation and ordinary discipline. We accepted as authoritative the orders of the senior officer in the prison, and this officer associated with him two or three men who divided up between them responsibilities for keeping order, for assigning quarters, for adjusting difficulties, etc. Our general went through the form, and it was not much more than a form, of appointing on his staff a commissary. It was the duty of this officer to receive from the prison sergeant the daily ration and to arrange for an equitable distribution of such ration among the prison messes. We had, for the convenience of such distribution, been divided into groups of six or eight. The so-called commissary had, of course, nothing to issue but the ration that was brought in. His office reminded me of the description given by the young showman in the menagerie, "this is the jackal what perwides for the lion always perwiding that there is anything to perwide." The Libby ration in these last months of 1864 comprised soup made out of inconspicuous little beans, and a chunk of corn bread. During the close of our sojourn in Libby, the soup part was cut off and the ration reduced itself to the corn bread. The corn bread as baked was marked out into squares, but for some reason which I never had explained to me, each square of corn bread was a ration not for one but for two. The messes, therefore, were subdivided into pairs and the chums had to arrange between themselves each morning for the division of the flat chunk into two portions. My chum and myself took turns in cutting that chunk into two pieces. On one piece was laid the broken knife and the man who had done the cutting then called to the other fellow, who stood with his back to the cake, to say whether he would have it "with" or "without" (the knife). Whichever piece one got, the other always looked a little bigger. We regretted to part with the black bean soup, although we had not been fond of it. It contained about as many bugs as there were beans, the taste was abominable, and the nourishment probably slight. I understood later when I was on parole in Richmond, that the beans and corn-meal issued to the prisoners had been rejected by the commissaries as unfit for their own troops. I should not venture to estimate with any precision the size or the weight of the chunk of corn bread which came to us once a day. My memory is, however, quite clear on the point that it was absurdly small. Some of us went through the form of cutting our chunk into three pieces with the idea that we would make three meals out of it; but it was very difficult to avoid eating up the three meals within the first hour even though we knew that we should have to wait until eleven o'clock the next morning for another chunk. Large or small, the chunk was not even nourishing throughout. The cake as baked contained other things besides corn-meal. Pieces of the corn-cob were ground up indiscriminately and we also found in the cake cockroaches and other insects and occasionally pieces of mice that had lost their way in the meal-bins. In reply to complaints that were from time to time submitted, the prison officers had nothing to say but that it was the best they had and that the Yankees had better be thankful that they got anything. I judge that by December 9, 1864, it must have been a very difficult task indeed for the rebel commissary-general to secure by his two lines of single track roads, one of which was from time to time being cut by our raiders, sufficient food to supply the army and the townspeople. It was not surprising that the fare remaining for the prisoners should have been inconsiderable in amount and abominable in quality. The stupid brutality of the whole business was in keeping prisoners at all in Richmond during the last winter of the war; for that stupidity which, as it meant the loss of many lives, may fairly be described by the simpler word of murder, the responsibility must rest with Jefferson Davis, Commissioner Ould, and General Winder.

The abiding place through the night and through the greater part of the day was, as said, the strip of floor allotted to each. It is my memory that at this time Libby was not so crowded but that each man could have the advantage of putting his head back against the wall. Later, when we were transferred to Danville, the arrangement of space required four rows of sleepers, two with their heads to the wall and two with their heads to the centre. The wall spaces were, of course, in demand. At the point of the wall in Libby where my own head rested (more or less restlessly) I found scratched (apparently with the point of a nail) on the two or three bricks the names of previous occupants of the quarters, names representing in most cases men who had "joined the majority." I naturally added, in order to complete the record, my own name on a brick a corner of which was still free. Some years after the war, a correspondent wrote to me from Richmond that he could if I wished send me this autographed brick in consideration of the payment of $5.00. As, however, there would have been no difficulty in scratching my name on another brick, I did not think the purchase worth while. That brick and its companions are now resting somewhere in Ashtabula County, Ohio. Some of you will recall that the Libby building was purchased by some speculators to be put up in Chicago for exhibition. It was a stupid plan, for the historic interest of the building was properly to be connected with its location, and there was something repellent in the thought of using as a show place a structure which represented so much of pathetic tragedy. I was myself not at all displeased to learn that the train carrying the timbers and the bricks of Libby had been wrecked at Ashtabula, and the materials scattered over the surrounding fields. The timbers were, I believe, finally taken to Chicago, but I understood that in place of going to the labour of picking up the scattered bricks, they utilised in reconstructing the building, old bricks available in Chicago. Whether or not they undertook to replace the scratched names of the dead veterans I do not know.

The ship-chandlery of William Libby & Son was, as we all know, placed close to the edge of the James River, so that goods could be landed directly on the Libby pier. Looking across the river from the back windows of the prison, we were able, during the nights of December, to see from time to time the flashes of the guns from the lines of the Army of the James. We used to make our artillery officers study out the line of fire and give us their opinion as to whether they did not believe the flashes were getting nearer. I suppose the distance was something over six miles, and if I am wrong in this calculation, there are veterans from the Army of the James who will set me right.

The prison had by this winter been so protected that there was no chance of any further attempts at escape by tunnelling. The cellar floor through which Rose and his associates had dug their tunnel in 1863 had been masoned over and under the later arrangement of the guards it would have been impracticable in any case to secure admission to this floor without observation. A most important part of the protection, however, was given by the addition to the prison guard of a magnificent blood-hound. The sergeant marched in front of the guard and the hound in the rear, and looking from the prison windows we could see him cock up his eye at us as he passed, as if he very fully understood the nature of his responsibilities. From time to time, the hound would also, either under orders or possibly of his own motion, make the circuit of the building, sniffing around its foundations. There would have been no chance of an undiscovered tunnel while that dog was within reach. I had trouble with that dog some months later when I was on parole in Richmond. I had been told that the intelligence of the blood-hound enabled him to be taught all kinds of things, but that it was very difficult, if not impossible, to unteach him anything. This hound had been taught "to go for" anybody wearing blue cloth. At this later time, I had secured clean clothes from home and the blue was, therefore, really blue instead of the nondescript colour of my much-worn prison garments. I had occasion from time to time to go to Castle Thunder, where the dog was kept, and the sergeant of the prison guard amused himself by putting the dog on a long leash to see how near he could get to the little Yankee adjutant without quite "chawing" him up. I complained in due form to the captain of the guard that the jaws of the hound did not constitute a fair war risk. He accepted my view and had the dog put on a shorter leash so that I was able to get past him into the prison door. I was told that when Weitzel's troops entered Richmond, the dog was captured and was later brought to New York and sold at auction on the steps of the Astor House. If the buyer permitted any of his home circle to wear army blue, there must certainly have been trouble.

On the first Tuesday in November, it was decided to hold in the prison a presidential election. I may admit to having shared the doubt expressed by some others as to the wisdom of the attempt. There was among the prisoners a dissatisfaction, which might be called a well-founded dissatisfaction, at the way in which they had been neglected, or appeared to have been neglected, by the authorities in Washington. At this time, the exchange had been blocked for more than six months and when in the following February, exchange arangements were finally resumed, there had in fact been no general exchange for nearly twelve months. As the war progressed and the resources of the Confederates were diminished, it was impossible for them to make appropriate provision for the care of prisoners, at least as far as the prisons of Northern Virginia were concerned. Even if there had been an honest desire on their part to save the lives or to protect the health of the helpless men for whom they were responsible, the task would have been difficult; but it was quite evident that there was no such desire. I remember among the war correspondence that is in print a letter from Commissioner Ould to President Davis, written in the winter of 1864–65, urging the policy of a prompt renewal of the exchange arrangements. It is evident, writes the commissioner (I am quoting only the substance of the letter and therefore do not use quotation marks), that we need for our depleted ranks all the fighting men that can be secured. The men who are returned to us from the Northern prisons are for the most part able-bodied and fit for service; while but few of the fellows that we should send North in the exchange will be permitted by their surgeons again to handle muskets.

I realised some months later the truth of Commissioner Ould's observations. The men who came out of Libby and Danville in February, 1865, were, with hardly an exception, unfit for service. The Confederates whom we met on the steamboats coming to Richmond as we went down the James, looked to be in good working and good fighting condition. By November, 1864, the mortality in the Virginia prisons had become serious. The men who were not entirely broken down were, through lack of food and through the exposure to cold from lack of clothing, physically discouraged and depressed although they did maintain for the most part will power. I could not but fear, therefore, that in an election which was to indicate their approval or their disapproval of the management of the authorities in Washington and of the inaction in regard to the renewal of the exchange, a majority of their votes might naturally be cast against the re-election of Lincoln. The men who had planned this test election trusted their comrades, and their confidence proved to be justified. When the vote was counted, it was found that we had re-elected Lincoln by about three to one. Years afterwards, I learned from Robert Lincoln that the report of this vote in Libby Prison, reaching his father months later, was referred to by the President as the most satisfactory and encouraging episode in the presidential campaign. His words were in effect: we can trust our soldiers. The votes had of course no part in the official count but they were, as Lincoln understood, important, as showing the persistent courage and devotion of the men. My own ballot would in any case have been illegal as I was but twenty years of age, but I have always felt that it was on the whole the most important vote I ever cast.

One night late in December, we had an interruption which, while at the time fatiguing, gave ground for encouragement. We were ordered up at two o'clock in the morning and were hurried across the town and packed into box cars for Danville. We gathered, from the exchange of a word or two with the guards who permitted themselves to talk, that there was a scare at headquarters about the advance of our lines. The journey was exhausting partly because, in the hurry of getting rations for us, the authorities had found nothing more convenient than salt fish and the train was allowed to stop but seldom. But thirsty and tired as we were, we were happy with the thought that perhaps our men really were getting into Richmond. They really were, but it took five months more to accomplish the task.

RUTH PUTNAM

The Purchase of New York

[*The story, so persistent as the basis of an infinite variety of jests, that the original Dutch settlers bought Manhattan Island from the Indians for twenty-four dollars ("and were gypped by the redskins," so one of the many puny vaudeville gags goes), was long believed by many historians to be a baseless legend. And, as is the way with historians who copy one another, some still write their histories under the dogmatic delusion that the story of the purchase is pure fantastic invention.*

As it turns out, the popular story of the purchase (and of the price paid) is not a fiction but a fact.

Ruth Putnam, a daughter of George Palmer and Victorine (Haven) Putnam, emulated her famous father in his passion for facts. Miss Putnam, having been graduated from Cornell University, one of the first co-educational schools in America, in 1878, specialized in Dutch history and wrote biographies of William the Silent and Charles the Bold, which won her international renown and membership in the Society of Dutch Letters at Leiden.

As a mere by-product of her infinite capacity for research among the libraries and archives of Holland, Ruth Putnam came across the document here described. Her discovery, with the succinct descriptive matter, appeared in the revived Putnam's Monthly *in 1909.*

The clean and scrupulous Dutchmen who settled Manhattan Island in 1624 wished to be on good terms with the Iroquois Indians, with whom they had to deal in the fur-trade of the Dutch West India Company. So, instead of forcing their will upon the natives by slaughter and intimidation as the English were wont to do, they, having decided they wanted Manhattan Island as headquarters, asked the Iroquois to name a price for free and untrammeled possession of the island. The island is 13½ miles long and, at its greatest breadth (14th Street), it is 2¼ miles wide. In a depression year, 1931, the real estate assessment of this parcel of land was eighteen and half billion dollars and the personal property assessment was $807,161,935.

The British saw that the Dutch had something in New Amsterdam, so in 1664 they sent over a fighting fleet and muscled in, in the name of His Britannic

Majesty Charles II, who ceded the looted city to his brother the Duke of York. Hence the present name, New York City.... It is a pleasure to record that neither Charles II nor the Duke of York (later James II) ever profited by the hold-up. Charles was broke, always on the lam, and soon so much in hock to Louis XIV that not even his marriage for money to Catharine of Braganza could get him out of the red. His reign was absolute for a while but was coincident with the Great Plague of London, the Great Fire of London, the "Popish Plot," the "Rye House Plot" and other disagreeable events.... His successor, James II, lasted only a brief spell as king, fled to France when things got hot, got some backing and thought he could mop up in Ireland, landed there and marched on Londonderry, and got the living daylights kicked out of him by the Irish and William III at the Battle of the Boyne. He fled again to France. That was about the last one hears or wants to hear of New York City's namesake.]

WHEN the following letter announcing the purchase for 60 *guilders* ($24) of the 11,000 *morgens* of land constituting Manhattan Island, was read in the Assembly of the States-General, on November 7, 1626, it was resolved that "No action is necessary on this information." Had their High Mightinesses possessed prevision, how strenuous might have been the resolution passed, that the newly acquired island should be kept forever under their control. Nor was the West India Company, that money-making trust which ventured this first speculation in wheat and in lands in the long line of enterprises known to Manhattan, more alive to the excellence of their investment. More than ten times the sum paid over to the Indians for about 22,000 acres, according to their estimate, has since been paid for a single square foot of New York soil! Probably there is no other sale on record where the advance in value has been so great.

Both the contents and the form of this letter were revealed to Americans by Mr. Brodhead over half a century ago; and the original itself still tells its own tale, as it hangs in The Hague Archives, giving testimony that is incontestable even though unsupported by any other contemporary evidence. At least so it would seem; but the statement that all Manhattan then passed from the aborigines direct to the West India Company does not go unchallenged. A tradition exists among the descendants of Sarah Rapelye, the first white child born within New Amsterdam's bounds, that the entire island was once in the possession of her family. Again, it is clear that Schaghen does not name Peter Minuit as a party to the transaction; but histories of New York repeat the statement, one from the other, that he made the purchase, and the latest book on the subject contains a view of him in the very act of paying the Indians!

Perhaps it *is* worth while to look back to our sources, from time to time. At this tercentenary period the letter must be interesting to many of the dwellers on Manhattan, though so few of to-day's millions trace their pedigree to Dutch roots.

Translation of Peter Schaghen's Report to the States-General.

Received 7 November, 1626.

High and Mighty Lords:

Yesterday the Ship the Arms of Amsterdam arrived here, having sailed from New Netherland, out of the River Mauritius, on the 23 September. They report that our people are in good heart and live in peace there; and, too, the women have borne children there. They have purchased the Island Manhattes from the Indians for the value of 60 guilders; 't is 11,000 morgens in size. They had all their grain sowed by the middle of May, and reaped by the middle of August. They sent thence samples of summer grain; such as wheat, rye, barley, oats, buckwheat, canary seed, beans and flax.

The cargo of the aforesaid ship is:

7246	beaver skins
178½	otter skins
675	otter skins
48	mink skins
36	wild cat skins
33	minks
34	rat skins

Considerable oak, timber and hickory.

Herewith, High and Mighty Lords, be commended to the mercy of the Almighty.

In Amsterdam, the 5th November, A.D. 1626.

Your high Mightinesses' obedient
(Signed) P. Schaghen

Received 7th November, 1626.

The address was as follows:

High and Mighty Lords,
My Lords the States-General at The Hague.

THOMAS SPENCER JEROME

Ancient Rome and Modern America

Classical history touches the modern world so intimately and at so many points that it often seems less ancient in reality than much of mediæval history. The Middle Ages, although not nearly so dark as they are commonly painted, are still remote from us in spirit and content. Cæsar is nearer to us than Charlemagne, and Seneca complains of social ills that are our own. The *Res Publica* of the Romans is the antecedent, politically as well as linguistically, of our own *Republic* and with the name we have also inherited certain characteristic traits. The long struggle between democracy and aristocracy, the transition from an agricultural community to an Empire, the crass materialism of a society founded on wealth, the social unrest which led to revolutions in politics and morals—all these mark the modernity of Rome.

A sketch of social development, applicable indifferently to either Rome or America, would show that this people—whichever we prefer—grew from an admixture of several similar stocks and that for many generations its members were predominantly small freehold farmers. They were not, in their early days, an urban folk, nor, it must be added, were they altogether urbane. Foreigners, coming in contact with them, remarked deficiencies in the manners and graces of social life. Indeed, they were rather hard and severe, as well as suspicious and censorious, not only towards neighbouring communities but also towards one another; and a keenly intrusive and meddlesome intolerance, manifesting itself in their social relations, was directed against departures from their somewhat narrow code of approved habits and customs. Partly as a result, perhaps, of this pressure towards uniformity, they produced but few striking individualities; but competence they had, and common sense, and—so it seemed to unsympathetic observers—commonplaceness. Towards distinctive characters, perhaps even towards personal distinction, they showed a jealous distrust and even hostility which easily led, through early revolutionary movements, to a highly prized, republican form of government, to a detestation of the name "king," and eventually to elaborate counterchecked democratic institutions.

They were not eminent in the domain of pure intellect, for they were especially occupied in applying intelligence to the practical side of life. A very important part of their activities lay in the acquisition of wealth. In the field of æsthetics they were distinctly weak, not regarding the beautiful as entitled to an existence independent of the materially useful or the ethically laudable. Their literary products showed little originality and long remained relatively unimportant, while their achievements in the other arts were even more imitative and subordinate.

Their morals, tinged with asceticism, occupied a large share in their consciousness. Mere amusement and delight in life seemed to them generally to deserve some reprobation, while gravity, even to the degree of austerity, was highly esteemed. Although they probably overestimated the righteousness of their conduct, they were, no doubt, on the whole a sedate and serious people, and so actively reprehended breaches of their strict if somewhat narrow ethical code as to render a measure of moral hypocrisy inevitable. Strong volitional powers are quite as often the cause as they are the result of stern moral ideals, and it is not surprising that both the Romans and the Americans showed abundant self-reliance and self-confidence which, especially in unimportant matters and in conjunction with a limited intellectual purview, tended to degenerate into vanity and boastfulness. As a result, unsympathetic observers marked only the defects of their qualities and failed to evaluate the real excellence of their achievements.

With what appeared to outsiders a ruthless disregard of the rights of others, they continually extended their dominions, though their military exploits were probably not so glorious as their patriotic historians loved to assert. Indeed, their Capital was once easily occupied and destroyed by an invading army under circumstances not wholly creditable to the defenders. But even this event did not check their progress or diminish their self-confidence. A great war menaced the national existence of both peoples—the second Punic War that of Rome, and the Civil War that of America. By indomitable perseverance the crisis was overcome, and the national life was quickened by the victory won and the ensuing peace and prosperity. But the war brought also economic changes destined to affect profoundly the social and political character of the people. Immigration to new and fertile lands recently opened for settlement had been in progress for some time but now became accentuated. Free farms were given actual settlers and new regions grew peopled and prosperous, while complaints of depopulation were heard from some of the long-settled localities. The immigration of foreign born persons of inferior economic status was also augmented, and their notable acquisition of wealth and prominence, together with their reception into the body politic in large numbers, awakened apprehensions. At the same time a noteworthy tendency to urbanism appeared and problems incident to city life developed, with the consequent change in many of the distinctive qualities of the people.

Another very important influence in the social development of the people was the rapid growth of great private fortunes following the definite establishment of national solidity. Hence resulted an era of ostentatious luxury and the vulgar extravagances of the *nouveaux riches* with their full-blown genealogical trees—and the satires on them. The taste for luxury, without the means to satisfy it, produced parasitism among the abject and disgust among those who were unwilling to fawn. Contact with riper foreign civilizations both by travel and by the importation of works of art often produced a pseudo-culture which had neither the skill to produce nor the taste to appreciate. The art of living had lost, largely, the simple virility of the older native folk and had not yet won the refined elegance of the new models.

In the older days, the women had been remarkably competent and devoted wives and mothers. With the increase of wealth came more attention to the ornamental side of life. The tedium of a life devoid of duties and devoted to self-indulgence drove them into a restless search for some means, not always clearly apprehended, of imparting a satisfying flavor to existence. As women of the wealthier classes became progressively more decorative than useful, there became evident on the part of some men a distaste to form matrimonial connections with women of their own class or to tolerate bonds which proved irksome. This preference for celibacy on the one side, and on the other the disinclination to interrupt the pursuit of pleasure by the bearing and nurture of children, coöperated to cause a marked diminution in the birth-rate among the wealthier classes. In families with children the employment of nurses, generally springing from a more primitive or sometimes from a decadent social *milieu*, tended to abolish family discipline and to alter the traditional characteristics of the nation. This condition of affairs attracted the complaints of moralists and the censure of statesmen.

The number of those who became feverish from their sudden glut of wealth and devoted themselves to the cult of pleasure by the manifestation of "conspicuous idleness and conspicuous waste" was probably at no time very great, but they loomed large in the eyes of superficial, that is to say, of most, observers. The few who vociferate make more stir than the many who keep silent. In the eyes of onlookers they excited not so much the disapprobation due to blatant folly as the craving arising from unsatisfied desire. The aim of the rich was pleasure, and that of the poor was to be rich. When the most conspicuous class of a community seems to be making the things purchasable by money the principal end of life, those who lack money feel that there is something wrong with the cosmos. Not many are reckless enough to blame Providence, and still less are they inclined to blame themselves; hence the third possible culprit is charged with responsibility, and the many came to feel that the few in some way, by force or by guile, had elbowed them out of their place in the sun. So with the growth of class consciousness came an increase of class jealousy, exacerbated by the bitterness of a sense of injustice.

The prejudices of the many were continually stimulated by the railing of satirists and the wailing of sentimentalists who have in all ages easily found imperfections in human affairs. The tendency of both Romans and Americans to exalt extravagantly the virtues of their ancestors gave moralists opportunities to paint moving pictures of decay. The position of the great mass of the smaller property owners was uncertain and changeable. Their dislike of the rich prevented their having plutocratic sympathies, while their detestation of the indigent kept them from any real union with the proletariat. In time, their desire for quiet and order contributed powerfully to the final pacification.

Under these conditions it is not surprising that demagogues found fertile fields for their labors. Then as now, most of them advocated in one form or another some homeopathic plan by which the evils thought to spring from the unearned and undeserved possession of property on the part of the few were to be cured by general donations to the many of equally unearned and undeserved advantages. Indiscriminate attacks and the consciousness of their own numerical inferiority drove the rich to an equally indiscriminating defense. Clever "bosses" organized and manipulated the voters. Aristocratic demagogues arose who sought to placate the people by doles, and the large gratifications bestowed upon the veterans of armed civil strife helped to spread the idea of getting something for nothing. Under a complicated framework of government, the political and social institutions came to be inharmonious with the facts of social life, and some parts of the machine, originally designed for a small homogeneous people, could hardly be kept in successful operation when the State had grown vastly larger, and the character of the people had greatly changed.

There is never much danger of the dispossession of the wealthy unless property has passed by inheritance into the hands of weaklings or unless those who profit by the existing order fail to stand together; but both these elements of weakness began to appear. Causes for unsatisfactory conditions were discovered in the malign activities of individuals, and the result was disorder. But disorder in the long run satisfies nobody, and after this fact had finally been made clear, general rearrangements of political affairs were effected to assure at least external domestic tranquillity and to force the chronic feeling of discontent into a different channel.

But our sketch has now gone a step or two beyond the point reached by the modern parallel. Abandoning, therefore, a chronological narrative, we shall consider the general personal characteristics shown by the citizens of the late Republic and early Empire. Here we find many peculiarities which are now again manifesting themselves in the more advanced societies of Europe and America. To attempt an exhaustive survey of them is beyond our scope, but in a general way some similarities may be suggested.

One aspect of this resemblance, namely, that of religion, is noted by Sir Leslie Stephen in these words: "We should perhaps find the best guidance, in any attempt at prophesying the future of religion, from studying the history of the last great revolution of faith. The analogy between the present age and that which witnessed the introduction of Christianity is too striking to have been missed by very many observers. The most superficial acquaintance with the general facts shows how close a parallel might be drawn by a competent historian. There are none of the striking manifestations of the present day to which it would not be easy to produce an analogy, though in some respects on a smaller scale. Now, as then, we can find mystical philosophers trying to evolve a satisfactory creed by some process of logical legerdemain out of theosophical moonshine; and amiable and intelligent persons labouring hard to prove that the old mythology could be forced to accept a rationalistic interpretation—whether in regard to the inspection of entrails or prayers for fine weather; and philosophers framing systems of morality entirely apart from the ancient creeds, and sufficiently satisfactory to themselves, while hopelessly incapable of impressing the popular mind; and politicians, conscious that the basis of social order was being sapped by the decay of the faith in which it had arisen, and therefore attempting the impossible task of galvinising dead creeds into some semblance of vitality; and strange superstitions creeping out of their lurking-places, and gaining influence in a luxurious society whose intelligence was an ineffectual safeguard against the most grovelling errors; and a dogged adherence of formalists and conservatives to ancient ways, and much empty profession of barren orthodoxy; and, beneath all, a vague disquiet, a breaking-up of ancient social and natural bonds, and a blind groping toward some more cosmopolitan creed and some deeper satisfaction for the emotional needs of mankind." [1]

Perhaps the most fundamental characteristic which in protean forms manifested itself in all the aspects of Roman life during the years under consideration, was a general unrest and a dissatisfaction with existing conditions. The world had acquired a great capacity for *ennui,* and many travelled from place to place, blind to the truth of Horace's sage line: *caelum non animum mutant qui trans mare currunt.*[2] Various psycho-neuroses seem to have been increasing, or at least to have been attracting more attention. Seneca, especially, was much occupied in giving advice regarding conditions of mind and nerves which we can now recognize as distinctly pathological. For it is now known that a feeling of unrest and *malaise* is the result of a generally disordered coenesthesis. Similarly, many, if not most, commentators on modern life refer to our restless superficiality, our incapacity for simple repose of mind and body: we are easily bored and we fidget. We seem to be losing a capacity for calm leisure, and if we may judge from imaginative literature, we are prone to manifest a heartache about—it is not always very clear what it is about, but we feel none the less distressed over the matter.

To what degree the gentle melancholy of Virgil and Marcus Aurelius, the timorous despair of Seneca, the shrill railing of Juvenal, and the lurid horror which casts a baleful glare over Tacitus's writings present a correct picture of Roman conditions, is not our present concern. We are now observing merely the fact of the similarity of Roman and modern societies and one of the similarities is that we have similar accounts of them. "Taking account of these various groups of undoubted facts," says Alfred Russel Wallace, "many of which are so gross, so terrible, that they cannot be overstated, it is not too much to say that our whole system of society is rotten from top to bottom, and the Social Environment as a whole, in relation to our possibilities

---

[1] Sir Leslie Stephen, *An Agnostic's Apology* (London, 1893), pp. 353, 354.
[2] *Epistulæ* I, 11, 27.

and our claims, is the worst that the world has ever seen."[3] Such indictments are a prominent and not altogether trustworthy characteristic of both civilizations, and are much alike whether we have them in the literary form of Roman satire or the cruder shape of modern "muck-raking." From the point of view of the psychiatrist, these manifestations of morbid emotivity are easily referable to pathological, psychic states. Feelings of this nature tend naturally to establish congruent beliefs, and to find persons or personified abstractions, either malignant dæmons, or Society, Capitalism and Vested Interests, against whom the disordered emotions discharge themselves.

Other indications of similar general psychological states in the men of old times and of the present may be found in an efflorescence of pity, philanthropy and kindred feelings which evidence the consciousness of certain defects in organized society. The lot of the poor, especially, then as now, attracted increasing attention. While the direct gift of food to the Roman poor was carried further, although not primarily for charitable reasons, than is the case in any modern state, yet we spend, no doubt, a sum relatively as large in the relief—and manufacture—of poverty. With the slackening of individual effort, the humbler classes of Roman society seemed to become less able to care for their own needs, and after generations of peace, and in fertile parts of Italy, the emperors felt called upon to enter into large schemes of loaning money to freehold farmers. "Rural credits," it will appear, are not altogether a modern economic measure. Again, we are trying, rather fitfully, to be sure, to readjust society in the interests of the weak. Enormous charitable gifts, some wise and some foolish, were made, then as now, with the vague idea of buying popularity and mental peace. That the gifts were sometimes looked upon as "tainted money" is clear from Lucian.[4]

It would be easy to extend almost indefinitely these suggestions of similar conditions in the societies of ancient Rome and the modern world. Some of them have been noted by Ferrero in his *Characters and Events of Roman History*.[5] But there are, of course, many and obvious differences between Roman and contemporary civilizations. Foremost among these is the great unlikeness in political organization. The Roman theory of government suggested by the word *imperium* is something unfamiliar to us. The Romans'

---

[3] *Social Environment and Moral Progress* (New York, 1913), p. 169.

[4] Lucian, *Phalaris*, I, II; see also S. Dill, *Roman Society from Nero to Marcus Aurelius* (London, 1905), pp. 192ff., 223, 245.

[5] Putnam's (New York, 1909), p. 243ff. The subject is treated with greater detail in Ferrero's *Ancient Rome and Modern America*, Putnam's (New York, 1914), a work which appeared after Mr. Jerome's death.—Editor.

failure to develop a system of representative institutions; their notion of the intimate relation between the soldier and his general; their idea of the tribunicial power; their easy acceptance of the exercise of a magistracy by two or more persons possessing full power, everyone, and not acting as a board; their failure to utilize the power that seems to us to be inherent in the control of the public purse; their conception of judicial authority; their legal theory of the family with its *patria potestas;* their institution of slavery with the ensuing bond between patron and freedman; and, above all, the fact that Rome as a city state at a relatively early time so decisively transcended all possible rivals in power as to become overlord of an awe-struck world—all these and many more differences make it clear that there are very important dissimilarities between the two societies, especially in structure, form, and function. But these differences, it will be observed, lie in the domain of institutions, where historical analogy, from the very nature of things, can be neither close nor convincing.

Quite apart from them, Rome, with her great social problems of proletariat and patricians, of wealth and poverty, of urbanism and the decline of agriculture, has a message for the modern world. The Middle Ages, with their monasticism, their feudal wars, and their conception of the individual, are infinitely more remote from us than the City of the Seven Hills. In a very real sense, she is for us the synthesis of human life. Embracing a larger variety of men, politics, and conditions, all brought into direct relations with a focal point than is the case with any other country of the past, and including in simple, well-defined lines all the important aspects of human societies, Rome has this further advantage, that while her influence continues potent in the world, her career as a political organism is finished. And we may learn from her; to quote Eduard Meyer,[6] it is "just because here (*i.e.*, antiquity) the development has come to an end, because ancient history is finished and gone, and lies before our eye complete and entire, that we may put questions to it and derive lessons from it such as are possible in no other part of history." We can see what happened. We can observe Rome emerging, as it were, from the inane, simple in government and in social life; we can follow, almost step by step, her evolution into a fully developed, complex coherent heterogeneity, and then we can witness the long decline, while the complicated social and political structure slowly disintegrates and finally disappears, leaving mankind to readjust itself in the Ages called Dark, but which never quite lost the saving memory of Rome.

[6] *Kleine Schriften* (Halle, 1910), p. 217.

This is the greatest backward step in the life of humanity of which history affords any clear record. That a civilization so like our own in many respects should fail to endure, should, in fact, succumb to a barbarism which camped among its ruins, is a reflection likely to give rise, at times, to a vague fear that our boasted modern society may further resemble the ancient in the manner of its dissolution. The incredible has once happened, and the history of the past does not justify a facile optimism.

CHARLES A. LINDBERGH

The Flight to Paris

On the morning of May 19th, a light rain was falling and the sky was overcast. Weather reports from land stations and ships along the great circle course were unfavorable and there was apparently no prospect of taking off for Paris for several days at least. In the morning I visited the Wright plant at Paterson, New Jersey, and had planned to attend a theatre performance in New York that evening. But at about six o'clock I received a special report from the New York Weather Bureau. A high pressure area was over the entire North Atlantic and the low pressure over Nova Scotia and Newfoundland was receding. It was apparent that the prospects of the fog clearing up were as good as I might expect for some time to come. The North Atlantic should be clear with only local storms on the coast of Europe. The moon had just passed full and the percentage of days with fog over Newfoundland and the Grand Banks was increasing so that there seemed to be no advantage in waiting longer.

We went to Curtiss Field as quickly as possible and made arrangements for the barograph to be sealed and installed, and for the plane to be serviced and checked.

We decided partially to fill the fuel tanks in the hangar before towing the ship on a truck to Roosevelt Field, which adjoins Curtiss on the east, where the servicing would be completed.

I left the responsibility for conditioning the plane in the hands of the men on the field while I went into the hotel for about two and one-half hours of rest; but at the hotel there were several more details which had to be completed and I was unable to get any sleep that night.

I returned to the field before daybreak on the morning of the twentieth. A light rain was falling which continued until almost dawn; consequently we did not move the ship to Roosevelt Field until much later than we had planned, and the take-off was delayed from daybreak until nearly eight o'clock.

At dawn the shower had passed, although the sky was overcast, and occasionally there would be some slight precipitation. The tail of the plane was lashed to a truck and escorted by a number of motorcycle police. The slow trip from Curtiss to Roosevelt was begun.

The ship was placed at the extreme west end of the field heading along the east and west runway, and the final fueling commenced.

About 7:40 A.M. the motor was started and at 7:52 I took off on the flight for Paris.

The field was a little soft due to the rain during the night and the heavily loaded plane gathered speed very slowly. After passing the half-way mark, however, it was apparent that I would be able to clear the obstructions at the end. I passed over a tractor by about fifteen feet and a telephone line by about twenty, with a fair reserve of flying speed. I believe that the ship would have taken off from a hard field with at least five hundred pounds more weight.

I turned slightly to the right to avoid some high trees on a hill directly ahead, but by the time I had gone a few hundred yards I had sufficient altitude to clear all obstructions and throttled the engine down to 1750 R.P.M. I took up a compass course at once and soon reached Long Island Sound where the Curtiss Oriole with its photographer, which had been escorting me, turned back.

The haze soon cleared and from Cape Cod through the southern half of Nova Scotia the weather and visibility were excellent. I was flying very low, sometimes as close as ten feet from the trees and water.

On the three hundred mile stretch of water between Cape Cod and Nova Scotia I passed within view of numerous fishing vessels.

The northern part of Nova Scotia contained a number of storm areas and several times I flew through cloudbursts.

As I neared the northern coast, snow appeared in patches on the ground and far to the eastward the coastline was covered with fog.

For many miles between Nova Scotia and Newfoundland the ocean was covered with caked ice but as I approached the coast the ice disappeared entirely and I saw several ships in this area.

I had taken up a course for St. Johns, which is south of the great Circle from New York to Paris, so that there would be no question of the fact that I had passed Newfoundland in case I was forced down in the north Atlantic.

I passed over numerous icebergs after leaving St. Johns, but saw no ships except near the coast.

Darkness set in about 8:15 New York time and a thin, low fog formed through which the white bergs showed up with surprising clearness. This fog became thicker and increased in height until within two hours I was just skimming the top of storm clouds at about ten thousand feet. Even at this altitude there was a thick haze through which only the stars directly overhead could be seen.

There was no moon and it was very dark. The tops of some of the storm clouds were several thousand feet above me and at one time, when I attempted to fly through one of the larger clouds, sleet started to collect on the plane and I was forced to turn around and get back into clear air immediately and then fly around any clouds which I could not get over.

The moon appeared on the horizon after about two hours of darkness; then the flying was much less complicated.

Dawn came at about 1 A.M. New York time and the temperature had risen until there was practically no remaining danger of sleet.

Shortly after sunrise the clouds became more broken although some of them were far above me and it was often necessary to fly through them, navigating by instruments only.

As the sun became higher, holes appeared in the fog. Through one the open water was visible, and I dropped down until less than a hundred feet above the waves. There was a strong wind blowing from the northwest and the ocean was covered with white caps.

After a few miles of fairly clear weather the ceiling lowered to zero and for nearly two hours I flew entirely blind through the fog at an altitude of about 1500 feet. Then the fog raised and the water was visible again.

On several more occasions it was necessary to fly by instruments for short periods; then the fog broke up into patches. These patches took on forms of every description. Numerous shorelines appeared, with trees perfectly outlined against the horizon. In fact, the mirages were so natural that, had I not been in mid-Atlantic and known that no land existed along my route, I would have taken them to be actual islands.

As the fog cleared I dropped down closer to the water, sometimes flying within ten feet of the waves and seldom higher than two hundred.

There is a cushion of air close to the ground or water through which a plane flies with less effort than when at a higher altitude, and for hours at a time I took advantage of this factor.

Also, it was less difficult to determine the wind drift near the water. During the entire flight the wind was strong enough to produce white caps on the waves. When one of these formed, the foam would be blown off, showing the wind's direction and approximate velocity. This foam remained on the water long enough for me to obtain a general idea of my drift.

During the day I saw a number of porpoises and a few birds but no ships, although I understand that two different boats reported me passing over.

The first indication of my approach to the European Coast was a small fishing boat which I first noticed a few miles ahead and slightly to the south of my course. There were several of these fishing boats grouped within a few miles of each other.

I flew over the first boat without seeing any signs of life. As I circled over the second, however, a man's face appeared, looking out of the cabin window.

I had carried on short conversations with people on the ground by flying low with throttled engine, shouting a question, and receiving the answer by some signal. When I saw this fisherman I decided to try to get him to point towards land. I had no sooner made the decision than the futility of the effort became apparent. In all likelihood he could not speak English, and even if he could he would undoubtedly be far too astounded to answer. However, I circled again and closing the throttle as the plane passed within a few feet of the boat I shouted, "Which way is Ireland?" Of course the attempt was useless, and I continued on my course.

Less than an hour later a rugged and semi-mountainous coastline appeared to the northeast. I was flying less than two hundred feet from the water when I sighted it. The shore was fairly distinct and not over ten or fifteen miles away. A light haze coupled with numerous local storm areas had prevented my seeing it from a long distance.

The coastline came down from the north, curved over towards the east. I had very little doubt that it was the southwestern end of Ireland but in order to make sure I changed my course towards the nearest point of land.

I located Cape Valentia and Dingle Bay, then resumed my compass course towards Paris.

After leaving Ireland I passed a number of steamers and was seldom out of sight of a ship.

In a little over two hours the coast of England appeared. My course passed over Southern England and a little south of Plymouth; then across the English Channel, striking France over Cherbourg.

The English farms were very impressive from the air in contrast to ours in America. They appeared extremely small and unusually neat and tidy with their stone and hedge fences.

I was flying at about a fifteen hundred foot altitude over England and as I crossed the Channel and passed over Cherbourg, France, I had probably seen more of that part of Europe than many native Europeans. The visibility was good and the country could be seen for miles around.

People who have taken their first flight often remark that no one knows what the locality he lives in is like until he has seen it from above. Countries take on different characteristics from the air.

The sun went down shortly after passing Cherbourg and soon the beacons along the Paris-London airway became visible.

I first saw the lights of Paris a little before ten P.M., or five P.M. New York time, and a few minutes later I was circling the Eiffel Tower at an altitude of about four thousand feet.

The lights of Le Bourget were plainly visible, but appeared to be very close to Paris. I had understood that the field was farther from the city, so continued out to the northeast into the country for four or five miles to make sure that there was not another field farther out which might be Le Bourget. Then I returned and spiralled down closer to the lights. Presently I could make out long lines of hangars, and the roads appeared to be jammed with cars.

I flew low over the field once, then circled around into the wind and landed.

PERIOD PIECES

T HE SELECTIONS *in the following section are chosen more for their extrinsic than for their intrinsic merits, less for their literary style or distinction than for their sentimental value, less for the sort of literary history than gets into the learned literary commentaries than for precisely the sort of literary history that is left out of such treatises and commentaries. There are antimacassars here and lavender and old lace, some whatnots and museum pieces. But they are the emotional and intellectual actualities that the mass of the people—rich or poor, fat or lean, bright or dumb, cultivated or just-growed—lived with and had their being in, at various periods during the past hundred years in America.*

As a museum place, I would cite you, for instance, Elliott Flower's "A Stranger in New York." It was written for, or at least bought by, Putnam's Monthly *and has never been reprinted, so far as I can discover. Yet it is a generic piece. It is the grand-daddy, the Adam indeed, of all the thousands of stories, articles and squibs that have since appeared. For years the late O. O. McIntyre, living in New York and never going back where he came from, made over $75,000 a year playing slight variations of this same tune, over and over again in his syndicated column, "Day by Day." It is the gag that New York is a village with a false-front, a Cecil de Mille movie set, pretty to look at but thin and soulless and nothing but a painted canvas and papier-maché and two-by-fours holding it up; that the town is full of swindlers, crooks, dopes and deadbeats; and that "it's all right for a visit; but I wouldn't want to live here."* ...

And take Myrtle Reed. Thirty years ago, come December, she had run up a sale of two million five hundred thousand copies of her eleven books and an untold number of copies of "Pickaback Songs" for which she had written the words and Eva Cruzen Hart had written the music. What was the reason for this popularity? The publishers knew, I think (female readers like to have a good cry now and then and even hard-boiled tough-mugs in fetid night-clubs break down and weep into their beer on no more provocation than hearing some tenth-rate performer give a bad imitation of Fannie Brice singing "He Was My Man." Might as well ask: What is the secret of Al Jolson's popularity when he gets down on his knees in a prayerful attitude and yells 'Mammy' at the top of his voice), but it was good "promotion" to try to find out. They held a Prize Review Competition. The sole judge was Miss Jeanette L. Gilder, one of the editors of Putnam's Monthly *and a notable blue-stocking of her day. Fifty dollars was offered as the first prize, $25 as the second. (In looking over the list of unsuccessful contestants I see that Louise Driscoll, the poet, novelist and librarian was among them, unless there were two Louise Driscolls in Catskill, N. Y. at that time. Miss Driscoll, the poet, was a little later awarded a prize of $100 by* Poetry: A Magazine of Verse.) *The first prize in the Myrtle Reed contest was awarded to Ethel Grace Pike of Ames, Iowa. The secret of Miss Reed's popularity, it seems, was:*

"There is a genuine wholesomeness in her plots which is refreshing, indeed, in this day of the so-called 'Problem Novel.' [*Where have you heard that one before? Or rather where haven't you heard it? How can one escape from hearing or reading it? That's the problem. It is the average reviewer's dodge of saying something is good because it isn't like something else the reviewer doesn't like.—Ed.*] There is no airing of family scandals and divorces; no daring and disgraceful episodes of affinities; no tragic hours and midnight suicides because of inherited vices. [*Miss Ames had been reading Reginald Wright Kauffman, Robert Herrick, and Upton Sinclair, obviously. Their books were selling well, too.—Ed.*] Her heroes and heroines are not the freaks, fanatics or moral degenerates that are to be found in some of the late novels.... Myrtle Reed does not moralize and yet there are sermons in every volume. What a beautiful and helpful philosophy of life do we find in "A Spinner in the Sun"! The cheerful atmosphere of this story leaves one with the feeling that this is a beautiful world and that, as long as there is one of God's creatures in it to be helped, it is a 'world worth living in.'... Myrtle Reed's characters are real. They are so real that the reader at once feels a homelike atmosphere about the story, as if he were meeting old friends.... Myrtle Reed is an artist as well as a prose poet. She seems to delight in beautifully tinted backgrounds.... Every woman, however practical she may claim to be, loves romance, whether it occurs in fiction or in life. Men like it, too...."

I think that settles the question. All but those last twenty-three words of Miss Pike's essay are superfluous....

In going through the issues of the revived Putnam's Monthly *of the decade before the world war I found myself singularly fascinated by the short notes and comments and pictures, written by the editor or the editors, under the department head "The Lounger." It is impossible to identify the authorship because there were several editors. However, Miss Gilder or her brother Joseph B. Gilder seem to have been responsible for the selections I have made. This stuff brings back old memories, sometimes with a shock. How many remember what it meant to Fletcherize? Fletcherizing was a fad that made one out of five, who was past thirty-five and even a lot who were younger, look as though he or she were chewing their cud. Horace Fletcher, the apostle of slow-eating, had over 200,000 certified adherents to his gospel. Something like the Vitamin craze today, only cheaper. I was especially interested in the day's menu of a Fletcher disciple who on this diet, which cost her only 26 cents a day, escaped from invalidism and developed perfect health. I think I'll cut out my order for Vitamins and take up Fletcherism....*

The literature combating European and especially British sneers at American culture was enormous and reached its apogee in James Russell Lowell's magnificent exercise in sustained irony, "On a Certain Condescension among Foreigners"; but of the lesser lights there was no more vigorous or more persistent a fighter in defense of American culture and the American scene than George Palmer Putnam, as the two interesting selections from his "American Facts" will show. Moreover, Putnam, having written it primarily for the instruction of the British (although the book was a big success in this country), took his book over to England, shoved it under British noses and made them like it....

There is a slight inconsistency, of the proper kind, of course, in G. P. Putman's valiant press-agentry of American manners and culture in the two selections from the famous "Potiphar Papers," written by George William Curtis. When the original Putnam's Magazine *was founded, the publisher had the enthusiastic moral support of the best authors then available, including Lowell, Bryant, Melville, Charles F. Briggs, Frederick Cozzens, John Greenleaf Whittier, Nathaniel Hawthorne and George William Curtis.*

Curtis was a humorist and satirist and in the "Potiphar Papers" he unmercifully lambasted the "best" society of the period. His humor still holds up, I think.... Lowell's "Fable for Critics" is famous, of course, but it is a period piece that is still worth studying.... The Chappell, Barton and White selections are contemporary period pieces of light humor. Barton was a cartoonist and lexicographer, and authority on dictionaries as well as a humorist. White's "Farewell to Model T" first appeared in The New Yorker, *a magazine which admirably reflects the sophisticated and rather bored but nice-tempered humor of the day.*

WASHINGTON IRVING

The People of Connecticut

I. FAITHFULLY DESCRIBING THE INGENIOUS PEOPLE OF CONNECTICUT AND THEREABOUTS — SHOWING, MOREOVER, THE TRUE MEANING OF LIBERTY OF CONSCIENCE, AND A CURIOUS DEVICE AMONG THESE STURDY BARBARIANS TO KEEP UP A HARMONY OF INTERCOURSE, AND PROMOTE POPULATION

THAT my readers may the more fully comprehend the extent of the calamity, at this very moment impending over the honest, unsuspecting province of Nieuw Nederlandts, and its dubious governor, it is necessary that I should give some account of a horde of strange barbarians, bordering upon the eastern frontier.

Now so it came to pass, that many years previous to the time of which we are treating, the sage cabinet of England had adopted a certain national creed, a kind of public walk of faith, or rather a religious turnpike, in which every loyal subject was directed to travel to Zion,—taking care to pay the *toll-gatherers* by the way.

Albeit a certain shrewd race of men, being very much given to indulge their own opinions on all manner of subjects (a propensity exceedingly offensive to your free governments of Europe), did most presumptuously dare to think for themselves in matters of religion, exercising what they considered a natural and unextinguishable right—the liberty of conscience.

As, however, they possessed that ingenuous habit of mind which always thinks aloud, which rides cock a hoop on the tongue, and is forever galloping into other people's ears, it naturally followed that their liberty of conscience likewise implied *liberty of speech,* which being freely indulged, soon put the country in a hubbub, and aroused the pious indignation of the vigilant fathers of the Church.

The usual methods were adopted to reclaim them, which in those days were considered efficacious in bringing back stray sheep to the fold; that is to say, they were coaxed, they were admonished, they were menaced, they were buffeted,—line upon line, precept upon precept, lash upon lash, here a little and there a great deal, were exhorted without mercy and without success,—until the worthy pastors of the Church, wearied out by their unparalleled stubbornness, were driven, in the excess of their tender mercy, to adopt the Scripture text, and literally to "heap live embers on their heads."

Nothing, however, could subdue that independence of the tongue which has ever distinguished this singular race, so that, rather than subject that heroic member to further tyranny, they one and all embarked for the wilderness of America, to enjoy, unmolested, the inestimable right of talking. And, in fact, no sooner did they land upon the shore of this free-spoken country, than they all lifted up their voices, and made such a clamor of tongues, that we are told they frightened every bird and beast out of the neighborhood, and struck such mute terror into certain fish, that they have been called *dumb-fish* ever since.

This may appear marvellous, but it is nevertheless true; in proof of which I would observe, that the dumb-fish has ever since become an object of superstitious reverence, and forms the Saturday's dinner of every true Yankee.

The simple aborigines of the land for a while contemplated these strange folk in utter astonishment; but discovering that they wielded harmless though noisy weapons, and were a lively, ingenious, good-humored race of men they became very friendly and sociable, and gave them the name of *Yanokies,* which in the Mais-Tchusaeg (or Massachusetts) language signifies *silent men,*—a waggish appellation, since shortened into the familiar epithet of YANKEES, which they retain unto the present day.

True it is, and my fidelity as an historian will not allow me to pass over the fact, that, having served a regular apprenticeship in the school of persecution, these ingenious people soon showed that they had become masters of the art. The great majority were of one particular mode of thinking in matters of religion; but, to their great surprise and indignation, they found that divers Papists, Quakers, and Anabaptists were springing up among them, and all claiming to use the liberty of speech. This was at once pronounced a daring abuse of the liberty of conscience, which they now insisted was nothing more than the liberty to think as one pleased in matters of religion—provided one thought right; for otherwise it would be giving a latitude to damnable heresies. Now as they, the majority, were convinced that they alone thought right, it consequently followed, that whoever thought different from them thought wrong,—and whoever thought wrong, and obstinately persisted in not being convinced and converted, was a flagrant violator of the inestimable liberty of conscience, and a corrupt and infectious member of the body politic, and deserved to be lopped off and cast into the fire. The consequence of all which was a fiery persecution of divers sects, and especially of Quakers.

Now I'll warrant there are hosts of my readers, ready at once to lift up their hands and eyes, with that virtuous indignation with which we contemplate the faults and errors of our neighbors, and to exclaim at the preposterous idea of convincing the mind by tormenting the body, and establishing the doctrine of charity and forbearance by intolerant persecution. But in simple truth what are we doing at this very day, and in this very enlightened nation, but acting upon the very same principle in our political controversies? Have we not within but a few years released ourselves from the shackles of a government which cruelly denied us the privilege of governing ourselves, and using in full latitude that invaluable member, the tongue? and are we not at this very moment striving our best to tyrannize over the opinions, tie up the tongues, and ruin the fortunes of one another? What are our great political societies, but mere political inquisitions,—our pot-house committees, but little tribunals of denunciation,—our newspapers, but mere whipping-posts and pillories, where unfortunate individuals are pelted with rotten eggs, —and our council of appointment, but a grand *auto-da-fé,* where culprits are annually sacrificed for their political heresies?

Where, then, is the difference in principle between our measures and those you are so ready to condemn among the people I am treating of? There is none; the difference is merely circumstantial. Thus we *denounce,* instead of banishing,—we *libel,* instead of scourging,—we *turn out of office,* instead of hanging,—and where they burnt an offender in proper person, we either tar and feather, or *burn him in effigy,*—this political persecution being, somehow or other, the grand palladium of our liberties, and an incontrovertible proof that this is a *free country!*

But notwithstanding the fervent zeal with which this holy war was prosecuted against the whole race of unbelievers, we do not find that the population of this new colony was in any wise hindered thereby; on the contrary, they multiplied to a degree which would be incredible to any man unacquainted with the marvellous fecundity of this growing country.

This amazing increase may, indeed, be partly ascribed to a singular custom prevalent among them, commonly known by the name of *bundling,—*a superstitious rite observed by the young people of both sexes, with which they usually terminated their festivities, and which was kept up with religious strictness by the more bigoted part of the community. This ceremony was likewise, in those primitive times, considered as an indispensable preliminary to matrimony, their courtships commencing where ours usually finish,—by which means they acquired that intimate acquaintance with each other's good qualities before marriage, which has been pronounced by philosophers the sure basis of a happy union. Thus early did this cunning and ingenious people display a shrewdness of making a bargain, which has ever since distinguished them,—and a strict adherence to the good old vulgar maxim about "buying a pig in a poke."

To this sagacious custom, therefore, do I chiefly attribute the unparalleled increase of the Yanokie or Yankee race; for it is a certain fact, well authenticated by court records and parish registers, that, wherever the practice of bundling prevailed, there was an amazing number of sturdy brats annually born unto the State, without the licence of the law, or the benefit of clergy. Neither did the irregularity of their birth operate in the least to their disparagement. On the contrary, they grew up a long-sided, raw-boned, hardy race of whoreson whalers, wood-cutters, fisherman, and peddlers, and strapping corn-fed wenches,—who by their united efforts tended marvellously towards peopling those notable tracts of country called Nantucket, Piscataway, and Cape Cod.

2. HOW THESE SINGULAR BARBARIANS TURNED OUT TO BE NOTORIOUS SQUATTERS – HOW THEY BUILT AIR-CASTLES, AND ATTEMPTED TO INITIATE THE NEDERLANDERS INTO THE MYSTERY OF BUNDLING

IN THE LAST chapter I have given a faithful and unprejudiced account of the origin of that singular race of people inhabiting the country eastward of the Nieuw Nederlandts; but I have yet to mention certain peculiar habits which rendered them exceedingly annoying to our ever-honored Dutch ancestors.

The most prominent of these was a certain rambling propensity, with which, like the sons of Ishmael, they seem to have been gifted by heaven, and which continually goads them on to shift their residence from place to place, so that a Yankee farmer is in a constant state of migration, *tarrying* occasionally here and there, clearing lands for other people to enjoy, building houses for others to inhabit, and in a manner may be considered the wandering Arab of America.

His first thought, on coming to years of manhood, is to *settle* himself in the world,—which means nothing more nor less than to begin his rambles. To this end he takes unto himself for a wife some buxom country heiress, passing rich in red ribbons, glass beads, and mock tortoise-shell combs, with a white gown and morocco shoes for Sunday, and deeply skilled in the mystery of making apple-sweetmeats, long sauce, and pumpkin-pie.

Having thus provided himself, like a peddler with a heavy knapsack, wherewith to regale his shoulders through the journey of life, he literally sets out on the peregrination. His whole family, household-furniture, and farming utensils are hoisted into a covered cart, his own and his wife's wardrobe packed up in a firkin,—which done, he shoulders his axe, takes staff in hand, whistles "Yankee Doodle," and trudges off to the woods, as confident of the protection of Providence, and relying as cheerfully upon his own resources, as ever did a patriarch of yore when he journeyed into a strange country of the Gentiles. Having buried himself in the wilderness, he builds himself a log hut, clears away a corn-field and potato patch, and, Providence smiling upon his labors, is soon surrounded by a snug farm and some half a score of flaxen-headed urchins, who, by their size, seem to have sprung all at once out of the earth, like a crop of toadstools.

But it is not the nature of this most indefatigable of speculators to rest contented with any state of sublunary enjoyment: *improvement* is his darling passion; and having thus improved his lands, the next care is to provide a mansion worthy the residence of a landholder. A huge palace of pine boards immediately springs up in the midst of the wilderness, large enough for a parish church, and furnished with windows of all dimensions, but so rickety and flimsy withal, that every blast gives it a fit of the ague.

By the time the outside of this mighty air-castle is completed, either the funds or the zeal of our adventurer is exhausted, so that he barely manages to furnish one room within, where the whole family burrow together,—while the rest of the house is devoted to the curing of pumpkins, or storing of carrots and potatoes, and is decorated with fanciful festoons of dried apples and peaches. The outside, remaining unpainted, grows venerably black with time; the family wardrobe is laid under contribution for old hats, petticoats, and breeches, to stuff into the broken windows, while the four winds of heaven keep up a whistling and howling about this aerial palace, and play as many unruly gambols as they did of yore in the cave of old Æolus.

The humble log hut, which whilom nestled this *improving* family snugly within its narrow but comfortable walls, stands hard by, in ignominious contrast, degraded into a cow-house or pig-sty; and the whole scene reminds one forcibly of a fable, which I am surprised has never been recorded, of an aspiring snail, who abandoned his humble habitation, which he had long filled with great respectability, to crawl into the empty shell of a lobster,— where he would no doubt have resided with great style and splendor, the envy and the hate of all the painstaking snails in the neighborhood, had he not perished with cold in one corner of his stupendous mansion.

Being thus completely settled, and, to use his own words, "to rights," one would imagine that he would begin to enjoy the comforts of his situation,— to read newspapers, talk politics, neglect his own business, and attend to the affairs of the nation, like a useful and patriotic citizen; but now it is that his wayward disposition begins again to operate. He soon grows tired of a spot where there is no longer any room for improvement,—sells his farm, air-castle, petticoat windows and all, reloads his cart, shoulders his axe, puts himself at the head of his family, and wanders away in search of new lands,—again to fell trees,—again to clear corn-fields,—again to build a shingle palace, and again to sell off and wander. Such were the people of Connecticut, who bordered upon the eastern frontier of New Netherlands; and my readers may easily imagine what uncomfortable neighbors this light-hearted but restless tribe must have been to our tranquil progenitors. If they cannot, I would ask them if they have ever known one of our regular, well-organized Dutch families, whom it hath pleased heaven to afflict with the neighborhood of a French boarding-house? The honest old burgher cannot take his afternoon's pipe on the bench before his door, but he is persecuted with the scraping of fiddles, the chattering of women, and the squalling of children; he cannot sleep at night for the horrible melodies of some amateur, who chooses to serenade the moon, and display his terrible proficiency in *execution,* on the clarionet, hautboy, or some other soft-toned instrument; nor can he leave the street-door open, but his house is defiled by the unsavory visits of a troop of pup-dogs, who even sometimes carry their loathsome ravages into the *sanctum sanctorum,* the parlor!

If my readers have ever witnessed the sufferings of such a family, so situated, they may form some idea how our worthy ancestors were distressed by their mercurial neighbors of Connecticut.

Gangs of these marauders, we are told, penetrated into the New Netherland settlements, and threw whole villages into consternation by their unparalleled volubility and their intolerable inquisitiveness,—two evil habits hitherto unknown in those parts, or only known to be abhorred; for our ancestors were noted as being men of truly Spartan taciturnity, and who neither knew nor cared aught about anybody's concerns but their own. Many enormities were committed on the highways, where several unoffending burghers were brought to a stand, and tortured with questions and guesses, —which outrages occasioned as much vexation and heart-burning as does the modern right of search on the high seas.

Great jealousy did they likewise stir up, by their intermeddling and successes among the divine sex; for, being a race of brisk, likely, pleasant-tongued varlets, they soon seduced the light affections of the simple damsels from their ponderous Dutch gallants. Among other hideous customs, they attempted to introduce among them that of *bundling,* which the Dutch lasses of the Nederlandts, with that eager passion for novelty and foreign fashions natural to their sex, seemed very well inclined to follow, but that their mothers, being more experienced in the world, and better acquainted with men and things, strenuously discountenanced all such outlandish innovations.

But what chiefly operated to embroil our ancestors with these strange folk, was an unwarrantable liberty which they occasionally took of entering in hordes into the territories of the New Netherlands, and settling themselves down, without leave or licence, to *improve* the land, in the manner I have before noticed. This unceremonious mode of taking possession of *new land* was technically termed *squatting,* and hence is derived the appellation of *squatters,*—a name odious in the ears of all great land-holders, and which is given to those enterprising worthies who seize upon land first, and take their chance to make good their title to it afterwards.

All these grievances, and many others which were constantly accumulating, tended to form that dark and portentous cloud, which, as I observed in a former chapter, was slowly gathering over the tranquil province of New Netherlands. The pacific cabinet of Van Twiller, however, as will be perceived in the sequel, bore them all with a magnanimity that redounds to their immortal credit, becoming by passive endurance inured to this increasing mass of wrongs,—like that mighty man of old, who, by dint of carrying about a calf from the time it was born, continued to carry it without difficulty when it had grown to be an ox.

GEORGE PALMER PUTNAM

Literature in America

THE promiscuous introduction into the United States of the works of English authors, unrestricted by international laws of copyright, has had the tendency, unquestionably, of checking the progress there of a native literature. It is thought, however, that those who suppose that American literature has thus been utterly extinguished, or that no such thing ever existed, are somewhat in error—or are at least too much influenced by prejudice and incredulity.

Mr. Alison's argument that "European habits and ideas" are decisively "necessary" for the "due development" of even the best American works, because "they are all published in London," is rather illogical and fallacious. The works of the writers he mentions (Channing, Cooper, and Irving), with the exception of a single book, were all first "developed" at home, where the authors have received the just compensation for their labours, arising from the American demand for their books. Neither of them was compelled to come to Europe for a publisher; and in the case of one, although there have been seven rival editions of his works in England, the author was none the richer, in money, for his European fame. The other two have probably been well remunerated by London publishers, for the simultaneous publication of their works; but it is scarcely a fair sequence that, because it is sometimes found profitable to reprint American works in London, therefore those works are neglected at home. The learned historian's inference might be thus fairly parodied: "the works of Byron, Scott, and Dickens, are all published at Boston; a decisive proof that American habits and ideas are necessary for their due development."

Reference has already been made to the American historical publications and collections of materials for history. As illustrative of the demand in the United States for *original* works of this character, it may be repeated, that of Mr. Prescott's 'Ferdinand and Isabella,' in three expensive octavos, *nine editions* were called for in four years; and of his 'Conquest of Mexico,' 5000 copies were printed as the *first* edition from the stereotype plates. Each of these works is elegantly printed, and costs about a guinea and a half per copy.

The first volume of Bancroft's 'History of the United States,' was published in 1834; and the last edition, was the *tenth*. The three volumes cost the same as Prescott's.

The writings of Washington, collected by Mr. Sparks, form twelve illustrated octavos—an expensive set; those of Franklin fill ten large volumes; yet no less than 6500 sets [1] of the former, and 4500 of the latter, have actually been printed, and purchased by the not ungrateful countrymen of those two great men.

A similar taste and demand exist for good books of travels.

The first two works of Stephens, although published anonymously, and the subject not very novel, had an immediate and extensive sale worthy of their subsequent reputation; and no less than 12,000 copies of his expensive work on Central America were called for in less than three years.[2]

Of Dr. Robinson's Biblical Researches in Palestine, in three octavos, which even the 'Quarterly' was ready to praise, the first edition consisted of 2500 copies.

The great work on the Government Exploring Expedition to the South Seas, speaks for itself. It is in five large volumes, with an atlas, magnificently published, at a very heavy cost; and this work and the expedition itself shew that the government has done something for the advancement of science, as well as of commerce.

The Journal of the American Oriental Society gives a list of sixty-three volumes of American works on Asia, Africa, and the South Seas.

All these, be it observed, are instances of original American works, the copyright of which yields the authors a suitable and handsome compensation—though the publishers might reprint foreign works for nothing.

To prove that science is not utterly neglected, it may be mentioned that Dr. Bowditch, the self-taught, *ci-devant* cabin boy, translated and published, in four large quartos, La Place's *Mécanique Céleste,* adding a commentary of abstruse calculations and problems, about equal in bulk to the text. The

---

[1] Formerly under-estimated. These are the numbers given by Mr. Sparks himself.

[2] The London editions of this work, and 'Yucatan,' for which the liberal publisher handsomely pays the author, are entirely printed at New York, and are the same as the New York editions.

legislature of New York appropriated 200,000 dollars (40,000*l*.) for the preparation of the 'Natural History' of that State, in twelve quarto volumes. Professor Silliman, as already stated, has continued his quarterly *'Journal of Science'* more than a quarter of a century; the Franklin Institute of Philadelphia, has, for nineteen years, issued a monthly 'Journal' of their transactions; Mr. Audubon, whom Americans are proud to mention as their countryman, had, in Boston, United States, alone, twelve subscribers for his great work on Birds, at 180 guineas each; and 800 American subscribers to the smaller work, at about 24*l*. each; and is now producing a splendid work on Quadrupeds, beautifully executed at Philadelphia, and costing sixty guineas per copy: the American Philosophical Society sends forth ten quartos on Science; and other societies and individuals have contributed many works of much scientific value.

In poetry, about 120 original works; and in fiction about the same number, were published chiefly between 1830 and 1842.

In biblical, theological, and classical literature, it is well known that many valuable contributions have been made in the United States; and many excellent German works have been there first put into English. The only translations in English of the several biblical and classical works of Eschenburg, Buttmann, Gesenius, Jahn, Ramshorn, Hengstenberg, Giesler, Winer, etc., are those of American scholars. The Seminary at Andover has done much in this department; and the labours of its professors, Robinson, Stuart, Edwards, Park, Woods, and others; and those of Nordheimer, Gibbs, Bush, Hodge, etc., are made extensively available by English students as well as those at home. Probably, in Hebrew literature, and in some other departments, much more has been done of late years in the United States than in England. The attention paid to the study may be estimated by the demand for text-books. Of Stuart's Hebrew Grammer, *six editions* had been printed up to 1841; of Professor Bush's, two editions; and of Nordheimer's, in two volumes, 1500 copies were sold in three years. Two editions, consisting together of 6000 copies, of Dr. Robinson's Gesenius' Hebrew Lexicon, have been printed in Boston—the first in 1836, the second in 1844. Three rival editions of Professor Robinson's Greek Lexicon, and one of Professor Stuart's Hebrew Grammar, were reprinted in England.

Nearly all the classical works used by the 16,000 students annually are American editions, with original notes, by the instructors in the colleges at home. Herodotus, Xenophon, Livy, Sallust, Cæsar, Tacitus; Homer, Sophocles, Euripides, Aristophanes; Horace, Ovid, Plautus, Terence, Juvenal,

Plutarch, Seneca, Cicero, Quintilian, Longinus—and even a work of Plato,—are thus made accessible to tens of thousands, in the original text, enriched by ample modern illustrations. These for students: while the general reader of the most moderate means is supplied in his own language with all the best works of the "sages of antiquity."

Ethical and political philosophy receive some little attention in the United States as would appear by booksellers' lists. The works of President Edwards (whose name as a metaphysician has been heard of abroad), and those of recent writers, such as Upham, Tappan, Schmucker, Rauch, Wayland, Marsh, Day, Bowen, Adams, and Emerson, may afford some proofs that Americans occasionally indulge in 'speculation' of another sort, than that for mere money-getting. Added to these *original* treatises, are original translations of the works of Cousin, Jouffroy, De Wette, Gall, Speurzheim, and others: and it is a rather curious fact, that Americans have *first* collected and *first* printed complete editions of the works of such English writers as Cudworth, Bolingbroke, Burke, Paley, and Dugald Stewart; and first printed in a book form the essays and reviews of Carlyle, Macaulay,[3] Jeffrey, Talfourd, Stephens, and Professor Wilson. They have also reprinted the works of Bacon, Dr. Brown, Reid, Coleridge, Bentham, Abercrombie, Dymond, Adam Smith, Chalmers, Isaac Taylor; and yet a learned historian, already quoted, says that in America "works on the higher branches of speculation and philosophy are *unknown*."

Some useful contributions to the science of political economy may be mentioned—such as those of the late Matthew Carey, of Henry C. Carey (the publisher), of President Wayland, Condy Raguet, Vethake, Gallatin, Rae, Sedgewick, Tucker, etc. The 'Federalist,' written by Hamilton, Madison, and Jay, was one of the earliest American works on political science and contributed largely to the adoption of the present constitution, which was ably defended also by a work of the elder Adams. A large number of books and tracts on public economy were published by the philanthropic Matthew Carey; and the chief work of his son, on that subject, is elaborate and of high character.

Dr. Lieber, of South-Carolina College, a German by birth, but one whom America has been proud to adopt as one of her most intelligent, able, and discriminating citizens, has enriched the American stock of political learn-

---

[3] The whole of Macaulay's Essays, in two volumes, are sold in New York for 50 cents (2*s.* sterling). This is giving *literature* "to the million."— 5000 copies, at least, have been circulated.

ing by a profound work on political ethics, and a treatise on political hermeneutics. He also edited the Encyclopædia Americana.

The demand for theological literature, both native and foreign, is remarkable, considering the whole number of readers: biblical commentaries are largely called for: that of Scott, a voluminous and costly work, has been multiplied to the extent of 60,000 copies; that of Henry nearly as much. Even the ponderous work of Patrick, Lowth and Whitby, is distributed in thousands; while of original works, it is an authentic fact that 150,000 volumes of a series on the New Testament were printed in nine years; and 100,000 large volumes of original compilations on biblical literature were sent forth from one little village in the State of Vermont.[4] Thus, nearly every family, rich and poor, not only has its Bible, but its 'Commentary' and illustration of the Scripture text.

The statistics of book-making in the United States are not accessible in a complete form, owing to the deficiency of a general register. A list for about twelve years, ending 1842, gives the following particulars, viz.—

SUBJECTS	ORIGINAL AMERICAN	REPRINTS
Biography	106	122
American History and Geography	118	20
Foreign History and Geography	91	195
Literary History	—	12
Ethics	19	31
Poetry (in separate volumes)	103	76
Novels and Tales	115	—[5]
Greek and Latin Classics, with notes	36	none
———————— translated	—	36
Greek, Latin, and Hebrew text books	35	none

Medical, law, and miscellaneous—not ascertained.

In the year 1834, the proportion was thus:—

	ORIGINAL AMERICAN	REPRINTS
Education	73	9
Divinity	37	18
Novels and Tales	19	95
History and Biography	19	17

[4] Brattleboro. The same building receives rags at one door, and sends them forth as bound books at the other.
[5] Not ascertained, but a large number.

Jurisprudence	20	3
Poetry	8	3
Travels	8	10
Fine Arts	8	—
Miscellaneous	59	43
Total	251	198

which shews that the United States do not entirely rely upon foreign sources for their intellectual sustenance, and especially not for their school-books. The editions are usually larger than in England, and oftener repeated. The capital invested in the book and paper business, in 1840, was 10,619,054 dollars.

Several American works may be mentioned which have been pronounced by English critics as superior to any others in their departments.

American authors are not always deprived of just remuneration for their writing. The Harpers, of New York, are said to have paid Mr. Prescott 7500 dollars (1500*l.*) for the *first* edition of his 'Conquest of Mexico,' and to have offered double that sum (which was declined) for the entire copyright. In two years the sale of 'Barnes' Notes' yielded the author alone more than 5000 dollars. President Day has received more than 25,000 dollars (5000*l.*) for an Algebra; and Dr. Webster had about the same sum from a spelling-book (!); and all these yet retained their copyright in future editions. A Philadelphia publisher paid to authors 135,000 dollars in five years. These are certainly peculiar instances; but much more proof could be given, that native literary genius and useful talent are not neglected, but receive a fair amount of encouragement from American publishers and the public.

The various periodicals in the United States diffuse altogether an immense amount of reading, a large proportion of which may be said to contain sound and useful knowledge. The North American Review has existed about thirty years, and has always been conducted with a dignity and courtesy worthy of imitation. The literary magazines are very numerous, and their articles have often proved available in more ways than one. Some of these magazines have a circulation of from 20,000 to 30,000 copies. There are in all 227 periodicals, 138 daily newspapers, and 1266 weekly or semi-weekly papers.[6]

[6] *See* Part II.—Newspapers.

It is to be hoped that the literary relations of the United States and the 'mother country,' will ere long be placed on a just and proper footing by a law of international copyright. There are difficulties in the way of this measure which are not thought of by many of those writers who have so indignantly and coarsely denounced 'American pirates;' and this sort of intemperate zeal and unwarrantable insult is not well calculated to accomplish the desired object. That American publishers, as a body, are not the opposers of it, but are ready to pay the foreign author for his works, is evident from the fact that the writer of this, in 1843, personally procured the signatures of ninety-seven of the principal publishers, printers, and bookbinders, in the American cities, to a petition to Congress "in favour of international copyright." [7] This petition was referred to select committees in each house of Congress, which are understood to favour the measure, but various causes have delayed its progress.

Whatever may be the culpability of American publishers in reprinting English books, and in sometimes adding to, or abridging them, we never heard of a single instance there, of dishonest *concealment* of the *origin* of a book by an alteration of the title and preface, or the suppression of the author's name. Yet several instances have been quoted of this practice in England. Two or three articles from the North American Review, at different times, have been appropriated entire, as *original,* in the pages of a London Review, whose age and respectability should have discountenanced such an act. The transplanting of American magazine articles into English periodicals, frequently in so disguised a shape that the exotic loses its identity, has become an ordinary occurrence. Some works of fiction, in their new names and English dress, would scarcely be recognised by their own fathers. The transformations of 'Burton' into 'Quebec and New York;' of 'The Infidel' into 'The Fall of Mexico;' of 'Probus' into 'The Last Days of Aurelian;' and 'Letters from Palmyra' into 'Zenobia' herself; of 'Young Maiden' into 'English Maiden;' and 'American Traveller' into 'African Traveller,' are as sudden and ingenious as the changes of a pantomime.

[7] While so engaged, the writer happened to visit a student at an institution in a country village, and found him engaged in a discussion at the regular meeting of one of the Societies of the Students. This meeting was in an appropriate hall, adjoining the library of the society. The subject of debate was "International Copyright." It was conducted in due form and order, the President checking the speakers the moment the time for each expired. The arguments were really able and ingenious on both sides, and would have edified Freemason's Hall. This was at a quiet country town in Connecticut.

'Charcoal Sketches' jump into the *middle* of London orthodox 'three-volumes,' and leave their own name and their father's on the other side of the ocean. The Londoners take a Natural History from Dr. Harris, a translation of Heeren from Mr. Bancroft, a Greek Grammar from Mr. Everett, and a Law of Bailments from Judge Story, not only with no "by your leave," but with a false assumption of paternal honours. And more recently a bulky Greek Lexicon of high standing, by an Edinburgh professor, has copied page after page from the American work of Mr. Pickering, without so much as alluding to the existence of such a work in its list of authorities.[8]

In these, and other similar cases, the American author is not only *minus* pecuniary advantage, but loses also the credit or fame (if there be any), which is justly his due; and what author is wholly indifferent to the "bubble reputation?"

As the law now stands, English publishers have clearly a right to reprint foreign works if they choose, and Americans have as clearly the same right. "*We* claim reprisals," says the English—be it so—the claim is undisputed; and some of the transatlantic *literati* will even thank you for the attention: but while the *practice* of each party recognises this '*right*,' is it not folly for them to pelt each other with hard words, because they mutually exercise it? Print from each other on each side: and the more the merrier—but let the author have his fair chance for what *credit* he may earn; and do not bandy 'beams' and 'motes' about the rest.

The number of American books reprinted in England is much greater than is usually supposed, because many a one gives no indication of its origin. "Who reads an American book?" was asked by the witty Sydney Smith, in the 'Edinburgh,' perhaps twenty years since; and he had no *unfriendly* doubts. *Now*, many *do* read these outlandish books, without being themselves aware of it. In about ten years, the 'London Catalogue' chronicled in the same list with their English brethren, the following English reprints from the American:

[8] On the other side, an American author was charged bitterly with bad faith, for quoting as his authority 'Cyclopædia of Useful Knowledge,——vols., London,' instead of 'Penny Cyclopædia.' This should not have been so; but those who know the gentleman and the facts, know well that there was no sort of intention of deception or disguise. The work referred to was by many currently called the 'Cyclopædia of Useful Knowledge,' *i. e.* 'The Cyclopædia of the Society of Useful Knowledge,' briefly expressed. We venture to say that there were very few who possessed the work mentioned who did not know at once *what* Cyclopædia was quoted.

Theology	68 works	Poetry	12 works
Fiction	66 "	Ethics	11 "
Juvenile	56 "	Philology	10 "
Travels	52 "	Science	9 "
Education	41 "	Law	9 "
Biography	26 "		
History	22 "	Total	382 works

Of some of these,—such as books by Abbott, Channing, Stephens, Peter Parley, Barnes, Dana, etc., many thousands have been printed. There were three or four rival editions of Dana's 'Two Years before the Mast' and the sale of *one* of them reached 15,000 copies; and yet scarcely any of these writers received a penny out of their own country.

GEORGE PALMER PUTNAM

Culture in America

Many of the pictures of American Society and Manners, by British tourists, have been wrongly drawn and coloured in three particulars. They have been taken (far too much for a fair average), 1. From the travelling population. 2. From the large sea-ports, where are centred the poverty and vices of the worst class of European emigrants. 3. From the Western and South-western borders and the backwoods—far distant from the older States and more cultivated society—a region yet in a state of fermentation, and shewing its crude and unsettled materials on the surface.

It is always better to 'start fair.' The last thing I expect to do, is to prove that society and manners in the 'new world' are universally pure, polished, and unexceptionable. No American of common sense is so presumptuous as that.

Let the disagreeable superfluities of tobacco chewing and spitting be scourged as they deserve, and more than one American will say—Amen! I can sympathize in the most hearty antipathy to such practices, without assuming a self-righteous fastidiousness.

Vulgarity and rudeness of manners are not *necessary* consequences of 'free and enlightened republicanism,' or one might well desire less freedom and more civilization. For one, I will not quarrel with the most caustic satire, or with the broadest burlesque, which would hold the mirror up to any American propensity offensive to good manners or good taste, in any way which would cure it. Let the castigation be ever so severe to sensitive nerves —if given in a right spirit, it will do no harm. Even the caricatures of Mrs. Trollope (whose writings are themselves not overloaded with refinement) were taken on the whole in very good part. Americans would forget her Western bazaar speculation and its *irritable* consequences, and thank her for another dose. Her name is a very scarecrow to all evil-doers. Let an unlucky wight in the boxes of a theatre but innocently turn his back for a moment to the pit, and Trollope! Trollope! Trollope! from the 'gods' and 'groundlings,' soon brings him to his senses. Such watchwords are useful in public places. Their 'moral suasion' is immense. No sanguinary enactments of a Draco would now be so much feared by an American backwoods' audience, as this terrible 'Trollope!' buzzed from a hundred tongues.

But though there is a want of refinement among the masses, which is to be lamented, and though their manners and customs might graze roughly against the fastidiousness of one accustomed to the more quiet, dignified, and polished circles among the wealthy of the Old world,—and though this noted sin of 'expectoration' is so offensive and so prevalent in certain quarters,—I still maintain that the English popular pictures of American popular manners represent the *whole* subject about as fairly as the 'fore and aft' passengers of a Thames steamer on a Sunday would represent *English society*: life in Bethnal Green, or Spitalfields, or Billingsgate, would just as truly be Life in London.

To revert to the specifications of error. Let it be considered that a foreigner who makes a short stay, and a rapid run over a country, must necessarily come in contact with *out-of-door people,* rather than people at their own homes. This is especially the case in the United States, where visitors fly over thousands of miles in the same time they would take for hundreds, or tens, in Europe. And besides this, they forget that in the United States *everybody travels,* and everybody travels in the same stage-coach, the same railroad car, the same steamboat cabin. With the exception of the actual labourer or needy emigrant on the deck, there is no separation or classification. Your neighbour at table may be a senator, a bootmaker, or a blacksmith,—and yet, for the time being, you are all on a level of rights and privileges. English ideas will naturally revolt at the system; but as such *is* the system, it is needless to expect from *all* your fellow-travellers as much considerateness and refinement, as if you were in the 'first class' Birmingham carriage, with a strong partition between you and the three lower grades bound on the same journey.

But consider, on the other hand, what a variously assorted cargo you are packed with—the men who make the shoes, as well as the men who make the laws,—and wonder at the general good order, harmony, and mutual forebearance, rather than carp at minor annoyances which you may encounter for the first time. Consider too that, though you may be talking to an actual labouring farmer, he is yet the *owner of the soil he cultivates,* and therefore naturally assumes a brusquer and more forward air than would be ventured upon by an European *tenant,* or serf, who has very little he can call *his own.* And there is much in those words.

The rush to the dinner-table in hotels and steamers, and the almost equally rapid rush *away* from it, are justly lashed by foreigners, and are far too peculiarly American habits. Let such habits be dosed till cured. The eager mechanic or man of business is unfortunately apt to be governed by the hurrying principle, even at his meals; and more quiet people are too prone to fall into the ranks—for in this age of screw-propellers no one likes to be the last.[1]

As to the crudities and disorders of the sea-ports, let the records of the prisons and almshouses tell in figures what proportion of their inmates are natives of the country, and for how many we are indebted to our friends from Europe. The tale, if fully told, would be instructive to both hemispheres. And an almost equally instructive moral might be gleaned from an accurate return of the relative influences at work in sustaining or degrading the public faith and the pecuniary engagements of the several States. I have no wish to screen or excuse the sins of the defaulters, or to suggest an unfair shirking of the responsibility; but the fact is too notorious to be doubted, that the chief part of the opposition in Pennsylvania and elsewhere to energetic measures for sustaining the public faith by direct taxation, has been made—*not* by *Americans* properly so called—not by the descendants of those who founded and freed the nation; but by 'citizens' of yesterday—the unsettled and needy population which has *recently* been bestowed upon us by Europe—the same Europe that now stigmatizes 'repudiation' and insolvency as peculiarly republican sins.

An English quarterly critic has recently pronounced judgment upon the excellence and impartiality of some recent 'Excursions,' because the author

[1] Remember this is in promiscuous *tables d'hote* of public conveyances and hotels. We are inclined to believe that American private life is somewhat different. And here may be mentioned a very common English mistake about domestic service in the United States. At an English dinner-party recently, a lady commiserated a gentleman from New York, with "How do you manage with your servants?—it must be so odd to have your servants sitting at your own table!" The lady was scarcely convinced, even by quotations from English writers, that a dinner or evening party in New York, Boston, or most large towns, is as civilised and 'fashionable' as the same thing in Marylebone or St. Pancras—we won't say May-fair, for in the Republic, gold plate and livery are rather scarce. In New England villages, where all American girls and boys aspire to something higher, there is certainly a dry air of independence in domestic servants—if they *are* American,—which must grate harshly on the nice *classical* perceptions of an Englishman: but the lady in question had evidently been reading, not even of country life in older States, but of life in the backwoods—the manners and customs of 'Montacute,' or a 'New Purchase.'

was not a transient visitor, but a twenty years' resident. The inference is natural, but not infallible. Did the author live twenty years in or near the places he describes?—or ten years, or one year? Oh, no; his residence was only distant a thousand miles or so. He is an unimpeachable witness, for he was there twenty years, says the critic. A *full* account of his twenty years' experience would be decidedly interesting to his former friends and neighbours. Unfortunately he buries all of *them* in oblivion, and, in search of more picturesque materials, he excursionises over the continent to the frontiers. He happened there, twelve years ago, to witness scenes which excited as much horror through the United States as they would anywhere else; and lo! in 1844 (his famous 'redline'-tempest-in-a-teapot having blown over meanwhile, and left his antipathies harmless), this twelve-year-old drama of gamblers and lynchers forms the staple of a couple of octavos, printed and reviewed as the last new work on American Society!

Such are some of the materials for the one-sided and dark-shaded drawings of life in the New world. And for others, a bare landing in Boston, a step to New York, a run to Niagara, a sail of one or two thousand miles on the Mississippi, a chase among the wild men of the woods and prairies, and a 'railing' and steaming back to New York, and the note-book is full.

I have seen more than one intelligent man 'using up' the subject in this way. A gentleman of sense and information, and (I believe) of high family, landed with me a year or two since at New York. We were both on a visit—he to a foreign country—I to my native land. In three or four days he had disappeared in a Hudson-river steamer. About five weeks after, I met him again at Hartford, in Connecticut, where he stopped—to dine. "You will stay here a day or two?" "No, I go on in ten minutes. I have been to Niagara, and across the Alleghanies, and I sail in the Liverpool steamer next week." "But this is a nice sort of a village—you should see it: did you stop at New Haven?" "No; only passed through it—it seemed a pretty little place,—but I had no time to spare." Now, in these two places, *par exemple,* an intelligent traveller who had come 3000 miles to look at the country, saw a steam-boat landing, a rail-road car, a bar room, and a stage-house dinner—the usual materials. And what had he omitted? In New Haven, he might have seen a flourishing institution of learning, with its 400 students, its valuable mineral cabinet and laboratory, its picture gallery; and he would have found among its professors, men who would do honour to any such institution, and who would gladly have received him with the hospitality due to a liberal and intelligent Englishman. If he had cared for popular instruction, he might have visited in this little town, eleven schools for boys, and ten female seminaries, and he would have been surprised at the number and extent of their studies. And in this little town, scarcely as large as Greenwich, he would have found twenty churches and places for public worship; nine printing-offices; two daily newspapers; two tri-weekly, and five weekly papers; and four magazines or periodicals.

In Hartford, two-thirds as large, he would have found another flourishing college, with a botanical garden; an extensive asylum for the deaf and dumb, and another for the insane, both on an admirable plan; an Athenæum, historical society, young men's institute; gallery of paintings; a museum; an arsenal, twelve churches; fourteen newspapers; six periodicals, and publishers of books to the amount of 50,000*l.* per annum. In both of these places he would have found a large proportion of neat, and some even elegant, private residences; all indicating comfort, taste, and competence. If he had visited the firesides of the people, he would have found those people, I venture to say, intelligent, respectable, energetic, thriving; and ready to give the right hand of hearty hospitality to an inquiring visitor from the land of their forefathers. But my English friend had heard of 'nothing particular' in those places; and so he saw the bar-rooms, dined, and—pushed on.

I again overtook him at Boston, and proposed to shew him some of the numerous public institutions, literary and benevolent, of that city—a city unsurpassed, in these particulars, by any other town of its size in either hemisphere. He glanced from its State-house dome over the panorama of cultivated environs with their neat villages, and at the fine harbour and bay studded with the white flag of commerce from every part of the world; looked at the navy yard and the *walls* of the university, and the steamer was ready, and he was gone.

I visited other places. At Providence, a manufacturing town of Rhode Island, perhaps as large as Dover, I found another university respectably endowed for giving a sound classical education to 150 students; an 'Athenæum' with 15,000 volumes, including such works as Denon's great folios on Egypt. At Andover, I visited a theological seminary, which for efficiency and the ability of its professors is highly distinguished both at home and abroad. At Worcester, I saw the hall of an antiquarian society (founded half a century ago), with its curious library of 6000 volumes. At Salem, a town equal in size to the English Portsmouth, there was the usual 'Athenæum,' in which one may consult 'Philosophical Transactions,' 'Asiatic Researches,' or any 'such branches of learning;' and an interesting museum of curiosities, brought home from India, China, and the South Seas, by the town's own navigators; and here are *merchants,* worthy of the name, whose wealth and leisure permit them to cultivate the study of science and art. At Portsmouth, Portland, and many smaller places, I found invariably a lyceum, or public library, filled with standard useful books. Lowell, with its cotton mills and steam-engines, has also its lyceum and scientific lecture-room, and its Mechanics Library Association. In the valley of the Connecticut, I found town after town outvying each other in the neatness, taste, and independence displayed in every dwelling. Such were Springfield, and Northampton, Amherst, Brattleboro, Hanover.

In excursions through all the six States of New England, and in a great part of the State of New York, while I saw everywhere an industrious, thriving, and orderly population, and abundant proofs also of the general diffusion of intelligence; I did not see a single person intoxicated, a single beggar, or even a single case of extreme destitution. Now, if after ample opportunities of seeing and studying the condition of the masses in Europe, an American compares it deliberately and reflectively for the third and fourth time, with that of the people of New England, and finds such results, must *all* his love for his native land be placed to the account of ignorance, prejudice, and national vanity? Or may he not venture to think of a part, at least, of his own country, that if she has not reached the Old World's refinement, luxury, grandeur, and destitution, she has yet something desirable in the intelligent and contented faces around her own firesides?

A common English charge against Americans is that of excessive love of money, inordinate greediness for gain. There is, doubtless, too much of this. Dollars *are* sought for and talked about. The people of all grades find dollars useful; they think of them, work for them, plan out schemes on large and small scales for obtaining them; with many, indeed this is the chief occupation. And dollars have been discussed in drawing-rooms, sometimes—much to the detriment of good taste. This spirit and practice is changing however; and, it is to be hoped, will be radically cured. But, although the word 'dollar' is so commonly current, and projects for gain are so staple a part of the conversation of many people, and the spirit of gain is strongly enough developed, I should doubt whether there is any more *sordidness* or greediness in all this, than is common to all commercial people. Money is sought, *for the use of it;* because it gives the *the means of enjoying life*: and very seldom for the purpose of mere accumulation. If earnestly sought for, it is also usually as freely and liberally spent. A *miser* in the United States is a *rara avis*. Mere wealth, without a liberal disposition to devote it to some useful or tasteful purpose, would there excite little respect. I honestly think that though there may be in England less of that 'talking of dollars' there is no less of the same motives and principles at work for the acquirement of gain.

I have suggested instances in which travelling visitors take away impressions of a town from a passing glance at its inn, its coach-office, and its bar-room. These bar-rooms, by the way, are rapidly vanishing into thin air. If travellers will write the rest into non-existence, ninety-nine out of one hundred will say, Amen! Capt. Hall, fifteen years ago, complained that the people in stage-coaches drank so much brandy as to be quite offensive. Mr. Dickens, in 1842, complained of temperance being so general, that, on more than one occasion, he could not obtain a glass of brandy at a public-house. The writer, in 1843, dined at some fifty different *tables d'hote,* in different States—some of them of the first class, with abundant specimens of French cookery; and he can confidently say, that of *all* the guests at these fifty tables, not one in ten drank *anything* but water.

GEORGE WILLIAM CURTIS

"Our Best Society"

IF GILT were only gold, or sugar-candy common sense, what a fine thing our society would be! If to lavish money upon *objets de vertu,* to wear the most costly dresses, and always to have them cut in the height of the fashion; to build houses thirty feet broad, as if they were palaces; to furnish them with all the luxurious devices of Parisian genius; to give superb banquets, at which your guests laugh, and which make you miserable; to drive a fine carriage and ape European liveries, and crests, and coats-of-arms; to resent the friendly advances of your baker's wife, and the lady of your butcher (you being yourself a cobbler's daughter); to talk much of the "old families" and of your aristocratic foreign friends; to despise labour; to prate of "good society"; to travesty and parody, in every conceivable way, a society which we know only in books and by the superficial observation of foreign travel, which arises out of a social organization entirely unknown to us, and which is opposed to our fundamental and essential principles; if all this were fine, what a prodigiously fine society would ours be!

This occurred to us upon lately receiving a card of invitation to a brilliant ball. We were quietly ruminating over our evening fire, with Disraeli's Wellington speech, "all tears," in our hands, with the account of a great man's burial, and a little man's triumph across the channel. So many great men gone, we mused. and such great crises impending! This democratic movement in Europe; Kossuth and Mazzini waiting for the moment to give the word; the Russian bear watchfully sucking his paws; the Napoleonic empire redivivus; Cuba, and annexation, and slavery; California and Australia, and the consequent considerations of political economy; dear me! exclaimed we, putting on a fresh hodful of coal, we must look a little into the state of parties.

As we put down the coal-scuttle there was a knock at the door. We said, "come in," and in came a neat Alhambra-watered envelope, containing the announcement that the queen of fashion was "at home" that evening week. Later in the evening, came a friend to smoke a cigar. The card was lying upon the table, and he read it with eagerness. "You'll go, of course," said he, "for you will meet all the 'best society.'"

Shall we, truly? Shall we really see the "best society of the city," the picked flower of its genius, character, and beauty? What makes the "best society" of men and women? The noblest specimens of each, of course. The men who mould the time, who refresh our faith in heroism and virtue, who make Plato, and Zeno, and Shakspeare, and all Shakspeare's gentlemen, possible again. The women, whose beauty, and sweetness, and dignity, and high accomplishment, and grace, make us understand the Greek Mythology, and weaken our desire to have some glimpse of the most famous women of history. The "best society" is that in which the virtues are most shining, which is the most charitable, forgiving, long-suffering, modest, and innocent. The "best society" is, in its very name, that in which there is the least hypocrisy and insincerity of all kinds, which recoils from, and blasts, artificiality, which is anxious to be all that it is possible to be, and which sternly reprobates all shallow pretence, all coxcombry and foppery, and insists upon simplicity as the infallible characteristic of true worth. That is the "best society," which comprises the best men and women.

Had we recently arrived from the moon, we might, upon hearing that we were to meet the "best society," have fancied that we were about to enjoy an opportunity not to be overvalued. But unfortunately we were not so freshly arrived. We had received other cards, and had perfected our toilette many times, to meet this same society, so magnificently described, and had found it the least "best" of all. Who compose it? Whom shall we meet if we go to this ball?

We shall meet three classes of persons: first, those who are rich, and who have all that money can buy; second, those who belong to what are technically called "the good old families," because some ancestor was a man of mark in the state or country, or was very rich, and has kept the fortune in the family; and, thirdly, a swarm of youths who can dance dexterously, and who are invited for that purpose. Now these are all arbitrary and factitious distinctions upon which to found so profound a social difference as that which exists in American, or, at least, in New York society. First, as a general rule, the rich men of every community who make their own money are not the most generally intelligent and cultivated. They have a shrewd talent which secures a fortune, and which keeps them closely at the work of amassing from their youngest years until they are old. They are sturdy men of simple tastes often. Sometimes, though rarely, very generous, but necessarily with an altogether false and exaggerated idea of the importance of money. They are a rather rough, unsympathetic, and, perhaps, selfish class, who, themselves, despise purple and fine linen, and still prefer a cot-bed and a bare room, although they may be worth millions. But they are married to scheming, or ambitious, or disappointed women, whose life is a prolonged pageant, and they are dragged hither and thither in it, are bled of their golden blood, and forced into a position they do not covet and which they despise. Then there are the inheritors of wealth. How many of them inherit the valiant genius and hard frugality which built up their fortunes; how many acknowledge the stern and heavy responsibility of their opportunities; how many refuse to dream their lives away in a Sybarite luxury; how many are smitten with the lofty ambition of achieving an enduring name by works of a permanent value; how many do not dwindle into dainty dilettanti, and dilute their manhood with factitious sentimentality instead of a hearty, human sympathy; how many are not satisfied with having the fastest horses and the "crackest" carriages, and an unlimited wardrobe, and a weak affectation and puerile imitation of foreign life?

And who are these of our secondly, these "old families"? The spirit of our time and of our country knows no such thing, but the habitué of "society" hears constantly of "a good family." It means simply, the collective mass of children, grandchildren, nephews, nieces, and descendants of some man who deserved well of his country, and whom his country honors. But sad is the heritage of a great name! The son of Burke will inevitably be measured by Burke. The niece of Pope must show some superiority to other women (so to speak), or her equality is inferiority. The feeling of men attributes some magical charm to blood, and we look to see the daughter of Helen as fair as her mother, and the son of Shakspeare musical as his sire. If they are not so, if they are merely names, and common persons—if there is no Burke, nor Shakspeare, nor Washington, nor Bacon, in their words, or actions, or lives, then we must pity them, and pass gently on, not upbraiding them, but regretting that it is one of the laws of greatness that it dwindles all things in its vicinity, which would otherwise show large enough. Nay, in our regard for the great man, we may even admit to a compassionate honor, as pensioners upon our charity, those who bear and transmit his name. But if these heirs should presume upon that fame, and claim any precedence of living men and women because their dead grandfather was a hero,—they must be shown the door directly. We should dread to be born a Percy, or a Colonna, or a Bonaparte. We should not like to be the second Duke of Wellington, nor Charles Dickens, Jr. It is a terrible thing, one would say, to a mind of honorable feeling, to be pointed out as somebody's son, or uncle, or granddaughter, as if the excellence were all derived. It must be a little humiliating to reflect that if your great uncle had not been somebody, you would be nobody,—that, in fact, you are only a name, and that, if you should consent to change it for the sake of a fortune, as is sometimes done, you would cease to be any thing but a rich man. "My father was President, or Governor of the State," some pompous man may say. But, by Jupiter! king of gods and men, what are *you?* Is the instinctive response. Do you not see, our pompous friend, that you are only pointing your own unimportance? If your father was Governor of the State, what right have you to use that fact only to fatten your self-conceit? Take care, good care; for whether you say it by your lips or by your life, that withering response awaits you,—"then what are *you?*" If your ancestor was great, you are under bonds to greatness. If you are small, make haste to learn it betimes, and, thanking Heaven that your name has been made illustrious, retire into a corner and keep it, at least, untarnished.

Our thirdly, is a class made by sundry French tailors, bootmakers, dancing-masters, and Mr. Brown. They are a corps-de-ballet, for the use of private entertainments. They are fostered by society for the use of young debutantes, and hardier damsels, who have dared two or three years of the "tight" polka. They are cultivated for their heels, not their heads. Their life begins at ten o'clock in the evening, and lasts until four in the morning. They go home and sleep until nine; then they reel, sleepy, to counting-houses and offices, and doze on desks until dinner-time. Or, unable to do that, they are actively at work all day, and their cheeks grow pale, and their lips thin, and their eyes bloodshot and hollow, and they drag themselves home at evening to catch a nap until the ball begins, or to dine and smoke at their club, and be very manly with punches and coarse stories; and then to rush into hot and glittering rooms, and seize very *décolleté* girls closely around the waist, and dash with them around an area of stretched linen, saying in the panting pauses. "How very hot it is!" "How very pretty Miss Podge looks!" "What a good redowa!" "Are you going to Mrs. Potiphar's?"

Is this the assembled flower of manhood and womanhood, called "best society," and to see which is so envied a privilege? If such are the elements, can we be long in arriving at the present state, and necessary future condition of parties?

"Vanity Fair" is peculiarly a picture of modern society. It aims at English follies, but its mark is universal, as the madness is. It is called a satire, but after much diligent reading, we cannot discover the satire. A state of society not at all superior to that of "Vanity Fair" is not unknown to our experience; and, unless truth-telling be satire; unless the most tragically real portraiture be satire; unless scalding tears of sorrow, and the bitter regret of a manly mind over the miserable spectacle of artificiality, wasted powers, misdirected energies, and lost opportunities, be satirical; we do not find satire in that sad story. The reader closes it with a grief beyond tears. It leaves a vague apprehension in the mind, as if we should suspect the air to be poisoned. It suggests the terrible thought of the enfeebling of moral power, and the deterioration of noble character, as a necessary consequence of contact with "society." Every man looks suddenly and sharply around him, and accosts himself and his neighbors, to ascertain if they are all parties to this corruption. Sentimental youths and maidens, upon velvet sofas, or in calf-bound libraries, resolve that it is an insult to human nature—are sure that their velvet and calf-bound friends are not like the dramatis personæ of "Vanity Fair," and that the drama is therefore hideous and unreal. They should remember, what they uniformly and universally forget, that we are not invited, upon the rising of the curtain, to behold a cosmorama, or picture of the world, but a representation of that part of it called Vanity Fair. What its just limits are—how far its poisonous purlieus reach—how much of the world's air is tainted by it, is a question which every thoughtful man will ask himself, with a shudder, and look sadly around, to answer. If the sentimental objectors rally again to the charge, and declare that, if we wish to improve the world, its virtuous ambition must be piqued and stimulated by making the shining heights of "the ideal" more radiant; we reply, that none shall surpass us in honoring the men whose creations of beauty inspire and instruct mankind. But if they benefit the world, it is no less true that a vivid apprehension of the depths into which we are sunken or may sink, nerves the soul's courage quite as much as the alluring mirage of the happy heights we may attain. "To hold the mirror up to Nature," is still the most potent method of shaming sin and strengthening virtue.

If "Vanity Fair" is a satire, what novel of society is not? Are "Vivian Grey," and "Pelham," and the long catalogue of books illustrating English, or the host of Balzacs, Sands, Sues, and Dumas, that paint French society, any less satires? Nay, if you should catch any dandy in Broadway, or in Pall-Mall, or upon the Boulevards, this very morning and write a coldly true history of his life and actions, his doings and undoings, would it not be the most scathing and tremendous satire?—if by satire you mean the consuming melancholy of the conviction, that the life of that pendant to a moustache, is an insult to the possible life of a man?

We have read of a hypocrisy so thorough, that it was surprised you should think it hypocritical; and we have bitterly thought of the saying, when hearing one mother say of another mother's child, that she had "made a good match," because the girl was betrothed to a stupid boy whose father was rich. The remark was the key of our social feeling.

Let us look at it a little, and, first of all, let the reader consider the criticism, and not the critic. We may like very well, in our individual capacity, to partake of the delicacies prepared by our hostess's *chef,* we may not be averse to *paté* and myriad *objets de goût,* and if you caught us in a corner at the next ball, putting away a fair share of *dinde aux truffes,* we know you would have at us in a tone of great moral indignation, and wish to know why we sneaked into great houses, eating good suppers, and drinking choice wines, and then went away with an indigestion, to write dyspeptic disgusts at society.

We might reply that it is necessary to know something of a subject before writing about it, and that if a man wished to describe the habits of South Sea Islanders, it is useless to go to Greenland; we might also confess a partiality for *paté,* and a tenderness for *truffes,* and acknowledge that, considering our single absence would not put down extravagant, pompous parties, we were not strong enough to let the morsels drop into unappreciating mouths; or we might say, that if a man invited us to see his new house, it would not be ungracious nor insulting to his hospitality, to point out whatever weak parts we might detect in it, nor to declare our candid conviction, that it was built upon wrong principles and could not stand. He might believe us if we had been in the house, but he certainly would not, if we had never seen it. Nor would it be a very wise reply upon his part, that we might build a better if we didn't like that. We are not fond of David's pictures, but we certainly could never paint half so well; nor of Pope's poetry, but posterity will never hear of our verses. Criticism is not construction, it is observation. If we could surpass in its own way every thing which displeased us, we should make short work of it, and instead of showing what fatal blemishes deform our present society, we should present a specimen of perfection, directly.

We went to the brilliant ball. There was too much of every thing. Too much light, and eating, and drinking, and dancing, and flirting, and dressing, and feigning, and smirking, and much too many people. Good taste insists first upon fitness. But why had Mrs. Potiphar given this ball? We inquired industriously, and learned it was because she did not give one last year. Is it then essential to do this thing biennially? inquired we with some trepidation. "Certainly," was the bland reply, "or society will forget you." Every body was unhappy at Mrs. Potiphar's, save a few girls and boys, who danced violently all the evening. Those who did not dance walked up and down the rooms as well as they could, squeezing by non-dancing ladies, causing them to swear in their hearts as the brusque broadcloth carried away the light out-works of gauze and gossamer. The dowagers, ranged in solid phalanx, occupied all the chairs and sofas against the wall, and fanned themselves until supper-time, looking at each other's diamonds, and criticising the toilettes of the younger ladies, each narrowly watching her peculiar Polly Jane, that she did not betray too much interest in any man who was not of a certain fortune. It is the cold, vulgar truth, madam, nor are we in the slightest degree exaggerating. Elderly gentlemen, twisting single gloves in a very wretched manner, came up and bowed to the dowagers, and smirked, and said it was a pleasant party, and a handsome house, and then clutched their hands behind them, and walked miserably away, looking as affable as possible. And the dowagers made a little fun of the elderly gentlemen, among themselves, as they walked away.

Then came the younger non-dancing men—a class of the community who wear black cravats and waistcoats, and thrust their thumbs and forefingers in their waistcoat pockets, and are called "talking men." Some of them are literary, and affect the philosopher; have, perhaps, written a book or two, and are a small species of lion to very young ladies. Some are of the *blasé* kind; men who affect the extremest elegance, and are reputed "so aristocratic," and who care for nothing in particular, but wish they had not been born gentlemen, in which case they might have escaped ennui. These gentlemen stand with hat in hand, and coats and trowsers most unexceptionable. They are the "so gentlemanly" persons of whom one hears a great deal, but which seems to mean nothing but cleanliness. Vivian Grey and Pelham are the models of their ambition, and they succeed in being Pendennis. They enjoy the reputation of being "very clever," and "very talented fellows," "smart chaps," &c., but they refrain from proving what is so generously conceded. They are often men of a certain cultivation. They have travelled, many of them,—spending a year or two in Paris, and a month or two in the rest of

Europe. Consequently they endure society at home, with a smile, and a shrug, and a graceful superciliousness, which is very engaging. They are perfectly at home, and they rather despise Young America, which, in the next room, is diligently earning its invitation. They prefer to hover about the ladies who did not come out this season, but are a little used to the world, with whom they are upon most friendly terms, and who criticise together very freely all the great events in the great world of fashion.

These elegant Pendennises we saw at Mrs. Potiphar's, but not without a sadness which can hardly be explained. They had been boys once, all of them, fresh and frank-hearted, and full of a noble ambition. They had read and pondered the histories of great men; how they resolved, and struggled, and achieved. In the pure portraiture of genius, they had loved and honoured noble women, and each young heart was sworn to truth and the service of beauty. Those feelings were chivalric and fair. Those boyish instincts clung to whatever was lovely, and rejected the specious snare, however graceful and elegant. They sailed, new knights, upon that old and endless crusade against hypocrisy and the devil, and they were lost in the luxury of Corinth, nor longer seek the difficult shores beyond. A present smile was worth a future laurel. The ease of the moment was worth immortal tranquillity. They renounced the stern worship of the unknown God, and acknowledged the deities of Athens. But the seal of their shame is their own smile at their early dreams, and the high hopes of their boyhood, their sneering infidelity of simplicity, their skepticism of motives and of men. Youths, whose younger years were fervid with the resolution to strike and win, to deserve, at least, a gentle remembrance, if not a dazzling fame, are content to eat, and drink, and sleep well; to go to the opera and all the balls; to be known as "gentlemanly," and "aristocratic," and "dangerous," and "elegant"; to cherish a luxurious and enervating indolence, and to "succeed," upon the cheap reputation of having been "fast" in Paris. The end of such men is evident enough from the beginning. They are snuffed out by a "great match," and become an appendage to a rich woman; or they dwindle off into old roués, men of the world in sad earnest, and not with elegant affectation, *blasé;* and as they began Arthur Pendennises, so they end the Major. But, believe it, that old fossil heart is wrung sometimes by a mortal pang, as it remembers those squandered opportunities and that lost life.

From these groups we passed into the dancing-room. We have seen dancing in other countries, and dressing. We have certainly never seen gentlemen dance so easily, gracefully and well as the American. But the *style* of dancing, in its whirl, its rush, its fury, is only equalled by that of the masked balls at the French opera, and the balls at the *Salle Valentino,* the *Jardin Mabille,* the *Chateau Rouge,* and other favourite resorts of Parisian Grisettes and Lorettes. We saw a few young men looking upon the dance very soberly, and, upon inquiry, learned that they were engaged to certain ladies of the corps-de-ballet. Nor did we wonder that the spectacle of a young woman whirling in a *décolleté* state, and in the embrace of a warm youth, around a heated room, induced a little sobriety upon her lover's face, if not a sadness in his heart. Amusement, recreation, enjoyment! There are no more beautiful things. But this proceeding falls under another head. We watched the various toilettes of these bounding belles. They were rich and tasteful. But a man at our elbow, of experience and shrewd observation, said, with a sneer, for which we called him to account, "I observe that American ladies are so rich in charms that they are not at all chary of them. It is certainly generous to us miserable black coats. But, do you know, it strikes me as a generosity of display that must necessarily leave the donor poorer in maidenly feeling." We thought ourselves cynical, but this was intolerable; and in a very crisp manner we demanded an apology.

"Why," responded our friend with more of sadness than of satire in his tone, "why are you so exasperated? Look at this scene! Consider that this is, really, the life of these girls. This is what they 'come out' for. This is the end of their ambition. They think of it, dream of it, long for it. Is it amusement? Yes, to a few, possibly. But listen, and gather, if you can, from their remarks (when they make any) that they have any thought beyond this, and going to church very rigidly on Sunday. The vigor of polking and church-going are proportioned; as is the one so is the other. My young friend, I am no ascetic, and do not suppose a man is damned because he dances. But Life is not a ball (more's the pity, truly, for these butterflies), nor is its sole duty and delight, dancing. When I consider this spectacle,—when I remember what a noble and beautiful woman is, what a manly man,—when I reel, dazzled by this glare, drunken with these perfumes, confused by this alluring music, and reflect upon the enormous sums wasted in a pompous profusion that delights no one,—when I look around upon all this rampant vulgarity in tinsel and Brussels lace, and think how fortunes go, how men struggle and lose the bloom of their honesty, how women hide in a smiling pretence, and eye with caustic glances their neighbor's newer house, diamonds, or porcelain, and observe their daughters, such as these,—why, I tremble and tremble, and this scene to-night, every 'crack' ball this winter will be, not the pleasant society of men and women, but—even in this young country—an orgie such as rotting Corinth saw, a frenzied festival of Rome in its decadence."

There was a sober truth in this bitterness, and we turned away to escape the sombre thought of the moment. Addressing one of the panting Houris who stood melting in a window, we spoke (and confess how absurdly) of the Düsseldorf Gallery. It was merely to avoid saying how warm the room was, and how pleasant the party was; facts upon which we had already sufficiently enlarged. "Yes, they are pretty pictures; but la! how long it must have taken Mr. Düsseldorf to paint them all"; was the reply.

By the Farnesian Hercules! no Roman sylph in her city's decline would ever have called the sun-god, Mr. Apollo. We hope that Houri melted entirely away in the window, but we certainly did not stay to see.

Passing out toward the supper-room we encountered two young men. "What, Hal," said one, *"you* at Mrs. Potiphar's?" It seems that Hal was a sprig of one of the "old families." "Well, Joe," said Hal, a little confused, "it *is* a little strange. The fact is I didn't mean to be here, but I concluded to compromise by coming, *and not being introduced to the host."* Hal could come, eat Potiphar's supper, drink his wines, spoil his carpets, laugh at his fashionable struggles, and affect the puppyism of a foreign Lord, because he disgraced the name of a man who had done some service somewhere, while Potiphar was only an honest man who made a fortune.

The supper-room was a pleasant place. The table was covered with a chaos of supper. Every thing sweet and rare, and hot and cold, solid and liquid, was there. It was the very apotheosis of gilt gingerbread. There was a universal rush and struggle. The charge of the guards at Waterloo was nothing to it. Jellies, custard, oyster-soup, ice-cream, wine and water, gushed in profuse cascades over transparent precipices of *tulle,* muslin, gauze, silk, and satin. Clumsy boys tumbled against costly dresses and smeared them with preserves,—when clean plates failed, the contents of plates already used were quietly "chucked" under the table—heel-taps of champagne were poured into the oyster tureens or overflowed upon plates to clear the glasses—wine of all kinds flowed in torrents, particularly down the throats of very young men, who evinced their manhood by becoming noisy, troublesome, and disgusting, and were finally either led, sick, into the hat room, or carried out of the way, drunk. The supper over, the young people attended by their matrons descended to the dancing-room for the "German." This is a dance commencing usually at midnight or a little after, and continuing indefinitely toward daybreak. The young people were attended by their matrons, who were there to supervise the morals and manners of their charges. To secure the performance of this duty, the young people took good care to sit where the matrons could not see them, nor did they, by any chance, look toward the quarter in which the matrons sat. In that quarter, through all the varying mazes of the prolonged dance, to two o'clock, to three, to four, sat the bediamonded dowagers, the mothers, the matrons,—against nature, against common sense. They babbled with each other, they drowsed, they dozed. Their fans fell listless into their laps. In the adjoining room, out of the waking sight, even, of the then sleeping mammas, the daughters whirled in the close embrace of partners who had brought down bottles of champagne from the supper-room, and put them by the side of their chairs for occasional refreshment during the dance. The dizzy hours staggered by—"Azalia, you *must* come now," had been already said a dozen times, but only as by the scribes. Finally it was declared with authority. Azalia went,—Amelia—Arabella. The rest followed. There was prolonged cloaking, there were lingering farewells. A few papas were in the supper-room, sitting among the *débris* of game. A few young non-dancing husbands sat beneath gas unnaturally bright, reading whatever chance book was at hand, and thinking of the young child at home waiting for mamma who was dancing the "German" below. A few exhausted matrons sat in the robing-room, tired, sad, wishing Jane would come up; assailed at intervals by a vague suspicion that it was not quite worth while; wondering how it was they used to have such good times at balls; yawning, and looking at their watches; while the regular beat of the music below, with sardonic sadness, continued. At last Jane came up, had had the most glorious time, and went down with mamma to the carriage, and so drove home. Even the last Jane went—the last noisy youth was expelled, and Mr. and Mrs. Potiphar having duly performed their biennial social duty, dismissed the music, ordered the servants to count the spoons, and an hour or two after daylight went to bed. Enviable Mr. and Mrs. Potiphar!

We are now prepared for the great moral indignation of the friend who saw us eating our *dinde aux truffes* in that remarkable supper-room. We are waiting to hear him say in the most moderate and "gentlemanly" manner, that it is all very well to select flaws and present them as specimens, and to learn from him, possibly with indignant publicity, that the present condition of parties is not what we have intimated. Or, in his quiet and pointed way, he may smile at our fiery assault upon edged flounces and nuga pyramids, and the kingdom of Lilliput in general.

Yet, after all, and despite the youths who are led out, and carried home, or who stumble through the "German," this is a sober matter. My friend told us we should see the "best society." But he is a prodigious wag. Who make this country? From whom is its character of unparalleled enterprise, heroism and success derived? Who have given it its place in the respect and the fear of the world? Who, annually, recruit its energies, confirm its progress, and secure its triumph? Who are its characteristic children, the pith, the sinew, the bone of its prosperity? Who found, and direct, and continue its manifold institutions of mercy and education? Who are, essentially, Americans? Indignant friend, these classes, whoever they may be, are the "best society," because they alone are the representatives of its character and cultivation. They are the "best society" of New York, of Boston, of Baltimore, of St. Louis, of New Orleans, whether they live upon six hundred or sixty thousand dollars a year—whether they inhabit princely houses in fashionable streets (which they often do), or not—whether their sons have graduated at Celarius' and the *Jardin Mabille,* or have never been out of their fathers' shops— whether they have "air" and "style," and are "so gentlemanly" and "so aristocratic," or not. Your shoemaker, your lawyer, your butcher, your clergyman—if they are simple and steady, and, whether rich or poor, are unseduced by the sirens of extravagance and ruinous display, help make up the "best society." For that mystic communion is not composed of the rich, but of the worthy; and is "best" by its virtues, and not by its vices. When Johnson, Burke, Goldsmith, Garrick, Reynolds, and their friends, met at supper in Goldsmith's rooms, where was the "best society" in England? When George the Fourth outraged humanity and decency in his treatment of Queen Caroline, who was the first scoundrel in Europe?

Pause yet a moment, indignant friend. Whose habits and principles would ruin this country as rapidly as it has been made? Who are enamored of a puerile imitation of foreign splendors? Who strenuously endeavor to graft the questionable points of Parisian society upon our own? Who pass a few years in Europe and return skeptical of republicanism and human improvement, longing and sighing for more sharply emphasized social distinctions? Who squander with profuse recklessness the hard-earned fortunes of their sires? Who diligently devote their time to nothing, foolishly and wrongly supposing that a young English nobleman has nothing to do? Who, in fine, evince by their collective conduct, that they regard their Americanism as a misfortune, and are so the most deadly enemies of their country? None but what our wag facetiously termed "the best society."

If the reader doubts, let him consider its practical results in any great emporium of "best society." Marriage is there regarded as a luxury, too expensive for any but the sons of rich men, or fortunate young men. We once heard an eminent divine assert, and only half in sport, that the rate of living was advancing so incredibly, that weddings in his experience were perceptibly diminishing. The reasons might have been many and various. But we all acknowledge the fact. On the other hand, and about the same time, a lovely damsel (ah! Clorinda!) whose father was not wealthy, who had no prospective means of support, who could do nothing but polka to perfection, who literally knew almost nothing, and who constantly shocked every fairly intelligent person by the glaring ignorance betrayed in her remarks, informed a friend at one of the Saratoga balls, whither he had made haste to meet "the best society," that there were "not more than three good matches in society!" *La Dame aux Camélias,* Marie Duplessis, was, to our fancy, a much more feminine, and admirable, and moral, and human person, than the adored Clorinda. And yet what she said was the legitimate result of the state of our fashionable society. It worships wealth, and the pomp which wealth can purchase, more than virtue, genius, or beauty. We may be told that it has always been so in every country, and that the fine society of all lands is as profuse and flashy as our own. We deny it, flatly. Neither English, nor French, nor Italian, nor German society, is so unspeakably barren as that which is technically called "society" here. In London, and Paris, and Vienna, and Rome, all the really eminent men and women help make up the mass of society. A party is not a mere ball, but it is a congress of the wit, beauty, and fame of the capital. It is worth while to dress, if you shall meet Macaulay, or Hallam, or Guizot, or Thiers, or Landseer, or Delaroche,—Mrs. Norton, the Misses Berry, Madame Recamier, and all the brilliant women and famous foreigners. But why should we desert the pleasant pages of those men, and the recorded gossip of those women, to be squeezed flat against a wall, while young Doughface pours oyster-gravy down our shirt-front, and Caroline Pettitoes wonders at "Mr. Düsseldorf's" industry?

If intelligent people decline to go, you justly remark, it is their own fault. Yes, but if they stay away it is very certainly their great gain. The elderly people are always neglected with us, and nothing surprises intelligent strangers more, than the tyrannical supremacy of Young America. But we are not surprised at this neglect. How can we be if we have our eyes open? When Caroline Pettitoes retreats from the floor to the sofa, and instead of a "polker" figures at parties as a matron, do you suppose that "tough old

Joes" like ourselves, are going to desert the young Caroline upon the floor, for Madame Pettitoes upon the sofa? If the pretty young Caroline, with youth, health, freshness, a fine, budding form, and wreathed in a semi-transparent haze of flounced and flowered gauze, is so vapid that we prefer to accost her with our eyes alone, and not with our tongues, is the same Caroline married into a Madame Pettitoes, and fanning herself upon a sofa,—no longer particularly fresh, nor young, nor pretty, and no longer budding but very fully blown,—likely to be fascinating in conversation? We cannot wonder that the whole connection of Pettitoes, when advanced to the matron state, is entirely neglected. Proper homage to age we can all pay at home, to our parents and grandparents. Proper respect for some persons is best preserved by avoiding their neighborhood.

And what, think you, is the influence of this extravagant expense and senseless show upon these same young men and women? We can easily discover. It saps their noble ambition, assails their health, lowers their estimate of men and their reverence for women, cherishes an eager and aimless rivalry, weakens true feeling, wipes away the bloom of true modesty, and induces an ennui, a satiety, and a kind of dilettante misanthropy, which is only the more monstrous because it is undoubtedly real. You shall hear young men of intelligence and cultivation, to whom the unprecedented circumstances of this country offer opportunities of a great and beneficent career, complaining that they were born within this blighted circle—regretting that they were not bakers and tallow-chandlers, and under no obligation to keep up appearances—deliberately surrendering all the golden possibilities of that Future which this country, beyond all others, holds before them—sighing that they are not rich enough to marry the girls they love, and bitterly upbraiding fortune that they are not millionnaires—suffering the vigor of their years to exhale in idle wishes and pointless regrets—disgracing their manhood by lying in wait behind their "so gentlemanly" and "aristocratic" manners, until they can pounce upon a "fortune" and ensnare an heiress into matrimony: and so having dragged their gifts, their horses of the sun, into a service which shames out of them all their native pride and power, they sink in the mire, and their peers and emulators exclaim that they have "made a good thing of it."

Are these the processes by which a noble race is made and perpetuated? At Mrs. Potiphar's we heard several Pendennises longing for a similar luxury, and announcing their firm purpose, never to have wives nor houses, until they could have them as splendid as jewelled Mrs. Potiphar, and her palace, thirty feet front. Where were their heads and their hearts, and their arms? How looks this craven despondency, before the stern virtues of the ages we call dark? When a man is so voluntarily imbecile as to regret he is not rich, if that is what he wants, before he has struck a blow for wealth; or so dastardly as to renounce the prospect of love, because, sitting sighing, in velvet dressing-gown and slippers, he does not see his way clear to ten thousand a year; when young women coiffed *à merveille,* of unexceptionable "style," who, with or without a prospective penny, secretly look down upon honest women who struggle for a livelihood, like noble and Christian beings, and, as such, are rewarded; in whose society a man must forget that he has ever read, thought or felt; who destroy in the mind, the fair ideal of woman, which the genius of art and poetry, and love, their inspirer, has created; then it seems to us, it is high time that the subject should be regarded not as a matter of breaking butterflies upon the wheel, but as a sad and sober question, in whose solution, all fathers and mothers, and the state itself, are interested. When keen observers, and men of the world, from Europe, are amazed and appalled at the giddy whirl and frenzied rush of our society—a society singular in history, for the exaggerated prominence it assigns to wealth, irrespective of the talents that amassed it, they and their possessor being usually hustled out of sight—is it not quite time to ponder a little upon the Court of Louis XIV., and the "merrie days" of King Charles II.? Is it not clear that, if what our good wag, with caustic irony, called "best society," were really such, every thoughtful man would read upon Mrs. Potiphar's softly-tinted walls, the terrible "mene, mene" of an imminent destruction?

Venice in her purple prime of luxury, when the famous law was passed, making all gondolas black, that the nobles should not squander fortunes upon them, was not more luxurious than New York to-day. Our hotels have a superficial splendor, derived from a profusion of gilt and paint, wood and damask. Yet, in not one of them can the traveller be so quietly comfortable as in an English Inn, and nowhere in New York can the stranger procure a dinner, at once so neat and elegant, and economical, as at scores of Cafés in Paris. The fever of display has consumed comfort. A gondola plated with gold was no easier than a black wooden one. We could well spare a little gilt upon the walls, for more cleanliness upon the public table; nor is it worth while to cover the walls with mirrors to reflect a want of comfort. One prefers a wooden bench to a greasy velvet cushion, and a sanded floor to a soiled and threadbare carpet. An insipid uniformity is the

Procrustes-bed, upon which "society" is stretched. Every new house is the counterpart of every other, with the exception of more gilt, if the owner can afford it. The interior arrangement, instead of being characteristic, instead of revealing something of the tastes and feelings of the owner, is rigorously conformed to every other interior. The same hollow and tame complaisance rules in the intercourse of society. Who dares say precisely what he thinks upon a great topic? What youth ventures to say sharp things, of slavery, for instance, at a polite dinner-table? What girl dares wear curls, when Martelle prescribes puffs or bandeaux? What specimen of Young America dares have his trowsers loose or wear straps to them? We want individuality, heroism, and, if necessary, an uncompromising persistence in difference.

This is the present state of parties. They are wildly extravagant, full of senseless display; they are avoided by the pleasant and intelligent, and swarm with reckless regiments of "Brown's men." The ends of the earth contribute their choicest products to the supper, and there is every thing that wealth can purchase, and all the spacious splendor that thirty feet front can afford. They are hot, and crowded, and glaring. There is a little weak scandal, venomous, not witty, and a stream of weary platitude, mortifying to every sensible person. Will any of our Pendennis friends intermit their indignation for a moment, and consider how many good things they have said or heard during the season? If Mr. Potiphar's eyes should chance to fall here, will he reckon the amount of satisfaction and enjoyment he derived from Mrs. Potiphar's ball, and will that lady candidly confess what she gained from it beside weariness and disgust? What eloquent sermons we remember to have heard in which the sins and the sinners of Babylon, Jericho and Gomorrah were scathed with holy indignation. The cloth is very hard upon Cain, and completely routs the erring kings of Judah. The Spanish Inquisition, too, gets frightful knocks, and there is much eloquent exhortation to preach the gospel in the interior of Siam. Let it be preached there, and God speed the word. But also let us have a text or two in Broadway and the Avenue.

The best sermon ever preached upon society, within our knowledge, is "Vanity Fair." Is the spirit of that story less true of New York than of London? Probably we never see Amelia at our parties, nor Lieutenant George Osborne, nor good gawky Dobbin, nor Mrs. Rebecca Sharp Crawley, nor old Steyne. We are very much pained, of course, that any author should take such dreary views of human nature. We, for our parts, all go to Mrs. Potiphar's to refresh our faith in men and women. Generosity, amiability, a catholic charity, simplicity, taste, sense, high cultivation, and intelligence, distinguish our parties. The statesman seeks their stimulating influence; the literary man, after the day's labour, desires the repose of their elegant conversation; the professional man and the merchant hurry up from down town to shuffle off the coil of heavy duty, and forget the drudgery of life in the agreeable picture of its amenities and graces presented by Mrs. Potiphar's ball. Is this account of the matter, or "Vanity Fair," the satire? What are the prospects of any society of which that tale is the true history?

There is a picture in the Luxembourg gallery at Paris, "The Decadence of the Romans," which made the fame and fortune of Couture, the painter. It represents an orgie in the court of a temple, during the last days of Rome. A swarm of revellers occupy the middle of the picture, wreathed in elaborate intricacy of luxurious posture, men and women intermingled; their faces, in which the old Roman fire scarcely flickers, brutalized with excess of every kind; their heads of dishevelled hair bound with coronals of leaves, while, from goblets of an antique grace, they drain the fiery torrent which is destroying them. Around the bacchanalian feast stand, lofty upon pedestals, the statues of old Rome, looking with marble calmness and the severity of a rebuke beyond words upon the revellers. A youth of boyish grace, with a wreath woven in his tangled hair, and with red and drowsy eyes, sits listless upon one pedestal, while upon another stands a boy, insane with drunkenness, and proffering a dripping goblet to the marble mouth of the statue. In the corner of the picture, as if just quitting the court—Rome finally departing—is a group of Romans with care-worn brows, and hands raised to their faces in melancholy meditation. In the foreground of the picture, which is painted with all the sumptuous splendor of Venetian art, is a stately vase, around which hangs a festoon of gorgeous flowers, its end dragging upon the pavement. In the background, between the columns, smiles the blue sky of Italy—the only thing Italian not deteriorated by time. The careful student of this picture, if he has been long in Paris, is some day startled by detecting, especially in the faces of the women represented, a surprising likeness to the women of Paris, and perceives, with a thrill of dismay, that the models for this picture of decadent human nature are furnished by the very city in which he lives.

GEORGE WILLIAM CURTIS

A Meditation by Paul Potiphar, Esq.

WELL, my new house is finished—and so am I. I hope Mrs. Potiphar is satisfied. Everybody agrees that it is "palatial." The daily papers have had columns of description, and I am, evidently, according to their authority, "munificent," "tasteful," "enterprising," and "patriotic." Amen! but what business have I with palatial residences? What more can I possibly want, than a spacious, comfortable house? Do *I* want buhl *escritoires?* Do I want *or molu* things? Do I know any thing about pictures and statues? In the name of heaven do I want rose-pink bed-curtains to give my grizzly old phiz a delicate "auroral hue," as Cream Cheese says of Mrs. P.'s complexion? Because I have made fifty thousand this last year in Timbuctoo bonds, must I convert it all into a house, so large that it will not hold me comfortably,—so splendid that I might as well live in a porcelain vase, for the trouble of taking care of it,—so prodigiously "palatial" that I have to skulk into my private room, put on my slippers, close the door, shut myself up with myself, and wonder why I married Mrs. Potiphar?

This house is her doing. Before I married her, I would have worn yellow silk breeches on 'Change if she had commanded me—for love. Now I would build her two houses twice as large as this, if she required it—for peace. It's all over. When I came home from China I was the desirable Mr. Potiphar, and every evening was a field-day for me, in which I reviewed all the matrimonial forces. It is astonishing, now I come to think of it, how skilfully Brigadier-General Mrs. Pettitoes deployed those daughters of hers; how vigorously Mrs. Tabby led on her forlorn hope; and how unweariedly, Murat-like, Mrs. De Famille charged at the head of her cavalry. They deserve to be made Marshals of France, all of them. And I am sure, that if women ought ever to receive honorary testimonials, it is for having "married a daughter well."

That's a pretty phrase! The mammas marry, the misses are married.

And yet, I don't see why I say so. I fear I am getting sour. For certainly, Polly's mother didn't marry Polly to me. I fell in love with her; the rest followed. Old Gnu says that it's true Polly's mother didn't marry her, but she did marry herself, to me.

"Do you really think, Paul Potiphar," said he, a few months ago, when I was troubled about Polly's getting a livery, "that your wife was in love with you, a dry old chip from China? Don't you hear her say whenever any of her friends are engaged, that they 'have done very well!' and made a 'capital match!' and have you any doubt of her meaning? Don't you know that this is the only country in which the word 'money' must never be named in the young female ear; and in whose best society—not universally nor without exception, of course not; Paul, don't be a fool—money makes marriages? When you were engaged, 'the world' said that it was a 'capital thing' for Polly. Did that mean that you were a good, generous, intelligent, friendly, and patient man, who would be the companion for life she ought to have? You know, as well as I do, and as all the people who said it know, that it meant you were worth a few hundred thousands, that you could build a splendid house, keep horses and chariots, and live in style. You and I are sensible men, Paul, and we take the world as we find it; and know that if a man wants a good dinner he must pay for it. We don't quarrel with this state of things. How can it be helped? But we need not virtuously pretend it's something else. When my wife, being then a gay girl, first smiled at me, and looked at me, and smelt at the flowers I sent her in an unutterable manner, and proved to me that she didn't love me by the efforts she made to show that she did, why, I was foolishly smitten with her, and married her. I knew that she did not marry me, but sundry shares in the Patagonia and Nova Zembla Consolidation, and a few hundred house lots upon the island. What then? I wanted her, she was willing to take me,—being sensible enough to know that the stock and the lots had an incumbrance. *Voilà tout,* as young Boosey says. Your wife wants you to build a house. You'd better build it. It's the easiest way. Make up your mind to Mrs. Potiphar, my dear Paul, and thank heaven you've no daughters to be married off by that estimable woman."

Why does a man build a house? To live in, I suppose—to have a home. But is a fine house a home? I mean, is a "palatial residence," with Mrs. Potiphar at the head of it, the "home" of which we all dream more or less, and for which we ardently long as we grow older? A house, I take it, is a retreat to which a man hurries from business, and in which he is compensated by the tenderness and thoughtful regard of a woman, and the play of his children, for the rough rubs with men. I know it is a silly view of the case, but I'm getting old and can't help it. Mrs. Potiphar is perfectly right when she says:

"You men are intolerable. After attending to your own affairs all day, and being free from the fuss of housekeeping, you expect to come home and shuffle into your slippers, and snooze over the evening paper—if it were possible to snooze over the exciting and respectable evening journal you take—while we are to sew, and talk with you if you are talkative, and darn the stockings, and make tea. You come home tired, and likely enough, surly, and gloom about like a thundercloud if dinner isn't ready for you the instant you are ready for it, and then sit mum and eat it; and snap at the children, and show yourselves the selfish, ugly things you are. Am *I* to have no fun, never go to the opera, never go to a ball, never have a party at home? Men are tyrants, Mr. Potiphar. They are ogres who entice us poor girls into their castles, and then eat up our happiness, and scold us while they eat."

Well, I suppose it is so. I suppose I am an ogre and enticed Polly into my castle. But she didn't find it large enough, and teased me to build another. I suppose she does sit with me in the evening, and sew, and make tea, and wait upon me. I suppose she does, but I've not a clear idea of it. I know it is unkind of me, when I have been hard at work all day, trying to make and secure the money that gives her and her family every thing they want, and which wearies me body and soul, to expect her to let me stay at home, and be quiet. I know I ought to dress and go into Gnu's house, and smirk at his wife, and stand up in a black suit before him attired in the same way, and talk about the same stocks that we discussed down town in the morning in colored trowsers. That's a social duty, I suppose. And I ought to see various slight young gentlemen whirl my wife around the room, and hear them tell her when they stop, that it's very warm. That's another social duty, I suppose. And I must smile when the same young gentlemen put their elbows into my stomach, and hop on my feet in order to extend the circle of the dance. I'm sure Mrs. P. is right. She does very right to ask, "Have we no social duties, I should like to know?"

And when we have performed these social duties in Gnu's house, how mean it is, how "it looks," not to build a larger house for him and Mrs. Gnu to come and perform their social duties in. I give it up. There's no doubt of it.

One day Polly said to me:

"Mr. Potiphar, we're getting down town."

"What do you mean, my dear?"

"Why, every body is building above us, and there are actually shops in the next street. Singe, the pastry-cook, has hired Mrs. Crœsus's old house."

"I know it. Old Crœsus told me so some time ago; and he said how sorry he was to go. 'Why, Potiphar,' said he, 'I really hoped when I built there, that I should stay, and not go out of the house, finally, until I went into no other. I have lived there long enough to love the place, and have some associations with it; and my family have grown up in it, and love the old house too. It was our *home*. When any of us said 'home,' we meant not the family only, but the house in which the family lived, where the children were all born, and where two have died, and my old mother, too. I'm in a new house now, and have lost my reckoning entirely. I don't know the house; I've no associations with it. The house is new, the furniture is new, and my feelings are new. It's a farce for me to begin again, in this way. But my wife says it's all right, that every body does it, and wants to know how it can be helped; and, as I don't want to argue the matter, I look amen.' That's the way Mr. Crœsus submits to his new house, Mrs. Potiphar."

She doesn't understand it. Poor child! how should she? She, and Mrs. Crœsus, and Mrs. Gnu, and even Mrs. Settum Downe, are all as nomadic as Bedouin Arabs. The Rev. Cream Cheese says, that he sees in this constant migration from one house to another, a striking resemblance to the "tents of a night," spoken of in Scripture. He imparts this religious consolation to me when I grumble. He says, that it prevents a too-closely clinging affection to temporary abodes. One day, at dinner, that audacious wag, Boosey, asked him if the "many manthuns" mentioned in the Bible, were not as true of mortal as of immortal life. Mrs. Potiphar grew purple, and Mr. Cheese looked at Boosey in the most serious manner over the top of his champagne-glass. I am glad to say that Polly has properly rebuked Gauche Boosey for his irreligion, by not asking him to her Saturday evening *matinées dansantes*.

There was no escape from the house, however. It must be built. It was not only Mrs. Potiphar that persisted, but the spirit of the age and of the country. One can't live among shops. When Pearl street comes to Park Place, Park Place must run for its life up to Thirtieth street. I know it can't be helped, but I protested, and I will protest. If I've got to go, I'll have my grumble. My wife says:

"I'm ashamed of you, Potiphar. Do you pretend to be an American, and not give way willingly to the march of improvement? You had better talk with Mr. Cream Cheese upon the 'genius of the country.' You are really unpatriotic, you show nothing of the enterprising spirit of your time." "Yes," I answer. "That's pretty from you; you are patriotic, are n't you, with your liveries and illimitable expenses, and your low bows to money, and your immense intimacy with all lords and ladies that honor the city by visiting it. You are prodigiously patriotic with your inane imitations of a splendor impossible to you in the nature of things. You are the ideal American woman, aren't you, Mrs. Potiphar."

Then I run, for I'm afraid of myself, as much as of her. I am sick of this universal plea of patriotism. It is used to excuse all the follies that outrage it. I am not patriotic if I don't do this and that, which, if done, is a ludicrous caricature of something foreign. I am not up to the time if I persist in having my own comfort in my own way. I try to resist the irresistible march of improvement, if I decline to build a great house, which, when it is built, is a puny copy of a bad model. I am very unpatriotic if I am not trying to outspend foreign noblemen, and if I don't affect, without education, or taste, or habit, what is only beautiful, when it is the result of the three.

However, this is merely my grumble. I knew, the first morning Mrs. Potiphar spoke of a new house, that I must build it. What she said was perfectly true; we were getting down town, there was no doubt of the growing inconvenience of our situation. It was becoming a dusty, noisy region. The congregation of the Rev. Far Niente had sold their church and moved up town. Now doesn't it really seem as if were a cross between the Arabs who dwell in tents and those who live in cities, for we are migratory in the city? A directory is a more imperative annual necessity here than in any other civilized region. My wife says it is a constant pleasure to her to go round and see the new houses and the new furniture of her new friends, every year. I saw that I must submit. But I determined to make little occasional stands against it. So one day I said:

"Polly, do you know that the wives of all the noblemen who will be your very dear and intimate friends and models when you go abroad, always live in the same houses in London, and Paris, and Rome, and Vienna? Do you know that Northumberland House is so called because it is the hereditary town mansion of the Duke, and that the son and daughter-in-law of Lord Londonderry will live after him in the house where his father and mother lived before him? Did that ever occur to you, my dear?"

"Mr. Potiphar," she replied, "do you mean to go by the example of foreign noblemen? I thought you always laughed at me for what you call 'aping.'"

"So I do, and so I will continue to do, Mrs. Potiphar; only I thought that, perhaps, you would like to know the fact, because it might make you more lenient to me when I regretted leaving our old house here. It has an aristocratic precedent."

Poor, dear little Mrs. P.! It didn't take as I meant it should, and I said no more. Yet it does seem to me a pity that we lose all the interest and advantage of a homestead. The house and its furniture become endeared by long residence, and by their mute share in all the chances of our life. The chair in which some dear old friend so often sat—father and mother, perhaps—and in which they shall sit no more; the old-fashioned table with the cuts and scratches that generations of children have made upon it; the old bookcases; the heavy sideboard; the glass, from which such bumpers sparkled for those who are hopelessly scattered now, or for ever gone; the doors they opened; the walls that echoed their long-hushed laughter,—are we wise when we part with them all, or, when compelled to do so, to leave them eagerly?

I remember my brother James used to say:

"What is our envy for our country friends, but that their homes are permanent and characteristic? Their children's children may play in the same garden. Each annual festival may summon them to the old hearth. In the meeting-house they sit in the wooden pews where long ago they sat and dreamed of Jerusalem, and now as they sit there, that long ago is fairer than the holy city. Through the open window they see the grass waving softly in the summer air, over old graves dearer to them than many new houses. By a thousand tangible and visible associations they are still, with a peculiar sense of actuality, near to all they love."

Polly would call it a sentimental whim—if she could take Mrs. Crœsus's advice before she spoke of it—but what then? When I was fifteen, I fell desperately in love with Lucy Lamb. "Pooh, pooh," said my father, "you are romantic, it's all a whim of yours."

And he succeeded in breaking it up. I went to China, and Lucy married old Firkin, and lived in a splendid house, and now lies in a splendid tomb of Carrara marble, exquisitely sculptured.

When I was forty, I came home from China, and the old gentleman said, "I want you to marry Arabella Bobbs, the heiress. It will be a good match."

I said to him.

"Pooh, pooh, my dear father, you are mercenary; it's all a whim of yours."

"My dear son, I know it," said he, "the whole thing is whim. You can live on a hundred dollars a year, if you choose. But you have the whim of a good dinner, of a statue, of a book. Why not? Only be careful in following your whims, that they really come to something. Have as many whims as you please, but don't follow them all."

"Certainly not," said I; and fell in love with the present Mrs. Potiphar, and married her, off-hand. So, if she calls this genuine influence of association a mere whim—let it go at that. She is a whim, too. My mistake simply was in not following out the romantic whim, and marrying Lucy Lamb. At least it seems to me so, this morning. In fact, sitting in my very new "palatial residence," the whole business of life seems to me rather whimsical.

For here I am, come into port at last. No longer young,—but worth a good fortune,—master of a great house,—respected down town,—husband of Mrs. Potiphar,—and father of Master Frederic ditto. Per contra; I shall never be in love again,—in getting my fortune I have lost my real life,—my house is dreary,—Mrs. Potiphar is not Lucy Lamb,—and Master Frederic—is a good boy.

The game is all up for me, and yet I trust I have good feeling enough left to sympathize with those who are still playing. I see girls as lovely and dear as any of which poets have sung—as fresh as dew-drops, and beautiful as morning. I watch their glances, and understand them better than they know —for they do not dream that "old Potiphar" does any thing more than pay Mrs. P.'s bills. I see the youths nervous about neckcloths, and anxious that their hair shall be parted straight behind. I see them all wear the same tie, the same trowsers, the same boots. I hear them all say the same thing, and dance with the same partners in the same way. I see them go to Europe and return—I hear them talk slang to show that they have exhausted human life in foreign parts, and observe them demean themselves according to their idea of the English nobleman. I watch them go in strongly for being "manly," and "smashing the spoonies"—asserting intimacies with certain uncertain women in Paris, and proving it by their treatment of ladies at home. I see them fuddle themselves on fine wines and talk like cooks, play heavily and lose, and win, and pay, and drink, and maintain a conservative position in politics, denouncing "Uncle Tom's Cabin," as a false and fanatical tract; and declaring that our peculiar institutions are our own affair, and that John Bull had better keep his eyes at home to look into his coal mines. I see this vigorous fermentation subside, and much clear character deposited—and, also, much life and talent muddled for ever.

It is whimsical, because this absurd spectacle is presented by manikins who are made of the same clay as Plutarch's heroes—because, deliberately, they prefer cabbages to roses. I am not at all angry with them. On the contrary, when they dance well I look on with pleasure. Man ought to dance, but he ought to do something else, too. All genial gentlemen in all ages have danced. Who quarrels with dancing? Ask Mrs. Potiphar if I ever objected to it. But then, people must dance at their own risk. If Lucy Lamb, by dancing with young Boosey when he is tipsy, shows that she has no self-respect, how can I, coolly talking with Mrs. Lamb in the corner, and gravely looking on, respect the young lady? Lucy tells me that if she dances with James she must with John. I cannot deny it, for I am not sufficiently familiar with the regulations of the mystery. Only this; if dancing with sober James makes it necessary to dance with tipsy John—it seems to me, upon a hasty glance at the subject, that a self-respecting Lucy would refrain from the dance with James. Why it should be so, I cannot understand. Why Lucy must dance with every man who asks her, whether he is in his senses, or knows how to dance, or is agreeable to her or not, is a profound mystery to Paul Potiphar. Here is a case of woman's wrongs, decidedly. We men cull the choicest partners, make the severest selections, and the innocent Lucys gracefully submit. Lucy loves James, and a waltz with him (as P. P. knows very well from experience) is "a little heaven below" to both. Now, dearest Lucy, why must you pay the awful penance of immediately waltzing with John, against whom your womanly instinct rebels? And yet the laws of social life are so stern, that Lucy must make the terrible decision, whether it is better to waltz with James or worse to waltz with John! "Whether," to put it strongly with Father Jerome, "heaven is pleasanter than hell is painful."

I say that I watch these graceful gamesters, without bitter feeling. Sometimes it is sad to see James woo Lucy, win her, marry her, and then both discover that they have made a mistake. I don't see how they could have helped it; and when the world, that loves them both so tenderly, holds up its pure hands of horror, why, Paul Potiphar goes quietly home to Mrs. P., who is dressing for Lucy's ball, and says nothing. He prefers to retire into his private room, and his slippers, and read the last number of *Bleak House,* or a chapter in *Vanity Fair*. If Mrs. Potiphar catches him at the latter, she is sure to say:

"There it is again; always reading those exaggerated sketches of society.

Odious man that he is. I am sure he never knew a truly womanly woman."

"Polly, when he comes back in September I'll introduce him to you," is the only answer I have time to make, for it is already half past ten, and Mrs. P. must be off to the ball.

I know that our set is not the world, nor the country, nor the city. I know that the amiable youths who are in league to crush spooneyism are not many, and well I know, that in our set (I mean Mrs. P.'s) there are hearts as noble and characters as lofty as in any time and in any land. And yet, as the father of a family (viz. Frederic, our son), I am constrained to believe that our social tendency is to the wildest extravagance. Here, for instance, is my house. It cost me eighty-five thousand dollars. It is superbly furnished. Mrs. P. and I don't know much about such things. She was only stringent for buhl, and the last Parisian models, so we delivered our house into the hands of certain eminent upholsterers to be furnished, as we send Frederic to the tailor's to be clothed. To be sure, I asked what proof we had that the upholsterer was possessed of taste. But Mrs. P. silenced me, by saying that it was his business to have taste, and that a man who sold furniture, naturally knew what was handsome and proper for my house.

The furnishing was certainly performed with great splendor and expense. My drawing-rooms strongly resemble the warehouse of an ideal cabinet-maker. Every whim of table—every caprice of chair and sofa, is satisfied in those rooms. There are curtains like rainbows, and carpets, as if the curtains had dripped all over the floor. There are heavy cabinets of carved walnut, such as belong in the heavy wainscotted rooms of old palaces, set against my last French pattern of wall paper. There are lofty chairs, like the thrones of archbishops in Gothic cathedrals, standing by the side of the elaborately gilded frames of mirrors. Marble statues of Venus and the Apollo support my mantels, upon which *or molu* Louis Quatorze clocks ring the hours. In all possible places there are statues, statuettes, vases, plates, teacups, and liquor-cases. The wood-work, when white, is elaborated in Moresco carving—when oak and walnut, it is heavily moulded. The contrasts are pretty, but rather sudden. In truth, my house is a huge curiosity-shop of valuable articles,—clustered without taste, or feeling, or reason. They are there, because my house was large and I was able to buy them; and because, as Mrs. P. says, one must have buhl and *or molu,* and new forms of furniture, and do as well as one's neighbors, and show that one is rich, if he is so. They are there, in fact, because I couldn't help it. I didn't want them, but then I don't know what I did want. Somehow I don't feel as if I had a home, merely because orders were given to the best upholsterers and fancy-men in town to send a sample of all their wares to my house. To pay a morning call at Mrs. Potiphar's is, in some ways, better than going shopping. You see more new and costly things in a shorter time. People say, "What a love of a chair!" "What a darling table!" "What a heavenly sofa!" and they all go and tease their husbands to get things precisely like them. When Kurz Pacha, the Sennaar minister, came to a dinner at my house, he said:

"Bless my soul! Mr. Potiphar, your house is just like your neighbor's."

I know it. I am perfectly aware that there is no more difference between my house and Crœsus's, than there is in two ten-dollar bills of the same bank. He might live in my house and I in his, without any confusion. He has the same curtains, carpets, chairs, tables, Venuses, Apollos, busts, vases, &c. And he goes into his room, and thinks it's all a devilish bore, just as I do. We have each got to refurnish every few years, and therefore have no possible opportunity for attaching ourselves to the objects about us. Unfortunately Kurz Pacha particularly detested precisely what Mrs. P. most liked, because it is the fashion to like them. I mean the Louis Quatorze and the Louis Quinze things.

"Taste, dear Mrs. Potiphar," said the Pacha, "was a thing not known in the days of those kings. Grace was entirely supplanted by grotesqueness, and now, instead of pure and beautiful Greek forms, we must collect these hideous things. If you are going backward to find models, why not go as far as the good ones? My dear madam, an *or molu* Louis Quatorze clock would have given Pericles a fit. Your drawing-rooms would have thrown Aspasia into hysterics. Things are not beautiful because they cost money; nor is any grouping handsome without harmony. Your house is like a woman dressed in Ninon de l'Enclos's bodice, with Queen Anne's hooped skirt, who limps in Chinese shoes, and wears an Elizabethan ruff round her neck, and a Druse's horn on her head. My dear madam, this is the kind of thing we go to see in museums. It is the old stock joke of the world."

By Jove! how mad Mrs. Potiphar was! She rose from table, to the great dismay of Kurz Pacha, and I could only restrain her by reminding her that the Sennaar Minister had but an imperfect idea of our language, and that in Sennaar people probably said what they thought when they conversed.

"You'd better go to Sennaar, then, yourself, Mr. Potiphar," said my wife, as she smoothed her rumpled feathers.

" 'Pon my word, madam, it's my own opinion," replied I.

Kurz Pacha, who is a philosopher (of the Sennaar school), asks me if people have no ideas of their own in building houses. I answer, none, that I know of, except that of getting the house built. The fact is, it is as much as Paul Potiphar can do, to make the money to erect his palatial residence, and then to keep it going. There are a great many fine statues in my house, but I know nothing about them; I don't see why we should have such heathen images in reputable houses. But Mrs. P. says:

"Pooh! have you no love for the fine arts?"

There it is! It doesn't do not to love the fine arts; so Polly is continually cluttering up the halls and staircases with marble, and sending me heavy bills for the same.

When the house was ready, and my wife had purchased the furniture, she came and said to me:

"Now, my dear P., there is one thing we haven't thought of."

"What's that?"

"Pictures, you know, dear."

"What do you want pictures for?" growled I, and rather surlily, I am afraid.

"Why to furnish the walls; what do you suppose we want pictures for?"

"I tell you, Polly," said I, "that pictures are the most extravagant kind of furniture. Pshaw! a man rubs and dabbles a little upon a canvas two feet square, and then coolly asks three hundred dollars for it."

"Dear me, Pot," she answered, "I don't want home-made pictures. What an idea! Do you think I'd have pictures on my walls that were painted in this country?—No, my dear husband, let us have some choice specimens of the old masters. A landscape by Rayfel, for instance; or one of Angel's fruit pieces, or a cattle scene by Verynees, or a Madonna of Giddo's, or a boar-hunt of Hannibal Crackkey's."

What was the use of fighting against this sort of thing? I told her to have it her own way. Mrs. P. consulted Singe the pastry cook, who told her his cousin had just come out from Italy with a lot of the very finest pictures in the world, which he had bribed one of the Pope's guard to steal from the Vatican, and which he would sell at a bargain.

They hang on my walls now. They represent nothing in particular; but in certain lights, if you look very closely, you can easily recognize something in them that looks like a lump of something brown. There is one very ugly woman with a convulsive child in her arms, to which Mrs. P. directly takes all her visitors, and asks them to admire the beautiful Shay douver of Giddo's. When I go out to dinner with people that talk pictures and books, and that kind of thing, I don't like to seem behind, so I say, in a critical way, that Giddo was a good painter. None of them contradict me, and one day when somebody asked, "Which of his pictures do you prefer?" I answered straight, "His Shay douver," and no more questions were asked.

They hang all about the house now. The Giddo is in the dining-room. I asked the Sennaar Minister if it wasn't odd to have a religious picture in the dining-room. He smiled, and said that it was perfectly proper if I liked it, and if the picture of such an ugly woman didn't take away my appetite.

"What difference does it make," said he, in the Sennaar manner, "it would be equally out of keeping with every other room in your house. My dear Potiphar, it is a perfectly unprincipled house, this of yours. If your mind were in the condition of your house, so ill-assorted, so confused, so overloaded with things that don't belong together, you would never make another cent. You have order, propriety, harmony, in your dealings with the Symmes's Hole Bore Co., and they are the secrets of your success. Why not have the same elements in your house? Why pitch every century, country, and fashion, higgledy-piggledy into your parlors and dining-room? Have every thing you can get, in heaven's name, but have every thing in its place. If you are a plodding tradesman, knowing and caring nothing about pictures, or books, or statuary, or *objets de vertu;* don't have them. Suppose your neighbor chooses to put them in his house. If he has them merely because he had the money to pay for them, he is the butt of every picture and book he owns.

"When I meet Mr. Crœsus in Wall street, I respect him as I do a king in his palace, or a scholar in his study. He is master of the occasion. He commands like Nelson at the Nile. I, who am merely a diplomatist, skulk and hurry along, and if Mr. Crœsus smiles, I inwardly thank him for his charity. Wall street is Crœsus's sphere, and all his powers play there perfectly. But when I meet him in his house, surrounded by objects of art, by the triumphs of a skill which he does not understand, and for which he cares nothing,— of which, in fact, he seems afraid, because he knows any chance question about them would trip him up,—my feeling is very much changed. If I should ask him what *or molu* is, I don't believe he could answer, though his splendid *or molu* clock rang, indignant, from the mantel. But if I should say, 'Invest me this thousand dollars,' he would secure me eight per cent. It certainly isn't necessary to know what *or molu* is, nor to have any other *objet de vertu* but your wife. Then why should you barricade yourself behind all these things that you really cannot enjoy, because you don't understand?

If you could not read Italian, you would be a fool to buy Dante, merely because you knew he was a great poet. And, in the same way, if you know nothing about matters of art, it is equally foolish for you to buy statues and pictures, although you hear on all sides, that, as Mrs. P. says, one must love art.

"As for learning from your own pictures, you know, perfectly well, that until you have some taste in the matter, you will be paying money for your pictures, blindly, so that the only persons upon whom your display of art would make any impression, will be the very ones to see that you know nothing about it.

"In Sennaar, a man is literally 'the master of the house.' He isn't surrounded by what he does not understand; he is not obliged to talk book, and picture, when he knows nothing about these matters. He is not afraid of his parlor, and you feel instantly upon entering the house, the character of the master. Please, my dear Mr. Potiphar, survey your mansion and tell me what kind of a man it indicates. If it does not proclaim (in your case) the President of the Patagonia Junction, a man shrewd, and hard and solid, without taste or liberal cultivation, it is a painted deceiver. If it tries to insinuate by this chaotic profusion of rich and rare objects, that you are a cultivated, accomplished, tasteful, and generous man, it is a bad lie, because a transparent one. Why, my dear old Pot., the moment your servant opens the front door, a man of sense perceives the whole thing. You and Mrs. Potiphar are bullied by all the brilliancy you have conjured up. It is the old story of the fisherman and the genii. And your guests all see it. They are too well-bred to speak of it; but I come from Sennaar, where we do not lay so much stress upon that kind of good breeding. Mr. Paul Potiphar, it is one thing to have plenty of money, and quite another, to know how to spend it."

Now, as I told him, this kind of talk may do very well in Sennaar, but it is absurd in a country like ours. How are people to know that I'm rich, unless I show it? I'm sorry for it, but how shall I help it, having Mrs. P. at hand?

"How about the library?" said she one day.

"What library?" inquired I.

"Why, our library, of course."

"I haven't any."

"Do you mean to have such a house as this without a library?"

"Why," said I plaintively, "I don't read books—I never did, and I never shall; and I don't care any thing about them. Why should I have a library?"

"Why, because it's part of a house like this."

"Mrs. P., are you fond of books?"

"No, not particularly. But one must have some regard to appearances. Suppose we are Hottentots, you don't want us to look so, do you?"

I thought that it was quite as barbarous to imprison a lot of books that we should never open, and that would stand in gilt upon the shelves, silently laughing us to scorn, as not to have them if we didn't want them. I proposed a compromise.

"Is it the looks of the thing, Mrs. P.?" said I.

"That's all," she answered.

"Oh! well, I'll arrange it."

So I had my shelves built, and my old friends Matthews and Rider furnished me with complete sets of handsome gilt covers to all the books that no gentleman's library should be without, which I arranged, carefully, upon the shelves, and had the best-looking library in town. I locked 'em in, and the key is always lost when any body wants to take down a book. However, it was a good investment in leather, for it brings me in the reputation of a reading man and a patron of literature.

Mrs. P. is a religious woman—the Rev. Cream Cheese takes care of that—but only yesterday she proposed something to me that smells very strongly of candlesticks.

"Pot.," I want a *prieu-dieu."*

"Pray-do what?" answered I.

"Stop, you wicked man. I say I want a kneeling-chair."

"A kneeling-chair?" I gasped, utterly confused.

"A *prie-dieu*—a *prie-dieu*—to pray in, you know."

My Sennaar friend, who was at table, choked. When he recovered, and we were sipping the "blue seal," he told me that he thought Mrs. Potiphar in a *prie-dieu* was rather a more amusing idea than Giddo's Madonna in the dining-room.

"She will insist upon its being carved handsomely in walnut. She will not pray upon pine. It is a romantic, not a religious, whim. She'll want a missal next; vellum or no prayers. This is piety of the 'Lady Alice' school. It belongs to a fine lady and a fine house precisely as your library does, and it will be precisely as genuine. Mrs. Potiphar in a *prie-dieu* is like that blue morocco Comus in your library. It is charming to look at, but there's nothing in it. Let her have the *prie-dieu* by all means, and then begin to build a chapel. No gentleman's house should be without a chapel. You'll have to come to it,

Potiphar. You'll have to hear Cream Cheese read morning prayers in a purple chasuble,—*que sais-je?* You'll see religion made a part of the newest fashion in houses, as you already see literature and art, and with just as much reality and reason."

Privately, I am glad the Sennaar minister has gone out of town. It's bad enough to be uncomfortable in your own house without knowing why; but to have a philosopher of the Sennaar school show you why you are so, is cutting it rather too fat. I am gradually getting resigned to my house. I've got one more struggle to go through next week in Mrs. Potiphar's musical party. The morning soirées are over for the season, and Mrs. P. begins to talk of the watering places. I am getting gradually resigned; but only gradually.

Oh! dear me, I wonder if this is the "home, sweet home" business the girls used to sing about! Music does certainly alter cases. I can't quite get used to it. Last week I was one morning in the basement breakfast-room, and I heard an extra cried. I ran out of the area door—dear me!—before I thought what I was about, I emerged bareheaded from under the steps, and ran a little way after the boy. I know it wasn't proper. I am sorry, very sorry. I am afraid Mrs. Crœsus saw me; I know Mrs. Gnu told it all about that morning; and Mrs. Settum Downe called directly upon Mrs. Potiphar, to know if it were really true that I had lost my wits, as every body was saying. I don't know what Mrs. P. answered. I am sorry to have compromised her so. I went immediately and ordered a pray-do of the blackest walnut. My resignation is very gradual. Kurz Pacha says they put on gravestones in Sennaar three Latin words—do you know Latin? if you don't, come and borrow some of my books. The words are: *ora pro me!*

JAMES RUSSELL LOWELL

A Fable for Critics

READER! *walk up at once (it will soon be too late) and
buy at a perfectly ruinous rate*
A
FABLE FOR CRITICS;
OR, BETTER,
(*I like, as a thing that the reader's first fancy may strike,
an old-fashioned title-page,
such as presents a tabular view of the volume's contents*)
A GLANCE
AT A FEW OF OUR LITERARY PROGENIES
(*Mrs. Malaprop's word*)
FROM
THE TUB OF DIOGENES;
A VOCAL AND MUSICAL MEDLEY
THAT IS,
A SERIES OF JOKES
By A Wonderful Quiz,
*who accompanies himself with a rub-a-dub-dub, full of spirit and grace,
on the top of the tub.*
SET FORTH IN
October, the 21st day, in the year '48:
G. P. PUTNAM, BROADWAY.

PHŒBUS, sitting one day in a laurel-tree's shade
   Was reminded of Daphne, of whom it was made,
   For the god being one day too warm in his wooing,
She took to the tree to escape his pursuing;
Be the cause what it might, from his offers she shrunk,
And, Ginevra-like, shut herself up in a trunk;
And, though 'twas a step into which he had driven her,
He somehow or other had never forgiven her;
Her memory he nursed as a kind of a tonic,
Something bitter to chew when he'd play the Byronic,

And I can't count the obstinate nymphs that he brought over,
By a strange kind of smile he put on when he thought of her.
"My case is like Dido's," he sometimes remark'd,
"When I last saw my love, she was fairly embark'd;
Let hunters from me take this saw when they need it,
—You're not always sure of your game when you've tree'd it.
Just conceive such a change taking place in one's mistress!
What romance would be left?—who can flatter or kiss trees?
And for mercy's sake, how could one keep up a dialogue
With a dull wooden thing that will live and will die a log,
Not to say that the thought would forever intrude
That you've less chance to win her the more she is wood?
Ah! it went to my heart, and the memory still grieves,
To see those loved graces all taking their leaves;
Those charms beyond speech, so enchanting but now,
As they left me forever, each making its bough!
If her tongue *had* a tang sometimes more than was right,
Her new bark is worse than ten times her old bite."

   Now, Daphne,—before she was happily treeified,—
Over all other flowers the lily had deified,
And when she expected the god on a visit,
('Twas before he had made his intentions explicit,)
Some buds she arranged with a vast deal of care,
To look as if artlessly twined in her hair,
Where they seemed, as he said, when he paid his addresses,
Like the day breaking through the long night of her tresses;
So, whenever he wished to be quite irresistible,
Like a man with eight trumps in his hand at a whist-table,
(I feared me at first that the rhyme was untwistable,
Though I might have lugged in an allusion to Cristabel,)—
He would take up a lily, and gloomily look in it,
As I shall at the ——, when they cut up my book in it.

   Well, here, after all the bad rhyme I've been spinning,
I've got back at last to my story's beginning:
Sitting there, as I say, in the shade of his mistress,
As dull as a volume of old Chester mysteries,
Or as those puzzling specimens, which, in old histories,

We read of his verses—the Oracles, namely,—
(I wonder the Greeks should have swallowed them tamely,
For one might bet safely whatever he has to risk,
They were laid at his door by some ancient Miss Asterisk,
And so dull that the men who retailed them out-doors
Got the ill name of 'augurs,' because they were bores,)—
First, he mused what the animal substance or herb is
Would induce a moustache, for you know he's *imberbis;*
Then he shuddered to think how his youthful position
Was assailed by the age of his son the physician;
At some poems he glanced, had been sent to him lately,
And the metre and sentiment puzzled him greatly;
"Mehercle! I'd make such proceedings felonious,—
Have they all of them slept in the cave of Trophonius?
Look well to your seat, 'tis like taking an airing
On a corduroy road, and that out of repairing;
It leads one, 'tis true, through the primitive forest,
Grand natural features—but, then, one has no rest;
You just catch a glimpse of some ravishing distance,
When a jolt puts the whole of it out of existence,—
Why not use their ears, if they happen to have any?"
—Here the laurel-leaves murmured the name of poor Daphne.

"O, weep with me, Daphne," he sighed, "for you know it's
A terrible thing to be pestered with poets!
But, alas, she is dumb, and the proverb holds good,
She never will cry till she's out of the wood!
What wouldn't I give if I never had known of her?
'Twere a kind of relief had I something to groan over;
If I had but some letters of hers, now, to toss over,
I might turn for the nonce a Byronic philosopher,
And bewitch all the flats by bemoaning the loss of her.
One needs something tangible, though, to begin on—
A loom, as it were, for the fancy to spin on;
What boots all your grist? it can never be ground
Till a breeze makes the arms of the windmill go round,
(Or, if 'tis a water-mill, alter the metaphor,
And say it won't stir, save the wheel be well wet afore,

Or lug in some stuff about water "so dreamily,"—
It is not a metaphor, though, 'tis a simile;)
A lily, perhaps, would set *my* mill agoing,
For just at this season, I think, they are blowing,
Here, somebody, fetch one, not very far hence
They're in bloom by the score, 'tis but climbing a fence;
There's a poet hard by, who does nothing but fill his
Whole garden, from one end to t'other, with lilies;
A very good plan, were it not for satiety,
One longs for a weed here and there, for variety;
Though a weed is no more than a flower in disguise,
Which is seen through at once, if love give a man eyes.

   Now there happened to be among Phœbus's followers,
A gentleman, one of the omnivorous swallowers
Who bolt every book that comes out of the press,
Without the least question of larger or less,
Whose stomachs are strong at the expense of their head,—
For reading new books is like eating new bread,
One can bear it at first, but by gradual steps he
Is brought to death's door of a mental dyspepsy.
On a previous stage of existence, our Hero
Had ridden outside, with the glass below zero;
He had been, 'tis a fact you may safely rely on,
Of a very old stock a most eminent scion,—
A stock all fresh quacks their fierce boluses ply on,
Who stretch the new boots Earth's unwilling to try on,
Whom humbugs of all shapes and sorts keep their eye on,
Whose hair's in the mortar of every new Zion,
Who, when whistles are dear, go directly and buy one,
Who think slavery a crime that we must not say fie on,
Who hunt, if they e'er hunt at all, with the lion,
(Though they hunt lions also, whenever they spy one,)
Who contrive to make every good fortune a wry one,
And at last choose the hard bed of honor to die on,
Whose pedigree traced to earth's earliest years,
Is longer than any thing else but their ears;—

In short, he was sent into life with the wrong key,
He unlocked the door, and stept forth a poor donkey.
Though kicked and abused by his bipedal betters,
Yet he filled no mean place in the kingdom of letters;
Far happier than many a literary hack,
He bore only paper-mill rags on his back;
(For it makes a vast difference which side the mill
One expends on the paper his labor and skill;)
So, when his soul waited a new transmigration,
And Destiny balanced 'twixt this and that station,
Not having much time to expend upon bothers,
Remembering he'd had some connexion with authors,
And considering his four legs had grown paralytic,—
She set him on two, and he came forth a critic.

   Through his babyhood no kind of pleasure he took
In any amusement but tearing a book;
For him there was no intermediate stage,
From babyhood up to straight-laced middle age;
There were years when he didn't wear coat-tails behind,
But a boy he could never be rightly defined;
Like the Irish Good Folk, though in length scarce a span,
From the womb he came gravely, a little old man;
While other boys' trowsers demanded the toil
Of the motherly fingers on all kinds of soil,
Red, yellow, brown, black, clayey, gravelly, loamy,
He sat in a corner and read Viri Romæ.
He never was known to unbend or to revel once
In base, marbles, hockey, or kick up the devil once;
He was just one of those who excite the benevolence
Of old prigs who sound the soul's depth with a ledger,
And are on the look out for some young men to "edger-
-cate," as they call it, who won't be too costly,
And who'll afterward take to the ministry mostly;
Who always wear spectacles, always look bilious,
Always keep on good terms with each *mater-familias*
Throughout the whole parish, and manage to rear
Ten boys like themselves, on four hundred a year;

Who, fulfilling in turn the same fearful conditions,
Either preach through their noses, or go upon missions.

In this way our hero got safely to College,
Where he bolted alike both his commons and knowledge;
A reading-machine, always wound up and going,
He mastered whatever was not worth the knowing,
Appeared in a gown, and a vest of black satin,
To spout such a Gothic oration in Latin,
That Tully could never have made out a word in it,
(Though himself was the model the author preferred in it,)
And grasping the parchment which gave him in fee,
All the mystic and so-forths contained in A. B.,
He was launched (life is always compared to a sea,)
With just enough learning, and skill for the using it,
To prove he'd a brain, by forever confusing it.
So worthy Saint Benedict, piously burning
With the holiest zeal against secular learning,
Nesciensque scienter, as writers express it,
Indoctusque sapienter à Româ recessit.

'Twould be endless to tell you the things that he knew,
All separate facts, undeniably true,
But with him or each other they'd nothing to do;
No power of combining, arranging, discerning,
Digested the masses he learned into learning;
There was one thing in life he had practical knowledge for,
(And this, you will think, he need scarce go to college for,)
Not a deed would he do, nor a word would he utter,
Till he'd weighed its relations to plain bread and butter.
When he left Alma Mater, he practised his wits
In compiling the journals' historical bits,—
Of shops broken open, men falling in fits,
Great fortunes in England bequeathed to poor printers,
And cold spells, the coldest for many past winters,—
Then, rising by industry, knack, and address,
Got notices up for an unbiassed press,

With a mind so well poised, it seemed equally made for
Applause or abuse, just which chanced to be paid for;
From this point his progress was rapid and sure,
To the post of a regular heavy reviewer.

And here I must say, he wrote excellent articles
On the Hebraic points, or the force of Greek particles,
They filled up the space nothing else was prepared for,
And nobody read that which nobody cared for;
If any old book reached a fiftieth edition,
He could fill forty pages with safe erudition;
He could gauge the old books by the old set of rules,
And his very old nothings pleased very old fools;
But give him a new book, fresh out of the heart,
And you put him at sea without compass or chart,—
His blunders aspired to the rank of an art;
For his lore was engraft, something foreign that grew in him,
Exhausting the sap of the native and true in him,
So that when a man came with a soul that was new in him,
Carving new forms of truth out of Nature's old granite,
New and old at their birth, like Le Verrier's planet,
Which, to get a true judgment, themselves must create
In the soul of their critic the measure and weight,
Being rather themselves a fresh standard of grace,
To compute their own judge, and assign him his place,
Our reviewer would crawl all about it and round it,
And, reporting each circumstance just as he found it,
Without the least malice,—his record would be
Profoundly æsthetic as that of a flea,
Which, supping on Wordsworth, should print, for our sakes,
Recollections of nights with the Bard of the Lakes,
Or, borne by an Arab guide, ventured to render a
General view of the ruins at Denderah.

As I said, he was never precisely unkind,
The defect in his brain was mere absence of mind;
If he boasted, 'twas simply that he was self-made,
A position which I, for one, never gainsaid,

My respect for my Maker supposing a skill
In his works which our hero would answer but ill;
And I trust that the mould which he used may be cracked, or he,
Made bold by success, may make broad his phylactery,
And set up a kind of a man-manufactory,
An event which I shudder to think about, seeing
That Man is a moral, accountable being.

He meant well enough, but was still in the way,
As a dunce always is, let him be where he may;
Indeed, they appear to come into existence
To impede other folks with their awkward assistance;
If you set up a dunce on the very North pole,
All alone with himself, I believe, on my soul,
He'd manage to get betwixt somebody's shins,
And pitch him down bodily, all in his sins,
To the grave polar bears sitting round on the ice,
All shortening their grace, to be in for a slice;
Or, if he found nobody else there to pother,
Why, one of his legs would just trip up the other,
For there's nothing we read of in torture's inventions,
Like a well-meaning dunce, with the best of intentions.

A terrible fellow to meet in society,
Not the toast that he buttered was ever so dry at tea;
There he'd sit at the table and stir in his sugar,
Crouching close for a spring, all the while, like a cougar;
Be sure of your facts, of your measures and weights,
Of your time—he's as fond as an Arab of dates;—
You'll be telling, perhaps, in your comical way,
Of something you've seen in the course of the day;
And, just as you're tapering out the conclusion,
You venture an ill-fated classic allusion,—
The girls have all got their laughs ready, when, whack!
The cougar comes down on your thunderstruck back;
You had left out a comma,—your Greek's put in joint,
And pointed at cost of your story's whole point.

In the course of the evening, you venture on certain
Soft speeches to Anne, in the shade of the curtain;
You tell her your heart can be likened to *one* flower,
"And that, oh most charming of women, 's the sunflower,
Which turns"—here a clear nasal voice, to your terror,
From outside the curtain, says "that's all an error."
As for him, he's—no matter, he never grew tender,
Sitting after a ball, with his feet on the fender,
Shaping somebody's sweet features out of cigar smoke,
(Though he'd willingly grant you that such doings are smoke;)
All women he damns with *mutabile semper,*
And if ever he felt something like love's distemper,
'Twas toward a young lady who spoke ancient Mexican,
And assisted her father in making a lexicon;
Though I recollect hearing him get quite ferocious
About one Mary Clausum, the mistress of Grotius,
Or something of that sort,—but, no bore to bore ye
With character-painting, I'll turn to my story.

Now, Apollo, who finds it convenient sometimes
To get his court clear of the makers of rhymes,
The *genus,* I think it is called, *irritabile,*
Every one of whom thinks himself treated most shabbily,
And nurses a—what is it?—*immedicabile,*
Which keeps him at boiling-point, hot for a quarrel,
As bitter as wormwood, and sourer than sorrel,
If any poor devil but looks at a laurel;—
Apollo, I say, being sick of their rioting,
(Though he sometimes acknowledged their verse had a quieting
Effect after dinner, and seemed to suggest a
Retreat to the shrine of a tranquil siesta,)
Kept our Hero at hand, who, by means of a bray,
Which he gave to the life, drove the rabble away;
And if that wouldn't do, he was sure to succeed,
If he took his review out and offered to read;
Or, failing in plans of this milder description,
He would ask for their aid to get up a subscription,

Considering that authorship wasn't a rich craft,
To print the "American drama of Witchcraft."
"Stay, I'll read you a scene,"—but he hardly began,
Ere Apollo shrieked "Help!" and the authors all ran:
And once, when these purgatives acted with less spirit,
And the desperate case asked a remedy desperate,
He drew from his pocket a foolscap epistle,
As calmly as if 'twere a nine-barelled pistol,
And threatened them all with the judgment to come,
Of "A wandering Star's first impressions of Rome."
"Stop! stop!" with their hands o'er their ears screamed the Muses,
"He may go off and murder himself, if he chooses,
'Twas a means self-defence only sanctioned his trying,
'Tis mere massacre now that the enemy's flying;
If he's forced to 't again, and we happen to be there,
Give us each a large handkerchief soaked in strong ether."

  I called this a "Fable for Critics;" you think it's
More like a display of my rhythmical trinkets;
My plot, like an icicle, 's slender and slippery,
Every moment more slender, and likely to slip awry,
And the reader unwilling *in loco desipere,*
Is free to jump over as much of my frippery
As he fancies, and, if he's a provident skipper, he
May have an Odyssean sway of the gales,
And get safe into port, ere his patience all fails;
Moreover, although 'tis a slender return
For your toil and expense, yet my paper will burn,
And, if you have manfully struggled thus far with me,
You may e'en twist me up, and just light your cigar with me:
If too angry for that, you can tear me in pieces,
And my *membra disjecta* consign to the breezes,
A fate like great Ratzau's, whom one of those bores,
Who beflead with bad verses poor Louis Quatorze,
Describes, (the first verse somehow ends with *victoire,*)
As *dispersant partout et ses membres et sa gloire;*
Or, if I were over-desirous of earning
A repute among noodles for classical learning,

I could pick you a score of allusions, I wis,
As new as the jests of *Didaskalos tis;*
Better still, I could make out a good solid list
From recondite authors who do not exist,—
But that would be naughty: at least, I could twist
Something out of Absyrtus, or turn your inquiries
After Milton's prose metaphor, drawn from Osiris;—
But, as Cicero says he won't say this or that,
(A fetch, I must say, most transparent and flat,)
After saying whate'er he could possibly think of,—
I simply will state that I pause on the brink of
A mire, ankle-deep, of deliberate confusion,
Made up of old jumbles of classic allusion,
So, when you were thinking yourselves to be pitied,
Just conceive how much harder your teeth you'd have gritted,
An 'twere not for the dulness I've kindly omitted.

I'd apologize here for my many digressions,
Were it not that I'm certain to trip into fresh ones,
('Tis so hard to escape if you get in their mesh once;)
Just reflect, if you please, how 'tis said by Horatius,
That Mæonides nods now and then, and, my gracious!
It certainly does look a little bit ominous
When he gets under way with *ton d'apameibomenos.*
(Here a something occurs which I'll just clap a rhyme to,
And say it myself, ere a Zoilus has time to,—
Any author a nap like Van Winkle's may take,
If he only contrive to keep readers awake,
But he'll very soon find himself laid on the shelf,
If *they* fall a nodding when he nods himself.)

Once for all, to return, and to stay, will I, nill I—
When Phœbus expressed his desire for a lily,
Our hero, whose homœopathic sagacity
With an ocean of zeal mixed his drop of capacity,
Set off for the garden as fast as the wind,
(Or, to take a comparison more to my mind,
As a sound politician leaves conscience behind,)

And leaped the low fence, as a party hack jumps
O'er his principles, when something else turns up trumps.

  He was gone a long time, and Apollo meanwhile,
Went over some sonnets of his with a file,
For of all compositions, he thought that the sonnet
Best repaid all the toil you expended upon it;
It should reach with one impulse the end of its course,
And for one final blow collect all of its force;
Not a verse should be salient, but each one should tend
With a wave-like up-gathering to burst at the end,—
So, condensing the strength here, there smoothing a wry kink,
He was killing the time, when up walked Mr. ——;
At a few steps behind him, a small man in glasses,
Went dodging about, muttering "murderers! asses!"
From out of his pocket a paper he'd take,
With the proud look of martyrdom tied to its stake,
And, reading a squib at himself, he'd say, "Here I see
'Gainst American letters a bloody conspiracy,
They are all by my personal enemies written;
I must post an anonymous letter to Britain,
And show that this gall is the merest suggestion
Of spite at my zeal on the Copyright question,
For, on this side of the water, 'tis prudent to pull
O'er the eyes of the public their national wool,
By accusing of slavish respect to John Bull,
All American authors who have more or less
Of that anti-American humburg—success,
While in private we're always embracing the knees
Of some twopenny editor over the seas,
And licking his critical shoes, for you know 'tis
The whole aim of our lives to get one English 'notice',
My American puffs I would willingly burn all,
(They're all from one source, monthly, weekly, diurnal,)
To get but a kick from a transmarine journal!"

  So, culling the gibes of each critical scorner
As if they were plums, and himself were Jack Horner,
He came cautiously on, peeping round every corner,

And into each hole where a weasel might pass in,
Expecting the knife of some critic assassin,
Who stabs to the heart with a caricature,
Not so bad as those daubs of the Sun, to be sure,
Yet done with a dagger-ò-type, whose vile portraits
Disperse all one's good, and condense all one's poor traits.

   Apollo looked up, hearing footsteps approaching,
And slipped out of sight the new rhymes he was broaching,—
"Good day, Mr. ——, I'm happy to meet
With a scholar so ripe, and a critic so neat,
Who through Grub-street the soul of a gentleman carries,—
What news from that suburb of London and Paris
Which latterly makes such shrill claims to monopolize
The credit of being the New World's metropolis!"

   "Why, nothing of consequence, save this attack
On my friend there, behind, by some pitiful hack,
Who thinks every national author a poor one,
That isn't a copy of something that's foreign,
And assaults the American Dick—"
                               "Nay, 'tis clear
That your Damon there's fond of a flea in his ear,
And, if no one else furnished them gratis, on tick
He would buy some himself, just to hear the old click;
Why, I honestly think, if some fool in Japan
Should turn up his nose at the 'Poems on Man,'
Your friend there by some inward instinct would know it,
Would get it translated, reprinted, and show it;
As a man might take off a high stock to exhibit
The autograph round his own neck of the gibbet;
Nor would let it rest so, but fire column after column,
Signed Cato, or Brutus, or something as solemn,
By way of displaying his critical crosses,
And tweaking that poor transatlantic proboscis,
His broadsides resulting (and this there's no doubt of,)
In successively sinking the craft they're fired out of.
Now nobody knows when an author is hit,
If he don't have a public hysterical fit;

Let him only keep close in his snug garret's dim ether,
And nobody'd think of his critics—or him either;
If an author have any least fibre of worth in him,
Abuse would but tickle the organ of mirth in him,
All the critics on earth cannot crush with their ban,
One word that's in tune with the nature of man."

"Well, perhaps so; meanwhile I have brought you a book,
Into which if you'll just have the goodness to look,
You may feel so delighted, when you have got through it,
As to think it not unworth your while to review it,
And I think I can promise your thoughts, if you do,
A place in the next Democratic Review."

"The most thankless of gods you must surely have tho't me,
For this is the forty-fourth copy you've brought me,
I have given them away, or at least I have tried,
But I've forty-two left, standing all side by side,
(The man who accepted that one copy, died,)—
From one end of a shelf to the other they reach,
'With the author's respects' neatly written in each.
The publisher, sure, will proclaim a Te Deum,
When he hears of that order the British Museum
Has sent for one set of what books were first printed
In America, little or big,—for 'tis hinted
That this is the first truly tangible hope he
Has ever had raised for the sale of a copy.
I've thought very often 'twould be a good thing
In all public collections of books, if a wing
Were set off by itself, like the seas from the dry lands,
Marked *Literature suited to desolate islands,*
And filled with such books as could never be read
Save by readers of proofs, forced to do it for bread,—
Such books as one's wrecked on in small country-taverns,
Such as hermits might mortify over in caverns,
Such as Satan, if printing had then been invented,
As the climax of woe, would to Job have presented,
Such as Crusoe might dip in, although there are few so
Outrageously cornered by fate as poor Crusoe;

And since the philanthropists just now are banging
And gibbeting all who're in favor of hanging,—
(Though Cheever has proved that the Bible and Altar
Were let down from Heaven at the end of a halter,
And that vital religion would dull and grow callous,
Unrefreshed, now and then, with a sniff of the gallows,)—
And folks are beginning to think it looks odd,
To choke a poor scamp for the glory of God;
And that He who esteems the Virginia reel
A bait to draw saints from their spiritual weal,
And regards the quadrille as a far greater knavery
Than crushing His African children with slavery,—
Since all who take part in a waltz or cotillion
Are mounted for hell on the Devil's own pillion,
Who, as every true orthodox Christian well knows,
Approaches the heart through the door of the toes,—
That He, I was saying, whose judgments are stored
For such as take steps in despite of his word,
Should look with delight on the agonized prancing
Of a wretch who has not the least ground for his dancing,
While the State, standing by, sings a verse from the Psalter
About offering to God on his favorite halter,
And, when the legs droop from their twitching divergence,
Sells the clothes to a Jew, and the corpse to the surgeons;—

  Now, instead of all this, I think I can direct you all
To a criminal code both humane and effectual;—
I propose to shut up every doer of wrong
With these desperate books, for such term, short or long,
As by statute in such cases made and provided,
Shall be by your wise legislators decided
Thus:—Let murderers be shut, to grow wiser and cooler,
At hard labor for life on the works of Miss ———;
Petty thieves, kept from flagranter crimes by their fears,
Shall peruse Yankee Doodle a blank term of years,—
That American Punch, like the English, no doubt—
Just the sugar and lemons and spirit left out.

"But stay, here comes Tityrus Griswold, and leads on
The flocks whom he first plucks alive, and then feeds on,—
A loud cackling swarm, in whose feathers warm-drest,
He goes for as perfect a—swan, as the rest.

"There comes Emerson first, whose rich words, every one,
Are like gold nails in temples to hang trophies on,
Whose prose is grand verse, while his verse, the Lord knows,
Is some of it pr——No, 'tis not even prose;
I'm speaking of metres; some poems have welled
From those rare depths of soul that have ne'er been excelled;
They're not epics, but that doesn't matter a pin,
In creating, the only hard thing's to begin;
A grass-blade 's no easier to make than an oak,
If you've once found the way, you've achieved the grand stroke;
In the worst of his poems are mines of rich matter,
But thrown in a heap with a crush and a clatter;
Now it is not one thing nor another alone
Makes a poem, but rather the general tone,
The something pervading, uniting the whole,
The before unconceived, unconceivable soul,
So that just in removing this trifle or that, you
Take away, as it were, a chief limb of the statue;
Roots, wood, bark, and leaves, singly perfect may be,
But, clapt hodge-podge together, they don't make a tree.

"But, to come back to Emerson, (whom by the way,
I believe we left waiting,)—his is, we may say,
A Greek head on right Yankee shoulders, whose range
Has Olympus for one pole, for t'other the Exchange;
He seems, to my thinking, (although I'm afraid
The comparison must, long ere this, have been made,)
A Plotinus-Montaigne, where the Egyptian's gold mist
And the Gascon's shrewd wit cheek-by-jowl co-exist;
All admire, and yet scarcely six converts he's got
To I don't (nor they either) exactly know what;
For though he builds glorious temples, 'tis odd
He leaves never a doorway to get in a god.

'Tis refreshing to old-fashioned people like me,
To meet such a primitive Pagan as he,
In whose mind all creation is duly respected
As parts of himself—just a little projected;
And who's willing to worship the stars and the sun,
A convert to—nothing but Emerson.
So perfect a balance there is in his head,
That he talks of things sometimes as if they were dead;
Life, nature, love, God, and affairs of that sort,
He looks at as merely ideas; in short,
As if they were fossils stuck round in a cabinet,
Of such vast extent that our earth's a mere dab in it;
Composed just as he is inclined to conjecture her,
Namely, one part pure earth, ninety-nine parts pure lecturer;
You are filled with delight at his clear demonstration,
Each figure, word, gesture, just fits the occasion,
With the quiet precision of science he'll sort 'em,
But you can't help suspecting the whole a *post mortem*.

"There are persons, mole-blind to the soul's make and style,
Who insist on a likeness 'twixt him and Carlyle;
To compare him with Plato would be vastly fairer,
Carlyle's the more burly, but E. is the rarer;
He sees fewer objects, but clearlier, truelier,
If C.'s as original, E.'s more peculiar;
That he's more of a man you might say of the one,
Of the other he's more of an Emerson;
C.'s the Titan, as shaggy of mind as of limb,—
E. the clear-eyed Olympian, rapid and slim;
The one's two-thirds Norseman, the other half Greek,
Where the one's most abounding, the other's to seek;
C.'s generals require to be seen in the mass,—
E.'s specialties gain if enlarged by the glass;
C. gives nature and God his own fits of the blues,
And rims common-sense things with mystical hues,—
E. sits in a mystery calm and intense,
And looks coolly around him with sharp common-sense;

C. shows you how every-day matters unite
With the dim transdiurnal recesses of night,—
While E., in a plain, preternatural way,
Makes mysteries matters of mere every day;
C. draws all his characters quite *à la* Fuseli,—
He don't sketch their bundles of muscles and thews illy,
But he paints with a brush so untamed and profuse,
They seem nothing but bundles of muscles and thews;
E. is rather like Flaxman, lines strait and severe,
And a colorless outline, but full, round, and clear;—
To the men he thinks worthy he frankly accords
The design of a white marble statue in words.
C. labors to get at the centre, and then
Take a reckoning from there of his actions and men;
E. calmly assumes the said centre as granted,
And, given himself, has whatever is wanted.

"He has imitators in scores, who omit
No part of the man but his wisdom and wit,—
Who go carefully o'er the sky-blue of his brain,
And when he has skimmed it once, skim it again;
If at all they resemble him, you may be sure it is
Because their shoals mirror his mists and obscurities,
As a mud-puddle seems deep as heaven for a minute,
While a cloud that floats o'er is reflected within it.

"There comes ——, for instance; to see him's rare sport,
Tread in Emerson's tracks with legs painfully short;
How he jumps, how he strains, and gets red in the face,
To keep step with the mystagogue's natural pace!
He follows as close as a stick to a rocket,
His fingers exploring the prophet's each pocket.
Fie, for shame, brother bard; with good fruit of your own,
Can't you let neighbor Emerson's orchards alone?
Besides, 'tis no use, you'll not find e'en a core,—
—— has picked up all the windfalls before.
They might strip every tree, and E. would never catch 'em,
His Hesperides have no rude dragon to watch 'em;
When they send him a dishfull, and ask him to try 'em,

He never suspects how the sly rogues came by 'em;
He wonders why 'tis there are none such his trees on,
And thinks 'em the best he has tasted this season.

"Yonder, calm as a cloud, Alcott stalks in a dream,
And fancies himself in thy groves, Academe,
With the Parthenon nigh, and the olive-trees o'er him,
And never a fact to perplex him or bore him,
With a snug room at Plato's, when night comes, to walk to,
And people from morning till midnight to talk to,
And from midnight till morning, nor snore in their listening;—
So he muses, his face with the joy of it glistening,
For his highest conceit of a happiest state is
Where they'd live upon acorns, and hear him talk gratis;
And indeed, I believe, no man ever talked better—
Each sentence hangs perfectly poised to a letter;
He seems piling words, but there's royal dust hid
In the heart of each sky-piercing pyramid.
While he talks he is great, but goes out like a taper,
If you shut him up closely with pen, ink, and paper;
Yet his fingers itch for 'em from morning till night,
And he thinks he does wrong if he don't always write;
In this, as in all things, a lamb among men,
He goes to sure death when he goes to his pen.

"Close behind him is Brownson, his mouth very full
With attempting to gulp a Gregorian bull;
Who contrives, spite of that, to pour out as he goes
A stream of transparent and forcible prose;
He shifts quite about, then proceeds to expound
That 'tis merely the earth, not himself, that turns round,
And wishes it clearly impressed on your mind,
That the weather-cock rules and not follows the wind;
Proving first, then as deftly confuting each side,
With no doctrine pleased that's not somewhere denied,
He lays the denier away on the shelf,
And then—down beside him lies gravely himself.

He's the Salt River boatman, who always stands willing
To convey friend or foe without charging a shilling,
And so fond of the trip that, when leisure's to spare,
He'll row himself up, if he can't get a fare.
The worst of it is, that his logic's so strong,
That of two sides he commonly chooses the wrong;
If there *is* only one, why, he'll split it in two,
And first pummel this half, then that, black and blue.
That white's white needs no proof, but it takes a deep fellow
To prove it jet-black, and that jet-black is yellow.
He offers the true faith to drink in a sieve,—
When it reaches your lips there's naught left to believe
But a few silly- (syllo-, I mean,) -gisms that squat 'em
Like tadpoles, o'erjoyed with the mud at the bottom.

"There is Willis, so *natty* and jaunty and gay,
Who says his best things in so foppish a way,
With conceits and pet phrases so thickly o'erlaying 'em,
That one hardly knows whether to thank him for saying 'em;
Over-ornament ruins both poem and prose,
Just conceive of a muse with a ring in her nose!
His prose had a natural grace of its own,
And enough of it, too, if he'd let it alone;
But he twitches and jerks so, one fairly gets tired,
And is forced to forgive where he might have admired;
Yet whenever it slips away free and unlaced,
It runs like a stream with a musical waste,
And gurgles along with the liquidest sweep;—
'Tis not deep as a river, but who'd have it deep?
In a country where scarcely a village is found
That has not its author sublime and profound,
For some one to be slightly shoal is a duty,
And Willis's shallowness makes half his beauty.
His prose winds along with a blithe, gurgling error,
And reflects all of Heaven it can see in its mirror.
'Tis a narrowish strip, but it is not an artifice,—
'Tis the true out-of-doors with its genuine hearty phiz;

It is Nature herself, and there's something in that,
Since most brains reflect but the crown of a hat.
No volume I know to read under a tree,
More truly delicious than his A l' Abri,
With the shadows of leaves flowing over your book,
Like ripple-shades netting the bed of a brook;
With June coming softly your shoulder to look over,
Breezes waiting to turn every leaf of your book over,
And Nature to criticise still as you read,—
The page that bears that is a rare one indeed.

"He's so innate a cockney, that had he been born
Where plain bare-skin's the only full-dress that is worn,
He'd have given his own such an air that you'd say
'T had been made by a tailor to lounge in Broadway.
His nature's a glass of champagne with the foam on't,
As tender as Fletcher, as witty as Beaumont;
So his best things are done in the flush of the moment,
If he wait, all is spoiled; he may stir it and shake it,
But, the fixed air once gone, he can never re-make it.
He might be a marvel of easy delightfulness,
If he would not sometimes leave the *r* out of sprightfulness;
And he ought to let Scripture alone—'tis self-slaughter,
For nobody likes inspiration-and-water.
He'd have been just the fellow to sup at the Mermaid,
Cracking jokes at rare Ben, with an eye to the bar-maid,
His wit running up as Canary ran down,—
The topmost bright bubble on the wave of The Town.

"Here comes Parker, the Orson of parsons, a man
Whom the Church undertook to put under her ban,—
(The Church of Socinus, I mean)—his opinions
Being So- (ultra) -cinian, they shocked the Socinians;
They believed—faith I'm puzzled—I think I may call
Their belief a believing in nothing at all,
Or something of that sort; I know they all went
For a general union of total dissent:

He went a step farther; without cough or hem,
He frankly avowed he believed not in them;
And, before he could be jumbled up or prevented,
From their orthodox kind of dissent he dissented.
There was heresy here, you perceive, for the right
Of privately judging means simply that light
Has been granted to *me,* for deciding on *you,*
And, in happier times, before Atheism grew,
The deed contained clauses for cooking you, too.
Now at Xerxes and Knut we all laugh, yet our foot
With the same wave is wet that mocked Xerxes and Knut;
And we all entertain a sincere private notion,
That our *Thus far!* will have a great weight with the ocean.
'Twas so with our liberal Christians: they bore
With sincerest conviction their chairs to the shore;
They brandished their worn theological birches,
Bade natural progress keep out of the Churches,
And expected the lines they had drawn to prevail
With the fast-rising tide to keep out of their pale;
They had formerly dammed the Pontifical See,
And the same thing, they thought, would do nicely for P.;
But he turned up his nose at their murmuring and shamming,
And cared (shall I say?) not a d— for their damming;
So they first read him out of their Church, and next minute
Turned round and declared he had never been in it.
But the ban was too small or the man was too big,
For he recks not their bells, books, and candles a fig;
(He don't look like a man who would *stay* treated shabbily,
Sophroniscus' son's head o'er the features of Rabelais;)—
He bangs and bethwacks them,—their backs he salutes
With the whole tree of knowledge torn up by the roots;
His sermons with satire are plenteously verjuiced,
And he talks in one breath of Confutzee, Cass, Zerduscht,
Jack Robinson, Peter the Hermit, Strap, Dathan,
Cush, Pitt (not the bottomless, *that* he's no faith in,)
Pan, Pillicock, Shakspeare, Paul, Toots, Monsieur Tonson,
Aldebaran, Alcander, Ben Khorat, Ben Jonson,

Thoth, Richter, Joe Smith, Father Paul, Judah Monis,
Musæus, Muretus, hem,—μ Scorpionis,
Maccabee, Maccaboy, Mac—Mac—ah! Machiavelli,
Condorcet, Count d'Orsay, Conder, Say, Ganganelli,
Orion, O'Connell, the Chevalier D'O,
(Whom the great Sully speaks of,) τo $\pi a \nu$, the great toe
Of the statue of Jupiter, now made to pass
For that of Jew Peter by good Romish brass,—
(You may add for yourselves, for I find it a bore,
All the names you have ever, or not, heard before,
And when you've done that—why, invent a few more.)
His hearers can't tell you on Sunday beforehand,
If in that day's discourse they'll be Bibled or Koraned,
For he's seized the idea (by his martyrdom fired,)
That all men, (not orthodox) *may be* inspired;
Yet, though wisdom profane with his creed he may weave in,
He makes it quite clear what he *doesn't* believe in,
While some, who decry him, think all Kingdom Come
Is a sort of a, kind of a, species of Hum,
Of which, as it were, so to speak, not a crumb
Would be left, if we didn't keep carefully mum,
And, to make a clean breast, that 'tis perfectly plain
That *all* kinds of wisdom are somewhat profane;
Now P.'s creed than this may be lighter or darker,
But in one thing, 'tis clear, he has faith, namely—Parker;
And this is what makes him the crowd-drawing preacher,
There's a back-ground of god to each hard-working feature,
Every word that he speaks has been fierily furnaced
In the blast of a life that has struggled in earnest:
There he stands, looking more like a ploughman than priest,
If not dreadfully awkward, not graceful at least,
His gestures all downright and same, if you will,
As of brown-fisted Hobnail in hoeing a drill,
But his periods fall on you, stroke after stroke,
Like the blows of a lumberer felling an oak,
You forget the man wholly, you're thankful to meet
With a preacher who smacks of the field and the street,

And to hear, you're not over-particular whence,
Almost Taylor's profusion, quite Latimer's sense.

"There is Bryant, as quiet, as cool, and as dignified,
As a smooth, silent iceberg, that never is ignified,
Save when by reflection 'tis kindled o' nights
With a semblance of flame by the chill Northern Lights.
He may rank (Griswold says so) first bard of your nation,
(There's no doubt that he stands in supreme ice-olation,)
Your topmost Parnassus he may set his heel on,
But no warm applauses come, peal following peal on,—
He's too smooth and too polished to hang any zeal on:
Unqualified merits, I'll grant, if you choose, he has 'em,
But he lacks the one merit of kindling enthusiasm;
If he stir you at all, it is just, on my soul,
Like being stirred up with the very North Pole.

"He is very nice reading in summer, but *inter
Nos,* we don't want *extra* freezing in winter;
Take him up in the depth of July, my advice is,
When you feel an Egyptian devotion to ices.
But, deduct all you can, there's enough that's right good in him,
He has a true soul for field, river, and wood in him;
And his heart, in the midst of brick walls, or where'er it is,
Glows, softens, and thrills with the tenderest charities,—
To you mortals that delve in this trade-ridden planet?
No, to old Berkshire's hills, with their limestone and granite.
If you're one who *in loco* (add *foco* here) *desipis,*
You will get of his outermost heart (as I guess) a piece;
But you'd get deeper down if you came as a precipice,
And would break the last seal of its inwardest fountain,
If you only could palm yourself off for a mountain.
Mr. Quivis, or somebody quite as discerning,
Some scholar who's hourly expecting his learning,
Calls B. the American Wordsworth; but Wordsworth
Is worth near as much as your whole tuneful herd's worth.
No, don't be absurd, he's an excellent Bryant;
But, my friends, you'll endanger the life of your client,
By attempting to stretch him up into a giant:

If you choose to compare him, I think there are two per-
-sons fit for a parallel—Thomson and Cowper;[1]
I don't mean exactly,—there's something of each,
There's T.'s love of nature, C.'s penchant to preach;
Just mix up their minds so that C.'s spice of craziness
Shall balance and neutralize T.'s turn for laziness,
And it gives you a brain cool, quite frictionless, quiet,
Whose internal police nips the buds of all riot,—
A brain like a permanent strait-jacket put on
The heart which strives vainly to burst off a button,—
A brain which, without being slow or mechanic,
Does more than a larger less drilled, more volcanic;
He's a Cowper condensed, with no craziness bitten,
And the advantage that Wordsworth before him has written.

"But, my dear little bardlings, don't prick up your ears,
Nor suppose I would rank you and Bryant as peers;
If I call him an iceberg, I don't mean to say
There is nothing in that which is grand, in its way;
He is almost the one of your poets that knows
How much grace, strength, and dignity lie in Repose;
If he sometimes falls short, he is too wise to mar
His thought's modest fulness by going too far;
'Twould be well if your authors should all make a trial
Of what virtue there is in severe self-denial,
And measure their writings by Hesiod's staff,
Which teaches that all has less value than half.

"There is Whittier, whose swelling and vehement heart
Strains the strait-breasted drab of the Quaker apart,
And reveals the live Man, still supreme and erect
Underneath the bemummying wrappers of sect;
There was ne'er a man born who had more of the swing
Of the true lyric bard and all that kind of thing;

[1] To demonstrate quickly and easily how per-
-versely absurd 'tis to sound this name *Cowper*,
As people in general call him named *super*,
I just add that he rhymes it himself with horse-trooper.

And his failures arise, (though perhaps he don't know it,)
From the very same cause that has made him a poet,—
A fervor of mind which knows no separation
'Twixt simple excitement and pure inspiration,
As my Pythoness erst sometimes erred from not knowing
If 'twere I or mere wind through her tripod was blowing;
Let his mind once get head in its favorite direction
And the torrent of verse bursts the dams of reflection,
While, borne with the rush of the metre along,
The poet may chance to go right or go wrong,
Content with the whirl and delirium of song;
Then his grammar's not always correct, nor his rhymes,
And he's prone to repeat his own lyrics sometimes,
Not his best, though, for those are struck off at white heats
When the heart in his breast like a trip-hammer beats,
And can ne'er be repeated again any more
Than they could have been carefully plotted before:
Like old what's-his-name there at the battle of Hastings,
(Who, however, gave more than mere rhythmical bastings.)
Our Quaker leads off metaphorical fights
For reform and whatever they call human rights,
Both singing and striking in front of the war
And hitting his foes with the mallet of Thor;
Anne haec, one exclaims, on beholding his knocks,
Vestis filii tui, O, leather-clad Fox?
Can that by thy son, in the battle's mid din,
Preaching brotherly love and then driving it in
To the brain of the tough old Goliath of sin,
With the smoothest of pebbles from Castaly's spring
Impressed on his hard moral sense with a sling?

"All honor and praise to the right-hearted bard
Who was true to The Voice when such service was hard,
Who himself was so free he dared sing for the slave
When to look but a protest in silence was brave;
All honor and praise to the women and men
Who spoke out for the dumb and the down-trodden then!

I need not to name them, already for each
I see History preparing the statue and niche;
They were harsh, but shall *you* be so shocked at hard words
Who have beaten your pruning-hooks up into swords,
Whose rewards and hurrahs men are surer to gain
By the reaping of men and of women than grain?
Why should *you* stand aghast at their fierce wordy war, if
You scalp one another for Bank or for Tariff?
Your calling them cut-throats and knaves all day long
Don't prove that the use of hard language is wrong;
While the World's heart beats quicker to think of such men
As signed Tyranny's doom with a bloody steel-pen,
While on Fourth-of-Julys beardless orators fright one
With hints at Harmodius and Aristogeiton,
You need not look shy at your sisters and brothers
Who stab with sharp words for the freedom of others;—
No, a wreath, twine a wreath for the loyal and true
Who, for sake of the many, dared stand with the few,
Not of blood-spattered laurel for enemies braved,
But of broad, peaceful oak-leaves for citizens saved!

"Here comes Dana, abstractedly loitering along,
Involved in a paulo-post-future of song,
Who'll be going to write what'll never be written
Till the Muse, ere he thinks of it, gives him the mitten,—
Who is so well aware of how things should be done,
That his own works displease him before they're begun,—
Who so well all that makes up good poetry knows,
That the best of his poems is written in prose;
All saddled and bridled stood Pegasus waiting,
He was booted and spurred, but he loitered debating,
In a very grave question his soul was immersed,—
Which foot in the stirrup he ought to put first;
And, while this point and that he judicially dwelt on,
He, somehow or other, had written Paul Felton,
Whose beauties or faults, whichsoever you see there,
You'll allow only genius could hit upon either.

That he once was the Idle Man none will deplore,
But I fear he will never be any thing more;
The ocean of song heaves and glitters before him,
The depth and the vastness and longing sweep o'er him,
He knows every breaker and shoal on the chart,
He has the Coast Pilot and so on by heart,
Yet he spends his whole life, like the man in the fable,
In learning to swim on his library-table.

"There swaggers John Neal, who has wasted in Maine
The sinews and chords of his pugilist brain,
Who might have been poet, but that, in its stead, he
Preferred to believe that he was so already;
Too hasty to wait till Art's ripe fruit should drop,
He must pelt down an unripe and colicky crop;
Who took to the law, and had this sterling plea for it,
It required him to quarrel, and paid him a fee for it;
A man who's made less than he might have, because
He always has thought himself more than he was,—
Who, with very good natural gifts as a bard,
Broke the strings of his lyre out by striking too hard,
And cracked half the notes of a truly fine voice,
Because song drew less instant attention than noise.
Ah, men do not know how much strength is in poise,
That he goes the farthest who goes far enough,
And that all beyond that is just bother and stuff.
No vain man matures, he makes too much new wood;
His blooms are too thick for the fruit to be good;
'Tis the modest man ripens, 'tis he that achieves,
Just what's needed of sunshine and shade he receives;
Grapes, to mellow, require the cool dark of their leaves;
Neal wants balance; he throws his mind always too far,
And whisks out flocks of comets, but never a star;
He has so much muscle, and loves so to show it,
That he strips himself naked to prove he's a poet,
And, to show he could leap Art's wide ditch, if he tried,
Jumps clean o'er it, and into the hedge t'other side.

He has strength, but there's nothing about him in keeping;
One gets surelier onward by walking than leaping;
He has used his own sinews himself to distress,
And had done vastly more had he done vastly less;
In letters, too soon is as bad as too late,
Could he only have waited he might have been great,
But he plumped into Helicon up to the waist,
And muddied the stream ere he took his first taste.

"There is Hawthorne, with genius so shrinking and rare
That you hardly at first see the strength that is there;
A frame so robust, with a nature so sweet,
So earnest, so graceful, so solid, so fleet,
Is worth a descent from Olympus to meet;
'Tis as if a rough oak that for ages had stood,
With his gnarled bony branches like ribs of the wood,
Should bloom, after cycles of struggle and scathe,
With a single anemone trembly and rathe;
His strength is so tender, his wildness so meek,
That a suitable parallel sets one to seek,—
He's a John Bunyan Fouqué, a Puritan Tieck;
When Nature was shaping him, clay was not granted
For making so full-sized a man as she wanted,
So, to fill out her model, a little she spared
From some finer-grained stuff for a woman prepared,
And she could not have hit a more excellent plan
For making him fully and perfectly man.
The success of her scheme gave her so much delight,
That she tried it again, shortly after, in Dwight;
Only, while she was kneading and shaping the clay,
She sang to her work in her sweet childish way,
And found, when she'd put the last touch to his soul,
That the music had somehow got mixed with the whole.

"Here's Cooper, who's written six volumes to show
He's as good as a lord: well, let's grant that he's so;
If a person prefer that description of praise,
Why, a coronet's certainly cheaper than bays;

But he need take no pains to convince us he's not
(As his enemies say) the American Scott.
Choose any twelve men, and let C. read aloud
That one of his novels of which he's most proud,
And I'd lay any bet that, without ever quitting
Their box, they'd be all, to a man, for acquitting.
He has drawn you one character, though, that is new,
One wildflower he's plucked that is wet with the dew
Of this fresh Western world, and, the thing not to mince,
He has done naught but copy it ill ever since;
His Indians, with proper respect be it said,
Are just Natty Bumpo daubed over with red,
And his very Long Toms are the same useful Nat,
Rigged up in duck pants and a sou'-wester hat,
(Though, once in a Coffin, a good chance was found
To have slipt the old fellow away underground.)
All his other men-figures are clothes upon sticks,
The *dernier chemise* of a man in a fix,
(As a captain besieged, when his garrison's small,
Sets up caps upon poles to be seen o'er the wall;)
And the women he draws from one model don't vary,
All sappy as maples and flat as a prairie.
When a character's wanted, he goes to the task
As a cooper would do in composing a cask;
He picks out the staves, of their qualities heedful,
Just hoops them together as tight as is needful,
And, if the best fortune should crown the attempt, he
Has made at the most something wooden and empty.

"Don't suppose I would underrate Cooper's abilities,
If I thought you'd do that, I should feel very ill at ease;
The men who have given to *one* character life
And objective existence, are not very rife;
You may number them all, both prose-writers and singers,
Without overrunning the bounds of your fingers,
And Natty won't go to oblivion quicker
Than Adams the parson or Primrose the vicar.

"There is one thing in Cooper I like, too, and that is
That on manners he lectures his countrymen gratis;
Not precisely so either, because, for a rarity,
He is paid for his tickets in unpopularity.
Now he may overcharge his American pictures,
But you'll grant there's a good deal of truth in his strictures;
And I honor the man who is willing to sink
Half his present repute for the freedom to think,
And, when he has thought, be his cause strong or weak,
Will risk t'other half for the freedom to speak,
Caring naught for what vengeance the mob has in store,
Let that mob be the upper ten thousand or lower.

"There are truths you Americans need to be told,
And it never'll refute them to swagger and scold;
John Bull, looking o'er the Atlantic, in choler
At your aptness for trade, says you worship the dollar;
But to scorn such i-dollar-try's what very few do,
And John goes to that church as often as you do.
No matter what John says, don't try to outcrow him,
'Tis enough to go quietly on and outgrow him;
Like most fathers, Bull hates to see Number One
Displacing himself in the mind of his son,
And detests the same faults in himself he'd neglected
When he sees them again in his child's glass reflected;
To love one another you're too like by half,
If he is a bull, you're a pretty stout calf,
And tear your own pasture for naught but to show
What a nice pair of horns you're beginning to grow.

"There are one or two things I should just like to hint,
For you don't often get the truth told you in print;
The most of you (this is what strikes all beholders)
Have a mental and physical stoop in the shoulders;
Though you ought to be free as the winds and the waves,
You've the gait and the manners of runaway slaves;
Tho' you brag of your New World, you don't half believe in it,
And as much of the Old as is possible weave in it;

Your goddess of freedom, a tight, buxom girl,
With lips like a cherry and teeth like a pearl,
With eyes bold as Herè's, and hair floating free,
And full of the sun as the spray of the sea,
Who can sing at a husking or romp at a shearing,
Who can trip through the forests alone without fearing,
Who can drive home the cows with a song through the grass,
Keeps glancing aside into Europe's cracked glass,
Hides her red hands in gloves, pinches up her lithe waist,
And makes herself wretched with transmarine taste;
She loses her fresh country charm when she takes
Any mirror except her own rivers and lakes.

"You steal Englishmen's books and think Englishmen's thought,
With their salt on her tail your wild eagle is caught;
Your literature suits its each whisper and motion
To what will be thought of it over the ocean;
The cast clothes of Europe your statesmanship tries
And mumbles again the old blarneys and lies;—
Forget Europe wholly, your veins throb with blood
To which the dull current in hers is but mud;
Let her sneer, let her say your experiment fails,
In her voice there's a tremble e'en now while she rails,
And your shore will soon be in the nature of things
Covered thick with gilt driftwood of runaway kings,
Where alone, as it were in a Longfellow's Waif,
Her fugitive pieces will find themselves safe.
O, my friends, thank your God, if you have one, that he
'Twixt the Old World and you set the gulf of a sea;
Be strong-backed, brown-handed, upright as your pines,
By the scale of a hemisphere shape your designs,
Be true to yourselves and this new nineteenth age,
As a statue by Powers, or a picture by Page,
Plough, dig, sail, forge, build, carve, paint, make all things new,
To your own New-World instincts contrive to be true,
Keep your ears open wide to the Future's first call,
Be whatever you will, but yourselves first of all,

Stand fronting the dawn on Toil's heaven-scaling peaks,
And become my new race of more practical Greeks.—
Hem! your likeness at present, I shudder to tell o't,
Is that you have your slaves, and the Greek had his helot."

Here a gentleman present, who had in his attic
More pepper than brains, shrieked—"The man's a fanatic,
I'm a capital tailor with warm tar and feathers,
And will make him a suit that'll serve in all weathers;
But we'll argue the point first, I'm willing to reason 't,
Palaver before condemnation 's but decent,
So, through my humble person, Humanity begs
Of the friends of true freedom a loan of bad eggs."
But Apollo let one such a look of his show forth
As when ἤιε νύχτι ἐοιχώς, and so forth,
And the gentleman somehow slunk out of the way,
But, as he was going, gained courage to say,—
"At slavery in the abstract my whole soul rebels,
I am as strongly opposed to't as any one else."
"Ay, no doubt, but whenever I've happened to meet
With a wrong or a crime, it is always concrete,"
Answered Phœbus severely; then turning to us,
"The mistakes of such fellows as just made the fuss
Is only in taking a great busy nation
For a part of their pitiful cotton-plantation.—
But there comes Miranda, Zeus! where shall I flee to?
She has such a penchant for bothering me too!
She always keeps asking if I don't observe a
Particular likeness 'twixt her and Minerva;
She tells me my efforts in verse are quite clever;—
She's been travelling now, and will be worse than ever;
One would think, though, a sharp-sighted noter she'd be
Of all that's worth mentioning over the sea,
For a woman must surely see well, if she try,
The whole of whose being's a capital **I**:
She will take an old notion, and make it her own,
By saying it o'er in her Sybilline tone,
Or persuade you 'tis something tremendously deep,

By repeating it so as to put you to sleep;
And she well may defy any mortal to see through it,
When once she has mixed up her infinite *me* through it.
There is one thing she owns in her own single right,
It is native and genuine—namely, her spite:
Though, when acting as censor, she privately blows
A censor of vanity 'neath her own nose."

Here Miranda came up, and said, "Phœbus! you know
That the infinite Soul has its infinite woe,
As I ought to know, having lived cheek by jowl,
Since the day I was born, with the Infinite Soul;
I myself introduced, I myself, I alone,
To my Land's better life authors solely my own,
Who the sad heart of earth on their shoulders have taken,
Whose works sound a depth by Life's quiet unshaken,
Such as Shakspeare, for instance, the Bible, and Bacon,
Not to mention my own works; Time's nadir is fleet,
And, as for myself, I'm quite out of conceit,"—

"Quite out of conceit! I'm enchanted to hear it,"
Cried Appollo aside, "Who'd have thought she was near it?
To be sure one is apt to exhaust those commodities
He uses too fast, yet in this case as odd it is
As if Neptune should say to his turbots and whitings,
'I'm as much out of salt as Miranda's own writings,'
(Which, as she in her own happy manner has said,
Sound a depth, for 'tis one of the functions of lead.)
She often has asked me if I could not find
A place somewhere near me that suited her mind;
I know but a single one vacant, which she,
With her rare talent that way, would fit to a T.
And it would not imply any pause or cessation
In the work she esteems her peculiar vocation,—
She may enter on duty to-day, if she chooses,
And remain Tiring-woman for life to the Muses."

(Miranda meanwhile has succeeded in driving
Up into a corner, in spite of their striving,

A small flock of terrified victims, and there,
With an I-turn-the-crank-of-the-Universe air
And a tone which, at least to *my* fancy, appears
Not so much to be entering as boxing your ears,
Is unfolding a tale (of herself, I surmise,)
For 'tis dotted as thick as a peacock's with I's.)
Apropos of Miranda, I'll rest on my oars
And drift through a trifling digression on bores,
For, though not wearing ear-rings *in more majorum,*
Our ears are kept bored just as if we still wore 'em.
There was one feudal custom worth keeping, at least,
Roasted bores made a part of each well-ordered feast,
And of all quiet pleasures the very *ne plus*
Was in hunting wild bores as the tame ones hunt us.
Archæologians, I know, who have personal fears
Of this wise application of hounds and of spears,
Have tried to make out, with a zeal more than wonted,
'Twas a kind of wild swine that our ancestors hunted;
But I'll never believe that the age which has strewn
Europe o'er with cathedrals, and otherwise shown
That it knew what was what, could by chance not have known,
(Spending, too, its chief time with its buff on, no doubt,)
Which beast 'twould improve the world most to thin out.
I divide bores myself, in the manner of rifles,
Into two great divisions, regardless of trifles;—
There's your smooth-bore and screw-bore, who do not much vary
In the weight of cold lead they respectively carry.
The smooth-bore is one in whose essence the mind
Not a corner nor cranny to cling by can find;
You feel as in nightmares sometimes, when you slip
Down a steep slated roof where there's nothing to grip,
You slide and you slide, the blank horror increases,
You had rather by far be at once smashed to pieces,
You fancy a whirlpool below white and frothing,
And finally drop off and light upon—nothing.
The screw-bore has twists in him, faint predilections
For going just wrong in the tritest directions;

When he's wrong he is flat, when he's right he can't show it,
He'll tell you what Snooks said about the new poet,[2]
Or how Fogrum was outraged by Tennyson's Princess;
He has spent all his spare time and intellect since his
Birth in perusing, on each art and science,
Just the books in which no one puts any reliance,
And though *nemo*, we're told, *horis omnibus sapit,*
The rule will not fit him, however you shape it,
For he has a perennial foison of sappiness;
He has just enough force to spoil half your day's happiness,
And to make him a sort of mosquito to be with,
But just not enough to dispute or agree with.

These sketches I made (not to be too explicit)
From two honest fellows who made me a visit,
And broke, like the tale of the Bear and the Fiddle,
My reflections on Halleck short off by the middle;
I shall not now go into the subject more deeply,
For I notice that some of my readers look sleep'ly,
I will barely remark that, 'mongst civilized nations,
There's none that displays more exemplary patience
Under all sorts of boring, at all sorts of hours,
From all sorts of desperate persons, than ours.
Not to speak of our papers, our State legislatures,
And other such trials for sensitive natures,
Just look for a moment at Congress,—appalled,
My fancy shrinks back from the phantom it called;
Why, there's scarcely a member unworthy to frown
'Neath what Fourier nicknames the Boreal crown;
Only think what that infinite bore-pow'r could do
If applied with a utilitarian view;
Suppose, for example, we shipped it with care
To Sahara's great desert and let it bore there,
If they held one short session and did nothing else,
They'd fill the whole waste with Artesian wells.
But 'tis time now with pen phonographic to follow
Through some more of his sketches our laughing Appollo:—

[2] (If you call Snooks an owl, he will show by his looks
That he's morally certain you're jealous of Snooks.)

"There comes Harry Franco, and, as he draws near,
You find that's a smile which you took for a sneer;
One half of him contradicts t'other, his wont
Is to say very sharp things and do very blunt;
His manner's as hard as his feelings are tender,
And a *sortie* he'll make when he means to surrender;
He's in joke half the time when he seems to be sternest,
When he seems to be joking, be sure he's in earnest;
He has common sense in a way that's uncommon,
Hates humbug and cant, loves his friends like a woman,
Builds his dislikes of cards and his friendships of oak,
Loves a prejudice better than aught but a joke,
Is half upright Quaker, half downright Come-outer,
Loves Freedom too well to go stark mad about her,
Quite artless himself is a lover of Art,
Shuts you out of his secrets and into his heart,
And though not a poet, yet all must admire
In his letters of Pinto his skill on the liar.

"There comes Poe with his raven, like Barnaby Rudge,
Three-fifths of him genius and two-fifths sheer fudge,
Who talks like a book of iambs and pentameters,
In a way to make people of common-sense damn metres,
Who has written some things quite the best of their kind,
But the heart somehow seems all squeezed out by the mind,
Who—but hey-day! What's this? Messieurs Mathews and Poe,
You mustn't fling mud-balls at Longfellow so,
Does it make a man worse that his character's such
As to make his friends love him (as you think) too much?
Why, there is not a bard at this moment alive
More willing than he that his fellows should thrive;
While you are abusing him thus, even now
He would help either one of you out of a slough;
You may say that he's smooth and all that till you're hoarse,
But remember that elegance also is force;
After polishing granite as much as you will,
The heart keeps its tough old persistency still;

Deduct all you can that still keeps you at bay,—
Why, he'll live till men weary of Collins and Gray;
I'm not over-fond of Greek metres in English,
To me rhyme's a gain, so it be not too jinglish,
And your modern hexameter verses are no more
Like Greek ones than sleek Mr. Pope is like Homer;
As the roar of the sea to the coo of a pigeon is,
So, compared to your moderns, sounds old Melesigenes;
I may be too partial, the reason, perhaps, o't is
That I've heard the old blind man recite his own rhapsodies,
And my ear with that music impregnate may be,
Like the poor exiled shell with the soul of the sea,
Or as one can't bear Strauss when his nature is cloven
To its deeps within deeps by the stroke of Beethoven;
But, set that aside, and 'tis truth that I speak,
Had Theocritus written in English, not Greek,
I believe that his exquisite sense would scarce change a line
In that rare, tender, virgin-like pastoral Evangeline.
That's not ancient nor modern, its place is apart
Where time has no sway, in the realm of pure Art,
'Tis a shrine of retreat from Earth's hubbub and strife
As quiet and chaste as the author's own life.

"There comes Philothea, her face all a-glow,
She has just been dividing some poor creature's woe,
And can't tell which pleases her most, to relieve
His want, or his story to hear and believe;
No doubt against many deep griefs she prevails,
For her ear is the refuge of destitute tales;
She knows well that silence is sorrow's best food,
And that talking draws off from the heart its black blood,
So she'll listen with patience and let you unfold
Your bundle of rags as 'twere pure cloth of gold,
Which, indeed, it all turns to as soon as she's touched it,
And, (to borrow a phrase from the nursery,) *muched* it,
She has such a musical taste, she will go
Any distance to hear one who draws a long bow;

She will swallow a wonder by mere might and main
And thinks it geometry's fault if she's fain
To consider things flat, inasmuch as they're plain;
Facts with her are accomplished, as Frenchmen would say,
They will prove all she wishes them to—either way,
And, as fact lies on this side or that, we must try,
If we're seeking the truth, to find where it don't lie;
I was telling her once of a marvellous aloe
That for thousands of years had looked spindling and sallow,
And, though nursed by the fruitfullest powers of mud,
Had never vouchsafed e'en so much as a bud,
Till its owner remarked, as a sailor, you know,
Often will in a calm, that it never would blow,
For he wished to exhibit the plant, and designed
That its blowing should help him in raising the wind;
At last it was told him that if he should water
Its roots with the blood of his unmarried daughter,
(Who was born, as her mother, a Calvinist said,
With a Baxter's effectual call on her head,)
It would blow as the obstinate breeze did when by a
Like decree of her father died Iphigenia;
At first he declared he himself would be blowed
Ere his conscience with such a foul crime he would load,
But the thought, coming oft, grew less dark than before,
And he mused, as each creditor knocked at his door,
If *this* were but done they would dun me no more;
I told Philothea his struggles and doubts,
And how he considered the ins and the outs
Of the visions he had, and the dreadful dyspepsy,
How he went to the seer that live at Po'keepsie,
How the seer advised him to sleep on it first
And to read his big volume in case of the worst,
And further advised he should pay him five dollars
For writing HUM, HUM, on his wristbands and collars;
Three years and ten days these dark words he had studied
When the daughter was missed, and the aloe had budded;
I told how he watched it grow large and more large,
And wondered how much for the show he should charge,—

She had listened with utter indifference to this, till
I told how it bloomed, and discharging its pistil
With an aim the Eumenides dictated, shot
The botanical filicide dead on the spot;
It had blown, but he reaped not his horrible gains,
For it blew with such force as to blow out his brains,
And the crime was blown also, because on the wad,
Which was paper, was writ 'Visitation of God,'
As well as a thrilling account of the deed
Which the coroner kindly allowed me to read.

"Well, my friend took this story up just, to be sure,
As one might a poor foundling that's laid at one's door;
She combed it and washed it and clothed it and fed it,
And as if 'twere her own child most tenderly bred it,
Laid the scene (of the legend, I mean,) far away a-
mong the green vales underneath Himalaya.
And by artist-like touches, laid on here and there,
Made the whole thing so touching, I frankly declare
I have read it all thrice, and, perhaps I am weak,
But I found every time there were tears on my cheek.

"The pole, science tells us, the magnet controls,
But she is a magnet to emigrant Poles,
And folks with a mission that nobody knows,
Throng thickly about her as bees round a rose;
She can fill up the *carets* in such, make their scope
Converge to some focus of rational hope,
And, with sympathies fresh as the morning, their gall
Can transmute into honey,—but this is not all;
Not only for those she has solace, oh, say,
Vice's desperate nursling adrift in Broadway,
Who clingest, with all that is left of thee human,
To the last slender spar from the wreck of the woman,
Hast thou not found one shore where those tired drooping feet
Could reach firm mother-earth, one full heart on whose beat
The soothed head in silence reposing could hear
The chimes of far childhood throb thick on the ear?

Ah, there's many a beam from the fountain of day
That to reach us unclouded, must pass, on its way,
Through the soul of a woman, and hers is wide ope
To the influence of Heaven as the blue eyes of Hope;
Yes, a great soul is hers, one that dares to go in
To the prison, the slave-hut, the alleys of sin,
And to bring into each, or to find there, some line
Of the never completely out-trampled divine;
If her heart at high floods swamps her brain now and then,
'Tis but richer for that when the tide ebbs agen,
As, after old Nile has subsided, his plain
Overflows with a second broad deluge of grain;
What a wealth would it bring to the narrow and sour
Could they be as a Child but for one little hour!

"What! Irving? thrice welcome, warm heart and fine brain,
You bring back the happiest spirit from Spain,
And the gravest sweet humor, that ever were there
Since Cervantes met death in his gentle despair;
Nay, don't be embarrassed, nor look so beseeching,—
I shan't run directly against my own preaching,
And, having just laughed at their Raphaels and Dantes,
Go to setting you up beside matchless Cervantes;
But allow me to speak what I honestly feel,—
To a true poet-heart add the fun of Dick Steele,
Throw in all of Addison, *minus* the chill,
With the whole of that partnership's stock and good will,
Mix well, and while stirring, hum o'er, as a spell,
The fine *old* English Gentleman, simmer it well,
Sweeten just to your own private liking, then strain,
That only the finest and clearest remain,
Let it stand out of doors till a soul it receives
From the warm lazy sun loitering down through green leaves,
And you'll find a choice nature, not wholly deserving
A name either English or Yankee,—just Irving.

"There goes,—but *stet nominis umbra*,—his name
You'll be glad enough, some day or other, to claim,

And will all crowd about him and swear that you knew him
If some English hack-critic should chance to review him;
The old *procos ante ne projiciatis*
MARGARITAS, for him you have verified gratis;
What matters his name? Why, it may be Sylvester,
Judd, Junior, or Junius, Ulysses, or Nestor,
For aught *I* know or care; 'tis enough that I look
On the author of 'Margaret,' the first Yankee book
With the *soul* of Down East in't, and things farther East,
As far as the threshold of morning, at least,
Where awaits the fair dawn of the simple and true,
Of the day that comes slowly to make all things new.
'T has a smack of pine woods, of bare field and bleak hill
Such as only the breed of the Mayflower could till;
The Puritan's shown in it, touch to the core,
Such as prayed, smiting Agag on red Marston moor;
With an unwilling humor, half-choked by the drouth
In brown hollows about the inhospitable mouth;
With a soul full of poetry, though it has qualms
About finding a happiness out of the Psalms;
Full of tenderness, too, though it shrinks in the dark,
Hamadryad-like, under the coarse, shaggy bark;
That sees visions, knows wrestlings of God with the Will,
And has its own Sinais and thunderings still."—

Here, "Forgive me, Apollo," I cried, "while I pour
My heart out to my birth-place: O, loved more and more
Dear Baystate, from whose rocky bosom thy sons
Should suck milk, strong-will-giving, brave, such as runs
In the veins of old Graylock,—who is it that dares
Call thee pedler, a soul wrapt in bank books and shares?
It is false! She's a Poet! I see, as I write,
Along the far railroad the steam-snake glide white,
The cataract-throb of her mill-hearts I hear,
The swift strokes of trip-hammers weary my ear,
Sledges ring upon anvils, through logs the saw screams,
Blocks swing up to their place, beetles drive home the beams:—

It is songs such as these that she croons to the din
Of her fast-flying shuttles, year out and year in,
While from earth's farthest corner there comes not a breeze
But wafts her the buzz of her gold-gleaning bees:
What though those horn hands have as yet found small time
For painting and sculpture and music and rhyme?
These will come in due order, the need that pressed sorest
Was to vanquish the seasons, the ocean, the forest,
To bridle and harness the rivers, the steam,
Making that whirl her mill-wheels, this tug in her team,
To vassalize old tyrant Winter, and make
Him delve surlily for her on river and lake;—
When this New World was parted, she strove not to shirk
Her lot in the heirdom, the tough, silent Work,
The hero-share ever, from Herakles down
To Odin, the Earth's iron sceptre and crown;
Yes, thou dear, noble Mother! if ever men's praise
Could be claimed for creating heroical lays,
Thou hast won it; if ever the laurel divine
Crowned the Maker and Builder, that glory is thine!
Thy songs are right epic, they tell how this rude
Rock-rib of our earth here was tamed and subdued;
Thou hast written them plain on the face of the planet
In brave, deathless letters of iron and granite;
Thou hast printed them deep for all time; they are set
From the same runic type-fount and alphabet
With thy stout Berkshire hills and the arms of thy Bay,—
They are staves from the burly old Mayflower lay.
If the drones of the Old World, in querulous ease,
Ask thy Art and thy Letters, point proudly to these,
Or, if they deny these are Letters and Art,
Toil on with the same old invincible heart;
Thou art rearing the pedestal broad-based and grand
Whereon the fair shapes of the Artist shall stand,
And creating, through labors undaunted and long,
The true theme for all Sculpture and Painting and Song!

"But my good mother Baystate wants no praise of mine,
She learned from *her* mother a precept divine
About something that butters no parsnips, her *forte*
In another direction lies, work is her sport,
(Though she'll curtsey and set her cap straight, that she will,
If you talk about Plymouth and one Bunker's hill.)
The dear, notable goodwife! by this time of night,
Her hearth is swept clean, and her fire burning bright,
And she sits in a chair (of home plan and make) rocking,
Musing much, all the while, as she darns on a stocking,
Whether turkeys will come pretty high next Thanksgiving,
Whether flour'll be so dear, for, as sure as she's living,
She will use rye-and-injun then, whether the pig
By this time ain't got pretty tolerable big,
And whether to sell it outright will be best,
Or to smoke hams and shoulders and salt down the rest,—
At this minute, she'd swop all my verses, ah, cruel!
For the last patent stove that is saving of fuel;
So I'll just let Apollo go on, for his phiz
Shows I've kept him awaiting too long as it is."

"If our friend, there, who seems a reporter, is through
With his burst of emotion, our theme we'll pursue,"
Said Apollo; some smiled, and, indeed, I must own
There was something sarcastic, perhaps, in his tone;—

"There's Holmes, who is matchless among you for wit;
A Leyden-jar always full-charged, from which flit
The electrical tingles of hit after hit;
In long poems 'tis painful sometimes and invites
A thought of the way the new Telegraph writes,
Which pricks down its little sharp sentences spitefully
As if you got more than you'd title to rightfully,
And if it were hoping its wild father Lightning
Would flame in for a second and give you a fright'ning.
He has perfect sway of what *I* call a sham metre,
But many admire it, the English hexameter,

And Campbell, I think, wrote most commonly worse,
With less nerve, swing, and fire in the same kind of verse,
Nor e'er achieved aught in't so worthy of praise
As the tribute of Holmes to the grand *Marseillaise*.
You went crazy last year over Bulwer's New Timon;—
Why, if B., to the day of his dying, should rhyme on,
Heaping verses on verses and tomes upon tomes,
He could ne'er reach the best point and vigor of Holmes.
His are just the fine hands, too, to weave you a lyric
Full of fancy, fun, feeling, or spiced with satyric
In so kindly a measure, that nobody knows
What to do but e'en join in the laugh, friends and foes.

"There is Lowell, who's striving Parnassus to climb
With a whole bale of *isms* tied together with rhyme,
He might get on alone, spite of brambles and boulders,
But he can't with that bundle he has on his shoulders,
The top of the hill he will ne'er come nigh reaching
Till he learns the distinction 'twixt singing and preaching;
His lyre has some chords that would ring pretty well,
But he'd rather by half make a drum of the shell,
And rattle away till he's old as Methusalem,
At the head of a march to the last new Jerusalem.

"There goes Halleck, whose Fanny's a pseudo Don Juan,
With the wickedness out that gave salt to the true one,
He's a wit, though, I hear, of the very first order,
And once made a pun on the words soft Recorder;
More than this, he's a very great poet, I'm told,
And has had his works published in crimson and gold,
With something they call 'Illustrations,' to wit,
Like those with which Chapman obscured Holy Writ,[3]
Which are said to illustrate, because, as I view it,
Like *lucus a non,* they precisely don't do it;
Let a man who can write what himself understands
Keep clear, if he can, of designing men's hands,

[3] (Cuts rightly called wooden, as all must admit.)

Who bury the sense, if there's any worth having,
And then very honestly call it engraving.
But, to quit *badinage,* which there isn't much wit in,
No doubt Halleck's better than all he has written;
In his verse a clear glimpse you will frequently find,
If not of a great, of a fortunate mind,
Which contrives to be true to its natural loves
In a world of back-offices, ledgers and stoves.
When his heart breaks away from the brokers and banks,
And kneels in its own private shrine to give thanks,
There's a genial manliness in him that earns
Our sincerest respect, (read, for instance, his "Burns,")
And we can't but regret (seek excuse where we may)
That so much of a man has been peddled away.

"But what's that? a mass-meeting? No, there come in lots
The American Disraelis, Bulwers, and Scotts,
And in short the American everything-elses,
Each charging the others with envies and jealousies;—
By the way, 'tis a fact that displays what profusions
Of all kinds of greatness bless free institutions,
That while the Old World has produced barely eight
Of such poets as all men agree to call great,
And of other great characters hardly a score,
(One might safely say less than that rather than more,)
With you every year a whole crop is begotten,
They're as much of a staple as corn, or as cotton;
Why, there's scarcely a huddle of log-huts and shanties
That has not brought forth its own Miltons and Dantes;
I myself know ten Byrons, one Coleridge, three Shelleys,
Two Raphaels, six Titians, (I think) one Apelles,
Leonardos and Rubenses plenty as lichens,
One (but that one is plenty) American Dickens,
A whole flock of Lambs, any number of Tennysons,—
In short, if a man has the luck to have any sons,
He may feel pretty certain that one out of twain
Will be some very great person over again.

There is one inconvenience in all this which lies
In the fact that by contrast we estimate size,[4]
And, where there are none except Titans, great stature
Is only a simple proceeding of nature.
What puff the strained sails of your praise shall you furl at, if
The calmest degree that you know is superlative?
At Rome, all whom Charon took into his wherry must,
As a matter of course, be well *issimus*ed and *errimus*ed,
A Greek, too, could feel, while in that famous boat he tost,
That his friends would take care he wa ιστοϛed and ωταιοϛed,
And formerly we, as through grave-yards we past,
Thought the world went from bad to worse fearfully fast;
Let us glance for a moment, 'tis well worth the pains,
And note what an average grave-yard contains;
There lie levellers levelled, duns done up themselves,
There are booksellers finally laid on their shelves,
Horizontally there lie upright politicians,
Dose-a-dose with their patients sleep faultless physicians,
There are slave-drivers quietly whipt under-ground,
There bookbinders, done up in boards, are fast bound,
There card-players wait till the last trump be played,
There all the choice spirits get finally laid,
There the babe that's unborn is supplied with a berth,
There men without legs get their six feet of earth,
There lawyers repose, each wrapt up in his case,
There seekers of office are sure of a place,
There defendant and plaintiff get equally cast,
There shoemakers quietly stick to the last,
There brokers at length become silent as stocks,
There stage-drivers sleep without quitting their box,
And so forth and so forth and so forth and so on,
With this kind of stuff one might endlessly go on;

[4] That is in most cases we do, but not all,
Past a doubt, there are men who are innately small,
Such as Blank, who, without being 'minished a tittle,
Might stand for a type of the Absolute Little.

To come to the point, I may safely assert you
Will find in each yard every cardinal virtue; [5]
Each has six truest patriots: four discoverers of ether,
Who never had thought on't nor mentioned it either:
Ten poets, the greatest who ever wrote rhyme:
Two hundred and forty first men of their time:
One person whose portrait just gave the least hint
Its original had a most horrible squint:
One critic, most (what do they call it?) reflective,
Who never had used the phrase ob- or subjective:
Forty fathers of Freedom, of whom twenty bred
Their sons for the rice-swamps, at so much a head,
And their daughters for—faugh! thirty mothers of Gracchi:
Non-resistants who gave many a spiritual black-eye:
Eight true friends of their kind, one of whom was a jailor:
Four captains almost as astounding as Taylor:
Two dozen of Italy's exiles who shoot us his
Kaisership daily, stern pen-and-ink Brutuses,
Who, in Yankee back-parlors, with crucified smile,[6]
Mount serenely their country's funereal pile:
Ninety-nine Irish heroes, ferocious rebellers
'Gainst the Saxon in cis-marine garrets and cellars,
Who shake their dread fists o'er the sea and all that,—
As long as a copper drops into the hat:
Nine hundred Teutonic republicans stark
From Vaterland's battles just won—in the Park,
Who the happy profession of martyrdom take
Whenever it gives them a chance at a steak:
Sixty-two second Washingtons: two or three Jacksons:
And so many everything else that it racks one's
Poor memory too much to continue the list,
Especially now they no longer exist;—
I would merely observe that you've taken to giving
The puffs that belong to the dead to the living,

[5] (And at this just conclusion will surely arrive,
That the goodness of earth is more dead than alive.)
[6] Not forgetting their tea and their toast, though, the while.

And that somehow your trump-of-contemporary-doom's tones
Is tuned after old dedications and tombstones."—

Here the critic came in and a thistle presented [7]—
From a frown to a smile the god's features relented,
As he stared at his envoy, who, swelling with pride,
To the god's asking look, nothing daunted, replied,
"You're surprised, I suppose, I was absent so long,
But your godship respecting the lilies was wrong;
I hunted the garden from one end to t'other,
And got no reward but vexation and bother,
Till, tossed out with weeds in a corner to wither,
This one lily I found and made haste to bring hither."

"Did he think I had given him a book to review?
I ought to have known what the fellow would do,"
Muttered Phœbus aside, "for a thistle will pass
Beyond doubt for the queen of all flowers with an ass;
He has chosen in just the same way as he'd choose
His specimens out of the books he reviews
And now, as this offers an excellent text,
I'll give 'em some brief hints on criticism next."
So, musing a moment, he turned to the crowd,
And, clearing his voice, spoke as follows aloud,—

"My friends, in the happier days of the muse,
We were luckily free from such things as reviews;
Then naught came between with its fog to make clearer
The heart of the poet to that of his hearer;
Then the poet brought heaven to the people, and they
Felt that they, too, were poets in hearing his lay;
Then the poet was prophet, the past in his soul
Pre-created the future, both parts of one whole;
Then for him there was nothing too great or too small,
For one natural deity sanctified all;
Then the bard owned no clipper and meter of moods
Save the spirit of silence that hovers and broods
O'er the seas and the mountains, the rivers and woods;

[7] Turn back now to page—goodness only knows what,
And take a fresh hold on the thread of my plot.

He asked not earth's verdict, forgetting the clods,
His soul soared and sang to an audience of gods;
'Twas for them that he measured the thought and the line,
And shaped for their vision the perfect design,
With as glorious a foresight, a balance as true,
As swung out the worlds in the infinite blue;
Then a glory and greatness invested man's heart,
The universal, which now stands estranged and apart,
In the free individual moulded, was Art;
Then the forms of the Artist seemed thrilled with desire,
For something as yet unattained, fuller, higher,
As once with her lips, lifted hands, and eyes listening,
And her whole upward soul in her countenance glistening,
Eurydice stood—like a beacon unfired,
Which, once touchd with flame, will leap heave'nward inspired—
And waited with answering kindle to mark
The first gleam of Orpheus that pained the red Dark;
Then painting, song, sculpture, did more than relieve
The need that men feel to create and believe,
And as, in all beauty, who listens with love,
Hears these words oft repeated—'beyond and above,'
So these seemed to be but the visible sign
Of the grasp of the soul after things more divine;
They were ladders the Artist erected to climb
O'er the narrow horizon of space and of time,
And we see there the footsteps by which men had gained
To the one rapturous glimpse of the never-attained,
As shepherds could erst sometimes trace in the sod
The last spurning print of a sky-cleaving god.

"But now, on the poet's dis-privacied moods
With *do this* and *do that* the pert critic intrudes;
While he thinks he's been barely fulfilling his duty
To interpret 'twixt men and their own sense of beauty,
And has striven, while others sought honor or pelf,
To make his kind happy as he was himself,
He finds he's been guilty of horrid offences
In all kinds of moods, numbers, genders, and tenses;

He's been *ob* and *sub*jective, what Kettle calls Pot,
Precisely, at all events, what he ought not,
You have done this, says one judge; *done that,* says another
You should have done this, grumbles one; *that,* says t'other;
Never mind what he touches, one shrieks out *Taboo!*
And while he is wondering what he shall do,
Since each suggests opposite topics for song,
They all shout together *you're right!* or *you're wrong!*

"Nature fits all her children with something to do,
He who would write and can't write, can surely review,
Can set up a small booth as critic and sell us his
Petty conceit and his pettier jealousies;
Thus a lawyer's apprentice, just out of his teens,
Will do for the Jeffrey of six magazines;
Having read Johnson's lives of the poets half through,
There's nothing on earth he's not competent to;
He reviews with as much nonchalance as he whistles,—
He goes through a book and just picks out the thistles,
It matters not whether he blame or commend,
If he's bad as a foe, he's far worse as a friend;
Let an author but write what's above his poor scope,
And he'll go to work gravely and twist up a rope,
And, inviting the world to see punishment done,
Hang himself up to bleach in the wind and the sun;
'Tis delightful to see, when a man comes along
Who has any thing in him peculiar and strong,
Every cockboat that swims clear its fierce (pop-) gundeck at him
And make as he passes its ludicrous Peck at him,"—

Here, Miranda came up and began, "As to that,"—
Apollo at once seized his gloves, cane, and hat,
And, seeing the place getting rapidly cleared,
I, too, snatched my notes and forthwith disappeared.

CHARLES F. BRIGGS
("HARRY FRANKO")

Uncle Tomitudes

HERE is a miracle! or something, at least, that has not happened before, and consequently, for which the world was not prepared; for the belief of King Solomon still prevails, that nothing will be which has not already been, and every new thing is incredible until it has been duplicated. Uncle Tom, therefore, is a miracle, his advent had not been foreseen nor foretold, and nobody believes in him now that he has come, and made good his claim to be considered somebody. But, Uncle Tom's superiors were not believed in at first, and he can well afford to bide his time.

Never since books were first printed has the success of Uncle Tom been equalled; the history of literature contains nothing parallel to it, nor approaching it; it is, in fact, the first real success in book-making, for all other successes in literature were failures when compared with the success of Uncle Tom. And it is worth remembering that this first success in a field which all the mighty men of the earth have labored in, was accomplished by an American woman. Who reads an American book, did you inquire, Mr. Smith? Why, your comfortable presence should have been preserved in the world a year or two longer, that you might have asked, as you would have done, "who does not?"

There have been a good many books which were considered popular on their first appearance, which were widely read and more widely talked about. But, what were they all, compared with Uncle Tom, whose honest countenance now overshadows the reading world, like the dark cloud with a silver lining. Don Quixote was a popular book on its first coming out, and so was Gil Blas, and Richardson's Pamela, and Fielding's Tom Jones, and Hannah More's Cœlebs, and Gibbon's Decline and Fall; and so were the Vicar of Wakefield, and Rasselas, and the Tale of a Tub, and Evelina, the Lady of the Lake, Waverley, the Sorrows of Werter, Childe Harold, the Spy, Pelham, Vivian Grey, Pickwick, the Mysteries of Paris, and Macaulay's History. These are among the most famous books that rose suddenly in popular esteem on their first appearance, but the united sale of the whole of them, within the first nine months of their publication, would not equal the sale of Uncle Tom in the same time.

But this success does not, by any means, argue that Uncle Tom is superior to all other books; but it is an unmistakable indication that it is a live book, and that it will continue to live when many other books which have been pronounced immortal, shall be dead and buried in an oblivion, from which there is no resurrection.

Uncle Tom is not only a miracle of itself, but it announces the commencement of a miraculous Era in the literary world. A dozen years ago, Uncle Tom would have been a comparative failure—there might not have been more than a million copies sold in the first year of its publication. Such a phenomenon as its present popularity could have happened only in the present wondrous age. It required all the aid of our new machinery to produce the phenomenon; our steam-presses, steam-ships, steam-carriages, iron roads, electric telegraphs, and universal peace among the reading nations of the earth. But beyond all, it required the readers to consume the books, and these have never before been so numerous; the next year, they will be more numerous still, and Uncle Tom may be eclipsed by the shadow of a new comer in the reading world. It is not Uncle Tom alone who has made the way for himself; the road to popularity has been preparing for him, ever since the birth of Cadmus; he has only proclaimed the fact that the great avenues of literature are all open, wide, and well paved, and free to all who have the strength to travel in them. Hereafter, the book which does not circulate to the extent of a million of copies, will be regarded as a failure. What the first edition of a popular novel will be by-and-by, when the telegraphic wires will be printing it simultaneously, in New-York, St. Petersburgh, San Francisco, Pekin and the intermediate cities, it is not easy to estimate. Then, when an international copyright shall secure the whole world to the popular author, for his market, authorship, we imagine, will be a rather more lucrative employment than it happens to be at present. The possibility of such a time does not appear half so improbable now, as the actualities of Uncle Tom would have sounded in the earlier days of the Edinburgh Review.

It is but nine months since this Iliad of the blacks, as an English reviewer calls Uncle Tom, made its appearance among books, and already its sale has exceeded a million of copies; author and publisher have made fortunes out of it, and Mrs. Stowe, who was before unknown, is as familiar a name in all parts of the civilized world as that of Homer or Shakspeare. Nearly two hundred thousand copies of the first edition of the work have been sold in the United States, and the publishers say they are unable to meet the growing demand. The book was published on the 20th of last March, and on the 1st of December there had been sold one hundred and twenty thousand sets of the edition in two volumes, fifty thousand copies of the cheaper edition in one, and three thousand copies of the costly illustrated edition. The publishers have kept four steam-presses running, night and day, Sundays only excepted, and at double the ordinary speed, being equal to sixteen presses worked ten hours a day at the usual speed. They keep two hundred hands constantly employed in binding Uncle Tom, and he has consumed five thousand reams of white paper, weighing seventy-five tons. They have paid to the author twenty thousand three hundred dollars as her share of the profits on the actual cash sales of the first nine months. But it is in England where Uncle Tom has made his deepest mark. Such has been the sensation produced by the book there, and so numerous have been the editions published, that it is extremely difficult to collect the statistics of its circulation with a tolerable degree of exactness. But we know of twenty rival editions in England and Scotland, and that millions of copies have been produced. Bentley has placed it among his standard novels. Routledge issues a handsome edition of it with a preface by the Earl of Carlisle; and this virtuous nobleman, with the blood of all the Howards in his veins, sees nothing out of the way in venting his indignation against American Slavery, in the preface of a book which is stolen from its author and published without her consent. Bentley also tacks on an "indignant preface" to his edition, but it is stated that he gives a percentage on the sale to the author, which gives him a right to be indignant, if he chooses. But the Earl of Carlisle and Routledge might have reserved their indignation against slavery, it strikes us until they had taken to honest courses themselves. Another publisher in London issues an edition and proposes to share profits with the author, while a penny subscription has been got up as a testimonial to her from all the readers of the work in Great Britain and Ireland. We have seen it stated that there were thirty different editions published in London within six months of the publication of the work here, and one firm keeps four hundred men employed in printing and binding it. There have been popular editions published also, in Edinburgh and in Glasgow; and it has been dramatized and produced on the boards of nearly every theatre in the Kingdom. Uncle Tom was played in six different theatres in London at the same time. An illustrated edition is now publishing in London by a bookseller named Cassell, the illustrations being furnished by the famous and inimitable George Cruikshank. The same publisher has issued an Uncle Tom Almanac, with designs by some of the most eminent artists of London. The whole Beecher family, of which Mrs. Stowe is a member, have been glorified in the English periodicals, and are exciting as much attention just now, as the Napoleonic family, to which they bear great resemblance; one being a family of Kings and Queens, and the other of preachers and authors—sovereigns in the intellectual world.

Uncle Tom was not long in making his way across the British Channel, and four rival editions are claiming the attention of the Parisians, one under the title of *le Père Tom,* and another of *la Case de l'Oncle Tom.* But the fresh racy descriptions of the author lose their vigor and force when rendered into French, though the interest of the narrative remains. The book reads better in German than in French, and makes a deeper impression on the Teuton than upon the Gallic mind.

The *Allgemein Zeitung,* of Augsburg, says of it in the course of a long review:

"We confess that in the whole modern romance literature of Germany, England and France, we know of no novel to be called equal to this. In comparison with this glowing eloquence, that never fails of its purpose, this wonderful truth to nature, the largeness of these ideas, and the artistic faultlessness of the machinery in this book, George Sand, with her *Spiridion* and *Claudie,* appears to us untrue and artificial; Dickens, with his but too faithful pictures from the popular life of London, petty; Bulwer, hectic and self-conscious. It is like a sign of warning from the New World to the Old. In recent times a great deal has been said about an intervention of the youthful American Republic in the affairs of Europe. In literature, the symptoms of such an intellectual intervention are already perceptible."

This is rather stronger praise than any of the French critics have bestowed upon Uncle Tom, one of whom thinks it inferior to Hildreth's Archy Moore. But Mrs. Stowe's epic is more read in Paris, just now, than any other book, and it is said to have a greater success than any similar production since the publication of Paul and Virginia.

Uncle Tom has found its way into Italy, where there are more American travellers than American books. Our *chargé,* at Sardinia, reports that it is making its mark there, as in other parts of Europe, in a manner that astonishes the people. Two editions in Italian have been published in Turin, and one of the daily papers was publishing it as a *feuilleton,* after the manner of the Paris press.

What progress Uncle Tom has made in the other northern nations of Europe, in Russia, Sweden, Denmark, Poland and Lapland, we have not been informed; but it is undoubtedly drawing its tears from the eyes of the hyperboreans, as well as from the inhabitants of the mild south. India and Mexico, and South America, have yet to be Uncle Tomitised, for we have not heard of any editions of Mrs. Stowe's great romance among the descendants of the Aztecs, the Gauchos, or the Brazilians. It must spread over the whole earth, like the cholera, only reversing its origin and the order of its progress. One of our newspaper critics compares the Uncle Tomific, which the reading world is now suffering from, to the yellow fever, which does not strike us as a very apt comparison, because the yellow fever is confined wholly to tropical climes, while Uncle Tom, like the cholera, knows no distinction of climate or race. He is bound to go; and future generations of Terra-del Fuegians and Esquimaux, will be making Christmas presents at this season of the year, of Uncle Tom's Cabin in holiday bindings.

Not the least remarkable among the phenomena that have attended the publication of Uncle Tom has been the numerous works written expressly to counteract the impressions which the book was supposed likely to make. This is something entirely new in literature. It is one of the most striking testimonials to the intrinsic merit of the work that it should be thought necessary to neutralize its influence by issuing other romances to prove that Uncle Tom is a fiction. Nothing of the kind was ever before deemed necessary. When Mrs. Radcliffe was bewitching the novel-reading world with her stories of haunted Castles there were no romances written to prove that ruined Castles were not haunted. But Uncle Tom had scarcely seen the light when dozens of steel pens were set at work to prove him an impostor, and his author an ignoramus. Some dozens of these anti-Uncle Tom romances have been published and many more of them remain in obscure manuscript. We have had the pleasure of looking over a score or two, which were seeking a publisher, and nearly all of them were written by women, upon the principle of *similia similibus.* The writer of one of these unpublished anti-Tom novels had made a calculation, the innocent ingenuity of which tickled our very midriff. She had ascertained that one hundred and fifty thousand copies of Uncle Tom's Cabin had been sold, and she calculated that every reader of that romance would be anxious to hear the other side of the story of domestic slavery, and her romance being the silver lining of the Southern institution, she came to a publisher with a modest proposal based upon a certain sale of one hundred and fifty thousand copies of her work. But this good lady had not made a greater mistake than the majority of our reviewers who have assumed that the "golden joys" of Mrs. Stowe's authorship were all owing to her having sung of Africa. Most unaccountably they imagine that it is the subject, and not the manner of its treatment, that has fascinated the reading public. But a more effete subject, one of which the public were more heartily wearied, which was more unwelcome to ears polite than that of slavery, it would not have been easy to select. Whoever touched it was sure of that cruelest of all martyrdoms, contemptuous neglect. The martyr age of anti-slavery, as Harriet Martineau called it, had passed away, and the more fatal age of indifference and contempt had succeeded. The public had been inundated and surfeited with anti-slavery sentiment in all possible forms, from the fierce denunciations of the Pilsbury Garrison school, down to the mild objurgations of Lucretia Mott. Every possible form of literary composition and pictorial embellishment had been devoted to the subject, and no one either needed, or desired, any further enlightenment about it, when Uncle Tom's Cabin was announced to the world of novel readers. The chances were a thousand to one against the success of the book. And yet it has succeeded beyond all other books that were ever written. And the cause is obvious; but, because it was obvious and lay upon the surface, it has been overlooked, there being an opinion among most men that truth must be a long way out of reach.

"When I am reading a book," says Dean Swift, in his Thoughts on Various Subjects, "whether wise or silly, it seems to me to be alive and talking to me." This is the secret of the success of Uncle Tom's Cabin; it is a live book, and it talks to its readers as if it were alive. It first awakens their attention, arrests their thoughts, touches their sympathies, rouses their curiosity, and creates such an interest in the story it is telling, that they cannot let it drop until the whole story is told. And this is done, not because it is a tale of slavery, but in spite of it. If it were the story of a Russian Serf, an evicted Milesian, a Manchester weaver, or an Italian State prisoner, the result would be the same. It is the consummate art of the story teller that has given popularity to Uncle Tom's Cabin, and nothing else. The anti-slavery sentiment obtruded by the author in her own person, upon the notice of the reader, must be felt by every one, to be the great blemish of the book; and it is one of the proofs of its great merits as a romance, that it has succeeded in spite of this defect. If Mrs. Stowe would permit some judicious friend to run his pen through these excrescences, and to obliterate a flippant attempt at Pickwickian humor, here and there, Uncle Tom's Cabin would be a nearly perfect work of art, and would deserve to be placed by the side of the greatest romances the world has known. It has often been spoken of by critics as deficient in artistic ability, but it is to its masterly construction, or artistic quality, that it is indebted for its popularity. The overplus of popularity given to the work by its anti-slavery sentiment is not much greater than the loss of readers from the same source; but the evangelical sentiment of the book, the conversions to holiness through the influence of Uncle Tom's preaching, which the *London Times* cavilled at, is a greater cause of its popularity with the religious classes, we imagine, than the anti-slavery sentiment which it contains. For the religious sentiment of Uncle Tom is in strict accordance with the theology of nine-tenths of the Christian world. In all the great requisites of a romance it is decidedly superior to any other production of an American pen.

There are not, in Uncle Tom's Cabin, any of the delicacies of language which impart so great a charm to the writings of Irving and Hawthorne, nor any descriptions of scenery such as abound in the romances of Cooper, nor any thing like the bewildering sensuousness of Typee Melville; but there are broader, deeper, higher and holier sympathies than can be found in our other romances; finer delineations of character, a wider scope of observation, a more purely American spirit, and a more vigorous narrative faculty. We can name no novel, after Tom Jones, that is superior to Uncle Tom in constructive ability. The interest of the narrative begins in the first page and is continued with consummate skill to the last. In this respect Thackeray is the first of contemporary English novelists, and Bulwer deserves the next mention. But the commencement of all of Thackeray's stories is dull and uninviting, while Bulwer, who opens briskly, and excites the attention of the reader in the beginning, flags and grows dull at the close. Mrs. Stowe, like Fielding, seizes upon the attention at the outset, and never lets it go for a moment until the end. It matters not by what means this is done, it is the chief object aimed at by the romancer, and the greatest artist is he who does it in the most effectual manner; if the writer of fiction fails in this point, he fails altogether. And the same may be said of every other writer; the mind must first be amused before it can be instructed.

In no other American book that we have read are there so many well-delineated American characters; the greater part of them are wholly new in fiction. The mischievous little imp Topsy, is a sort of infantine Caliban, and all the other darkies are delineated with wonderful skill and freedom; and each page of the book is like a cartoon of charcoal sketches. It has been objected to Uncle Tom, that all the whites are impossibly wicked, and all the blacks are impossibly good. But nothing could be further from the truth than such an assertion; the most amiable of the characters are some of the slave owners, while the most degraded and vile are, of course, the slaves. There is no partisanship apparent in the narrative proper, and if the author did not, occasionally, address the reader in her own person, greatly to her own prejudice, we should hardly suspect her of anti-slavery leanings.

An ingenious writer in the *Literary World* has done Mrs. Stowe the favor to point out an instance of undeniable, but, we presume, unconscious plagiarism, on her part, for which she should feel herself under great obligations to him. He proves pretty clearly, that the weakest part of Uncle Tom has been borrowed from Mrs. Sherwood. Little Eva is, unquestionably, nothing more than an adaptation of the Little Henry of the English Lady; and, for our own part, we think it very creditable to Mrs. Stowe that such is the case. The little Nells, little Pauls, little Henrys, and little Evas, are a class of people for which we care but little. Dickens has much to answer for in popularizing the brood of little impossibilities, who are as destitute of the true qualities of childhood as the crying babies which are hung up in the windows of toy-shops. One Topsy is worth a dozen little Evas. But it is a proof of the genius of the author, that every character she introduces into her story is invested with such a distinct individuality that we remember it as a new acquaintance, and feel a strong interest in its fate.

We have heard of almost innumerable instances of the power of Uncle Tom, but one of the finest compliments that has been ever paid to its fascinations was from a Southern Senator and a slave-holder. Somebody had persuaded him to read the book, and, on being asked what he thought of it, he merely replied that he should be very sorry for his wife to read it. A friend of ours was sleeping one night in a strange house, and being annoyed by hearing somebody in the adjoining chamber alternately groaning and laughing, he knocked upon the wall and said, "Hallo, there! What's the matter? Are you sick, or reading Uncle Tom's Cabin?" The stranger replied that he was reading Uncle Tom.

Apart from all considerations of the subject, or motive, of Uncle Tom's

Cabin, the great success of the book shows what may be accomplished by American authors who exercise their genius upon American subjects. Imitations of foreign and classical literature, though equal to the originals, will not command success. The American author or artist who is ambitious of success must confine himself to the illustration of American subjects. Cooper made his first essay upon foreign ground and failed. He then came back to America, with no better talent than he carried abroad, and succeeded, having first secured a reputation by the use of a home subject, and then succeeded with foreign materials. But Irving always wrote as an American even when his theme was foreign. There is yet remaining an uncultivated but rich field for American genius. Our first novel of society has yet to be written. We are daily looking for the appearance of our native novelist who shall take his place by the side of Irving, of Cooper, of Melville, and Hawthorne, and Mrs. Stowe. Like the sister of Fatima, we can see a cloud in the distance, but we cannot make out the form of the approaching genius. There are steam-presses and paper-mills now erecting to welcome him. Our aborigines and sailors, and transcendentalists, and heroes, and slaves, have all had their Iliad, but our men and women of society are yet looking for their Fielding, their Bulwer, or their Thackeray.

Some of the foreign correspondents of our daily papers, in commenting on the popularity of Uncle Tom in Europe, account for it by saying that the English are glad of an opportunity to circulate a book which shows up our country to disadvantage. But we do not perceive the force of this argument. We do not think that any degree of hatred to our institutions could induce the people of Great Britain to read a dull book. Besides, there have been dozens of books published about slavery, which throw Uncle Tom's Cabin completely in the shade in their pictures of our domestic institutions. In fact, Mrs. Stowe's book gives a much more agreeable picture of Southern slavery than any of the works we have seen which profess to give the right side of the tapestry. A desire to degrade America surely cannot be the reason why the representation of dramatic scenes in Uncle Tom have proved so attractive in our own theatres. For our part, we think that the actual effect of Mrs. Stowe's romance will be to create a much more indulgent and forgiving spirit towards the people of the South than has prevailed in England heretofore. Our last presidential election certainly did not afford any reason to believe that the minds of our countrymen had been at all influenced by Mrs. Stowe's enchantments.

"ELIZABETH WETHERELL"
(SUSAN WARNER)

Christmas With the Chaunceys

He that loses any thing, and gets wisdom by it, is a gainer by the loss.
L'Estrange

Left alone in the strange room with the flickering fire, how quickly Ellen's thoughts left Ventnor and flew over the sea. They often travelled that road it is true, but now perhaps the very home look of every thing, where yet *she* was not at home, might have sent them. There was a bitter twinge or two, and for a minute Ellen's head drooped. "Tomorrow will be Christmas eve—last Christmas eve—oh mamma!"

Little Ellen Chauncey soon came back, and sitting down beside her on the foot of the bed began the business of undressing.

"Don't you love Christmas time?" said she; "I think it's the pleasantest in all the year; we always have a houseful of people, and such fine times. But then in summer I think *that's* the pleasantest. I s'pose they're all pleasant. Do you hang up your stocking?"

"No," said Ellen.

"Don't you! why I always did ever since I can remember. I used to think, when I was a little girl you know," said she laughing,—"I used to think that Santa Claus came down the chimney, and I used to hang up my stocking as near the fireplace as I could; but I know better than that now; I don't care where I hang it. You know who Santa Claus is, don't you?"

"He's nobody," said Ellen.

"O yes he is—he's a great many people—he's whoever gives you any thing. *My* Santa Claus is mamma, and grandpapa, and grandmamma, and aunt Sophia, and aunt Matilda; and I thought I should have had uncle George too this Christmas, but he couldn't come. Uncle Howard never gives me any thing. I am sorry uncle George couldn't come; I like him the best of all my uncles."

"I never had any body but mamma to give me presents," said Ellen, "and she never gave me much more at Christmas than at other times."

"I used to have presents from mamma and grandpapa too, both Christmas and New Year, but now I have grown so old mamma only gives me something Christmas and grandpapa only New Year. It would be too much, you know, for me to have both when my presents are so big. I don't believe a stocking will hold 'em much longer. But O! we've got such a fine plan in our heads," said little Ellen, lowering her voice and speaking with open eyes and great energy,—"*we* are going to make presents this year!—we children—won't it be fine?—we are going to make what we like for any body we choose, and let nobody know any thing about it; and then New Year's morning, you know, when the things are all under the napkins we will give ours to somebody to put where they belong, and nobody will know any thing about them till they see them there. Won't it be fine? I'm so glad you are here, for I want you to tell me what I shall make."

"Who is it for?" said Ellen.

"O mamma; you know I can't make for every body, so I think I had rather it should be for mamma. I *thought* of making her a needlebook with white backs, and getting Gilbert Gillespie to paint them—he can paint beautifully,—and having her name and something else written very nicely inside—how do you think that would do?"

"I should think it would do very nicely," said Ellen,—"very nicely indeed."

"I wish uncle George was at home though to write it for me,—he writes so beautifully; I can't do it well enough."

"I am afraid I can't either," said Ellen. "Perhaps somebody else can."

"I don't know who. Aunt Sophia scribbles and scratches, and besides I don't want her to know any thing about it. But there's another thing I don't know how to fix, and that's the edges of the leaves—the leaves for the needles—they must be fixed—somehow."

"I can show you how to do that," said Ellen brightening; "mamma had a needlebook that was given to her that had the edges beautifully fixed; and I wanted to know how it was done, and she showed me. I'll show you that. It takes a good while, but that's no matter."

"O thank you; how nice that is. O no that's no matter. And then it will do very well, won't it? Now if I can only catch Gilbert in a good humour—he isn't my cousin—he's Marianne's cousin—that big boy you saw down stairs—he's so big he won't have any thing to say to me sometimes, but I guess I'll get him to do this. Don't you want to make something for somebody?"

Ellen *had* had one or two feverish thoughts on this subject since the beginning of the conversation; but she only said,—

"It's no matter—you know I haven't got any thing here; and besides I shall not be here till New Year."

"Not here till New Year! yes you shall," said little Ellen, throwing herself upon her neck; "indeed you aren't going away before that. I *know* you aren't—I heard grandmamma and aunt Sophia talking about it. Say you will stay here till New Year—do!"

"I should like to very much indeed," said Ellen, "if Alice does."

In the midst of half a dozen kisses with which her little companion rewarded this speech, somebody close by said pleasantly,—

"What time of night do you suppose it is?"

The girls started;—there was Mrs. Chauncey.

"O mamma," exclaimed her little daughter, springing to her feet, "I hope you haven't heard what we have been talking about?"

"Not a word," said Mrs. Chauncey, smiling, "but as to-morrow will be long enough to talk in, hadn't you better go to bed now?"

Her daughter obeyed her immediately, after one more hug to Ellen and telling her she was *so* glad she had come. Mrs. Chauncey stayed to see Ellen in bed and press one kind motherly kiss upon her face, so tenderly that Ellen's eyes were moistened as she withdrew. But in her dreams that night the rosy sweet face, blue eyes, and little plump figure of Ellen Chauncey played the greatest part.

She slept till Alice was obliged to waken her the next morning; and then got up with her head in a charming confusion of pleasures past and pleasures to come,—things known and unknown to be made for every body's New Year presents,—linen collars and painted needlebooks; and no sooner was breakfast over than she was showing and explaining to Ellen Chauncey a particularly splendid and mysterious way of embroidering the edges of needlebook leaves. Deep in this they were still an hour afterwards, and in the comparative merits of purple and rose-colour, when a little hubbub arose at the other end of the room on the arrival of a new-comer. Ellen Chauncey looked up from her work, then dropped it, exclaiming, "There she is!—now for the bag!"—and pulled Ellen along with her towards the party. A young lady was in the midst of it, talking so fast that she had not time to take off her cloak and bonnet. As her eye met Ellen's however she came to a sudden pause. It was Margaret Dunscombe. Ellen's face certainly showed no pleasure; Margaret's darkened with a very disagreeable surprise.

"My goodness!—Ellen Montgomery!—how on earth did you get *here?*"

"Do you know her?" asked one of the girls, as the two Ellens went off after "aunt Sophia."

"Do I know her? Yes—just enough,—exactly. How did she get here?"

"Miss Humphreys brought her."

"Who's Miss Humphreys?"

"Hush!" said Marianne, lowering her tone,—"that's her brother in the window."

"Whose brother?—hers or Miss Humphreys'?"

"Miss Humphreys'. Did you never see her? she is here, or has been here, a great deal of the time. Grandma calls her her fourth daughter; and she is just as much at home as if she was; and she brought her here."

"And she's at home too, I suppose. Well, it's no business of mine."

"What do you know of her?"

"O enough—that's just it—don't want to know any more."

"Well, you needn't; but what's the matter with her?"

"O I don't know—I'll tell you some other time—she's a conceited little piece. We had the care of her coming up the river, that's how I come to know about her; 'ma said it was the last child she would be bothered with in that way."

Presently the two girls came back, bringing word to clear the table, for aunt Sophia was coming with the moroccos. As soon as she came Ellen Chauncey sprang to her neck and whispered an earnest question. "Certainly!" aunt Sophia said, as she poured out the contents of the bag; and her little niece delightedly told Ellen *she* was to have her share as well as the rest.

The table was now strewn with pieces of morocco of all sizes and colours, which were hastily turned over and examined with eager hands and sparkling eyes. Some were mere scraps, to be sure; but others showed a breadth and length of beauty which was declared to be "first-rate," and "fine"; and one beautiful large piece of blue morocco in particular was made up in imagination by two or three of the party in as many different ways. Marianne wanted it for a book-cover; Margaret declared she could make a lovely reticule with it; and Ellen could not help thinking it would make a very pretty needle-box, such a one as she had seen in the possession of one of the girls, and longed to make for Alice.

"Well, what's to be done now?" said Miss Sophia,—"or am I not to know?"

"Oh you're not to know—you're not to know, aunt Sophy," cried the girls;—"you mustn't ask."

"I'll tell you what they are going to do with 'em," said George Walsh coming up to her with a mischievous face, and adding in a loud whisper, shielding his mouth with his hand,—"they're going to make pr——"

He was laid hold of forcibly by the whole party screaming and laughing, and stopped short from finishing his speech.

"Well then I'll take my departure," said Miss Sophia;—"but how will you manage to divide all these scraps?"

"Suppose we were to put them in the bag again, and you hold the bag, and we were to draw them out without looking," said Ellen Chauncey,—"as we used to do with the sugar-plums."

As no better plan was thought of this was agreed upon; and little Ellen shutting up her eyes very tight stuck in her hand and pulled out a little bit of green morocco about the size of a dollar. Ellen Montgomery came next; then Margaret, then Marianne, then their mutual friend Isabel Hawthorn. Each had to take her turn a great many times; and at the end of the drawing the pieces were found to be pretty equally divided among the party, with the exception of Ellen, who besides several other good pieces had drawn the famous blue.

"That will do very nicely," said little Ellen Chauncey;—"I am glad you have got that, Ellen. Now, aunt Sophy!—one thing more—you know the silks and ribbons you promised us."

"Bless me! I haven't done yet, eh? Well you shall have them, but we are all going out to walk now; I'll give them to you this afternoon. Come! put these away and get on your bonnets and cloaks."

A hard measure! but it was done. After the walk came dinner! after dinner aunt Sophia had to be found and waited on, till she had fairly sought out and delivered to their hands the wished-for bundles of silks and satins. It gave great satisfaction.

"But how shall we do about dividing these?" said little Ellen; "shall we draw lots again?"

"No, Ellen," said Marianne, "that won't do, because we might every one get just the thing we do not want. I want one colour or stuff to go with my morocco, and you want another to go with yours; and you might get mine and I might get yours. We had best each choose in turn what we like, beginning at Isabel."

"Very well," said little Ellen, "I'm agreed."

"Any thing for a quiet life," said George Walsh.

But this business of choosing was found to be very long and very difficult, each one was so fearful of not taking the exact piece she wanted most. The elder members of the family began to gather for dinner, and several came and stood round the table where the children were; little noticed by them, they were so wrapped up in silks and satins. Ellen seemed the least interested person at table, and had made her selections with the least delay and difficulty; and now as it was not her turn sat very soberly looking on with her head resting on her hand.

"I declare it's too vexatious!" said Margaret Dunscombe;—"here I've got this beautiful piece of blue satin, and can't do any thing with it; it just matches that blue morocco—it's a perfect match—I could have made a splendid thing of it, and I have got some cord and tassels that would just do—I declare it's too bad."

Ellen's colour changed.

"Well, choose, Margaret," said Marianne.

"I don't know what to choose—that's the thing. What can one do with red and purple morocco and blue satin? I might as well give up. I've a great notion to take this piece of yellow satin and dress up a Turkish doll to frighten the next young one I meet with."

"I wish you would, Margaret, and give it to me when it's done," cried little Ellen Chauncey.

" 'Tain't made yet," said the other dryly.

Ellen's colour had changed and changed; her hand twitched nervously, and she glanced uneasily from Margaret's store of finery to her own.

"Come choose, Margaret," said Ellen Chauncey; "I dare say Ellen wants the blue morocco as much as you do."

"No, I don't!" said Ellen abruptly, throwing it over the table to her;—"take it, Margaret,—you may have it."

"What do you mean?" said the other astounded.

"I mean you may have it," said Ellen,—"I don't want it."

"Well, I'll tell you what," said the other,—"I'll give you yellow satin for it—or some of my red morocco?"

"No,—I had rather not," repeated Ellen;—"I don't want it—you may have it."

"Very generously done," remarked Miss Sophia; "I hope you'll all take a lesson in the art of being obliging."

"Quite a noble little girl," said Mrs. Gillespie.

Ellen crimsoned. "No, ma'am, I am not, indeed," she said, looking at them with eyes that were filling fast,—"please don't say so,—I don't deserve it."

"I shall say what I think, my dear," said Mrs. Gillespie smiling, "but I am glad you add the grace of modesty to that of generosity; it is the more uncommon of the two."

"I am not modest! I am not generous; you mustn't say so," cried Ellen. She struggled; the blood rushed to the surface, suffusing every particle of skin that could be seen;—then left it, as with eyes cast down she went on—"I don't deserve to be praised,—it was more Margaret's than mine. I oughtn't to have kept it at all—for I saw a little bit when I put my hand in. I didn't mean to, but I did!"

Raising her eyes hastily to Alice's face, they met those of John, who was standing behind her. She had not counted upon him for one of her listeners; she knew Mrs. Gillespie, Mrs. Chauncey, Miss Sophia, and Alice had heard her; but this was the one drop too much. Her head sunk; she covered her face a moment, and then made her escape out of the room before even Ellen could follow her.

There was a moment's silence. Alice seemed to have some difficulty not to follow Ellen's example. Margaret pouted; Mrs. Chauncey's eyes filled with tears, and her little daughter seemed divided between doubt and dismay. Her first move however was to run off in pursuit of Ellen. Alice went after her.

"Here's a beautiful example of honour and honesty for you!" said Margaret Dunscombe, at length.

"I think it is," said John, quietly.

"An uncommon instance," said Mrs. Chauncey.

"I am glad every body thinks so," said Margaret, sullenly; "I hope I sha'n't copy it, that's all."

"I think you are in no danger," said John, again.

"Very well!" said Margaret, who between her desire of speaking and her desire of concealing her vexation did not know what to do with herself;—"every body must judge for himself, I suppose; I've got enough of her, for my part."

"Where did you ever see her before?" said Isabel Hawthorn.

"O she came up the river with us—mamma had to take care of her—she was with us two days."

"And didn't you like her?"

"No, I guess I didn't! she was a perfect plague. All the day on board the steamboat she scarcely came near us; we couldn't pretend to keep sight of her; mamma had to send her maid out to look after her I don't know how many times. She scraped acquaintance with some strange man on board and liked his company better than ours, for she stayed with him the whole blessed day, waking and sleeping; of course mamma didn't like it at all. She didn't go to a single meal with us; you know of course that wasn't proper behaviour."

"No indeed," said Isabel.

"I suppose," said John, coolly, "she chose the society she thought the pleasantest. Probably Miss Margaret's politeness was more than she had been accustomed to."

Margaret coloured, not quite knowing what to make of the speaker or his speech.

"It would take much to make me believe," said gentle Mrs. Chauncey, "that a child of such refined and delicate feeling as that little girl evidently has, could take pleasure in improper company."

Margaret had a reply at her tongue's end, but she had also an uneasy feeling that there were eyes not far off too keen of sight to be baffled; she kept silence till the group dispersed and she had an opportunity of whispering in Marianne's ear that *"that* was the very most disagreeable man she had ever seen in her life."

"What a singular fancy you have taken to this little pet of Alice's, Mr. John," said Mrs. Marshman's youngest daughter. "You quite surprise me."

"Did you think me a misanthrope, Miss Sophia?"

"O no, not at all; but I always had a notion you would not be easily pleased in the choice of favourites."

"*Easily!* When a simple intelligent child of twelve or thirteen is a common character, then I will allow that I am easily pleased."

"Twelve or thirteen!" said Miss Sophia; "what are you thinking about? Alice says she is only ten or eleven."

"In years—perhaps."

"How gravely you take me up!" said the young lady, laughing. "My dear Mr. John, 'in years perhaps,' you may call yourself twenty, but in every thing else you might much better pass for thirty or forty."

As they were called to dinner Alice and Ellen Chauncey came back; the former looking a little serious, the latter crying, and wishing aloud that all the moroccos had been in the fire. They had not been able to find Ellen. Neither was she in the drawing-room when they returned to it after dinner; and a second search was made in vain. John went to the library which was separate from the other rooms, thinking she might have chosen that for a hiding-place. She was not there; but the pleasant light of the room where only the fire was burning, invited a stay. He sat down in the deep window, and was musingly looking out into the moonlight, when the door softly opened and Ellen came in. She stole in noiselessly, so that he did not hear her, and *she* thought the room empty; till in passing slowly down toward the fire she came upon him in the window. Her start first let him know she was there; she would have run, but one of her hands was caught, and she could not get it away.

"Running away from your brother, Ellie!" said he, kindly; "what is the matter?"

Ellen shrunk from meeting his eye and was silent.

"I know all, Ellie," said he, still very kindly,—"I have seen all;—why do you shun me?"

Ellen said nothing; the big tears began to run down her face and frock.

"You are taking this matter too hardly, dear Ellen," he said, drawing her close to him;—"you did wrong, but you have done all you could to repair the wrong;—neither man nor woman can do more than that."

But though encouraged by his manner, the tears flowed faster than ever.

"Where have you been? Alice was looking for you, and little Ellen Chauncey was in great trouble. I don't know what dreadful thing she thought you had done with yourself. Come!—life up your head and let me see you smile again."

Ellen lifted her head, but could not her eyes, though she tried to smile.

"I want to talk to you a little about this," said he. "You know you gave me leave to be your brother,—will you let me ask you a question or two?"

"O yes—whatever he pleased," Ellen said.

"Then sit down here," said he, making room for her on the wide window-seat, but still keeping hold of her hand and speaking very gently. "You said you saw when you took the morocco—I don't quite understand—how was it?"

"Why," said Ellen, "we were not to look, and we had gone three times round and nobody had got that large piece yet, and we all wanted it; and I did not mean to look at all, but I don't know how it was, just before I shut my eyes I happened to see the corner of it sticking up, and then I took it."

"With your eyes open?"

"No, no, with them shut. And I had scarcely got it when I was sorry for it and wished it back."

"You will wonder at me perhaps, Ellie," said John, "but I am not very sorry this has happened. You are no worse than before;—it has only made you see what you are—very, very weak,—quite unable to keep yourself right without constant help. Sudden temptation was too much for you—so it has many a time been for me, and so it has happened to the best men on earth. I suppose if you had had a minute's time to think you would not have done as you did?"

"No, indeed!" said Ellen. "I was sorry a minute after."

"And I dare say the thought of it weighed upon your mind ever since?"

"Oh yes!" said Ellen;—"it wasn't out of my head a minute the whole day."

"Then let it make you very humble, dear Ellie, and let it make you in future keep close to our dear Saviour, without whose help we cannot stand a moment."

Ellen sobbed; and he allowed her to do so for a few minutes, then said, "But you have not been thinking much about Him, Ellie."

The sobs ceased; he saw his words had taken hold.

"Is it right," he said softly, "that we should be more troubled about what people will think of us, than for having displeased or dishonoured Him?"

Ellen now looked up, and in her look was all the answer he wished.

"You understand me, I see," said he. "Be humbled in the dust before him—the more the better; but whenever we are greatly concerned, for our own sakes, about other people's opinion, we may be sure we are thinking too little of God and what will please him."

"I am very sorry," said poor Ellen, from whose eyes the tears began to drop again,—"I am very wrong—but I couldn't bear to think what Alice would think—and you—and all of them—"

"Here's Alice to speak for herself," said John.

As Alice came up with a quick step and knelt down before her, Ellen sprang to her neck, and they held each other very fast indeed. John walked up and down the room. Presently he stopped before them.

"All's well again," said Alice, "and we are going in to tea."

He smiled and held out his hand, which Ellen took, but he would not leave the library, declaring they had a quarter of an hour still. So they sauntered up and down the long room, talking of different things, so pleasantly that Ellen near forgot her troubles. Then came in Miss Sophia to find them, and then Mr. Marshman, and Marianne to call them to tea; so the going into the drawing-room was not half so bad as Ellen thought it would be.

She behaved very well; her face was touchingly humble that night; and all the evening she kept fast by either Alice or John, without budging an inch. And as little Ellen Chauncey and her cousin George Walsh chose to be where she was, the young party was quite divided; and not the least merry portion of it was that mixed with the older people. Little Ellen was half beside herself with spirits; the secret of which perhaps was the fact, which she several times in the course of the evening whispered to Ellen as a great piece of news, that "it was Christmas eve!"

FREDERICK G. COZZENS

Living in the Country

A COUNTRY FIRE-PLACE — LARES AND PENATES — SENTIMENT — SPRING VEGETABLES IN THE GERM — A GARDEN ON PAPER — WARM WEATHER — A FESTA, AND IRRUPTION OF NOSEOLOGISTS — CONSTITUTIONAL LAW, AND SO FORTH.

It is a good thing to have an old-fashioned fire-place in the country; a broad-breasted, deep-chested chimney-piece, with its old-fashioned fender, its old-fashioned andirons, its old-fashioned shovel and tongs, and a goodly show of cherry-red hickory, in a glow, with its volume of blue smoke curling up the thoracic duct. "Ah! Mrs. Sparrowgrass, what would the country be without a chimney corner and a hearth? Do you know," said I "the little fairies dance upon the hearth-stone when an heir is born in a house?" Mrs. Sparrowgrass said she did not know it, but, she said, she wanted me to stop talking about such things. "And the cricket," said I, "how cheerful its carol on the approach of winter." Mrs. S. said the sound of a cricket made her feel melancholy. "And the altar and the hearth-stone: symbols of religion and of home! Before one the bride—beside the other the wife! No wonder, Mrs. Sparrowgrass, they are sacred things; that mankind have ever held them inviolable, and preserved them from sacrilege, in all times, and in all countries. Do you know," said I, "how dear this hearth is to me?" Mrs. Sparrowgrass said, with hickory wood at eight dollars a cord, it did not surprise her to hear me grumble. "If wood were twenty dollars a cord I would not complain. Here we have everything—

"———content,
Retirement, rural quiet, friendship, books,
Ease and alternate labor, useful life;"

"and as I sit before our household altar," said I, placing my hand upon the mantel, "with you beside me, Mrs. S., I feel that all the beautiful fables of poets are only truths in parables when they relate to the hearth-stone—the heart-stone, I may say, of home!"

This fine sentiment did not move Mrs. Sparrowgrass a whit. She said she was sleepy. After all I begin to believe sentiment is a poor thing in the country. It does very well in books, and on the stage, but it will not answer for the rural districts. The country is too genuine and honest for it. It is a pretty affectation, only fit for artificial life. Mrs. Peppergrass may wear it with her rouge and diamonds in a drawing room, but it will not pass current here; any more than the simulated flush of her cheeks can compare with that painted in those of a rustic beauty by the sun and air.

"Mrs. Sparrowgrass," said I, "let us have some nuts and apples, and a pitcher of Binghamton cider; we have a good cheerful fire to-night, and why should we not enjoy it?"

When Mrs. Sparrowgrass returned from giving directions about the fruit and cider, she brought with her a square paper box full of garden seed. To get good garden seed is an important thing in the country. If you depend upon an agricultural warehouse you may be disappointed. The way to do is, to select the best specimens from your own raising: then you are sure they are fresh, at least. Mrs. Sparrowgrass opened the box. First she took out a package of seeds, wrapped up in a newspaper—then she took out another package tied up in brown paper—then she drew forth a bundle that was pinned up—then another that was taped up—then another twisted up—then out came a bursted package of watermelon seeds—then a withered ear of corn—then another package of watermelon seeds from another melon—then a handful of split okra pods—then handsful of beans, peas, squash seeds, melon seeds, cucumber seeds, sweet corn, evergreen corn, and other germs. Then another bursted paper of watermelon seeds. There were watermelon seeds enough to keep half the country supplied with this refreshing article of luxury. As the treasures were spread out on the table, there came over me a feeling that reminded me of Christmas times, when the young ones used to pant down stairs, before dawn, lamp in hand, to see the kindly toy-gifts of Santa Claus. Then the Mental Gardener, taking Anticipation by the hand, went forth into the future garden; the peas sprouted out in round leaves, tomato put forth his aromatic spread; sweet corn thrust his green blades out of many a hillock; lettuce threw up his slender spoons; beans shouldered their way into the world, like Æneases, with the old beans on their backs; and watermelon and cucumber, in voluptuous play, sported over the beds like truant school-boys.

"Here are sweet peas, on tiptoe for a flight:
With wings of gentle flush o'er delicate white,
And taper fingers catching at all things,
To bind them all about with tiny rings."

Now," said I, "Mrs. Sparrowgrass, let us arrange these in proper order; I will make a chart of the garden on a piece of paper, and put everything down with a date, to be planted in its proper time." Mrs. Sparrowgrass said she thought that an excellent plan. "Yes," I replied, tasting the cider, "we will make a garden to-night on paper, a ground plan, as it were, and plant from that; now, Mrs. S., read off the different packages." Mrs. Sparrowgrass took up a paper and laid it aside, then another, and laid it aside. "I think," said she, as the third paper was placed upon the table, "I did not write any names on the seeds, but I believe I can tell them apart; these," said she, "are watermelons." "Very well, what next?" "The next," said Mrs. S., "is either musk-melon or cucumber seed." "My dear," said I, "we want plenty of melons, for the summer, but I do not wish to plant half an acre of pickles by mistake; can't you be sure about the matter?" Mrs. Sparrowgrass said she could not. "Well, then, lay the paper down and call off the next." "The next are not radishes, I know," said Mrs. S., "they must be summer cabbages." "Are you sure now, Mrs. Sparrowgrass," said I, getting a little out of temper. Mrs. Sparrowgrass said she was sure of it, because cabbage seed looked exactly like turnip seed. "Did you save turnip seed also," said I. Mrs. Sparrowgrass replied, that she had provided some, but they must be in another paper. "Then call off the next; we will plant them for cabbages, whether or no." "Here *is* a name," said Mrs. Sparrowgrass, brightening up. "Read it," said I, pen in hand. "Watermelons—not so good," said Mrs. S. "Lay that paper with the rest and proceed." "Corn," said Mrs. Sparrowgrass, with a smile. "Variety?" "Pop, I am sure." "Good, now we begin to see daylight." "Squash," said Mrs. Sparrowgrass. "Winter or Summer?" "Both." "Lay that paper aside, my dear." "Tomato." "Red or yellow?" Mrs. Sparrowgrass said she had pinned up the one and tied up the other, to distinguish them, but it was so long ago, she had forgotten which was which. "Never mind," said I, "there is one comfort, they cannot bear without showing their colors." "Now for the next." Mrs. Sparrowgrass said upon tasting the tomato seed, she was sure they were bell-peppers. "Very well, so much is gained, we are sure of the capsicum. The next." "Beans," said Mrs. Sparrowgrass.

There is one kind of bean, in regard to which I have a prejudice. I allude to the asparagus bean, a sort of long-winded esculent, inclined to be prolific in strings. It does not climb very high on the pole, but crops out in an abundance of pods, usually not shorter than a bill of extras, after a contract; and although interesting as a curious vegetable, still not exactly the bean likely to be highly commended by your city guests, when served up to them at table. When Mrs. Sparrowgrass, in answer to my question, as to the particular species of bean referred too, answered, "Limas," I felt relief at once. "Put the Limas to the right with the sheep, Mrs. S., and as for the rest of the seeds, sweep them into the refuse basket. I will add another stick to the fire, pare an apple for you, and an apple for me, light a cigar, and be comfortable. What is the use of fretting about a few seeds more or less? But, next year, we will mark all the packages with *names,* to prevent mistakes, won't we, Mrs. Sparrowgrass?"

There has been a great change in the atmosphere within a few days. The maple twigs are all scarlet and yellow fringes, the sod is verdurous and moist; in the morning a shower of melody falls from the trees around us, where blue birds and "pewees" are keeping an academy of music. Off on the river there is a long perspective of shad-poles, apparently stretching from shore to shore, and, here and there, a boat, with picturesque fishermen, at work over the gill-nets. Now and then a shad is held up; in the distance it has a star-like glitter, against the early morning sun. The fruit-trees are bronzed with buds. Occasionally a feeble fly creeps along, like a valetudinarian too early in the season at a watering-place. The marshes are all a-whistle with dissipated bull-frogs, who keep up their revelry at unseemly hours. Our great Polander is in high cluck, and we find eggs in the hens' nests. IT IS SPRING! It is a good thing to have spring in the country. People grow young again in the spring in the country. The world, the old globe itself, grows young in the spring, and why not Mr. and Mrs. Sparrowgrass? The city, in the spring, is like the apples of Sodom, "fair and pleasant to behold, but dust and ashes within." But who shall sing or say what spring is in the country?

> "——To what shall I compare it?
> It has a glory, and naught else can share it:
> The thought thereof is awful, sweet, and holy,
> Chasing away all worldliness and folly."

"Mrs. Sparrowgrass," said I, "the weather is beginning to be very warm and spring-like; how would you like to have a little *festa?*" Mrs. Sparrowgrass said that, in her present frame of mind, a fester was not necessary for her happiness. I replied, "I meant a *festa,* not a fester; a little fête, a few friends, a few flowers, a mild sort of spring dinner, if you please; some music, claret, fresh lettuce, lamb and spinach, and a breakfast of eggs fresh laid in the morning, with rice cakes and coffee." Mrs. Sparrowgrass said she was willing. "Then," said I, "Mrs. S., I will invite a few old friends, and we will have an elegant time." So from that day we watched the sky very cleverly for a week, to ascertain the probable course of the clouds, and consulted the thermometer to know what chance there was of having open windows for the occasion. The only drawback that stood in the way of perfect enjoyment was, our lawn had been half rooted out of existence by an irruption of predatory pigs. It was vexatious enough to see our lawn bottom-side up on a festive occasion. But I determined to have redress for it. Upon consulting with the best legal authority in the village, I was told that I could obtain damages by identifying the animals, and commencing suit against the owner. As I had not seen the animals, I asked Mrs. Sparrowgrass if she could identify them. She said she could not. "Then," said I to my legal friend, "what can I do?" He replied that he did not know. "Then," said I, "if they come again, and I catch them in the act, can I fire a gun among them?" He said I could; but that I would be liable for whatever damages was done them. "That," said I, "would not answer; my object is to make the owner suffer, not the poor quadrupeds." He replied that the only sufferers would probably be the pigs and myself. Then I asked him, if the owner recovered against me, whether I could bring a replevin suit against him. He said that, under the Constitution of the United States, such a suit could be brought. I asked him if I could recover. He said I could not. Then I asked him what remedy I could have. He answered that if I found the pigs on my grounds, I could drive them to the pound, then call upon the fence viewers, get them to assess the damages done, and by this means mulct the owner for the trespass. This advice pleased me highly; it was practical and humane. I determined to act upon it, and slept soundly upon the resolution. The next day our guests came up from town. I explained the lawn to them, and having been fortified on legal points, instructed them as to remedy for trespass. The day was warm and beautiful; our doors and windows were thrown wide open. By way of offset to the appearance of the lawn, I had contrived, by purchasing an expensive little bijou of a vase, and filling it with sweet breathing flowers, to spread a rural air of fragrance throughout the parlor. The doors of the bay-window open on the piazza; in one doorway stood a tray of delicate confections, upon two slender quartette tables. These were put in the shade to keep cool. I had suborned an Italian to bring them up by hand, in pristine sharpness and beauty of outline. I was taking a glass of sherry with our old friend Capt. Bacon, of the U. S. Navy, when suddenly our dogs commenced barking. We keep our dogs chained up by daylight. Looking over my glass of sherry, I observed a detachment of the most villainous looking pigs rooting up my early pea-patch. "Now," said I, "Captain," putting down my glass deliberately, "I will show you some fun; excuse me for a few minutes;" and with that I bowed significantly to our festal guests. They understood at once that etiquette must give way when the pea-patch was about being annihilated. I then went out, unchained the dogs, and commenced driving the pigs out of the garden. After considerable trampling of all my early vegetables, under the eyes of my guests, I managed to get the ringleader of the swinish multitude into my parlor. He was a large, powerful looking fellow, with a great deal of comb, long legs, mottled complexion, and ears pretty well dogged. He stood for a moment at bay against the sofa, then charged upon the dogs, ran against the centre table, which he accidentally upset, got headed off by Captain Bacon, who came to the rescue, darted under our quartette tables,—making a general distribution of confectionery, and finally got cornered in the piazza.

By this time I was so much exasperated that I was capable of taking the life of the intruder, and probably should have done so had my gun not been at the gunsmith's. In striking at him with a stick, I accidently hit one of the dogs such a blow as to disable him. But I was determined to capture the destroyer and put him in the pound. After some difficulty in getting him out of the piazza, I drove him into the library and finally out in the ground. The rest of his confederates were there, quietly feeding on the remains of the garden. Finally I found myself on the hot, high road, with all my captives and one dog, in search of the pound. Not knowing where the pound was, after driving them for a quarter of a mile, I made inquiry of a respectable looking man, whom I met in corduroy breeches, on the road. He informed me that he did not know. I then fell in with a colored boy who told me the only pound was at Dobb's Ferry. Dobb's Ferry is a thriving village about seven miles north of the Nepperhan. I made a bargain with the colored boy for three dollars, and by his assistance the animals were safely lodged in the pound. By this means I was enabled to return to my guests. Next day I found out the owner. I got the fence-viewers to estimate the damages.

The fence-viewers looked at the broken mahogany and estimated. I spoke of the vase, the flowers, [greenhouse flowers] and the confectionery. These did not appear to strike them as damageable. I think the fence-viewers are not liberal enough in their views. The damages done to a man's temper and constitution shall be included, if ever I get to be fence-viewer; to say nothing of exotics trampled under foot, and a beautiful dessert ruthlessly destroyed by unclean animals. Besides that, we shall not have a pea until everybody else in the village has done with peas. We shall be late in the season with our early peas. At last an advertisement appeared in the county paper, which contained the decision of the fence-viewers, to wit:—

WESTCHESTER COUNTY.
TOWN OF YONKERS. } ss.

WE, THE SUBSCRIBERS, fence-viewers of said town, having been applied to by Samson Sparrowgrass of said town to appraise the damages done by nine hogs, five wintered, [four spotted and one white,] and four spring pigs, [two white] distrained by him doing damage on his lands, and having been to the place, and viewed and ascertained the damages, do hereby certify the amount thereof to be three dollars, and that the fees for our services are two dollars. Given under our hands, this —— day of ——, 185—.

DANIEL MALMSEY,
PETER ASSMANSHAUSER.
Fence-viewers.

The above hogs are in the Pound at Dobb's Ferry.

CORNELIUS CORKWOOD,
Pound Master.

"Under the circumstances," said I, "Mrs. Sparrowgrass, what do you think of the pound as a legal remedy?" Mrs. S. said it was shameful. "So I think, too; but why should we repine? the birds sing, the sky is blue, the grass is green side up, the trees are full of leaves, the air is balmy, and the children, God bless them! are happy. Why should we repine about trifles? If we want early peas we can buy them, and as for the vase flowers, and confectionery, they would have been all over with, by this time, if the pigs had not been here. There is no use to cry, like Alexander, for another world; let us enjoy the one we have, Mrs. Sparrowgrass."

MYRTLE REED

The Roses and the Song

THERE had been a lover's quarrel and she had given him back his ring. He thrust it into his pocket and said, unconcernedly, that there were other girls who would be glad to wear it.

Her face flushed, whether in anger or pain he did not know, but she made no reply. And he left her exulting in the thought that the old love was dead.

As the days went by, he began to miss her. First, when his chum died in a far-off country, with no friend near. He remembered with a pang how sweetly comforting she had always been, never asking questions, but soothing his irritation and trouble with her gentle womanly sympathy.

He know just what she would do if he could tell her that Tom was dead. She would put her soft cheek against his own rough one, and say: "I am so sorry dear. I'm not much, I know, but you've got me, and nothing, not even death can change that."

"Not even death"—yes, it was quite true. Death changes nothing.—It is only life that separates utterly.

He began to miss the afternoon walks, the lingering in book store and art galleries, and the quiet evenings at home over the blazing fire, when he sat with his arm around her and told her how he had spent the time since they last met. Every thought was in some way of her, and the emptiness of his heart without her seemed strange in connection with the fact that the old love was dead.

He saw by a morning paper that there was to be a concert for the benefit of some charitable institution, and on the program, printed beneath the announcement, was her name. He smiled grimly. How often he had gone with her when she sang in public! He remembered every little detail of every evening. He always waited behind the scenes, because she said she could sing better when he was near her. And whatever the critics might say, she was sure of his praise.

It was on the way home from one of these affairs that he had first told her that he loved her. Through the rose-leaf rain that fell from her hair and bosom at his touch he had kissed her for the first time, and the thrill of her sweet lips was with him still. How short the ride had been that night and why was the coachman in such an unreasonable hurry to get home?

He made up his mind that he would not go to the concert that night, but somehow, he bought a ticket and was there before the doors opened. So he went out to walk around a little. People who went to concerts early were his especial detestation.

In a florist's window he saw some unusually beautiful roses. He had always sent her roses before, to match her gown, and it seemed queer not to buy them for her now.

Perhaps he really ought to send her some to show her that he cherished no resentment. Anyone could send her flowers over the footlights. The other men that she knew would undoubtedly remember her, and he didn't want to seem unfriendly.

So he went in. "Four dozen La France roses," he said, and the clerk speedily made the selection. He took a card out of his pocket, and chewed the end of his pencil meditatively.

It was strange that he should have selected that particular kind, he thought. That other night, after he had gone home, he had found a solitary pink petal clinging to his scarf-pin. He remembered with a flush of tenderness that it had come from one of the roses—his roses—on her breast. He had kissed it passionately and hidden it in a book—a little book which she had given him.

With memory came heartache, his empty life and her wounded love. The words shaped themselves under his pencil:

"You know what the roses mean. Will you wear one when you sing the second time? Forgive me and love me again—my sweetheart."

He tied the card himself into the centre of the bunch, so it was half hidden by the flowers. He gave them to the usher with a queer tremolo note in his voice. "After her first number, understand?"

There was a piano solo, and then she appeared. What she sang he did not know, but her deep contralto, holding heaven in its tones, he both knew and understood. She did not sing as well as usual. Her voice lacked warmth and sincerity and her intonation was faulty. The applause was loud but not spontaneous although many of her friends were there. His were the only flowers she received.

When she came out the second time, he looked at her anxiously, but there was never a sign of a rose. He sank down in his chair with a sigh and covered his face with his hand.

This time she sang as only *she* could sing. Oh, that glorious contralto! Suggestions of twilight and dawn, of suffering and joy, of love and its renunciation.

There was no mistaking her success and the great house rang with plaudits from basement to roof. He, only, was silent; praying in mute agony for a sign.

She willingly responded to the encore and a hush fell upon the audience with the first notes of Tosti's "Good-Bye."

Falling leaf, and fading tree.

Oh, why should she sing that? He writhed as if in bodily pain, but the beautiful voice went on and on.

Good-bye, summer, good-bye, good-bye!

How cruel she seemed! Stately, imperious, yet womanly, she held her listeners spellbound, but every word cut into his heart like a knife.

All the to-morrows shall be as to-day

The tears came and his lips grew white. Then some way into the cruel magnificence of her voice came a hint of pity as she sang:

"Good-bye to hope, good-bye, good-bye!"

There was a hush, then she began again:

What are we waiting for, Oh, my heart?
Kiss me straight on the brows, and part!

All the love in her soul surged into her song; the joy of happy love; the agony of despairing love; the pleading cry of doubting love; the dull suffering of hopeless love; and then her whole strength was merged into a passionate prayer for the lost love, as she sang the last words:

Good-bye forever, good-bye forever!
Good-bye, good-bye, good—bye—!

She bowed her acknowledgments again and again, and when the clamour was over, he hastened into the little room behind the stage where she was putting on her wraps. She was alone but her carriage was waiting.

As he entered, she started in surprise, then held out her hand.

"Dear," he said, "if this is the end, won't you let me kiss you *once* for the sake of our old happiness? We were so much to each other—you and I. Even if you wouldn't wear the rose, won't you let me hold you just a minute as I used to do?"

"Wear the rose," she repeated, "what do you mean?"

"Didn't you see my card?"

"No," she answered, "I couldn't look at them—they are—La—France—you know—and——"

She reached out trembling fingers and found the card. She read the tender message twice—the little message which meant so much, then looked up into his face.

"If I could," she whispered, "I'd pin them all on."

Someway she slipped into her rightful place again, and very little was said as they rolled home. But when he lit the gas in his own room he saw something queer in the mirror, and found, clinging to his scarf-pin, the petal of a La France rose.

ELLIOTT FLOWER

A Stranger in New York

I MET him in New York in "the good old summer time." He was from the West, and so was I. In this there was a bond of fellowship. He was lonely, and so was I. In this there was another bond. He was thirsty, and so was I. Here was a third bond; and it followed naturally that we drifted into conversation as soon as the waiter had attended to our immediate wants.

"Never again," he remarked gloomily.

"Never again what?" I inquired.

"Never again will you see me in this home of the big graft unless I bring a section of the West with me."

"It's a pretty good town," I argued, although I was wishing myself back home at that very moment.

"Oh, the town's good enough," he conceded, "if it wasn't for the people. I could make something nice out of this town if they'd let me populate it."

"We happen to be here at the wrong time," I suggested. "Nothing doing in New York in the summer, you know."

"Plenty doing," he retorted, "but it isn't worth doing."

"Suppose," I said, mindful of the fact that New York's complacency is so great that it finds entertainment in all criticisms that come from west of the Hudson, "suppose you tell me what's the matter with New York and let me pass it on to the benighted souls that live here."

"You don't need to be told; you know."

"How do you know I know?"

"Because you don't live here."

"Is the truth, as you see it, open to every stranger that comes to New York?" I queried.

"No" he answered. "If you had a title or fifty million dollars they'd keep the truth from you until they'd hitched you up to some New York girl or found some other way of making you sorry. What you see through a champagne-glass looks pretty good, you know; but a headache and a whole lot of regret usually follows."

"All of which convinces me," I said, "that you have an interesting message for New York, and I should like nothing better than to deliver it. New York is always looking for diversion, is always willing to pay for it, and always finds the remarks of such insignificant mortals as you and me highly diverting. I know of no other town that will pay to be roasted. Let us, therefore, get even with New York by taking away some of its coin in exchange for such 'hot ones' as we are able to pass out."

"Son, I'm with you," he declared. "The money don't tempt me—you'd know I wasn't a New Yorker by that—but there's relief and relaxation in the job."

"I'll interview you," I suggested. "You're a distinguished stranger, just arrived, and I'm a reporter. Now, what do you think of New York?"

"I try not to think of it," he replied promptly, "because I can't reduce my general impressions and feelings to language without jeopardizing my immortal soul."

"But you must think of it," I insisted. "Eliminate your personal feelings and you may be able to speak without danger to your soul. Now, blaze away."

He beckoned to the waiter first. Then, being strengthened for the task, he leaned back in his chair and thoughtfully released these remarks: "Every time that New York looks in the glass she thinks she sees all there is to North America. That is the main fault, briefly stated; but there are others. New York is the only city in the world, so far as I know, that invests money in lemons. The rest of us have lemons handed to us occasionally, but New York buys them—the sourest of financial lemons. Then, when she finds that she has tied up all the cash in her possession—most of which did not belong to her—she goes into hysterics and frantically calls upon the rest of the country to provide her with pocket money. The sole mission of the rest of the country, in her opinion, is to furnish her with cash for her financial eccentricities, and the rest of the country has usually done it. And she isn't even grateful. She is so accustomed to having other people's money to play with that she has come to look upon it as her own. Therefore, instead of being grateful to us, she demands gratitude from us when she lets us have the necessary cash to move the crops. But it's mostly our money—the money that our banks have kept on deposit here and that she has been using in her financial operations. Why, hang it all! New York relies on our cash to do business! If you don't believe it, just note the fit she has whenever we decide to keep our money at home. New York is the spoiled child of the nation; she gets so reckless at times that we have to shut down on the cash until she promises to be good; and, through it all, except in moments of dire need, she is superciliously patronizing.

"Very good," I commended, "but somewhat too general. I am seeking a phase of this great subject upon which you can talk with real feeling—something based upon your personal experience. Let us tackle the New York that we, as strangers, know instead of the New York we read about."

"Easy enough," he returned. "New York is the loneliest spot on earth for the stranger. The only people disposed to be friendly are those who will take away your reputation or your cash—very likely both. Every man here will warn you against most other men and all women, if he condescends to recognize you at all. That shows New York's opinion of New York."

"Have you no friends at all here?" I asked.

"Not a one. I thought I had two or three, but I was mistaken. They're very friendly when they're in my part of the country, but here they give me only the telephone glad hand, which is easy and cheap. You've been up against that, of course."

"Possibly," I admitted doubtfully.

"Sure you have." He rattled along with the confidence of one who knew his subject thoroughly. "Everybody gets it here. I had it passed out to me the first day, when I gleefully called up a man I'd been clever to out our way. He was mighty glad to hear I was in town—tickled to death. 'But I haven't a minute to spare to-day, old man,' he said, 'I'll be up to your hotel in the morning.' That was five days ago, and I haven't even found his card in my key-box. He might at least have taken the trouble to bribe the clerk to put his card in the box some time when I was out, don't you think?"

I agreed that a man was entitled to that much consideration, and then asked how he explained this disinclination to see him.

"He's afraid of my 'graft,'" was the prompt reply. "I haven't any, but no New York man can understand that."

"Still," I persisted, "there's the Great White Way. No other city has a street like Broadway."

"And it's a good thing," he retorted. "There isn't another street in the world as superficial and insincere as Broadway. You can't believe anything that you hear on Broadway, and mighty little that you see: even the figures are mostly made by dressmakers and tailors, Nature apparently having slipped a cog in the making. And you've got to be *blasé* or you get fooled. 'The child died,' was a remark that caught my attention—in a café, of course. You have to get into a café to hear anything on Broadway, except the newsboys and the cable-cars. Anyhow, I heard that the child died, and I was mighty sorry about it. 'He carried himself splendidly in the scene that followed,' was the next thing that drifted to my ears. One of the little tragedies of life, I thought, and I was tempted to ask if there was anything I could do. 'After that,' the man went on, 'he thought he ought to get more. You see, he was only getting $25 in real money and $100 on the bills, so he kicked for a raise, and the manager gave him the boot." That's Broadway—a vaudeville continuous."

"There's more to New York than Broadway," I suggested.

"Not if you let a New York man tell it."

"Nevertheless, there is."

"Well, there's the subway," he grumbled. "That has its advantages, one of which is the relief you feel when you get out of it. Then it makes some of the Broadway musical productions sound pretty good, too: anything sounds good after you've heard a subway train rounding a curve. And its history is a complete treatise on the art of handing lemons to unsophisticated investors."

I beckoned to a waiter, feeling that my comrade from the West deserved some slight tribute for his masterly presentation of New York's attractions for the stranger.

"You should try Coney Island," I then ventured doubtfully, fearing that he might weaken.

"I have," he returned promptly; "I went down to Coney for a swim, and came back to New York for a bath. I needed the bath. I went down on the sunny side of a boat because I failed to board the boat the day before to reserve a shady spot, and I came back on an 'express train' that made about ten unscheduled stops between stations. A fat man stood on my toes most of the time. Oh, I know all about Concy. I spent a good part of my time down there waiting for somebody to come out of the ocean so that there would be room for me to get in."

I lured him on by suggesting that there is lots to do there, anyhow.

"Sure, sure," he agreed. "You can buy things you don't want all day long; there are more opportunities to buy what you don't need than anywhere else on earth. Then you can look for a place where you can sit down without having to buy a drink and tip the waiter. That's an interesting occupation, but unprofitable, for you can't escape the tip there any more than you can in New York. The tip is one of the big items hereabouts; you have to add about twenty-five per cent. to your estimate of expenses to cover it. They say that ten per cent. is enough, but that's safe only when you're sure you'll never have the same waiter again."

"Still," I persisted, "I think the waiters here say 'Thank you' better than they do anywhere else."

"They ought to. Look at the rate per word they get for it."

"Let's get back to Coney," I said.

"Sure. I learned the Coney Island game for $4.75, which was cheap. Anybody will tell you that. It has cost some people so much that they have had to swim back. I just wanted to sit down somewhere, even at the cost of a glass of beer and a tip. I sat down. Then I paid $3 for a small bottle. I don't know what it contained; I know what I paid for, but I don't know what I got. Nobody ever knows that at Coney. Add $1.50 for a bottle of Rhine wine—alleged. The waiter got only a quarter because the situation was such that I was rather anxious to be thrown out. What! Oh, I guess the girl got a commission on the sale. She wanted me to pay the manager to let her skip her turn and help me reduce the visible supply of small bottles, but I wouldn't so she went back on the stage and sang that touching ballad, 'He told me that he loved me, but I found his name was Punk.' It was my chance to escape."

"Did you try Brighton?"

"Both Brighton and Manhattan. A little higher prices for the things you don't need, that's all."

"You should try Rockaway."

"I have—Rockaway and Far Rockaway. Got a highball and a light lunch at Far Rockaway, and a financial stringency set in immediately thereafter. I was glad I took my swim first—while I had money. The *risqué* bathing suits at these beaches—and Coney—are all on the picture postals, which was a disappointment. One of the things I learned is that mighty few girls look well in bathing suits. They'd wear 'em on Broadway if they did. Still there seemed to be compensations. Father Neptune is the originator and general manager of the greatest public hugging-matches in the world, no holds barred and many of the young men were very busy picking girls out of the waves. I tried it myself. You can tell whether you are *persona grata* in the matter by the promptness with which she permits herself to be upset again. What! No, my girl didn't do it again. You see, I lacked practice in this sport, so I inadvertently caught her by the wrong end, got her feet above water first, and she had a hole in her stocking. That settled me. So I came back to New York with the rest of the population, and just as lonely as ever."

I beckoned for the waiter again.

"No, son," he interposed, "this is on me."

"But you have been entertaining me," I urged.

"Entertaining you!" he snorted. "Well, you've been a regular escape-valve for me; I had to let off steam or bust. And I've got to linger here another week. Think of that! Another week in this supercilious, superficial, self-complacent home of graft and lemons."

"You'll never come back, of course."

"Never, that is— Well, son, that's the funny part of it! I have an idea I'll come scooting back here at the very first opportunity. How about you?"

"I'm with you," I said, "from start to finish. You have sized New York up in a way that makes my heart go out to you—you see the town as I see it —but I'll be looking for an excuse to come back within a month after I get away. I wonder what the secret of it is."

"Let us," said my western comrade, "look for it in the bottom of the glass."

We searched industriously, but found it not.

NOTES FROM "THE LOUNGER"

(From "Putnam's Monthly," 1906-1910)

MASTER MASTICATOR

MR. FLETCHER has been preaching the gospel of slow eating and thorough mastication for many years, and his disciples—members of the Chew-Chew Club, as they might be called—are said to number 200,000.

What Mr. Fletcher says is, in the main, as sound as it is simple. He teaches us to eat slowly, and to chew our food as the cow chews her—calmly and deliberately. We all knew this before Mr. Fletcher told us. We learned it in our nursery rhymes; for there we were cautioned against gluttony, with frightful examples of the fate of gluttons ever before us. In his books Mr. Fletcher gives us the scientific reasons on which his theories are based, and when we come to put them into practice, we find that they are wise, and are conscious of feeling the better for their observance. For many years a traveller, Mr. Fletcher at last settled in Venice, choosing as his home the Palazzo Saibante, on the Grand Canal. I should hardly choose Venice for my home if I wanted to make fruit and vegetables the chief of my diet, for they are so hard to get fresh from the tree or the earth in that islanded city. On the other hand, Venice has her counterbalancing advantages, the chief of which is, that she is Venice!

Mr. Fletcher is in New York now teaching the people of the East Side how to eat. He occupies an apartment in the so-called "Phipps Tenement No. 1," in East 31st Street, and a mighty nice apartment it is. Another apartment, on the floor below, he has fitted up as a sort of dietetic laboratory, where his pupils will be trained.

For the benefit of those who may wish to know on how little per day a Fletcherite can live, without going hungry, I quote the bill-of-fare written down by one of his young lady disciples:

"I never spend more than thirty cents a day—that is my extreme limit. Here is my exact menu. You must remember that I buy altogether in First Avenue, where prices are low":

BREAKFAST:
    Toasted corn flakes (one 10 cent box lasts two weeks) .... .00 5/7
    Juice one half grape fruit on corn flakes (grape fruit, 5 cents) .. .02 1/2
    2 cups hot water .... .00
    1 spoonful sugar .... ?
    2 slices dry toast .... .01

    Approximate total .... .04 9/14

LUNCHEON at a restaurant down-town:
    1 or 2 slices graham bread and butter,
    1 bowl soup,
    1 small dish ice-cream .... .12
    Note.—This luncheon may be obtained at these prices at the Princess Club, in Nassau Street.

DINNER:
    1 dish of vegetables, such as carrots and cauliflower .... .07
    Milk .... .04
    Bread .... .01

    Total .... .12

or:
    Fruit salad .... .07
    Bread .... .01
    Milk .... .04

    Total .... .12

    Total for entire day .... .28 3/4

"I am perfectly satisfied," she continued.
"My health has greatly improved. I was ill when I began."

As for Mr. Fletcher himself, when he puts up at the Waldorf-Astoria his food costs him only one dollar a day. If, however, it be true that Mr. Boldt, the proprietor of that hostelry, says that the cost of food is twenty-seven cents a day per capita, he could not lose on Mr. Fletcher. Everything beyond twenty-seven cents that his guests spend on their meals goes toward paying the general expenses of the hotel.

MRS. O. H. P. B.

Mrs. O. H. P. Belmont knew how to attract the mob when she threw Marble House open for examination at five dollars a head. It was all for the cause of suffrage, for which cause it was a great day. Marble House is rather an unimaginative name for one's home. I should as soon think of calling my home Brick House, or Board House, or Concrete House. A house might be known to the public by a name so practical and descriptive, but one would scarcely expect the owner to give it such a name in baptism.

CLYDE FITCH

Clyde Fitch was on the top wave of his popularity at the time of his death. His plays were never in greater demand in this country, and he had just come into his own in England. With the exception of Sardou, he was the most popular playwright of his time. Of the sixty or more plays that he wrote, scarcely one was a failure. It was no unusual thing for four "Fitch plays" to be running in New York at one time, and the same is getting to be true of London. Mr. Fitch was a rapid writer. He could dash off a play in a few weeks, because he had it all worked out in his head before he began to write. But his work did not end when the play was finished. It had barely begun. He worked as hard over the production as though that were his only business. Every detail of stage setting, of costuming, was arranged by him. As for the actors, he usually selected them before the play was written. He could pick a stage winner as a horse man can pick a winning horse. If Clyde Fitch had not been a playwright he would have been a novelist. He was a keen observer of men and women, particularly of women, and he could have put them into books as well as he did into plays. He had a woman's love for beauty and luxury, and his surroundings indicated the indulgence of expensive tastes. Pictures and bric-a-brac were to him what gambling and drinking are to some men. He could not resist them, and his houses in town and country were overloaded with objects that he had collected in his travels along the beaten paths or in out-of-the-way places.

That Clyde Fitch was the cleverest American playwright goes without saying. It will be many a long day before we have one as prolific and as evenly good. He was born to write for the theatre, for he knew human nature and he knew the stage. The New York *Times* does not exaggerate when it says of Clyde Fitch:

> He will surely rank with Augier and not below Farquhar and Vanbrugh, if not with Congreve and Sheridan. The author of the first and second acts of "The Climbers," the first half of "The Truth," two or three scenes in "The Girl with the Green Eyes" and the love scenes of "Barbara Frietchie," certainly did something well worth doing for American fiction, quite apart from his material service to the contemporary stage.

Just now we are a little too near him to place him without prejudice. Posterity, however, will do him justice.

WILLIAM WINTER GETS THE SACK

So we are not longer to see "W. W." signed to the dramatic reviews in the *Tribune*. Even when I was a youngster I have read Mr. Winter's criticisms and enjoyed them, whether I agreed with them or not. They were as much a feature of the *Tribune* as were Horace Greeley's agricultural editorials. The trouble was in the counting-room. Mr. Winter dared speak his mind, and this interfered with the advertising accounts of the theatres; so off came his head. More than forty years of honorable and valuable service counted for nothing. Mr. Winter's copy was "blue-pencilled," and Mr. Winter resigned. That was not so strange as that his resignation should have been accepted. Something similar is said to have happened a year or so ago with Mr. W. P. Eaton and the *Sun*. Interfere with the cash receipts at your peril! Critics may go just so far but no farther. They can hit the small fry as hard as they like, thus showing their independence to a doubting world; but let them hit "higher up," and they might as well resign, for they will be asked to if they don't.

The *Outlook* speaks its mind freely on this subject, and it expresses the views of thousands of people. It quotes part of a letter written by the editor of the *Tribune* to Mr. Winter, of which there can be but one interpretation:

> It is my opinion that the theatrical news published on Sunday should not be condemnatory.... That a play is well attended, that there has, or has not, been a change in the cast, etc., etc.—these are facts which can be properly stated, whether the play is good or bad.

If we understand the English language, this is a clear statement that in the *Tribune,* at least in its Sunday edition, there must appear no criticism which will offend any of its theatrical advertisers. We have no wish to interfere in the private affairs of our neighbors, but this does not seem to us to be a private affair. The public has a right to know whether the theatrical criticisms which it reads are the opinions of competent and impartial critics, or are dictated by the theatrical managers. There have been of late a few American plays of dramatic and literary power, and more plays which, though ephemeral and unliterary, touched pertinently public and social questions. Yet there is a general feeling that the American stage has in very recent years degenerated, and that the American playwright is too often, not a literary and dramatic artist, but a hack employee of the great managers. Is it any wonder that the stage is looked upon with distrust and contempt by free and enlightened people when its dominant spirits in this country are able and willing to dictate the kind of criticism that shall be published in a paper of such a distinguished literary and artistic history as the New York *Tribune?* The editors of some of our great metropolitan newspapers indulge occasionally in a good deal of lofty talk about the glories of "a free press" and the danger to our institutions if we make our libel laws so severe that the editors may occasionally be restrained by the courts. What kind of a free press have we when the receipts of the counting-room determine the opinions of the editorial room?

MARK TWAIN'S DAUGHTER MARRIES

The wedding of Miss Clara Clemens to Mr. Ossip Gabrilowitsch at the bride's home, "Stormfield," Redding, Conn., was as picturesque as the story of the courtship and wedding of these two musicians could possibly suggest. I have spoken of Mr. Clemens's country home more than once in these pages, and it has been pictured here as well. A more romantic setting for a romantic wedding could not possibly be imagined. It was a small wedding (only the immediate friends of the family were present), and it took place in the drawing-room of the house. The bride, as is the wont of brides, was dressed in white, and so was Mr. Clemens, who gave his daughter away. He wore one of his famous white flannel suits topped by the scarlet cap and gown which he wore when his degree was conferred upon him by Oxford University. Mr. Clemens could no more help being humorous, no matter what the occasion, than he could help breathing, and the wedding of his daughter was no exception to the rule. To "avoid any delays at the ceremony" he prepared an interview which was given to the Press:

> Clara and Gabrilowitsch were pupils together under Leschetizky, in Vienna, ten years ago. We have known him intimately ever since. It's not new—the engagement. It was made and dissolved twice, six years ago. Recovering from a perilous surgical operation, two or three months passed by him here in the house ended a week or ten days days ago in a renewal. The wedding had to be sudden, for Gabrilowitsch's European season is ready to begin. The pair will sail a fortnight from now. The first engagements are in Germany. They have taken a house in Berlin.

When impertinently asked whether the marriage pleased him, Mr. Clemens replied:

> Yes, fully as much as any marriage could please me or perhaps any other father. There are two or three tragically solemn things in this life, and a happy marriage is one of them, for the terrors of life are all to come. A funeral is a solemn office, but I go to them with a spiritual uplift, thankful that the dead friend has been set free. That which follows is to me tragic and awful—the burial. I am glad of this marriage, and Mrs. Clemens would be glad, for she always had a warm affection for Gabrilowitsch, but all the same it is a tragedy, since it is a happy marriage with its future before it, loaded to the Plimsoll line with uncertainties.

When interviewed about the Mark Twain Library at Redding, Mr. Clemens referred to the various means that had been adopted for raising money for it, and made reference to a recent concert that had netted something less than four hundred dollars for the good work. It might have netted a great deal more if the prices had been higher, for it was an "all-star performance," including Miss Clemens, Mr. Gabrilowitsch and Mr. David Bispham, not to mention Mr. Clemens, who spoke a few words of introduction. I don't remember all that Mr. Clemens said, but I do remember that he said that it was hardly necessary for him to introduce Mr. Bispham or Mr. Gabrilowitsch to any audience, they were too well-known, but his daughter, who was not so well-known, was handsomer. Then he went on to say, that he did not see why he should have made these introductory remarks anyway, except that he had promised to do so, and he always believed in keeping a promise, although he was not quite sure whether that was the thing to do. He said there were times when a man was sorely tempted not to keep a promise. For instance: If he was about to be hanged and the sheriff should tell him that he could go home and visit his family, if he would return at the end of that two weeks to be hanged; for the sake of the reprieve the man would give his promise to return, but when the time came, it would be a pretty hard thing for him to do. "I know just how it feels," said Mr. Clemens, "as I made such a promise once myself,—but I didn't keep it."

Notwithstanding the fact that this was an all-star performance, the tickets were only fifty, seventy-five cents, and one dollar. They might just as well have been two or three times as much, for the cause was a good one, and the attractions certainly unusual. In New York it would have cost anywhere from one dollar and a half to two dollars to hear either one of these artists alone, but to hear them together, and with such a setting, was worth even more money, and would have been gladly paid if it had been asked.

"HANNELE" BANNED

Miss Ethel Barrymore, now playing in "Lady Frederick," has accepted the invitation of the University of California to appear in the Greek Theatre at Berkeley in the title role in the "Elektra" of Euripides. A translation of the tragedy has been made for her by Professor Gilbert Murray of Oxford University. The Greek Theatre at Berkeley is an open-air affair, seating seven thousand people. It was here in the summer of 1906 that Mme. Bernhardt played Racine's "Phedre" before an excited audience. Miss Barrymore has not Mme. Bernhardt's art, but she has youth and beauty and a fine voice, which, it is said, may some day be heard in grand opera.

Some fifteen years ago an attempt was made to give Gerhart Hauptmann's "Hannele" in this city, but public sentiment was bitterly opposed to it and the Mayor was called upon to prevent its performance. This he did not succeed in doing, but Commodore Gerry, President of the Society for the Prevention of Cruelty to Children, interfered and prevented a girl of fifteen from impersonating the heroine of the play. He argued that the play was calculated to injure the morals of a child, to say nothing of its effect upon her nervous system. The management secured an older actress for the part, but the public was not interested, and the play, notwithstanding the advertising it had received, failed to attract and after a few performances was withdrawn.

During the past winter "Hannele" has been given more than once at the New Deutsches Theatre, and no one has made any objection, not even Commodore Gerry. Is this because the play was given in German? Indeed, no. It is because of "The Servant in the House." Mr. Charles Rann Kennedy's modern morality play turned the tide. In this play, which has been running for two seasons, the Christ is boldly impersonated, and no one seems to mind it. Once in a while I have heard an expression of distaste from some one who has seen it, more often from some one who has not; but on the whole it has been very much praised and financially has been a great success. It is not only because of the character of Manson (Son of Man), but for the tone of socialism pervading the play. Our plutocrats like this—on the stage—and delight to be seen applauding the sentiments of the socialistic drain-digger. There is no denying that the play teaches a moral lesson, that it is well written and admirably acted.

STEPHEN PHILLIPS BANKRUPT

The rumor that Stephen Phillips was in a bad way financially was shown to be founded on fact, by his going into bankruptcy. His debts, it appears, amount to £614 ($3070), with no assets. His income consists of five percent royalties on plays written for various theatrical managers. Here is the trouble. Mr. Phillips should have put himself in the hands of a theatrical agent. No business manager of a playwright should allow him to accept five percent royalty. He might let him begin at that, but he would work up to twenty percent on a sliding scale. A great deal has been published about Mr. Phillips and his unbusinesslike methods, and he has frequently been compared with Harold Skimpole. It is a pity, for few poets ever started with better prospects, few having been dramatists as well as writers of verse.

THE NEW THEATRE

Mr. Henry Miller does not seem to like the New Theatre. He thinks the idea "un-American," and calls the building "a gilded incubator," and says that "it won't hatch any great drama." Mr. Miller said this immediately on his return from London, where he played in "The Great Divide," with perhaps not as much success as in this country. He had a bad voyage and was not feeling any too optimistic when he landed here; and then, I dare say, he ran amuck of the Customs, which is enough to make a pessimist of the worst kind out of the most pronounced optimist. "In charge of the actors of the New Theatre," he said, "they put a man who gives the information that he knows how to fire actors; it might be well for them to have some one who would know first how to hire the actors." Perhaps Mr. Miller misinterpreted the meaning of Mr. Ames's remark, if it was Mr. Ames's remark, that he knows how to "fire actors." Instead of firing them in the sense of throwing them out, he may have meant inspiring them. Indeed, it seems to me that Mr. Miller must have had a very rough voyage and a very hard time with the Customs, for he is so very severe on the New Theatre, which he thinks, sooner or later, will go to smash. It will be rather later than sooner, if at all, for Mr. W. K. Vanderbilt is reported to have said, at a meeting of the Directors, that he will pay any deficit out of his own pocket for the next ten years—though Mr. Ames and Mr. Corbin ask only five years in which to prove what the New Theatre can do.

I cannot say that I admire the New Theatre's selection of plays. I think that "Antony and Cleopatra" was an unfortunate one for the opening. If they had given us Miss Marlowe and Mr. Sothern in a Shakespearian comedy, "Much Ado" or "As You Like It," the result would have been more satisfactory. That was the first mistake. "The Cottage in the Air" was the second, for the play is not of sufficient importance or novelty for the New Theatre; while "The Nigger" is the third and biggest mistake the management have made. Mr. Edward Sheldon, the author of this play, is a clever young playwright, and some day may do something that will live; but he is too young and too inexperienced a dramatist to handle such a subject as he tackles in "The Nigger." If a plot such as this can be acted out before a New York audience in a theatre that is supposed to stand for the best, the finest, and the most decent, then it is futile to criticize the plays that make Broadway odorous. If a story whose plot hinges on an unspeakable crime can be acted before audiences of young men and young women, or even old men and old women, then there is no line to be drawn. Every playwright who writes unpleasant plays, argues that he has a moral lesson to teach, and that he is depicting life as it is, but this argument will not hold. There are other things in life than Tenderloin episodes and the most hideous side of the negro question. There are times when I think a censor would not be a bad thing!

EARLY SHAVIANISMS

Mr. Charles Frohman invited several English dramatists to spend their Christmas in this country, among them Mr. George Bernard Shaw. The others who were invited probably accepted or declined the invitation in a private letter to Mr. Frohman. Not so Mr. Shaw. The opportunity for advertising was too great. He had his declination cabled from the other side to the extent of half a column in the *Sun*. It is amusing reading, for Mr. Shaw is never dull, and there is some truth in what he says:

Why should any one who is in London go to America? You can understand any one in America coming to London. They all make a rush to do so. I might change my attitude if the stream were setting the other way and it were the dream of every Londoner the moment he had saved money to go to America. As it is, I am in the right place. Americans are in the wrong place. At least they seem to think so. Why should I move?

The Americans may be mistaken. I notice they never know anything about their own country. They are always astounded if you tell them what is going on there.

For instance, they are ignorant of the fact that liberty does not exist, there. I could be arrested the moment I landed on the charge of inciting the women of America to immorality by my good looks. I could be imprisoned for suggesting reform of the marriage laws or for questioning the story about Elisha and the bears....

I do not want to see the Statue of Liberty in New York harbor. Even my appetite for irony does not go as far as that.

To go to America is to go back a century in civilization. The manner of living in America today is simply that of two centuries ago, complicated with certain developments of industrial brigandage peculiar to the twentieth century.

Mr. Shaw's modesty was never more apparent than in his final reason for not coming to America. If he visited us he thinks that "everything else would stop. The people will cease to be interested in politics, commerce, art or anything else. Nicaragua may shoot all the Americans it likes; then the shots will not be heard in the din of silly talk about Bernard Shaw." Let me correct this last remark to "in the din of silly talk *by* Bernard Shaw."

GEORGE S. CHAPPELL
("DR. WALTER E. TRAPROCK")

The Fatu-liva Bird

I SHALL never forget the day when my bride and I sat on the edge of the lagoon after our matinal dip in its pellucid waters. It was a perfect September morn. So was she.

"My dear," I said suddenly, "Hatiaa Kappa eppe taue."

It sounds like a college fraternity but really means, "My woodlark, what is your name?"

I had been married over a week and I did not know my wife's name.

"Kippiputuonaa," she murmured musically.

"Taro ititi aa moieha ephaa lihaha?" I questioned, which, freely translated, is "What?"

"Kippiputuonaa."

Then, throwing back her head with its superb aureole of hair she softly crooned the words and music of the choral which the community chorus had sung on our wedding night.

> *Hooio-hooio uku hai unio*
> *Kippiputunonaa aaa titi huti*
> *O tefi tapu, O eio hoki*
> *Hooio-hooio, one naani-tui.*

How it all came back to me! Leaning towards her, I gently pressed the lobe of her ear with my chin, the native method of expressing deep affection. Her dusky cheeks flushed and with infinite shyness she lifted her left foot and placed it on my knee. Tattooed the length of the roseleaf sole in the graceful ideographic lettering of the islands I read—

"Kippiputuonaa," (Daughter of Pearl and Coral).

"What an exquisite name!" I murmured, "and so unusual!"

I was awed. I felt as if this superb creature, my mate, had revealed to me the last, most hidden of her secrets. I had heard of Mother of Pearl,—but of the Daughter—never ... and I was married to her!

"And you," she whispered, "are Naani-Tui, Face-of-the-Moon!"

I liked that. Frankly I was a bit set up about it. It sounded so much better than Moon-face.

I thrust out my left foot, bare of any inscription, and she tickled it playfully with a blade of *haro*. Radiant Kippiputuonaa—whom I soon called "Kippy" for short—your name shall ever remain a blessed memory, the deepest and dearest wound in my heart.

Kippy proposed that I should be marked for identification in the usual manner, but I shuddered at the thought. I was far too ticklish; I should have died under the needle.

What days of joyous romping we had! One morning a little crowd of us, just the Swanks, Whinneys and ourselves, met on the beach for a pillow-fight. It was a rare sport, and, as the pillows were eighteen-inch logs of *rapiti-wood,* not without its element of danger. A half-hour of this and we lay bruised and panting on the beach listening to the hoarse bellowing of the *wak-waks*.

The *wak-wak* is without exception the most outrageous creature that ploughs the deep in fishy guise. For man-eating qualities he had the shark skinned a nautical mile.

Whinney made a true remark to me one night,—one of the few he ever made. The ocean was particularly audible that evening.

"Listen to that surf," I remarked. "I never heard it grumble like that before."

"You'd grumble, if you were full of *wak-waks*," he said.

The *wak-wak* has a mouth like a subway entrance and I was told that so great was his appetite for human flesh that when, as occasionally happened, some unfortunate swimmer had been eaten by a shark, a *wak-wak* was sure to come rushing up and bolt shark, man and all. Consequently I did most of my swimming in the lagoon.

Speaking of the lagoon reminds me of an absurd bit of information I picked up from Kippy that made me feel as flat as a pressed fern. We were wandering along the shore one morning and she suddenly pointed to the *Kawa* and said laughingly.

"Why Tippi-litti (Triplett) bring Tree-with-Wings over *Hoopoi* (cocoanuts)?"

"Why not swim?" she asked. "Look see. Big hole."

I looked and saw. A whole section of the atoll near where we were standing was movable. Kippy jumped up and down on it and it rocked like a raft. At the edges I saw that it was lashed to the near-by trees with vines! Cheap? You could have bought me for a bad clam. As I thought of the days we had sweated over those damned cocoanuts, of Triplett's peril, of the danger to the yawl, while our very families looked on and laughed, thinking it was a game, and we might have slipped out the movable lock-gate and simply eased through—well, for the first time in my married life I was mad. Kippy was all tenderness in an instant.

"Face-of-Moon, no rain," she begged, "Daughter of Pearl and Coral eat clouds."

She chinned my ear passionately, and I was disarmed in an instant.

I hated to tell Triplett—it seemed to dim his glory, but I needn't have worried.

"Good business," he exclaimed. "We can get her out inter the open an' have some sailin' parties. I'd like to catch one of them *wak-waks*."

That was the sort Triplett was. He'd done his trick and there was an end of it. The next day he had William Henry Thomas busy re-rigging the *Kawa*. William Henry Thomas, by the way, insisted on living on board in happy but unholy wedlock, and Whinney, Swank and I felt that it was better so. Somehow we considered him the village scandal.

During these peaceful days I wrote a great deal, posting up my diary as far as we had gone and jotting down a lot of valuable material. Swank had got his impedimenta off the boat and began daubing furiously, landscapes, seascapes, monotypes, ideographs, everything. Most of them were hideously funny, but he did one thing,—inspired by love, I suppose—a portrait of his wife that was a hummer. She was a lovely little thing with a lovely name, Lupoba-Tilaana, "Mist-on-the-Mountain."

"Swank," I said, "that's a ten-strike. The mountain is a little out of focus but the mist is immense!"

He squirted me with yellow ochre.

Whinney was in his element. Ornithology, botany, ethulology, he took them all on single-handed.

"Listen to that," he said to me one night as we were strolling back from a friendly game of *Kahooti* with Baahaabaa and some of our friends.

I listened. It was the most unearthly and at the same time the most beautiful bird-song I have ever heard.

"What is it?" I asked, as the cry resounded again, a piercing screech of pain ending in a long yowl of joy.

"It is the motherhood cry of the *fatu-liva*," he said. "She has just laid an egg."

"But why the note of suffering?" I queried.

"The eggs of the *fatu-liva* are square," said Whinney, and I was silenced.

Motherhood is indeed the great mystery. Little did I realize that night how much I was to owe to the *fatu-liva* and her strange maternal gift which saved my life in one of the weirdest adventures that has ever befallen mortal man.

It was a placid day on the sea and Kippy and I were returning from a ten-mile swim to a neighboring island whither I had been taken to be shown off to some relatives.

"*Wak-wak*," I had said when she first proposed the expedition, but she had laughed gaily and nodded her head to indicate that there was not the slightest danger, and, shamed into it, we had set forth and made an excellent crossing.

On the return trip, midway between the two islands, I was floating lazily, supported by a girdle of inflated dew-fish bladders and towed by Kippy. She had propped over my head her verdant *taa-taa* without which the natives never swim for fear of the tropical sun, and I think I must have dozed off for I was suddenly roused by a hoarse Klaxon-bellow "Kaaraschaa-gha!" which told me all too plainly that I was in the most hideous peril.

"*Wak-wak!*" I barked, and all my past life began to unfold before me.

It was a horrid sight—the *wak-wak*, I mean. He was swimming on the surface, and at ten feet I saw his great jaws open, lined with row upon row of teeth that stretched back into his interior as far as the eye could reach and farther. Mixed up with this dreadful reality were visions of my past. I seemed to be peering into one of those vast, empty auditoriums that had greeted my opera, "Jumping Jean," when it was finally produced, privately.

"Help! Help!" I screamed, reverting to English.

Suddenly Kippy seized the *taa-taa* from my nerveless grasp. Half closing it, she swam directly toward the monster into whose widening throat she thrust the sharp-pointed instrument, in, in, until I thought she herself would follow it. And then, as she had intended, the points pierced the *wak-wak's* tonsil.

With a shriek of pain his jaws began to close and, on the instant, Kippy yanked the handle with all her might, opening the *taa-taa* to its full extent in the beast's very narrows.

Choked though he was, unable for the moment to bite or expel the outer air and submerge, the brute was still dangerous. Kippy was towing me shoreward at a speed which caused the sea to foam about my bladders but the *wak-wak* still pursued us. A second time my dauntless mate rose to the occasion.

With amazing buoyancy she lifted herself to a half-seated position on the surface of the water and poured forth the most astounding imitation of the motherhood cry of the *fatu-liva*.

"Biloo-ow-ow-ow-ow-zing-aaa!"

Again, and yet again, it rang across the waters, and in the distance, flying at incredible speed, I saw the rainbow host of *fatu-livas* coming towards us!

Gallant fowl! Shall I ever forget how they circled about us. One of their clan, as they supposed, was in dire danger and they functioned as only a *fatu-liva* can. Flying at an immense height, in battle formation, they began laying eggs with marvelous precision. The first two struck the *wak-wak* square on the nose and he screamed with pain. The third, landing corner-wise, put out his right eye and he began to thrash in helpless circles. The fourth was a direct hit on my left temple. "Face-of-the-Moon" passed over the horizon into oblivion whence he emerged to find himself in a tree, his brow eased with an *alova-leaf* poultice, his heart comforted by Daughter of Pearl and Coral.

RALPH BARTON

Science in Rhyme without Reason

ASTRONOMY

Astronomy (from *astron,* star,
   And *nemo,* to arrange)
Examines what is passing far
   And more than passing strange.

It deals with Martian polar frost,
   And inter-stellar space,
And wonders why the moon has lost
   The sets from out its face.

Astronomers of gentle mien
   Can give particulars
About the distances between
   Three thousand million stars.

But, if you asked the distance to
   The nearest movie-show,
It's likely one would answer you,
   "I really do not know."

BACTERIOLOGY

You have better sense, I hope,
Than to keep a microscope
   To inspect the odd behavior of Bacterium.
Once I looked through one of these
At a tiny bit of cheese.
   Now, instead of having cheese, I have delirium.

What I saw did not incite
An untroubled appetite;
   Now I disinfect my food before it's edible.
I'm afraid to breath the air;
I see microbes everywhere!
   Oh, the joy I miss in life is quite incredible!

BIOLOGY

In college, Windermere de Vere was beautiful and tall;
He won the girls who wouldn't look at Elmer Hobbs at all.
His fancy waistcoats fitted well, his eyes were dark and sad;
While Hobbs was small and diffident, and wore a thorax pad.

In after years, de Vere became a famous movie star,
And all the ladies in the world adored him from afar.
They followed him about the streets and begged for autographs;
Poor Hobbs took up the tombstone trade and chisled epitaphs.

And all the papers, ninety books, and every magazine
Proclaimed de Vere by far the Greatest Lover on the screen.
For him, Queens left their husbands and stenographers their jobs;
But no one seemed to care about the whereabouts of Hobbs.

When both the men had reached the age when tums resemble tubs,
They chanced to meet in one of our most fashionable clubs
"Well, Solomon—" Hobbs hailed de Vere, in mocking metaphor;
"Don't call me that!" de Vere exclaimed, "I am a bachelor!"

Poor, gentle Hobbs, in meek surprise, surveyed the movie star,
Then asked him if he would honor him by taking a cigar.
"Today," said Hobbs, "my ninth wife had my thirty-seventh child;
I trust that you will find the weed exceptionally mild."

BOTANY

I went into a florist's booth,
  To learn a little botany;
And asked them for the flower of youth,
  But found they hadn't got any.

I then required forget-me-not;
  They said it wasn't likely.
I wheeled about and quit the spot,
  Perhaps a bit obliquely.

LEE STROUT WHITE

Farewell to Model T

I see by the new Sears Roebuck catalogue that it is still possible to buy an axle for a 1909 Model T Ford, but I am not deceived. The great days have faded, the end is in sight. Only one page in the current catalogue is devoted to parts and accessories for the Model T; yet everyone remembers springtimes when the Ford gadget section was larger than men's clothing, almost as large as household furnishings. The last Model T was built in 1927, and the car is fading from what scholars call the American scene—which is an understatement, because to a few million people who grew up with it, the old Ford practically *was* the American scene.

It was the miracle God had wrought. And it was patently the sort of thing that could only happen once. Mechanically uncanny, it was like nothing that had ever come to the world before. Flourishing industries rose and fell with it. As a vehicle, it was hard-working, commonplace, heroic; and it often seemed to transmit those qualities to the persons who rode in it. My own generation identifies it with Youth, with its gaudy, irretrievable excitements; before it fades into the mist, I would like to pay it the tribute of the sigh that is not a sob, and set down random entries in a shape somewhat less cumbersome than a Sears Roebuck catalogue.

The Model T was distinguished from all other makes of cars by the fact that its transmission was of a type known as planetary—which was half metaphysics, half sheer friction. Engineers accepted the word "planetary" in its epicyclic sense, but I was always conscious that it also meant "wandering," "erratic." Because of the peculiar nature of this planetary element, there was always, in Model T, a certain dull rapport between engine and wheels, and even when the car was in a state known as neutral, it trembled with a deep imperative and tended to inch forward. There was never a moment when the bands were not faintly egging the machine on. In this respect it was like a horse, rolling the bit on its tongue, and country people brought to it the same technique they used with draft animals.

Its most remarkable quality was its rate of acceleration. In its palmy days the Model T could take off faster than anything on the road. The reason was simple. To get under way, you simply hooked the third finger of the right hand around a lever on the steering column, pulled down hard, and shoved your left foot forcibly against the low-speed pedal. These were simple, positive motions; the car responded by lunging forward with a roar. After a few seconds of this turmoil, you took your toe off the pedal, eased up a mite on the throttle, and the car, possessed of only two forward speeds, catapulted directly into high with a series of ugly jerks and was off on its glorious errand. The abruptness of this departure was never equalled in other cars of the period. The human leg was (and still is) incapable of letting in a clutch with anything like the forthright abandon that used to send Model T on its way. Letting in a clutch is a negative, hesitant motion, depending on delicate nervous control; pushing down the Ford pedal was a simple, country motion—an expansive act, which came as natural as kicking an old door to make it budge.

The driver of the old Model T was a man enthroned. The car, with top up, stood seven feet high. The driver sat on top of the gas tank, brooding it with his own body. When he wanted gasoline, he alighted, along with everything else in the front seat; the seat was pulled off, the metal cap unscrewed, and a wooden stick thrust down to sound the liquid in the well. There were always a couple of these sounding sticks kicking around in the ratty subcushion regions of a flivver. Refuelling was more of a social function then, because the driver had to unbend, whether he wanted to or not. Directly in front of the driver was the windshield—high, uncompromisingly erect. Nobody talked about air resistance, and the four cylinders pushed the car through the atmosphere with a simple disregard of physical law.

There was this about a Model T; the purchaser never regarded his purchase as a complete, finished product. When you bought a Ford, you figured you had a start—a vibrant, spirited framework to which could be screwed an almost limitless assortment of decorative and functional hardware. Driving away from the agency, hugging the new wheel between your knees, you were already full of creative worry. A Ford was born naked as a baby, and a flourishing industry grew up out of correcting its rare deficiencies and combatting its fascinating diseases. Those were the great days of lily-painting.

I have been looking at some old Sears Roebuck catalogues, and they bring everything back so clear.

First you bought a Ruby Safety Reflector for the rear, so that your posterior would glow in another car's brilliance. Then you invested thirty-nine cents in some radiator Moto Wings, a popular ornament which gave the Pegasus touch to the machine and did something godlike to the owner. For nine cents you bought a fan-belt guide to keep the belt from slipping off the pulley.

You bought a radiator compound to stop leaks. This was as much a part of everybody's equipment as aspirin tablets are of a medicine cabinet. You bought special oil to prevent chattering, a clamp-on dash light, a patching outfit, a tool box which you bolted to the running board, a sun visor, a steering-column brace to keep the column rigid, and a set of emergency containers for gas, oil, and water—three thin, disclike cans which reposed in a case on the running board during long, important journeys—red for gas, gray for water, green for oil. It was only a beginning. After the car was about a year old, steps were taken to check the alarming disintegration. (Model T was full of tumors, but they were benign.) A set of anti-rattlers (98¢) was a popular panacea. You hooked them on to the gas and spark rods, to the brake pull rod, and to the steering-rod connections. Hood silencers, of black rubber, were applied to the fluttering hood. Shock-absorbers and snubbers gave "complete relaxation." Some people bought rubber pedal pads, to fit over the standard metal pedals. (I didn't like these, I remember.) Persons of a suspicious or pugnacious turn of mind bought a rear-view mirror; but most Model T owners weren't worried by what was coming from behind because they would soon enough see it out in front. They rode in a state of cheerful catalepsy. Quite a large mutinous clique among Ford owners went over to a foot accelerator (you could buy one and screw it to the floor board), but there was a certain madness in these people, because the Model T, just as she stood, had a choice of three foot pedals to push, and there were plenty of moments when both feet were occupied in the routine performance of duty and when the only way to speed up the engine was with the hand throttle.

Gadget bred gadget. Owners not only bought ready-made gadgets, they invented gadgets to meet special needs. I myself drove my car directly from the agency to the blacksmith's, and had the smith affix two enormous iron brackets to the port running board to support an army trunk.

People who owned closed models built along different lines: they bought ball grip handles for opening doors, window anti-rattlers, and de-luxe flower vases of the cut-glass anti-splash type. People with delicate sensibilities garnished their car with a device called the Donna Lee Automobile Disseminator—a porous vase guaranteed, according to Sears, to fill the car with a "faint clean odor of lavender."

The gap between open cars and closed cars was not as great then as it is now: for $11.95, Sears Roebuck converted your touring car into a sedan and you went forth renewed. One agreeable quality of the old Fords was that they had no bumpers, and their fenders softened and wilted with the years and permitted the driver to squeeze in and out of tight places.

Tires were 30x3½, cost about twelve dollars, and punctured readily. Everybody carried a Jiffy patching set, with a nutmeg grater to roughen the tube before the goo was spread on. Everybody was capable of putting on a patch, expected to have to, and did have to.

During my association with Model T's, self-starters were not a prevalent accessory. They were expensive and under suspicion. Your car came equipped with a serviceable crank, and the first thing you learned was how to Get Results. It was a special trick, and until you learned it (usually from another Ford owner, but sometimes by a period of appalling experimentation) you might as well have been winding up an awning. The trick was to leave the ignition switch off, proceed to the animal's head, pull the choke (which was a little wire protruding through the radiator), and give the crank two or three nonchalant upward lifts. Then, whistling as though thinking about something else, you would saunter back to the driver's cabin, turn the ignition on, return to the crank, and this time, catching it on the down stroke, give it a quick spin with plenty of That. If this procedure was followed, the engine almost always responded—first with a few scattered explosions, then with a tumultuous gunfire, which you checked by racing around to the driver's seat and retarding the throttle. Often, if the emergency brake hadn't been pulled all the way back, the car advanced on you the instant the first explosion occurred and you would hold it back by leaning your weight against it. I can still feel my old Ford nuzzling me at the curb, as though looking for an apple in my pocket.

In zero weather, ordinary cranking became an impossibility, except for giants. The oil thickened, and it became necessary to jack up the rear wheels, which, for some planetary reason, eased the throw.

The lore and legend that governed the Ford were boundless. Owners had their own theories about everything; they discussed mutual problems in that wise, infinitely resourceful way old women discuss rheumatism. Exact knowledge was pretty scarce, and often proved less effective than superstition. Dropping a camphor ball into the gas tank was a popular expedient; it seemed to have a tonic effect on both man and machine. There wasn't much to base exact knowledge on. The Ford driver flew blind. He didn't know the temperature of his engine, the speed of his car, the amount of his fuel, or the pressure of his oil (the old Ford lubricated itself by what was amiably described as the "splash system"). A speedometer cost money and was an extra, like a windshield-wiper. The dashboard of the early models was bare save for an ignition key; later models, grown effete, boasted an ammeter which pulsated alarmingly with the throbbing of the car. Under the dash was a box of coils, with vibrators which you adjusted, or thought you adjusted. Whatever the driver learned of his motor, he learned not through instruments but through sudden developments. I remember that the timer was one of the vital organs about which there was ample doctrine. When everything else had been checked, you "had a look" at the timer. It was an extravagantly odd little device, simple in construction, mysterious in function. It contained a roller, held by a spring, and there were four contact points on the inside of the case against which, many people believed, the roller rolled. I have had a timer apart on a sick Ford many times, but I never really knew what I was up to—I was just showing off before God.

There were almost as many schools of thought as there were timers. Some people, when things went wrong, just clenched their teeth and gave the timer a smart crack with a wrench. Other people opened it up and blew on it. There was a school that held that the timer needed large amounts of oil; they fixed it by frequent baptism. And there was a school that was positive it was meant to run dry as a bone; these people were continually taking it off and wiping it. I remember once spitting into a timer; not in anger, but in a spirit of research. You see, the Model T driver moved in the realm of metaphysics. He believed his car could be hexed.

One reason the Ford anatomy was never reduced to an exact science was that, having "fixed" it, the owner couldn't honestly claim that the treatment had brought about the cure. There were too many authenticated cases of Fords fixing themselves—restored naturally to health after a short rest. Farmers soon discovered this, and it fitted nicely with their draft-horse philosophy: "Let 'er cool off and she'll snap into it again."

A Ford owner had Number One Bearing constantly in mind. This bearing, being at the front end of the motor, was the one that always burned out, because the oil didn't reach it when the car was climbing hills. (That's what I was always told, anyway.) The oil used to recede and leave Number One dry as a clam flat; you had to watch that bearing like a hawk. It was like a weak heart—you could hear it start knocking, and that was when you stopped and let her cool off. Try as you would to keep the oil supply right, in the end Number One always went out. "Number One Bearing burned out on me and I had to have her replaced," you would say, wisely; and your companions always had a lot to tell about how to protect and pamper Number One to keep her alive.

Sprinkled not too liberally among the millions of amateur witch doctors who drove Fords and applied their own abominable cures were the heaven-sent mechanics who could really make the car talk. These professionals turned up in undreamed-of-spots. One time, on the banks of the Columbia River in Washington, I heard the rear end go out of my Model T when I was trying to whip it up a steep incline onto the deck of a ferry. Something snapped; the car slid backward into the mud. It seemed to me like the end of the trail. But the captain of the ferry, observing the withered remnant, spoke up.

"What's got her?" he asked.

"I guess it's the rear end," I replied, listlessly. The captain leaned over the rail and stared. Then I saw that there was a hunger in his eyes that set him off from other men.

"Tell you what," he said, carelessly, trying to cover up his eagerness, "let's pull the son of a bitch up onto the boat, and I'll help you fix her while we're going back and forth on the river."

We did just this. All that day I plied between the towns of Pasco and Kennewick, while the skipper (who had once worked in a Ford garage) directed the amazing work of resetting the bones of my car.

Springtime in the heyday of the Model T was a delirious season. Owning a car was still a major excitement, roads were still wonderful and bad. The Fords were obviously conceived in madness; any car which was capable of going from forward into reverse without any perceptible mechanical hiatus was bound to be a mighty challenging thing to the human imagination. Boys used to veer them off the highway into a level pasture and run wild with them, as though they were cutting up with a girl.

Most everybody used the reverse pedal quite as much as the regular foot brake—it distributed the wear over the bands and wore them all down evenly. That was the big trick, to wear all the bands down evenly, so that the final chattering would be total and the whole unit scream for renewal.

The days were golden, the nights were dim and strange. I still recall with trembling those loud, nocturnal crises when you drew up to a signpost and raced the engine so the lights would be bright enough to read destinations by. I have never been really planetary since. I suppose it's time to say good-bye. Farewell, my lovely!

ESSAYS

THE SELECTION of *American essays presented herewith gives, I think, a pretty fair cross-section of the essay form as it has been developed at its best. An Englishman almost invariably thinks (wrong word; skip it) that an essay is something like something Charles Lamb might have written, and that above all it must be gentle and whimsical; and, because that kind of writing requires no thought at all nor even a subject, every English writer at some time or another commits a book of "essays." They all sound like something by somebody who is under the delusion that he is following in the footsteps of the gentle Lamb. He is; but like a white-wing. Sometimes you find an Englishman who is of a different school, the ponderous school, of opinion as to what an essay is like. He thinks an essay is like something by Dr. Johnson. So he imagines he is following in the footsteps of Dr. Johnson.... The image-idea is still the same; but the scene is the circus.*

Henry David Thoreau quit paying taxes, got thrown into jail and then went to live like a hermit in the woods in protest against the idea of the Boston Brahmins that an essay was something like something Charles Lamb might write. One might imagine that he took up the pencil-making trade because he couldn't stomach "The Autocrat of the Breakfast Table" or "The Professor at the Breakfast Table" and he was sure Holmes wrote with a quill. ... But genius that he was, Thoreau, he could not help attracting followers among precisely the type of person he was trying to get away from.... Paul Elmer More even followed him into the woods, by example. More was the sort of man who could seriously argue in one of his Shelburne Essays that private property, however obtained, was a more sacred thing than human life. It is a good thing Thoreau didn't live to see that essay and "A Hermit's Notes on Thoreau": he would have gone stark, raving crazy—or whetted up a broad-axe....

Elbert Hubbard was as peculiarly an American phenomenon as P. T. Barnum and he had something of the same sort of genius Barnum had. But Barnum did more than play practical jokes on the boobery with stuff like "This way to the Egress!"; he created the modern circus, a great cultural institution. And Elbert Hubbard did more than wear his hair long, sell the "Rubaiyat" in fancy limp-leather bindings, and lumber up thousands of

American homes with almost immovably heavy furniture suitable only for the courtyards of early California missions. In the horse-and-buggy days, he challenged the snobbish idea that knowledge and a taste for reading the best in literature was a thing for only the few, went upon the vaudeville stage (good showman that he was) and proved that vaudeville audiences like ideas and things of the mind and spirit as much as, if not better than, they like jugglers and trained seals. The intellectual snobs had scared self-made men, geniuses without formal education, such as Thomas A. Edison, Harvey Firestone, Henry Ford and other geniuses of a kind, into an active state of resentment against the very idea of what the Mores called culture. Hubbard brought them out of this; they became his friends. Hubbard also brought mental stimulations through his Philistine and his rather gaudy Fra to thousands of towns where there were no bookstores, no libraries—because he learned how to merchandize his product and distribute his magazine and how to keep interest in his magazine up. He wrote in a vigorous and lively style, in the American idiom, instead of in a desiccated and embalmed style cultivated by the snobs of literature....

One of the most waspish geniuses of all time was the etcher, painter and professional dandy, James McNeill Whistler, who, being a crack-shot at repartee himself, inevitably ran afoul of his only rival in the rapier thrust of words, Oscar Wilde. Their duel was historic. The selections include practically all the source material that constitute the anecdotes you hear at any party when the name of Wilde or Whistler comes up....

Donald Culross Peattie, after a rather disheartening attempt to write salable fiction (he had published three novels), wrote "An Almanac for Moderns" in 1935. On its publication in the spring of 1936 it was hailed by competent critics as a work of genius, but it was a unique book of essays by a naturalist in which a distinguished prose-poetic style conveyed the curious, exact information of an all-round, natural, but modest scientist. In the fall of 1936 "An Almanac for Moderns" was chosen by a symposium of reviewers and critics from all over the country as being "the contemporary work by an American writer produced during 1935 most likely to become a classic." The final board of judges consisted of Carl Van Doren, chairman, Harry Hansen of the New York World-Telegram, Joseph Wood Krutch of The Nation, and Burton Rascoe. A gold medal was struck and awarded to Don Peattie by the Limited Editions Club; a beautifully designed and illustrated edition of the book was sent to the club's subscribers; George Macy, president of the Limited Editions Club, gave a magnificent breakfast to Peattie in *the Waldorf-Astoria, inviting several hundred people including critics, reviewers, and newspaper reporters. . . . And the resulting publicity stimulated the already booming trade sale of "An Almanac for Moderns" and sent it rolling toward fame and fortune for the author.*

Mark Van Doren, the poet and amateur naturalist, wrote of "An Almanac for Moderns": "Not merely is it the best of its kind that I have read in years; it is one of the best I ever read." And I, writing in Esquire *before Van Doren, Krutch, Hansen and I made the award, saluted the book as "a classic." "An Almanac for Moderns" is about birds and bees and frogs and the visible aspects of nature, but it is also life seen under the microscope—and about Man and his relation to the universe about him. There is an essay for each day in the year, beginning with March 21st, which is the beginning of the reign of Aries in the signs of the Zodiac. It is from Aries that I have made a selection from this extraordinary book.*

HENRY DAVID THOREAU

An Excursion to Canada

"New England is by some affirmed to be an island, bounded on the north with the river Canada (so called from Monsieur Cane)."—Josselyn's Rareties

I. CONCORD TO MONTREAL

I FEAR that I have not got much to say about Canada, not having seen much; what I got by going to Canada was a cold. I left Concord, Massachusetts, Wednesday morning, Sept. 25th, ——, for Quebec. Fare seven dollars there and back; distance from Boston, five hundred and ten miles; being obliged to leave Montreal on the return as soon as Friday, Oct. 4th, or within ten days. I will not stop to tell the reader the names of my fellow-travellers; there were said to be fifteen hundred of them. I wished only to be set down in Canada, and take one honest walk there as I might in Concord woods of an afternoon.

The country was new to me beyond Fitchburg. In Ashburnham and afterward, as we were whirled rapidly along, I noticed the woodbine (*ameplopsis quinquefolia*), its leaves now changed, for the most part on dead trees, draping them like a red scarf. It was a little exciting, suggesting bloodshed, or or at least a military life, like an epaulet or sash, as if it were dyed with the blood of the trees whose wounds it was inadequate to stanch. For now the bloody autumn was come, and an Indian warfare was waged through the forest. These military trees appeared very numerous, for our rapid progress connected those that were even some miles apart. Does the woodbine prefer the elm? The first view of Monadnoc was obtained five or six miles this side of Fitzwilliam, but nearest and best at Troy and beyond. Then there were the Troy cuts and embankments. Keen-street strikes the traveller favorably, it is so wide, level, straight and long. I have heard one of my relatives who was born and bred there, say, that you could see a chicken run across it a mile off. I have also been told that when this town was settled they laid out a street four rods wide, but at a subsequent meeting of the proprietors one rose and remarked, "We have plenty of land, why not make the street eight rods wide?" and so they voted that it should be eight rods wide, and the town is known far and near for its handsome street. It was a cheap way of securing comfort, as well as fame, and I wish that all new towns would take pattern from this. It is best to lay our plans widely in youth, for then land is cheap, and it is but too easy to contract our views afterward. Youths so laid out, with broad avenues and parks, that they may make handsome and liberal old men! Show me a youth whose mind is like some Washington city of magnificent distances, prepared for the most remotely successful and glorious life after all, when those spaces shall be built over, and the idea of the founder be realized. I trust that every New England boy will begin by laying out a Keen-street through his head, eight rods wide. I know one such Washington city of a man, whose lots as yet are only surveyed and staked out, and except a cluster of shanties here and there, only the capitol stands there for all structures, and any day you may see from afar his princely idea borne coachwise along the spacious but yet empty avenues. Keen is built on a remarkably large and level interval, like the bed of a lake, and the surrounding hills, which are remote from its street, must afford some good walks. The scenery of mountain towns is commonly too much crowded. A town which is built on a plain of some extent, with an open horizon, and surrounded by hills at a distance, affords the best walks and views.

As we travel north-west up the country, sugar-maples, beeches, birches, hemlocks, spruce, butternuts and ash trees, prevail more and more. To the rapid traveller the number of elms in a town is the measure of its civility. One man in the cars has a bottle full of some liquor. The whole company smile whenever it is exhibited. I find no difficulty in containing myself. The Westmoreland country looked attractive. I heard a passenger giving the very obvious derivation of this name, West-more-land, as if it were purely American, and he had made a discovery; but I thought of "my cousin Westmoreland" in England. Every one will remember the approach to Bellows' Falls, under a high cliff which rises from the Connecticut. I was disappointed in the size of the river here; it appeared shrunk to a mere mountain stream. The water was evidently very low. The rivers which we had crossed this forenoon possessed more of the character of mountain streams than those in the vicinity of Concord, and I was surprised to see everywhere traces of recent freshets, which had carried away bridges and injured the railroad, though I had heard nothing of it. In Ludlow, Mount Holly, and beyond, there is interesting mountain scenery, not rugged and stupendous, but such as you could easily ramble over—long narrow mountain vales through which to see the horizon. You are in the midst of the Green Mountains. A few more elevated blue peaks are seen from the neighborhood of Mount Holly, perhaps Killington Peak is one. Sometimes, as on the Western railroad, you are whirled over mountainous embankments, from which the scared horses in the valleys appear diminished to hounds. All the hills blush; I think that autumn must be the best season to journey over even the *Green* Mountains. You frequently exclaim to yourself, what *red* maples! The sugar maple is not so red. You see some of the latter with rosy spots or cheeks only, blushing on one side like fruit, while all the rest of the tree is green, proving either some partiality in the light or frosts, or some prematurity in particular branches. Tall and slender ash trees, whose foliage is turned to a dark mulberry color, are frequent. The butternut, which is a remarkably spreading tree, is turned completely yellow, thus proving its relation to the hickories. I was also struck by the bright yellow tints of the yellow-birch. The sugar-maple is remarkable for its clean ankle. The groves of these trees looked like vast forest sheds, their branches stopping short at a uniform height, four or five feet from the ground, like eaves, as if they had been trimmed by art, so that you could look under and through the whole grove with its leafy canopy, as under a tent whose curtain is raised.

As you approach Lake Champlain you begin to see the New-York mountains. The first view of the Lake at Vergennes is impressive, but rather from association than from any peculiarity in the scenery. It lies there so small (not appearing in that proportion to the width of the State that it does on the map), but beautifully quiet, like a picture of the Lake of Lucerne on a music box, where you trace the name Lucerne among the foliage; far more ideal than ever it looked on the map. It does not say, "Here I am, Lake Champlain," as the conductor might for it, but having studied the geography thirty years, you crossed over a hill one afternoon and beheld it. But it is only a glimpse that you get here. At Burlington you rush to a wharf and go on board a steamboat, two hundred and thirty-two miles from Boston. We left Concord at twenty minutes before eight in the morning, and reached Burlington about six at night, but too late to see the Lake. We got our first fair view of the Lake at dawn, just before reaching Plattsburg, and saw blue ranges of mountains on either hand, in New-York, and in Vermont, the former especially grand. A few white schooners, like gulls, were seen in the distance, for it is not waste and solitary like a lake in Tartary; but it was such a view as leaves not much to be said; indeed I have postponed Lake Champlain to another day.

The oldest reference to these waters that I have yet seen, is in the account of Cartier's discovery and exploration of the St. Lawrence in 1535. Samuel Champlain actually discovered and paddled up the Lake in July, 1609, eleven years before the settlement of Plymouth, accompanying a war-party of the Canadian Indians against the Iroquois. He describes the islands in it as not inhabited, although they are pleasant, on account of the continual wars of the Indians, in consequence of which they withdrew from the rivers and lakes into the depths of the land, that they may not be surprised. "Continuing our course," says he, "in this Lake, on the western side, viewing the country, I saw on the eastern side very high mountains, where there was more on the summit. I inquired of the savages if those places were inhabited. They replied that they were, and that they were Iroquois, and that in those places there were beautiful valleys and plains fertile in corn, such as I have eaten in this country, with an infinity of other fruits." This is the earliest account of what is now Vermont.

The number of French Canadian gentlemen and ladies among the passengers, and the sound of the French language, advertised us by this time, that we were being whirled towards some foreign vortex. And now we have left Rouse's Point, and entered the Sorel river, and passed the invisible barrier between the States and Canada. The shores of the Sorel, Richelieu or St. John's river, are flat and reedy, where I had expected something more rough and mountainous for a natural boundary between two nations. Yet I saw a difference at once, in the few huts, in the pirogues on the shore, and as it were, in the shore itself. This was an interesting scenery to me, and the very reeds or rushes in the shallow water, and the tree-tops in the swamps, have left a pleasing impression. We had still a distant view behind us of two or three blue mountains in Vermont and New-York. About nine o'clock in the forenoon we reached St. John's, an old frontier post three hundred and six miles from Boston and twenty-four from Montreal. We now discovered that we were in a foreign country, in a station-house of another nation. This building was a barn-like structure, looking as if it were the work of the villagers combined, like a log-house in a new settlement. My attention was caught by the double advertisements in French and English fastened to its posts, by the formality of the English, and the covert or open reference to their queen and the British lion. No gentlemanly conductor appeared, none whom you would know to be the conductor by his dress and demeanor; but, ere long we began to see here and there a solid, red-faced, burly-looking Englishman, a little pursy perhaps, who made us ashamed of ourselves and our thin and nervous countrymen—a grandfatherly personage, at home in his great-coat, who looked as if he might be a stage proprietor, certainly a railroad director, and knew, or had a right to know when the cars did start. Then there were two or three pale-faced, black-eyed, loquacious Canadian French gentlemen there, shrugging their shoulders; pitted as if they had all had the small-pox. In the meanwhile some soldiers, red-coats, belonging to the barracks near by, were turned out to be drilled. At every important point in our route the soldiers showed themselves ready for us; though they were evidently rather raw recruits here, they manœuvred far better than our soldiers; yet, as usual, I heard some Yankees speak as if they were as great shakes, and they had seen the Acton Blues manœuvre as well. The officers spoke sharply to them, and appeared to be doing their part thoroughly. I heard one, suddenly coming to the rear, exclaim, "Michael Donothy, take his name!" Though I could not see what the latter did or omitted to do, it was whispered that Michael Donothy would have to suffer for that. I heard some of our party discussing the possibility of their driving these troops off the field with their umbrellas. I thought that the Yankee, though undisciplined, had this advantage at least, that he especially is a man who, everywhere and under all circumstances, is fully resolved to better his condition essentially, and therefore he could afford to be beaten at first; while the virtue of the Irishman, and to a great extent the Englishman, consists in merely maintaining his ground or condition. The Canadians here, a rather poor-looking race, clad in grey homespun, which gave them the appearance of being covered with dust, were riding about in caleches and small one-horse carts called charettes. The Yankees assumed that all the riders were racing, or at least exhibiting the paces of their horses, and saluted them accordingly. We saw but little of the village here, for nobody could tell us when the cars would start; that was kept a profound secret, perhaps for political reasons; and therefore we were tied to our seats. The inhabitants of St. John's and vicinity are described by an English traveller as "singularly unprepossessing," and before completing his period he adds, "besides, they are generally very much disaffected to the British crown." I suspect that that "besides" should have been a because.

At length, about noon, the cars began to roll towards La Prairie. The whole distance of fifteen miles was over a remarkably level country, resembling a western prairie, with the mountains about Chambly visible in the north-east. This novel, but monotonous scenery, was exciting. At La Prairie we first took notice of the tinned roofs, but above all, of the St. Lawrence, which looked like a lake; in fact it is considerably expanded here; it was nine miles across diagonally to Montreal. Mount Royal in the rear of the city and the island of St. Helen's opposite to it, were now conspicuous. We could also see the Sault St. Louis about five miles up the river, and the Sault Vorruan still farther eastward. The former are described as the most considerable rapids in the St. Lawrence; but we could see merely a gleam of light there as from a cobweb in the sun. Soon the city of Montreal was discovered with its tin roofs shining afar. Their reflections fell on the eye like a clash of cymbals on the ear. Above all the church of Notre Dame was conspicuous, and anon the Bonsecours market-house, occupying a commanding position on the quay, in the rear of the shipping. This city makes the more favorable impression from being approached by water, and also being built of stone, a grey limestone found on the island. Here, after travelling directly inland the whole breadth of New England, we had struck upon a city's harbor—it made on me the impression of a seaport—to which ships of six hundred tons can ascend, and where vessels drawing fifteen feet lie close to the wharf, five hundred and forty miles from the Gulf; the St. Lawrence being here two miles wide. There was a great crowd assembled on the ferry-boat wharf, and on the quay, to receive the Yankees, and flags of all colors were streaming from the vessels to celebrate their arrival. When the gun was fired, the gentry hurrahed again and again, and then the Canadian caleche drivers, who were most interested in the matter, and who, I perceived, were separated from the former by a fence, hurrahed their welcome; first the broadcloth, then the homespun.

It was early in the afternoon when we stepped ashore, with a single companion I soon found my way to the church of Notre Dame. I saw that it was of great size and signified something. It is said to be the largest ecclesiastical structure in North America, and can seat ten thousand. It is two hundred and fifty-five and a half feet long, and the groined ceiling is eighty feet above your head. The Catholic are the only churches which I have seen worth remembering, which are not almost wholly profane. I do not speak only of the rich and splendid like this, but of the humblest of them as well. Coming from the hurrahing mob and the rattling carrriages, we pushed aside the listed door of this church, and found ourselves instantly in an atmosphere which might be sacred to thought and religion, if one had any. There sat one or two women who had stolen a moment from the concerns of the day, as they were passing; but, if there had been fifty people there, it would still have been the most solitary place imaginable. They did not look up at us, nor did one regard another. We walked softly down the broad-aisle with our hats in our hands. Presently came in a troop of Canadians, in their homespun, who had come to the city in the boat with us, and one and all kneeled down in the aisle before the high altar to their devotions, somewhat awkwardly, as cattle prepare to lie down, and there we left them. As if you were to catch some farmer's sons from Marlboro', come to cattle-show, silently kneeling in Concord meeting-house some Wednesday! Would there not soon be a mob peeping in at the windows? It is true, these Roman Catholics, priests and all, impress me as a people who have fallen far behind the significance of their symbols. It is as if an ox had strayed into a church and were trying to bethink himself. Nevertheless, they are capable of reverence; but we Yankees are a people in whom this sentiment has nearly died out, and in this respect we cannot bethink ourselves even as oxen. I did not mind the pictures nor the candles, whether tallow or tin. Those of the former which I looked at appeared tawdry. It matters little to me whether the pictures are by a neophyte of the Algonquin or the Italian tribe. But I was impressed by the quiet religious atmosphere of the place. It was a great cave in the midst of a city; and what were the altars and the tinsel but the sparkling stalactics, into which you entered in a moment, and where the still atmosphere and the sombre light disposed to serious and profitable thought? Such a cave at hand, which you can enter any day, is worth a thousand of our churches which are open only Sundays—hardly long enough for an airing—and then filled with a bustling congregation—a church where the priest is the least part, where you do your own preaching, where the universe preaches to you and can be heard.... In Concord, to be sure, we do not need such. Our forests are such a church, far grander and more sacred. We dare not leave *our* meeting-houses open for fear they would be profaned. Such a cave, such a shrine, in one of our groves, for instance, how long would it be respected? for what purposes would it be entered, by such baboons as we are? I think of its value not only to religion, but to philosophy and to poetry; besides a reading room, to have a thinking room in every city! Perchance the time will come when every house even will have not only its sleeping rooms, and dining room, and talking room or parlor, but its thinking room also, and the architects will put it into their plans. Let it be furnished and ornamented with whatever conduces to serious and creative thought. I should not object to the holy water, or any other simple symbols if it were consecrated by the imagination of the worshippers.

I heard that some Yankees bet that the candles were not wax, but tin. A European assured them that they were wax; but, inquiring of the sexton, he was surprised to learn that they were tin filled with oil. The church was too poor to afford wax. As for the Protestant churches, here or elsewhere, they did not interest me, for it is only as caves that churches interest me at all, and in that respect they were inferior.

Montreal makes the impression of a larger city than you had expected to find, though you may have heard that it contains nearly sixty thousand inhabitants. In the newer parts it appeared to be growing fast like a small New-York, and to be considerably Americanized. The names of the squares reminded you of Paris—the Champ de Mars, the Place d'Armes, and others, and you feel as if a French revolution might break out any moment. Glimpses of Mount Royal rising behind the town, and the names of some streets in that direction make one think of Edinburgh. That hill sets off this city wonderfully. I inquired at a principal book-store for books published in Montreal. They said that there were none but school-books and the like; they got their books from the States. From time to time we met a priest in the streets, for they are distinguished by their dress like the *civil* police. Like clergymen generally, with or without the gown, they made on us the impression of effeminacy. We also met some Sisters of Charity, dressed in black, with Shaker-shaped black bonnets and crosses, and cadaverous faces, who looked as if they had almost cried their eyes out, their complexions parboiled with scalding tears; insulting the daylight by their presence, having taken an oath not to smile. By cadaverous I mean that their faces were like the faces of those who have been dead and buried for a year, and then untombed, with the life's grief upon them, and yet, for some unaccountable reason, the process of decay arrested.

> "Truth never fails her servant, sir, nor leaves him
> With the day's shame upon him."

They waited demurely on the sidewalk while a truck laden with raisins was driven in at the seminary of St. Sulpice, never once lifting their eyes from the ground.

The soldier here, as every where in Canada, appeared to be put forward, and by his best foot. They were in the proportion of the soldiers to the laborers in an African ant-hill. The inhabitants evidently rely on them in a great measure for music and entertainment. You would meet with them pacing back and forth before some guard-house or passage-way, guarding, regarding and disregarding all kinds of law by turns, apparently for the sake of the discipline to themselves, and not because it was important to exclude any body from entering that way. They reminded me of the men who are paid for piling up bricks and then throwing them down again. On every prominent ledge you could see England's hands holding the Canadas, and I judged by the redness of her knuckles that she would soon have to let go. In the rear of such a guardhouse, in a large gravelled square or parade ground, called the Champ de Mars, we saw a large body of soldiers being drilled, we being as yet the only spectators. But they did not appear to notice us any more than the devotees in the church, but were seemingly as indifferent to fewness of spectators as the phenomena of nature are, whatever they might have been thinking under their helmets, of the Yankees that were to come. Each man wore white kid gloves. It was one of the most interesting sights which I saw in Canada. The problem appeared to be how to smooth down all individual protuberances or idiosyncrasies, and make a thousand men move as one man, animated by one central will, and there was some approach to success. They obeyed the signals of a commander who stood at a great distance, wand in hand, and the precision, and promptness, and harmony of their movements could not easily have been matched. The harmony was far more remarkable than that of any quire or band, and obtained, no doubt, at a greater cost. They made on me the impression, not of many individuals, but of one vast centipede of a man, good for all sorts of pulling down; and why not then for some kinds of building up? If men could combine thus earnestly, and patiently, and harmoniously to some really worthy end, what might they not accomplish! They now put their hands, and partially perchance their heads, together, and the result is that they are the imperfect tools of an imperfect and tyrannical government. But if they could put their hands and heads, and hearts and all together, such a co-operation and harmony would be the very end and success for which government now exists in vain—a government, as it were, not only with tools, but stock to trade with.

I was obliged to frame some sentences that sounded like French in order to deal with the market women, who, for the most part, cannot speak English. According to the guide-book the relative population of this city stands nearly thus: two-fifths are French Canadian; nearly one-fifth British Canadian; one-and-a-half-fifth English, Irish, and Scotch; somewhat less than one-half-fifth Germans, United States people, and others. I saw nothing like pie for sale, and no good cake to put in my bundle, such as you can easily find in our towns, but plenty of fair-looking apples, for which Montreal Island is celebrated, and also pears, cheaper, and I thought better than ours, and peaches, which, though they were probably brought from the South, were as cheap as they commonly are with us. So imperative is the law of demand and supply that, as I have been told, the market of Montreal is sometimes supplied with green apples from the State of New York some weeks even before they are ripe in the latter place. I saw here the spruce wax which the Canadians chew, done up in little silvered papers, a penny a roll; also a small and shrivelled fruit which they called *cérises* mixed with many little stems somewhat like raisins, but I soon returned what I had bought, finding them rather insipid, only putting a sample in my pocket. Since my return, I find on comparison that it is the fruit of the sweet viburnum (*viburnum lentago*), which with us rarely holds on till it is ripe.

I stood on the deck of the steamer John Munn, late in the afternoon, when the second and third ferry-boats arrived from La Prairie, bringing the remainder of the Yankees. I never saw so many caleches, cabs, charettes, and similar vehicles collected before, and doubt if New York could easily furnish more. The handsome and substantial stone quay, which stretches a mile along the river side, and protects the street from the ice, was thronged with the citizens who had turned out on foot and in carriages to welcome or to behold the Yankees. It was interesting to see the caleche drivers dash up and down the slope of the quay with their active little horses. They drive much faster than in our cities. I have been told that some of them came nine miles into the city every morning and return every night, without changing their horses during the day. In the midst of the crowd of carts, I observed one deep one loaded with sheep with their legs tied together, and their bodies piled one upon another, as if the driver had forgotten that they were sheep and not yet mutton. A sight, I trust, peculiar to Canada, though I fear that it is not.

II. QUEBEC AND MONTMORENCI

About six o'clock we started for Quebec, one hundred and eighty miles distant by the river; gliding past Longueil and Boucherville on the right, and *Pointe aux Trembles,* "so called from having been originally covered with aspens," and *Bout de l'Isle,* or the end of the island, on the left. I repeat these names not merely for want of more substantial facts to record, but because they sounded singularly poetic to my ears. There certainly was no lie in them. They suggested that some simple, and, perchance, heroic human life might have transpired there. There is all the poetry in the world in a name. It is a poem which the mass of men hear and read. What is poetry in the common sense, but a string of such jingling names? I want nothing better than a good word. The name of a thing may easily be more than the thing itself to me. Inexpressibly beautiful appears the recognition by man of the least natural fact, and the allying his life to it. All the world reiterating this slender truth, that aspens once grew there; and the swift inference is, that men were there to see them. And so it would be with the names of our native and neighboring villages, if we had not profaned them.

The daylight now failed us, and we went below; but I endeavored to console myself for being obliged to make this voyage by night, by thinking that I did not lose a great deal, the shores being low and rather unattractive, and that the river itself was much the more interesting object. I heard something in the night about the boat being at William Henry, Three Rivers, and in the Richelieu Rapids, but I was still where I had been when I lost sight of *Pointe aux Trembles.* To hear a man who has been waked up at midnight in the cabin of a steamboat, inquiring, "Waiter, where are we now?" is, as if at any moment of the earth's revolution round the sun, or of the system round its centre, one were to raise himself up and inquire of one of the deck hands, "Where are we now?"

I went on deck at daybreak, when we were thirty or forty miles above Quebec. The banks were now higher and more interesting. There was an "uninterrupted succession of white-washed cottages" on each side of the river. This is what every traveller tells. But it is not to be taken as an evidence of the populousness of the country in general, hardly even of the river banks. They have presented a similar appearance for a hundred years. The Swedish traveller and naturalist, Kalm, who descended this river in 1749, says, "It could really be called a village, beginning at Montreal and ending at Quebec, which is a distance of more than one hundred and eighty miles; for the farmhouses, are never above five arpents, and sometimes but three asunder, a few places excepted." Even in 1684 Hontan said that the houses were not more than a gunshot apart at most. Ere long we passed Cape Rouge, eight miles above Quebec, the mouth of the Chaudière on the opposite or south side, New Liverpool Cove with its lumber rafts and some shipping; then Sillery and Wolfe's Cove and the Heights of Abraham on the north, with now a view of Cape Diamond, and the citadel in front. The approach to Quebec was very imposing. It was about six o'clock in the morning when we arrived. There is but a single street under the cliff on the south side of the cape, which was made by blasting the rocks and filling up the river. Three-story houses did not rise more than one-fifth or one-sixth the way up the nearly perpendicular rock, whose summit is three hundred and forty-five feet above the water. We saw, as we glided past, the sign on the side of the precipice, part way up, pointing to the spot where Montgomery was killed in 1775. Formerly it was the custom for those who went to Quebec for the first time, to be ducked, or else pay a fine. Not even the Governor General escaped. But we were too many to be ducked, even if the custom had not been abolished.

Here we were, in the harbor of Quebec, still three hundred and sixty miles from the mouth of the St. Lawrence, in a basin two miles across, where the greatest depth is twenty-eight fathoms, and though the water is fresh, the tide rises seventeen to twenty-four feet, a harbor "large and deep enough," says a British traveller " to hold the English navy." I may as well state that in 1844 the county of Quebec contained about forty-five thousand inhabitants, (the city and suburbs having about forty-three thousand); about twenty-eight thousand being Canadians of French origin; eight thousand British; over seven thousand natives of Ireland; one thousand five hundred natives of England; the rest Scotch and others. Thirty-six thousand belong to the Church of Rome.

Separating ourselves from the crowd, we walked up a narrow street, thence ascended by some wooden steps, called the Break-neck Stairs, into another steep, narrow, and zig-zag street, blasted through the rock, which last led through a low massive stone portal, called Prescott Gate, the principal thoroughfare into the Upper Town. This passage was defended by cannon, with a guard-house over it, a sentinel at his post, and other soldiers at hand ready to relieve him. I rubbed my eyes to be sure that I was in the nineteenth century, and was not entering one of those portals which sometimes adorn the frontispieces of new editions of old black-letter volumes. I thought it would be a good place to read Froissart's Chronicles. It was such a reminiscence of the middle ages as Scott's novels. Men apparently dwelt there for security. Peace be unto them! As if the inhabitants of New-York were to go over to Castle William to live! What a place it must be to bring up children! Being safe through the gate we naturally took the street which was steepest, and after a few turns found ourselves on the Durham Terrace, a wooden platform on the site of the old castle of St. Louis, still one hundred and fifteen feet below the summit of the citadel, overlooking the Lower Town, the wharf where we had landed, the harbor, the Isle of Orleans, and the river and surrounding country to a great distance. It was literally a *splendid* view. We could see six or seven miles distant, in the northeast, an indentation in the lofty shore of the northern channel, apparently on one side of the harbor, which marked the mouth of the Montmorenci, whose celebrated fall was only a few rods in the rear.

At a shoe-shop, whither we were directed for this purpose we got some of our American money changed into English. I found that American hard money would have answered as well, excepting cents, which fell very fast before their pennies, it taking two of the former to make one of the latter, and often the penny, which had cost us two cents did us the service of one cent only. Moreover, our robust cents were compelled to meet on even terms a crew of vile half-penny tokens, and bung-town coppers, which had more brass in their composition, and so perchance made their way in the world. Wishing to get into the citadel, we were directed to the Jesuits' Barracks,—a good part of the public buildings here are barracks,—to get a pass of the Town Major. We did not heed the sentries at the gate, nor did they us, and what under the sun they were placed there for, unless to hinder a free circulation of the air, was not apparent. There we saw soldiers eating their breakfasts in their mess room, from bare wooden tables in camp fashion. We were continually meeting with soldiers in the streets, carrying funny little tin pails of all shapes, even semicircular, as if made to pack conveniently. I supposed that they contained their dinners, so many slices of bread and butter to each, perchance. Sometimes they were carrying some kind of military chest on a sort of bier or hand-barrow, with a springy, undulating, military step, all passengers giving way to them, even the charette drivers stopping for them to pass—as if the battle were being lost from an inadequate supply of powder. There was a regiment of Highlanders, and, as I understood, of Royal Irish, in the city; and by this time there was a regiment of Yankees also. I had already observed, looking up even from the water, the head and shoulders of some General Poniatowsky, with an enormous cocked hat and gun, peering over the roof of a house, away up where the chimney caps commonly are with us, as it were a caricature of war and military awfulness; but I had not gone far up St. Louis street before my riddle was solved, by the apparition of a real live Highlander under a cocked hat, and with his knees out, standing and marching sentinel on the ramparts, between St. Louis and St. John's Gate. (It must be a holy war that is waged there.) We stood close by without fear and looked at him. His legs were somewhat tanned, and the hair had begun to grow on them, as some of our wise men predict that it will in such cases, but I did not think they were remarkable in any respect. Notwithstanding all his warlike gear, when I inquired of him the way to the Plains of Abraham, he could not answer me without betraying some bashfulness through his broad Scotch. Soon after, we passed another of these creatures standing sentry at the St. Louis Gate, who let us go by without shooting us, or even demanding the countersign. We then began to go through the gate, which was so thick and tunnel-like, as to remind me of those lines in Claudian's Old Man of Verona, about the getting out of the gate being the greater part of a journey;—as you might imagine yourself crawling through an architectural vignette *at the end* of a black-letter volume. We were then reminded that we had been in a fortress, from which we emerged by numerous zig-zags in a ditch-like road, going a considerable distance to advance a few rods, where they could have shot us two or three times over, if their minds had been disposed as their guns were. The greatest, or rather the most prominent, part of this city was constructed with the design to offer the deadliest resistance to leaden and iron missiles, that might be cast against it. But it is a remarkable meteorological and psychological fact, that it is rarely known to rain lead with much violence, except on places so constructed. Keeping on about a mile we came to the Plains of Abraham,—for having got through with the Saints, we come next to the Patriarchs. Here the Highland regiment was being reviewed, while the band stood on one side and played,—methinks it was "La Claire Fontaine," the national air of the Canadian French. This is the site where a real battle once took place, to commemorate which they have had a sham fight here almost every day since. The Highlanders manœuvred very well, and if the precision of their movements was less remarkable, they did not appear so stiffly erect as the English or Royal Irish, but had a more elastic and graceful gait, like a herd of their own red deer, or as if accustomed to stepping down the sides of mountains. But they made a sad impression on the whole, for it was obvious that all true manhood was in the process of being drilled out of them. I have no doubt that soldiers well drilled are, as a class, peculiarly destitute of originality and independence. The officers appeared like men dressed above their condition. It is impossible to give the soldier a good education, without making him a deserter. His natural foe is the government that drills him. What would any philanthropist, who felt an interest in these men's welfare, naturally do, but first of all teach them so to respect themselves, that they could not be hired for this work, whatever might be the consequences to this government or that;— not drill a few, but educate all. I observed one older man among them, gray as a wharf-rat, and supple as an eel, marching lock-step with the rest who would have to pay for that elastic gait.

We returned to the citadel along the heights, plucking such flowers as grew there. There was an abundance of succory still in blossom, broad-leaved golden-rod, butter-cups, thorn-bushes, Canada thistles, and ivy, on the very summit of Cape Diamond. I also found the bladder-campion in the neighborhood. We there enjoyed an extensive view, which I will describe in another place. Our pass, which stated that all the rules were "to be strictly enforced," as if they were determined to keep up the resemblance of reality to the last gasp, opened to us the Dalhousie Gate, and we were conducted over the citadel by a bare-legged Highlander in cocked hat and full regimentals. He told us that he had been here about three years, and had formerly been stationed at Gibraltar. As if his regiment, having perchance been nestled amid the rocks of Edinburgh Castle, must flit from rock to rock thenceforth over the earth's surface, like a bald eagle, or other bird of prey, from eyrie to eyrie. As we were going out, we met the Yankees coming in, in a body, headed by a red-coated officer called the commandant, and escorted by many citizens, both English and French Canadian. I therefore immediately fell into the procession, and went round the citadel again with more intelligent guides, carrying, as before, all my effects with me. Seeing that nobody walked with the red-coated commandant, I attached myself to him, and though I was not what is called well-dressed, he did not know whether to repel me or not, for I talked like one who was not aware of any deficiency in that respect. Probably there was not one among all the Yankees who went to Canada this time, who was not more splendidly dressed than I was. It would have been a poor story if I had not enjoyed some distinction. I had on my "bad-weather clothes," like Olaf Trygresson the Northman, when he went to the Thing in England, where, by the way, he won his bride. As we stood by the thirty-two-pounder on the summit of Cape Diamond, which is fired three times a day, the commandant told me that it would carry to the Isle of Orleans, four miles distant, and that no hostile vessel could come round the island. I now saw the subterranean or, rather, "casemated barracks" of the soldiers, which I had not noticed before, though I might have walked over them. They had very narrow windows, serving as loop-holes for musketry, and small iron chimneys rising above the ground. There we saw the soldiers at home and in an undress, splitting wood —I looked to see whether with swords or axes—and in various ways endeavoring to realize that their nation was now at peace with this part of the world. A part of each regiment, chiefly officers, are allowed to marry. A grandfatherly, would-be-witty Englishman, could give a Yankee whom he was patronizing, no reason for the bare knees of the Highlanders, other than oddity. The rock within the citadel is a little convex, so that shells falling on it would roll toward the circumference, where the barracks of the soldiers and officers are; it has been proposed, therefore, to make it slightly concave, so that they may roll into the centre, where they would be comparatively harmless; and it is estimated that to do this would cost twenty thousand pounds sterling. It may be well to remember this when I build my next house, and have the roof "all correct" for bomb-shells.

At mid-afternoon we made haste down *Sault au Matelot-street,* towards the Falls of Montmorenci, about eight miles down the St. Lawrence, on the north side, leaving the further examination of Quebec till our return. On our way, we saw men in the streets sawing logs pit-fashion, and afterward, with a common wood-saw and horse, cutting the planks into squares for paving the streets. This looked very shiftless, especially in a country abounding in water-power, and reminded me that I was no longer in Yankee land. I found, on inquiry, that the excuse for this was, that labor was so cheap; and I thought, with some pain, how cheap men are here! I have since learned that the English traveller, Warburton, remarked, soon after landing at Quebec, that every thing was cheap there but men. That must be the difference between going thither from New and from Old England. I had already observed the dogs harnessed to their little milk-carts, which contain a single large can, lying asleep in the gutters, regardless of the houses, while they rested from their labors, at different stages of the ascent in the Upper Town. I was surprised at the regular and extensive use made of these animals for drawing, not only milk, but groceries, wood, &c. It reminded me that the dog commonly is not put to any use. Cats catch mice; but dogs only worry the cats. Kalm, a hundred years ago, saw sledges here for ladies to ride in, drawn by a pair of dogs. He says, "A middle-sized dog is sufficient to draw a single person, when the roads are good;" and he was told by old people, that horses were very scarce in their youths, and almost all the land-carriage was then effected by dogs. They made me think of the Esquimaux, who, in fact, are the next people on the north. Charlevoix says, that the first horses were introduced in 1665.

We crossed Dorchester Bridge, over the St. Charles, the little river in which Cartier, the discoverer of the St. Lawrence, put his ships, and spent the winter of 1535, and found ourselves on an excellent macadamized road, called *Le Chemin de Beauport*. We had left Concord Wednesday morning, and we endeavored to realize that now, Friday morning, we were taking a walk in Canada, in the Seigniory of Beauport, a foreign country, which a few days before had seemed almost as far off as England and France. Instead of rambling to Flint's Pond or the Sudbury Meadows, we found ourselves, after being a little detained in cars and steamboats—after spending half a night at Burlington, and half a day at Montreal—taking a walk down the bank of the St. Lawrence to the Falls of Montmorenci and elsewhere. Well, I thought to myself, here I am in a foreign country; let me have my eyes about me, and take it all in. It already looked and felt a good deal colder than it had in New England, as we might have expected it would. I realized fully that I was four degrees nearer the pole, and shuddered at the thought; and I wondered if it were possible that the peaches might not be all gone when I returned. It was an atmosphere that made me think of the fur-trade, which is so interesting a department in Canada, for I had for all head covering a thin palm-leaf hat without lining, that cost twenty-five cents, and over my coat one of those unspeakably cheap, as well as thin, brown linen sacks of the Oak Hall pattern, which every summer appear all over New England, thick as the leaves upon the trees. It was a thoroughly Yankee costume, which some of my fellow-travellers wore in the cars to save their coats a dusting. I wore mine, at first, because it looked better than the coat it covered, and last, because two coats were warmer than one, though one was thin and dirty. I never wear my best coat on a journey, though perchance I could show a certificate to prove that I have a more costly one, at least, at home, if that were all that a gentleman required. It is not wise for a traveller to go dressed. I should no more think of it than of putting on a clean dicky and blacking my shoes to go a fishing; as if you were going out to dine, when, in fact, the genuine traveller is going out to work hard, and fare harder—to eat a crust by the way-side whenever he can get it. Honest travelling is about as dirty work as you can do, and a man needs a pair of overalls for it. As for blacking my shoes in such a case, I should as soon think of blacking my face. I carry a piece of tallow to preserve the leather, and keep out the water; that's all; and many an officious shoe-black, who carried off my shoes when I was slumbering, mistaking me for a gentleman, has had occasion to repent it before he produced a gloss on them.

My pack, in fact, was home-made, for I keep a short list of those articles which, from frequent experience, I have found indispensable to the foot traveller; and when I am about to start, I have only to consult that, to be sure that nothing is omitted, and, what is more important, nothing superfluous inserted. Most of my fellow-travellers carried carpet-bags, or valises. Sometimes one had two or three ponderous yellow valises in his clutch, at each pitch of the cars, as if we were going to have another rush for seats; and when there was a rush in earnest, and there were not a few, I would see my man in the crowd, with two or three affectionate lusty fellows along each side of his arm, between his shoulder and his valises, which last held them tight to his back, like the nut on the end of a screw. I could not help asking in my mind—what so great cause for showing Canada to those valises, when perhaps your very nieces had to stay at home for want of an escort? I should have liked to be present when the custom-house officer came aboard of him, and asked him to declare upon his honor if he had any thing but wearing apparel in them. Even the elephant carries but a small trunk on his journeys. The perfection of travelling is to travel without baggage. After considerable reflection and experience, I have concluded, that the best bag for the foot traveller is made with a handkerchief, or, if he study appearances, a piece of stiff brown paper, well tied up, with a fresh piece within to put outside when the first is torn. That is good for both town and country, and none will know but you are carrying home the silk for a new gown for your wife, when it may be a dirty shirt. A bundle which you can carry literally under your arm, and which will shrink and swell with its contents. I never found the carpet-bag of equal capacity which was not a bundle of itself. We styled ourselves the knights of the umbrella and the bundle; for wherever we went, whether to Notre Dame or Mount Royal, or the Champ-de-Mars, to the Town Major's or the Bishop's Palace, to the Citadel, with a bare-legged Highlander for our escort, or to the Plains of

Abraham, to dinner or to bed, the umbrella and the bundle went with us; for we wished to be ready to digress at any moment. We made it our home nowhere in particular, but everywhere where our umbrella and bundle were. It would have been an amusing circumstance, if the Mayor of one of those cities had politely inquired where we were staying. We could only have answered, that we were staying with his honor for the time being. I was amused when, after our return, some green ones inquired if we found it easy to get accommodated; as if we went abroad to get accommodated, when we can get that at home.

We met with many charettes, bringing wood and stone to the city. The most ordinary-looking horses travelled faster than ours, or, perhaps they were ordinary-looking, because, as I am told, the Canadians do not use the curry-comb. Moreover, it is said, that on the approach of winter, their horses acquire an increased quantity of hair, to protect them from the cold. If this be true, some of our horses would make you think winter were approaching, even in mid-summer. We soon began to see women and girls at work in the fields, digging potatoes alone, or bundling up the grain which the men cut. They appeared in rude health, with a great deal of color in their cheeks, and, if their occupation had made them coarse, it impressed me as better in its effects than making shirts at fourpence a piece, or doing nothing at all; unless it be chewing slate pencils, with still smaller results. They were much more agreeable objects, with their great broad-brimmed hats and flowing dresses, than the men and boys. We afterward saw them doing various other kinds of work; indeed, I thought that we saw more women at work out of doors than men. On our return, we observed in this town a girl with Indian boots, nearly two feet high, taking the harness off a dog. The purity and transparency of the atmosphere were wonderful. When we had been walking an hour, we were surprised, on turning round, to see how near the city, with its glittering tin roofs, still looked. A village ten miles off did not appear to be more than three or four. I was convinced that you could see objects distinctly there much farther than here. It is true, the villages are of a dazzling white, but the dazzle is to be referred, perhaps, to the transparency of the atmosphere, as much as to the whitewash.

We were now fairly in the village of Beauport, though there was still but one road, the houses stood close upon this, without any front-yards, and at any angle with it, as if they had dropped down, being set with more reference to the road which the sun travels. It being about sundown, and the Falls not far off, we began to look round for a lodging, for we preferred to put up at a private house, that we might see more of the inhabitants. We inquired first at the most promising looking houses, if indeed any were promising. When we knocked, they shouted some French word for come in, perhaps *entrez*, and we asked for a lodging in English; but we found, unexpectedly, that they spoke French only. Then we went along and tried another house, being generally saluted by a rush of two or three little curs, which readily distinguished a foreigner, and which we were prepared now to hear bark in French. Our first question would be, *Parlez-vous Anglais?* but the invariable answer was, *Non, monsieur;* and we soon found that the inhabitants were exclusively French Canadians, and nobody spoke English at all, any more than in France; that, in fact, we were in a foreign country, where the inhabitants uttered not one familiar sound to us. Then we tried by turns to talk French with them, in which we succeeded sometimes pretty well, but for the most part, pretty ill. *Pouvez-vous nous donner un lit cette nuit?* we would ask, and then they would answer with French volubility, so that we could catch only a word here and there. We could understand the women and children generally better than the men, and they us; and thus, after a while, we would learn that they had no more beds than they used.

So we were compelled to inquire: *Ya-t'il une maison publique ici?* (*auberge* we should have said perhaps, for they seemed never to have heard of the other,) and they answered at length that there was no tavern, unless we could get lodgings at the mill, *le moulin,* which we had passed; or they would direct us to a grocery, and almost every house had a small grocery at one end of it. We called on the public notary or village lawyer, but he had no more beds nor English than the rest. At one house, there was so good a misunderstanding at once established through the politeness of all parties, that we were encouraged to walk in and sit down, and ask for a glass of water; and having drank their water, we thought it was as good as to have tasted their salt. When our host and his wife spoke of their poor accommodations, meaning for themselves, we assured them that they were good enough, for we thought that they were only apologizing for the poorness of the accommodations they were about to offer us, and we did not discover our mistake till they took us up a ladder into a loft, and showed to our eyes what they had been laboring in vain to communicate to our brains through our ears, that they had but that one apartment with its few beds for the whole family. We made our *a-dieus* forthwith, and with gravity, perceiving the literal signification of that word. We were finally taken in at a sort of public-house, whose master worked for Patterson, the proprietor of the extensive saw-mills driven by a portion of the Montmorenci stolen from the fall, whose roar we now heard. We here talked, or murdered French all the evening, with the master of the house and his family, and probably had a more amusing time than if we had completely understood one another. At length they showed us to a bed in their best chamber, very high to get into, with a low wooden rail to it. It had no cotton sheets, but coarse home-made, dark colored linen ones. Afterward, we had to do with sheets still coarser than these, and nearly the color of our blankets. There was a large open buffet loaded with crockery, in one corner of the room, as if to display their wealth to travellers, and pictures of scripture scenes, French, Italian, and Spanish, hung around. Our hostess came back directly to inquire if we would have brandy for breakfast. The next morning, when I asked their names, she took down the temperance pledges of herself and husband, and children, which were hanging against the wall. They were Jean Baptiste Binet, and his wife, Genevieve Binet, Jean Baptiste is the sobriquet of the French Canadians.

After breakfast we proceeded to the fall, which was within half a mile, and at this distance its rustling sound, like the wind among the leaves, filled all the air. We were disappointed to find that we were in some measure shut out from the west side of the fall by the private grounds and fences of Patterson, who appropriates not only a part of the water for his mill, but a still larger part of the prospect, so that we were obliged to trespass. This gentleman's mansion-house and grounds were formerly occupied by the Duke of Kent, father to Queen Victoria. It appeared to me in bad taste for an individual, though he were the father of Queen Victoria, to obtrude himself with his land titles, or at least his fences, on so remarkable a natural phenomenon, which should, in every sense, belong to mankind. Some falls should even be kept sacred from the intrusion of mills and factories, as water-privileges in another than the millwright's sense. This small river falls perpendicularly nearly two hundred and fifty feet at one pitch. The St. Lawrence falls only 164 feet at Niagara. It is a very simple and noble fall, and leaves nothing to be desired; but the most that I could say of it would only have the force of one other testimony to assure the reader that it is there. We looked directly down on it from the point of a projecting rock, and saw far below us, on a low promontory, the grass kept fresh and green by the perpetual drizzle, looking like moss. The rock is a kind of slate, in the crevices of which grew ferns and golden-rods. The prevailing trees on the shores were spruce and arbor-vitæ, the latter very large and now full of fruit, also aspens, alders, and the mountain ash with its berries. Every emigrant who arrives in this country by way of the St. Lawrence, as he opens a point of the Isle of Orleans, sees the Montmorenci tumbling into the Great River thus magnificently in a vast white sheet, making its contribution with emphasis. Roberval's pilot, Jean Alphonse, saw this fall thus, and described it in 1542. It is a splendid introduction to the scenery of Quebec. Instead of an artificial fountain in its square, Quebec has this magnificent natural waterfall to adorn one side of its harbor. Within the mouth of the chasm below, which can be entered only at ebb tide, we had a grand view at once of Quebec and of the fall. Kalm says that the noise of the fall is sometimes heard at Quebec, about eight miles distant, and is a sign of a north-east wind. The side of this chasm of soft and crumbling slate too steep to climb, was among the memorable features of the scene. In the winter of 1829 the frozen spray of the fall descending on the ice of the St. Lawrence, made a hill one hundred and twenty-six feet high. It is an annual phenomenon which some think may help explain the formation of glaciers.

In the vicinity of the fall we began to notice what looked like our red-fruited thorn bushes, grown to the size of ordinary apple-trees, very common, and full of large red or yellow fruit, which the inhabitants called *pommettes*, but I did not learn that they were put to any use.

III. ST. ANNE

BY THE MIDDLE of the forenoon, though it was a rainy day, we were once more on our way down the north bank of the St. Lawrence, in a north-easterly direction, toward the Falls of St. Anne, which are about thirty miles from Quebec. The settled, more level, and fertile portion of Canada East, may be described rudely as a triangle, with its apex slanting toward the north-east, about one hundred miles wide at its base, and from two to three, or even four hundred miles long, if you reckon its narrow north-eastern extremity; it being the immediate valley of the St. Lawrence and its tributaries, rising by a single or by successive terraces toward the mountains on either hand. Though the words Canada East on the map, stretch over many rivers and lakes and unexplored wildernesses, the actual Canada, which might be the colored portion of the map, is but a little clearing on the banks of the river, which one of those syllables would more than cover. The banks of the St. Lawrence are rather low from Montreal to the Richelieu Rapids, about forty miles above Quebec. Thence they rise gradually to Cape Diamond, or Quebec. Where we now were, eight miles north-east of Quebec, the mountains which form the northern side of this triangle were only five or six miles distant from the river, gradually departing further and further from it, on the west, till they reach the Ottawa, and making haste to meet it on the east, at Cape Tourmente, now in plain sight about twenty miles distant. So that we were travelling in a very narrow and sharp triangle between the mountains and the river, tilted up toward the mountains on the north, never losing sight of our great fellow-traveller on our right. According to Bouchette's Topographical Description of the Canadas, we were in the Seigniory of the Côte de Beaupre, in the County of Montmorenci, and the District of Quebec; in that part of Canada which was the first to be settled, and where the face of the country and the population have undergone the least change from the beginning, where the influence of the States and of Europe is least felt, and the inhabitants see little or nothing of the world over the walls of Quebec. This Seigniory was granted in 1636, and is now the property of the Seminary of Quebec. It is the most mountainous one in the province. There are some half-a-dozen parishes in it, each containing a church, parsonage-house, grist-mill, and several saw-mills. We were now in the most westerly parish called Ange Gardien, or the Guardian Angel, which is bounded on the west by the Montmorenci. The north bank of the St. Lawrence here is formed on a grand scale. It slopes gently, either directly from the shore, or from the edge of an interval, till at the distance of about a mile, it attains the height of four or five hundred feet. The single road runs along the side of the slope two or three hundred feet above the river at first, and from a quarter of a mile to a mile distant from it, and affords fine views of the north channel, which is about a mile wide, and of the beautiful Isle of Orleans, about twenty miles long by five wide, where grow the best apples and plums in the Quebec District.

Though there was but this single road, it was a continuous village for as far as we walked this day and the next, or about thirty miles down the river, the houses being as near together all the way as in the middle of one of our smallest straggling country villages, and we could never tell by their number when we were on the skirts of a parish, for the road never ran through the fields or woods. We were told that it was just six miles from one parish church to another. I thought that we saw every house in Ange Gardien. Therefore, as it was a muddy day, we never got out of the mud, nor out of the village, unless we got over the fence; then indeed, if it was on the north side, we were out of the civilized world. There were sometimes a few more houses near the church, it is true, but we had only to go a quarter of a mile from the road to the top of the bank to find ourselves on the verge of the uninhabited, and, for the most part, unexplored wilderness stretching toward Hudson's Bay. The farms accordingly were extremely long and narrow, each having a frontage on the river. Bouchette accounts for this peculiar manner of laying out a village by referring to "the social character of the Canadian peasant, who is singularly fond of neighborhood," also to the advantage arising from a concentration of strength in Indian times. Each farm, called *terre,* he says, is, in nine cases out of ten, three arpents wide by thirty deep, that is, very nearly thirty-five by three hundred and forty-nine of our rods; sometimes one-half arpent by thirty, or one to sixty; sometimes in fact a few yards by half a mile. Of course it costs more for fences. A remarkable difference between the Canadian and the New England character appears from the fact that in 1745, the French government were obliged to pass a law forbidding the farmers or *censitaires* building on land less than one and a half arpents front by thirty or forty deep, under a certain penalty, in order to compel emigration, and bring the seigneurs' estates all under cultivation; and it is thought that they have now less reluctance to leave the paternal roof than formerly, "removing beyond the sight of the parish spire, or the sound of the parish bell." But I find that in the previous or 17th century, the complaint, often renewed, was of a totally opposite character, namely, that the inhabitants dispersed and exposed themselves to the Iroquois. Accordingly, about 1664, the king was obliged to order that "they should make no more clearings except one next to another, and that they should reduce their parishes to the form of the parishes in France as much as possible. The Canadians of those days at least, possessed a roving spirit of adventure which carried them further, in exposure to hardship and danger, than ever the New England colonist went, and led them, though not to clear and colonize the wilderness, yet to range over it as *coureurs de bois,* or runners of the woods, or as Houtan prefers to call them, *coureurs de risques,* runners of risks; to say nothing of their enterprising priesthood; and Charlevoix thinks that if the authorities had taken the right steps to prevent the youth from ranging the woods (*de courir les bois*) they would have had an excellent militia to fight the Indians and English.

The road, in this clayey looking soil, was exceedingly muddy in consequences of the night's rain. We met an old woman directing her dog, which was harnessed to a little cart, to the least muddy part of the road. It was a beggarly sight. But harnessed to the cart as he was, we heard him barking after we had passed, though we looked any where but to the cart to see where the dog was that barked. The houses commonly fronted the south, whatever angle they might make with the road; and frequently they had no door nor cheerful window on the roadside. Half the time, they stood fifteen to forty rods from the road, and there was no very obvious passage to them, so that you would suppose that there must be another road running by them; they were of stone, rather coarsely mortared, but neatly white-washed, almost invariably one story high, and long in proportion to their height, with a shingled roof, the shingles being pointed, for ornament, at the eaves, like the pickets of a fence, and also, one row half way up the roof. The gables sometimes projected a foot or two at the ridge-pole only. Yet they were very humble and unpretending dwellings. They commonly had the date of their erection on them. The windows opened in the middle, like blinds, and were frequently provided with solid shutters. Sometimes, when we walked along the back side of a house, which stood near the road, we observed stout stakes leaning against it, by which the shutters, now pushed half open, were fastened at night; within, the houses were neatly ceiled with wood not painted. The oven was commonly out of doors, built of stone and mortar, frequently on a raised platform of planks. The cellar was often on the opposite side of the road, in front of or behind the houses, looking like an ice-house with us, with a lattice door for summer. The very few mechanics whom we met had an old-Bettyish look, in their aprons and *bonnets rouges,* like fools' caps. The men wore commonly the same *bonnet rouge,* or red woollen, or worsted cap, or sometimes blue or gray, looking to us as if they had got up with their nightcaps on, and in fact, I afterwards found that they had. Their clothes were of the cloth of the country, *étoffe du pays,* gray or some other plain color. The women looked stout, with gowns that stood out stiffly, also, for the most part, apparently of some home-made stuff. We also saw some specimens of the more characteristic winter dress of the Canadian, and I have since frequently detected him in New England by his coarse gray home-spun capote and picturesque red sash, and his well furred cap, made to protect his ears against the severity of his climate.

It drizzled all day, so that the roads did not improve. We began now to meet with wooden crosses frequently, by the road-side, about a dozen feet high, often old and toppling down, sometimes standing in a square wooden platform, sometimes in a pile of stones, with a little niche containing a picture of the virgin and child, or of Christ alone, sometimes with a string of beads, and covered with a piece of glass to keep out the rain, with the words, *pour la vierge,* or *Inri,* on them. Frequently, on the cross-bar, there would be quite a collection of knick-knacks, looking like an Italian's board; the representation in wood of a hand, a hammer, spikes, pincers, a flask of vinegar, a ladder, &c., the whole perchance surmounted by a weathercock; but I could not look at an honest weathercock in this walk, without mistrusting that there was some covert reference in it to St. Peter. From time to time we passed a little one story chapel-like building, with a tin-roofed spire, a shrine, perhaps it would be called, close to the path-side, with a lattice door, through which we could see an altar, and pictures about the walls; equally open, through rain and shine, though there was no getting into it. At these places the inhabitants kneeled and perhaps breathed a short prayer. We saw one school-house in our walk, and listened to the sounds which issued from it; but it appeared like a place where the process, not of enlightening, but of obfuscating the mind was going on, and the pupils received only so much light as could penetrate the shadow of the Catholic church. The churches were very picturesque, and their interior much more showy than the dwelling houses promised. They were of stone, for it was ordered in 1699, that that should be their material. They had tinned spires, and quaint ornaments. That of l'Ange Gardien had a dial on it, with the middle age Roman numerals on its face, and some images in niches on the outside. Probably its counterpart has existed in Normandy for a thousand years. At the church of Chateau Richer, which is the next parish to l'Ange Gardien, we read, looking over the wall, the inscriptions in the adjacent church-yard, which began with, *"Ici git"* or *"repose,"* and one over a boy contained, *"Priez pour lui."* This answered as well as Pére la Chaise. We knocked at the door of the curé's house here, when a sleek friar-like personage, in his sacerdotal robe appeared to our *Parlez-vous Anglais?* Even he answered, *"Non, Monsieur;"* but at last we made him understand what we wanted. It was to find the ruins of the old chateau. *"Ah! oui! oui!"* he exclaimed, and donning his coat, hastened forth, and conducted us to a small heap of rubbish which we had already examined. He said that fifteen years before, it was *plus considérable.* Seeing at that moment three little red birds fly out of a crevice in the ruins, up into an arbor-vitæ tree, which grew out of them, I asked him their names, in such French as I could muster, but he neither understood me, nor ornithology; he only inquired where we had *appris à parler Français;* we told him, *dans les Etats-Unis;* and so we bowed him into his house again. I was surprised to find a man wearing a black coat, and with apparently no work to do, even in that part of the world.

The universal salutation from the inhabitants whom we met was *bon jour*, at the same time touching the hat; with *bon jour*, and touching your hat, you may go smoothly through all Canada East. A little boy, meeting us would remark, "*Bon jour, Monsieur; le chemin est mauvais:*" Good morning, sir; it is bad walking. Sir Francis Head says that the immigrant is forward to "appreciate the happiness of living in a land in which the old country's servile custom of touching the hat does not exist," but he was thinking of Canada West, of course. It would, indeed, be a serious bore to be obliged to touch your hat several times a day. A Yankee has not leisure for it.

We saw peas, and even beans, collected into heaps in the fields. The former are an important crop here, and, I suppose, are not so much infested by the weevil as with us. They were plenty of apples, very fair and sound, by the road-side, but they were so small as to suggest the origin of the apple in the crab. There was also a small red fruit which they called *snells*, and another also red and very acid, whose name a little boy wrote for me "pinbéna." It is probably the same with, or similar to the *pembina* of the voyageurs, a species of viburnum, which, according to Richardson, has given its name to many of the rivers of Rupert's Land. The forest trees were spruce, arbor-vitæ, firs, birches, beeches, two or three kinds of maple, bass-wood, wild-cherry, aspens, &c., but no pitch pines (*pinus rigida*). I saw very few, if any, trees which had been set out for shade or ornament. The water was commonly running streams or springs in the bank by the road-side, and was excellent. The parishes are commonly separated by a stream, and frequently the farms. I noticed that the fields were furrowed or thrown into beds seven or eight feet wide to dry the soil.

At the *Rivière du Sault à la Puce,* which, I suppose, means the River of the Fall of the Flea, was advertised in English, as the sportsmen are English, "the best snipe-shooting grounds," over the door of a small public-house. These words being English affected me as if I had been absent now ten years from my country, and for so long had not heard the sound of my native language, and every one of them was as interesting to me as if I had been a snipe-shooter, and they had been snipes. The prunella or self-heal, in the grass here, was an old acquaintance. We frequently saw the inhabitants washing, or cooking for their pigs, and in one place hackling flax by the road side. It was pleasant to see these usually domestic operations carried on out of doors, even in that cold country.

At twilight we reached a bridge over a little river, the boundary between Chateau Richer and St. Anne, *le premier pont de St. Anne,* and at dark the church of *La Bonne St. Anne.* Formerly vessels from France, when they came in sight of this church, gave "a general discharge of their artillery," as a sign of joy that they had escaped all the dangers of the river. Though all the while we had grand views of the adjacent country far up and down the river, and, for the most part, when we turned about, of Quebec in the horizon behind us, and we never beheld it without new surprise and admiration; yet, throughout our walk, the Great River of Canada on our right hand was the main feature in the landscape, and this expands so rapidly below the Isle of Orleans, and creates such a breadth of level horizon above its waters in that direction, that, looking down the river as we approached the extremity of that island, the St. Lawrence seemed to be opening into the ocean, though we were still about three hundred and twenty-five miles from what can be called its mouth.

When we inquired here for a *maison publique* we were directed apparently to that private house where we were most likely to find entertainment. There were no guide-boards where we walked, because there was but one road; there were no shops nor signs, because there were no artisans to speak of, and the people raised their own provisions; and there were no taverns because there were no travellers. We here bespoke lodging and breakfast. They had, as usual, a large old-fashioned, two-storied box stove in the middle of the room, out of which, in due time, there was sure to be forthcoming a supper, breakfast, or dinner. The lower half held the fire, the upper the hot air, and as it was a cool Canadian evening, this was a comforting sight to us. Being four or five feet high it warmed the whole person as you stood by it. The stove was plainly a very important article of furniture in Canada, and was not set aside during the summer. Its size, and the respect which was paid to it, told of the severe winters which it had seen and prevailed over. The master of the house, in his long-pointed, red woollen cap, had a thoroughly antique physiognomy of the old Norman stamp. He might have come over with Jacques Cartier. His was the hardest French to understand of any we had heard yet, for there was a great difference between one speaker and another, and this man talked with a pipe in his mouth beside, a kind of tobacco French. I asked him what he called his dog. He said *Brock!* At Binet's they called the cat *min*—min! min! min! I inquired if we could cross the river here to the Isle of Orleans, thinking to return that way when we had been to the Falls. He answered, *"S'il ne fait pas un trop grand vent."*

If there is not too much wind, they use small boats or pirogues, and the waves are often too high for them. He wore, as usual, something between a moccasin and a boot, which he called *bottes Indiennes,* Indian boots, and had made himself. The tops were of calf or sheep-skin, and the soles of cowhide turned up like a moccasin. They were yellow or reddish, the leather never having been tanned nor colored. The women wore the same. He told us that he had travelled ten leagues due north into the bush. He had been to the Falls of St. Anne, and said that they were more beautiful, but not greater, than Montmorenci, *plus bel mais non plus grand que Montmorenci.* As soon as we had retired the family commenced their devotions. A little boy officiated, and for a long time we heard him muttering over his prayers.

In the morning, after a breakfast of tea, maple sugar, bread and butter, and what I suppose is called a *potage* (potatoes and meat boiled with flour), the universal dish as we found, perhaps the national one, I ran over to the Church of La Bonne St. Anne, whose matin bell we had heard, it being Sunday morning. Our books said that this church had "long been an object of interest, from the miraculous cures said to have been wrought on visitors to the shrine." There was a profusion of gilding, and I counted more than twenty-five crutches suspended on the walls, some for grown persons, some for children, which it was to be inferred so many sick had been able to dispense with; but they looked as if they had been made to order by the carpenter who made the church. There were one or two villagers at their devotions at that early hour, who did not look up, but when they had sat a long time with their little book before the picture of one saint, went to another. Our whole walk was through a thoroughly Catholic country, and there was no trace of any other religion. I doubt if there are any more simple and unsophisticated Catholics any where. Emery de Caen, Champlain's contemporary, told the Huguenot sailors that "Monseigneur, the Duke de Ventadour (Viceroy), did not wish that they should sing psalms in the Great River."

On our way to the falls, we met the habitants coming to the Church of La Bonne St. Anne, walking or riding in charettes by families. I remarked that they were universally of small stature. The toll-man at the bridge, over the St. Anne, was the first man we had chanced to meet since we left Quebec, who could speak a word of English. How good French the inhabitants of this part of Canada speak, I am not competent to say; I only know that it is not made impure by being mixed with English. I do not know why it should not be as good as is spoken in Normandy. Charlevoix, who was here a hundred years ago, observes, "the French language is nowhere spoken with greater purity, there being no accent perceptible;" and Potherie said "they had no dialect, which, indeed, is generally lost in a colony."

The falls, which we were in search of, are three miles up the St. Anne. We followed for a short distance a foot-path up the east bank of this river, through handsome sugar-maple and arbor-vitæ groves. Having lost the path which led to a house where we were to get further directions, we dashed at once into the woods, steering by guess and by compass, climbing directly through woods, a steep hill, or mountain, five or six hundred feet high, which was, in fact, only the bank of the St. Lawrence. Beyond this we by good luck fell into another path, and following this or a branch of it, at our discretion, through a forest consisting of large white pines,—the first we had seen in our walk,—we at length heard the roar of falling water, and came out at the head of the Falls of St. Anne. We had descended into a ravine or cleft in the mountain, whose walls rose still a hundred feet above us, though we were near its top, and we now stood on a very rocky shore, where the water had lately flowed a dozen feet higher, as appeared by the stones and drift-wood, and large birches twisted and splintered as a farmer twists a withe. Here the river, one or two hundred feet wide, came flowing rapidly over a rocky bed out of that interesting wilderness which stretches toward Hudson's Bay and Davis's Straits. Ha-ha Bay, on the Saguenay, was about one hundred miles north of where we stood. Looking on the map, I find that the first country on the north which bears a name, is that part of Rupert's Land called East Main. This river, called after the holy Anne, flowing from such a direction, here tumbled over a precipice, at present by three channels, how far down I do not know, but far enough for all our purposes, and to as good a distance as if twice as far. It matters little whether you call it one, or two, or three hundred feet; at any rate, it was a sufficient water-privilege for us. I crossed the principal channel directly over the verge of the fall, where it was contracted to about fifteen feet in width, by a dead tree which had been dropped across and secured in a cleft of the opposite rock, and a smaller one a few feet higher, which served for a hand-rail. This bridge was rotten as well as small and slippery, being stripped of bark, and I was obliged to seize a moment to pass when the falling water did not surge over it, and midway, though at the expense of wet feet, I looked down probably more than a hundred feet, into the mist and foam below. This gave me the freedom of an island of precipitous rock, by which I descended as by giant steps, the rock being composed of large cubical masses, clothed with delicate, close-hugging lichens of various colors, kept fresh and bright by the moisture, till I viewed the first fall from the front, and looked down still deeper to where the second and third channels fell into a remarkably large circular basin worn in the stone. The falling water seemed to jar the very rocks, and the noise to be ever increasing. The vista down stream was through a narrow and deep cleft in the mountain, all white suds at the bottom; but a sudden angle in this gorge prevented my seeing through to the bottom of the fall. Returning to the shore, I made my way down stream through the forest to see how far the fall extended, and how the river came out of that adventure. It was to clamber along the side of a precipitous mountain of loose mossy rocks, covered with a damp primitive forest, and terminating at the bottom in an abrupt precipice over the stream. This was the east side of the fall. At length, after a quarter of a mile, I got down to still water, and on looking up through the winding gorge, I could just see to the foot of the fall which I had before examined; while from the opposite side of the stream, here much contracted, rose a perpendicular wall, I will not venture to say how many hundred feet, but only that it was the highest perpendicular wall of bare rock that I ever saw. In front of me tumbles in from the summit of the cliff a tributary stream, making a beautiful cascade, which was a remarkable fall in itself, and there was a cleft in this precipice, apparently four or five feet wide, perfectly straight up and down from top to bottom, which from its cavernous depth and darkness, appeared merely as *a black streak*. This precipice is not sloped, nor is the material soft and crumbling slate as at Montmorenci, but it rises perfectly perpendicular, like the side of a mountain fortress, and is cracked into vast cubical masses of gray and black rock shining with moisture, as if it were the ruin of an ancient wall built by Titans. Birches, spruces, mountain-ashes with their bright red berries, arbor-vitæs, white pines, alders, &c., overhung this chasm on the very verge of the cliff and in the crevices, and here and there were buttresses of rock supporting trees part way down, yet so as to enhance, not injure, the effect of the bare rock. Take it altogether, it was a most wild and rugged and stupendous chasm, so deep and narrow where a river had worn itself a passage through a mountain of rock, and all around was the comparatively untrodden wilderness.

This was the limit of our walk down the St. Lawrence. Early in the afternoon we began to retrace our steps, not being able to cross the north channel and return by the Isle of Orleans, on account of the *trop grand vent,* or too great wind. Though the waves did run pretty high, it was evident that the inhabitants of Montmorenci County were no sailors, and made but little use of the river. When we reached the bridge, between St. Anne and Chateau Richer, I ran back a little way to ask a man in the field the name of the river which we were crossing, but for a long time I could not make out what he said, for he was one of the more unintelligible Jacques Cartier men. At last it flashed upon me that it was *La Rivière au Chien,* or the Dog River, which my eyes beheld, which brought to my mind the life of the Canadian *voyageur* and *coureur de bois,* a more western and wilder Arcadia, methinks, than the world has ever seen; for the Greeks, with all their wood and river gods, were not so qualified to name the natural features of a country; as the ancestors of these French Canadians; and if any people had a right to substitute their own for the Indian names, it was they. They have preceded the pioneer on our own frontiers, and named the prairie for us. *La Rivière au Chien* cannot, by any license of language, be translated into Dog River, for that is not such a giving it to the dogs, and recognizing their place in creation as the French implies. One of the tributaries of the St. Anne is named, *La Rivière de la Rose;* and further east are, *La Rivière de la Blondelle,* and *La Rivière de la Friponne.* Their very *rivière* meanders more than our *river.*

Yet the impression which this country made on me, was commonly different from this. To a traveller from the Old World, Canada East may appear like a new country, and its inhabitants like colonists, but to me, coming from New England, and being a very green traveller withal—notwithstanding what I have said about Hudson's Bay,—it appeared as old as Normandy itself, and realized much that I had heard of Europe and the Middle Ages. Even the names of humble Canadian villages affected me as if they had been those of the renowned cities of antiquity. To be told by a habitan, when I asked the name of a village in sight, that it is *St. Fercole* or *St. Anne,* the *Guardian Angel* or the *Holy Joseph's,* or of a mountain, that it was *Bélangé,* or *St. Hyacinthe!* As soon as you leave the States, these saintly names begin. *St. John* is the first town you stop at (fortunately we did not see it), and thenceforward, the names of the mountains and streams, and villages, reel, if I may so speak, with the intoxication of poetry;—*Chambly, Longueil, Pointe aux Trembles, Bartholomy,* &c., &c.; as if it needed only a little foreign accent, a few more liquids and vowels perchance in the language, to make us locate our ideals at once. I began to dream of Provence and the Troubadours, and of places and things which have no existence on the earth. They veiled the Indian and the primitive forest, and the woods toward Hudson's Bay, were only as the forests of France and Germany. I could not at once bring myself to believe that the inhabitants who pronounced daily those beautiful, and to me, significant names, lead as prosaic lives as we of New England. In short, the Canada which I saw, was not merely a place for railroads to terminate in, and for criminals to run to.

When I asked the man to whom I have referred, if there were any falls on the *Rivière au Chien,* for I saw that it came over the same high bank with the Montmorenci and St. Anne; he answered that there were. How far? I inquired; *Trois quatres lieue.* How high? *Je pense, quatre-vingt-dix pieds;* that is, ninety feet. We turned aside to look at the falls of the *Rivière du Sault à la Puce,* half a mile from the road, which before we had passed in our haste and ignorance, and we pronounced them as beautiful as any that we saw; yet they seemed to make no account of them there, and when first we inquired the way to the Falls, directed us to Montmorenci, seven miles distant. It was evident that this was the country for waterfalls; that every stream that empties into the St. Lawrence, for some hundreds of miles, must have a great fall or cascade on it, and in its passage through the mountains, was, for a short distance, a small Saguenay, with its upright walls. This fall of La Puce, the least remarkable of the four which we visited in this vicinity, we had never heard of till we came to Canada, and yet, so far as I know, there is nothing of the kind in New England to be compared with it.

At a house near the western boundary of Chateau Richer, whose master was said to speak a very little English, having recently lived at Quebec, we got lodging for the night. As usual, we had to go down a lane to get round to the south side of the house where the door was, away from the road. For these Canadian houses have no front door, properly speaking. Every part is for the use of the occupant exclusively, and no part has reference to the traveller or to travel. Every New England house, on the contrary, has a front and principal door opening to the great world, though it may be on the cold side, for it stands on the highway of nations, and the road which runs by it, comes from the Old World and goes to the Far West; but the Canadian's door opens into his back yard and farm alone, and the road which runs behind his house leads only from the church of one saint to that of another. We found a large family, hired men, wife, and children, just eating their supper. They prepared some for us afterwards. The hired men were a merry crew of short black-eyed fellows, and the wife a thin-faced, sharp-featured French Canadian woman. Our host's English staggered us rather more than any French we had heard yet; indeed, we found that even we spoke better French than he did English, and we concluded that a less crime would be committed on the whole, if we spoke French with him, and in no respect aided or abetted his attempts to speak English. We had a long and merry chat with the family this Sunday evening in their spacious kitchen. While my companion smoked a pipe and parlez-vous'd with one party, I parleyed and gesticulated to another. The whole family was enlisted, and I kept a little girl writing what was otherwise unintelligible. The geography getting obscure, we called for chalk, and the greasy oiled table-cloth having been wiped,—for it needed no French, but only a sentence from the universal language of looks on my part, to indicate that it needed it,—we drew the St. Lawrence with its parishes thereon, and thenceforward went on swimmingly, by turns handling the chalk and committing to the table-cloth what would otherwise have been left in a limbo of unintelligibility. This was greatly to the entertainment of all parties. I was amused to hear how much use they made of the word *oui* in conversation with one another. After repeated single insertions of it one would suddenly throw back his head at the same time with his chair, and exclaim rapidly, *oui! oui! oui! oui!* like a Yankee driving pigs. Our host told us that the farms thereabouts were generally two acres, or three hundred and sixty French feet wide, by one and a half leagues (?) or a little more than four and a half of our miles deep. This use of the word acre as long measure, arises from the fact that the French acre or arpent, the arpent of Paris, makes a square of ten perches of eighteen feet each on a side, a Paris foot being equal to 1.06575 English feet. He said that the wood was cut off about one mile from the river. The rest was "bush," and beyond that the "Queen's bush." Old as the country is, each landholder bounds on the primitive forest, and fuel bears no price. As I had forgotten the French for sickle, they went out in the evening to the barn and got one, and so clenched the certainty of our understanding one another. Then, wishing to learn if they used the cradle, and not knowing any French word for this instrument, I set up the knives and forks on the blade of the sickle to represent one; at which they all exclaimed that they knew and had used it. When *snells* were mentioned they went out in the dark and plucked some. They were pretty good. They said that they had three kinds of plums growing wild, blue, white, and red, the two former much alike, and the best. Also they asked me if I would have *des pommes,* some apples, and got me some. They were exceedingly fair and glossy, and it was evident that there was no worm in them, but they were as hard almost as a stone, as if the season was too short to mellow them. We had seen no soft and yellow apples by the road-side. I declined eating one, much as I admired it, observing that it would be good *dans le printemps,* in the spring. In the morning when the mistress had set the eggs a frying, she nodded to a thick-set jolly-looking fellow, who rolled up his sleeves, seized the long-handled griddle, and commenced a series of revolutions and evolutions with it, ever and anon tossing its contents into the air, where they turned completely topsy-turvey and came down t'other side up; and this he repeated till they were done. That appeared to be his duty when eggs were concerned. I did not chance to witness this performance, but my companion did, and he pronounced it a master-piece in its way.

PAUL ELMER MORE

A Hermit's Notes on Thoreau

NEAR the secluded village of Shelburne that lies along the peaceful valley of the Androscoggin, I took upon myself to live two years as a hermit after a mild Epicurean fashion of my own. Three maiden aunts wagged their heads ominously; my nearest friend inquired cautiously whether there was any taint of insanity in the family; an old grey-haired lady, a veritable saint who had not been soured by her many deeds of charity, admonished me on the utter selfishness and godlessness of such a proceeding. But I clung heroically to my resolution. Summer tourists in that pleasant valley may still see the little red house among the pines,— empty now, I believe; and I dare say gaudy coaches still draw up at the door, as they used to do, when the gaudier bonnets and hats exchanged wondering remarks on the cabalistic inscription over the lintel, or spoke condescendingly to the great dog lying on the steps. As for the hermit within, having found it impossible to educe any meaning from the tangled habits of mankind while he himself was whirled about in the imbroglio, he had determined to try the efficacy of undisturbed meditation at a distance. So deficient had been his education that he was actually better acquainted with the aspirations and emotions of the old dwellers on the Ganges than with those of the modern toilers by the Hudson or the Potomac. He had been deafened by the "indistinguishable roar" of the streets, and could make no sense of the noisy jargon of the market place. But—shall it be confessed?— although he discovered many things during his contemplative sojourn in the wilderness, and learned that the attempt to criticise and not to create literature was to be his labour in this world, nevertheless he returned to civilisation as ignorant, alas, of its meaning as when he left it.

However, it is not my intention to justify the saintly old lady's charge of egotism by telling the story of my exodus to the desert; that, perhaps, may come later and at a more suitable time. I wish now only to record the memories of one perfect day in June, when woods and mountains were as yet a new delight.

The fresh odours of morning were still swaying in the air when I set out on this particular day; and my steps turned instinctively to the great pine forest, called the Cathedral Woods, that filled the valley and climbed the hill slopes behind my house. There, many long roads that are laid down in no map wind hither and thither among the trees, whose leafless trunks tower into the sky and then meet in evergreen arches overhead. There,

> The tumult of the times disconsolate

never enters, and no noise of the world is heard save now and then, in winter, the ringing strokes of the woodchopper at his cruel task. How many times I have walked those quiet cathedral aisles, while my great dog paced faithfully on before! Underfoot the dry, purple-hued moss was stretched like a royal carpet; and at intervals a glimpse of the deep sky, caught through an aperture in the groined roof, reminded me of the other world, and carried my thoughts still farther from the desolating memories of this life. Nothing but pure odours were there, sweeter than cloistral incense; and murmurous voices of the pines, more harmonious than the chanting of trained choristers; and in the heart of the wanderer nothing but tranquillity and passionless peace.

Often now the recollection of those scenes comes floating back upon his senses when, in the wakeful seasons of a summer night, he hears the wind at work among the trees; even in barren city streets some sound or spectacle can act upon him as a spell, banishing for a moment the hideous contention of commerce, and placing him beneath the restful shadows of the pines. May his understanding cease its function, and his heart forget to feel, when the memory of those days has utterly left him and he walks in the world without this consolation of remembered peace.

Nor can I recollect that my mind, in these walks, was much called away from contemplation by the petty curiosities of the herbalist or birdlorist, for I am not one zealously addicted to scrutinising into the minuter secrets of Nature. It never seemed to me that a flower was made sweeter by knowing the construction of its ovaries, or assumed a new importance when I learned its trivial or scientific name. The wood thrush and the veery sing as melodiously to the uninformed as to the subtly curious. Indeed, I sometimes think a little ignorance is wholesome in our communion with Nature, until we are ready to part with her altogether. She is feminine in this as in other respects, and loves to shroud herself in illusions, as the Hindus taught in their books. For they called her Mâyâ, the very person and power of deception, whose sway over the beholder must end as soon as her mystery is penetrated.

Dear as the sound of the wood thrush's note still is to my ears, something of charm and allurement has gone from it since I have become intimate with the name and habits of the bird. As a child born and reared in the city, that wild, ringing call was perfectly new and strange to me when, one early dawn, I first heard it during a visit to the Delaware Water Gap. To me, whose ears had grown familiar only with the rumble of paved streets, the sound was like a reiterated unearthly summons inviting me from my narrow prison existence out into a wide and unexplored world of impulse and adventure. Long afterwards I learned the name of the songster whose note had made so strong an impression on my childish senses, but still I associate the song with the grandiose scenery, with the sheer forests and streams and the rapid river of the Water Gap. I was indeed almost a man—though the confession may sound incredible in these days—before I again heard the wood thrush's note, and my second adventure impressed me almost as profoundly as the first. In the outer suburbs of the city where my home had always been, I was walking one day with a brother, when suddenly out of a grove of laurel oaks sounded, clear and triumphant, the note which I remembered so well, but which had come to have to my imagination the unreality and mystery of a dream of long ago. Instantly my heart leapt within me. "It is the fateful summons once more!" I cried; and, with my companion who was equally ignorant of bird-lore, I ran into the grove to discover the wild trumpeter. That was a strange chase in the fading twilight, while the unknown songster led us on from tree to tree, ever deeper into the woods. Many times we saw him on one of the lower boughs, but could not for a long while bring ourselves to believe that so wondrous a melody should proceed from so plain a minstrel. And at last, when we had satisfied ourselves of his identity, and the night had fallen, we came out into the road with a strange solemnity hanging over us. Our ears had been opened to the unceasing harmonies of creation, and our eyes had been made aware of the endless drama of natural life. We had been initiated into the lesser mysteries; and if the sacred pageantry was not then, and never was to be, perfectly clear to our understanding, the imagination was nevertheless awed and purified.

If the knowledge and experience of years have made me a little more callous to these deeper influences, at least I have not deliberately closed the door to them by incautious prying. Perhaps a long course of wayward reading has taught me to look upon the world with eyes quite different from those of the modern exquisite searchers into Nature. I remember the story of Prometheus, and think his punishment is typical of the penalty that falls upon those who grasp at powers and knowledge not intended for mankind,—some nemesis of a more material loneliness and a more barren pride torturing them because they have turned from human knowledge to an alien and forbidden sphere. Like Prometheus, they shall in the end cry out in vain:—

> O air divine, and O swift-wingëd winds!
> Ye river fountains, and thou myriad-twinkling
> Laughter of ocean waves! O mother earth!
> And thou, O all-discerning orb o' the sun!—
> To you, I cry to you; behold what I,
> A god, endure of evil from the gods.

Nor is the tale of Prometheus alone in teaching this lesson of prudence, nor was Greece the only land of antiquity where reverence was deemed more salutary than curiosity. The myth of the veiled Isis passed in those days from people to people, and was everywhere received as a symbol of the veil of illusion about Nature, which no man might lift with impunity. And the same idea was, if anything, intensified in the Middle Ages. The common people, and the Church as well, looked with horror on such scholars as Pope Gerbert, who was thought, for his knowledge of Nature, to have sold himself to the devil; and on such discoverers as Roger Bacon, whose wicked searching into forbidden things cost him fourteen years in prison. And even in modern times did not the poet Blake say: "I fear Wordsworth loves nature, and nature is the work of the Devil. The Devil is in us as far as we are nature"? It has remained for an age of scepticism to substitute investigation for awe. After all, can any course of study or open-air pedagogics bring us into real communion with the world about us? I fear much of the talk about companionship with Nature that pervades our summer life is little better than cant and self-deception, and he best understands the veiled goddess who most frankly admits her impenetrable secrecy. The peace that comes to us from contemplating the vast panorama spread out before us is due rather to the sense of a great passionless power entirely out of our domain than to any real intimacy with the hidden deity. It was John Woolman, the famous New Jersey Quaker, who wrote, during a journey through the wilderness of Pennsylvania: "In my travelling on the road, I often felt a cry rise from the centre of my mind, thus, 'O Lord, I am a stranger on the earth, hide not thy face from me.'"

But I forget that I am myself travelling on the road; and all this long disquisition is only a chapter of reminiscences, due to the multitudinous singing of the thrushes on this side and that, as we—I and my great dog—trod the high cathedral aisles. After a while the sound of running water came to us above the deeper diapason of the pines, and, turning aside, we clambered down to a brook which we had already learned to make the terminus of our walks. Along this stream we had discovered a dozen secret nooks where man and dog might lie or sit at ease, and to-day I stretched myself on a cool, hollow rock, with my eyes looking up the long, leafy chasm of the brook. Just above my couch the current was dammed by a row of mossy boulders, over which the waters poured with a continual murmur and plash. My head was only a little higher than the pool beyond the boulders, and, lying motionless, I watched the flies weaving a pattern over the surface of the quiet water, and now and then was rewarded by seeing a greedy trout leap into the sunlight to capture one of the winged weavers. Surely, if there is any such thing as real intimacy with Nature, it is in just such secluded spots as this; for the grander scenes require of us a moral enthusiasm which can come to the soul only at rare intervals and for brief moments. From these chosen mountain retreats, one might send to a scientist, busy with his books and instruments and curious to pry into the secret powers of Nature, some such an appeal as this:—

>Brother, awhile your impious engines leave;
> Nor always seek with flame-compelling wires
>Out of the palsied hand of Zeus to reave
> His dear celestial fires.
>
>What though he drowse upon a tottering bench,
> Forgetful how his random bolts are hurled!
>Are you to blame? or is it yours to quench
> The thunders of the world?
>
>Come learn with me through folly to be wise:
> Think you by cunning laws of optic lore
>To lend the enamelled fields or burning skies
> One splendour lacked before?

A wizard footrule to the waves of sound
  You lay,—hath measure in the song of bird
Or ever in the voice of waters found
  One melody erst unheard?

Ah, for a season close your magic books,
  Your rods and crystals in the closet hide;
I know in covert ways a hundred nooks,
  High on the mountain side,

Where through the golden hours that follow noon,
  Under the greenwood shadows you and I
May talk of happy lives, until too soon
  Night's shadows fold the sky.

And while like incense blown among the leaves
  Our fragrant smoke ascends from carven bowl,
We'll con the lesser wisdom that deceives
  The Questioner in the soul,

And laugh to hoodwink where we cannot rout:—
  Did Bruno of the Stubborn heart outbrave,
Or could the mind of Galileo flout
  The folly of the Grave?

So it seemed to me that the lesser wisdom of quiet content before the face of Nature's mysteries might be studied in the untrained garden of my hermitage. But I have been dreaming and moralising on the little life about me and the greater life of the world too long. So lying near the level of the still pool I began to read. The volume chosen was the most appropriate to the time and place that could be imagined,—Thoreau's *Walden;* and having entered upon an experiment not altogether unlike his, I now set myself to reading the record of his two years of solitude. I learned many things from that morning's perusal. Several times I had read the *Odyssey* within sight of the sea; and the murmur of the waves on the beach, beating through the rhythm of the poem, had taught me how vital a thing a book might be, and how it could acquire a peculiar validity from harmonious surroundings; but now the reading of Thoreau in that charmed and lonely spot emphasised this commonplace truth in a special manner. *Walden* studied in the closet, and *Walden* mused over under the trees, by running water, are two quite different books. And then, from Thoreau, the greatest by far of our writers on Nature, and the creator of a new sentiment in literature, my mind turned to the long list of Americans who have left, or are still composing, a worthy record of their love and appreciation of the natural world. Our land of multiform activities has produced so little that is really creative in literature or art! Hawthorne and Poe, and possibly one or two others, were masters in their own field; yet even they chose not quite the highest realm for their genius to work in. But in one subject our writers have led the way and are still pre-eminent: Thoreau was the creator of a new manner of writing about Nature. In its deeper essence his work is inimitable, as it is the voice of a unique personality; but in its superficial aspects it has been taken up by a host of living writers, who have caught something of his method, even if they lack his genius and singleness of heart. From these it was an easy transition to compare Thoreau's attitude of mind with that of Wordsworth and the other great poets of his century who went to Nature for their inspiration, and made Nature-writing the characteristic note of modern verse. What is it in Thoreau that is not to be found in Byron and Shelley and Wordsworth, not to mention old Izaak Walton, Gilbert White of Selborne, and a host of others? It was a rare treat, as I lay in that leafy covert, to go over in memory the famous descriptive passages from these authors, and to contrast their spirit with that of the book in my hand.

As I considered these matters, it seemed to me that Thoreau's work was distinguished from that of his American predecessors and imitators by just these qualities of awe and wonder which we, in our communings with Nature, so often cast away. Mere description, though it may at times have a scientific value, is after all a very cheap form of literature; and, as I have already intimated, too much curiosity of detail is likely to exert a deadening influence on the philosophic and poetic contemplation of Nature. Such an influence is, as I believe, specially noticeable at the present time, and even Thoreau was not entirely free from its baneful effect. Much of his writing, perhaps the greater part, is the mere record of observation and classification, and has not the slightest claim on our remembrance, —unless, indeed, it possesses some scientific value, which I doubt. Certainly the parts of his work having permanent interest are just those chapters where he is less the minute observer, and more the contemplative philosopher. Despite the width and exactness of his information, he was far from having the truly scientific spirit; the acquisition of knowledge, with him, was in the end quite subordinate to his interest in the moral significance of Nature, and the words he read in her obscure scroll were a language of strange mysteries, oftentimes of awe. It is a constant reproach to the prying, self-satisfied habits of small minds to see the reverence of this great-hearted observer before the supreme goddess he so loved and studied.

Much of this contemplative spirit of Thoreau is due to the soul of the man himself, to that personal force which no analysis of character can explain. But, besides this, it has always seemed to me that, more than in any other descriptive writer of the land, his mind is the natural outgrowth, and his essays the natural expression, of a feeling deep-rooted in the historical beginnings of New England; and this foundation in the past gives a strength and convincing force to his words that lesser writers utterly lack. Consider the new life of the Puritan colonists in the strange surroundings of their desert home. Consider the case of the adventurous Pilgrims sailing from the comfortable city of Leyden to the unknown wilderness over the sea. As Governor Bradford wrote, "the place they had thoughts on was some of those vast & unpeopled countries of America, which are frutfull & fitt for habitation, being devoyd of all civill inhabitants, wher ther are only salvage and brutish men, which range up and downe, little otherwise than ye wild beasts of the same." In these vast and unpeopled countries, where beast and bird were strange to the eye, and where "salvage" men abounded,—men who did not always make the land so "fitt" for new inhabitants as Bradford might have desired,—it was inevitable that the mind should be turned to explore and report on natural phenomena and on savage life. It is a fact that some of the descriptions of sea and land made by wanderers to Virginia and Massachusetts have a directness and graphic power, touched occasionally with an element of wildness, that render them even to-day agreeable reading.

This was before the time of Rousseau, and before Gray had discovered the beauty of wild mountain scenery; inevitably the early American writers were chiefly interested in Nature as the home of future colonists, and their books are for the most part semi-scientific accounts of what they studied from a utilitarian point of view. But the dryness of detailed description in the New World was from the first modified and lighted up by the wondering awe of men set down in the midst of the strange and often threatening forces of an untried wilderness; and this sense of awful aloofness, which to a certain extent lay dormant in the earlier writers, did nevertheless sink deep into the heart of New England, and when, in the lapse of time, the country entered into its intellectual renaissance, and the genius came who was destined to give full expression to the thoughts of his people before the face of Nature, it was inevitable that his works should be dominated by just this sense of poetic mystery.

It is this New World inheritance, moreover,—joined, of course, with his own inexplicable personality, which must not be left out of account,—that makes Thoreau's attitude toward Nature something quite distinct from that of the great poets who just preceded him. There was in him none of the fiery spirit of the revolution which caused Byron to mingle hatred of men with enthusiasm for the Alpine solitudes. There was none of the passion for beauty and the voluptuous self-abandonment of Keats; these were not in the atmosphere he breathed at Concord. He was not touched with Shelley's unearthly mysticism, nor had he ever fed

> on the aërial kisses
> Of shapes that haunt thought's wildernesses;

his moral sinews were too stark and strong for that form of mental dissipation. Least of all did he, after the manner of Wordsworth, hear in the voice of Nature any compassionate plea for the weakness and sorrow of the downtrodden. Philanthropy and humanitarian sympathies were to him a desolation and a woe. "Philanthropy is almost the only virtue which is sufficiently appreciated by mankind. Nay, it is greatly overrated; and it is our selfishness which overrates it," he writes. And again: "The philanthropist too often surrounds mankind with the remembrance of his own cast-off griefs as an atmosphere, and calls it sympathy." Similarly his reliance on the human will was too sturdy to be much perturbed by the inequalities and sufferings of mankind, and his faith in the individual was too unshaken to be led into humanitarian interest in the masses. "Alas! this is the crying sin of the age," he declares, "this want of faith in the prevalence of a man."

But the deepest and most essential difference is the lack of pantheistic reverie in Thoreau. It is this brooding over the universal spirit embodied in the material world which almost always marks the return of sympathy with Nature, and which is particularly noticeable in the writers of the past century. So Lord Byron, wracked and broken by his social catastrophes, turns for relief to the fair scenes of Lake Leman, and finds in the high mountains and placid waters a consoling spirit akin to his own.

> Are not the mountains, waves, and skies, a part
> Of me and of my soul, as I of them?

he asks; and in the bitterness of his human disappointment he would "be alone, and love Earth only for its earthly sake." Shelley, too, "mixed awful talk" with the "great parent," and heard in her voice an answer to all his vague dreams of the soul of universal love. No one, so far as I know, has yet studied the relation between Wordsworth's pantheism and his humanitarian sympathies, but we need only glance at his lines on Tintern Abbey to see how closely the two feelings were interknit in his mind. It was because he felt this

> sense sublime
> Of something far more deeply interfused,
> Whose dwelling is the light of setting suns,
> And the round ocean, and the living air,
> And the blue sky, and in the mind of man;

it was because the distinctions of the human will and the consequent perception of individual responsibility were largely absorbed in this dream of the universal spirit, that he heard in Nature "the still, sad music of humanity," and reproduced it so sympathetically in his own song. Of all this pantheism, whether attended with revolt from responsibility or languid reverie or humanitarian dreams, there is hardly a trace in Thoreau. The memory of man's struggle with the primeval woods and fields was not so lost in antiquity that the world had grown into an indistinguishable part of human life. If Nature smiled upon Thoreau at times, she was still an alien creature who succumbed only to his force and tenderness, as she had before given her bounty, though reluctantly, to the Pilgrim Fathers. A certain companionship he had with the plants and wild beasts of the field, a certain intimacy with the dumb earth; but he did not seek to merge his personality in their impersonal life, or look to them for a response to his own inner moods; he associated with them as the soul associates with the body.

More characteristic is his sense of awe, even of dread, toward the great unsubdued forces of the world. The loneliness of the mountains such as they appeared to the early adventurers in a strange, unexplored country; the repellent loneliness of the barren heights frowning down inhospitably upon the pioneer who scratched the soil at their base; the loneliness and terror of the dark, untrodden forests, where the wanderer might stray away and be lost forever, where savage men were more feared than the wild animals, and where superstition saw the haunt of the Black Man and of all uncleanness,— all this tradition of sombre solitude made Nature to Thoreau something very different from the hills and valleys of Old England. "We have not seen pure Nature," he says, "unless we have seen her thus vast and drear and inhuman.... Man was not to be associated with it. It was matter, vast, terrific,—not his Mother Earth that we have heard of, not for him to tread on, or be buried in,—no, it were being too familiar even to let his bones lie there, —the home, this, of Necessity and Fate." After reading Byron's invocation to the Alps as the palaces of Nature; or the ethereal mountain scenes in Shelley's *Alastor,* where all the sternness of the everlasting hills is dissolved into rainbow hues of shifting light as dainty as the poet's own soul; or Wordsworth's familiar musings in the vale of Grasmere,—if, after these, we turn to Thoreau's account of the ascent of Mount Katahdin, we seem at once to be in the home of another tradition. I am tempted to quote a few sentences of that account to emphasise the point. On the mountain heights, he says of the beholder:

He is more lone than you can imagine. There is less of substantial thought and fair understanding in him than in the plains where men inhabit. His reason is dispersed and shadowy, more thin and subtile, like the air. Vast, Titanic, inhuman Nature has got him at disadvantage, caught him alone, and pilfers him of some of his divine faculty. She does not smile on him as in the plains. She seems to say sternly, Why came ye here before your time? This ground is not prepared for you. Is it not enough that I smile in the valleys? I have never made this soil for thy feet, this air for thy breathing, these rocks for thy neighbours. I cannot pity nor fondle thee here, but forever relentlessly drive thee hence to where I *am* kind.

I do not mean to present the work of Thoreau as equal in value to the achievement of the great poets with whom I have compared him, but wish merely in this way to bring out more definitely his characteristic traits. Yet if his creative genius is less than theirs, I cannot but think his attitude toward Nature is in many respects truer and more wholesome. Pantheism, whether on the banks of the Ganges or of the Thames, seems to bring with it a spreading taint of effeminacy; and from this the mental attitude of our Concord naturalist was eminently free. There is something tonic and bracing in his intercourse with the rude forces of the forest; he went to Walden Pond because he had "private business to transact," not for relaxation and mystical reverie. "To be a philosopher," he said, "is not merely to have subtle thoughts, nor even to found a school, but so to love wisdom as to live according to its dictates, a life of simplicity, independence, magnanimity, and trust;" and by recurring to the solitudes of Nature he thought he could best develop in himself just these manly virtues. Nature was to him a discipline of the will as much as a stimulant to the imagination. He would, if it were possible, "combine the hardiness of the savages with the intellectualness of the civilised man;" and in this method of working out the philosophical life we see again the influence of long and deep-rooted tradition. To the first settlers, the red man was as much an object of curiosity and demanded as much study as the earth they came to cultivate; their books are full of graphic pictures of savage life, and it should seem as if now in Thoreau this inherited interest had received at last its ripest expression. When he travelled in the wilderness of Maine, he was as much absorbed in learning the habits of his Indian guides as in exploring the woods. He had some innate sympathy or perception which taught him to find relics of old Indian life where others would pass them by, and there is a well-known story of his answer to one who asked him where such relics could be discovered: he merely stooped down and picked an arrowhead from the ground.

And withal his stoic virtues never dulled his sense of awe, and his long years of observation never lessened his feeling of strangeness in the presence of solitary Nature. If at times his writing descends into the cataloguing style of the ordinary naturalist, yet the old tradition of wonder was too strong in him to be more than temporarily obscured. Unfortunately, his occasional faults have become in some of his recent imitators the staple of their talent; but Thoreau was pre-eminently the poet and philosopher of his school, and I cannot do better than close these desultory notes with the quotation of a passage which seems to me to convey most vividly his sensitiveness to the solemn mystery of the deep forest:

> We heard [he writes in his *Chesuncook*], come faintly echoing, or creeping from afar, through the moss-clad aisles, a dull, dry, rushing sound, with a solid core to it, yet as if half smothered under the grasp of the luxuriant and fungus-like forest, like the shutting of a door in some distant entry of the damp and shaggy wilderness. If we had not been there, no mortal had heard it. When we asked Joe [the Indian guide] in a whisper what it was, he answered,—"Tree fall."

MOSES COIT TYLER

The Literary Strivings of Mr. Joel Barlow

I

During the earlier months of the year 1779, there was living at Yale College an alert young man, Joel Barlow by name, ostensibly devoting himself to graduate studies there, but really absorbed in the not incongruous employments of cultivating poetry, the affections of a certain young lady in the town, and his own fond hopes of a college-tutorship. In the July of the previous year he had taken at the college his first degree, and on that occasion had won for himself a quite exhilarating tea-pot reputation by a poem which, from the midst of all the clouds and clamors of that low-spirited war, celebrated "The Prospects of Peace." He was already in his twenty-fifth year, his small patrimony spent, his eyes anxiously turned for some scholar-like employment which would permit him to take speedily unto himself the wife of his choice, and to set about the writing of a certain huge, patriotic, and philosophic poem with which his soul was even then uneasily swelling. So, on the 30th of January, of this year 1779, he poured out his heart by letter to his class-mate, Noah Webster, then plodding as a schoolmaster in a country-town in Connecticut:—"You and I are not the first in the world who have broken loose from college without friends and without fortune to push us into public notice. Let us show the world a few more examples of men standing upon their own merit and rising in spite of obstacles.... I am yet at a loss for an employment for life, and unhappy in this state of suspense. The American Republic is a fine theatre for the display of merit of every kind. If ever virtue is to be rewarded, it is in America. Literary accomplishments will not be so much noticed till sometime after the settlement of peace, and the people become more refined. More blustering characters must bear sway at present, and the hardy veterans must retire from the field before the philosopher can retire to the closet. I don't feel as if ever I should enter upon either of the learned professions for a livelihood." [1]

As the months slipped away, his hope of the tutorship slipped away likewise; and to the brotherly heart of Noah Webster he once more spoke out his solicitude: "At present, I must own, my prospects are clouded. Mr. Perkins ... advises me to go into business for a living, and make poetry only an amusement for leisure hours.... These leisure hours will never come to me, after I am buried in business for life." [2]

Then a whole year passed. The tutorship never came; but instead of it, there dawned upon him the plan of finding a livelihood, together with some literary leisure, by going into the army as a chaplain. Of all this situation, a contemporary glimpse is given in a letter written to General Greene from New Haven, on the 10th of April, 1780, by Barlow's brother-poet, Captain David Humphreys: "There is a hopeful genius ... in this town, who is so far gone in poetry, that there is no hope of reclaiming and making him attentive to anything else. To be more serious about the matter, the person intended is a young gentleman by the name of Barlow, who I could wish was introduced to your notice. He is certainly a very great genius, and has undertaken a work which, I am persuaded, will do honor to himself and his country—if he is enabled to prosecute it in the manner he has proposed. It is entitled the 'Vision of Columbus' and in the course of the poem will bring into view upon a large scale all the great events that have or will take place on the continent. From a sight of the first book, which he has nearly finished, I have conceived an exceeding high idea of the performance. But the difficulty is, it will be a labor of three years at least; and his patrimony, which consisted in continental bills, is by no means sufficient to support him." [3]

II

As a result of all these conferences over his affairs, it turned out that in the September following, with much reluctance and even with some desperation, he accepted a chaplaincy in the army,—not as having any sort of vocation to

[1] "Life and Letters of Joel Barlow," by Charles Burr Todd, 18-19. My study of the published writings of Barlow was finished before the appearance of this capital book, in the preparation of which its author had the use of the great collection of Barlow papers made with so much perseverance by the late Lemuel G. Olmsted. The book has been of much use to me for personal items concerning Barlow, and especially for many passages from his private correspondence previously existing only in manuscript.
[2] "Life and Letters," etc., 20.
[3] "Humphrey's Family in America," 155-156.

the sacred ministry, but only as having present need of bread, and the willingness to earn it, in this capacity of extemporized and amateur parson, by putting to pulpit uses his capacity to compose sonorous sentences and to declaim them. In a letter to his beloved, written on the 11th of September from the camp near Paramus in New Jersey, he sets forth, in entirely secular language, his earliest experience of the sacred office: "Did not arrive at camp till Saturday night. I lodged in a tent on a bed of bark that wet night.... Monday, the army marched ... a few miles ... On Thursday evening I began to open my mouth, which is none of the smallest and out of it there went a noise which the brigade received as the duty of my office. On Sunday ... I gave them a preachment, and ... was flattered afterward by some of the most sensible hearers with the great merit of the performance. I know you will ask me how I made out: I really did well, far beyond my expectations, and I find it all a joke, as much as Cassius did, to be in awe of such a thing as myself."[4]

Presently, compliments for his sermons were succeeded by other agreeable things, marked civilities from great generals, the sight of imposing military pageants, even the place of honor at dinner with Washington himself,—all tending to convince our large-mouthed young evangelist, that his irruption into the sacred office, as amateur parson, was turning out no bad speculation after all. On the 23d of September, 1780, writing as usual to his beloved, he says: "This is Saturday afternoon. I have fixed my magazine for to-morrow, and my thoughts are at liberty to dwell upon their favorite object, the centre of all my happiness. We have to-day made a move back from Hackensack to an old encampment here near the river, where I have taken lodgings in an old Dutchman's bedroom.... The worst difficulty is, the Sabbath days come rather too thick."[5] As this comfortable young chaplain, snugly sitting there in the "old Dutchman's bedroom," scribbled away merrily to his sweetheart, little knew he of a great thing that had been happening but a few hours before, and not many miles off, just across the Hudson,—a deed of hell baffled, a deed of sorrow begun, through the arrest by three militiamen on the high-road near Tarrytown, of a handsome young gentleman, journeying southward on horseback, and found, after close investigation, to be carrying precious documents in his boots,—not the least precious document of them all being the man himself who wore the boots, to wit, Major John André, Adjutant-General of the British army. Even on the subsequent Monday

[4] "Life and Letters," etc., 31-32.
[5] Ibid., 33-34.

morning, the news of Arnold's treachery and of André's arrest seems not to have reached Barlow's camp; for the careless strain of his love-letter still holds: "My dear, it is now Monday morning. I have left that blank in the line for Sunday, when I had no feelings worth communicating, except a few anxious thoughts about the preachment, which I made in a great Dutch barn. This is the third sermon I have given them, and I feel pretty well about it." [6]

The ink that formed those words could hardly have been dry on the paper, when Rumor, blowing furiously upon all her winds the names of Arnold and André, stormed into Barlow's quarters with her now prodigious babblement; and, just one week later, Barlow himself had something very unusual to write about. On the morning of that day, Monday, the 2d of October, riding a few miles northward to Tappan, he had seen a ghastly sight—a new-made gallows and the handsome young spy hanged thereon. Coming back to his quarters, he wrote to his confidante: "I have been since to attend the execution of Major André, Adjutant-General of the British army, hanged as a spy. A politer gentleman, or a greater character of his age, is not alive. He was twenty-eight years old. He was dressed completely, and suffered with calmness and cheerfulness. With an appearance of philosophy and heroism, he observed that he was buoyed above the fear of death by the consciousness that every action of his life had been honorable, that in a few minutes he should be out of all pleasure or pain. Whether he has altered his mind, or whether he has any mind, is now best known to himself." [7]

After this rather pagan conclusion respecting poor André, thus ignobly impelled into that state wherein he was to ascertain what truth there might be in our dim earth-dream of a disembodied mind, the young chaplain reverts, by a natural and somewhat habitual transition, to the greater and more attractive subject of himself: "My situation in the army grows more and more agreeable. I am as hearty and as healthy as I can be in your absence. I gave them a preachment yesterday for the fourth time—a flaming political sermon, occasioned by the treachery of Arnold. I had a number of gentlemen from the other brigades, and I am told it did me great honor.... I had a billet last week from General Greene to dine with him." [8]

It is obvious that the temporarily Reverend Joel Barlow was now getting on in the world; and one observes without displeasure how, all along that

---

[6] "Life and Letters," etc., 34.
[7] *Ibid.*, etc., 35.
[8] *Ibid.*, etc., 35.

period, his letters ripple with intimations of his own consciousness of the fact. Above all things, in the expected military inactivity of the approaching winter, he was glad to see his way to leisure for that huge patriotic and philosophic poem, which was struggling to break forth from within the brain of him, and which was to blazon in deathless verse the triumph of human freedom and of human nature then insupportably advancing toward its stately consummation in America. On the 18th of October, from Notaway, he writes: "My prospects for my poem are better now than ever. I shall have more leisure than I expected, and in winter shall have scarcely any interruption if I choose to pursue the plan. I intend to take winter quarters in the vicinity of camp, wherever it may be, and set Quamminy [9] to work like a sprite all winter. I will tell you more about it when I see you. Yesterday, the Reverend Mr. Claremont [10] had a billet from General Washington to dine. How do you think I felt when the greatest man on earth placed me at his right hand, with Lord Sterling at his left, at table? ... Since the preaching of my sermon on the treason of Arnold and the glory of America, several gentlemen who did not hear it, and some who did, have been to read it. They talk of printing it. Colonel Humphreys has made me promise to loan him the plan and the first book of my poem to read at headquarters." [11]

III

The poem, of which Barlow thus early in his life began to dream, and which proved to be, likewise, the one absorbing task and inspiration of nearly all his remaining years on earth, was originally named by him The "Vision of Columbus." It was to be "rather of the philosophic than epic kind." Moreover, it was "on the subject of America at large," and was "to exhibit the importance of this country in every point of view as the noblest and most elevated part of the earth, and reserved to be [the] last and greatest theatre for the improvement of mankind in every article in which they are capable of improvement." [12]

Whether this, our not over-bashful prophet Joel, whilom of Connecticut, hath truly within him, in any sufficient measure, the heaven-born vision and the strength for so mighty an argument of song, is doubtless a thing that may be very easily called into question. Meantime, no one can justly

---

[9] A nickname for himself.
[10] Another of his jocose aliases.
[11] "Life and Letters," etc., 36-37.
[12] *Ibid.*, etc., 15.

fail to note the sincerity of his early enthusiasm for a most noble idea, and the persistence of the same through all the toils, and distractions, and disenchantments of a busy and a conspicuous life. By the autumn of 1782, using sturdily whatsoever leisure he could pluck from his duties and diversions as military parson, he had got the poem so far advanced as to be able, after the manner of those days, to invite subscriptions for its immediate publication. Luckily, the public eagerness for the poem seems to have been expressed in a manner so temperate as to indicate to the author that any delay which he might choose to interpose in its publication, would probably be borne by mankind with becoming fortitude.

A delay of five years was, in fact, so interposed,—five years of extremely laborious and miscellaneous occupation on the part of Joel Barlow. He had been married in 1781; and having in 1783 established his home in Hartford, and having ceased to maintain any longer the tiresome farce of being a preacher, he went into the business of keeping a printing-office and of editing a weekly newspaper; he likewise undertook and performed the job of revising, for the Congregational churches of Connecticut, Watts's version of The Psalms, himself adding new metrical paraphrases of fourteen [13]; he also studied law, and was admitted to the bar; finally, according to his biographer he "wrote a great deal of poetry, annuals, New Year's verses, bon mots, political squibs, and satires," [14]—of the latter, the most notable being his contributions to "The Anarchiad."

Not until the spring of the year 1787, was he able to give to the public the great poem upon which he had been so long engaged, and even then in a form which he afterward characterized as a mere "sketch." In a small octavo volume, with a dedication to America's gracious ally, "His Most Christian Majesty, Louis the Sixteenth, King of France and Navarre," and with an appendix containing a list of nearly eight hundred subscribers in Europe and in America, "The Vision of Columbus," a philosophical poem in nine books and in nearly five thousand lines, made its entrance into the world, receiving, it is said, a not unfriendly reception in America, in England, and in France, and procuring for its author a leading position as an American man of letters.[15]

---

[13] In the Mass. Hist. Society's Library is a small volume, given by George Ticknor, and containing the contributions made by Barlow to the book of Psalms and Hymns of which he was editor. His translations of the Psalms are numbers 28, 43, 52, 53, 54, 59, 70, 79, 88, 113, 118, 137, 138, and 140. His hymns are as follows: numbers 63, 65, 66, 67, 68.

[14] Todd, in "Life and Letters," etc., 46.

[15] "Life and Letters," etc., 54.

Even then, however, the poem failed to relieve the author of his burden,—his still unspeakable conception of the magnificent part which America was then playing, and was destined to play, in the development of mankind throughout all the world, and throughout all time; and the subsequent twenty years of his life—years passed chiefly in France, and in no obscure relation to some of the great men and great events of that mighty time—were given by him consciously or unconsciously, to the reconstruction, recomposition, and enlargement of this poem. In 1807, having then returned to America, and being possessed of ample wealth as well as of a considerable name in the world, he issued the work, in its final form, under the title of "The Columbiad."

Probably no book, at once so ambitious in design, so imposing in bulk, and so superb in all the physical accessories of paper, type, illustration, and binding, had ever before proceeded from an American press. It contains twelve full-paged steel engravings, from designs painted expressly for the book by Fulton and Smirke. In place of the original dedication to King Louis the Sixteenth, whom the author in the meantime had indirectly helped to dethrone and to decapitate, the work is inscribed to the American inventor of steam navigation. Then follows a preface in explanation of the poetic form, as well as of the poetic and the moral objects, of the work. This, again, is followed by an elaborate introduction, rehearsing in clear and stately prose the leading facts in the career of Columbus, after which the impetuous reader is no longer withheld from access to "The Columbiad" itself.

IV

The poem opens with a night-scene in Valladolid,—the palace of King Ferdinand dimly discovered through "the drizzly fogs," and beneath one of its towers, a dungeon, in which Columbus, old, sick, ruined, disheartened, lies in chains. Here, starting feverishly from a troubled sleep, the hapless old man moans to his dungeon walls the story of his life,—a life of vast, high-hearted endeavor and of world-enriching achievement, all basely rewarded by poverty, imprisonment, pain, and shame. At the end of his sorrowful monologue,

"A thundering sound
Roll'd thro' the shuddering walls and shook the ground;
O'er all the dungeon, where black arches bend,
The roofs unfold, and streams of light descend;

> The growing splendor fills the astonish'd room,
> And gales ethereal breathe a glad perfume.
> Robed in the radiance, moved a form serene,
> Of human structure, but of heavenly mien;
> Near to the prisoner's couch he takes his stand,
> And waves, in sign of peace, his holy hand.
> Tall rose his statue; youth's endearing grace
> Adorn'd his limbs and brighten'd in his face;
> Loose o'er his locks the star of evening hung,
> And sounds melodious moved his cheerful tongue." [16]

This resplendent and gracious visitor, who enters the dungeon in the midst of such supernatural demonstrations, is of the ancient race of Titans, Hesper by name, the brother of Atlas, himself the guardian genius of the western regions of the earth, and especially of those enormous twin-continents to which Columbus had at last opened the way. To Columbus, in this his uttermost misery, has Hesper come with a message and a mission of comfort; he assures the broken-hearted old man that, although he is thus ignobly treated by an age in which the rewards of life are dealt out by "blinded faction," an age in which the millions are "awed into slaves," while

> —"blood-stained steps lead upward to a throne,"

yet the future has in store for him a boundless recompense, and of this he promises to give him an immediate vision. At the word of Hesper,

> —"Columbus raised his head;
> His chains dropt off; the cave, the castle fled";

while together they walked forth from the prison. Steep before them stretched "a heaven-illumined road" leading up a mountain, of a height so enormous that it could overlook all the earth, even its summit being fragrant with the breath of flowers. This is the mount from which, for his consolation, the vision of distant lands, and of distant ages, and of people and civilizations unborn, is to be enrolled before the eyes of the weary and dying old man:

> "Led by the Power, the hero gain'd the height;
> New strength and brilliance flush'd his mortal sight;
> When calm before them flow'd the western main,
> Far stretch'd, immense, a sky-encircled plain.

[16] Book i., 127-140.

No sail, no isle, no cloud invests the bound,
Nor billowy surge disturbs the vast profound;
Till, deep in distant heavens, the sun's blue ray
Topt unknown cliffs and call'd them up to day;
Slow glimmering into sight wide regions drew,
And rose and brighten'd on the expanding view;
Fair sweep the waves, the lessening ocean smiles,
In misty radiance loom a thousand isles;
Near and more near the long drawn coasts arise,
Bays stretch their arms and mountains lift the skies;
The lakes, high mounded, point the streams their way,
Slopes, ridges, plains their spreading skirts display,
The vales branch forth, high walk approaching groves,
And all the majesty of nature moves." [17]

From this miraculous altitude, therefore, and by the aid of this miraculous conductor, does Columbus now look abroad over all that portion of the world which "his daring sail descried," his eyes being suddenly clothed, for that stupendous undertaking, with the gift of piercing alike into distance and into futurity; and what he thus sees, as regards nature and man and man's doing, is then reported, with eager and unflagging energy, and likewise in the conventional rhymed pentameters of eighteenth century English verse, through the generous profusion of these ten books. Over all that new-found hemisphere, do the anointed eyes of Columbus travel, on their swift and heart-thrilling quest, from land to land, from age to age, taking inventory of what those far-off realms contain: the lavish amplitude on which all things there are builded,—mountains, rivers, cataracts, forests, plains; the beauty and the benignity and the costliness which dwell there in earth and sky and sea; and the myriad tokens that there indeed were felt the last culminating, and most bountiful, and most tender, touches of the divine workmanship in the act of creation:

"For here great nature, with a bolder hand,
Roll'd the broad stream, and heaved the lifted land;
And here, from finsh'd earth, triumphant trod
The last ascending steps of her creating God." [18]

[17] Book i., 197-214.
[18] Ibid., 357-360.

After this colossal topographical survey of the hemisphere he had discovered, Columbus is enabled by the same resplendent and all-competent cicerone to look forth on the various tribes and nations that dwell there, to learn the story of their origin, and to inspect the cities which they had founded,—especially lingering over the romantic and pathetic history of Peru. From the past, Hesper now turns to the future, giving to Columbus, in the first place, a vision of the maleficent, dire catastrophe brought upon Peru in consequence of its invasion and conquest by his own successors; whereat recoiling in grief from so dreadful a result of the great deed of his life, he begs to be permitted to see no more. To assuage this burst of grief, Hesper then causes all Europe to be displayed before the eyes of Columbus, exhibiting to him the manifold and magnificent effects which mankind was to experience from the discovery of America,—commerce quickened, letters revived, religion reformed, government ameliorated, and finally the enormous exodus of the western nations from Europe to America begun, particularly the establishment of England's colonies in the northern continent. Thenceforward, through several books of the poem, the vision is confined to that continent, and to the unfolding of its colonial experience; the sharp and fatal antithesis there developed between the colonies of England and those of France; the outbreak of war between them; Braddock's last battle, and the apparition of Washington on that field of slaughter; the actions of Abercrombie, of Amherst, of Wolfe; finally, peace. Now, the English colonies, freed from the appalling danger which had so long menaced them from their French rivals, seem about to enter on their golden age, when lo, dark clouds gather over the eastern seas, and roll westward, and bury the continent in their black folds. Upon sight of this dismal eclipse, Hesper explains to Columbus its meaning. "Here," he tells him, "march the troublous years," during which the colonies, in order to save themselves from "lawless rule," are forced to repudiate their allegiance to England, and to assert an untrammelled national life. Then, as Columbus continues to gaze into the darkness, the central cloud bursts and moves away, giving to him a sudden view of the continental congress in full session in the "throng'd city" of Penn, of the several free-minded and indomitable communities which its members represent, and of "their endeavors to arrest the violence of England." As these endeavors prove futile, "the demon War" is seen "stalking over the ocean," leading against America the English forces:

"Slow, dark, portentous, as the meteors sweep,
And curtain black the illimitable deep,
High stalks, from surge to surge, a demon Form,
That howls thro' heaven and breaths a billowing storm.
His head is hung with clouds; his giant hand
Flings a blue flame far flickering to the land;
His blood-stain'd limbs drip carnage as he strides,
And taint with gory glume the staggering tides;
Like two red suns his quivering eyeballs glare,
His mouth disgorges all the stores of war,
Pikes, muskets, mortars, guns, and globes of fire,
And lighted bombs that fusing trails expire.
Perch'd on his helmet, two twin sisters rode,
The favorite offspring of the murderous god,—
Famine and Pestilence; ...
Then earth convulsive groan'd, high shriek'd the air,
And hell in gratulation call'd him War.
Behind the fiend, swift hovering for the coast,
Hangs o'er the wave Britannia's sail-wing'd host;
They crowd the main, they spread their sheets abroad,
From the wide Lawrence to the Georgian flood,
Point their black batteries to the peopled shore,
And spouting flames commence the hideous roar." [19]

As Columbus and his conductor continue to gaze upon this far-off scene of havoc, of gigantic destruction, of portentous cruelty, they witness what proves to be a prophetic rehearsal of all the great events of the American Revolutionary War,—the conflagration of towns along the coast from Falmouth to Norfolk; the Battle of Bunker Hill; the arrival of Washington to take command of the American forces before Boston; the death of Montgomery under the walls of Quebec; the loss of New York; Washington's retreat across the Delaware; his brilliant and victorious exploit in return; the cruelties inflicted on American prisoners by the British in their prison ships; Burgoyne's invasion, defeat, surrender; the interposition of France, and the renewal of the struggle under her assistance; finally, the investiture of Yorktown, and the surrender of Lord Cornwallis and his army. At the end of all this military tumult, blending "the groans of death and battle's bray," "the

[19] Book v., 471-498.

drum's rude clang, the war wolf's hideous howl,"—the description of which fills three books,—the author, as a matter of course, addresses a hymn to Peace, proclaiming his own delight in the privilege, at last, of celebrating her victories.

But not at once is the poet permitted to yield his verse to the service of merely joyous and unimperilled peace; and addressing in his own person his fellow-countrymen as they emerge from the Revolutionary War, he says:

> "Think not, my friends, the patriot's task is done,
> Or Freedom safe, because the battle's won." [20]

Peace, he tells them, hath her responsibilities and her dangers, no less than her delights; and the treasure of civic freedom which they have now gained through so much suffering, they may lose again through too much confidence and through too little care. He solemnly summons them to the exercise of the highest virtues of men and of patriots; and he implores them above all things to enquire whether they, Americans, the loud-voiced champions before all the world, of the principle of freedom for man, are not themselves, even then, guilty of a most atrocious and a most damning violation of that vaunted principle. At this reference to the ineffable crime then perpetrated by Americans upon Africans, there follows a passage of genuine poetic sublimity: it is the tremendous expostulation of Atlas, the guardian-genius of Africa, addressed to Hesper, the guardian-genius of America:

> "Hark! a dread voice, with heaven-astounding strain,
> Swells like a thousand thunders o'er the main.
>   .   .   .   .
> ———'t is Atlas, throned sublime,
> Great brother guardian of old Afric's clime;
> High o'er his coast he rears his frowning form,
> O'erlooks and calms his sky-borne fields of storm,
> Flings off the clouds that round his shoulders hung,
> And breaks from clogs of ice his trembling tongue;
> While far thro' space with rage and grief he glares,
> Heaves his hoar head and shakes the heaven he bears:
> —'Son of my sire! Oh latest brightest birth
> That sprang from his fair spouse, prolific Earth!

[20] Book viii., 79-80.

> Great Hesper, say what sordid ceaseless hate
> Impels thee thus to mar my elder state.
> Our sire assign'd thee thy more glorious reign,
> Secured and bounded by our laboring main,—
> That main (tho' still my birthright name it bear)
> Thy sails o'ershadow, thy brave children share.
> I grant it thus; while air surrounds the ball,
> Let breezes blow, let oceans roll for all.
> But thy proud sons, a strange ungenerous race,
> Enslave my tribes, and each fair world disgrace,
> Provoke wide vengeance in their lawless land,
> The bolt ill placed in thy forbearing hand.'"

As he continues to describe and to denounce the insolence and the inhumanity of the vast institutional crime perpetrated, age after age, upon the people of Africa by America's "strange ungenerous race," the angry Titan waxes every moment angrier and still more angry, under the effects of his own eloquence; and his ever-accumulating wrath explodes in a series of grim, huge taunts—such, indeed, as any right-minded Titan would very naturally give way to—over the contrast then to be seen, between the lofty political pretensions of the American patriots, and that most foul performance of theirs in actual life:

> "Enslave my tribes! then boast their cantons free,
> Preach faith and justice, bend the sainted knee,
> Invite all men their liberty to share?
>
> . . . . . .
>
> Enslave my tribes! what half mankind imban,
> Then read, expound, enforce the rights of man?
> Prove plain and clear how nature's hand of old
> Cast all men equal in her human mould?
>
> . . . . . .
>
> Write, speak, avenge, for ancient sufferings feel,
> Impale each tyrant on their pens of steel,
> Declare how freemen can a world create,
> And slaves and masters ruin every state?
> Enslave my tribes! and think with dumb disdain,
> To 'scape this arm and prove my vengeance vain?

> But look! methinks beneath my foot I ken
> A few chain'd things that seem no longer men,—
> Thy sons, perchance, whom Barbary's coast can tell
> The sweets of that loved scourge they wield so well." [21]

The hint, lurking in those four lines, of some bitter retaliation in kind to be inflicted by Africa upon America, leads up to a vivid prophecy of the sufferings of American captives at the hands of the Barbary pirates. If, however, this retaliation be not sufficient, it shall prove, continues the Titan, but the beginning of a penal vengeance that will certainly be subject to no imputation of incompleteness:

> "Nor shall these pangs atone the nation's crime;
> Far heavier vengeance in the march of time,
> Attends them still, if still they dare debase
> And hold enthrall'd the millions of my race,—
> A vengeance that shall shake the world's deep frame,
> That heaven abhors, and hell might shrink to name." [22]

The threat of final and all-sufficing vengeance, which the guardian genius of Africa then hurls across the ocean at his offending brother, the guardian genius of America, has indeed a very impressive energy and sublimity. Deep down "in earth's mid caves," where the very bases of the Alps and of the Andes meet together, and "lock their granite feet," are already "cauldron'd floods of fire,"—which fire, says Atlas:

> "Waits but the fissure that my wave shall find,
> To force the foldings of the rocky rind,
> Crash your curst continent, and wheel on high
> The vast avulsion vaulting thro' the sky,
> Fling far the bursting fragments, scattering wide
> Rocks, mountains, nation o'er the burning tide."

So complete shall be this avenging cataclysm, that the whole continental barrier hitherto interposed between the Atlantic and the Pacific Oceans, shall be devoured, and nothing be left visible save

[21] Book viii., 214-240.
[22] *Ibid.,* 261-266.

> "Two oceans dasht in one—that climbs and roars,
> And seeks in vain the exterminated shores."

Nothing shall be left visible, indeed, of all that proud, crime-enacting continent, except a single, solitary crag jutting out above the desolate fury of the waters:

> "A dim lone island in the watery waste
> Mourns all his minor mountains wreck'd and hurl'd,
> Stands the sad relic of a ruin'd world,
> Attests the wrath our Mother kept in store,
> And rues her judgments on the race she bore."

And in this void and desolation, henceforth, no living thing shall stir, save only that imperial Eagle which the people thus annihilated had once dared to claim as their own:

> "His own bald Eagle skims alone the sky,
> Darts from all points of heaven her searching eye,
> Kens thro' the gloom her ancient rock of rest,
> And finds her cavern'd crag, her solitary nest." [23]

At the conclusion of this prodigous protest against the crime of American slavery,—a protest, the conception of which is in a very high degree majestic and poetic,—the author speaks once more in his real character; and with a nóble intensity of passion, he implores his fellow-countrymen, themselves just emerging in triumph from a war for freedom, not to deny to others that freedom which they had so well won for themselves:

> "Fathers and friends, I know the boding fears
> Of angry genii and of rending spheres
> Assail not souls like yours, whom Science bright
> Thro' shadowy nature leads with surer light;
> For whom she strips the heavens of love and hate,
> Strikes from Jove's hand the brandisht bolt of fate,
> Gives each effect its own indubious cause,
> Divides her moral from her physic laws,
> Shows where the virtues find their nurturing food,
> And men their motives to be just and good.

[23] Book viii., 271-304.

> You scorn the Titan's threat; nor shall I strain
> The powers of pathos in a task so vain
> As Afric's wrongs to sing; for what avails
> To harp for you these known familiar tales?
> To tongue mute misery, and re-rack the soul
> With crimes oft copied from that bloody scroll
> Where Slavery pens her woes?—tho' 't is but there
> We learn the weight that moral pain can bear.
> The tale might startle still the accustomed ear.
>
> Melt every heart, and thro' the nation gain
> Full many a voice to break the barbarous chain." [24]

But not alone to the compassion of his brethren will he appeal, but rather and especially to their self-respect, and to their homage for that ancient and unpitying law whereunder he who takes freedom from another, takes it likewise from himself:

> "Tyrants are never free; and, small and great,
> All masters must be tyrants soon or late;
> So nature works; and oft the lordling knave
> Turns out at once a tyrant and a slave.
>
> . . . .
>
> Ah! would you not be slaves, with lords and kings,
> Then be not masters,—there the danger springs.
> The whole crude system that torments the earth,
> Of rank, privation, privilege of birth,
> False honor, fraud, corruption, civil jars,
> The rage of conquest and the curse of wars,
> Pandora's total shower, all ills combined
> That erst o'erwhelm'd and still distress mankind,
> Box'd up secure in your deliberate hand,
> Wait your bequest, to fix or fly this land.
> Equality of Right is nature's plan;
> And following nature is the march of man." [25]

---

[24] Book viii., 309-330.
[25] *Ibid.*, 335-364.

Rallying from this strong and not inharmonious digression, the poem once more resumes its natural course, and flows on and on to its many-membered close, through two more books,—during which our most affable, erudite, and philosophical Titan reveals to Columbus the gradual advancement of mankind in all the great elements and attributes of civilization; likewise explains to him nature's law of progress, "from the birth of the universe to the present state of the earth and its inhabitants"; and after much more instructive discourse on politics, philosophy, history, chemistry, physics, constitutional law, and mechanical inventions, not altogether omitting the Hanseatic league, Copernicus, Kepler, Galileo, Newton, Herschel, Descartes, Bacon, the magnetic needle, and the printing-press, he exhibits to him with a limning of quite undisturbed optimism, the complete success of the federal system in America, the extension of that system over all the earth, and at last, in one august dissolving view, the millenium of cosmopolitan statesmanship through "a general congress of all nations, assembled to establish the political harmony of mankind." [26]

V

However great may be the faults to be found with the execution of this poem, it is hardly possible to deny that its idea, at any rate, is both poetic and noble; it is to connect, in a work of high imaginative literature, all that is beneficent and soul-stirring in the aggregate contribution made by America to the general stock of the world's welfare, with all that is heroic and pathetic in the career of him, the undismayed idealist, the saint, the admiral of boundless faith and sorrow, who made America known to the rest of the world.

Barlow's earlier and less ambitious project for his poem, as seen in his draft written in 1779, was the wiser one: "The poem will be rather of the philosophic than epic kind." [27] Even eight years afterward, at the time of its first publication, he still saw that, as the stupendous consequences of the discovery of America could be represented to Columbus only in vision,[28] so such representation would be likely to produce, not a real story, but merely a succession of scenes painted on the air, too impalpable and flitting, as well as too disconnected, for the purposes of an epic. No title for the poem, therefore, could have been better than its first title, "The Vision of

[26] Book x., Argument.
[27] "Life and Letters," etc., 15.
[28] "The Vision of Columbus," Introd., 20, fifth ed. London: 1794.

Columbus"; because, being perfectly accurate, it was also quite unpretentious, and involved no hazards by a challenge which might result in discomfiture and derision. Unfortunately, in his final reconstruction of the poem, this sane thought seems to have yielded to the cravings of an inordinate literary ambition; and by the new title which he gave to his work, and by its new prelude, and by its new supernatural machinery of river gods and other clumsy and incongruous imitations of Homer and Virgil, he claimed for his poem the awful honors of an epic, and thereby invoked upon it literary comparisons and critical tests which it could not endure. Nay, it may perhaps be said, that the very pomp and opulence of typographical costume which attended its re-entrance into the world, its grandiose and too prosperous equipment, even its physical magnitude—its arrogant and preposterous bigness, as a mere book,—all had the effect of averting sympathy and of inviting scorn, as though it were an attempt by mere bulk and bravado and good clothes to overawe the sentinels who guard the approaches to Parnassus.

Better would it have been, both for the poem and for the poet, if, in his later revision of the work, he had attempted no change in its essential character. A philosophical poem exhibiting, under the device of a vision seen by the discoverer of America, the vast and benign function assigned to the New World in the development of mankind, might have deserved and received in our literature the homage at least of serious consideration. Of course, never upon any plan could the poem have taken rank as a work of genius, or have escaped the penalties of the author's great literary defects. Under any character, it would have had no tender or delicate qualities, no lightness of touch, no flashes of beauty, not a ripple of humor, no quiet and dainty charm; a surfeit, rather, of vehemence and proclamation,—sonorous, metallic, rhetorical; forced description, manufactured sentiment, sublimity generated of pasteboard and starch; an ever-rolling tattoo of declamation, invective, eulogy; big, gaudy flowers of poetry which are also flowers of wax. Moreover, not even genius could have saved this poem from the literary disaster involved in its adoption of that conventional poetic diction and of that worn-out metrical form from which, after a whole century of favor, English literature was just then turning away in a recoil of weariness and disgust.

And yet, with all his limitations as a poet, the author of "The Columbiad" is entitled to the praise due to a sturdy and effective ethical teacher in verse. In didactic expression, the poem is often epigrammatic, trenchant, and strong; nay, in strenuous moral exposition and enforcement, it is at times even noble and impressive. Everywhere is the author faithful to the great object of his poem, namely, "to inculcate the love of rational liberty, and to discountenance the deleterious passion for violence and war; to show that on the basis of the republican principle all good morals, as well as good government and hopes of permanent peace, must be founded; and to convince the student in political science that the theoretical question of the future advancement of human society ... is held in dispute and still unsettled only because we have had too little experience of organized liberty in the government of nations, to have well considered its effects." [29] Everywhere in the poem one finds an invincible hope for human liberty, for the victories of reason, for the ultimate conquest of moral evil in the world. It represents, too, the manifold intellectual aspirations of the time in which he lived, its scientific progress, its mechanical ingenuity and daring, its wish to reject all degrading forms of faith, the unquenchable confidence of human nature in the final and happy solution of all those problems that then pained the earth with their unutterable menace. Finally, there breathes through the poem the most genuine love of country. In the eyes of this writer America is, by favor of Heaven, the superior land of all the earth. His love for America is something more than a clannish instinct, something better than the mere greed of provincialism; and this huge political and philosophical essay in verse, the writing of which formed the one real business of Barlow's life, may be accepted by us, whether we are proud of the fact or not, as an involuntary expression, for that period, of the American national consciousness and even of the American national character itself, as sincere, and as unfliching as were, in their different ways, the renowned state-paper of Jefferson, the constitution of 1789, and Washington's farewell address.

VI

Respecting the minor writings of Joel Barlow, we may note, in passing, two products of his callow academic muse: "An Elegy on the late Honorable Titus Hosmer, Esquire," in 1780;[30] and "A Poem" spoken at the Public Commencement at Yale College, in 1781.[31] Eleven years after the latter date, when he had acquired something like reputation by his "Vision of

---

[29] "The Columbiad," Preface, x.
[30] "American Poems," 108-117.
[31] *Ibid.*, 94-107.

Columbus," and something like notoriety by his active political radicalism in England and in France, he published a poetical diatribe entitled "The Conspiracy of Kings."[32] The poem is of the kind called satire; attempts to catch the tone of Juvenal; aims to be very exasperating, even appalling; somehow succeeds in being only abusive; emits mere howls of metrical vituperation against those unhappy gentlemen—

> "for blood and plunder famed,
> Sultans, or Kings, or Czars, or Emp'rors named,"

and especially against their triumphant literary champion, Edmund Burke.

Late in the year 1792, Barlow, who had been made by the National Convention a citizen of France—an honor then bestowed on no other American except Washington and Hamilton—went by invitation into Savoy, in the hope of being returned for the new Department of Mont Blanc as one of its deputies in the National Convention. At Chambery he remained several weeks, captivated by its scenery, finding great refreshment in the simple life of its people, and every day, amid its green mountain slopes and its pretty farmhouses, reminded of his own early life among the hills of western Connecticut. Writing to his wife, he said: "With you and a little farm among these romantic mountains and valleys, I could be happy, content; I would care no more for the pleasures of the plain. But America—the word is sweetness to my soul; it awakens all the tenderness of my nature."[33] In this mood of patriotic reminiscence and of longing for home, it happened to him, one evening, as he sat down to supper "under the smoky rafters of a Savoyard inn," to find steaming hot upon the table the favorite dish of his own New England—"Hasty-Pudding,"—a dish for which he had many a time enquired in vain in London and Paris. The exile's heart was touched; and with genuine enthusiasm, and in lucky disregard of his usual poetic stilts, he then produced the one really popular poem he ever wrote,—the famous mock pastoral which bears the name of the dish that had so inspired him, and which in its opening lines preserves a glimpse of the romantic Italian scene wherein it was written, even as it is pervaded throughout by the homely tones and tints of domestic life in colonial New England:

---

[32] "The Columbian Muse," 1-10, where it is printed without the "Preface" and "Note on Mr. Burke," both of which are given in "the Political Writings of Joel Barlow," 237-258.
[33] "Life and Letters," etc., 99.

"Ye Alps audacious, through the heavens that rise,
To cramp the day and hide me from the skies;
Ye Gallic flags that, o'er their heights unfurled,
Bear death to kings and freedom to the world,
I sing not you. A softer theme I choose,
A virgin theme, unconscious of the Muse,
But fruitful, rich, well suited to inspire
The purest frenzy of poetic fire.

. . . .

Dear Hasty-Pudding, what unpromised joy
Expands my heart to meet thee in Savoy!
Doomed o'er the world through devious paths to roam,
Each clime my country, and each house my home,
My soul is soothed, my cares have found an end,
I greet my long-lost, unforgotten friend.

   For thee through Paris, that corrupted town,
How long in vain I wandered up and down,
Where shameless Bacchus, with his drenching hoard
Cold from his cave, usurps the morning board.
London is lost in smoke, and steeped in tea;
No Yankee there can lisp the name of thee.
The uncouth word, a libel on the town,
Would call a proclamation from the Crown.

. . . .

But here, though distant from our native shore,
With mutual glee we meet and laugh once more.
The same! I know thee by that yellow face,
That strong complexion of true Indian race,
Which time can never change, nor soil impair,
Nor Alpine snows, nor Turkey's morbid air;

. . . .

My song, resounding in its grateful glee,
No merit claims,—I praise myself in thee.
My father loved thee through his length of days!
For thee his fields were shaded o'er with maize;

>From thee what health, what vigor he possessed,
>Ten sturdy freemen from his loins attest.
>Thy constellation ruled my natal morn,
>And all my bones were made of Indian corn.
>Delicious grain; whatever from it take,
>To roast or boil, to smother or to bake,
>In every dish 't is welcome still to me,
>But most, my Hasty-Pudding! most in thee." [34]

VII

The field of literature in which Barlow seems to have been capable of real mastership was that of prose,—particularly in the forms of history and argumentative discussion; and his laborious and life-long devotion to poetry merely illustrates a tendency occasionally to be seen in the history of men of letters—the tendency to mistake the whispers of ambition for the invitations of genius. Certainly Barlow was a robust, sagacious, and very able man; he had wide and enlightened sympathies, an extraordinary capacity for practical affairs either in finance, politics, or diplomacy, and a many-sidedness of intellectual activity and accomplishment which might, perhaps, justify the title of "universal genius," which an eminent historian has lately given to him;[35] but, as a man of letters, his real aptitude lay in a direction in which his work, at the time of his premature death, had been only incidental. Had his life been spared—and it was laid down deliberately in the cause of his country and for the peace of the world—he would probably have found his true literary vocation in the writing of that history of the American Revolution, which Jefferson had long urged him to undertake.

Perhaps the two least significant specimens of his work as a prose writer are a pair of orations, which were produced under special temptations to rhetorical effusion and aridity,—the one for the Fourth of July, 1787,[36] the other for the Fourth of July, 1809.[37]

During his long residence abroad, he had two or three periods of activity as a prose writer, and chiefly in the discussion of political questions. His

---

[34] "Life and Letters," etc., 99-108, where the poem is given entire. A better copy, as having the "Preface" and the original division into three Cantos, may be read in Burton, "Cyclopædia of Wit and Humor," i., 19-22.

[35] H. Adams, "Hist. U. S.," i., 110-111.

[36] Niles, "Prin. and Acts," etc., 384-389.

[37] Pamphlet, 1809.

year of greatest productiveness seems to have been 1792, during which he wrote portions of the notes, and perhaps the preface, for a London edition of Trumbull's "M'Fingal"; likewise, "Advice to the Privileged Orders in the Several States of Europe, resulting from the Necessity and Propriety of a General Revolution in the Principle of Government,"[38]—the most elaborate, and upon the whole, the ablest of his prose writings; also, "A Letter to the National Convention of France, on the Defects in the Constitution of 1791, and the Extent of the Amendments which ought to be Applied;"[39] finally, "A Letter to the People of Piedmont, on the Advantages of the French Revolution, and the Necessity of adopting its Principles in Italy."[40]

Toward the close of the last decade of the eighteenth century, his mind seems to have turned with uncommon interest to the affairs of his own country, as is shown, for example, by his pamphlet published in London in 1800, entitled "A View of the Public Debt, Receipts, and Expenditures of the United States," as well as by his first and second "Letter from Paris to the Citzens of the United States," the one in 1800 and the other in 1801.

In 1806, after his return to America, he published "Prospectus of a National Institution to be established in the United States,"[41]—an ably written and a very impressive scheme for a grand national university, to be founded at the capital, with the most enlightened and liberal provision both for original research and for instruction.

Perhaps nowhere else in his writings does Barlow appear to better advantage than he does in nearly the last product of his pen,—his "Letter to Henry Gregoire, Bishop, Senator, Compte of the Empire, and Member of the Institute of France, in reply to his Letter on the Columbiad."[42] This brochure, which is an expression of the author's whole mind and character at a time when both had reached their highest point of ripeness and of gentle wisdom, can hardly fail to renew and to enlarge one's impression, not only of Barlow's intellectual ability, but of the breadth and beauty of his spirit. It is a model, also, of courteous theological discussion, furnishing,

---

[38] Part I., London, 1792. Part II., though written in 1792, was not published, owing to the interference of the government, until 1795, when it was "Printed and Sold by Daniel Isaac Eaton, Printer and Bookseller to the Supreme Majesty of the People, at the Cock and Swine, No. 74 Newgate Street." Part II. did not complete the work. A copy is in "The Political Writings of Joel Barlow," pp. iii.-xvi., 17-157.

[39] London, 1792. Also in Barlow's "Political Writings," 156-198.

[40] Barlow's "Political Writings," 199-235.

[41] Pamphlet, printed anonymously. Washington, 1806.

[42] Washington, D. C., 1809; and reprinted, though without the full title, in "Life and Letters," etc., 221-233.

as he himself said, "one example of the calmness and candor with which a dispute may be conducted, even on the subject of religion." [43] Moreover, it is of especial interest for the authentic indications it affords as to Barlow's attitude toward Christianity,—a matter upon which he had been greatly misrepresented. He avows himself as still adhering, "from a conviction that they are right," to the religious sect in which he was born and educated; [44] and he solemnly denies the charges of religious apostasy which had been made against him in America by his political enemies. "It has even been said and published.... that I went to the bar of your Convention, when it was the fashion so to do, and made a solemn recantation of my Christian faith, declaring myself an atheist or deist, or some other anti-Christian apostate. ... Now, as an active member of that Convention, a steady attendant at their sittings, and my most intimate friend, you know that such a thing could not have been done without your knowledge; you know therefore that it was not done; you know I never went but once to the bar of that Convention, which was on the occasion to which you allude in the letter now before me, to present an address from the Constitutional Society in London, of which I was a member. You know I always sympathized in your grief, and partook of all your resentment, while such horrors and blasphemies were passing, of which these typographical cannibals of reputation have made me a participant." [45] "You will see that I have nothing to do with the unbelievers who have attacked the Christian system, either before the French Revolution, or during, or since that monumental period. I am not one of them." [46]

[43] "Life and Letters," etc., 233.
[44] *Ibid.*, 223.
[45] *Ibid.*, etc., 230-231.
[46] *Ibid.*, 228.

FREDERICK BEECHER PERKINS

Connecticut Georgics

I "FARMED IT" two summers, when I was eleven and twelve years old. I had been brought up within a paved city; was lean, white, slender, school-worn, bookish. Analyzing now the phases of interior life which I only experienced then, I seem to have been impregnated with city associations; or rather the boy's soul in me was paved over with brick and stone, like the walls whose hot reflections smote my eyes in summer, and girded me in always. I can remember how I shed a shrunken epidermis, as it were, like a moulting crab, as if I really grew inwardly by the fresh fulness of the country. I found that, besides the side of human life on which I had theretofore been gazing; dry and scaly with brick and stone, dead and still on Sundays, dinning and resounding all the week with the clash of pavements under armed heel and hoof, with rattle and groan of wheels—the unrelenting and desperate onwardness of the great Yankee dollar-chase;—that, besides this, there was another—infinite, calm, peaceful, sun-lighted, dewy, free, full of life, unconstrained, fresh, vigorous—the world of God; as the city is the world of men—and of devils.

I was to enter upon my agricultural novitiate under the tutorship of an uncle, a farmer near the south shore of Connecticut. I departed for my destination early one morning in the end of Spring, from my city home in the interior of the State, riding in the wagon of a certain landholder from my uncle's vicinity, who had come thither on business in his private conveyance. All the day I rode southward, through town and village, wood and field, in the absorbing trance of deep delight which a child enjoys in any discursive or adventurous enterprise, however humble. Every thing was enjoyable. The steady, binary progression of the old farm-horse's persistent trot; the rattling of the bones of the hard-seated and springless wagon; the boundless woods, full of new forms and colors, on rocks, branches and leaves; sprinkled on surface, and permeated through unfathomable depths, with sparkling specks of sunlight; the occasional chip squirrel, provincially called "chip-munk," jerking or gliding along the fences; sometimes a "very magnificent three-tailed bashaw"—a red or gray compeer of the rodent tribe—a beast which I was almost as much surprised to see, at least outside of a rotatory tin gymnasium, as if he had been a giraffe or an ornithorhynchus; the wide, open fields, with their "industrial regiments" on active service, in undress uniform; the twisting and writhing trout-brooks; the quiet and composed rivers; the steep hills, and deep, still ponds, of each of which the neighbors aver with pride that the bottom has never been found—a fact, perhaps, to be accounted for by its never having been considered worth looking after; all were new, all overflowing with light, and life, and joy.

I was startled at being vanquished by my companion in a strife, with whose weapons I had presumed him unacquainted. I began to "tell stories," and at first acquitted myself to my satisfaction; but soon I found that I had met my match. Mr. N.'s talents as a *raconteur* were infinitely above my own. Not only were his stories funnier than mine, but whenever I boggled, he kindly suggested the missing matter; and when I did not boggle, he invariably furnished an improved catastrophe.

We stopped to dine at the house of a farmer. And then and there—with shame I tell it— did I first feel the excitement of the intoxicating cup. That excitement, however, did not in the present instance exhibit itself in the gorgeous colors poetically supposed to clothe it. The flowing bowl was represented, upon the pine "mahogany" of our Connecticut Amphitryon, by a broken-nosed earthen pitcher; and the mighty wine, by equally mighty cider, of so hard a texture that our host stated that it could only with great difficulty be bitten off by the partaker, at the end of his draught. Of this seductive fluid I drank two tumblers-full; and to me, unconscious and verdant, it tasted good, as sour things are wont to do to children. But a quick retribution came upon me. The puckery stuff began to bite like a serpent, and sting like an adder, with a promptitude not adverted to by Solomon.

We came safe to our journey's end; arriving, as the evening fell, at the farmstead, my summer home. Darkness was already gathering among the thick shadowing of great elms and prim locusts in the wide dooryard. Piles of saw-mill slabs fortified the woodpile, which, paved with chips, the mangled remains of slaughtered King Log, spread before the "stoop"; a façade of lofty barns—the "old" barn and the "new"—were ranged across the background in the north, sheltering the lane, into which we had driven, and which, leaving woodpile and stoop to the east, led northward to the abutting front of the two barnyards. A wood-shed, opening to the south, ran out from the house, displaying, within, a vast and miscellaneous concourse of firewood, lumber, tools, and all the mechanico-agricultural apparatus of a farmer's tinkering shop. Entering the house, after greeting due, and a proper refection for my inner boy, I was speedily asleep; and, next morning early, was enrolled in the ranks of industry, and detailed for skirmishing and outpost service: in other words, I was promoted to the captaincy over a platoon of "milky mothers," whose daily march to and from near and distant pastures I was to guard and guide. By appropriate degrees, I was led deeper and deeper within the agricultural mysteries of planting and hoeing, and the aftercoming work of haying and harvest.

Perhaps descriptions of a few separate days' experience will best portray what manner of life I led.

THE FRESH MEADOW

With empty cart and full dinner-pails, we set out early for the assault upon the June grass. The "fresh meadow" was a level intervale, the road to which ran through a large upland mowing lot, descended through a secret chasm in a ledge of rocks crowned with trees, and led us out into the open sunny meadow behind, like the downward paths by which princes in fairy tales descend into realms of underground loveliness, ruled by expectant queens.

In such expeditions I took my first lessons in the ox-compelling art. The mysteries of "haw" and "gee," of "hwo" and "hwish"—the last an outlandish Vermontese barbarism, signifying "back," were duly explained. The cartwhip exercise was demonstrated; whose adaptation to the intellectual capacities of the bovine race is marked by the simplicity of genius. For the single lesson taught the ox appeals with metaphysical truth to the desire of happiness common to beasts with men; and with practical wisdom develops in a ultilitarian direction his natural instinct to get away from what hurts him. If, therefore, I wish him to go forward, I "flick" him *à posteriori;* if I would have him retrogress, I pound his nose with the whip-stock; if he should come towards me, I touch him up on the further side with the lash, and if he should go from me, I prod his hither ribs with the butt. These manœuvres having been accompanied with dexterous intonations of the four aforesaid sounds, together with "go 'lang!" "what are ye 'ba-a-a-ut?" and other interjections hortatory, mandatory, and sometimes, I grieve to say, imprecatory, all developed by skilful teamsters into many wonderful, intricate, and imaginative variations executed through the nose, the intelligent beast gradually learns to do, at the sound alone, what he did at first, at the sound accompanied with action. Some imagine that herein is the true solution of the myth of Amphion's song, viz.: He played—a Greek prototype of the great Italian fiddler—a pagan Paganini—upon a one-stringed πλέκτρον, plectrum, or whip (comp. *plago, plagare,* to scourge), which he accompanied with the voice, probably in the Lydian mode; and as he worked powerfully upon the feelings of his cattle, by his vigorous instrumental performance, executed *fortissimo, forestissimo, sforzando,* and *confuoco molto,* so, when he performed as vocal solos these impassioned variations upon one string, the vivid recollections of his masterly instrumentation induced his cattle to manœuver with such remarkable agility, as to give rise to the present slightly varied account, that he played *to* the beasts, instead of *on* them. This, however, is a digression, for which, now that I have followed it out to my satisfaction, I ask pardon.

Theory such as I have adverted to was imparted to me; and very soon I flourished the pliant hickory, and bawled out the scientific monosyllables with a nasality as easy and workmanlike as that of any Bill or Joe, to the manner born.

The meadow is entered; the cart left in a corner, resting on its wheels and long nose, like that Australian bird who locates himself, for his ease, tripod-wise upon his two legs and his bill; the dinner-pails are sheltered in its shadow; scythes are hung and whetted, and "forward four." The best man goes foremost; and the strong-backed scythemen, each with "rifle" or whetstone in his red right hand, girded low and tight, stepping wide and bending forward, seem to gesture the falling grass into the long straight swaths which grow close under and after the left hand of each.

> "And forward, and forward,
> Resistlessly they go;
> For strong arms wave the long keen glaive
> That vibrates down below."

Is any thing more inspiring than the "rhythmic sweep" of a platoon of mowers? They seem to beat the time to some mysterious marching music. Strength is magnificently shown; no labor will better test the thews and sinews of a man. The same indescribable joy arises from the simultaneous steady movement that pulsates out from the heavy tread of marching men, and the symmetrical involutions of a hall of dancers. And there is rapid and continual progress. Abundant conditions of excitement are in the operations of a band of mowers. If strength, action, rhythm, simultaneity, and success, in concrete and vivid presentation, will not stir pulses of deep pleasure in a man's soul, he should be kicked out of decent society as an undoubted treasoner and incendiary, or sent to the School for the Training and Teaching of Idiots, as a pitiable instance of that anticlimax of mental negation whose two higher degrees are (see Dr. S. G. Howe's Reports) simpleton and fool— as a fully undeveloped idiot.

Away go the mowers, halfway round the field; and now they stand erect, and the ringing reduplicating clash of the whetstones comes back upon their steps. But I too must perform my office. With ardor I inquire, like the revolutionary orator, "Why stand we here idle?" and with a "peaked stick" I descend in fury upon the slain. The red-top and daisies are tossed abroad upon the four winds; and with an ennobling consciousness of power, and working out certain dim conceptions of a grand military march, by brandishing my stick in unison with the alternation of advancing steps, I sweep up and down the field in a centrifugacious halo of scattered gramineæ, feeling, as nearly as I can judge, very much like a cyclone.

But over what tremendous volcanoes of thinly covered agonies and horrid throes of pain are all hollow human exultations enacted! In the midst of my stormful march, a frightful dart of Eblis, a sharp sudden stroke, precipitated as by diabolical propulsion from some far distant sphere of malignant wrath, smites me full upon the forehead. A shrieking diphthongal OU! and a lofty *entrechat* are the involuntary introductories of my *debut* as "*Le danseur malgré lui.*" Several millions of minute yellow devils, with black stripes and a "voice and hideous hum," stimulate me into an inconceivably rapid and intricate war-dance, accompanied by a solo *obligato* upon the human voice. I have, in short, trodden upon a yellow hornets' nest. The Briarean evolutions of my hands knock off my hat. An enterprising "bird" forthwith ensconces himself among my locks, and proceeds to harpoon me at his leisure. I seem to scrub out every hair, such is the promptitude and velocity of the friction which I apply. But I despair of maintaining my position, the enemy having made a lodgment within the citadel. I run as nobody ever ran before, and suddenly turn and flee at a sharp angle to my first course, in order that the momentum of my foes may throw them off my track. But they turn as quickly as I sticking much closer than either a friend or a brother would do.

I see the brook before me, I go headforemost, splash! into a deep hole, where I stumble, fall, choke, and am picked out by the mowers, who are nearly helpless with laughter. I have swallowed several quarts of warm brook-water, screeched until I cannot whisper, expended more strength and breath than it seems possible that I should ever recover; have endured and am enduring more pain than ten hydrophobiacs; and with one eye fast shut and swelled into a hard red lump of agony, and sundry abnormal "organs" extemporizing cranial evidence of a most unsymmetrical character, I lie helpless, blind, sopping, and sobbing in a swath of fresh, cool, green grass, until time, salt, and plantain leaves assuage most of the pain. I know what hornets are, at least in their foreign relations; but the single item of knowledge is no equivalent for the difficulties under which it was pursued. What fiends they are! Did the Inquisition ever try hornets on any particularly refractory captive?

Soon comes the dinner time, indicated to the observant farmers, by the proportions of shadow and sunlight, upon the roof of a certain barn. We made a nest in bushes and long grass, within the shadow of great trees, and squatted Turk-like around a service of tin crockery, brown paper and bark, whereon were displayed salt beef, cold boiled potatoes, bread and butter, and a specimen of rye ginger-bread, which, for weight and tenacity, might be a mass of native copper, from Lake Superior. The food disappears rapidly, under the direction of jack-knives and one-pronged forks, whittled from sticks. The jug clucks and chuckles to the affectionate kisses of the thirsty workmen, and much refreshed they take a short "nooning" to tell stories, gossip or sleep, and go to work again.

Haymakers cure in the afternoon what they kill in the morning. At two or three o'clock the mowing ceases, and the raking begins. In this operation, the weakest goes first, that the strongest man may take the heaviest raking; so I am *ex officio* leader. I must fall smartly to, to keep ahead, or my rear-rank man will rake my heels off; and for a while I go bravely on. But the peculiar hold, and sliding manipulation of the "rake's-tail" soon tell on my city-bred hands. The insides of my thumbs, and the space between them and my fingers, is first red and then raw; and by the time that the grass lies in winrows, I have done enough. Before sunset the winrows are rolled into cocks, which are shaped conewise, and skilfully shingle-laid for shedding of rain; and with a small load of new hay, hastily pitched upon the cart, for immediate use, we return home.

Close after sunset is milking; after milking, supper; after supper, prayers;

and after prayers, sleep, which, indeed, had made an irruption from its legitimate domain, in the chambers above, and taken me at a disadvantage—when I was "down," on my knees, as in duty bound. The steady unmodulated evenness of my uncle's reading—for the family was Episcopalian—and the full melody of the words, put me quickly asleep, and I reluctantly rise, retire, and undress; reluctantly, because the motion charms away the drowsy god into whose embrace I sank so softly, and leaves me broad awake to lie down in bed. But I soon forget that and every other trouble, and know no more until daybreak.

THE SALT MEADOW

Salt is good. Men like it, and beasts. To cattle, however, near the sea, is often given an allowance of "salt hay," instead of the pure condiment. Salt hay is of two principal sorts, called, where my information was obtained, "salt grass" and "black-grass." There is also a sedge, which grows along the river-sides and in ditches and marshes; a coarse, sword-shaped grass, used for thatching or litter. The salt-grass, and black-grass, are fine short grasses, growing upon the level surfaces called "salt meadows." These are alluvial deposits of a strange unctuous marine mud, stretching along the coast in recesses, and up river valleys; a curious half vegetable earth, soft, black, slippery. A twenty-foot pole may be often thrust down into it without finding bottom. Indeed, it sometimes does a very fair business in the quicksand line. Somewhere under the surface of a very smooth-faced salt-meadow, a little east of New Haven, are the duplicate and triplicate of some furlongs of embankment, swallowed down by an unexpected abyss beneath, at the expense and to the chagrin of the New Haven and New London Railroad Company.

The salt grass is of a bright yellowish green;—a beautiful hue in healthy vegetation, although elsewhere peculiarly sickly—and the black-grass, as its name imports, of a very dark green. The stretches of meadow are like great patches of particolored velvet, so soft is the tone of color given by the fineness of the grass and the delicacy of its tints. Rocks, and patches of upland called islands by the farmers, stand out here and there, above the level line of the salt land, as distinctly as any sea-island from the water; and as into the sea, points and promontories of upland project into it.

The salt haying is later than the upland haying and in sundry details varies from it. The day in the salt meadow was an adventurous expedition to me; for we had to start early and return late, living several miles up the country. The scene of action, too, was strange and new; open to the sea on one side, swept by the salt breezes, looked in upon by the silent ships that all day long went trooping by, haunted by queer shore-birds and odd reptiles, covered and edged by grotesque plants; a whole new world to an up-country boy. My work was light, for the grass was thin and easy to spread; and I used to spend much of the day in the desultory wanderings that children love. I strolled among the sedge and sought muscles; poked sticks down by the "fiddlers'" holes, and caught the odd occupant by his single claw, as he fled up from the supposed earthquake; chased the said fiddler—a small gray one-clawed crab, who scuttles and dodges about as jerkingly and nimbly as a fiddler's elbow, whence his name—as he ran about the banks; raked out oysters from the river-bed close by, and learned the inhuman art of eating them raw; investigated the scabby patches of naked mud, which lie here and there among the grass; rheumy sore-looking places, plantless, crusted over with dry scales, as if a cutaneous disease had destroyed the life of the surface, from an excess, perhaps, of salt, causing humors in the ground, and exanthematous disorders. Or I watched the boatmen, who occasionally "dropped kellick" in the river channel, and plied the oyster-tongs. These are a ferocious hybrid between an iron-toothed rake and a pair of scissors; having the long handles, cross-head and teeth of the former, and the pivotal interduplication of the latter; so that at fifteen or twenty feet under water, the iron teeth bite between each other, like the fingers of clasped hands, griping firmly whatever is between them. Or I rambled off to one of the tree-crowned "islands" afore mentioned—I always fancied that they were not standing still, but slowly gliding along the meadow, wandering off down to the sea—and explored their nooks and corners. The day waned pleasantly, under strange influences. A vague and dreamy feeling of exploratory desire pervaded the atmosphere. The level land, the level sea, the bright horizon afar over the water, the wide and open views, the dancing of the distance in the hot air, the silent motion of the winged ships, the sighing of the steady wind, as if it felt relief at gliding unbroken over the expanse; the notion of vastness and the dim suggestion of the distance, spoke to all the melancholy longings, and questioning, yearning thoughts that sleep in children's minds—but are too often murdered by ungenial training before they wake.

Then there were curious inventions of husbandry. The meadow is often too soft to bear the loaded cart. Sometimes the elastic greasy crust unexpectedly lets through the wheel, or the feet of the cattle. Then the lofty load careens, and slides off; the oxen kick and plunge while the meadow holds them fast by the heels, or sink to their bellies, and stand still until unyoked, and left to crawl unimpeded out. Sometimes all the chains in the meadow are hitched to the cart-tongue, leading to firm ground; and half-a-dozen teams united drag the distant load ashore. But if the danger of the muddy depths has been wisely foreseen, a "meadow sled" carries the burden safely over. This is a stout drag, consisting of two wide runners well framed together, and so made as to fit under the axle-tree without lifting the wheels from the ground. It is chained to its place, like a peddler's bull-dog; and on this additional bearing, the cart goes securely sliding about over smooth grass and slimy mud, almost as easily as over snow. If even that precaution is judged insufficient, the hay is "poled out." Two stout "hay poles" are thrust beneath the heap, and two men, one behind and one before, carrying it, as upon a sedan, to terra firma. This is sometimes a troublesome business. Mosquitoes are terrifically rife in some parts of the salt meadows. They will rise on one's track almost in a solid mass, and pursue with a wolfishly, bloodthirsty pertinacity, which is pretty sure to result in anger, slaps, and blood. This may not be absolutely unendurable, so long as the hands are free to slap; but when you have a heavy hay cock squatting on the poles, of which you carry one end, you are pinned; and then, of the above mixtures, slaps being unavailable, there remains only the anger and the blood; of which you monopolize the former, and the gentleman with the "little bill" the latter. There is another ugly insect, rarely seen, at least in Connecticut, except upon the salt meadows. It is an enormous black fly, half as large again as a "bull bumble-bee," and a great deal more troublesome. He is a bloody villain, and a truculent. He carries in his snout a machine compounded of a bradawl and a pump, with which he perforates and depletes his victims; and he sings bass. One of these rascals will make a horse or a yoke of oxen nearly crazy. They will bear tolerably well to be all speckled over with mosquitoes or "green-heads," if they can't get rid of them; but this monster carries too many guns. They cannot stand so deliberate and extensive a stab as his; and unless he is forthwith dispatched or driven off, they may be expected to execute antics more energetic than useful.

THE WHITEFISHING

Such was a day in the salt meadows. But the pleasantest days of my farming, were days of fishing. The sea is an inexhaustible storehouse of fertilizers to the farmers of the coast. Rockweed, seaweed, mud, shells and whitefish, are carted up the country as far as eight or ten miles, and spread upon the land, or deposited in the barn-yard. Thus the bounty of the sea balances the sterility of the granite formation along the sound.

The whitefish is a herring-like fish, very bony and oily, which comes in the summer in shoals, called by the fishermen "schools," from unknown regions toward the ever mysterious East, out of the realms of the sea. They are caught by millions and sold by thousands; and are a st—— smell, I mean, in the nostrils of those who flee by railroad from the stifling city to Sachem's Head, and to the other shoreward haunts of the "upper ten." But they make corn and potatoes grow nicely: and I found that after working a day or two among their unburied remains, I was not affected either mentally, by the ghastly appearance of the defunct, or physically, by their exhalations.

They come up into harbors and coves to feed, as is supposed—for I don't know that any body has actually seen them at it—and while they are at table, a long seine is dropped round them, and they are ensnared. But all this does not give the history of my day.

We rise in advance of the regular hours, for the "fish-house" is five miles away, and the day must needs be long. Well provisioned in stomach and basket, we set out before light, afoot. Our way lies for some distance along one side of a river valley, down a crooked straggling country road, dodging about through patches of woods, round and hard-headed rocky ledges, and passing here and there a solitary house yet alone in the perfect stillness of early morning. The trampling steps and rustic voices of our party broke rudely forward into the yet unviolated silence of the night; which seemed to flee along wood and field, and always to be couching shyly before us, hoping to rest at last undisturbed. We came to a cross-road, at which our former path ended; but our veteran leader unfalteringly guided us across it, through a barn-yard opposite, around the cow-shed, down the lane, through a pair of bars under an apple-tree; and we entered upon one of the footpaths that mark up all country neighborhoods—sneaking about under mysterious shades and remote hill sides, or edging along by pasture fences, and disappearing under a log, or tapering off into a mouse track; but which lead the initiated to many a destination much to be desired for work or for sport. This one led us under an orchard of apple-trees all drenched in dew, through a mowing-lot or two, over a ridge thinly set with trees, and out upon the last swell of the sinking upland, where it sloped away into the wide open level of the salt meadows, and looked out upon the sea beyond, which gleamed out from under the morning mists (for by this time the sun looked out upon the landscape), and came brimming up in the fulness of the flood-tide to the limit of the low beach, as if meditating a good run and roll across the meadow. Now we could see the river again, all swollen and black with the regorged salt water, creeping half choked and crookedly about in the meadow, between two narrow edgings of sedge, as you may see a burly face within a slender rim of whisker. As we descended upon the salt alluvium, the plague of mosquitoes arose upon us. After every man, as after Fergus MacIvor Vich Ian Vohr, went a tail of devoted followers; and like his, ours proposed to make a living out of their leader. Content now dwelt in cowhide boots; much grumbling and some blood came from those whose ankles were yarn-defended only; and an irregular fire of slaps did considerable execution among the foe, as they came piping and singing to the onset, like Milton's devils. Thus escorted, in the style of Bon Gaultier's Thairshon—

"With four and twenty men,
And five and twenty pipers,"

we crossed the marsh to the stygian seeming river, crossed the river in a stygian seeming skiff, rickety and patched, which was dislodged from a cunning concealment in a sedgy ditch and "sculled" (not an inappropriate motive power for the skiff of the dead; undoubtedly Charon's method of propulsion) with one hand by our dextrous chief, and resumed our dreary and slippery walk on the other side. Now the fish-house loomed up on the neighboring beach, looking on its solitary rocky perch, as large as a farm-house, but shrinking as we approached, until as we entered it, it became definitely about twelve feet square, and seven feet "between joints." It was fitted up with half a dozen bunks filled with salt hay for bedding, a table and chairs rather halt, a fire-place, a closet, an attic, a kettle, a fryingpan, sundry other cooking utensils, and an extensive assortment of antique and grotesque garments. Hats consisting of a large hole edged with a narrow rim, great rusty boots, trowsers such as if a young tornado had worn and torn them, and horrid red shirts, sat, stood, lay and hung, on floor, chairs, bedside or rafters, as though a troop of imps had been rioting up and down in them, and at the opening of the door by mortal men, had instantaneously jumped out and fled.

The provisions were stored in the closet, and the members of the "fish-gang" disguised themselves in piratical outfits from the aforesaid ready-made stock, leaving their decent clothes for their return home, and becoming, in their wild and ragged gear, entirely independent of moisture and of mud. Next, they hauled up the boat—a great clumsy, flat-bottomed, heavy-sterned scow, equipped with a capstan forward and a platform aft to carry the seine—and having beached her in front of the reel, proceeded to unreel and ship the seine, ready for setting. We boys armed ourselves with old hoes and tin pots, and marched off to dig long clams, with an eye to a stew at home, and to the inveigling of certain blackfish, sea-bass, and other of the Neptunian herds, understood to be lurking and wandering around the rocks in front of the fish-house, at proper times of tide. When the seine was all aboard, the fishermen sat down on the sand and rocks, and one climbed the signal-pole, to look out for a "school" of fish.

The fish-house was on a point at the western end of a somewhat shallow bay, whose shore, a silver-sanded beach, ran curving round to the point on the other side. The fish, as before mentioned, always come from the eastward; working up into the shallows, skittering and skimming in sport along the surface, or fleeing in haste before the sharks or porpoises or other great fish who follow after them for their meals: and the wide dark ripple of the whole shoal, the racing spatter of a frightened few, or the bay all dotted with the quietly emergent little black black-fins, or tails flourishing aloft preparatory to a dive after lunch, are the signs that betray his booty to the fisherman's eye. "I see a *flag!*" sings out an ardent youth. Flag is, metaphorically, tail, from its flaunting display by the ambitious owner. The experienced elders don't see it, probably because the young man saw it first; but immediately the great "school" with one consent deploys upon the smooth surface of the bay, and ten thousand back fins and tails dot the quiet water, which ripples and rustles with the glancing mass of life within its bosom. Hoes and tin pots are cast aside, as we rush to see the sport; for the fishermen have sprung for the boat, in excitement intense, but repressed for fear of alarming the timid fish. They launch their awkward craft, and softly pull away to seaward, amid smothered prophecies of from ten to a hundred and fifty thousand fish, and under the captaincy of steady old Uncle Jim Langdon, who stands in the stern-sheets to direct the rowers and to deliver over the net. He guides the boat by ordering the oarsmen; not with the salt phrases of oceanic seaman-ships, but with the same words that rule old Buck and Bright, at his farmstead up by the East Woods. "Haw now, Bill, a little; haw, I tell you; there, go 'long." Now he lifts off the wide net, as the "warp," left fastened to the capstan ashore, under the reel, drags it silently down into the water, and the lengthening line of floats, bobs and wavers upon the sea. "Haw a little; haw boat; pull now; pull! Con-found their darned picters," says Uncle Jim, in a sudden revulsion of wrath, for all the fish have suddenly sunk, and there is danger that they will disgracefully sneak out under the lower edge of the net while it hangs in deep water, and walk away each with his tongue in his cheek, leaving the fishermen only "fisherman's luck." "There, there they are ag'in," says the old man, as the black points stick out once more:—"Go it. Come, pull ahead." And the heavy boat sweeps slowly round the fish, until the whole seine, eighty rods long, just a quarter of a mile, hangs in the sea around them.

"Unconscious of their fate, the little victims play,"

and the fishermen beach the boat at the other side of the bay, carry the warp at that end to the further capstan, and prepare to haul. Now there is need of "all hands and the cook"; for the sooner the warp can be wound in upon the capstans, the sooner the net will range up into shallow water, where the danger of losing fish under the lead-line will be over. Both capstans are manned, and boys and men shove round the bars on the "keen jump," until soon the staff at either end of the net comes riding up the beach. Now comes hard pulling; for the rest of the net must be drawn in by hand, and it holds many fish and much water, besides the drag of the corks on the surface and of the lead-line on the bottom. Slowly and steadily come the two ends of the net, hand over hand, piled up as it comes in on the beach. A fish or two appears, hung by the gills in the meshes. A troop of innocent-looking fellows come darting along from the middle of the net, having just discovered that they are inside of something. Now the fact becomes universally known among the ensnared; and they dart backward and forward by hundreds and by fifties, seeking escape. There is none. They are crowded closer and closer within their narrowing prison-house. The water thickens, rustles, boils with them. And now, a great throbbing slippery mass, they lie squeezed up together in the bag of the net, while two exultant captors run for baskets. And a boathook; for Uncle Jim points out a long black thong like a carter's whip, slung out once or twice above the seething whitefish, announcing the dreaded stingray; and certain wallops elsewhere advise of the presence of a shark. The baskets come. Two men take each, dip them full of flapping fish, carry them up the beach, and throw them down to die, between hot sun and hotter sand. After twenty minutes of such work, the dippers dip carefully, lest they get a stroke from the ray, who has sunk quietly to the bottom, or a nip from his cousin the "sea-attorney." Somebody has hit the "stinger," as they call him, and he wallops up to the surface, and snaps his long tail about. Suddenly a bold young fellow grips the extremity of it, and with both hands holds tight singing out sharply, while the great flat clumsy fish wabbles and "flops" this way and that way, nearly hauling his captor over upon his nose among the fish, "*Jab* the boat-hook into him, quick, will ye?" Chunk! It goes, fairly into the creature's back; four men seize the hook-staff and walk the big sting-ray bodily out ashore, his first friend steering him behind by the tail. Poor old ray! he lies wounded and bleeding on the dry, hot sand, guggling and choking, helpless and doomed. I run and jump up before him, whereupon he unexpectedly gives a strange loud watery snort, and wallops almost off the ground, as if, like Mr. Briggs' pickerel (see London Punch), he were going to "fly at me, and bark like a dog." It scares me, until I reflect upon his locomotive disadvantages, and so I repeat my irritating gambadoes, until the monster is too dead to notice them. He weighs at least five hundred pounds; and is long enough and broad enough to cover a table for six. His three "stings" are cut off and given me to scrape, wash and preserve, with strict cautions from the friendly fishermen against allowing the sharp points or barbs, or the poisonous black slime adhering to them, to get through my skin. These "stings" are tapering two-edged daggers of hard white bone, set flatwise one over the other upon the upper side of the ray's tail, and so jointed on that they can be erected and made to stand out like three fingers stretched apart. The ends, and the barbs that point backwards along the sides, are as sharp as needles, and will inflict a frightful ragged cut. No wound is more dangerous or more dreaded. The slimy black venom which sticks all over the stings lodges in the lesion, and the unlucky recipient of the ray's blow is in imminent danger of lock-jaw. A friend of mine was hit by one of these ugly things in the ankle. The barbed blade caught among the sinews, and drew one of them fairly out from the leg—a red and white string a foot long. He was laid up long with the consequent inflammation and fever; had lock-jaw; almost died; and halts yet upon the leg which the "stinger" stung. Of the three stings which the fishermen gave me, I send one to the Editor of Putnam's Monthly with these sheets.

The whitefish are all deposited upon the beach, in silvery, sliddering heaps;

choking, gasping and jumping; or curling into shuddering, agonized rings for a moment, and then quietly straightening out to die. Last of all, the sneaking shark, who had nosed off to the furthest corner and wound himself up in the net, hoping to be hidden, is hauled up, and turned, kicking and kicked, out from the twisted meshes, to share the fate of those he had desired to destroy. It is pitiful to see the little whitefish gape and tumble and bounce about in innocent agony. The clumsy ray never troubles any body except in self-defence, and gets some sympathy; but nobody sympathizes with the pig-eyed, shovel-nosed villain who now spats the sand, and winks and nips with his three rows of thorny teeth, as he feels his thievish life slipping away from him. I sarcastically hint that he must be hungry, since he opens his mouth so wide; and I cautiously insert therein a whitefish or two, and set them well down with a stick. He has no appetite, after all, and spits them out; and, as I renew my attentions, he gathers himself up in a rage, and springs at me so strongly that the grinning jaws snap together within an inch of my fist. A little more strength in the old scoundrel's tail, and I should have repented me of catering for the shark. I recommend nobody to feed sharks from his fingers.

The net is empty—all but sundry non-descripts of the sea which stick here and there upon the meshes. A "sea-spider" or two, like a large mouldy acorn with six long legs; red starfish; varieties of seaweed; a stick and a fragment of old rope, are all. Half the hands count the fish, putting them in piles of four or five thousands each, and the rest replace the seine upon the boat, in readiness for another haul.

Dinner is cooked in a great iron pot. It is a chowder, of course—fisherman's food; what should it be?—Not the "old, original" chowder, the codfish aristocrat of chowders, whose idea is consecrated by the masterly manipulations and majestic name of the mighty man of Marshfield—the "Republican King"—but still a chowder, a delicious dish to appetites sharpened by sea air and sea water. It is a many-sided dish; of pork and fish, potatoes and bread, and onions and turnips—"all compact"—"chequits" and sea-bass, blackfish, long clams, "pumpkin-seeds," and an accidental eel, all contribute. Pepper and salt, but especially hunger, are the seasoning: and I firmly believe that no such flavorous food ever slid tickling down mortal throat, as plopped out from the canted chowder-kettle in the solitary fish-house by the sea.

Late at night we returned home; the gain to the fishers being about a hundred thousand fish worth some forty or fifty dollars, and the gain to me being a store of happy memories; not so salable, perhaps, as the fish, but lasting longer and fresher, neither by me willingly to be exchanged for any ordinary tangible commodity.

Such was my life with the farmers by the sea. The time and space fail me to tell of the rockweeding expeditions; the wanderings after lost cattle in the woods; the wood-cutting in the same; the whortleberry parties; the numberless delightful and adventurous occupations in which my farming summers passed. It was pleasure unspeakable. And not that only, but I gained a store of strength, and hardy habits to keep it good, which subsequent years of study and confinement have not hitherto exhausted. I never can see a thin, white-faced schoolboy of twelve or fifteen, that I do not long to exile him; to expatriate him for a year or two from the pie and cake, the coddling and cookery of home, the weary, brain-baking of his school, out into the healthy world of the workers in the soil. His parents would be glad, however indignant or sorrowful at the parting, when he should return, as brown as a berry, straight, strong and hearty, almost able to eat his former self, if he were forthcoming.

I also gained an invaluable agricultural bias; so that I am ready, when my expected competence shall have been accumulated, to betake myself to the shadow of my trees and vines, and to the sunshine of my tilled land, and there in peace to end my days, living in the world of God, among the trees, the plants, the dumb beasts, the earth, the infinitude of beauty and vigor and youth, designed by him; as much superior to architectural and artistic parrotries of stone and canvas, as the pure, mystic beauty of Mont Blanc, the glories of the sea, of storms, and of the evening clouds, are superior to the gorgeous drapery and gilt gingerbread of a hotel bridal-chamber.

ELBERT HUBBARD

Whitman

I

Max Nordau wrote a book—wrote it with his tongue in his cheek, a dash of vitriol in the ink, and with a pen that scratched.

And the first critic who seemed to place a just estimate on the work was Mr. Zangwill (who has no Christian name). Mr. Zangwill made an attempt to swear out a *writ de lunatico inquirendo* against his Jewish brother, on the ground that the first symptom of insanity is often the delusion that others are insane; and this being so, Dr. Nordau was not a safe subject to be at large. But the Assize of Public Opinion denied the petition and the dear people bought the book at from three to five dollars per copy. Printed in several languages, its sales have mounted to a hundred thousand volumes, and the author's net profit is full forty thousand dollars. No wonder is it that, with pockets full to bursting, Dr. Nordau goes out behind the house and laughs uproariously whenever he thinks of how he has worked the world!

If Dr. Talmage is the Barnum of Theology, surely we may call Dr. Nordau the Barnum of Science. His agility in manipulating facts is equal to Hermann's now-you-see-it and now-you-don't with pocket handkerchiefs. Yet Hermann's exhibition is worth the admittance fee and Nordau's book (seemingly written in collaboration with Jules Verne and Mark Twain) would be cheap for a dollar. But what I object to is Prof. Hermann's disciples posing as Sure-Enough Materializing Mediums and Prof. Lombroso's followers calling themselves Scientists, when each goes forth without scrip or purse with no other purpose than to supply themselves with both.

Yet it was Barnum himself who said that the public delights in being humbugged, and strange it is that we will not allow ourselves to be thimble-rigged without paying for the privilege.

Nordau's success hinged on his audacious assumption that the public knew nothing of the Law of Antithesis. Yet Plato explained that the opposite of things look alike, and sometimes *are* alike, and that was quite a while ago.

The multitude answered: "Thou hast a devil"; Many of them said: "He hath a devil and is mad"; Festus said with a loud voice: "Paul, thou art beside thyself." And Nordau shouts in a voice more heady than that of Pilate, more throaty than that of Festus—"Mad—Whitman was—mad beyond the cavil of a doubt!"

In 1862, Lincoln, looking out of a window (before lilacs last in the dooryard bloomed) on one of the streets of Washington, saw a workingman in shirt sleeves go by. Turning to a friend, the President said: "There goes a *man!"* The explanation sounds singularly like that of Napoleon on meeting Goethe. But the Corsican's remark was intended for the poet's ear, while Lincoln did not know who his man was, although he came to know him afterward.

Lincoln in his early days was a workingman—an athlete, and he never quite got the idea out of his head (and I am glad) that he was still a hewer of wood. He once told George William Curtis that he more than half expected yet to go back to the farm and earn his daily bread by the work that his hands found to do; he dreamed of it nights, and whenever he saw a splendid toiler, he felt like hailing the man as brother and striking hands with him. When Lincoln saw Whitman strolling majestically past, he took him for a stevedore or possibly the foreman of a construction gang.

Whitman was fifty-one years old then. His long flowing beard was snow white and the shock that covered his Jove-like head was iron grey. His form was that of an Apollo who had arrived at years of discretion. He weighed even two hundred pounds and was just six feet high. His plain check cotton shirt was open at the throat to the breast; and he had an independence, a self-sufficiency, and withal a cleanliness, a sweetness, a gentleness, that told that, although he had a giant's strength, he did not use it like a giant. Whitman used no tobacco, neither did he apply hot and rebellious liquors to his blood and with unblushing forehead woo the means of debility and disease. Up to his fifty-third year he had never known a sick day, although at thirty his hair had begun to whiten. He had the look of age in his youth and the look of youth in his age that often marks the exceptional man.

But at fifty-three his splendid health was crowded to the breaking strain. How? Through caring for wounded, sick, and dying men: hour after hour, day after day, through the long silent watches of the night. From 1864 to the day of his death in 1892, physically, he was a man in ruins. But he did not wither at the top. Through it all he held the healthy optimism of boyhood, carrying with him the perfume of the morning and the lavish heart of youth.

Doctor Bucke, who was superintendent of a hospital for the insane for fifteen years, and the intimate friend of Whitman all the time, has said: "His build, his stature, his exceptional health of mind and body, the size and form of his features, his cleanliness of mind and body, the grace of his movements and gestures, the grandeur, and especially the magnetism of his presence; the charm of his voice, his genial kindly humor; the simplicity of his habits and tastes, his fredom from convention, the largeness and beauty of his manner; his calmness and majesty; his charity and forbearance—his entire unresentfulness under whatever provocation; his liberality, his universal sympathy with humanity in all ages and lands, his broad tolerance, his catholic friendliness, and his unexampled faculty of attracting affection, all prove his perfectly proportioned manliness."

But Whitman differed from the disciple of Lombroso in two notable particulars: He had no quarrel with the world, and he did not wax rich. "One thing thou lackest, O Walt Whitman!" we might have said to the poet, "you are not a financier." He died poor. But this is not proof of degeneracy save on 'Change. When the children of Count Tolstoy endeavored to have him adjudged insane, the Court denied the application and voiced the wisest decision that ever came out of Russia: A man who gives away his money is not necessarily more foolish than he who saves it.

And with Mr. Horace L. Traubel I say: Whitman was the sanest man I ever saw.

II

Some men make themselves homes; and others there be who rent rooms. Walt Whitman was essentially a citizen of the world: the world was his home and mankind were his friends. There was a quality in the man peculiarly universal: a strong, virile poise that asked for nothing, but took what it needed.

He loved men as brothers, yet his brothers after the flesh understood him not; he loved children—they turned to him instinctively—but he had no children of his own; he loved women and yet this strongly sexed and manly man never loved a woman. And I might here say as Philip Gilbert Hamerton said of Turner, "He was lamentably unfortunate in this: throughout his whole life he never came under the ennobling and refining influence of a good woman."

It requires two to make a home. The first home was made when a woman, cradling in her loving arms a baby, crooned a lullaby. All the tender sentimentality we throw around a place is the result of the sacred thought that we live there with someone else. It is *our* home. The home is a tryst—the place where we retire and shut the world out. Lovers make a home just as birds make a nest, and unless a man knows the spell of the divine passion I hardly see how he can have a home at all. He only rents a room.

Camden is separated from the city of Philadelphia by the Delaware River. Camden lies low and flat—a great sandy, monotonous waste of straggling buildings. Here and there are straight rows of cheap houses, evidently erected by staid, broad-brimmed speculators from across the river, with eyes on the main chance. But they reckoned ill, for the town did not boom. Some of these houses have marble steps and white barn door shutters, that might withstand a siege. When a funeral takes place in one of these houses the shutters are tied with strips of mournful black alpaca for a year and a day. Engineers, dockmen, express drivers, and mechanics largely make up citizens of Camden. Of course, Camden has its smug corner where prosperous merchants most do congregate: where they play croquet in the front yards, and have window boxes, and a piano and veranda chairs and terra cotta statuary, but for the most part the houses of Camden are rented, and rented cheap.

Many of the domiciles are frame and have the happy tumble-down look of the back streets in Charleston or Richmond—those streets where white trash merges off into prosperous colored aristocracy. Old hats do duty in keeping out the fresh air where providence has interfered and broken out a pane; blinds hang by a single hinge; bricks on the chimney tops threaten the passers-by; stringers and posts mark the place where proud picket fences once stood—the pickets having gone for kindling long ago. In the warm summer evenings men in shirt-sleeves sit on the front steps and stolidly smoke, while children pile up sand in the streets and play in the gutters.

Parallel with Mickle Street, a block away, are railway tracks. There noisy switch engines, that never keep Sabbath, puff back and forth, day and night, sending showers of soot and smoke when the wind is right (and it usually is) straight over Number 328, where, according to John Addington

Symonds and William Michael Rossetti, lived the mightiest seer of the century—the man whom they rank with Socrates, Epictetus, St. Paul, Michael Angelo, and Dante.

It was in August of 1883 that I first walked up that little street—a hot sultry summer evening. There had been a shower that turned the dust of the unpaved roadway to mud. The air was close and muggy. The houses, built right up to the side-walks, over which in little gutters the steaming sewage ran, seemed to have discharged their occupants into the street to enjoy the cool of the day. Barefooted children by the score paddled in the mud. All the steps were filled with loungers; some of the men had discarded not only coats but shirts as well and now sat in flaming red underwear, holding babies.

They say that "woman's work is never done," but to the women of Mickle Street this does not apply, but stay! perhaps their work *is* never done. Anyway, I remember that women sat on the curbs in calico dresses or leaned out the windows, and all seemed supremely free from care.

"Can you tell me where Mr. Whitman lives?" I asked a portly dame who was resting her elbows on a window-sill.

"Who?"

"Mr. Whitman!"

"You mean Walt Whitman?"

"Yes."

"Show the gentleman, Molly, he'll give you a nickel, I'm sure!"

I had not seen Molly. She stood behind me, but as her mother spoke she seized tight hold of one of my fingers, claiming me as her lawful prey, and all the other children looked on with envious eyes as little Molly threw at them glances of scorn and marched me off. Molly was five, going on six, she told me. She had bright red hair, a grimy face and little chapped feet that made not a sound as we walked. She got her nickel and carried it in her mouth and this made conversation difficult. After going one block she suddenly stopped, squared me around and pointing said, "Them is he!" and disappeared.

In a wheeled rattan chair, in the hallway, a little back from the door of a plain weather-beaten house, sat the coatless philosopher, his face and head wreathed in a tumult of snow white hair.

I had a little speech, all prepared weeks before and committed to memory, that I intended to repeat, telling him how I had read his poems and admired them. And further I had stored away in my mind a few blades from *Leaves of Grass* that I proposed to bring out at the right time as a sort of certificate of character. But when that little girl jerked me right-about-face and heartlessly deserted me, I stared dumbly at the man whom I had come a hundred miles to see. I began angling for my little speech but could not fetch it.

"Hello!" called the philosopher, out of the white aureole; "Hello! come here, boy!"

He held out his hand and as I took it there was a grasp with meaning in it.

"Don't go yet, Joe," he said to a man seated on the step smoking a cob pipe.

"The old woman's calling me," said the swarthy Joe. Joe evidently held truth lightly. "So long, Walt!"

"Good-bye, Joe. Sit down, lad, sit down!"

I sat in the doorway at his feet.

"Now isn't it queer—that fellow is a regular philosopher and works out some great problems, but he's ashamed to express 'em. He could no more give you his best than he could fly. Ashamed I s'pose, ashamed of the best that is in him. We are all a little that way—all but me—I try to write my best, regardless of whether the thing sounds ridiculous or not—regardless of what others think or say or have said. Ashamed of our holiest, truest, and best! Is it not too bad?

"You are twenty-five now? well boy, you may grow until you are thirty and then you will be as wise as you ever will be. Haven't you noticed that men of sixty have no clearer vision than men of forty? One reason is that we have been taught that we know all about life and death and the mysteries of the grave. But the main reason is that we are ashamed to shove out and be ourselves. Jesus expressed His own individuality perhaps more than any man we know of, and so He wields a wider influence than any other. And this though we only have a record of just twenty-seven days of His life.

"Now that fellow that just left is an engineer, and he dreams some beautiful dreams, but he never expresses them to any one, only hints them to me, and this only at twilight. He is like a weasel or mink or a whip-poor-will, he comes out only at night.

" 'If the weather was like this all the time people would never learn to read and write,' said Joe to me just as you arrived. And isn't that so? Here we can count a hundred people up and down this street, and not one is reading, not one but that is just lolling about, except the children and they are only happy when playing in the dirt. Why if this tropical weather should continue we would all slip back into South Sea Islanders! You can only raise good men in a little strip around the North Temperate Zone—when you get out of the track of the glacier a tender hearted, sympathetic man of brains is an accident."

Then the old man suddenly ceased and I imagined that he was following the thought out in his own mind. We sat silent for a space. The twilight fell, and a lamp-lighter lit the street lamp on the corner. He stopped an instant to cheerily salute the poet as he past. The man sitting on the door-step, across the street, smoking, knocked the ashes out of his pipe on his boot heel and went indoors. Women called their children, who did not respond, but still played on. Then the creepers were carried in, to be fed their bread and milk and put to bed; and shortly shrill feminine voices ordered the older children indoors, and some obeyed.

The night crept slowly on.

I heard old Walt chuckle behind me, talking incoherently to himself, and then he said:

"You are wondering why I live in such a place as this?"

"Yes, that is exactly what I was thinking of!"

"You think I belong in the country, in some quiet shady place. But all I have to do is to shut my eyes and go there. No man loves the woods more than I—I was born within sound of the sea—down on Long Island and I know all the songs that the sea-shell sings. But this babble and babel of voices pleases me better especially since my legs went on a strike, for although I can't walk, you see I still mix with the throng, so I suffer no loss. In the woods a man must be all hands and feet. I like the folks, the plain, ignorant unpretentious folks; and the youngsters that come and slide on my cellar door do not disturb me a bit. I'm different from Carlyle—you know he had a noise-proof room where he locked himself in. Now when a huckster goes by, crying his wares I open the blinds, and often wrangle with the fellow over the price of things. But the rogues have got into a way lately of leaving truck for me and refusing pay. To-day an Irishman passed in three quarts of berries and walked off pretending to be mad because I offered to pay. When he was gone, I beckoned to the babies over the way—they came over and we had a feast.

"Yes, I like the folks around here; I like the women, and I like the men, and I like the babies, and I like the youngsters that play in the alley and make mud pies on my steps. I expect to stay here until I die."

"You speak of death as a matter of course—you are not afraid to die?"

"Oh, no, my boy, death is as natural as life, and a deal kinder. But it is all good—I accept it all and give thanks—you have not forgotten my chant to death?"

"Not I!"

I repeated a few lines from *Drum Taps*.

He followed me, rapping gently with his cane on the floor, and with little interjectory remarks of "That's so!" "Very true!" "Good, good!" And when I faltered and lost the lines he picked them up where "The voice of my spirit tallied the song of the bird." In a strong clear voice but a voice full of sublime feeling he repeated:

Come, lovely and soothing Death,
Undulate round the world, serenely arriving, arriving,
In the day, in the night, to all, to each,
Sooner or later, delicate Death.
Praised be the fathomless universe
For life and joy, and for objects and knowledge curious,
And for love, sweet love—but praise! praise! praise
For the sure enwinding arms of cool, enfolding Death.
Dark Mother, always gliding near with soft feet,
Have none chanted for thee a chant of fullest welcome?
Then I chant for thee, I glorify thee above all,
I bring thee a song that when thou must indeed come, come unfalteringly
Approach, strong deliveress,
When it is so, when thou hast taken them
I joyously sing the dead,
Lost in the loving, floating ocean of thee,
Laved in the flood of thy bliss, O Death.
From me to thee glad serenades,
Dances for thee I propose, saluting thee, adornments and feastings for thee,
And the sights of the open landscape and the high spread sky are fitting,
And life and the fields, and the huge and thoughtful night.
The night in silence under many a star,
The ocean shore and the husky whispering wave whose voice I know,
And the soul turning to thee, O vast and well veil'd Death,
And the body gratefully nestling close to thee.
Over the tree-tops I float thee a song,

Over the rising and sinking waves, over the myriad fields and the prairies wide,
Over the dense-packed cities all, and the teeming wharves, and ways,
I float this carol with joy, with joy to thee O Death.

The last playing youngster had silently disappeared from the streets. The doorsteps were deserted—save where across the way a young man and maiden sat in the gloaming conversing in low monotone.

The clouds had drifted away.

A great yellow star shone out above the chimney tops in the east.

I arose to go.

"I wish you'd come oftener—I see you so seldom, lad," said the old man, half plaintively.

I did not explain that we had never met before—that I had come from New York purposely to see him. He thought he knew me. And so he did—as much as I could impart. The rest was irrelevant. As to my occupation or name, what booted it?—he had no curiosity concerning me. I grasped his outstretched hand in both of my own.

He said not a word; neither did I.

I turned and made my way to the ferry—past the whispering lovers on the doorsteps, and over the railway tracks where the noisy engines puffed. As I walked on board the boat the wind blew up cool and fresh from the west. The star in the east grew brighter, and other stars came out, reflecting themselves like gems in the dark blue of the Delaware.

There was a soft sublimity in the sound of the bells that came echoing over the waters. My heart was very full for I had felt the thrill of being in the presence of a great and loving soul.

It was the first time and the last that I ever saw Walt Whitman.

III

Most writers bear no message: they carry no torch. Sometimes they excite wonder, or they amuse and divert—divert us from our work. To be diverted to a certain degree may be well, but there is a point where earth ends and cloudland begins, and even great poets occasionally befog the things which they would reveal.

Homer was seemingly blind to much simple truth; Virgil carries you away from earth; Horace was undone without his Macænas; Dante makes you an exile; Shakespeare was singularly silent concerning the doubts, difficulties, and common lives of common people; Byron's Corsair life does not help you in your toil, and in his fight with English Bards and Scotch Reviewers we crave neutrality; to be caught in the meshes of Pope's *Dunciad* is not pleasant; and Lowell's *Fable for Critics* is only another *Dunciad*. But above all poets who have ever lived the author of *Leaves of Grass* was the poet of humanity.

Milton knew all about Heaven, and Dante conducts us through Hell, but it was left for Whitman to show us Earth. His voice never goes so high that it breaks an impotent falsetto, neither does it growl and snarl at things it does not understand and not understanding does not like. He was so great that he had no envy, and his insight was so sure that he had no prejudice. He never boasted that he was higher, nor claimed to be less than any of the other sons of men. He met all on terms of absolute equality, mixing with the poor, the lowly, the fallen, the oppressed, the cultured, the rich—simply as brother with brother. And when he said to the outcast, "Not till the sun excludes you will I exclude you," he voiced a sentiment worthy of a god.

He was brother to the elements, the mountains, the seas, the clouds, the sky. He loved them all and partook of them all in his large, free, unselfish, untrammelled nature. His heart knew no limits, and feeling his feet mortis'd in granite and his footsteps tenon'd in infinity he knew the amplitude of time.

Only the great are generous; only the strong are forgiving. Like Lot's wife, most poets look back over their shoulders; and those who are not looking backward insist that we shall look into the future, and the vast majority of the whole scribbling rabble accept the precept, "Man never is, but always to be blest."

We grieve for childhood's happy days, and long for sweet rest in Heaven and sigh for mansions in the skies. And the people about us seem so indifferent, and our friends so lukewarm, and really no one understands us, and our environment queers our budding spirituality and the frost of jealousy nips our aspirations: "O Paradise, O Paradise, the world is growing old; who would not be at rest and free where love is never cold." So sing the fearsome dyspeptics of the stylus. O anæmic he, you bloodless she, nipping at crackers, sipping at tea, why not consider that although the evolutionists tell us where we came from, and the theologians inform us where we are going to, yet the only thing we are really sure of is that we are here!

The present is the perpetually moving spot where history ends and prophecy begins. It is our only possession: the past we reach through lapsing memory, halting recollection, hearsay, and belief; we pierce the future by wistful faith or anxious hope, but the present is beneath our feet.

Whitman sings the beauty and the glory of the present. He rebukes our groans and sighs—bids us look about on every side at the wonders of creation, and at the miracles within our grasp. He lifts us up, restores us to our own, introduces us to man and Nature and thus infuses into us courage, manly pride, self-reliance, and the strong faith that comes when we feel our kinship with God.

He was so mixed with the universe that his voice took on the sway of elemental integrity and candor. Absolutely honest, this man was unafraid and unashamed, for Nature has neither apprehension, shame nor vain-glory. In *Leaves of Grass* Whitman speaks as all men have ever spoken who believe in God and in themselves—oracular, without apology, without abasement—fearlessly. He tells of the powers and mysteries that pervade and guide all life, all death, all purpose. His work is masculine, as the sun is masculine; for the Prophetic voice is as surely masculine as the lullaby and lyric cry are feminine.

Whitman brings the warmth of the sun to the buds of the heart so that they open and bring forth form, color, perfume. He becomes for them aliment and dew; so these buds become blossoms, fruits, tall branches, and stately trees that cast refreshing shadows.

There are men who are to other men as the shadow of a mighty rock in a weary land—such is Walt Whitman.

JAMES McNEILL WHISTLER

The Ruskin Affair

PROLOGUE

"For Mr. Whistler's own sake, no less than for the protection of the purchaser, Sir Coutts Lindsay ought not to have admitted works into the gallery in which the ill-educated conceit of the artist so nearly approached the aspect of wilful imposture. I have seen, and heard, much of cockney impudence before now; but never expected to hear a coxcomb ask two hundred guineas for flinging a pot of paint in the public's face."

JOHN RUSKIN

Professor John Ruskin in *Fors Clavigera*, July 2, 1877

THE ACTION

IN THE Court of Exchequer Division on Monday, before Baron Huddleston and a special jury, the case of Whistler *v.* Ruskin came on for hearing. In this action the plaintiff claimed £1000 damages.

Mr. Serjeant Parry and Mr. Petheram appeared for the plaintiff; and the Attorney-General and Mr. Bowen represented the defendant.

Mr. SERJEANT PARRY, in opening the case on behalf of the plaintiff, said that Mr. Whistler had followed the profession of an artist for many years, both in this and other countries. Mr. Ruskin, as would be probably known to the gentlemen of the jury, held perhaps the highest position in Europe

Lawsuit for Libel against Mr. Ruskin, Nov. 15, 1878

and America as an art critic, and some of his works were, he might say, destined to immortality. He was, in fact, a gentleman of the highest reputation. In the July number of *Fors Clavigera* there appeared passages in which Mr. Ruskin criticised what he called "the modern school," and then followed the paragraph of which Mr. Whistler now complained, and which was. "For Mr. Whistler's own sake, no less than for the protection of the purchaser, Sir Coutts Lindsay ought not to have admitted works into the gallery in which the ill-educated conceit of the artist so nearly approached the aspect of wilful imposture. I have seen, and heard, much of cockney impudence before now; but never expected to hear a coxcomb ask two hundred guineas for flinging a pot of paint in the public's face." That passage, no doubt, had been read by thousands, and so it had gone forth to the world that Mr. Whistler was an ill-educated man, an impostor, a cockney pretender, and an impudent coxcomb.

Mr. WHISTLER, cross-examined by the ATTORNEY-GENERAL, said: "I have sent pictures to the Academy which have not been received. I believe that is the experience of all artists.... The nocturne in black and gold is a night piece, and represents the fireworks at Cremorne."

"Not a view of Cremorne?"

"If it were called a view of Cremorne, it would certainly bring about nothing but disappointment on the part of the beholders. (*Laughter*.) It is an artistic arrangement. It was marked two hundred guineas."

"Is not that what we, who are not artists, would call a stiffish price?"

"I think it very likely that that may be so."

"But artists always give good value for their money, don't they?"

"I am glad to hear that so well established. (*A laugh*.) I do not know Mr. Ruskin, or that he holds the view that a picture should only be exhibited when it is finished, when nothing can be done to improve it, but that is a correct view; the arrangement in black and gold was a finished picture, I did not intend to do anything more to it."

"Now, Mr. Whistler. Can you tell me how long it took you to knock off that nocturne?"

"I beg your pardon?" (*Laughter*.)

"Oh! I am afraid that I am using a term that applies rather perhaps to my own work. I should have said, 'How long did you take to paint that picture?'"

"Oh, no! permit me, I am too greatly flattered to think that you apply, to work of mine, any term that you are in the habit of using with reference to your own. Let us say then how long did I take to 'knock off,' I think that is it—to knock off that nocturne; well, as well as I remember, about a day."

"Only a day?"

"Well, I won't be quite positive; I may have still put a few more touches to it the next day if the painting were not dry. I had better say then, that I was two days at work on it."

"Oh, two days! The labour of two days, then, is that for which you ask two hundred guineas!"

"No;—I ask it for the knowledge of a lifetime." (*Applause*.)

"You have been told that your pictures exhibit some eccentricities?"

"Yes; often." (*Laughter*.)

"You send them to the galleries to incite the admiration of the public?"

"That would be such vast absurdity on my part, that I don't think I could." (*Laughter*.)

"You know that many critics entirely disagree with your views as to these pictures?"

"It would be beyond me to agree with the critics."

"You don't approve of criticism then?"

"I should not disapprove in any way of technical criticism by a man whose whole life is passed in the practice of the science which he criticises; but for the opinion of a man whose life is not so passed I would have as little regard as you would, if he expressed an opinion on law."

"You expect to be criticised?"

"Yes; certainly. And I do not expect to be affected by it, until it becomes a case of this kind. It is not only when criticism is inimical that I object to it, but also when it is incompetent. I hold that none but an artist can be a competent critic."

"You put your pictures upon the garden wall, Mr. Whistler, or hang them on the clothes-line, don't you—to mellow?"

"I do not understand."

"Do you not put your paintings out into the garden?"

"Oh! I understand now. I thought, at first, that you were perhaps again using a term that you are accustomed to yourself. Yes; I certainly do put the canvases into the garden that they may dry in the open air while I am painting, but I should be sorry to see them 'mellowed.'"

"Why do you call Mr. Irving 'an arrangement in black'?" (*Laughter*.)

Mr. Baron Huddleston: "It is the picture, and not Mr. Irving, that is the arrangement."

A discussion ensued as to the inspection of the pictures, and incidentally Baron Huddleston remarked that a critic must be competent to form an opinion, and bold enough to express that opinion in strong terms if necessary.

The Attorney-General complained that no answer was given to a written application by the defendant's solicitors for leave to inspect the pictures which the plaintiff had been called upon to produce at the trial. The Witness replied that Mr. Arthur Severn had been to his studio to inspect the paintings, on behalf of the defendant, for the purpose of passing his final judgment upon them and settling that question for ever.

Cross-examination continued: "What was the subject of the nocturne in blue and silver belonging to Mr. Grahame?"

"A moonlight effect on the river near old Battersea Bridge."

"What has become of the nocturne in black and gold?"

"I believe it is before you." (*Laughter*.)

The picture called the nocturne in blue and silver was now produced in Court.

"That is Mr. Grahame's picture. It represents Battersea Bridge by moonlight."

Baron Huddleston: "Which part of the picture is the bridge?" (*Laughter*.)

His Lordship earnestly rebuked those who laughed. And witness explained to his Lordship the composition of the picture.

"Do you say that this is a correct representation of Battersea Bridge?"

"I did not intend it to be a 'correct' portrait of the bridge. It is only a moonlight scene, and the pier in the centre of the picture may not be like the piers at Battersea Bridge as you know them in broad daylight. As to what the picture represents, that depends upon who looks at it. To some persons it may represent all that is intended; to others it may represent nothing."

"The prevailing colour is blue?"

"Perhaps."

"Are those figures on the top of the bridge intended for people?"

"They are just what you like."

"Is that a barge beneath?"

"Yes. I am very much encouraged at your perceiving that. My whole scheme was only to bring about a certain harmony of colour."

"What is that gold-coloured mark on the right of the picture like a cascade?"

"The 'cascade of gold' is a firework."

A second nocturne in blue and silver was then produced.

WITNESS: "That represents another moonlight scene on the Thames looking up Battersea Reach. I completed the mass of the picture in one day."

The Court then adjourned. During the interval the jury visited the Probate Court to view the pictures which had been collected in the Westminster Palace Hotel.

After the Court had re-assembled the "Nocturne in Black and Gold" was again produced, and Mr. WHISTLER was further cross-examined by the ATTORNEY-GENERAL: "The picture represents a distant view of Cremorne with a falling rocket and other fireworks. It occupied two days, and is a finished picture. The black monogram on the frame was placed in its position with reference to the proper decorative balance of the whole."

"You have made the study of Art your study of a lifetime. Now, do you think that anybody looking at that picture might fairly come to the conclusion that it had no peculiar beauty?"

"I have strong evidence that Mr. Ruskin did come to that conclusion."

"Do you think it fair that Mr. Ruskin should come to that conclusion?"

"What might be fair to Mr. Ruskin I cannot answer."

"Then you mean, Mr. Whistler, that the initiated in technical matters might have no difficulty in understanding your work. But do you think now that you could make *me* see the beauty of that picture?"

The witness then paused, and examining attentively the Attorney-General's face and looking at the picture alternately, said, after apparently giving the subject much thought, while the Court waited in silence for his answer:

"No! Do you know I fear it would be as hopeless as for the musician to pour his notes into the ear of a deaf man. (*Laughter*.)

"I offer the picture, which I have conscientiously painted, as being worth two hundred guineas. I have known unbiased people express the opinion that it represents fireworks in a night-scene. I would not complain of any person who might simply take a different view."

The Court then adjourned.

The ATTORNEY-GENERAL, in resuming his address on behalf of the defendant on Tuesday, said he hoped to convince the jury, before his case closed, that Mr. Ruskin's criticism upon the plaintiff's pictures was perfectly fair and *bonâ fide;* * and that, however severe it might be, there was nothing that could reasonably be complained of..... Let them examine the nocturne in blue and silver, said to represent Battersea Bridge. What was that structure in the middle? Was it a telescope or a fire-escape? Was it like Battersea Bridge? What were the figures at the top of the bridge? And if they were horses and carts, how in the name of fortune were they to get off? Now, about these pictures, if the plaintiff's argument was to avail, they must not venture publicly to express an opinion, or they would have brought against them an action for damages.

After all, Critics had their uses.† He should like to know what would become of Poetry, of Politics, of Painting, if Critics were to be extinguished? Every Painter struggled to obtain fame.

* "Enter now the great room with the Veronese at the end of it, for which the painter (*quite rightly*) was summoned before the Inquisition of State."—Prof. JOHN RUSKIN: *Guide to Principal Pictures, Academy of Fine Arts, Venice.*

† "I have now given up ten years of my life to the single purpose of enabling myself to judge rightly of art... earnestly desiring to ascertain, and *to be able to teach*, the truth respecting art; also knowing that this truth was *by time and labour* definitely ascertainable."—Prof. RUSKIN: *Modern Painters*, Vol. III.

No artist could obtain fame, except through criticism.*

....As to these pictures, they could only come to the conclusion that they were strange fantastical conceits not worthy to be called works of Art.

....Coming to the libel, the Attorney-General said it had been contended that Mr. Ruskin was not justified in interfering with a man's livelihood. But why not? Then it was said, "Oh! you have ridiculed Mr. Whistler's pictures." If Mr. Whistler disliked ridicule, he should not have subjected himself to it by exhibiting publicly such productions. If a man thought a picture was a daub † he had a right to say so, without subjecting himself to a risk of an action.

He would not be able to call Mr. Ruskin, as he was far too ill to attend; but, if he had been able to appear, he would have given his opinion of Mr. Whistler's work in the witness-box.

He had the highest appreciation for *completed pictures* ‡ and he required from an artist that he should possess something more than a few flashes of genius! §

Mr. Ruskin entertaining those views, it was not wonderful that his attention should be attracted to

---

* "Canaletto, had he been a great painter, might have cast his reflections wherever he chose... but he is a little and a bad painter."—Mr. RUSKIN, Art Critic.

"I repeat there is nothing but the work of Prout which is true, living, or right in its general impression, and nothing, therefore, so inexhaustively *agreeable"* (sic). —J. RUSKIN, Art Professor; *Modern Painters.*

† "Now it is evident that in Rembrandt's system, while the contrasts are not more right than with Veronese, the colours are all wrong from beginning to end."—JOHN RUSKIN, Art Authority.

"Thirdly, that TRUTHS OF COLOUR ARE THE LEAST IMPORTANT OF ALL TRUTHS."— Mr. RUSKIN, Prof. of Art: *Modern Painters,* Vol. I. Chap. V.

"And that colour is indeed a most unimportant characteristic of objects, would be further evident on the slightest consideration. The colour of plants is constantly changing with the season... but the nature and essence of the thing are independent of these changes. An oak is an oak, whether green with spring, or red with winter; a dahlia is a dahlia, whether it be yellow or crimson; and if some monster hunting florist should ever frighten the flower blue, still it will be a dahlia; but not so if the same arbitrary changes could be effected in its form. Let the roughness of the bark and the angles of the boughs be smoothed or diminished, and the oak ceases to be an oak; but let it retain its universal structure and outward form, and though its leaves grow white, or pink, or blue, or tri-colour, it would be a white oak, or a pink oak, or a republican oak, but an oak still."—JOHN RUSKIN, Esq., M.A., Teacher and Slade Prof. of Fine Arts: *Modern Painters.*

REFLECTION:

'In conduct and conversation,
 It did a sinner good to hear
 Him deal in ratiocination!'

‡ I was pleased by a little unpretending modern German picture at Dusseldorf, by Bosch, representing a boy carving a model of his sheep dog in wood."—J. RUSKIN: *Modern Painters.*

§ I have just said that every class of rock, earth, and cloud must be known by the painter with geologic and meteorologic accuracy."—Slade Prof. RUSKIN: *Modern Painting.*

JAMES M'NEILL WHISTLER

Mr. Whistler's pictures. He subjected the pictures, if they chose,* to ridicule and contempt. Then Mr. Ruskin spoke of "the ill-educated † conceit of the artist, so nearly approaching the action of imposture." If his pictures were mere extravagances, how could it redound to the credit of Mr. Whistler to send them to the Grosvenor Gallery to be exhibited? Some artistic gentleman from Manchester, Leeds, or Sheffield might perhaps be induced to buy one of the pictures because it was a Whistler, and what Mr. Ruskin meant was that he might better have remained in Manchester, Sheffield, or Leeds, with his money in his pocket. It was said that the term "ill-educated conceit" ought never to have been applied to Mr. Whistler, who had devoted the whole of his life to educating himself in Art; ‡ but Mr. Ruskin's views § as to his success did not accord with those of Mr. Whistler. The libel complained of said also, "I never expected to hear a coxcomb ask two hundred guineas for flinging a pot of paint in the public's face." What was a coxcomb? He had looked the word up, and found that it came from the old idea of the licensed jester who wore a cap and bells with a cock's comb in it, who went about making jests for the amusement of his master and family. If that were the true definition, then Mr. Whistler should not complain, because his pictures had afforded a most amusing jest! *He did not know when so much amusement had been afforded to the || British Public as by Mr. Whistler's pictures.* He had now finished. Mr. Ruskin had lived a long life without being attacked, and no one had attempted to control his pen through the medium of a jury. Mr. Ruskin said, through him, as his counsel, that he did not retract one syllable of his criticism, believing it was right. Of course, if they found a verdict against Mr. Ruskin, he would have

---

* "Vulgarity, dulness, or impiety will indeed always express themselves through art, in brown and gray, as in Rembrandt."—Prof. JOHN RUSKIN: *Modern Painters.*

† "It is physically impossible, for instance, rightly to draw certain forms of the upper clouds with a brush; nothing will do it but the palette knife with loaded white after the blue ground is prepared."—JOHN RUSKIN, Prof. of Painting.

‡ "And thus we are guided, almost forced, by the laws of nature, to do right in art. Had granite been white and marble speckled (and why should this not have been, but by the definite Divine appointment for the good of man?), the huge figures of the Egyptian would have been as oppressive to the sight as cliffs of snow, and the Venus de Medicis would have looked like some exquisitely graceful species of frog."—Slade Professor JOHN RUSKIN.

§ "The principal object in the foreground of Turner's 'Building of Carthage' is a group of children sailing toy boats. The exquisite choice of this incident... is quite as appreciable when it is told, as when it is seen—it has nothing to do with the technicalities of painting;... such a thought as this is something far above all art."—JOHN RUSKIN, Art Professor: *Modern Painters.*

REFLECTION:

"Be not righteous overmuch, neither make thyself overwise; why shouldest thou destroy thyself?"

|| "It is especially to be remembered that drawings of this simple character [Prout's and W. Hunt's] were made for these same middle classes,

exclusively; and even for the second order of middle classes, more accurately expressed by the term 'bourgeoisie.' They gave an unquestionable tone of liberalmindedness to a suburban villa, and were the cheerfullest possible decorations for a moderate-sized breakfast parlour, opening on a nicely mown lawn."—JOHN RUSKIN, Art Professor: *Notes on S. Prout and W. Hunt.*

* "It seems to me, and seemed always probable, that I might have done much more good in some other way."—Prof. JOHN RUSKIN, Art Teacher: *Modern Painters,* Vol. V.

† "Give thorough examination to the wonderful painting, *as such,* in the great Veronese ... and then, for contrast with its reckless power, and for final image to be remembered of sweet Italian art in its earnestness ... the Beata Catherine Vigri's St. Ursula, ... I will only say in closing, as I said of the Vicar's picture in beginning, that it would be well if any of us could do such things nowadays:—and more especially if our vicars and young ladies could."— JOHN RUSKIN, Prof. of Fine Art: *Guide to Principal Pictures, Academy of Fine Arts, Venice.*

"Of the estimate which shall be formed of Mr. Jones's own work...

"His work, first, is simply the only art-work at present produced in England which will be received by the future as 'classic' in its kind—the best that has been or could be."—Prof. RUSKIN: *Fors Clavigera,* July 2, 1877.

to cease writing,* but it would be an evil day for Art, in this country, when Mr. Ruskin would be prevented from indulging in legitimate and proper criticism, by pointing out what was beautiful and what was not.†

Evidence was then called on behalf of the defendant. Witnesses for the defendant, Messrs. Edward Burne-Jones, Frith, and Tom Taylor.

Mr. EDWARD BURNE-JONES called.

Mr. BOWEN, by way of presenting him properly to the consideration of the Court, proceeded to read extracts of eulogistic appreciation of this artist from the defendant's own writings.

The examination of witness then commenced; and in answer to Mr. BOWEN, Mr. JONES said: "I am a painter, and have devoted about twenty years to the study. I have painted various works, including the 'Days of Creation' and 'Venus's Mirror,' both of which were exhibited at the Grosvenor Gallery in 1877. I have also exhibited 'Deferentia,' 'Fides,' 'St. George,' and 'Sybil.' I have one work, 'Merlin and Vivian,' now being exhibited in Paris. In my opinion complete finish ought to be the object of all artists. A picture ought not to fall short of what has been for ages considered complete finish.

Mr. BOWEN: "Do you see any art quality in that nocturne, Mr. Jones?"

Mr. JONES: "Yes .... I must speak the truth, you know" .... (*Emotion.*)

Mr. BOWEN: ... "Yes. Well, Mr. Jones, what quality do you see in it?"

Mr. JONES: "Colour. It has fine colour, and atmosphere."

Mr. BOWEN: "Ah. Well, do you consider detail and composition essential to a work of Art?"

Mr. JONES: "Most certainly I do."

Mr. BOWEN: "Then what detail and composition do you find in this nocturne?"

Mr. Jones: "Absolutely none." *

Mr. Bowen: "Do you think two hundred guineas a large price for that picture?"

Mr. Jones: "Yes. When you think of the amount of earnest work done for a smaller sum."

Examination continued: "Does it show the finish of a complete work of art?"

"Not in any sense whatever. The picture representing a night scene on Battersea Bridge is good in colour, but bewildering in form; and it has no composition and detail. A day or a day and a half seems a reasonable time within which to paint it. It shows no finish—it is simply a sketch. The nocturne in black and gold has not the merit of the other two pictures, and it would be impossible to call it a serious work of art. Mr. Whistler's picture is only one of the thousand failures to paint night. The picture is not worth two hundred guineas."

Mr. Bowen here proposed to ask the witness to look at a picture of Titian,† in order to show what finish was.‡

Mr. Serjeant Parry objected.

Mr. Baron Huddleston: "You will have to prove that it is a Titian."

Mr. Bowen: "I shall be able to do that."

Mr. Baron Huddleston: "That can only be by repute. I do not want to raise a laugh, but there is a well-known case of 'an undoubted' Titian being purchased with a view to enabling students and others to find out how to produce his wonderful colours. With that object the picture was rubbed down, and they found a red surface, beneath which they thought was the secret, but on continuing the rubbing they discovered a full-length portrait of George III. in uniform!"

The witness was then asked to look at the picture, and he said: "It is a portrait of Doge Andrea Gritti, and I believe it is a real Titian. It shows

REFLECTION:

* There is a cunning condition of mind that *requires to know*. On the Stock Exchange this insures safe investment. In the painting trade this would induce certain picture-makers to cross the river at noon, in a boat, before negotiating a Nocturne, in order to make sure of detail on the bank, that honesty the purchaser might exact, and out of which he might have been tricked by the Night!

"The action of imagination of the highest power in Burne-Jones, under the conditions of scholarship, of social beauty, and of social distress, which necessarily aid, thwart, and colour it in the nineteenth century, are alone in art,—unrivalled in their kind; and I *know* that these will be immortal, as the best things the mid-nineteenth century in England could do, in such true relations as it had, through all confusion, retained with the paternal and everlasting Art of the world."—John Ruskin, LL.D.: *Fors Clavigera*, July 2, 1877.

† "I believe the world may see another Titian, and another Raffaelle, before it sees another Rubens."—Mr. Ruskin.

‡ . "The Butcher's Dog, in the corner of Mr. Mulready's 'Butt' displays, perhaps, the most wonderful, because the most dignified, finish... and assuredly the most perfect unity of drawing and colour which the entire range of ancient and modern art can exhibit. Albert Durer is, indeed, the only rival who might be suggested."—John Ruskin, Slade Professor of Art: *Modern Painters*.

finish. It is a very perfect sample of the highest finish of ancient art.* The flesh is perfect, the modelling of the face is round and good. That is an 'arrangement in flesh and blood!'"

The witness having pointed out the excellences of that portrait, said: "I think Mr. Whistler had great powers at first, which he has not since justified. He has evaded the difficulties of his art, because the difficulty of an artist increases every day of his professional life."

Cross-examined: "What is the value of this picture of Titian?"—"That is a mere accident of the saleroom."

"Is it worth one thousand guineas?"—"It would be worth many thousands to me."

Mr. FRITH was then examined: "I am an R.A.; and have devoted my life to painting. I am a member of the Academies of various countries. I am the author of the 'Railway Station,' 'Derby Day,' and 'Rake's Progress.' I have seen Mr. Whistler's pictures, and in my opinion they are not serious works of art. The nocturne in black and gold is not a serious work to me. I cannot see anything of the true representation of water and atmosphere in the painting of 'Battersea Bridge.' There is a pretty colour which pleases the eye, but there is nothing more. To my thinking, the description of moonlight is not true. The picture is not worth two hundred guineas. Composition and detail are most important matters in a picture. In our profession men of equal merit differ as to the character of a picture. One may blame, while another praises, a work. I have not exhibited at the Grosvenor Gallery. I have read Mr. Ruskin's works."

Mr. Frith here got down.

Mr. TOM TAYLOR—Poor Law Commissioner, Editor of *Punch,* and so forth—and so forth: "I am an art critic of long standing. I have been engaged

---

*..."I feel entitled to point out that the picture by Titian, produced in the case of Whistler *v.* Ruskin is an early specimen of that master, and does not represent adequately the style and qualities which have obtained for him his great reputation—one obvious point of difference between this and his more mature work being the far greater amount of finish—I do not say completeness—exhibited in it... and as the picture was brought forward with a view to inform the jury as to the nature of the work of the greatest painter, and more especially as to the high finish introduced in it, it is evident that it was calculated to produce an erroneous impression on their minds, if indeed any one present at the inquiry can hold that those gentlemen were in any way fitted to understand the issues raised therein.—I am, Sir, your obedient servant,
            "A. MOORE.
"Nov. 28."
    Extract of a letter to the Editor of the *Echo.*

"It was just a toss up whether I became an Artist or an Auctioneer."—W. P. FRITH, R.A.

in this capacity by the *Times,* and other journals, for the last twenty years. I edited the 'Life of Reynolds,' and 'Haydon.' I have *always* studied art. I have seen these pictures of Mr. Whistler's when they were exhibited at the Dudley and the Grosvenor Galleries. The 'Nocturne' in black and gold I do not think a serious work of art." The witness here took from the pockets of his overcoat copies of the *Times,* and, with the permission of the Court, read again with unction his own criticism, to every word of which he said he still adhered. "All Mr. Whistler's work is unfinished. It is sketchy. He no doubt possesses artistic qualities, and he has got appreciation of qualities of tone, but he is not complete, and all his works are in the nature of sketching. I have expressed, and still adhere to the opinion, that these pictures only come 'one step nearer pictures than a delicately tinted wall-paper.' "

This ended the case for the defendant.

Verdict for plaintiff. Damages one farthing.

PROFESSOR RUSKIN'S GROUP

My dear Sambourne,—I know I shall be only charmed, as I always am, by your work, and if I am myself its subject, I shall only be flattered in addition.

Punch in person sat upon me in the box; why should not the most subtle of his staff have a shot? Moreover, whatever delicacy and refinement Tom Taylor may still have left in his pocket (from which, in Court, he drew his ammunition) I doubt not he will urge you to use, that it may not be wasted. Meanwhile you must not throw away sentiment upon what you call "this trying time."

To have brought about an "Arrangement in Frith, Jones, *Punch* and Ruskin, with a touch of Titian," is a joy! and in itself sufficient to satisfy even my craving for curious "combinations."—Ever yours

REFLECTION:
He must have tossed up.

REFLECTION:
A decidedly honest man—I have not heard of him since.

REFLECTION:
To perceive in Ruskin's army Tom Taylor, his champion—whose opinion he prizes—Mr. Frith, his ideal—was gratifying. But to sit and look at Mr. Burne-Jones, in common cause with Tom Taylor—whom he esteems, and Mr. Frith—whom he respects — conscientiously appraising the work of a *confrère*—was a privilege!

The World, Dec. 11, 1878. A pleasant *résumé* of the situation—in reply to Mr. Sambourne's expressed hope that his historical cartoon in *Punch* might not offend.

Altercation with Oscar

"RENGAINES!"

LAST NIGHT, at Prince's Hall, Mr. Whistler made his first public appearance as a lecturer on Art..... There were some arrows .... shot off .... and (O, *mea culpa!*) at dress reformers most of all..... That an artist will find beauty in ugliness, *le beau dans l'horrible,* is now a commonplace of the schools..... I differ entirely from Mr. Whistler. An Artist is not an isolated fact; he is the resultant of a certain *milieu* and a certain *entourage,* and can no more be born of a nation that is devoid of any sense of beauty than a fig can grow from a thorn or a rose blossom from a thistle..... The poet is the supreme Artist, for he is the master of colour and of form, and the real musician besides, and is lord over all life and all arts; and so to the poet beyond all others are these mysteries known; to Edgar Allan Poe and Baudelaire, not to Benjamin West and Paul Delaroche.....

Oscar Wilde

Pall Mall Gazette,
Feb. 21, 1885

REFLECTION:
It is not enough that our simple Sunflower thrive on his "thistle"—he has now grafted Edgar Poe on the "rose" tree of the early American Market in "a certain milieu" of dry goods and sympathy; and "a certain entourage" of worship and wooden nutmegs.

Born of a Nation, not absolutely "devoid of any sense of beauty"—Their idol—cherished—listened to—and understood.

Foolish Baudelaire!—Mistaken Mallarmé!

TENDERNESS IN TITE STREET

TO THE POET:
OSCAR,—I have read your exquisite article in the *Pall Mall.* Nothing is more delicate, in the flattery of "the Poet" to "the Painter," than the *naïveté* of "the Poet," in the choice of his Painters—Benjamin West and Paul Delaroche!

You have pointed out that "the Painter's mission is to find *"le beau dans l'horrible,"* and have left to "the Poet" the discovery of *"l'horrible" dans "le beau"!*

Chelsea,

The World.

TO THE PAINTER:

DEAR Butterfly,—By the aid of a biographical dictionary, I made the discovery that there were once two painters, called Benjamin West and Paul Delaroche, who rashly lectured upon Art. As of their works nothing at all remains, I conclude that they explained themselves away.

Be warned in time, James; and remain, as I do, incomprehensible. To be great is to be misunderstood. *Tout à vous,* Oscar Wilde

The World.

REFLECTION:

I do know a bird, who, like Oscar, with his head in the sand, still believes in the undiscovered!

TO THE COMMITTEE OF THE
"NATIONAL ART EXHIBITION"

GENTLEMEN,—I am naturally interested in any effort made among Painters to prove that they are alive—but when I find, thrust in the van of your leaders, the body of my dead 'Arry, I know that putrefaction alone can result. When, following 'Arry, there comes on Oscar, you finish in farce, and bring upon yourselves the scorn and ridicule of your *confrères* in Europe.

What has Oscar in common with Art? except that he dines at our tables and picks from our platters the plums for the pudding he peddles in the provinces. Oscar—the amiable, irresponsible, esurient Oscar—with no more sense of a picture than of the fit of a coat, has the courage of the opinions ... of others!

With 'Arry and Oscar you have avenged the Academy.

I am, Gentlemen, yours obediently,

It to be misunderstood is to be great, it was rash in Oscar to reveal the source of his inspirations: the *"Biographical Dictionary!"*

Letter read at a meeting of this Society, associated for purposes of Art reform.

The World, Nov. 17, 1888.

QUAND MÊME!

ATLAS, this is very sad! With our James vulgarity begins at home, and should be allowed to stay there.
—*A vous,* Oscar Wilde

TO WHOM:

"A poor thing," Oscar!—"but," for once, I suppose "your own."

Enclosed to the Poet, with a line, "Oscar, you must really keep outside 'the radius'!"

The World, Nov. 24, 1886.

Oscar Again

THE HABIT OF SECOND NATURES

Truth, Jan. 2, 1890.

MOST VALIANT *Truth*,—Among your ruthless exposures of the shams of to-day, nothing, I confess, have I enjoyed with keener relish than your late tilt at that arch-impostor and pest of the period—the all-pervading plagiarist!

I learn, by the way, that in America he may, under the "Law of '84," as it is called, be criminally prosecuted, incarcerated, and made to pick oakum, as he has hitherto picked brains—and pockets!

How was it that, in your list of culprits, you omitted that fattest of offenders—our own Oscar?

His methods are brought again freshly to my mind, by the indefatigable and tardy Romeike, who sends me newspaper cuttings of "Mr. Herbert Vivian's Reminiscences," in which, among other entertaining anecdotes, is told at length, the story of Oscar simulating the becoming pride of author, upon a certain evening, in the club of the Academy students, and arrogating to himself the responsibility of the lecture, with which, at his earnest prayer, I had, in good fellowship, crammed him, that he might not add deplorable failure to foolish appearance, in his anomalous position, as art-expounder, before his clear-headed audience.

He went forth, on that occasion, as my St. John—but, forgetting that humility should be his chief characteristic, and unable to withstand the unaccustomed respect with which his utterances were received, he not only trifled with my shoe, but bolted with the latchet!

Mr. Vivian, in his book, tells us, further on, that lately, in an article in the *Nineteenth Century* on the "Decay of Lying," Mr. Wilde has deliberately and incautiously incorporated, "without a word of comment," a portion of the well-remembered letter in which, after admitting his rare appreciation and amazing memory, I acknowledge that "Oscar has the courage of the opinions.... of others!"

My recognition of this, his latest proof of open admiration, I send him in the following little note, which I fancy you may think *à propos* to publish, as an example to your readers, in similar circumstances, of noble generosity in sweet reproof, tempered, as it should be, to the lamb in his condition:—

"Oscar, you have been down the area again, I see!

"I had forgotten you, and so allowed your hair to grow over the sore place. And now, while I looked the other way, you have stolen *your own scalp!* and potted it in more of your pudding.

"Labby has pointed out that, for the detected plagiarist, there is still one way to self-respect (besides hanging himself, of course), and that is for him boldly to declare, *"Je prends mon bien là où je le trouve.'*

"You, Oscar, can go further, and with fresh effrontery, that will bring you the envy of all criminal *confrères,* unblushingly boast, 'Moi, pe prends son bien là où je le trouve!' "
Chelsea

IN THE MARKET PLACE

Truth, Jan. 9, 1890.

SIR,—I can hardly imagine that the public are in the very smallest degree interested in the shrill shrieks of "Plagiarism" that proceed from time to time out of the lips of silly vanity or incompetent mediocrity.

However, as Mr. James Whistler has had the impertinence to attack me with both venom and vulgarity in your columns, I hope you will allow me to state that the assertions contained in his letters are as deliberately untrue as they are deliberately offensive.

The definition of a disciple as one who has the courage of the opinions of his master is really too old even for Mr. Whistler to be allowed to claim it, and as for borrowing Mr. Whistler's ideas about art, the only thoroughly original ideas I have ever heard him express have had reference to his own superiority as a painter over painters greater than himself.

It is a trouble for any gentleman to have to notice the lucubrations of so ill-bred and ignorant a person as Mr. Whistler, but your publication of his insolent letter left me no option in the matter.—I remain, Sir, faithfully yours,

Oscar Wilde

PANIC

Truth, Jan. 16, 1890.

O TRUTH!—Cowed and humiliated, I acknowledge that our Oscar is at last original. At bay, and sublime in his agony, he certainly has, for once, borrowed from no living author, and comes out in his own true colours—as his own "gentleman."

How shall I stand against his just anger, and his damning allegations! for it must be clear to your readers, that, beside his clean polish, as prettily set forth in his epistle, I, alas! am but the "ill-bred and ignorant person," whose "lucubrations" "it is a trouble" for him "to notice."

Still will I, desperate as is my condition, point out that though "impertinent," "venomous," and "vulgar," he claims me as his "master"—and, in the dock, bases his innocence upon such relation between us.

In all humility, therefore, I admit that the outcome of my "silly vanity and incompetent mediocrity," must be the incarnation: "Oscar Wilde." *Mea culpa!* the Gods may perhaps forgive and forget.

To you, *Truth*—champion of the truth—I leave the brave task of proclaiming again that the story of the lecture to the students of the Royal Academy was, as I told it to you, no fiction.

In the presence of Mr. Waldo Story did Oscar make his prayer for preparation; and at his table was he entrusted with the materials for his crime.

You also shall again unearth, in the *Nineteenth Century Review* of Jan. 1889, page 37, the other appropriated property, slily stowed away, in an article on "The Decay of Lying"—though why Decay!

To shirk this matter thus is craven, doubtless; but I am awe-stricken and tremble, for truly, "the rage of the sheep is terrible!"

JUST INDIGNATION

OSCAR,—How dare you! What means this disguise?

Restore those things to Nathan's, and never again let me find you masquerading the streets of my Chelsea in the combined costumes of Kossuth and Mr. Mantalini!

Upon perceiving the Poet, in Polish cap and green overcoat, befrogged, and wonderfully befurred.

AN ADVANCED CRITIC

TO THE EDITOR:

SIR,—I find myself obliged to notice the critical review of the "Ten o'Clock," that appeared in your paper (March 6).

In the interest of my publishers, I beg to state formally that the work has not as yet been issued at all—and I would point out that what is still in

Pall Mall Gazette,
March 28, 1888.

the hands of the printer, cannot possibly have fallen into the fingers of your incautious contributor!

The early telegram is doubtless the ambition of this smart, though premature and restless one—but he is wanting in habit, and unhappy in his haste!—What will you? The *Pall Mall* and the people have been imposed upon.

Be good enough, Sir, to insert this note, lest the public suppose, upon your authority, that the "Ten o'Clock," as yet unseen in the window of Piccadilly, has, in consequence of this sudden summing up, been hurriedly withdrawn from circulation.—I am, Sir,

THE ADVANTAGE OF EXPLANATION

Pall Mall Gazette,
March 31, 1888.

TO THE EDITOR:

SIR,—Just three weeks after publication Mr. Whistler "finds himself obliged to notice the critical review of the 'Ten o'Clock' that appeared in your paper." He points out that "what is still in the hands of the printer cannot possibly have fallen into the fingers of your incautious contributor." I do not pretend to be acquainted with the multitudinous matters that may be in the hands of his publishers' printers. But I can declare—and you, Sir, will corroborate me—that a printed copy of Mr. Whistler's smart but misleading lecture was placed in my hands for review, and, moreover, that the notice did not appear until the pamphlet was duly advertised by Messrs. Chatto and Windus as ready. It is, of course, a matter of regret to me if, as Mr. Whistler suggests, his publishers' interests are likely to suffer from the review; but if an author's work, in the reviewer's opinion, be full of rash statement and mischievous doctrine, the publishers must submit to the risk of frank criticism. But it will be observed that Mr. Whistler is merely seeking to create an impression that your Reviewer never saw the work he criticized, which is surely not a creditable position to take up, even by a sensitive man writhing under adverse criticism.—I am, Sir, most obediently,

Your Reviewer

TESTIMONY

TO THE EDITOR:

Pall Mall Gazette,
April 7, 1888.

SIR,—My apologies, I pray you, to the much disturbed gentleman, "Your Reviewer," who complains that I have allowed "just three weeks" to go by without noticing his writing.

Let me hasten, lest he be further offended, to acknowledge his answer, in Saturday's paper.

After much matter, he comes unexpectedly upon a clear understanding of my letter—"It will be observed," he says naïvely, "that Mr. Whistler is merely seeking to create an impression that your Reviewer never saw the work he criticized,"—herein he is completely right, this is absolutely the impression I did seek to create—"which," he continues, "is surely not a creditable position to take up"— again I agree with him, and admit the sad spectacle a "Reviewer" presents in such position.

He further "declares," and calls upon you, Sir, to "corroborate" him, "that a printed copy of Mr. Whistler's misleading lecture was placed in my hands for review"—and moreover, that "the notice did not appear until the pamphlet was duly advertised by Messrs. Chatto and Windus as ready."

Pausing to note that if the lecture had not seemed misleading to him, it would surely not have been worth uttering at all, I come to the copy in question—this could only have been a printed proof, quaintly acquired—as will be seen by the following letter from Messrs. Chatto and Windus, which I

must beg you, Sir, to publish, with this note—as it deals also with the remaining point, the advertisement of the pamphlet,
And, I am, Sir,

The following is the letter from Mr. Whistler's publishers:—

DEAR SIR,—In reply to your question we have to say that we certainly have not sent out any copy of the "Ten o'Clock" to the press, or to anybody else excepting yourself. The work is still in the printers' hands, and we have for a long time past been advertising it only as "shortly" to be published; indeed, only a few proofs have so far been taken from the type.
Yours faithfully,
Chatto and Windus

THEODORE ROOSEVELT

"The Man with the Muck-Rake"

["On April 14th, 1906, Mr. Roosevelt delivered, at the laying of the cornerstone of the Office Building of the House of Representatives, an address which attracted a very large measure of attention. The speaker had in his mind two main topics: first, the tendency to exaggeration on the part of journals, and on the part of the public generally, in criticizing public evils and the actions of officials and of others in responsibility; and, secondly, the accountability to the community of those who have accumulated large property. The address was reported in the press throughout the country, and its publication brought about a more general discussion than any of the President's previous utterances. The author during the past five months has given due consideration to the expressions of unfavorable criticism, as well as to those of approval, of the conclusions and suggestions that he presented in his address; and he now reports that he finds occasion for no material modifications in these conclusions. He has made a careful revision of the text, and has added certain material. The questions which were under consideration last April are still pending questions; and they are likely to be discussed for years to come. It has seemed to the editors of Putnam's *that the address in its revised and final text is likely to prove of interest to their readers, and deserves preservation in this more permanent form.—Editors."*

The above is the explanatory matter accompanying the first revised and definitive text of one of the most sensational public speeches ever delivered by "T.R.", a vigorous and colorful personality whose integrity was so unquestioned and whose intelligence was so naively limited that he never doubted for a moment that he was not only the President and representative of the United States but that he was the United States.

He defied the Constitution and exercised more dictatorial power than all the other presidents put together, Abraham Lincoln included. He threatened war without Congressional mandate, put the fear of God into the withered-armed, warplumaged braggart Wilhelm II, King of Prussia and German emperor (whom for a long time he admired), laid down the law (his) to Venezuela, Colombia and to Moroccan tribal bandits, issued an order excluding Japanese laborers on the Pacific Coast in sublime disregard of the power granted a President of the

United States and not only invaded state's rights and municipal rights by an order dismissing suits against the San Francisco school board but thereby put himself above the Supreme Court and all the judicial and legislative functions of the republic.... He did all this with a violence of temper which was not selfishly motivated but out of a deep, impersonal, patriotic concern with the welfare of the nation and so he was forgiven those trespasses.... But although "T.R." was quick to attack public evils of all sorts and did not fear to blast and make tremble the money kings and robber barons whom he characterized as "certain malefactors of great wealth," he was acutely sensitive to criticism himself and was strangely impatient with journalists such as Lincoln Steffens, Upton Sinclair, Samuel Hopkins Adams, S. S. McClure and other agents of reform. He apparently wanted all reform notions to originate from himself. And so, when exposé literature was in full blast and the magazines which sponsored it were reaping a full harvest in circulation, advertising and prestige, "T.R." chose a routine and unimportant occasion—a corner-stone laying—to detonate one of his most elaborate caches of dynamite.

The nervously energetic and resourceful dictator-demagogue who could electrify and charm his voting constituency by calling his enemies "polecats" and "skunks" could also play all the tremolo stops of the biblical style. He could thrill the boobery down to their boots with stuff like "We stand at Armageddon and we battle for the Lord!" but he could also pull the same rheorical trick to discomfit others who not only thought they were standing at Armageddon and battling for the Lord but that they were on the same side "T.R." was on. That was their mistake: Teddy was his own side—pitcher, catcher, first baseman, infield, outfield and umpire. He disposed of them by pulling out all the organ stops and doing a weepy variation on a theme from Pilgrim's Progress,—"The Man With the Muck-Rake."... For a long time henceforth any magazine or newspaper editor, with civic pride, justice and circulation in his mind, had only to try to exercise them to be labeled a "muck-raker," a term which came to have connotations of the utmost opprobrium—and therefore left the field open for Teddy to do all the muck-raking himself, without any chance of his being called a "muck-racker"; for it would have been very ineffectual for the men he had denigrated by calling them "muck-rakers" to reply: "Yah! You're another!"... "T.R.," having adroitly dipped into the muck and swished it all over the men who were also trying to do some cleaning up, set vigorously to work mopping up the muck to which his attention had been called.... As you will see when you read the following article, which, printed in the first issue of the revived Putnam's Monthly *in 1906, was a slightly revised and amended version, it was one of the most sensational public utterances ever made by perhaps the most colorful of all our American presidential personalities.]*

Over a century ago Washington laid the corner-stone of the Capitol in what was then little more than a tract of wooded wilderness here beside the Potomac. We now find it necessary to provide by great additional buildings for the business of the Government. This growth in the need for the housing of the Government is but a proof and example of the way in which the Nation has grown and the sphere of action of the National Government has grown. We now administer the affairs of a Nation in which the extraordinary growth of population has been out stripped by the growth of wealth and the growth in complex interests. The material problems that face us to-day are not such as they were in Washington's time, but the underlying facts of human nature are the same now as they were then. Under altered external form we war with the same tendencies toward evil that were evident in Washington's time, and are helped by the same tendencies for good. It is about some of these that I wish to say a word to-day.

In Bunyan's "Pilgrims' Progress' you may recall the description of the Man with the Muck-rake, the man who could look no way but downward, with the muck-rake in his hand; who was offered a celestial crown for his muck-rake, but who would neither look up nor regard the crown he was offered, but continued to rake to himself the filth of the floor.

In "Pilgrim's Progress" the Man with the Muck-rake is set forth as the example of him whose vision is fixed on carnal instead of on spiritual things. Yet he also typifies the man who in this life consistently refuses to see aught that is lofty, and fixes his eyes with solemn intentness only on that which is vile and debasing. Now, it is very necessary that we should not flinch from seeing what is vile and debasing. There is filth on the floor, and it must be scraped up with the muck-rake: and there are times and places where this service is the most needed of all the services that can be performed. But the man who never does anything else, who never thinks or speaks or writes save of his feats with the muck-rake, speedily becomes, not a help to society, not an incitement to good, but one of the most potent forces for evil.

There are, in the body politic, economic, and social, many and grave evils, and there is urgent necessity for the sternest war upon them. There should be relentless exposure of and attack upon every evil man, whether politician or business man, every evil practice, whether in politics, in business, or in social life. I hail as a benefactor every writer or speaker, every man who, on the platform, or in book, magazine, or newspaper, with merciless severity makes such attack, provided always that he in his turn remembers that the attack is of use only if it is absolutely truthful. The liar is no whit better than the thief, and if his mendacity takes the form of slander, he may be worse than most thieves. It puts a premium upon knavery untruthfully to attack an honest man, or even with hysterical exaggeration to assail a bad man with untruth. An epidemic of indiscriminate assault upon character does no good, but very great harm. The soul of every scoundrel is gladdened whenever an honest man is assailed, or even when a scoundrel is untruthfully assailed.

Now, it is easy to twist out of shape what I have just said, easy to affect to misunderstand it, and, if it is slurred over in repetition, not difficult really to misunderstand it. Some persons are sincerely incapable of understanding that to denounce mud-slinging does not mean the indorsement of whitewashing; and both the interested individuals who need whitewashing, and those others who practise mudslinging, like to encourage such confusion of ideas. One of the chief counts against those who make indiscriminate assault upon men in business or men in public life is that they invite a reaction which is sure to tell powerfully in favor of the unscrupulous scoundrel who really ought to be attacked, who ought to be exposed, who ought, if possible, to be put in the penitentiary. If Aristides is praised overmuch as just, people get tired of hearing it; and overcensure of the unjust finally and from similar reasons results in their favor.

Any excess is almost sure to invite a reaction; and, unfortunately, the reaction, instead of taking the form of punishment of those guilty of the excess, is very apt to take the form either of punishment of the unoffending or of giving immunity, and even strength, to offenders. The effort to make financial or political profit out of the destruction of character can only result in public calamity. Gross and reckless assaults on character, whether on the stump or in newspaper, magazine, or book, create a morbid and vicious public sentiment, and at the same time act as a profound deterrent to able men of normal sensitiveness and tend to prevent them from entering the public service at any price. As an instance in point, I may mention that one serious difficulty encountered in getting the right type of men to dig the Panama Canal is the certainty that they will be exposed, both without, and, I am sorry to say, sometimes within, Congress, to utterly reckless assaults on their character and capacity.

At the risk of repetition let me say again that my plea is, not for immunity to but for the most unsparing exposure of the politician who betrays his trust, of the big business man who makes or spends his fortune in illegitimate or corrupt ways. There should be a resolute effort to hunt every such man out of the position he has disgraced. Expose the crime, and hunt down the criminal; but remember that even in the case of crime, if it is attacked in sensational, lurid, and untruthful fashion, the attack may do more damage to the public mind than the crime itself. It is because I feel that there should be no rest in the endless war against the forces of evil that I ask that the war be conducted with sanity as well as with resolution. The men with the muck-rakes are often indispensable to the well-being of society; but only if they know when to stop raking the muck, and to look upward to the celestial crown above them, to the crown of worthy endeavor. There are beautiful things above and round about them; and if they gradually grow to feel that the whole world is nothing but muck, their power of usefulness is gone. If the whole picture is painted black, there remains no hue whereby to single out the rascals for distinction from their fellows. Such painting finally induces a kind of moral color-blindness; and people affected by it come to the conclusion that no man is really black, and no man really white, but that all are gray. In other words, they believe neither in the truth of the attack, nor in the honesty of the man who is attacked; they grow as suspicious of the accusation as of the offence; it becomes well-nigh hopeless to stir them either to wrath against wrong-doing or to enthusiasm for what is right; and such a mental attitude in the public gives hope to every knave, and is the despair of honest men.

To assail the great and admitted evils of our political and industrial life with such crude and sweeping generalizations as to include decent men in the general condemnation means the searing of the public conscience. There results a general attitude either of cynical belief in and indifference to public corruption or else of a distrustful inability to discriminate between the good and the bad. Either attitude is fraught with untold damage to the country as a whole. The fool who has not sense to discriminate between what is good and what is bad is well-nigh as dangerous as the man who does discriminate and yet chooses the bad. There is nothing more distressing to every good patriot, to every good American, than the hard, scoffing spirit which treats the allegation of dishonesty in a public man as a cause for laughter. Such laughter is worse than the crackling of thorns under a pot, for it denotes not merely the vacant mind, but the heart in which high emotions have been choked before they could grow to fruition.

There is any amount of good in the world, and there never was a time when loftier and more disinterested work for the betterment of mankind was being done than now. The forces that tend for evil are great and terrible but the forces of truth and love and courage and honesty and generosity and sympathy are also stronger than ever before. It is a foolish and timid, no less than a wicked thing, to blink the fact that the forces of evil are strong, but it is even worse to fail to take into account the strength of the forces that tell for good. Hysterical sensationalism is the very poorest weapon wherewith to fight for lasting righteousness. The men who, with stern sobriety and truth, assail the many evils of our time, whether in the public press, or in magazines, or in books, are the leaders and allies of all engaged in the work for social and political betterment. But if they give good reason for distrust of what they say, if they chill the ardor of those who demand truth as a primary virtue, they thereby betray the good cause, and play into the hands of the very men against whom they are nominally at war.

In his "Ecclesiastical Polity" that fine old Elizabethan divine, Bishop Hooker, wrote:

> He that goeth about to persuade a multitude that they are not so well governed as they ought to be shall never want attentive and favorable hearers, because they know the manifold defects whereunto every kind of regimen is subject; but the secret lets and difficulties, which in public proceedings are innumerable and inevitable, they have not ordinarily the judgment to consider.

This truth should be kept constantly in mind by every free people desiring to preserve the sanity and poise indispensable to the permanent success of self-government. Yet, on the other hand, it is vital not to permit this spirit of sanity and self-command to degenerate into mere mental stagnation. Bad though a state of hysterical excitement is, and evil though the results are which come from the violent oscillations such excitement invariably produces, yet a sodden acquiescence in evil is even worse. At this moment we are passing through a period of great unrest—social, political, and industrial unrest. It is of the utmost importance for our future that this should prove to be not the unrest of mere rebelliousness against life, of mere dissatisfaction with the inevitable inequality of conditions, but the unrest of a resolute and eager ambition to secure the betterment of the individual and the Nation. So far as this movement of agitation throughout the country takes the form of a fierce discontent with evil, of a determination to punish the authors of evil, whether in industry or politics, the feeling is to be heartily welcomed as a sign of healthy life.

If, on the other hand, it turns into a mere crusade of appetite against appetite, a contest between the brutal greed of the "have-nots" and the brutal greed of the "haves," then it has no significance for good, but only for evil. If it seeks to establish a line of cleavage, not along the line which divides good men from bad, but along that other line, running at right angles thereto, which divides those who are well off from those who are less well off, then it will be fraught with immeasurable harm to the body politic.

We can no more and no less afford to condone evil in the man of capital than evil in the man of no capital. The wealthy man who exults because there is a failure of justice in the effort to bring some trust magnate to an account for his misdeeds is as bad as, and no worse than, the so-called labor leader who clamorously strives to excite a foul class feeling on behalf of some other labor leader who is implicated in murder. One attitude is as bad as the other and no worse; in each case the accused is entitled to exact justice; and in neither case is there need of action by others which can be construed into an expression of sympathy for crime. There is nothing more anti-social in a democratic republic like ours than such vicious class-consciousness. The multimillionaires who band together to prevent the enactment of proper laws for the supervision of the use of wealth, or to assail those who resolutely enforce such laws, or to exercise a hidden influence upon the political destinies of parties or individuals in their own personal interest, are a menace to the whole community; and a menace at least as great is offered by those laboring men who band together to defy the law, and by their openly used influence to coerce law-upholding public officials. The apologists for either class of offenders are themselves enemies of good citizenship; and incidentally they are also, to a peculiar degree, the enemies of every honest-dealing corporation and every law-abiding labor union.

It is a prime necessity that if the present unrest is to result in permanent good the emotion shall be translated into action, and that the action shall be marked by honesty, sanity, and self-restraint. There is mighty little good in a mere spasm of reform. The reform that counts is that which comes through steady, continuous growth; violent emotionalism leads to exhaustion.

It is important to this people to grapple with the problems connected with the amassing of enormous fortunes, and the use of those fortunes, both corporate and individual, in business. We should discriminate in the sharpest way between fortunes well won and fortunes ill won; between those gained as an incident to performing great services to the community as a whole, and those gained in evil fashion by keeping just within the limits of mere law-honesty. Of course no amount of charity in spending such fortunes in any way compensates for misconduct in making them. As a matter of personal conviction, and without pretending to discuss the details or formulate the system, I feel that we shall ultimately have to consider the adoption of some such scheme as that of a progressive tax on all fortunes, beyond a certain amount, either given in life or devised or bequeathed upon death to any individual—a tax so framed as to put it out of the power of the owner of one of these enormous fortunes to hand on more than a certain amount to any one individual; the tax, of course, to be imposed by the National and not the State Government. Such taxation should, of course, be aimed merely at the inheritance or transmission in their entirety of those fortunes swollen beyond all healthy limits.

Again, the National Government must in some form exercise supervision over corporations engaged in inter-State business—and all large corporations are engaged in inter-State business,—whether by license or otherwise, so as to permit us to deal with the far-reaching evils of over-capitalization. This year we are making a beginning in the direction of serious effort to settle some of these economic problems by the railway rate legislation. Such legislation, if so framed, as I am sure it will be, as to secure definite and tangible results, will amount to something of itself; and it will amount to a great deal more in so far as it is taken as a first step in the direction of a policy of superintendence and control over corporate wealth engaged in inter-State commerce, this superintendence and control not to be exercised in a spirit of malevolence toward the men who have created the wealth, but with the firm purpose both to do justice to them and to see that they in their turn do justice to the public at large.

The first requisite in the public servants who are to deal in this shape with corporations, whether as legislators or as executives, is honesty. This honesty can be no respecter of persons. There can be no such thing as unilateral honesty. The danger is not really from corrupt corporations: it springs from the corruption itself, whether exercised for or against corporations.

The eighth commandment reads, "Thou shalt not steal." It does not read, "Thou shalt not steal from the rich man." It does not read, "Thou shalt not steal from the poor man." It reads simply and plainly, "Thou shalt not steal." No good whatever will come from that warped and mock morality which denounces the misdeeds of men of wealth and forgets the misdeeds practised at their expense; which denounces bribery, but blinds itself to blackmail; which foams with rage if a corporation secures favors by improper methods, and merely leers with hideous mirth if the corporation is itself wronged. The only public servant who can be trusted honestly to protect the rights of the public against the misdeeds of a corporation is that public man who will just as surely protect the corporation itself from wrongful aggression. If a public man is willing to yield to popular clamor and do wrong to the men of wealth or to rich corporations, it may be set down as certain that if the opportunity comes he will secretly and furtively do wrong to the public in the interest of a corporation.

But, in addition to honesty, we need sanity. No honesty will make a public man useful if that man is timid or foolish, if he is a hot-headed zealot or an impracticable visionary. As we strive for reform we find that it is not at all merely the case of a long uphill pull. On the contrary, there is almost as much of breeching work as of collar work; to depend only on traces means that there will soon be a runaway and an upset. The men of wealth who to-day are trying to prevent the regulation and control of their business in the interest of the public by the proper Government authorities will not succeed, in my judgment, in checking the progress of the movement. But if they did succeed they would find that they had sown the wind and would surely reap the whirlwind, for they would ultimately provoke the violent excesses which accompany a reform coming by convulsion instead of by steady and natural growth.

On the other hand, the wild preachers of unrest and discontent, the wild agitators against the entire existing order, the men who act crookedly, whether because of sinister design or from mere puzzle-headedness, the men who preach destruction without proposing any substitute for what they intend to destroy, or who propose a substitute which would be far worse than the existing evils—all these men are the most dangerous opponents of real reform. If they get their way, they will lead the people into a deeper pit than any into which they could fall under the present system. If they fail to get their way, they will still do incalculable harm by provoking the kind of reaction which, in its revolt against the senseless evil of their teaching would enthrone more securely than ever the very evils which their misguided followers believe they are attacking.

More important than aught else is the development of the broadest sympathy of man for man. The welfare of the wage-worker, the welfare of the tiller of the soil—upon this depends the welfare of the entire country;

their good is not to be sought in pulling down others; but their good must be the prime object of all our statesmanship.

Materially we must strive to secure a broader economic opportunity for all men, so that each shall have a better chance to show the stuff of which he is made. Spiritually and ethically we must strive to bring about clean living and right thinking. We appreciate that the things of the body are important; but we appreciate also that the things of the soul are immeasurably more important. The foundation stone of national life is, and ever must be, the high individual character of the average citizen.

APPENDIX

Five months have gone by since I made this speech. I have reread it, and having added a few sentences strengthening one paragraph. I believe more strongly than ever, if that is possible, in all that I have therein said.

THEODORE ROOSEVELT

Sept. 20th, 1906.
Sagamore Hill

JOSIAH ROYCE

Provincialism

I AM PREACHING no new doctrine in emphasizing the importance of the provincial spirit for our whole national life. But I may next try to explain a little more clearly just what I mean by provincialism.

By provincialism, as you remember, I mean, in general, the devotion of each community to the cherishing of its own peculiar social life, and of its own unique ideals. Provincialism, as you thus see, stands in a certain contrast to national patriotism. Sometimes, of course, the two tendencies in the past have stood in direct conflict with each other. When provincialism opposes, or perhaps assails, national ideals, we call it sectionalism. Of the sectionalism that leads toward disunion, you and I have all of us a very well founded horror. But provincialism does not necessarily take the form of sectionalism. Nor, when sectionalism is overcome in a given community, does provincialism, in its other and better aspects, tend to decline. On the contrary, in European countries, you can see many instances where provincialism has long survived the very high development of a love of the national unity of great peoples, and has even prospered by reason of the very fact that the consciousness of membership in a great nation is closely bound up, in each community, with a genuine local patriotism. Scotland and Germany are both of them countries where provincialism flourishes. Both of them are regions where, in the past, sectionalism was long predominant, and where the results of sectionalism were disastrous. In both of them, moreover, the consciousness of membership in a great nation has triumphed over the older sectionalism. And in both of them the wiser provincialism, surviving, is still a source of strength, both to the single community and to the nation itself. What more loyal and effective servants has the British Empire than are furnished to her by the better sorts of Scotchmen? And who is to the very depths of his strongly individual soul more provincial, who is more a lover of the social ideals of his own home, than is the Scot? As for Germany,—wherein lies the strongest safeguard of her national future? In her navy? In her colonial ambitions? In her foreign policy? No, I should say, in her fondness for retaining and cultivating the better traditions and the manifold ideals of her provinces. If the Imperial power and the military discipline of her great army unify her national consciousness, she needs all the more the retention and the training of the local consciousness of her various communities. Nobody who knows anything of German life and literature can doubt that if Luther's Bible and the unity of language and of literature have been essential to the formation of the German nation, the health of that nation also depends upon the strength and the warmth of the local affections and ideals of her numerous and various communities.

As such instances remind us, the difference between sectionalism and the higher forms of provincialism is analogous to the difference which, in individuals, makes selfishness so markedly contrasted with self-respect. The provincialism for which I am pleading is the self-respect of the community, not its sectional selfishness. And of the idealized forms of self-respect no community can possess too much, just as no individual can set his personal ideals too high.

The provincial self-respect depends, first in any one instance, upon observing that each community must indeed live its own life, and that therefore a community cannot wisely live if it merely takes over the customs of other people, unchanged and hence unassimilated. The provincial self-respect depends secondly upon insisting that the stranger, the newcomer, the alien, must win his social place, if at all then, through his willingness to conform in due measure to the characteristic social standards which the community sets. Every community needs new blood, new life, progress. But the new blood must become its own blood. The new life must circulate in the veins of the community. That is, provincial self-respect forbids the community to be at the mercy of the social standards of transient visitors, or of intruders. The community must emphasize its own ideals. Until a new community thus wins some sort of spiritual authority over its new-comers and its transient folk, it has not yet become provincial, but remains, like an early California mining camp, a community where individuals indeed have souls, and may have noble souls, but where the social order has no soul. For the wiser provincialism is the soul of the community, seeking expression in word, in custom, and good works. By this soul the stranger's soul must be judged before he can find his due place. But an older community that, once having been thus provincial, has dwindled in soul until it has lost control over its incoming or over its transient population of strangers, so that its summer visitors or its foreign immigrants can henceforth make of it what they will,—well, such a community is in great danger of moral death. Its old home then becomes a sort of abandoned farm in the spiritual world. And in the spiritual world, where there is always so much good soil to till, abandoned farms are always out of place.

And so these three factors in every healthy sort of provincial self-respect I emphasize: First, the determination of the community to live its own life, not in isolation, not in sectional selfishness, but through preserving the integrity of its individual ideals and customs. Second, the authority, the gentle but firm social authority which the community exercises towards newcomers and sojourners,—not repelling them, not despising them, but insisting that the soul of the community has its dignity to assert over the souls of all those wayward individuals who have not yet learned to appreciate its meaning. And third, the local patriotism which loves to make this authority beautiful and winning, by idealizing the province, by adorning it, by glorifying it through legend and song and good works, and kindly provision for the needs of its inhabitants. Wherever these three factors, provincial independence of spirit, provincial authority, and provincial love for making this authority beautiful and winning co-operate, there you have the genuine self-respect of the province awakened. There you have what ought to survive when sectionalism passes away. There you find what the whole nation needs to get through and from the province.

And herewith I come directly to the most important aspect of provincialism,—an aspect which I have indicated all along, but which I must now, if only by means of a word or two, especially emphasize. Provincialism, of the sort that I have just described, is good for the province. But it is still more good for the nation as a whole. In a former essay upon this subject,—an essay that I long since put into print,—I stated at length the special reasons why I hold this view. The modern nation tends from its very vastness to become self-estranged, incomprehensible to its citizens, the prey of vast and fatally irresistible social forces. Economic tendencies more and more lead to a crushing of individual initiative, to a levelling of social interests and to a corresponding decrease of the spirit of true loyalty. When certain forms of popular excitement appear, as for example when the newspapers begin to preach some unholy war or other, the nation is too much in danger of falling prey to the mob-spirit. Under these conditions our national safety lies in cultivating that spirit of calm and clear considerateness which only a highly developed provincial self-respect can keep permanently alive. Repeatedly of late years we have seen how much the national safety depends upon the silent voters,—the voters whom the newspapers that most cater to the mob, and that circulate most widely, cannot influence,—the voters who care little how long the shouting lasted at this or at that national convention, and who are at once conservative and docile, critical and practical, thoughtful and decisive. We still have this vast silent vote, this body of considerate and prudent electors to depend upon. Nobody knows upon which side these electors will vote when next we come to decide great national issues; but we have good reason still to hope that no agitators will be powerful enough wholly to mislead them, that no political bosses are crafty enough permanently to enslave their judgment, that no popular magazines will have so large a circulation as to control them, that no newspapers can be noisy enough to deafen their ears to the voice of wisdom.

Now, how shall we keep this body of silent and thoughtful voters? I answer, through the cultivation of a wholesome provincial spirit. In provincial life the small social group of those who take counsel together, the town meeting, the local association, the club, can be kept alive, and the use of the clear reason in local affairs can be wisely cultivated, while the loyal practical instincts of the well-knit community can prevent that fantastic misuse of the reason which gives birth to schemes of wild reform, and which deceives the multitude by the mere show of argument. The province is the place for cultivating coolness of judgment side by side with intense and homely devotion.

JOHN DEWEY

Man and Art

By one of the ironic perversities that often attend the course of affairs, the existence of the works of art upon which formation of an esthetic theory depends has become an obstruction to theory about them. For one reason, these works are products that exist externally and physically. In common conception, the work of art is often identified with the building, book, painting, or statue in its existence apart from human experience. Since the actual work of art is what the product does with and in experience, the result is not favorable to understanding. In addition, the very perfection of some of these products, the prestige they possess because of a long history of unquestioned admiration, creates conventions that get in the way of fresh insight. When an art product once attains classic status, it somehow becomes isolated from the human conditions under which it was brought into being and from the human consequences it engenders in actual life-experience.

When artistic objects are separated from both conditions of origin and operation in experience, a wall is built around them that renders almost opaque their general significance, with which esthetic theory deals. Art is remitted to a separate realm, where it is cut off from that association with the materials and aims of every other form of human effort, undergoing, and achievement. A primary task is thus imposed upon one who undertakes to write upon the philosophy of the fine arts. This task is to restore continuity between the refined and intensified forms of experience that are works of art and the everyday events, doings, and sufferings that are universally recognized to constitute experience. Mountain peaks do not float unsupported; they do not even just rest upon the earth. They *are* the earth in one of its manifest operations. It is the business of those who are concerned with the theory of the earth, geographers and geologists, to make this fact evident in its various implications. The theorist who would deal philosophically with fine art has a like task to accomplish.

If one is willing to grant this position, even if only by way of temporary experiment, he will see that there follows a conclusion at first sight surprising. In order to understand the meaning of artistic products, we have to forget them for a time, to turn aside from them and have recourse to the ordinary forces and conditions of experience that we do not usually regard as esthetic. We must arrive at the theory of art by means of a detour. For theory is concerned with understanding, insight, not without exclamations of admiration, and stimulation of that emotional outburst often called appreciation. It is quite possible to enjoy flowers in their colored form and delicate fragrance without knowing anything about plants theoretically. But if one sets out to *understand* the flowering of plants, he is committed to finding out something about the interactions of soil, air, water and sunlight that condition the growth of plants.

By common consent, the Parthenon is a great work of art. Yet it has esthetic standing only as the work becomes an experience for a human being. And, if one is to go beyond personal enjoyment into the formation of a theory about that large republic of art of which the building is one member, one has to be willing at some point in his reflections to turn from it to the bustling, arguing, acutely sensitive Athenian citizens, with civic sense identified with a civic religion, of whose experience the temple was an expression, and who built it not as a work of art but as a civic commemoration. The turning to them is as human beings who had needs that were a demand for the building and that were carried to fulfillment in it; it is not an examination such as might be carried on by a sociologist in search for material relevant to his purpose. The one who sets out to theorize about the esthetic experience embodied in the Parthenon must realize in thought what the people into whose lives it entered had in common, as creators and as those who were satisfied with it, with people in our own homes and on our own streets.

In order to *understand* the esthetic in its ultimate and approved forms, one must begin with it in the raw; in the events and scenes that hold the attentive eye and ear of man, arousing his interest and affording him enjoyment as he looks and listens: the sights that hold the crowd—the fire-engine rushing by; the machines excavating enormous holes in the earth; the human-fly climbing the steeple-side; the men perched high in air on girders, throwing and catching red-hot bolts. The sources of art in human experience will be learned by him who sees how the tense grace of the ball-player infects the onlooking crowd; who notes the delight of the housewife in tending her plants, and the intent interest of her goodman in tending the patch of green in front of the house; the zest of the spectator in poking the wood burning on the hearth and in watching the darting flames and crumbling coals. These people, if questioned as to the reason for their actions, would doubtless return reasonable answers. The man who poked the sticks of burning wood would say he did it to make the fire burn better; but he is none the less fascinated by the colorful drama of change enacted before his eyes and imaginatively partakes in it. He does not remain a cold spectator. What Coleridge said of the reader of poetry is true in its way of all who are happily absorbed in their activities of mind and body: "The reader should be carried forward, not merely or chiefly by the mechanical impulse of curiosity, not by a restless desire to arrive at the final solution, but by the pleasurable activity of the journey itself."

The intelligent mechanic engaged in his job, interested in doing well and finding satisfaction in his handiwork, caring for his materials and tools with genuine affection, is artistically engaged. The difference between such a worker and the inept and careless bungler is as great in the shop as it is in the studio. Oftentimes the product may not appeal to the esthetic sense of those who use the product. The fault, however, is oftentimes not so much with the worker as with the conditions of the market for which his product is designed. Were conditions and opportunities different, things as significant to the eye as those produced by earlier craftsmen would be made.

So extensive and subtly pervasive are the ideas that set Art upon a remote pedestal, that many a person would be repelled rather than pleased if told that he enjoyed his casual recreations, in part at least, because of their esthetic quality. The arts which today have most vitality for the average person are things he does not take to be arts: for instance, the movie, jazzed music, the comic strip, and, too frequently, newspaper accounts of love-nests, murders, and exploits of bandits. For, when what he knows as art is relegated to the museum and gallery, the unconquerable impulse towards experiences enjoyable in themselves finds such outlet as the daily environment provides. Many a person who protests against the museum conception of art, still shares the fallacy from which that conception springs. For the popular notion comes from a separation of art from the objects and scenes of ordinary experience that many theorists and critics pride themselves upon holding and even elaborating. The times when select and distinguished objects are closely connected with the products of usual vocations are the times when appreciation of the former is most rife and most keen. When, because of their remoteness, the objects acknowledged by the cultivated to be works of fine art seem anemic to the mass of people, esthetic hunger is likely to seek the cheap and the vulgar.

The factors that have glorified fine art by setting it upon a far-off pedestal did not arise within the realm of art nor is their influence confined to the arts. For many persons an aura of mingled awe and unreality encompasses the "spiritual" and the "ideal" while "matter" has become by contrast a term of depreciation, something to be explained away or apologized for. The forces at work are those that have removed religion as well as fine art from the scope of the common or community life. The forces have historically produced so many of the dislocations and divisions of modern life and thought that art could not escape their influence. We do not have to travel to the ends of the earth nor return many millennia in time to find peoples for whom everything that intensifies the sense of immediate living is an object of intense admiration. Bodily scarification, waving feathers, gaudy robes, shining ornaments of gold and silver, of emerald and jade, formed the contents of esthetic arts, and, presumably, without the vulgarity of class exhibitionism that attends their analogues today. Domestic utensils, furnishings of tent and house, rugs, mats, jars, pots, bows, spears, were wrought with such delighted care that today we hunt them out and give them places of honor in our art museums. Yet in their own time and place, such things were enhancements of the processes of everyday life. Instead of being elevated to a niche apart, they belonged to display of prowess, the manifestation of group and clan membership, worship of gods, feasting and fasting, fighting, hunting, and all the rhythmic crises that punctuate the stream of living.

Dancing and pantomime, the sources of the art of the theater, flourished as part of religious rites and celebrations. Musical art abounded in the fingering of the stretched string, the beating of the taut skin, the blowing with reeds. Even in the caves, human habitations were adorned with colored pictures that kept alive to the senses experiences with the animals that were so closely bound with the lives of humans. Structures that housed their gods and the instrumentalities that facilitated commerce with the higher powers were wrought with especial fineness. But the arts of the drama, music, painting, and architecture thus exemplified had no peculiar connection with theaters, galleries, museums. They were part of the significant life of an organized community.

The collective life that was manifested in war, worship, the forum, knew no division between what was characteristic of these places and operations, and the arts that brought color, grace, and dignity, into them. Painting and sculpture were organically one with architecture, as that was one with the social purpose that buildings served. Music and song were intimate parts of the rites and ceremonies in which the meaning of group life was consummated. Drama was a vital reënactment of the legends and history of group life. Not even in Athens can such arts be torn loose from this setting in direct experience and yet retain their significant character. Athletic sports, as well as drama, celebrated and enforced traditions of race and group, instructing the people, commemorating glories, and strengthening their civic pride.

Under such conditions, it is not surprising that the Athenian Greeks, when they came to reflect upon art, formed the idea that it is an act of reproduction, or imitation. There are many objections to this conception. But the vogue of the theory is testimony to the close connection of the fine arts with daily life; the idea would not have occurred to any one had art been remote from the interests of life. For the doctrine did not signify that art was a literal copying of objects, but that it reflected the emotions and ideas that are associated with the chief institutions of social life. Plato felt this connection so strongly that it led him to his idea of the necessity of censorship of poets, dramatists, and musicians. Perhaps he exaggerated when he said that a change from the Doric to the Lydian mode in music would be the sure precursor of civic degeneration. But no contemporary would have doubted that music was an integral part of the ethos and the institutions of the community. The idea of "art for art's sake" would not have been even understood.

There must then be historic reasons for the rise of the compartmental conception of fine art. Our present museums and galleries to which works of fine art are removed and stored illustrate some of the causes that have operated to segregate art instead of finding it an attendant of temple, forum, and other forms of associated life. An instructive history of modern art could be written in terms of the formation of the distinctively modern institutions of museum and exhibition gallery. I may point to a few outstanding facts. Most European museums are, among other things, memorials of the rise of nationalism and imperialism. Every capital must have its own museum of painting, sculpture, etc., devoted in part to exhibiting the greatness of its artistic past, and, in other part, to exhibiting the loot gathered by its monarchs in conquest of other nations; for instance, the accumulations of the spoils of Napoleon that are in the Louvre. They testify to the connection between the modern segregation of art and nationalism and militarism. Doubtless this connection has served at times a useful purpose, as in the case of Japan, who, when she was in the process of westernization, saved much of her art treasures by nationalizing the temples that contained them.

The growth of capitalism has been a powerful influence in the development of the museum as the proper home for works of art, and in the promotion of the idea that they are apart from the common life. The *nouveaux riches,* who are an important by-product of the capitalist system, have felt especially bound to surround themselves with works of fine art which, being rare, are also costly. Generally speaking, the typical collector is the typical capitalist. For evidence of good standing in the realm of higher culture, he amasses paintings, statuary, and artistic *bijoux,* as his stocks and bonds certify to his standing in the economic world.

Not merely individuals, but communities and nations, put their cultural good taste in evidence by building opera houses, galleries, and museums. These show that a community is not wholly absorbed in material wealth, because it is willing to spend its gains in patronage of art. It erects these buildings and collects their contents as it now builds a cathedral. These things reflect and establish superior cultural status, while their segregation from the common life reflects the fact that they are not part of a native and spontaneous culture. They are a kind of counterpart of a holier-than-thou attitude, exhibited not toward persons as such but toward the interests and occupations that absorb most of the community's time and energy.

Modern industry and commerce have an international scope. The contents of galleries and museums testify to the growth of economic cosmopolitanism. The mobility of trade and of populations, due to the economic system, has weakened or destroyed the connection between works of art and the *genius loci* of which they were once the natural expression. As works of art have lost their indigenous status, they have acquired a new one—that of being specimens of fine art and nothing else. Moreover, works of art are now produced, like other articles, for sale in the market. Economic patronage by wealthy and powerful individuals has at many times played a part in the encouragement of artistic production. Probably many a savage tribe had its Maecenas. But now even that much of intimate social connection is lost in the impersonality of a world market. Objects that were in the past valid and significant because of their place in the life of a community now function in isolation from the conditions of their origin. By that fact they are also set apart from common experience, and serve as insignia of taste and certificates of special culture.

Because of changes in industrial conditions the artist has been pushed to one side from the main streams of active interest. Industry has been mechanized and an artist cannot work mechanically for mass production. He is less integrated than formerly in the normal flow of social services. A peculiar esthetic "individualism" results. Artists find it incumbent upon them to betake themselves to their work as an isolated means of "self-expression." In order not to cater to the trend of economic forces, they often feel obliged to exaggerate their separateness to the point of eccentricity. Consequently artistic products take on to a still greater degree the air of something independent and esoteric.

Put the action of all such forces together, and the conditions that create the gulf which exists generally between producer and consumer in modern society operate to create also a chasm between ordinary and esthetic experience. Finally we have, as the record of this chasm, accepted as if it were normal, the philosophies of art that locate it in a region inhabited by no other creature, and that emphasize beyond all reason the merely contemplative character of the esthetic. Confusion of values enters in to accentuate the separation. Adventitious matters, like the pleasure of collecting, of exhibiting, of ownership and display, simulate esthetic values. Criticism is affected. There is much applause for the wonders of appreciation and the glories of the transcendent beauty of art indulged in without much regard to capacity for esthetic perception in the concrete.

My purpose, however, is not to engage in an economic interpretation of the history of the arts, much less to argue that economic conditions are either invariably or directly relevant to perception and enjoyment, or even to interpretation of individual works of art. It is to indicate that *theories* which isolate art and its appreciation by placing them in a realm of their own, disconnected from other modes of experiencing, are not inherent in the subject-matter but arise because of specifiable extraneous conditions. Embedded as they are in institutions and in habits of life, these conditions operate effectively because they work so unconsciously. Then the theorist assumes they are embedded in the nature of things. Nevertheless, the influence of these conditions is not confined to theory. As I have already indicated, it deeply affects the practice of living, driving away esthetic perceptions that are necessary ingredients of happiness, or reducing them to the level of compensating transient pleasurable excitations.

Even to readers who are adversely inclined to what has been said, the implications of the statements that have been made may be useful in defining the nature of the problem: that of recovering the continuity of esthetic experience with normal processes of living. The understanding of art and of its rôle in civilization is not furthered by setting out with eulogies of it nor by occupying ourselves exclusively at the outset with great works of art recognized as such. The comprehension which theory essays will be arrived at by a detour; by going back to experience of the common or mill run of things to discover the esthetic quality such experience possesses. Theory can start with and from acknowledged works of art only when the esthetic is already compartmentalized, or only when works of art are set in a niche apart instead of being celebrations, recognized as such, of the things of ordinary experience. Even a crude experience, if authentically an experience, is more fit to give a clue to the intrinsic nature of esthetic experience than is an object already set apart from any other mode of experience. Following this clue we can discover how the work of art develops and accentuates what is characteristically valuable in things of everyday enjoyment. The art product will then be seen to issue from the latter, when the full meaning of ordinary experience is expressed, as dyes come out of coal tar products when they receive special treatment.

Many theories about art already exist. If there is justification for proposing yet another philosophy of the esthetic, it must be found in a new mode of approach. Combinations and permutations among existing theories can easily be brought forth by those so inclined. But, to my mind, the trouble with existing theories is that they start from a ready-made compartmentalization, or from a conception of art that "spiritualizes" it out of connection with the objects of concrete experience. The alternative, however, to such spiritualization is not a degrading and Philistinish materialization of works of fine art, but a conception that discloses the way in which these works idealize qualities found in common experience. Were works of art placed in a directly human context in popular esteem, they would have a much wider appeal than they can have when pigeon-hole theories of art win general acceptance.

A conception of fine art that sets out from its connection with discovered qualities of ordinary experience will be able to indicate the factors and forces that favor the normal development of common human activities into matters of artistic value. It will also be able to point out those conditions that arrest its normal growth. Writers on esthetic theory often raise the question of whether esthetic philosophy can aid in cultivation of esthetic appreciation.

The question is a branch of the general theory of criticism, which, it seems to me, fails to accomplish its full office if it does not indicate what to look for and what to find in concrete esthetic objects. But, in any case, it is safe to say that a philosophy of art is sterilized unless it makes us aware of the function of art in relation to other modes of experience, and unless it indicates why this function is so inadequately realized, and unless it suggests the conditions under which the office would be successfully performed.

The comparison of the emergence of works of art out of ordinary experiences to the refining of raw materials into valuable products may seem to some unworthy, if not an actual attempt to reduce works of art to the status of articles manufactured for commercial purposes. The point, however, is that no amount of ecstatic eulogy of finished works can of itself assist the understanding or the generation of such works. Flowers can be enjoyed without knowing about the interactions of soil, air, moisture, and seeds of which they are the result. But they cannot be *understood* without taking just these interactions into account—and theory is a matter of understanding. Theory is concerned with discovering the nature of the production of works of art and of their enjoyment in perception. How is it that the everyday making of things grows into that form of making which is genuinely artistic? How is it that our everyday enjoyment of scenes and situations develops into the peculiar satisfaction that attends the experience which is emphatically esthetic? These are the questions theory must answer. The answers cannot be found, unless we are willing to find the germs and roots in matters of experience that we do not currently regard as esthetic. Having discovered these active seeds, we may follow the course of their growth into the highest forms of finished and refined art.

It is a commonplace that we cannot direct, save accidentally, the growth and flowering of plants, however lovely and enjoyed, without understanding their causal conditions. It should be just a commonplace that esthetic understanding—as distinct from sheer personal enjoyment—must start with the soil, air, and light out of which things esthetically admirable arise. And these conditions are the conditions and factors that make an ordinary experience complete. The more we recognize this fact, the more we shall find ourselves faced with a problem rather than with a final solution. *If* artistic and esthetic quality is implicit in every normal experience, how shall we explain how and why it so generally fails to become explicit? Why is it that to multitudes art seems to be an importation into experience from a foreign country and the esthetic to be a synonym for something artificial?

We cannot answer these questions any more than we can trace the development of art out of everyday experience, unless we have a clear and coherent idea of what is meant when we say "normal experience." Fortunately, the road to arriving at such an idea is open and well marked. The nature of experience is determined by the essential conditions of life. While man is other than bird and beast, he shares basic vital functions with them and has to make the same basal adjustments if he is to continue the process of living. Having the same vital needs, man derives the means by which he breathes, moves, looks and listens, the very brain with which he coördinates his senses and his movements, from his animal forbears. The organs with which he maintains himself in being are not of himself alone, but by the grace of struggles and achievements of a long line of animal ancestry.

Fortunately a theory of the place of the esthetic in experience does not have to lose itself in minute details when it starts with experience in its elemental form. Broad outlines suffice. The first great consideration is that life goes on in an environment; not merely *in* it but because of it, through interaction with it. No creature lives merely under its skin; its subcutaneous organs are means of connection with what lies beyond its bodily frame, and to which, in order to live, it must adjust itself, by accommodation and defence but also by conquest. At every moment, the living creature is exposed to dangers from its surroundings, and at every moment, it must draw upon something in its surroundings to satisfy its needs. The career and destiny of a living being are bound up with its interchanges with its environment, not externally but in the most intimate way.

The growl of a dog crouching over his food, his howl in time of loss and loneliness, the wagging of his tail at the return of his human friend are expressions of the implication of a living in a natural medium which includes man along with the animal he has domesticated. Every need, say hunger for fresh air or food, is a lack that denotes at least a temporary absence of adequate adjustment with surroundings. But it is also a demand, a reaching out into the environment to make good the lack and to restore adjustment by building at least a temporary equilibrium. Life itself consists of phases in which the organism falls out of step with the march of surrounding things and then recovers unison with it—either through effort or by some happy chance. And, in a growing life, the recovery is never mere return to a prior state, for it is enriched by the state of disparity and resistance through which it has successfully passed. If the gap between organism and environment is too wide, the creature dies. If its activity is not enhanced by the temporary alienation, it merely subsists. Life grows when a temporary falling out is a transition to a more extensive balance of the energies of the organism with those of the conditions under which it lives.

These bilogical commonplaces are something more than that; they reach to the roots of the esthetic in experience. The world is full of things that are indifferent and even hostile to life; the very processes by which life is maintained tend to throw it out of gear with its surroundings. Nevertheless, if life continues and if in continuing it expands, there is an overcoming of factors of opposition and conflict; there is a transformation of them into differentiated aspects of a higher powered and more significant life. The marvel of organic, of vital, adaptation through expansion (instead of by contraction and passive accommodation) actually takes place. Here in germ are balance and harmony attained through rhythm. Equilibrium comes about not mechanically and inertly but out of, and because of, tension.

There is in nature, even below the level of life, something more than mere flux and change. Form is arrived at whenever a stable, even though moving, equilibrium is reached. Changes interlock and sustain one another. Wherever there is this coherence there is endurance. Order is not imposed from without but is made out of the relations of harmonious interactions that energies bear to one another. Because it is active (not anything static because foreign to what goes on) order itself develops. It comes to include within its balanced movement a greater variety of changes.

Order cannot but be admirable in a world constantly threatened with disorder—in a world where living creatures can go on living only by taking advantage of whatever order exists about them, incorporating it into themselves. In a world like ours, every living creature that attains sensibility welcomes order with a response of harmonious feeling whenever it finds a congruous order about it.

For only when an organism shares in the ordered relations of its environment does it secure the stability essential to living. And when the participation comes after a phase of disruption and conflict, it bears within itself the germs of a consummation akin to the esthetic.

The rhythm of loss of integration with environment and recovery of union not only persists in man but becomes conscious with him; its conditions are material out of which he forms purposes. Emotion is the conscious sign of a break, actual or impending. The discord is the occasion that induces reflection. Desire for restoration of the union converts mere emotion into interest in objects as conditions of realization of harmony. With the realization, material of reflection is incorporated into objects as their meaning. Since the artist cares in a peculiar way for the phase of experience in which union is achieved, he does not shun moments of resistance and tension. He rather cultivates them, not for their own sake but because of their potentialities, bringing to living consciousness an experience that is unified and total. In contrast with the person whose purpose is esthetic, the scientific man is interested in problems, in situations wherein tension between the matter of observation and of thought is marked. Of course he cares for their resolution. But he does not rest in it; he passes on to another problem using an attained solution only as a stepping stone from which to set on foot further inquiries.

The difference between the esthetic and the intellectual is thus one of the place where emphasis falls in the constant rhythm that marks the interaction of the live creature with his surroundings. The ultimate matter of both emphases in experience is the same, as is also their general form. The odd notion that an artist does not think and a scientific inquirer does nothing else is the result of converting a difference of tempo and emphasis into a difference in kind. The thinker has his esthetic moment when his ideas cease to be mere ideas and become the corporate meanings of objects. The artist has his problems and thinks as he works. But his thought is more immediately embodied in the object. Because of the comparative remoteness of his end, the scientific worker operates with symbols, words and mathematical signs. The artist does his thinking in the very qualitative media he works in, and the terms lie so close to the object that he is producing that they merge directly into it.

The live animal does not have to project emotions into the objects experienced. Nature is kind and hateful, bland and morose, irritating and comforting, long before she is mathematically qualified or even a congeries of "secondary" qualities like colors and their shapes. Even such words as long and short, solid and hollow, still carry to all, but those who are intellectually specialized, a moral and emotional connotation. The dictionary will inform any one who consults it that the early use of words like sweet and bitter was not to denote qualities of sense as such but to discriminate things as favorable and hostile. How could it be otherwise? Direct experience comes from nature and man interacting with each other. In this interaction, human energy gathers, is released, dammed up, frustrated and victorious. There are rhythmic beats of want and fulfillment, pulses of doing and being withheld from doing.

All interactions that effect stability and order in the whirling flux of change are rhythms. There is ebb and flow, systole and diastole: ordered change. The latter moves within bounds. To overpass the limits that are set is destruction and death, out of which, however, new rhythms are built up. The proportionate interception of changes establishes an order that is spatially, not merely temporally patterned: like the waves of the sea, the ripples of sand where waves have flowed back and forth, the fleecy and the black-bottomed cloud. Contrast of lack and fullness, of struggle and achievement, of adjustment after consummated irregularity, form the drama in which action, feeling, and meaning are one. The outcome is balance and counterbalance. These are not static nor mechanical. They express power that is intense because measured through overcoming resistance. Environing objects avail and counteravail.

There are two sorts of possible worlds in which esthetic experience would not occur. In a world of mere flux, change would not be cumulative; it would not move toward a close. Stability and rest would have no being. Equally is it true, however, that a world that is finished, ended, would have no traits of suspense and crisis, and would offer no opportunity for resolution. Where everything is already complete, there is no fulfillment. We envisage with pleasure Nirvana and a uniform heavenly bliss only because they are projected upon the background of our present world of stress and conflict. Because the actual world, that in which we live, is a combination of movement and culmination, or breaks and re-unions, the experience of a living creature is capable of esthetic quality. The live being recurrently loses and reëstablishes equilibrium with his surroundings. The moment of passage from disturbance into harmony is that of intensest life. In a finished world, sleep and waking could not be distinguished. In one wholly perturbed, conditions could not even be struggled with. In a world made after the pattern of ours, moments of fulfillment punctuate experience with rhythmically enjoyed intervals.

Inner harmony is attained only when, by some means, terms are made with the environment. When it occurs on any other than an "objective" basis, it is illusory—in extreme cases to the point of insanity. Fortunately for variety in experience, terms are made in many ways—ways ultimately decided by selective interest. Pleasures may come about through chance contact and stimulation; such pleasures are not to be despised in a world full of pain. But happiness and delight are a different sort of thing. They come to be through a fulfillment that reaches to the depths of our being—one that is an adjustment of our whole being with the conditions of existence. In the process of living, attainment of a period of equilibrium is at the same time the initiation of a new relation to the environment, one that brings with it potency of new adjustments to be made through struggle. The time of consummation is also one of beginning anew. Any attempt to perpetuate beyond its term the enjoyment attending the time of fulfillment and harmony constitutes withdrawal from the world. Hence it marks the lowering and loss of vitality. But, through the phases of perturbation and conflict, there abides the deep-seated memory of an underlying harmony, the sense of which haunts life like the sense of being founded on a rock.

Most mortals are conscious that a split often occurs between their present living and their past and future. Then the past hangs upon them as a burden; it invades the present with a sense of regret, of opportunities not used, and of consequences we wish undone. It rests upon the present as an oppression, instead of being a storehouse of resources by which to move confidently forward. But the live creature adopts its past; it can make friends with even its stupidities, using them as warnings that increase present wariness. Instead of trying to live upon whatever may have been achieved in the past, it uses past successes to inform the present. Every living experience owes its richness to what Santayana well calls "hushed reverberations."[1]

To the being fully alive, the future is not ominous but a promise; it surrounds the present as a halo. It consists of possibilities that are felt as a possession of what is now and here. In life that is truly life, everything overlaps and merges. But all too often we exist in apprehensions of what the future may bring, and are divided within ourselves. Even when not overanxious, we do not enjoy the present because we subordinate it to that which is absent. Because of the frequency of this abandonment of the present to the past and future, the happy periods of an experience that is now complete because it absorbs into itself memories of the past and anticipations of the past, come to constitute an esthetic ideal. Only when the past ceases to trouble and anticipations of the future are not perturbing is a being wholly united with his environment and therefore fully alive. Art celebrates with

---

[1] "These familiar flowers, these well-remembered bird-notes, this sky with its fitful brightness, these furrowed and grassy fields, each with a sort of personality given to it by the capricious hedge, such things as these are the mother tongue of our imagination, the language that is laden with all the subtle inextricable associations the fleeting hours of our childhood left behind them. Our delight in the sunshine on the deep-bladed grass today might be no more than the faint perception of wearied souls, if it were not for the sunshine and grass of far-off years, which still live in us and transform our perception into love." George Eliot in "The Mill on the Floss."

peculiar intensity the moments in which the past reënforces the present and in which the future is a quickening of what now is.

To grasp the sources of esthetic experience it is, therefore, necessary to have recourse to animal life below the human scale. The activities of the fox, the dog, and the thrush may at least stand as reminders and symbols of that unity of experience which we so fractionize when work is labor, and thought withdraws us from the world. The live animal is fully present, all there, in all of its actions: in its wary glances, its sharp sniffings, its abrupt cocking of ears. All senses are equally on the *qui vive*. As you watch, you see motion merging into sense and sense into motion—constituting that animal grace so hard for man to rival. What the live creature retains from the past and what it expects from the future operate as directions in the present. The dog is never pedantic nor academic; for these things arise only when the past is severed in consciousness from the present and is set up as a model to copy or a storehouse upon which to draw. The past absorbed into the present carries on; it presses forward.

There is much in the life of the savage that is sodden. But, when the savage is most alive, he is most observant of the world about him and most taut with energy. As he watches what stirs about him, he, too, is stirred. His observation is both action in preparation and foresight of the future. He is as active through his whole being when he looks and listens as when he stalks his quarry or stealthily retreats from a foe. His senses are sentinels of immediate thought and outposts of action, and not, as they so often are with us, mere pathways along which material is gathered to be stored away for a delayed and remote possibility.

It is mere ignorance that leads then to the supposition that connection of art and esthetic perception with experience signifies a lowering of their significance and dignity. Experience in the degree in which it *is* experience is heightened vitality. Instead of signifying being shut up within one's own private feelings and sensations, it signifies active and alert commerce with the world; at its height it signifies complete interpenetration of self and the world of objects and events. Instead of signifying surrender to caprice and disorder, it affords our sole demonstration of a stability that is not stagnation but is rhythmic and developing. Because experience is the fulfillment of an organism in its struggles and achievements in a world of things, it is art in germ. Even in its rudimentary forms, it contains the promise of that delightful perception which is esthetic experience.

THOMAS SPENCER JEROME

The Credibility of Testimony

THE STUDENT of Roman history is confronted at the outset by the general problem of the degree of confidence which may justly be felt regarding information based on human testimony. There have been many indeed who have gloomily questioned the extent of our knowledge of the past of human societies. Motley asserted that "the record of our race is essentially unwritten. What we call history is but made up of a few scattered fragments, while it is scarcely given to human intelligence to comprehend the great whole."[1] And Froude, with what some scholars would call his own method in mind, declared that "it often seems to me as if History was like a child's box of letters, with which we can spell any word we please. We have only to pick out such letters as we want, arrange them as we like, and say nothing about those which do not suit our purpose."[2]

The scholar is bound to weigh his evidence with the utmost care, for the testimony may be either deliberately or unconsciously falsified. It is evident, for example, that Weems, the Plutarch-like biographer of Washington, invented out of whole cloth the tale of the cherry tree, and that, being animated by the same exalted principles as his amiable Greek predecessor, his intention was not "to give information about George Washington but to suggest virtuous conduct to young Americans."[3] The president of the American Historical Association in 1909 devoted a considerable part of his annual address to certain striking cases of fraudulent evidence deliberately manufactured to support various historical theses, with results that may well produce dismay in the moralist and caution in the student. He refers to the men of the Middle Ages and Renaissance busily and joyously engaged in

---

[1] *The United Netherlands* (New York, 1868), vol. III, p. 477.
[2] J. A. Froude, *Short Studies on Great Subjects* (*The Science of History*), vol. I (New York, 1876), p. 1.
[3] A. B. Hart, *American Historical Review*, vol. XV (1910), p. 242.

fabricating books which purported to come from the ancients; to that master of imaginative historians, George Psalmanazar, who in 1704 evolved from his inner consciousness a *Historical and Geographical Description of Formosa;* to Lucas, the nineteenth century jobber in spurious letters, who palmed off on avid customers 27,000 autograph epistles, among which were those of Sir Isaac Newton, Shakespeare, Rabelais, Strabo, Plato, Lazarus, and Judas Iscariot, to Ingulf's *History of the Abbey of Croyland,* and Simonides's *History of Egypt* by Uranius; to the so-called *Letters of Montcalm,* the *Travels* of Jonathan Carver, Gordon's *History of the Revolution,* and to Buell's recent life of John Paul Jones, with its entertaining but spurious "original documents." [4]

In addition to evidence thus deliberately manufactured, there is also testimony which has been unconsciously falsified through defects of observation, imagination, and memory. For instance, in 1911 there appeared in a small English magazine, which shall remain unnamed, a description by an eyewitness of the eruption of Vesuvius in 1906. The most interesting feature of this article was that it contained, with the exception of the eruption and of the writer's presence in Capri, practically not a single correct statement of the events observed; and the defect extended to very simple matters of fact about which there ought to have been no question of interpretation. It was said, for example, that just before the eruption the volcano seemed on the point of extinction, whereas the "smoke" had been gradually increasing for three years; that the sea became too rough to permit crossing to Naples, and that for over a week no mail or news was received from the mainland. As a matter of fact, no day passed without at least one mail boat, and the weather was continuously calm. Capri, the writer of the article went on to say, was buried under the volcanic ash; "our roof and garden were covered to the depth of half a metre;" whereas the fall of ash would have been considerably overestimated if put at half an inch. And yet the article, I have reason to believe, was written by a young man whose good faith was not open to question. If the memory could thus go wrong in five years, we cannot wholly avoid the suspicion that the famous letters of Pliny the Younger, written some twenty-five or thirty years after the catastrophe which overwhelmed Pompeii, may contain elements due to a similar defective recollection.

But selected episodes, however valuable they may be as illustrations of an established proposition, possess little probative force; at most they serve to indicate merely that many false stories obtain currency—a matter of common

[4] A. B. Hart, *op. cit.,* pp. 227-251.

knowledge. What is needed for our purposes is a class of cases obtained under strict control from identical objective data, and sufficiently numerous to furnish us with averages and percentages, so that we may see, not simply that human minds are sometimes inaccurate—everyone knows that—but rather in what proportion such inaccuracies exist, and how profound they are. Such cases should also have the characteristic of relation to minds which for the time being had no motive to misstate and presumably were endeavoring to bear true testimony as to simple objective facts.

For material of this sort recourse must be taken to the researches of certain scholars, chiefly Continental, who of late years have made careful investigations into the psychology of testimony. A glance at the results obtained in a few cases will furnish some idea of the difficulties which beset a student whose material is derived from human testimony.

One of the simplest experiments was that carried out by M. Binet with children.[5] A new reddish-brown French two centimes stamp together with some other simple objects—we confine our attention to the stamp—was pasted on a piece of cardboard and shown to twenty-four children for a space of twelve seconds, and they were then separately interrogated about what had been exhibited. Four questions were asked about the stamp. All but three of the children said it was a French and not a foreign stamp. Only nine, however, stated its color correctly, although either red or brown was taken as a correct answer. The false answers were with one exception given positively. The blue of the fifteen centimes stamp was perhaps most familiar to the children, and six of them declared this stamp was blue; three said green; four said rose, and even white had its witness. Nine out of the twenty-four gave the correct denomination of the stamp, which was plainly marked on it. There was noticed a correlation between mistakes of color and of denomination. Thirteen answered correctly that the stamp was an unused one. One intelligent boy declared it was a used stamp; and being asked how he had reached this opinion, said that he saw that the gum had been removed; yet the stamp was pasted upon a card. Four asserted positively that it had been used, alleging that they were able to see distinctly the cancelling stamp, and they described its location. One of the

---

[5] *L'Année Psychologique,* vol. XII (1906), p. 161ff; XI (1905), p. 128ff. Dr. Gross, after a careful examination of the subject, reached the conclusion that a healthy child, at least a boy, is one of the best witnesses to simple events, and that the errors of children, while different from those of adults, are neither more gross nor more frequent than those of their elders. See H. Gross, *Zur Frage der Zeugenaussage, Archiv für Kriminal-Anthropologie und Kriminalistik,* vol. XXXVI (1910), pp. 372-382.

older pupils even saw the letters "RIS"—the last letters of the word Paris—in the cancelling mark. The experimenter calls attention to the precision of these false memories as showing that a very positive statement given without the least hesitation can be entirely false. So also the descriptions were generally exact on one point and false on another: few were erroneous in all particulars. When experiments of this sort were carried on by means of leading questions, the percentage of errors was much greater, and similar results were obtained with students from sixteen to nineteen years of age. Where a written description of an object seen was required, only one-sixth of the observers made no mistakes. It was abundantly shown in all these cases that positiveness on the part of the witness and presence of detail in his answers gave no assurances whatever of their correctness.

One of Stern's tests was slightly more complicated.[6] He had three simple pictures in black and white, which he exhibited for forty-five seconds each to about thirty cultivated adults who immediately wrote down what they had seen in each picture, and thereafter at certain intervals of time again submitted written statements. Such parts of their depositions as they were willing to take oath upon were indicated by underlining. Without going into details, it may be said that the results were not of a nature calculated to give one great confidence in the value of testimony. Error was not the exception, but the rule. Out of two hundred and eighty-two depositions only seventeen were entirely correct; and of these seventeen, fifteen were among the statements written down immediately. By the fifth day even, the proportion of misstatements reached about a quarter of all the details submitted. In the depositions containing indications of matters on which the observer was willing to take an oath, only thirteen out of sixty-three failed to contain false statements, to all of which however the witnesses were prepared to swear. Many of these were cases of the introduction of elements which were absolutely absent from the picture. So one student wrote three weeks after the event: "The picture shows an old man seated on a wooden bench. A small boy is standing at his left. *He is looking at the old man who is feeding a pigeon. On the roof is perched another pigeon which is preparing to fly to the ground to get its share of the food.*" The italicized statements were wholly incorrect: there were no pigeons in the picture. Perhaps the figure of a cat in the scene may have suggested the idea of a bird to the observer. In this, as in other cases, the testimony of women revealed more, but less exact, remembrance than that of men.

[6] Compare *L'Année Psychologique*, vol. XII (1906), p. 168ff.

A third class of experiments is that of a representation before spectators who do not suspect the fictitious character of the scene, of a short but striking event carefully prepared beforehand. For instance, at a Psychological Congress at Göttingen before witnesses who were psychologists, jurists, and physicians, and therefore presumably more skilled in observation and statement than ordinary persons, the following carefully prepared experiment was tried:

"Not far from the hall of meeting of the Congress, a public festival and masquerade ball were in progress. Suddenly the door of the hall opened and a clown rushed madly in, pursued by a negro with a revolver in his hand. They stopped in the middle of the hall, reviled one another; the clown fell, the negro leaped upon him, fired, and then suddenly both ran out of the room. The whole affair had lasted barely twenty seconds. The presiding officer requested the members present to write out, severally, statements of the affair, since doubtless there would be a judicial investigation. Forty reports were made out. Only one had less than twenty per cent of errors, fourteen had from twenty to forty per cent of errors, twelve from forty to fifty per cent, and thirteen more than fifty per cent. Furthermore, in twenty-four reports, ten per cent of the details were pure inventions, and the proportion of inventions surpassed that figure in ten other reports.... It goes without saying that the entire scene had been arranged and even photographed in advance. The ten false reports are then to be put in the category of fables and legends, the twenty-four are semi-legendary, and six only can be regarded as having approximately the value of exact testimony. But with an ordinary public, the proportions are different, and one may estimate the percentage of pure inventions at fifty per cent at least." [7]

It will appear from these and similar experiments that erroneous testimony was given in simple matters of direct, personal observation by witnesses who were not influenced by any conscious preëxisting emotion or prepossession, and who were actuated by a desire to give an exact and truthful narrative. Yet the results were not encouraging. It is evident, as scholars who have conducted or studied such experiments have shown, that good faith, the desire to tell the truth, and the certainty that the testimony is true, as well as the opportunity to secure correct information, and the absence of prepossessions, are far from affording adequate guarantees that the truth will be told. The most honest witness may misstate; the worst may tell the truth. Entirely faithful testimony is not the rule but rather a rare exception. If such

[7] A. van Gennep, *La Formation des Légendes* (Paris, 1910), pp. 158-159.

then are the distortions which appear in testimony when there is a desire to give a precise and accurate narrative, we cannot be surprised at any result where the feelings are less scientific in character, as is the case with most of Roman historical material.

The fact is that the human mind considered as an instrument for the attainment and enunciation of correct knowledge of the external world leaves much to be desired. The average mind remains essentially primitive. And inasmuch as most of our historical information regarding the later Republic and the early Empire has come down to us through several minds and presumably been affected in the process, it is worth while, before scrutinizing the evidence in detail, to gain some general idea of the defects of the agents whereby the evidence has been transmitted.

In the first place we are forced to recognize the fact that in their general mental characteristics, most people are and always have been not very far removed from their earliest ancestors.[8] Sir Henry Maine declares that even after the ages of change which separate the civilized man from the savage or barbarian, the difference between them is not so great as the vulgar opinion would have it. There is much of the savage in our contemporaries. Many occupations, pursuits, and tastes are common to them and their primitive ancestors. "Like the savage, the Englishman, Frenchman, or American makes war; like the savage, he hunts; like the savage, he dances; like the savage he indulges in endless deliberation; like the savage, he sets an extravagant value on rhetoric; like the savage, he is a man of party, with a newspaper for a totem, instead of a mark on his forehead or arm; and, like a savage, he is apt to make of his totem, his God."[9]

All this will appear perfectly natural if it be remembered that biologically speaking the mental attainments of one generation do not pass on to the next by inheritance. Each infant comes into the world quite as ignorant as every other of his contemporaries, or of his predecessors. What we ordinarily call his education is mainly devoted to teaching him a few things received by him on authority—many of them far from true—and to giving him some ability to read and write so that he may come in touch with other minds, most of which are not more advanced than his own. An ocean of knowledge lies before him, but it is bitter to his taste. The necessities of remunerative employment force him to learn more or less, sometimes a good deal, about

---

[8] See review of L. Lévy-Bruhl, *Les fonctions mentales dans les sociétés inférieures* (Paris, 1910), in *Revue Philosophique*, vol. LXX (1910), pp. 279-291.

[9] Sir Henry Maine, *Popular Government* (New York, 1886), p. 144.

some one limited field of human achievement. If it be farming, he may come to know the succession, coördination, and inevitability of a certain class of natural phenomena; he knows that he must sow to reap. But when he gets away from his farm, the first confidence man can persuade him that he can reap in some unfamiliar field without sowing.

It is necessary, then, to examine the nature of this common mind, which has shown itself *semper ubique et ab omnibus idem,* in order to ascertain in what ways it is an imperfectly and inaccurately functioning machine, and how these imperfections and inaccuracies manifest themselves in matters which are of special concern to students of history.

The unity of the human mind renders all schemes of classification of psychological phenomena particularly misleading. As a matter of mere convenience in orderly exposition, we may find it possible to distinguish difficulties in obtaining truthful and accurate evidence into those arising out of:

(1) The general inherent imperfections in the thinking mechanism. (2) The effects of the general principle apparent in all manifestations of force, which may be called "the law of least effort." The forms assumed by this principle bear different names as it is related to different sorts of dynamics; in human action it is often termed indolence.[10] (3) The controlling influence of the primary organic and effective life of the organism on the secondary and derivative activities of thought, belief, and expression.

In an analytical treatise, in which mental phenomena could be viewed at some particular angle, split up into their elements, and segregated, such a classification might answer; but we are dealing with actual, complex manifestations resulting in most cases from these three causes acting together in various combinations. Consequently a less neat division is preferable. Starting, then, from the proposition that there is an effective element in all thinking, we may first examine those mental imperfections which may coexist with any sort of desire or feeling, and hence may impair testimony even when there is a wish and intention to give a simple, straightforward, and truthful narrative; and secondly, the conscious or subconscious perturbations caused by a desire on the part of the narrator to please, annoy, persuade, or otherwise affect the auditor in a way not calculated to give him correct and complete information.

The mental imperfections referred to under the first head may be sepa-

---

[10] Compare Th. Ribot, *Le Moindre Effort en Psychologie,* in *Revue Philosophique,* vol. LXX (1910), pp. 361-386; *ibid.,* LXXI (1911), pp. 164-167; Sir Leslie Stephen, *An Agnostic's Apology,* p. 324.

rated, to some extent, into those inherent in the mechanism and those due to its defective operation under "the law of least effort," although no sharp line of demarcation is possible between the two. In considering the perturbation caused by a desire to affect the auditor in a special, but improper, way, we shall have occasion to observe the power of the feelings to produce not only mendacious assertions but also honest, although erroneous, beliefs supporting the dominant sentiment; beliefs which give rise to judgments of fact probative of the beliefs and justificatory of the primary, emotional state.

Viewed in a general way, the main and perhaps the only function played by the neural and cerebral organism is to put man in touch with his environment as a basis for adaptive reactions on his part. The various forms of activity of the nerves and brain are parts of the mechanism by which this end is accomplished. This function, the last human power to be developed in evolution and the first to disappear in involution may be termed "the function of the real," which "consists in the apprehension of reality in all its forms," in that "attention to the present life, of which M. Bergson speaks in a metaphysical work which often seems to foresee the results of psychological observations."[11]

In its simplest form the matter may be stated thus: the physiological process which is expressed on the psychological side as a thought or an idea may be initiated by a stimulus coming either from the organs of sense directly or by revivals in memory, or originating in some other brain cell; as if, let us say, a bell had several bell-pulls attached to it. In case of a complete mistake as to the source of the stimulus, the result is an hallucination. The well-developed mind is able to discriminate promptly and surely as to the source, but in a primitive mind this power is very feeble. A child up to about his seventh year at least does not clearly distinguish between the real and the imaginary.[12] He may in play begin by pretending that a well-known skin before the fireplace is a bear, and suddenly become frightened by the purely imaginary qualities which he has just given it. A savage constructs a fetich in much the same way. A metaphysician hypostasizes concepts, until the Platonic Idea of Chair seems to become more real to him than the chair in which he sits. In sleep it is not the emotions, the memory, the imagination, or the reasoning that ceases activity, but it is the synthetic function of the

---

[11] P. Janet, *Les Obsessions et la Psychasthénie* (Paris, 1908), vol. I, p. 477. The reference to Bergson is *Matière et Mémoire* (Paris, 1896), p. 190. See further Janet, *op. cit.*, vol. I, p. 443ff; 470ff; II, p. 29ff; 461.

[12] See *Revue Philosophique*, vol. LXVII (1909), p. 658.

real. In those suffering from psychopathies, the most characteristic symptom is that their feelings, thoughts, and acts become unrelated to reality.

The most difficult mental synthesis to make, that requiring what has been called the "highest mental tension," and possessing the greatest richness of content of thought, is a *real* situation. Imagining or reasoning about unreal things is far simpler: it is easier, as M. Bergson has remarked, to read a novel than a history. Utopian dreams and idealistic speculations are well within the powers of a psychasthenic, even of a lunatic: it is only the fully developed man, however, who can grasp the world as it is, and because he can, dares grasp it. But minds of even fair general precision are instruments which few possess, and one who cannot see things as they are, cannot, *a fortiori,* narrate them as they are.

It is not to be supposed that a fundamental human characteristic like the "function of the real" has been reserved for modern scholars to discover. The ability of a living organism to make a wide and accurate synthesis of the facts of its environment, correctly perceived and remembered and put into proper relation with one another, and then to react upon it in such a way as to promote the welfare of the organism, is nothing more than sound common sense. In civil or military affairs we call it a genius for statesmanship or generalship; in biology we know it is the power of adaptation; in historiography it means clear vision, critical acumen, fearless independence and complete veracity.

The basis of all right knowledge about anything is accuracy and completeness of observation. A highly developed power of ratiocination, if not based on precise and correct data, is simply an additional cause of error, since it is more misleading to take the wrong path and follow it rigorously than to keep on making errors which may, and sometimes do, cancel one another, and eventually bring one out into the right path. But precision and accuracy require a mental effort which fatigues and pains one unaccustomed to it. "It is," as Spencer says, "impossible to get accuracy from undeveloped minds; and undeveloped minds dislike prescribed ways of obtaining accuracy. Cooks hate weights and scales—prefer handfuls and pinches; and consider it an imputation on their skill if you suggest that definite measures would be better. There are uneducated men who trust their own sensations rather than the scale of a thermometer—will even sometimes say that the thermometer is wrong, because it does not agree with their sensations. The like holds with language. You cannot get uncultivated people, or indeed the great mass of people called cultivated, to tell you neither more nor less than the fact. Always they either overstate or understate, and regard criticism or qualification of their strong words as rude or perverse." [13]

These qualities of vagueness and inaccuracy are painfully frequent in most of our authorities.[14] Polybius and Livy present rather full statements regarding Hannibal's route across the Alps, but it is impossible to identify with any certainty the pass which was actually used; and nearly all ancient geographical information is equally unsatisfactory. The Romans had available a great mass of statistical material in their census lists, but with rare exceptions they carefully kept away from it when they wrote books. Cassius Dio seems to apologize for making an exact statement of an important date, as if precision were a blemish.[15] We should never suspect from literary sources that much of the agricultural land of Italy was cut up into small holdings, as the inscriptions indicate; while the sources from which we endeavor to solve questions of population, commerce, or finance seem to be perversely deficient in breadth, depth, and precision. A great part of our material bears about the same relation to fact as do old maps or plans to the real topography, or old prints to the landscape which they purport to represent.[16]

These are some of the difficulties in the way of obtaining trustworthy reports from the promptly written narratives of eye-witnesses; but only a very small part of our historical material was set down forthwith from personal observation. Even when participants in events composed descriptions of them, it was frequently after the lapse of many years, and, as the experiments described have shown, testimony rapidly becomes more defective with the passing of time.

For memory, as is well known, is a common source of error. There are extensive *lacunæ* in it which are filled in by subconscious imagination. "We meet with a blank or a chaos in traversing the particular field of remembrance from which the events have lapsed; but this will often be filled with some conjectured events which rapidly become attached to the adjacent parts, and form, in conjunction with them, a consolidated but fallacious fragment in memory;" or it "may be that the edges of the *lacunæ* close up—events

---

[13] Herbert Spencer, *The Principles of Psychology*, section 416, Appleton edition (New York, vol. II, 1910), p. 388.

[14] See Langlois et Seignobos, *Introduction aux Études Historiques*, pp. 48ff; 102ff.

[15] Cassius Dio, LI, 1.

[16] Compare James Thomson Shotwell, article *History* in *Encyclopædia Britannica*, 11th edition, vol. XIII, p. 532.

originally separated by a considerable interval are now *remembered* vividly in immediate juxtaposition, and there is no trace of the piecing." [17] If one has wide general intelligence and sound common sense, and if the subject matter is familiar, this completion and reconstruction of the memory may be done with substantial accuracy; but otherwise it is not so. In any case, the reconstruction is purposive and selective.

Another significant factor in impairing the validity of testimony is that of language. The failure on the part of a writer to interpret correctly events of another age and sometimes of another *milieu,* frequently rests upon the imprecision of language. Words often change their meaning with the lapse of years, and expressions which are figurative or symbolic may mislead the commentator of a later day.[18] It is evident that later writers on religion went astray in their interpretations of earlier religious thought,[19] and it is probable that in the controversy between Gaius and the Jews each party misinterpreted the other's language.[20] We should know more than we do now about the Roman census, if we were quite sure of the exact meaning of such expressions as *capite censi*. Beloch, indeed, bases his discussion of the population of ancient Italy on the theory that the phrase *civium capita* quite changed its meaning between the years 70 and 28 B.C.[21] Ferrero has pointed out that what a Roman writer calls corruption, we generally call progress.[22] Again, had the word *tyrant* possessed a distinct and unchanging significance, certain pages of ancient history would have been less misunderstood. Language, indeed, often obscures rather than elucidates the facts lying back of it; for, as Hobbes says: "words are wise men's counters, they do but reckon by them: but they are the mony of fooles." [23]

The credulous acceptance of statements made by others, due to a tendency to shirk mental effort, is another serious defect in many historical sources. Livy, for example, frequently accepted on authority of the older annalists statements which he could easily have corrected by consulting official documents extant in his day. Especially slavish is such credulity when the state-

---

[17] Dr. R. Hodgson quoted by F. Podmore, *Studies in Psychical Research* (London, 1897), p. 99.

[18] See E. B. Tylor, *Primitive Culture,* vol. II (5th edit., London, 1913), p. 445ff; Langlois et Seignobos, *op. cit.,* pp. 122ff., 190, 230; Le Bon, *Les Opinions et les Croyances* (Paris, 1911), p. 145ff.

[19] See below, p. 167.

[20] See below, p. 417.

[21] J. Beloch, *Die Bevölkerung der griechisch-römischen Welt* (Leipzig, 1886), p. 374ff.

[22] Ferrero, *Characters and Events in Roman History,* pp. 3-35.

[23] T. Hobbes, *Leviathan,* I, 4.

ment reported harmonizes with one's emotional prepossessions. One readily accepts scandal about a person whom one dislikes.[24] But credulity does not stop at accepting statements of fact. The "law of least effort" leads most men to avoid all mental exercise necessary to form an opinion about any matter, and to accept *in toto* the statements of others in regard to beliefs and judgments. To the mind of a primitive type every mental presentation, whether of internal or external origin, appears to be true unless the mind is already possessed by some contradictory idea. Where the contradiction between two ideas cannot be ignored, it is explained by some fanciful theory, such as a metamorphosis. It is so much easier to admit than to deny, for the act of criticism essential to denial involves an effort. Many shirk this effort to such an extent that a bold assertion often prevails in the face of its obvious absurdity, even in the face of clear evidence of the senses. In its extreme form, this process leads to hypnosis.

So feeble was the critical spirit in Roman times, so relatively unimportant was it to many of our authorities whether a thing was true or not, so little interested were they in independent, scientific research, that unmitigated credulity as to the most incredible assertions was their commonest as well as perhaps their most blighting defect. What exacerbates the situation is the fact that they seldom mention their sources, or even indicate that they have any. As a result, we are left quite uncertain whether the writer from whom a statement is derived was capable of affording honest information.

The foregoing are some of the difficulties which beset the mind in the correct ascertainment of facts; but there are further difficulties to be encountered before a truthful narrative emerges. The mind is not a phonograph which repeats in testimony what it takes in from the senses; and in the manipulation and transformation which experience undergoes before it reappears in evidence, there participates a whole brood of sophistries and fallacies, blunders and botches of intellection, which play their part in distorting and confusing the original facts. In much of what commonly passes for reasoning there is less logic than dreaming.[25] Careful reflection and close reasoning require too much effort. Men "guess at results," said Spencer. "They will not deliberately examine premises and conclusions.... Just in proportion as their ability to reason is small, they resent any attempt to bring their conclusion, or any part of their argument, to the test."[26] The

---

[24] See Tacitus, *Histories*, I, 34: *et facilius de odio creditur*.
[25] See J. Jastrow, *The Subconscious* (Boston, 1906), p. 85.
[26] Herbert Spencer, *The Principles of Psychology*, section 416, vol. II, p. 388.

trouble with a slovenly reasoner is not primarily intellectual; it is rather volitional and affective. He does not care enough about perfecting himself to take the trouble and make the effort involved in rigorous mental processes. It is much easier to argue from extreme facts than to weigh carefully and to avoid hasty generalizations. This is a sturdy and shameless fallacy, much esteemed by controversialists, and ancient writers afford some striking instances of it. Many of them were prone to confuse judgments of facts with judgments of value, and to present what were really only expressions of personal tastes, ideals, or interests, in the guise of objective facts.[27]

We are thus led to consider the second point involved in the falsification of evidence, namely, the conscious or sub-conscious perturbations caused by the narrator's desire to affect the reader or auditor in some special way.

It is necessary to bear in mind from the outset that there is "no thinking without desire, intention, or purpose. 'The one thing that stands out,' says, for instance, Professor Dewey, is 'that thinking is inquiry, and knowledge as science is the outcome of systematically directed inquiry.' Thought absolutely undirected would be not even a dream—mere meaningless, chaotic atoms of thought. It is *the intention, the purpose,* which makes thought what it is; that is to say, significant. We think because we will. Thought does not exist for itself; it is the instrument of desire. To discover ways and means of gratifying proximate or distant desires, needs, cravings, is the function of intelligence." [28]

"Every pulse of consciousness is psychically compounded of will, feeling, and thought." No one of these elements can be absent, although at successive stages of consciousness they differ in relative intensity. "The unit of conscious life is neither thought, nor feeling, nor will, but all three in movement towards an object." [29]

Thinking, then, has for its sole function that of assisting the organism to adjust itself to the exigencies of the social or physical environment in such a way, if possible, as to bring about results agreeable to its feelings and corresponding to its desires. It is a bit of mechanism to accomplish our wishes, to gratify our sentiments, as well as may be in view of its defects.[30]

Without attempting an analytical sketch of the thinking process, we may say that after the mind has been directed to a subject, and some progress has

[27] For judgments of value, compare G. Fonsegrive, *Revue Philosophique,* vol. LXIX (1910), p. 553ff; vol. LXX (1910), p. 44ff.
[28] J. H. Leuba, *The Psychological Origin and the Nature of Religion* (London, 1909), p. 6.
[29] *Ibid.,* pp. 7, 8.
[30] See W. McDougall, *An Introduction to Social Psychology* (London, 1908), p. 44.

been made in choosing, congruent to the directing impulse, the various images, memories, and ideas that have swarmed into consciousness, a sort of auto-criticism comes into play and a judgment of the present results of thinking is made.[31] This is not primarily a judging of the results of our thinking with reference to the objective world, but with reference to the relation of the results to the initial and continuing stimulus of thinking, that is, the feeling of desire. If the result of the thinking appears to accord with the desire, and if the action based upon it seems to satisfy the feelings, the point at which most men stop thinking has been reached. But in a complete thinking out of a problem the mind necessarily takes a broader survey of the situation. The conclusion arrived at will then be developed in imagination and its projected results will be held up for comparison with two groups of things, one subjective and the other objective.

In the first place the conclusion with its probable results is scrutinized with reference to the elements of the affective and volitional life other than the particular feeling and desire which have hitherto been directing the operation; since the conclusion, while congruous to one feeling and desire, may be incongruous to others which are stronger, or to a complexus whose aggregate is stronger. It may be realized, for instance, that the conclusion arrived at by the thinking will gratify our hate but compromise our safety. In such a case the thinking process is repeated in the search for a result which will be more generally satisfactory.

But in the second place, when the mind has accumulated a stock of experiences, it has learned that the arrangement and order of thoughts do not always correspond to the arrangement and order of objective things. It is at this point that the desire of the bard to please the assembled warriors by singing of their extraordinary prowess, or of the historian to inculcate virtue by glorifying the records of his race, or of the witness in the box to save his case, leads to what may fairly be called mendacity. Indeed, so ingrained is the practice of gratifying the feeling and desire which initiate thinking that conventional fictions are apt to be less misleading than scrupulously exact statements. We may imagine the misunderstandings which would be caused by a refusal to adopt the common mendacities of polite society. In the more serious field of statecraft, Bismarck is said to have found that nothing so deceived his adversaries as to tell them the truth.

In conclusion, the matter comes down to this, that the human mind is not

[31] For a fuller discussion of this process, compare A. Binet and Th. Simon, *L'Année Psychologique*, vol. XV (1909), p. 128ff.

primarily an organ by which man determines the real objective truth of things and gives utterance to it, but is rather a tool by which one accomplishes one's desires. As this intelligence grows, man comes to know to a greater or less degree that inanimate nature, as well as the lower animals, has uniform modes of reaction, and that his desires in regard to them can be effected only by real knowledge; hence he abandons magic for science when dealing with them and tries to think clearly and accurately. But his fellow men he finds more complex problems. They can be deceived to his profit; they can be entertained by fictions to his profit; they can be coerced by threats to his profit; and in these various ways of extracting profit from them, his language will be guided by dominating principles other than a desire to give them truthful information. He finds furthermore that there are various sorts of obligations laid upon him to refrain from truth-telling under divers penalties. He is a member of a state, a church, a party, a class, a clique, a family, and in all these relations he is virtually obliged to see things as they are not, and to speak that which is false, under penalties varying from execution down to mere inarticulate unpopularity, most difficult to be borne. Acting in these various capacities he is constantly trained in juggling testimony, in judicious blindness, in expressing opinions he does not feel, in bringing his words and actions and thoughts, if possible, into conformity with something other than real facts; and all the while he sees those who are most completely and skilfully disingenuous reaping rewards, or what he has been taught to regard as such, in private and public life. Apart from certain occupations where he is brought into contact with something other than human nature, he finds little to encourage resolute veracity of thought and speech; and many forms of declension from this ideal he is taught to hold as very precious virtues—many aspects of loyalty and patriotism, or of orthodoxy, much of conventional morality, politeness, tact, *savoir faire,* and the like. He started with a cerebro-neural system which was far from perfect, and his training is usually not of a kind to lead him to struggle against its defects, or to seek after an ideal of veracity.

So when he comes to write a letter or a book which deals with his human relations, he is not only confronted with the facts which he must judge, but also with an abundance of interests, likes, dislikes, and beliefs relating to the facts. Towards his reader he is possessed by a desire to interest, entertain, to persuade, or to dissuade; and his auto-criticism is directed toward one or more of these ends rather than toward the end of giving accurate and unbiased instruction. The sentiments of those whom he is addressing are satisfied by his supporting and stimulating them, not by his putting them to confusion and forcing them to fight for their beliefs.

Enough of these perturbations arise about the threshold of consciousness, but many more lurk beneath and affect what is said and written, even when there is a desire to tell the simple truth. Fortunately, mixed up with them is a great measure of truth which, hostile to dominant prepossessions, has been thrust into the background, but which nevertheless frequently crops out to give the lie to mendacity itself. It is the problem of the historical student to identify these unconscious fidelities to fact, and to extract them from the mass of conscious or unconscious perversions, clear them up, link them together, and establish the real situation. And the first principle to be observed is that when a document from the distant past is under consideration, we have not made the first step towards its interpretation until we have recognized that although it is in a learned tongue, it is none the less a human document. Only so can we dismiss from our minds the powerful prepossession of man's childhood—a blind reverence for the written word.

EARNEST ALBERT HOOTON

Apology for Man

Introduction

Lest any one of my readers has forgotten his Greek, I remind you that *anthropos* in that language means "man" and that anthropology is, therefore, the science of man. However, after nearly a quarter of a century of study of that science, I have decided that the proper function of the anthropologist is to apologize for man. In its primary meaning an "apology" signifies a "defense or vindication from charge or aspersion." Accepting this meaning, I rise to defend our species. However, in commoner usage an apology is understood as "a frank acknowledgment, by way of reparation, of offense given" (Oxford Dictionary). In this sense, I think, the need of an apologist for man is even more urgent. Brashly, perhaps, I venture to volunteer.

To some of you, indeed, it may never have occurred that an apology in behalf of man is required; to others of you, more thoughtful, it may seem that for man no apology is possible. In point of fact, man usually either considers himself a self-made animal and consequently adores his maker, or assumes himself to be the creation of a supreme intelligence, for which the latter is alternately congratulated and blamed. An attitude of humility, abasement, contrition, and apology for its shortcomings is thoroughly uncharacteristic of the species *Homo sapiens,* except as a manifestation of religion. I am convinced that this most salutary of religious attitudes should be carried over into science. Man should confess his evolutionary deficiencies, and resolve that, in future, he will try to be a better animal.

The defensive apology which I propose to offer in behalf of man, pertains to his appearance, physique, and biological habits. But an apology ought not to be broadcast aimlessly into the circumambient ether. It ought to be offered to someone to whom it is due. I suggest that the only proper recipients of an apology for man's appearance would be the anthropoid apes, whom man sometimes claims as his nearest relatives. In the absence of such suitable auditors, I venture, without any insolent implication, to submit this defense to a probably more sympathetic assemblage—and to one which is, at any rate, more intelligent.

The second and penitential apology is offered for man's behavior—for his use of the gift of articulate speech, for his attempts to control nature, for his social habits and his systems of ethics. Such an apology cannot be a complete defense or vindication, but only an acknowledgment of wrong with the plea of certain extenuating circumstances. It is owed to man himself, to Nature, to God, and to the universe. The apology for man's physical appearance I undertake with a certain confidence; that for his behavior with full realization that it is the espousal of a lost cause.

APOLOGY FOR MAN'S PHYSIQUE

His Nakedness

If you were respectable anthropoid apes catching your first glimpse of a specimen of man, your modesty would be shocked by the spectacle of his obscene nakedness. Indeed, even to man himself it is a well-nigh insupportable sight, unless he be a savage devoid of culture, or a nudist devoid of sensibility. For here is a mammalian anomaly which lacks the customary covering of fur or hair and displays only clumps and tufts disgustingly sprouting from inappropriate areas. What strange capillary blight has afflicted this animal so as to denude his body of the hairy coat which protects the tender skin from bruises and abrasions, insulates the vital organs, and prevents too rapid loss of heat or scorching of the tissues by the actinic rays of the sun? Why has man retained abundant hair only in places where it is relatively useless—such as the brain case which is already adequately protected by a thick shell of bone, and the face where whiskers merely interfere with feeding? To cover his bodily nakedness, man has been forced to slay more fortunate animals so that he may array himself in their furs, or to weave fabrics from their shorn hair or from vegetable fibers wherewith to make inconvenient, unhygienic, and generally ridiculous garments. On the other hand, in order to get rid of the superfluous and entangling hair on his face and head, man has been driven to invent many contrivances for eradicating, cutting, and shaving. The adult male White has experimented unhappily through several millennia, trying everything from a flint flake to an electric lawn mower in order to clear his face from hirsute entanglement without flaying himself. Each morning he immolates himself for ten minutes upon the altar of evolutionary inefficiency, until, at the age of three-score-and-ten, he has paid his full tribute of some 3047 hours of suffering—physical torture, if self-inflicted; both physical and mental, if he has patronized a barber. And even this staggering total is exclusive of hair-cuts.

Probably most theories advanced to explain the vagaries of human hair growth have been evolved by scientists during their matutinal shaving periods. We may dismiss summarily the naïve supposition that parts of the body have been denuded of hair by the friction of clothing. The least amount of body hair growth is found, on the one hand, in Negroid stocks which have gone naked, presumably for at least 30,000 years, and, on the other hand, in Mongoloids, who have probably sewed themselves up for the winter during a considerable part of that period. I do not recall the origin of the suggestion that human hairlessness was evolved in the tropics to enable man to rid himself of the external parasites commonly called lice. It need be remarked only that, if such was the case, the evolutionary device has been singularly unsuccessful.

Darwin applied his vigorous mind to the task of explaining man's irregular and disharmonious hair growth by his theory of sexual selection. He supposed that nakedness of the skin could not be a direct advantage to man and therefore that his body could not have been divested of hair through natural selection. He observed that in several species of monkeys the posterior end of the body has been denuded of hair, and that these naked surfaces are brilliantly colored. It appeared to him that the hair had been removed in order more effectively to display the bright skin color and thus to attract the opposite sex. Darwin noted further that the female in man, and even, to some extent, among the anthropoid apes, is less hairy than the male, and suggested that denudation began earlier in that sex—far back in the prehuman period. He imagined that the process was completed by the incipiently hairless mothers transmitting the new characteristic to their offspring of both sexes, and exercising both for themselves and for their comparatively naked daughters a discriminatory choice of mates. The smooth-skinned suitor would be preferred to the shaggy and hirsute. Thus Darwin, like Adam, blamed it on the woman.

The great evolutionist made a rather feeble attempt to explain the excessive growth of head hair in women and of beards in men. He suggested that long hair is greatly admired, alleged that in North American Indians a chief was selected solely on account of the length of his hair, and finally fell back upon St. Paul's statement, "if a woman have long hair, it is a glory to her." He entirely suppressed the preceding verse of St. Paul's epistle which reads: "Doth not even nature itself teach you, that, if a man have long hair, it is a shame unto him?"[1] Darwin toyed with but rejected, the theory that the beard of the male serves to protect his throat in fighting, and cogently remarked that the mustache, which presumably had the same origin, could serve no such practical purpose.[2] In the end he had to resort once more to the aesthetic preference of the mating female. His assumption of the dominating role of the capricious and fastidious female, a sort of prehuman Delilah, is far from convincing. Abundant body hair in the male is traditionally and probably physiologically associated with an excess of strength and virility, and the prehuman female probably liked her man hairy. In any case, zoölogical studies of the habits of contemporary subhuman primates indicate in no indecisive fashion that the female is not asked, but taken; that she is passive, acquiescent, and devoid of aesthetic perception. She does not choose, but only stands and waits. Darwin might have done better with his subject if he himself had formed the habit of shaving. Perhaps he had built up a defense around an inferiority complex with respect to his beard.

Recent students have ascribed more importance to nutrition and glandular functioning in explaining human hair growth than to the romantic theory of sexual selection. Thus Sir Arthur Keith has pointed out that the human baby is not only less hairy than the anthropoid baby, but also considerably more plump. The secretions of the thyroid gland probably affect both the nourishment of the skin and the hair. If man's ancestors at an early time obtained command of an adequate food supply, hairlessness might have been one of the first effects of incipient human culture.[3] As man waxed fat his hairiness waned. The layer of subcutaneous fat would discourage the growth of the hair follicles and take over the insulating function of the hairy coat.

There are other theories to account for this deplorably glabrous condition of man, but none which would satisfy a critical anthropoid ape. Chivalry, as well as common sense, dictates a rejection of the blame-it-on-your-wife theory. I adhere rather to the supposition that we have retained a foetal condition,

---

[1] Darwin, Charles, *The Descent of Man*, Part III, Chapter XX, pp. 915-922, especially p. 921. Cf. St. Paul, I Corinthians, 11, 14-15.

[2] Darwin, *op. cit.*, p. 811.

[3] Keith, Arthur, *The Human Body*, p. 205, London, 1912.

normal in the third month of pre-natal development, and, on the whole, disadvantageous, but correlated with other persistent foetal features which have a positive survival value. Thus we stand naked, and not unashamed, but claiming that we have done our best to remedy a situation which is not of our making.

His Body Build and Posture

The second aspect of man which would revolt the gazing anthropoid is the monstrous elongation of his legs, his deformed feet with their misshapen and useless toes, his feeble and abbreviated arms, and his extraordinary posture and gait. Beginning with the juncture of the lower limbs and trunk and avoiding indelicate details, a scrutinizing anthropoid would comment unfavorably upon the excessive protrusion of the human buttocks. He would judge the architecture of man's rear elevation to be inept, bizarre, and rococo. The anthropoid gaze, hastily lowered to the thighs, would be further offended by monstrous bulges of muscle, knobby knee-pans, razor-crested shin bones, insufficiently covered in front and unduly padded behind, heels projecting like hammers, humped insteps, terminating in vestigial digits—a gross spatulate great toe, devoid of grasping power; lesser toes, successively smaller and more misshapen until the acme of degeneracy is reached in the little toe, a sort of external vermiform appendix.

Planting these mutilated slabs flat upon the ground, man advances upon his grotesque hind legs, protruding his thorax, his belly, and those organs which in quadrupeds are modestly suspended beneath a concealing body bulk. This coarse and inelegant description could hardly shock the most refined of my readers as painfully as the reality shocks an anthropoid ape. Let us endeavor, for once, to see ourselves as other primates see us.

It now devolves upon me to attempt a defense of these human deviations from the norm of mammalian posture and proportions. The ancestors of man and of the gorilla, chimpanzee, and orang-utan probably started "from scratch" as generalized apes at least as far back as the Upper Miocene Period, perhaps seven million years ago. They were already giant primates, perhaps as large as they are today, and all were mainly tree-dwellers who progressed from bough to bough, principally by a method of arm-swinging which is called brachiation. Their food was largely plant products, mostly plucked in the trees, but partly collected on the ground, to which they frequently ventured. Their arms were somewhat elongated and over-developed by their method of locomotion, but not to the exaggerated extent characteristic of the modern orang-utan. Their legs were comparatively short and weak, equipped with mobile, grasping feet, in which the great toes were separated from the long outer digits by a wide interval, so that the former could be opposed to the latter—a movement essential for encircling a bough. When on the ground, these generalized anthropoids moved on all fours, supporting themselves on the knuckles of the fingers and upon the outer borders of their half-clenched, loose-jointed feet. This quadrupedal progression was awkward and slow. Occasionally they reared up and tottered a few paces on their hind legs. They were more "at home" in the trees.

At this critical juncture of prehuman and anthropoid affairs, man's forebears seem to have abandoned arboreal life and taken to the ground. I diverge from orthodox anthropological opinion in crediting this epochal event to their superior intelligence and initiative rather than to some environmental accident, such as a deforestation of the ancestral abode. Tree-dwelling is advantageous and safe only for small and agile animals. Gravitation and the inadequacy of an arboreal diet joined forces with an innate capacity for grasping environmental opportunities to urge the adventurers to seek a more abundant livelihood on the ground. The bodily adaptations which followed this radical change can be inferred with some certainty.

In the first place, the newly terrestrial proto-humans were confronted with two alternatives of posture and gait: either to go down on all fours like baboons, or to attempt an erect stance and method of progression on the precarious support of their hind limbs. The former was by all odds the easier and the more natural, since it offered greater possibilities of speed and stability. But it sentenced its user to the fate of an earth-bound quadruped, nosing through life with all four extremities devoted to support and locomotion. Bipedal gait and upright posture, on the contrary, provided the inestimable advantages of increased stature, the ability to see wider horizons, and of an emancipated pair of prehensile limbs wherewith to explore, to contrive weapons and tools, to gather food and to convey it to the mouth. Here, forsooth, the ape with human destiny was at the very cross-roads of evolution, and he took the right turning. He chose the difficult path which led upward toward humanity.

Now almost all of man's anomalies of gait and proportion were necessitated by that supremely intelligent choice. The quadruped had to be remade, by dint of all sorts of organic shifts and compromises. The axis of the trunk had to be shifted from the horizontal to the vertical—a result effected by a sharp bending forward of the spine in the lumbar region, between the ribcage and the bony pelvic girdle. The pelvis itself underwent a process of flattening, increase in width, tilting, and other changes necessary to adapt it for the transmission of the entire weight of the body to the legs and for the extension and shift of the muscular attachments essential for the balanced erect posture. The whole lower limb became enormously hypertrophied and elongated in response to its amplified function; more leverage was necessary for speed and for support; a complete straightening or extension of the legs upon the thighs was indispensable to a standing posture which should bring their vertical axes into line with the axis of the head and trunk.

However, the most profound modifications were effected in the foot, at that time a loose-jointed prehensile member, with a great toe stuck out like a thumb, long recurving outer digits, little development of the heel, and a flat instep. The great toe was brought into line with the long axis of the foot, so that it was directed forward rather than inward; the lesser toes, no longer needed for grasping, began to shrink; the loose, mobile bones of the instep (tarsus) were consolidated into a strong but elastic vault, capable of resisting the shocks and stresses of weight-bearing; the heel was enlarged and extended backward to afford more leverage for the great calf muscles which lift the body weight in walking. Thus a mobile, prehensile foot was transformed into a stable supporting organ, beautifully adapted for its new but restricted function. If it looks awkward and carries a few vestigial and useless parts left over from its inheritance, it is nevertheless much more serviceable than in its unmodified ancestral form. One needs only to look at an anthropoid ape on the ground to realize that the prehensile foot is an inadequate support for an erect biped.

Further, the seemingly grotesque abbreviation of man's arms becomes intelligible if one considers the disadvantages which would attend upon elongated, trailing arms for an animal with upright stance and bipedal gait. The creature would be in continual danger of stepping on his own fingers, and, in order to feed himself or to perform other and more skilled manual movements, would be forced to move the segments of his upper extremity through vast arcs, slowly and awkwardly because of the length of the levers, and with considerable waste of space on account of excessive wing spread. Lifting your hand to scratch your nose would involve a major gymnastic effort. Taking it all in all, man's present posture and bodily proportions are by no means the sorry result of trying to make the best of a bad business, but rather the supremely successful end product of the reconstruction of a thoroughly obsolete mechanism. This series of adaptations may be credited to natural selection's brilliant choice of the fittest variations of an animal which was forever trying to increase his own efficiency.

Of course, if this defense of human posture and proportions seems inadequate, there are other explanations. J. R. de la H. Marett attributes these human anomalies to mineral deficiency in certain early simians. It seems that in the Miocene Period the inland area of the Eurasiatic continent suffered a progressive desiccation. The trees disappeared and the able-bodied, progressive, arboreal anthropoids followed the migrating forests into the well-watered tropics. There remained, crawling in the grass, or shuffling through the sand, the weaker sisters. These inferior apes became adapted and survived by utilizing the surplus of calcium in the arid, alkaline soils. The cartilages at the ends of their long bones grew, thus providing more material to be calcified. Since their arms had already undergone a process of shrinkage, owing to the lack of boughs from which to suspend the body weight, the calcium deposition and growth were concentrated in the lower extremity. Hence the arms lagged and the legs grew enormously, involving the perplexed prehumans in a postural dilemma. They had their choice of progressing in a pyramidal, quadrupedal posture, with the nose barely off the ground and what ought to be the base of the trunk elevated toward the inhospitable skies, or of attempting to balance upon their hypertrophied hind legs and to wabble through life on an unstable and shifting base of support. Owing to certain difficulties with the law of gravity encountered in depressing the intaking end of the digestive tract below the outgoing, these creatures stood up, thereby exposing a vast area of vulnerable front to a hostile world. We need not accept this theory of the evolution of human posture through mineral deficiency, but the revelation of anatomical difficulties encountered cannot fail to evoke the sympathetic understanding of our anthropoid ape critics.

His Face and Teeth, His Brain

Doubtless, to the superior anthropoid ape, man's most unsightly deformity would be his head. Wherefore the swollen brain-case, and the dwarfed face, receding beneath bulging brows, with a fleshy excrescence protruded in the middle, and with degenerative hairy growths pendent from feeble jowls? What of the charnelhouse exposed when man opens his mouth—the inadequately whitened sepulchre of a decaying dentition?

Plausible, if somewhat rationalized, explanations of the course of evolution of the primate brain have been offered by the late Sir Grafton Elliot Smith and by Professor F. Wood Jones. The lowliest and most primitive animals of the Primate Order (which includes lemurs, tarsiers, monkeys, apes, and man) possessed potentialities of brain development far in excess of those of other mammals. Primates are inherently "brainy." The impetus toward brain growth in the early and simple forms of primates was furnished by the utilization of their natural organic equipment in the favoring arboreal environment. Tree life put a premium upon the development of the visual sense in preference to the more primitive senses of smell and hearing. It encouraged agility, balance, and muscular co-ordination. However, no great evolutionary advance would have resulted from these stimuli had not the primates been possessed of sensitive, grasping hands and feet—each with five digits terminating in flat nails instead of claws, and with great toes and thumbs capable of rotation so that they could be opposed to the outer digits. This movement of opposition, originating in the encircling grasp of boughs, is the essential prerequisite for every skilled manual act. It enables that ultimate primate, man, to fabricate tools and thus to achieve a material culture which is his unique possession. The early primates were diminutive, long-snouted, small-brained creatures which ran along the boughs on all fours, feeding on every edible which their tree abodes offered. The first step toward higher evolution occurred when some of the more progressive forms, called tarsiers, began to sit up in the trees, thus specializing their hind limbs for support, and what is infinitely more important, releasing from the duty of support and locomotion the upper pair of prehensile limbs. These, equipped with their pentadactyl hands, could be used for plucking food, conveying it to the mouth, bringing objects before the eyes for examination, and for general tactile exploration of the animal's own body and of everything else within reach.

Now, it is a well known biological principle that the greater the demands put upon an organ, the larger it becomes. The movements of the hands are controlled by motor areas in the nervous covering of the forebrain. These areas expand in response to increasing use and complexity of the movements of the members which they direct. Greater use of the brain demands a larger blood supply, which in turn promotes growth. By tactile exploration and visual examination there grow up, adjacent to the respective motor areas in the cortical surface of the brain, areas which picture the movements of the parts concerned, so that the animal is enabled to visualize actions which are to be carried out and to recall those which have been performed. Further elaborations of the neopallium, or new nervous cortex which mantles the brain, probably provide for association areas, in which, according to Wood Jones, the impressions from different receptive centers are blended, and the memories and experiences derived from the several senses are formed, sorted, and stored.[4] In short, this functional theory of the evolution of the primate brain assumes a sort of physiological perpetual motion, in which emancipated hands continually call for more nervous area in the brain to govern their increasing movements and to store up their multiplying impressions, while the expanding and active brain, on its part, devises ever more mischief still for idle hands to do.

But what of our shrunken face, the remnant of a once projecting mammalian snout? Here again the brain functionalists offer a seductive explanation. The elongate muzzle of the lower animals subserves a triple purpose. It provides the structural setting of the apparatus of mastication; by its extreme forward extension it allows the grazing animal to bite off food whilst the eyes, set well back, are still enabled to see what is eaten and to view the landscape o'er for potential enemies. Finally, the snout terminates in the nose, which is not only a sensitive tactile organ in quadrupeds, but also is the principal receptor of the olfactory sense, which, in the selection of food and in the detection of enemies, is the paramount sensory asset—far more important than vision.

Now the emancipation of the prehensile forelimbs from the duties of support and locomotion permits them to be used for hand-feeding, thus relieving the snout of its grazing function. Again, the hands not only pluck the food, but begin to use sticks and stones as weapons, and ultimately, as tools. The free use of the hands and fists deprives the jaws of yet another function— that of defense and offense. Generally in primates, great tusk-like canine teeth at the anterior corners of the jaws serve the double duty of fighting appurtenances and blades for shearing through the tough rinds of fruits and through vegetable fibers.

Just as increased function of a bodily part results in its development, so diminished use causes shrinkage. Consequently, the new utilization of the liberated hands results in a recession of the jaws. The dental arches grow smaller; the projecting canine teeth are reduced to the level of their fellows; the outthrust facial skeleton is bent down below the expanding brain-case; the nose, still a respiratory organ and the seat of the sense of smell, is left—a forlorn fleshy promontory overhanging the reduced mouth cavity. To put it concisely, the brain has expanded because greater and greater demands have

[4] Jones F. Wood, *Arboreal Man*, p. 191. London, 1916.

been made upon it, and the jaws have shrunk because the majority of their functions have been taken over by the hands and the extra-organic objects used as implements.

Of course, an anthropoid ape with an orthodox biological training might reject the foregoing explanation on the ground that it reeks of Lamarckianism—a wish-fulfillment interpretation of evolution which commands little support nowadays. Such doubting Thomases may regard as futile man's attempt to correlate with superior intelligence that vast malignancy which surmounts his spinal cord. For these there remains the endocrine theory of J. R. Marett, who points out that iodine deficiency, arising from life in the arid plains, is often associated with a waterlogging of the body tissues and cranial expansion, due not to increase of gray matter, but to water on the brain or hydrocephaly. It may be interpreted in part as an effort of an overworked and goiterous thyroid gland to counteract bodily acidity—in short, "to alkalize." If indeed remote inland humanoids suffered from hydrocephaly, subsequent increases in actual brain mass may then be due merely to nature's abhorrence of a vacuum—a compensatory growth designed to fill the space left empty by the receding flood of cerebro-spinal fluid, and in no way related to cerebration. However, I am inclined to regard unfavorably this morbid theory of human evolution. I doubt that disease has kicked an inadequate ape upstairs to humanity. Our huge brains, however little utilized at present, are, at least in part, an ancestral achievement, and our flat faces measure our recession from the brute beast.

APOLOGY FOR MAN'S BEHAVIOR

For at least 30,000 years, and quite probably for thrice that period of time, man has existed at his modern anatomical status, erect, accomplished in bipedal stance and gait, with free hands almost unlimited in the variety and precision of their movements, with an enormous and highly organized brain, capable not only of directing, controlling, and co-ordinating bodily activity, but also of storing up and recalling past impressions, of visualizing the future, of deliberating, planning, and formulating abstract concepts. With this superior evolutionary endowment, what has been the achievement of *Homo sapiens?*

An apology for man's behavior should be addressed to some impartial group of superhuman intelligence; anthropoid apes can be invoked only as occasional critics of the broadly zoölogical aspects of man's social activities. I must ask *you* therefore to attempt to dissociate yourselves from the human species and to serve as dispassionate and critical judges, before whom I am to plead in behalf of man.

Man's Gift of Articulate Speech

Man frequently distinguishes himself from other animals by what he proudly calls "the gift of articulate speech." Some years ago, when the late William Jennings Bryan was crusading against evolution, I was inveigled into introducing him to an undergraduate audience. I managed to avoid serving as the target of his wit and satire by suggesting that, if articulate speech be taken as the criterion of distinction between man and ape, Mr. Bryan of all human beings could most justly disclaim a simian ancestry.

To an anthropoid ape the range, quality, and volume of human vocalization would not be remarkable. A gorilla, for example, can both outscream a woman and roar in a deep bass roll like distant thunder, which can be heard for three or four miles. Even the small gibbon has a voice described by a musician as "much more powerful than that of any singer he had ever heard." As a matter of fact, the anthropoid apes have laryngeal sacs which are extensions of the voice-box, capable of inflation and use as resonance chambers. There is also ample evidence that the voice as an organ for the expression of emotion is utilized by the great apes with a variation and efficacy in no whit inferior to that manifested by the human voice, and with far greater power. In fact, one might conclude that an anthropoid ape would regard a Metropolitan opera star as next-door to dumb.

The ape, unimpressed with the range and volume of the human voice, would nevertheless be appalled at its incessant utilization. Lacking, presumably, the ability to fabricate lofty and complicated thoughts, he would not understand man's continuous compulsion to communicate these results of his cerebration to his fellows, whether or not they care to listen. In fact, it would probably not occur to an ape that the ceaseless waves of humanly vocalized sound vibrating against his ear drums are intended to convey thoughts and ideas. Nor would he be altogether wrong. Man's human wants are not radically dissimilar to those of other animals. He wakes and sleeps, eats, digests, and eliminates, makes love and fights, sickens and dies, in a thoroughly mammalian fashion. Why, then, does he eternally discuss his animalistic affairs, preserving a decent silence but once a year, for two minutes, on Armistice Day? "But," I say (in my rôle of apologist), "human culture is based upon the communication of knowledge through the medium of speech." This is, of course, a statement which no anthropoid ape is in a position to contradict. It is probably true. However, it may be pointed out that the record of human culture is far more ancient than that of language, possibly because no material evidence of the existence of the latter is available before the invention of writing. Nevertheless, beginning with the dawn of the Pleistocene, perhaps one million years ago, we possess an almost unbroken sequence of man-made stone tools, which manifest a continuous and ever improving tradition of craftsmanship. These ancient implements doubtless represent only the few elements which have survived because of the durability of the material used. Pleistocene human culture must have included much more than stone axes and scrapers. It is a fact that many competent anatomists who have examined the various fragmentary skulls and brain cases of the earliest known fossil men—undoubtedly the fabricators of some of the more advanced types of implements—have questioned their ability to employ articulate speech. I myself disagree with this view and think that Pithecanthropus, for example, was probably excessively garrulous, though undoubtedly incoherent and nonsensical in most of his linguistic offerings. I should think that man originated from an irrepressibly noisy and babbling type of ape.

However, it seems possible that most of the transmission of culture was effected through watching and through imitation in the early days of human evolution, rather than by linguistic communication. Even today there exist in the Congo forest region of Africa primitive pygmy Negritos, who possess a very simple culture of their own, but apparently no language. They use the speech of their neighbors, which they must have borrowed after the production of their own culture. However, this may be a somewhat trivial and academic discussion.

It is more pertinent to inquire whether man's use of language has not contributed as much to destruction of himself and his civilization as to his preservation and its upbuilding. Although language is the universal possession of all races of *Homo sapiens,* the diversification of speech has been so extensive and so rapid that the world's population from prehistoric times has consisted of many smaller or larger groups whose articulate and written communications are, for the most part, mutually unintelligible. Thus, whereas the common possession of speech might be expected to unite all men, inasmuch as it enables them to understand each other's thoughts, motives, and culture, the reverse is the case. Language erects more barriers than bridges. There is, apparently, in man an ineradicable tendency to dislike, to distrust, and to judge as inferior the individual or group which speaks a language unintelligible to him. We consider apes to be lower animals because, as far as we know, they have no language. In a lesser degree we rate those men our inferiors who do not use our own language. Since, within the unified linguistic group, culture is now largely transmitted through the instrumentality of speech and language, the differentiation of the latter carries with it to a great extent the diversifying of the former. And, to some extent, the greater the cultural differences between two groups, the more marked their mutual antipathies become, if they are in competition.

It is the common practice of larger and more powerful groups to attempt to impose their own languages upon alien-speaking peoples with whom they come into contact. Such linguistic servitude not only awakens a bitter resentment in the vanquished, but tends to destroy their culture without giving them in exchange an understanding of, and participation in, the culture of their conquerors. In other words, the Indian who is forced to learn English sacrifices his own culture without getting a fair equivalent. It therefore may be argued that, in a broad sense, language has destroyed as much of culture as it has produced. It is also conceivable that imperfect and garbled translations from one language to another have produced more misunderstanding and discord than would have arisen between groups with mutually unintelligible languages, or without any languages at all.

It may be possible today for an inhabitant of Mars to listen to the thousands of humanly made sounds and vocalizations which, in nearly every part of the earth, are amplified and projected into space. What would he hear? He would hear the pseudo-cultured voices of radio announcers murdering the King's English in mendacious statements about the merits of commercial products; he would hear the raucous voices of newspaper reporters broadcasting sordid crimes, the horrors of war, and political misinformation; he would hear the glutinous tones of the female cosmetic tout, the nasal whine of the degenerate crooner, the blaring cacophonies of a hundred "swing" bands, and the platitudinous insincerities of bawling demagogues. He might hear the monarch of the world's greatest empire announcing his ignominious abdication to an audience of two hundred and fifty million mortals (including I know not how many snivelling sympathizers). He might not, unless endowed with superhuman patience, listen long enough to hear anything which would justify man's gift of articulate speech.

His Attempts to Control Nature

Man's attempts to control nature would undoubtedly evoke the awe and admiration of any anthropoid ape and might even command the respect of critical appraisers of human conduct. Certainly it is in the field of material culture that the human species has accomplished its most substantial achievement. Man is preëminently an animal good at gadgets. There is, however, grave reason for doubting his judgment in their utilization.

Perhaps the first chemical process which man employed for his own service was combustion. Presumably its earliest utilization was to shed heat upon naked and chilled bodies. It was then discovered to be a most effective means of scaring off nocturnal beasts of prey, as well as an illuminant indispensable in the hours of darkness, a labor-saving means of sharpening wooden implements, and an admirable agent for the preparation and preservation of food. Much later came the discovery that fire could be used in extracting and working metals, and, last of all, that it could be employed to generate power. The destructive power of fire was early experienced by man and was deliberately employed in clearing land for tillage. In comparatively ancient times man began to use fire as a weapon in warfare, beginning with incendiary torches and arrows, proceeding to gunpowder, and thence to explosives, which have been developed principally and most efficiently for the destruction of human beings and their works.

However, man has never been able completely to control fire, largely because he fails to use it with proper caution. It continues to get beyond his check and to destroy him and his property and vast quantities of natural products now as in primitive times. His inadequacy in its handling is evinced by his universal fear of fire.

In the control and utilization of gases, the achievements of our species have not been commendable. One might begin with air, which man breathes in common with other terrestrial vertebrates. He differs from other animals in that he seems incapable of selecting the right kind of air for breathing. Man is forever doing things which foul the air, and thus poisoning himself by his own stupidity. He pens himself up in a limited air space and suffocates; he manufactures noxious gases which accidentally or intentionally displace the air and remove him from the ranks of the living; he has been completely unable to filter the air of the disease germs which he breathes to his detriment; he and all of his works are powerless to prevent a hurricane or to withstand its force. Man has indeed been able to utilize the power of moving air currents to a limited extent by sails and windmills, and to imitate the flight of birds, with the certainty of eventually breaking his neck if he tries it. By dint of much experimentation, man has also succeeded in producing many gases other than the natural air, mostly lethal and useful only for destroying his fellow beings.

Man uses water much in the same way as other animals; he has to drink it constantly, washes in it frequently, and drowns in it occasionally—probably oftener than other terrestrial vertebrates. Without water he dies as miserably as any other beast; and with too much of it, as in floods, he is equally unable to cope. However, he excels other animals in that he has learned to utilize water-power. He has also been comparatively successful in the physical manipulation of this compound for his own use, and in purifying it, as well as in mixing it in a great variety of more or less harmful concoctions, which he uses as beverages.

Critics of man would be forced to admit that he is clever in his ability to domesticate other animals and plants, so that he may live upon them, their work, and their products. They might, however, comment unfavorably upon the small number of the animal species thus domesticated and the fact that virtually no additions to this useful list have been made since prehistoric times. It might be observed also that man has unintentionally domesticated a considerable number of noxious animals, such as rats, mice, lice, cockroaches, flies, and other undesirable companions which do him inestimable damage. It is of some interest also to reflect that in his attempts to domesticate the members of his own Primate order—monkeys and apes—who are presumably of a higher intelligence than most other mammals, man has failed ignominiously. He has had no luck at all with insects, except bees, and very little with fish. In the domestication of plants he has been, on the whole, more skillful and more successful. Nevertheless, among the cultivated species, commercially produced and distributed, he has included a not inconsiderable number of plants, the use of which has been, and is, a major cause of human deterioration.

Of man's attempts to control micro-organisms, it need be said only that they are incipient, and, as yet, comparatively futile. Surveying the whole situation, however, it might be concluded that man as an animal has shown a good deal of intelligence and ingenuity in attempting to control and to manipulate nature.

It is rather man's lack of judgment in the exercise of control of natural resources which would disgust critics of higher intelligence, although it would not surprise the apes. Man observes that the wood of trees is serviceable for constructing habitations and other buildings. He straightway and recklessly denudes the earth of forests in so far as he is able. He finds that the meat and skins of the bison are valuable and immediately goes to work to exterminate the bison. He allows his grazing animals to strip the turf from the soil so that it is blown away and fertile places become deserts. He clears for cultivation and exhausts the rich land by stupid planting. He goes into wholesale production of food, cereals, fruit, and livestock and allows the fruits of his labors to rot or to starve, because he has not provided any adequate method of distributing them, or because no one can pay for them. He invents machines which do the work of many men, and is perplexed by the many men who are out of work. It would be hard to convince judges of human conduct that man is not an economic fool.

His Attempts to Control Himself

Man's efforts to control himself individually and in society might impel a gorilla to thump his chest and roar with laughter. Let us consider the probable reactions of the chimpanzee to familial functions as performed by modern man. As a matter of fact there is very little in the family life of the most primitive type of modern savage, such as the native Australian, which would appeal to a chimpanzee as in any wise unnatural or extraordinary. But he would find the family conduct of civilized man somewhat eccentric.

Birth is accomplished much the same way in anthropoid and human species, although the ape mother performs for herself the duty of midwife, biting off the cord, cleaning the infant, and seeing that its lungs are cleared. The ape is the more self-reliant. The anthropoid baby is suckled, carried, and cared for by its mother, and by her is assisted in its first efforts to walk. It gets little or no paternal care and attention—which however are only occasional and superfluous features of human infancy. The ape child begins to fend for itself at an early age, gathering its food, consorting with its age mates, and depending upon the adults of the group only for occasional companionship and protection. An anthropoid would not understand the domestic custom whereby the young are maintained as economic parasites by their parents for two decades or more of their lives, long after they have reached sexual maturity and adult size. The ape might doubt whether our practice in this matter, from the general zoölogical point of view, is beneficial to the species. In ape society a young male does not acquire a mate until he is able to take her by beating off his rivals and to make good his possession. The female is, of course, always self-supporting. The situation of the young man who could not marry his girl because they couldn't live with her folks, because her folks were still living with their folks, would not arise in anthropoid society.

While available evidence does not indicate that apes are more restrained in their sexual life than human beings, they appear to manage the number of their progeny with such discretion that no mother produces new offspring while she is still burdened with the care of previous infants. Furthermore, the size of any ape group seems to be restricted by the ability of its members to gain a livelihood in the collecting of food, whereas in human society the less economic capacity, the more numerous the offspring. Again, the weak, sickly, and constitutionally unfit among the anthropoid apes are eliminated, either through neglect or deliberately, doubtless because our cousins are insufficiently intelligent to have developed those humanitarian sentiments which demand the preservation of life, however painful it is to its possessors and however useless to society. No anthropoid ape has ever heard of natural selection, but that ruthless surgeon continually operates to excise from the stock any malignant growth. Finally, the anthropoid ape whose physical powers are waning is no longer able to dominate the group and tends to go off by himself and lead a solitary existence.

Now I am by no means disposed to admit that other primate societies necessarily regulate all of their affairs better than do human groups. I am merely calling attention to certain obvious contrasts between a natural primate social organization and one that is highly artificial.

A critic who had surveyed the great advances which man has made in his material culture—his homes and his buildings, his means of transportation, his utilization of the energy pent up in natural resources, his extraordinary facility in devising methods of communication—might examine with high expectation the extent to which man has applied his intelligence to the improvement of his health and biological status. An animal which aspires to split the atom and to measure the universe, might conceivably extend his own life to a degree commensurate with the extension of his knowledge, might improve his organism as he has improved his tools and weapons.

The ordinary animal tries to protract his individual existence only by eating, fighting, running away, and hiding, and his species' existence by breeding and by some exercise of parental care. Otherwise his organism survives only through its inherent capacities and its luck with environmental hazards. Primitive man has improved markedly all these natural methods of maintaining life and has even attempted to add another preservative—medical care. The medical science of the savage is, however, compounded of magic and superstition and includes few remedies of actual value. It seems probable that, on the whole, the doctor at the primitive stage of culture kills oftener than he cures. He merely adds to the strain upon a long-suffering organism exerted by the pressure of a ruthless natural selection. Actually man's ignorance of his own anatomy and physiology and of the pathological agents which invade his organism has been so crass that medical skill has been a negligible factor in the increase of human populations up to the last century, even in the most civilized societies. Now, however, advance in medical knowledge, together with public hygiene and sanitation, have radically reduced the mortality at the beginning of the life span and literally have taken the graves out from under the feet of the aging. In the United States the death rate of males born alive during the first year has been reduced from 12.7 per cent to 6.2 per cent in 30 years, and the expectation of life from the beginning of the century has increased from 48 to 59 years in males, and from 51 to 63 years in females. Short of homicide, a man has practically no chance of outliving his wife; females, after attaining a certain age, become almost immortal.

Now, it is perfectly obvious to intelligent judges of man's behavior that this preservation and prolongation of life largely increases the proportion among the living population of the constitutionally inferior—the lame, the halt, and the blind. It also makes for a world peopled increasingly with the immature and the senile, of those who have not yet developed their mental powers and their judgment, and of those who are in process of losing both. If medical science were able to make whole the bodies and minds it preserves, one might find little to criticize in the age shift in composition of the population. But it is unfortunately true that we have succeeded all too well in keeping the engine running, but have been quite unable to repair the steering gear. Since the immature are not granted a voice in the government and the decrepit are not denied it, we may expect ever-increasing social ructions as a result of senile decay dominating dementia præcox, in a world of diminishing average intelligence.

One of the human institutions for which apology is required is government. Undoubtedly an anthropoid ape would appreciate and understand government by dictatorship; he might even realize the advantages of a communistic regime. But a superhuman critic of man's affairs would be puzzled by a democracy. He would have to be informed that democracy involves the essential principle that all law-abiding adults have equal rights and privileges and an equal voice in the government. Such a democratic government implies, or should imply, an approximate parity of intelligence in the electorate, or a majority of individuals of superior intelligence, if it is to function capably and successfully. There can be no miracle whereby the group intelligence transcends the possibly moronic mean of its constituent members. Therefore, a democracy becomes a better or worse social instrument as the mean intelligence of its population rises or falls.

Now, on the whole, there is a marked positive association between bodily health and mental health. A ten-year study of American criminals and insane has convinced me that there is an even stronger correlation between mental and social inadequacy and biological inferiority. Since civilized men are preserving the unfit in body, it follows that they are depreciating their intelligence currency. There are plenty of indirect evidences of a decline in the national intelligence of civilized countries, but I am apologizing in behalf of man and not voluntarily contributing evidence which might be used against him.

Judges of human behavior, informed of modern preparations for warfare and of the methods which are employed to destroy human life, might easily leap to an erroneous conclusion with respect to the purpose and function of this highly developed institution. They would probably reason as follows: "Men are too soft-hearted to keep their populations down to the right numbers by birth control or infanticide. They love babies, and like to care for the sick and helpless. Therefore, when the weak, the unfit, and the useless grow to adult years and become a menace to the common good, nations conspire mutually to start patriotic crusades, whereby their superfluous and inferior populations destroy each other in a high atmosphere of heroism and devotion to public duty. 'Dulce et decorum est pro patria mori.' But is this not a very expensive method of population control?"

As the protagonist of the human race, I must admit that in warfare, on the contrary, we select as the victims for sacrifice, not the bodily and mentally unfit, but those adjudged to be, on every scientific test, the flower of each nation. Nor do I know how to answer the inevitable retort that man's right hand certainly does not know what his left hand is doing, when with the one he preserves the worst of his kind, and with the other destroys the best.

I should probably try to divert attention from this issue by descanting upon the grandeur of human conceptions of justice, the wonderful mechanism whereby it is administered, the sanctity of the law, and how we strenuously organize efficient police systems to prevent its infraction; how we are learning to regard the criminal, not as a vicious brute to be exterminated without ruth, but as a wayward and possibly sick child to be rehabilitated and cured by patient and loving care, and ultimately to be returned again to society with the Christly admonition, "Go, and sin no more." I should point out how, at each Christmas season, our wise and noble governors bestow upon their happy states the priceless gift of a goodly parcel of liberated murderers, thieves, and other convicted felons. I should wax eloquent upon our democratic belief that ignorance and social maladjustment is at the root of all crime, that a proper and more extensive education of the young—perhaps extending to middle age—together with a wise reorganization of our social and economic institutions, could eradicate this evil forever.

I fear, however, that all of the ape members of the investigating body, if any remained upon the judicial bench, would resign and take to the nearest trees. For no animal society tolerates the outlaw. The anti-social animal is killed or driven out. Judges of superior intelligence, however, would take a broader-minded viewpoint and put some pertinent questions. "Is it not true that education at the public expense has been extended these many years to nearly every class of person in the United States, and that facilities for more and better learning have increased almost immeasurably during the last quarter of a century?"

To this the protagonist of human behavior, with rejuvenated spirit, proudly answers, "Yes."

"Is it true that in recent times the noble-spirited and socially minded, who in bygone days concerned themselves with the salvation of men's souls, have now, for the most part, turned to the reform of human society and are no longer attempting to prepare men for heaven, but rather to rescue them for a very present and man-made hell?" The answer is again in the affirmative.

"Have not hosts of intelligent and highly educated men and women—penologists, sociologists, phycologists, psychiatrists, jurists, and sheer philanthropists—labored at prison reform and refined the treatment of the delinquent until it may be said that the convicted felon receives more social consideration than the law-abiding working man?" That would be a question which would not justify an unequivocal answer on the part of counsel for the defense.

"Is it not true that, in spite of the advance of education and all the substantial progress in methods of social amelioration, crime is still increasing enormously, and that the discharged convict continues to return to his crime, like a dog to his vomit?" And finally, "Is it not therefore apparent, in the light of the evidence here presented, that modern man is selling his biological birthright for a mess of morons; that the voice may be the voice of democracy, but the hands are the hands of apes?"

LOUIS KRONENBERGER

The Eighteenth Century Attitude

THE EIGHTEENTH CENTURY, like the Renaissance, appeals more to the imagination than to the memory. It has, for those who admire it, an atmosphere if not indeed an aura, in part no doubt because of a character so unusually marked, but in even greater part because of a character so completely vanished. If one thinks of it with any emotion at all, one can hardly think of it without nostalgia, nor fail to call to mind those memorials which kindle glamour—powdered hair, coaches-and-four, minuets. The felicity of those who think this way is probably intemperate; but then, the century which has the greatest reputation for being rational has almost never called forth a rational response. People like it either too well or too little: one school, which finds its spokesmen among the Dobsons and the Stracheys, cannot be parted for even a single day from Walpole or Pope; the other and more populous school simply regards eighteenth-century England as a bore. It depends, no doubt, on whether you prefer a way of life to life itself.

I cannot personally see much sense in the attitude of either school. It requires a peculiarly sentimental and unadventurous nature to sigh over the departed splendours of an era long since buried, and to impute to it so much glamour; and it implies, not a critic's or a sociologist's interest, but an antiquary's. It is all too easy and misleading to think only of Georgian houses and Gainsborough portraits, Pope's grotto and Walpole's Gothic, the rotunda at Ranelagh and the pumproom at Bath, Addison holding forth at the Kit-Cat and Johnson at the Cheshire Cheese, the Duchess of Marlborough defying Queen Anne and Flora Macdonald shielding the Young Pretender. That, plainly, is mere façade; although that is perhaps as far in mental perspective as Dobson ever got in composing his *Eighteenth-Century Vignettes*. An uncorrected impression of the eighteenth century as surpassing all others in brilliance and lustre and gallantry would pretty closely resemble nonsense; though it is nonsense subscribed to by many sensible and sensitive people.

It does not take any clear-eyed student of the period very long to see that John Wesley or Samuel Richardson was a much more influential figure than the Earl of Chesterfield or the Duchess of Devonshire, and that Newgate outranked Ranelagh to the same considerable extent that it outlasted it. Nor does it require really taxing research to discover that much eighteenth-century brilliance was shallow if not empty, that its breeding was often confused with formality, and that all but the best of its wit stands open to impeachment.

But even if its glamour has been magnified at will, there is no justice in the assertion that the century was dull. It is, to begin with, one of the great pivotal and transitional eras of all time. England in 1700 was possibly the most advanced nation in Europe, yet the England of 1700 was a nest of brainless superstitions, blind bigotries, rancorous plots and vicious prejudices. The political scene was not only coarse and clandestine—it always is—but was darkened by the most barefaced corruption, the most medieval practices, the most barbarous injustice. The religious atmosphere was if anything worse: every kind of nonconformist, freethinker, papist and Jew stood in danger of corporal and even capital punishment; prejudice was rife; bigotry was rampant; all the bishops were politicians; most of the vicars were heels; and a denominational trifle could provoke a national explosion. The penal laws were flagitious: people went to prison almost for singing out of tune, and the prisons they went to were everything vile that graft, inhumanity and negligence could make them. Men expired of disease on bug-ridden beds rotting from the water that drenched the cells. Science, medicine, sanitation were all in their infancy, and worse mistakes were committed in their name than had used to be committed under the heading of ignorance. It is to be added furthermore, as no mere coincidence, that never was there a comparable breed of greatly-endowed, evilly-principled statesmen and leaders, men who misused great gifts in their thirst for great position, nearly all of them careerists, tricksters, time-servers, double-dealers. I instance Bolingbroke, Harley, Marlborough, Robert Walpole, men who ruled England in the first decades of the eighteenth century, and who sank her character to the level of their own.

It was *that* England which in the course of a hundred years espoused so much wiser rule, so much cleaner—though unclean—politics, religion so much more flexible and human; which abolished all the worst of its penal laws, grew conscientious about philanthropy, made headway in science and sanitation; and produced, in less formidable men, better and wiser public servants. It was *that* century which, beginning in darkness, culminated in the French Revolution; and a century so pivotal cannot by any standards be considered dull. But there are other reasons for discrediting its 'dullness.' This much glamour can justly be imputed, over and above the snuffboxes and the flowered waistcoats, to eighteenth-century England: it abounded with flashing and glittering personalities. Its people, as individuals, are stamped with a really glowing dye; their minds, even when arid, are watered with wit; their gestures are at once vivid and impeccable; their words, if you care for turns of phrase and the incantation of rhythms, are among the most distinguished ever uttered. The nineteenth century produced, it is possible, better minds, but personalities nowhere so good. Whether we think of such magnificent bullies as Johnson and Swift, of a dazzling trickster like Bolingbroke, of so superb a stuffed shirt as Gibbon, of Pope combining psychopathic venom with Mozartean grace, of a polite trifler like George Selwyn, of an artist in gossip like Horace Walpole, of dirty, witty, worldlywise Lady Mary, of Fox losing fortunes at faro but, amidst caste pleasures, supporting both the American and the French Revolutions: whether we think of these, or of dozens of other eighteenth-century Englishmen, we must be aware that this highly rational, faintly idiotic breed of men were not, and are not, dull. Some of them were perhaps a little inhuman, or a little misshapen, or a little eccentric, or a little ridiculous (indeed, it rather shocks one to find so many irrational offshoots of rationalism); some, I fear, were even more than a little grotesque: but they were not dull. They are, at worst, interesting museum-pieces, as in some respects the eighteenth century itself was the greatest of all museums.

The truth, then, would seem to me to lie somewhere between the sentimentalist's notion of glamour and the skeptic's certainty of dullness. What it comes down to in the end, if I may risk being glib, is that the eighteenth century had a temperament and did not have a soul. It was a very worldly age, or would have been had it not taken such naive pride in its worldliness. It was an age of very great assurance: it not only knew what it wanted, but thought it knew what was good for it; and it decided that there was only one right way of doing everything. All this tended to sharpen and refine its sensibilities, so that at sniffing, sipping, grazing it stands without a peer; as for really smelling, drinking and feeling, the age thought these might be a little vulgar. So frightened were eighteenth-century people of artistic excess, that without knowing it they sometimes cultivated privation. This does not apply, to be sure, to their coarser appetites; one scarcely needs to be reminded that almost everybody in the eighteenth century (except the very numerous poor) was a glutton and (including the very numerous poor) a drunkard and a lecher. It applies, rather, to their mincing esthetics, to their gingerly life of the spirit, and to their minds which resembled formally laid out gardens. They were a very self-conscious race and, because they were, they never came to a full growth.

Yet if this was the general truth, there are so many exceptions to it that it hardly seems true. For the age, however soulless, produced ceaselessly and perdurably. The England of those years was commencing her grand cycle; and looking back, we see a century in which the tempo of things is just rapid enough to make for considerable advancement, and yet slow enough to reveal itself without confusion. In 1700 England still stood, half-scared out of her wits, under the threat of Louis XIV's France; in 1800, thanks to great generals and great administrators and great thieves, England was a mistress of empire: India was hers, Canada was hers, Australia was hers; she more than ever ruled the waves; she piloted her industries far and wide; and among the arts, though music had passed out of her forever with Purcell, in a century she had produced the first of the world's great masters of fiction; masters of essay-writing, masters of letter-writing, a handful of brilliant second-rate painters, a first-rate painter, and a great painter-poet. The Industrial Revolution was accomplished and at hand; thanks to the Sir Robert Walpoles, a nation of shopkeepers was prospering handsomely; and—one minute more, now, and the touch will forevermore be lost—she had brought to full flower what we must always refer to, and proudly refer to, as eighteenth-century prose.

That prose has been the despair of all those coming after. It is not so much that every word of it is precious, or every rhythm right, as that never again, I think, a nation will speak with one voice, uncovering its temperament and its lack of soul. *Le style c'est du siècle* is a truer way of putting it than *le style c'est del l'homme*. It has its own tight little bouquet, its own dry-sherry taste in the mouth, this prose the secret of which belongs as exclusively to the eighteenth century as that of making stained glass to the Middle Ages. We are never so conscious of the differences in style among the English writers of that day as of the likenesses; every last one of them is the child of a tradition which he understands and to which he assents. It is by no means odd that these men, expressing themselves so lucidly and reasonably, should forever represent an Age of Reason. And the celebrated rationalism of their century is more truly in their prose than in what that prose went on to say.

They are the eternal foes of all the dada, the ha ha, the blah-blah of the human race; they despised obscurity, unseemly laughter and emotional mucilage with all their hearts; they asked of writing that it be highbred and low-pitched, that it stand for what they preened themselves on being; that it be an art form as they desired their life be an art form; and in that prose they produced a marvelous wish-fulfillment. Let us not be deceived. These men led lives as grubby and untidy as our own; they satisfy no one's definition of what composes a great gentleman; but they dressed as he might dress, and they wrote as he might write.

As for the celebrated rationalism, I distrust it. It has a very real place, of course, in the history of philosophy and of political thought. The seventeenth century, topheavy with superstition and supernaturalism, was to lose everything at the hands of Locke, Bolingbroke, Hume, Diderot, Tom Paine and a dozen others; the freethinker of Johnson's day was no worse outlawed than the speakeasy proprietor in ours; deism was fashionable rather than not; even in Queen Anne's reign Marlborough's son-in-law Sunderland boasted that he was a 'republican'; and educated men looked on such uncontroversial matters as life and death with all the enlightenment born of reason. But in a social sense the high skepticism of the eighteenth century was adulterated by misdoubts less lofty; and that shoulder-shrugging which, to some, has always seemed the last word in wisdom was, whatever the age might aver to the contrary, the key to its tone. The pseudo-classicism which operated so rigorously in literature was not without its purchase on life. In poetry, Horace by way of Boileau had handed over the Word to Pope; and in life Horace was transmitting his complacent, tabloid philosophy to all of Pope's contemporaries. For them, as recently for Mr. James Branch Cabell, Horace was 'the most wise and most durable of human poets.' They might strew their prose and their conversation with weightier names, but they were in practice no profounder, and no more classical, than the Roman.

Yet there was another mentor of an influence perhaps equal to Horace's. This was the Duc de la Rochefoucauld whose cold-blooded maxims, engendered by life at Louis XIV's court, won acceptance in the satellite highlife of eighteenth-century England. Any idealism that might have survived Horace's knowing smile was done to death by Rochefoucauld's piercing eye. Swift somewhere chose as a motto the Duke's pulverizing dictum, 'We all of us have strength enough to endure the misfortune of others,' and Chesterfield assented to the even more damaging dictum, 'In the misfortunes of our best friends we often find something that is not exactly displeasing.' But Rochefoucauld's whole barrage of cynicism—'Vanity is the greatest of all flatterers'; 'We often forgive those who bore us, but we cannot forgive those whom we bore'; 'To establish oneself in the world one does all one can to seem established there'; 'Hypocrisy is the homage that vice renders to virtue'; 'Pride does not wish to owe and vanity does not wish to pay'—his whole barrage of cynicism, ascribing all our conduct in life to self-love, went further toward destroying what latent generous feeling existed among eighteenth-century men. Their much applauded skepticism degenerates really into the killing frost of cynicism: the main evil of which is, not the truth that plainly resides in the cynicism, but the indifference of cynicism toward any worthier kind of truth than its own. Thus Chesterfield's *Letters*, directly descended from Rochefoucauld's *Maxims*, are spiritually the key to the highlife of the age; or to be fair, to the highlife of any age. Only, in other ages an attitude like Chesterfield's has been something to dissemble rather than imitate.

The run, then, of eighteenth-century rationalism is of a degrading, almost misanthropic sort, and not to be compared with the humanism of freer and warmer epochs. Even under the silly morality of Victorian days, unctuous mouthing produced some show of heart, some noble acts in the hope that they would be recognized as noble; to be good was a greater social asset than to be graceful. But in a time of capricious patrons and debtors' prisons and the boss rule of a dozen great Whig families; in a time of hard drinking and high gambling and furious political animosities; in an age, that is, when it was remarkably difficult to keep one's countenance, the keeping it was the supreme virtue. Well, the men of those days did not labour in vain. They have had their wish; they have come down to posterity with a reputation for having kept their countenances. They have come down as men and women who regarded social intercourse as nothing impromptu, but as something that demanded toil and imposed responsibility. Above everything else one must please in life. Chesterfield, Walpole, Lady Mary—how many of them apologize, for example, for talking about themselves! How necessary it was to be well-groomed, well-mannered, well-spoken; and what greater sin, in an age so quickly bored, than to prove boring? They went to school every day of their lives, and rehearsed in private what they performed in public. They had tone, they had grace, they had glitter; all this they have still, when we revert to them; and if we found out they did not have it, perhaps we should feel even worse cheated than they.

But it told on them, and they could not quite keep up the pretence. They wanted other things: in spite of Lord Chesterfield's decree that no gentleman ever laughs aloud, they wanted to laugh aloud; in spite of a whole century's aversion to tears, they wanted to shed floods of them; in spite of their horror of vulgarity, they wanted to roll in the mud; in spite of their defence of reason, they had a craving for grotesquerie. And so, after doing a generation's duty at the Italian opera, they went mad over the rollicking, boisterous high spirits of *The Beggar's Opera,* and *The Beggar's Opera* became the greatest dramatic success of the entire century. Not less did the woes of servant girls and suchlike things, in Richardson's sentimental tomes, break down their austere reserves. 'This Richardson is a strange fellow,' wrote callous Lady Mary to her daugher. 'I heartily despise him, and eagerly read him, nay, sob over his works in a most scandalous manner.' Richardson became the best-seller of his age. Scarcely less did they throw themselves pell-mell into the imbecilic horrors of the Gothic romance, where everything clanks and creaks and groans, and maidens are even purer than they are desperate, and dungeons are discouragingly deep, and moats discouragingly wide. What oceans of nonsense did not *The Castle of Otranto* give rise to, as Mrs. Radcliffe and so many others took up Walpole's well-rewarded hint? Our eighteenth-century friends were careful, of course, to sanction all these excrescences by thinking of them as fads, but what a glimpse they offer us of the price they paid for going around, emotionally, in clothes a size too small for them.

Thus, though the main literary tradition of the century follows the real spirit of the century and produces a Pope, a Chesterfield, a Gibbon, there still was room and to spare for the bounce of Gay, the weepiness of Richardson, the prettier tears of Sterne, the fake Gothic of Walpole; and there emerged too, in uncongenial ground, a mystic and humanitarian like Blake who beckons us on, as who does not know, to the great flowering of the Romantic Revival.

In the following pages we can sample, I believe, almost all the styles together with almost all the art-forms, of eighteenth-century literature. If some great names of the age are wanting, at least none that are present fall far short of distinction. Despite any amount of fault-finding and investigation, in the end we must admit that we are in good company. We are among productions which somehow give the lie to any generalizations, my own not least, about eighteenth-century writing. For, to repeat, we are among vivid personalities whose reaction to life no amount of Zeitgeist can blot out, and whose talents break through even their beliefs. For it is true, and much to the eighteenth century's credit, that its tight little bouquet has not evaporated and can still be smelt, where the cascades of strong Victorian perfume have all been drained away, or lost their power of allure. Even Chesterfield's *Letters,* for all their cynicism and—a point much less commented upon—for all their touches of absurdity, somehow retain their gloss. Among the works included here, only *The Castle of Otranto* has been outraged by time; perhaps I have included it as an object lesson.

We can hardly forget that the groundwork for the *major* eighteenth-century tradition was laid by geniuses sick in mind and body like Swift and Pope. But if their characters contain little of the philosophic calm, the balance, the sanity of an Age of Reason, their art reveals the control which their lives failed in. Swift we shall advert to later as a man above mere tradition, when we have finished with the men who created or acquiesced in the formulas of the period; but Pope is one of its lawgivers. Through a supreme manipulation of the heroic couplet he was able to terrify his own generation, to enslave the poets of the generations which followed, and to delight and disgust posterity. It was his instinct to take offense, and he made it his trade. Ranging literature where we will, we cannot find another man so purely venomous; and his brilliant couplets ring all the changes of a morbid hate. But Pope, though he might not have prospered had his age sneered and wrangled and conspired less, was all the same the victim of his age. He was at bottom a man of sentiment, and the age was hard; of vanity, and the age was cruel; of sensibility, and the age was coarse. Hence the deformed, disabled poet with his biting tongue fell in with the practices of the day, and in settling private scores became the most formidable of satirists. His work is a lasting model in its kind; for the vomitings of his mean mind and crushed-out soul turned, like objects in a fairy-tale, into verses really patrician in their grace, really dazzling in their brilliance.

The Dunciad is hardly Pope's finest production: but it surely ranks next after *The Rape* and one or two of the *Epistles;* and after flaying—perhaps incontinently—dullness and dullards through many cantos, it concludes almost sublimely. It is of Pope's most mature versifying, and I suspect that its mastery over form accounts for the dilated nature of its substance, and for its foolish determination to go a full fifteen rounds after winning by a knockout long before the end. Even Pope was not above being dull, at times, about dullness. It is more to the point, however, to ask who else has treated dullness so brilliantly? And where else, I am forced to add, shall we find more uncharitable sneering, on the part of a successful author tripping it with the great, toward the 'sons of a day,' the hungry hacks who slept unwashed upon bulks?

'These are—ah, no! these *were*—the gazetteers.'

As an artist, Pope was right in demolishing mediocre art. But as a man he was wrong for despising mediocre artists merely as men. He preferred the great world to humanity, like Chesterfield and Gibbon and Walpole and so many others of his century; that attitude, indeed, is part of the ideology of the century; it is part of what was wrong with the century. And with it there went, despite much poise, a lack of human dignity.

Turning to Chesterfield, we are in the high midsummer of the eighteenth century. Despite everything that can be said against him, I suspect that his era is very deep in his debt for the picture he has drawn of a society so polished, so fastidious, so possessed, as he says, 'by the graces'; a society in which the bumpkin, the pedant, the parvenu, the bore, the killjoy have no place, and where one may be supposed to have sat down to dinner more elegantly than any one has ever sat, not Petronius himself. But there is no evidence that the social world of Chesterfield's ideal ever existed, even among Chesterfield's friends—though it came closer to existing then than at any time thereafter. But the precepts rammed down young Philip Stanhope's throat were truly enough what the then English upper classes aspired to practise; and we may not, perhaps, be utter fools sometimes to imagine brilliant gatherings where, under the unnumbered candles of lustrous chandeliers, every gesture was graceful, every woman charming, every voice melodious, and every answer witty. Chesterfield's injunctions are at any rate precise, and tell us what the eighteenth century wanted, whether or not it ever got its wish. But of course there is as much of the caste spirit in these letters as there is of the aristocratic, and much more of worldliness than of wisdom. It is now somewhat the fashion to defend Chesterfield against the allegations of a hundred and fifty years, and to assert that he is better than cynical and more than clever. This is not so. He holds up well enough as a privileged worldling; his cynicism is supportable because it proceeds from experience of a corrupt society; but he shatters even his own mould of form by being a nag and a little something of a fool. I have mitigated the nagging, here, by so greatly reducing the bulk; but Chesterfield's foolish side is ineradicable. It reveals an imperfect taste, deriving in turn from too meagre and narrow values, from a want of the finest feelings and broadest sympathies. Why need playing the fiddle put 'a gentleman in a very frivolous, contemptible light'; why was 'a merry fellow never yet a respectable man'; and what of the command to young Stanhope that since he had increased his girth, he should make haste to add to his height? The truth is, that for all his contempt of pedantry, Chesterfield within his own dominions was a pedant; and one may suspect that in writing the letters his aim was a little less to instruct the pupil than to exhibit the master.

The wonder is, perhaps, that the *Letters* read as well as they do. Certainly today something of our comic sense is aroused, and not least because the boy that Chesterfield laboured to make into a paragon remained, till the very end, a lump. But even today we must render homage to prose at once so sleek and so sturdy; to the vigorously expressed personality that holds the pen; and find instructive these dissertations which are simultaneously a conception, a defence, and an indictment of a way of life. No man ever, in a way, put a meaner value on human nature than this accomplished society cynic; it was indeed because the meat of life seemed so worthless to him that he concentrated so untiringly on the sauce.

The great name of Gibbon hangs over the century like a fixed star, but the Gibbon of the *Autobiography* differs from the Gibbon of the *Decline and Fall* in trying to do for himself what posterity, with a sense of privilege, has done for the *History*. Gibbon, as much as Chesterfield, is the creature of his era; and if in Chesterfield we have no careless conception of the eighteenth-century man of fashion, in Gibbon we have the gravest possible delineation of the man of parts. His memoirs are perhaps the high-water mark of the 'classical' idea. Self-esteem flows out of them quietly and pellucidly in a beautiful jet of words: the self-esteem of a man who has mastered the formula imposed upon him by his period. It would not be possible now to conquer life as Gibbon conquered it, and it would not seem wise. To write as Gibbon wrote of himself, even retrospectively, one must never have known the temptations of mortality; but only have lived with a genius for work and an equal genius for aloofness. From the *Decline and Fall* we know that he had the one, and from the *Autobiography* that he had the other. What composure! He abandoned love for all time in one short celebrated sentence: 'I sighed as a lover, I obeyed as a son.' He passed up pretty nearly everything else, I suspect, for the same reason that he passed up romance: because he did not want it. He traveled and read extensively; sat in Parliament inconspicuously; and mingled on terms of discreet good fellowship with the very best company, at home and abroad, of his day. There is nothing more to be said of him except that the wrote a very great book, the *History of the Decline and Fall of the Roman Empire.*

Yet the *Autobiography* is almost the last production that one would seek to belittle. It is first of all a perfect piece of prose. It is secondly a perfect piece of portraiture, in which a cautious, painstaking, brilliant man gives himself the symmetry, the whiteness, and the public character of a monument. If there was never anything so pompous, there was never, all the same, anything so delightful. Half march, half minuet, the book is *all* manner, the life story, as someone has said, of a man who mistook himself for the Roman Empire. The printed page seems inadequate; nothing less than marble, one feels, will do for Gibbon describing his gout. Yet, such is he as a writer that, using dry means, he makes a dry life into something that is not dry. And among other things there is the reward of coming upon many famous and many flawless sentences—as, to mention one that is both, the breath-taking compliment to *Tom Jones.*

Of our authors, Sheridan is the last chronicler of society life: for the Walpole of the *Letters,* probably the greatest of all its chroniclers, cannot be detected in the author of *Otranto.* And even with Sheridan we have passed the crest—Pope's lack of charity, Chesterfield's hardness, Gibbon's reserve are tinctured now with something else, and the gates of sentiment are beginning to swing open. Where Congreve, seventy-five years before, took the abuses of society for granted and held them up to nature for what they were, Sheridan goes now to work against them. Both men used a medium even more artificial than the life it hit off, and stylized their approach to fit a narrow frame and achieve an effect too unified for the whole truth. But Congreve's undutifulness to the laws of nature is due solely to his appreciation of the laws of comedy, whereas Sheridan is diverted both by the laws of comedy and the desires of morality and sentiment. Thus Congreve, unlike Sheridan, is not edifying; but neither is he, unlike Sheridan, false. The author of *The School for Scandal* returns without demur to a theatre of heroes and villains, of endings that reconcile happiness with virtue.

Sheridan is not so penetrating or brilliant as Congreve, but he is much more skilful and, simply as a playwright, more accomplished. *The School for Scandal* has more motion and continuity than the Restoration drama because it has more plot and less incident, more characters whose fortunes are at stake and fewer characters that express a point of view. Congreve is precise where Sheridan is pat; the one knew the world and the other knew his trade. But so well did Sheridan know his trade, so amusing are his scandal-mongers, so lively is their scandal, so witty is their talk, that after a hundred and fifty years a bloom lies still upon this play. Even its sentiment is not displeasing. And though we may question whether in life the issues are so happily decided, the fact remains that Charles Surface is a lovable fellow, and Joseph Surface an odious one.

Pope, Chesterfield, Gibbon and Sheridan are in the main tradition: would-be, and often truly, classical; would-be, and often truly, aristocratic. All of them except Sheridan take chief pride in standing apart, in having delicate sensibilities, and none of the enthusiasm and heartiness—they would have called it grossness—of other men. But we can scarcely read a page of *The Drapier's Letters,* or of almost anything else by Swift, without feeling a profound difference in tone. On the surface, to be sure, the style is equally dry; and deeper down we can detect something of the same tradition and temperament. Nor is it that Swift held social position and all that went with it in contempt, or felt a deep human kinship with the masses. He wanted very much to be treated like a lord (I suppose because he was not one) and to him all anonymous and submerged humanity was a despicable rabble. Yet Swift, who was indeed the misanthrope he is reputed to be, was moved by what he saw of life to passionate indignation. He well knew that the lords he bullied and fellowshipped with were corrupt leaders in a corrupt society, and that life was a selfish, predatory affair of a few masters and a multitude of victims. The sum of all his preaching is that only wisdom and virtue should have any credit in the world; the sum of all his experience is that wisdom and virtue barely exist. Thus the man, warped from birth, passed through stages of frustration, bitterness, contempt and disgust to one of intense, militant loathing—a most improper eighteenth-century emotion. And out of that loathing, which rather is the mark of a tormented mind than a magnanimous heart, Swift employed all his huge genius to fight for mankind. The combat he waged was too magnificent for it to matter that he was warring against his own resentments no less than other men's. Aroused by the poverty, the suffering, the helplessness in life, and particularly of the downtrodden Irish he lived among and personally despised, he fought tyranny and corruption tooth and nail. No one can forget that greatest of all short ironical blasts, the *Modest Proposal.* If *The Drapier's Letters* shows something less of genius in defending the same exploited race, it shows genius enough, and can claim among other things to have actually halted an outrage. Wood's halfpence never came to Ireland.

It matters little today that some of Swift's logic was defective, and that the halfpence themselves need not have bowed Ireland lower under the yoke. The point is, and always was, that the patent which Wood obtained was part of the spoils of a disgraceful system, and that a man was practising for gain what the state should have provided for nothing.

Though *The Drapier's Letters* have fallen somewhat into neglect, they are worth a fresh perusal. Here, assuredly, is great pamphleteering: and we need not recognize all Swift's references nor follow all his arguments to feel the heat of his indignation, the cut of his wit, the persuasiveness of his brilliant argument *ad hominem*. And we can feel too something of a man who, in the long run, only can be *felt,* since ten generations of critics have not succeeded in clearly explaining him. That being so, I need not apologize for eschewing an 'explanation' in a page or two.

Gay was Swift's—and Pope's—contemporary, an amiable fellow always in hot water. Though the aristocracy took him up, half affectionately, half contemptuously, he never hardened into the mould they scrupulously cultivated. One need not feel that *The Beggar's Opera* is very much as literature in order to credit its peculiarly honest and unflattering picture of the times. Here again the century's defenses are down, and in the burlesquing of a man of heart we may observe the heartlessness implicit in a reign of privilege. The play is high-spirited, noisy, absurd; its lyrics were sung to tunes long familiar to the English people; its purpose is plainly entertainment. But here hardboiledness and knavery seem to protest against themselves, and the W. S. Gilbert of George II's day gives us a good sample of the underworld which George II refused to worry about. In Macheath the author caricatured the public and private doings and misdoings of the prime minister, Robert Walpole; and Walpole was acute enough to see that a nation's songs might damage him as a nation's sermons could not. He therefore refused a license to Gay's sequel, *Polly;* but *The Beggar's Opera* has flourished till the present day. However highly or seriously we may choose to regard it, this we can hardly deny: that on a smaller scale it does what Swift and Defoe and sometimes Fielding did: it shows us an age in déshabillé. This has its value when we stop to recall that the age worried above everything else about appearances.

Sterne is not in the prevailing tradition either, though no one more than he expressed what lay just below the eighteenth-century surface. The man of feeling goes back at least as far as Richard Steele who had, besides a warm heart, the moral heat of a repentant sinner. Steele's forgotten plays are in a direction away from the untempered cynicism of the Restoration drama, and are the first signs of a recrudescence of sentiment. By Richardson's time feeling has begun to assert itself in earnest. Sterne follows close on Richardson's heels, but the two men are poles apart in temperament: what could be less like Richardson's earnestness than Sterne's playful, subtle, arch sentimentality? Much, perhaps too much, has been written about the merits and charm of *Tristram Shandy* and *A Sentimental Journey,* and there has always been a suggestion of cult about Sterne's warmest admirers. For my part, *Shandy* is as full of longueurs as of felicities, and is enough of a classic to take care of itself without being overpraised, or praised for the wrong things. But there are not many books of as short span as *A Sentimental Journey* which can claim to be as good. Yorick's travels move at exactly the right tempo, alternating between a saunter and a trot; every episode is diverting or touching or alive; we see French life through eyes not in the least conventional; we wrap ourselves in a haze of artful, pleasantly insincere gallantry; and there is nowhere better to go looking for that rarest of things in a book, the perfect sentence. It is scarcely necessary to repeat that Sterne's curiously nervous style is the product of studious, almost affected, care. Here indeed we are in the presence of a temperament—a temperament exploited up to the hilt. Here feeling and fancy are balked of higher aspirations to serve us merely as ornament. I *will* be charming, Yorick says; and despite his faults, he is.

The faults are well-known enough: the lingering archness which often grows transparent; the playfulness not unlikely to turn cute; the smirking and ogling of an English vicar who would but dares not; the over-indulgence of sentiment and personality. These are traits which disfigure an otherwise irresistible scene, but thanks to the artist in Sterne, do not disfigure it too badly. From a reading of Sterne's letters I should think that I would have disliked the man, and found him quite intolerable at times in a drawing-room. But because, while pretending to be, he was *not* artless; because, while aspiring to be, he was *not* lovable, he saves himself in his best work. There he takes no chances on his natural charm, but works like a galley-slave to bring about, by every device of cunning, the miracle. Yorick is as much better than Laurence Sterne as sound artistry can make a man.

No sooner had sentiment come out of its eighteenth-century hiding than imagination began again to beat its wings. It appeared in the peculiar form of the Gothic romance which, during two generations, served as watered pap to a fancy-starved reading public; and it was Walpole's *Castle of Otranto* which began a vogue that was to flourish until laughed out of sight by *Northanger Abbey*. It is hard today to decide which of the two books is the better parody. Certainly no one now will sleep the worse for reading *The Castle of Otranto* in bed at night, but to Walpole's contemporaries it was presumably a book of spells and horrors, and the figure of the gigantic hat, the nocturnal scenes in the chapel, the very atmosphere of the Middle Ages itself, made one's hair stand on end, thereby jarring an eighteenth-century peruke. Today we risk no part of our reputations by calling the book mere nonsense. Today, when laughter is no longer supposed unseemly, we may give way to it while turning the pages of Walpole's romance. But once, let us remember, it made grown up people shiver, and started a great vogue.

I have not included here something so close to claptrap without reason. To begin with, *Otranto* headed a movement which, by indirect and grotesque means, liberated the pent-up English imagination. Deviating from the fixed eighteenth-century pattern, *Otranto* finally destroyed that pattern; it is the mountain brook which became at last the great river of the Romantic Revival. So great was Scott's debt to the book that—I hope gratiture was his reason—he praised it. Indeed, it was a kind of disguised Frankenstein which in the end blasted all the prissy Horace Walpoles off the earth. But there are other reasons for bringing Walpole's shocker into the company of its betters. It is always useful to examine a certain amount of trash, the more so if it is trash that a former generation took seriously; it is pleasant to read trash which, whatever it may not be, yet is readable; and it is perhaps expedient to read trash which still goes by the name of a classic. And this volume of stale bogeys remains, somehow, a classic. At any rate I have just had a look at it, and was not bored. There is still some merit in the prose, some cleverness in the story-telling, some interest in the story. And Walpole, to my mind, was not much worse a sorcerer than Arthur Machen.

But it is like coming out of a lumber-room into the open air to pass from Walpole to Blake. It is hard, of course, to think of Blake as belonging to any century, least of all the eighteenth. Where Walpole discharged a blank cartridge from a popgun, Blake let fly fire itself from a cannon; fire that took lofty and fantastic shapes as it darted between air and earth. Here was a true romantic, a true mystic, a true revolutionary; and for all his sieges of madness, a great human being. Instead of Walpole's haunted world he gives us a haunting one of his own, which, lest it fail to cast a spell upon our sight, has too a bewitching music. Here there are no fake horrors of vaults and moonlight, but the naked mysteries of worlds beyond worlds, the woes of little lost children, and the terrors of unanchored souls. Blake, like a true friend of God—a God he saw vividly amid a hierarchy of angels —speaks out of his heart, and pauses among his dreams to ask, with the stern voice of reality, Why? We have not yet answered his ardent, rebellious question concerning the miseries in life; but the images and symbols he used with such haunting effect will not, among honest people, brook an evasion.

This naive and wonderful poetry of Blake's may serve to show us that all reigns must end, even the reign of reason and of Pope. For it was but a few years after the *Songs of Innocence* and the *Songs of Experience* that Wordsworth and Coleridge proclaimed their manifesto which is the century's death-warrant if not its very funeral. It is a century with which we as good citizens today should choose to have as little as possible in common; yet how distinguished it was in its fashion, how satisfying are its merits and, for that matter, how edifying its blunders. With its misplaced devotion to art, its narrowly patrician standards, its stream of wit, its love and show of brilliance, it was a supremely *literary* century. Men have never written better prose than they did in that hundred years. Some of the best of it will be found in these pages giving expression, it so happens, to some of the best traits that made up eighteenth-century life, and to some of the worst. I do not claim that because this is a miscellany of classics it is a miscellany of masterpieces. But here, at the very least, is worthy reading-matter that provides the key to an age. Any one who reads this book (with the proper care and diligence) can voice an opinion, without risking his good name, as to what it must have felt like to live when Swift, and after him Sterne and Sheridan, were alive.

DONALD CULROSS PEATTIE

Aries

MARCH TWENTY-FIRST

On this chill uncertain spring day, toward twilight, I have heard the first frog quaver from the marsh. That is a sound that Pharaoh listened to as it rose from the Nile, and it blended, I suppose, with his discontents and longings, as it does with ours. There is something lonely in that first shaken and uplifted trilling croak. And more than lonely, for I hear a warning in it, as Pharaoh heard the sound of plague. It speaks of the return of life, animal life, to the earth. It tells of all that is most unutterable in evolution—the terrible continuity and fluidity of protoplasm, the irrepressible forces of reproduction—not mystical human love, but the cold batrachian jelly by which we vertebrates are linked to the things that creep and writhe and are blind yet breed and have being. More than half it seems to threaten that when mankind has quite thoroughly shattered and eaten and debauched himself with his own follies, that voice may still be ringing out in the marshes of the Nile and the Thames and the Potomac, unconscious that Pharaoh wept for his son.

It always seems to me that no sooner do I hear the first frog trill than I find the first cloud of frog's eggs in a wayside pool, so swiftly does the emergent creature pour out the libation of its cool fertility. There is life where before there was none. It is as repulsive as it is beautiful, as silvery-black as it is slimy. Life, in short, raw and exciting, life almost in primordial form, irreducible element.

MARCH TWENTY-SECOND

For the ancients the world was a little place, bounded between Ind and Thule. The sky bent very low over Olympus, and astronomers had not yet taken the friendliness out of the stars. The shepherd kings of the desert called them by the names Job knew, Al-Debaran, Fomalhaut, Mizar, Al-Goth, Al-Tair, Deneb and Achernar. For the Greeks the glittering constellations made pictures of their heroes and heroines, and of beasts and birds. The heavenly truth of their Arcadian mythology blazed nightly in the skies for the simplest clod to read.

Through all this celestial splendor the sun plowed yearly in a broad track that they called the zodiac. As it entered each constellation a new month with fresh significances and consequences was marked down by a symbol. Lo, in the months when the rains descended, when the Nile and the Tigris and Yangtse rose, the sun entered the constellations that were like fishes, and like Water Carriers! In the hot dry months it was in the constellation that is unmistakably a scorpion, bane of the desert. Who could say that the stars in their orderly procession did not sway a man's destiny?

Best of all, the year began with spring, with the vernal equinox. It was a natural, a pastoral, a homely sort of year, which a man could take to his heart and remember; he could tell the date by the feeling in his bones. It is the year which green things, and the beasts and birds in their migrations, all obey, a year like man's life, from his birth cry to the snows upon the philosopher's head.

MARCH TWENTY-THIRD

The old almanacs have told off their years, and are dead with them. The weather-wisdom and the simple faith that cropped up through them as naturally as grass in an orchard, are withered now, and their flowers of homely philosophy and seasonable prediction and reflection are dry, and only faintly, quaintly fragrant. The significance of the Bull and the Crab and the Lion are not more dead, for the modern mind, than the Nature philosophy of a generation ago. This age has seen the trees blasted to skeletons by the great guns, and the birds feeding on men's eyes. Pippa has passed.

It is not that man alone is vile. Man is a part of Nature. So is the atomic disassociation called high explosive. So are violent death, rape, agony, and rotting. They were all here, and quite natural, before our day, in the sweet sky and the blowing fields.

There is no philosophy with a shadow of realism about it, save a philosophy based upon Nature. It turns a smiling face, a surface easily conquered by the gun, the bridge, the dynamite stick. Yet there is no obedience but to its laws. Hammurabi spoke and Rameses commanded, and the rat gnawed and the sun shone and the hive followed its multiplex and golden order. Flowers pushed up their child faces in the spring, and the bacteria slowly took apart the stuff of life. Today the Kremlin commands, the Vatican speaks. And tomorrow the rat will still be fattening, the sun be a little older, and the bacteria remain lords of creation, whose subtraction would topple the rest of life.

Now how can a man base his way of thought on Nature and wear so happy a face? How can he take comfort from withering grass where he lays his head, from a dying sun to which he turns his face, from a mortal woman's head pressed on his shoulder? To say how that might be, well might he talk the year around.

MARCH TWENTY-FOURTH

Perhaps in Tempe the wild lawns are thick with crocuses, and narcissus blows around Paestum, but here on this eastern shore of a western world, spring is a season of what the embittered call realism, by which they mean the spoiling of joy. Joy will come, as the joy of a child's birth comes—after the pains. So dry cold winds still walk abroad, under gray skies.

It is not that nothing blooms or flies; the honey bees were out for an hour, the one hour of sunlight, and above the pools where the salamander's eggs drift in inky swirls, the early midges danced. Down the runs and rills I can hear the calling of a red-bird entreating me to come and find him, come and find him! There is a black storm of grackles in the tree limbs where the naked maple flowers are bursting out in scarlet tips from their bud scales, and a song-sparrow sits on an alder that dangles out its little gold tails.

We are so used to flowers wrapped up in the pretty envelopes of their corollas and calyces, so softened in our taste for the lovely in Nature, that we scarcely rate an alder catkin as a flower at all. Yet it is nothing else— nothing but the male antlers, sowing the wind with their freight of fertilizing pollen. The small, compact female flowers, like tiny cones, wait in the chill wild air for the golden cargo.

So does our spring begin, in a slow flowering on the leafless wood of the bough of hazel and alder and poplar and willow, a hardy business, a spawning upon the air, like the spawning in the ponds, a flowering so primitive that it carries us back to ancient geologic times, when trees that are now fossils sowed the wind like these, their descendants—an epoch when the world, too, was in its naked springtime.

MARCH TWENTY-FIFTH

The beginnings of spring, the true beginnings, are quite unlike the springtides of which poets and musicians sing. The artists become conscious of spring in late April, or May, when it is not too much to say that the village idiot would observe that birds are singing and nesting, that fields bear up their freight of flowering and ants return to their proverbial industry.

But the first vernal days are younger. Spring steals in shyly, a tall, naked child in her pale gold hair, amidst us the un-innocent, skeptics in wool mufflers, prudes in gumshoes and Grundies with head-colds. Very secretly the old field cedars sow the wind with the freight of their ancient pollen. A grackle in the willow croaks and sings in the uncertain, ragged voice of a boy. The marshes brim, and walking is a muddy business. Oaks still are barren and secretive. On the lilac tree only the twin buds suggest her coming maturity and flowering. But there in the pond float the inky masses of those frogs' eggs, visibly life in all its rawness, its elemental shape and purpose. Now is the moment when the secret of life could be discovered, yet no one finds it.

MARCH TWENTY-SIXTH

Out of the stoa, two thousand years ago, strode a giant to lay hold on life and explain it. He went down to the "primordial slime" of the seashore to look for its origin. There if anywhere he would find it, he thought, where the salt water and the earth were met, and the mud quivered like a living thing, and from it emerged strange shapeless primitive beings, themselves scarce more than animate bits of ooze. To Aristotle it seemed plain enough that out of the dead and the inanimate is made the living, and back to death are turned the bodies of all things that have lived, to be used over again. So nothing was wasted; all moved in a perpetual cycle. Out of vinegar, he felt certain, came vinegar eels, out of dung came blow-flies, out of decaying fruit bees were born, and out of the rain pool frogs spawned.

But the eye of even Aristotle was purblind in its nakedness. Of the spore and the sperm he never dreamed; he guessed nothing of bacteria. Now man can peer down through the microscope, up at the revealed stars. And behold, the lens has only multiplied the facts and deepened the mystery.

For now we know that spontaneous generation never takes place. Life comes only from life. Was not the ancient Hindu symbol for it a serpent with a tail in its mouth? Intuitive old fellows, those Aryan brothers of ours, wise in their superstitions, like old women. Life, we discover, is a closed, nay, a charmed circle. Wherever you pick it up, it has already begun; yet as soon as you try to follow it, it is already dying.

MARCH TWENTY-SEVENTH

First to grasp biology as a science, Aristotle thought that he had also captured the secret of life itself. From the vast and original body of his observation, he deduced a cosmology like a pure Greek temple, symmetrical and satisfying. For two millenniums it housed the serene intelligence of the race.

Here was an absolute philosophy; nothing need be added to it; detraction was heretical. It traced the ascent of life from the tidal ooze up to man, the plants placed below the animals, the animals ranged in order of increasing intelligence. Beyond man nothing could be imagined but God, the supreme intelligence. God was all spirit; the lifeless rock was all matter. Living beings on this earth were spirit infusing matter.

Still this conception provides the favorite text of poet or pastor, praising the earth and the fullness thereof. It fits so well with the grandeur of the heavens, the beauty of the flowers at our feet, the rapture of the birds! The Nature lover of today would ask nothing better than that it should be true.

Aristotle was sure of it. He points to marble in a quarry. It is only matter; then the sculptor attacks it with his chisel, with a shape in his mind. With form, soul enters into the marble. So all living things are filled with soul, some with more, some with less. But even a jellyfish is infused with that which the rock possesses not. Thus existence has its origin in supreme intelligence, and everything has an intelligent cause and serves its useful purpose. That purpose is the development of higher planes of existence. Science, thought its Adam, had but to put the pieces of the puzzle together, to expose for praise the cosmic design, all beautiful.

MARCH TWENTY-EIGHTH

The hook-nosed Averroës, the Spanish Arab born in Cordova in 1126, and one time cadi of Seville, shook a slow dissenting head. He did not like this simile of Aristotle's, of the marble brought to life and form by the sculptor. The simile, he keenly perceived, would be applicable at best if the outlines of the statute were already performed in the marble as it lay in the quarry. For that is precisely how we find life. The tree is preformed in the seed; the future animal already exists in the embryo. Wherever we look we find form, structure, adaptation, already present. Never has it been vouchsafed to us to see pure creation out of the lifeless.

And Galileo, also, ventured to shake the pillars of the Schoolmen's Aristotelian temple. Such a confirmed old scrutinizer was not to be drawn toward inscrutable will. The stars, nearest of all to Aristotle's God, should have moved with godlike precision, and Galileo, peering, found them erring strangely all across heaven. He shrugged, but was content. Nature itself was the miracle. Nature with all its imperfections. Futile for science to try to discover what the forces of Nature are; it can only discover how they operate.

MARCH TWENTY-NINTH

Comforting, sustaining, like the teat to the nursling, is Aristotle's beautiful idea that everything serves a useful purpose and is part of the great design. Ask, for instance, of what use is grass. Grass, the pietist assures us, was made in order to nourish cows. Cows are here on earth to nourish men. So all flesh is grass, and grass was put here for man.

But of what use, pray, is man? Would anybody, besides his dog, miss him if he were gone? Would the sun cease to shed its light because there were no human beings here to sing the praises of sunlight? Would there be sorrow among the little hiding creatures of the underwood, or loneliness in the hearts of the proud and noble beasts? Would the other simians feel that their king was gone? Would God, Jehovah, Zeus, Allah, miss the sound of hymns and psalms, the odor of frankincense and flattery?

There is no certainty vouchsafed us in the vast testimony of Nature that the universe was designed for man, nor yet for any purpose, even the bleak purpose of symmetry. The courageous thinker must look the inimical aspects of his environment in the face, and accept the stern fact that the universe is hostile and deathy to him save for a very narrow zone where it permits him, for a few eons, to exist.

MARCH THIRTIETH

Archaic and obsolete sounds the wisdom of the great old Greek. Life, his pronouncement ran, is soul pervading matter. What, soul in a jellyfish, an oyster, a burdock? Then by soul he could not have meant that moral quality which Paul of Tarsus or Augustine of Hippo were to call soul. Aristotle is talking rather about that undefined but essential and precious something that just divides the lowliest microörganism from the dust; that makes the ugly thousand-legged creature flee from death; that makes the bird pour out its heart in morning rapture; that makes the love of man for woman a holy thing sacred to the carrying on of the race.

But what is this but life itself? In every instance Aristotle but affirms that living beings are matter pervaded by a noble, a palpitant and thrilling thing called life. This is the mystery, and his neat cosmology solves nothing of it. But it is not Aristotle's fault that he did not give us the true picture of things. It is Nature herself, as we grow in comprehension of her, who weans us from our early faith.

MARCH THIRTY-FIRST

Aristotle's rooms in the little temple of the Lyceum were the first laboratory, where dissection laid bare the sinews and bones of life. The Lyceum was a world closer to the marine biological station at Woods Hole, Massachusetts, than it was to its neighbor the Parthenon. Its master did for marine biology what Euclid did for geometry; his work on the embryology of the chick still stands as a nearly perfect monograph of biological investigation. The originality, the scope of his works, the magnificence of his dream for biology as an independent science, have probably never been surpassed by any one who has lived since.

Unlike many of the more timid or less gifted investigators of today, Aristotle could not help coming to conclusions about it all. For his cosmology it should be said that it was the best, perhaps the only possible, philosophy of the origin and nature of life which the times permitted. We can all feel in our bones how agreeable it were to accept the notion of design, symmetry, purpose, an evolution toward a spiritual godhead such as Aristotle assures us exists.

But as it was Aristotle himself who taught us to observe, investigate, deduce what facts compel us to deduce, so we must concede that it is Nature herself, century after century—day after day, indeed, in the whirlwind progress of science—that propels us farther and farther away from Aristotelian beliefs. At every point she fails to confirm the grand old man's cherished picture of things. There are persons so endowed by temperament that they will assert that if Nature has no "soul," purpose, nor symmetry, we needs must put them in the picture, lest the resulting composition be scandalous, intolerable, and maddening. To such the scientist can only say, "Believe as you please."

APRIL FIRST

I say that it touches a man that his blood is sea water and his tears are salt, that the seed of his loins is scarcely different from the same cells in a seaweed, and that of stuff like his bones are coral made. I say that physical and bio logic law lies down with him, and wakes when a child stirs in the womb, and that the sap in a tree, uprushing in the spring, and the smell of the loam, where the bacteria bestir themselves in darkness, and the path of the sun in the heaven, these are facts of first importance to his mental conclusions, and that a man who goes in no consciousness of them is a drifter and a dreamer, without a home or any contact with reality.

APRIL SECOND

Each year, and above all, each spring, raises up for Nature a new generation of lovers—and this quite irrespective of the age of the new votary. As I write this a boy is going out to the marshes to watch with field glasses the mating of the red-winged blackbirds, rising up in airy swirls and clouds. Or perhaps he carries some manual to the field, and sits him down on an old log, to trace his way through Latin names, that seem at first so barbarous and stiff. There is no explaining why the boy has suddenly forsaken the ball and bat, or finds a kite less interesting in the spring skies than a bird. For a few weeks, or a few seasons, or perhaps for a lifetime, he will follow this bent with passion.

And at the same time there will be a man who all his life has put away this call, or never heard it before, who has come to the easier, latter end of life, when leisure is his own. And he goes out in the woods to collect his first botanical specimen and to learn that he has much to learn for all his years.

They are never to be forgotten—that first bird pursued through thicket and over field with serious intent, not to kill but to know it, or that first plant lifted reverently and excitedly from the earth. No spring returns but that I wish I might live again through the moment when I went out in the woods and sat down with a book in my hands, to learn not only the name, but the ways and the range and the charm of the windflower, *Anemone quinquefolia*.

APRIL THIRD

It was on this day in 1837 that there was born in the Catskill country the sage of "Slabsides," John Burroughs. Friend, in his youth, to Whitman, with whom he made hospital rounds in Washington in the Civil War, he was linked in our minds in his latter days with Edison and Henry Ford and John Muir as one of the grand old men. To the doors of "Slabsides" and "Riverby" and "Woodchuck Lodge" trooped interviewers, fellow loafers, naturalists young and old to see the raiser of bees, the husbandman of grapes. He was anything but the hermit that Thoreau had been.

The recluse of Walden, of course, was one of John's models, at least in his early years—along with Emerson and Audubon and Wordsworth. One of his first essays submitted to the *Atlantic Monthly* sent William Dean Howells to running through Emerson's works to see if it were not plagiarized. Burroughs modeled himself throughout upon the lines of genius and succeeded in giving a good imitation of it. If he was only partially rated as a naturalist in scientific circles, that is simply because he discovered but little new—except as it was new to him.

But John was honest; he never pretended even to himself that he was a scientist. He was an appreciator, and in a wide sense, a poet of science, but a poet who would take no license. With Roosevelt he made war upon nature fakers; more than any other writer he forced Darwin, and the idea of evolution, upon a sentimental and still fundamentalist America—an America that would never have accepted such heresies from one who looked and spake less like Elijah.

APRIL FOURTH

The life of John Burroughs cannot be told alone in its outward events. Its greatest significance lies in the changes that went on inside the man himself, for they reflect the changes of an age which began with such stirring, idealistic democrats as Lincoln and Gladstone, Whitman and Emerson, underwent the racking controversy between religion and science, submitted to the triumph of the German mechanists, saw the vanishing of the American wilderness, the waning popularity of the essay, of contemplation and simplicity, and ended in the fiery hells of the World War.

It was as a penman, a loafer, a buoyant talker that John began his career. A delightful humanizer, a popularizer accepted on face value from the start, Burroughs was at first a slipshod observer. He had a positive distaste for exactitude. But he was always sensitive to bigger men about him. Darwin's painstaking work on the movements of plants, and the observations of Fabre —"the Sherlock Holmes of insects" as Burroughs aptly called him—brought him in middle life to serious study. He dropped Wordsworth and Tennyson from his shelves and gave place to Carlyle and Fiske and Bergson. He grew steadily more muscular.

A little more, and Burroughs might have become a scientist. But the World War was too crushing a blow for the man who had once stood in the crowd to hear Lincoln's Second Inaugural speech. In his hatred of Germany and the soul-less thought which she embodied for him, he became, as he declared, "a savage old man." Never a thorough convert to methodic science, he recanted in horror, only to find that he could no longer read the gentle poets.

APRIL FIFTH

Everywhere spring unfurls her slim green standards—here a freshening of the dun grass and there a rush of vivid life to the twigs of the sassafras saplings that line the country roads. The onion grass is shooting up, spindling and strong-scented in the woods. Sulphurous hellebore leaves, inviting but poisonous, expand in the cress beds around the springs and little rills. The crumpled rank leaf of skunk cabbage opens out, a sultry color one might expect to see rather in a tropical rain forest.

In the stagnant ponds and the cross-country ditches through the low meadows by the river the green scum has appeared. It is Algae, of different sorts, each with its shade of the new dominant color. A brilliant primal green is

Spirogyra, so exquisite under the microscope; there is an unwholesome blue-green of a more primitive, slimier alga, and a yellow-green one I cannot name at all. These are the colors of the first green things that ever grew upon an uninhabited earth, for from the fresh water Algae all plant life must be descended.

And on the tree trunks Algae of deep moss-green and soft grass-green are freshening after the rains. So everywhere the color of life returns to the earth, returns to gladden the eye that was hungry for it. Not all of these greens are pretty or quite *nice,* as the tender golden green haze of leaves in the tulip trees is lovely in the landscape now. But all of life is not nice—perhaps the most of it and even the best of it is not.

APRIL SIXTH

The last fling of winter is over, save for tingling nights and dawns rimed with a silver frost. Everywhere I hear the metallic clinking of the cricket frogs, the trilling of the toads, the gabble of the grackles. Today the first dragonflies have emerged to dart about in an afternoon sunshine that in the leafless thickets seemed as intense as a summer day, and over the swell of the fields, still high with their brown and yellow stands of grass and weeds, the heat waves shimmer. The earth, the soil itself, has a dreaming quality about it. It is warm now to the touch; it has come alive; it hides secrets that in a moment, in a little while, it will tell. Some of them are bursting out already—the first leaves of windflowers uncurling, the spears of mottled adder's tongue leaves and the furled up flags of bloodroot. Old earth is great with her children, the bulb and the grub, and the sleepy mammal and the seed.

APRIL SEVENTH

It was the way of seers of old to read in the flight of birds and the entrails of a ram, destiny's intentions. Prophets there are today—economists, social theorists, iconoclasts and makers of new ikons for old—who read the doom of this and predict the rise of that, in the configuration of events as they fly overhead, or in the investigation of the past's cold carcass.

Man's ultimate fate is not written in the works of Spengler or Veblen or Marx, but in the nucleus of his own cells; his end, if it be predestined, is in the death of a star, or in a rising of the bacteria. He will do well to have a heed to the nature of life, for of life there is but one kind. Man shares it with the corn and the crow, the oak and the mayfly. Therefore in such natural things may he well search for auguries.

On any clear-skied day of the year I may be found engrossed in nothing weightier than watching an anthill or gathering inedible fungi, to all appearance strayed from the argument of my philosophy. But in truth it is philosophy that has a weakness toward straying; the facts upon which it is builded rest firm, and impel the philosopher to seek them, even aside, down the bypaths, under the bracken, in the small, anonymous places. Even here, escaped from all but a bright bird eye, all sound of traffic but the brook's over its stones, man is not rid of his crying inner query. And the smiling woodland silence falls knowledgeably upon his ears.

APRIL EIGHTH

There is something classic about the study of the little world that is made up by our first spring flowers—all those which bloom not later than April. They are delightfully easy to learn, in case you do not already know them, for there are so few of them that any local manual of the spring flowers will swiftly make you friends for life with them. Happy are those who this year, for the first time, go wood wandering to find them, who first crack open the new manual, smelling of fresh ink, and rejoice in the little new pocket lens. And many, many are the feet that have trod that way before, the boy Linnæus, the young Asa Gray, the child prodigies like Rafinesque and Haller, the wearied great scholars seeking rest and distraction, like Jacob Grimm and John Stuart Mill.

So great names lend their luster to this innocent delight. But the classicism of the earliest wildflowers derives also from the fact that they fall into a few families, the lily, pink, buttercup, crucifer, rose, violet, umbellifer, heath and composite families, whose unmistakable ear-marks are as decisive as the national traits of Greeks, Persians, Hindus, Englishmen and Norsemen. Characteristic of the northern hemisphere, these give us blossoms that turn up to us the dainty face upon the delicate stalk. They mean to us all that is brave and fresh and frail in the name of spring. Summer flowers distract us with well upon a hundred families, with a strong tropical element; autumnal flowers are confined almost wholly to the tall rank composites. But something in the spring flora, perfect in its simplicity and unity, carries us back to Arcady.

APRIL NINTH

Whenever I walk in the marshy ground I find the spikes of Equisetum thrusting up in a pale, almost a fleshy turret, soft and moist to the touch, and hollow like a pipe. Like the cinnamon fern, this fern-ally throws up a strange spore-bearing frond almost devoid of coloring matter, quite unlike the purely vegetative green shoot that rises beside it.

Somewhere in the now scattered fragments of the great evolutionary line of the ferns, through Equisetum to the clubmosses and Selaginella, the lost trace of the flowering plants must have branched away, through stages that we shall never know, through families whose unreal fossils take us step by step toward the cycads and the pines. The odd thing is that these emergent groups should be gone from the world, never again to know the grip of the earth between their roots, the warmth of sunlight on their fronds.

But, each spring, little ancient Equisetum pushes up again, to enjoy the old, old sunshine and bare its spores to the wind. It is like some wizened antique race of men whose stature is cretin, whose language is cryptic, that has been driven down into the marshes, isolated, decimated, and spared at last because time has simply forgotten to finish it off.

APRIL TENTH

After the long spell of bad weather the birds, who were banked up, I fancy, somewhere in the Carolinas, are coming through in a torrent. There are so many that I can keep but the most delirious count of them. My records are carried away in fluttering confusion, like a wind gauge in a hurricane. Every time I approach the marsh I hear the warning cries of the herons, like the drop of an old chain on its own coils, and from beyond the cat-tail lances the snaky neck and archaic head of the bittern is turned to look at me, with the astonished and disapproving gaze that Archæopteryx might have turned on an anachronistic human.

In the wet maple woods, where the skunk cabbage leaf is expanding in its unabashed ugliness, the grackles are already quieting, and in their place I hear, morning and evening, the first sounds of mourning doves. Along the runs and rills kingfishers are setting up their riparian claims with loud cries, like the whirling of a boy's wooden rattle. I have simply lost all account of the order of arrival of the sparrow tribe, of the swallows, vireos and warblers and wrens. There is no order; they all seemed to come on the same day, and continue to arrive in increasing numbers every day.

Now is the moment when the novice at bird-gazing needs a friend. Flowers are best identified, if one is a neophyte, by one's self. The mere exercise of tracking them to their names will fix them in the memory. But with the birds, a guide, a friend by the side, to point out what you ought to have seen, to pass you the binoculars and whisper eagerly in your ear, is worth a shelf of books.

APRIL ELEVENTH

Some call them fiddle heads, those first elvish green coils of fern that are pushing up in the woods, breaking a wet and sullen sod as mushrooms do. Compare them if you like to the scrolled head of a fiddle, or call them bishop's staves. But as soon as the coil is half expanded, then from the cunningly involuted roll begin to shoot the tendrily side branches of the frond, the pinnæ that may again be divided into pinnules. Now they are called lady's fingers, from their dainty charm, but as they grope upwards as if they were reaching for the pale sunlight, their name is dead men's hands. Truly, out of the darkness, where forever the stems of our little northern ferns are hid, the frond reaches up an eager hand for the blessed sunlight.

In the tropics there are ferns, tree ferns, with true stems, but a moment's thoughtful glance will show any one that the apparent stem of a fern is but a leaf stalk. Most of the plant lives a mole's existence in this harsher clime. Only a leaf or two, a spore-bearing frond, is ever thrown up to the light and air.

All that concerns the fern has filled the human mind with thoughts of mystery and dread. Martagon and lunary, moonwort and rattlesnake fern, male fern and lady fern, these names suggest the mingled confusion and superstition which they roused in the antique mind. Witches allegedly gathered fern seed to work their spells. It is safe to suppose that none but supernatural folk could do so, since ferns have no seeds. In this, perhaps, lay their quality of evil for the medieval mind.

> "Fern, that vile, unuseful weed
> That grows equivocally without seed."

APRIL TWELFTH

There came a moment in this chill, palely green afternoon, as all the world was watery with running ponds, and the river boiling high and yellow, when I stood among the uncoiling fronds of the cinnamon ferns and listened to the first piping of the tree frog. I used not to distinguish him from the pond frogs, but my ear at last is attuned to the difference. A pond frog is a coarse and booming creature compared with the eery, contented and yet lonely little tree frog thrilling the light airs with its song.

It is strange how a note that must assuredly bespeak contentment, almost in this case a hymn of domestic felicity, can so trouble the heart of the listener. For the song rises over the creak-crack of the swamp frogs with an unearthly soaring wail, a note of keening that the country folk will say foretells a coming rain. And they are right in this. The tree frog never cries but a soft, oppressive dampness hangs upon the air, and spring thunder speaks in the western sky. Just so, in summer, do the cicadas, early in the morning, foretell a blazing day, and crickets in the autumn grass predict their deaths of frost.

APRIL THIRTEENTH

First, a frog's egg is encircled vertically by a single groove—the future right and left of the animal. Then another longitudinal line cuts it at right angles, and by the third day if not sooner, there always appears that horizontal slice, a girdle round the egg not at its equator but above it—half way to the egg's north pole. Significant inequality that divides the body from the head! Splendid injustice that we may thank for all the brains that we possess!

Now the original grant of life is broken up by an intricate inheritance into cells increasingly fine, increasingly significant. Small matter if you no longer follow all the events in strict detail for the division proceeds internally, with dazzling swiftness. On the fourth day the low-power microscope is needed, and a few days later the high-power lens, with which one may see the first rush of blood along the veins.

But still the naked eye can distinguish externally the ridge of the nerve cord, that so swiftly vanishes in the shroud of flesh. Then the gills rush out, only themselves to be buried. The awkward head takes shape, the tail, like the legs of a man in a sack, struggles to expand itself, and so at last, with a sort of horror and delight, we watch the animal shouldering potently about in the prison of its larval state as it prepares to emerge upon the year with all its hungers, its needs and its cries.

APRIL FOURTEENTH

The tadpoles in the quiet bay of the brook are now far past the stage of inky black little wrigglers attached by their two little sticky pads to any stick or leaf, merely breathing through their gills, and lashing with their hair-fine cilia. A dark brown skin—really gold spots mottling the black—now proclaims the leopard frogs they will become. Now the hunger of the open mouths is insatiable; a tadpole, when not resting in sheer exhaustion, will not (and I suppose could not safely) cease for one moment to eat. They all scrape the slime from the sticks and stones; they nibble the water weeds; they are launched upon life with all its appetites and delights and perils.

And what perils! The water is now alive with treacherous, fiercely biting back-swimmers and their cousins the giant water bugs with ugly sucking mouths. The dragonfly nymphs emerge as if perfectly timed to live upon a banquet of frog larvæ prepared for them, tigers of the ponds with legs that snatch, and jaws that devour. Fish, turtles, and water birds might all well die in early spring but for the monstrous fertility of the female leopard frog. She must spawn enough children to pay tribute to hundreds of merciless ogre overlords and still more, so that by good fortune June shall hear the marshes rattling with her children's hymns.

So already the contest is begun, not, in reality the battle between death and life, but life locked naked with life, in a sort of terrible mating of substances, dissolving and fusing from one species into another, one instant palpitant batrachian jelly and the next the wry croak of a stilted shorebird.

APRIL FIFTEENTH

There is one spot in my neighborhood where I can literally wade into the very medium of life itself, and that is the marsh and the pond. With a net—or with nothing better than my hands, if need be, I can scoop up the teeming stuff of it—the decaying twigs bearing fresh-water sponges, the shard of a crayfish that went to make a meal for a bittern, the strands of the first Algae, a handful of mud out of which small nameless things come kicking and twisting. Here is the world of the fairy shrimp, of the thin tubifex worms poised for retreat into their mud chimneys, the caddis-fly larvæ, like centaurs with their dragging cases hampering half their bodies, of the transparent Leptodora, the phantom snatcher of that netherworld.

All about me rise the cries of the redwings, sweet gurgling watery whistles, and the angry *peent, peent* when I come too near their nesting places. The waters lap the tiny shores of this impermanent sea; the ancient sunlight warms me, and dances on the ripples. The feel of life, the joy of it, the thrill and the warmth of it are in my bones, and the same sensations penetrate, I know, to the very bottom of the pond.

APRIL SIXTEENTH

Upon the bottom of any pond in spring are pastured its tiny grazing animals, its pollywogs and snails, its microscopic flagellates, each one of which will produce a thousand descendants in a month, its rotifers of which each, seventy hours after hatching from the egg, becomes itself a spawning factory. Just above them wait and prowl the small creatures of prey, the crayfish and the tigerish dragonfly nymphs, the nymphs of the mayflies, agile as minnows. Voracity awaits these too; they are destined to vanish down greater jaws and bills and gullets. Life in the casual pond, like life in the sea or the jungle, is like a pyramid with the multiplex and miniform for the broad base.

A bucketful of water may support ten thousand copepods; but a water snake may require a marsh to himself, as a whale needs league upon league of sea, or a bear the half of a mountainside. It is a question if there be any biologic advantage in mastering your environment when you need such a quantity of it to support you. Necessity presses just as sternly on the great beasts as on the small. The problem of population and food is the same, and the increased consciousness of the so-called higher forms is harshly compensated for by their increased capacity for suffering. True, it were pleasanter to eat than be eaten, but in the end even kings must come to dust.

APRIL SEVENTEENTH

You can never tell what they will be teaching next, but when I was a student they taught that plant life began in the fresh-water ponds, and not in the sea, as many people suppose. For the fresh-water Algae, the little green and bluegreen pond scums, are not only, upon the face of it, the simplest green plants alive today, but their fossil record is buried in the ancient rocks. From the fresh water the Algae invaded the sea, and so the seaweeds came into being. The story of evolution runs from the fresh water to the sea, and from the sea to the land, and, oddly enough, one part of the tale runs from the land back into the pond.

The pond, of course, contains animals and plants that have been aquatic since the beginning of their time on earth, but the great majority of its inhabitants have re-entered the water from the land. The insects in these April waters must be considered as erstwhile air-breathing, flying creatures of the upper world, that have had to learn through ages of evolution to swim, to breathe through gills or carry their air supply with them. They are under the water only by virtue of a tremendous amount of adaptation to the liquid airless medium. The turtle on the log, the muskrat with his home in the bank, these too have chosen water life and display adaptation to it—the streamline form, the lifted snout and eye so perfectly adapted to swimming just at the surface, the feet fit either for burrowing or a flipperlike swimming. And creatures who go back to life's earlier, watery home return equipped with all the advantages that the harshly competitive life on land or in the air brought out in them.

APRIL EIGHTEENTH

The ancient forms from which today's world evolved have not become impotent with age. From the old stumps new shoots spring up. Primitive as they are, those clouds of diatoms that fill the ponds in the first days of spring are new; they are modern Algae adapted to the cold seas and the frozen ponds of our barely post-glacial era, little hard infrangible atoms carven as it were out of silicon crystals. Those bacteria that prey exclusively upon men and the higher animals cannot be anything but recent developments. Everywhere is flow and flux.

So far from being a steady progress in our exalted direction, evolution for the most is tending quite otherwheres. It may troop joyfully backwards (or it looks backward from our view point) toward simplification, toward a successful laziness. Parasitism, for example, is a highly lucrative mode of life that has probably never been more abundant than in the present.

In short, evolution is not so much progress as it is simply change. It does not leave all its primitive forms behind. It carries them over from age to age, well knowing that they are the precious base of the pyramid on which the more fantastic and costly experiments must be carried.

APRIL NINETEENTH

If progress is an increasing power to master and mold environment, then there is a strong current of progress in evolution. A one-celled flagellate certainly has but the dullest awareness of its environment as it bumps aimlessly about, but the redwinged blackbird hanging its nest on the cat-tails and the muskrat digging crafty passages into and out of his home—these highly sentient, motile, instinctive and often intelligent creatures are a world and many ages beyond the blind and stupid flagellate. And last, in his majesty comes man, who if he does not like the marsh, will dig ditches and drain it off. In a year he will be turning a furrow there, sowing his domesticated crop, the obedient grain; he will drive out every animal and plant that does not bow down to him.

Man—man has the world in the hollow of his hand. He is a standing refutation of an old superstition like predestination—or a new one like determinism. His chances seem all but boundless, and boundless might be his optimism if he had not already thrown away so many of his opportunities. That very marsh was the home of waterfowl as valuable as they were beautiful. Now they must die, because in this world all breeding grounds are already crammed full. When he slays the birds, he lets loose their prey, and his worst enemy, the insects. He wastes his forests faster than he replaces them, and slaughters the mink and the beaver and the seal. He devours his limited coal supply ever faster; he fouls the rivers, invents poison gases and turns his destruction even on his own kind. And in the end he may present the spectacle of some Brobdingnagian spoiled baby, gulping down his cake and howling for it too.

POEMS

POETRY *speaks for itself. The following selection made from the list of one publishing house, about covers the whole field of poetry and mere verse, from the unique Edgar Allan Poe to the jolly newspaper columnist, the late Jake Falstaff.*

George Haven Putnam in "George Palmer Putnam, a Memoir" tells one story concerning his father's relations with Poe which is of curious importance to those who would still try to solve the Poe enigma. Putnam relates that Poe wrote "Eureka" in three days, at a desk in Putnam's office. Not that Putnam wanted him there, because Poe was drunk as a hoot-owl all those three days, unkempt and reeking with alcohol; but because Poe had a meticulous sense of honor, and having extracted $14 from Putnam in advance for the wildest notion among the many wild notions he had proposed to Putnam—and had written them according to plan when Putnam forked over an advance, Poe meant to finish up the job, then and there, for which he had been paid.

Putnam tells that Poe came staggering into the office, wild-eyed, one day and said he had just discovered the solution to the riddle of the universe, that he was going to write it out, that it would sell a million copies—and that he needed fourteen dollars. That amount, Putnam says, was the equivalent of about two weeks' board and room at the lodging house where Poe was staying. When Putnam gave him the money, Poe wrote a receipt in his etching-like penmanship as carefully worded as to particulars as an over-conscientious lawyer might write it. Then he called for pen and paper, sat down and started to write the "prose poem." He came back punctually the next morning and the next morning and finished the exceedingly long work in the third day.

The "prose poem" didn't sell to the extent of a million copies immediately. It took about ten years to dispose of 750 copies.

But the strange thing about it is that Paul Valéry, the French poet and philosopher, who succeeded to Anatole France's chair in the French Academy, says in an essay on "Eureka" that it is just what Poe told Putnam it was that day—a key to the door of the unknown, a solution or at least the suggestion to a solution of the riddle of the universe. Valéry contends that this "prose poem" not only anticipates Bergson and Einstein but that it is the greatest single exercise of the mind and imagination the world has ever seen. And, in time, in various reprints, editions and translations, "Eureka" has sold many times over a million copies.

EDGAR ALLAN POE

The Raven

Once upon a midnight dreary, while I pondered, weak and weary,
Over many a quaint and curious volume of forgotten lore,—
While I nodded, nearly napping, suddenly there came a tapping,
As of some one gently rapping,—rapping at my chamber door,
" 'Tis some visitor," I muttered, "tapping at my chamber door,—
    Only this, and nothing more."

Ah, distinctly I remember it was in the bleak December,
And each separate dying ember wrought its ghost upon the floor,
Eagerly I wished the morrow;—vainly I had sought to borrow
From my books surcease of sorrow,—sorrow for the lost Lenore,—
For the rare and radiant maiden whom the angels name Lenore,—
    Nameless here for evermore.

And the silken sad uncertain rustling of each purple curtain
Thrilled me—filled me—with fantastic terrors never felt before;
So that now, to still the beating of my heart, I stood repeating
" 'Tis some visitor entreating entrance at my chamber door,—
Some late visitor entreating entrance at my chamber door.
    That it is, and nothing more."

Presently my soul grew stronger: hesitating then no longer,
"Sir," said I, "or Madam, truly your forgiveness I implore:
But the fact is I was napping, and so gently you came rapping,
And so faintly you came tapping, tapping at my chamber door,
That I scarce was sure I heard you." Here I opened wide the door.
    Darkness there, and nothing more.

Deep into that darkness peering, long I stood there, wondering, fearing,
Doubting, dreaming dreams no mortal ever dared to dream before.
But the silence was unbroken, and the stillness gave no token,
And the only word there spoken was the whispered word, "Lenore!"
This I whispered, and an echo murmured back the word, "Lenore!"
    Merely this, and nothing more.

Back into the chamber turning, all my soul within me burning,
Soon again I heard a tapping, something louder than before.
"Surely," said I, "surely that is something at my window-lattice:
Let me see, then, what thereat is, and this mystery explore,—
Let my heart be still a moment, and this mystery explore:
    'Tis the wind, and nothing more."

Open here I flung the shutter, when, with many a flirt and flutter,
In there stepped a stately Raven of the saintly days of yore.
Not the least obeisance made he,—not a minute stopped or stayed he,
But, with mien of lord or lady, perched above my chamber door,—
Perched upon a bust of Pallas just above my chamber door,—
    Perched, and sat, and nothing more.

Then this ebon bird beguiling my sad fancy into smiling,
By the grave and stern decorum of the countenance it wore,
"Though thy crest be shorn and shaven, thou," I said, "art sure no craven,
Ghastly, grim, and ancient Raven, wandering from the Nightly shore.
Tell me what thy lordly name is on the Night's Plutonian shore!"
    Quoth the Raven, "Nevermore."

Much I marvelled this ungainly fowl to hear discourse so plainly,
Though its answer little meaning—little relevancy bore;
For we cannot help agreeing that no living human being
Ever yet was blessed with seeing bird above his chamber door,—
Bird or beast upon the sculptured bust above his chamber door,
    With such name as "Nevermore."

But the Raven, sitting lonely on that placid bust, spoke only
That one word, as if his soul in that one word he did outpour.
Nothing further then he uttered; not a feather then he fluttered,—

Till I scarcely more than muttered, "Other friends have flown before!
On the morrow *he* will leave me, as my hopes have flown before!"
    Then the bird said "Nevermore."

Startled at the stillness broken by reply so aptly spoken,
"Doubtless," said I, "what it utters is its only stock and store,
Caught from some unhappy master whom unmerciful Disaster
Followed fast and followed faster till his songs one burden bore,—
Till the dirges of his Hope that melancholy burden bore
    Of 'never,—nevermore!' "

But the Raven still beguiling all my sad soul into smiling,
Straight I wheeled a cushioned seat in front of bird and bust and door;
Then, upon the velvet sinking, I betook myself to linking
Fancy unto fancy, thinking what this ominous bird of yore—
What this grim, ungainly, ghastly, gaunt and ominous bird of yore
    Meant in croaking "Nevermore."

This I sat engaged in guessing, but no syllable expressing
To the fowl whose fiery eyes now burned into my bosom's core:
This and more I sat divining, with my head at ease reclining
On the cushion's velvet lining that the lamplight gloated o'er,
But whose velvet violet lining, with the lamplight gloating o'er,
    She shall press, ah, nevermore!

Then, methought, the air grew denser, perfumed from an unseen censer
Swung by Seraphim whose footfalls tinkled on the tufted floor.
"Wretch!" I cried, "thy God hath lent thee—by these angels he hath sent thee
Respite—respite and nepenthe from thy memories of Lenore!
Quaff, oh quaff this kind nepenthe, and forget the lost Lenore!"
    Quoth the Raven, "Nevermore."

"Prophet!" cried I, "thing of evil!—prophet still, if bird or devil!—
Whether Tempter sent, or whether tempest tossed thee here ashore,
Desolate yet all undaunted, on this desert land enchanted—
On this Home by horror haunted—tell me truly, I implore—
Is there—*is* there balm in Gilead? Tell me!—tell me, I implore!"
    Quoth the Raven, "Nevermore."

"Prophet!" cried I, "thing of evil!—prophet still, if bird or devil!—
By that Heaven that bends above us—by that God we both adore!—
Tell this soul with sorrow laden, if, within the distant Aidenn,
It shall clasp a sainted maiden whom the angels name Lenore,—
Clasp a rare and radiant maiden whom the angels name Lenore."
    Quoth the Raven, "Nevermore."

"Be that word our sign of parting, bird or fiend!" I shrieked, upstarting.
"Get thee back into the tempest and the Night's Plutonian shore!
Leave no black plume as a token of that lie thy soul hath spoken!
Leave my loneliness unbroken!—quit the bust above my door!
Take thy beak from out my heart, and take thy form from off my door!"
    Quoth the Raven, "Nevermore."

And the Raven, never flitting, still is sitting, still is sitting
On the pallid bust of Pallas, just above my chamber door;
And his eyes have all the seeming of a demon's that is dreaming,
And the lamplight o'er him streaming throws his shadow on the floor;
And my soul from out that shadow that lies floating on the floor
    Shall be lifted—nevermore!

Lenore

Ah, broken is the golden bowl!—the spirit flown forever!—
Let the bell toll!—a saintly soul floats on the Stygian river;
And, Guy De Vere, hast *thou* no tear?—weep now, or never more!

See, on yon drear and rigid bier low lies thy love, Lenore!
Come, let the burial rite be read,—the funeral song be sung!—
An anthem for the queenliest dead that ever died so young,—
A dirge for her the doubly dead in that she died so young.

"Wretches! ye loved her for her wealth and hated her for her pride!
And when she fell in feeble health, ye blessed her—that she died!
How *shall* the ritual, then, be read?—the requiem how be sung
By you—by yours, the evil eye,—by yours, the slanderous tongue
That did to death the innocence that died, and died so young?"

Peccavimus! But rave not thus, and let a Sabbath song
Go up to God so solemnly the dead may feel no wrong!
The sweet Lenore hath "gone before," with Hope, that flew beside,
Leaving thee wild for the dear child that should have been thy bride!—
For her, the fair and *debonair,* that now so lowly lies,
The life upon her yellow hair, but not within her eyes,—
The life still there, upon her hair,—the death upon her eyes.

"Avaunt! To-night my heart is light! No dirge will I upraise,
But waft the angel on her flight with a pæan of old days!
Let *no* bell toll!—lest her sweet soul, amid its hallowed mirth,
Should catch the note, as it doth float up from the damned Earth!
To friends above, from fiends below, the indignant ghost is riven,—
From Hell unto a high estate far up within the Heaven,—
From grief and groan to a golden throne, beside the King of Heaven."

Israfel[*]

IN HEAVEN a spirit doth dwell,
  "Whose heartstrings are a lute."
None sing so wildly well
As the angel, Israfel,
And the giddy stars (so legends tell),
Ceasing their hymns attend the spell
  Of his voice, all mute.

Tottering above,
  In her highest noon,
  The enamoured moon
Blushes with love,—
  While, to listen, the red levin
  (With the rapid Pleiades, even,
  Which were seven,)
  Pauses in heaven.

[*] And the angel Israfel, whose heartstrings are a lute, and who has the sweetest voice of all God's creatures.—KORAN

And they say (the starry choir
   And the other listening things)
That Israfeli's fire
Is owing to that lyre
   By which he sits and sings,
The trembling living wire
   Of those unusual strings.

But the skies that angel trod,
   Where deep thoughts are a duty—
Where Love's a grown-up god,—
   Where the Houri glances are
   Imbued with all the beauty
   Which we worship in a star.

Therefore, thou are not wrong,
   Israfeli, who despisest
An unimpassioned song:
To thee the laurels belong,
   Best bard, because the wisest!
Merrily live, and long!

The ecstasies above
   With thy burning measures suit
Thy grief, thy joy, thy hate, thy love,
   With the fervour of thy lute:
   Well may the stars be mute!

Yes, heaven is thine; but this
   Is a world of sweets and sours:
   Our flowers are merely—flowers,
And the shadow of thy perfect bliss
   Is the sunshine of ours.

If I could dwell
Where Israfel
   Hath dwelt, and he where I,

He might not sing so wildly well
 A mortal melody,—
While a bolder note than this might swell
 From my lyre within the sky.

HENRY WADSWORTH LONGFELLOW

The Two Angels

Two angels, one of Life and one of Death,
 Passed o'er the village as the morning broke;
The dawn was on their faces, and beneath,
 The sombre houses hearsed with plumes of smoke.

Their attitude and aspect were the same,
 Alike their features and their robes of white;
But one was crowned with amaranth, as with flame,
 And one with asphodels, like flakes of light.

I saw them pause on their celestial way;
 Then said I, with deep fear and doubt oppressed:
"Beat not so loud, my heart, lest thou betray
 The place where thy beloved are at rest!"

And he, who wore the crown of asphodels,
 Descending, at my door began to knock,
And my soul sank within me, as in wells
 The waters sink before an earthquake's shock.

I recognized the nameless agony,
 The terror and the tremor and the pain,
That oft before had filled and haunted me,
 And now returned with threefold strength again.

The door I opened to my heavenly guest,
   And listened, for I thought I heard God's voice;
And knowing whatsoe'er he sent was best,
   Dared neither to lament nor to rejoice.

Then with a smile, that filled the house with light,
   "My errand is not Death, but Life," he said;
And ere I answered, passing out of sight
   On his celestial embassy he sped.

'Twas at thy door, O friend! and not at mine,
   The angel with the amaranthine wreath,
Pausing descended, and with voice divine,
   Whispered a word that had a sound like Death.

Then fell upon the house a sudden gloom,
   A shadow on those features fair and thin;
And softly, from that hushed and darkened room,
   Two angels issued, where but one went in.

All is of God! If He but wave His hand
   The mists collect, the rain falls thick and loud,
Till with a smile of light on sea and land,
   Lo! he looks back from the departing cloud.

Angels of Life and Death alike are His;
   Without his leave they pass no threshold o'er;
Who, then, would wish or dare, believing this,
   Against his messengers to shut the door?

My Lost Youth

Often I think of the beautiful town
   That is seated by the sea;
Often in thought go up and down
The pleasant streets of that dear old town,
   And my youth comes back to me.

      And a verse of a Lapland song
        Is haunting my memory still:
      "A boy's will is the wind's will,
And the thoughts of youth are long, long thoughts."

I can see the shadowy lines of its trees,
    And catch, in sudden gleams,
The sheen of the far-surrounding seas,
And islands that were the Hesperides
    Of all my boyish dreams.
      And the burden of that old song,
        It murmurs and whispers still:
      "A boy's will is the wind's will,
And the thoughts of youth are long, long thoughts."

I remember the black wharves and the slips,
    And the sea-tides tossing free;
And Spanish sailors with bearded lips,
And the beauty and mystery of the ships,
    And the magic of the sea.
      And the voice of that wayward song
        Is singing and saying still:
      "A boy's will is the wind's will,
And the thoughts of youth are long, long thoughts."

I remember the bulwarks by the shore,
    And the fort upon the hill;
The sunrise gun, with its hollow roar,
The drum-beat repeated o'er and o'er,
    And the bugle wild and shrill.
      And the music of that old song
        Throbs in my memory still:
      "A boy's will is the wind's will,
And the thoughts of youth are long, long thoughts."

I remember the sea-fight far away,
    How it thundered o'er the tide!
And the dead captains, as they lay
In their graves, o'erlooking the tranquil bay
    Where they in battle died.

And the sound of that mournful song
  Goes through me with a thrill:
"A boy's will is the wind's will,
And the thoughts of youth are long, long thoughts."

I can see the breezy dome of groves,
  The shadows of Deering's Woods;
And the friendships old and the early loves
Come back with a Sabbath sound, as of doves
  In quiet neighborhoods.
    And the verse of that sweet old song,
    It flutters and murmurs still:
    "A boy's will is the wind's will,
And the thoughts of youth are long, long thoughts."

I remember the gleams and glooms that dart
  Across the school-boy's brain;
The song and the silence in the heart,
That in part are prophecies, and in part
  Are longings wild and vain.
    And the voice of that fitful song
    Sings on, and is never still:
    "A boy's will is the wind's will,
And the thoughts of youth are long, long thoughts."

There are things of which I may not speak;
  There are dreams that cannot die;
There are thoughts that make the strong heart weak,
And bring a pallor into the cheek,
  And a mist before the eye.
    And the words of that fatal song
    Come over me like a chill:
    "A boy's will is the wind's will,
And the thoughts of youth are long, long thoughts."

Strange to me now are the forms I meet
  When I visit the dear old town;
But the native air is pure and sweet,
And the trees that o'ershadow each well known street,
  As they balance up and down,

    Are singing the beautiful song,
    Are sighing and whispering still:
    "A boy's will is the wind's will,
And the thoughts of youth are long, long thoughts."

And Deering's Woods are fresh and fair,
    And with joy that is almost pain
My heart goes back to wander there,
And among the dreams of the days that were,
    I find my lost youth again.
    And the strange and beautiful song,
    The groves are repeating it still:
    "A boy's will is the wind's will,
And the thoughts of youth are long, long thoughts."

JAMES RUSSELL LOWELL

Without and Within

My coachman in the moonlight, there,
    Looks through the side light of the door;
I hear him with his brethren swear,
    As I could do,—but only more.

Flattening his nose against the pane
    He envies me my brilliant lot,
And blows his aching fists in vain,
    And wishes me a place more hot.

He sees me to the supper go,
    A silken wonder by my side,
Bare arms, bare shoulders, and a row
    Of flounces, for the door too wide.

He thinks, how happy is my arm
   'Neath its white-gloved and jewelled load,
And wishes me some dreadful harm,
   Hearing the merry corks explode.

Meanwhile I inly curse the bore
   Of hunting still the same old coon,
And envy him, outside the door,
   In golden quiets of the moon.

The winter wind is not so cold
   As the bright smiles he sees me win,
Nor our host's oldest wine so old
   As our poor gabble—watery—thin.

I envy him the ungyved prance
   By which his freezing feet he warms,
And drag my lady's-chains and dance
   The galley slave of dreary forms.

O! could he have my share of din
   And I his quiet!—past a doubt
'Twould still be one man bored within,
   And just another bored without.

GEORGE WILLIAM CURTIS

Spring or Summer?

SWIFTLY the young Spring came,—
   Love is not dearer—
Whispered the Summer's name
   As ever nearer.

Swiftly the young Spring fled,
 Dawn is not fleeter,—
Promiser or promiséd,—
 Heart! which was sweeter?

Gondola Songs

I

Rushes lean over the water,
 Shells lie on the shore,
And thou, the blue ocean's daughter,
 Sleep'st soft in the song of its roar.

Clouds sail over the ocean,
 White gusts fleck its calm,
But never its wildest motion
 Thy beautiful rest should harm.

White feet on the edge of the billow
 Mock its smooth-seething cream;
Hard ribs of beach sand thy pillow,
 And a noble lover thy dream.

Like tangles of sea-weed streaming
 Over a perfect pearl,
Thy fair hair fringes thy dreaming,
 O sleeping Lido girl!

II

Girl on the marble riva,
 You watch the gondolas glide;
The gondoliers are silent,
 The lovers sit side by side.

The gondoliers are silent,
  The lovers have all to say;
The cheek of the blushing lady
  Is paled by the dying day.

Her long fair hair is braided,
  Yours falls in a midnight shower;
Her face from the sun is shaded,
  Your bloom is a sun-bronzed flower.

The whispering lovers see you,
  As they glide by the marble shores;
You are the shade of their picture,
  And they are the light of yours.

You do not glide in a gondola,
  Nor lie on a lover's breast;
You stand in the palace shadow,
  And look on the sunset West.

There glitter your proud pavilions,
  And, breathing a summer air,—
Dark girl on the lonely riva,
  The lover awaits you there.

WILLIAM CULLEN BRYANT

Robert of Lincoln

Merrily swinging on briar and weed,
    Near to the nest of his little dame,
Over the mountain-side or mead,
    Robert of Lincoln is telling his name;

   Bob-o'-Link, bob-o'-link,
    Spink, spank, spink;
Snug and safe is that nest of ours,
Hidden among the summer flowers.
     Chee, chee, chee.

Robert of Lincoln is gaily drest,
  Wearing a bright black wedding coat;
White are his shoulders and white his crest,
  Hear him call in his merry note,—
   Bob-o'-link, bob-o'-link,
    Spink, spank, spink;
Look, what a nice new coat is mine,
Sure there was never a bird so fine.
     Chee, chee, chee.

Robert of Lincoln's Quaker wife,
  Pretty and quiet, with plain brown wings,
Passing at home a patient life,
  Broods in the grass while her husband sings
   Bob-o'-link, bob-o'-link,
    Spink, spank, spink;
Brood, kind creature; you need not fear
Thieves and robbers while I am here.
     Chee, chee, chee.

Modest and shy as a nun is she;
  One weak chirp is her only note.
Braggart and prince of braggarts is he,
  Pouring boasts from his little throat,—
   Bob-o'-link, bob-o'-link,
    Spink, spank, spink;
Never was I afraid of man;
Catch me, cowardly knaves, if you can.
     Chee, chee, chee.

Six white eggs on a bed of hay,
  Flecked with purple, a pretty sight!

There as the mother sits all day
  Robert is singing with all his might
    Bob-o'link, bob-o'-link,
      Spink, spank, spink;
Nice good wife, that never goes out,
Keeping house while I frolic about.
        Chee, chee, chee.

Soon as the little ones chip the shell
  Six wide mouths are open for food;
Robert of Lincoln bestirs him well,
  Gathering seeds for the hungry brood.
    Bob-o'link, bob-o'-link,
      Spink, spank, spink;
This new life is likely to be
Hard for a gay young fellow like me.
        Chee, chee, chee.

Robert of Lincoln at length is made
  Sober with work, and silent with care;
Off is his holiday garment laid,
  Half forgotten that merry air,
    Bob-o'-link, bob-o'-link,
      Spink, spank, spink;
Nobody knows but my mate and I
Where our nest and our nestlings lie.
        Chee, chee, chee.

Summer wanes; the children are grown;
  Fun and frolic no more he knows;
Robert of Lincoln's a humdrum crone;
  Off he flies, and we sing as he goes
    Bob-o'-link, bob-o'-link,
      Spink, spank, spink;
When you can pipe that merry old strain
Robert of Lincoln come back again.
        Chee, chee, chee.

WILLIAM HENRY HURLBERT

Sehnsucht

Come, beauteous day!
Never did lover on his bridal night
So chide thine over-eager light
　As I thy long delay!

Bring me my rest!
Never can these sweet thorny roses
Whereon my heart reposes
　Be into slumber pressed!

Day be my night!
Night hath no stars to rival with her eyes,
Night hath no peace like his who lies
　Upon her bosom white.

She did transmute
This my poor cell into a paradise,
Gorgeous with blossoming lips and dewy eyes
　And all her beauty's fruit.

Nor dull nor gray
Seems to mine eyes this dim and wintry morn.
Ne'er did the rosy banners of the Dawn
　Herald a brighter day!

Come, beauteous day!
Come, or in sunny light, or storm eclipse!
Bring me to the immortal summer of her lips,
　Then have thy way!

WALT WHITMAN

Song of the Open Road

1

AFOOT and light-hearted, I take to the open road,
Healthy, free, the world before me,
The long brown path before me, leading wherever I choose.

Henceforth I ask not good-fortune—I myself am good fortune;
Henceforth I whimper no more, postpone no more, need nothing,
Strong and content, I travel the open road.

The earth—that is sufficient;
I do not want the constellations any nearer;
I know they are very well where they are;
I know they suffice for those who belong to them.

(Still here I carry my old delicious burdens;
I carry them, men and women—I carry them with me wherever I go;
I swear it is impossible for me to get rid of them;
I am fill'd with them, and I will fill them in return.)

2

You road I enter upon and look around! I believe you are not all that is here;
I believe that much unseen is also here.

Here the profound lesson of reception, neither preference or denial;
The black with his woolly head, the felon, the diseas'd, the illiterate person, are not denied;
The birth, the hasting after the physician, the beggar's tramp, the drunkard's stagger, the laughing party of mechanics,
The escaped youth, the rich person's carriage, the fop, the eloping couple,

The early market-man, the hearse, the moving of furniture into the town, the
    return back from the town,
They pass—I also pass—anything passes—none can be interdicted;
None but are accepted—none but are dear to me.

3

You air that serves me with breath to speak!
You objects that call from diffusion my meanings, and give them shape!
You light that wraps me and all things in delicate equable showers!
You paths worn in the irregular hollows by the roadsides!
I think you are latent with unseen existences—you are so dear to me.

You flagg'd walks of the cities! you strong curbs at the edges!
You ferries! you planks and posts of wharves! you timber-lined sides! you
    distant ships!
You rows of houses! you window-pierc'd façades! you roofs!
You porches and entrances! you copings and iron guards!
You windows whose transparent shells might expose so much!
You doors and ascending steps! you arches!
You gray stones of interminable pavements! you trodden crossings!
From all that has been near you, I believe you have imparted to yourselves,
    and now would impart the same secretly to me;
From the living and the dead I think you have peopled your impassive sur-
    faces, and the spirits thereof would be evident and amicable with me.

4

The earth expanding right hand and left hand,
The picture alive, every part in its best light,
The music falling in where it is wanted, and stopping where it is not
    wanted,
The cheerful voice of the public road—the gay fresh sentiment of the road.

O highway I travel! O public road! do you say to me, *Do not leave me?*
Do you say, *Venture not? If you leave me, you are lost?*
Do you say, *I am already prepared—I am well-beaten and undenied—
    adhere to me?*

O public road! I say back, I am not afraid to leave you—yet I love you;
You express me better than I can express myself;
You shall be more to me than my poem.

I think heroic deeds were all conceiv'd in the open air, and all great poems also;
I think I could stop here myself, and do miracles;
(My judgments, thoughts, I henceforth try by the open air, the road;)
I think whatever I shall meet on the road I shall like, and whoever beholds me shall like me;
I think whoever I see must be happy.

5

From this hour, freedom!
From this hour I ordain myself loos'd of limits and imaginary lines,
Going where I list, my own master, total and absolute,
Listening to others, and considering well what they say,
Pausing, searching, receiving, contemplating,
Gently, but with undeniable will, divesting myself of the holds that would hold me.

I inhale great draughts of space;
The east and the west are mine, and the north and the south are mine.

I am larger, better than I thought;
I did not know I held so much goodness.

All seems beautiful to me;
I can repeat over to men and women, You have done such good to me, I would do the same to you.

I will recruit for myself and you as I go;
I will scatter myself among men and women as I go;
I will toss the new gladness and roughness among them;
Whoever denies me, it shall not trouble me;
Whoever accepts me, he or she shall be blessed, and shall bless me.

6

Now if a thousand perfect men were to appear, it would not amaze me;
Now if a thousand beautiful forms of women appear'd, it would not astonish me.

Now I see the secret of the making of the best persons,
It is to grow in the open air, and to eat and sleep with the earth.

Here a great personal deed has room;
A great deed seizes upon the hearts of the whole race of men,
Its effusion of strength and will overwhelms law, and mocks all authority and all argument against it.

Here is the test of wisdom;
Wisdom is not finally tested in schools;
Wisdom cannot be pass'd from one having it, to another not having it;
Wisdom is of the Soul, is not susceptible of proof, is its own proof,
Applies to all stages and objects and qualities, and is content,
Is the certainty of the reality and immotality of things, and the excellence of things;
Something there is in the float of the sight of things that provokes it out of the Soul.

Now I reëxamine philosophies and religions,
They may prove well 'n lecture-rooms, yet not prove at all under the spacious clouds, and along the landscape and flowing currents.

Here is realization;
Here is a man tallied—he realizes here what he has in him;
The past, the future, majesty, love—if they are vacant of you, you are vacant of them.

Only the kernel of every object nourishes;
Where is he who tears off the husks for you and me?
Where is he that undoes stratagems and envelopes for you and me?

Here is adhesiveness—it is not previously fashion'd—it is apropos;
Do you know what it is, as you pass, to be loved by strangers?
Do you know the talk of those turning eye-balls?

7

Here is the efflux of the Soul;
The efflux of the Soul comes from within, through embower'd gates, ever provoking questions:
These yearnings, why are they? These thoughts in the darkness, why are they?
Why are there men and women that while they are nigh me, the sun-light expands my blood?
Why, when they leave me, do my pennants of joy sink flat and lank?
Why are there trees I never walk under, but large and melodious thoughts descend upon me?
(I think they hang there winter and summer on those trees, and always drop fruit as I pass;)
What is it I interchange so suddenly with strangers?
What with some driver, as I ride on the seat by his side?
What with some fisherman, drawing his seine by the shore, as I walk by, and pause?
What gives me to be free to a woman's or man's good-will? What gives them to be free to mine?

8

The efflux of the Soul is happiness—here is happiness;
I think it pervades the open air, waiting at all times;
Now it flows unto us—we are rightly charged.

Here rises the fluid and attaching character;
The fluid and attaching character is the freshness and sweetness of man and woman;
(The herbs of the morning sprout no fresher and sweeter every day out of the roots of themselves, than it sprouts fresh and sweet continually out of itself.)

Toward the fluid and attaching character exudes the sweat of the love of young and old;
From it falls distill'd the charm that mocks beauty and attainments;
Toward it heaves the shuddering longing ache of contact.

9

Allons! whoever you are, come travel with me!
Traveling with me, you find what never tires.

The earth never tires;
The earth is rude, silent, incomprehensible at first—Nature is rude and incomprehensible at first;
Be not discouraged—keep on—there are divine things, well envelop'd;
I swear to you there are divine things more beautiful than words can tell

Allons! we must not stop here!
However sweet these laid-up stores—however convenient this dwelling, we cannot remain here;
However shelter'd this port, and however calm these waters, we must not anchor here;
However welcome the hospitality that surrounds us, we are permitted to receive it but a little while.

10

Allons! the inducements shall be greater;
We will sail pathless and wild seas;
We will go where winds blow, waves dash, and the Yankee clipper speeds by under full sail.

Allons! with power, liberty, the earth, the elements!
Health, defiance, gayety, self-esteem, curiosity;
Allons! from all formules!
From your formules, O bat-eyed and materialistic priests!

The stale cadaver blocks up the passage—the burial waits no longer.

Allons! yet take warning!
He traveling with me needs the best blood, thews, endurance;
None may come to the trial, till he or she bring courage and health.

Come not here if you have already spent the best of yourself;
Only those may come, who come in sweet and determin'd bodies;
No diseas'd person—no rum-drinker or venereal taint is permitted here.

I and mine do not convince by arguments, similes, rhymes;
We convince by our presence.

11

Listen! I will be honest with you;
I do not offer the old smooth prizes, but offer rough new prizes;
These are the days that must happen to you:

You shall not heap up what is call'd riches,
You shall scatter with lavish hand all that you earn or achieve,
You but arrive at the city to which you were destin'd—you hardly settle yourself to satisfaction, before you are call'd by an irresistible call to depart,
You shall be treated to the ironical smiles and mockings of those who remain behind you;
What beckonings of love you receive, you shall only answer with passionate kisses of parting,
You shall not allow the hold of those who spread their reach'd hands toward you.

12

Allons! after the GREAT COMPANIONS! and to belong to them!
They too are on the road! they are the swift and majestic men; they are the greatest women.

Over that which hinder'd them—over that which retarded—passing impediments large or small,
Committers of crimes, committers of many beautiful virtues,
Enjoyers of calms of seas, and storms of seas,
Sailors of many a ship, walkers of many a mile of land,
Habitués of many distant countries, habitués of far-distant dwellings,

Trusters of men and women, observers of cities, solitary toilers,
Pausers and contemplators of tufts, blossoms, shells of the shore,
Dancers at wedding-dances, kissers of brides, tender helpers of children, bearers of children,
Soldiers of revolts, standers by gaping graves, lowerers down of coffins,
Journeyers over consecutive seasons, over the years—the curious years, each emerging from that which preceded it,
Journeyers as with companions, namely, their own diverse phases,
Forth-steppers from the latent unrealized baby-days,
Journeyers gayly with their own youth—Journeyers with their bearded and well grain'd manhood,
Journeyers with their womanhood, ample, unsurpass'd, content,
Journeyers with their own sublime old age of manhood or womanhood,
Old age, calm, expanded, broad with the haughty breadth of the universe,
Old age, flowing free with the delicious near-by freedom of death.

13

Allons! to that which is endless, as it was beginningless,
To undergo much, tramps of days, rests of nights,
To merge all in the travel they tend to, and the days and nights they tend to,
Again to merge them in the start of superior journeys;
To see nothing anywhere but what you may reach it and pass it,
To conceive no time, however distant, but what you may reach it and pass it,
To look up or down no road but it stretches and waits for you—however long, but it stretches and waits for you;
To see no being, not God's or any, but you also go thither,
To see no possession but you may possess it—enjoying all without labor or purchase—abstracting the feast, yet not abstracting one particle of it;
To take the best of the farmer's farm and the rich man's elegant villa, and the chaste blessings of the well-married couple, and the fruits of orchards and flowers of gardens,
To take to your use out of the compact cities as you pass through,
To carry buildings and streets with you afterward wherever you go,
To gather the minds of men out of their brains as you encounter them— to gather the love out of their hearts,

To take your lovers on the road with you, for all that you leave them behind you,
To know the universe itself as a road—as many roads—as roads for traveling souls.

14

The Soul travels;
The body does not travel as much as the soul;
The body has just as great a work as the soul, and parts away at last for the journeys of the soul.

All parts away for the progress of souls;
All religion, all solid things, arts, governments,—all that was or is apparent upon this globe or any globe, falls into niches and corners before the procession of Souls along the grand roads of the universe.

Of the progress of the souls of men and women along the grand roads of the universe, all other progress is the needed emblem and sustenance.

Forever alive, forever forward,
Stately, solemn, sad, withdrawn, baffled, mad, turbulent, feeble, dissatisfied,
Desperate, proud, fond, sick, accepted by men, rejected by men,
They go! they go! I know that they go, but I know not where they go;
But I know that they go toward the best—toward something great.

15

Allons! whoever you are! come forth!
You must not stay sleeping and dallying there in the house, though you built it, or though it has been built for you.
Allons! out of the dark confinement!
It is useless to protest—I know all, and expose it.

Behold, through you as bad as the rest,
Through the laughter, dancing, dining, supping, of people,
Inside of dresses and ornaments, inside of those wash'd and trimm'd faces,
Behold a secret silent loathing and despair.

No husband, no wife, no friend, trusted to hear the confession;
Another self, a duplicate of every one, skulking and hiding it goes,
Formless and wordless through the streets of the cities, polite and bland in the parlors,
In the cars of rail-roads, in steamboats, in the public assembly,
Home to the houses of men and women, at the table, in the bed-room, everywhere,
Smartly attired, countenance smiling, form upright, death under the breast-bones, hell under the skull-bones,
Under the broadcloth and gloves, under the ribbons and artificial flowers,
Keeping fair with the customs, speaking not a syllable of itself,
Speaking of anything else, but never of itself.

16

Allons! through struggles and wars!
The goal that was named cannot be countermanded.

Have the past struggles succeeded?
What has succeeded? yourself? your nation? nature?
Now understand me well—It is provided in the essence of things, that from any fruition of success, no matter what, shall come forth something to make a greater struggle necessary.

My call is the call of battle—I nourish active rebellion;
He going with me must go well arm'd;
He going with me goes often with spare diet, poverty, angry enemies, desertions.

17

Allons! the road is before us!
It is safe—I have tried it—my own feet have tried it well.

Allons! be not detain'd!
Let the paper remain on the desk unwritten, and the book on the shelf unopen'd!

Let the tools remain in the workshop! let the money remain unearn'd!
Let the school stand! mind not the cry of the teacher!
Let the preacher preach in his pulpit! let the lawyer plead in the court, and the judge expound the law.

Mon enfant! I give you my hand!
I give you my love, more precious than money,
I give you myself, before preaching or law;
Will you give me yourself? will you come travel with me?
Shall we stick by each other as long as we live?

EDMUND CLARENCE STEDMAN

Amavi

I LOVED: and in the morning sky
   How fairy-like the castle grew!
Proud turrets ever pointing high,
   Like minarets, to the dreamy blue;
   Bright fountains leaping through and through
The golden sunshine; on the air
   Gay banners streaming;—never drew
Painter or poet scene more fair!

And in that castle I would live,
   And in that castle I would die;
And there, in curtained bowers, would give
   Heart-warm responses—sigh for sigh;
   There, when but one sweet face was nigh,
The orient hours should glide along,
   Charmed by the magic of her eye,
Like stanzas of an antique song.

O foolish heart! O young Romance,
   That faded with the noon-day sun!
Alas for gentle dalliance,
   For burning pleasures never won!
   Oh, for a season dead and gone—
A wizard time, that then did seem
   Only a prelude, leading on
To sweeter portions of the dream!

I loved: but withered are Love's flowers;
   No longer, in the morning sky,
That fairy castle lifts its towers—
   Like minarets, ever pointing high;
   Torn are the bannerets, and dry
The silver fountains in its halls.
   But the wild sea, with endless sigh,
Moans round and over the crumbled walls!

RICHARD HENRY STODDARD

Threnody

Early or late, come when it will,
   At midnight or at noon,
Promise of good, or threat of ill,
   Death always comes too soon.
To the child who is too young to know,
   (Pray heaven he never may!)
   This life of ours is more than play,—
A debt contracted long ago
   Which he perforce must pay;
   And the man whose head is gray,

And sad, is fain to borrow,
Albeit with added pain and sorrow,
  The comfort of delay;
  Only let him live to-day—
There will be time to die to-morrow!
Now there is not an hour to spare,
  Under the uncertain sky,
Save to pluck roses for the hair
Of the loving and the fair,
And the kisses following these,
Like a swarming hive of bees
  That soar on high,
Till, drunken with their own sweet wine,
  They fall and die.
When dear words have all been said
  And bright eyes no longer shine
  (Ah, not thine!)
  Close these weary eyes of mine,
And bear me to the lonely bed
  Where unhonored I shall lie,
  While the tardy years go by,
  Without question or reply
From the long-forgotten dead.

RICHARD WATSON GILDER

Milton

VOICE archangelical, supreme, sublime;
  Most dedicate and rapt of all the quire
Of singers since humanity and time
Were fashioned from the sempiternal fire!

None of the laureled race with thee hath name
  Save him, the bard austere and benedight,
  Who, like thee, traversed the infernal flame

And dared the dread and Everlasting Light.
Milton! the reverberate centuries but bring
  Thy presence nearer; thou dost mightier loom
  Even as thy day recedes; yea, thou dost sing
  With accent more divine, sounding the doom
Of base, infectious and unholy thought,
While upward climbs the world by one high spirit taught.

WILLIAM WINTER

The Rubicon

I

ONE OTHER bitter drop to drink,
    And then—no more!
One little pause upon the brink,
    And then—go o'er!
One sigh—and then the lib'rant morn
    Of perfect day,
When my free spirit, newly born,
    Will soar away!

II

One pang—and I shall rend the thrall
    Where grief abides,
And generous Death will show me all
    That now he hides;

And, lucid in that second birth,
   I shall discern
What all the sages of the earth
   Have died to learn.

III

One motion—and the stream is crost,
   So dark, so deep!
And I shall triumph, or be lost
   In endless sleep.
Then, onward! Whatsoe'er my fate,
   I shall not care!
Nor Sin nor Sorrow, Love nor Hate
   Can touch me there.

RICHARD HOVEY

His Submission

You will betray me—Oh, deny it not!
   What right have I alas, to say you nay?
I, traitor of ten loves, what shall I say
To plead with you that I be not forgot?
My love has not been squandered jot by jot
In little loves that perish with the day.
My treason has been ever to the sway
Of Queens—my faith has known no petty blot.
You will betray me as I have betrayed
And I shall kiss the hand that does me wrong,
And oh, not pardon—I need pardon more,
But in proud torment, dumb and unafraid,
Burn in my hell nor cease the bitter song
Your beauty triumphs in for evermore.

ROBERT LOVEMAN

Rose Song

I

Yellow rose, go to her,
   Breathe all my woe to her,
Mellow rose, tell her my hope and despair;
Swear my wild vow of her
To the calm brow of her,
Drawn in tempestuous deeps of her hair.

II

Crush'd in the arms of her,
Thou shalt know balms of myrrh,
Rose, O rare rose, to my Lady, away!
Waft, where I wait for her,
Love, and love's fate for her,
Haste thee, rose, haste, to my Lady, I pray!

MADISON CAWEIN

My Romance

If it befalls that the midnight hovers
   In mist no moonlight breaks,
The leagues of years my spirit covers,
   And myself myself forsakes.

And I live in a land of stars and flowers,
  White cliffs by a silver sea;
And the pearly points of her opal towers
  From the mountains beckon me.

And I think that I know that I hear her calling
  From a casement bathed with light—
The music of waters in waters falling
  To palms from a rocky height.

And I feel that I think my love's awaited
  By the romance of her charms;
That her feet are early and mine belated
  In a world that chains my arms.

But I break my chains and the rest is easy—
  In the shadow of the rose
Snow-white, that blooms in her garden breezy,
  We meet and no one knows.

To dream sweet dreams and kiss sweet kisses;
  The world—it may live or die;
The world that forgets, the soul that misses
  The life that has long gone by.

We speak old vows that have long been spoken,
  And weep a long-gone woe,—
For you must know our hearts were broken
  Hundreds of years ago.

A Niello

I

It is not early spring and yet
  Of lamb's-tongue banks above the stream,
And blotted banks of violet
    My heart will dream.

Is it because the wind-flower apes
The beauty that was once her brow,
That the white thought of it still shapes
    The April now?

Because the wild-rose learned to blush
In tune with cheeks of maidenhood,
I find full Junetide in bare brush
    And empty wood?

Why will I think how young she died!—
Straight, barren death stalks down the trees,
The hard-eyed hours by his side
    That kill and freeze.

II

When orchards are in bloom again
My heart will bound, my blood will beat,
To hear the red-bird so repeat
   On apple boughs his strain;
His blithe, loud song, heard through the rain
In summer, now among the bloom,—
Where all the bees and hornets boom,—
   Inviting to remain.

When orchards are in bloom once more,
Evasions of dear dreams will draw
My feet, like some persistent law,
   Through blossoms to her door:
And I shall ask her, as before,
"To let me help her at the well";
And fill her pail; and long to tell
   My secret, o'er and o'er.

I shall not speak until we quit
The farm-gate, buried in its stain
Of orchards all in bloom again,
   And see the wood-dove sit

And call; and through the blossoms flit
The cat-bird crying while he flies;
Then bashfully I'll praise her eyes,
   And cheeks with gladness lit.

And it may be that she will place
Her trust in me as once before,—
When orchards are in bloom once more,
   With all her sweet girl grace:
And we shall tarry till a trace
Of sunset dyes the heaven, and then—
To tell her all; and bend again
   To kiss her quiet face!

And homeward, humming, I shall go
Along the cricket-chirring ways,
When all the west, one crimson blaze,
   Blooms as if orchards blow
Piled petals in it. I shall know
Glad youth once more and have her here,
Who has been dead this many a year,
   To make my old heart glow.

III

I would not die when Springtime lifts
   The white world to her maiden mouth,
And heaps its cradle with gay gifts,
   Breeze-blown from out the singing south:
Too glad for death the wind and rain;
   Too heedless for earth's wildest woe
The young hypocrisy of pain
   That will not let you know.

I would not die when Summer shakes
   Her daisied locks below her hips,
And, naked as a star that takes
   A cloud, into the water slips:

Too rich were earth for my poor needs
   In egotism of loveliness;
The apathy that never heeds
   If grief be more or less.

But I would die when Autumn goes,
   The wild rain dripping from her hair,
Through forests where the wild wind blows
   Death and the red wreck everywhere:
Sweet as love's last farewells and tears
   To fall asleep in the sad days,
With patience and with faith that nears
   The mist that God shall raise.

The Idyl of the Standing-Stone

THE teasel and the horsemint spread
   The hillsides with pink sunset thrown
   On earth around The Standing-Stone
That ripples in its rocky bed:
   There are no treasuries that hold
   Gold richer than the daisies' gold
That crowd its mouth and head.

Deep harvest, and a mower stands
   Among the morning wheat and whets
   His scythe, and for a space forgets
The labor of the ripened lands;
   Then bends, and through the dewy grain
   His cradle hisses, and again
He swings it in his hands.

And she beholds him where he mows
   On acres whence the water sends
   Faint music of reflecting bends
And falls that interblend with flows;
   She stands among the old bee-gums,
   Where all the apiary hums,
A simple bramble-rose.

She hears him whistling as he leans
  To circling sweeps the rabbits fly,
  And sighs and smiles and knows not why,
Nor what her heart's sweet secret means:
  He rests upon his scythe and sees
  Her smiling 'mid the hives of bees
Beneath the flowering-beans.

The peacock-purple lizard creeps
  Along the fence-rail; and the drone
  Of insects makes the country lone
With dreaming where the water sleeps:
  She hears him singing as he swings
  His scythe; he thinks of other things
Than toil and, singing, reaps.

GUY WETMORE CARRYL

When the Great Gray Ships Come In

(NEW YORK HARBOR, AUGUST 20, 1898)

To eastward ringing, to westward winging, o'er mapless miles of sea,
  On winds and tides the gospel rides that the furthermost isles are free;
And the furthermost isles make answer, harbor, and height, and hill,
Breaker and beach cry, each to each, " 'T is the Mother who calls! Be still!"
Mother! new-found, beloved, and strong to hold from harm,
Stretching to these across the seas the shield of her sovereign arm,
Who summoned the guns of her sailor sons, who bade her navies roam,
Who calls again to the leagues of main, and who calls them this time home!

And the great gray ships are silent, and the weary watchers rest;
The black cloud dies in the August skies, and deep in the golden west

Invisible hands are limning a glory of crimson bars,
And far above is the wonder of a myriad wakened stars!
Peace! As the tidings silence the strenuous cannonade,
Peace at last! is the bugle-blast the length of the long blockade;
And eyes of vigil weary are lit with the glad release,
From ship to ship and from lip to lip it is "Peace! Thank God for peace!"

Ah, in the sweet hereafter Columbia still shall show
The sons of these who swept the seas how she bade them rise and go;
How, when the stirring summons smote on her children's ear,
South and North at the call stood forth, and the whole land answered "Here!"
For the soul of the soldier's story and the heart of the sailor's song
Are all of those who meet their foes as right should meet with wrong,
Who fight their guns till the foeman runs, and then, on the decks they trod,
Brave faces raise, and give the praise to the grace of their country's God!

Yes, it is good to battle, and good to be strong and free,
To carry the hearts of a people to the uttermost ends of sea,
To see the day steal up the bay, where the enemy lies in wait,
To run your ship to the harbor's lip and sink her across the strait:—
But better the golden evening when the ships round heads for home,
And the long gray miles slip swiftly past in a swirl of seething foam,
And the people wait at the haven's gate to greet the men who win!
Thank God for peace! Thank God for peace, when the great gray ships come in!

"The Winds and the Sea Obey Him"

W
Who once hath heard the sea above her graves
Sing to the stars her requiem, and on whom
Her spell is laid of shoreward-sliding waves,
    Alternate gleam and gloom,
In reverent mood and silent, standing where
    Her hundred throats their diapason raise,
Hath found the very perfectness of prayer
    And plenitude of praise.

Thenceforward is his hope a thing apart
  From man's perplexing dogmas, good or ill;
Deep in the sacred silence of his heart
    His faith abideth, still:—
A faith that fails not, steadfast, humble, kind,
  Amid a vexing multitude of creeds
That bend and break with every passing wind,
    Like tempest-trampled reeds.
The tide of man's belief may ebb or flow;
  Its swift mutations, many though they be,
He heedeth not who once hath come to know
    The anthem of the sea.
From sages and their blindly fashioned lore
  He turns, to watch with reverential eyes
The seas men fear serve ceaselessly before
    The God whom men despise!
Through length of days and year succeeding year
  Earth's strongest power serves Heaven's still stronger one,
And all the winds, in holy-hearted fear,
    To do His bidding run.
Ah, likewise serving, restless hearts, be still,
  And learn, like little children, of the way—
Secure in Him, Whose strong enduring will
    The winds and sea obey!

The Debutante

To-day dawned not upon the earth as other days have done:
A throng of little virgin clouds stood waiting for the sun,
Till the herald-winds aligned them, and they blushed, and stood aside,
As the marshals of the morning flung the eastern portals wide.
So Nature lit her playhouse for the play that May begins,
And the twigs of honeysuckle sawed like little violins:
In the dawn there dwelt a whisper of a presence that was new,
For the slender Spring was at the wing, and waiting for her cue!

As yet I could not see her, and the stage was wide and bare;
As yet the Winter's chorus echoed faintly on the air
With a dying wail of tempest, and of dry and tortured trees,
But a promise of new music lent enchantment to the breeze.
In the scene's secluded corners lay the snow-drifts, still secure;
But the murmur of their melting sang another overture
Than the brooks of brown November, and I listened, and I knew
That blue-eyed Spring was at the wing, and waiting for her cue!

The world was all attention, and the hemlocks stood, a-row,
Ushers, never changing costume through the Seasons' wonder-show,
While the day, below the hillside, tried her colors, one by one,
On the clouds experimenting, till the coming of the sun.
In the vines about my window, where the sparrows all convene,
They were practising the chorus that should usher in the Queen,
And the sod-imprisoned flowers craved the word to shoulder through:
Green-girdled Spring was at the wing, and waiting for her cue!

She shall enter to the clarion of the crystal-ringing brooks,
She shall tread on frail arbutus in the moist and mossy nooks;
She shall touch the bleak drop-curtain of the Winter with her wand
Till it lifts, and shows the wonder of the apple blooms beyond!
Yet with all her golden sunlight, and her twilights of perfume,
Yet with all the mystic splendor of her nights of starlit gloom,
She shall bring no sweeter moment than this one in which I knew
That laughing Spring was at the wing, and waiting for her cue!

The Fog

THE fog slunk down from Labrador, stealthy, sure, and slow,
Southwardly shifting, far inshore, so never a man might know
How the sea it trod with feet soft-shod, watching the distance dim,
Where the fishing-fleet to the eastward beat, white dots on the ocean's rim.
Feeling the sands with its furtive hands, fingering cape and cove,
Where the sweet salt smells of the nearer swells up the sloping hillside rove;
Where the whimpering sea-gulls swoop and soar, and the great king-herons
    go,
The fog slunk down from Labrador, stealthy, sure, and slow!

Then a stillness fell on crag and cliff, on beach and breaker fell,
As the sea-breeze brought on its final whiff the note of a distant bell,
One faint, far sound, and the fog unwound its mantle across the lea,
Joined hand in hand with a wind from land, and the twain went out to sea.
And the wind that rose spoke soft, of those who watch on the cliffs at dawn,
And the fog's white lips, of sinking ships where the tortured tempests spawn,
As, each to each, they told once more such things as fishers know,
When the fog slinks down from Labrador, stealthy, sure, and slow!

Oh, the wan, white hours go limping by, when that pall comes in between
The great, blue bell of the cloudless sky and the ocean's romping green!
Nor sane young day, nor swirl of spray, as the cat's-paws lunge and lift;—
On sad, slow waves, like the mounds of graves, the fishermen's dories drift.
For the fishing-craft that leapt and laughed are swallowed in ghostly gray:
Only God's eyes may see where lies the lap of the sheltered bay,
So their dories grope, for lost their lore, witlessly to and fro,
When the fog slinks down from Labrador, stealthy, sure, and slow!

Oh, men of the fleet, 'tis ye who learn, of the white fog's biting breath,
That life may hang on the way ye turn, or the way ye turn be death!
Though they on the lea look out to sea for the woe or the weal of you,
The ominous East, like a hungry beast, is waiting your tidings, too.
A night and a day, mayhap, ye stray; a day and a night, perchance,
The dory is led toward Marblehead, or pointed away for France;
The shore may save, or the sea may score, in the unknown final throw,
When the fog slinks down from Labrador, stealthy, sure, and slow!

Ah, God of the Sea, what joy there lies in that first faint hint of sun!—
When the pallid curtains sulking rise, and the reaches wider run,
When a wind from the west on the sullen breast of the waters shoulders near,
And the blessed blue of the sky looks through, as the fog-wreaths curl and clear.
Ah, God, what joy when the gallant buoy, swung high on a sudden swell,
Puts fear to flight like a dream of night with its calm, courageous bell,
And the dory trips the sea's wide floor with the verve 'twas wont to know,
And the fog slinks back to Labrador, stealthy, sure, and slow!

JAMES OPPENHEIM

At Twilight

All things move slowly at this hallowed hour—
    O twilight, teach my heart your simple spell,
  That I, returning to Mankind, may tell
Humanity the purity and power
Of Silence! Every leaf and every blade
    Shine with their clearest beauty, and the sky
    Deepens and deepens through Eternity,
And even the least bird is unafraid!

Life's in the hands of God, and moves forever
    Safe near His heart; lo, at the hour of dusk
    The Spirit, as the fruit breaks through its husk,
Lifts, and is swept in the eternal river,
    Vast in the realms that know no human chart,
    Yet calm, because it pulses with God's heart!

SARA TEASDALE

Song

You bound strong sandals on my feet,
  You gave me bread and wine,
And bade me out, 'neath sun and stars,
  For all the world was mine.
Oh, take the sandals off my feet,
  You know not what you do;
For all my world is in your arms,
  My sun and stars are you.

Less than the Cloud to the Wind

Less than the cloud to the wind,
  Less than the foam to the sea,
Less than the rose to the storm
  Am I to thee.

More than the star to the night,
  More than the rain to the lea,
More than heaven to earth
  Art thou to me.

The Wayfarer

Love entered in my heart one day,
  A sad, unwelcome guest;
But when he begged that he might stay,
  I let him wait and rest.

He broke my sleep with sorrowing,
  And shook my dreams with tears,
And when my heart was fain to sing,
  He stilled its joy with fears.

But now that he has gone his way,
  I miss the old sweet pain,
And sometimes in the night I pray
  That he may come again.

The Song for Colin

I sang a song at dusking time
  Beneath the evening star,
And Terence left his latest rhyme
  To answer from afar.

Pierrot laid down his lute to weep,
   And sighed, "She sings for me,"
But Colin slept a careless sleep
   Beneath an apple tree.

DON MARQUIS

October

Cease to call him sad or sober,
   Merriest of months, October!

Patron of the bursting bins,
Reveller in wayside inns,—
I can nowhere find a trace
Of the pensive in his face;
There is mingled wit and folly,
But the mad-cap lacks the grace
Of a thoughtful melancholy.
Spendthrift of the season's gold,
How he loves to fling about
Treasure filched from Summertime!—
Never ruffling squire of old
Better loved a tavern bout
When Prince Hal was in his prime.

Doublet slashed with gold and green;
Cloak of crimson, changeful sheen,
Opulently opaline,
Of the dews that gem his breast;
Frosty lace about his throat;
Scarlet plumes that flirt and float

Backward in a gay unrest—
Where's another gallant drest
With such tricksy gayety,
Such unlessoned vanity?

With his amber afternoons
And his pendant poets' moons—
With his twilights dashed with rose
From the red-lipped afterglows—
With his vocal airs at dawn
Breathing hints of Helicon—
With the winding of the horn
Where his huntsmen meet the morn—
Bacchanalian bees that sip
Where his cider-presses drip—
With his every piping breeze
Shaking from familiar trees
Apples of Hesperides—
With the chuckle, chirp, and trill
Of his jolly brooks that spill
Mirth in tangled madrigals
Down pebble-dappled waterfalls;
Brooks that laugh and make escape
Through wild arbors where the grape
Purples with a promise of
Racy vintage rare as love—
With his merry wanton air,
Mirth and vanity and folly,
Why should he be made to bear
Burden of some melancholy
Song that swoons and sinks with care?

O cease to sing him sad or sober—
He's a jolly dog, October!

THEODOSIA GARRISON

At the Road's End

SOMETIMES the road was a twisted riddle
  Where one might stray for a crooked mile,
But O, she danced to the pipes and fiddle
  Most of the while, most of the while.

Sometimes the wind and the rain together
  Blurred the hill that she needs must climb,
But O, she tripped it in primrose weather
  Most of the time, most of the time.

Who may say that the journey tried her?
  Never a Romany went as gay,
Seeing that true love walked beside her
  All of the way, all of the way.

The House in Trouble

As we rode through the village, the houses every one
  Were open to the west wind and merry with the sun;
All except the one house, shuttered from the day,
Like a soul in sorrow who hides his face away.

As we rode past the village it would not quit my mind—
The little house in trouble that we had left behind;
Smoke lifted from the chimney, but the closed door cried,
"Oh, hurry by, oh, hurry by, nor seek the grief I hide."

O little house in trouble, when back again I ride,
God grant I see your windows shine, your door flung wide,
And all your new-grown garden tremulous with Spring,
Like a face that smiles again through peace of comforting.

Cophetua's Queen

MY NECK was never bowed before I hung a jewel on it,
    My hands were always free until I weighted them with rings.
Till I found the golden robe and the pride to don it,
    Till I wore the silken shoon with their silver strings,
    I ran free and ragged with the world's wild things.

Yet honour is a jewel, and one is proud to bear it,
    And duty makes the rings I wear and one would keep them bright,
A King's love is a golden robe and glad am I to wear it,
    And I must walk in careful paths to keep my shoon aright.

I wonder how the brook would feel to naked feet tonight!

CALE YOUNG RICE

The Winter is Long

Low autumn clouds and a wind to take them anywhere.
    Wild flying leaves, that do not know they are dead,
Because the limbs they have fallen from are unforgotten,
    And all spring said.

Rain is coming, and with it cold, the traveller,
Out of the north, to harden the earth with frost.
Then those children of death, the leaves, will lie down quietly,
No longer wind-tossed.

This has happened before. This will happen forever.
The old habits of earth are strange and strong.
Turn monk or faun, then—and pray, or rove the woods joyfully.
The winter is long.

On Farms

The brook by Jardine's wood
Ought to have known that the wheat
Did not need to be flooded,
It should have kept its bed—
Instead of breaking the weir down
And leaving the wheat muddied,
Each green blade clotted with clay
Or drowned in pools as red.

But that is the way on farms.
Nor will complaining serve:
It's always a little silly
To take things up with God.
For somehow you will find
That the seasons, willy-nilly,
Come without compulsion—
And go at no one's nod.

Katharsis

Cool in his bed, with limbs straight and quiet,
He heard the wind lifting the dark leaves
And swathing the tall wheat in the wet night without
Smoothly into momentary sheaves.
"If there is any passion better than coolness
After rain and sleep," he said, "or any sound
Sweeter than leaves whispering to an awaker
Who knows himself no more by passion bound,
Let it be mine when I am worthy of living
Unfeveredly upon the fevered earth,
Or when I have won the right to lie dying
Without a doubt of all living was worth.
Let it be mine.—But ask me not whether
A broken heart will mend in any weather."

CAROLYN CROSBY WILSON

Mid Winter

If I were God, I'd mould hills rolling low
Smooth them and shape them, sift them deep with snow,
And scatter them with furze that they might lie
Softly, against the wide deep-tinted sky.
In slow caress my forming hand would linger,
Then a swift finger,
Down some long slope, half carelessly would break
A jagged course for melting snows to take,
The outscooped valley's length they'd run, and then,
Skirting new hills, go slipping out of ken;
And distanced far, a low-hung sun I'd light,
And paint blue shadows on the rose-touched white;
Then, wearied, put aside my colours and my clay
And fashion paradise and man on some less perfect day.

Roads

Roads do not run, they only lie,
Each inch beneath its inch of sky
Chained endlessly, although they yearn
To race beyond a tempting turn.
Rain, falling leaves, and grinding wheel
Their patient, upturned faces feel,
Dreaming all day, as dream roads must,
Of unreturning bits of dust.

One Lack I Have

One lack I have, one dream not satisfied,
(And will it ever be?) to make you know
What never silence, speech, caress can show,
The depths of love which once I sought to hide,

Now grown so great that like a rising tide,
Thwarted, they beat upon me with their flow
Of ecstasy, and every day I go
Seeking some key to set my flood gates wide.

Yet in my heart, I know that this is best;
Love grows not dull that still is love in quest.
That want is dearest that finds scanty food,
And love were little were it understood.
Our souls would shrivel in us could we dare
Full, sudden sight of all the love we bear.

On the Arrogance of Lovers

Lovers have said joy never was begun
    Till love was learned; O Chanteclers of bliss,
Was there no glorious rising of the sun
Unlicensed by the summons of your kiss?
Have you not tracked still waters with white foam,
Walked with a brown road to its dusty end,
Heard music, read an uncut book at home,
Or sat before the hearth-fire with a friend?

I am a lover too; yet in my thought
Linger the hundred happy hours I stored
From all the placid years before you brought
This last and crowning treasure to my hoard.
And often I recall, half wistfully,
The morning vigour that's in going free.

DAVID MORTON

Wooden Ships

They are remembering forests where they grew,—
  The midnight quiet, and the giant dance;
And all the murmuring summers that they knew
  Are haunting still their altered circumstance.
Leaves they have lost, and robins in the nest,
  Tug of the goodly earth denied to ships,
These, and the rooted certainties, and rest,—
  To gain a watery girdle at the hips.

Only the wind that follows ever aft,
  They greet not as a stranger on their ways;
But this old friend, with whom they drank and laughed,
  Sits in the stern and talks of other days
When they had held high bacchanalias still,
Or dreamed among the stars on some tall hill.

Revelation

Walking these long, late twilights of the Spring,
  Where all the fret of life seems nothing worth,
And grief, itself, a half-forgotten thing,
  Less keen than these cool odours of the earth,—
I sometimes think we find the secret gate
  That gives on gardens of enchanted light,
Restoring glories that we lost of late,
  To quiet wisdom and more certain sight.

A holier mood will haunt our stubborn will,
  Till we shall see revealments through the grass,
And stop, abashed, before a daffodil,
  A shining weed, a stone on ways we pass,
Stand with bared head before the evening star,
And know these holy things for what they are.

Moonflowers

These frail, white blooms have lit the Summer night
    Like ghosts of beauty that had gone too soon,—
With something less than any glimmering light
    That sways and faints and trembles in the moon.
I think the Earth, grown half-regretful, now,
    Of faces that were lovely of old time,
Lifts here again dim hands and hair and brow,
    In loveliness more fragile than a rhyme.

So that the listening night has somehow learned
    A way of prescient waiting through the dark,
For half-forgotten loveliness returned,—
    Too frail and dim for eyes like ours to mark
More than a ghostly glimmer on the air,
That once was lighted brows and hands and hair.

Noon of Summer

Always the summer heaps upon the heart
This drowning sweetness through the slow, hot days...
Here pairs of butterflies will drift and part
On airy cruises down uncharted ways,
From weed to stirless weed... but otherwise
The world is spell and stillness and a swoon
That through a dream of yellow butterflies
Is heavy with the hot, sweet breath of noon.

The red-top clover bends beneath the bee
That rides her to the earth and slumbers there,
And all but drowns—aye, even such as he...
In this long sweetness on the drowsy air
That merges thought... and butterfly... and dreaming...
And swoon... and bee... and sober sight, and seeming.

Prescience

I turn my back on goldenrod today;
It is too early... it is not the season...
And train my eyes to look another way,
And in my walking I invent a reason
For taking, here, an unaccustomed turn,
And so avoid the meadow, by a mile,
Where these inordinate flames have come to burn
The fields that yet are summer for a while.

Heart that I bear across the summer flood,
Watching the green wood, or the curving sky,
What is it, now, that you are troubled by,
That there should be this slow sense, in the blood,
Of blue smoke rising... and the short days come...
And tall, blurred lanterns on the pathway home?

MARGARET EMERSON BAILEY

Close to the Earth

Let the brown lark fly
That has wings to fly.
The ant, the beetle,
The mole, and I
Keep close to the earth
Where we like to lie.

For close to the earth a beetle may trundle
Its treasure below in a claw-clipped bundle;
And close to the earth an ant may funnel
Earth-work in turrets the length of its tunnel;

And close to the earth the secret mole
May fit to its body its cool, dark hole;
And I, who have never a wish to climb
The sky with a lilt or a whistling rhyme,
May stoop, and listen, and mark the time
Of surer songs than a bird ever sings—
Songs slow with the pulse at the root of things.

Requiem

No man wishes
Body and soul
Of a woman. Either
Outweighs the whole.

For both together
Well may be
Less than he bargained for,
Separately.

One gives to the other
Till there is
Left from neither
What he'd call his.

And he shows wisdom
When all's said and done,
Of her body or soul
To have martyred one.

But while he wishes
A half, not the whole,
God rest her body—
God save her soul.

Encounter

Strange it is
To meet with a face
That tugs Time back
To a secret place;
That tugs Time back
Through bush and bracken
To the cross-road's fork
And the wrong road taken;
Yet never a sign upon that face
Of the share-and-share
In a secret place.

White Christmas

This is December, and zero weather;
This is the season of less, not more.
But better get ready the empty manger,
Pitch-fork hay on the draughty floor.

A pretty time for a cow to be calving.
What does she think will become of her young?
But bolt the door from the flying snowflakes.
Slam it to where the sill has sprung.

Am I to fetch clover as I fetch water,
With ice on the pasture, ice on the sedge?
But cold as a barn, this needn't be colder.
Stuff an old shirt in the window ledge.

You'd think she'd know there was nothing to grow on,
That frosty hay is poor fodder for milk.
But lift the oil lamp to the furthermost corner—
Eyes like stars and a coat like silk.

Where has the heart of winter a warm spot
For any creature so newly born?
But look at the milk-white breath of the cattle;
The warm, white breath of the lowing cattle,
Taking the chill off of Christmas morn.

JAKE FALSTAFF

Beautiful Sunday

It was such a bright morning
That the cows, coming out of the cool dark barns feeling a good deal better,
Stood for a while and blinked,
And the young heifers said to each other,
"Oh my!
I never saw such a pretty day!
Let's jump over fences!
Let's go running up and down lanes with our tails in the air."
And the old sisterly Jerseys
Thought to themselves, "That patch of white clover
Over in the corner where the woodchucks are
Ought to be about ready for a good going over."

Well, you never saw anything in your life like the way the young ducks were acting.
They were tearing in and out of the water
Making enough noise to be heard all over the township;
Even the robins were scandalized
And sat around in the trees looking sideways and one-eyed at them.

All the crawdads in that part of the creek
Picked up and moved, and the sober old snake
Slipped off his rock and went for a walk in the briars.

The ghosts of dead spiders
Had been busy all night, and every few feet along the road
There was a rope of gossamer.
The old white horse taking two old gray people to meeting
Held up his head and said to himself,
"Look at those ropes!
Watch me bust them!
Whammy, there goes another one!
Doggone, I'll bet there isn't another horse in 42 counties
Can run along a road pulling a buggy and busting ropes and cables."
And all of a sudden he felt so good
That he threw up his hindquarters and gave a big two-legged kick,
And the old gray woman said, "Well, I swan to gracious,"
And the old gray man got all tangled up with the lines
And nearly fell out of the buggy reaching for the whip.
"Whoa, there," he said. "Whoa, there, Roosevelt!
Hold on now! What in the Sam Hill is into you?"

About 14 hundred May apple stems,
With their parasols up, marched down the hill
And all the spring beauties turned up their pale, peaked noses
And said, "Don't them May apples
Think they're somebody
With their bumbershoots up!"

Oh, it was a grand day, a specially grand day,
And all the flowers were so sweet
That the butterflies sneezed,
And the young goats and the lambs
Couldn't think of anything special enough
In the way of capers and didoes,
So they just stood still and looked wise.

The Elfin Wife

GRAVELY she goes about her little duties:
  Smiling to show them she does not mind them:
Gravely she genuflects to small gnome beauties
  Wheresoever she may find them.

She pauses in her sweeping to make herself some wishes:
  She sits on her legs and thinks about the grate:
She feels a dear well-being when she does the dishes
  Because of the smoothness of a china plate.

Whether it is linens, clean-smelling, piled,
  Whether it is chairs or rugs or dresses,
She goes among them like a dreamy child
  Playing with the things she loves and possesses.

Can you not see her, cool eyes shady,
  Cool hands gentle, cool cheeks white?
Can you not see her, my love's lady,
  Doing the duties of her grave delight?

Valedictory

(NEW YORK, JUNE 25, 1929)

FORGIVE me, hearty and amiable city,
  If, having beheld your beauty,
I go back to my own places.

If, having seen you as the barbarians saw Semiramis
On the wall of her undefended city,
I do not put down my arms and come,
Beating my breast for madness
And shouting for ecstasy,
To be your servitor.

It is not because I have seen nymphs,
Although I have seen nymphs.

It is not because I have drunk dew,
Though I have been dew-drunken.

It is because I have stood in the evening
At the beginning of a fat valley.
It is because I have opened a barndoor
On an evening in winter.

If I stay, I am too far from the place where I shall lie down
When the time comes to lie down.
I shall lie there a long time
Until I become a part of that fertility.
It will be wise for me to know the clod well
Before I go to sleep upon it;
I am not comfortable in a strange bed.

You are splendid; you are nameless because there is no name great enough
    for you;
You are as beautiful with madness as the queen that rode upon the brow of
    an elephant into the fountain courts of Solomon;
But I must go back to my own places;
I must go back to the bitter crows of autumn
And the brooks flowing northward in spring
Bearing ice in their currents.
I must go back to the wind screaming in winter
And the heat flickering in summer.
I must go back to my own places—
To wedding and childbed and patriarchal death.

FICTION

ON OCTOBER 1, 1852, *George Palmer Putnam mailed from his office at 10 Park Place, New York City, a number of letters, all in the same wording, to a select list of American writers, stating that he proposed to issue a literary magazine of a high standard of quality and asking the recipient if he had on hand any fiction or articles that might be available for use in the magazine and, if not, could the publisher have the recipient's permission to use his name, as a probable contributor, in the prospectus and other advertising matter concerning the magazine.*

It is significant to observe that in this letter Mr. Putnam made it clear that "We plan to make it (the magazine) as essentially an organ of American thought as possible."

The intellectual patriot and battler for an International Copyright agreement, who had written, assembled and published "American Facts" for the edification of the British, was not going to fill his new magazine with articles and stories pirated from English magazines, as so many other American magazine publishers were doing at the time: his magazine was going to be written by Americans for Americans. And the material was to be paid for.

Among those who received copies of this letter were: Richard H. Dana, Jr., Henry W. Longfellow, R. W. Emerson, O. W. Holmes, H. James (father of Henry James and William James).

Putnam had already enlisted Washington Irving, William Cullen Byrant, Nathaniel Hawthorne, Herman Melville, Parke Godwin, Frederick S. Cozzens, Bayard Taylor, and John P. Kennedy and George W. Curtis. Editorship of the magazine was placed in the hands of Charles F. Briggs. Minimum payment for material was established at $3 and the maximum at $5 per page. The size of the magazine was set at 144 pages, two columns to the page. Enough subscriptions were received for the first issue to subsidize printing and paper costs for an edition of 12,000. The only cash outlay was for the contributions, which Putnam paid for on acceptance, *an innovation in itself. The first issue was brought out on January 2, 1853, under the title* Putnam's Monthly Magazine *and was a financial as well as a literary success from the start. The circulation grew to a high of 20,000, at about which figure it was stabilized until the panic of 1857 interrupted its career.*

Herman Melville was a contributor from the start both as an anonymous book reviewer and as a writer of some of the stories which later appeared in book form under the title "Piazza Tales." When in his writings Melville left the sea for land, his stories lacked life and luster, so some of these piazza tales are very heavy going. But during 1855 Melville's masterpiece in the novelette form, "Benito Cereno," appeared serially in Putnam's Monthly Magazine. Lewis Mumford in his biographical study "Herman Melville" rightly says that "Benito Cereno" "marked the culmination of Melville's power as a short-story writer, as "Moby Dick" marked his triumph as an epic poet." Mumford says that Melville boldly took the story from a book of voyages by Captain Amasa Delano, but Melville made it Melville. "One can mark Melville's literary powers," writes Mumford, "in the complete transformation of Delano's patent story: he adds a score of details to heighten the mystery and deepen the sinister aspect of the scene; and by sheer virtuosity he transfers the reader's sympathies to the Spanish captain, who in the original story is far more cruel, barbarous, and unprincipled than the forces he contends against. . . . The moral of the original tale is that ingratitude, stirred by cupidity, may follow the most generous act, and that American captains had better beware of befriending too whole-heartedly a foreign vessel. In "Benito Cereno" the point is that noble conduct and good will . . . may seem sheer guile; and further, that there is an inscrutable evil that makes the passage of fine souls through the world an endless Calvary." . . .

In 1851 Putnam published "Mosses from an Old Manse" by Nathaniel Hawthorne, an author almost unknown at the time. The book was so complete a flop that when, after it had been on sale for two years, the publisher could report a sale of less than 750 copies, Hawthorne was so discouraged that he put the completed manuscript of "The Scarlet Letter" in the drawer of his desk in the Custom House at Salem, where he was a clerk, and left it there for two years. But Hawthorne had read the manuscript to his wife and a few friends and word of "The Scarlet Letter" finally came to the ears of James T. Fields of the Boston publishing firm of Ticknor & Fields, who journeyed to Salem, read the manuscript, and thereupon contracted with Hawthorne for book publication of all of Hawthorne's work. "The Scarlet Letter" was a success.

The fame of "The Scarlet Letter" attracted the attention of readers and critics to "Mosses from an Old Manse," which as every school-boy knows, rather to his regret, is now a text-book in the English literature course of practically every public school in the land, as an American classic. The stories and sketches are excellent; but I think that teachers of English *should realize that some of that puzzlement which adult readers experienced upon first encountering "Mosses from an Old Manse" is a natural phenomenon with a fourteen-year-old boy or girl and I suggest that, instead of complicating the child's tedium in trying to read Hawthorne by exasperating questionnaires, they pitch "Mosses from an Old Manse" out of the curriculum and give the kids something easier. I have here chosen good Hawthorne but not the ones which perennially appear in anthologies....*

Ambrose Bierce, a spectacular figure in American literary life and the subject of endless speculation as to whether he is alive or dead since his disappearance in Mexico a quarter of a century ago, enlisted as a private with the Union forces during the Civil War and emerged as a Major, like his publisher, George Haven Putnam. A huge and sanguinary man, eager to pick quarrels and ready to fight at the drop of a hat—in personal encounters—he had a violent revulsion against the mass murder of war. In "Chickamauga," his masterpiece as a short-story writer, he has expressed that revulsion in one of the most gruesome and ingenious stories ever written to depict the obscene horror of the aftermath of battle....

Remy de Gourmont in his "Promenades Littéraires" wrote that Edgar Allan Poe was the "most American writer" that America had ever produced and cited "The Great Balloon Hoax" as a particular example of what he meant. He said that nowhere else except in America, "land of extravagance and excess," would a writer think of perpetrating an intellectual joke like that one. This is a refutation of the opinion expressed by many critics that Poe's genius is alien in character and that his literary derivations are French, an opinion doubtless based upon the fact that Baudelaire so superbly translated "Tales of the Grotesque and the Arabesque" that they became French classics, Mallarmé translated "The Raven" into verse of astonishing beauty and truth to the original, and the French mystery story has grown directly from the seeds of Poe's inventions. The selection herewith is Poe at his most fascinating best as a creator of moods and of a sense of a mysterious world and mysterious forces we wot not of....

Although Washington Irving was an American, he lived for some time in England, and his style, though graceful enough, never was energized by the American idiom. Most of his essays and his tales with an American setting might just as well have been written by a talented English writer of the period. It is only in his humorous stuff that we get a touch of the American spirit.... When G. P. Putnam became Irving's publisher, Irving was convinced that his popularity had played out and that he could no longer earn a living by writing; he had settled down to his work as a state servant in the diplomatic corps. He was sixty-five years of age and although he was a celebrated personage fêted by the literary and ambassadorial big-wigs on both sides of the water, his Philadelphia publishers had allowed his works to go out of print, because there was no call for them. Putnam gave Irving a new contract and persuaded him to start writing again. Moreover, he bought and had shipped up to Irving's estate at Sunnyside, N. Y., one of those new-fangled roll-top desks, so much the fashion, on which to do this writing. A little later Putnam went up to Sunnyside, eyes beaming with his own beneficence and expectantly awaiting Irving's expression of gratitude. Instead Irving was in a rage. He greeted Putnam with the angry exclamation, "You have ruined my work! I have placed my papers in these confounded pigeon-holes and I can't remember where a single paper is! I've had the girls in here all morning trying to help me find things! I'll never be able to finish 'Washington' for you on this new-fangled piece of furniture!" ... Just a typical author....

Although Henry James' father was a frequent contributor of papers on various subjects to the old Putnam's Monthly Magazine, *Henry James was never a Putnam author, except as a contributor to the revived* Putnam's Monthly. *The selection given herewith is Jamesian and is one of his lesser known short novels. It ran as a serial....*

One of those co-incidental accidents of publishing was responsible for the vast success of John Erskine's "The Private Life of Helen of Troy" and the comparative failure of Emily James Putnam's "Candaules' Wife and Other Old Stories." Both Erskine and Mrs. Putnam had had, unknown to each other, practically the same literary idea at the same time. This idea was a fictional treatment, in modern, sophisticated, and realistico-satiric terms, of the story of Helen of Troy. Erskine's novel was published about the same time Mrs. Putnam's short story, "Helen in Egypt" appeared in The Atlantic Monthly. *By the time her story was included in a book of short stories, all on related Greek themes, she could not use the title "Helen in Egypt" because Erskine had, in a way, preëmpted its use. Booksellers are, moreover, reluctant to stock books of short stories owing to an ancient myth (somewhat justified in spite of Kipling, Bierce, O. Henry, Maupassant, Lardner, Hemingway, et al.), that "books of short stories do not sell." So "Candaules' Wife and Other Stories" fell among those many fine "neglected" books which bibliophiles stumble onto years after publication.*

Yet "Helen in Egypt" is a modern short story which I do not believe those who care for literary craftsmanship of a very high order will willingly let die. There are, as most Greek scholars know, many legends about Helen besides the Homeric and familiar one. One of these legends, treated by Euripides and later dramatists, is that after the fall of Troy, Helen escaped or was taken captive, to Egypt and there rounded out a full life. Mrs. Putnam, a notable Greek and Latin scholar, former Dean of Barnard College (before her marriage to Major George Haven Putnam), and author of that classic work "The Lady," took this later legend and made a superb and amusingly human story out of it.

HERMAN MELVILLE

Benito Cereno

PART I

IN THE YEAR 1799, Captain Amasa Delano, of Duxbury, in Massachusetts, commanding a large sealer and general trader, lay at anchor, with a valuable cargo, in the harbor of St. Maria—a small, desert, uninhabited island toward the southern extremity of the long coast of Chili. There he had touched for water.

On the second day, not long after dawn, while lying in his berth, his mate came below, informing him that a strange sail was coming into the bay. Ships were then not so plenty in those waters as now. He rose, dressed, and went on deck.

The morning was one peculiar to that coast. Everything was mute and calm; everything gray. The sea, though undulated into long roods of swells, seemed fixed, and was sleeked at the surface like waved lead that has cooled and set in the smelter's mold. The sky seemed a gray mantle. Flights of troubled gray fowl, kith and kin with flights of troubled gray vapors among which they were mixed, skimmed low and fitfully over the waters, as swallows over meadows before storms. Shadows present, foreshadowing deeper shadows to come.

To Captain Delano's surprise, the stranger, viewed through the glass, showed no colors; though to do so upon entering a haven, however uninhabited in its shores, where but a single other ship might be lying, was the custom among peaceful seamen of all nations. Considering the lawlessness and loneliness of the spot, and the sort of stories, at that day, associated with those seas, Captain Delano's surprise might have deepened into some uneasiness had he not been a person of a singularly undistrustful good nature, not liable, except on extraordinary and repeated excitement, and hardly then, to indulge in personal alarms, any way involving the imputation of malign evil in man. Whether, in view of what humanity is capable, such a trait implies, along with a benevolent heart, more than ordinary quickness and accuracy of intellectual perception, may be left to the wise to determine.

But whatever misgivings might have obtruded on first seeing the stranger, would almost, in any seaman's mind, have been dissipated by observing that, the ship, in navigating into the harbor, was drawing too near the land, for her own safety's sake, owing to a sunken reef making out off her bow. This seemed to prove her a stranger, indeed, not only to the sealer, but the island; consequently, she could be no wonted freebooter on that ocean. With no small interest, Captain Delano continued to watch her—a proceeding not much facilitated by the vapors partly mantling the hull, through which the far matin light from her cabin streamed equivocally enough; much like the sun—by this time crescented on the rim of the horizon, and apparently, in company with the strange ship, entering the harbor—which, wimpled by the same low, creeping clouds, showed not unlike a Lima intriguante's one sinister eye peering across the Plaza from the Indian loophole of her dusk *saya-y-manta*.

It might have been but a deception of the vapors, but, the longer the stranger was watched, the more singular appeared her maneuvers. Ere long it seemed hard to decide whether she meant to come in or no—what she wanted, or what she was about. The wind, which had breezed up a little during the night, was now extremely light and baffling, which the more increased the apparent uncertainty of her movements.

Surmising, at last, that it might be a ship in distress, Captain Delano ordered his whale-boat to be dropped, and, much to the wary opposition of his mate, prepared to board her, and, at the least, pilot her in. On the night previous, a fishing-party of the seamen had gone a long distance to some detached rocks out of sight from the sealer, and, an hour or two before day-break, had returned, having met with no small success. Presuming that the stranger might have been long off soundings, the good captain put several baskets of the fish, for presents, into his boat, and so pulled away. From her continuing too near the sunken reef, deeming her in danger, calling to his men, he made all haste to apprise those on board of their situation. But, some time ere the boat came up, the wind, light though it was, having shifted, had headed the vessel off, as well as partly broken the vapors from about her.

Upon gaining a less remote view, the ship, when made signally visible on the verge of the leaden-hued swells, with the shreds of fog here and there raggedly furring her, appeared like a white-washed monastery after a thunder-storm, seen perched upon some dun cliff among the Pyrenees. But it was no purely fanciful resemblance which now, for a moment, almost led Captain Delano to think that nothing less than a ship-load of monks was before him. Peering over the bulwarks were what really seemed, in the hazy distance, throngs of dark cowls; while, fitfully revealed through the open portholes, other dark moving figures were dimly descried, as of Black Friars pacing the cloisters.

Upon a still nigher approach, this appearance was modified, and the true character of the vessel was plain—a Spanish merchantman of the first class; carrying negro slaves, amongst other valuable freight, from one colonial port to another. A very large, and, in its time, a very fine vessel, such as in those days were at intervals encountered along that main; sometimes superseded Acapulco treasure-ships, or retired frigates of the Spanish king's navy, which, like superannuated Italian palaces, still, under a decline of masters, preserved signs of former state.

As the whale-boat drew more and more nigh, the cause of the peculiar pipe-clayed aspect of the stranger was seen in the slovenly neglect pervading her. The spars, ropes, and great part of the bulwarks, looked woolly, from long unacquaintance with the scraper, tar, and the brush. Her keel seemed laid, her ribs put together, and she launched, from Ezekiel's Valley of Dry Bones.

In the present business in which she was engaged, the ship's general model and rig appeared to have undergone no material change from their original warlike and Froissart pattern. However, no guns were seen.

The tops were large, and were railed about with what had once been octagonal net-work, all now in sad disrepair. These tops hung overhead like three ruinous aviaries, in one of which was seen perched, on a ratlin, a white noddy, a strange fowl, so called from its lethargic, somnambulistic character, being frequently caught by hand at sea. Battered and mouldy, the castellated forecastle seemed some ancient turret, long ago taken by assault, and then left to decay. Toward the stern, two high-raised quarter galleries—the balustrades here and there covered with dry, tindery sea-moss—opening out from the unoccupied state-cabin, whose dead lights, for all the mild weather, were hermetically closed and calked—these tenantless balconies hung over the sea as if it were the grand Venetian canal. But the principal relic of faded grandeur was the ample oval of the shield-like stern-piece, intricately carved with the arms of Castile and Leon, medallioned about by groups of mythological or symbolical devices; uppermost and central of which was a dark satyr in a mask, holding his foot on the prostrate neck of a writhing figure, likewise masked.

Whether the ship had a figure-head, or only a plain beak, was not quite certain, owing to canvas wrapped about that part, either to protect it while undergoing a re-furbishing, or else decently to hide its decay. Rudely painted or chalked, as in a sailor freak, along the forward side of a sort of pedestal below the canvas, was the sentence, *"Seguid vuestro jefe,"* (follow your leader); while upon the tarnished head-boards, near by, appeared, in stately capitals, once gilt, the ship's name, "SAN DOMINICK," each letter streakingly corroded with tricklings of copper-spike rust; while, like mourning weeds, dark festoons of sea-grass slimily swept to and fro over the name, with every hearse-like roll of the hull.

As at last the boat was hooked from the bow along toward the gangway amidship, its keel, while yet some inches separated from the hull, harshly grated as on a sunken coral reef. It proved a huge bunch of conglobated barnacles adhering below the water to the side like a wen; a token of baffling airs and long calms passed somewhere in those seas.

Climbing the side, the visitor was at once surrounded by a clamorous throng of whites and blacks, but the latter outnumbering the former more than could have been expected, negro transportation-ship as the stranger in port was. But, in one language, and as with one voice, all poured out a common tale of suffering; in which the negresses, of whom there were not a few, exceeded the others in their dolorous vehemence. The scurvy, together with a fever, had swept off a great part of their number, more especially the Spaniards. Off Cape Horn, they had narrowly escaped shipwreck; then, for days together, they had lain tranced without wind; their provisions were low; their water next to none; their lips that moment were baked.

While Captain Delano was thus made the mark of all eager tongues, his one eager glance took in all the faces, with every other object about him.

Always upon first boarding a large and populous ship at sea, especially a foreign one, with a nondescript crew such as Lascars or Manilla men, the impression varies in a peculiar way from that produced by first entering a strange house with strange inmates in a strange land. Both house and ship, the one by its walls and blinds, the other by its high bulwarks like ramparts, hoard from view their interiors till the last moment; but in the case of the ship there is this addition; that the living spectacle it contains, upon its sudden and complete disclosure, has, in contrast with the blank ocean which zones it, something of the effect of enchantment. The ship seems unreal; these strange costumes, gestures, and faces, but a shadowy tableau just emerged from the deep, which directly must receive back what it gave.

Perhaps it was some such influence as above is attempted to be described, which, in Captain Delano's mind, hightened whatever, upon a staid scrutiny, might have seemed unusual; especially the conspicuous figures of four elderly grizzled negroes, their heads like black, doddered willow tops, who, in venerable contrast to the tumult below them, were couched sphynx-like, one on the starboard cat-head, another on the larboard, and the remaining pair face to face on the opposite bulwarks above the main-chains. They each had bits of unstranded old junk in their hands, and, with a sort of stoical self-content, were picking the junk into oakum, a small heap of which lay by their sides. They accompanied the task with a continuous, low, monotonous chant; droning and druling away like so many gray-headed bag-pipers playing a funeral march.

The quarter-deck rose into an ample elevated poop, upon the forward verge of which, lifted, like the oakum-pickers, some eight feet above the general throng, sat along in a row, separated by regular spaces, the cross-legged figures of six other blacks; each with a rusty hatchet in his hand, which, with a bit of brick and a rag, he was engaged like a scullion in scouring; while between each two was a small stack of hatchets, their rusted edges turned forward awaiting a like operation. Though occasionally the four oakum-pickers would briefly address some person or persons in the crowd below, yet the six hatchet-polishers neither spoke to others, nor breathed a whisper among themselves, but sat intent upon their task, except at intervals, when, with the peculiar love in negroes of uniting industry with pastime, two and two they sideways clashed their hatchets together, like cymbals, with a barbarous din. All six, unlike the generality, had the raw aspect of unsophisticated Africans.

But that first comprehensive glance which took in those ten figures, with scores less conspicuous, rested but an instant upon them, as, impatient of the hubbub of voices, the visitor turned in quest of whomsoever it might be that commanded the ship.

But as if not unwilling to let nature make known her own case among his suffering charge, or else in despair of restraining it for the time, the Spanish captain, a gentlemanly, reserved-looking, and rather young man to a stranger's eye, dressed with singular richness, but bearing plain traces of recent sleepless cares and disquietudes, stood passively by, leaning against the main-mast, at one moment casting a dreary, spiritless look upon his excited people, at the next an unhappy glance toward his visitor. By his side stood a black of small stature, in whose rude face, as occasionally, like a shepherd's dog, he mutely turned it up into the Spaniard's, sorrow and affection were equally blended.

Struggling through the throng, the American advanced to the Spaniard, assuring him of his sympathies, and offering to render whatever assistance might be in his power. To which the Spaniard returned, for the present, but grave and ceremonious acknowledgments, his national formality dusked by the saturnine mood of ill health.

But losing no time in mere compliments, Captain Delano returning to the gangway, had his baskets of fish brought up; and as the wind still continued light, so that some hours at least must elapse ere the ship could be brought to the anchorage, he bade his men return to the sealer, and fetch back as much water as the whale-boat could carry, with whatever soft bread the steward might have, all the remaining pumpkins on board, with a box of sugar, and a dozen of his private bottles of cider.

Not many minutes after the boat's pushing off, to the vexation of all, the wind entirely died away, and the tide turning, began drifting back the ship helplessly seaward. But trusting this would not long last, Captain Delano sought with good hopes to cheer up the strangers, feeling no small satisfaction that, with persons in their condition he could—thanks to his frequent voyages along the Spanish main—converse with some freedom in their native tongue.

While left alone with them, he was not long in observing some things tending to highten his first impressions; but surprise was lost in pity, both for the Spaniards and blacks, alike evidently reduced from scarcity of water and provisions; while long-continued suffering seemed to have brought out the less good-natured qualities of the negroes, besides, at the same time, impairing the Spaniard's authority over them. But, under the circumstances, precisely this condition of things was to have been anticipated. In armies, navies, cities, or families, in nature herself, nothing more relaxes good order than misery. Still, Captain Delano was not without the idea, that had Benito Cereno been a man of greater energy, misrule would hardly have come to the present pass. But the debility, constitutional or induced by the hardships, bodily and mental, of the Spanish captain, was too obvious to be overlooked. A prey to settled dejection, as if long mocked with hope he would not now indulge it, even when it had ceased to be a mock, the prospect of that day or evening at furthest, lying at anchor, with plenty of water for his people, and a brother captain to counsel and befriend, seemed in no perceptible degree to encourage him. His mind appeared unstrung, if not still more seriously affected. Shut up in these oaken walls, chained to one dull round of command, whose unconditionality cloyed him, like some hypochondriac abbot he moved slowly about, at times suddenly pausing, starting, or staring, biting his lip, biting his finger-nail, flushing, paling, twitching his beard, with other symptoms of an absent or moody mind. This distempered spirit was lodged, as before hinted, in as distempered a frame. He was rather tall, but seemed never to have been robust, and now with nervous suffering was almost worn to a skeleton. A tendency to some pulmonary complaint appeared to have been lately confirmed. His voice was like that of one with lungs half gone, hoarsely suppressed, a husky whisper. No wonder that, as in this state he tottered about, his private servant apprehensively followed him. Sometimes the negro gave his master his arm, or took his handkerchief out of his pocket for him; performing these and similar offices with that affectionate zeal which transmutes into something filial or fraternal acts in themselves but menial; and which has gained for the negro the repute of making the most pleasing body servant in the world; one, too, whom a master need be on no stiffly superior terms with, but may treat with familiar trust; less a servant than a devoted companion.

Marking the noisy indocility of the blacks in general, as well as what seemed the sullen inefficiency of the whites, it was not without humane satisfaction that Captain Delano witnessed the steady good conduct of Babo.

But the good conduct of Babo, hardly more than the ill-behavior of others, seemed to withdraw the half-lunatic Don Benito from his cloudy languor. Not that such precisely was the impression made by the Spaniard on the mind of his visitor. The Spaniard's individual unrest was, for the present, but noted as a conspicuous feature in the ship's general affliction. Still, Captain Delano was not a little concerned at what he could not help taking for the time to be Don Benito's unfriendly indifference towards himself. The Spaniard's manner, too, conveyed a sort of sour and gloomy disdain, which he seemed at no pains to disguise. But this the American in charity ascribed to the harassing effects of sickness, since, in former instances, he had noted that there are peculiar natures on whom prolonged physical suffering seems to cancel every social instinct of kindness; as if forced to black bread themselves, they deemed it but equity that each person coming nigh them should, indirectly, by some slight or affront, be made to partake of their fare.

But ere long Captain Delano bethought him that, indulgent as he was at the first, in judging the Spaniard, he might not, after all, have exercised charity enough. At bottom it was Don Benito's reserve which displeased him; but the same reserve was shown towards all but his personal attendant. Even the formal reports which, according to sea-usage, were, at stated times, made to him by some petty underling, either a white, mulatto or black, he hardly had patience enough to listen to, without betraying contemptuous aversion. His manner upon such occasions was, in its degree, not unlike that which might be supposed to have been his imperial countryman's, Charles V., just previous to the anchoritish retirement of that monarch from the throne.

This splenetic disrelish of his place was evinced in almost every function pertaining to it. Proud as he was moody, he condescended to no personal mandate. Whatever special orders were necessary, their delivery was delegated to his body-servant, who in turn transferred them to their ultimate destination, through runners, alert Spanish boys or slave boys, like pages or pilot-fish within easy call continually hovering round Don Benito. So that to have beheld this undemonstrative invalid gliding about, apathetic and mute, no landsman could have dreamed that in him was lodged a dictatorship beyond which, while at sea, there was no earthly appeal.

Thus, the Spaniard, regarded in his reserve, seemed as the involuntary victim of mental disorder. But, in fact, his reserve might, in some degree, have proceeded from design. If so, then in Don Benito was evinced the unhealthy climax of that icy though conscientious policy, more or less adopted by all commanders of large ships, which, except in signal emergencies, obliterates alike the manifestation of sway with every trace of sociality; transforming the man into a block, or rather into a loaded cannon, which, until there is call for thunder, has nothing to say.

Viewing him in this light, it seemed but a natural token of the perverse habit induced by a long course of such hard self-restraint, that, notwithstanding the present condition of his ship, the Spaniard should still persist in a demeanor, which, however harmless, or, it may be, appropriate, in a well appointed vessel, such as the San Dominick might have been at the outset of the voyage, was anything but judicious now. But the Spaniard perhaps thought that it was with captains as with gods: reserve, under all events, must still be their cue. But more probably this appearance of slumbering dominion might have been but an attempted disguise to conscious imbecility—not deep policy, but shallow device. But be all this as it might, whether Don Benito's manner was designed or not, the more Captain Delano noted its pervading reserve, the less he felt uneasiness at any particular manifestation of that reserve towards himself.

Neither were his thoughts taken up by the captain alone. Wonted to the quiet orderliness of the sealer's comfortable family of a crew, the noisy confusion of the San Dominick's suffering host repeatedly challenged his eye. Some prominent breaches not only of discipline but of decency were observed. These Captain Delano could not but ascribe, in the main, to the absence of those subordinate deck-officers to whom, along with higher duties, is entrusted what may be styled the police department of a populous ship. True, the old oakum-pickers appeared at times to act the part of monitorial constables to their countrymen, the blacks; but though occasionally succeeding in allaying trifling outbreaks now and then between man and man, they could do little or nothing toward establishing general quiet. The San Dominick was in the condition of a transatlantic emigrant ship, among whose multitude of living freight are some individuals, doubtless, as little troublesome as crates and bales; but the friendly remonstrances of such with their ruder companions are of not so much avail as the unfriendly arm of the mate. What the San Dominick wanted was, what the emigrant ship has, stern superior officers. But on these decks not so much as a fourth mate was to be seen.

The visitor's curiosity was roused to learn the particulars of those mishaps which had brought about such absenteeism, with its consequences; because, though deriving some inkling of the voyage from the wails which at the first moment had greeted him, yet of the details no clear understanding had been had. The best account would, doubtless, be given by the captain. Yet at first the visitor was loth to ask it, unwilling to provoke some distant rebuff. But plucking up courage, he at last accosted Don Benito, renewing the expression of his benevolent interest, adding, that did he (Captain Delano) but know the particulars of the ship's misfortunes, he would, perhaps, be better able in the end to relieve them. Would Don Benito favor him with the whole story?

Don Benito faltered; then, like some somnambulist suddenly interfered with, vacantly stared at his visitor, and ended by looking down on the deck. He maintained this posture so long, that Captain Delano, almost equally disconcerted, and involuntarily almost as rude, turned suddenly from him, walking forward to accost one of the Spanish seamen for the desired information. But he had hardly gone five paces, when with a sort of eagerness Don Benito invited him back, regretting his momentary absence of mind, and professing readiness to gratify him.

While most part of the story was being given, the two captains stood on the after part of the main-deck, a privileged spot, no one being near but the servant.

"It is now a hundred and ninety days," began the Spaniard, in his husky whisper, "that this ship, well officered and well manned, with several cabin passengers—some fifty Spaniards in all—sailed from Buenos Ayres bound to Lima, with a general cargo, Paraguay tea and the like—and," pointing forward, "that parcel of negroes, now not more than a hundred and fifty, as you see, but then numbering over three hundred souls. Off Cape Horn we had heavy gales. In one moment, by night, three of my best officers, with fifteen sailors, were lost, with the main-yard; the spar snapping under them in the slings, as they sought, with heavers, to beat down the icy sail. To lighten the hull, the heavier sacks of mata were thrown into the sea, with most of the water-pipes lashed on deck at the time. And this last necessity it was, combined with the prolonged detentions afterwards experienced, which eventually brought about our chief causes of suffering. When——"

Here there was a sudden fainting attack of his cough, brought on, no doubt, by his mental distress. His servant sustained him, and drawing a cordial from his pocket placed it to his lips. He a little revived. But unwilling to leave him unsupported while yet imperfectly restored, the black with one arm still encircled his master, at the same time keeping his eye fixed on his face, as if to watch for the first sign of complete restoration, or relapse, as the event might prove.

The Spaniard proceeded, but brokenly and obscurely, as one in a dream.

—"Oh, my God! rather than pass through what I have, with joy I would have hailed the most terrible gales; but——"

His cough returned and with increased violence; this subsiding, with reddened lips and closed eyes he fell heavily against his supporter.

"His mind wanders. He was thinking of the plague that followed the gales," plaintively sighed the servant; "my poor, poor master!" wringing one hand, and with the other wiping the mouth. "But be patient, Señor," again turning to Captain Delano, "these fits do not last long; master will soon be himself."

Don Benito reviving, went on; but as this portion of the story was very brokenly delivered, the substance only will here be set down.

It appeared that after the ship had been many days tossed in storms off the Cape, the scurvy broke out, carrying off numbers of the whites and blacks. When at last they had worked round into the Pacific, their spars and sails were so damaged, and so inadequately handled by the surviving mariners, most of whom were become invalids, that, unable to lay her northerly course by the wind, which was powerful, the unmanageable ship for successive days and nights was blown northwestward, where the breeze suddenly deserted her, in unknown waters, to sultry calms. The absence of the water pipes now proved as fatal to life as before their presence had menaced it. Induced, or at least aggravated, by the more than scanty allowance of water, a malignant fever followed the scurvy; with the excessive heat of the lengthened calm, making such short work of it as to sweep away, as by billows, whole families of the Africans, and a yet larger number, proportionably, of the Spaniards, including, by a luckless fatality, every officer on board. Consequently, in the smart west winds eventually following the calm, the already rent sails having to be simply dropped, not furled, at need, had been gradually reduced to the beggar's rags they were now. To procure substitutes for his lost sailors, as well as supplies of water and sails, the captain at the earliest opportunity had made for Baldivia, the southermost civilized port of Chili and South America; but upon nearing the coast the thick weather had prevented him from so much as sighting that harbor. Since which period, almost without a crew, and almost without canvas and almost without water, and at intervals giving its added dead to the sea, the San Dominick had been battle-dored about by contrary winds, inveigled by currents, or grown weedy in calms. Like a man lost in woods, more than once she had doubled upon her own track.

"But throughout these calamities," huskily continued Don Benito, painfully turning in the half embrace of his servant, "I have to thank those negroes you see, who, though to your inexperienced eyes appearing unruly, have, indeed, conducted themselves with less of restlessness than even their owner could have thought possible under such circumstances."

Here he again fell faintly back. Again his mind wandered: but he rallied, and less obscurely proceeded.

"Yes, their owner was quite right in assuring me that no fetters would be needed with his blacks; so that while, as is wont in this transportation, those negroes have always remained upon deck—not thrust below, as in the

Guineamen—they have, also, from the beginning, been freely permitted to range within given bounds at their pleasure."

Once more the faintness returned—his mind roved—but, recovering, he resumed:

"But it is Babo here to whom, under God, I owe not only my own preservation, but likewise to him, chiefly, the merit is due, of pacifying his more ignorant brethren, when at intervals tempted to murmurings."

"Ah, master," sighed the black, bowing his face, "don't speak of me; Babo is nothing; what Babo has done was but duty."

"Faithful fellow!" cried Capt. Delano. "Don Benito, I envy you such a friend; slave I cannot call him."

As master and man stood before him, the black upholding the white, Captain Delano could not but bethink him of the beauty of that relationship which could present such a spectacle of fidelity on the one hand and confidence on the other. The scene was hightened by the contrast in dress, denoting their relative positions. The Spaniard wore a loose Chili jacket of dark velvet; white small clothes and stockings, with silver buckles at the knee and instep; a high-crowned sombrero, of fine grass; a slender sword, silver mounted, hung from a knot in his sash; the last being an almost invariable adjunct, more for utility than ornament, of a South American gentleman's dress to this hour. Excepting when his occasional nervous contortions brought about disarray, there was a certain precision in his attire, curiously at variance with the unsightly disorder around; especially in the belittered Ghetto, forward of the main-mast, wholly occupied by the blacks.

The servant wore nothing but wide trowsers, apparently, from their coarseness and patches, made out of some old topsail; they were clean, and confined at the waist by a bit of unstranded rope, which, with his composed, deprecatory air at times, made him look something like a begging friar of St. Francis.

However unsuitable for the time and place, at least in the blunt-thinking American's eyes, and however strangely surviving in the midst of all his afflictions, the toilette of Don Benito might not, in fashion at least, have gone beyond the style of the day among South Americans of his class. Though on the present voyage sailing from Buenos Ayres, he had avowed himself a native and resident of Chili, whose inhabitants had not so generally adopted the plain coat and once plebeian pantaloons; but, with a becoming modification, adhered to their provincial costume, picturesque as any in the world. Still, relatively to the pale history of the voyage, and his own pale face, there seemed something so incongruous in the Spaniard's apparel, as almost to suggest the image of an invalid courtier tottering about London streets in the time of the plague.

The portion of the narrative which, perhaps, most excited interest, as well as some surprise, considering the latitudes in question, was the long calms spoken of, and more particularly the ship's so long drifting about. Without communicating the opinion, of course, the American could not but impute at least part of the detentions both to clumsy seamanship and faulty navigation. Eying Don Benito's small, yellow hands, he easily inferred that the young captain had not got into command at the hawse-hole, but the cabin-window; and if so, why wonder at incompetence, in youth, sickness, and aristocracy united? Such was his democratic conclusion.

But drowning criticism in compassion, after a fresh repetition of his sympathies, Captain Delano having heard out his story, not only engaged, as in the first place, to see Don Benito and his people supplied in their immediate bodily needs, but, also, now further promised to assist him in procuring a large permanent supply of water, as well as some sails and rigging; and, though it would involve no small embarrassment to himself, yet he would spare three of his best seamen for temporary deck officers; so that without delay the ship might proceed to Conception, there fully to refit for Lima, her destined port.

Such generosity was not without its effect, even upon the invalid. His face lighted up; eager and hectic, he met the honest glance of his visitor. With gratitude he seemed overcome.

"This excitement is bad for master," whispered the servant, taking his arm, and with soothing words gently drawing him aside.

When Don Benito returned, the American was pained to observe that his hopefulness, like the sudden kindling in his cheek, was but febrile and transient.

Ere long, with a joyless mien, looking up towards the poop, the host invited his guest to accompany him there, for the benefit of what little breath of wind might be stirring.

As during the telling of the story, Captain Delano had once or twice started at the occasional cymballing of the hatchet-polishers, wondering why such an interruption should be allowed, especially in that part of the ship, and in the ears of an invalid; and moreover, as the hatchets had anything but an attractive look, and the handlers of them still less so, it was, therefore, to tell the truth, not without some lurking reluctance, or even shrinking, it may be, that Captain Delano, with apparent complaisance, acquiesced in his host's invitation. The more so, since with an untimely caprice of punctilio, rendered distressing by his cadaverous aspect, Don Benito, with Castilian bows, solemnly insisted upon his guest's preceding him up the ladder leading to the elevation; where, one on each side of the last step, sat for armorial supporters and sentries two of the ominous file. Gingerly enough stepped good Captain Delano between them, and in the instant of leaving them behind, like one running the gauntlet, he felt an apprehensive twitch in the calves of his legs.

But when, facing about, he saw the whole file, like so many organ-grinders, still stupidly intent on their work, unmindful of everything beside, he could not but smile at his late fidgeting panic.

Presently, while standing with Don Benito, looking forward upon the decks below, he was struck by one of those instances of insubordination previously alluded to. Three black boys, with two Spanish boys, were sitting together on the hatches, scraping a rude wooden platter, in which some scanty mess had recently been cooked. Suddenly, one of the black boys, enraged at a word dropped by one of his white companions, seized a knife, and though called to forbear by one of the oakum-pickers, struck the lad over the head, inflicting a gash from which blood flowed.

In amazement, Captain Delano inquired what this meant. To which the pale Benito dully muttered, that it was merely the sport of the lad.

"Pretty serious sport, truly," rejoined Captain Delano. "Had such a thing happened on board the Bachelor's Delight, instant punishment would have followed."

At these words the Spaniard turned upon the American one of his sudden, staring, half-lunatic looks; then relapsing into his torpor, answered, "Doubtless, doubtless, Señor."

Is it, thought Captain Delano, that this helpless man is one of those paper captains I've known, who by policy wink at what by power they cannot put down? I know no sadder sight than a commander who has little of command but the name.

"I should think, Don Benito," he now said, glancing towards the oakum-picker who had sought to interfere with the boys, "that you would find it advantageous to keep all your blacks employed, especially the younger ones, no matter at what useless task, and no matter what happens to the ship. Why, even with my little band, I find such a course indispensable. I once kept a crew on my quarter-deck thrumming mats for my cabin, when, for three days, I had given up my ship—mats, men, and all—for a speedy loss, owing to the violence of a gale, in which we could do nothing but helplessly drive before it."

"Doubtless, doubtless," muttered Don Benito.

"But," continued Captain Delano, again glancing upon the oakum-pickers and then at the hatchet-polishers, near by, "I see you keep some at least of your host employed."

"Yes," was again the vacant response.

"Those old men there, shaking their pows from their pulpits," continued Captain Delano, pointing to the oakum-pickers, "seem to act the part of old dominies to the rest, little heeded as their admonitions are at times. Is this voluntary on their part, Don Benito, or have you appointed them shepherds to your flock of black sheep?"

"What posts they fill, I appointed them," rejoined the Spaniard, in an acrid tone, as if resenting some supposed satiric reflection.

"And these others, these Ashantee conjurors here," continued Captain Delano, rather uneasily eying the brandished steel of the hatchet-polishers, where in spots it had been brought to a shine, "this seems a curious business they are at, Don Benito?"

"In the gales we met," answered the Spaniard, "what of our general cargo was not thrown overboard was much damaged by the brine. Since coming into calm weather, I have had several cases of knives and hatchets daily brought up for overhauling and cleaning."

"A prudent idea, Don Benito. You are part owner of ship and cargo, I presume; but not of the slaves, perhaps?"

"I am owner of all you see," impatiently returned Don Benito, "except the main company of blacks, who belonged to my late friend, Alexandro Aranda."

As he mentioned this name, his air was heart-broken; his knees shook: his servant supported him.

Thinking he divined the cause of such unusual emotion, to confirm his surmise, Captain Delano, after a pause, said, "And may I ask, Don Benito, whether—since awhile ago you spoke of some cabin passengers—the friend, whose loss so afflicts you at the outset of the voyage accompanied his blacks?"

"Yes."

"But died of the fever?"

"Died of the fever.—Oh, could I but——"

Again quivering, the Spaniard paused.

"Pardon me," said Captain Delano slowly, "but I think that, by a sympathetic experience, I conjecture, Don Benito, what it is that gives the keener edge to your grief. It was once my hard fortune to lose at sea a dear friend, my own brother, then supercargo. Assured of the welfare of his spirit, its departure I could have borne like a man; but that honest eye, that honest hand—both of which had so often met mine—and that warm heart; all, all—like scraps to the dogs—to throw all to the sharks! It was then I vowed never to have for fellow-voyager a man I loved, unless, unbeknown to him, I had provided every requisite, in case of a fatality, for embalming his mortal part for interment on shore. Were your friend's remains now on board this ship, Don Benito, not thus strangely would the mention of his name affect you."

"On board this ship?" echoed the Spaniard. Then, with horrified gestures, as directed against some specter, he unconsciously fell into the ready arms of his attendant, who, with a silent appeal toward Captain Delano, seemed beseeching him not again to broach a theme so unspeakably distressing to his master.

This poor fellow now, thought the pained American, is the victim of that sad superstition which associates goblins with the deserted body of man, as ghosts with an abandoned house. How unlike are we made! What to me, in like case, would have been a solemn satisfaction, the bare suggestion, even, terrifies the Spaniard into this trance. Poor Alexandro Aranda! what would you say could you here see your friend—who, on former voyages, when you for months were left behind, has, I dare say, often longed, and longed, for one peep at you—now transported with terror at the least thought of having you anyway nigh him.

At this moment, with a dreary graveyard toll, betokening a flaw, the ship's forecastle bell, smote by one of the grizzled oakum-pickers, proclaimed ten o'clock through the leaden calm; when Captain Delano's attention was caught by the moving figure of a gigantic black, emerging from the general crowd below, and slowly advancing towards the elevated poop. An iron collar was about his neck, from which depended a chain, thrice wound round his body; the terminating links padlocked together at a broad band of iron, his girdle.

"How like a mute Atufal moves," murmured the servant.

The black mounted the steps of the poop, and, like a brave prisoner, brought up to receive sentence, stood in unquailing muteness before Don Benito, now recovered from his attack.

At the first glimpse of his approach, Don Benito had started, a resentful shadow swept over his face; and, as with the sudden memory of bootless rage, his white lips glued together.

This is some mulish mutineer, thought Captain Delano, surveying, not without a mixture of admiration, the colossal form of the negro.

"See, he waits your question, master," said the servant.

Thus reminded, Don Benito, nervously averting his glance, as if shunning, by anticipation, some rebellious response, in a disconcerted voice, thus spoke:—

"Atufal, will you ask my pardon now?"

The black was silent.

"Again, master," murmured the servant, with bitter upbraiding eyeing his countryman, "Again, master; he will bend to master yet."

"Answer," said Don Benito, still averting his glance, "say but the one word *pardon,* and your chains shall be off."

Upon this, the black, slowly raising both arms, let them lifelessly fall, his links clanking, his head bowed; as much as to say, "no, I am content."

"Go," said Don Benito, with inkept and unknown emotion.

Deliberately as he had come, the black obeyed.

"Excuse me, Don Benito," said Captain Delano, "but this scene surprises me; what means it, pray?"

"It means that that negro alone, of all the band, has given me peculiar cause of offense. I have put him in chains; I——"

Here he paused; his hand to his head, as if there were a swimming there, or a sudden bewilderment of memory had come over him; but meeting his servant's kindly glance seemed reassured, and proceeded:—

"I could not scourge such a form. But I told him he must ask my pardon. As yet he has not. At my command, every two hours he stands before me."

"And how long has this been?"

"Some sixty days."

"And obedient in all else? And respectful?"

"Yes."

"Upon my conscience, then," exclaimed Captain Delano, impulsively, "he has a royal spirit in him, this fellow."

"He may have some right to it," bitterly returned Don Benito, "he says he was king in his own land."

"Yes," said the servant, entering a word, "those slits in Atufal's ears once held wedges of gold; but poor Babo here, in his own land, was only a poor slave; a black man's slave was Babo, who now is the white's."

Somewhat annoyed by these conversational familiarities, Captain Delano turned curiously upon the attendant, then glanced inquiringly at his master; but, as if long wonted to these little informalities, neither master nor man seemed to understand him.

"What, pray, was Atufal's offense, Don Benito?" asked Captain Delano; "if it was not something very serious, take a fool's advice, and, in view of his general docility, as well as in some natural respect for his spirit, remit him his penalty."

"No, no, master never will do that," here murmured the servant to himself; "proud Atufal must first ask master's pardon. The slave there carries the padlock, but master here carries the key."

His attention thus directed, Captain Delano now noticed for the first time that, suspended by a slender silken cord, from Don Benito's neck hung a key. At once, from the servant's muttered syllables divining the key's purpose, he smiled and said:—"So, Don Benito—padlock and key—significant symbols, truly."

Biting his lip, Don Benito faltered.

Though the remark of Captain Delano, a man of such native simplicity as to be incapable of satire or irony, had been dropped in playful allusion to the Spaniard's singularly evidenced lordship over the black; yet the hypochondriac seemed in some way to have taken it as a malicious reflection upon his confessed inability thus far to break down, at least, on a verbal summons, the entrenched will of the slave. Deploring this supposed misconception, yet despairing of correcting it, Captain Delano shifted the subject; but finding his companion more than ever withdrawn, as if still slowly digesting the lees of the presumed affront above-mentioned, by-and-by Captain Delano likewise became less talkative, oppressed, against his own will, by what seemed the secret vindictiveness of the morbidly sensitive Spaniard. But the good sailor himself, of a quite contrary disposition, refrained, on his part, alike from the appearance as from the feeling of resentment, and if silent, was only so from contagion.

Presently the Spaniard, assisted by his servant, somewhat discourteously crossed over from Captain Delano; a procedure which, sensibly enough, might have been allowed to pass for idle caprice of ill-humor, had not master and man, lingering round the corner of the elevated skylight, began whispering together in low voices. This was unpleasing. And more: the moody air of the Spaniard, which at times had not been without a sort of valetudinarian stateliness, now seemed anything but dignified; while the menial familiarity of the servant lost its original charm of simple-hearted attachment.

In his embarrassment, the visitor turned his face to the other side of the ship. By so doing, his glance accidentally fell on a young Spanish sailor, a coil of rope in his hand, just stepped from the deck to the first round of the mizzen-rigging. Perhaps the man would not have been particularly noticed, were it not that, during his ascent to one of the yards, he, with a sort of covert intentness, kept his eye fixed on Captain Delano, from whom, presently, it passed, as if by a natural sequence, to the two whisperers.

His own attention thus redirected to that quarter, Captain Delano gave a slight start. From something in Don Benito's manner just then, it seemed as if the visitor had, at least partly, been the subject of the withdrawn consultation going on—a conjecture as little agreeable to the guest as it was little flattering to the host.

The singular alternations of courtesy and ill-breeding in the Spanish captain were unaccountable, except on one of two suppositions—innocent lunacy, or wicked imposture.

But the first idea, though it might naturally have occurred to an indifferent observer, and, in some respect, had not hitherto been wholly a stranger to Captain Delano's mind, yet, now that, in an incipient way, he began to regard the stranger's conduct something in the light of an intentional affront, of course the idea of lunacy was virtually vacated. But if not a lunatic, what then? Under the circumstances, would a gentleman, nay, any honest boor, act the part now acted by his host? The man was an imposter. Some low-born adventurer, masquerading as an oceanic grandee; yet so ignorant of the first requisites of mere gentlemanhood as to be betrayed into the present remarkable indecorum. That strange ceremoniousness, too, at other times evinced, seemed not uncharacteristic of one playing a part above his real level. Benito Cereno—Don Benito Cereno—a sounding name. One, too, at that period, not unknown, in the surname, to supercargoes and sea captains trading along the Spanish Main, as belonging to one of the most enterprising and extensive mercantile families in all those provinces; several members of it having titles; a sort of Castilian Rothschild, with a noble brother, or cousin, in every great trading town of South America. The alleged Don Benito was in early manhood, about twenty-nine or thirty. To assume a sort of roving cadetship in the maritime affairs of such a house, what more likely scheme for a young knave of talent and spirit? But the Spaniard was a pale invalid. Never mind. For even to the degree of simulating mortal disease, the craft of some tricksters had been known to attain. To think that, under the aspect of infantile weakness, the most savage energies might be couched—those velvets of the Spaniard but the velvet paw to his fangs.

From no train of thought did these fancies come; not from within, but from without; suddenly, too, and in one throng, like hoar frost; yet as soon to vanish as the mild sun of Captain Delano's good-nature regained its meridian.

Glancing over once more towards Don Benito—whose side-face, revealed above the skylight, was now turned towards him—Captain Delano was struck by the profile, whose clearness of cut was refined by the thinness incident to ill-health, as well as ennobled about the chin by the beard. Away with suspicion. He was a true off-shoot of a true hidalgo Cereno.

Relieved by these and other better thoughts, the visitor, lightly humming a tune, now began indifferently pacing the poop, so as not to betray to Don Benito that he had at all mistrusted incivility, much less duplicity; for such mistrust would yet be proved illusory, and by the event; though, for the present, the circumstance which had provoked that distrust remained unexplained. But when that little mystery should have been cleared up, Captain Delano thought he might extremely regret it, did he allow Don Benito to become aware that he had indulged in ungenerous surmises. In short, to the Spaniard's black-letter text, it was best, for awhile, to leave open margin.

Presently, his pale face twitching and overcast, the Spaniard, still supported by his attendant, moved over towards his guest, when, with even more than his usual embarrassment, and a strange sort of intriguing intonation in his husky whisper, the following conversation began:—

"Señor, may I ask how long you have lain at this isle?"

"Oh, but a day or two, Don Benito."

"And from what port are you last?"

"Canton."

"And there, Señor, you exchanged your seal-skins for teas and silks, I think you said?"

"Yes. Silks, mostly."

"And the balance you took in specie, perhaps?"

Captain Delano, fidgeting a little, answered—

"Yes; some silver; not a very great deal, though."

"Ah—well. May I ask how many men have you on board, Señor?"

Captain Delano slightly started, but answered—

"About five-and-twenty, all told."

"And at present, Señor, all on board, I suppose?"

"All on board, Don Benito," replied the Captain, now with satisfaction.

"And will be to-night, Señor?"

At this last question, following so many pertinacious ones, for the soul of him Captain Delano could not but look very earnestly at the questioner, who, instead of meeting the glance, with every token of craven discomposure dropped his eyes to the deck; presenting an unworthy contrast to his servant, who, just then, was kneeling at his feet, adjusting a loose shoe-buckle; his disengaged face meantime, with humble curiosity, turned openly up into his master's downcast one.

The Spaniard, still with a guilty shuffle, repeated his question:—

"And—will be to-night, Señor?"

"Yes, for aught I know," returned Captain Delano,—"but nay," rallying himself into fearless truth, "some of them talked of going off on another fishing party about midnight."

"Your ships generally go—go more or less armed, I believe, Señor?"

"Oh, a six-pounder or two, in case of emergency," was the intrepidly indifferent reply, "with a small stock of muskets, sealing-spears, and cutlasses, you know."

As he thus responded, Captain Delano again glanced at Don Benito, but the latter's eyes were averted; while abruptly and awkwardly shifting the subject, he made some peevish allusion to the calm, and then, without apology, once more, with his attendant, withdrew to the opposite bulwarks, where the whispering was resumed.

At this moment, and ere Captain Delano could cast a cool thought upon what had just passed, the young Spanish sailor before mentioned was seen descending from the rigging. In act of stooping over to spring inboard to the deck, his voluminous, unconfined frock, or shirt, of coarse woollen, much spotted with tar, opened out far down the chest, revealing a soiled undergarment of what seemed the finest linen, edged, about the neck, with a narrow blue ribbon, sadly faded and worn. At this moment the young sailor's eye was again fixed on the whisperers, and Captain Delano thought he observed a lurking significance in it, as if silent signs of some Freemason sort had that instant been interchanged.

This once more impelled his own glance in the direction of Don Benito, and, as before, he could not but infer that himself formed the subject of the conference. He paused. The sound of the hatchet-polishing fell on his ears. He cast another swift side-look at the two. They had the air of conspirators. In connection with the late questionings and the incident of the young sailor, these things now begat such return of involuntary suspicion, that the singular guilelessness of the American could not endure it. Plucking up a gay and humorous expression, he crossed over to the two rapidly, saying:—"Ha, Don Benito, your black here seems high in your trust; a sort of privy-counselor, in fact."

Upon this, the servant looked up with a good-natured grin, but the master started as from a venomous bite. It was a moment or two before the Spaniard sufficiently recovered himself to reply; which he did, at last, with cold constraint:—"Yes, Señor, I have trust in Babo."

Here Babo, changing his previous grin of mere animal humor into an intelligent smile, not ungratefully eyed his master.

Finding that the Spaniard now stood silent and reserved, as if involuntarily, or purposely giving hint that his guest's proximity was inconvenient just then, Captain Delano, unwilling to appear uncivil even to incivility itself, made some trivial remark and moved off; again and again turning over in his mind the mysterious demeanor of Don Benito Cereno.

He had descended from the poop, and, wrapped in thought, was passing near a dark hatchway, leading down into the steerage, when, perceiving motion there, he looked to see what moved. The same instant there was a sparkle in the shadowy hatchway, and he saw one of the Spanish sailors prowling there hurriedly placing his hand in the bosom of his frock, as if hiding something. Before the man could have been certain who it was that was passing, he slunk below out of sight. But enough was seen of him to make it sure that he was the same young sailor before noticed in the rigging.

What was that which so sparkled? thought Captain Delano. It was no lamp—no match—no live coal. Could it have been a jewel? But how come sailors with jewels?—or with silk-trimmed under-shirts either? Has he been robbing the trunks of the dead cabin passengers? But if so, he would hardly wear one of the stolen articles on board ship here. Ah, ah—if now that was, indeed, a secret sign I saw passing between this suspicious fellow and his captain awhile since; if I could only be certain that in my uneasiness my senses did not deceive me, then——

Here, passing from one suspicious thing to another, his mind revolved the point of the strange questions put to him concerning his ship.

By a curious coincidence, as each point was recalled, the black wizards of Ashantee would strike up with their hatchets, as in ominous comment on the white stranger's thoughts. Pressed by such enigmas and portents, it would have been almost against nature, had not, even into the least distrustful heart, some ugly misgivings obtruded.

Observing the ship now helplessly fallen into a current, with enchanted sails, drifting with increased rapidity seaward; and noting that, from a lately intercepted projection of the land, the sealer was hidden, the stout mariner began to quake at thoughts which he barely durst confess to himself. Above all, he began to feel a ghostly dread of Don Benito. And yet when he roused himself, dilated his chest, felt himself strong on his legs, and coolly considered it—what did all these phantoms amount to?

Had the Spaniard any sinister scheme, it must have reference not so much to him (Captain Delano) as to his ship (the Bachelor's Delight). Hence the present drifting away of the one ship from the other, instead of favoring any such possible scheme, was, for the time at least, opposed to it. Clearly any suspicion, combining such contradictions, must need be delusive. Beside, was it not absurd to think of a vessel in distress—a vessel by sickness almost dismanned of her crew—a vessel whose inmates were parched for water—was it not a thousand times absurd that such a craft should, at present, be of a piratical character; or her commander, either for himself or those under him, cherish any desire but for speedy relief and refreshment? But then, might not general distress, and thirst in particular, be affected? And might not that same undiminished Spanish crew, alleged to have perished off to a remnant, be at that very moment lurking in the hold? On heart-broken pretense of entreating a cup of cold water, fiends in human form had got into lonely dwellings, nor retired until a dark deed had been done. And among the Malay pirates, it was no unusual thing to lure ships after them into their treacherous harbors, or entice boarders from a declared enemy at sea, by the spectacle of thinly manned or vacant decks, beneath which prowled a hundred spears with yellow arms ready to upthrust them through the mats. Not that Captain Delano had entirely credited such things. He had heard of them—and now, as stories, they recurred. The present destination of the ship was the anchorage. There she would be near his own vessel. Upon gaining that vicinity, might not the San Dominick, like a slumbering volcano, suddenly let loose energies now hid?

He recalled the Spaniard's manner while telling his story. There was a gloomy hesitancy and subterfuge about it. It was just the manner of one making up his tale for evil purposes, as he goes. But if that story was not true, what was the truth? That the ship had unlawfully come into the Spaniard's possession? But in many of its details, especially in reference to the more calamitous parts, such as the fatalities among the seamen, the consequent prolonged beating about, the past sufferings from obstinate calms, and still continued suffering from thirst; in all these points, as well as others, Don Benito's story had corroborated not only the wailing ejaculations of the indiscriminate multitude, white and black, but likewise—what seemed impossible to be counterfeit—by the very expression and play of every human feature, which Captain Delano saw. If Don Benito's story was throughout an invention, then every soul on board, down to the youngest negress, was his carefully drilled recruit in the plot: an incredible inference. And yet, if there was ground for mistrusting the Spanish captain's veracity, that inference was a legitimate one.

In short, scarce an uneasiness entered the honest sailor's mind but, by a subsequent spontaneous act of good sense, it was ejected. At last he began to laugh at these forebodings; and laugh at the strange ship for, in its aspect someway siding with them, as it were; and laugh, too, at the odd-looking blacks, particularly those old scissors-grinders, the Ashantees; and those bed-ridden old knitting-women, the oakum-pickers; and, in a human way, he almost began to laugh at the dark Spaniard himself, the central hobgoblin of all.

For the rest, whatever in a serious way seemed enigmatical, was now good-naturedly explained away by the thought that, for the most part, the poor invalid scarcely knew what he was about; either sulking in black vapors, or putting random questions without sense or object. Evidently, for the present, the man was not fit to be entrusted with the ship. On some benevolent plea withdrawing the command from him Captain Delano would yet have to send her to Conception, in charge of his second mate, a worthy person and good navigator—a plan which would prove no wiser for the San Dominick than for Don Benito; for, relieved from all anxiety, keeping wholly to his cabin, the sick man, under the good nursing of his servant, would probably, by the end of the passage, be in a measure restored to health, and with that he should also be restored to authority.

Such were the American's thoughts. They were tranquilizing. There was a difference between the idea of Don Benito's darkly pre-ordaining Captain Delano's fate, and Captain Delano's lightly arranging Don Benito's. Nevertheless, it was not without something of relief that the good seaman presently perceived his whale-boat in the distance. Its absence had been prolonged by unexpected detention at the sealer's side, as well as its returning trip lengthened by the continual recession of the goal.

PART II

THE ADVANCING SPECK was observed by the blacks. Their shouts attracted the attention of Don Benito, who, with a return of courtesy, approaching Captain Delano, expressed satisfaction at the coming of some supplies, slight and temporary as they must necessarily prove.

Captain Delano responded; but while doing so, his attention was drawn to something passing on the deck below; among the crowd climbing the landward bulwarks, anxiously watching the coming boat, two blacks, to all appearances accidentally incommoded by one of the sailors, flew out against him with horrible curses, which the sailor someway resenting, the two blacks dashed him to the deck and jumped upon him, despite the earnest cries of the oakum-pickers.

"Don Benito," said Captain Delano quickly, "do you see what is going on there? Look!"

But, seized by his cough, the Spaniard staggered, with both hands to his face, on the point of falling. Captain Delano would have supported him, but the servant was more alert, who, with one hand sustaining his master, with the other applied the cordial. Don Benito restored, the black withdrew his support, slipping aside a little, but dutifully remaining within call of a whisper. Such discretion was here evinced as quite wiped away, in the visitor's eyes, any blemish of impropriety which might have attached to the attendant, from the indecorous conferences before mentioned; showing, too, that if the servant were to blame, it might be more the master's fault than his own, since when left to himself he could conduct thus well.

His glance thus called away from the spectacle of disorder to the more pleasing one before him, Captain Delano could not avoid again congratulating Don Benito upon possessing such a servant, who, though perhaps a little too forward now and then, must upon the whole be invaluable to one in the invalid's situation.

"Tell me, Don Benito," he added, with a smile—"I should like to have your man here myself—what will you take for him? Would fifty doubloons be any object?"

"Master wouldn't part with Babo for a thousand doubloons," murmured the black, overhearing the offer, and taking it in earnest, and, with the strange vanity of a faithful slave appreciated by his master, scorning to hear so paltry a valuation put upon him by a stranger. But Don Benito, apparently hardly yet completely restored, and again interrupted by his cough, made but some broken reply.

Soon his physical distress become so great, affecting his mind, too, apparently, that, as if to screen the sad spectacle, the servant gently conducted his master below.

Left to himself, the American, to while away the time till his boat should arrive, would have pleasantly accosted some one of the few Spanish seamen he saw; but recalling something that Don Benito had said touching their ill conduct, he refrained, as a ship-master indisposed to countenance cowardice or unfaithfulness in seamen.

While, with these thoughts, standing with eye directed forward towards that handful of sailors, suddenly he thought that some of them returned the glance and with a sort of meaning. He rubbed his eyes, and looked again; but again seemed to see the same thing. Under a new form, but more obscure than any previous one, the old suspicions recurred, but, in the absence of Don Benito, with less of panic than before. Despite the bad account given of the sailors, Captain Delano resolved forthwith to accost one of them. Descending the poop, he made his way through the blacks, his movement drawing a queer cry from the oakum-pickers, prompted by whom, the negroes, twitching each other aside, divided before him; but, as if curious to see what was the object of this deliberate visit to their Ghetto, closing in behind, in tolerable order, followed the white stranger up. His progress thus proclaimed as by mounted kings-at-arms, and escorted as by a Caffre guard of honor, Captain Delano, assuming a good humored, off-handed air, continued to advance; now and then saying a blithe word to the negroes, and his eye curiously surveying the white faces, here and there sparsely mixed in with the blacks, like stray white pawns venturously involved in the ranks of the chess-men opposed.

While thinking which of them to select for his purpose, he chanced to observe a sailor seated on the deck engaged in tarring the strap of a large block, with a circle of blacks squatted round him inquisitively eying the process.

The mean employment of the man was in contrast with something superior in his figure. His hand, black with continually thrusting it into the tar-pot held for him by a negro, seemed not naturally allied to his face, a face which would have been a very fine one but for its haggardness. Whether this haggardness had aught to do with criminality, could not be determined; since, as intense heat and cold, though unlike, produce like sensations, so innocence and guilt, when, through casual association with mental pain, stamping any visible impress, use one seal—a hacked one.

Not again that this reflection occurred to Captain Delano at the time, charitable man as he was. Rather another idea. Because observing so singular a haggardness to be combined with a dark eye, averted as in trouble and shame, and then, however illogically, uniting in his mind his own private suspicions of the crew with the confessed ill-opinion on the part of their Captain, he was insensibly operated upon by certain general notions, which, while disconnecting pain and abashment from virtue, as invariably link them with vice.

If, indeed, there be any wickedness on board this ship, thought Captain Delano, be sure that man there has fouled his hand in it, even as now he fouls it in the pitch. I don't like to accost him. I will speak to this other, this old Jack here on the windlass.

He advanced to an old Barcelona tar, in ragged red breeches and dirty night cap, cheeks trenched and bronzed, whiskers dense as thorn hedges. Seated between two sleepy-looking Africans, this mariner, like his younger shipmate, was employed upon some rigging—splicing a cable—the sleepy-looking blacks performing the inferior function of holding the outer parts of the ropes for him.

Upon Captain Delano's approach, the man at once hung his head below its previous level; the one necessary for business. It appeared as if he desired to be thought absorbed, with more than common fidelity, in his task. Being addressed, he glanced up, but with what seemed a furtive, diffident air, which sat strangely enough on his weather-beaten visage, much as if a grizzly bear, instead of growling and biting, should simper and cast sheep's eyes. He was asked several questions concerning the voyage, questions purposely referring to several particulars in Don Benito's narrative, not previously corroborated by those impulsive cries greeting the visitor on first coming on board. The questions were briefly answered, confirming all that remained to be confirmed of the story. The negroes about the windlass joined in with the old sailor, but, as they became talkative, he by degrees became mute, and at length quite glum, seemed morosely unwilling to answer more questions, and yet, all the while, this ursine air was somehow mixed with his sheepish one.

Despairing of getting into unembarrassed talk with such a centaur, Captain Delano, after glancing round for a more promising countenance, but seeing none, spoke pleasantly to the blacks to make way for him; and so, amid various grins and grimaces, returned to the poop, feeling a little strange at first, he could hardly tell why, but upon the whole with regained confidence in Benito Cereno.

How plainly, thought he, did that old whiskerando yonder betray a consciousness of ill-desert. No doubt, when he saw me coming, he dreaded lest I, apprised by his Captain of the crew's general misbehavior, came with sharp words for him, and so down with his head. And yet—and yet, now that I think of it, that very old fellow, if I err not, was one of those who seemed so earnestly eying me here awhile since. Ah, these currents spin one's head round almost as much as they do the ship. Ha, there now's a pleasant sort of sunny sight; quite sociable, too.

His attention had been drawn to a slumbering negress, partly disclosed through the lace-work of some rigging, lying, with youthful limbs carelessly disposed, under the lee of the bulwarks, like a doe in the shade of a woodland rock. Sprawling at her lapped breasts was her wide-awake fawn, stark naked, its black little body half lifted from the deck, crosswise with its dam's; its hands, like two paws, clambering upon her; its mouth and nose ineffectually rooting to get at the mark; and meantime giving a vexatious half-grunt, blending with the composed snore of the negress.

The uncommon vigor of the child at length roused the mother. She started up, at distance facing Captain Delano. But as if not at all concerned at the attitude in which she had been caught, delightedly she caught the child up, with maternal transports, covering it with kisses.

There's naked nature, now; pure tenderness and love, thought Captain Delano, well pleased.

This incident prompted him to remark the other negresses more particularly than before. He was gratified with their manners; like most uncivilized women, they seemed at once tender of heart and tough of constitution; equally ready to die for their infants or fight for them. Unsophisticated as leopardesses; loving as doves. Ah! thought Captain Delano, these perhaps are some of the very women whom Mungo Park saw in Africa, and gave such a noble account of.

These natural sights somehow insensibly deepened his confidence and ease. At last he looked to see how his boat was getting on; but it was still pretty remote. He turned to see if Don Benito had returned; but he had not.

To change the scene, as well as to please himself with a leisurely observation of the coming boat, stepping over into the mizzen-chains he clambered his way into the starboard quarter-gallery; one of those abandoned Venetian-looking water-balconies previously mentioned; retreats cut off from the deck. As his foot pressed the half-damp, half-dry sea-mosses matting the place, and a chance phantom cats-paw—an islet of breeze, unheralded, unfollowed—as this ghostly cats-paw came fanning his cheek, as his glance fell upon the row of small, round dead-lights, all closed like coppered eyes of the coffined, and the state-cabin door, once connecting with the gallery, even as the dead-lights had once looked out upon it, but now calked fast like a sarcophagus lid, to a purple-black, tarred-over panel, threshold, and post; and he bethought him of the time, when that state-cabin and this state-balcony had heard the voices of the Spanish king's officers, and the forms of the Lima viceroy's daughters had perhaps leaned where he stood—as these and other images flitted through his mind, as the cats-paw through the calm, gradually he felt rising a dreamy inquietude, like that of one who alone on the prairie feels unrest from the repose of the noon.

He leaned against the carved balustrade, again looking off toward his boat; but found his eye falling upon the ribboned grass, trailing along the ship's water-line, straight as a border of green box; and parterres of sea-weed, broad ovals and crescents, floating nigh and far, with what seemed long formal alleys between, crossing the terraces of swells, and sweeping round as if leading to the grottoes below. And overhanging all was the balustrade by his arm, which, partly stained with pitch and partly embossed with moss, seemed the charred ruin of some summer-house in a grand garden long running to waste.

Trying to break one charm, he was but becharmed anew. Though upon the wide sea, he seemed in some far inland country; prisoner in some deserted château, left to stare at empty grounds, and peer out at vague roads, where never wagon or wayfarer passed.

But these enchantments were a little disenchanted as his eye fell on the corroded main-chains. Of an ancient style, massy and rusty in link, shackle and bolt, they seemed even more fit for the ship's present business than the one for which probably she had been built.

Presently he thought something moved nigh the chains. He rubbed his eyes, and looked hard. Groves of rigging were about the chains; and there, peering from behind a great stay, like an Indian from behind a hemlock, a Spanish sailor, a marlingspike in his hand, was seen, who made what seemed an imperfect gesture towards the balcony, but immediately, as if alarmed by some advancing step along the deck within, vanished into the recesses of the hempen forest, like a poacher.

What meant this? Something the man had sought to communicate, unbeknown to any one, even to his captain. Did the secret involve aught unfavorable to his captain? Were those previous misgivings of Captain Delano's about to be verified? Or, in his haunted mood at the moment, had some random, unintentional motion of the man, while busy with the stay, as if repairing it, been mistaken for a significant beckoning?

Not unbewildered, again he gazed off for his boat. But it was temporarily hidden by a rocky spur of the isle. As with some eagerness he bent forward, watching for the first shooting view of its beak, the balustrade gave way before him like charcoal. Had he not clutched an outreaching rope he would have fallen into the sea. The crash, though feeble, and the fall, though hollow, of the rotten fragments, must have been overheard. He glanced up. With sober curiosity peering down upon him was one of the old oakum-pickers, slipped from his perch to an outside boom; while below the old negro, and, invisible to him, reconnoitering from a port-hole like a fox from the mouth of its den, crouched the Spanish sailor again. From something suddenly suggested by the man's air, the mad idea now darted into Captain Delano's mind, that Don Benito's plea of indisposition, in withdrawing below, was but a pretense: that he was engaged there maturing some plot, of which the sailor, by some means gaining an inkling, had a mind to warn the stranger against; incited, it may be, by gratitude for a kind word on first boarding the ship. Was it from foreseeing some possible interference like this, that Don Benito had, beforehand, given such a bad character of his sailors, while praising the negroes; though, indeed, the former seemed as docile as the latter the contrary? The whites, too, by nature, were the shrewder race. A man with some evil design, would he not be likely to speak well of that stupidity which was blind to his depravity, and malign that intelligence from which it might not be hidden? Not unlikely, perhaps. But if the whites had dark secrets concerning Don Benito, could then Don Benito be any way in complicity with the blacks? But they were too stupid. Besides, who ever heard of a white so far a renegade as to apostatize from his very species almost, by leaguing in against it with negroes? These difficulties recalled former ones. Lost in their mazes, Captain Delano, who had now regained the deck, was uneasily advancing along it, when he observed a new face; an aged sailor seated cross-legged near the main hatchway. His skin was shrunk up with wrinkles like a pelican's empty pouch; his hair frosted; his countenance grave and composed. His hands were full of ropes, which he was working into a large knot. Some blacks were about him obligingly dipping the strands for him, here and there, as the exigencies of the operation demanded.

Captain Delano crossed over to him, and stood in silence surveying the knot; his mind, by a not uncongenial transition, passing from its own entanglements to those of the hemp. For intricacy such a knot he had never seen in an American ship, or indeed any other. The old man looked like an Egyptian priest, making gordian knots for the temple of Ammon. The knot seemed a combination of double-bowline-knot, treble-crown-knot, back-handed-well-knot, knot-in-and-out-knot, and jamming-knot.

At last, puzzled to comprehend the meaning of such a knot, Captain Delano addressed the knotter:—

"What are you knotting there, my man?"

"The knot," was the brief reply, without looking up.

"So it seems; but what is it for?"

"For some one else to undo," muttered back the old man, plying his fingers harder than ever, the knot being now nearly completed.

While Captain Delano stood watching him, suddenly the old man threw the knot towards him, saying in broken English,—the first heard in the ship,—something to this effect—"Undo it, cut it, quick." It was said lowly, but with such condensation of rapidity, that the long, slow words in Spanish, which had preceded and followed, almost operated as covers to the brief English between.

For a moment, knot in hand, and knot in head, Captain Delano stood mute; while, without further heeding him, the old man was now intent upon other ropes. Presently there was a slight stir behind Captain Delano. Turning, he saw the chained negro, Atufal, standing quietly there. The next moment the old sailor rose, muttering, and, followed by his subordinate negroes, removed to the forward part of the ship, where in the crowd he disappeared.

An elderly negro, in a clout like an infant's, and with a pepper and salt head, and a kind of attorney air, now approached Captain Delano. In tolerable Spanish, and with a good-natured, knowing wink, he informed him that the old knotter was simple-witted, but harmless; often playing his old tricks. The negro concluded by begging the knot, for of course the stranger would not care to be troubled with it. Unconsciously, it was handed to him. With a sort of congé, the negro received it, and turning his back, ferreted into it like a detective Custom House officer after smuggled laces. Soon, with some African word, equivalent to pshaw, he tossed the knot overboard.

All this is very queer now, thought Captain Delano, with a qualmish sort of emotion; but as one feeling incipient sea-sickness, he strove, by ignoring the symptoms, to get rid of the malady. Once more he looked off for his boat. To his delight, it was now again in view, leaving the rocky spur astern.

The sensation here experienced, after at first relieving his uneasiness, with unforseen efficiency, soon began to remove it. The less distant sight of that well-known boat—showing it, not as before, half blended with the haze, but with outline defined, so that its individuality, like a man's, was manifest; that boat, Rover by name, which, though now in strange seas, had often pressed the beach of Captain Delano's home, and, brought to its threshold for repairs, had familiarly lain there, as a Newfoundland dog; the sight of that household boat evoked a thousand trustful associations, which, contrasted with previous suspicions, filled him not only with lightsome confidence, but somehow with half humorous self-reproaches at his former lack of it.

"What, I, Amasa Delano—Jack of the Beach, as they called me when a lad—I, Amasa; the same that, duck-satchel in hand, used to paddle along the waterside to the school-house made from the old hulk;—I, little Jack of the Beach, that used to go berrying with cousin Nat and the rest; I to be murdered here at the ends of the earth, on board a haunted pirate-ship by a horrible Spaniard?—Too nonsensical to think of it! Who would murder Amasa Delano? His conscience is clean. There is some one above. Fie, fie, Jack of the Beach! you are a child indeed; a child of the second childhood, old boy; you are beginning to dote and drule, I'm afraid."

Light of heart and foot, he stepped aft, and there was met by Don Benito's servant, who, with a pleasing expression, responsive to his own present feelings, informed him that his master had recovered from the effects of his coughing fit, and had just ordered him to go present his compliments to his good guest, Don Amasa, and say that he (Don Benito) would soon have the happiness to rejoin him.

There now, do you mark that? again thought Captain Delano, walking the poop. What a donkey I was. This kind gentleman who here sends me his kind compliments, he, but ten minutes ago, dark-lantern in hand, was dodging round some old grind-stone in the hold, sharpening a hatchet for me, I thought. Well, well; these long calms have a morbid effect on the mind, I've often heard, though I never believed it before. Ha! glancing towards the boat; there's Rover; good dog; a white bone in her mouth. A pretty big bone though, seems to me.—What? Yes, she has fallen afoul of the bubbling tide-rip there. It sets her the other way, too, for the time. Patience.

It was now about noon, though, from the grayness of everything, it seemed to be getting towards dusk.

The calm was confirmed. In the far distance, away from the influence of land, the leaden ocean seemed laid out and leaded up, its course finished, soul gone, defunct. But the current from landward, where the ship was, increased; silently sweeping her further and further towards the tranced waters beyond.

Still, from his knowledge of those latitudes, cherishing hopes of a breeze, and a fair and fresh one, at any moment, Captain Delano, despite present prospects, buoyantly counted upon bringing the San Dominick safely to anchor ere night. The distance swept over was nothing; since, with a good wind, ten minutes' sailing would retrace more than sixty minutes drifting. Meantime, one moment turning to mark "Rover" fighting the tide-rip, and the next to see Don Benito approaching, he continued walking the poop.

Gradually he felt a vexation arising from the delay of his boat; this soon merged into uneasiness; and at last, his eye falling continually, as from a stage-box into the pit, upon the strange crowd before and below him, and by and by recognising there the face—now composed to indifference—of the Spanish sailor who had seemed to beckon from the main chains, something of his old trepidations returned.

Ah, thought he—gravely enough—this is like the ague: because it went off, it follows not that it won't come back.

Though ashamed of the relapse, he could not altogether subdue it; and so, exerting his good nature to the utmost, insensibly he came to a compromise.

Yes, this is a strange craft; a strange history, too, and strange folks on board. But—nothing more.

By way of keeping his mind out of mischief till the boat should arrive, he tried to occupy it with turning over and over, in a purely speculative sort of way, some lesser peculiarities of the captain and crew. Among others, four curious points recurred.

First, the affair of the Spanish lad assailed with a knife by the slave boy; an act winked at by Don Benito. Second, the tyranny in Don Benito's treatment of Atufal, the black; as if a child should lead a bull of the Nile by the ring in his nose. Third, the trampling of the sailor by the two negroes; a piece of insolence passed over without so much as a reprimand. Fourth, the cringing submission to their master of all the ship's underlings, mostly blacks; as if by the least inadvertence they feared to draw down his despotic displeasure.

Coupling these points, they seemed somewhat contradictory. But what then, thought Capain Delano, glancing towards his now nearing boat,—what then? Why, Don Benito is a very capricious commander. But he is not the first of the sort I have seen; though it's true he rather exceeds any other. But as a nation—continued he in his reveries—these Spaniards are all an odd set; the very word Spaniard has a curious, conspirator, Guy-Fawkish twang to it. And yet, I dare say, Spaniards in the main are as good folks as any in Duxbury, Massachusetts. Ah good! At last "Rover" has come.

As, with its welcome freight, the boat touched the side, the oakum-pickers, with venerable gestures, sought to restrain the blacks, who, at the sight of three gurried water-casks in its bottom, and a pile of wilted pumpkins in its bow, hung over the bulwarks in disorderly raptures.

Don Benito with his servant now appeared; his coming, perhaps, hastened by hearing the noise. Of him Captain Delano sought permission to serve out the water, so that all might share alike, and none injure themselves by unfair excess. But sensible, and, on Don Benito's account, kind as this offer was, it was received with what seemed impatience; as if aware that he lacked energy as a commander, Don Benito, with the true jealousy of weakness, resented as an affront any interference. So, at least, Captain Delano inferred.

In another moment the casks were being hoisted in, when some of the eager negroes accidentally jostled Captain Delano, where he stood by the gangway; so that, unmindful of Don Benito, yielding to the impulse of the moment, with good-natured authority he bade the blacks stand back; to enforce his words making use of a half-mirthful, half-menacing gesture. Instantly the blacks paused, just where they were, each negro and negress suspended in his or her posture, exactly as the word had found them—for a few seconds continuing so—while, as between the responsive posts of a telegraph, an unknown syllable ran from man to man among the perched oakum-pickers. While Captain Delano's attention was fixed by this scene, suddenly the hatchet-polishers half rose, and a rapid cry came from Don Benito.

Thinking that at the signal of the Spaniard he was about to be massacred, Captain Delano would have sprung for his boat, but paused, as the oakum-pickers, dropping down into the crowd with earnest exclamations, forced every white and every negro back, at the same moment, with gestures friendly and familiar, almost jocose, bidding him, in substance, not be a fool. Simultaneously the hatchet-polishers resumed their seats, quietly as so many tailors, and at once, as if nothing had happened, the work of hoisting in the casks was resumed, whites and blacks singing at the tackle.

Captain Delano glanced towards Don Benito. As he saw his meager form in the act of recovering itself from reclining in the servant's arms, into which the agitated invalid had fallen, he could not but marvel at the panic by which himself had been surprised on the darting supposition that such a commander, who upon a legitimate occasion, so trivial, too, as it now appeared, could lose all self-command, was, with energetic iniquity, going to bring about his murder.

The casks being on deck, Captain Delano was handed a number of jars and cups by one of the steward's aids, who, in the name of Don Benito, entreated him to do as he had proposed: dole out the water. He complied, with republican impartiality as to this republican element, which always seeks one level, serving the oldest white no better than the youngest black; excepting, indeed, poor Don Benito, whose condition, if not rank, demanded an extra allowance. To him, in the first place, Captain Delano presented a fair pitcher of the fluid; but, thirsting as he was for fresh water, Don Benito quaffed not a drop until after several grave bows and salutes. A reciprocation of courtesies which the sight-loving Africans hailed with clapping of hands.

Two of the less wilted pumpkins being reserved for the cabin table, the residue were minced up on the spot for the general regalement. But the soft bread, sugar, and bottled cider, Captain Delano would have given the Spaniards alone, and in chief Don Benito; but the latter objected; which disinterestedness, on his part, not a little pleased the American; and so mouthfuls all around were given alike to whites and blacks; excepting one bottle of cider, which Babo insisted upon setting aside for his master.

Here it may be observed that as, on the first visit of the boat, the American had not permitted his men to board the ship, neither did he now; being unwilling to add to the confusion of the decks.

Not uninfluenced by the peculiar good humor at present prevailing, and for the time oblivious of any but benevolent thoughts, Captain Delano, who from recent indications counted upon a breeze within an hour or two at furthest, dispatched the boat back to the sealer with orders for all the hands that could be spared immediately to set about rafting casks to the watering-place and filling them. Likewise he bade word be carried to his chief officer, that if against present expectation the ship was not brought to anchor by sunset, he need be under no concern, for as there was to be a full moon that night, he (Captain Delano) would remain on board ready to play the pilot, should the wind come soon or late.

As the two Captains stood together, observing the departing boat—the servant as it happened having just spied a spot on his master's velvet sleeve, and silently engaged rubbing it out—the American expressed his regrets that the San Dominick had no boats; none, at least, but the unseaworthy old hulk of the long-boat, which, warped as a camel's skeleton in the desert, and almost as bleached, lay pot-wise inverted amidships, one side a little tipped, furnishing a subterraneous sort of den for family groups of the blacks, mostly women and small children; who, squatting on old mats below, or perched above in the dark dome, on the elevated seats, were descried, some distance within, like a social circle of bats, sheltering in some friendly cave; at intervals, ebon flights of naked boys and girls, three or four years old, darting in and out of the den's mouth.

"Had you three or four boats now, Don Benito," said Captain Delano, "I think that, by tugging at the oars, your negroes here might help along matters some.—Did you sail from port without boats, Don Benito?"

"They were stove in the gales, Señor."

"That was bad. Many men, too, you lost then. Boats and men.—Those must have been hard gales, Don Benito."

"Past all speech," cringed the Spaniard.

"Tell me, Don Benito," continued his companion with increased interest, "tell me, were these gales immediately off the pitch of Cape Horn?"

"Cape Horn?—who spoke of Cape Horn?"

"Yourself did, when giving me an account of your voyage," answered Captain Delano with almost equal astonishment at this eating of his own words, even as he ever seemed eating his own heart, on the part of the Spaniard. "You yourself, Don Benito, spoke of Cape Horn," he emphatically repeated.

The Spaniard turned, in a sort of stooping posture, pausing an instant, as one about to make a plunging exchange of elements, as from air to water.

At this moment a messenger-boy, a white, hurried by, in the regular performance of his function carrying the last expired half hour forward to the forecastle, from the cabin time-piece, to have it struck at the ship's large bell.

"Master," said the servant, discontinuing his work on the coat sleeve, and addressing the rapt Spaniard with a sort of timid apprehensiveness, as one charged with a duty, the discharge of which, it was foreseen, would prove irksome to the very person who had imposed it, and for whose benefit it was intended, "master told me never mind where he was, or how engaged, always to remind him, to a minute, when shaving-time comes. Miguel has gone to strike the half-hour afternoon. It is *now*, master. Will master go into the cuddy?"

"Ah—yes," answered the Spaniard, starting, somewhat as from dreams into realities; then turning upon Captain Delano, he said that ere long he would resume the conversation.

"Then if master means to talk more to Don Amasa," said the servant, "why not let Don Amasa sit by master in the cuddy, and master can talk, and Don Amasa can listen, while Babo here lathers and strops."

"Yes," said Captain Delano, not unpleased with this sociable plan, "yes, Don Benito, unless you had rather not, I will go with you."

"Be it so, Señor."

As the three passed aft, the American could not but think it another strange instance of his host's capriciousness, this being shaved with such uncommon punctuality in the middle of the day. But he deemed it more than likely that the servant's anxious fidelity had something to do with the matter, inasmuch as the timely interruption served to rally his master from the mood which had evidently been coming upon him.

The place called the cuddy was a light deck-cabin formed by the poop, a sort of attic to the large cabin below. Part of it had formerly been the quarters of the officers; but since their death all the partitionings had been thrown down, and the whole interior converted into one spacious and airy marine hall; for absence of fine furniture and picturesque disarray, of odd appurtenances, somewhat answering to the wide, cluttered hall of some eccentric bachelor-squire in the country, who hangs his shooting-jacket and tobacco-pouch on deer antlers, and keeps his fishing-rod, tongs, and walking-stick in the same corner.

The similitude was heightened, if not originally suggested, by glimpses of the surrounding sea; since, in one aspect, the country and the ocean seem cousins-german.

The floor of the cuddy was matted. Overhead, four or five old muskets were stuck into horizontal holes along the beams. On one side was a claw-footed old table lashed to the deck; a thumbed missal on it, and over it a small, meager crucifix attached to the bulkhead. Under the table lay a dented cutlass or two, with a hacked harpoon, among some melancholy old rigging, like a heap of poor friar's girdles. There were also two long, sharp-ribbed settees of malacca cane, black with age, and uncomfortable to look at as inquisitors' racks, with a large, misshapen arm-chair, which, furnished with a rude barber's crutch at the back, working with a screw, seemed some grotesque, middle-age engine of torment. A flag locker was in one corner, open, exposing various colored bunting, some rolled up, others half unrolled, still others tumbled. Opposite was a cumbrous wash-stand, of black mahogany, all of one block, with a pedestal, like a font, and over it a railed shelf, containing combs, brushes, and other implements of the toilet. A torn hammock of stained grass swung near; the sheets tossed, and the pillow wrinkled up like a brow, as if whoever slept here slept but illy, with alternate visitations of sad thoughts and bad dreams.

The further extremity of the cuddy, overhanging the ship's stern, was pierced with three openings, windows or port holes, according as men or cannon might peer, socially or unsocially, out of them. At present neither men nor cannon were seen, though huge ring-bolts and other rusty iron fixtures of the wood-work hinted of twenty-four-pounders.

Glancing towards the hammock as he entered, Captain Delano said, "You sleep here, Don Benito?"

"Yes, Señor, since we got into mild weather."

"This seems a sort of dormitory, sitting-room, sail-loft, chapel, armory, and private closet all together, Don Benito," added Captain Delano, looking round.

"Yes, Señor; events have not been favorable to much order in my arrangements."

Here the servant, napkin on arm, made a motion as if waiting his master's good pleasure, Don Benito signified his readiness, when, seating him in the malacca arm-chair, and for the guest's convenience drawing opposite it one of the settees, the servant commenced operations by throwing back his master's collar and loosening his cravat.

There is something in the negro which, in a peculiar way, fits him for avocations about one's person. Most negroes are natural valets and hairdressers; taking to the comb and brush congenially as to the castinets, and flourishing them apparently with almost equal satisfaction. There is, too, a smooth tact about them in this employment, with a marvelous, noiseless, gliding briskness, not ungraceful in its way, singularly pleasing to behold, and still more so to be the manipulated subject of. And above all is the great gift of good humor. Not the mere grin or laugh is here meant. Those were unsuitable. But a certain easy cheerfulness, harmonious in every glance and gesture; as though God had set the whole negro to some pleasant tune.

When to all this is added the docility arising from the unaspiring contentment of a limited mind, and that susceptibility of blind attachment sometimes inhering in indisputable inferiors, one readily perceives why those hypochondriacs, Johnson and Byron—it may be something like the hypochondriac, Benito Cereno—took to their hearts, almost to the exclusion of the entire white race, their serving men, the negroes, Barber and Fletcher. But if there be that in the negro which exempts him from the inflicted sourness of the morbid or cynical mind, how, in his most prepossessing aspects, must he appear to a benevolent one? When at ease with respect to exterior things, Captain Delano's nature was not only benign, but familiarly and humorously so. At home, he had often taken rare satisfaction in sitting in his door, watching some free man of color at his work or play. If on a voyage he chanced to have a black sailor, invariably he was on chatty, and half-gamesome terms with him. In fact, like most men of a good, blithe heart, Captain Delano took to negroes, not philanthropically, but genially, just as other men to Newfoundland dogs.

Hitherto the circumstances in which he found the San Dominick had repressed the tendency. But in the cuddy, relieved from his former uneasiness, and, for various reasons, more sociably inclined than at any previous period of the day, and seeing the colored servant, napkin on arm, so debonair about his master, in a business so familiar as that of shaving, too, all his old weakness for negroes returned.

Among other things, he was amused with an odd instance of the African love of bright colors and fine shows, in the black's informally taking from the flag-locker a great piece of bunting of all hues, and lavishly tucking it under his master's chin for an apron.

The mode of shaving among the Spaniards is a little different from what it is with other nations. They have a basin, specifically called a barber's basin, which on one side is scooped out, so as accurately to receive the chin, against which it is closely held in lathering; which is done, not with a brush, but with soap dipped in the water of the basin and rubbed on the face.

In the present instance salt-water was used for lack of better; and the parts lathered were only the upper lip, and low down under the throat, all the rest being cultivated beard.

The preliminaries being somewhat novel to Captain Delano, he sat curiously eying them, so that no conversation took place, nor for the present did Don Benito appear disposed to renew any.

Setting down his basin, the negro searched among the razors, as for the sharpest, and having found it, gave it an additional edge by expertly strapping it on the firm, smooth, oily skin of his open palm; he then made a gesture as if to begin, but midway stood suspended for an instant, one hand elevating the razor, the other professionally dabbling among the bubbling suds on the Spaniard's lank-neck. Not unaffected by the close sight of the gleaming steel, Don Benito nervously shuddered, his usual ghastliness was hightened by the lather, which lather, again, was intensified in its hue by the contrasting sootiness of the negro's body. Altogether the scene was somewhat peculiar, at least to Captain Delano, nor, as he saw the two thus postured, could he resist the vagary, that in the black he saw a headsman, and in the white, a man at the block. But this was one of those antic conceits, appearing and vanishing in a breath, from which, perhaps, the best regulated mind is not free.

Meantime the agitation of the Spaniard had a little loosened the bunting from around him, so that one broad fold swept curtain-like over the chair-arm to the floor, revealing, amid a profusion of armorial bars and ground-colors—black, blue, and yellow—a closed castle in a blood-red field diagonal with a lion rampant in a white.

"The castle and the lion," exclaimed Captain Delano—"why, Don Benito, this is the flag of Spain you use here. It's well it's only I, and not the King, that sees this," he added with a smile, "but"—turning towards the black,—"it's all one, I suppose, so the colors be gay;" which playful remark did not fail somewhat to tickle the negro.

"Now, master," he said, readjusting the flag, and pressing the head gently further back into the crotch of the chair; "now master," and the steel glanced nigh the throat.

Again Don Benito faintly shuddered.

"You must not shake so, master.—See, Don Amasa, master always shakes when I shave him. And yet master knows I never yet have drawn blood, though it's true, if master will shake so, I may some of these times. Now master," he continued. "And now, Don Amasa, please go on with your talk about the gale, and all that, master can hear, and between times master can answer."

"Ah yes, these gales," said Captain Delano; "but the more I think of your voyage, Don Benito, the more I wonder, not at the gales, terrible as they must have been, but at the disastrous interval following them. For here, by your account, have you been these two months and more getting from Cape Horn to St. Maria, a distance which I myself, with a good wind, have sailed in a few days. True, you had calms, and long ones, but to be becalmed for two months, that is, at least, unusual. Why, Don Benito, had almost any other gentleman told me such a story, I should have been half disposed to a little incredulity."

Here an involuntary expression came over the Spaniard, similar to that just before on the deck, and whether it was the start he gave, or a sudden gawky roll of the hull in the calm, or a momentary unsteadiness of the servant's hand; however it was, just then the razor drew blood, spots of which stained the creamy lather under the throat; immediately the black barber drew back his steel, and remaining in his professional attitude, back to Captain Delano, and face to Don Benito, held up the trickling razor, saying, with a sort of half humorous sorrow, "See, master,—you shook so—here's Babo's first blood."

No sword drawn before James the First of England, no assassination in that timid King's presence, could have produced a more terrified aspect than was now presented by Don Benito.

Poor fellow, thought Captain Delano, so nervous he can't even bear the sight of barber's blood; and this unstrung, sick man, is it credible that I should have imagined he meant to spill all my blood, who can't endure the sight of one little drop of his own? Surely, Amasa Delano, you have been beside yourself this day. Tell it not when you get home, sappy Amasa. Well, well, he looks like a murderer, doesn't he? More like as if himself were to be done for. Well, well, this day's experience shall be a good lesson.

Meantime, while these things were running through the honest seaman's mind, the servant had taken the napkin from his arm, and to Don Benito had said—"But answer Don Amasa, please, master, while I wipe this ugly stuff off the razor, and strop it again."

As he said the words, his face was turned half round, so as to be alike visible to the Spaniard and the American, and seemed by its expression to hint, that he was desirous, by getting his master to go on with the conversation, considerately to withdraw his attention from the recent annoying accident. As if glad to snatch the offered relief, Don Benito resumed, rehearsing to Captain Delano, that not only were the calms of unusual duration, but the ship had fallen in with obstinate currents; and other things he added, some of which were but repetitions of former statements, to explain how it came to pass that the passage from Cape Horn to St. Maria had been so exceedingly long, now and then mingling with his words, incidental praises, less qualified than before, to the blacks, for their general good conduct.

These particulars were not given consecutively, the servant now and then using his razor, and so, between the intervals of shaving, the story and panegyric went on with more than usual huskiness.

To Captain Delano's imagination, now again not wholly at rest, there was something so hollow in the Spaniard's manner, with apparently some reciprocal hollowness in the servant's dusky comment of silence, that the idea flashed across him, that possibly master and man, for some unknown purpose, were acting out, both in word and deed, nay, to the very tremor of Don Benito's limbs, some juggling play before him. Neither did the suspicion of collusion lack apparent support, from the fact of those whispered conferences before mentioned. But then, what could be the object of enacting this play of the barber before him? At last, regarding the notion as a whimsy, insensibly suggested, perhaps, by the theatrical aspect of Don Benito in his harlequin ensign, Captain Delano speedily banished it.

The shaving over, the servant bestirred himself with a small bottle of scented waters, pouring a few drops on the head, and then diligently rubbing; the vehemence of the exercise causing the muscles of his face to twitch rather strangely.

His next operation was with comb, scissors and brush; going round and round, smoothing a curl here, clipping an unruly whisker-hair there, giving a graceful sweep to the temple-lock, with other impromptu touches evincing the hand of a master; while, like any resigned gentleman in barber's hands, Don Benito bore all, much less uneasily, at least, than he had done the razoring; indeed, he sat so pale and rigid now, that the negro seemed a Nubian sculptor finishing off a white statute-head.

All being over at last, the standard of Spain removed, tumbled up, and tossed back into the flag-locker, the negro's warm breath blowing away any stray hair which might have lodged down his master's neck; collar and cravat readjusted; a speck of lint whisked off the velvet lapel; all this being done; backing off a little space, and pausing with an expression of subdued self-complacency, the servant for a moment surveyed his master, as, in toilet at least, the creature of his own tasteful hands.

Captain Delano playfully complimented him upon his achievement; at the same time congratulating Don Benito.

But neither sweet waters, nor shampooing, nor fidelity, nor sociality, delighted the Spaniard. Seeing him relapsing into forbidding gloom, and still remaining seated, Captain Delano, thinking that his presence was undesired just then, withdrew, on pretense of seeing whether, as he had prophecied, any signs of a breeze were visible.

Walking forward to the mainmast, he stood awhile thinking over the scene, and not without some undefined misgivings, when he heard a noise near the cuddy, and turning, saw the negro, his hand to his cheek. Advancing, Captain Delano perceived that the cheek was bleeding. He was about to ask the cause, when the negro's wailing soliloquy enlightened him.

"Ah, when will master get better from his sickness; only the sour heart that sour sickness breeds made him serve Babo so; cutting Babo with the razor, because, only by accident, Babo had given master one little scratch; and for the first time in so many a day, too. Ah, ah, ah," holding his hand to his face.

Is it possible, thought Captain Delano; was it to wreak in private his Spanish spite against this poor friend of his, that Don Benito, by his sullen manner, impelled me to withdraw? Ah, this slavery breeds ugly passions in man—Poor fellow!

He was about to speak in sympathy to the negro, but with a timid reluctance he now reëntered the cuddy.

Presently master and man came forth; Don Benito leaning on his servant as if nothing had happened.

But a sort of love-quarrel, after all, thought Captain Delano.

He accosted Don Benito, and they slowly walked together. They had gone but a few paces, when the steward—a tall rajah-looking mulatto, orientally set off with a pagoda turban formed by three or four Madras handkerchiefs wound about his head, tier on tier—approaching with a salaam, announced lunch in the cabin.

On their way thither, the two Captains were preceded by the mulatto, who, turning round as he advanced, with continual smiles and bows, ushered them in, a display of elegance which quite completed the insignificance of the small bare-headed Babo, who, as if not unconscious of inferiority, eyed askance the graceful steward. But in part, Captain Delano imputed his jealous watchfulness to that peculiar feeling which the full-blooded African entertains for the adulterated one. As for the steward, his manner, if not bespeaking much dignity of self-respect, yet evidenced his extreme desire to please; which is doubly meritorious, as at once Christian and Chesterfieldian.

Captain Delano observed with interest that while the complexion of the mulatto was hybrid, his physiognomy was European; classically so.

"Don Benito," whispered he, "I am glad to see this usher-of-the-golden-rod of yours; the sight refutes an ugly remark once made to me by a Barbadoes planter; that when a mulatto has a regular European face, look out for him; he is a devil. But see, your steward here has features more regular than King George's of England; and yet there he nods, and bows, and smiles; a king, indeed—the king of kind hearts and polite fellows. What a pleasant voice he has, too?"

"He has, Señor."

"But, tell me, has he not, so far as you have known him, always proved a good, worthy fellow?" said Captain Delano, pausing, while with a final genuflexion the steward disappeared into the cabin; "come, for the reason just mentioned, I am curious to know."

"Francesco is a good man," sort of sluggishly responded Don Benito, like a phlegmatic appreciator, who would neither find fault nor flatter.

"Ah, I thought so. For it were strange indeed, and not very creditable to us white-skins, if a little of our blood mixed with the African's, should, far from improving the latter's quality, have the sad effect of pouring vitriolic acid into black broth; improving the hue, perhaps, but not the wholesomeness."

"Doubtless, doubtless, Señor, but"—glancing at Babo—"not to speak of negroes, your planter's remark I have heard applied to the Spanish and Indian intermixtures in our provinces. But I know nothing about the matter," he listlessly added.

And here they entered the cabin.

The lunch was a frugal one. Some of Captain Delano's fresh fish and pumpkins, biscuit and salt beef, the reserved bottle of cider, and the San Dominick's last bottle of Canary.

As they entered, Francesco, with two or three colored aids, was hovering over the table giving the last adjustments. Upon perceiving their master they withdrew, Francesco making a smiling congé, and the Spaniard, without condescending to notice it, fastidiously remarking to his companion that he relished not superfluous attendance.

Without companions, host and guest sat down, like a childless married couple, at opposite ends of the table, Don Benito waving Captain Delano to his place, and, weak as he was, insisting upon that gentleman being seated before himself.

The negro placed a rug under Don Benito's feet, and a cushion behind his back, and then stood behind, not his master's chair, but Captain Delano's. At first, this a little surprised the latter. But it was soon evident that, in taking his position, the black was still true to his master; since by facing him he could the more readily anticipate his slightest want.

"This is an uncommonly intelligent fellow of yours, Don Benito," whispered Captain Delano across the table.

"You say true, Señor."

During the repast, the guest again reverted to parts of Don Benito's story, begging further particulars here and there. He inquired how it was that the scurvy and fever should have committed such wholesale havoc upon the whites, while destroying less than half of the blacks. As if this question reproduced the whole scene of plague before the Spaniard's eyes, miserably reminding him of his solitude in a cabin where before he had had so many friends and officers round him, his hand shook, his face became hueless, broken words escaped; but directly the same memory of the past seemed replaced by insane terrors of the present. With starting eyes he stared before him at vacancy. For nothing was to be seen but the hand of his servant pushing the Canary over towards him. At length a few sips served partially to restore him. He made random reference to the different constitution of races, enabling one to offer more resistance to certain maladies than another. The thought was new to his companion.

Presently Captain Delano, intending to say something to his host concerning the pecuniary part of the business he had undertaken for him, especially—since he was strictly accountable to his owners—with reference to the new suit of sails, and other things of that sort; and naturally preferring to conduct such affairs in private, was desirous that the servant should withdraw; imagining that Don Benito for a few minutes could dispense with his attendance. He, however, waited awhile; thinking that, as the conversation proceeded, Don Benito, without being prompted, would perceive the propriety of the step.

But it was otherwise. At last catching his host's eye, Captain Delano, with a slight backward gesture of his thumb, whispered, "Don Benito, pardon me, but there is an interference with the full expression of what I have to say to you."

Upon this the Spaniard changed countenance; which was imputed to his resenting the hint, as in some way a reflection upon his servant. After a moment's pause, he assured his guest that the black's remaining with them could be of no disservice; because since losing his officers he had made Babo (whose original office, it now appeared, had been captain of the slaves) not only his constant attendant and companion, but in all things his confidant.

After this, nothing more could be said; though, indeed, Captain Delano could hardly avoid some little tinge of irritation upon being left ungratified in so inconsiderable a wish, by one, too, for whom he intended such solid services. But it is only his querulousness, thought he; and so filling his glass he proceeded to business.

The price of the sails and other matters was fixed upon. But while this was being done, the American observed that, though his original offer of assistance had been hailed with hectic animation, yet now when it was reduced to a business transaction, indifference and apathy were betrayed. Don Benito, in fact, appeared to submit to hearing the details more out of regard to common propriety, than from any impression that weighty benefit to himself and his voyage was involved.

Soon, this manner became still more reserved. The effort was vain to seek to draw him into social talk. Gnawed by his splenetic mood, he sat twitching his beard, while to little purpose the hand of his servant, mute as that on the wall, slowly pushed over the Canary.

Lunch being over, they sat down on the cushioned transom; the servant placing a pillow behind his master. The long continuance of the calm had now affected the atmosphere. Don Benito sighed heavily, as if for breath.

"Why not adjourn to the cuddy," said Captain Delano; "there is more air there." But the host sat silent and motionless.

Meantime his servant knelt before him, with a large fan of feathers. And Francesco coming in on tiptoes, handed the negro a little cup of aromatic waters, with which at intervals he chafed his master's brow; smoothing the hair along the temples as a nurse does a child's. He spoke no word. He only rested his eye on his master's, as if, amid all Don Benito's distress, a little to refresh his spirit by the silent sight of fidelity.

Presently the ship's bell sounded two o'clock; and through the cabin-windows a slight rippling of the sea was discerned; and from the desired direction.

"There," exclaimed Captain Delano, "I told you so, Don Benito, look!"

He had risen to his feet, speaking in a very animated tone, with a view the more to rouse his companion. But though the crimson curtain of the stern-window near him that moment fluttered against his pale cheek, Don Benito seemed to have even less welcome for the breeze than the calm.

Poor fellow, thought Captain Delano, bitter experience has taught him that one ripple does not make a wind, any more than one swallow a summer. But he is mistaken for once. I will get his ship in for him, and prove it.

Briefly alluding to his weak condition, he urged his host to remain quietly where he was, since he (Captain Delano) would with pleasure take upon himself the responsibility of making the best use of the wind.

Upon gaining the deck, Captain Delano started at the unexpected figure of Atufal, monumentally fixed at the threshold, like one of those sculptured porters of black marble guarding the porches of Egyptian tombs.

But this time the start was, perhaps, purely physical. Atufal's presence, singularly attesting docility even in sullenness, was contrasted with that of the hatchet-polishers, who in patience evinced their industry; while both spectacles showed, that lax as Don Benito's general authority might be, still whenever he chose to exert it, no man so savage or colossal but must, more or less, bow.

Snatching a trumpet which hung from the bulwarks, with a free step Captain Delano advanced to the forward edge of the poop, issuing his orders in his best Spanish. The few sailors and many negroes, all equally pleased, obediently set about heading the ship towards the harbor.

While giving some directions about setting a lower stu'n'-sail, suddenly Captain Delano heard a voice faithfully repeating his orders. Turning, he saw Babo, now for the time acting, under the pilot, his original part of captain of the slaves. This assistance proved valuable. Tattered sails and warped yards were soon brought into some trim. And no brace or halyard was pulled but to the blithe songs of the inspirited negroes.

Good fellows, thought Captain Delano, a little training would make fine sailors of them. Why see, the very women pull and sing too. These must be some of those Ashantee negresses that make such capital soldiers, I've heard. But who's at the helm. I must have a good hand there.

He went to see.

The San Dominick steered with a cumbrous tiller, with large horizontal pullies attached. At each pully-end stood a subordinate black, and between them, at the tiller-head, the responsible post, a Spanish seaman, whose countenance evinced his due share in the general hopefulness and confidence at the coming of the breeze.

He proved the same man who had behaved with so shame-faced an air on the windlass.

"Ah,—it is you, my man," exclaimed Captain Delano—"well, no more sheep's-eyes now;—look straightforward and keep the ship so. Good hand, I trust? And want to get into the harbor, don't you?"

"Sí, Señor," assented the man with an inward chuckle, grasping the tiller-head firmly. Upon this, unperceived by the American, the two blacks eyed the sailor askance.

Finding all right at the helm, the pilot went forward to the forecastle, to see how matters stood there.

The ship now had way enough to breast the current. With the approach of evening, the breeze would be sure to freshen.

Having done all that was needed for the present, Captain Delano, giving his last orders to the sailors, turned aft to report affairs to Don Benito in the cabin; perhaps additionally incited to rejoin him by the hope of snatching a moment's private chat while his servant was engaged upon deck.

From opposite sides, there were, beneath the poop, two approaches to the cabin; one further forward than the other, and consequently communicating with a longer passage. Marking the servant still above, Captain Delano, taking the nighest entrance—the one last named, and at whose porch Atufal still stood—hurried on his way, till, arrived at the cabin threshold, he paused an instant, a little to recover from his eagerness. Then, with the words of his intended business upon his lips, he entered. As he advanced toward the Spaniard, on the transom, he heard another footstep, keeping time with his. From the opposite door, a salver in hand, the servant was likewise advancing.

"Confound the faithful fellow," thought Captain Delano; "what a vexatious coincidence."

Possibly, the vexation might have been something different, were it not for the buoyant confidence inspired by the breeze. But even as it was, he felt a slight twinge, from a sudden involuntary association in his mind of Babo with Atufal.

"Don Benito," said he, "I give you joy; the breeze will hold, and will increase. By the way, your tall man and time-piece, Atufal, stands without. By your order, of course?"

Don Benito recoiled, as if at some bland satirical touch, delivered with such adroit garnish of apparent good-breeding as to present no handle for retort.

He is like one flayed alive, thought Captain Delano; where may one touch him without causing a shrink?

The servant moved before his master, adjusting a cushion; recalled to civility, the Spaniard stiffly replied: "You are right. The slave appears where you saw him, according to my command; which is, that if at the given hour I am below, he must take his stand and abide my coming."

"Ah now, pardon me, but that is treating the poor fellow like an ex-king denied. Ah, Don Benito," smiling, "for all the license you permit in some things, I fear lest, at bottom, you are a bitter hard master."

Again Don Benito shrank; and this time, as the good sailor thought, from a genuine twinge of his conscience.

Conversation now became constrained. In vain Captain Delano called attention to the now perceptible motion of the keel gently cleaving the sea; with lack-lustre eye, Don Benito returned words few and reserved.

By-and-by, the wind having steadily risen, and still blowing right into the harbor, bore the San Dominick swiftly on. Rounding a point of land, the sealer at distance came into open view.

Meantime Captain Delano had again repaired to the deck, remaining there some time. Having at last altered the ship's course, so as to give the reef a wide berth, he returned for a few moments below.

I will cheer up my poor friend, this time, thought he.

"Better and better, Don Benito," he cried as he blithely reëntered; "there will soon be an end to your cares, at least for awhile. For when, after a long, sad voyage, you know, the anchor drops into the haven, all its vast weight seems lifted from the captain's heart. We are getting on famously, Don Benito. My ship is in sight. Look through this side-light here; there she is; all a-taunt-o! The Bachelor's Delight, my good friend. Ah, how this wind braces one up. Come, you must take a cup of coffee with me this evening. My old steward will give you as fine a cup as ever any sultan tasted. What say you, Don Benito, will you?"

At first, the Spaniard glanced feverishly up, casting a longing look towards the sealer, while with mute concern his servant gazed into his face. Suddenly the old ague of coldness returned, and dropping back to his cushions he was silent.

"You do not answer. Come, all day you have been my host; would you have hospitality all on one side?"

"I cannot go," was the response.

"What? it will not fatigue you. The ships will lie together as near as they can, without swinging foul. It will be little more than stepping from deck to deck; which is but as from room to room. Come, come, you must not refuse me."

"I cannot go," decisively and repulsively repeated Don Benito.

Renouncing all but the last appearance of courtesy, with a sort of cadaverous sullenness, and biting his thin nails to the quick, he glanced, almost glared, at his guest; as if impatient that a stranger's presence should interfere with the full indulgence of his morbid hour. Meantime the sound of the parted waters came more and more gurglingly and merrily in at the windows; as reproaching him for his dark spleen; as telling him that, sulk as he might, and go mad with it, nature cared not a jot; since, whose fault was it, pray?

But the foul mood was now at its depth, as the fair wind at its hight.

There was something in the man so, far beyond any mere unsociality or sourness previously evinced, that even the forbearing good-nature of his guest could no longer endure it. Wholly at a loss to account for such demeanor, and deeming sickness with eccentricity, however extreme, no adequate excuse, well satisfied, too, that nothing in his own conduct could justify it, Captain Delano's pride began to be roused. Himself became reserved. But all seemed one to the Spaniard. Quitting him, therefore, Captain Delano once more went to the deck.

The ship was now within less than two miles of the sealer. The whaleboat was seen darting over the interval.

To be brief, the two vessels, thanks to the pilot's skill, ere long in neighborly style lay anchored together.

PART III

BEFORE RETURNING to his own vessel, Captain Delano had intended communicating to Don Benito the practical details of the proposed services to be rendered. But, as it was, unwilling anew to subject himself to rebuffs, he resolved, now that he had seen the San Dominick safely moored, immediately to quit her, without further allusion to hospitality or business. Indefinitely postponing his ulterior plans, he would regulate his future actions according to future circumstances. His boat was ready to receive him; but his host still tarried below. Well, thought Captain Delano, if he has little breeding, the more need to show mine. He descended to the cabin to bid a ceremonious, and, it may be, tacitly rebukeful adieu. But to his great satisfaction, Don Benito, as if he began to feel the weight of that treatment with which his slighted guest had, not indecorously, retaliated upon him, now supported by his servant, rose to his feet, and grasping Captain Delano's hand, stood tremulous; too much agitated to speak. But the good augury hence drawn was suddenly dashed, by his resuming all his previous reserve, with augmented gloom, as, with half-averted eyes, he silently reseated himself on his cushions. With a corresponding return of his own chilled feelings, Captain Delano bowed and withdrew.

He was hardly midway in the narrow corridor, dim as a tunnel, leading from the cabin to the stairs, when a sound, as of the tolling for execution in some jail-yard, fell on his ears. It was the echo of the ship's flawed bell, striking the hour, drearily reverberated in this subterranean vault. Instantly, by a fatality not to be withstood, his mind, responsive to the portent, swarmed with superstitious suspicions. He paused. In images far swifter than these sentences, the minutest details of all his former distrusts swept through him.

Hitherto, credulous good-nature had been too ready to furnish excuses for reasonable fears. Why was the Spaniard, so superfluously punctilious at times, now heedless of common propriety in not accompanying to the side his departing guest? Did indisposition forbid? Indisposition had not forbidden more irksome exertion that day. His last equivocal demeanor recurred. He had risen to his feet, grasped his guest's hand, motioned toward his hat; then, in an instant, all was eclipsed in sinister muteness and gloom. Did this imply one brief, repentent relenting at the final moment, from some iniquitous plot, followed by remorseless return to it? His last glance seemed to express a calamitous, yet acquiescent farewell to Captain Delano forever. Why decline the invitation to visit the sealer that evening? Or was the Spaniard less hardened than the Jew, who refrained not from supping at the board of him whom the same night he meant to betray? What imported all those day-long enigmas and contradictions, except they were intended to mystify, preliminary to some stealthy blow? Atufal, the pretended rebel, but punctual shadow, that moment lurked by the threshold without. He seemed a sentry, and more. Who, by his own confession, had stationed him there? Was the negro now lying in wait?

The Spaniard behind—his creature before: to rush from darkness to light was the involuntary choice.

The next moment, with clenched jaw and hand, he passed Atufal, and stood unarmed in the light. As he saw his trim ship lying peacefully at her anchor, and almost within ordinary call; as he saw his household boat, with familiar faces in it, patiently rising and falling on the short waves by the San Dominick's side; and then, glancing about the decks where he stood, saw the oakum-pickers still gravely plying their fingers; and heard the low, buzzing whistle and industrious hum of the hatchet-polishers, still bestirring themselves over their endless occupation; and more than all, as he saw the benign aspect of nature, taking her innocent repose in the evening; the screened sun in the quiet camp of the west shining out like the mild light from Abraham's tent; as his charmed eye and ear took in all these, with the chained figure of the black, the clenched jaw and hand relaxed. Once again he smiled at the phantoms which had mocked him, and felt something like a tinge of remorse, that, by indulging them even for a moment, he should, by implication, have betrayed an almost atheist doubt of the ever-watchful Providence above.

There was a few minutes' delay, while, in obedience to his orders, the boat was being hooked along to the gangway. During this interval, a sort of saddened satisfaction stole over Captain Delano, at thinking of the kindly offices he had that day discharged for a stranger. Ah, thought he, after good actions one's conscience is never ungrateful, however much so the benefited party may be.

Presently, his foot, in the first act of descent into the boat, pressed the first round of the side-ladder, his face presented inward upon the deck. In the same moment, he heard his name courteously sounded; and, to his pleased surprise, saw Don Benito advancing—an unwonted energy in his air, as if, at the last moment, intent upon making amends for his recent discourtesy. With instinctive good feeling, Captain Delano, revoking his foot, turned and reciprocally advanced. As he did so, the Spaniard's nervous eagerness increased, but his vital energy failed; so that, the better to support him, the servant, placing his master's hand on his naked shoulder, and gently holding it there, formed himself into a sort of crutch.

When the two captains met, the Spaniard again fervently took the hand of the American, at the same time casting an earnest glance into his eyes, but, as before, too much overcome to speak.

I have done him wrong, self-reproachfully thought Captain Delano; his apparent coldness has deceived me; in no instance has he meant to offend.

Meantime, as if fearful that the continuance of the scene might too much unstring his master, the servant seemed anxious to terminate it. And so, still presenting himself as a crutch, and walking between the two captains, he advanced with them towards the gangway; while still, as if full of kindly contrition, Don Benito would not let go the hand of Captain Delano, but retained it in his, across the black's body.

Soon they were standing by the side, looking over into the boat, whose crew turned up their curious eyes. Waiting a moment for the Spaniard to relinquish his hold, the now embarrassed Captain Delano lifted his foot, to overstep the threshold of the open gangway; but still Don Benito would not let go his hand. And yet, with an agitated tone, he said, "I can go no further; here I must bid you adieu. Adieu, my dear, dear Don Amasa. Go—go!" suddenly tearing his hand loose, "go, and God guard you better than me, my best friend."

Not unaffected, Captain Delano would now have lingered; but catching the meekly admonitory eye of the servant, with a hasty farewell he descended into his boat, followed by the continual adieus of Don Benito, standing rooted in the gangway.

Seating himself in the stern, Captain Delano, making a last salute, ordered the boat shoved off. The crew had their oars on end. The bowsman pushed the boat a sufficient distance for the oars to be lengthwise dropped. The instant that was done, Don Benito sprang over the bulwarks, falling at the feet of Captain Delano; at the same time, calling towards his ship, but in tones so frenzied, that none in the boat could understand him. But, as if not equally obtuse, three Spanish sailors, from three different and distant parts of the ship, splashed into the sea, swimming after their captain, as if intent upon his rescue.

The dismayed officer of the boat eagerly asked what this meant. To which, Captain Delano, turning a disdainful smile upon the unaccountable Benito Cereno, answered that, for his part, he neither knew nor cared; but it seemed as if the Spaniard had taken it into his head to produce the impression among his people that the boat wanted to kidnap him. "Or else—give way for your lives," he wildly added, starting at a clattering hubbub in the ship, above which rang the tocsin of the hatchet polishers; and seizing Don Benito by the throat, he added, "this plotting pirate means murder!" Here, in apparent verification of the words, the servant, a dagger in his hand, was seen on the rail overhead, poised, in the act of leaping, as if with desperate fidelity to befriend his master to the last; while, seemingly to aid the black, the three Spanish sailors were trying to clamber into the hampered bow. Meantime, the whole host of negroes, as if inflamed at the sight of their jeopardized captain, impended in one sooty avalanche over the bulwarks.

All this, with what preceded, and what followed, occurred with such involutions of rapidity, that past, present, and future seemed one.

Seeing the negro coming, Captain Delano had flung the Spaniard aside, almost in the very act of clutching him, and, by the unconscious recoil, shifting his place, with arms thrown up, so promptly grappled the servant in his descent, that with dagger presented at Captain Delano's heart, the black seemed of purpose to have leaped there as to his mark. But the weapon was wrenched away, and the assailant dashed down into the bottom of the boat, which now, with disentangled oars, began to speed through the sea.

At this juncture, the left hand of Captain Delano, on one side, again clutched the half-reclined Don Benito, heedless that he was in a speechless faint, while his right foot, on the other side, ground the prostrate negro; and his right arm pressed for added speed on the after oar, his eye bent forward, encouraging his men to their utmost.

But here, the officer of the boat, who had at last succeeded in beating off the towing Spanish sailors, and was now, with face turned aft, assisting the bowsman at his oar, suddenly called to Captain Delano, to see what the black was about; while a Portuguese oarsman shouted to him to give heed to what the Spaniard was saying.

Glancing down at his feet, Captain Delano saw the freed hand of the servant aiming with a second dagger—a small one, before concealed in his wool —with this he was snakishly writhing up from the boat's bottom, at the heart of his master, his countenance lividly vindictive, expressing the centred purpose of his soul; while the Spaniard, half-choked, was vainly shrinking away, with husky words, incoherent to all but the Portuguese.

That moment, across the long-benighted mind of Captain Delano, a flash of revelation swept, illuminating in unanticipated clearness Benito Cereno's whole mysterious demeanor, with every enigmatic event of the day, as well as the entire past voyage of the San Dominick. He smote Babo's hand down, but his own heart smote him harder. With infinite pity he withdrew his hold from Don Benito. Not Captain Delano, but Don Benito, the black, in leaping into the boat, had intended to stab.

Both the black's hands were held, as, glancing up towards the San Dominick, Captain Delano, now with the scales dropped from his eyes, saw the negroes, not in misrule, not in tumult, not as if frantically concerned for Don Benito, but with mask torn away, flourishing hatchets and knives, in ferocious piratical revolt. Like delirious black dervishes, the six Ashantees danced on the poop. Prevented by their foes from springing into the water, the Spanish boys were hurrying up to the topmost spars, while such of the few Spanish sailors, not already in the sea, less alert, were descried, helplessly mixed in, on deck, with the blacks.

Meantime Captain Delano hailed his own vessel, ordering the ports up, and the guns run out. But by this time the cable of the San Dominick had been cut; and the fag-end, in lashing out, whipped away the canvas shroud about the beak, suddenly revealing, as the bleached hull swung round towards the open ocean, death for the figurehead, in a human skeleton; chalky comment on the chalked words below, *"Follow your leader."*

At the sight, Don Benito, covering his face, wailed out: " 'Tis he, Aranda! my murdered, unburied friend!"

Upon reaching the sealer, calling for ropes, Captain Delano bound the negro, who made no resistance, and had him hoisted to the deck. He would then have assisted the now almost helpless Don Benito up the side; but Don Benito, wan as he was, refused to move, or be moved, until the negro should have been first put below out of view. When, presently assured that it was done, he no more shrank from the ascent.

The boat was immediately dispatched back to pick up the three swimming sailors. Meantime, the guns were in readiness, though, owing to the San Dominick having glided somewhat astern of the sealer, only the aftermost one could be brought to bear. With this, they fired six times; thinking to cripple the fugitive ship by bringing down her spars. But only a few inconsiderable ropes were shot away. Soon the ship was beyond the guns' range, steering broad out of the bay; the blacks thickly clustering round the bowsprit, one moment with taunting cries towards the whites, the next with upthrown gestures hailing the now dusky expanse of ocean—cawing crows escaped from the hand of the fowler.

The first impulse was to slip the cables and give chase. But, upon second thoughts, to pursue with whale-boat and yawl seemed more promising.

Upon inquiring of Don Benito what fire arms they had on board the San Dominick, Captain Delano was answered that they had none that could be used; because, in the earlier stages of the mutiny, a cabin-passenger, since dead, had secretly put out of order the locks of what few muskets there were. But with all his remaining strength, Don Benito entreated the American not to give chase, either with ship or boat; for the negroes had already proved themselves such desperadoes, that, in case of a present assault, nothing but a total massacre of the whites could be looked for. But, regarding this warning as coming from one whose spirit had been crushed by misery, the American did not give up his design.

The boats were got ready and armed. Captain Delano ordered twenty-five men into them. He was going himself when Don Benito grasped his arm.

"What! have you saved my life, señor, and are you now going to throw away your own?"

The officers also, for reasons connected with their interests and those of the voyage, and a duty owing to the owners, strongly objected against their commander's going. Weighing their remonstrances a moment, Captain Delano felt bound to remain; appointing his chief mate—an athletic and resolute man, who had been a privateer's man, and, as his enemies whispered, a pirate—to head the party. The more to encourage the sailors, they were told, that the Spanish captain considered his ship as good as lost; that she and her cargo, including some gold and silver, were worth upwards of ten thousand doubloons. Take her, and no small part should be theirs. The sailors replied with a shout.

The fugitives had now almost gained an offing. It was nearly night; but the moon was rising. After hard, prolonged pulling, the boats came up on the ship's quarters, at a suitable distance laying upon their oars to discharge their muskets. Having no bullets to return, the negroes sent their yells. But, upon the second volley, Indian-like, they hurtled their hatchets. One took off a sailor's fingers. Another struck the whale-boat's bow, cutting off the rope there, and remaining stuck in the gunwale like a woodman's axe. Snatching it, quivering from its lodgment, the mate hurled it back. The returned gauntlet now stuck in the ship's broken quarter-gallery, and so remained.

The negroes giving too hot a reception, the whites kept a more respectful distance. Hovering now just out of reach of the hurtling hatchets, they, with a view to the close encounter which must soon come, sought to decoy the blacks into entirely disarming themselves of their most murderous weapons in a hand-to-hand fight, by foolishly flinging them, as missiles, short of the mark, into the sea. But ere long perceiving the stratagem, the negroes desisted, though not before many of them had to replace their lost hatchets with handspikes; an exchange which, as counted upon, proved in the end favorable to the assailants.

Meantime, with a strong wind, the ship still clove the water; the boats alternately falling behind, and pulling up, to discharge fresh volleys.

The fire was mostly directed towards the stern, since there, chiefly, the negroes, at present, were clustering. But to kill or maim the negroes was not the object. To take them, with the ship, was the object. To do it, the ship must be boarded; which could not be done by boats while she was sailing so fast.

A thought now struck the mate. Observing the Spanish boys still aloft, high as they could get, he called to them to descend to the yards, and cut adrift the sails. It was done. About this time, owing to causes hereafter to be shown, two Spaniards, in the dress of sailors and conspicuously showing themselves, were killed; not by volleys, but by deliberate marksman's shots; while, as it afterwards appeared, by one of the general discharges, Atufal, the black, and the Spaniard at the helm likewise were killed. What now, with the loss of the sails, and loss of leaders, the ship became unmanageable to the negroes. With creaking masts, she came heavily round to the wind; the prow slowly swinging, into view of the boats, its skeleton gleaming in the horizontal moonlight, and casting a gigantic ribbed shadow upon the water. One extended arm of the ghost seemed beckoning the whites to avenge it.

"Follow your leader!" cried the mate; and, one on each bow, the boats boarded. Scaling-spears and cutlasses crossed hatchets and hand-spikes. Huddled upon the long-boat amidships, the negresses raised a wailing chant, whose chorus was the clash of the steel.

For a time, the attack wavered; the negroes wedging themselves to beat it back; the half-repelled sailors, as yet unable to gain a footing, fighting as troopers in the saddle, one leg sideways flung over the bulwarks, and one without, plying their cutlasses like carters' whips. But in vain. They were almost overborne, when, rallying themselves into a squad as one man, with a huzza, they sprang inboard; where, entangled, they involuntarily separated again. For a few breaths' space, there was a vague, muffled, inner sound, as of submerged sword-fish rushing hither and thither through shoals of blackfish. Soon, in a reunited band, and joined by the Spanish seamen, the whites came to the surface, irresistibly driving the negroes toward the stern. But a barricade of casks and sacks, from side to side, had been thrown up by the mainmast. Here the negroes faced about, and though scorning peace or truce, yet fain would have had a respite. But, without pause, overleaping the barrier, the unflagging sailors again closed. Exhausted, the blacks now fought in despair. Their red tongues lolled, wolf-like, from their black mouths. But the pale sailors' teeth were set; not a word was spoken; and, in five minutes more, the ship was won.

Nearly a score of the negroes were killed. Exclusive of those by the balls, many were mangled; their wounds—mostly inflicted by the long-edged scaling-spears—resembling those shaven ones of the English at Preston Pans, made by the poled scythes of the Highlanders. On the other side, none were killed, though several were wounded; some severely, including the mate.

The surviving negroes were temporarily secured, and the ship, towed back into the harbor at midnight, once more lay anchored.

Omitting the incidents and arrangements ensuing, suffice it that, after two days spent in refitting, the two ships sailed in company for Conception, in Chili, and thence for Lima, in Peru; where, before the vice-regal courts, the whole affair, from the beginning, underwent investigation.

Though, midway on the passage, the ill-fated Spaniard, relaxed from constraint, showed some signs of regaining health with free-will; yet, agreeably to his own foreboding, shortly before arriving at Lima, he relapsed, finally becoming so reduced as to be carried ashore in arms. Hearing of his story and plight, one of the many religious institutions of the City of Kings opened an hospitable refuge to him, where both physician and priest were his nurses, and a member of the order volunteered to be his one special guardian and consoler, by night and by day.

The following extracts, translated from one of the official Spanish documents, will it is hoped, shed light on the preceding narrative, as well as, in the first place, reveal the true port of departure and true history of the San Dominick's voyage, down to the time of her touching at the island of St. Maria.

But, ere the extracts come, it may be well to preface them with a remark.

The document selected, from among many others, for partial translation, contains the deposition of Benito Cereno; the first taken in the case. Some disclosures therein were, at the time, held dubious for both learned and natural reasons. The tribunal inclined to the opinion that the deponent, not undisturbed in his mind by recent events, raved of some things which could never have happened. But subsequent depositions of the surviving sailors, bearing out the revelations of their captain in several of the strangest particulars, gave credence to the rest. So that the tribunal, in its final decision, rested its capital sentences upon statements which, had they lacked confirmation, it would have deemed it but duty to reject.

I, Don Jose de Abos and Padilla, His Majesty's Notary for the Royal Revenue, and Register of this Province, and Notary Public of the Holy Crusade of this Bishopric, etc.

Do certify and declare, as much as is requisite in law, that, in the criminal cause commenced the twenty-fourth of the month of September, in the year seventeen hundred and ninety-nine, against the Senegal negroes of the ship San Dominick, the following declaration before me was made.

Declaration of the first witness, DON BENITO CERENO.

The same day, and month, and year, His Honor, Doctor Juan Martinez de Rozas, Councilor of the Royal Audience of this Kingdom, and learned in the law of this Intendency, ordered the captain of the ship San Dominick, Don Benito Cereno, to appear; which he did in his litter, attended by the monk Infelez; of whom he received, before Don José de Abos and Padilla, Notary Public of the Holy Crusade, the oath, which he took by God, our Lord, and a sign of the Cross; under which he promised to tell the truth of whatever he should know and should be asked;—and being interrogated agreeably to the tenor of the act commencing the process, he said, that on the twentieth of May last, he set sail with his ship from the port of Valparaiso, bound to that of Callao; loaded with the produce of the country and one hundred and sixty blacks, of both sexes, mostly belonging to Don Alexandro Aranda, gentleman, of the city of Mendoza; that the crew of the ship consisted of thirty-six men, beside the persons who went as passengers; that the negroes were in part as follows:

[*Here, in the original, follows a list of some fifty names, descriptions, and ages, compiled from certain recovered documents of Aranda's, and also from recollections of the deponent, from which portions only are extracted.*]

—One, from about eighteen to nineteen years, named José, and this was the man that waited upon his master, Don Alexandro, and who speaks well the Spanish, having served him four or five years; * * * a mulatto, named Francesco, the cabin steward, of a good person and voice, having sung in the Valparaiso churches, native of the province of Buenos Ayres, aged about thirty-five years. * * * A smart negro, named Dago, who had been for many years a grave-digger among the Spaniards, aged forty-six years. * * * Four old negroes, born in Africa, from sixty to seventy, but sound, calkers by trade, whose names are as follows:—the first was named Muri, and he was killed (as was also his son named Diamelo); the second, Nacta; the third, Yola, likewise killed; the fourth, Ghofan; and six full grown negroes, aged from thirty to forty-five, all raw, and born among the Ashantees—Matiluqui, Yan, Lecbe, Mapenda, Yambaio, Akim; four of whom were killed; * * * a powerful negro named Atufal, who, being supposed to have been a chief in Africa, his owners set great store by him. * * * And a small negro of Senegal, but some years among the Spaniards, aged about thirty, which negro's name was Babo; * * * that he does not remember the names of the others, but that still expecting the residue of Don Alexandro's papers will be found, will then take due account of them all, and remit to the court; * * * and thirty-nine women and children of all ages.

[*After the catalogue, the deposition goes on as follows:*]

* * * That all the negroes slept upon deck, as is customary in this navigation, and none wore fetters, because the owner, his friend Aranda, told him that they were all tractable; * * * that on the seventh day after leaving port, at three o'clock in the morning, all the Spaniards being asleep except the two officers on the watch, who were the boatswain, Juan Robles, and the carpenter, Juan Bautista Gayete, and the helmsman and his boy, the negroes revolted suddenly, wounded dangerously the boatswain and the carpenter, and successively killed eighteen men of those who were sleeping upon deck, some with hand-spikes and hatchets, and others by throwing them alive overboard, after tying them; that of the Spaniards upon deck, they left about seven, as he thinks, alive and tied, to manœuvre the ship, and three or four more, who hid themselves, remained also alive. Although in the act of revolt the negroes made themselves masters of the hatchway, six or seven wounded went through it to the cockpit, without any hindrance on their part; that in the act of revolt, the mate and another person, whose name he does not recollect, attempted to come up through the hatchway, but having been wounded at the onset, they were obliged to return to the cabin; that the deponent resolved at break of day to come up the companionway, where the negro Babo was, being the ringleader, and Atufal, who assisted him, and having spoken to them, exhorted them to cease committing such atrocities, asking them, at the same time, what they wanted and intended to do, offering, himself, to obey their commands; that, notwithstanding this, they threw, in his presence, three men, alive and tied, overboard; that they told the deponent to come up, and that they would not kill him; which having done, the negro Babo asked him whether there were in those seas any negro countries where they might be carried, and he answered them. No; that the negro Babo afterwards told him to carry them to Senegal, or to the neighboring islands of St. Nicholas; and he answered, that this was impossible, on account of the great distance, the necessity involved of rounding Cape Horn, the bad condition of the vessel, the want of provisions, sails, and water; but that the negro Babo replied to him he must carry them in any way, that they would do and conform themselves to everything the deponent should require as to eating and drinking; that after a long conference, being absolutely compelled to please them, for they threatened him to kill all the whites if they were not, at all events, carried to Senegal, he told them that what was most wanting for the voyage was water; that they would go near the coast to take it, and thence they would proceed on their course; that the negro Babo agreed to it; and the deponent steered towards the intermediate ports, hoping to meet some Spanish or foreign vessel that would save them; that within ten or eleven days they saw the land, and continued their course by it in the vicinity of Nasca; that the deponent observed that the negroes were now restless and mutinous, because he did not effect the taking in of water, the negro Babo having required, with threats, that it should be done, without fail, the following day; he told him he saw plainly that the coast was steep, and the rivers designated in the maps were not to be found, with other reasons suitable to the circumstances; that the best way would be to go to the island of Santa Maria, where they might water and victual easily, it being a desert island, as the foreigners did; that the deponent did not go to Pisco, that was near, nor make any other port of the coast, because the negro Babo had intimated to him several times, that he would kill all the whites the very moment he should perceive any city, town, or settlement of any kind on the shores to which they should be carried: that having determined to go to the island of Santa Maria, as the deponent had planned, for the purpose of trying whether, in the passage or in the island itself, they could find any vessel that should favor them, or whether he could escape from it in a boat to the neighboring coast of Arruco; to adopt the necessary means he immediately changed his course, steering for the island; that the negroes Babo and Atufal held daily conferences, in which they discussed what was necessary for their design of returning to Senegal, whether they were to kill all the Spaniards, and particularly the deponent; that eight days after parting from the coast of Nasea, the deponent being on the watch a little after day-break, and soon after the negroes had their meeting, the negro Babo came to the place where the deponent was, and told him that he had determined to kill his master, Don Alexandro Aranda, both because he and his companions could not otherwise be sure of their liberty, and that, to keep the seamen in subjection, he wanted to prepare a warning of what road they should be made to take did they or any of them oppose him; and that, by means of the death of Don Alexandro, that warning would best be given; but, that what this last meant, the deponent did not at the time comprehend, nor could not, further than that the death of Don Alexandro was intended; and moreover, the negro Babo proposed to the deponent to call the mate Raneds, who was sleeping in the cabin, before the thing was done, for fear, as the deponent understood it, that the mate, who was a good navigator, should be killed with Don Alexandro and the rest; that the deponent, who was the friend, from youth, of Don Alexandro, prayed and conjured, but all was useless; for the negro Babo answered him that the thing could not be prevented, and that all the Spaniards risked their death if they should attempt to frustrate his will in this matter, or any other; that, in this conflict, the deponent called the mate, Raneds, who was forced to go apart, and immediately the negro Babo commanded the Ashantee Matiluqui and the Ashantee Lecbe to go and commit the murder; that those two went down with hatchets to the berth of Don Alexandro; that, yet half alive and mangled, they dragged him on deck; that they were going to throw him overboard in that state, but the negro Babo stopped them, bidding the murder be completed on the deck before him, which was done, when, by his orders, the body was carried below, forward; that nothing more was seen of it by the deponent for three days; * * * that Don Alonzo Sidonia, an old man, long resident at Valparaiso, and lately appointed to a civil office in Peru, whither he had taken passage, was at the time sleeping in the berth opposite Don Alexandro's; that, awakening at his cries, surprised by them, and at the sight of the negroes with their bloody hatchets in their hands, he threw himself into the sea through a window which was near him, and was drowned, without it being in the power of the deponent to assist or take him up; * * * that, a short time after killing Aranda, they brought upon deck his german-cousin, of middle-age, Don Francisco Masa, of Mendoza, and the young Don Joaquin, Marques de Aramboalaza, then lately from Spain, with his Spanish servant Ponce, and the three young clerks of Aranda, José Mozairi, Lorenzo Bargas, and Hermenegildo Gandix, all of Cadiz; that Don Joaquin and Hermenegildo Gandix, the negro Babo for purposes hereafter to appear, preserved alive; but Don Francisco Masa, José Mozairi, and Lorenzo Bargas, with Ponce the servant, beside the boatswain, Juan Robles, the boatswain's mates, Manuel Viscaya and Roderigo Hurta, and four of the sailors, the negro Babo ordered to be thrown alive into the sea, although they made no resistance, nor begged for anything else but mercy; that the boatswain, Juan Robles, who knew how to swim, kept the longest above water, making acts of contrition, and, in the last words he uttered, charged this deponent to cause mass to be said for his soul to our Lady of Succor: * * * that, during the three days which followed, the deponent, uncertain what fate had befallen the remains of Don Alexandro, frequently asked the negro Babo where they were, and, if still on board, whether they were to be preserved for interment ashore, entreating him so to order it; that the negro Babo answered nothing till the fourth day, when at sunrise, the deponent coming on deck, the negro Babo showed him a skeleton, which had been substituted for the ship's proper figure-head, the image of Christopher Colon, the discoverer of the New World; that the negro Babo asked him whose skeleton that was, and whether, from its whiteness, he should not think it a white's; that, upon his covering his face, the negro Babo, coming close, said words to this effect: "Keep faith with the blacks from here to Senegal, or you shall in spirit, as now in body, follow your leader," pointing to the prow; * * * that the same morning the negro Babo took by succession each Spaniard forward, and asked him whose skeleton that was, and whether, from its whiteness, he should not think it a white's; that each Spaniard covered his face; that then to each the negro Babo repeated the words in the first place said to the deponent; * * * that they (the Spaniards), being then assembled aft, the negro Babo harangued them, saying that he had now done all; that the deponent (as navigator for the negroes) might pursue his course, warning him and all of them that they should, soul and body, go the way of Don Alexandro if he saw them (the Spaniards) speak or plot anything against them (the negroes)—a threat which was repeated every day; that, before the events last mentioned, they had tied the cook to throw him overboard, for it is not known what thing they heard him speak, but finally the negro Babo spared his life, at the request of the deponent; that a few days after, the deponent, endeavoring not to omit any means to preserve the lives of the remaining whites, spoke to the negroes peace and tranquillity, and agreed to draw up a paper, signed by the deponent and the sailors who could write, as also by the negro Babo, for himself and all the blacks, in which the deponent obliged himself to carry them to Senegal, and they not to kill any more, and he formally to make over to them the ship, with the cargo, with which they were for that time satisfied and quieted. * * * But the next day, the more surely to guard against the sailors' escape, the negro Babo commanded all the boats to be destroyed but the long-boat, which was unseaworthy, and another, a cutter in good condition, which, knowing it would yet be wanted for lowering the water casks, he had it lowered down into the hold.

※　　※　　※　　※　　※　　※　　※

[*Various particulars of the prolonged and perplexed navigation ensuing here follow, with incidents of a calamitous calm, from which portion one passage is extracted, to wit:*]

—That on the fifth day of the calm, all on board suffering much from the heat, and want of water, and five having died in fits, and mad, the negroes became irritable, and for a chance gesture, which they deemed suspicious—though it was harmless—made by the mate, Raneds, to the deponent, in the act of handing a quadrant, they killed him; but that for this they afterwards were sorry, the mate being the only remaining navigator on board, except the deponent.

* * * * * * *

—That omitting other events, which daily happened, and which can only serve uselessly to recall past misfortunes and conflicts, after seventy-three days' navigation, reckoned from the time they sailed from Nasca, during which they navigated under a scanty allowance of water, and were afflicted with the calms before mentioned, they at last arrived at the island of Santa Maria, on the seventeenth of the month of August, at about six o'clock in the afternoon, at which hour they cast anchor very near the American ship, Bachelor's Delight, which lay in the same bay, commanded by the generous Captain Amasa Delano; but at six o'clock in the morning, they had already descried the port, and the negroes became uneasy, as soon as at distance they saw the ship, not having expected to see one there; that the negro Babo pacified them, assuring them that no fear need be had; that straightway he ordered the figure on the bow to be covered with canvas, as for repairs, and had the decks a little set in order; that for a time the negro Babo and the negro Atufal conferred; that the negro Atufal was for sailing away, but the negro Babo would not, and, by himself, cast about what to do; that at last he came to the deponent, proposing to him to say and do all that the deponent declares to have said and done to the American captain; * * *

* * * that the negro Babo warned him that if he varied in the least, or uttered any word, or gave any look that should give the least intimation of the past events or present state, he would instantly kill him, with all his companions, showing a dagger, which he carried hid, saying something which, as he understood it, meant that that dagger would be alert as his eye; that the negro Babo then announced the plan to all his companions, which pleased them; that he then, the better to disguise the truth, devised many expedients, in some of them uniting deceit and defense; that of this sort was the device of the six Ashantees before named, who were his bravoes; that them he stationed on the break of the poop, as if to clean certain hatchets (in cases, which were part of the cargo), but in reality to use them, and distribute them at need, and at a given word he told them that, among other devices, was the device of presenting Atufal, his right-hand man, as chained, though in a moment the chains could be dropped; that in every particular he informed the deponent what part he was expected to enact in every device, and what story he was to tell on every occasion, always threatening him with instant death if he varied in the least: that, conscious that many of the negroes would be turbulent, the negro Babo appointed the four aged negroes, who were calkers, to keep what domestic order they could on the decks; that again and again he harangued the Spaniards and his companions, informing them of his intent, and of his devices, and of the invented story that this deponent was to tell, charging them lest any of them varied from that story; that these arrangements were made and matured during the interval of two or three hours, between their first sighting the ship and the arrival on board of Captain Amasa Delano; that this happened about half-past seven o'clock in the morning, Captain Amasa Delano coming in his boat, and all gladly receiving him; that the deponent, as well as he could force himself, acting then the part of principal owner, and a free captain of the ship, told Captain Amasa Delano, when called upon, that he came from Buenos Ayres, bound to Lima, with three hundred negroes; that off Cape Horn, and in a subsequent fever, many negroes had died; that also, by similar casualties, all the sea officers and the greatest part of the crew had died.

* * * * * * *

[*And so the deposition goes on, circumstantially recounting the fictitious story dictated to the deponent by Babo, and through the deponent imposed upon Captain Delano; and also recounting the friendly offers of Captain Delano, with other things, but all of which is here omitted. After the fictitious, strange story, etc., the deposition proceeds:*]

* * * * * * *

—That the generous Captain Amasa Delano remained on board all the day, till he left the ship anchored at six o'clock in the evening, deponent speaking to him always of his pretended misfortunes, under the fore-mentioned principles, without having had it in his power to tell a single word, or give him the least hint, that he might know the truth and state of things; because the negro Babo, performing the office of an officious servant with all the appearance of submission of the humble slave, did not leave the deponent one moment; that this was in order to observe the deponent's actions and words, for the negro Babo understands well the Spanish; and besides, there were thereabout some others who were constantly on the watch, and likewise understood the Spanish; * * * that upon one occasion, while deponent was standing on the deck conversing with Amasa Delano, by a secret sign the negro Babo drew him (the deponent) aside, the act appearing as if originating with the deponent; that then, he being drawn aside, the negro Babo proposed to him to gain from Amasa Delano full particulars about his ship, and crew, and arms; that the deponent asked "For what?" that the negro Babo answered he might conceive; that, grieved at the prospect of what might overtake the generous Captain Amasa Delano, the deponent at first refused to ask the desired questions, and used every argument to induce the negro Babo to give up this new design; that the negro Babo showed the point of his dagger; that, after the information had been obtained, the negro Babo again drew him aside, telling him that that very night he (the deponent) would be captain of two ships, instead of one, for that, great part of the American's ship's crew being to be absent fishing, the six Ashantees, without any one else, would easily take it; that at this time he said other things to the same purpose; that no entreaties availed; that, before Amasa Delano's coming on board, no hint had been given touching the capture of the American ship: that to prevent this project the deponent was powerless; * * * —that in some things his memory is confused, he cannot distinctly recall every event; * * * —that as soon as they had cast anchor at six of the clock in the evening, as has before been stated, the American Captain took leave to return to his vessel; that upon a sudden impulse, which the deponent believes to have come from God and his angels, he, after the farewell had been said, followed the generous Captain Amasa Delano as far as the gunwale, where he stayed, under pretense of taking leave, until Amasa Delano should have been seated in his boat; that on shoving off, the deponent sprang from the gunwale into the boat, and fell into it, he knows not how, God guarding him; that—

*   *   *   *   *   *   *

[Here, in the original, follows the account of what further happened at the escape, and how the San Dominick was retaken, and of the passage to the coast; including in the recital many expressions of "eternal gratitude" to the "generous Captain Amasa Delano." The deposition then proceeds with *recapitulatory remarks, and a partial renumeration of the negroes, making record of their individual part in the past events, with a view to furnishing, according to command of the court, the data whereon to found the criminal sentences to be pronounced. From this portion is the following:*]

—That he believes that all the negroes, though not in the first place knowing to the design of revolt, when it was accomplished, approved it. * * * That the negro, José, eighteen years old, and in the personal service of Don Alexandro, was the one who communicated the information to the negro Babo, about the state of things in the cabin, before the revolt; that this is known, because, in the preceding midnight, he use to come from his berth, which was under his master's, in the cabin, to the deck where the ringleader and his associates were, and had secret conversations with the negro Babo, in which he was several times seen by the mate; that, one night, the mate drove him away twice; * * * that this same negro José, was the one who, without being commanded to do so by the negro Babo, as Lecbe and Martinqui were, stabbed his master, Don Alexandro, after he had been dragged half-lifeless to the deck; * * * that the mulatto steward, Francisco, was of the first band of revolters, that he was, in all things, the creature and tool of the negro Babo, that, to make his court, he, just before a repast in the cabin, proposed, to the negro Babo, poisoning a dish for the generous Captain Amasa Delano; this is known and believed, because the negroes have said it; but that the negro Babo, having another design, forbade Francisco; * * * that the Ashantee Lecbe was one of the worst of them; for that, on the day the ship was retaken, he assisted in the defense of her, with a hatchet in each hand, with one of which he wounded, in the breast, the chief mate of Amasa Delano, in the first act of boarding; this all knew; that, in sight of the deponent, Lecbe struck, with a hatchet, Don Francisco Masa when, by the negro Babo's orders, he was carrying him to throw him overboard, alive; beside participating in the murder, before mentioned, of Don Alexandro Aranda, and others of the cabin passengers; that, owing to the fury with which the Ashantees fought in the engagement with the boats, but this Lecbe and Yan survived; that Yan was bad as Lecbe; that Yan was the man who, by Babo's command, willingly prepared the skeleton of Don Alexandro, in a way the negroes afterwards told the deponent, but which he, so long as reason is left him, can never divulge; that Yan and Lecbe were the two who, in a calm by night, riveted the skeleton to the bow; this also the negroes told him; that the negro Babo was he who traced the inscription below it;

that the negro Babo was the plotter from first to last; he ordered every murder, and was the helm and keel of the revolt; that Atufal was his lieutenant in all; but Atufal, with his own hand, committed no murder; nor did the negro Babo; * * * that Atufal was shot, being killed in the fight with the boats, ere boarding; * * * that the negresses, of age, were knowing to the revolt, and testified themselves satisfied at the death of their master, Don Alexandro; that, had the negroes not restrained them, they would have tortured to death, instead of simply killing, the Spaniards slain by command of the negro Babo; that the negresses used their utmost influence to have the deponent made away with; that, in the various acts of murder, they sang songs and danced—not gaily, but solemnly; and before the engagement with the boats, as well as during the action, they sang melancholy songs to the negroes, and that this melancholy tone was more inflaming than a different one would have been, and was so intended; that all this is believed, because the negroes have said it.

—That of the thirty-six men of the crew exclusive of the passengers, (all of whom are now dead), which the deponent had knowledge of, six only remained alive, with four cabin-boys and ship-boys, not included with the crew; * * * —that the negroes broke an arm of one of the cabin-boys and gave him strokes with hatchets.

[*Then follow various random disclosures referring to various periods of time. The following are extracted:*]

—That during the presence of Captain Amasa Delano on board, some attempts were made by the sailors, and one by Hermenegildo Gandix, to convey hints to him of the true state of affairs; but that these attempts were ineffectual, owing to fear of incurring death, and furthermore owing to the devices which offered contradictions to the true state of affairs; as well as owing to the generosity and piety of Amasa Delano incapable of sounding such wickedness; * * * that Luys Galgo, a sailor about sixty years of age, and formerly of the king's navy, was one of those who sought to convey tokens to Captain Amasa Delano; but his intent, though undiscovered, being suspected, he was, on a pretense, made to retire out of sight, and at last into the hold, and there was made away with. This the negroes have since said; * * * that one of the ship-boys feeling, from Captain Amasa Delano's presence, some hopes of release, and not having enough prudence, dropped some chance-word respecting his expectations, which being overheard and understood by a slave-boy with whom he was eating at the time, the latter struck him on the head with a knife, inflicting a bad wound, but of which the boy is now healing; that likewise, not long before the ship was brought to anchor, one of the seamen, steering at the time, endangered himself by letting the blacks remark a certain unconscious hopeful expression in his countenance, arising from some cause similar to the above; but this sailor, by his heedful after conduct, escaped; * * * that these statements are made to show the court that from the beginning to the end of the revolt, it was impossible for the deponent and his men to act otherwise than they did; * * *—that the third clerk, Hermenegildo Gandix, who before had been forced to live among the seamen, wearing a seaman's habit, and in all respects appearing to be one for the time; he, Gandix, was killed by a musket-ball fired through a mistake from the American boats before boarding; having in his fright ran up the mizzen-rigging, calling to the boats—"don't board," lest upon their boarding the negroes should kill him; that this inducing the Americans to believe he some way favored the cause of the negroes, they fired two balls at him, so that he fell wounded from the rigging, and was drowned in the sea; * * *—that the young Don Joaquin, Marques de Arambaolaza, like Hermenegildo Gandix, the third clerk, was degraded to the office and appearance of a common seaman; that upon one occasion when Don Joaquin shrank, the negro Babo commanded the Ashantee Lecbe to take tar and heat it, and pour it upon Don Joaquin's hands; * * *—that Don Joaquin was killed owing to another mistake of the Americans, but one impossible to be avoided, as upon the approach of the boats, Don Joaquin, with a hatchet tied edge out and upright to his hand, was made by the negroes to appear on the bulwarks; whereupon, seen with arms in his hands and in a questionable attitude, he was shot for a renegade seaman; * * *—that on the person of Don Joaquin was found secreted a jewel, which, by papers that were discovered, proved to have been meant for the shrine of our Lady of Mercy in Lima; a votive offering, beforehand prepared and guarded, to attest his gratitude, when he should have landed in Peru, his last destination, for the safe conclusion of his entire voyage from Spain; * * *—that the jewel, with the other effects of the late Don Joaquin, is in the custody of the brethren of the Hospital de Sacerdotes, awaiting the decision of the honorable court; * * *—that, owing to the condition of the deponent, as well as the haste in which the boats departed for the attack, the Americans were not forewarned that there were, among the apparent crew, a passenger and one of the clerks disguised by the negro Babo; * * *—that, beside the negroes killed in the action, some were killed after the capture and re-anchoring at night, when shackled to the ring-bolts on deck; that these deaths were committed by the sailors, ere they could be prevented. That so soon as informed of it, Captain Amasa Delano used all his authority, and, in particular with his own hand, struck down Martinez Gola, who, having found a razor in the pocket of an old jacket of his, which one of the shackled negroes had on, was aiming it at the negro's throat; that the noble Captain Amasa Delano also wrenched from the hand of Bartholomew Barlo, a dagger secreted at the time of the massacre of the whites, with which he was in the act of stabbing a shackled negro, who, the same day, with another negro, had thrown him down and jumped upon him; * * * —that, for all the events, befalling through so long a time, during which the ship was in the hands of the negro Babo, he cannot here give account; but that, what he has said is the most substantial of what occurs to him at present, and is the truth under the oath which he has taken; which declaration he affirmed and ratified, after hearing it read to him.

He said that he is twenty-nine years of age, and broken in body and mind; that when finally dismissed by the court, he shall not return home to Chili, but betake himself to the monastery on Mount Agonia without; and signed with his honor, and crossed himself, and, for the time, departed as he came, in his litter, with the monk Infelez, to the Hospital de Sacerdotes.

BENITO CERENO

DOCTOR ROZAS

If the deposition of Benito Cereno has served as the key to fit into the lock of the complications which preceded it, then, as a vault whose door has been flung back, the San Dominick's hull lies open to-day.

Hitherto the nature of this narrative, besides rendering the intricacies in the beginning unavoidable, has more or less required that many things, instead of being set down in the order of occurrence, should be retrospectively, or irregularly given; this last is the case with the following passages, which will conclude the account:

During the long, mild voyage to Lima, there was, as before hinted, a period during which Don Benito a little recovered his health, or, at least in some degree, his tranquillity. Ere the decided relapse which came, the two captains had many cordial conversations—their fraternal unreserve in singular contrast with former withdrawments.

Again and again, it was repeated, how hard it had been to enact the part forced on the Spaniard by Babo.

"Ah, my dear Don Amasa," Don Benito once said, "at those very times when you thought me so morose and ungrateful, nay, when, as you now admit, you half thought me plotting your murder, at those very times my heart was frozen; I could not look at you, thinking of what, both on board this ship and your own, hung, from other hands, over my kind benefactor. And as God lives, Don Amasa, I know not whether desire for my own safety alone could have nerved me to that leap into your boat, had it not been for the thought that, did you, unenlightened, return to your ship, you, my best friend, with all who might be with you, stolen upon, that night, in your hammocks, would never in this world have wakened again. Do but think how you walked this deck, how you sat in this cabin, every inch of ground mined into honey-combs under you. Had I dropped the least hint, made the least advance towards an understanding between us, death, explosive death—yours as mine—would have ended the scene."

"True, true," cried Captain Delano, starting, "you saved my life, Don Benito, more than I yours; saved it, too, against my knowledge and will."

"Nay, my friend," rejoined the Spaniard, courteous even to the point of religion, "God charmed your life, but you saved mine. To think of some things you did—those smilings and chattings, rash pointings and gesturings. For less than these, they slew my mate, Raneds; but you had the Prince of Heaven's safe conduct through all ambuscades."

"Yes, all is owing to Providence, I know; but the temper of my mind that morning was more than commonly pleasant, while the sight of so much suffering, more apparent than real, added to my good nature, compassion, and charity, happily interweaving the three. Had it been otherwise, doubtless, as you hint, some of my interferences with the blacks might have ended unhappily enough. Besides that, those feelings I spoke of enabled me to get the better of momentary distrust, at times when acuteness might have cost me my life, without saving another's. Only at the end did my suspicions get the better of me, and you know how wide of the mark they then proved."

"Wide, indeed," said Don Benito, sadly; "you were with me all day; stood with me, sat with me, talked with me, looked at me, ate with me, drank with me; and yet, your last act was to clutch for a villain, not only an innocent man, but the most pitiable of all men. To such degree may malign machinations and deceptions impose. So far may even the best men err, in judging the conduct of one with the recesses of whose condition he is not acquainted. But you were forced to it; and you were in time undeceived. Would that, in both respects, it was so ever, and with all men."

"I think I understand you; you generalize, Don Benito; and mournfully enough. But the past is passed; why moralize upon it? Forget it. See, yon bright sun has forgotten it all, and the blue sea, and the blue sky; these have turned over new leaves."

"Because they have no memory," he dejectedly replied; "because they are not human."

"But these mild trades that now fan your cheek, Don Benito, do they not come with a human-like healing to you? Warm friends, steadfast friends are the trades."

"With their steadfastness they but waft me to my tomb, señor," was the foreboding response.

"You are saved, Don Benito," cried Captain Delano, more and more astonished and pained; "you are saved; what has cast such a shadow upon you?"

"The negro."

There was silence, while the moody man sat, slowly and unconsciously gathering his mantle about him, as if it were a pall.

There was no more conversation that day.

But if the Spaniard's melancholy sometimes ended in muteness upon topics like the above, there were others upon which he never spoke at all; on which, indeed, all his old reserves were piled. Pass over the worst, and, only to elucidate, let an item or two of these be cited. The dress so precise and costly, worn by him on the day whose events have been narrated, had not willingly been put on. And that silver-mounted sword, apparent symbol of despotic command, was not, indeed, a sword, but the ghost of one. The scabbard, artificially stiffened, was empty.

As for the black—whose brain, not body, had schemed and led the revolt, with the plot—his slight frame, inadequate to that which it held, had at once yielded to the superior muscular strength of his captor, in the boat. Seeing all was over, he uttered no sound, and could not be forced to. His aspect seemed to say, since I cannot do deeds, I will not speak words. Put in irons in the hold, with the rest, he was carried to Lima. During the passage Don Benito did not visit him. Nor then, nor at any time after, would he look at him. Before the tribunal he refused. When pressed by the judges he fainted. On the testimony of the sailors alone rested the legal identity of Babo. And yet the Spaniard would, upon occasion, verbally refer to the negro, as has been shown; but look on him he would not, or could not.

Some months after, dragged to the gibbet at the tail of a mule, the black met his voiceless end. The body was burned to ashes; but for many days, the head, that hive of subtlety, fixed on a pole in the Plaza, met, unabashed, the gaze of the whites; and across the Plaza looked towards St. Bartholomew's church, in whose vaults slept then, as now, the recovered bones of Aranda; and across the Rimac bridge looked towards the monastery, on Mount Agonia without; where, three months after being dismissed by the court, Benito Cereno, borne on the bier, did, indeed, follow his leader.

EDGAR ALLAN POE

William Wilson

> What say of it? what say CONSCIENCE grim,
> That spectre in my path?
>   —*Chamberlain's Pharronida.*

Let me call myself, for the present, William Wilson. The fair page now lying before me need not be sullied with my real appellation. This has been already too much an object for the scorn—for the horror—for the detestation of my race. To the uttermost regions of the globe have not the indignant winds bruited its unparalled infamy? Oh, outcast of all outcasts most abandoned!—to the earth art thou not for ever dead? to its honors, to its flowers, to its golden aspirations?—and a cloud, dense, dismal, and limitless, does it not hang eternally between thy hopes and heaven?

I would not, if I could, here or today, embody a record of my later years of unspeakable misery and unpardonable crime. This epoch—these later years—took unto themselves a sudden elevation in turpitude, whose origin alone it is my present purpose to assign. Men usually grow base by degrees. From me, in an instant, all virtue dropped bodily as a mantle. From comparatively trivial wickedness I passed, with the stride of a giant, into more than the enormities of an Elah Gabalus. What chance—what one event brought this evil thing to pass, bear with me while I relate. Death approaches; and the shadow which foreruns him has thrown a softening influence over my spirit. I long, in passing through the dim valley, for the sympathy—I had nearly said for the pity—of my fellow men. I would fain have them believe that I have been, in some measure, the slave of circumstances beyond human control. I would wish them to seek out for me, in the details I am about to give, some little oasis of *fatality* amid a wilderness of error. I would have them allow—what they cannot refrain from allowing—that, although temptation may have ere-while existed as great, man was never thus, at least, tempted before—certainly, never *thus* fell. And is it therefore that he has never thus suffered? Have I not indeed been living in a dream? And am I not now dying a victim to the horror and the mystery of the wildest of all sublunary visions?

I am the descendant of a race whose imaginative and easily excitable tempermanent has at all times rendered them remarkable; and, in my earliest infancy, I gave evidence of having fully inherited the family character. As I advanced in years it was more strongly developed; becoming, for many reasons, a cause of serious disquietude to my friends, and of positive injury to myself. I grew self-willed, addicted to the wildest caprices, and a prey to the most ungovernable passions. Weak minded, and beset with constitutional infirmities akin to my own, my parents could do but little to check the evil propensities which distinguished me. Some feeble and ill-directed efforts resulted in complete failure on their part, and, of course, in total triumph on mine. Thenceforward my voice was a household law; and at an age when few children have abandoned their leading-strings, I was left to the guidance of my own will, and became, in all but name, the master of my own actions.

My earliest recollections of a school-life, are connected with a large, rambling, Elizabethan house, in a misty-looking village of England, where were a vast number of gigantic and gnarled trees, and where all the houses were excessively ancient. In truth, it was a dream-like and spirit-soothing place, that venerable old town. At this moment, in fancy, I feel the refreshing chilliness of its deeply-shadowed avenues, inhale the fragrance of its thousand shrubberies, and thrill anew with undefinable delight, at the deep hollow note of the church-bell, breaking, each hour, with sullen and sudden roar, upon the stillness of the dusky atmosphere in which the fretted Gothic steeple lay imbedded and asleep.

It gives me, perhaps, as much of pleasure as I can now in any manner experience, to dwell upon minute recollections of the school and its concerns. Steeped in misery as I am—misery, alas! only too real—I shall be pardoned for seeking relief, however slight and temporary, in the weakness of a few rambling details. These, moreover, utterly trivial, and even ridiculous in themselves, assume, to my fancy, adventitious importance, as connected with a period and a locality when and where I recognize the first ambiguous monitions of the destiny which afterward so fully overshadowed me. Let me then remember.

The house, I have said, was old and irregular. The grounds were extensive, and a high and solid brick wall, topped with a bed of mortar and broken glass, encompassed the whole. This prison-like rampart formed the limit of our domain; beyond it we saw but thrice a week—once every Saturday afternoon, when, attended by two ushers, we were permitted to take brief walks in a body through some of the neighboring fields—and twice during Sunday, when we were paraded in the same formal manner to the morning and evening service in the one church in the village. Of this church the principal of our school was pastor. With how deep a spirit of wonder and perplexity was I wont to regard him from our remote pew in the gallery, as, with step solemn and slow, he ascended the pulpit! This reverend man, with countenance so demurely benign, with robes so glossy and so clerically flowing, with wig so minutely powdered, so rigid and so vast,—could this be he who, of late, with sour visage, and in snuffy habiliments, administered, ferule in hand, the Draconian Laws of the academy? Oh, gigantic paradox, too utterly monstrous for solution!

At an angle of the ponderous wall frowned a more ponderous gate. It was riveted and studded with iron bolts, and surmounted with jagged iron spikes. What impressions of deep awe did it inspire! It was never opened save for the three periodical egressions and ingressions already mentioned; then, in every creak of its mighty hinges, we found a plenitude of mystery—a world of matter for solemn remark, or for more solemn meditation.

The extensive enclosure was irregular in form, having many capacious recesses. Of these, three or four of the largest constituted the play-ground. It was level, and covered with fine hard gravel. I well remember it had no trees, nor benches, nor any thing similar within it. Of course it was in the rear of the house. In front lay a small parterre, planted with box and other shrubs, but through this sacred division we passed only upon rare occasions indeed—such as a first advent to school or final departure thence, or perhaps, when a parent or friend having called for us, we joyfully took our way home for the Christmas or Midsummer holidays.

But the house!—how quaint an old building was this!—to me how veritable a palace of enchantment! There was really no end to its windings—to its incomprehensible subdivisions. It was difficult, at any given time, to say with certainty upon which of its two stories one happened to be. From each room to every other there were sure to be found three or four steps either in ascent or descent. Then the lateral branches were innumerable—inconceivable—and so returning in upon themselves, that our most exact ideas in regard to the whole mansion were not very far different from those with which we pondered upon infinity. During the five years of my residence here,

I was never able to ascertain with precision, in what remote locality lay the little sleeping apartment assigned to myself and some eighteen or twenty other scholars.

The school-room was the largest in the house—I could not help thinking, in the world. It was very long, narrow, and dismally low, with pointed Gothic windows and a ceiling of oak. In a remote and terror-inspiring angle was a square enclosure of eight or ten feet, comprising the *sanctum*, "during hours," of our principal, the Reverend Dr. Bransby. It was a solid structure, with massy door, sooner than open which in the absence of the "Dominie," we would all have willingly perished by the *peine forte et dure*. In other angles were two other similar boxes, far less reverenced, indeed, but still greatly matters of awe. One of these was the pulpit of the "classical" usher, one of the "English and mathematical." Interspersed about the room, crossing and recrossing in endless irregularity, were innumerable benches and desks, black, ancient, and time-worn, piled desperately with much bethumbed books, and so beseamed with initial letters, names at full length, grotesque figures, and other multiplied efforts of the knife, as to have entirely lost what little of original form might have been their portion in days long departed. A huge bucket with water stood at one extremity of the room, and a clock of stupendous dimensions at the other.

Encompassed by the massy walls of this venerable academy, I passed, yet not in tedium or disgust, the years of the third lustrum of my life. The teeming brain of childhood requires no external world of incident to occupy or amuse it; and the apparently dismal monotony of a school was replete with more intense excitement than my riper youth has derived from luxury, or my full manhood from crime. Yet I must believe that my first mental development had in it much of the uncommon—even much of the *outre*. Upon mankind at large the events of very early existence rarely leave in mature age any definite impression. All is gray shadow—a weak and irregular remembrance—an indistinct regathering of feeble pleasures and phantasmagoric pains. With me this is not so. In childhood I must have felt with the energy of a man what I now find stamped upon memory in lines as vivid, as deep, and as durable as the *exergues* of the Carthaginian medals.

Yet in fact—in the fact of the world's view—how little was there to remember! The morning's awakening, the nightly summons to bed; the connings, the recitations; the periodical half-holidays, and perambulations; the play-ground, with its broils, its pastimes, its intrigues;—these, by a mental sorcery long forgotten, were made to involve a wilderness of sensation, a world of rich incident, a universe of varied emotion, of excitement, the most passionate and spirit-stirring. *"Oh, le bon temps que se siecle de fer!"*

In truth, the ardor, the enthusiasm, and the imperiousness of my disposition, soon rendered me a marked character among my schoolmates, and by slow, but natural gradations, gave me an ascendancy over all not greatly older than myself;—over all with a single exception. This exception was found in the person of a scholar, who, although no relation, bore the same christian and surname as myself;—a circumstance, in fact, little remarkable; for notwithstanding a noble descent, mine was one of those every-day appellations which seem, by prescriptive right, to have been, time out of mind, the common property of the mob. In this narrative I have therefore designated myself as William Wilson—a fictitious title not very dissimilar to the real. My namesake alone, of those who in school phraseology constituted "our set," presumed to compete with me in the studies of the class—in the sports and broils of the play-ground—to refuse implicit belief in my assertions, and submission to my will—indeed, to interfere with my arbitrary dictation in any respect whatsoever. If there is on earth a supreme and unqualified despotism, it is the despotism of a master-mind in boyhood over the less energetic spirits of its companions.

Wilson's rebellion was to me a source of the greatest embarrassment; the more so as, in spite of the bravado with which in public I made a point of treating him and his pretensions, I secretly felt that I feared him, and could not help thinking the equality which he maintained so easily with myself, a proof of his true superiority; since not to be overcome cost me a perpetual struggle. Yet this superiority—even this equality—was in truth acknowledged by no one but myself; our associates, by some unaccountable blindness, seemed not even to suspect it. Indeed, his competition, his resistance, and especially his impertinent and dogged interference with my purposes, were not more pointed than private. He appeared to be destitute alike of the ambition which urged, and of the passionate energy of mind which enabled me to excel. In his rivalry he might have been supposed actuated solely by a whimsical desire to thwart, astonish, or mortify myself; although there were times when I could not help observing, with a feeling made up of wonder, abasement, and pique, that he mingled with his injuries, his insults, or his contradictions, a certain most inappropriate, and assuredly most unwelcome *affectionateness* of manner. I could only conceive this singular behavior to arise from a consummate self-conceit assuming the vulgar airs of patronage and protection.

Perhaps it was this latter trait in Wilson's conduct, conjoined with our identity of name, and the mere accident of our having entered the school upon the same day, which set afloat the notion that we were brothers, among the senior class in the academy. These do not usually inquire with much strictness into the affairs of their juniors. I have before said, or should have said, that Wilson was not, in a most remote degree, connected with my family. But assuredly if we *had* been brothers we must have been twins; for, after leaving Dr. Bransby's, I casually learned that my namesake was born on the nineteenth of January, 1813—and this is a somewhat remarkable coincidence; for the day is precisely that of my own nativity.

It may seem strange that in spite of the continual anxiety occasioned me by the rivalry of Wilson, and his intolerable spirit of contradiction, I could not bring myself to hate him altogether. We had, to be sure, nearly every day a quarrel in which, yielding me publicly the palm of victory, he, in some manner, contrived to make me feel that it was he who had deserved it; yet a sense of pride on my part, and a veritable dignity on his own, kept us always upon what are called "speaking terms," while there were many points of strong congeniality in our tempers, operating to wake in me a sentiment which our position alone, perhaps, prevented from ripening into friendship. It is difficult, indeed, to define, or even to describe, my real feelings toward him. They formed a motley and heterogeneous admixture;—some petulant animosity, which was not yet hatred, some esteem, more respect, much fear, with a world of uneasy curiosity. To the moralist it will be necessary to say, in addition, that Wilson and myself were the most inseparable of companions.

It was no doubt the anomalous state of affairs existing between us, which turned all my attacks upon him, (and there were many, either open or covert) into the channel of banter or practical joke (giving pain while assuming the aspect of mere fun) rather than into a more serious and determined hostility. But my endeavors on this head were by no means uniformly successful, even when my plans were the most wittily concocted; for my namesake had much about him, in character, of that unassuming and quiet austerity which, while enjoying the poignancy of its own jokes, has no heel of Achilles in itself, and absolutely refuses to be laughed at. I could find, indeed, but one vulnerable point, and that, lying in a personal peculiarity, arising, perhaps, from constitutional disease, would have been spared by any antagonist less at his wit's end than myself;—my rival had a weakness in the facial or guttural organs, which precluded him from raising his voice at any time *above a very low whisper*. Of this defect I did not fail to take what poor advantage lay in my power.

Wilson's retaliations in kind were many; and there was one form of his practical wit that disturbed me beyond measure. How his sagacity first discovered at all that so petty a thing would vex me, is a question I never could solve; but having discovered, he habitually practised the annoyance. I had always felt aversion to my uncourtly patronymic, and its very common, if not plebeian prænomen. The words were venom in my ears; and when, upon the day of my arrival, a second William Wilson came also to the academy, I felt angry with him for bearing the name, and doubly disgusted with the name because a stranger bore it, who would be the cause of its two-fold repetition, who would be constantly in my presence, and whose concerns, in the ordinary routine of the school business, must inevitably, on account of the detestable coincidence, be often confounded with my own.

The feeling of vexation thus engendered grew stronger with every circumstance tending to show resemblance, moral or physical, between my rival and myself. I had not then discovered the remarkable fact that we were of the same age; but I saw that we were of the same height, and I perceived that we were even singularly alike in general contour of person and outline of feature. I was galled, too, by the rumor touching a relationship, which had grown current in the upper forms. In a word, nothing could more seriously disturb me, (although I scrupulously concealed such disturbance), than any allusion to a similarity of mind, person, or condition existing between us. But, in truth, I had no reason to believe that (with the exception of the matter of relationship, and in the case of Wilson himself), this similarity had ever been made a subject of comment, or even observed at all by our schoolfellows. That *he* observed it in all its bearings, and as fixedly as I, was apparent; but that he could discover in such circumstances so fruitful a field of annoyance, can only be attributed, as I said before, to his more than ordinary penetration.

His cue, which was to perfect an imitation of myself, lay both in words and in actions; and most admirably did he play his part. My dress it was an easy matter to copy; my gait and general manner were without difficulty, appropriated; in spite of his constitutional defect, even my voice did not escape him. My louder tones were, of course, unattempted, but then the key,—it was identical; *and his singular whisper, it grew the very echo of my own.*

How greatly this most exquisite portraiture harassed me (for it could not justly be termed a caricature), I will not now venture to describe. I had but one consolation—in the fact that the imitation, apparently, was noticed by myself alone, and that I had to endure only the knowing and strangely sarcastic smiles of my namesake himself. Satisfied with having produced in my bosom the intended effect, he seemed to chuckle in secret over the sting he had inflicted, and was characteristically disregardful of the public applause which the success of his witty endeavors might have so easily elicited. That the school, indeed, did not feel his design, perceive its accomplishment, and participate in his sneer, was, for many anxious months, a riddle I could not resolve. Perhaps the *gradation* of his copy rendered it not readily perceptible; or, more possibly, I owed my security to the masterly air of the copyist, who, disdaining the letter (which in a painting is all the obtuse can see), gave but the full spirit of his original for my individual contemplation and chagrin.

I have already more than once spoken of the disgusting air of patronage which he assumed toward me, and of his frequent officious interference with my will. This interference often took the ungracious character of advice; advice not openly given, but hinted or insinuated. I received it with a repugnance which gained strength as I grew in years. Yet, at this distant day, let me do him the simple justice to acknowledge that I can recall no occasion when the suggestions of my rival were on the side of those errors or follies so usual to his immature age and seeming inexperience; that his moral sense, at least, if not his general talents and worldly wisdom, was far keener than my own; and that I might, to-day, have been a better and thus a happier man, had I less frequently rejected the counsels embodied in those meaning whispers which I then but too cordially hated and too bitterly despised.

As it was I at length grew restive in the extreme under his distasteful supervision, and daily resented more and more openly, what I considered his intolerable arrogance. I have said that, in the first years of our connection as schoolmates, my feelings in regard to him might have been easily ripened into friendship; but, in the latter months of my residence at the academy, although the intrusion of his ordinary manner had, beyond doubt, in some measure, abated, my sentiments, in nearly similar proportion, partook very much of positive hatred. Upon one occasion he saw this, I think, and afterward avoided, or made a show of avoiding me.

It was about the same period, if I remember aright, that, in an altercation of violence with him, in which he was more than usually thrown off his guard, and spoke and acted with an openness of demeanor rather foreign to his nature, I discovered, or fancied I discovered, in his accent, in his air, and general appearance, a something which first startled, and then deeply interested me, by bringing to mind dim visions of my earliest infancy—wild, confused, and thronging memories of a time when memory herself was yet unborn. I cannot better describe the sensation which oppressed me, than by saying that I could with difficulty shake off the belief of my having been acquainted with the being who stood before me, at some epoch very long ago—some point of the past even infinitely remote. The delusion, however, faded rapidly as it came; and I mention it at all but to define the day of the last conversation I there held with my singular namesake.

The huge old house, with its countless sub-divisions, had several large chambers communicating with each other, where slept the greater number of the students. There were, however (as must necessarily happen in a building so awkwardly planned), many little nooks or recesses, the odds and ends of the structure; and these the economic ingenuity of Dr. Bransby had also fitted up as dormitories; although, being the merest closets, they were capable of accommodating but a single individual. One of these small apartments was occupied by Wilson.

One night, about the close of my fifth year at the school, and immediately after the altercation just mentioned, finding every one wrapped in sleep, I arose from bed, and, lamp in hand, stole through a wilderness of narrow passages, from my own bedroom to that of my rival. I had long been plotting one of those ill-natured pieces of practical wit at his expense in which I had hitherto been so uniformly unsuccessful. It was my intention, now, to put my scheme in operation and I resolved to make him feel the whole extent of the malice with which I was imbued. Having reached his closet, I noiselessly entered, leaving the lamp, with a shade over it, on the outside. I advanced a step and listened to the sound of his tranquil breathing. Assured of his being asleep, I returned, took the light, and with it again approached the bed. Close curtains were around it, which, in the prosecution of my plan, I slowly and quietly withdrew, when the bright rays fell vividly upon the sleeper, and my eyes at the same moment, upon his countenance. I looked;—and a numbness, an iciness of feeling instantly pervaded my frame. My breast heaved, my knees tottered, my whole spirit became possessed with an abjectless yet intolerable horror. Gasping for breath, I lowered the lamp in still nearer proximity to the face. Were these—*these* the lineaments of William Wilson? I saw, indeed, that they were his, but I shook as if with a fit of the ague, in fancying they were not. What *was* there about them to confound me in this manner? I gazed;—while my brain reeled with a multitude of incoherent thoughts. Not thus he appeared—assuredly not *thus*—in the vivacity of his waking hours. The same name! the same contour of person! the same day of arrival at the academy! And then his dogged and meaningless imitation of my gait, my voice, my habits, and my manner! Was it, in truth, within the bounds of human possibility, that *what I now saw* was the result, merely, of the habitual practise of this sarcastic imitation? Awe-stricken, and with a creeping shudder, I extinguished the lamp, passed silently from the chamber, and left, at once, the halls of that old academy, never to enter them again.

After a lapse of some months, spent at home in mere idleness, I found myself a student at Eton. The brief interval had been sufficient to enfeeble my remembrance of the events at Dr. Bransby's, or at least to effect a material change in the nature of the feelings with which I remembered them. The truth—the tragedy—of the drama was no more. I could now find room to doubt the evidence of my senses; and seldom called up the subject at all but with wonder at the extent of human credulity, and a smile at the vivid force of the imagination which I hereditarily possessed. Neither was this species of skepticism likely to be diminished by the character of the life I led at Eton. The vortex of thoughtless folly into which I there so immediately and so recklessly plunged, washed away all but the froth of my past hours, ingulfed at once every solid or serious impression, and left to memory only the veriest levities of a former existence.

I do not wish, however, to trace the course of my miserable profligacy here —a profligacy which set at defiance the laws, while it eluded the vigilance of the institution. Three years of folly, passed without profit, had but given me rooted habits of vice, and added, in a somewhat unusual degree, to my bodily stature, when, after a week of soulless dissipation, I invited a small party of the most dissolute students to a secret carousal in my chambers. We met at a late hour of the night; for our debaucheries were to be faithfully protracted until morning. The wine flowed freely, and there were not wanting other and perhaps more dangerous seductions; so that the gray dawn had already faintly appeared in the east while our delirious extravagance was at its height. Madly flushed with cards and intoxication, I was in the act of insisting upon a toast of more than wonted profanity, when my attention was suddenly diverted by the violent, although partial, unclosing of the door of the apartment, and by the eager voice of a servant from without. He said that some person, apparently in great haste, demanded to speak with me in the hall.

Wildly excited with wine, the unexpected interruption rather delighted than surprised me. I staggered forward at once, and a few steps brought me to the vestibule of the building. In this low and small room there hung no lamp; and now no light at all was admitted, save that of the exceedingly feeble dawn which made its way through the semi-circular window. As I put my foot over the threshold, I became aware of the figure of a youth about my own height, and habited in a white kerseymere morning frock, cut in the novel fashion of the one I myself wore at the moment. This the faint light enabled me to perceive; but the features of his face I could not distinguish. Upon my entering, he strode hurriedly up to me, and, seizing me by the arm with a gesture of petulant impatience, whispered the words "William Wilson" in my ear.

I grew perfectly sober in an instant.

There was that in the manner of the stranger, and in the tremulous shake of his uplifted finger, as he held it between my eyes and the light, which filled me with unqualified amazement; but it was not this which had so violently moved me. It was the pregnancy of solemn admonition in the singular, low, hissing utterance; and, above all, it was the character, the tone, *the key,* of those few, simple, and familiar, yet *whispered* syllables, which came with a thousand thronging memories of by-gone days, and struck upon my soul with the shock of a galvanic battery. Ere I could recover the use of my senses he was gone.

Although this event failed not of a vivid effect upon my disordered imagination, yet was it evanescent as vivid. For some weeks, indeed, I busied myself in earnest enquiry, or was wrapped in a cloud of morbid speculation. I did not pretend to disguise from my perception the identity of the singular individual who thus perseveringly interfered with my affairs, and harassed me with his insinuated counsel. But who and what was this Wilson?—and whence came he?—and what were his purposes? Upon neither of these points could I be satisfied—merely ascertaining, in regard to him, that a sudden accident in his family had caused his removal from Dr. Bransby's academy on the afternoon of the day in which I myself had eloped. But in a brief period I ceased to think upon the subject, my attention being all absorbed in a contemplated departure for Oxford. Thither I soon went, the uncalculating vanity of my parents furnishing me with an outfit and annual establishment, which would enable me to indulge at will in the luxury already so dear to my heart—to vie in profuseness of expenditure with the haughtiest heirs of the wealthiest earldoms in Great Britain.

Excited by such appliances to vice, my constitutional temperament broke forth with redoubled ardor, and I spurned even the common restraints of decency in the mad infatuation of my revels. But it were absurd to pause in the detail of my extravagance. Let it suffice, that among spendthrifts I out-Heroded Herod, and that, giving name to a multitude of novel follies, I added no brief appendix to the long catalogue of vices then usual in the most dissolute university in Europe.

It could hardly be credited, however, that I had, even here, so utterly fallen from the gentlemanly estate, as to seek acquaintance with the vilest arts of the gambler by profession, and, having become an adept in his despicable science, to practice it habitually as a means of increasing my already enormous income at the expense of the weak-minded among my fellow-collegians. Such, nevertheless, was the fact. And the very enormity of this offence against all manly and honorable sentiment proved, beyond doubt, the main if not the sole reason of the impunity with which it was committed. Who, indeed, among my most abandoned associates, would not rather have disputed the clearest evidence of his senses, than have suspected of such courses, the gay, the frank, the generous William Wilson—the noblest and most liberal commoner at Oxford—him whose follies (said his parasites) were but the follies of youth and unbridled fancy—whose errors but inimitable whim—whose darkest vice but a careless and dashing extravagance?

I had been now two years successfully busied in this way, when there came to the university a young *parvenu* nobleman, Glendenning—rich, said report, as Herodes Atticus—his riches, too, as easily acquired. I soon found him of weak intellect, and, of course, marked him as a fitting subject for my skill. I frequently engaged him in play, and contrived, with the gambler's usual art, to let him win considerable sums, the more effectually to entangle him in my snares. At length, my schemes being ripe, I met him (with the full-intention that this meeting should be final and decisive) at the chambers of a fellow-commoner (Mr. Preston), equally intimate with both, but who, to do him justice, entertained not even a remote suspicion of my design. To give this a better coloring, I had contrived to have assembled a party of some eight or ten, and was solicitously careful that the introduction of cards should appear accidental, and originate in the proposal of my contemplated dupe himself. To be brief upon a vile topic, none of the low finesse was omitted, so customary upon similar occasions, that it is a just matter for wonder how any are still found so besotted as to fall its victim.

We had protracted our sitting far into the night, and I had at length effected the manœuvre of getting Glendenning as my sole antagonist. The game, too, was my favorite *écarte*. The rest of the company, interested in the extent of our play, had abandoned their own cards, and were standing around us as spectators. The *parvenu,* who had been induced by my artifices in the early part of the evening, to drink deeply, now shuffled, dealt, or played, with a wild nervousness of manner for which his intoxication, I thought, might partially, but could not altogether account. In a very short period he had become my debtor to a large amount, when, having taken a long draught of port, he did precisely what I had been coolly anticipating— he proposed to double our already extravagant stakes. With a well-feigned show of reluctance, and not until after my repeated refusal had seduced him into some angry words which gave a color of *pique* to my compliance, did I finally comply. The result, of course, did but prove how entirely the prey was in my toils: in less than an hour he had quadrupled his debt. For some time his countenance had been losing the florid tinge lent it by the wine; but now, to my astonishment, I perceived that it had grown to a pallor truly fearful. I say, to my astonishment. Glendenning had been represented to my eager inquiries as immeasurably wealthy; and the sums which he had as yet lost, although in themselves vast, could not, I supposed, very seriously annoy, much less so violently affect him. That he was overcome by the wine just swallowed, was the idea which most readily presented itself; and, rather with a view to the preservation of my own character in the eyes of my associates, than from any less interested motive, I was about to insist, peremptorily, upon a discontinuance of the play, when some expressions at my elbow from among the company, and an ejaculation evincing utter despair on the part of Glendenning, gave me to understand that I had effected his total ruin under circumstances which, rendering him an object for the pity of all, should have protected him from the ill offices even of a fiend.

What now might have been my conduct it is difficult to say. The pitiable condition of my dupe had thrown an air of embarrassed gloom over all; and, for some moments, a profound silence was maintained, during which I could not help feeling my cheeks tingle with the many burning glances of scorn or reproach cast upon me by the less abandoned of the party. I will even own that an intolerable weight of anxiety was for a brief instant lifted from my bosom by the sudden and extraordinary interruption which ensued. The wide, heavy folding doors of the apartment were all at once thrown open, to their full extent, with a vigorous and rushing impetuosity that extinguished, as if by magic, every candle in the room. Their light in dying, enabled us just to perceive that a stranger had entered, about my own height, and closely muffled in a cloak. The darkness, however, was not total; and we could only *feel* that he was standing in our midst. Before any one of us could recover from the extreme astonishment into which this rudeness had thrown all, we heard the voice of the intruder.

"Gentlemen," he said, in a low, distinct, and never-to-be-forgotten *whisper* which thrilled to the very marrow of my bones, "gentlemen, I make an apology for this behavior, because in thus behaving, I am fulfilling a duty. You are, beyond doubt, uninformed of the true character of the person who has to-night won at *écarte* a large sum of money from Lord Glendenning. I will therefore put you upon an expeditious and decisive plan of obtaining this very necessary information. Please to examine, at your leisure, the inner linings of the cuff of his left sleeve, and the several little packages which may be found in the somewhat capacious pockets of his embroidered morning wrapper."

While he spoke, so profound was the stillness that one might have heard a pin drop upon the floor. In ceasing, he departed at once, and as abruptly as he had entered. Can I—shall I describe my sensations? Must I say that I felt all the horrors of the damned? Most assuredly I had a little time for reflection. Many hands roughly seized me upon the spot, and lights were immediately reproduced. A search ensued. In the lining of my sleeve were found all the court cards essential in *ecarte,* and, in the pockets of my wrapper, a number of packs, fac-similes of those used at our sittings, with the single exception that mine were of the species called, technically, *arron-dees;* the honors being slightly convex at the sides. In this disposition, the dupe who cuts, as customary, at the length of the pack, will invariably find that he cuts his antagonist an honor; while the gambler, cutting at the breadth, will, as certainly, cut nothing for his victim which may count in the records of the game.

Any burst of indignation upon this discovery would have affected me less than the silent contempt, or the sarcastic composure, with which it was received.

"Mr. Wilson," said our host, stooping to remove from beneath his feet an exceedingly luxurious cloak of rare furs, "Mr. Wilson, this is your property." (The weather was cold; and, upon quitting my own room, I had thrown a cloak over my dressing wrapper, putting it off upon reaching the scene of play.) "I presume it is supererogatory to seek here (eyeing the folds of the garment with a bitter smile) for any farther evidence of your skill. Indeed, we have had enough. You will see the necessity, I hope, of quitting Oxford— at all events, of quitting instantly my chambers."

Abased, humbled to the dust as I then was, it is probable that I should have resented this galling language by immediate personal violence, had not my whole attention been at the moment arrested by a fact of the most startling character. The cloak which I had worn was of a rare description of fur; how rare, how extravagantly costly, I shall not venture to say. Its fashion, too, was of my own fantastic invention; for I was fastidious to an absurd degree of coxcombry, in matters of this frivolous nature. When, therefore, Mr. Preston reached me that which he had picked up upon the floor, and near the folding-doors of the apartment, it was with an astonishment nearly bordering upon terror, that I perceived my own already hanging on my arm, (where I had no doubt unwittingly placed it,) and that the one presented me was but its exact counterpart in every, in even the minutest possible particular. The singular being who had so disastrously exposed me, had been muffled, I remembered, in a cloak; and none had been worn at all by any of the members of our party, with the exception of myself. Retaining some presence of mind, I took the one offered me by Preston; placed it, unnoticed, over my own; left the apartment with a resolute scowl of defiance; and, next morning ere dawn of day, commenced a hurried journey from Oxford to the continent, in a perfect agony of horror and of shame.

I fled in vain. My evil destiny pursued me as if in exultation, and proved, indeed, that the exercise of its mysterious dominion had as yet only begun. Scarcely had I set foot in Paris, ere I had fresh evidence of the detestable interest taken by this Wilson in my concerns. Years flew, while I experienced no relief. Villain!—at Rome, with how untimely, yet with how spectral an officiousness, stepped he in between me and my ambition! at Vienna, too—at Berlin—and at Moscow! Where, in truth, had I *not* bitter cause to curse him within my heart? From his inscrutable tyranny did I at length flee, panic-stricken, as from a pestilence; and to the very ends of the earth *I fled in vain.*

And again, and again, in secret communion with my own spirit, would I demand the questions "Who is he?—whence came he?—and what are his objects?" But no answer was there found. And now I scrutinized, with a minute scrutiny, the forms, and the methods, and the leading traits of his impertinent supervision. But even here there was very little upon which to base a conjecture. It was noticeable, indeed, that, in no one of the multiplied instances in which he had of late crossed my path, had he so crossed it except to frustrate those schemes, or to disturb those actions, which, if fully carried out, might have resulted in bitter mischief. Poor justification this, in truth, for an authority so imperiously assumed! Poor indemnity for natural rights of self-agency so pertinaciously, so insultingly denied!

I had also been forced to notice that my tormentor, for a very long period of time, (while scrupulously and with miraculous dexterity maintaining his whim of an identity of apparel with myself,) had so contrived it, in the execution of his varied interference with my will, that I saw not, at any moment, the features of his face. Be Wilson what he might, *this,* at least, was but the veriest of affectation, or of folly. Could he, for an instant, have supposed that, in my admonisher at Eton—in the destroyer of my honor at Oxford,—in him who thwarted my ambition at Rome, my revenge at Paris, my passionate love at Naples, or what he falsely termed my avarice in Egypt, —that in this, my arch-enemy and evil genius, I could fail to recognize the William Wilson of my school-boy days,—the name-sake, the companion, the rival,—the hated and dreaded rival at Dr. Bransby's? Impossible!—But let me hasten to the last eventful scene of the drama.

Thus far I had succumbed supinely to this imperious domination. The sentiment of deep awe with which I habitually regarded the elevated character, the majestic wisdom, the apparent omnipresence and omnipotence of Wilson, added to a feeling of even terror, with which certain other traits in his nature and assumptions inspired me, had operated, hitherto, to impress me with an idea of my own utter weakness and helplessness, and to suggest an implicit, although bitterly reluctant submission to his arbitrary will. But, of late days, I had given myself up entirely to wine; and its maddening influence upon my hereditary temper rendered me more and more impatient of control. I began to murmur,—to hesitate,—to resist. And was it only fancy which induced me to believe that, with the increase of my own firmness, that of my tormentor underwent a proportional diminution? Be this as it may, I now began to feel the inspiration of a burning hope, and at length nurtured in my secret thoughts a stern and desperate resolution that I would submit no longer to be enslaved.

It was at Rome, during the Carnival of 18—, that I attended a masquerade in the palazzo of the Neapolitan Duke Di Broglio. I had indulged more freely than usual in the excesses of the wine-table; and now the suffocating atmosphere of the crowded rooms irritated me beyond endurance. The difficulty, too, of forcing my way through the mazes of the company contributed not a little to the ruffling of my temper; for I was anxiously seeking (let me not say with what unworthy motive) the young, the gay, the beautiful wife of the aged and doting Di Broglio. With a too unscrupulous confidence she had previously communicated to me the secret of the costume in which she would be habited, and now, having caught a glimpse of her person, I was hurrying to make my way into her presence. At this moment I felt a light hand placed upon my shoulder, and that ever-remembered, low, damnable *whisper* within my ear.

In an absolute frenzy of wrath, I turned at once upon him who had thus interrupted me, and seized him violently by the collar. He was attired, as I had expected, in a costume altogether similar to my own; wearing a Spanish cloak of blue velvet, begirt about the waist with a crimson belt sustaining a rapier. A mask of black silk entirely covered his face.

"Scoundrel!" I said, in a voice husky with rage, while every syllable I uttered seemed as new fuel to my fury; "scoundrel! impostor! accursed villain! you shall not—you *shall not* dog me unto death! Follow me, or I stab you where you stand!"—and I broke my way from the ball-room into a small ante-chamber adjoining, dragging him unresistingly with me as I went.

Upon entering, I thrust him furiously from me. He staggered against the wall, while I closed the door with an oath, and commanded him to draw. He hesitated but for an instant; then, with a slight sigh, drew in silence, and put himself upon his defence.

The contest was brief indeed. I was frantic with every species of wild excitement, and felt within my single arm the energy and power of a multitude. In a few seconds I forced him by sheer strength against the wainscotting, and thus, getting him at mercy, plunged my sword, with brute ferocity, repeatedly through and through his bosom.

At that instant some person tried the latch of the door. I hastened to prevent an intrusion, and then immediately returned to my dying antagonist. But what human language can adequately portray *that* astonishment, *that* horror which possessed me at the spectacle then presented to view? The brief moment in which I averted my eyes had been sufficient to produce, apparently, a material change in the arrangements at the upper or farther end of the room. A large mirror,—so at first it seemed to me in my confusion—now stood where none had been perceptible before; and as I stepped up to it in extremity of terror, mine own image, but with features all pale and dabbled in blood, advanced to meet me with a feeble and tottering gait.

Thus it appeared, I say, but was not. It was my antagonist—it was Wilson, who then stood before me in the agonies of his dissolution. His mask and cloak lay, where he had thrown them, upon the floor. Not a thread in all his raiment—not a line in all the marked and singular lineaments of his face which was not, even in the most absolute identity, *mine own!*

It was Wilson; but he spoke no longer in a whisper, and I could have fancied that I myself was speaking while he said:

"*You have conquered, and I yield. Yet henceforward art thou also dead— dead to the World, to Heaven, and to Hope! In me didst thou exist—and, in my death, see by this image, which is thine own, how utterly thou hast murdered thyself.*"

NATHANIEL HAWTHORNE

Young Goodman Brown

YOUNG GOODMAN BROWN came forth at sunset, into the street of Salem village, but put his head back, after crossing the threshold, to exchange a parting kiss with his young wife. And Faith, as the wife was aptly named, thrust her own pretty head into the street, letting the wind play with the pink ribbons of her cap, while she called to Goodman Brown.

"Dearest heart," whispered she, softly and rather sadly, when her lips were close to his ear, "pr'ythee, put off your journey until sunrise, and sleep in your own bed to-night. A lone woman is troubled with such dreams and such thoughts, that she's afeard of herself, sometimes. Pray, tarry with me this night, dear husband, of all nights in the year!"

"My love and my Faith," replied young Goodman Brown, "of all nights in the year, this one night must I tarry away from thee. My journey, as thou callest it, forth and back again, must needs be done 'twixt now and sunrise. What, my sweet, pretty wife, dost thou doubt me already, and we but three months married!"

"Then God bless you!" said Faith, with the pink ribbons, "and may you find all well, when you come back."

"Amen!" cried Goodman Brown. "Say thy prayers, dear Faith, and go to bed at dusk, and no harm will come to thee."

So they parted; and the young man pursued his way, until, being about to turn the corner by the meeting-house, he looked back and saw the head of Faith still peeping after him, with a melancholy air, in spite of her pink ribbons.

"Poor little Faith!" thought he, for his heart smote him. "What a wretch am I, to leave her on such an errand! She talks of dreams, too. Methought, as she spoke, there was trouble in her face, as if a dream had warned her what work is to be done to-night. But, no, no! 'twould kill her to think it.

Well; she's a blessed angel on earth; and after this one night, I'll cling to her skirts and follow her to Heaven.

With this excellent resolve for the future, Goodman Brown felt himself justified in making more haste on his present evil purpose. He had taken a dreary road, darkened by all the gloomiest trees of the forest, which barely stood aside to let the narrow path creep through, and closed immediately behind. It was all as lonely as could be; and there is this peculiarity in such a solitude, that the traveller knows not who may be concealed by the innumerable trunks and the thick boughs overhead; so that, with lonely footsteps, he may yet be passing through an unseen multitude.

"There may be a devilish Indian behind every tree," said Goodman Brown to himself; and he glanced fearfully behind him, as he added, "What if the devil himself should be at my very elbow!"

His head being turned back, he passed a crook of the road, and looking forward again, beheld the figure of a man, in grave and decent attire, seated at the foot of an old tree. He arose, at Goodman Brown's approach, and walked onward, side by side with him.

"You are late, Goodman Brown," said he. "The clock of the Old South was striking, as I came through Boston; and that is full fifteen minutes agone."

"Faith kept me back awhile," replied the young man, with a tremor in his voice, caused by the sudden appearance of his companion, though not wholly unexpected.

It was now deep dusk in the forest, and deepest in that part of it where these two were journeying. As nearly as could be discerned, the second traveller was about fifty years old, apparently in the same rank of life as Goodman Brown, and bearing a considerable resemblance to him, though perhaps more in expression than features. Still, they might have been taken for father and son. And yet, though the elder person was as simply clad as the younger, and as simple in manner too, he had an indescribable air of one who knew the world, and would not have felt abashed at the governor's dinner-table, or in King William's court, were it possible that his affairs should call him thither. But the only thing about him, that could be fixed upon as remarkable, was his staff, which bore the likeness of a great black snake, so curiously wrought, that it might almost be seen to twist and wriggle itself like a living serpent. This, of course, must have been an ocular deception, assisted by the uncertain light.

"Come, Goodman Brown!" cried his fellow-traveller, "this is a dull pace for the beginning of a journey. Take my staff, if you are so soon weary."

"Friend," said the other, exchanging his slow pace for a full stop, "having kept covenant by meeting thee here, it is my purpose now to return whence I came. I have scruples, touching the matter thou wot'st of."

"Sayest thou so?" replied he of the serpent, smiling apart. "Let us walk on, nevertheless, reasoning as we go, and if I convince thee not, thou shalt turn back. We are but a little way in the forest, yet."

"Too far, too far!" exclaimed the goodman, unconsciously resuming his walk. "My father never went into the woods on such an errand, nor his father before him. We have been a race of honest men and good Christians, since the days of the martyrs. And shall I be the first of the name of Brown, that ever took this path and kept"—

"Such company, thou wouldst say," observed the elder person, interrupting his pause. "Well said, Goodman Brown! I have been as well acquainted with your family as with ever a one among the Puritans; and that's no trifle to say. I helped your grandfather, the constable, when he lashed the Quaker woman so smartly through the streets of Salem. And it was I that brought your father a pitch-pine knot, kindled at my own hearth, to set fire to an Indian village, in king Philip's war. They were my good friends, both; and many a pleasant walk have we had along this path, and returned merrily after midnight. I would fain be friends with you, for their sake."

"If it be as thou sayest," replied Goodman Brown, "I marvel they never spoke of these matters. Or, verily, I marvel not, seeing that the least rumor of the sort would have driven them from New England. We are a people of prayer, and good works to boot, and abide no such wickedness."

"Wickedness or not," said the traveller with the twisted staff, "I have a very general acquaintance here in New England. The deacons of many a church have drunk the communion wine with me; the selectmen, of divers towns, make me their chairman; and a majority of the Great and General Court are firm supporters of my interest. The governor and I, too—but these are state secrets."

"Can this be so!" cried Goodman Brown, with a stare of amazement at his undisturbed companion. "Howbeit, I have nothing to do with the governor and council; they have their own ways, and are no rule for a simple husbandman like me. But, were I to go on with thee, how should I meet the eye of that good old man, our minister, at Salem village? Oh, his voice would make me tremble, both Sabbath-day and lecture-day!"

Thus far, the elder traveller had listened with due gravity, but now burst into a fit of irrepressible mirth, shaking himself so violently, that his snake-like staff actually seemed to wriggle in sympathy.

"Ha! ha! ha!" shouted he, again and again; then composing himself, "Well, go on, Goodman Brown, go on; but, prithee, don't kill me with laughing!"

"Well, then, to end the matter at once," said Goodman Brown, considerably nettled, "there is my wife, Faith. It would break her dear little heart; and I'd rather break my own!"

"Nay, if that be the case," answered the other, "e'en go thy ways, Goodman Brown. I would not, for twenty old women like the one hobbling before us, that Faith should come to any harm."

As he spoke, he pointed his staff at a female figure on the path, in whom Goodman Brown recognized a very pious and exemplary dame, who had taught him his catechism in youth, and was still his moral and spiritual adviser, jointly with the minister and Deacon Gookin.

"A marvel, truly, that Goody Cloyse should be so far in the wilderness, at night-fall!" said he. "But, with your leave, friend, I shall take a cut through the woods, until we have left this Christian woman behind. Being a stranger to you, she might ask whom I was consorting with, and whither I was going."

"Be it so," said his fellow-traveller. "Betake you to the woods, and let me keep the path."

Accordingly, the young man turned aside, but took care to watch his companion, who advanced softly along the road, until he had come within a staff's length of the old dame. She, meanwhile, was making the best of her way, with singular speed for so aged a woman, and mumbling some indistinct words, a prayer, doubtless, as she went. The traveller put forth his staff, and touched her withered neck with what seemed the serpent's tail.

"The devil!" screamed the pious old lady.

"Then Goody Cloyse knows her old friend?" observed the traveller, confronting her, and leaning on his writhing stick.

"Ah, forsooth, and is it your worship, indeed?" cried the good dame. "Yea, truly it is, and in the very image of my old gossip, Goodman Brown, the grandfather of the silly fellow that now is. But, would your worship believe it? my broomstick hath strangely disappeared, stolen, as I suspect, by that unhanged witch, Goody Cory, and that, too, when I was all anointed with the juice of smallage and cinque-foil and wolf's-bane"—

"Mingled with fine wheat and the fat of a new-born babe," said the shape of old Goodman Brown.

"Ah, your worship knows the recipe," cried the old lady, cackling aloud. "So, as I was saying, being all ready for the meeting, and no horse to ride on, I made up my mind to foot it; for they tell me, there is a nice young man to be taken into communion to-night. But now your good worship will lend me your arm, and we shall be there in a twinkling."

"That can hardly be," answered her friend. "I may not spare you my arm, Goody Cloyse, but here is my staff, if you will."

So saying, he threw it down at her feet, where, perhaps, it assumed life, being one of the rods which its owner had formerly lent to the Egyptian Magi. Of this fact, however, Goodman Brown could not take cognizance. He had cast up his eyes in astonishment, and looking down again, beheld neither Goody Cloyse nor the serpentine staff, but his fellow-traveller alone, who waited for him as calmly as if nothing had happened.

"That old woman taught me my catechism!" said the young man; and there was a world of meaning in this simple comment.

They continued to walk onward, while the elder traveller exhorted his companion to make good speed and persevere in the path, discoursing so aptly, that his arguments seemed rather to spring up in the bosom of his auditor, than to be suggested by himself. As they went, he plucked a branch of maple, to serve for a walking-stick, and began to strip it of the twigs and little boughs, which were wet with evening dew. The moment his fingers touched them, they became strangely withered and dried up, as with a week's sunshine. Thus the pair proceeded, at a good free pace, until suddenly, in a gloomy hollow of the road, Goodman Brown sat himself down on the stump of a tree, and refused to go any farther.

"Friend," said he, stubbornly, "my mind is made up. Not another step will I budge on this errand. What if a wretched old woman do choose to go to the devil, when I thought she was going to Heaven! Is that any reason why I should quit my dear Faith, and go after her?"

"You will think better of this by-and-by," said his acquaintance, composedly. "Sit here and rest yourself awhile; and when you feel like moving again, there is my staff to help you along."

Without more words, he threw his companion the maple stick, and was as speedily out of sight as if he had vanished into the deepening gloom. The young man sat a few moments by the road-side, applauding himself greatly, and thinking with how clear a conscience he should meet the minister, in his morning-walk, nor shrink from the eye of good old Deacon Gookin. And what calm sleep would be his, that very night, which was to have been spent so wickedly, but purely and sweetly now, in the arms of Faith! Amidst these pleasant and praiseworthy meditations, Goodman Brown heard the tramp of horses along the road, and deemed it advisable to conceal himself within the verge of the forest, conscious of the guilty purpose that had brought him thither, though now so happily turned from it.

On came the hoof-tramps and the voices of the riders, two grave old voices, conversing soberly as they drew near. These mingled sounds appeared to pass along the road, within a few yards of the young man's hiding-place; but owing, doubtless, to the depth of the gloom, at that particular spot, neither the travellers nor their steeds were visible. Though their figures brushed the small boughs by the way-side, it could not be seen that they intercepted, even for a moment, the faint gleam from the strip of bright sky, athwart which they must have passed. Goodman Brown alternately crouched and stoop on tip-toe, pulling aside the branches, and thrusting forth his head as far as he durst, without discerning so much as a shadow. It vexed him the more, because he could have sworn, were such a thing possible, that he recognized the voices of the minister and Deacon Gookin, jogging along quietly, as they were wont to do, when bound to some ordination or ecclesiastical council. While yet within hearing, one of the riders stopped to pluck a switch.

"Of the two, reverend Sir," said the voice like the deacon's, "I had rather miss an ordination-dinner than to-night's meeting. They tell me that some of our community are to be here from Falmouth and beyond, and others from Connecticut and Rhode Island; besides several of the Indian powows, who, after their fashion, know almost as much deviltry as the best of us. Moreover, there is a goodly young woman to be taken into communion."

"Mighty well, Deacon Gookin!" replied the solemn old tones of the minister. "Spur up, or we shall be late. Nothing can be done, you know, until I get on the ground."

The hoofs clattered again, and the voices, talking so strangely in the empty air, passed on through the forest, where no church had ever been gathered, nor solitary Christian prayed. Whither then, could these holy men be journeying, so deep into the heathen wilderness? Young Goodman Brown caught hold of a tree, for support, being ready to sink down on the ground, faint and overburthened with the heavy sickness of his heart. He looked up to the sky, doubting whether there really was a Heaven above him. Yet, there was the blue arch, and the stars brightening in it.

"With Heaven above, and Faith below, I will yet stand firm against the devil!" cried Goodman Brown.

While he still gazed upward, into the deep arch of the firmament, and had lifted his hands to pray, a cloud, though no wind was stirring, hurried across the zenith, and hid the brightening stars. The blue sky was still visible, except directly overhead, where this black mass of cloud was sweeping swiftly northward. Aloft in the air, as if from the depths of the cloud, came a confused and doubtful sound of voices. Once, the listener fancied that he could distinguish the accents of town's-people of his own, men and women, both pious and ungodly, many of whom he had met at the communion-table, and had seen others rioting at the tavern. The next moment, so indistinct were the sounds, he doubted whether he had heard aught but the murmur of the old forest, whispering without a wind. Then came a stronger swell of those familiar tones, heard daily in the sunshine, at Salem village, but never, until now, from a cloud of night. There was one voice, of a young woman, uttering lamentations, yet with an uncertain sorrow, and entreating for some favor, which, perhaps, it would grieve her to obtain. And all the unseen multitude, both saints and sinners, seemed to encourage her onward.

"Faith!" shouted Goodman Brown, in a voice of agony and desperation; and the echoes of the forest mocked him, crying—"Faith! Faith!" as if bewildered wretches were seeking her, all through the wilderness.

The cry of grief, rage, and terror, was yet piercing the night, when the unhappy husband held his breath for a response. There was a scream, drowned immediately in a louder murmur of voices, fading into far-off laughter, as the dark cloud swept away, leaving the clear and silent sky above Goodman Brown. But something fluttered lightly down through the air, and caught on the branch of a tree. The young man seized it, and beheld a pink ribbon.

"My Faith is gone!" cried he, after one stupefied moment. "There is no good on earth; and sin is but a name. Come, devil! for to thee is this world given."

And maddened with despair, so that he laughed loud and long, did Goodman Brown grasp his staff and set forth again, at such a rate, that he seemed to fly along the forest-path, rather than to walk or run. The road grew wilder and drearier, and more faintly traced, and vanished at length, leaving him in the heart of the dark wilderness, still rushing onward, with the instinct that guides mortal man to evil. The whole forest was peopled with frightful sounds; the creaking of the trees, the howling of wild beasts, and the yell of Indians; while, sometimes the wind tolled like a distant church-bell, and sometimes gave a broad roar around the traveller, as if all Nature were laughing him to scorn. But he was himself the chief horror of the scene, and shrank not from its other horrors.

"Ha! ha! ha!" roared Goodman Brown, when the wind laughed at him. "Let us hear which will laugh loudest! Think not to frighten me with your deviltry! Come witch, come wizard, come Indian powow, come devil himself! and here comes Goodman Brown. You may as well fear him as he fear you!"

In truth, all through the haunted forest, there could be nothing more frightful than the figure of Goodman Brown. On he flew, among the black pines, brandishing his staff with frenzied gestures, now giving vent to an inspiration of horrid blasphemy, and now shouting forth such laughter, as set all the echoes of the forest laughing like demons around him. The fiend in his own shape is less hideous, than when he rages in the breast of man. Thus sped the demoniac on his course, until, quivering among the trees, he saw a red light before him, as when the felled trunks and branches of a clearing have been set on fire, and throw up their lurid blaze against the sky, at the hour of midnight. He paused, in a lull of the tempest that had driven him onward, and heard the swell of what seemed a hymn, rolling solemnly from a distance, with the weight of many voices. He knew the tune; It was a familiar one in the choir of the village meeting-house. The verse died heavily away, and was lengthened by a chorus, not of human voices, but of all the sounds of the benighted wilderness, pealing in awful harmony together. Goodman Brown cried out; and his cry was lost to his own ear, by its unison with the cry of the desert.

In the interval of silence, he stole forward, until the light glared full upon his eyes. At one extremity of an open space, hemmed in by the dark wall of the forest, arose a rock, bearing some rude, natural resemblances either to an altar or a pulpit, and surrounded by four blazing pines, their tops a flame, their stems untouched, like candles at an evening meeting. The mass of foliage, that had overgrown the summit of the rock, was all on fire, blazing high into the night, and fitfully illuminating the whole field. Each pendant twig and leafy festoon was in a blaze. As the red light arose and fell, a numerous congregation alternately shone forth, then disappeared in shadow, and again grew, as it were, out of the darkness, peopling the heart of the solitary woods at once.

"A grave and dark-clad company!" quoth Goodman Brown.

In truth, they were such. Among them, quivering to-and-fro, between gloom and splendor, appeared faces that would be seen, next day, at the council-board of the province, and others which, Sabbath after Sabbath, looked devoutly heavenward, and benignantly over the crowded pews, from the holiest pulpits in the land. Some affirm, that the lady of the governor was there. At least, there were high dames well known to her, and wives of honored husbands, and widows, a great multitude, and ancient maidens, all of excellent repute, and fair young girls, who trembled lest their mothers should espy them. Either the sudden gleams of light, flashing over the obscure field, bedazzled Goodman Brown, or he recognized a score of the church-members of Salem village, famous for their especial sanctity. Good old Deacon Gookin had arrived, and waited at the skirts of that venerable saint, his reverend pastor. But, irreverently consorting with these grave, reputable, and pious people, these elders of the church, these chaste dames and dewy virgins, there were men of dissolute lives and women of spotted fame, wretches given over to all mean and filthy vice, and suspected even of horrid crimes. It was strange to see, that the good shrank not from the wicked, nor were the sinners abashed by the saints. Scattered, also, among their pale-faced enemies, were the Indian priests, or powows, who had often scared their native forest with more hideous incantations than any known to English witchcraft.

"But, where is Faith?" thought Goodman Brown; and, as hope came into his heart, he trembled.

Another verse of the hymn arose, a slow and mournful strain, such as the pious love, but joined to words which expressed all that our nature can conceive of sin, and darkly hinted at far more. Unfathomable to mere mortals is the lore of fiends. Verse after verse was sung, and still the chorus of the desert swelled between, like the deepest tone of a mighty organ. And, with the final peal of that dreadful anthem, there came a sound, as if the roaring wind, the rushing streams, the howling beasts, and every other voice of the unconverted wilderness, were mingling and according with the voice of guilty man, in homage to the prince of all. The four blazing pines threw up a loftier flame, and obscurely discovered shapes and visages of horror on the smoke-wreaths, above the impious assembly. At the same moment, the fire on the rock shot redly forth, and formed a glowing arch above its base, where now appeared a figure. With reverence be it spoken, the apparition bore no slight similitude, both in garb and manner, to some grave divine of the New England churches.

"Bring forth the converts!" cried a voice, that echoed through the field and rolled into the forest.

At the word, Goodman Brown stepped forth from the shadow of the trees, and approached the congregation, with whom he felt a loathful brotherhood, by the sympathy of all that was wicked in his heart. He could have well nigh sworn, that the shape of his own dead father beckoned him to advance, looking downward from a smoke-wreath, while a woman, with dim features of despair, threw out her hand to warn him back. Was it his mother? But he had no power to retreat one step, nor to resist, even in thought, when the minister and good old Deacon Gookin seized his arms, and led him to the blazing rock. Thither came also the slender form of a veiled female, led between Goody Cloyse, that pious teacher of the catechism, and Martha Carrier, who had received the devil's promise to be queen of hell. A rampant hag was she! And there stood the proselytes, beneath the canopy of fire.

"Welcome, my children," said the dark figure, "to the communion of your race! Ye have found, thus young, your nature and your destiny. My children, look behind you!"

They turned; and flashing forth, as it were, in a sheet of flame, the fiend-worshippers were seen; the smile of welcome gleamed darkly on every visage.

"There," resumed the sable form, "are all whom ye have reverenced from youth. Ye deemed them holier than yourselves, and shrank from your own sin, contrasting it with their lives of righteousness, and prayerful aspirations heavenward. Yet, here are they all, in my worshipping assembly! This night it shall be granted you to know their secret deeds; how hoary-bearded elders of the church have whispered wanton words to the young maids of their households; how many a woman, eager for widow's weeds, has given her husband a drink at bed-time, and let him sleep his last sleep in her bosom; how beardless youths have made haste to inherit their father's wealth; and how fair damsels—blush not, sweet ones!—have dug little graves in the garden, and bidden me, the sole guest, to an infant's funeral. By the sympathy of your human hearts for sin, ye shall scent out all the places—whether in church, bed-chamber, street, field, or forest—where crime has been committed, and shall exult to behold the whole earth one stain of guilt, one mighty blood-spot. Far more than this! It shall be yours to penetrate, in every bosom, the deep mystery of sin, the fountain of all wicked arts, and which inexhaustibly supplies more evil impulses than human power—than my power, at its utmost!—can make manifest in deeds. And now, my children, look upon each other."

They did so; and, by the blaze of the hell-kindled torches, the wretched man beheld his Faith, and the wife her husband, trembling before that unhallowed altar.

"Lo! there ye stand, my children," said the figure, in a deep and solemn tone, almost sad, with its despairing awfulness, as if his once angelic nature could yet mourn for our miserable race. "Depending upon one another's hearts, ye had still hoped that virtue were not all a dream! Now are ye undeceived!—Evil is the nature of mankind. Evil must be your only happiness. Welcome, again, my children, to the communion of your race!"

"Welcome!" repeated the fiend-worshippers, in one cry of despair and triumph.

And there they stood, the only pair, as it seemed, who were yet hesitating on the verge of wickedness, in this dark world. A basin was hollowed, naturally, in the rock. Did it contain water, reddened by the lurid light? or was it blood? or, perchance, a liquid flame? Herein did the Shape of Evil dip his hand, and prepare to lay the mark of baptism upon their foreheads, that they might be partakers of the mystery of sin, more conscious of the secret guilt of others, both in deed and thought, than they could now be of their own. The husband cast one look at his pale wife, and Faith at him. What polluted wretches would the next glance show them to each other, shuddering alike at what they disclosed and what they saw!

"Faith! Faith!" cried the husband. "Look up to Heaven, and resist the Wicked One!"

Whether Faith obeyed, he knew not. Hardly had he spoken, when he found himself amid calm night and solitude, listening to a roar of the wind, which died heavily away through the forest. He staggered against the rock, and felt it chill and damp, while a hanging twig, that had been all on fire, besprinkled his cheek with the coldest dew.

The next morning, young Goodman Brown came slowly into the street of Salem village, staring around him like a bewildered man. The good old minister was taking a walk along the graveyard, to get an appetite for breakfast and meditate his sermon, and bestowed a blessing, as he passed, on Goodman Brown. He shrank from the venerable saint, as if to avoid an anathema. Old Deacon Gookin was at domestic worship, and the holy words of his prayer were heard through the open window. "What God doth the wizard pray to?" quoth Goodman Brown. Goody Cloyse, that excellent old Christian, stood in the early sunshine, at her own lattice, catechising a little girl, who had brought her a pint of morning's milk. Goodman Brown snatched away the child, as from the grasp of the fiend himself. Turning the corner by the meeting-house, he spied the head of Faith, with the pink ribbons, gazing anxiously forth, and bursting into such joy at sight of him, that she skipt along the street, and almost kissed her husband before the whole village. But Goodman Brown looked sternly and sadly into her face, and passed on without a greeting.

Had Goodman Brown fallen asleep in the forest, and only dreamed a wild dream of a witch-meeting?

Be it so, if you will. But, alas! it was a dream of evil omen for young Goodman Brown. A stern, a sad, a darkly meditative, a distrustful, if not a desperate man, did he become, from the night of that fearful dream. On the Sabbath-day, when the congregation were singing a holy psalm, he could not listen, because an anthem of sin rushed loudly upon his ear, and drowned all the blessed strain. When the minister spoke from the pulpit, with power and fervid eloquence, and with his hand on the open bible, of the sacred truths of our religion, and of saint-like lives and trumphant deaths, and of future bliss or misery unutterable, then did Goodman Brown turn pale, dreading lest the roof should thunder down upon the grey blasphemer and his hearers. Often, awaking suddenly at midnight, he shrank from the bosom of Faith, and at morning or eventide, when the family knelt down at prayer, he scowled, and muttered to himself, and gazed sternly at his wife, and turned away. And when he had lived long, and was borne to his grave, a hoary corpse, followed by Faith, an aged woman, and children and grandchildren, a goodly procession, besides neighbors, not a few, they carved no hopeful verse upon his tombstone; for his dying hour was gloom.

NATHANIEL HAWTHORNE

The Celestial Railroad

Not a great while ago, passing through the gate of dreams, I visited that region of the earth in which lies the famous city of Destruction. It interested me much to learn that, by the public spirit of some of the inhabitants, a railroad has recently been established between this populous and flourishing town, and the Celestial City. Having a little time upon my hands, I resolved to gratify a liberal curiosity to make a trip thither. Accordingly, one fine morning, after paying my bill at the hotel, and directing the porter to stow my luggage behind a coach, I took my seat in the vehicle and set out for the Station-house. It was my good fortune to enjoy the company of a gentleman—one Mr. Smooth-it-away—who, though he had never actually visited the Celestial City, yet seemed as well acquainted with its laws, customs, policy, and statistics, as with those of the city of Destruction, of which he was a native townsman. Being, moreover, a director of the railroad corporation, and one of its largest stockholders, he had it in his power to give me all desirable information respecting that praiseworthy enterprise.

Our coach rattled out of the city, and, at a short distance from its outskirts, passed over a bridge, of elegant construction, but somewhat too slight, as I imagined, to sustain any considerable weight. On both sides lay an extensive quagmire, which could not have been more disagreeable either to sight or smell, had all the kennels of the earth emptied their pollution there.

"This," remarked Mr. Smooth-it-away, "is the famous Slough of Despond—a disgrace to all the neighborhood; and the greater, that it might so easily be converted into firm ground."

"I have understood," said I, "that efforts have been made for that purpose, from time immemorial. Bunyan mentions that above twenty thousand cartloads of wholesome instructions had been thrown in here, without effect."

"Very probably!—and what effect could be anticipated from such unsubstantial stuff?" cried Mr. Smooth-it-away. "You observe this convenient bridge. We obtained a sufficient foundation for it by throwing into the Slough some editions of books of morality, volumes of French philosophy and German rationalism, tracts, sermons, and essays of modern clergymen, extracts from Plato, Confucius, and various Hindoo sages, together with a few ingenious commentaries upon texts of Scripture—all of which, by some scientific process, have been converted into a mass like granite. The whole bog might be filled up with similar matter."

It really seemed to me, however, that the bridge vibrated and heaved up and down in a very formidable manner; and, spite of Mr. Smooth-it-away's testimony to the solidity of its foundation, I should be loth to cross it in a crowded omnibus; especially, if each passenger were encumbered with as heavy luggage as that gentleman and myself. Nevertheless, we got over without accident, and soon found ourselves at the Station-house. This very neat and spacious edifice is erected on the site of the little Wicket-gate, which formerly, as all old pilgrims will recollect, stood directly across the highway, and, by its inconvenient narrowness, was a great obstruction to the traveller of liberal mind and expansive stomach. The reader of John Bunyan will be glad to know, that Christian's old friend, Evangelist, who was accustomed to supply each pilgrim with a mystic roll, now presides at the ticket office. Some malicious persons, it is true, deny the identity of this reputable character with the Evangelist of old times, and even pretend to bring competent evidence of an imposture. Without involving myself in a dispute, I shall merely observe, that, so far as my experience goes, the square pieces of pasteboard, now delivered to passengers, are much more convenient and useful along the road, than the antique roll of parchment. Whether they will be as readily received at the gate of the Celestial City, I decline giving an opinion.

A large number of passengers were already at the Station-house, awaiting the departure of the cars. By the aspect and demeanor of these persons, it was easy to judge that the feelings of the community had undergone a very favorable change, in reference to the celestial pilgrimage. It would have done Bunyan's heart good to see it. Instead of a lonely and ragged man, with a huge burthen on his back, plodding along sorrowfully on foot, while the whole city hooted after him, here were parties of the first gentry and most respectable people in the neighborhood, setting forth towards the Celestial City, as cheerfully as if the pilgrimage were merely a summer tour. Among the gentlemen were characters of deserved eminence, magistrates, politicians, and men of wealth, by whose example religion could not but be greatly recommended to their meaner brethren. In the ladies' apartment, too, I rejoiced to distinguish some of those flowers of fashionable society, who are so well fitted to adorn the most elevated circles of the Celestial City. There was much pleasant conversation about the news of the day, topics of business, politics, or the lighter matters of amusement; while religion, though indubitably the main thing at heart, was thrown tastefully into the back-ground. Even an infidel would have heard little or nothing to shock his sensibility.

One great convenience of the new method of going on pilgrimage, I must not forget to mention. Our enormous burthens, instead of being carried on our shoulders, as had been the custom of old, were all snugly deposited in the baggage-car, and, as I was assured, would be delivered to their respective owners at the journey's end. Another thing, likewise, the benevolent reader will be delighted to understand. It may be remembered that there was an ancient feud between Prince Beelzebub and the keeper of the Wicket-Gate, and that the adherents of the former distinguished personage were accustomed to shoot deadly arrows at honest pilgrims, while knocking at the door. This dispute, much to the credit as well of the illustrious potentate above-mentioned, as of the worthy and enlightened Directors of the railroad, has been pacifically arranged, on the principle of mutual compromise. The Prince's subjects are now pretty numerously employed about the Station-house, some in taking care of the baggage, others in collecting fuel, feeding the engines, and such congenial occupations; and I can conscientiously affirm, that persons more attentive to their business, more willing to accommodate, or more generally agreeable to the passengers, are not to be found on any railroad. Every good heart must surely exult at so satisfactory an arrangement of an immemorial difficulty.

"Where is Mr. Great-heart?" inquired I. "Beyond a doubt, the Directors have engaged that famous old champion to be chief conductor on the railroad?"

"Why, no," said Mr. Smooth-it-away, with a dry cough. "He was offered the situation of brake-man; but, to tell you the truth, our friend Great-heart has grown preposterously stiff and narrow in his old age. He has so often guided pilgrims over the road, on foot, that he considers it a sin to travel in any other fashion. Besides, the old fellow had entered so heartily into the ancient feud with Prince Beelzebub, that he would have been perpetually at blows or ill language with some of the prince's subjects, and thus have embroiled us anew. So, on the whole, we were not sorry when honest Great-heart went off to the Celestial City in a huff, and left us at liberty to choose a more suitable and accommodating man. Yonder comes the conductor of the train. You will probably recognize him at once."

The engine at this moment took its station in advance of the cars, looking, I must confess, much more like a sort of mechanical demon that would hurry us to the infernal regions, than a laudable contrivance for smoothing our way to the Celestial City. On its top sat a personage almost enveloped in smoke and flame, which—not to startle the reader—appeared to gush from his own mouth and stomach, as well as from the engine's brazen abdomen.

"Do my eyes deceive me?" cried I. "What on earth is this! A living creature?—if so, he is own brother to the engine he rides upon!"

"Poh, poh, you are obtuse!" said Mr. Smooth-it-away, with a hearty laugh. "Don't you know Apollyon, Christian's old enemy, with whom he fought so fierce a battle in the Valley of Humiliation? He was the very fellow to manage the engine; and so we have reconciled him to the custom of going on pilgrimage, and engaged him as chief conductor."

"Bravo, bravo!" exclaimed I, with irrepressible enthusiasm, "this shows the liberality of the age; this proves, if anything can, that all musty prejudices are in a fair way to be obliterated. And how will Christian rejoice to hear of this happy transformation of his old antagonist! I promise myself great pleasure in informing him of it, when we reach the Celestial City."

The passengers being all comfortably seated, we now rattled away merrily, accomplishing a greater distance in ten minutes than Christian probably trudged over in a day. It was laughable while we glanced along, as it were, at the tail of a thunderbolt, to observe two dusty foot-travellers, in the old pilgrim-guise, with cockle-shell and staff, their mystic rolls of parchment in their hands, and their intolerable burthens on their backs. The preposterous obstinacy of these honest people, in persisting to groan and stumble along the difficult pathway, rather than take advantage of modern improvements, excited great mirth among our wiser brotherhood. We greeted the two pilgrims with many pleasant gibes and a roar of laughter; whereupon, they gazed at us with such woeful and absurdly compassionate visages, that our merriment grew tenfold more obstreperous. Apollyon, also, entered heartily into the fun, and contrived to flirt the smoke and flame of the engine, or of his own breath, into their faces, and envelope them in an atmosphere of scalding steam. These little practical jokes amused us mightily, and doubtless afforded the pilgrims the gratification of considering themselves martyrs.

At some distance from the railroad, Mr. Smooth-it-away pointed to a large, antique edifice, which, he observed, was a tavern of long standing, and had formerly been a noted stopping-place for pilgrims. In Bunyan's roadbook it is mentioned as the Interpreter's House.

"I have long had a curiosity to visit that old mansion," remarked I.

It is not one of our stations, as you perceive," said my companion. "The keeper was violently opposed to the railroad; and well he might be, as the track left his house of entertainment on one side, and thus was pretty certain to deprive him of all his reputable customers. But the foot-path still passes his door; and the old gentleman now and then receives a call from some simple traveller, and entertains him with fare as old-fashioned as himself."

Before our talk on this subject came to a conclusion, we were rushing by the place where Christian's burthen fell from his shoulders, at the sight of the Cross. This served as a theme for Mr. Smooth-it-away, Mr. Live-for-the-world, Mr. Hide-sin-in-the-heart, Mr. Scaly-conscience, and a knot of gentlemen from the town of Shun-repentance, to descant upon the inestimable advantages resulting from the safety of our baggage. Myself, and all the passengers indeed, joined with great unanimity in this view of the matter; for our burthens were rich in many things esteemed precious throughout the world; and especially, we each of us possessed a great variety of favorite Habits, which we trusted would not be out of fashion, even in the polite circles of the Celestial City. It would have been a sad spectacle to see such an assortment of valuable articles tumbling into the sepulchre. Thus pleasantly conversing on the favorable circumstances of our position, as compared with those of past pilgrims, and of narrow-minded ones at the present day, we soon found ourselves at the foot of the Hill Difficulty. Through the very heart of this rocky mountain a tunnel has been constructed, of most admirable architecture, with a lofty arch and a spacious double-track; so that, unless the earth and rocks should chance to crumble down, it will remain an eternal monument of the builder's skill and enterprise. It is a great though incidental advantage, that the materials from the heart of the Hill Difficulty have been employed in filling up the Valley of Humiliation; thus obviating the necessity of descending into that disagreeable and unwholesome hollow.

"This is a wonderful improvement, indeed," said I. "Yet I should have been glad of an opportunity to visit the Palace Beautiful, and be introduced to the charming young ladies—Miss Prudence, Miss Piety, Miss Charity, and the rest—who have the kindness to entertain pilgrims there."

"Young ladies!" cried Mr. Smooth-it-away, as soon as he could speak for laughing. "And charming young ladies! Why, my dear fellow, they are old maids, every soul of them—prim, starched, dry, and angular—and not one of them, I will venture to say, has altered so much as the fashion of her gown, since the days of Christian's pilgrimage."

"Ah, well," said I, much comforted, "then I can very readily dispense with their acquaintance."

The respectable Apollyon was now putting on the steam at a prodigious rate; anxious, perhaps, to get rid of the unpleasant reminiscences connected with the spot where he had so disastrously encountered Christian. Consulting Mr. Bunyan's road-book, I perceived that we must now be within a few miles of the Valley of the Shadow of Death; into which doleful region, at our present speed, we should plunge much sooner than seemed at all desirable. In truth, I expected nothing better than to find myself in the ditch on one side, or the quag on the other. But on communicating my apprehensions to Mr. Smooth-it-away, he assured me that the difficulties of this passage, even in its worst condition, had been vastly exaggerated, and that, in its present state of improvement, I might consider myself as safe as on any railroad in Christendom.

Even while we were speaking, the train shot into the entrance of this dreaded Valley. Though I plead guilty to some foolish palpitations of the heart, during our headlong rush over the causeway here constructed, yet it were unjust to withhold the highest encomiums on the boldness of its original conception, and the ingenuity of those who executed it. It was gratifying, likewise, to observe how much care had been taken to dispel the everlasting gloom, and supply the defect of cheerful sunshine; not a ray of which has ever penetrated among these awful shadows. For this purpose, the inflammable gas, which exudes plentifully from the soil, is collected by means of pipes, and thence communicated to a quadruple row of lamps, along the whole extent of the passage. Thus a radiance has been created, even out of the fiery and sulphurous curse that rests for ever upon the Valley; a radiance hurtful, however, to the eyes, and somewhat bewildering, as I discovered by the changes which it wrought in the visages of my companions. In this respect, as compared with natural daylight, there is the same difference as between truth and falsehood; but if the reader have ever travelled through the dark Valley, he will have learned to be thankful for any light that he could get; if not from the sky above, then from the blasted soil beneath. Such was the red brilliancy of these lamps, that they appeared to build walls of fire on both sides of the track, between which we held our course at lightning speed, while a reverberating thunder filled the Valley with its echoes. Had the engine run off the track—a catastrophe, it is whispered, by no means unprecedented—the bottomless pit, if there be any such place, would undoubtedly have received us. Just as some dismal fooleries of this nature had made my heart quake, there came a tremendous shriek, careering along the Valley as if a thousand devils had burst their lungs to utter it, but which proved to be merely the whistle of the engine, on arriving at a stopping-place.

The spot, where we had now paused, is the same that our friend Bunyan —truthful man, but infected with many fantastic notions—has designated, in terms plainer than I like to repeat, as the mouth of the infernal region. This, however, must be a mistake; inasmuch as Mr. Smooth-it-away, while we remained in the smoky and lurid cavern, took occasion to prove that Tophet has not even a metaphorical existence. The place, he assured us, is no other than the crater of a half-extinct volcano, in which the Directors had caused forges to be set up, for the manufacture of railroad iron. Hence, also, is obtained a plentiful supply of fuel for the use of the engines. Whoever had gazed into the dismal obscurity of the broad cavern-mouth, whence ever and anon darted huge tongues of dusky flame,—and had seen the strange, half-shaped monsters, and visions of faces horribly grotesque, into which the smoke seemed to wreathe itself,—and had heard the awful murmurs, and shrieks, and deep shuddering whispers of the blast, sometimes forming themselves into words almost articulate,—would have seized upon Mr. Smooth-it-away's comfortable explanation, as greedily as we did. The inhabitants of the cavern, moreover, were unlovely personages, dark, smoke-begrimed, generally deformed, with mis-shapen feet, and a glow of dusky redness in their eyes; as if their hearts had caught fire, and were blazing out of the upper windows. It struck me as a peculiarity, that the laborers at the forge, and those who brought fuel to the engine, when they began to draw short breath, positively emitted smoke from their mouth and nostrils.

Among the idlers about the train, most of whom were puffing cigars which they had lighted at the flame of the crater, I was perplexed to notice several who, to my certain knowledge, had heretofore set forth by railroad for the Celestial City. They looked dark, wild, and smoky, with a singular resemblance, indeed, to the native inhabitants; like whom, also, they had a disagreeable propensity to ill-natured gibes and sneers, the habit of which had wrought a settled contortion of their visages. Having been on speaking terms with one of these persons—an indolent, good-for-nothing fellow, who went by the name of Take-it-easy—I called him, and inquired what was his business there.

"Did you not start," said I, "for the Celestial City?"

"That's a fact," said Mr. Take-it-easy, carelessly puffing some smoke into my eyes. "But I heard such bad accounts, that I never took pains to climb the hill, on which the city stands. No business doing—no fun going on—nothing to drink, and no smoking allowed—and a thrumming of church-music from morning till night! I would not stay in such a place, if they offered me house-room and living free."

"But, my good Mr. Take-it-easy," cried I, "why take up your residence here, of all places in the world?"

"Oh," said the loafer, with a grin, "it is very warm hereabouts, and I meet with plenty of old acquaintances, and altogether the place suits me. I hope to see you back again, some day soon. A pleasant journey to you!"

While he was speaking, the bell of the engine rang, and we dashed away, after dropping a few passengers, but receiving no new ones. Rattling onward through the Valley, we were dazzled with the fiercely gleaming gas-lamps, as before. But sometimes, in the dark of intense brightness, grim faces, that bore the aspect and expression of individual sins, or evil passions, seemed to thrust themselves through the veil of light, glaring upon us, and stretching forth a great dusky hand, as if to impede our progress. I almost thought, that they were my own sins that appalled me there. These were freaks of imagination—nothing more, certainly,—mere delusions, which I ought to be heartily ashamed of—but, all through the Dark Valley, I was tormented, and pestered, and dolefully bewildered, with the same kind of waking dreams. The mephitic gases of that region intoxicate the brain. As the light of natural day, however, began to struggle with the glow of the lanterns, these vain imaginations lost their vividness, and finally vanished with the first ray of sunshine that greeted our escape from the Valley of the Shadow of Death. Ere we had gone a mile beyond it, I could well nigh have taken my oath, that this whole gloomy passage was a dream.

At the end of the Valley, as John Bunyan mentions, is a cavern, where, in his days, dwelt two cruel giants, Pope and Pagan, who had strewn the ground about their residence with the bones of slaughtered pilgrims. These vile old troglodytes are no longer there; but in their deserted cave another terrible giant has thrust himself, and makes it his business to seize upon honest travellers, and fat them for his table with plentiful meals of smoke, mist, moonshine, raw potatoes, and saw-dust. He is a German by birth, and is called Giant Transcendentalist; but as to his form, his features, his substance, and his nature generally, it is the chief peculiarity of this huge miscreant, that neither he for himself, nor anybody for him, has ever been able to describe them. As we rushed by the cavern's mouth, we caught a hasty glimpse of him, looking somewhat like an ill-proportioned figure, but considerably more like a heap of fog and duskiness. He shouted after us but in so strange a phraseology, that we knew not what he meant, nor whether to be encouraged or affrighted.

It was late in the day, when the train thundered into the ancient city of Vanity, where Vanity Fair is still at the height of prosperity, and exhibits an epitome of whatever is brilliant, gay, and fascinating, beneath the sun. As I purposed to make a considerable stay here, it gratified me to learn that there is no longer the want of harmony between the townspeople and pilgrims, which impelled the former to such lamentably mistaken measures as the persecution of Christian, and the fiery martyrdom of Faithful. On the contrary, as the new railroad brings with it great trade and a constant influx of strangers, the lord of Vanity Fair is its chief patron, and the capitalists of the city are among the largest stockholders. Many passengers stop to take their pleasure or make their profit in the Fair, instead of going onward to the Celestial City. Indeed, such are the charms of the place, that people often affirm it to be the true and only heaven; stoutly contending that there is no other, that those who seek further are mere dreamers, and that, if the fabled brightness of the Celestial City lay but a bare mile beyond the gates of Vanity, they would not be fools enough to go thither. Without subscribing to these, perhaps, exaggerated encomiums, I can truly say, that my abode in the city was mainly agreeable, and my intercourse with the inhabitants productive of much amusement and instruction.

Being naturally of a serious turn, my attention was directed to the solid advantages derivable from a residence here, rather than to the effervescent pleasures, which are the grand object with too many visitors. The Christian reader, if he have had no accounts of the city later than Bunyan's time, will be surprised to hear that almost every street has its church, and that the reverend clergy are nowhere held in higher respect than at Vanity Fair. And well do they deserve such honorable estimation; for the maxims of wisdom and virtue which fall from their lips, come from as deep a spiritual source, and tend to as lofty a religious aim, as those of the sagest philosophers of old. In justification of this high praise, I need only mention the names of the Rev. Mr. Shallow-deep; the Rev. Mr. Stumble-at-Truth; that fine old clerical character, the Rev. Mr. This-to-day, who expects shortly to resign his pulpit to the Rev. Mr. That-to-morrow; together with the Rev. Mr. Bewilderment; the Rev. Mr. Clog-the-spirit; and, last and greatest, the Rev. Dr. Wind-of-doctrine. The labors of these eminent divines are aided by those of innumerable lecturers, who diffuse such a various profundity, in all subjects of human or celestial science, that any man may acquire an omnigenous erudition, without the trouble of even learning to read. Thus literature is etherealized by assuming for its medium the human voice; and knowledge, depositing all its heavier particles—except, doubtless, its gold—becomes exhaled into a sound, which forthwith steals into the ever-open ear of the community. These ingenious methods constitute a sort of machinery, by which thought and study are done to every person's hand, without his putting himself to the slightest inconvenience in the matter. There is another species of machine for the wholesale manufacture of individual morality. This excellent result is effected by societies for all manner of virtuous purposes; with which a man has merely to connect himself, throwing, as it were, his quota of virtue into the common stock; and the president and directors will take care that the aggregate amount be well applied. All these, and other wonderful improvements in ethics, religion, and literature, being made plain to my comprehension, by the ingenious Mr. Smooth-it-away, inspired me with a vast admiration of Vanity Fair.

It would fill a volume, in an age of pamphlets, were I to record all my observations in this great capital of human business and pleasure. There was an unlimited range of society—the powerful, the wise, the witty, and the famous in every walk of life—princes, presidents, poets, generals, artists, actors, and philanthropists, all making their own market at the Fair, and deeming no price too exorbitant for such commodities as hit their fancy. It was well worth one's while, even if he had no idea of buying or selling, to loiter through the bazaars, and observe the various sorts of traffic that were going forward.

Some of the purchasers, I thought, made very foolish bargains. For instance, a young man having inherited a splendid fortune, laid out a considerable portion of it in the purchase of diseases, and finally spent all the rest for a heavy lot of repentance and a suit of rags. A very pretty girl bar-tered a heart as clear as crystal, and which seemed her most valuable possession, for another jewel of the same kind, but so worn and defaced as to be utterly worthless. In one shop, there were a great many crowns of laurel and myrtle, which soldiers, authors, statesmen, and various other people, pressed eagerly to buy; some purchased these paltry wreaths with their lives; others by a toilsome servitude of years; and many sacrificed whatever was most valuable, yet finally slunk away without the crown. There was a sort of stock or scrip, called Conscience, which seemed to be in great demand, and would purchase almost anything. Indeed, few rich commodities were to be obtained without paying a heavy sum in this particular stock, and a man's business was seldom very lucrative, unless he knew precisely when and how to throw his hoard of Conscience into the market. Yet as this stock was the only thing of permanent value, whoever parted with it was sure to find himself a loser, in the long run. Several of the speculations were of a questionable character. Occasionally, a member of Congress recruited his pocket by the sale of his constituents; and I was assured that public officers have often sold their country at very moderate prices. Thousands sold their happiness for a whim. Gilded chains were in great demand, and purchased with almost any sacrifice. In truth, those who desired, according to the old adage, to sell anything valuable for a song, might find customers all over the Fair; and there were innumerable messes of pottage, piping hot, for such as chose to buy them with their birthrights. A few articles, however, could not be found genuine at Vanity Fair. If a customer wished to renew his stock of youth, the dealers offered him a set of false teeth and an auburn wig; if he demanded peace of mind, they recommended opium or a brandy-bottle.

Tracts of land and golden mansions, situate in the Celestial City, were often exchanged, at very disadvantageous rates, for a few years' lease of small, dismal, inconvenient tenements in Vanity Fair. Prince Beelzebub himself took great interest in this sort of traffic, and sometimes condescended to meddle with smaller matters. I once had the pleasure to see him bargaining with a miser for his soul, which, after much ingenious skirmishing on both sides, his Highness succeeded in obtaining at about the value of sixpence. The prince remarked, with a smile, that he was a loser by the transaction.

Day after day, as I walked the streets of Vanity, my manners and deportment became more and more like those of the inhabitants. The place began to seem like home; the idea of pursuing my travels to the Celestial City was almost obliterated from my mind. I was reminded of it, however, by the sight of the same pair of simple pilgrims at whom we had laughed so heartily, when Apollyon puffed smoke and steam into their faces, at the commencement of our journey. There they stood amid the densest bustle of Vanity—the dealers offering them their purple, and fine linen, and jewels; the men of wit and humor gibing at them; a pair of buxom ladies ogling them askance; while the benevolent Mr. Smooth-it-away whispered some of his wisdom at their elbows, and pointed to a newly-erected temple,—but there were these worthy simpletons, making the scene look wild and monstrous, merely by their sturdy repudiation of all part in its business or pleasures.

One of them—his name was Stick-to-the-right—perceived in my face, I suppose, a species of sympathy and almost admiration, which, to my own great surprise, I could not help feeling for this pragmatic couple. It prompted him to address me.

"Sir," inquired he, with a sad, yet mild and kindly voice, "do you call yourself a pilgrim?"

"Yes," I replied, "my right to that appellation is indubitable. I am merely a sojourner here in Vanity Fair, being bound to the Celestial City by the new railroad."

"Alas, friend," rejoined Mr. Stick-to-the-right, "I do assure you, and beseech you to receive the truth of my words, that that whole concern is a bubble. You may travel on it all your lifetime, were you to live thousands of years, and yet never get beyond the limits of Vanity Fair! Yea; though you should deem yourself entering the gates of the Blessed City, it will be nothing but a miserable delusion."

"The Lord of the Celestial City," began the other pilgrim, whose name was Mr. Foot-it-to-Heaven, "has refused, and will ever refuse, to grant an act of incorporation for this railroad; and unless that be obtained, no passenger can ever hope to enter his dominions. Wherefore, every man, who buys a ticket, must lay his account with losing the purchase-money—which is the value of his own soul."

"Poh, nonsense!" said Mr. Smooth-it-away, taking my arm and leading me off, "these fellows ought to be indicted for a libel. If the law stood as it once did in Vanity Fair, we should see them grinning through the iron bars of the prison window."

This incident made a considerable impression on my mind, and contributed with other circumstances to indispose me to a permanent residence in the city of Vanity; although, of course, I was not simple enough to give up my original plan of gliding along easily and commodiously by railroad. Still, I grew anxious to be gone. There was one strange thing that troubled me; amid the occupations or amusements of the fair, nothing was more common than for a person—whether at a feast, theatre, or church, or trafficking for wealth and honors, or whatever he might be doing, and however unseasonable the interruption—suddenly to vanish like a soap-bubble, and be never more seen of his fellows; and so accustomed were the latter to such little accidents, that they went on with their business, as quietly as if nothing had happened. But it was otherwise with me.

Finally, after a pretty long residence at the Fair, I resumed my journey towards the Celestial City, still with Mr. Smooth-it-away at my side. At a short distance beyond the suburbs of Vanity, we passed the ancient silver mine, of which Demas was the first discoverer, and which is now wrought to great advantage, supplying nearly all the coined currency of the world. A little further onward was the spot where Lot's wife had stood for ages, under the semblance of a pillar of salt. Curious travellers have long since carried it away piecemeal. Had all regrets been punished as rigorously as this poor dame's were, my yearning for the relinquished delights of Vanity Fair might have produced a similar change in my own corporeal substance, and left me a warning to future pilgrims.

The next remarkable object was a large edifice, constructed of moss-grown stone, but in a modern and airy style of architecture. The engine came to a pause in its vicinity with the usual tremendous shriek.

"This was formerly the castle of the redoubted giant Despair," observed Mr. Smooth-it-away; "but, since his death, Mr. Flimsy-faith has repaired it, and now keeps an excellent house of entertainment here. It is one of our stopping-places."

"It seems but slightly put together," remarked I, looking at the frail, yet ponderous walls. "I do not envy Mr. Flimsy-faith his habitation. Some day it will thunder down upon the heads of the occupants."

"We shall escape, at all events," said Mr. Smooth-it-away, "for Apollyon is putting on the steam again."

The road now plunged into a gorge of the Delectable Mountains, and traversed the field where, in former ages, the blind men wandered and stumbled among the tombs. One of these ancient tomb-stones had been thrust across the track, by some malicious person, and gave the train of cars a terrible jolt. Far up the rugged side of a mountain, I perceived a rusty iron door, half overgrown with bushes and creeping plants, but with smoke issuing from its crevices.

"Is that," inquired I, "the very door in the hill-side, which the shepherds assured Christian was a by-way to Hell?"

"That was a joke on the part of the shepherds," said Mr. Smooth-it-away, with a smile. "It is neither more nor less than the door of a cavern, which they use as a smoke-house for the preparation of mutton hams."

My recollections of the journey are now, for a little space, dim and confused, inasmuch as a singular drowsiness here overcame me, owing to the fact that we were passing over the enchanted ground, the air of which encourages a disposition to sleep. I awoke, however, as soon as we crossed the borders of the pleasant land of Beulah. All the passengers were rubbing their eyes, comparing watches, and congratulating one another on the prospect of arriving so seasonably at the journey's end. The sweet breezes of this happy clime came refreshingly to our nostrils; we beheld the glimmering gush of silver fountains, overhung by trees of beautiful foliage and delicious fruit, which were propagated by grafts from the celestial gardens. Once, as we dashed onward like a hurricane, there was a flutter of wings, and the bright appearance of an angel in the air, speeding forth on some heavenly mission. The engine now announced the close vicinity of the final Stationhouse, by one last and horrible scream, in which there seemed to be distinguishable every kind of wailing and woe, and bitter fierceness of wrath, all mixed up with the wild laughter of a devil or a madman. Throughout our journey, at every stopping-place, Apollyon had exercised his ingenuity in screwing the most abominable sounds out of the whistle of the steam-engine; but in this closing effort he outdid himself, and created an infernal uproar, which, besides disturbing the peaceful inhabitants of Beulah, must have sent its discord even through the celestial gates.

While the horrid clamor was still ringing in our ears, we heard an exulting strain, as if a thousand instruments of music, with height, and depth, and sweetness in their tones, at once tender and triumphant, were struck in unison, to greet the approach of some illustrious hero, who had fought the good fight and won a glorious victory, and was come to lay aside his battered arms for ever. Looking to ascertain what might be the occasion of this glad harmony, I perceived, on alighting from the cars, that a multitude of shining ones had assembled on the other side of the river, to welcome two poor pilgrims, who were just emerging from its depths. They were the same whom Apollyon and ourselves had persecuted with taunts and gibes, and scalding steam, at the commencement of our journey—the same whose unworldly aspect and impressive words had stirred my conscience, amid the wild revellers of Vanity Fair.

"How amazingly well those men have got on!" cried I to Mr. Smooth-it-away. "I wish we were secure of as good a reception."

"Never fear—never fear!" answered my friend. "Come—make haste; the ferry-boat will be off directly; and in three minutes you will be on the other side of the river. No doubt you will find coaches to carry you up to the city gates."

A steam ferry-boat, the last improvement on this important route, lay at the river side, puffing, snorting, and emitting all those other disagreeable utterances, which betoken the departure to be immediate. I hurried on board with the rest of the passengers, most of whom were in great perturbation; some bawling out for their baggage; some tearing their hair and exclaiming that the boat would explode or sink; some already pale with the heaving of the stream; some gazing affrighted at the ugly aspect of the steersman; and some still dizzy with the slumberous influences of the Enchanted Ground. Looking back to the shore, I was amazed to discern Mr. Smooth-it-away waving his hand in token of farewell!

"Don't you go over to the Celestial City?" exclaimed I.

"Oh, no!" answered he with a queer smile, and that same disagreeable contortion of visage which I had remarked in the inhabitants of the Dark Valley. "Oh, no! I have come thus far only for the sake of your pleasant company. Good bye! We shall meet again."

And then did my excellent friend, Mr. Smooth-it-away, laugh outright; in the midst of which cachinnation, a smoke-wreath issued from his mouth and nostrils, while a twinkle of lurid flame darted out of either eye, proving indubitably that his heart was all of a red blaze. The impudent fiend! To deny the existence of Tophet, when he felt its fiery tortures raging within his breast! I rushed to the side of the boat, intending to fling myself on shore. But the wheels, as they began their revolutions, threw a dash of spray over me, so cold—so deadly cold, with the chill that will never leave those waters, until Death be drowned in his own river—that, with a shiver and a heart-quake, I awoke. Thank heaven, it was a Dream!

WASHINGTON IRVING

Guests from Gibbet Island

A LEGEND OF COMMUNIPAW

FOUND AMONG THE KNICKERBOCKER PAPERS AT WOLFERT'S ROOST

Whoever has visited the ancient and renowned village of Communipaw may have noticed an old stone building, of most ruinous and sinister appearance. The doors and window-shutters are ready to drop from their hinges; old clothes are stuffed in the broken panes of glass, while legions of half-starved dogs prowl about the premises, and rush out and bark at every passer-by, for your beggarly house in a village is most apt to swarm with profligate and ill-conditioned dogs. What adds to the sinister appearance of this mansion is a tall frame in front, not a little resembling a gallows, and which looks as if waiting to accommodate some of the inhabitants with a well-merited airing. It is not a gallows, however, but an ancient sign-post; for this dwelling in the golden days of Communipaw was one of the most orderly and peaceful of village taverns, where public affairs were talked and smoked over. In fact, it was in this very building that Oloffe the Dreamer and his companions concerted that great voyage of discovery and colonization in which they explored Buttermilk Channel, were nearly shipwrecked in the strait of Hell Gate, and finally landed on the island of Manhattan, and founded the great city of New Amsterdam.

Even after the province had been cruelly wrested from the sway of their High Mightinesses by the combined forces of the British and the Yankees, this tavern continued its ancient loyalty. It is true, the head of the Prince of Orange disappeared from the sign, a strange bird being painted over it, with the explanatory legend of "DIE WILDE GANS," or, The Wild Goose; but this all the world knew to be a sly riddle of the landlord, the worthy Teunis Van Gieson, a knowing man, in a small way, who laid his finger beside his nose and winked, when any one studied the signification of his sign, and observed that his goose was hatching, but would join the flock whenever they flew over the water; an enigma which was the perpetual recreation and delight of the loyal but fat-headed burghers of Communipaw.

Under the sway of this patriotic, though discreet and quiet publican, the tavern continued to flourish in primeval tranquillity, and was the resort of true-hearted Nederlanders, from all parts of Pavonia; who met here quietly and secretly, to smoke and drink the downfall of Briton and Yankee, and success to Admiral Van Tromp.

The only drawback on the comfort of the establishment was a nephew of mine host, a sister's son, Yan Yost Vanderscamp by name, and a real scamp by nature. This unlucky whipster showed an early propensity to mischief, which he gratified in a small way by playing tricks upon the frequenters of the Wild Goose,—putting gunpowder in their pipes, or squibs in their pockets, and astonishing them with an explosion, while they sat nodding around the fireplace in the bar-room; and if perchance a worthy burgher from some distant part of Pavonia lingered until dark over his potation, it was odds but young Vanderscamp would slip a brier under his horse's tail, as he mounted, and send him clattering along the road, in neck-or-nothing style, to the infinite astonishment and discomfiture of the rider.

It may be wondered at, that mine host of the Wild Goose did not turn such a graceless varlet out of doors; but Teunis Van Gieson was an easy-tempered man, and, having no child of his own, looked upon his nephew with almost parental indulgence. His patience and good-nature were doomed to be tried by another inmate of his mansion. This was a cross-grained curmudgeon of a negro, named Pluto, who was a kind of enigma in Communipaw. Where he came from, nobody knew. He was found one morning, after a storm, cast like a sea-monster on the strand, in front of the Wild Goose, and lay there, more dead than alive. The neighbors gathered round, and speculated on this production of the deep; whether it were fish or flesh, or a compound of both, commonly yclept a merman. The kind-hearted Teunis Van Gieson, seeing that he wore the human form, took him into his house, and warmed him into life. By degrees, he showed signs of intelligence, and even uttered signs very much like language, but which no one in Communipaw could understand. Some thought him a negro just from Guinea, who had either fallen overboard, or escaped from a slave-ship. Nothing, however, could ever draw from him any account of his origin. When questioned on the subject, he merely pointed to Gibbet Island, a small rocky islet which lies in the open bay, just opposite Communipaw, as if that were his native place, though everybody knew it had never been inhabited.

In the process of time, he acquired something of the Dutch language; that is to say, he learnt all its vocabulary of oaths and maledictions, with just words sufficient to string them together. *"Donder en blicksem!"* (thunder and lightning) was the gentlest of his ejaculations. For years he kept about the Wild Goose, more like one of those familiar spirits, or household goblins, we read of, than like a human being. He acknowledged allegiance to no one, but performed various domestic offices, when it suited his humor; waiting occasionally on the guests, grooming the horses, cutting wood, drawing water; and all this without being ordered. Lay any command on him, and the stubborn sea-urchin was sure to rebel. He was never so much at home, however, as when on the water, plying about in skiff or canoe, entirely alone, fishing, crabbing, or grabbing for oysters, and would bring home quantities for the larder of the Wild Goose, which he would throw down at the kitchen-door, with a growl. No wind nor weather deterred him from launching forth on his favorite element; indeed, the wilder the weather, the more he seemed to enjoy it. If a storm was brewing, he was sure to put off from shore; and would be seen far out in the bay, his light skiff dancing like a feather on the waves, when sea and sky were in a turmoil, and the stoutest ships were fain to lower their sails. Sometimes on such occasions he would be absent for days together. How he weathered the tempest, and how and where he subsisted, no one could divine, nor did any one venture to ask, for all had an almost superstitious awe of him. Some of the Communipaw oystermen declared they had more than once seen him suddenly disappear, canoe and all, as if plunged beneath the waves, and after a while come up again, in quite a different part of the bay; whence they concluded that he could live under water like that notable species of wild-duck commonly called the hell-diver. All began to consider him in the light of a foul-weather bird, like the Mother Carey's chicken, or stormy petrel; and whenever they saw him putting far out in his skiff, in cloudy weather, made up their minds for a storm.

The only being for whom he seemed to have any liking was Yan Yost Vanderscamp, and him he liked for his very wickedness. He in a manner took the boy under his tutelage, prompted him to all kinds of mischief, aided him in every wild harum-scarum freak, until the lad became the complete scapegrace of the village, a pest to his uncle and to every one else. Nor were his pranks confined to the land; he soon learned to accompany old Pluto on the water. Together these worthies would cruise about the broad bay, and all the neighboring straits and rivers; poking around in skiffs and canoes; robbing the set nets of the fishermen; landing on remote coasts, and laying waste orchards and water-melon patches; in short, carrying on a complete system of piracy, on a small scale. Piloted by Pluto, the youthful Vanderscamp soon became acquainted with all the bays, rivers, creeks, and inlets of the watery world around him; could navigate from the Hook to Spiting Devil on the darkest night, and learned to set even the terrors of Hell Gate at defiance.

At length negro and boy suddenly disappeared, and days and weeks elapsed, but without tidings of them. Some said they must have run away and gone to sea; others jocosely hinted that old Pluto, being no other than his namesake in disguise, had spirited away the boy to the nether regions. All, however, agreed in one thing, that the village was well rid of them.

In the process of time, the good Teunis Van Gieson slept with his fathers, and the tavern remained shut up, waiting for a claimant, for the next heir was Yan Yost Vanderscamp, and he had not been heard of for years. At length, one day, a boat was seen pulling for shore, from a long, black, rakish-looking schooner, that lay at anchor in the bay. The boat's crew seemed worthy of the craft from which they debarked. Never had such a set of noisy, roistering, swaggering varlets landed in peaceful Communipaw. They were outlandish in garb and demeanor, and were headed by a rough, burly, bully ruffian, with fiery whiskers, a copper nose, a scar across his face, and a great Flaunderish beaver slouched on one side of his head, in whom, to their dismay, the quiet inhabitants were made to recognize their early pest, Yan Yost Vanderscamp. The rear of this hopeful gang was brought up by old Pluto, who had lost an eye, grown grizzly-headed, and looked more like a devil than ever. Vanderscamp renewed his acquaintance with the old burghers, much against their will, and in a manner not at all to their taste. He slapped them familiarly on the back, gave them an iron grip of the hand, and was hail-fellow well met. According to his own account, he had been all the world over, had made money by bags full, had ships in every sea, and now meant to turn the Wild Goose into a country-seat, where he and his comrades, all rich merchants from foreign parts, might enjoy themselves in the interval of their voyages.

Sure enough, in a little while there was a complete metamorphose of the Wild Goose. From being a quiet, peaceful Dutch public-house, it became a most riotous, uproarious private dwelling; a complete rendezvous for boisterous men of the seas, who came here to have what they called a "blow-out" on dry land, and might be seen at all hours, lounging about the door, or lolling out of the windows, swearing among themselves, and cracking rough jokes on every passer-by. The house was fitted up, too, in so strange a manner: hammocks slung to the walls, instead of bedsteads; odd kinds of furniture, of foreign fashion; bamboo couches, Spanish chairs; pistols, cutlasses, and blunderbusses, suspended on every peg; silver crucifixes on the mantelpieces, silver candlesticks and porringers on the tables, contrasting oddly with the pewter and Delf ware of the original establishment. And then the strange amusements of these sea-monsters! Pitching Spanish dollars, instead of quoits; firing blunderbusses out of the window; shooting at a mark, or at any unhappy dog, or cat, or pig, or barndoor fowl, that might happen to come within reach.

The only being who seemed to relish their rough waggery was old Pluto; and yet he led but a dog's life of it, for they practised all kinds of manual jokes upon him, kicked him about like a foot-ball, shook him by his grizzly mop of wool, and never spoke to him without coupling a curse, by way of adjective, to his name, and consigning him to the infernal regions. The old fellow, however, seemed to like them the better the more they cursed him, though his utmost expression of pleasure never amounted to more than the growl of a petted bear, when his ears are rubbed.

Old Pluto was the ministering spirit at the orgies of the Wild Goose; and such orgies as took place there! Such drinking, singing, whooping, swearing; with an occasional interlude of quarrelling and fighting. The noisier grew the revel, the more old Pluto plied the potations, until the guests would become frantic in their merriment, smashing everything to pieces, and throwing the house out of the windows. Sometimes, after a drinking bout, they sallied forth and scoured the village, to the dismay of the worthy burghers, who gathered their women within doors, and would have shut up the house. Vanderscamp, however, was not to be rebuffed. He insisted on renewing acquaintance with his old neighbors, and on introducing his friends, the merchants, to their families; swore he was on the lookout for a wife, and meant, before he stopped, to find husbands for all their daughters. So, will-ye, nill-ye, sociable he was; swaggered about their best parlors, with his hat on one side of his head; sat on the good-wife's nicely waxed mahogany table, kicking his heels against the carved and polished legs; kissed and tousled the young *vrows;* and, if they frowned and pouted, gave them a gold rosary, or a sparkling cross, to put them in good-humor again.

Sometimes nothing would satisfy him, but he must have some of his old neighbors to dinner at the Wild Goose. There was no refusing him, for he had the complete upper hand of the community, and the peaceful burghers all stood in awe of him. But what a time would the quiet, worthy men have, among these rake-hells, who would delight to astound them with the most extravagant gunpowder tales, embroidered with all kinds of foreign oaths, clink the can with them, pledge them in deep potations, bawl drinking-songs in their ears, and occasionally fire pistols over their heads, or under the table, and then laugh in their faces, and ask them how they liked the smell of gunpowder.

Thus was the little village of Communipaw for a time like the unfortunate wight possessed with devils; until Vanderscamp and his brother merchants would sail on another trading voyage, when the Wild Goose would be shut up, and everything relapse into quiet, only to be disturbed by his next visitation.

The mystery of all these proceedings gradually dawned upon the tardy intellects of Communipaw. These were the times of the notorious Captain Kidd, when the American harbors were the resorts of piratical adventurers of all kinds, who, under pretext of mercantile voyages, scoured the West Indies, made plundering descents upon the Spanish Main, visited even the remote Indian Seas, and then came to dispose of their booty, have their revels, and fit out new expeditions in the English colonies.

Vanderscamp had served in this hopeful school, and, having risen to importance among the buccaneers, had pitched upon his native village and early home, as a quiet, out-of-the-way, unsuspected place, where he and his comrades, while anchored at New York, might have their feasts, and concert their plans, without molestation.

At length the attention of the British government was called to these piratical enterprises, that were becoming so frequent and outrageous. Vigorous measures were taken to check and punish them. Several of the most noted freebooters were caught and executed, and three of Vanderscamp's chosen comrades, the most riotous swash-bucklers of the Wild Goose, were hanged in chains on Gibbet Island, in full sight of their favorite resort. As to Vanderscamp himself, he and his man Pluto again disappeared, and it was hoped by the people of Communipaw that he had fallen in some foreign brawl, or been swung on some foreign gallows.

For a time, therefore, the tranquillity of the village was restored; the worthy Dutchmen once more smoked their pipes in peace, eyeing with peculiar complacency their old pests and terrors, the pirates, dangling and drying in the sun, on Gibbet Island.

This perfect calm was doomed at length to be ruffled. The fiery persecution of the pirates gradually subsided. Justice was satisfied with the examples that had been made, and there was no more talk of Kidd, and the other heroes of like kidney. On a calm summer evening, a boat, somewhat heavily laden, was seen pulling into Communipaw. What was the surprise and disquiet of the inhabitants to see Yan Yost Vanderscamp seated at the helm, and his man Pluto tugging at the oar! Vanderscamp, however, was apparently an altered man. He brought home with him a wife, who seemed to be a shrew, and to have the upper hand of him. He no longer was the swaggering, bully ruffian, but affected the regular merchant, and talked of retiring from business, and settling down quietly, to pass the rest of his days in his native place.

The Wild Goose mansion was again opened, but with diminished splendor, and no riot. It is true, Vanderscamp had frequent nautical visitors, and the sound of revelry was occasionally overheard in his house; but everything seemed to be done under the rose, and old Pluto was the only servant that officiated at these orgies. The visitors, indeed, were by no means of the turbulent stamp of their predecessors; but quiet mysterious traders; full of nods, and winks, and hieroglyphic signs, with whom, to use their cant phrase, "everything was smug." Their ships came to anchor at night, in the lower bay; and, on a private signal, Vanderscamp would launch his boat, and, accompanied solely by his man Pluto, would make them mysterious visits. Sometimes boats pulled in at night, in front of the Wild Goose, and various articles of merchandise were landed in the dark, and spirited away, nobody knew whither. One of the more curious of the inhabitants kept watch, and caught a glimpse of the features of some of these night visitors, by the casual glance of a lantern, and declared that he recognized more than one of the freebooting frequenters of the Wild Goose, in former times; whence he concluded that Vanderscamp was at his old game, and that this mysterious merchandise was nothing more nor less than piratical plunder. The more charitable opinion, however, was, that Vanderscamp and his comrades, having been driven from their old line of business by the "oppressions of government," had resorted to smuggling to make both ends meet.

Be that as it may, I come now to the extraordinary fact which is the butt-end of this story. It happened, late one night, that Yan Yost Vanderscamp was returning across the broad bay, in his light skiff, rowed by his man

Pluto. He had been carousing on board of a vessel, newly arrived, and was somewhat obfuscated in intellect, by the liquor he had imbibed. It was a still, sultry night; a heavy mass of lurid clouds was rising in the west, with the low muttering of distant thunder. Vanderscamp called on Pluto to pull lustily, that they might get home before the gathering storm. The old negro made no reply, but shaped his course so as to skirt the rocky shores of Gibbet Island. A faint creaking overhead caused Vanderscamp to cast up his eyes, when, to his horror, he beheld the bodies of his three pot companions and brothers in iniquity dangling in the moonlight, their rags fluttering, and their chains creaking, as they were slowly swung backward and forward by the rising breeze.

"What do you mean, you blockhead!" cried Vanderscamp, "by pulling so close to the island?"

"I thought you'd be glad to see your old friends once more," growled the negro; "you were never afraid of a living man, what do you fear from the dead?"

"Who's afraid?" hiccoughed Vanderscamp, partly heated by liquor, partly nettled by the jeer of the negro; "who's afraid? Hang me, but I would be glad to see them once more, alive or dead, at the Wild Goose. Come, my lads in the wind!" continued he, taking a draught, and flourishing the bottle above his head, "here's fair weather to you in the other world; and if you should be walking the rounds to-night, odds fish! but I'll be happy if you will drop in to supper."

A dismal creaking was the only reply. The wind blew loud and shrill, and as it whistled round the gallows, and among the bones, sounded as if they were laughing and gibbering in the air. Old Pluto chuckled to himself, and now pulled for home. The storm burst over the voyagers, while they were yet far from shore. The rain fell in torrents, the thunder crashed and pealed, and the lightning kept up an incessant blaze. It was stark midnight before they landed at Communipaw.

Dripping and shivering, Vanderscamp crawled homeward. He was completely sobered by the storm, the water soaked from without having diluted and cooled the liquor within. Arrived at the Wild Goose, he knocked timidly and dubiously at the door; for he dreaded the reception he was to experience from his wife. He had reason to do so. She met him at the threshold, in a precious ill-humor.

"Is this a time," said she, "to keep people out of their beds, and to bring home company, to turn the house upside down?"

"Company?" said Vanderscamp, meekly; "I have brought no company with me, wife?"

"No, indeed! they have got here before you, but by your invitation; and blessed-looking company they are, truly!"

Vanderscamp's knees smote together. "For the love of heaven, where are they, wife?"

"Where?—why in the blue room, up-stairs, making themselves as much at home as if the house were their own."

Vanderscamp made a desperate effort, scrambled up to the room, and threw open the door. Sure enough, there at a table, on which burned a light as blue as brimstone, sat the three guests from Gibbet Island, with halters round their necks, and bobbing their cups together, as if they were hob-or-nobbing, and trolling the old Dutch freebooter's glee, since translated into English:—

> "For three merry lads be we,
> And three merry lads be we;
> I on the land, and thou on the sand,
> And Jack on the gallows-tree."

Vanderscamp saw and heard no more. Starting back with horror, he missed his footing on the landing-place, and fell from the top of the stairs to the bottom. He was taken up speechless, either from the fall or the fright, and was buried in the yard of the little Dutch church at Bergen, on the following Sunday.

From that day forward the fate of the Wild Goose was sealed. It was pronounced a *haunted house,* and avoided accordingly. No one inhabited it but Vanderscamp's shrew of a widow and old Pluto, and they were considered but little better than its hobgoblin visitors. Pluto grew more and more haggard and morose, and looked more like an imp of darkness than a human being. He spoke to no one, but went about muttering to himself; or, as some hinted, talking with the devil, who, though unseen, was ever at his elbow. Now and then he was seen pulling about the bay alone in his skiff, in dark weather, or at the approach of nightfall; nobody could tell why, unless on an errand to invite more guests from the gallows. Indeed, it was affirmed that the Wild Goose still continued to be a house of entertainment for such guests, and that on stormy nights the blue chamber was occasionally illuminated, and sounds of diabolical merriment were overheard, mingling with the howling of the tempest. Some treated these as idle stories, until on one such night, it was about the time of the equinox, there was a horrible uproar in the Wild Goose, that could not be mistaken. It was not so much the sound of revelry, however, as strife, with two or three piercing shrieks, that pervaded every part of the village. Nevertheless, no one thought of hastening to the spot. On the contrary, the honest burghers of Communipaw drew their nightcaps over their ears, and buried their heads under the bedclothes, at the thoughts of Vanderscamp and his gallows companions.

The next morning some of the bolder and more curious undertook to reconnoitre. All was quiet and lifeless at the Wild Goose. The door yawned wide open, and had evidently been open all night, for the storm had beaten into the house. Gathering more courage from the silence and apparent desertion, they gradually ventured over the threshold. The house had indeed the air of having been possessed by devils. Everything was topsy-turvy; trunks had been broken open, and chests of drawers and corner cupboards turned inside out, as in a time of general sack and pillage; but the most woful sight was the widow of Yan Yost Vanderscamp, extended a corpse on the floor of the blue chamber, with the marks of a deadly gripe on the windpipe.

All now was conjecture and dismay at Communipaw; and the disappearance of old Pluto, who was nowhere to be found, gave rise to all kinds of wild surmises. Some suggested that the negro had betrayed the house to some of Vanderscamp's buccaneering associates, and that they had decamped together with the booty; others surmised that the negro was nothing more nor less than a devil incarnate, who had now accomplished his ends, and made off with his dues.

Events, however, vindicated the negro from this last imputation. His skiff was picked up, drifting about the bay, bottom upward, as if wrecked in a tempest; and his body was found, shortly afterward, by some Communipaw fishermen, stranded among the rocks of Gibbet Island, near the foot of the pirates' gallows. The fishermen shook their heads, and observed that old Pluto had ventured once too often to invite Guests from Gibbet Island.

AMBROSE BIERCE

Chickamauga

ONE SUNNY autumn afternoon a child strayed away from its rude home in a small field and entered a forest unobserved. It was happy in a new sense of freedom from control, happy in the opportunity of exploration and adventure; for this child's spirit, in bodies of its ancestors, had for thousands of years been trained to memorable feats of discovery and conquest—victories in battles whose critical moments were centuries, whose victors' camps were cities of hewn stone. From the cradle of its race it had conquered its way through two continents and passing a great sea had penetrated a third, there to be born to war and dominion as a heritage.

The child was a boy aged about six years, the son of a poor planter. In his younger manhood the father had been a soldier, had fought against naked savages and followed the flag of his country into the capital of a civilized race to the far South. In the peaceful life of a planter the warrior-fire survived; once kindled, it is never extinguished. The man loved military books and pictures and the boy had understood enough to make himself a wooden sword, though even the eye of his father would hardly have known it for what it was. This weapon he now bore bravely, as became the son of an heroic race, and pausing now and again in the sunny space of the forest assumed, with some exaggeration, the postures of aggression and defense that he had been taught by the engraver's art. Made reckless by the ease with which he overcame invisible foes attempting to stay his advance, he committed the common enough military error of pushing the pursuit to a dangerous extreme, until he found himself upon the margin of a wide but shallow brook, whose rapid waters barred his direct advance against the flying foe that had crossed with illogical ease. But the intrepid victor was not to be baffled; the spirit of the race which had passed the great sea burned unconquerable in that small breast and would not be denied. Finding a place where some bowlders in the bed of the stream lay but a step or a leap apart, he made his way across and fell again upon the rear-guard of his imaginary foe, putting all to the sword.

Now that the battle had been won, prudence required that he withdraw to his base of operations. Alas; like many a mightier conqueror, and like one, the mightiest, he could not

> curb the lust for war,
> Nor learn that tempted Fate will leave the loftiest star.

Advancing from the bank of the creek he suddenly found himself confronted with a new and more formidable enemy: in the path that he was following, sat, bolt upright, with ears erect and paws suspended before it, a rabbit! With a startled cry the child turned and fled, he knew not in what direction, calling with inarticulate cries for his mother, weeping, stumbling, his tender skin cruelly torn by brambles, his little heart beating hard with terror—breathless, blind with tears—lost in the forest! Then, for more than an hour, he wandered with erring feet through the tangled undergrowth, till at last, overcome by fatigue, he lay down in a narrow space between two rocks, within a few yards of the stream and still grasping his toy sword, no longer a weapon but a companion, sobbed himself to sleep. The wood birds sang merrily above his head; the squirrels, whisking their bravery of tail, ran barking from tree to tree, unconscious of the pity of it, and somewhere far away was a strange, muffled thunder, as if the partridges were drumming in celebration of nature's victory over the son of her immemorial enslavers. And back at the little plantation, where white men and black were hastily searching the fields and hedges in alarm, a mother's heart was breaking for her missing child.

Hours passed, and then the little sleeper rose to his feet. The chill of the evening was in his limbs, the fear of the gloom in his heart. But he had rested, and he no longer wept. With some blind instinct which impelled to action he struggled through the undergrowth about him and came to a more open ground—on his right the brook, to the left a gentle acclivity studded with infrequent trees; over all, the gathering gloom of twilight. A thin, ghostly mist rose along the water. It frightened and repelled him; instead of recrossing, in the direction whence he had come, he turned his back upon it, and went forward toward the dark inclosing wood. Suddenly he saw before him a strange moving object which he took to be some large animal—a dog, a pig—he could not name it; perhaps it was a bear. He had seen pictures of bears, but knew of nothing to their discredit and had vaguely wished to meet one. But something in form or movement of this object—something in the awkwardness of its approach—told him that it was not a bear, and curiosity was stayed by fear. He stood still and as it came slowly on gained courage every moment, for he saw that at least it had not the long, menacing ears of the rabbit. Possibly his impressionable mind was half conscious of something familiar in its shambling, awkward gait. Before it had approached near enough to resolve his doubts he saw that it was followed by another and another. To right and to left were many more; the whole open space about him was alive with them—all moving toward the brook.

They were men. They crept upon their hands and knees. They used their hands only, dragging their legs. They used their knees only, their arms hanging idle at their sides. They strove to rise to their feet, but fell prone in the attempt. They did nothing naturally, and nothing alike, save only to advance foot by foot in the same direction. Singly, in pairs and in little groups, they came on through the gloom, some halting now and again while others crept slowly past them, then resuming their movement. They came by dozens and by hundreds; as far on either hand as one could see in the deepening gloom they extended and the black wood behind them appeared to be inexhaustible. The very ground seemed in motion toward the creek. Occasionally one who had paused did not again go on, but lay motionless. He was dead. Some, pausing, made strange gestures with their hands, erected their arms and lowered them again, clasped their heads; spread their palms upward, as men are sometimes seen to do in public prayer.

Not all of this did the child note; it is what would have been noted by an elder observer; he saw little but that these were men, yet crept like babes. Being men, they were not terrible, though unfamiliarly clad. He moved among them freely, going from one to another and peering into their faces with childish curiosity. All their faces were singularly white and many were streaked and gouted with red. Something in this—something too, perhaps, in their grotesque attitudes and movements—reminded him of the painted clown whom he had seen last summer in the circus, and he laughed as he watched them. But on and ever on they crept, these maimed and bleeding men, as heedless as he of the dramatic contrast between his laughter and their own ghastly gravity. To him it was a merry spectacle. He had seen his father's negroes creep upon their hands and knees for his amusement—had ridden them so, "making believe" they were his horses. He now approached one of these crawling figures from behind and with an agile movement mounted it astride. The man sank upon his breast, recovered, flung the small boy fiercely to the ground as an unbroken colt might have done, then turned upon him a face that lacked a lower jaw—from the upper teeth to the throat was a great red gap fringed with hanging shreds of flesh and splinters of bone. The unnatural prominence of nose, the absence of chin, the fierce eyes, gave this man the appearance of a great bird of prey crimsoned in throat and breast by the blood of its quarry. The man rose to his knees, the child to his feet. The man shook his fist at the child; the child, terrified at last, ran to a tree near by, got upon the farther side of it and took a more serious view of the situation. And so the clumsy multitude dragged itself slowly and painfully along in hideous pantomime—moved forward down the slope like a swarm of great black beetles, with never a sound of going—in silence profound, absolute.

Instead of darkening, the haunted landscape began to brighten. Through the belt of trees beyond the brook shone a strange red light, the trunks and branches of the trees making a black lacework against it. It struck the creeping figures and gave them monstrous shadows, which caricatured their movements on the lit grass. It fell upon their faces, touching their whiteness with a ruddy tinge, accentuating the stains with which so many of them were freaked and maculated. It sparkled on buttons and bits of metal in their clothing. Instinctively the child turned toward the growing splendor and moved down the slope with his horrible companions; in a few moments had passed the foremost of the throng—not much of a feat, considering his advantages. He placed himself in the lead, his wooden sword still in hand, and solemnly directed the march, conforming his pace to theirs and occasionally turning as if to see that his forces did not straggle. Surely such a leader never before had such a following.

Scattered about upon the ground now slowly narrowing by the encroachment of this awful march to water, were certain articles to which, in the leader's mind, were coupled no significant associations: an occasional blanket, tightly rolled lengthwise, doubled and the ends bound together with a string; a heavy knapsack here, and there a broken rifle—such things, in short, as are found in the rear of retreating troops, the "spoor" of men flying from their hunters. Everywhere near the creek, which here had a magin of lowland, the earth was trodden into mud by the feet of men and horses. An observer of better experience in the use of his eyes would have noticed that these footprints pointed in both directions; the ground had been twice passed over—in advance and in retreat. A few hours before, these desperate, stricken men, with their more fortunate and now distant comrades, had penetrated the forest in thousands. Their successive battalions, breaking into swarms and re-forming in lines, had passed the child on every side—had almost trodden on him as he slept. The rustle and murmur of their march had not awakened him. Almost within a stone's throw of where he lay they had fought a battle; but all unheard by him were the roar of the musketry, the shock of the cannon, "the thunder of the captains and the shouting." He had slept through it all, grasping his little wooden sword with perhaps a tighter clutch in unconscious sympathy with his martial environment, but as heedless of the grandeur of the struggle as the dead who had died to make the glory.

The fire beyond the belt of woods on the farther side of the creek, reflected to earth from the canopy of its own smoke, was now suffusing the whole landscape. It transformed the sinuous line of mist to the vapor of gold. The water gleamed with dashes of red, and red, too, were many of the stones protruding above the surface. But that was blood; the less desperately wounded had stained them in crossing. On them, too, the child now crossed with eager steps; he was going to the fire. As he stood upon the farther bank he turned about to look at the companions of his march. The advance was arriving at the creek. The stronger had already drawn themselves to the brink and plunged their faces into the flood. Three or four who lay without motion appeared to have no heads. At this the child's eyes expanded with wonder; even his hospitable understanding could not accept a phenomenon implying such vitality as that. After slaking their thirst these men had not had the strength to back away from the water, nor to keep their heads above it. They were drowned. In rear of these, the open spaces of the forest showed the leader as many formless figures of his grim command as at first; but not nearly so many were in motion. He waved his cap for their encouragement and smilingly pointed with his weapon in the direction of the guiding light—a pillar of fire to this strange exodus.

Confident of the fidelity of his forces, he now entered the belt of woods, passed through it easily in the red illumination, climbed a fence, ran across a field, turning now and again to coquet with his responsive shadow, and so approached the blazing ruin of a dwelling. Desolation everywhere! In all the wide glare not a living thing was visible. He cared nothing for that; the spectacle pleased, and he danced with glee in imitation of the wavering flames. He ran about, collecting fuel, but every object that he found was too heavy for him to cast in from the distance to which the heat limited his approach. In despair he flung in his sword—a surrender to the superior forces of nature. His military career was at an end.

Shifting his position, his eyes fell upon some outbuildings which had an oddly familiar appearance, as if he had dreamed of them. He stood considering them with wonder, when suddenly the entire plantation, with its inclosing forest, seemed to turn as if upon a pivot. His little world swung half around; the points of the compass were reversed. He recognized the blazing building as his own home!

For a moment he stood stupefied by the power of the revelation, then ran with stumbling feet, making a half-circuit of the ruin. There, conspicuous in the light of the conflagration, lay the dead body of a woman—the white face turned upward, the hands thrown out and clutched full of grass, the clothing deranged, the long dark hair in tangles and full of clotted blood. The greater part of the forehead was torn away, and from the jagged hole the brain protruded, overflowing the temple, a frothy mass of gray, crowned with clusters of crimson bubbles—the work of a shell.

The child moved his little hands, making wild, uncertain gestures. He uttered a series of inarticulate and indescribable cries—something between the chattering of an ape and the gobbling of a turkey—a startling, soulless, unholy sound, the language of a devil. The child was a deaf mute.

Then he stood motionless, with quivering lips, looking down upon the wreck.

MELVILLE DAVISSON POST

The Men of the Jimmy

I

"Parks," said Randolph Mason, "has Leslie Wilder a country place on the Hudson?"

"Yes, sir," replied the bald little clerk. "It is at Cliphmore, I think, sir."

"Well," said Mason, "here is his message, Parks, asking that I come to him immediately. It seems urgent and probably means a will. Find out what time a train leaves the city and have a carriage."

The clerk took the telegram, put on his coat, and went down on the street. It was cold and snowing heavily. The wind blew up from the river, driving the snow in great, blinding sheets. The melancholy Parks pulled his hat down over his face, walked slowly round the square, and came back to the entrance of the office building. Instead of taking the elevator he went slowly up the steps into the outer office. Here he took off his coat and went over to the window, and stood for some minutes looking out at the white city.

"At any rate he will not suspect me," he muttered, "and we must get every dollar possible while we can. He won't last always."

At this moment a carriage drove up and stopped by the curb. Parks turned round quickly and went into Mason's private office. "Sir," he said, "your train leaves at six ten, and the carriage is waiting."

When Randolph Mason stepped from the train at the little Cliphmore station, it was pitch dark, and the snow was sweeping past in great waves. He groped his way to the little station-house and pounded on the door. There was no response. As he turned round a man stepped up on the platform, pulled off his cap, and said, "Excuse me, sir, de carriage is over here, sir." Mason followed the man across the platform, and up what seemed to be a gravel road for perhaps twenty yards. Here they found a closed carriage. The man threw open the door, helped Mason in, and closed it, forcing the handle carefully. Then he climbed up in front, struck the horses, and drove away.

For perhaps half an hour the carriage rattled along the gravel road, and Mason sat motionless. Suddenly he leaned over, turned the handle of the carriage door, and jerked it sharply. The door did not open. He tucked the robes around him and leaned back in the seat, like a man who had convinced himself of the truth of something that he suspected. Presently the carriage began to wobble and jolt as though upon an unkept country road. The driver pulled up his horses and allowed them to walk. The snow drifted up around him and he seemed to have great difficulty in keeping to the road. Presently he stopped, climbed down from the box and attempted to open the door. He apparently had some difficulty, but finally threw it back and said: "Dis is de place, sir."

Randolph Mason got out and looked around him. "This may be the place," he said to the man, "but this is not Wilder's."

"I said dis here is de place," answered the man, doggedly.

"Beyond a doubt," said Mason, "and since you are such a cunning liar I will go in."

The driver left the horses standing and led the way across what seemed to be an unkept lawn, Mason following. A house loomed up in the dark before them. The driver stopped and rapped on the door. There was no light visible and no indication of any inhabitant. The driver rapped again without getting any response. Then he began to curse, and to kick the door violently.

"Will you be quiet?" said a voice from the inside, and the door opened. The hall-way was dark, and the men on the outside could not see the speaker.

"Here is de man, sir," said the driver.

"That is good," replied the voice; "come in."

The two men stepped into the house. The man who had bid them enter closed the door and bolted it. Then he took a lantern from under his coat and led them back through the hall to the rear of the building. The house was dilapidated and old, and had the appearance of having been deserted for many years.

The man with the lantern turned down a side hall, opened a door, and ushered Mason into a big room, where there was a monster log fire blazing. This room was dirty and bare. The windows were carefully covered from the inside, so as to prevent the light from being seen. There was no furniture except a broken table and a few old chairs. At the table sat an old man smoking a pipe. He had on a cap and overcoat, and was studying a newspaper spread out before him. He seemed to be spelling out the words with great difficulty, and did not look up. Randolph Mason took off his great-coat, threw it over a chair, and seated himself before the fire. The man with the lantern placed it on the mantel-shelf, took up a short pipe, and seating himself on a box by the hearth corner, began to smoke. He was a powerful man, perhaps forty years old, clean and decently dressed. His forehead was broad. His eyes were unusually big and blue. He seemed to be of considerable intelligence, and his expression, taken all in all, was innocent and kindly.

For a time there was nothing said. The driver went out to look after his horses. The old man at the table labored on at his newspaper, and Randolph Mason sat looking into the fire. Suddenly he turned to the man at his left. "Sir," said he "to what difficulty am I indebted for this honor?"

"Well," said the man, putting his pipe into his pocket, "the combination is too high for us this time! we can't crack it. We knew about you and sent for you."

"Your plan for getting me here does little credit to your wits," said Mason; "the trick is infantile and trite."

"But it got you here anyhow," replied the man.

"Yes," said Mason, "when the dupe is willing to be one. But suppose I had rather concluded to break with your driver at the station? It is likewise dangerous to drive a man locked in a carriage when he may easily kill you through the window."

"Trow on de light, Barker," said the old man at the table; "what is de use of gropin'?"

"Well," said the younger man, "the fact is simply this: The Boss and Leary and a 'supe' were cracking a safe out in the States. They were tunnelling up early in the morning, when the 'supe' forced a jimmy through the floor. The bank janitor saw it, and they were all caught and sent up for ten years. We have tried every way to get the boys out, but have been unable to do anything at all, until a few days ago we discovered that one of the guards could be bribed to pass in a kit, and to hit the 'supe' if there should be any shooting, if we could put up enough stuff. He was to be discharged at the end of his month anyway, and he did not care.

But he would not move a finger under four thousand dollars. We have been two weeks trying to raise the money, and have now only twelve hundred. The guard has only a week longer, and another opportunity will not occur perhaps in a lifetime. We have tried everything, and cannot raise another hundred, and it is our only chance to save the Boss and Leary."

"Dat is right," put in the old man; "it don't go at all wid us, we is gittin' trowed on it, and dat is sure unless dis gent knows a good ting to push, and dat is what he is here fur, to name de good ting to push. Dat is right, dat's what we 's got to have, and we 's got to have it now. We don't keer no hell-room fur de 'supe,' it 's de Boss and Leary we wants."

Randolph Mason got up and stood with his back to the fire. The lines of his face grew deep and hard. Presently he thrust out his jaw, and began to walk backward and forward across the room.

"Barker," muttered the old man, looking up for the first time, "de guy has jimmy iron in him."

The blue-eyed man nodded and continued to watch Mason curiously. Suddenly, as he passed the old man at the table, Mason stopped short and put his finger down on the newspaper. The younger man leaped up noiselessly, and looking over Mason's shoulder read the head-lines under his finger. "Kidnapped," it ran. "The youngest son of Cornelius Rockham stolen from the millionaire's carriage. Large rewards offered. No clew."

"Do you know anything about this?" said Mason, shortly.

"Dat 's de hell," replied the old man, "we does n't."

Mason straightened up and swung round on his heel. "Sir," he said to the man Barker, "are you wanted in New York?"

"No," he replied, "I am just over; they don't know me."

"Good," said Mason, "it is as plain as a blue print. Come over here."

The two crossed to the far corner of the room. There Mason grasped the man by the shoulder and began to talk to him rapidly, but in a voice too low to be heard by the old man at the table. "Smoove guy, dis," muttered the old man. "He may be fly in de nut, but he takes no chances on de large audejence."

For perhaps twenty minutes Randolph Mason talked to the man at the wall. At first the fellow did not seem to understand, but after a time his face lighted up with wonder and eagerness, and his assurance seemed to convince the speaker, for presently they came back together to the fire.

"You," said Mason to the old man, "what is your name?"

"It cuts no ice about de label," replied the old man, pulling at his pipe. "Fur de purposes of dis seeyance I am de Jook of Marlbone."

"Well," said Mason, putting on his coat, "Mr. Barker will tell your lordship what you are to do."

The big blue-eyed man went out and presently returned with the carriage driver. "Mr. Mason," he said, "Bill will drive you to the train and you will be in New York by twelve."

"Remember," said Mason, savagely, turning around at the door, "it must be exactly as I have told you, word for word."

11

"I tell you," said Cornelius Rockham, "it is the most remarkable proposition that I have ever heard."

"It is strange," replied the Police Chief, thoughtfully. "You say the fellow declared that he had a proposition to make in regard to the child, and that he refused to make it save in the presence of witnesses."

"Yes, he actually said that he would not speak with me alone or where he might be misunderstood, but that he would come here to-night at ten and state the matter to me and such reliable witnesses as I should see fit to have, not less than three in number; that a considerable sum of money might be required, and that I would do well to have it in readiness; that if I feared robbery or treachery, I should fill the house with policemen, and take any and every precaution that I thought necessary. In fact, he urged that I should have the most reliable men possible for witnesses, and as many as I desired, and that I must avail myself of every police protection in order that I might feel amply and thoroughly secure."

"Well," said the Police Chief, "if the fellow is not straight he is a fool. No living crook would ever make such a proposition."

"So I am convinced," replied Mr. Rockham. "The precautions he suggests certainly prove it. He places himself absolutely in our hands, and knows that if any crooked work should be attempted we have everything ready to thwart it; that there is nothing that he could accomplish, and he would only be placing himself helplessly in the grasp of the police. However, we will not fail to avail ourselves of his suggestion. You will see to it, Chief?"

"Yes," said the officer, rising and putting on his coat. "We will give him no possible chance. It is now five. I will send the men in an hour."

At ten o'clock that night, the palatial residence of Cornelius Rockham was in a state of complete police blockade. All the approaches were carefully guarded. The house itself, from the basement to the very roof, literally swarmed with the trusted spies of the police. The Chief felt indeed that his elaborate precautions were in a vast measure unnecessary. He was not a quick man, but he was careful after a ponderous method, and trusted much to precautionary safeguards.

Cornelius Rockham, the Chief, and two sergeants in citizen's dress, were waiting. Presently the bell rang and a servant ushered a man into the room. He was big and plainly dressed. His hair was brown and his eyes were blue, frank and kindly and his expression was pleasant and innocent, almost infantile.

"Good-evening, gentlemen," he said, "I believe I am here by appointment with Mr. Rockham."

"Yes," replied Cornelius Rockham, rising, "pray be seated, sir. I have asked these gentlemen to be present, as you suggested."

"Your time is valuable, no doubt," said the man, taking the proffered chair, "and I will consume as little of it as possible. My name is Barker. I am a comparative stranger in this city, and by pure accident am enabled to make the proposition which I am going to make. Your child has been missing now for several days, I believe, without any clew whatever. I do not know who kidnapped it, nor any of the circumstances. It is now half-past ten o'clock. I do not know where it is at this time, and I could not now take you to it. At eleven o'clock to-night, I shall know where it is, and I shall be able to take you to it. But I need money, and I must have five thousand dollars to compensate me for the information."

The man paused for a moment, and passed his hand across his forehead. "Now," he went on, "to be perfectly plain. I will not trust you, and you, of course, will not trust me. In order to insure good faith on both sides, I must ask that you pay me the money here, in the presence of these witnesses, then handcuff me to a police officer, and I will take you to the child at eleven o'clock. You may surround me with all the guards you think proper, and take every precaution to insure your safety and prevent my escape. You will pardon my extreme frankness, but business is business, and we all know that matters of this kind must be arranged beforehand. Men are too indifferent after they get what they want." Barker stopped short, and looked up frankly at the men around him.

Cornelius Rockham did not reply, but his white, haggard face lighted up hopefully. He beckoned to the Police Chief, and the two went into an adjoining room.

"What do you think?" said Rockham, turning to the officer.

"That man," replied the Chief, "means what he says, or else he is an insane fool, and he certainly bears no indication of the latter. It is evident that he will not open his mouth until he gets the money, for the reason that he is afraid that he will be ignored after the child is recovered. I do not believe there is any risk in paying him now, and doing as he says; because he cannot possibly escape when fastened to a sergeant, and if he proves to be a fake, or tries any crooked work, we will return the money to you and lock him up."

"I am inclined to agree with you," replied Rockham; "the man is eccentric and suspicious, but he certainly will not move until paid, and we have no charge as yet upon which to arrest him. Nor would it avail us anything if we did. There is little if any risk, and much probability of learning something of the boy. I will do it."

He went down to the far end of the hall and took a package of bills from a desk. Then the two men returned to the drawing-room.

"Sir," said Rockham to Barker, "I accept your proposition, here is the money, but you must consider yourself utterly in our hands. I am willing to trust you, but I am going to follow your suggestion."

"A contract is a contract," replied Barker, taking the money and counting it carefully. When he had satisfied himself that the amount was correct he thrust the roll of bills into his outside coat pocket.

"It is now fifteen minutes until eleven," said the Police Chief, stepping up to Barker's chair, "and if you are ready we will go."

"I am ready," said the man, getting up.

The Police Chief took a pair of steel handcuffs from his pocket, locked one part of them carefully on Barker's left wrist and fastened the other to the right wrist of the sergeant. Then they went out of the house and down the steps to the carriages.

The Police Chief, Barker, and the sergeant climbed into the first carriage, and Mr. Rockham and the other officer into the second.

"Have your man drive to the Central Park entrance," said Barker to the Chief. The officer called to the driver and the carriages rolled away. At the west entrance to Central Park the men alighted.

"Now, gentlemen," said Barker, "we must walk west to the second corner and wait there until a cab passes from the east. The cab will be close curtained and will be drawn by a sorrel cob. As it passes you will dart out, seize the horse, and take possession of the cab. You will find the child in the cab, but I must insist for my own welfare, that you make every appearance of having me under arrest and in close custody."

The five men turned down the street in the direction indicated. Mr. Rockham and one of the officers in the front and the other two following with Barker between them. For a time they walked along in silence. Then the Police Chief took some cigars from his pocket, gave one to the sergeant, and offering them to Barker said, "Will you smoke, sir?"

"Not a cigar, I thank you," replied the man, "but if you will permit me I will light my pipe."

The two men stopped. Barker took a short pipe and a pouch of tobacco from his pocket, filled the pipe and lighted it; as he was about to return the pouch to his coat pocket, an old apple-woman, hobbling past, caught the odor and stopped.

"Fur de love of Hivin, Mister," she drawled, "give me a pipe uv yer terbaccy?" Barker laughed, tossed her the pouch, and the three hurried on.

At the corner indicated the men stopped. The Police Chief examined the handcuffs carefully to see that they were all right; then they drew back in the shadow and waited for the cab. Eleven o'clock came and passed and the cab did not appear. Mr. Rockham paced the sidewalk nervously and the policemen gathered close around Barker.

At half-past eleven o'clock Barker straightened up, shrugged his shoulders, and turned to the Police Chief. "It is no use," he said, "they are not here and they never will come now."

"What!" cried the Police Chief savagely, "do you mean that we are fooled?"

"Yes," said Barker, "all of us. It is no use I tell you, the thing is over."

"It is not over with you, my man," growled the Chief. "Here, sergeant, get Mr. Rockham his money and let us lock this fellow up."

The sergeant turned and thrust his hand into Barker's outside coat pocket, then his chin dropped and he turned white. "It is gone!" he muttered.

"Gone!" shouted Rockham; "search the rascal!"

The sergeant began to go carefully over the man. Suddenly he stopped. "Chief," he muttered, "it was in that tobacco pouch."

The Police Chief staggered back and spun round on his heel. "Angels of

Hell!" he gasped, "it was a cute trick, and it threw us all, every one of us."

Rockham bounded forward and brought his hand down heavily on Barker's shoulder. "As for you, my fine fellow," he said, bitterly, "we have you all right and we will land you in Sing Sing."

Barker was silent. In the dark the men could not see that he was smiling.

III

The court-room of Judge Walter P. Wright was filled with an interested audience of the greater and unpunished criminals of New York. The application of Barker for a *habeas corpus,* on the ground that he had committed no crime, had attracted wide attention. It was known that the facts were not disputed, and the proceeding was a matter of wonder.

Some days before, the case had been submitted to the learned judge. The attorneys for the People had not been anxious enough to be interested, and looked upon the application as a farce. The young man who appeared for Barker announced that he represented one Randolph Mason, a counsellor, and was present only for the purpose of asking that Barker be discharged, and for the further purpose of filing the brief of Mason in support of the application. He made no argument whatever, and had simply handed up the brief, which the attorneys for the People had not thought it worth their while to examine.

Barker sat in the dock, grim and confident. The attorneys for the commonwealth were listless. The audience was silent and attentive. It was a vital matter to them. If Barker had committed no crime, what a rich, untramped field was open. The Judge laid his hand upon the books piled up beside him and looked down at the bar.

"This proceeding," he began, "is upon the application of one Lemuel Barker for a writ of *habeas corpus,* asking that he be discharged from custody, upon the ground that he has committed no crime punishable at common law or under the statutes of New York. An agreed state of facts has been submitted, upon which he stands charged by the commonwealth with having obtained five thousand dollars from one Cornelius Rockham by false pretences. The facts are, briefly, that on the 17th day of December Barker called at the residence of Rockham and said that he desired to make a proposition looking to the recovery of the lost child of said Rockham, but he desired to make it in the presence of witnesses, and would return at ten o'clock that night. Pursuant to his appointment, Barker again presented himself at the residence of said Rockham, and, in the presence of witnesses, declared, in substance, that at that time (then ten o'clock) he knew nothing of the said child, could not produce it, and could give no information in regard to it, but that at eleven o'clock he would know where the child was and would produce it; and that, if the said Rockham would then and there pay him five thousand dollars, he would at eleven o'clock take them to the lost child. The money was paid and the transaction completed.

"At eleven o'clock, Barker took the men to a certain corner in the upper part of this city, and it there developed that the entire matter was a scheme on his part for the purpose of obtaining the said sum of money, which he had in some manner disposed of; and that he in fact knew nothing of the child and never intended to produce it.

"The attorneys for the People considered it idle to discuss what they believed to be such a plain case of obtaining money under false pretences; and I confess that upon first hearing I was inclined to believe the proceeding a useless imposition upon the judiciary. I have had occasion to change my opinion."

The attorneys present looked at each other with wonder and drew their chairs closer to the table. The audience moved anxiously.

"The prisoner," continued the Judge, "has filed in his behalf the remarkable brief of one Randolph Mason, a counsellor. This I have read, first, with curiosity, then interest, then wonder, and, finally, conviction. In it the crime sought to be charged is traced from the days of the West Saxon Wights up to the present, beginning with the most ancient cases and ending with the later decisions of our own Court of Appeals. I have gone over these cases with great care, and find that the vital element of this crime is, and has ever been, the false and fraudulent representation or statement as to an *existing* or *past fact*. Hence, no representation, however false, in regard to a *future* transaction can be a crime. Nor can a false statement, *promissory* in its nature, be the subject of a criminal charge.

"To constitute this crime there must always be a false representation or statement as to a *fact,* and that *fact* must be a *past* or an *existing fact*. These are plain statements of ancient and well settled law, and laid here in this brief, almost in the exact language of our courts.

"In this case the vital element of crime is wanting. The evidence fails utterly to show false representation as to any *existing fact*. The prisoner, Barker, at the time of the transaction, positively disclaimed any knowledge of the child, or any ability to produce it. What he did represent was that he would know, and that he would perform certain things, in the future. The question of remoteness is irrelevant. It is immaterial whether the future time be removed minutes or years.

"The false representation complained of was wholly in regard to a future transaction, and essentially promissory in its nature, and such a wrong is not, and never has been, held to be the foundation of a criminal charge."

"But, if your Honor please," said the senior counsel for the People, rising, "is it not clearly evident that the prisoner, Barker, began with a design to defraud; that that design was present and obtained at the time of this transaction; that a representation was made to Rockham for the purpose of convincing him that there then existed a *bona fide* intention to produce his child; that money was obtained by false statements in regard to this intention then existing, when in fact such intention did not exist and never existed, and statements made to induce Rockham to believe that it did exist were all utterly false, fraudulent and delusive? Surely this is a crime."

The attorney sat down with the air of one who had propounded an unanswerable proposition. The Judge adjusted his eyeglasses and began to turn the pages of a report. "I read," he said, "from the syllabus of the case of The People of New York *vs*. John H. Blanchard. 'An indictment for false pretences may not be founded upon an assertion of an existing intention, although it did not in fact exist. There must be a false representation as to an existing fact.'

"Your statement, sir, in regard to intention, in this case is true, but it is no element of crime."

"But, sir," interposed the counsel for the People, now fully awake to the fact that Barker was slipping from his grasp, "I ask to hold this man for conspiracy and as a violator of the Statute of Cheats."

"Sir," said the Judge, with some show of impatience, "I call your attention to Scott's case and the leading case of Ranney. In the former, the learned Court announces that if the false and fraudulent representations are not criminal there can be no conspiracy; and, in the latter, the Court says plainly that false pretences in former statutes, and gross fraud or cheat in the more recent acts, mean essentially the same thing.

"You must further well know that this man could not be indicted at common law for cheat, because no false token was used, and because in respect to the instrumentality by which it was accomplished it had no special reference to the public interest.

"This case is most remarkable in that it bears all the marks of a gross and detestable fraud, and in morals is a vicious and grievous wrong, but under our law it is no crime and the offender cannot be punished."

"I understand your Honor to hold," said the baffled attorney, jumping to his feet, "that this man is guilty of no crime; that the dastardly act which he confesses to have done constitutes no crime, and that he is to go out of this court-room freed from every description of liability or responsibility to any criminal tribunal; that the law is so defective and its arm so short that it cannot pluck forth the offender and punish him when by every instinct of morality he is a criminal. If this be true, what a limitless field is open to the knave, and what a snug harbor for him is the great commonwealth of New York!"

"I can pardon your abruptness," said the Judge, looking down upon the angry and excited counsellor, "for the reason that your words are almost exactly the lament of presiding Justice Mullin in the case of Scott. But, sir, this is not a matter of sentiment; it is not a matter of morality; it is not even a matter of right. It is purely and simply a matter of law, and there is no law."

The Judge unconsciously arose and stood upright beside the bench. The audience of criminals bent forward in their seats.

"I feel," he continued, "for the first time the utter inability of the law to cope with the gigantic cunning of Evil. I appreciate the utter villainy that pervaded this entire transaction. I am convinced that it was planned with painstaking care by some master mind moved by Satanic impulse. I now know that there is abroad in this city a malicious intelligence of almost infinite genius, against which the machinery of the law is inoperative. Against every sentiment of common right, of common justice, I am compelled to decide that Lemuel Barker is guilty of no crime and stands acquit."

It was high noon. The audience of criminals passed out from the temple of so-called Justice, and with them went Lemuel Barker, unwhipped and brazen; now with ample means by which to wrest his fellows in villainy from the righteous wrath of the commonwealth. They were all enemies of this same commonwealth, bitter, never wearying enemies, and to-day they had learned much. How short-armed the Law was! Wondrous marvel that they had not known it sooner! To be sure they must plan so cunningly that only the Judge should pass upon them. He was a mere legal machine. He was only the hand applying the rigid rule of the law. The danger was with the jury; there lay the peril to be avoided. The jury! how they hated it and feared it! and of right, for none knew better than they that whenever, and wherever, and however men stop to probe for it, they always find, far down in the human heart, a great love of common right and fair dealing that is as deep-seated and abiding as the very springs of life.

EMILY JAMES PUTNAM

Helen in Egypt

The priests in answer to my inquiries on the subject of Helen informed me of the following particulars. When Alexander had carried off Helen from Sparta he took ship and sailed homewards. On his way across the Ægean a gale arose which drove him from his course and took him down to the sea of Egypt; hence, as the wind did not abate, he was carried on to the coast, when he went ashore, landing at the Salt Pans in that mouth of the Nile which is now called the Canopic. At this place there stood upon the shore a temple, which still exists, dedicated to Herakles. If a slave runs away from his master and taking sanctuary at this shrine gives himself up to the god, and receives certain sacred marks upon his person, whosoever his master may be he cannot lay hand on him. This law still remained unchanged to my time. Hearing therefore of the custom of the place, the attendants of Alexander deserted him, and fled to the temple where they sat as suppliants. While there, wishing to damage their master, they accused him to the Egyptians, narrating all the circumstances of the rape of Helen and the wrong done to Menelaus. These charges they brought not only before the priests but also before the warden of that mouth of the river whose name was Thonis.

As soon as he received the intelligence Thonis sent a message to Proteus, who was at Memphis, to this effect: "A stranger is arrived from Greece; he is by race a Teucrian and has done a wicked deed in the country from which he is come. Having beguiled the wife of the man whose guest he was, he carried her away with him, and much treasure also. Compelled by stress of weather, he has now put in here. Are we to let him depart as he came, or shall we seize what he has brought?"

Proteus replied, "Seize the man, be he who he may, that has dealt thus wickedly with his friend, and bring him before me that I may hear what he will say for himself."

Thonis on receiving these orders arrested Alexander and stopped the departure of his ships; then, taking with him Alexander, Helen, the treasures and also the fugitive slaves, he went up to Memphis. When all were arrived Proteus asked Alexander who he was and whence he had come. Alexander replied by giving his descent, the name of his country and a true account of his late voyage. Then Proteus questioned him as to how he got possession of Helen. In his reply Alexander became confused and diverged from the truth, whereon the slaves interposed, confuted his statements and told the whole story of the crime.

Finally Proteus delivered judgment as follows: "Did I not regard it as a matter of the utmost consequence that no stranger driven to my country by adverse winds should ever be put to death, I would certainly have avenged the Greek by slaying thee....I suffer thee to depart; but the woman and the treasures I shall not permit to be carried away. Here they must stay till the Greek stranger comes in person and takes them back with him. For thyself and thy companions, I command thee to begone from my land within the space of three days."...

Such is the account given by the Egyptian priests, and I am myself inclined to regard as true all that they say of Helen from the following considerations:—if Helen had been at Troy the inhabitants would I think have given her up to the Greeks, whether Alexander consented to it or no. For surely neither Priam nor his family could have been so infatuated as to endanger their own persons, their children and their city, merely that Alexander might possess Helen. The fact was that they had no Helen to deliver, and so they told the Greeks, but the Greeks would not believe what they said—divine providence, as I think, so willing that by their utter destruction it might be made evident to all men that when great wrongs are done the gods will surely visit them with great punishments.

Herodotus, Book II, Chapters 113, 114, 115, and 120

I

When the second morning dawned the north wind had increased in strength, an ugly sea was running and it was very cold. During the night the helmsman had been obliged to let the vessel fall off more and more until she was very nearly running before the gale.

Paris conferred in low tones with the sailing-master. He was haggard with sleeplessness, excitement and anxiety, and the motion of the vessel had affected him unpleasantly, but he was happy. If the worst should come, to drown with Helen seemed to him all a man could ask; in the meantime however he was grieved to the heart for her discomfort.

"We can't do it," he whispered to the master. "We can't cross with the wind like this. These northers sometimes last for days. We had better get under the lea of Crete and lie there till it blows out."

The master pointed over his shoulder to windward. "Do you see that gray cloud on the skyline to the northwest?"

"Yes."

"That is Crete. We passed it in the night."

"Good God," said Paris. "Then we are in the open Egyptian sea."

"Yes."

"There is nothing to do then but run before it till we run under."

"We shall not run under," said the master. "It will run over us."

"Supposing we float and the wind holds, how soon shall we see the coast?"

"I've no idea. I've never been down here. Some say it is five days' sail from Phæstus, and some say it is twenty."

Paris considered. "Food?" he asked.

"For about five days, spreading it rather thin," said the master.

Two men squatted at the tiller, one looking forward towards the scrap of sail and the horizon ahead, the other glancing back at the windward sky and the snarling seas. Every hour they were relieved from the crew who sat amidships at their oars, at the master's signal helping the helmsmen to dodge the more obvious perils.

The driest part of the boat was forward under the little triangle of deck. Here lay Helen, couched among the more perishable of the supplies. Soft skins and rugs were strewn beneath her, and during the first hours of the voyage her two handmaidens had taken turns in supporting her on their knees. But as the sea rose they had fallen sick, and Helen had turned them out into the open waist among the sailors.

"You will be better in the air," she said, and they, adoring her, murmured "how kind madam always is," and crept wretchedly forth to lie in the wash of the bilge, where the sailors laughed at them.

Helen knew as well as anyone that it is only plain women who are seasick, but she had overlooked this fact and had chosen on other principles the least lovely of her women to be her companions. She had herself slept soundly and she woke only when the sun was high. The strong air of the sea had brought color into her ivory cheeks and crisped her hair so that it stood out about her face in a soft cloud. Nor did she feel any fear of the wind or the sea. Far better than Paris and better than the master himself she was able to appreciate the buoyancy of the vessel. Moreover as she lay still for a while, unready to announce herself as awake, her mind, consciously busy with the emotional aspects of her situation, formed on a lower plane of attention the judgment that the gale had reached its height and would presently moderate. And to her adventurous temper the fact that they were scudding heaven knew whither through uncharted seas, a fact which appalled Paris and the master, was in itself a pleasant excitement.

But her enjoyment of the adventure was spoiled by the intrusion of another set of images. Vaguely before she fell asleep, clearly after she had waked, she had seen that the affair was taking a different shape from what she had pictured to herself. Not for a moment had she meant to participate in a mere vulgar elopement. She felt nothing in common with the great lovers of history. Io was a poor creature, a seducer's victim, driven to flight to hide her shame. Europa was a child, dazzled, amused, overwhelmed. Medea was a splendid woman no doubt, gifted and strong, but she had given all for love as simply as either of the others. Helen saw her own case as essentially different from any of these. She was a princess, passing from one throne to another. Paris had brought assurance from Priam his father that she should come to him as his daughter, that Troy should receive her as one that conferred honor, that the Trojans would hold and defend her though all Europe should come to carry her back. She had pictured a short passage over summer seas, the sailors singing at their garlanded oars, Menelaus and his insufferable dullness left behind forever, and a new world of devotion open before her. All was to be done with dignity. She had brought with her a quantity of comforts and valuables from Menelaus' house, having no mind to appear to her new admirers as a blowsy runaway. Naturally she had been obliged to leave secretly, a detail repugnant to her sense of decorum, but many a great captain had found it necessary to do the same. She had left a message for Menelaus putting the affair in its true light as an international event. To his slow mind the idea might be hard to grasp, but she felt sure Agamemnon would explain it to him. Of course Paris could not be left out altogether. His dignity was essential to her own and she had given him full weight; but she had felt that Menelaus would need no underlining of this passage. Paris was incredibly handsome and had a tact with women which Menelaus could appreciate though there was nothing corresponding to it in his own processes. Paris had seemed to her in every way fitted for his part, a fairy prince, deeply in love, chivalrous, brave, regretting the base aspects of his adventure and eager to fight for his lady once she was safely his.

But she no longer saw Paris quite like this. At dusk last night she had closed her eyes against the spectacle of a wilted Paris trying to be sick to windward. The sailing-master with an oath had lifted him bodily to the lee-rail....

A pair of blankets had been hung from the deck to screen Helen's bower, but one of them had blown away in the night. The sailors seated on thwarts through the boat strove to be discreet but often, peeping through her eyelashes, she saw bright dark eyes peering at her. She turned over to the protection of the remaining curtain, thus coming into contact with the packets stored at each side of the covered space. Some of the packets containing bread, others salt fish and others cheese. The aroma of each was distinctly perceptible. Helen had no contempt for any of these things. Indeed she meant to consume a portion of each for her breakfast. But that she, a queen, the most beautiful woman in the world, the daughter of Zeus, the favorite of Aphrodite, a cause of war to kings, should have to sleep where she could smell them touched her heart with a chilling sense of failure.

Meantime a new embarrassment opened before Paris. The seamen were beginning to grumble for their breakfast, and Helen was lying on the stores. Her women waited the signal to rouse her, but Paris frowned at them and came himself to the ragged entrance of the sorry bower. Softly he spoke her name, and softly and sweetly she answered him. He stooped and looked under the deck, dreading to see the signs of suffering; but there she lay glowing with such beauty as he had never yet seen her wear. Sweetly she smiled on him and he fell on his knees beside her. Never had he felt so keenly that she was a queen and he, though a prince, a shepherd. All night he had been upheld by the thought of a rapturous morning kiss behind the kindly curtains, but now he dared not kiss her. The wretched surroundings that his love had brought her to obliged him to an increased respect. He was rather proud of feeling thus, and it did not occur to him that Helen herself had a hand in it.

II

On the fourth day the wind hauled to the west and abated, so that on the fifth they made a propitious landfall on the coast of Egypt. Feeling his way along the skipper finally beached his boat safely within that mouth of the Nile called the Canopic, near the Salt Pans. On a little eminence thereby stood a temple of Herakles and thither the whole company bent their steps to give thanks for their escape. The seamen rudely pressed ahead. Helen, veiled, walked gravely with an arm resting on the shoulders of each of her maidens. Paris came last, carrying the more precious of her parcels.

When they reached the temple twenty minutes later than the men they found trouble. The master and the seamen stood in a grinning row beneath the porch of the temple and on the steps before them stood a smiling priest who rubbed his hands and welcomed the late-comers.

"Madam and sir," said he, "surely the gods have a special care of you, since you have come safely through a storm that has brought more than one wreck upon our shores. Enter and give thanks and let us minister to your wants."

The sailors made no offer to stand aside to let them pass and Paris raised his hand in anger.

"Slaves," he said, "make way." And as he glanced along the row of insolent faces he noted that each man had the sign of the swastika drawn in vermilion on his forehead.

"I must explain," said the priest, still smiling and rubbing his hands. He was clean-shaven, even his poll being razed, and he was clad in white linen from head to foot and shod with papyrus sandals. Paris thought he had never seen anyone look so clean or so repulsive.

"Noble sir," said the priest, "it is my duty to declare to every visitor of this temple, before permitting him to enter, that it is a sanctuary. If a slave enters and gives himself up to the god and receives the sacred sign upon his brow, he thenceforth has no mortal master. As my vows require, I made this announcement to this ship's company, and one and all they closed with the offer. From their anxiety to have the marking finished before your arrival I infer that you are their former master. I fear this may inconvenience you."

Paris sprang up the steps and drew his sword in such a red fog of anger that his hand was stayed a moment because he could not instantly decide whether to slay the priest first or go straight for the captain and the sailors. But in this second the priest stepped before him and held up a warning hand. He had stopped smiling and his voice was no longer honied but harsh.

"The gods alone can help you, my poor boy," he said. "I fear you have already sinned against them. Do not offend them further. And I may remark, on a lower plane, that I have fifty armed men within call."

Paris replaced his sword. Love was teaching him many things; for Helen's safety he renounced the beau geste.

"Holy one," he said, "what is this country and who is the king of it? In the name of Zeus who protects strangers I ask to be taken before him."

"This is the land of Egypt," said the priest. "It is ruled by King Proteus who lives in Memphis, two days' journey up the river. The warden of this port is Thonis, and it is my duty at once to take you before him with these sailors and this lady,—doubtless I should not exaggerate if I said this fair lady," and he saluted Helen with a bow of ironic reverence.

Paris, watching him with silent fury, saw his face change as he returned to the upright position, and looking to see what had caused this change he saw that Helen had raised her veil and was gazing into the eyes of the priest. Her expression was one of faint and almost amused interest and she seemed to be looking from a long way off.

The avidity that appeared in the priest's eyes and mouth was strange for so holy a man. It caused Paris to realize that going about the world in charge of the most beautiful woman in it would not be restful.

The priest bowed again. "Madam," he said, "forgive my levity and let me offer you the security of this shrine. Will you not take sanctuary here while this unhappy young man goes to give an account of his misdeeds?"

Gently Helen answered, still faintly amused. "Why should I take sanctuary? I am a free woman, guided by the gods in what I do. My companion is a prince in his own country and my trusted friend. I need no sanctuary unless we have fallen upon a barbarous land where strangers are ill-treated."

Paris took Helen's hand. "Thank you, dearest," he said. "Let us go. Thonis may be more sympathetic with us than this shaven celibate."

Helen softly pressed his hand. "Paris," she murmured, "it may be after all that we have done wrong. If we have we cannot hope for sympathy."

"For heaven's sake," cried Paris, "don't lose courage now! We went over that a hundred times. Come, we are together for better or for worse. We will tell our story frankly to this warden and win through to happiness or die together."

Helen gazed at him with lovely inscrutable eyes. Her look made his head swim with passion and admiration and yet it sent a pang of terror through him. Her eyes were like the eyes of a goddess.

"Come," she said, and they went forward, the priest showing them the way.

Paris, upborne by his great love, was strong in his belief that love justifies all. This woman was made for him. The gods in heaven had brought it to pass that she was his. Could anyone, god or man, condemn this marvel of the world to a lifetime with Menelaus? Paris was humble; he knew he was himself unworthy of her, but at least he loved her. Menelaus, honest, tiresome man, displayed the traits of the husband of all time. Perseus saving Andromeda could not have glowed with purer chivalry than did Paris in rescuing Helen from Menelaus. But far down beneath all this heady excitement a troublesome thought worked steadily, desperately, like an entombed miner. Why had he permitted Helen to bring away so many of Menelaus' goods? It was natural that she should want to come not quite empty-handed to her new kinsmen. He had understood the feeling and in fact admired her for it. Now that he saw an ugly side to the act he blamed himself, not her. But on the main issue his conscience was good and he longed to tell his story to this barbarian official, and indeed to all the world.

The warden of the port received them in a fine hall supported by many columns, quite different from Paris' notion of a barbarian's house. The man himself was gross, fat and dusky, and strangely dressed. He was playing at draughts with his clerk and black men fanned them. Paris sought Helen's eye for a silent exchange of impressions, but she stood a little behind him, sheltered by her maidens, and covertly studying the warden's face.

The priest told his story. The seamen had come to him declaring their master had committed a great crime. He had seduced the wife of his host and carried her off together with much treasure. The gods in their anger had nearly drowned them all and had driven them to the ends of the earth whence they could hardly hope to get home again.

Impassively the warden listened; then he motioned to Paris that he should speak, and Paris stepped forward glowing with good faith.

"Sir," said he, "I am Paris, son of Priam king of Troy. While I kept my father's flocks on Mount Ida, Zeus himself—for what reason who can say?—referred to me the dispute between the three greatest goddesses as to which is the most beautiful. As I am an honest man Aphrodite fairly won the prize. In gratitude to me she promised me the fairest woman in the world for my wife, Helen, called the daughter of Tyndareus king of Sparta but in fact the child of Zeus. Thus with the sanction of the gods and with my father's approval I went forth to win this lady. Doubtless it was by the good offices of Aphrodite that she loved me as I loved her. I am not worthy of her—what mortal could be?—but we belong to each other by the will of the gods, and I will give my life to maintain her honor and her happiness."

The warden listened to him quizzically and nudged his clerk. "Did you ever hear of all these kings and queens," he asked, "whose sons are shepherds and whose daughters are the children of somebody else?" And both men laughed.

"Prince," he said, addressing Paris, "this is all very pretty but is it true as these sailors say that the lady happens to be the wife of another man, that he was your unsuspicious host, and that you have carried off together with his wife a considerable amount of his property?"

"On the voyage to Sparta," said Paris, "my ship with all my goods was lost on a sandbank. This lady brought with her the simplest comforts to supply the loss and all will be returned fourfold to Menelaus when we reach Troy."

Another thought struck the warden. "Let us see the lady," he said.

Slowly the handmaids stepped aside, and slowly Helen moved forward, her head humbly bowed, her hands crossed suppliant-wise on her breast.

"Look up, look up, my dear," said the warden. "Nobody is going to hurt you."

And Helen looked up. She shot at the warden the drollest glance of confession and avoidance and the room was transformed by her smile, her fairness and her look of youth. You would not have supposed she was more than sixteen.

"Good God," said the warden, "who could blame him? Lady, we mortals are truly the playthings of the gods. It is not for me to judge your strange case. I must send you to Memphis to the king, together with this rather simple-minded and I fear unworthy young man and these sailors." And he forthwith gave orders that they should be conveyed to the capital in a style befitting their rank.

III

As they journeyed up the great river, driven by a breeze that blew always from the north, Paris noted, it is true, the many novelties of the country, the trim little rice-fields, the black men working in them, the tall trees like bouquets of fern on long stems, and the great deadly lizards on the sandbanks; but the real activity of his mind was devoted to the consideration of their plight and above all to the effort to understand Helen. Since they had landed she had given no sign that they were lovers. This grieved him but he did not accuse her of a cooling love. They were in danger and they must be discreet. But with a sharper pang he felt that she was disappointed in him; he had drawn her into a scrape and was not man enough to get her out. Her talismanic beauty, not his sword, was their defense.

In the evening the boat was moored to the bank for the night. The river flowed past them mighty as a sea and quiet as a pond. A great orange moon rose from behind the eastern hills, such a moon as was never seen in Troy or Greece. On such a night a man like Paris could no more keep his emotions to himself than the honeysuckle can hold back its scent. He seated himself by Helen and murmured, "Dearest, tell me your thoughts."

"I like this country," said Helen. "I am glad we have come here."

"It becomes you," said Paris. "I've been admiring you all day as you lie there more like a queen than a prisoner, served by these humble blacks, shaded from the sun with beautiful stuffs whose very name I do not know. Never will this great river—I salute him—bear anything so lovely again."

"Do you know, Paris," said Helen, "I am sometimes sorry to hear you dwell forever on this beauty of mine. It seems as though I had nothing else. Is it all you see in me?"

This attack seemed to Paris so unfair and so uncalled for that he spoke with more bitterness than he knew he had. "I know I am a fool," he said. "Perhaps you are getting tired of me altogether."

"Paris," said Helen, "are you turning against me?"

"Good heaven," cried Paris, "am I not your dog, your slave, your fool? Haven't you made me feel every hour of the day since we came to this cursed land that you are of the race of the gods rather than a human woman and my lover? Don't I know that when we appear before this leather-colored king he will only look at you once and acquit you of all wrong while I bear the blame? Of course I am willing to bear the blame," added poor Paris hastily. "There is no blame, but if there were it is mine. Only I cannot bear that you should separate yourself from me. You don't mean to, of course, but when men see your face they naturally give greater weight to what you say or even to what you don't say than to the words of a mere man. I ought to be our spokesman, but your beauty is more convincing than the plain truth."

"How little you know me," said Helen with a sigh. "No woman ever lived who needed beauty less than I do. See here, Paris, I will make you a promise. This barbarous king shall not see my face tomorrow until he has given judgment. I renounce the advantage you complain of and you shall have it all your own way. It may be the death of us both, and I may say some things that you won't like, but at least you can never feel that I saved myself by my poor face at your expense. I will tell you fairly in advance however what I think will happen. Unless they put us both to death we shall be parted."

"The difference between us," said Paris bitterly, "is that I would rather die with you than live without you."

"My poor Paris," said Helen, "life is always good."

Next morning a bend in the river revealed to them the columned temples and palaces of Memphis, the busy quays, the avenues of palms, the statues of dead kings towering to the sky, the multitude of inhabitants numerous as ants and very like ants in their activity and the strict division of them into carriers of burdens, soldiers and rulers. For a while Paris and Helen forgot their danger and their divided hearts, so insignificant did they seem. Paris was overwhelmed; how could he hope to get so much as a patient hearing from the king of such a city? But Helen carried her head high beneath her sheltering veil. "I like this place," she said again.

Without undue delay they were brought before the king. Half a dozen times they thought they had reached the presence, for each successive anteroom deceived them by its splendour. The audience-hall itself was like a park of trees with its interminable avenues of columns. The king sat upon a high chair on a raised platform. He wore a beard on his chin and a golden serpent on his head. His guards and attendants were past counting.

A chancellor called upon the sailors to tell their tale and they repeated what they had said to the priest and before Thonis.

Then Paris was bidden to reply. He blinked and swallowed and made the speech he had prepared. He repeated in the main what he had said before Thonis, but one statement he altered. "These men lie," he said. "They are slaves and badly frightened slaves. They believe I have brought them bad luck and they will say anything to blacken me. These goods of which they talk so much I brought from Troy as gifts from my father and my mother to my bride."

The king turned to the sailors. "Can you prove your words?" he asked.

"My lord," said the captain, "your scribe holds in his hand the writing of what the prince told the warden of the port. Will you graciously ask him to read it?"

And from a sheet of some thin tough stuff covered with dismal signs the scribe recited to Paris' amazement every word he had said to the warden, including the story of the shipwreck. This was mere magic to the unfortunate young man and he hung his head in shame and discouragement. Through the confusion of his thoughts he heard Helen's clear moving voice.

"O king, may I speak?" said she.

"Speak, madam," said the king, "but raise your veil."

Helen knelt at his feet. "'Let me keep to the custom of my simple country," she begged. "I could not speak if I beheld your greatness."

"As you will, my child," said the king.

Helen rose to her feet and spoke and all listened attentively, so compelling was her voice.

"All that this gentleman has said is true but for one thing, and what these men have said is true also, as far as their slave souls can know the truth. I am the daughter of Leda and of Zeus, though Tyndareus is called my father. He gave me in marriage when I was still a child to Menelaus and with me he gave a kingdom. From my birth Aphrodite has been my mistress and my friend. She it was who bade me leave my husband with the stranger prince and to take with me for my comfort and for my credit in a strange land some small part of the goods I brought to Menelaus. I thought I could do as I would with my own; but let them be sent back to Sparta. They are nothing. Surely some god at enmity with Aphrodite has driven us out of our course and brought us to this distress. Who can tell the mind of the gods that live forever? Far easier would it have been for me to live on quietly at Sparta with goodly Menelaus."

While Paris was marvelling at the adroitness with which Helen had conveyed the idea that her elopment was a duty rather than a pleasure and had avoided the plea of all-for-love which he now felt he had himself been somewhat undignified in urging, he was surprised to find that though she had herself made an excellent impression on the king, she had not done much for her friend.

"My child," said the king, "I see how your simplicity and ignorance of the world have been played upon by this young man who seems to be at the same time designing and incompetent. There are aspects of the case on which we should be wise to shed the light of a noble woman's mind"; and turning to an officer of the guard he said, "give her majesty my love and ask her if she will kindly attend me here."

This development was a thunderclap to Paris. Much as he disliked facing the idea, it had become clearer to him at every step that Helen, not he, would save them if they were to be saved. He detested the sight of her power over other men, yet he had come to count on it. He regarded it as demonstrated that no man would be severe with Helen, but what about a woman? He felt instinctively that the very sources of her strength with men would handicap her here. How fortunate that her face was veiled! In looking forward to their life in Troy he had always felt that Hector and his father would be Helen's best friends and might be obliged sometimes to protect her from the women of the family. And now this queen! What was she like, and how would Helen deal with her? He felt another pang of mingled pain and hope in the reflection that Helen's mind was dealing with the fresh problem far more clearly and rapidly than his own.

A disturbance in the hall told of the queen's arrival. She bowed before the king and seated herself on a vacant throne at his right. She had a strong somewhat stern face, in feature not unlike the king's own and she wore like him the royal asp. The king pointed out to her the parties to the suit and repeated in substance their various evidence.

"I refrain, my dear," said he, "from comment of my own as I wish your independent opinion."

The chancellor looked fixedly at the wall two hundred feet away; two courtiers exchanged a glance; the captain of the guard coughed behind his hand. It was clear to Paris that to the king's familiars there was something amusing in his speech.

"It seems quite clear," said the queen in a loud determined voice, "that the young man is a liar, a seducer and a thief and that the young woman is a lost creature."

"Madame," said Paris, "with your knowledge of the world you should realize that I am not a liar; if I were I should never have told so stupid a lie as this one. Nor am I thief. This lady has explained that she took only of her own. Let the goods go back to Menelaus at once. As she says, they are nothing. And least of all am I a seducer, if you mean by the word what it means to me."

"I suppose you are this woman's lover," said the queen.

"I love her, certainly," said Paris.

The queen looked at him malevolently. "I am not interested in the subtleties of illicit love," said she.

Helen had been slowly advancing inch by inch toward the queen. As these words were spoken she threw herself at the queen's feet with a little sob.

"Oh, Madam," she cried, "if I had only had a mother, a sister, a friend like you! Never has my unhappy lot brought into my life a woman so high-minded!"

"Tut, tut," said the queen; "what's all this?"

"I am not worthy, madam," sobbed Helen, "so much as to touch your robe, but let my sinful lips purify themselves thus," and she bent her lovely head and beneath her veil kissed the queen's sandal.

It was evident that the queen began to be interested. "Let me tell you all," Helen went on. "As you say such a story as mine is hardly fit for your ears, and yet I never knew until I saw you and heard your words how wicked I have been. I beg you, madam, of your goodness to take me apart where no man can hear us. I will tell you everything, just as it happened, and you shall tell me how to make atonement to gods and men."

A sort of smile tinctured the queen's grimness. "Your majesty," she said to the king, "I ask you to put this young woman in my charge. You will doubtless deal with the young man to the full extent of the law. Death, I should say, would meet his case."

"The trouble is, my dear," said the king, "that our laws absolutely forbid putting strangers to death. I am horrified as you are by his violation of the first principles of society, but what can I do? We can keep the lady and the goods and restore them when opportunity serves to the barbarous chief to whom they belong; but I can do nothing with the young man but give him a ship and send him home."

"It is a pity," said the queen. She rose to withdraw and directed that Helen should be brought to her. With parted lips and round eyes of wonder Paris watched them go.

IV

It was not until the following day that he saw Helen again, and he spent a restless night in wondering what her next move would be. It would be untrue to say that his confidence in Helen was unshaken. As he recalled their days of furtive lovemaking in Sparta when her passion and her amorous invention had excelled his as much as her cool diplomacy excelled his now, he could not quite convince himself that circumstances alone were changed; the change was in Helen herself. All that she had done for them both might have been an added bond, but it was in fact a barrier. She did not confide in him. She did not let him feel that their interests were one. It had not yet occurred to him that she might throw him over, but he realized wearily that she was not a simple person like himself, and that possession of her instead of being the great simplification he had expected was a complication perhaps too great for his powers.

Early in the morning a messenger brought him to her, and to his relief he was alone with her. It was the first time since they had left Sparta and he ran to her with open arms. But Helen checked him.

"Paris," she said, "I am on my honor. Be brave, my dear friend. This is our last talk together and we must be like brother and sister."

"What!" shouted Paris, standing before her, his arms still outstretched. "What do you mean? What have they done to you?"

"They have shown me," said Helen gently, "that we have done wrong. Love is not the only thing in the world. There are greater gods than Aphrodite."

"Good heavens," said Paris, "are you throwing me over?"

"You make it very hard," said Helen. "If we had planned together to rob a shrine, or to kill a defenseless person, and you had come to me and said 'Helen, we must not do this; it is wrong,' I should not have raged at you. I should have thought to myself 'Paris is an honorable man; there must be reason in what he says.' And I would have thought it over and if I came to agree with you I should have been grateful to you, and if I did not agree with you I should still believe you were acting for the best, to satisfy your own sense of what was right."

"Helen," said Paris, "you make me sick with your sense of what is right. There is only one right thing now for us, and that is to be true to each other. You have left everything for me; I have risked everything for you. We are man and woman grown; we knew the nature of our act and we knew the responsibility we undertook towards each other. Was it mere impulse that gave you to me in Sparta? I thought your whole life was in it as mine was. But you can't mean it; don't frighten me so; are there listeners for whom you are speaking?"

"I don't know whether there are listeners," said Helen. "Whether there are or not I can say but one thing. Some day, Paris you will see that I am right."

Once in his shepherd days Paris had killed a lioness who attacked the flock, and had found beside her a tiny whelp. This he brought to his hut and tended it and found it the prettiest of little pets. It grew more rapidly than he could have wished, but in spite of the warnings of his friends he kept the affectionate creature as his housemate. One day as he was teasing it in play it leaped straight at him with bared tooth and claw, and if comrades had not been at hand Paris' pet would have torn his throat out. The scene and its emotion flashed through his consciousness now.

"You are terrible," said he to Helen. "You are dangerous. You ought to be killed."

"Keep your hate alive, Paris, to help you to fight for Troy when the Greeks come."

"But the Greeks will not come if you are not there."

"I think they will," said Helen. "My husband's brother Agamemnon saw quite well what you and I were planning; why do you think he let us come away without hindrance? Simply because it would make a very convenient cause of war. The truth is, Paris, Agamemnon is going to take Troy because he believes the Greeks should control the Hellespont."

"The Greeks control the Hellespont!" shouted Paris. "My brother Hector will have a word or two to say to that!"

"I have no doubt," said Helen, "that Hector and Agamemnon will exchange many words on the windy plains of Troy, whether Helen is there or not. And doubtless Agamemnon will insist that I am there, and the stupid chiefs will believe him, and doubtless as long as men sing songs songs will be sung of how Troy fell for shameless Helen's sake, for a runaway princess is a more inspiring thing to fight for and to sing of than a trade route. But it will not be true.... Paris, they will not let us talk longer. The guard is at hand to take you to the sea. Forget me until you can think of me more kindly. As for me I shall stay with these good people and keep myself for Menelaus."

At this Paris' nerves were fairly overset and he burst into a horrible laugh. He flung his arm across his eyes and ran from the room and as he met the guard on the threshold he cried through his laughter, "She is keeping herself for Menelaus!"

Helen sat awhile pensive until a maiden came to summon her to the queen. "My dear," said the queen, "you have behaved nobly. Sit beside me with your work and tell me the story you hinted at yesterday of your ill-treatment at the hands of Theseus."

And the queen gave Helen a golden distaff and a silver basket that ran upon wheels, and the wheels were rimmed with gold.

HENRY JAMES

The Bench of Desolation

I

SHE had practically, he believed, conveyed the intimation, the horrid, brutal, vulgar menace, in the course of their last dreadful conversation, when, for whatever was left him of pluck or confidence—confidence in what he would fain have called a little more confidently the strength of his position—he had judged best not to take it up. But this time there was no question of not understanding, or of pretending he didn't; the ugly, the awful words, ruthlessly formed by her lips, were like the fingers of a hand that she might have thrust into her pocket for extraction of the monstrous object that would serve best for—what should he call it?—a gage of battle.

"If I haven't a very different answer from you within the next three days I shall put the matter into the hands of my solicitor, whom it may interest you to know I've already seen. I shall bring an action for 'breach' against you, Herbert Dodd, as sure as my name's Kate Cookham."

There it was, straight and strong—yet he felt he could say for himself, when once it had come, or even, already, just as it was coming, that it turned on, as if she had moved an electric switch, the very brightest light of his own very reasons. There *she* was, in all the grossness of her native indelicacy, in all her essential excess of will and destitution of scruple; and it was the woman capable of that ignoble threat who, his sharper sense of her quality having become so quite deterrent, was now making for him a crime of it that he shouldn't wish to tie himself to her for life. The vivid, lurid thing was the reality, all unmistakable, of her purpose; she had thought her case well out; had measured its odious, specious presentability; had taken, he might be sure, the very best advice obtainable at Properley, where there was always a first-rate promptitude of everything fourth-rate; it was disgustingly certain, in short, that she'd proceed. She was sharp and adroit, moreover—distinctly in certain ways a master hand; how otherwise, with her so limited mere attractiveness, should she have entangled him? He couldn't shut his eyes to the very probable truth that if she should try it she'd pull it off. She *knew* she would—precisely; and her assurance was thus the very proof of her cruelty. That she had pretended she loved him was comparatively nothing; other women had pretended it, and other women too had really done it; but that she had pretended he could possibly have been right and safe and blest in loving *her,* a creature of the kind who could sniff that squalor of the law-court, of claimed damages and brazen lies and published kisses, of love-letters read amid obscene guffaws, as a positive tonic to resentment, as a high incentive to her course—this was what put him so beautifully in the right. It was what it meant in a woman all through, he said to himself, the mere imagination of such machinery. Truly what a devilish conception and what an appalling nature! But there was no doubt, luckily, either, that he *could* plant his feet the firmer for his now intensified sense of these things. He was to live, it appeared, abominably worried, he was to live consciously rueful, he was to live perhaps even what a scoffing world would call abjectly exposed; but at least he was to live saved. In spite of his clutch of which steadying truth, however, and in spite of his declaring to her, with many other angry protests and pleas, that the line of conduct she announced was worthy of a vindictive barmaid, a lurking fear in him, too deep to counsel mere defiance, made him appear to keep open a little, till he could somehow turn round again, the door of possible composition. He had scoffed at her claim, at her threat, at her thinking she could hustle and bully him—"Such a way, my eye, to call back to life a dead love!"—yet his instinct was ever, prudentially but helplessly, for gaining time, even if time only more woefully to quake, and he gained it now by not absolutely giving for his ultimatum that he wouldn't think of coming round. He didn't in the smallest degree mean to come round, but it was characteristic of him that he could for three or four days breathe a little easier by having left her under the impression that he perhaps might. At the same time he could not have said—what had conduced to bring out, in retort, her own last word, the word on which they had parted—"Do you mean to say you yourself would now be *willing* to marry and live with a man of whom you could feel, the thing done, that he'd be all the while thinking of you in the light of a hideous coercion?" "Never you mind about *my* willingness," Kate had answered; "you've known what that has been for the last six months. Leave that to me, my willingness—I'll take care of it all right; and just see what conclusion you can come to about your own."

He was to remember afterwards how he had wondered whether, turned upon her in silence while her odious lucidity reigned unchecked, his face had shown her anything like the quantity of hate he felt. Probably not at all; no man's face *could* express that immense amount; especially the fair, refined, intellectual, gentlemanlike face which had had—and by her own more than once repeated avowal—so much to do with the enormous fancy she had originally taken to him. "Which—frankly now—would you personally *rather* I should do," he had at any rate asked her with an intention of supreme irony: "just sordidly marry you on top of this, or leave you the pleasure of your lovely appearance in court and of your so assured (since that's how you feel it) big haul of damages? Shan't you be awfully disappointed, in fact, if I don't let you get something better out of me than a poor, plain, ten-shilling gold ring and the rest of the blasphemous rubbish, as we should make it between us, pronounced at the altar? I take it, of course," he had swaggered on, "that your pretension wouldn't be for a moment that I should —after the act of profanity—take up my life with you."

"It's just as much my dream as it ever was, Herbert Dodd, to take up mine with *you!* Remember for me that I can do with it, my dear, that my idea is for even as much as that of you!" she had cried: "remember that for me, Herbert Dodd; remember, remember!"

It was on this she had left him—left him frankly under a mortal chill. There might have been the last ring of an appeal or a show of persistent and perverse tenderness in it, however preposterous any such matter; but in point of fact her large, clean, plain brown face—so much too big for her head, he now more than ever felt it to be, just as her head was so much too big for her body, and just as her hats had an irritating way of appearing to decline choice and conformity in respect to *any* of her dimensions—presented itself with about as much expression as his own shop-window when the broad, blank, sallow blind was down. He was fond of his shop-window with some good show on; he had a fancy for a good show and was master of twenty different schemes of taking arrangement for the old books and prints, "high-class rarities" his modest catalogue called them, in which he dealt and which his maternal uncle, David Geddes, had, as he liked to say, "handed down" to him (his widowed mother had screwed the whole thing, the stock and the connection and the rather bad little house in the rather bad little street, out of the ancient worthy, shortly before his death, in the name of the youngest and most interesting, the "delicate" one and the literary, of her five scattered and struggling children); he could enjoy his happiest collocations and contrasts and effects, his harmonies and varieties of toned and faded leather and cloth, his sought color-notes and the high clearnesses, here and there, of his white and beautifully figured price-labels, they could please him enough in themselves almost to console him for not oftener having to break, on a customer's insistence, into the balanced composition; but the dropped expanse of time-soiled canvas, the thing of Sundays and holidays, with just his name, "Herbert Dodd, Successor," painted on below his uncle's antique style, the feeble penlike flourishes already quite archaic, this ugly vacant mask, which might so easily be taken for the mask of failure, somehow always gave him a chill.

That had been just the sort of chill—the analogy was complete—of Kate Cookham's last look. He supposed people doing an awfully good and sure and steady business, in whatever line, could see a whole front turned to vacancy that way, and merely think of the hours off represented by it. Only for this—nervously to bear it, in other words, and Herbert Dodd, quite with the literary temperament himself, was capable of that amount of play of fancy, or even of morbid analysis—you had to be on some footing, you had to feel some confidence, pretty different from his own up to now. He had never *not* enjoyed passing his show on the other side of the street and taking it in thence with a casual obliquity; but he had never held optical commerce with the drawn blind for a moment longer than he could help. It *always* looked horribly final and as if it never would come up again. Big and bare, with his name staring at him from the middle, it thus offered in its grimness a turn of comparison for Miss Cookham's ominous visage. She never wore pretty, dotty, transparent veils, as Nan Drury did, and the words "Herbert Dodd"—save that she had sounded them at him there two or three times more like a Meg Merrilies or the bold bad woman in one of the melodramas of high life given during the fine season in the pavilion at the end of Properley Pier—were dreadfully, were permanently, seated on her lips. *She* was grim, no mistake.

That evening, alone in the back room above the shop, he saw so little what he could do that, consciously demoralised for the hour, he gave way to tears about it. Her taking a stand so incredibly "low," that was what he couldn't get over. The particular bitterness of his cup was his having let himself in for a struggle on such terms—the use, on her side, of the vulgarest process known to the law: the vulgarest, the vulgarest, he kept repeating that, clinging to the help rendered him by this imputation to his terrorist of the vice he sincerely believed he had ever, among difficulties (for oh he recognized the difficulties!) sought to keep most alien to him. He knew what he was, in a dismal, downtrodden sphere enough—the lean young proprietor of an old business that had itself rather shrivelled with age than ever grown fat, the purchase and sale of second-hand books and prints, with the back street of a long-fronted south-coast watering-place (Old Town by good luck) for the dusky field of his life. But he had gone in for all the education he could get—his educated customers would often hang about for more talk by the half-hour at a time, he actually feeling himself, and almost with a scruple, hold them there; which meant that he had had (he couldn't be blind to that) natural taste and had lovingly cultivated and formed it. Thus, from as far back as he could remember, there had been things all round him that he suffered from when other people didn't; and he had kept most of his suffering to himself—which had taught him, in a manner, *how* to suffer, and how almost to like to.

So, at any rate, he had never let go his sense of certain differences, he had done everything he could to keep it up—whereby everything that was vulgar was on the wrong side of his line. He had believed, for a series of strange, oppressed months, that Kate Cookham's manners and tone were on the right side; she had been governess—for young children—in two very good private families, and now had classes in literature and history for bigger girls who were sometimes brought by their mammas; in fact, coming in one day to look over his collection of students' manuals, and drawing it out, as so many did, for the evident sake of his conversation, she had appealed to him that very first time by her apparently pronounced intellectual side—goodness knew she didn't even then by the physical!—which she had artfully kept in view till she had entangled him past undoing. And it had all been but the cheapest of traps—when he came to take the pieces apart a bit—laid over a brazen avidity. What he now collapsed for, none the less—what he sank down on a chair at a table and nursed his weak, scared sobs in his resting arms for—was the fact that, whatever the trap, it held him as with the grip of sharp murderous steel. There he was, there he was; alone in the brown summer dusk—brown through *his* windows—he cried and he cried. He shouldn't get out without losing a limb. The only question was which of his limbs it should be.

Before he went out, later on—for he at last felt the need to—he could, however, but seek to remove from his face and his betraying eyes, over his washing-stand, the traces of his want of fortitude. He brushed himself up; with which, catching his stricken image a bit spectrally, in an old dim toilet-glass, he knew again, in a flash, the glow of righteous resentment. Who should be assured against coarse usage if a man of his really elegant, perhaps in fact a trifle over-refined appearance, his absolutely gentlemanlike type, couldn't be? He never went so far as to rate himself, with exaggeration, a gentleman; but he would have maintained against all comers, with perfect candor and as claiming a high advantage, that he was, in spite of that liability to blubber, "like" one; which he *was* no doubt, for that matter, at several points. Like what lady then, who could ever possibly have been taken for one, was Kate Cookham, and therefore how could one have anything—anything of the intimate and private order—out with her fairly and on the plane, the only possible one, of common equality? He might find himself crippled for life; he believed verily, the more he thought, that that was what was before him. But he ended by seeing this doom in the almost redeeming light of the fact that it would all have been because he was, comparatively, too gentlemanlike. Yes, a man in his station couldn't afford to carry that so far—it must sooner or later, in one way or another, spell ruin. Never mind—it was the only thing he could be. Of course he should exquisitely suffer—but when hadn't he exquisitely suffered? How was he going to get through life by *any* arrangement without that? No wonder such a woman as Kate Cookham had been keen to annex so rare a value. The right thing would have been that the highest price should be paid for it—by such a different sort of logic from this nightmare of *his* having to pay.

II

Which was the way, of course, he talked to Nan Drury—as he had felt the immediate wild need to do; for he should perhaps be able to bear it all somehow or other with *her*—while they sat together, when time and freedom served, on one of the very last, the far westward benches of the interminable sea-front. It wasn't everyone who walked so far, especially at that flat season—the only ghost of a bustle now, save for the gregarious, the obstreperous haunters of the fluttering, far-shining Pier, being reserved for the sunny Parade of midwinter. It wasn't everyone who cared for the sunsets (which you got awfully well from there and which were a particular strong point of the lower, the more "sympathetic" as Herbert Dodd liked to call it, Properley horizon) as he had always intensely cared, and as he had found Nan Drury care; to say nothing of his having also observed how little they directly spoke to Miss Cookham. He had taught this oppressive companion to notice them a bit, as he had taught her plenty of other things, but that was a different matter; for the reason that the "land's end" (stretching a point it carried off that name) had been, and had had to be, by their lack of more sequestered resorts and conveniences, the scene of so much of what she styled their wooing-time—or, to put it more properly, of the time during which she had made the straightest and most unabashed love to *him:* just as it could henceforth but render possible, under an equal rigor, that he should enjoy there periods of consolation from beautiful, gentle, tender-souled Nan, to whom he was now at last, after the wonderful way they had helped each other to behave, going to make love, absolutely unreserved and abandoned, absolutely reckless and romantic love, a refuge from poisonous reality, as hard as ever he might.

The league-long, paved, lighted, garden-plotted, seated and refuged Marina renounced its more or less celebrated attractions to break off short here; and an inward curve of the kindly westward shore almost made a wide-armed bay, with all the ugliness between town and country, and the further casual fringe of the coast, turning, as the day waned, to rich afternoon blooms of gray and brown and distant—it might fairly have been beautiful Hampshire—blue. Here it was that all that blighted summer, with Nan—from the dreadful Mayday on—he gave himself up to the reaction of intimacy with the *kind* of woman, at least, that he liked; even if of everything else that might make life possible he was to be, by what he could make out, forever starved. Here it was that—as well as on whatever other scraps of occasions they could manage—Nan began to take off and fold up and put away in her pocket her pretty, dotty, becoming veil; as under the logic of his having so tremendously ceased, in the shake of his dark storm-gust, to be engaged to another woman. Her removal of that obstacle to a trusted friend's assuring himself whether the peachlike bloom of her finer facial curves bore the test of such further inquiry into their cool sweetness as might reinforce a mere baffled gaze—her momentous, complete surrender of so much of her charm, let us say, both marked the change in the situation of the pair and established the record of their perfect observance of every propriety for so long before. They afterwards in fact could have dated it, their full clutch of their freedom and the bliss of their having so little henceforth to consider save their impotence, their poverty, their ruin; dated it from the hour of his recital to her of the—at the first blush—quite appalling upshot of his second and conclusive "scene of violence" with the mistress of his fortune, when the dire terms of his release had had to be formally, and oh! so abjectly, acceded to. She "compromised," the cruel brute, for Four Hundred Pounds down—for not a farthing less would she stay her strength from "proceedings." No jury in the land but would give her six, on the nail ("Oh she knew quite where she was, thank you") and he might feel lucky to get off with so whole a skin. This was the sum, then, for which he had grovellingly compounded—under an agreement sealed by a supreme exchange of remarks.

" 'Where in the name of lifelong ruin are you to *find* Four Hundred!' " Miss Cookham had mockingly repeated after him, while he gasped as from the twist of her grip on his collar. "That's *your* look-out, and I should have thought you'd have made sure you knew before you decided on your base perfidy." And then she had mouthed and minced, with ever so false a gentility, her consistent, her sickening conclusion. "Of course—I may mention again—if you too distinctly object to the trouble of looking, you know where to find *me*."

"I had rather starve to death than ever go within a mile of you!" Herbert described himself as having sweetly answered; and that was accordingly where *they* devotedly but desperately were—he and she, penniless Nan Drury. Her father, of Drury & Dean, was, like so far too many other of the anxious characters who peered through the dull window-glass of dusty offices at Properley, an Estate and House Agent, Surveyor, and Auctioneer; she was the prettiest Valuer of six, with two brothers, neither of the least use, but, thanks to the manner in which their main natural protector appeared to languish under the accumulation of his attributes, they couldn't be said very particularly or positively to live. Their continued collective existence was a good deal of a miracle even to themselves, though they had fallen into the way of not unnecessarily, or too nervously, exchanging remarks upon it, and had even in a sort, from year to year, got used to it. Nan's brooding pinkness when he talked to her, her so very parted lips, considering her pretty teeth, her so very parted eyelids, considering her pretty eyes, all of which might have been those of some waxen image of uncritical faith, cooled the heat of his helplessness very much as if he were laying his head on a tense silk pillow. She had, it was true, forms of speech, familiar watchwords, that affected him as small scratchy perforations of the smooth surface from within; but his pleasure in her and need of her were independent of such things and really almost altogether determined by the fact of the happy, even if all so lonely, forms and instincts in her which claimed kinship with his own. With her natural elegance stamped on her as by a die, with her dim and disinherited individual refinement of grace, which would have made any one wonder who she was anywhere—hat and veil and feather-boa and smart umbrella-knob and all—with her regular God-given distinction of type, in fine, she couldn't abide vulgarity much more than he could.

Therefore it didn't seem to him, under his stress, to matter particularly, for instance, if she *would* keep on referring so many things to the time, as she called it, when she came into his life—his own great insistence and contention being that she hadn't in the least entered there till his mind was wholly made up to eliminate his other friend. What that methodical fury was so fierce to bring home to him was the falsity to herself involved in the later acquaintance; whereas just his precious right to hold up his head to everything—before himself at least—sprang from the fact that she couldn't make dates fit anyhow. He hadn't so much as heard of his true beauty's existence (she had come back but a few weeks before from her two years with her terribly trying deceased aunt at Swindon, previous to which absence she had been an unnoticeable chit) till days and days, ever so many, upon his honor, after he had struck for freedom by his great first backing-out letter—the precious document, the treat for a British jury, in which, by itself, Miss Cookham's firm instructed her to recognize the prospect of a fortune. The way the ruffians had been "her" ruffians, it appeared as if she had posted them behind her from the first of her beginning her game, and the way "instructions" bounced out, with it, at a touch, larger than life, as if she had arrived with her pocket full of them! The date of the letter, taken with its other connections, and the date of *her* first give-away for himself, his seeing her get out of the Brighton train with Bill Frankle that day he had gone to make the row at the Station parcels' office about the miscarriage of the box from Wales—those were the facts it sufficed him to point to, as he had pointed to them for Nan Drury's benefit, goodness knew, often and often enough. If he didn't seek occasion to do so for anyone else's—in open court as they said—that was his own affair, or at least his and Nan's.

It little mattered, meanwhile, if on their bench of desolation, all that summer—and it may be added for summers and summers, to say nothing of winters, there and elsewhere, to come—she did give way to her artless habit of not contradicting him enough, which led to her often trailing up and down before him, too complacently, the untimely shreds and patches of his own glooms and desperations. "Well, I'm glad I *am* in your life, terrible as it is, however or whenever I did come in!" and *"Of course* you'd rather have starved—and it seems pretty well as if we shall, doesn't it?—than have bought her off by a false, abhorrent love, wouldn't you?" and "It isn't as if she hadn't made up to you the way she did before you had so much as looked at her, is it? or as if you hadn't shown her what you felt her really to be before you had so much as looked at *me,* is it either?" and "Yes, how on earth, pawning the shoes on your feet, you're going to raise another shilling—*that's* what you want to know, poor darling, don't you?"

III

His creditor, at the hour it suited her, transferred her base of operations to town, to which impenetrable scene she had also herself retired; and his raising of the first Two Hundred, during five exasperated and miserable months, and then of another Seventy piecemeal, bleedingly, after long delays and under the epistolary whiplash cracked by the London solicitor in his wretched ear even to an effect of the very report of Miss Cookham's tongue —these melancholy efforts formed a scramble up an arduous steep where steps were planted and missed, and bared knees were excoriated, and clutches at wayside tufts succeeded and failed, on a system to which poor Nan could have intelligently entered only if she had been somehow less ladylike. She kept putting into his mouth the sick quaver of where he should find the rest, the always inextinguishable rest, long after he had in silent rage fallen away from any further payment at all—at first, he had but too blackly felt, for himself, to the still quite possible non-exclusion of some penetrating ray of "exposure." He didn't care a two-penny damn now, and in point of fact, after he had by hook and by crook succeeded in being able to unload to the tune of Two-Hundred-and-Seventy, and then simply returned the newest reminder of his outstanding obligation unopened, this latter belated but real sign of fight, the first he had risked, remarkably caused nothing at all to happen; nothing at least but his being moved to quite tragically rueful wonder as to whether exactly some such demonstration mightn't have served his turn at an earlier stage.

He could by this time at any rate measure his ruin—with three fantastic mortgages on his house, his shop, his stock, and a burden of interest to carry under which his business simply stretched itself inanimate, without strength for a protesting kick, without breath for an appealing groan. Customers lingering for further enjoyment of the tasteful remarks he had cultivated the unobtrusive art of throwing in, would at this crisis have found plenty to repay them, might his wit have strayed a little more widely still, toward a circuitous egotistical outbreak, from the immediate question of the merits of this and that author or of the condition of this and that volume. He had come to be conscious through it all of strangely glaring at people when they tried to haggle—and not, as formerly, with the glare of derisive comment on their overdone humor, but with that of fairly idiotized surrender—as if they were much mistaken in supposing, for the sake of conversation, that he might take himself for savable by the difference between sevenpence and ninepence. He watched everything impossible and deplorable happen, as in an endless prolongation of his nightmare; watched himself proceed, that is, with the finest, richest incoherence, to the due preparation of his catastrophe. Everything came to seem *equally* part of this—in complete defiance of proportion; even his final command of detachment, on the bench of desolation (where each successive fact of his dire case regularly cut itself out, black, yet of senseless outline, against the red west) in respect to poor Nan's flat infelicities, which for the most part kept no pace with the years or with change, but only shook like hard peas in a child's rattle, the same peas always, of course, so long as the rattle didn't split open with usage or from somebody's act of irritation. They represented, or they had long done so, her contribution to the more superficial of the two branches of intimacy—the intellectual alternative, the one that didn't merely consist in her preparing herself for his putting his arm around her waist.

There were to have been moments, nevertheless, all the first couple of years, when she did touch in him, though to his actively dissimulating it, a more or less sensitive nerve—moments as they were too, to do her justice, when she treated him not to his own wisdom, or even folly, served up cold, but to a certain small bitter fruit of her personal, her unnatural, plucking. "I wonder that since *she* took legal advice so freely, to come down on you, you didn't take it yourself, a little, before being so sure you stood no chance. Perhaps *your* people would have been sure of something quite different—*perhaps,* I only say, you know." She "only" said it, but she said it, none the less, in the early time, about once a fortnight. In the later, and especially after their marriage, it had a way of coming up again to the exclusion, as it seemed to him, of almost everything else; in fact during the most dismal years, the three of the loss of their two children, the long stretch of sordid embarrassment ending in her death, he was afterwards to think of her as having generally said it several times a day. He was then also to remember that his answer, before she had learnt to discount it, had been inveterably at hand: "What would any solicitor have done or wanted to do but drag me just into the hideous public arena"—he had always so put it—"that it has been at any rate my pride and my honor, the one rag of self-respect covering my nakedness, to have loathed and avoided from every point of view?"

That had disposed of it so long as he cared, and by the time he had ceased to care for anything it had also lost itself in the rest of the vain babble of home. After his wife's death, during his year of mortal solitude, it awoke again as an echo of far-off things—far-off, very far-off, because he felt then not ten but twenty years older. That was by reason simply of the dead weight with which his load of debt had settled—the persistence of his misery dragging itself out. With all that had come and gone the bench of desolation was still there, just as the immortal flush of the westward sky kept hanging its indestructible curtain. He had never got away—everything had left him, but he himself had been able to turn his back on nothing—and now, his day's labor before a dirty desk at the Gas Works ended, he more often than not, almost any season at temperate Properley serving his turn, took his slow straight way to the Land's End and, collapsing there to rest, sat often for an hour at a time staring before him. He might in these sessions, with his eyes on the gray green sea, have been counting again and still recounting the beads, almost all worn smooth, of his rosary of pain—which had for the fingers of memory and the recurrences of wonder the same felt break of the smaller ones by the larger that would have aided a pious mumble in some dusky altar-chapel.

If it has been said of him that when once full submersion, as from far back, had visibly begun to await him, he watched himself, in a cold lucidity, *do* punctually and necessarily each of the deplorable things that were inconsistent with his keeping afloat, so at present again he might have been held agaze just by the presented grotesqueness of that vigil. Such ghosts of dead seasons were all he *had* now to watch—such a recaptured sense for instance as that of the dismal unavailing awareness that had attended his act of marriage. He had let submersion final and absolute become the signal for it— a mere minor determinant having been the more or less contemporaneously unfavorable effect on the business of Drury & Dean of the sudden disappearance of Mr. Dean with the single small tin box into which the certificates of the firm's credit had been found to be compressible. That had been his only form—or had at any rate seemed his only one. He couldn't not have married, no doubt, just as he couldn't not have suffered the last degree of humiliation and almost of want, or just as his wife and children couldn't not have died of the little he was able, under dire reiterated pinches, to do for them; but it *was* "rum," for final solitary brooding, that he hadn't appeared to see his way definitely to undertake the support of a family till the last scrap of his little low-browed, high-toned business and the last figment of "property" in the old tiled and timbered shell that housed it, had been sacrificed to creditors mustering six rows deep.

Of course what had counted too in the odd order was that even at the end of the two or three years he had "allowed" her, Kate Cookham, gorged with his unholy tribute, had become the subject of no successful seige on the part either of Bill Frankle or, by what he could make out, of anyone else. She had judged decent—he could do her that justice—to take herself personally out of his world, as he called it, for good and all, as soon as he had begun regularly to bleed; and, to whatever lucrative practice she might be devoting her great talents in London or elsewhere, he felt his conscious curiosity about her as cold, with time, as the passion of vain protest that she had originally left him to. He could recall but two direct echoes of her in all the bitter years—both communicated by Bill Frankle, disappointed and exposed and at last quite remarkable ingenuous sneak, who had also, from far back, taken to roaming the world, but who, during a period, used fitfully and ruefully to reappear. Herbert Dodd had quickly seen, at their first meeting— everyone met everyone sooner or later at Properley, if meeting it could always be called, either in the glare or the gloom of the explodedly attractive Embankment—that no silver stream of which he himself had been the remoter source could have played over the career of this all but repudiated acquaintance. That hadn't fitted with his first, his quite primitive raw vision of the probabilities, and he had further been puzzled when, much later on, it had come to him in a roundabout way that Miss Cookham was supposed to be, or to have been, among them for a few days "on the quiet," and that Frankle, who had seen her and who claimed to know more about it than he said, was cited as authority for the fact. But he hadn't himself at this juncture seen Frankle; he had only wondered, and a degree of mystification had even remained.

That memory referred itself to the dark days of old Drury's smash, the few weeks between his partner's dastardly flight and Herbert's own comment on it in the form of his standing up with Nan for the nuptial benediction of the Vicar of St. Bernard's on a very cold, bleak December morning and amid a circle of seven or eight long-faced, red-nosed and altogether dowdy persons. Poor Nan herself had struck him as red-nosed and dowdy by that time, but this only added, in his then, and indeed in his lasting view, to his general and his particular morbid bravery. He had cultivated ignorance, there were small inward immaterial luxuries he could scrappily cherish even among other, and the harshest, destitutions; and one of them was represented by this easy refusal of his mind to render to certain passages of his experience, to various ugly images, names, associations, the homage of continued attention. That served him, that helped him; but what happened when, a dozen dismal years having worn themselves away, he sat single and scraped bare again, as if his long wave of misfortune had washed him far beyond everything and then conspicuously retreated, was that, thus stranded by tidal action, deposited in the lonely hollow of his fate, he felt even sustaining pride turn to nought and heard no challenge from it when old mystifications, stealing forth in the dusk of the day's work done, scratched at the door of speculation and hung about, through the idle hours, for irritated notice.

The evenings of his squalid clerkship were all leisure now, but there was nothing at all near home on the other hand, for his imagination, numb and stiff from its long chill, to begin to play with. Voices from far off would quaver to him therefore in the stillness; where he knew for the most recurrent, little by little, the faint wail of his wife. He had become deaf to it in life, but at present, after so great an interval, he listened again, listened and listened, and seemed to hear it sound as by the pressure of some weak broken spring. It phrased for his ear her perpetual question, the one she had come to at the last as under the obsession of a discovered and resented wrong, a wrong withal that had its source much more in his own action than anywhere else. "That you didn't make *sure* she could have done anything, that you didn't make sure and that you were too afraid!"—this commemoration had ended by playing such a part in Nan's finally quite contracted consciousness as to exclude everything else.

At the time, somehow, he had made his terms with it; he had then more urgent questions to meet than that of the poor creature's taste in worrying pain; but actually it struck him—not the question, but the fact itself of the taste—as the one thing left over from all that had come and gone. So it was; nothing remained to him in the world, on the bench of desolation, but the option of taking up that echo—together with an abundance of free time for doing so. That he hadn't made sure of what might and what mightn't have been done to him, that he had been too afraid—had the proposition a possible bearing on his present apprehension of things? To reply indeed he would have had to be able to say what his present apprehension of things, left to itself, amounted to; an uninspiring effort indeed he judged it, sunk to so poor a pitch was his material of thought—though it might at last have been the feat he sought to perform as he stared at the gray-green sea.

IV

It was seldom Herbert Dodd was disturbed in any form of sequestered speculation, or that at his times of predilection, especially that of the long autumn blankness between the season of trippers and the season of Bathchairs, there were westward stragglers enough to jar upon his settled sense of priority. For himself his seat, the term of his walk, was consecrated; it had figured to him for years as the last (though there were others, not immediately near it, and differently disposed, that might have aspired to the title); so that he could invidiously distinguish as he approached, make out from a distance any accident of occupation, and never draw nearer while that unpleasantness lasted. What he disliked was to compromise on his tradition, whether for a man, a woman or a connoodling couple; it was to idiots of this last composition he most objected, he having sat there, in the past, alone, having sat there interminably with Nan, having sat there with—well, with other women when women, at hours of ease, could still care or count for him, but having never shared the place with any shuffling or snuffling stranger.

It was a world of fidgets and starts, however, the world of his present dreariness—he alone possessed in it, he seemed to make out, of the secret of the dignity of sitting still with one's fate; so that if he took a turn about or rested briefly elsewhere even foolish philanderers (though this would never have been his and Nan's way) ended soon by some adjournment as visibly pointless as their sprawl. Then, their backs turned, he would drop down on it, the bench of desolation—which was what he, and he only, made it, by sad adoption; where, for that matter, moreover, once he had settled at his end, it was marked that nobody else ever came to sit. He saw people, along the Marina, take this liberty with other resting presences; but his own struck them perhaps in general as either of too grim or just of too dingy a vicinage. He might have affected the fellow-lounger as a man evil, unsociable, possibly engaged in working out the idea of a crime; or otherwise, more probably—for on the whole he surely looked harmless—devoted to the worship of some absolutely unpractical remorse.

On a certain October Saturday he had got off, as usual, early; but the afternoon light, his pilgrimage drawing to its aim, could still show him, at long range, the rare case of an established usurper. His impulse was then, as by custom, to deviate a little and wait, all the more that the occupant of the bench was a lady, and that ladies, when alone were—at that austere end of the varied frontal stretch—markedly discontinuous; but he kept on at sight of this person's rising, while he was still fifty yards off, and proceeding, her back turned, to the edge of the broad terrace, the outer line of which followed the interspaced succession of seats and was guarded by an iron rail from the abruptly lower level of the beach. Here she stood before the sea, while our friend on his side, recognizing no reason to the contrary, sank into the place she had quitted. There were other benches, eastward and off by the course of the drive, for vague ladies. The lady indeed thus thrust upon Herbert's vision might have struck an observer either as not quite vague or as vague with a perverse intensity suggesting design.

Not that our own observer at once thought of these things; he only took in, and with no great interest, that the obtruded presence was a "real" lady; that she was dressed (he noticed such matters) with a certain elegance of propriety or intention of harmony; and that she remained perfectly still for a good many minutes; so many in fact that he presently ceased to heed her, and that as she wasn't straight before him, but as far to the left as was consistent with his missing her profile, he had turned himself to one of his sunsets again (though it wasn't quite one of his best) and let it hold him for a time that enabled her to alter her attitude and present a fuller view. Without other movement, but her back now to the sea and her face to the odd person who had appropriated her corner, she had taken a sustained look at him before he was aware she had stirred. On that apprehension, however, he became also promptly aware of her direct, her applied observation. As his sense of this quickly increased he wondered who she was and what she wanted—what, as it were, was the matter with her; it suggested to him, the next thing, that she had, under some strange idea, actually been waiting for him. Any idea about him to-day on the part of anyone could only *be* strange.

Yes, she stood there with the ample width of the Marina between them, but turned to him, for all the world, as to show frankly that she was concerned with him. And she *was*—oh yes—a real lady: a middle-aged person, of good appearance and of the best condition, in quiet but "handsome" black, save for very fresh white kid gloves, and with a pretty, dotty, becoming veil, predominantly white, adjusted to her countenance; which through it somehow, even to his imperfect sight, showed strong fine black brows and what he would have called on the spot character. But she was pale; her black brows were the blacker behind the flattering tissue; she still kept a hand, for support, on the terrace-rail, while the other, at the end of an extended arm that had an effect of rigidity, clearly pressed hard on the knob of a small and shining umbrella, the lower extremity of whose stick was equally, was sustainingly firm, on the walk. So this mature, qualified, important person stood and looked at the limp, undistinguished (oh his values of aspect now!), shabby man on the bench.

It was extraordinary, but the fact of her interest, by immensely surprising, by immediately agitating him, blinded him at first to her identity and, for the space of his long stare, diverted him from it; with which even then, when recognition did break, the sense of the shock, striking inward, simply consumed itself in gaping stillness. He sat there motionless and weak, fairly faint with surprise, and there was no instant, in all the succession of so many, at which Kate Cookham could have caught the special sign of his intelligence. Yet that she did catch something he saw—for he saw her steady herself, by her two supported hands, to meet it; while, after she had done so, a very wonderful thing happened, of which he could scarce, later on, have made a clear statement, though he was to think it over again and again. She moved toward him, she reached him, she stood there, she sat down near him, he merely passive and wonderstruck, unresentfully "impressed," gaping and taking it in—and all as with an open allowance on the part of each, so that they positively and quite intimately met in it, of the impertinence for their case, this case that brought them again, after horrible years, face to face, of the vanity, the profanity, the impossibility, of anything between them but silence.

Nearer to him, beside him at a considerable interval (oh she was immensely considerate!) she presented him, in the sharp terms of her transformed state —but thus the more amply, formally, ceremoniously—with the reasons that would serve him best for not having precipitately known her. She was simply another and a totally different person, and the exhibition of it to which she had proceeded with this solemn anxiety was all, obviously, for his benefit—once he had, as he appeared to be doing, provisionally accepted her approach. He had remembered her as inclined to the massive and cut off from the graceful; but this was a spare, fine, worn, almost wasted lady—who had repaired waste, it was true, however, with something he could only appreciate as a rich accumulation of manner. She was strangely older, so far as that went—marked by experience and as if many things had happened to her; her face had suffered, to its improvement, contraction and concentration; and if he had granted, of old and from the first, that her eyes were remarkable, had they yet ever had for him this sombre glow? Withal, something said, she had flourished—he felt it, wincing at it, as that; she had had a life, a career, a history—something that her present waiting air and nervous consciousness couldn't prevent his noting there as a deeply latent assurance. She had flourished, she had flourished—though to learn it after this fashion was somehow at the same time not to feel she flaunted it. It wasn't thus execration that she revived in him; she made in fact, exhibitively, as he could only have put it, the matter of long ago irrelevant and these extraordinary minutes of their reconstituted relation—how many? how few?—addressed themselves altogether to new possibilities.

Still it after a little awoke in him as with the throb of a touched nerve that his own very attitude was supplying a connection; he knew presently that he wouldn't have had her go, *couldn't* have made a sign to her for it (which was what she had been uncertain of) without speaking to him; and that therefore he was, as at the other, the hideous time, passive to whatever she might do. She was even yet, she was always, in possession of him; she had known how and where to find him and had appointed that he should see her, and, though he had never dreamed it was again to happen to him, he was meeting it already as if it might have been the only thing that the least humanly *could*. Yes, he had come back there to flop, by long custom, upon the bench of desolation *as* the man in the whole place, precisely, to whom nothing worth more than tuppence could happen; whereupon, in the gray desert of his consciousness, the very earth had suddenly opened and flamed. With this, further, it came over him that he hadn't been prepared and that his wretched appearance must show it. He wasn't fit to receive a visit—any visit; a flush for his felt misery, in the light of her opulence, broke out in his lean cheeks. But if he colored he sat as he was—she should at least, as a visitor, be satisfied. His eyes only, at last, turned from her and resumed a little their gaze at the sea. That, however, didn't relieve him, and he perpetrated in the course of another moment the odd desperate gesture of raising both his hands to his face and letting them, while he pressed it to them, cover and guard it. It was as he held them there that she at last spoke.

"I'll go away if you wish me to." And then she waited a moment. "I mean now—now that you've seen I'm here. I wanted you to know it, and I thought of writing—I was afraid of our meeting accidentally. Then I was afraid that if I wrote you might refuse. So I thought of this way—as I knew you must come out here." She went on with pauses, giving him a chance to make a sign. "I've waited several days. But I'll do what you wish. Only I should like in that case to come back." Again she stopped; but strange was it to him that he wouldn't have made her break off. She held him in boundless wonder. "I came down—I mean I came from town—on purpose. I'm staying on still, and I've a great patience and will give you time. Only may I say it's important? Now that I do see you," she brought out in the same way, "I see how inevitable it was—I mean that I should have wanted to come. But you must feel about it as you can," she wound up—"till you get used to the idea."

She spoke so for accommodation, for discretion, for some ulterior view already expressed in her manner, that, after taking well in, from behind his hands, that this was her very voice—oh ladylike!—heard, and heard in deprecation of displeasure, after long years again, he uncovered his face and freshly met her eyes. More than ever he couldn't have known her. Less and less remained of the figure, all the facts of which had long ago so hardened for him. She was a handsome, grave, authoritative, but refined and as it were, physically rearranged person—she, the outrageous vulgarity of whose prime assault had kept him shuddering so long as a shudder was in him. That atrocity in her was what everything had been built on, but somehow, all strangely, it was slipping from him; so that, after the oddest fashion conceivable, when he felt he mustn't let her go, it was as if he were putting out his hand to *save* the past, the hideous real unalterable past, exactly as she had been the cause of its being and the cause of his undergoing it. He should have been too awfully "sold" if he wasn't going to have been right about her.

"I don't mind," he heard himself at last say. Not to mind had seemed for the instant the length he was prepared to go; but he was afterwards aware of how soon he must have added: "You've come on purpose to see me?" He was on the point of putting to her further: "What then do you want of me?" But he would keep—yes, in time—from appearing to show he cared. If he showed he cared, where then would be his revenge? So he was already, within five minutes, thinking his revenge uncomfortably over instead of just comfortably knowing it. What came to him, at any rate, as they actually fell to talk was that, with such precautions, considerations, reduplications of consciousness, almost avowed feelings of her way on her own part, and light fingerings of his chords of sensibility, she was understanding, she *had* understood, more things than all the years, up to this strange eventide, had given him an inkling of. They talked, they went on—he hadn't let her retreat, to whatever it committed him and however abjectly it did so; yet keeping off and off, dealing with such surface facts as involved ancient acquaintance but kept abominations at bay. The recognition, the attestation that she *had* come down for him, that there would be reasons, that she had even hovered and watched, assured herself a little of his habits (which she managed to speak of as if, on their present ampler development, they were much to be deferred to), held them long enough to make vivid how, listen as stiffly or as serenely as he might, she sat there in fear, just as she had so stood there at first, and that her fear had really to do with her calculation of some sort of chance with him. What chance could it possibly be? Whatever it might have done, on this prodigious showing, with Kate Cookham, it made the present witness to the state of his fortunes simply exquisite: he ground his teeth secretly together as he saw he should have to take *that*. For what did it mean but that she would have liked to pity him if she could have done it with safety? Ah, however, he must give her no measure of safety!

By the time he had remarked, with that idea, that she probably saw few changes about them there that weren't for the worse—the place was going down, down and down, so fast that goodness knew where it would stop— and had also mentioned that in spite of this he himself remained faithful, with all its faults loving it still; by the time he had, after that fashion, superficially indulged her, adding a few further light and just sufficiently dry reflections on local matters, the disappearance of landmarks and important persons, the frequency of gales, the low policy of the town-council in playing down to cheap excursionists: by the time he had so acquitted himself, and she had observed, of her own motion, that she was staying at the Royal, which he knew for the time-honored, the conservative and exclusive hotel, he had made out for himself one thing at least, the amazing fact that he had been landed by his troubles, at the end of time, in a "social relation," of all things in the world, and that of that luxury he was now having unprecedented experience. He had but once in his life had his nose in the Royal, on the occasion of his himself delivering a parcel during some hiatus in his succession of impossible small boys, and meeting in the hall the lady who had bought of him, in the morning, a set of Crabbe, largely, he flattered himself, under the artful persuasion of his acute remarks on that author, gracefully associated by him, in this colloquy, he remembered, with a glance at Charles Lamb as well, and who went off, in a day or two, without settling, though he received her cheque from London three or four months later.

That hadn't been a social relation; and truly, deep within his appeal to himself to be remarkable, to be imperturbable and impenetrable, to be in fact quite incomparable now, throbbed the intense vision of his drawing out and draining dry the sensation he had begun to taste. He would do it, moreover —that would be the refinement of his art—not only without the betrayed anxiety of a single question, but just even by seeing her flounder (since she must, in a vagueness deeply disconcerting to her) as to her real effect on him. She was distinctly floundering by the time he had brought her—it had taken ten minutes—down to a consciousness of absurd and twaddling topics, to the reported precarious state, for instance, of the syndicate running the Bijou Theatre at the Pier-head—all as an admonition that she might want him to want to know why she was thus waiting on him, might want it for all she was worth, before he had ceased to be so remarkable as not to ask her. He didn't—and this assuredly was wondrous enough—want to do anything worse to her than let her flounder; but he was willing to do that so long as it mightn't prevent his seeing at least where *he* was. He seemed still to see where he was even at the minute that followed her final break-off, clearly intended to be resolute, from make-believe talk.

"I wonder if I might prevail on you to come to tea with me to-morrow at five."

He didn't so much as answer it—though he could scarcely believe his ears. To-morrow was Sunday, and the proposal referred, clearly, to the custom of "five-o'clock" tea, known to him only by the contemporary novel of manners and the catchy advertisement of table-linen. He had never in his life been present at any such luxurious rite, but he was offering practical indifference to it as a false mark of his sense that his social relation had already risen to his chin. "I gave up my very modest, but rather interesting little old book-business, perhaps you know, ever so long ago."

She floundered so that she could say nothing—meet *that* with no possible word; all the less too that his tone, casual and colorless, wholly defied any apprehension of it as a reverse. Silence only came; but after a moment she returned to her effort. "If you *can* come I shall be at home. To see you otherwise than thus was in fact what, as I tell you, I came down for. But I leave it," she returned, "to your feeling."

He had at this, it struck him, an inspiration; which he required however a minute or two to decide to carry out; a minute or two during which the shake of his foot over his knee became an intensity of fidget. "Of course I know I still owe you a large sum of money. If it's about *that* you wish to see me," he went on, "I may as well tell you just here that I shall be able to meet my full obligation in the future as little as I've met it in the past. I can never," said Herbert Dodd, "pay up that balance."

He had looked at her while he spoke, but on finishing looked off at the sea again and continued to agitate his foot. He knew now what he had done and why; and the sense of her fixed dark eyes on him during his speech and after didn't alter his small contentment. Yet even when she still said nothing he didn't turn round; he simply kept his corner as if *that* were his point made, should it even be the last word between them. It might have been, for that matter, from the way in which she presently rose, gathering herself, her fine umbrella and her very small smart reticule, in the construction of which shining gilt much figured, well together, and, after standing another instant, moved across to the rail of the terrace as she had done before and remained, as before, with her back to him, though this time, it well might be, under a different fear. A quarter of an hour ago she hadn't tried him, and had had that anxiety; now that she had tried him it wasn't easier—but she was thinking what she still could do. He left her to think—nothing in fact more interesting than the way she might decide had ever happened to him; but it was a part of this also that as she turned round and came nearer again he didn't rise, he gave her no help. If she got any, at least, from his looking up at her only, meeting her fixed eyes once more in silence, that was her own affair. "You must think," she said—"you must take all your time, but I shall be at home." She left it to him thus—she insisted, with her idea, on leaving him something too. And on her side as well she showed an art— which resulted, after another instant, in his having to rise to his feet. He flushed afresh as he did it—it exposed him so shabbily the more; and now if she took him in, with each of his seedy items, from head to foot, he didn't and couldn't and wouldn't know it, attaching his eyes hard and straight to something quite away from them.

It stuck in his throat to say he'd come, but she had so curious a way with her that he still less could say he wouldn't, and in a moment had taken refuge in something that was neither. "Are you married?"—he put it to her with that plainness, though it had seemed before he said it to do more for him that while she waited before replying.

"No, I'm not married," she said: and then had another wait that might have amounted to a question of what this had to do with it.

He surely couldn't have told her; so that he had recourse, a little poorly as he felt, but to an "Oh!" that still left them opposed. He turned away for it—that is for the poorness, which, lingering in the air, had almost a vulgar platitude; and when, he presently again wheeled about she had fallen off as for quitting him, only with a pause, once more, for a last look. It was all a bit awkward, but he had another happy thought, which consisted in his silently raising his hat as for a sign of dignified dismissal. He had cultivated of old, for the occasions of life, the right, the discriminated bow, and now, out of the gray limbo of the time when he could care for such things, this flicker of propriety leaped and worked. She might, for that matter, herself have liked it; since, receding further, only with her white face toward him, she paid it the homage of submission. He remained dignified, and she almost humbly went.

V

Nothing in the world, on the Sunday afternoon, could have prevented him from going; he was not after all destitute of three or four such articles of clothing as, if they wouldn't particularly grace the occasion, wouldn't positively dishonor it. That deficiency might have kept him away, but no voice of the spirit, no consideration of pride. It sweetened his impatience in fact—for he fairly felt it a long time to wait—that his pride would really most find its account in his acceptance of these conciliatory steps. From the moment he could put it in that way—that he couldn't refuse to hear what she might have, so very elaborately, to say for herself—he ought certainly to be at his ease; in illustration of which he whistled odd snatches to himself as he hung about on that cloud-dappled autumn Sunday, a mild private minstrelsy that his lips hadn't known since when? The interval of the twenty-four hours, made longer by a night of many more revivals than oblivions, had in fact dragged not a little; in spite of which, however, our extremely brushed-up and trimmed and polished friend knew an unprecedented flutter as he was ushered, at the Royal Hotel, into Miss Cookham's sitting-room. Yes, it was an adventure, and he had never had an adventure in his life; the term, for him, was essentially a term of high appreciation—such as disqualified for that figure, under due criticism, every single passage of his past career.

What struck him at the moment as qualifying in the highest degree this actual passage was the fact that at no great distance from his hostess in the luxurious room, as he apprehended it, in which the close of day had begun to hang a few shadows, sat a gentleman who rose as she rose, and whose name she at once mentioned to him. He had for Herbert Dodd all the air of a swell, the gentleman—rather red-faced and bald-headed, but moustachioed, waistcoated, neck-tied, to the highest pitch, with an effect of chains and rings, of shining teeth in a glassily monocular smile; a wondrous apparition to have been asked to "meet" him, as in contemporary fiction, or for him to have been asked to meet. "Captain Roper, Mr. Herbert Dodd"—their entertainer introduced them, yes; but with a sequel immediately afterwards more disconcerting apparently to Captain Roper himself even than to her second and more breathless visitor; a "Well then, good-bye till the next time," with a hand thrust straight out, which allowed the personage so addressed no alternative but to lay aside his tea-cup, even though Herbert saw there was a good deal left in it, and glare about him for his hat. Miss Cookham had had her tea tray on a small table before her, she had served Captain Roper while waiting for Mr. Dodd; but she simply dismissed him now, with a high sweet unmistakable decision, a knowledge of what she was about, as our hero would have called it, which enlarged at a stroke the latter's view of the number of different things and sorts of things, in the sphere of the manners and ways of those living at their ease, that a social relation would put before one. Captain Roper would have liked to remain, would have liked more tea, but Kate signified in this direct fashion that she had had enough of him. Herbert had seen things, in his walk of life—rough things, plenty; but never things smoothed with that especial smoothness, carried out as it were by the fine form of Captain Roper's own retreat, which included even a bright convulsed leave-taking cognisance of the plain, vague individual, of no lustre at all and with the very low-class guard of an old silver watch buttoned away under an ill-made coat, to whom he was sacrificed.

It came to Herbert as he left the place a shade less remarkable—though there was still wonder enough and to spare—that he had been even publicly and designedly sacrificed; exactly so that, as the door closed behind him, Kate Cookham, standing there to wait for it, could seem to say, across the room, to the friend of her youth, only by the expression of her fine eyes: "There—see what I do for you!" "For" him—that was the extraordinary thing, and not less so that he was already, within three minutes, after this fashion, taking it in as by the intensity of a new light; a light that was one somehow with this rich inner air of the plush-draped and much-mirrored hotel, where the firelight and the approach of evening confirmed together the privacy, and the loose curtains at the wide window were parted for a command of his old lifelong Parade—the field of life so familiar to him from below and in the wind and the wet, but which he had never in all the long years hung over at this vantage.

"He's an acquaintance, but a bore," his hostess explained in respect to Captain Roper. "He turned up yesterday, but I didn't invite him, and I had said to him before you came in that I was expecting a gentleman with whom I should wish to be alone. I go quite straight at my idea that way, as a rule; but you know," she now strikingly went on, "how straight I go. And he had had," she added, "his tea."

Dodd had been looking all round—had taken in, with the rest, the brightness, the distinguished elegance, as he supposed it, of the tea-service with which she was dealing and the variously tinted appeal of certain savory edibles on plates. "Oh but he *hadn't* had his tea!" he heard himself the next moment earnestly reply; which speech had at once betrayed, he was then quickly aware, the candor of his interest, the unsophisticated state that had survived so many troubles. If he was so interested how could he be proud, and if he was proud how could he be so interested?

He had made her at any rate laugh outright, and was further conscious, for this, both that it was the first time of that since their new meeting, and that it didn't affect him as harsh. It affected him, however, as free, for she replied at once, still smiling and as a part of it: "Oh, I think we shall get on!"

This told him he had made some difference for her, shown her the way, or something like it, that she hadn't been sure of yesterday; which moreover wasn't what he had intended—he had come armed for showing her nothing; so that after she had gone on with the same gain of gaiety, "You must at any rate comfortably have yours," there was but one answer for him to make.

His eyes played again over the tea-things—they seemed strangely to help him; but he didn't sit down. "I've come, as you see—but I've come, please, to understand; and if you require to be alone with me, and if I break bread with you, it seems to me I should first know exactly where I am and to what you suppose I so commit myself." He had thought it out and over and over, particularly the turn about breaking bread; though perhaps he didn't give it, in her presence—this was impossible, her presence altered so many things—quite the full sound or the weight he had planned.

But it had none the less come to his aid—it had made her perfectly grave. "You commit yourself to nothing. You're perfectly free. It's only I who commit myself."

On which, while she stood there as if all handsomely and deferentially waiting for him to consider and decide, he would have been naturally moved to ask her what she committed herself then *to*—so moved, that is, if he hadn't before saying it, thought more sharply still of something better. "Oh, that's another thing."

"Yes, that's another thing," Kate Cookham returned. To which she added, "So *now* won't you sit down?" He sank with deliberation into the seat from which Captain Roper had risen; she went back to her own and while she did so spoke again. "I'm *not* free. At least," she said over her tea-tray, "I'm free only for this."

Everything was there before them and around them, everything massive and shining, so that he had instinctively fallen back in his chair as for the wondering, the resigned acceptance of it; where her last words stirred in him a sense of odd depreciation. Only for "that"? "That" was everything, at this moment, to his long inanition, and the effect, as if she had suddenly and perversely mocked him, was to press the spring of a protest. "Isn't 'this' then riches?"

"Riches?" she smiled over, handing him his cup—for she had triumphed in having struck from him a question.

"I mean haven't you a lot of money?" He didn't care now that it was out; his cup was in his hand, and what was that but proved interest? He had succumbed to the social relation.

"Yes, I've money. Of course you wonder—but I've wanted you to wonder. It was to make you take that in that I came. So now you know," she said, leaning back where she faced him, but in a straighter chair and with her arms closely folded, after a fashion characteristic of her, as for some control of her nerves.

"You came to show you've money?"

"That's one of the things. Not a lot—not even very much. But enough," said Kate Cookham.

"Enough? I should think so!" he again couldn't help a bit crudely exhaling.

"Enough for what I wanted. I don't always live like this—not at all. But I came to the best hotel on purpose. I wanted to show you I could. Now," she asked, "do you understand?"

"Understand?" He only gaped.

She threw up her loosed arms which dropped again beside her. "I did it *for* you—I did it *for* you!"

" 'For' me—?"

"What I did—what I did here of old."

He stared, trying to see it. "When you made me pay you?"

"The Two Hundred and Seventy—all I could get from you, as you reminded me yesterday, so that I had to give up the rest. It was my idea," she went on—"it was my idea."

"To bleed me quite to death?" Oh, his ice was broken now!

"To make you raise money—since you could, you *could*. You did, you did—so what better proof?"

His hands fell from what he had touched; he could only stare—her own manner for it was different now too. "I did. I did indeed—!" And the woeful weak simplicity of it, which seemed somehow all that was left him, fell even on his own ear.

"Well then, here it is—it isn't lost!" she returned with a graver face.

"'Here' it is," he gasped, "my poor old money—my blood?"

"Oh, it's *my* blood too, you must know now!" She held up her head as not before—as for her right to speak of the thing to-day most precious to her. "I took it, but this—my being here this way—is what I've made of it! That was the idea I had!"

Her "ideas," as things to boast of, staggered him. "To have everything in the world, like this, at my wretched expense?"

She had folded her arms back again—grasping each elbow she sat firm; she knew he could see, and had known well from the first, what she had wanted to say, difficult, monstrous though it might be. "No more than at my own—but to do something with your money that you'd never do yourself."

"Myself, myself?" he wonderingly wailed. "Do you know—or don't you?—what my life has been?"

She waited, and for an instant, though the light in the room had failed a little more and would soon be mainly that of the flaring lamps on the windy Parade, he caught from her dark eye a silver gleam of impatience. "You've suffered and you've worked—which, God knows, is what I've done! *Of course* you've suffered," she said —"you inevitably had to! We have to," she went on, "to do or to be or to get anything."

"And pray what have I done or been or got?" Herbert Dodd found it almost desolately natural to demand.

It made her cover him again as with all she was thinking of. "Can you imagine nothing, or can't you conceive—?" And then as her challenge struck deeper in, deeper down than it had yet reached, and with the effect of a rush of the blood to his face, "It was *for* you, it was *for* you!" she again broke out—"and for what or whom else could it have been?"

He saw things to a tune now that made him answer straight: "I thought at one time it might be for Bill Frankle."

"Yes—that was the way you treated me," Miss Cookham as plainly replied.

But he let this pass; his thought had already got away from it. "What good then—it's having been for me—has that ever done me?"

"Doesn't it do you any good now?" his friend returned. To which she added, with another dim play of her tormented brightness, before he could speak: "But if you won't even have your tea——!"

He had in fact touched nothing and, if he could have explained, would have pleaded very veraciously that his appetite, keen when he came in, had somehow suddenly failed. It was beyond eating or drinking, what she seemed to want him to take from her. So if he looked, before him, over the array, it was to say, very grave and graceless: "Am I to understand that you offer to repay me?"

"I offer to repay you with interest, Herbert Dodd"—and her emphasis of the great word was wonderful.

It held him in his place a minute, and held his eyes upon her; after which, agitated too sharply to sit still, he pushed back his chair and stood up. It was as if mere distress or dismay at first worked in him, and was in fact a wave of deep and irresistible emotion which made him, on his feet, sway as in a great trouble and then, to correct it, throw himself stiffly toward the window, where he stood and looked out unseeing. The road, the wide terrace beyond, the seats, the eternal sea beyond that, the lighted lamps now flaring in the October night-wind, with the few dispersed people abroad at the tea-hour; these things, meeting and melting into the firelit hospitality at his elbow—or was it that portentous amenity that melted into *them?*—seemed to form round him and to put before him, all together, the strangest of circles and the newest of experiences, in which the unforgettable and the unimaginable were confoundingly mixed. "Oh, oh, oh!"—he could only almost howl for it.

And then, while a thick blur for some moments mantled everything, he knew she had got up, that she stood watching him, allowing for everything, again all "cleverly" patient with him, and he heard her speak again as with studied quietness and clearness. "I wanted to take care of you—it was what I first wanted—and what you first consented to. I'd have done it, oh I'd have done it, I'd have loved you and helped you and guarded you, and you'd have had no trouble, no bad blighting ruin, in all your easy, yes, just your quite jolly and comfortable life. I showed you and proved to you this—I brought it home to you, as I fondly fancied, and it made me briefly happy. You swore you cared for me, you wrote it and made me believe it—you pledged me your honor and your faith. Then you turned and changed suddenly from one day to another; everything altered, you broke your vows, you as good as told me you only wanted it off. You faced me with dislike, and in fact tried not to face me at all; you behaved as if you hated me—you had seen a girl, of great beauty, I admit, who made me a fright and a bore."

This brought him straight round. "No, Kate Cookham."

"Yes, Herbert Dodd." She but shook her head, calmly and nobly, in the now gathered dusk, and her memories and her cause and her character—or was it only her arch-subtlety, her line and her "idea"?—gave her an extraordinary large assurance.

She had touched, however, the treasure of his own case—his terrible own case that began to live again at once by the force of her talking of hers, and which could always all cluster about his great asseveration. "No, no, never, never; I had never seen her then and didn't dream of her; so that when you yourself began to be harsh and sharp with me, and to seem to want to quarrel, I could have but one idea—which was an appearance you didn't in the least, as I saw it then, account for or disprove."

"An appearance—?" Kate desired, as with high astonishment, to know which one.

"How *shouldn't* I have supposed you really to care for Bill Frankle?—as, thoroughly believing the motive of your claim for my money to be its help to your marrying him, since you couldn't marry me. I was only surprised when, time passing, I made out that that hadn't happened; and perhaps," he added the next instant with something of a conscious lapse from the finer style, "hadn't been in question."

She had listened to this only staring, and she was silent after he had said it, so silent for some instants that while he considered her something seemed to fail him, much as if he had thrown out his foot for a step and not found the place to rest it. He jerked round to the window again, and then she answered, but without passion unless it was that of her weariness for something stupid and forgiven in him, "Oh, the blind, the pitiful folly!"—to which, as it might perfectly have applied to her own behavior, he returned nothing. She had moreover at once gone on. "Put it then that there wasn't much to do—between your finding that you loathed me for another woman, or discovering only, when it came to the point, that you loathed me quite enough for myself."

Which, as she put it in that immensely effective fashion, he recognized that he must just unprotestingly and not so very awkwardly—not so *very!*—take from her; since, whatever he had thus come to her for, it wasn't to perjure himself with any pretence that, "another woman" or no other woman, he hadn't, for years and years, abhorred her. Now he was taking tea with her—or rather, literally, seemed not to be; but this made no difference, and he let her express it as she would while he distinguished a man he knew, Charley Coote, outside on the Parade, under favor of the empty hour and one of the flaring lamps, making up to a young woman with whom (it stuck out grotesquely in his manner) he had never before conversed. Dodd's own position was that of acquiescing in this recall of what had so bitterly been—but he hadn't come back to her, of himself, to stir up, to recall or to recriminate, and for *her* it could but be the very lesson of her whole present act that if she touched anything she touched everything. Soon enough she *was* indeed, and all overwhelmingly, touching everything—with a hand of which the boldness grew.

"But I didn't let *that,* even, make a difference in what I wanted—which was all," she said, "and had only and passionately been, to take care of you. I had *no* money whatever—nothing then of my own, not a penny to come by anyhow; so it wasn't with mine I could do it. But I could do it with yours," she amazingly wound up—"if I could once get yours out of you."

He faced straight about again—his eyebrows higher than they had ever been in his life. "Mine? What penny of it was mine? What scrap beyond a living had I ever pretended to have?"

She held herself still a minute, visibly with force; only her eyes consciously attached to the seat of a chair the back of which her hands, making it tilt toward her a little, grasped as for support. "You pretended to have enough to marry me—and that was all I afterwards claimed of you when you wouldn't." He was on the point of retorting that he had absolutely pretended to nothing—least of all to the primary desire that such a way of putting it fastened on him; he was on the point for ten seconds of giving her full in the face: "I never *had* any such dream till you yourself—infatuated with me as, frankly, you on the whole appeared to be—got round me and muddled me up and made me behave as if in a way that went against the evidence of my senses." But he was to feel as quickly that, whatever the ugly, the spent, the irrecoverable truth, he might better have bitten his tongue off: there beat on him there this strange and other, this so prodigiously different beautiful and dreadful truth that no far remembrance and no abiding ache of his own could wholly falsify, and that was indeed all out with her next words. "That—*using* it for you and using you yourself for your own future—was my motive. I've led my life, which has been an affair, I assure you; and, as I've told you without your quite seeming to understand —I've brought everything fivefold back to you."

The perspiration broke out on his forehead. "Everything's mine?" he quavered as for the deep piercing pain of it.

"Everything!" said Kate Cookham.

So it told him how she had loved him—but with the tremendous effect at once of its only glaring out at him from the whole thing that it was verily she, a thousand times over, who, in the exposure of his youth and his vanity, had, on the bench of desolation, the scene of yesterday's own renewal, left for him no forward steps to take. It hung there for him tragically vivid again, the hour she had first found him sequestered and accessible after making his acquaintance at his shop. And from this, by a succession of links that fairly clicked to his ear as with their perfect fitting, the fate and the pain and the payment of others stood together in a great grim order. Everything there then was *his*—to make him ask what had been Nan's, poor Nan's of the constant question of whether he need have collapsed. She was before him, she was between them, his little dead dissatisfied wife; across all whose final woe and whose lowly grave he was to reach out, it appeared, to take gifts. He saw them too, the gifts; saw them—she bristled with them—in his actual companion's brave and sincere and authoritative figure, her strangest of demonstrations. But the other appearance was intenser, as if their ghost had waved wild arms; so that half a minute hadn't passed before the one poor thing that remained of Nan, and that yet thus became a quite mighty and momentous poor thing, was sitting on his lips as for its sole opportunity.

"Can you give me your word of honor that I mightn't, under decent advice, have defied you?"

It made her turn very white; but now that she had said what she *had* said she could still hold up her head. "Certainly you might have defied me, Herbert Dodd."

"They would have told me you had no legal case?"

Well, if she was pale she was bold. "You talk of decent advice—!" She broke off, there was too much to say, and all needless. What she said instead was: "They would have told you I had nothing."

"I didn't so much as ask," her sad visitor remarked.

"Of course you didn't so much as ask."

"I couldn't be so outrageously vulgar," he went on.

"*I* could, by God's help!" said Kate Cookham.

"Thank you." He had found at his command a tone that made him feel more gentlemanlike than he had ever felt in his life or should doubtless ever feel again. It might have been enough—but somehow as they stood there with this immense clearance between them it wasn't. The clearance was like a sudden gap or great bleak opening through which there blew upon them a deadly chill. Too many things had fallen away, too many new rolled up and over him, and they made something within shake him to his base. It upset the full vessel, and though she kept her eyes on him he let that consequence come, bursting into tears, weakly crying there before her even as he had cried to himself in the hour of his youth when she had made him groundlessly fear. She turned away then—*that* she couldn't watch, and had presently flung herself on the sofa and, all responsively wailing, buried her own face on the cushioned arm. So for a minute their smothered sobs only filled the room. But he made out, through this disorder, where he had put down his hat; his stick and his new tan-colored gloves—they had cost two-and-thruppence and would have represented sacrifices—were on the chair beside it. He picked these articles up and all silently and softly—gasping, that is, but quite on tiptoe—reached the door and let himself out.

VI

Off there on the bench of desolation a week later she made him a more particular statement, which it had taken the remarkably tense interval to render possible. After leaving her at the hotel that last Sunday he had gone forth in his re-aggravated trouble and walked straight before him, in the teeth of the west wind, close to the iron rails of the stretched Marina and with his telltale face turned from persons occasionally met, and toward the surging sea. At the land's end, even in the confirmed darkness and the perhaps imminent big blow, his immemorial nook, small shelter as it yielded, had again received him; and it was in the course of this heedless session, no doubt, where the agitated air had nothing to add to the commotion within him, that he began to look his extraordinary fortune a bit straighter in the face and see it confess itself at once a fairytale and a nightmare. That, visibly, confoundingly, she was still attached to him (attached in fact was a mild word!) and that the unquestionable proof of it was in this offered pecuniary salve, of the thickest composition, for his wounds and sores and shames—these things were the fantastic fable, the tale of money in handfuls, that he seemed to have only to stand there and swallow and digest and feel himself full-fed by; but the whole of the rest was nightmare, and most of all nightmare his having thus to thank one through whom Nan and his little girls had known torture.

He didn't care for himself now, and this unextinguished, and apparently inextinguishable, charm by which he had held her was a fact incredibly romantic; but he gazed with a longer face than he had ever had for anything in the world at his potential acceptance of a great bouncing benefit from the person he intimately, if even in a manner indirectly, associated with the conditions to which his lovely wife and his little girls (who would have been so lovely too) had pitifully succumbed. He had accepted the social relation—which meant he had taken even that on trial—without knowing what it so dazzlingly masked; for a social relation it had become with a vengeance when it drove him about the place as now at his hours of freedom (and he actually and recklessly took, all demoralised and unstrung and unfit either for work or for anything else, other liberties that would get him into trouble) under this queer torment of irreconcilable things, a bewildered consciousness of tenderness and patience and cruelty, of great evident mystifying facts that were as little to be questioned as to be conceived or explained, and that were yet least, withal, to be lost sight of.

On that Sunday night he had wandered wild, incoherently ranging and throbbing, but this became the law of his next days as well, since he lacked more than ever all other resort or refuge and had nowhere to carry, to deposit or contractedly let loose and lock up, as it were, his swollen consciousness, which fairly split in twain the raw shell of his sordid little boarding-place. The arch of the sky and the spread of sea and shore alone gave him space; he could roam with himself anywhere, in short, far or near —he could only never take himself back. That certitude—that this was impossible to him even should she wait there among her plushes and bronzes ten years—was the thing he kept closest clutch of: it did wonders for what he would have called his self-respect. Exactly as he had left her so he would stand off—even though at moments when he pulled up sharp somewhere to put himself an intensest question his heart almost stood still. The days of the week went by, and as he had left her she stayed; to the extent, that is, of his having neither sight nor sound of her, and of the failure of every sign. It took nerve, he said, not to return to her, even for curiosity—since how, after all, in the name of wonder, had she invested the fruits of her extortion to such advantage, there being no chapter of all the obscurity of the years to beat that for queerness? But he dropped, tired to death, on benches, half-a-dozen times an evening—exactly on purpose to recognize that the nerve required was just the nerve he had.

As the days without a token from her multiplied he came in as well for hours—and these indeed mainly on the bench of desolation—of sitting stiff and stark in presence of the probability that he had lost everything forever. When he passed the Royal he never turned an eyelash, and when he met Captain Roper on the Front, three days after having been introduced to him, he "cut him dead"—another privileged consequence of a social relation —rather than seem to himself to make the remotest approach to the question of whether Miss Cookham had left Properley. He had cut people in the days of his life before, just as he had come to being himself cut—since there had been no time for him wholly without one or other face of that necessity— but had never effected such a severance as of this rare connection, which helped to give him thus the measure of his really precious sincerity. If he had lost what had hovered before him he had lost it, his only tribute to which proposition was to grind his teeth with one of those "scrunches," as he would have said, of which the violence fairly reached his ear. It wouldn't make him lift a finger, and in fact if Kate had simply taken herself off on the Tuesday or the Wednesday she would have reabsorbed again into the darkness from which she had emerged—and no lifting of fingers, the unspeakable chapter closed, would evermore avail. That at any rate was the kind of man he still was—even after all that had come and gone, and even if for a few dazed hours certain things had seemed pleasant. The dazed hours had passed, the surge of the old bitterness had dished him (shouldn't he have been shamed if it hadn't?) and he might sit there as before, as always, with nothing at all on earth to look to. He had therefore wrongfully believed himself to be degraded; and the last word about him would be that he *couldn't* then, it appeared, sink to vulgarity as he had tried to let his miseries make him.

And yet on the next Sunday morning, face to face with him again at the land's end, what she very soon came to was: "As if I believed you didn't *know* by what cord you hold me!" Absolutely too, and just that morning in fact, above all, he wouldn't, he quite couldn't have taken his solemn oath that he hadn't a sneaking remnant, as he might have put it to himself— a remnant of faith in tremendous things still to come of their interview. The day was sunny and breezy, the sea of a cold purple; he wouldn't go to church as he mostly went of Sunday mornings, that being, in its way too a social relation—and not least when two-and-thruppenny tan-colored gloves were new; which indeed he had the art of keeping them for ages. Yet he would dress himself as he scarce mustered resources for even to figure on the fringe of Society, local and transient, at St Bernard's, and in this trim he took his way westward; occupied largely, as he went, it might have seemed to any person pursuing the same course and happening to observe him, in a fascinated study of the motions of his shadow, the more or less grotesque shape projected, in front of him and mostly a bit to the right, over the blanched asphalt of the Parade and dangling and dancing at such a rate, shooting out and then contracting, that, viewed in themselves, its eccentricities might have formed the basis of an interesting challenge: "Find the state of mind, guess the nature of the agitation, possessing the person so remarkably represented!" Herbert Dodd, for that matter, might have been himself attempting to make by the sun's sharp aid some approach to his immediate horoscope.

It had at any rate been thus put before him that the dandling and dancing of his image occasionally gave way to perfect immobility, when he stopped and kept his eyes on it. "Suppose she should come, suppose she *should!*" it is revealed at least to ourselves that he had at these moments breathed to himself with the intensity of an arrest between hope and fear. It had glimmered upon him from early, with the look of the day, that, given all else that could happen, this would be rather, as he put it, in her line; and the possibility lived for him, as he proceeded, to the tune of a suspense almost sickening. It was, from one small stage of his pilgrimage to another, the "Forever, never!" of the sentimental case the playmates of his youth used to pretend to settle by plucking the petals of a daisy. But it came to his truly turning faint—so "queer" he felt—when, at the gained point of the long stretch from which he could always tell, he arrived within positive sight of his immemorial goal. His seat was taken and she was keeping it for him—it could only be *she* there in possession; whereby it shone out for Herbert Dodd that if he hadn't been quite sure of her recurrence she had at least been quite sure of his. *That* pulled him up to some purpose, where recognition began for them—or to the effect, in other words, of his pausing to judge if he could bear, for the sharpest note of their intercourse, this inveterate demonstration of her making him do what she liked. What settled the question for him then—and just while they avowedly watched each other, over the long interval, before closing, as if, on either side, for the major advantage—what settled it was this very fact that what she liked she liked so terribly. If it were simply to "use" him, as she had said the last time, and no matter to the profit of which of them she called it, one might let it go for that; since it could make her wait over, day after day, in that fashion, and with such a spending of money, on the hazard of their meeting again. How could she be the least sure he would ever again consent to it after the proved action on him, a week ago, of her last monstrous honesty? It was indeed positively as if he were now himself putting this influence—and for their common edification—to the supreme, to the finest test. He had a sublime, an ideal flight, which lasted about a minute. "Suppose, now that I see her there and what she has taken so characteristically for granted, suppose I just show her that she *hasn't* only confidently to wait or whistle for me, and that the length of my leash is greater than she measures, and that everything's impossible always?—show it by turning my back on her now and walking straight away. She won't be able not to understand *that!*"

Nothing had passed, across their distance, but the mute apprehension of each on the part of each; the whole expanse, at the church hour, was void of other life (he had scarce met a creature on his way from end to end), and the sun-seasoned gusts kept brushing the air and all the larger prospect clean. It was through this beautiful lucidity that he watched her watch him, as it were—watch him for what he would do. Neither moved at this high tension; Kate Cookham, her face fixed on him, only waited with a stiff appearance of leaving him, not for dignity but (to an effect of even deeper perversity) for kindness, free to choose. It yet somehow affected him at present, this attitude, as a gage of her *knowing too*—knowing, that is, that he wasn't really free, that this was the thinnest of vain parades, the poorest of hollow heroics, that his need, his solitude, his suffered wrong, his exhausted rancor, his foredoomed submission to any shown interest, all hung together too heavy on him to let the weak wings of his pride do more than vaguely tremble. They couldn't, they didn't carry him a single beat further away; according to which he stood rooted, neither retreating nor advancing, but presently correcting his own share of their bleak exchange by looking off at the sea. Deeply conscious of the awkwardness this posture gave him, he yet clung to it as the last shred of his honor, to the clear argument that it was one thing for him to have felt beneath all others, the previous days, that she was to be counted on, but quite as different for her to have felt that *he* was. His checked approach, arriving thus at no term, could in these odd conditions have established that he wasn't only if Kate Cookham had, as either of them might have said, taken it so—if she had given up the game at last by rising, by walking away and adding to the distance between them, and he had then definitely let her vanish into space. It became a fact that when she did finally rise—though after how long our record scarce takes on itself to say—it was not to confirm their separation, but to put an end to it; and this by slowly approaching him till she had come within earshot. He had wondered, once aware of it in spite of his averted face, what she would say and on what note, as it were, she would break their week's silence; so that he had to recognise anew, her voice reaching him, that remarkable quality in her which again and again came up for him as her art.

"There are twelve hundred and sixty pounds, to be definite, but I have it all down for you—and you've only to draw."

They lost themselves, these words, rare and exquisite, in the wide bright genial medium and the Sunday stillness, but even while that occurred and he was gaping for it she was herself there, in her battered ladylike truth, to answer for them, to represent them, and, if a further grace than their simple syllabled beauty were conceivable, almost embarrassingly to cause them to materialise. Yes, she let her smart and tight little reticule hang as if it bulged, beneath its clasp, with the whole portentous sum, and he felt himself glare again at this vividest of her attested claims. She might have been ready, on the spot, to open the store to the plunge of his hand, or, with the situation otherwise conceived, to impose on his pauperized state an acceptance of alms on a scale unprecedented in the annals of street-charity. Nothing so much counted for him, however, neither grave numeral nor elegant fraction, as the short, rich, rounded word that the breeze had picked up as it dropped and seemed now to blow about between them. "To draw—to draw?" Yes, he gaped it as if it had no sense; the fact being that even while he did so he was reading into her use of the term more romance than any word in the language had ever had for him. He, Herbert Dodd, was to live to "draw," like people, scarce hampered by the conditions of earth, whom he had remotely and circuitously heard about, and in fact when he walked back with her to where she had been sitting it was very much, for his strained nerves, as if the very bench of desolation itself were to be the scene of that exploit and he mightn't really live till he reached it.

When they had sat down together she did press the spring of her reticule, from which she drew, not a handful of gold nor a packet of crisp notes, but an oblong sealed letter, which she had thus waited on him she remarked, on purpose to deliver, and which would certify, with sundry particulars, to the credit she had opened for him at a London bank. He took it from her without looking at it, and held it, in the same manner, conspicuous and unassimilated, for most of the rest of the immediate time, appearing embarrassed with it, nervously twisting and flapping it, yet thus publicly retaining it even while aware, beneath everything, of the strange, the quite dreadful, wouldn't it be? engagement that such inaction practically stood for. He could accept money to that amount, yes—but not for nothing in return. For what then in return? He kept asking himself for what while she said other things and made above all, in her high, shrewd, successful way the point that, no, he needn't pretend that his conviction of her continued personal interest in him wouldn't have tided him over any question besetting him since their separation. She put it to him that the deep instinct of where he should at last find her must confidently have worked for him, since she confessed to her instinct of where she should find *him;* which meant—oh it came home to him as he fingered his sealed treasure!—neither more nor less than that she had now created between them an equality of experience. He wasn't to have done all the suffering, *she* was to have "been through" things he couldn't even guess at, and, since he was bargaining away his right ever again to allude to the unforgettable, so much there was of it, what her tacit proposition came to was that they were "square" and might start afresh.

He didn't take up her charge, as his so compromised "pride" yet in a manner prompted him, that he had enjoyed all the week all those elements of ease about her; the most he achieved for that was to declare, with an ingenuity contributing to float him no small distance further, that of course he had turned up at their old place of tryst, which had been, all the years, the haunt of his solitude and the goal of his walk any Sunday morning that seemed too beautiful for church; but that he hadn't in the least built on her presence there—since that supposition gave him, she would understand, wouldn't she? the air, disagreeable to him, of having come in search of her. Her quest of himself, once he had been seated there, would have been another matter—but in short "Of course after all you did come to me, just now, didn't you?" He felt himself, too, lamely and gracelessly grin, as for the final kick of his honor, in confirmation of the record that he had then yielded but to her humility. Her humility became for him at this hour and to this tune, on the bench of desolation, a quantity more prodigious and even more mysterious than that other guaranteed quantity the finger-tips of his left hand could feel the tap of by the action of his right; though what was in especial extraordinary was the manner in which she could keep making him such allowances and yet meet him again, at some turn, as with her residuum for her clever self so great.

"Come to you, Herbert Dodd?" She imperturbably echoed. "I've been coming to you for the last ten years!"

There had been for him, just before this, sixty supreme seconds of intensest aspiration—a minute of his keeping his certificate poised for a sharp thrust back at her, the thrust of the wild freedom of his saying: "No, no, I *can't* give them up; I can't simply sink them deep down in my soul forever, with no cross in all my future to mark *that* burial; so that if this is what our arrangement means I must decline to have anything to do with it." The words none the less hadn't come, and when she had herself, a couple of minutes later, spoken those others, the blood rose to his face as if, given his stiffness and her extravagance, he had just indeed saved himself.

Everything in fact stopped, even his fidget with his paper; she imposed a hush, she imposed at any rate the conscious decent form of one, and he couldn't afterwards have told how long, at this juncture, he must have sat simply gazing before him. It was so long, at any rate, that Kate herself got up—and quite indeed, presently, as if her own forms were now at an end. He had returned her nothing—so what was she waiting for? She had been on the two other occasions momentarily at a loss, but never so much so, no doubt, as was thus testified to by her leaving the bench and moving over once more to the rail of the terrace. She could carry it off, in a manner, with her resources, that she was waiting with so little to wait for; she could face him again, after looking off at the sea, as if this slightly stiff delay, not wholly exempt from awkwardness, had been but a fine scruple of her courtesy. She had gathered herself in; after giving him time to appeal she could take it that he had decided and that nothing was left for her to do. "Well then," she clearly launched at him across the broad walk—"well then, good-bye."

She had come nearer with it, as if he might rise for some show of express separation; but he only leaned back motionless, his eyes on her now—he kept her a moment before him. "Do you mean that we don't—that we don't—?" But he broke down.

"Do I 'mean'—?" She remained as for questions he might ask, but it was well-nigh as if there played through her dotty veil an irrepressible irony for that particular one. "I've meant, for long years, I think, all I'm capable of meaning. I've meant so much that I can't mean more. So there it is."

"But if you go," he appealed—and with a sense as of final flatness, however he arranged it, for his own attitude—"but if you go sha'n't I see you again?"

She waited a little, and it was strangely for him now as if—though at last so much more gorged with her tribute than she had ever been with his—something still depended on her. "Do you *like* to see me?" she very simply asked.

At this he did get up; that was easier than to say—at least with responsive simplicity; and again for a little he looked hard and in silence at his letter; which at last, however, raising his eyes to her own for the act, while he masked their conscious ruefulness, to his utmost, in some air of assurance, he slipped into the inner pocket of his coat, letting it settle there securely. "You're too wonderful." But he frowned at her with it as never in his life. "Where does it all come from?"

"The wonder of poor me?" Kate Cookham said. "It comes from *you*."

He shook his head slowly—feeling, with his letter there against his heart, such a new agility, almost such a new range of interest. "I mean so *much* money—so extraordinarily much."

Well, she held him a while blank. "Does it seem to you extraordinarily much—twelve-hundred-and-sixty? Because, you know," she added, "it's all."

"It's enough!" he returned with a slight thoughtful droop of his head to the right and his eyes attached to the far horizon as through a shade of shyness for what he was saying. He felt all her own lingering nearness somehow on his cheek.

"It's enough? Thank you then!" she rather oddly went on.

He shifted a little his posture. "It was more than a hundred a year—for you to get together."

"Yes," she assented, "that was what year by year I tried for."

"But that you could live all the while and save that—!" Yes, he was at liberty, as he hadn't been, quite pleasantly to marvel. All his wonderments in life had been hitherto unanswered—and didn't the change mean that here again was the social relation?

"Ah, I didn't live as you saw me the other day."

"Yes," he answered—and didn't he the next instant feel he must fairly have smiled with it?—"the other day you *were* going it!"

"For once in my life," said Kate Cookham. "I've left the hotel," she after a moment added.

"Ah, you're in—a—lodgings?" he found himself inquiring as for positive sociability.

She had apparently a slight shade of hesitation, but in an instant it was all right; as what he showed he wanted to know she seemed mostly to give him. "Yes—but far of course from here. Up on the hill." To which, after another instant, "At The Mount, Castle Terrace," she subjoined.

"Oh, I *know* The Mount. And Castle Terrace is awfully sunny and nice."

"Awfully sunny and nice," Kate Cookham took from him.

"So that if it isn't," he pursued, "like the Royal, why you're at least comfortable."

"I shall be comfortable anywhere now," she replied with a certain dryness. It was astonishing, however, what had become of his own. "Because I've accepted—?"

"Call it that!" she dimly smiled.

"I hope then at any rate," he returned, "you can now thoroughly rest." He spoke as for a cheerful conclusion and moved again also to smile, though as with a poor grimace, no doubt; since what he seemed most clearly to feel was that since he "accepted" he mustn't, for his last note, have accepted in sulkiness or gloom. With that, at the same time, he couldn't but know, in all his fibres, that with such a still-watching face as the dotty veil didn't disguise for him there was no possible concluding, at least on his part. On hers, on hers it was—as he had so often for a week had reflectively to pronounce things—another affair. Ah, somehow, both formidably and helpfully, her face concluded—yet in a sense so strangely enshrouded in things she didn't tell him. What *must* she, what mustn't she, have done? What she had said—and she had really told him nothing—was no account of her life; in the midst of which conflict of opposed recognitions, at any rate, it was as if, for all he could do, he himself now considerably floundered. "But I can't think—I can't think—!"

"You can't think I can have made so much money in the time and been honest?"

"Oh, you've been *honest!*" Herbert Dodd distinctly allowed.

It moved her stillness to a gesture—which, however, she had as promptly checked; and she went on the next instant as for further generosity to his failure of thought. "Everything was possible, under my stress, with my hatred."

"Your hatred—?" For she had paused as if it were after all too difficult.

"Of what I should for so long have been doing to you."

With this, for all his failures, a greater light than any yet shone upon him. "It made you think of ways—?"

"It made me think of everything. It made me work," said Kate Cookham. She added, however, the next moment: "But that's my story."

"And I mayn't hear it?"

"No—because I mayn't hear yours."

"Oh, mine—!" he said with the strangest, saddest, yet after all most resigned sense of surrender of it; which he tried to make sound as if he couldn't have told it, for its splendor of sacrifice and of misery, even if he would.

It seemed to move in her a little, exactly, that sense of the invidious. "Ah, mine too, I assure you—!"

He rallied at once to the interest. "Oh, we *can* talk then?"

"Never," she all oddly replied. "Never," said Kate Cookham.

They remained so, face to face; the effect of which for him was that he had after a little understood why. That was fundamental. "Well, I see."

Thus confronted they stayed; and then, as he saw with a contentment that came up from deeper still, it was indeed she who, with her worn fine face, would conclude. "But I can take care of you."

"You *have!*" he said as with nothing left of him but a beautiful appreciative candor.

"Oh, but you'll want it now in a way—!" she responsibly answered.

He waited a moment, dropping again on the seat. So, while she still stood, he looked up at her; with the sense somehow that there were too many things and that they were all together, terribly, irresistibly, doubtless blessedly, in her eyes and her whole person; which thus affected him for the moment as more than he could bear. He leaned forward, dropping his elbows to his knees and pressing his head on his hands. So he stayed, saying nothing; only, with the sense of her own sustained, renewed and wonderful action, knowing that an arm had passed round him and that he was held. She was beside him on the bench of desolation.

ADVENTURE

W*E have come a long way from Tom Paine's harangues urging American independence to Admiral Byrd's account of his flight to the South Pole, with which this section, and the book, ends. But that is the strange and unpredictable adventure in a hundred years of publishing.*

BELMORE BROWNE

The Climbing of Mount McKinley

Although the mountain was known among the pioneers along the Yukon, no news of it had as yet reached the outside world. W. A. Dickey, a young Princeton graduate, was destined to wake the mountain from its long sleep, and give it the prominence it deserved.

In 1896, with one companion, he "tracked" a boat up the Susitna River. He and Monks, his partner, were prospecting for gold, and in the course of time they reached a point where from some bare hills they got an open view of the Alaskan Range with Mount McKinley towering above it. With remarkable accuracy he estimated its height at 20,000 feet, and on his return to civilisation he wrote a newspaper article describing the location and grandeur of the great peak, which he called Mount McKinley.

A few years ago I asked Mr. Dickey why he named the mountain McKinley, and he answered that while they were in the wilderness he and his partner fell in with two prospectors who were rabid champions of free silver, and that after listening to their arguments for many weary days, he retaliated by naming the mountain after the champion of the gold standard.

After its rediscovery Mount McKinley again faded back into oblivion, for while it was known to a few prospectors who had pushed their way into the wilderness, no man had as yet reached its base.

* * *

We reached our base camp on the evening of the 24th of April and just four days later our advance on Mount McKinley began. Our idea was to make a reconnaissance in force with a dog team. What we would accomplish would depend entirely on the kind of "going" we found, but we figured that the dogs would be a help in pulling our freight up the glacier.

On reaching the head of "Glacier Pass" we decided to lie over until night came and to do our travelling then as the snow would be firmer. We had our fill of pemmican and tea at 10 P.M., and then we struck out over the frosted surface of the great glacier, which we called the McKinley Glacier. We had donned the mountain rope for good as the glacier was badly crevassed. I broke trail, followed by Professor Parker, who was in front of the dogs. La Voy was at the gee-pole of the sled.

Professor Parker was roped to La Voy, but we took care to keep the rope free from the sled as its weight was sufficient to carry us with it had it broken through the crust into a crevasse. About 11.30 the moon rose and its light looked almost golden against the deep blue shadows instead of silvery as it does in the Southland.

We crossed tracks of grizzly bears that were leaving their winter dens high up among the ice-falls of the upper glacier. We reached the base of the first serac at 3 A.M. and we were glad to rest as it was bitterly cold and we had made good progress. After a cat-nap La Voy and I made a trip to the top of the serac. We told Professor Parker that we would return in an hour, but we had not yet begun to appreciate the difficulties of travelling on the McKinley Glacier. There were countless crevasses and I was forced to sound every foot of our trail with my ice-axe, and although I used the greatest caution, I broke through into several ice caverns, but was saved by the rope from any serious accident. After we had been absent from camp for two hours, Professor Parker became worried, and thinking that the trail that La Voy and I had made would be perfectly safe, he started after us. He had only gone a short distance, however, when the trail itself caved in. Luckily, he caught himself with his hands as the crevasse was not wide, or he might have suffered a dangerous injury, or, probably, come to an end of his climbing career.

In the afternoon La Voy and I took the dogs and hauled a good load to the summit of the serac. Near the head of the ice-fall we were forced directly under the avalanche-polished walls of the Central North-Eastern Ridge, but when we had to cross areas that were swept by snow-slides we studied our chances carefully and crossed at the most favourable time.

The McKinley Glacier rises in steps, like a giant stairway. We rose about 1000 feet while climbing the first serac and then an almost level plain of snow lay before us. Crossing this blinding ice-field, we pitched our camp at the base of a tremendous serac that rose in two great cliffs with a narrow platform between. It was a wild-looking spot! Great blue cliffs of solid ice, scarred here and there by black rock, rose 4000 feet above us, and while we staked down our tent a snow-storm whirled down from the upper peaks, blotting everything from view and wrapping us in a white mantle. Moving cautiously in the storm, La Voy and I felt our way to the top of the first bench of the "great serac."

The western walls of this ice-fall were fed by the snow from the north peak of Mount McKinley, and we were thrilled by catching a glimpse of the main wall of the mountain hanging high above us. On May 3d, we advanced to the top of this first bench and brought up all our belongings. We had now reached an altitude of 8500 feet. We had a hellish morning; our tent was in an accursed spot and we feared to move a step without being tied to the rope.

La Voy fell into a crevasse when we were about to make camp. I made it a rule to lead as I was used to the treachery of the ice and being light of weight was less of a burden to handle if I broke into a crevasse. That morning, however, I felt an attack of snow-blindness coming on and asked La Voy to lead. He was very careful at first, but on reaching a level bench he became over-confident and swung rapidly along without sounding with his axe. Suddenly the snow broke through and the fact that he had reached the centre of the crevasse before he fell resulted in his dropping a good distance before the rope became taut. When his weight came on the rope, it did so with crushing force. I was in the middle of the rope and was unable to hold my feet, as my snowshoes slid on the crust. At the time of the shock on the rope Professor Parker was carrying a large coil in his left hand. This hand had been weakened by a gunshot wound on one of our former trips and when the rope came taut with a snap the loose coil was snatched from his hand and he was unable to help. I will never forget the few seconds that followed while La Voy's weight was pulling me towards the crevasse. I remember straining until my tendons cracked, and jabbing my ice-axe again and again into the hard crust. Just below we had had soft snow, but now, when soft snow would have been a boon, the crust had hardened so that I could not drive my axe home. I then braked with the head of my axe and when only six feet from the edge of the chasm I came to a stop. La Voy was almost at a standstill at the time and I thought that *I* had stopped him, but after calling several times, he finally answered and told me to give him more rope, as he was on a ledge of ice that protruded from the ice wall. I will always wonder whether I would have stopped him *without the aid of that ledge!* After anchoring myself firmly I had a talk with La Voy and he told me that he could follow the ledge upward to a point where he saw light coming through the snow. And while I paid out the rope he made the ascent and it was a welcome sight when he pushed his head through the snow some thirty feet to my left. I examined the crevasse as soon as he joined us; it was about six feet wide and as far as I could tell it extended to China.

After La Voy appeared, I took a photograph that shows him emerging from the crevasse, and we advanced thereafter with redoubled caution. We relayed our last load through driving snow and when nightfall came we were happy, for our altitude was now 8500 feet.

The day following was a "big day." The night before we had camped in driving snow and howling wind, surrounded by crevasses and a huge menacing serac rising one thousand feet sheer above us. Our chances of getting our dogs up the avalanche-scarred slopes looked slim indeed. The following day we made a reconnaissance in force and after I had broken into two crevasses we found a snow bridge across a yawning bergschrund, and after making sure that our dogs could cross, we reached the top. Then the sun came out. Our outside shirts were discarded, mitts thrown aside, and our benumbed feet came back to life under the blissful warmth. In the afternoon La Voy and I hauled two sled-loads to the top of the worst pitch and back-packed three hundred pounds over the bridge that spanned the bergschrund. While climbing the serac, Dewey and Fritz, our two "wheel-dogs," fell into a crevasse and they were unconscious by the time we pulled them out, although they recovered quickly when we loosened their collars. Strange as it may seem, the heat of the sun had little effect on the air temperature. On this day, when our faces were blistering and the glacier was a blinding glare of white, the temperature was 33°, *or only one degree above freezing!*

We were welcomed by another snow-storm when we camped at the summit of the "great serac." We did not know it then, as the driving snow shut out all sight of the surrounding mountains, but our labours to reach the head of the glacier were nearly over. When the clouds broke away on the following morning, we could see the grim walls of Mount McKinley high above our heads, and it was only about three miles to the end of the great amphitheatre where our glacier had its birth. We had risen 1175 feet in climbing the second step of the "great serac" and our camp was now at an altitude of 9675 feet, or nearly half-way up Mount McKinley.

We were not to have everything our own way, however, as a second snow-storm swept down the glacier and the new snow banked up by the ton on the mountainside made our returning under the great cliffs for our equipment a dangerous enterprise. Later, we were glad indeed that we had chosen the wiser course.

To understand the unpleasant side of what happened, one must have gone through the days of anxiety that we had known; we had fallen through treacherous snow into blue-black crevasses and edged breathlessly over precarious snow bridges, until we came to feel that we were never safe and that at any moment the snow might give beneath our feet with the familiar sickening feeling of a dropping elevator. Our position on the edge of the ice cliffs that fall away for more than a thousand feet added also to the terror of what happened.

It was after lunch; Professor Parker was sleeping and La Voy and I were talking in whispers while we listened to the rattle of storm-driven snow across the sides of our frail shelter. Suddenly we felt the glacier under us give a sickening heave and the nearby mountain thundered with avalanches. For an instant I thought that an ice cave had broken in with us, or that the serac was falling and taking us with it! But in a moment we were undeceived for another shock came, and as the thought *earthquake* flashed through my mind the air thundered and pulsated under the force of the countless avalanches. It was an awful and terrifying sound, and we were glad when the echoes ceased and we once more heard the dreary sound of wind and snow.

The following morning we awoke in a cloudy world, but it was clear enough for La Voy and myself to go down the back trail for our freight. The tent was thick with frost when we awoke, but we thought little of the cold until we began to travel and then our rubber shoe-packs froze. When we returned to camp an hour later the temperature had risen considerably but the thermometer still registered 10° below zero. We advanced immediately through a heavy snow-storm and broke a trail well up into the great gathering basin, and in the afternoon we hitched up the dogs and relayed a good load forward.

It cleared a little between snow flurries and on reaching the end of our morning's trail we left the dogs and broke forward to the top of the last serac on the McKinley Glacier.

We finally reached a point where we could study the whole sweep of the great North-Eastern Ridge and to our delight we saw a low col, or break in the ridge, that could be reached easily from our glacier and the ridge itself looked climbable all the way to the big basin between the two highest peaks of the big mountain.

We drew the following conclusions: As we had now attained an altitude of 11,000 feet, our camp on the col, or lowest portion of the ridge, would be close to 12,000 feet, which would leave us between three and five thousand feet of climbing before we reached the big basin between the north and south peaks.

We were highly elated by the promising appearance of the great ridge, and although we would lose some time in returning with the dogs, our chances were improving as the days were growing longer. Indeed, for the first time we felt confident of conquering the mountain. We were not so foolish as to belittle the task ahead of us, although we could see no natural climbing difficulties that we did not feel able to overcome. It was the "unknown dangers" that filled our minds with vague forebodings of hardships and difficulties. An altitude of 20,000 feet had never been attained so close to the Arctic circle, and we knew from previous experience that the hardships to be undergone at an altitude of only 10,000 feet on this northern giant were far more severe than those encountered in climbing a 20,000-foot peak in the Andes of South America. We knew that the severest weather conditions ever recorded occurred on Mount Washington only 6000 feet above the sea, when a wind of 180 miles an hour was noted with an accompanying temperature of 40° below zero! If these conditions could exist at 6000 feet, what might we not expect 20,000 feet up in the sky within 250 miles of the Arctic circle? It was this feeling of uncertainty as to what might happen that made our attempt on Mount McKinley as exciting a sporting proposition as the heart could desire.

On May 7th we awoke to another day of bitter cold, and snow squalls were sweeping across the glacier. La Voy and I drove the dogs to 11,000 feet through the storm and there we cached our trail sled, heavily loaded with food and mountain equipment, and securely lashed with ropes tautened over protecting caribou and mountain-sheep skins. As an added precaution I anchored the sled by driving an extra ice-axe between the forward braces deep into the snow.

The weather showed no signs of improving and as we would be unable to advance much farther with the dogs, and as every day of inaction meant just so many more rations of mountain food wasted, we decided to return to base camp at once. After a hasty lunch we packed up our belongings and started down the glacier.

For a short distance we had a faint trail to follow, but it disappeared at the base of the big serac. At first the dogs were able to follow it by scent, but they, too, were soon at fault.

Between the two cliffs of the great serac I had to begin sounding and trailbreaking and for seven hours we struggled against the worst glacier conditions that I have ever experienced. In the seven hours we crept down over six miles of ice and over the whole distance I sounded every foot that we advanced. On the middle serac the clouds closed down on us and then the snow fell, wrapping us in a chilling shroud and blotting out every mountain-side and landmark. Crevasses were the least of our troubles. On the edges of the seracs the ice had formed great caverns, and avalanches had covered these caverns with a treacherous layer of rotten snow.

The last serac we crept over in darkness. We were six miles from Glacier Pass, night had fallen, and the driving snow had turned us—men and dogs alike—to dim, white forms, so we decided to camp. We had only two hard-tack and one-eighth pound of pemmican between us. Luckily I had a piece of candle over which I melted a cup of snow water. After dividing our food scraps we rolled into our fur robes.

The next morning was brighter, and as our trail was downhill Professor Parker rode the sled and we jogged down to Glacier Pass in fine style. There we broached our cache and filled up on hardtack, tea, and sugar, and after a nap we struck out for base camp, which we reached in the evening of May 8th.

* * *

It was on the 5th day of June that we began our final attack on Mount McKinley. We took Arthur Aten and our dog team with us as far as the base of the first serac. It was a long, hard march and Aten remained all night, sharing my wolf robe. We awoke in a cloudy world and soon we were enveloped in a heavy snowstorm. Aten, fearful that he might be held by the storm, leaped on his sled and faded away into the white mist.

We now turned our minds toward back-packing our supplies to the head of the glacier where our sled and equipment were cached. Although we were travelling as light as we could we had all we could manage under the difficult conditions that we found on the glacier. The snow-storm continued for three days and we lay in our tent eating our valuable food and abusing the weather.

We were dumbfounded by the turn the weather had taken. All the mountains below us that had been practically free of snow when we arrived on the Clearwater River were now buried deep in snow. We knew it could not be the usual state of affairs for these same mountains were grass-covered. If every summer was a repetition of this one no grass could grow.

Under June 8th there is an interesting entry in my diary:

The glacier has been very noisy all day; it has groaned and cracked, and at short intervals there have been deep, powerful reports, sounding for all the world like the boom of big guns at a distance. We have been talking about this queer noise but are undecided as to its cause. It must be due to the settling of the great ice caverns under the tremendous weight of new snow.

It was not until we reached civilisation long afterwards that we found that the unusual booming sound had not come from the glacial caverns, but that it was made by Katmai in eruption three hundred miles away—Katmai, the volcano whose eruption buried Kodiak Island in ashes! Later we found these Katmai ashes in our teapot after we had melted snow, but again we accepted the easiest explanation and decided that the grit in our teacups was merely dust blown from the cliffs.

After the snow ceased falling we were held by good weather, for tons of snow hung poised on the steep cliffs and the route over the seracs under these avalanche-polished slopes was out of the question.

In order to make use of our time, La Voy and I snowshoed six miles to Glacier Pass and brought back an extra allowance of alcohol, sugar, pemmican, and hardtack. On our return we saw as fine an avalanche as it has been my luck to witness. It fell from the upper portions of the North-Eastern Ridge, for a distance of about three thousand feet, and when it struck the glacier it threw a snow cloud more than one thousand feet high. It was an awesome sight and we had to lower our tent quickly lest the terrific suction of air caused by the falling snow should do it damage.

After the snow had settled we commenced our arduous advance up the glacier. The new snow made travelling slow, and we were forced to break trail with light loads.

La Voy's "game knee" gave him trouble, and while climbing the second serac he fell through into a deep crevasse while following in my footsteps, and injured his knee again. But after a good rest he was able to advance once more.

At this time we were under a great nervous strain; the constant lookout for crevasses and avalanches had a depressing effect on us, but we were also in great fear that an avalanche might have buried our cache of mountain equipment. I will never forget the excitement we laboured under as we ploughed slowly up over the last serac. Suddenly a tiny speck of black showed in the snow ahead, and running wildly forward we came to our precious sled. The tip of the ice-axe with which we had anchored it was the only thing in sight, and on shovelling away the snow, we found that the sled had been turned on its side by the terrific wind caused by the avalanche that I had witnessed from the Caribou hills beyond our base camp. The discovery of our cache was a great stimulus to us. Besides the necessary food and equipment we recovered many longed-for luxuries such as mountain sheep and caribou skins to sleep on, reading matter, and a pocket chessboard.

Our cache was on the right-hand side of the final amphitheatre. Looking across the glacier we could see an easy route leading to the col of the North-Eastern Ridge. Where the ridge sagged, its summit was only five hundred feet above the floor of the glacier. We were held once more by a blizzard, but the rest was not unwelcome and when the weather cleared we lost no time in advancing to the top of the col. Here we shovelled deep into the steep snow slopes close to the summit of the ridge. As we dug deeper we made a wall of the blocks of hard snow, and when our labours were completed, we were protected from storms and wind.

When we moved our supplies from the glacier to the col camp we had a steep climb of five hundred feet to negotiate, and at this point La Voy found that on steep slopes of soft snow he could not depend on his knee. Now La Voy's strength was one of the most important factors in our attempt on the great peak, and as his courage was of the highest quality I knew that his knee was in a serious condition. In all the glacier work I broke trail as a matter of course as my light weight and long schooling in this work made it advisable. But La Voy's help on the great ridge was invaluable and as I looked up over the towering, knife-edge ridge, my heart sank at the possibility of his knee being seriously injured. There was only one thing to be done and that was to make the work as easy as possible for him, so I carried most of the dunnage, although he chafed under the new régime and amply made up for his lack of activity by shovelling out the deep holes in which we set our tent. It was in carrying an eighty-pound load from the glacier to our col camp that I first noticed the effect of our altitude, although it only made itself manifest by a slight acceleration of my breathing.

Our col camp was at an altitude of 11,800 feet, according to Professor Parker's Hicks and my Green aneroid barometer.

On June 19th we made our first reconnoissance on the ridge. Our plan was to climb to the Big Basin between the two great peaks and the reader will see how little we appreciated the immensity of the task that confronted us. We took with us ample food for six days, and in addition, extra clothing, films, cameras, glasses, compasses, barometers, a prismatic compass and level, anemometer, etc. The following account of our day's adventure is taken from my diary:

June 19th. Back from a very hard trip. We climbed to 13,200 feet through the softest of snow over as sensational a ridge as I have ever been on. Some of the slopes that we *traversed* were 60° or more, for I measured one that overhung a 2000-foot drop off that measured 50° on the clinometer, and there were many that I could not measure because we were afraid to stay on them longer than necessary. I broke and chopped our trail for five hours, and in places I had to first stamp down platforms in the soft snow before I could reach a firm footing.

La Voy's knee stopped us at 13,200 feet. Now the question is can he travel to-morrow? If he can and it's a good day we will take our camp outfit and climb to the Big Basin, and return for the food that we left on the ridge at 13,200 feet.

The above entry shows the optimistic view that I held concerning our reaching the basin. It was not until later that we realised to the full the gigantic size of the great mountain, as the next entry in my diary makes clear.

June 22d. Ridge Camp, altitude 13,600 feet. Much has happened in the last three days. On the morning of the 20th we started out in the firm belief that we would reach the edge of the Big Basin and camp before nightfall. It took us three hours to reach the point where we had left our packs on the first day. It was an impressive spot. The ridge was so sharp that I had to chop off the crest to make room for our feet.

On the left the ridge dropped away at a dizzy angle for 5000 feet to the surface of the east fork of the Muldrow Glacier, on the right it fell away almost straight for 2000 feet; you felt as if you were flying. In this narrow ridge we had chopped deep holes to insure the safety of our packs. From the packs onward there were no steps at all, and although I had had to remake a large proportion of our steps during the three preceding hours I started on confidently and we began to creep up the great knife edge of snow. As the time went on I began to feel the effects of the terrific labour. La Voy despite his willingness could not help me out as the steps were in soft snow and his knee was hurting him. After I had broken trail steadily for an hour, a rock that I had been working towards actually seemed farther away than when I started. As time went on the constant gazing upward along the white ridge into the sun's eye began to tell on me and by the end of the fifth hour I was snow-blind and completely done up. I saw no place level enough to camp and I supposed that we would find hard ice underlying the snow that would prevent our shovelling out a tent-site. I now knew that it would take hours to reach the basin, where we had figured in minutes, in fact I was beginning to realise what the mountain *is*—it is reared on such a gigantic scale that ice slopes that only look a few hundred feet high may be several thousand! At last I turned to my companions and told them that I was snow-blind and played out, and that I feared that I couldn't chop long enough to reach a camping place. About 100 feet above there was a slight sag in the snow slope below some rocks that were in their turn below the final rise of the ridge where it swoops up a thousand feet to join a rock peak that forms the southern gateway to the Big Basin.

After a council of war the Professor said, "Let's try to shovel a site in that sag above us." La Voy, who was fresh, went to work and to our unbounded joy he struck hard snow instead of ice, and in the course of two hours' hard work we had a shelter on the snow slope. We first picked the snow out with our ice-axes and then shovelled it out, the blocks rolling down 2000 feet from the little platform. While La Voy was finishing up Professor Parker and I descended for the packs we had left on the first day. The distance was close to 500 feet and *it had taken me two hours of heart-breaking toil to lead the way up!*

Went to bed suffering from my eyes, which La Voy doctored with boracic acid and zinc sulphate, and sick at heart, as I now knew that McKinley was too big for us with our present food supply of six days' rations. Marvellous sunset as we looked over a sea of clouds that stretched to the end of the earth.

The next entry tells of the final day when we were forced to change our plans and return for more food.

June 21st. Ridge Camp. Alt. 13,600 ft. Good day so we started (again) to pack some supplies into the Big Basin. After pounding down steps for an hour *we reached hard snow!* Oh! what a relief it was mentally as well as physically, for soft snow is treacherous stuff and on many of the steep *traverses* that we have made we have been afraid to *speak* for fear the reverberation of our voices would start the snow sliding. La Voy came forward generously and for eight hours we chopped alternately, each taking half-hour turns.

But the work was so difficult that after seven hours of continuous work with La Voy chopping half the time *we rose only 800 feet!* We were again forced to leave our packs on a knife-edged ridge at an altitude of 14,400 feet. We were close to the great peak that forms the south gateway and we could just begin to see into the Big Basin!

On our return to camp we talked the matter over, and we decided that there was only one thing to do—namely to return to our col camp and pack up ten days' rations. It was a hard blow to us as it meant hellish labour, but it had to be done.

All day we have been above a sea of clouds—that may mean that we are at last above the bad weather. No ill effects from altitude yet, am enjoying my smoke as usual. Min. tem. June 21st, 4° below zero. June 22d, 3° below zero.

On the following day—June 22d—we were awakened by the howling of the wind, and on emerging from our tent we found clouds about us. As all we had to do to reach our col camp was to follow the steps on the knife-edge ridge we started down for our extra supplies. It was strange to think as we descended through the grey pall that within a few inches of our feet the ridge dropped away between two thousand and four thousand feet. Many of our steps were filled in solidly with drifted snow, but it was far easier to remake them on our way downward than it would have been while ascending with loads.

We figured on twelve days' food from our ridge camp at 13,600 feet. Coming over the narrow arêtes we were struck by heavy "wullies" or wind squalls that blew the snow in clouds off into space. We could hardly see each other at times, and we drove our ice-axes deep into the snow, and moved cautiously; it was spectacular climbing.

By this time we were awful objects to look at; La Voy and I were always more or less snow-blind, from trail-chopping, and our eyes were swollen to slits and ran constantly; we were all almost black, unshaved, with our lips and noses swollen, cracked, and bleeding, our hands, too were swollen, cracked, and blood-stained. As La Voy said, we would have served "to frighten children into the straight and narrow path."

The following day was clear although the usual cloud carpet covered the lowlands. Taking our packs we again attacked the great ridge and nightfall found us triumphant at our ridge camp—we had dropped our loads under the "South Gateway Peak" at an elevation of 15,000 feet.

On the following day we advanced our camp to the shelter of the rocks, where I made the following entry in my diary:

"15,000-foot Camp."

We have packed up heavy loads from our ridge camp in a little more than three hours as the steps high up were not badly drifted. It was frightfully hard work and glad we are to be camped in the lee of some great granite slabs, with the sun warming our tent. This is the wildest and most desolate spot imaginable. We are on the very edge of the Big Basin that divides the two summits of Mount McKinley. Below us all is mist and clouds; it seems as if the earth, thinking we needed her no more, had withdrawn from our lives.

The Big Basin is glacier filled. There are three seracs, and between run easy snow slopes that promise an uneventful route to the base of the South Peak. All we have to do now is to traverse below the cliffs we are camped under, and we will be in the Big Basin.

It seems strange to realise that we are camped higher than Mount Tacoma or the Matterhorn! We left enough alcohol and pemmican at ridge camp to last us on our return. We are wearing our snow glasses inside the tent now, and my eyes are so bad that I sleep with glasses on.

In our 15,000-foot camp we were stormbound. An immense fall of snow occurred, and as we lay in our fur robes our ears were filled with the grandest natural music that I have ever heard, for during one entire morning the great amphitheatres thousands of feet below us thundered and boomed under the constant shock of avalanches, and through this awesome bass ran the shrill theme of shrieking wind.

Now up to our 15,000-foot camp we had noticed the altitude in one important respect only—Professor Parker and La Voy had been unable to eat their full ration of pemmican. Occasionally they let a meal go by without tasting it, and they attributed their inability to eat it to the fact that the pemmican was not good. I, however, suffered no inconvenience and ate as much as I wanted until I reached our 15,000-foot camp. On June 26th after the storm had passed we established a camp at 15,800 feet which we called our "16,000-foot camp." In the afternoon of the same day we advanced all our equipment with the exception of our camp outfit. That night I ate my ration of pemmican as usual, but a few hours after I began to suffer from abdominal cramps. The night was one long period of torture, and when morning came I made a vow that I would eat pemmican sparingly in the future. While the physical pain was bad enough the mental worry caused by our inability to eat pemmican was equally serious. Pemmican was our staff of life; on it we depended for strength and heat to carry us through the toil and cold of our high climb. Without it we would be reduced to a diet of tea, sugar, raisins, and a small allowance of chocolate, which was not enough to keep us warm, let alone furnish fuel for the hardest toil.

We were worn down to bone and sinew as it was and needed a strong food to give us strength; while we were as hard as iron we lacked the *rebound* that a well-fed man has—in the language of the training table "we had gone stale." We had learned too that it requires the same kind of energy to withstand bitter cold as it required in the accomplishment of hard physical work. Luckily, the average human being is an optimist; after worrying over the problem for an hour or two we decided that it was *uncooked* pemmican that disagreed with us and we dismissed the question after promising ourselves a pemmican pudding at our 16,000-foot camp.

Our progress upward through the Big Basin was uneventful except for the tremendous excitement we were labouring under. The cold too was intense. The leaves of my diary were so cold that I could not write without gloves. At our 16,000-foot camp with an alcohol stove going full blast and the warmth of our three bodies the temperature inside of our tent at 7.30 P.M. on the 26th of June was 5° below zero, and three hours later it was 19° below zero!

On the 27th of June we carried our packs in two relays to the top of the second serac between the two great peaks and camped just below the last serac that forms the highest point of the Big Basin. We arrived with our last loads after the sun had gone down, and I have never felt such savage cold as the ice-fields sent down to us. We were in a frigid hollow at an altitude (corrected reading) of 16,615 feet. On the north the great blue ice slopes led up at an almost unclimbable pitch between the granite buttresses of the Northern Peak. On the south frozen snow-fields swept gently to the rock-dotted sky-line of the Central North-East Ridge which led in an easy grade to the final or southern summit of the great mountain. La Voy went to work with our shovel while I picked away the hard snow with my ice-axe. Despite our labours our feet and hands were beginning to stiffen as we pitched the tent and started our stove, and we were seriously worried for fear Professor Parker would freeze. On the next day we devoted our time to resting and making the most careful preparations for the final climb. My diary entry for the day follows.

"17,000-foot Camp" (our barometers placed us close to that altitude but the final readings of our hypsometer compared with our base camp barometer readings placed this camp at an altitude of 16,615 feet). Bitterly cold. Professor Parker feels the altitude. If it is clear we will "hit" the summit to-morrow. We only have 3500 feet to climb. 3 P.M. same day—June 28th. Splendid loafing day—all well rested, and indications good for a fine climbing day to-morrow, but it has been blowing a gale on the upper snow-fields, although what few clouds have formed have been away below us. We will also be warm to-night as we will not get chilled making camp as we did yesterday. Have put in the spare time getting everything ready for the "big day." Last night was warm, only 8° below zero, so we are not so frightened by the weather, unless a blizzard strikes us, and then anything might happen. We feel somewhat like soldiers on the eve of a battle, for to-morrow promises to be a good day, and if it is it will be the final day of three seasons of endeavour and several years of thought, planning, and hoping. If we "get there" we will be happy men. There is nothing to stop us except a storm. The route is easy; direct from camp to some rocks that lead to the summit of the ridge 1000 feet above us, thence along the ridge for perhaps a mile to the final dome which will give us perhaps 2000 feet of ice-creeper climbing, and then our dream will be realised. Robert Louis Stevenson says that only one thing in life can be attained—Death; but Robert never climbed a high summit after years of failure! We will rise at 4 A.M. and start at 6, and we hope to make the climb at the rate of 500 feet an hour, or seven hours in all, and return in two—a nine-hour day.

8 P.M. same day. Beautiful night, have just come in from studying the peak and weather—can look out over the north-east end of the range and see each peak and valley—also blue washes that mean timber 15,000 feet below us; wish we had some here!

From our camp we saw the northern side of the horseshoe-shaped summit. The main ridge that we were to follow led up to the northern *heel* of of the horseshoe. There it rose to the almost level summit formed by the circular summit ridge. About one hundred yards from the very edge of the summit there was a slight rise, swelling, or hummock on the level ridge and this little hill is in all probability the highest point on the North American continent.

The morning of our final climb dawned clear as crystal. As I came out into the stabbing cold to report on the weather the whole expanse of country to the north-eastward stretched like a deep blue sea to where the rising sun was warming the distant horizon.

True to our schedule we left camp at 6 A.M. Not a sound broke the silence of this desolate amphitheatre. At first the snow was hard and required little chopping. We moved very quietly and steadily, conserving our strength for possible exertions to come. At regular half-hour intervals La Voy and I exchanged places, and the steady strokes of our axes went on with scarcely an intermission.

Between changes both Professor Parker and I checked off our rise in altitude and to our surprise we found that, although we thought we were making fairly good time, we were in reality climbing only 400 feet an hour. Close to the top of the big ridge 1000 feet above our camp we ran into soft snow and we fought against this unexpected handicap at frequent intervals during the day. When we reached 18,500 feet we stopped for an instant and congratulated each other joyfully for we had returned the altitude record of North America to America, by beating the Duke of the Abruzzi's record of 18,000 feet made on Mount St. Elias. Shortly afterward we reached the top of the big ridge. Sentiment, old associations, and a desire for a light second breakfast halted us in the lee of some granite boulders. We had long dreamed of this moment, because, for the first time, we were able to look down into our battle-ground of 1910, and see all the glaciers and peaks that we had hobnobbed with in the "old days." But the views looking northeastward along the Alaskan Range were even more magnificent. We could see the great wilderness of peaks and glaciers spread out below us like a map. On the northern side of the range there was not one cloud; the icy mountains blended into the rolling foothills which in turn melted into the dim blue of the timbered lowlands, that rolled away to the north, growing bluer and bluer until they were lost at the edge of the world.

As we advanced up the ridge we noticed a shortness of breath and Professor Parker's face was noticeably white but we made fast time and did not suffer in any other way. At a little less than 19,000 feet, we passed the last rock on the ridge and secured our first clear view of the summit. It rose as innocently as a tilted snow-covered tennis-court and as we looked it over we grinned with relief—we *knew* the peak was ours!

Just above us the first swell of the summit rose several hundred feet and we found hard crust and some glare ice where our ice-creepers for the first time began to be of use. Up to our highest camp we had used rubber "shoe-packs" with leather tops, but on our last climb we wore soft tanned moccasins covered with ice "creepers" of the Appalachian Mountain Club design.

During our ascent of the ridge and the first swell of the final summit the wind had increased, and the southern sky darkened until at the base of the final peak we were facing a snow-laden gale. As the storm had increased we had taken careful bearings, and as the snow slope was only moderately steep all we had to do was to "keep going uphill." The climbing was now about of the same steepness as that we encountered in scaling the ridge above our camp, and as the snow was driving in thicker clouds before the strengthening wind we cut good steps. The step chopping reduced our progress once more to the 400-foot an hour speed.

The slope we were attacking was a round dome that came to a point forming the top and beginning of the northern heel. Before the wind and snow blotted the upper snow-fields from view we had had a good view of the inside of the horseshoe which sloped down to wicked-looking seracs that overhung a snow-field far below. Our one thought therefore was to keep well to the north so that in case we got lost in a blizzard there would be less chance of our descending among the crevasses at the top of the drop off. To accomplish our desire we cut our steps in zigzags of about the same length.

When we started up the last slope above the first swell of the final dome we were at an altitude of 19,300 feet. At 19,300 feet La Voy had begun his turn of chopping and as the lower portion of the summit was less steep than the upper slopes we succeeded in rising 500 feet during our combined turns at leading.

As I again stepped ahead to take La Voy's place in the lead I realised for the first time that we were fighting a blizzard, for my companions loomed dimly through the clouds of ice-dust and the bitter wind stabbed through my "parka." Five minutes after I began chopping my hands began to freeze and until I returned to 18,000 feet I was engaged in a constant struggle to keep the frost from disabling my extremities. La Voy's gloves and mine became coated with ice in the chopping of steps.

The storm was so severe that I was actually afraid to get new, dry mittens out of my rucksack for I knew that my hands would be frozen in the process. The only thing to be done was to keep my fingers moving constantly inside of my leather-covered wool mittens.

When my second turn was three fourths finished Professor Parker's barometer registered 20,000 feet. It would have been possible for him to set back the dial and get a higher reading but beyond this point it would have been dangerous to read the instrument had he been able to. The fury of the storm and the lashing clouds of steel-like ice particles would have made it next to impossible to read the dial.

On reaching 19,000 feet my barometer had registered within 100 feet of Professor Parker's, but as we rose higher my instrument—probably due to false compensation—had dropped with great rapidity to 17,200 feet, or little higher than our camp between the two peaks! From then until I returned to camp it was useless, but on the following day it "recovered its composure" and registered the same as Professor Parker's. Professor Parker's barometer behaved with absolute regularity throughout our whole trip, and as we had been able to study the last slopes carefully and could approximate accurately our speed in climbing, our calculations would place the summit at 20,450 feet or 150 feet higher than the United States Government triangulation. On leaving, and returning to, our base camp, both our barometers and a third that Aten had read twice daily during our absence agreed closely; and furthermore all three agreed closely with Brooks's and Reaburn's contour lines.

After passing the 20,000-foot level the cold and the force of the wind began to tell on me. I was forced several times to stop and fight with desperate energy the deadly cold that was creeping up my hands and feet. My estimate at the time for the last quarter of my period was 50 feet. As I stepped aside to let La Voy pass me I saw from his face as he emerged from the snow cloud that he realised the danger of our position, but I knew too that the summit was near and determined to hold on to the last moment.

As Professor Parker passed me his lips were dark and his face showed white from cold through his "parka" hood, but he made no sign of distress and I will always remember the dauntless spirit he showed in our most trying hour. The last period of our climb on Mount McKinley is like the memory of an evil dream. La Voy was completely lost in the ice mist, and Professor Parker's frosted form was an indistinct blur above me. I worked savagely to keep my hands warm and as La Voy's period came to its close we moved slower and more slowly. Finally, I pulled my watch from my neck inside my "parka" hood, and its hands, and a faint hail from above, told me that my turn had come. In La Voy's period we had ascended about 250 feet.

As I reached La Voy I had to chop about twenty feet of steps before coming to the end of the rope. Something indistinct showed through the scud as I felt the rope tauten and a few steps more brought me to a little crack or *bergschrund*. Up to this time we had been working in the lee of the north heel of the horseshoe ridge, but as I topped the small rise made by the crack I was struck by the full fury of the storm. The breath was driven from my body and I held to my axe with stooped shoulders to stand against the gale; I couldn't go ahead. As I brushed the frost from my glasses and squinted upward through the stinging snow I saw a sight that will haunt me to my dying day. *The slope above me was no longer steep!* That was all I could see. What it meant I will never know for certain— all I can say is that we were close to the top!

As the blood congealed in my fingers I went back to La Voy. He was getting the end of the gale's whiplash and when I yelled that we couldn't stand the wind he agreed that it was suicide to try. With one accord we fell to chopping a seat in the ice in an attempt to shelter ourselves from the storm, but after sitting in a huddled group for an instant we all arose—we were beginning to freeze!

I turned to Professor Parker and yelled, "The game's up; we've got to get down!"

And he answered, "Can't we go on? I'll chop if I can." The memory of those words will always send a wave of admiration through my mind, but I had to answer that it was not a question of chopping and La Voy pointed out our back steps—or the place where our steps ought to be, for a foot below us everything was wiped out by the hissing snow.

Coming down from the final dome was as heartless a piece of work as any of us had ever done. Had I been blind, and I was nearly so from the trail chopping and stinging snow, I could not have progressed more slowly. Every foothold I found with my axe alone, for there was no sign of a step left. It took me nearly two hours to lead down that easy slope of one thousand feet! If my reader is a mountaineer he can complete the picture!

Never in my life have I been so glad to reach a place as I was when I reached the top of the first swell below the summit.

Had the cold that was creeping stealthily upward from the tips of La Voy's and my hands and feet once taken hold we would have frozen in a few minutes, and the worst part of our fight on the summit was the fact that we were fighting a cruel danger that was *unseen!* In the cañon of the Yentna in 1906, where Barrill and I had been forced to take our lives in our hands ten times in less than an hour, it was a fair open fight against the rushing water, but in a fight against a blizzard you are struggling blindfolded against a thousand stabbing ice daggers.

Our troubles were not over, however, when we reached the base of the final dome, for here there were no steps and in descending through the hissing clouds of ice-dust I was led by the wind alone. Again I might have accomplished as much while blinded for my only guide was the icy blast striking my right shoulder. Had the wind shifted we would have perished, but after what seemed hours a dim shape loomed through the storm—it was the highest rock on the great ridge and our route was now assured. Finding the first rock ended our first struggle on Mount McKinley's summit, for in descending we kept in the protecting lee of the great ridge. When the gale quieted enough to let us, we talked! We cursed the storm that had driven us back. La Voy said that we had done enough in getting on top of the mountain, and that we had climbed the peak because it was only a walk of a few minutes from our last steps to the final dome. This was true, but unfortunately there is a technicality in mountaineering that draws a distinction between a mountain top and *the* top of a mountain—we had not stood on *the top*—that was the only difference! We reached camp at 7.35 P.M. after as cruel and heart-breaking a day as I trust we will ever experience.

On the following day we could not climb. Almost all our wearing apparel down to our underclothes was filled with the frost particles that had been driven into our clothing by the gale.

Fate too ordained that the peak should be clear, although long "mares' tails" of snow stretching out to the north told us that the gale was still lashing the summit.

* * *

Throughout the long day after our fight with the summit we talked food and weather conditions. What had caused the storm on the summit? we asked each other. Was it a general storm sweeping in from the Susitna Valley, or was it a local *tourmente* caused by change of temperature? Similar questions filled our minds, and we decided to leave at 3 A.M. on our next attempt.

The following day, strengthened as far as our insipid food would allow, and with our eyes patched up by boracic acid, we started on our final attack.

The steps made on the previous day helped us and in four hours and a half or by 7.30 A.M. we had reached an altitude of 19,300 feet at the base of the final dome. From this point we could see our steps made on the first attempt leading up to the edge of the final dome, and from this point we also secured the photograph of the summit that appears in this book.

But our progress up the main ridge had been a race with a black cloud bank that was rolling up from the Susitna Valley, and as we started towards our final climb the clouds wrapped us in dense wind-driven sheets of snow.

We stood the exposure for an hour; now chopping a few steps aimlessly upwards, now stamping backward and forward on a little ledge we found, and when we had fought the blizzard to the limit of our endurance we turned and without a word stumbled downward to our ridge. I remember only a feeling of weakness and dumb despair; we had burned up and lived off our own tissue until we didn't care much what happened! In a crevice on the highest rock of the main ridge we left our minimum thermometer; it, a few cans of frozen pemmican, and our faithful old shovel, are the only traces of our struggle on the Big Mountain.

* * *

Although on account of climatic conditions I am unable to call this book, *The First Ascent of Mount McKinley,* we are equally proud of our conquest of the great peak, for from the point where our ice steps stopped, the climbing ceased; from there onward it was a short walk to the goal we gave so much to reach. If Mount McKinley is ever climbed to the final dome the men who climb it will follow the very trail we pioneered, until, weather permitting, they walk the short distance upward along the gently sloping ridge to the little snow knoll that forms the highest point on the continent. Were it not for this fact we would not have rested from the task we tried so long to accomplish.

WILLIAM BEEBE

April Twenty-sixth, Nineteen Hundred and Twenty-three

WHENEVER, as a boy, I read a book of exploration and adventure, I often wished that the author would, for a chapter, neglect the startling, ignore the high lights, the crisis of some mighty effort, or the thrilling dangers which either pass me by or are too soon forgotten to transcribe. I wanted the tale of an ordinary day, the happenings on the twenty-sixth of a month, which might well be confused with those of the twenty-fifth or the twenty-seventh. Hence this chapter.

At a quarter before six, when the first light of the mechanically regular tropical dawn came through the port holes, I awoke and sat up. This was my fiftieth morning in Cabin Number Seven of the *Noma,* and it had become home to me. For a few minutes I looked around and mentally compared this with other rooms and berths I had occupied; the carved cubby-hole in a Chinese junk, where I could never quite straighten out, with its ever changing wall pattern of blattids and heteropters which carried no scientific appeal; and again another memory, of a torture-shaped room where, I never quite understood how, four of us humans slept, shaved and in great storms clung, without knowing a word of one another's language, without an unpleasant thought or an infringement upon each person's individuality. I still remember with pleasure our method, on particularly vile weathered mornings, of passing the time. I would point and say "coat," and then, acting out the word, add "swinging coat." And three voices with three inconceivably different and comic accents would repeat the composite sound "swin-ging coa-at." Then I had to say the phrase, or whatever they thought I had meant, in three terrible tongues. Reoriented with the brief review of these and other memories, I looked around, and realized what a luxurious home was mine. I saw now with new eyes my little white cane headboard, mirror, bureau, closet, chest of drawers, couch and curtains of bright cretonne, soft carpet, six electric lights and fan, perfectly appointed bathroom. We were in an almost waterless country, and our stay depended on our supply, so as usual I used White Rock for tooth-brushing and shaving, a tumbler each, and bathed in clear salt water, which, now and then, the most delicate of tiny jelly-fish shared with me. I donned my regular tropical costume of tennis hat, woolen shirt, khaki shorts and sneakers. On the first deck the sailors were making that jolly noise of washing down, the shifting siss and rush of the hose mingling with the piston-like scrape and rub of brooms and holystones. I went up to the sun parlor which had now become our laboratory, with its ever familiar sight of myriads of vials, aquariums, stains, microscopes, books, and jars of fish, flesh, fowl and invertebrates.

A glance from the deck showed the wonderful panorama—southward the ascending green slopes of Indefatigable, with the highest crater, mysterious and quite unclimbed by man, wholly free from clouds; a few miles to the west Eden, our first love in the Galápagos and close at hand Daphne Islets, looking like the open mouth of a submerged bottle and its stopper. To port, stretched the long, low island of South Seymour, its white beaches sending an invitation which I would soon accept. The water was like a mirror, a flexible one which bowed now and then almost imperceptibly as a low silent roll slipped gently beneath the keel and on toward shore. As I settled to work, Wireless looked in, handed me the daily typewritten newssheet and asked if I had seen the last nine-foot shark which had been hooked late in the night.

I glanced at the sheet and read almost without interest that Berlin had denied something, Milwaukee boasted of I have forgotten what, the Giants were certain this year of . . . forty persons killed in a train wreck; bootleggers had a new scheme; and Saskatchewan—this I read twice, this held my attention:

"Saskatoon Saskatchewan . . . Carl Lynn world war veteran and one of the best known trappers and mushers in the North Country is believed to have lost his life in a death battle with a pack of timber wolves. Believed his body devoured by wolves after he had killed six."

So the world elsewhere was not all anæmic and inconsequential! Somewhere else in the world things were happening as in the days before Ruhr, prohibition, and Bolsheviks were coined. I ceased to resent the fake fire-place in the dining-saloon, with its transparent glass coal, and the wireless was not an anachronism in the Galápagos when it could bring a message such as the one from Saskatchewan.

With vial and forceps I went down over the side to investigate the shark. It was quite unhurt, and when we drew it up to the surface it almost demolished a small boat and myself. I went over its body and the great gills carefully for strange parasites. Weird beings live here, some of which take hold so firmly that they burrow down into the dermis, others skim swiftly over the rough shagreen surface, evading all efforts at capture. Some are recognizable as shrimp-like beings, others have lost almost all their organs except mouth, stomach and ovaries.

What a boon to the human race would be the tooth arrangement of a shark. Within the mouth is a deep groove with many rows of teeth lying flat, like shingles, upon one another. As the teeth in use on the edge of the jaw become worn or lost, others promptly rise up behind and take their place, and throughout the lifetime of the shark this supply never diminishes.

Soon after breakfast I went ashore. Long since I had learned to adapt myself to these islands in the matter of clothes,—in light tennis cap, bathing suit and thick soled canvas sneakers I could make my way slowly inland, along shore or into the water at will, without all the discomforts of seed-filled or soaked clothing. For a long time I sat on a new beach—a small personal beach of Seymour, where perhaps no one had ever sat before me. Here I fixed in my mind the surroundings of this islet so far out in the Pacific. Two miles away the yacht rode gracefully, almost eclipsing Eden, our first explored islet. The water before me was deep turquoise, darker blue along the horizon, paling imperceptibly into the clear emerald at my feet. The light fawn of the sand began at the alabaster line of gentle surf and stretched smoothly up to my seat. So far all was usual,—with less color it might have been a Long Island shore in mid-summer. But there are no shell-holes on Long Island beaches and I was sitting on the rim of one of the dozens scattered along in both directions. Not only in appearance, but in actual play on words these were veritable shell-holes, for each was the nest of a great sea-turtle, and at the bottom a litter of egg-shells from which the turtlelets had made their escape. Here was the transition to a tropical island.

And the windrows of shells flung along high storm mark were as beautiful and varied as in story-book islands. There were delicately lettered and shaded cowries, cassias voluted and stained with enamelled pigments; arca and wing-like valves of shell tissue, and fluted and cross-fluted super-clams. Limpets with scarlet circled keyholes became more brilliant as they decreased in size.

Over and against all this, jet black heads of lava rock were now revealed, now covered by the restless waves.

The first vegetation was timid growths, which dared much in sprouting close to high tide, clinging with fearful rootlets to the surface of the sand; here the myriad grey-green rosettes of *Caldenia*, whose tiny leaves were rich wine colour beneath, all frosted with a heavy coat of hairs. Beyond were equally prostrate *Amaranthus* and *Euphorbias*. Almost the first plant to raise its stems and tiny white flowers above the sand was a graceful *Heliotrope*, while farther behind me waved a small, orange-flowered *Lantana*, cousin to one of the world's tramps, which I have seen on the opposite side of the globe, on sandy shores of Ceylon, in the mud of the Straits Settlements, in my Jersey lowlands and along the country roads of England.

I stopped at this moment of writing, for a few inches beyond my paper I saw a three-foot snake creeping down the beach between my feet. Slowly I prepared and braced myself, and before he could escape I had him. He was probably as tame as the rest of the reptilian life, but he was too rare to take any chances with. He was dark brown above with two pale brown bands down each side, and beneath, the scales were a delicate pink; a harmless Galápagan native, feeding, as I found later, chiefly on grasshoppers.

I had scarcely packed up the snake when, with sudden darts, a beautiful male Tropidurus lizard approached, nodding violently with head and elbows when he caught sight of me. But my motionlessness resolved me in his eyes into a harmless bit of scenery, and he came and snatched a tiny ant from my shoe. Then a very young mocker flew over from the nearest bush, and the lizard flicked from view. This new youngster alighted on the sand, and another rustled the dry leaves behind me. One of them called, *peeent!* and I answered, when instantly I was struck full in the face by the young bird, who, on unsteady wing, had tried to alight on my hat but fluttered too low. For a moment he lay, spread-eagled, in my lap, both of us too surprised to move. Then he dived away and was called and fed by a parent.

Pelicans flew over and once from the sky a booby arrowed into the water, sending up a fountain of spray like a depth bomb. The pelicans made a great fuss over any fish captured, tossing it up and getting it just right for swallowing, but the booby rose from the water with closed beak, and at once beat steadily off as if the dip had been merely for a bath. This past-master angler was able to strike, capture, and swallow almost simultaneously.

The scarcity of sea birds in this great bay was a cause of constant surprise. In front of me, only four miles away, was Daphne Major, where as I knew were hundreds of nesting boobies, besides numerous tropicbirds, terns and shearwaters, yet it was a rare thing to the east or southward to see more than two or three boobies a day. Every tenant of Daphne, as I have said, must find its food far to the northward, out in the open water, and, at least at this breeding season, commute to and fro with almost no wanderings.

A slight shift of wind brought an odour to my nostrils,—an ancient fishy smell which would probably send most people down wind away from the source. But to a scientist such a hint is laden with hope of new things, and while it is true that a rose by any other name, etc., the converse is not at all equally true. To announce that chemical action, induced by the passing of time and by appropriate environment, is causing a certain accumulation of shell-contained matter to give off the gas H_2S, is to do away with much of the opprobrium attached to the bald statement, "The egg is rotten!"

The odour which was wafted my way made me sanguine of solving the mystery surrounding the deaths of the goats, and then there were always the byproducts of burying beetles and strange diptera. I shook off the sand and started down beach, when an object like a mottled stick caught my eye, projecting from a hole of a ghost crab, a few feet above the present tide level. I found it was a very beautifully marked moray-like eel, quite unhurt but lying motionless on the sand. When touched it came to life with a vengeance, and true to the reputation of its clan, made no effort to escape, but tried its best to reach and bite me. It was just two feet in length, rather stout, with a head like an arrow and a very short tail. The colour was pale buff with several alternating series of large mummy-brown spots, becoming smaller and paler on the head. The eyes were remarkable, being upturned in their sockets, so the very small slit-like pupils had vertical vision, while on the outer, lower part of the eyeball were several small, scarlet, hieroglyphic-like markings. Judging by the position and direction of the eyes and the character of the pupils, I should say the eel was nocturnal and a haunter of holes, or at least lived on the bottom, flounder-like, half hidden in the sand.

After a brief but active fight I got it into a collecting bag. Long afterward, when I learned its name, I realized that a scientific term could be apt—*Scytalichthys miurus*—the short-tailed viper fish. Nothing is known about its life or habits, for only two other specimens have ever been secured, both from Cape San Lucas at the extremity of Lower California, eighteen hundred miles northwest of my beach.

Having bagged my game, I again sniffed and started up wind. But as is so often the case, the side issue proved more important than the main object, for the scent led only to a pelican, hesitating between decay and desiccation. My by-product hopes were fulfilled, for as I turned it over, I saw a number of scurrying beetles. I collected about a dozen red-shouldered *Dermestes* closely related to our bacon or carpet beetles of the north, only here, lacking these human articles of diet, they have to turn to feathers and dried tendons. Darwin collected the same species on James Island. A tiny iridescent blue *Necrobia* or bone beetle was also captured.

Under a neighbouring stone I caught a pair of minute rove beetles, the male of which had a large horn on the thorax. It proved to be a new species. Also near by I found a group of half a dozen white toadstools, the only ones I saw in the whole archipelago.

The most abundant insects under stones were *Lepismids*, very appropriately in this land of ancient reptiles, for these are among the most primitive of insects, wingless because their race has never had wings, and we find them living today almost unchanged, going back as fossils in Baltic amber to the Lower Oligocene, a matter of about thirty-five million years. There were giant *Lepismids* on Seymour, one individual of which measured over three inches (78 mm.) from cerci to antennæ tips, but most of them were 50 to 60 mm. in total length. The body of the very large female was 26 mm. long. It was almost impossible to capture these entire, as they were injured at the slightest touch. This large species *Acrotelsa galapagœnsis*, was greyish black with a silvery sheen on the body scales, and with numerous tufts of short bristles.

I was attracted inland by a number of gulls and smaller birds which seemed to be feeding on a cloud of gnats. The latter proved to be grasshoppers, and the former lava gulls, purple martins and flycatchers. The giant grasshoppers had been in evidence since the first day I put foot on the Galápagos, but I had never seen so many as were gathered here on South Seymour. Hundreds flew up from the ground and grass as I walked along. They were feeding on the aromatic Bursera leaves, and many of these trees were completely denuded. On some branches there were many more insects than leaves and even the stems were lined. When I shook a limb, fifty or more would fly off into the air, and as many at once fly up to take their place. Hosts were continually flying high up into the air, and hovering like kestrels or fish hawks. Lava gulls were snatching the big females, while the lesser birds were taking the smallest males.

Except the dragonflies, and the feral so-called domestic animals such as pigs, donkeys, dogs and cattle, these grasshoppers were the wildest creatures living on the Galápagos. In early April at Harrison Cove they were courting, and every great female was the centre of three to five admiring males. I could not get near enough to observe much of the details of entreaty or selection, except that the males walked slowly back and forth in front of the females, on four legs, holding the third pair elevated to the fullest extent. The unusually brilliant colouring of this pair of legs may thus be of some secondary sexual significance. In this land so barren of insect voices, the clicking of the wings of these grasshoppers in flight was very noticeable.

These insects were as gay as butterflies, being intricately marked with yellow, scarlet and blue, the hind legs, as I have said, being especially brilliant, the upper leg banded red and black and the lower portions clear yellow. Only in the brightest coloured ones was the blue wholly dominant over the black, and equal in strength to the other primary colours. The females were often twice as large as the males, and at night, sometimes *against* a light breeze, the largest of the former sex would fly two miles out to the *Noma,* along the light beam from the searchlight, showing no signs of fatigue when they arrived. Although the males are full-winged I never knew one to come on board, even when we were anchored close to shore.

It was interesting to see the dominance of such strong fliers as these, for nearly eighty per cent of the orthopterous tenants of these islands are wingless or at least flightless. I did not find a single omnivorous or carnivorous reptile, bird or mammal which did not at one place or another have the remains of giant grasshoppers among its food. Even the mice fed on them and terns and gulls took them readily. Indeed, several times when an insect misjudged its direction and fell into the water, it was snapped up by some fish before it had a chance to struggle, and the tale of enemies seemed complete when one afternoon I saw two scarlet crabs pulling one apart between them.

Large dragonflies were hawking about, taking toll of the mosquitoes which I frightened out of the grass. I found it almost impossible to capture them in a net. They were far more difficult to approach than morpho butterflies in the jungle. So I resorted to an old method, and using a 22 calibre rifle, and shot cartridges, I shot at them at the outside range of effectiveness. My first attempt was amusing,—I only wounded my game, and after a somersault it regained its balance, and very much bent, flew very slowly to a high branch and there clung. The tip of the abdomen and one or two legs were injured. I had the same feeling that I have at the sight of a wounded animal, that I must put it out of its misery as soon as possible, so getting directly beneath I fired straight, and reduced it to a bedraggled pair of wings. My next half dozen shots were better, and I secured as many specimens almost uninjured, with perhaps a single wing broken, or some similarly unimportant injury. Going gunning for devil's darning needles seemed quite in place in this weird country, where seagulls fed on grasshoppers, and grasshoppers went to sea.

As if to emphasize this bizarre quality in the fauna, my next glance showed a full-sized, spotted-breasted, young mockingbird, perched with fluttering wings, actually being fed by a slender-billed, black, female cactus finch. Twice as I watched, this unnatural parent made trips and brought food to the young bird who was larger than the finch. After the second trip another cactus finch appeared, sang several times over *chur-wee! chur-wee! chur-wee!* and both flew away, leaving the young mocker to his fate.

I now made my way to the high veldt land where I had already studied and captured Conolophus. The single species of Galápagos hawk was abundant here, and at one time I saw twelve at once. They were rather sociable and four or five sometimes perched close together on a boulder or low tree. By walking very slowly I could come within two feet, and even when I had flushed them several times, they exhibited no signs of increased timidity. The martins did not quite approve of them, and occasionally swooped twittering at them when in flight. There was at least a single basis for this suspicion, for one hawk as I found by dissection had killed and eaten one of these birds. Although grasshoppers were flying about in all directions, the hawks seldom took one. Of four stomachs which I examined, only one had any remains of these insects. All had been feeding to repletion on giant red and black centipedes. I saw these striking creatures only rarely, and then it was the briefest glimpse as they disappeared into a pile of lava. Yet the hawks here and at least on two other islands, fed chiefly on a diet of centipedes, from six inches to a foot in length.

The martins to the number of about a dozen were hawking about, and occasionally swooping low down over the prostrate yellow-flowered *Tribulus*. I could not discern what attracted them, until later when I examined several and found that they had been feeding upon moths, one bird having eaten twelve, and another, twenty-one of these fuzzy-winged insects, among which were a number of day-flying sphinx moths.

The hawks did little or no hunting in the heat of the day, and often sat on the same perch, either in or out of the sun, for hours, preening their plumage, or nibbling parrot-like at the bark or leaves. They showed considerable curiosity, and as we photographed or chased the big lizards, they followed us about, perching in nearby trees. As a rule the hawks appeared to keep in trios, and occasionally the immaturity of the third bird was apparent. Now and then they called, the usual staccato or rolling scream, but not nearly as loud or prolonged as the note of our northern birds. On these low, open islands, where distances are so short they can see too easily for loud tones to be necessary. Two distinct phases of these hawks were common, dependent neither on sex nor age; one was dark blackish brown all over, the other was pale buff, below variegated with numerous large round spots.

The few sooty, ground finches present all flew up for a quick look at me, and then out of sight. They had almost no curiosity, and made their way about with a curious, slow, fluttering flight, the body held very steady and the wings beating with somewhat of an effort. Their notes were as simple as their garb, the usual song being *cu-wee! cu-wee! cu-wee!* Doves, small and short-tailed, flew past occasionally, less strongly and more slowly than doves in general, but with the same direct flight, and higher than any other land bird, twenty to fifty feet up.

A half hour after I reached the veldt I had a strange experience with a hawk. Desiring a specimen but not wishing to injure the skin, I backed away and at a considerable distance fired at it with fine shot in the third barrel of my gun. The bird turned a complete somersault, landed on the ground on its feet, lowered its head and ran full speed toward me and brought up exactly between my legs. I picked it up without resistance, placed it in a large basket and took it off to the yacht, where it readily took fish, preened itself and made no attempt to escape. Today, seven months later, it is living in good health at the New York Zoological Park.

I returned by way of the basaltic cliffs and found goats and small kids asleep here and there in the higher caves. On a flat rock I passed a big mother sea-lion nursing a thirty-pound youngster. She looked at me curiously, but made no movement until I rolled her off into the water, when she swam high out to see what next astonishing thing I would do. I took her pup and threw him as high into the air as I could. He fell into the water with a squawk and a splash and almost with a single movement of his tail shot himself out again upon the rock, looking at me and croaking, as if to say, "Please do it again." No tameness of horse or dog has ever impressed me with anything like the thrill which these wild creatures gave, in accepting the first human being they had ever seen as something which it was inconceivable could hurt them. I left the pup with his head bent over until it touched his back in an effort to watch me out of sight.

Returning to the *Noma* we trolled and caught two big, brown mottled groupers, and two of the very beautiful, gold-spotted Pacific mackeral *Scomberomorus sierra,* twenty inches long and fighters throughout their whole being.

Soon after lunch I went to the mainland of Indefatigable and made an impromptu attack on the interior. I had intended only describing a large half circle from one point of land to the next, but the going was so fair for the first half mile, that I took my bearings, lined up the first high craterlet with the great central peak and set out doggedly to cover ground. I have already described the gentle art of walking on Indefatigable on pages 67 and 79, so I need not repeat the details. As soon as the small basins of red earth appeared, the soft, waving grasses also materialized, and I began to gather the spiny seeds of *Cenchrus*. Gray, in his botany, describes a related species in our Southern States, under the name of hedgehog or bur-grass, and his final commentary is "a vile weed." I called it this also, among other epithets, which increased in power and sincerity as I encountered larger and larger fields. Simultaneously, the level ground began to be broken up into cross gullies and steep faults and canyons, necessitating wide detours, and, in place of the rather solid lava flows of the coast, there appeared acres of eternally balanced and eternally sliding slabs.

After the first two miles I seemed to get in the lee of the central ridge and every breath of air ceased. The clinker radiated heat until it seemed as if it had not yet cooled from the last eruption. Now and then I dipped down into a hollow floored with stagnant water, choked with green slime, and giving forth an aroma which seemed to thicken the still, superheated air into a denser medium—an invisible heavy fog of stench. At first I noticed occasional finches and doves and even caught any unusual insect, but soon my mind drew away from all casual objects, and my eyes, too tired to shift about, watched only my next perilous step, and now and then lifted to reorient my direction—headed ever for the mass of purple raincloud which had eclipsed the mountains. This was a better guide, quite as certain in direction and much higher. For mile after mile I rose hardly at all, only rarely from a red-hot knoll did I catch a glimpse of the bay behind me and the ever lessening *Noma*. Its decrease in size was the only warrant that I was making progress. The raincloud seemed as far as ever, and I had long since lost sight of my craterlet guide.

Several times I almost broke my ankle on slipping masses of lava, some of which must have weighed two or three hundred pounds, and which, once overbalanced, rolled and clanged down to the lowest levels. I think that if we had planned to return straight to Panama on the morrow, I would have kept on, for I could then have recuperated at will, but with the thought of three days on the wonder island of Tower I did not dare cripple myself too much, and after what I conservatively estimated at five miles, I gave up and rested. I climbed a thorny tree on the highest hill at hand, and saw at least two more miles of almost level going between me and the rather abrupt first rise of land.

I rested, squatting on my heels, for the lava was too hot to sit on for a moment. My tongue seemed three times its usual size, and I watched the blood slowly drip from the big gouges in my legs resulting from frequent falls.

Hardly a living thing was in sight. Two little moths fluttered about a flowerless, grey-green amaranthus, several ants appeared and waved their antennæ inquiringly in the direction of my gory limbs, and a great centipede crawled out of one crevice and into another. No movement of wind, no rustle of leaf, no voice of insect or bird troubled the vibrating waves of heat, or the sound of my pulse throbbing in my ears. Then just before I shifted, stretched and started back, a sulphur butterfly—most appropriately coloured for this particular bit of hell—drifted near, brushed against my face, rested its tattered wings on my knee for an instant, and fluttered on, headed where I could not follow—inland.

Half-way back my fatigue was momentarily forgotten when I caught a glimpse of some animal moving slowly along on the opposite side of a screen of weeds and cactus. In another moment I saw two dogs emerge—police dogs in appearance, one larger, brown with some white markings, and the second half-grown. The first one snarled silently at me, turned at once, and both galloped off over the broken ground.

About a mile from the coast I left my back-trail and struck direct, and soon skirted a good-sized salt lagoon on which I saw five Galápagos pintailed teal, three adults, a full-sized but flightless young bird and a solitary downy duckling which followed me for some distance, keeping a few feet from the land, as I stumbled along over the rough boulders.

When at last I reached the shore I was going very slowly, and as often as not with the aid of my hands to relieve my feet which were in rather bad shape. I lay down in the low surf, promptly had a severe cramp in my leg and foot, and went aboard the yacht. By dinner time I was all right again, but no trip on any other island, James, Albemarle or Tower, nor any all-day hunt I have ever made in the high Himalayas, has equalled this for sheer uncertain frightfulness of one step after another.

After dinner we made a quick trip to the mainland again. With some bird lime, John Tee-Van almost at once caught a mockingbird which is still thriving in the Zoological Park. In three hauls of the seine we took many fish, once a pure culture of half-beaks, almost two hundred, varying from one and a half to seven inches in length. The last time we examined the net a beautiful little eel-like blenny was found entangled, which proved to be a new species, *Runula albolinea*.

A little before six o'clock the mosquitoes rose in a grey mist out of the grass, and whenever we stood still for a moment we were the centre of a hazy aura, an almost ectoplasm, from which a thousand little needles pricked us. The insects were small, and carried very little poison with their bites, and of course in this humanless land, there was no danger of malaria.

On other evenings as long as there was light enough for us to see, we never failed to observe a host of dragonflies hawking back and forth, while now and then little yellow-bellied flycatchers would dive into the mass, their beaks snapping like castanets. This last night, eight mockingbirds made the most of this manna, so limited both temporarily and spatially. When at last we pushed off and leaped into the big lifeboat, we thrashed about with branches, nets and coats, endeavouring to clear the cock-pit and not infest the *Noma*.

Climbing to the topmost lookout deck, I saw that the sun had just dipped behind the distant rugged peaks of James. This, our last Indefatigable sunset, was a skyful of purest gold, enamelling with equal glory the scarcely rippled water, while the air was like cool velvet on my face. With my whole heart I hated to leave these no-man's wonderlands.

I turned toward Indefatigable and watched the great central peaks, having shed their purple coat of rain, slip for a brief time into their evening wrap of gorgeousness. Then as the grey-black garb of night began to be drawn about their dread, mysterious shoulders, I shuddered. Looking back now I can appreciate so well the farewell words of my shipwrecked taxi-driver,—"We didn't mind the days so much, we was busy and there was turtles to get and things to see, but the nights got us. Then we wondered could we drink blood in place of water for another day and week—and month—and suppose we got sick like Fred Jeff, and suppose a ship didn't ever come...."

For a few minutes the great searchlight played and flickered along the shore over two miles away, cutting a mighty swathe through the dusk. Even this brief minute of illumination was enough to attract a number of tiny moths who, soon after they settled on our canvas, steamed away with us from their natal island. Overside, the tide rushed along with the cool current, and with it was borne a world of delicate beings, some glowing with phosphorescence, others dark and invisible, while others were clearly outlined because they had swallowed uncounted hosts of the still glowing ones. A fish —a shark—a dolphin—struck ten million sparks out of the watery life as they rushed along.

The afterglow shot up in perfect imitation of the glowing flame and light of an active volcano, perhaps prophetic of the end of these peaks as it was of their beginning—peaks so lonely in mid-ocean, with their strange beings of scales and feathers, all now asleep somewhere out in the darkness. Somewhere the sulphur butterfly, the one which brushed against me far inland half-way to those dread peaks, was clinging upside down to a thorn, a Galápagos butterfly—like the volcanoes—asleep.

I went down into the glare of laboratory lights, and did many and various things, mostly ineffectively, with microscope and vials and forceps, paper and ink and words. Hours afterward, a sudden thrill ran through the ship; for the first time in many wonderful days, the *Noma* had awakened and throbbed with life. On the same lofty deck, at midnight, I watched alone. The anchor came up, the yacht slowly circled and gathered speed on her straight course toward Tower Island far to the northward; the nineteen hundred and twenty-third twenty-sixth-of-April had passed.

Daphne Major slipped by, the very ghost of an islet, a mere blotter-out of stars beyond, and not a sound came from all the birds fast asleep,—on the highest rim of the volcano, as well as upon the deep, hidden, unforgettable floor of the dead crater.

So had Orizaba once faded from view, and so the jungle of Borneo and the lights of Rangoon; so had been erased the last silhouette of Kinchinjunga and of Fuji. Tonight, with the passing of Indefatigable, there came the faint aromatic scent of Bursera leaves; but whether this, or the perfumed breeze which blows from the camphor groves of Kagoshima, or exciting odours drifting over Hoogly's waters from the Calcutta bazaars, or the scent of white jasmine in a Virginia garden, such memories are eternal, they are the saddest things in the world, and they pass all understanding.

ROY CHAPMAN ANDREWS

Finding the Baluchitherium

THE morning after our arrival at Tsagan Nor (the White Lake), Shackelford and I drove over to the Mongol village at the western end of the lake to call upon our neighbors. We found three groups of *yurts* facing a meadow. We were entertained in the *yurt* of the headman of the village, who gave us tea, cheese and *kumiss,* or fermented mare's milk, the simplest of home-brews, with a kick contributed by every mare. The headman's daughter, a charming little girl of seventeen, came up to me, shyly holding out her hand. The middle finger was green-black and terribly swollen—evidently from gangrene. That night she rode with her father to our camp, and I poulticed the finger. When the bandage was removed the following day, half the finger came off, to the terror of the poor little girl. But there was no inflammation in the rest of the hand, and in less than a fortnight the stump of the finger was completely healed.

Since I had cured the headman's daughter, he was ready to do anything we wished. I particularly asked him to keep his dogs tied up; for Shackelford wished to do a good deal of photographing in the vicinity of the *yurts*.

Because of a peculiar custom of the Mongols, the dogs are a great menace to human life. A corpse is the abode of evil spirits and therefore a most undesirable thing to have about the house; thus their chief desire is to dispose of the dead as quickly as possible.

Sometimes the body is placed upon a cart and driven rapidly across rough ground, so that it will fall off. The driver, fearful of attracting to himself the evil spirits that possess it, hurries on without looking back. Meanwhile dogs, birds and wolves make short work of the corpse. Only the bones, which every native will shun, are left. At the base of the hill upon which the lama city is built in Urga, there are hundreds of human skulls and bones, gruesome reminders to the living priests of what their own fate will be. Great black dogs slink about this "burial-ground" and fight over the bodies that are dragged out from the city. They live almost entirely upon human flesh and are terribly savage. It is certain death for a man to pass near this spot at night unless he is armed. Even in the daytime the dogs will attack a passer-by upon the slightest provocation, and if one of their own number is wounded, they seize and devour him. Berkey was attacked by three dogs at a *yurt* near Sain Noin Khan's and by shooting two of them with his revolver, just saved himself from being pulled down. My wife and I had a very narrow escape from death at Tuerin when we were lying in fur sleeping-bags near the motor-cars; the dogs thought we were dead Mongols and a pack of fourteen had gathered for a feast upon our unsuspecting bodies.

The Mongols object greatly to having anybody die within a *yurt,* and, when one member of a family is seriously ill, the others frequently decamp before the end comes. They run no risks of an encounter with a malign spirit. Once, when hunting on the plains, I found the skeleton of a woman lying beside the dead ashes of a fire, with a wooden bowl half filled with food. Twenty feet away was the circular mark where a *yurt* had stood. My Mongol guide explained that the woman was sick and had been left to die alone.

The routine of life in the *yurt* village near our camp might almost have been designed to please the eye of a photographer. Shackelford, companioned by his camera, was on hand at sunrise, when the men and boys drove camels and horses out to graze and the girls guided cattle, goats and sheep, and in midafternoon, when the herders brought their charges in to be milked. He saw the milk that was to yield a new supply of cheese and *kumiss* strained through perforated vessels half filled with matted hair and then poured into the goatskins that hung on the *yurt* walls. He watched the women making string or rope from camel's wool or repairing their summer garments of Chinese cotton. He recorded in motion-pictures the setting up of a *yurt* and the process of making felt.

One day when I was with him, we found several families engaged in the latter task. On the plain above the valley, where the ground was hard and flat, a strip of felt was spread. Upon it two old women put a thick layer of sheep's wool. This was thoroughly soaked with water and covered with a second felt layer. The "wool sandwich" was rolled up on a long pole, wrapped in a thin cloth and tightly bound, and ropes were fastened to the projecting ends of the pole. Then a Mongol mounted on a camel dragged the cylinder behind him over a smooth path for more than an hour. This rolling pressed the loose wool firmly together into a strip of felt, and all that remained was to dry it in the sun and bind the edges.

Shackelford and I were as pleased as children to show off our new headquarters at the White Lake to Bayard Colgate. He had reached the "Wild Ass Camp" on the evening of July 11, with mail for all the men except poor "Shack," whose letters were somewhere in the Gobi with others for the rest of us. Colgate made the run to Urga in two days and spent the same time on the return trip—altogether nearly eight hundred miles. He was away just nine days, an exceedingly creditable performance.

The Tsagan Nor region offered a fruitful field for my studies as a zoölogist. The lake and its shore swarmed with wild creatures. We found the beautiful bar-headed geese, so well known in India, breeding there in numbers. We also noticed swan-geese now and then, although they usually keep to the rivers, and in August, while sitting in my tent, I saw seven geese which were new to me. By wading into the water, with my gun held above my head, slowly I got within shooting distance and killed two. They proved to be greylags, geese which are common in Europe but extremely rare in northern China. Sheldrakes of two species, grebes and a multitude of shore-birds, waders, gulls and terns were always running about the beach in front of our camp. One night the taxidermists caught a shrew in their tent. This tiny insectivore is an inhabitant of damp, soft ground. Had I seen a wild elephant on the plains, I should hardly have been more surprised than to find this diminutive animal in the desert. Another curious insectivore was the hedgehog. Almost every evening Buckshot, one of our Chinese assistants, spent the first hours after dark along the lake-shore, hunting hedgehogs with a flash-light.

Shackelford adopted one of the little spiny fellows, and he became our most amusing pet. He was named "Johnny Tsagan Nor." He is now in the New York Zoölogical Park; for, on leaving China, Shackelford refused to be separated from him. The hedgehog, although not more than eight inches long, was a most voracious eater and did not limit himself to insects. A short time after our return to Peking, Clifford Pope brought a baby alligator about fifteen inches in length from the Yangtze River. The alligator and Johnny Tsagan Nor were left together overnight in a large packing-box in the laboratory. The next morning the reptile was dead and partly eaten. Johnny had been hungry.

Two genera of beautiful kangaroo-rats lived in the plains behind the tents. If a car came in at night, we could see them in the path of the headlights.

I often tried to catch one, but it could jump six or eight feet and always got over the ground faster than I could run. There were foxes in the long grass beside the water, antelopes and wild asses swarmed upon the plains behind camp and bighorn sheep and ibex roamed over Baga Bogdo.

In the land-locked lake itself there were fish, we knew from the good-sized swirls on the surface, but our hooks and lines yielded no results. By means of a twelve-foot net, however, we got numbers of minnows and small fish six or eight inches long. Several hundred specimens of these were preserved in formalin.

Tsagan Nor, which is fed by springs, is now three miles long by two miles wide, but evaporation is so rapid that the lake is becoming smaller. In 1925 it dried up entirely. Berkey and Morris counted seven ancient beach-marks, the highest of them twenty-eight feet above the present water-level. A depression that was evidently the old lake-floor extends for a long distance to the west. Colgate and I followed it for thirteen miles, and later we found that it reaches Orok Nor. Doubtless this was once a continuous body of water. On the south side of the basin, at the foot of the mountains, is a long, narrow belt of live sand-dunes. Very often in the afternoons we watched wind-storms sweeping over them and could see the sand streaming off the tops of the dunes like spray from gigantic waves.

Granger, Berkey and Morris never allowed themselves a moment's play, but I insisted that they all come to Tsagan Nor on July 18 to a field-meet that the Mongols were to hold under the direction of our friend, the head-man, whose daughter's hand I had treated. Two weeks before, he had sent out riders to invite the people from the various *yurts* within a radius of fifty miles. The programme included pony-races, wrestling, camel-races, roping and riding of wild horses and, best of all, a big feast of boiled mutton.

Because of their love of athletics and of life in the open, the Mongols seem to me less difficult than the Chinese for a Westerner to understand. Anybody with a sense of humor can get on well with the Mongols; for they too have that good quality along with their sportsmanlike point of view. They are fond of a practical joke and can appreciate it even when the laugh is on themselves. One day a Mongol rode up to my camp, carrying a big wooden pitcher of milk. Something frightened his pony, which began to buck like a western bronco. At every jump the milk splashed out, until finally it had drenched the Mongol from head to foot. It would have been a terrible loss of "face" to drop the pitcher, but when finally the pony was quieted and not a drop of milk remained, the Mongol himself laughed as hard as the rest of us. Many amusing stories are told of the Living Buddha's love of fun. It is related that, when he bought the first motor-car that came to Urga, his chief delight was to connect a wire with the batteries and stretch it across the courtyard, into which he could look from a window of the palace. There he would sit and roar with laughter when his visitors and ministers of state received a shock.

The geologists and Granger arrived a little after nine o'clock in the morning, and with the cameras set up in one of the Fulton trucks we went over to the village. A crowd of men and boys, dressed in red, yellow and plum-color, had gathered on the plain, so that it was a gorgeous assemblage. Fifty ponies had already gone five miles to the east, and, when we left camp, a Mongol rode off at full speed to start the race. I wanted them to run only two miles, but the Mongols would not consent to that. Their usual distance is from seven to fifteen miles, but we finally compromised on five miles. It is merely a question of a pony's endurance, because the Mongols have very little real understanding of horsemanship, although they are excellent riders and will start off at full speed even at the beginning of a race. At last we saw a cloud of dust in the distance and could distinguish the ponies, coming toward us in an irregular line. The riders were all boys, ten or twelve years old. A beautiful bay, ridden by a lama, came in an easy winner, and the little lama was the proudest child in all Mongolia. After the race the Mongols rode in a circle about a group of priests, chanting a barbaric song. The moving ponies and the brilliant colors made it seem like a "Wild West" show or an enormous circus.

The race of the camels interested us greatly for it was amazing to see how quickly the ungainly brutes got away on the start and what speed they could develop. At the finish a man on a fast pony had all he could do to keep abreast of them. The riding of wild horses was a bit disappointing, for only one animal gave the natives a really bad time of it. The Mongol pony does not know how to buck or "sunfish" as do our bronchos and contents himself with merely plunging.

The wrestling, in which some thirty men competed, was good sport. One burly fellow, who massaged himself thoroughly with saliva just before the match, won two falls with ease but was eliminated on the third, with great hurt to his pride. The winner received a frightful cut over the eye in his last bout but finally threw his man, although completely blinded by blood.

When the meet was ended, we all repaired to the headman's *yurt* for the feast. The Mongols obediently waited until Shackelford was ready with the camera. Then two huge wooden troughs containing six sheep were brought out. Nothing had been wasted. The fat and blood had been poured into the intestines and boiled to make enormous sausages. A most uninviting mess it was. As each of the two hundred men secured a chunk of mutton, he retired to a sunny corner, crammed his mouth full, and, as he began to chew, cut off the end of the meat close to his nose. We laughed until our sides ached while Shackelford recorded the choicest bits of this comedy on his film.

Berkey and Morris, who had returned to camp with all their duffle, left us on July 28 with three camels and three ponies besides a cook and two Mongols. Their destination was the southern side of the lake to complete their map to the foot of Baga Bogdo. Thus the Expedition was pretty well divided: Granger and Shackelford at the "Wild Ass Camp"; Colgate and I at Tsagan Nor; Berkey and Morris skipping about all over the south side of the lake. When planning the work in Peking, I had foreseen the need of such separations and had arranged three units for the Expedition; each one had its own chauffeur, cook and camp equipment and could operate independently.

The day after he joined Granger, Shackelford, while prospecting a riverbed, actually stumbled over a huge bone, which proved to be the head of the ulna, one of the lower bones of the fore limb, of a *Baluchitherium*. Berkey had discovered a calcaneum, or heel-bone, of the same beast at Iren Dabasu, but none of us had connected that fact with the report made by the Mongols that in the locality of the "Wild Ass Camp" there were bones as large as a man's body. Shackelford's discovery that this story was not mere native exaggeration set us all on edge with excitement. I went with Granger to the place where the ulna had been found, but no other fragments of the skeleton could be located, although we searched the dry stream-bed and the surrounding hills.

On August 3, just as Colgate and I had finished our dinner, we heard shouts and found that Berkey and Morris had arrived. From then until midnight we listened to the story of their wanderings and discoveries. They had been astounded at the tremendous scale of everything at Baga Bogdo. One of the alluvial fans, which they had ascended, was ten miles from base to crest and two thousand feet high. Others were much larger. Berkey said that in all his previous experience he had seen none that even approached them.

The mountain itself rose about twelve thousand feet above sea-level. It would be hardly possible to find a more varied and representative section of Mongolian topography. The two men had lived with it early and late for six weeks and had mapped eight hundred square miles. Yet when they stood on one of the lower peaks and looked across the vast panorama spread out below them, they felt that they had mapped only a postage-stamp.

The evening of the geologists' return was exciting enough to keep me awake long after the lights were out, but the next was still more memorable. Late in the afternoon there was a little rain and just at sunset a glorious rainbow stretched its fairy arch from the plain across the lake to the summit of Baga Bogdo. Below it the sky was ablaze with ragged tongues of flame; in the west billowy, gold-margined clouds, shot through with red, lay thick upon the desert. Wave after wave of light flooded the mountain across the lake—lavender, green and deepest purple—colors which blazed and faded almost before they could be named. We exclaimed breathlessly at first and then grew silent with awe. We felt that we should never see the like again. Suddenly a black car, with Granger and Shackelford in it, came out of the north and slipped quietly into camp. Even Shackelford's buoyant spirit was stilled by the grandeur of what was passing in the sky. Not until the purple twilight had settled over mountain, lake and desert, did the two men tell us why they had been so late. They had discovered parts of the skeleton of a *Baluchitherium!*

During the entire Mongolian expedition the best localities for fossils and the finest specimens were discovered when we were on the point of leaving a region for other fields. So it was with our greatest find, the *Baluchitherium*. On breaking camp Granger and Shackelford decided to walk through a still uninspected pocket in the bad lands and to have Wang, their Chinese chauffeur, drive their car ahead to a promontory two miles to the south. After a little, Wang, bored with waiting for them, decided to do some prospecting on his own account. Almost immediately he discovered a huge bone in the bottom of a gully that emptied into a ravine. Full of excitement, he climbed back into the car, and, when Granger and Shackelford arrived, proudly conducted them to the spot where he had found the fossil. It was the end of the humerus, or upper fore leg-bone, of a *Baluchitherium,* and other parts were visible, partially embedded in the earth. The most important of all was one whole side of the lower jaw. The bones were very well preserved and the men removed without difficulty all that they could discover. They searched the sides of the gully until the approaching sunset warned them to be on the way to Tsagan Nor if they wished to reach camp before dark.

I went to sleep very late that night, with my mind full of *Baluchitherium,* and had a vivid dream of finding the creature's skull in a canyon about fifteen miles from the spot where the jaw had been discovered the day before. When I asked Granger the next morning if he was sure that all the bones had been located in the somewhat hurried search, he said: "Well, it is possible that under the spot where we found the jaw there may be a skull or other bones not yet exposed by weathering." Since he himself was busy packing fossils to go by the caravan, which had reached Tsagan Nor and was making ready to start ahead of us, he suggested that Shackelford and I go to the "Wild Ass Camp" with Wang and dig up the bottom of the wash.

We did not leave till after tiffin; for it was only twenty miles—an hour's run for the car. On our arrival Shackelford and Wang set to work with shovels while I inspected the side of the gully, now and then sticking my pick into a bit of discolored earth. In about three minutes I reached the summit of the tiny ridge and looked down the other side. Instantly I saw a fragment of bone peeping out of the sand in the bottom of the wash. Its color was unmistakable. With a yell I leaped down the steep slope. When Shackelford and Wang came round the corner on the run, I was on my knees, scratching like a terrier. Already a huge chunk of bone had been unearthed and a dozen other fragments were visible in the sand. They were beautifully fossilized and so hard that we had no fear of breaking them. Laughing in hysterical excitement, we made the sand fly as we took out piece after piece of bone.

Suddenly my fingers struck a huge block. Shackelford followed it down and found the other end; then he produced a tooth. My dream had come true! We had discovered the skull of a *Baluchitherium!* One end of the block was loose and easily removed; the remainder appeared to extend indefinitely back into the earth. When Shackelford loosened the first tooth, I knew that it was time to stop if the wrath of the palæontologist was not to descend on our heads. Therefore we collected all the fragments and carried them up the slope to the car. No new-born baby ever was handled with more loving care than we bestowed upon those precious bones as we packed them in coats and bags, so that they would ride safely.

At six o'clock, while the men were having tea, we burst into camp, shouting like children. Granger has made so many interesting discoveries in his palæontological career that he is not easily stirred, but our story brought him up standing. Then silently and carefully he inspected the bones in the car.

We held a council over the largest of them, which was partly embedded in rock. It was difficult to identify at first; for we were dealing with an animal virtually unknown. At last Granger decided that the bone was the front of the skull. Then we made out two great incisor teeth and the bones of the maxillæ and premaxillæ. There was no doubt that we had also the posterior part of the skull; for I had identified the great occipital condyles and the neural canal, through which runs the spinal cord. Even though we had realized that the *Baluchitherium* was a colossal beast, the size of the bones left us absolutely astounded. The largest known rhinoceros was dwarfed in comparison; for the head of this animal was five feet long and his neck must have been of pillar-like proportions.

Early in the morning Colgate, Granger, Shackelford, Wang and I set merrily forth in one of the Fulton trucks for the scene of the great find. Shackelford and Walter lay back in camp-chairs, singing at the top of their voices. I suppose that fossils never were collected under happier circumstances.

When we arrived at the bottom of the gully, Granger and I made a careful examination of the skull. We decided that it was lying on its right side and that the left arch and tooth-row were gone. Later we found these conjectures to be correct.

Granger, Wang and I sifted every inch of the sand and gravel in the bottom of the wash, salvaging bits of bone and teeth. Granger carefully worked around the skull itself. While he whisked out the sand, grain by grain, the rest of us scattered over the surrounding bad lands to see if we could locate other bones. The skeleton had evidently lain near the summit of a ridge left between two gullies and had broken up as the earth weathered away and heavy rains fell. Part of it had gone down one side of the slope; this was what Wang had found the first day. The rest had rolled into the main wash, where I discovered it. And now Shackelford picked up a half-dozen important skull fragments, out on the plain at least three hundred yards from the ravine.

It took Granger four days to remove the skull; for it had to be encased in a shell of burlap and paste for safe transit by motor, camel, railroad and steamship, to New York.

In the meantime we made several short excursions. But it was already August 9 and, although the weather was still hot, geese and ducks were flocking and sand-grouse were flying eastward in countless thousands. I did not need these signs to tell me that winter was approaching and that it was time for us to take the trail. Yet we could not leave until we had spent a day at a grey bluff across the lake where Berkey and Morris had found Pliocene fossils. Cars could not possibly cross the sand-dunes; so on August 10 we set forth on camels.

The next afternoon the other men found some fine things in the grey beds, but I had the best luck of all. While inspecting a knoll of yellow gravel, I noticed a few fossil bits at the very base. Following them up, I came to a slight discoloration in the earth and saw a half-inch of bone exposed. Since I had found the calcaneum of a mastodon a few moments earlier, I thought that this was the end of a tusk, which very likely was fastened into the skull of a proboscidean. I scraped away the earth and soon realized that the fossil was not an elephant's trunk, but the antler of a stag —as perfect as if it had been dropped the day before instead of nearly a million years ago. I had long been interested in the living Asiatic wapiti because of its relationship to the elk of western America and to the red deer of Europe, and it was probable that in this very fossil we might have the ancestor of them both.

The actual removing of the antler was too delicate an undertaking for my pick-and-shovel methods; so I walked to the end of the knoll and fired three shots with my automatic pistol to bring up Granger and Shackelford, who, I knew, were somewhere in the maze of gullies below me. Before long they appeared, hot and puffing; for among the members of the Expedition such a signal meant that every man within hearing distance should not stand upon the order of his coming, but come as fast as his legs could carry him. Though it was then six o'clock, Granger was able to paste the antler with gum arabic and rice-paper and remove it.

As the sun was setting, we started for the long ride to camp. Before we had entered the dunes, darkness had fallen and a strong wind blew from the east. We urged our camels to their best speed; for it would have been decidedly dangerous to become lost in that drifting maze when a sandstorm was in progress. But before we left the last of the fantastic waves behind us, the wind dropped as suddenly as it had risen, the thickly piled clouds on the horizon disappeared and a glorious moon lighted us home.

stony shore under my feet, and the deep bog moss and the ferns that bordered it. Darkly appeared against the starlit sky the tossing silhouette of wind-torn trees; a mountain towered over me, immense and black. Snow was on the slopes not far away. It was cold, and the wind roared through the forest tops.

My soul was stirred by the vast glamour of that unseen wilderness, with fear of the terrific forces of the darkness, with wonder at what world the night concealed, with pride at the achievement of my being there, and with utter humility at my alien identity, diminutive, obscure, unseen in that boundless solitude beneath the stars.

With a strong fair wind we sailed next morning for the head of Admiralty Sound. The day was overcast and sullen; a dark sea lashed itself to gleaming foam against the frowning headlands of the coast. Sheer mountain sides here form the northern slope; they rise in cliffs a thousand feet in height, between whose pinnacled and spired summits pour streams and glaciers from a loftier snow-clad hinterland. It is a heartless, bleak coast; it was a tragic coast under that day's dark threat of storm.

The land at the head of Admiralty Sound is split by two valleys bearing easterly, a divided continuance of that chasm of the earth which is the sound. Between them, extending into the sound, to form two bays, stands Mount Hope, the western end of a ten-mile rocky range that terminates where the two valleys dip and join again to make the bed of the great inland lake, Fognano. Mount Hope appears from the sound to stand alone, a dome of rock detached from all the mountains of the region.

The southern bay lies open to the full fury of the west wind and the sea. A little treeless island two miles from the head, and near the shore, affords the only anchorage.

Although the wind was strong, to save manœuvring we jibbed to come about behind the island. And here, through my land-lubberly awkwardness in the handling of the congested intricacies of tiller and sheet at the cramped stern of our double-ender, the adventures of me nearly came to an untimely and inglorious end. The hurtling main-boom struck me with terrific force, hurling me backwards over the combing. I clutched and held to God knows what and hung, half in the water, a little more ashamed than scared, and far more scared than hurt.

However, we had come about, and continuing a little further on that tack we shot up into the wind and anchored in the calmer water of the island's lee.

On the shore of the bay, half a mile from where we lay, stood the buildings and enclosures of a sheep farm. Rowing ashore we proceeded there on foot. It was a small establishment, a house, a ramshackle shed or two, and the fenced corral and labyrinth of the dip. The surrounding plain was hidden with the charred stumps of a forest that had once stood there; and it was evidence of the short-sightedness of the human occupants of the place that the destruction of the trees had left the buildings exposed to the unbroken violence of the western gales. Over the sheep-cropped grass about the house was strewn a litter of filth and bones and rotting carcasses. Two condors left their carrion gorge as we approached and on huge wings raised themselves to mountain heights and soared away.

With the cold wind whistling about us, filling our eyes with drifting sand, we circled round the house in vain for signs of life within. Then, balked of that hospitality and the warm cup of coffee we had promised ourselves, we set off briskly for the head of the bay.

That southern valley in which we now were terminates at the sound in a broad, flat, sandy plain, that the pasturing of sheep has converted from a moss-grown waste into a close-cropped lawn of grass. A sand dune separates it from the shore and shelters it a little from prevailing winds. Between its northern border and the range of Mount Hope flows a deep, swift stream, broadening near its outlet so as to afford a roomy anchorage for a boat of the tonnage of ours; and it was with a view to shifting the *Kathleen* to that berth that we went to reconnoiter it.

It was high tide when we reached the river bank, and the sea having entered the lower reaches of the stream had deepened and broadened it and assimilated its current, so that we beheld a most inviting, almost land-locked, little harbor.

"Absolutely perfect!" we cried; and we hurried down to inspect the entrance.

This was not so good. It narrowed abruptly when it entered the sea to a passage not more than thirty feet in width, with a cliff on one side of it and a steep sand bank on the other. Outside, on one hand were reefs and on the other the long curved beach of the bay with the sea thundering along it. To all appearances, at that hour of high tide, with the surface of the water torn by the wind, there was depth enough outside for a straight approach. It was worth chancing in preference to continuing at the wind-raked anchorage where we lay.

On our return we found the tenant of the farm at home. And now, lest

ROCKWELL KENT

"Roll On"

WE TURNED out early, in that portentous hour that precedes the dawn. Above mountainous dark land the cloudless sky was luminous with stars; it was a breathless morning, clear and sweet. Then imperceptibly the daylight came and the gold of sunrise flung itself across the heavens, kindled the mountain peaks and overflowed the world. A gentle wind arose and bore us out. O fresh, clear, fair west wind! That day we blessed it, and the next and then for five interminable wind-bound weeks we cursed its obstinacy.

With the fair wind and freshening, and bright wind clouds streaming up across the sky, we sailed down Brenton Sound and passed the channel south of the Tucker Islands. Before us, due east by the compass, lay the green-blue length of Admiralty Sound, white-capped and swept by purple shadows. The sun shone dazzling bright on snowy peaks and glistening walls of rock, displaying all the details of the land in crystal clarity—bare golden hills, and shaded wonderlands of forest, and dark ravines that gushed out silver streams. It was a day so opulently beautiful that the pure exuberance of the wind and the sun induced intoxication.

Eastward of Cape Rowlett the land becomes increasingly abrupt and mountainous. Dwarfed, wind-worn forests, sparsely clothe the slopes. The naked structure of the land appears, rock faces broken sheer or glacier worn, vast slopes of ledge and gravel, stunted underbrush upon the middle heights, and plains of bog; and, on the summits, snow. Through gaps in that shore's mountain wall appear the lofty peaks and the snow-clad southern ranges, whose ice-choked valleys spill out glaciers down the hollows of the slopes.

At the head of Ainsworth Harbor there was visible to us, as we passed the entrance, a glacier huge as a frozen Mississippi. The eddies and churned currents of that ice stream score its broad surface with the forms of a flowing torrent. It breaks off at the water's edge in cliffs of translucent turquoise.

All day we sailed with a great wind astern that sometimes mounted to a gale. Those seas to our small boat were mountains high. They followed us as if to overwhelm us; they overtook and lifted us, and left us, foaming as they went.

There are few harbors along that precipitous shore, and in the miles between them scarcely a beach or sheltered point where one could land. Accordingly, when, with the afternoon not far advanced and the wind still holding strong, we elected to pass by Ainsworth Harbor and continue up the sound, we put before us a good two hours' sailing to reach the next anchorage, Parry Harbor. And that with a wind so fair and steady we should reach there in broad daylight we had no doubt. But wise men do not rely on the wind.

Within two hours it was calm, dead glassy calm; and in the long smooth swell of the subsiding sea we rocked and drifted helplessly about not two miles from the headland at the harbor's mouth. So on our helplessness the day went out; the shadow of the far-off western mountain sides extinguishing at last the highest flaming peaks. And night descended chill and bleak, and then the wind.

As we turned the headland the wind beat down in violent and variable squalls. It was impossible to see. We drove on into that darkness, trusting to what the chart obscurely showed of the coast's contour. For a few minutes we steered due south; then, estimating that we had come abreast of Stanley Cove, we proceeded to beat in short tacks straight at the abysmal midnight of the mountain side. Someone in speaking of this anchorage had told us of two rocks that we must pass between. With straining eyes we saw them straight before us. Sailing close hauled it seemed that by a narrow margin we could make the passage. Suddenly, with a howl of fury, the squall veered. We hung in stays a moment drifting onto the leeward rock. With swift presence of mind, the mate threw the tiller hard to windward. We slacked the sheet and bore away to clear the danger; we escaped that shipwreck by a fathom's clearance.

Somehow, aided by incessant sounding, we navigated safely that dark entrance to the cove, and, finding bottom at last, anchored in five fathoms of water.

While the mate set things on board to rights, I launched the skiff, and rowed out into that midnight to discover and explore the shore. I skirted the rocks for perhaps a quarter of a mile before encountering a landing place. There on a pebble beach, I drew the skiff ashore, and stood at last, after a voyage of near seven thousand miles, on grim Tierra del Fuego. I felt the these pages come to glow with that too kindly spirit of undiscriminating love for man, I permit myself the happiness of presenting this mealy-mouthed hypocrite as the pernicious scoundrel that he was.

There are all kinds of scoundrels. We have the individualists who, sinning against the law, get rich, or go to jail, or hang—and there's an end of them; there are the democratic scoundrels who, holding that one man is as good as another, sin against God, whose worship is "honoring his gifts, in other men, each according to his genius, and loving the greatest men best: those who envy or calumniate great men hate God." Irreverence is the *greatest* sin. But there remains that most inhuman sin of all, inhospitality.

If Gómez had been a weak, dyspeptic, suffering creature, whose own misery had poisoned the wells of kindness within him, there would have been cause enough, out of the hatefulness of life as he experienced it, to justify unbridled spleen against the world; but he was neither weak nor ill. He was a powerful and stocky fellow, brown skinned and bearded like a ruffian of romance. He hadn't mean and shifty eyes, but rather placid ox-like orbs that looked at me unfalteringly. Gómez was at peace with God and with himself, we came to know; and he observed his Christian fellowship with all the prayerful jumping, shouting, clapping, moaning, rolling, bouncing, sobbing imbecility of a Holy-jumper.

"Enter," said Gómez with a grimace of hospitality, when I had presented to him a warm letter of introduction from his employer, Señor Marcou, in which every attention and courtesy was bespoken. "We would ask you to partake of a meal with us, but we have so little to offer," and, ingratiatingly rubbing his hands, he proceeded to tell us that he abstained from wine and tobacco, and from the flesh of the "sinful" guanaco, and that he received four hundred pesos a month wages and free food and clothing. And all the while he talked we heard through the thin partition of the next room the incessant droning moaning of one praying aloud. Presently it ceased. There was the sound of a body bestirring itself and, with the great bulk filling the doorway, the prayerful one appeared.

"My dear wife," said Gómez, introducing her.

This saintly woman's face resembled a gorilla's; the eyes were small and close set, the nose was flat, and the whole skull projected toward an immense and shapeless orifice of mouth that opened and shut like a trap.

The house was untidy and unclean and almost empty. On the kitchen wall hung two framed Bible texts, and in the prayer-chamber bedroom was the broad, long, deep, soft couch of a voluptuary, laid with sheepskins, blankets, counterpanes, and the downy robes of sinful, wild guanacos.

"Very bad weather," said Gómez. "Very bad country; very bad pasture; very bad year for sheep; very bad men around here. Mulach at Lago Fognano very bad man, always drunk." (Muy mal hombre; siempre borracho!)

We questioned him about the anchorage in the river, telling him that we intended moving our boat to it. He laughed and, with obscure significance, shrugged his shoulders, avoiding a direct reply.

"Tomorrow," he said in obedience to a command in the letter I had presented, "I take you to the lake."

Both because of the tide's effect upon the river current and that it might favor us in the event of our running aground, we hoped to postpone the attempt to enter the river until the flood tide had set in. The day was, however, so overcast that at five o'clock, with darkness threatening, we hove anchor. The strong wind bore us with what seemed incredible speed toward the land, whose long, low shore appeared of unbroken extent, revealing nothing of the river's mouth save the cliff that marked it.

It had been high tide when we inspected the seaward approach, and the water had appeared to be of even and sufficient depth. Now, however, as we drew nearer to the land we observed breakers as far from shore as half a mile. Nevertheless, from what had been told us of the river, and particularly from Gómez' having mentioned no dangers, it seemed reasonable to continue; so, with white seas everywhere to starboard of us and reefs and a converging rocky shore to port, we held on straight for the narrow river mouth. Suddenly the water under us showed a pallid green. The mate leaped forward to observe the depth: it was too late. A long sea broke across our bows. There was no room to turn, nor time; we struck.

A foaming sea swept by us, grinding us along. Another followed, lifted us, and hurled us forward, clear. We gained new headway from the wind and shot ahead through a cauldron of white surf.

We struck again, were lifted by a bigger sea, carried two fathoms on its crest—and dropped so viciously that every fibre of the boat was strained. The stern swung round and we lay grounded, broadside to the wind and sea.

A squall struck, throwing us on our beam ends: in the wild tumult of the sea and wind we lowered sail and anchored.

We lay a quarter of a mile from shore. It was almost dark, and the falling tide soon left us in the very midst of breaking seas.

It was the work of some minutes to get the spare anchor out of the hold and bolt its uncouth parts together. The mate in this emergency became again a miracle of energy and strength and prompt obedience. With the white seas curling over the skiff's gunwale, he rowed the heavy anchor with its dragging weight of chain to windward, and at the chain's length dropped it. Then, taking advantage of every lift of the larger seas, we strained to draw the bow into the wind. Time and again without avail we pulled the anchor through the yielding sandy bottom, hove it aboard, replaced it in the skiff, and the mate carried it to sea again. The bow stuck fast. Finally, after an hour of exhausting labor, we worked the boat's stern into the wind and, with both anchors at their chain's and cable's lengths to windward, held her so, and went below to await the tide or dissolution.

Battening the companionway doors against the wind and the heavy seas that now and then boarded the stern, we rekindled the fire, that had burned out during our preoccupation, and settled down grimly to enjoy what dismal comfort was to be had.

Being, because of his youth and his wide experience of calamity, the more hopeful of us two, the mate was in this hour of misfortune the more dejected. The emotions trace a circle, with their cause as center and the radius the measure of disaster. While he sat overwhelmed by thought of the damage that our ship must suffer, I, with less hope, had already seen her thrown upon the shore, a total wreck. I had accepted this as an inevitable and therefore a finished episode. I had seen us stranded there—without a boat, to be sure, but quite alive and well. I had planned what we should save and, all in one moment of imagination, visioned our triumphant passage of the mountains southward. Out of the very all-eliminating completeness of disaster rose the sun upon a clean, new world. I laughed to see the mate so haggard and dispirited.

"Roll on, thou deep and dark blue ocean, roll!" I declaimed in tragically moving tones. And when, with lowered voice and the slow rhythm of the pendulum of destiny, I spoke these lines:

> *"He sinks into thy depths with bubbling groan,*
> *Without a grave, unknelled, uncoffined and unknown."*

the deep and bitter cup of the mate's misery bubbled over; he laughed. Nature, for both of us, had overdone its drama.

I remember years ago, when my older children were very little and we were all living in a tiny, one-room, abandoned schoolhouse in the Middle West, that they heard there, for the first time, thunder: and it was thunder so terrific that it seemed like a concussion of the universe about the little shell that held us. And the children were frightened. So we gave them each a tin pan and a heavy kitchen spoon.

"Take these," we said, "and when it thunders beat as hard as you can on the pans and see if you can make a bigger noise than the thunder. It's a game."

They did make a bigger noise, and loved it; and therewith ended forever the terrors of thunder.

No sound of nature could be more gruesomely harassing than that intermittent grinding, gnashing, thumping, creaking, groaning of our forlorn ship as she rolled and pounded in that sea. So I got out my beautiful, beloved silver flute and played upon it; and if it had never before imposed a mood of peace upon one human spirit—and that is possible—that day, by the incongruousness of its plaintive notes amid those sounds of wreck, it did.

Then, lo! as if the forces of destruction had grown discouraged in the face of our impressive nonchalance, the tides of the sea and of fortune turned to favor us. Instead of lifting on the crests of waves we floated free, and only pounded in the hollows.

With new energy and strength we went to work to improve our position, and in an hour's time, by pulling the vessel out to the anchors and carrying the anchors alternately out to sea, we reached a safe depth to lie in. It was an extremely rough and uncomfortable berth, but in the total darkness of that night it was out of the question to hoist canvas and look for another. Utterly exhausted, we turned in.

REAR ADMIRAL RICHARD E. BYRD

Flight to the South Pole

THANKSGIVING DAY, November 28th, brought what we wanted. At noon the Geological Party radioed a final weather report: "Unchanged. Perfect visibility. No clouds anywhere." Harrison finished with his balloon runs, Haines with his weather charts. The sky was still somewhat overcast, and the surface wind from the east southeast. Haines came into the library, his face grave. Together we went out for a walk and a last look at the weather. What he said exactly I have forgotten, but it was in effect: "If you don't go now, you may never have another chance as good as this." And that was that.

The mechanics, Bubier, Roth and Demas, went over the plane for the last time, testing everything with scrupulous care. A line of men passed five-gallon cans of gasoline to several men standing on the wing, who poured them into the wing tanks. Another line fed the stream of gear which flowed into the plane. Black weighed each thing before passing it on to McKinley and June, who were stowing the stuff in the cabin. Hanson went over the radio equipment. With de Ganahl I made a careful check of the sextant and the watches and chronometers, which were among the last things put aboard. For days de Ganahl and I had nursed the chronometers, checking them against the time tick broadcast every night from the United States. We knew their exact loss or gain.

The total weight was approximately 15,000 pounds.

Haines came up with a final report on the weather. "A twenty-mile wind from the south at 2,000 feet." I went into my office and picked up a flag weighted with a stone from Floyd Bennett's grave. It seemed fitting that something connected with the spirit of this noble friend, who stood with me over the North Pole, on May 9th, 1926, should rest as long as stone endures at the bottom of the world.

There were handshakes all around, and at 3:29 o'clock we were off. The skis were in the air after a run of 30 seconds—an excellent take-off. A calm expectation took hold of my mind.

Had you been there to glance over the cabin of this modern machine which has so revolutionized polar travel, I think you would have been impressed most of all—perhaps first of all—with the profusion of gear in the cabin. There was a small sledge, rolled masses of sleeping bags, bulky food sacks, two pressure gasoline stoves, rows of cans of gasoline packed about the main tank forward, funnels for draining gasoline and oil from the engines, bundles of clothing, tents and so on *ad infinitum*. There was scarcely room in which to move.

June had his radio in the after bulkhead on the port side. From time to time he flashed reports on our progress to the base. From the ear phones strapped to his helmet ran long cords so that he might move freely about the cabin without being obliged to take them off. His duties were varied and important. He had to attend to the motion picture camera, the radio and the complicated valves of the six gasoline tanks. Every now and then he relieved Balchen at the wheel, or helped him to follow the elusive trail.

McKinley had his mapping camera ready for action either on port or starboard side. It was for him and the camera he so sedulously served that the flight was made. The mapping of the corridor between Little America and the South Pole was one of the major objectives of the expedition.

Balchen was forward, bulking large in the narrow compartment, his massive hands on the wheel, now appraising the engines with a critical eye, now the dozen flickering fingers on the dials on the instrument board. Balchen was in his element. His calm fine face bespoke his confidence and sureness. He was anticipating the struggle at the "Hump" almost with eagerness.

It was quite warm forward, behind the engines. But a cold wind swept through the cabin, making one thankful for heavy clothes. When the skies cleared, a golden light poured into the cabin. The sound of the engines and propellers filled it. One had to shout to make oneself heard. From the navigation table aft, where my charts were spread out, a trolley ran to the control cabin. Over it I shot to Balchen the necessary messages and courses; he would turn and smile his understanding.

That, briefly, is the picture, and a startling one it makes in contrast with that of Amundsen's party, which had pressed along this same course eighteen years before. A wing, pistons and flashing propellers had taken the place of runner, dogs and legs. Amundsen was delighted to make 25 miles per day.

We had to average 90 miles per hour to accomplish our mission. We had the advantages of swiftness and comfort, but we had as well an enlarged fallibility. A flaw in a piece of steel, a bit of dirt in the fuel lines or carburetor jets, a few hours of strong head winds, fog or storm—these things, remotely beyond our control, could destroy our carefully laid plans and nullify our most determined efforts.

Still, it was not these things that entered our minds. Rather it was the thought of the "Hump," and how we should fare with it.

Soon after passing the crevasses we picked up again the vast escarpment to the right. More clearly than before we saw the white-blue streams of many glaciers discharging into the Barrier, and several of the higher snow-clad peaks glistened so brightly in the sun as to seem like volcanoes in eruption.

Now the Queen Maud Range loomed ahead. I searched again for the "appearance of land" to the east. Still the rolling Barrier—nothing else.

At 8:15 o'clock we had the Geological Party in sight—a cluster of beetles about two dark-topped tents. Balchen dropped overboard the photographs of the Queen Maud Range and the other things we had promised to bring. The parachute canopy to which they were attached fluttered open and fell in gentle oscillations, and we saw two or three figures rush out to catch it. We waved to them, and then prepared for a settlement of the issue at the "Hump."

Up to this time, the engines had operated continuously at cruising revolutions. Now Balchen opened them full throttle, and the Ford girded its loins for the long, fighting pull over the "Hump." We rose steadily. We were then about 60 miles north of the western portal of Axel Heiberg, and holding our course steadily on meridian 163° 45' W. with the sun compass.

I watched the altimeters, of which there were two in the navigation department. The fingers marched with little jumps across the face of the dial—3,000 feet, 3,500 4,000, 4,500. The Ford had her toes in, and was climbing with a vast, heaving effort.

Drawing nearer, we had edged 30° to the west of south, to bring not only Axel Heiberg but also Liv Glacier into view. This was a critical period. I was by no means certain which glacier I should choose for the ascent, I went forward and took a position behind the pilots.

The schemes and hopes of the next few minutes were beset by many uncertainties. Which would it be—Axel Heiberg or Liv Glacier?

There was this significant difference between flying and sledging: we could not pause long for decision or investigation. Minutes stood for gasoline, and gasoline was precious. The waste of so little as half an hour of fuel in a fruitless experiment might well overturn the mathematical balance on which the success of the flight depended. The execution of the plan hung on the proper choice of the route over the "Hump."

Yet, how well, after all, could judgment forecast the ultimate result? There were few facts on which we might base a decision. We knew, for example, from Amundsen's report, that the highest point of the pass of Axel Heiberg Glacier was 10,500 feet. We should know, in a very few minutes, after June had calculated the gasoline consumption, the weight of the plane. From that we could determine, according to the tables we had worked out and which were then before me, the approximate ceiling we should have. We should know, too, whether or not we should be able to complete the flight, other conditions being favorable.

These were the known elements. The unknown were burdened with equally important consequences. The structural nature of the head of the pass was of prime importance. We knew from Amundsen's descriptions and from what we could see with our own eyes, that the pass on both sides was surrounded by towering peaks, much higher than the maximum ceiling of the heavily loaded plane. But whether the pass was wide or narrow; whether it would allow us room to maneuver in case we could not rise above it; whether it would be narrow and running with a torrent of down-pressing wind which would dash a plane, already hovering near its service ceiling, to the glacier floor—these were things, naturally, we could not possibly know until the issue was directly at hand.

I stood beside Balchen, carefully studying the looming fortress, still wondering by what means we should attempt to carry it. With a gesture of the hand Balchen pointed to fog vapor rising from the black rock of the foothills which were Nansen's high priests—caused no doubt by the condensation of warm currents of air radiated from the sun-heated rocks. A thin layer of cloud seemed to cap Axel Heiberg's pass, and extended almost to Liv Glacier. But of this we were not certain. Perhaps it was the surface of the snow. If cloud, then our difficulties were already upon us. Even high clouds would be resting on the floor of the uplifted plateau.

There was, then, a gamble in the decision. Doubtless a flip of the coin would have served as well. In the end, we decided to choose Liv Glacier, the unknown pass to the right which Amundsen had seen far in the distance and named after Dr. Nansen's daughter. It seemed to be broader than Axel Heiberg, and the pass not quite so high.

A few minutes after 9 o'clock we passed near the intermediate base, which, of course, we could not see. Our altitude was then about 9,000 feet. At 9:15 o'clock we had the eastern portal on our left, and were ready to tackle the "Hump." We had discussed the "Hump" so often, had anticipated and maligned it so much, that now that it was in front of us and waiting in the flesh—in rock-ribbed, glacierized reality—it was like meeting an old acquaintance. But we approached it warily and respectfully, climbing steadily all the while with maximum power, to get a better view of its none too friendly visage.

June, wholly unaffected by the immediate perplexities, went about his job of getting the plane in fighting trim. He ripped open the last of the fuel cans, and poured the contents into the main tank. The empty tins he dropped overboard, through the trapdoor. Every tin weighed two pounds; and every pound dropped was to our gain. June examined the gauges of the five wing tanks, then measured with a graduated stick the amount of fuel in the main tank. He jotted the figures on a pad, made a few calculations and handed me the results. Consumption had thus far averaged between 55 and 60 gallons per hour. It had taken us longer to reach the mountains than we had expected, owing to head winds. However, the extra fuel taken aboard just before we left had absorbed this loss and we actually had a credit balance. We had, then, enough gasoline to take us to the Pole and back.

With that doubt disposed of, we went at the "Hump" confidently.

We were still rising, and the engines were pulling wonderfully well. The wind was about abeam, and, according to my calculations, not materially affecting the speed.

The glacier floor rose sharply, in a series of ice falls and terraces, some of which were well above the (then) altitude of the plane. These glacial waterfalls, some of which were from 200 to 400 feet high, seemed more beautiful than any precipitous stream I have ever seen. Beautiful yes, but how rudely and with what finality they would deal with steel and duralumin that crashed into them at 100 miles per hour.

Now the stream of air pouring down the pass roughened perceptibly. The great wing shivered and teetered as it balanced itself against the changing pressures. The wind from the left flowed against Fisher's steep flanks, and the constant, hammering bumps made footing uncertain in the plane. But McKinley steadily trained his 50-pound camera on the mountains to the left. The uncertainties of load and ceiling were not his concern. His only concern was photographs—photographs over which students and geographers might pore in the calm quiet of their studies.

The altimeters showed a height of 9,600 feet, but the figure was not necessarily exact. Nevertheless there were indications we were near the service ceiling of the plane.

The roughness of the air increased and became so violent that we were forced to swing slightly to the left, in search of calmer air. This brought us over a frightfully crevassed slope which ran up and toward Mount Nansen. We thus escaped the turbulent swirl about Fisher, but the down-surging currents here damped our climb. To the left we had the "blind" mountain glacier of Nansen in full view; and when we looked ahead we saw the plateau—a smooth, level plain of snow between Nansen and Fisher. The pass rose up to meet it.

In the center of the pass was a massive outcropping of snow-covered rocks, resembling an island, which protruded above and separated the descending stream of ice. Perhaps it was a peak or the highest eminence of a ridge connecting Fisher and Nansen which had managed through the ages to hold its head above the glacial torrent pouring down from the plateau. But its particular structure or relationship was of small moment then. I watched it only with reference to the climb of the plane; and realized, with some disgust and more consternation, that the nose of the plane, in spite of the fact that Balchen had steepened the angle of attack, did not rise materially above the outcropping. We were still climbing, but at a rapidly diminishing rate of speed. In the rarefied air the heavy plane responded to the controls with marked sluggishness. There is a vast difference between the plane of 1928 and the plane of 1937.

It was an awesome thing, creeping (so it seemed) through the narrow pass, with the black walls of Nansen and Fisher on either side, higher than the level of the wings, and watching the nose of the ship bob up and down across the face of that chunk of rock. It would move up, then slide down. Then move up, and fall off again. For perhaps a minute or two we deferred the decision; but there was no escaping it. If we were to risk a passage through the pass, we needed greater maneuverability than we had at that moment. Once we entered the pass, there would be no retreat. It offered no room for turn. If power was lost momentarily or if the air became excessively rough, we could only go ahead, or down. We had to climb, and there was only one way in which we could climb.

June, anticipating the command, already had his hand on the dump valve of the main tank. A pressure of the fingers—that was all that was necessary—and in two minutes 600 gallons of gasoline would gush out. I signaled to wait.

Balchen held to the climb almost to the edge of a stall. But it was clear to both of us that he could not hold it long enough. Balchen began to yell and gesticulate, and it was hard to catch the words in the roar of the engines echoing from the cliffs on either side. But the meaning was manifest. "Overboard—overboard—200 pounds!"

Which would it be—gasoline or food?

If gasoline, I thought, we might as well stop there and turn back. We could never get back to the base from the Pole. If food, the lives of all of us would be jeopardized in the event of a forced landing. Was that fair to McKinley, Balchen and June? It really took only a moment to reach the decision. The Pole, after all, was our objective. I knew the character of the three men. McKinley, in fact, had already hauled one of the food bags to the trapdoor. It weighed 125 pounds.

The brown bag was pushed out and fell, spinning, to the glacier. The improvement in the flying qualities of the plane was noticeable. It took another breath and resumed the climb.

Now the down-currents over Nansen became stronger. The plane trembled and rose and fell, as if struck bodily. We veered a trifle to the right, searching for helpful rising eddies. Balchen was flying shrewdly. He maintained flight at a sufficient distance below the absolute ceiling of the plane to retain at all times enough maneuverability to make him master of the ship. But he was hard pressed by circumstances; and I realized that, unless the plane was further lightened, the final thrust might bring us perilously close to the end of our reserve.

"More," Bernt shouted. "Another bag."

McKinley shoved a second bag through the trapdoor, and this time we saw it hit the glacier, and scatter in a soundless explosion. Two hundred and fifty pounds of food—enough to feed four men for a month—lay strewn on the barren ice.

The sacrifice swung the scales. The plane literally rose with a jump; the engines dug in, and we soon showed a gain in altitude of from 300 to 400 feet. It was what we wanted. We should clear the pass with about 500 feet to spare. Balchen gave a shout of joy. It was just as well. We could dump no more food. There was nothing left to dump except McKinley's camera. I am sure that, had he been asked to put it overboard, he would have done so instantly; and I am equally sure he would have followed the precious instrument with his own body.

The next few minutes dragged. We moved at a speed of 77 nautical miles per hour through the pass, with the black walls of Nansen on our left. The wing gradually lifted above them. The floor of the plateau stretched in a white immensity to the south. We were over the dreaded "Hump" at last. The Pole lay dead ahead over the horizon, less than 300 miles away. It was then about 9:45 o'clock (I did not note the exact time. There were other things to think about).

Gaining the plateau, we studied the situation a moment and then shifted course to the southward. Nansen's enormous towering ridge, lipped by the plateau, shoved its heavily broken sides into the sky. A whole chain of mountains began to parade across the eastern horizon. How high they are I cannot say, but surely some of them must be around 14,000 feet, to stand so boldly above the rim of the 10,000 foot plateau. Peak on peak, ridge on ridge, draped in snow garments which brilliantly reflected the sun, they extended in a solid array to the southeast. But can one really say they ran in that direction? The lines of direction are so bent in this region that 150 miles farther on, even were they to continue in the same general straight line, they must run north of east. This is what happens near the Pole.

We laid our line of flight on the 171st meridian.

Our altitude was then between 10,500 and 11,000 feet. We were "riding" the engines, conscious of the fact that if one should fail we must come down. Once the starboard engine did sputter a bit, and Balchen nosed down while June rushed to the fuel valves. But it was nothing; to conserve fuel, Balchen had "leaned" the mixture too much. A quick adjustment corrected the fault, and in a moment the engine took up its steady rhythm. Moments like this one make a pioneering flight anything but dull; one moment everything is lovely, and the next is full of forebodings.

The drift indicator showed a variable wind from the east. To compensate for it, we had to point the nose of the plane an average of about 12° to the east, in order to steer a straight course for the Pole. The influence of the drift on the course was always a bothersome element. It had to be watched carefully, and any change in the angle of drift detected at once, so as to make good a straight course south. Fitted in the floor of the plane was a drift indicator which McKinley used in connection with his photographic work, and during the flight he constantly checked the drift with me. Whenever I noted any change in the direction or strength of the wind, I would steady

Balchen on his course with the sun compass, first shaking the trolley line to attract his attention, then waving him on to the new course.

The character of the plateau surface varied from time to time. There were stretches of smooth, soft snow, colonies of domed haycocks and arrow-headed sastrugi. From the time we had first struck across the plateau its level appeared to slope gently toward the Pole; the altimeter showed that the *Floyd Bennett* was maintaining a fairly steady altitude at approximately 11,000 feet, and the plateau fell farther below. We had named the Ford after my gallant friend and companion on the North Pole flight.

While the mountains on the left were still in view, I attempted to shoot the sun with the sextant to get its altitude. This would give us a sun line which would cut our line of flight and at the point of intersection tell us what the sun had to say about our progress. The air, however, was fairly rough. The powerful center engine, laboring to keep the heavy load at an altitude of two miles, produced a weaving in the plane; and the most patient efforts failed to bring the sun and the bubble together long enough for a dependable sight. This was bothersome, but relatively unimportant at the time; we were quite confident as to the accuracy of the dead reckoning.

From time to time June "spelled" Balchen at the controls; and Balchen would walk back to the cabin, flexing his cramped muscles. There was little thought of food in any of us—a beef sandwich, stiff as a board from frost, and tea and coffee from a thermos bottle. It was difficult to believe that two decades or so before the most resolute men who had ever attempted to carry a remote objective, Scott and Shackleton, had plodded over this same plateau, a few miles each day, with hunger, fierce, unrelenting hunger, stalking them every step of the way.

Between 11:30 and 12:30 o'clock the mountains to the eastward began to disappear, dropping inperceptibly out of view, one after another. Not long after 12:30 o'clock the whole range had retreated from vision, and the plateau met the horizon in an indefinite line. The mountains to the right had long since disappeared.

The air finally turned smooth. At 12:38 o'clock I shot the sun. It hung, a ball of fire, just beyond *south* to the east, 21° above the horizon. So it was quite low, and we stared it in the eye. The sight gave me an approximate line of latitude, which placed us very near our position as calculated by dead reckoning. That dead reckoning and astronomy should check so closely was very encouraging. The position line placed us at Lat. 89° 4½′ S., or 55½ miles from the Pole. A short time later we reached an altitude of 11,000 feet. According to Amundsen's records, the plateau, which had risen to 10,300 feet, descended here to 9,600 feet. We were, therefore, about 1,400 feet above the plateau.

So the Pole was actually in sight. But I could not yet spare it so much as a glance. Chronometers, drift indicators and compasses are hard task-masters.

Relieved by June, Balchen came aft and reported that visibility was not as good as it had been. Clouds were gathering on the horizon off the port bow; and a storm, Balchen thought, was in the air. A storm was the last thing we wanted to meet on the plateau on the way back. It would be difficult enough to pass the Queen Maud Range in bright sunlight; in thick weather it would be suicidal. Conditions, however, were merely unpromising: not really bad, simply not good. If worse came to worst, we decided we could out-race the clouds to the mountains.

At six minutes after one o'clock, a sight of the sun put us a few miles ahead of our dead reckoning position. We were quite close now. At 1:14 o'clock, Greenwich civil time, our calculations showed that we were at the Pole.

I opened the trapdoor and dropped over the calculated position of the Pole the small flag which was weighted with the stone from Bennett's grave. Stone and flag plunged down together. The flag had been advanced 1,500 miles farther south than it had ever been advanced by any American or American expedition.

For a few seconds we stood over the spot where Amundsen had stood, December 14th, 1911; and where Scott had also stood, thirty-four days later, reading the note which Amundsen had left for him. In their honor, the flags of their countries were again carried over the Pole. There was nothing now to mark that scene: only a white desolation and solitude disturbed by the sound of our engines. The Pole lay in the center of a limitless plain. To the right, which is to say to the eastward, the horizon was covered with clouds. If mountains lay there, as some geologists believe, they were concealed and we had no hint of them.

And that, in brief, is all there is to tell about the South Pole. One gets there, and that is about all there is for the telling. It is the effort to get there that counts.

We put the Pole behind us and raced for home.

The mountains to the eastward came into view again, one by one. But whereas before the southernmost peaks had stood out clear and distinct, they were now confused by haze and clouds. The clouds were traveling fast, threatening to close in ahead of us; and, if we valued our skins, it behooved us to beat them to the pass.

We were then riding the 168th meridian to Axel Heiberg Glacier. It was my intention to return somewhat to the eastward of the original course, in order to bring within range as much new territory as was possible. McKinley, who had photographed the area to the eastward on the way to the Pole, was then mapping the area to the westward.

Time began to crawl. It was a case of hitting the pass of Axel Heiberg Glacier ahead of the clouds or being sorry. The wind was now astern and helping us considerably. Of course, its direction varied from time to time. Our speed increased. About two o'clock, seeking a still stronger wind aloft, we climbed several hundred feet and found a fairly stiff following wind. With that boosting us, we hurried over the plateau. At three o'clock Balchen opened the throttles wide and a short time later we climbed about 400 feet higher. At this level the wind was even stronger. We commenced to make better than 125 miles per hour. Our altitude was between 11,500 and 12,500 feet.

About 3:30 o'clock Balchen's face broke into a smile. Ruth Gade's conical turret was off to the starboard bow. There was Nansen off the port bow. Soon W. Christophersen came into view, a small rounded dome between Ruth Gade and Nansen. The charts, photographs and descriptions which I had culled from Amundsen's book, as well as the photographs which McKinley had taken on the base-laying flight, were before me; and as each new prominence appeared and fell neatly into its expected place, we were delighted. Our return course had been straight, and our position coincided with our dead reckoning position. The flight was almost done. Best of all, the pass was clear.

A few clouds were beginning to gather in the passes to the right and left, but we had outstripped the main advance,

By 3:50 o'clock we had passed over the head of the glacier, sinking lower all the time, and glided down the shattered terraces between the precipitous sides of Nansen and Don Pedro Christophersen. The air in places was very bumpy, and the loose gear in the plane was tossed about rather wildly.

We emerged from the glacier shortly after four o'clock.

June finished with his calculations of the fuel supply and reported there was a slight margin over needs. There was enough, then, to make further inquiry into Carmen Land; so we continued to the eastward. McKinley, I decided, ought to photograph this area.

We were now over the Barrier, and we could see how the shearing movements of the Barrier, where it pressed against the feet of the mountains, had produced deep and extensive crevasses in several areas. What mighty pressures must be at work, to rip that tough fabric as if it were silk. The extensions of the Queen Maud Range and the new mountains which we had seen on the base-laying flight were on our right, a solid rampart extending to the south or east. They were almost wholly covered with snow, and some were broken by glaciers of considerable size and beauty.

The flight proved what I already knew to be true: Carmen Land does not exist. McKinley photographed the Barrier where Amundsen believed it lay, and we then turned westward, landing presently at the base.

Taking the fuel aboard was quite a problem. Each can had to be broken open and poured, one by one, into the wing tanks, and we soon tired of lifting them to June, who was doing the pouring. It was 6 o'clock before we rose from the Barrier and headed north, on the last leg of the flight. By that time the outriders of the storm clouds were creeping over the mountain rim to the east.

We steered a straight course for Little America, and made no attempt to pick up the trail, which was to the east. But our course converged with the trail a few miles north of Little America. We flew by sun compass and drift indicator and made a perfect land fall. Again the sun compass had done its job.

We had Little America's radio spires in sight at 10 o'clock. A few minutes later we were over the Administration Building, swinging west to come in for a landing. A last survey showed that the Bay of Whales was still choked with ice, the northern edge of which extended almost to West Cape.

Sunday, Dec. 1

Well, it's done. We have seen the Pole. McKinley, Balchen and June have delivered the goods. They took the Pole in their stride, neatly, expeditiously, and undismayed. If I had searched the world I doubt if I could have found a better team. Theirs was the actual doing. But there is not a man in this camp who did not assist in the preparation for the flight. Whatever merit accrues to the accomplishment must be shared with them.

BIBLIOGRAPHICAL NOTES

BIBLIOGRAPHICAL NOTES

BY E. H. B.

HISTORY

Of the Origin and Design of Government in General
First chapter of "Common Sense." From "The Collected Writings of Thomas Paine." 1894.

The Drawing-up of the Declaration of Independence
From "The Autobiography of Thomas Jefferson." Edited, with an Introduction, by Paul Leicester Ford. 1892. A fragmentary memoir, written in Jefferson's old age, that is chiefly important for this account of the writing of one of the finest pieces of American prose.

Examination of the Constitution
Formation of the Constitution
The Republican Principle
On a Just Partition of Power
From "The Federalist." Edited by Henry Cabot Lodge. 1888. The Federalist Papers, written in 1788 by James Madison, Alexander Hamilton, and John Jay, to explain and urge the adoption of the new Constitution, set a literary standard of political pamphleteering that has not since been equalled. The papers reprinted here are Nos. XXXVII, XXXVIII, XXXIX, and LI.

Benjamin Franklin
From "Benjamin Franklin Self-Revealed." Copyright by William Cabell Bruce, 1917. This book was awarded the Pulitzer prize for biography. Mr. Bruce, later United States Senator from Maryland, is also the author of another distinguished two-volume biography, "John Randolph of Roanoke," published in 1923.

The Purchase of Louisiana; and Burr's Conspiracy
From "The Winning of the West." Copyright, 1889. Perhaps Theodore Roosevelt's greatest historical work, the result of his youthful enthusiasm for the West, an enthusiasm that was life-long.

Tippecanoe, and Tyler Too!
From "The Fabulous Forties." Copyright by Meade Minnigerode, 1924. A brilliant evocation of a gusty period in American history. Another section, concerning the Astor Place Opera House riot, is omitted only because of space limitations.

1016 AN AMERICAN READER

Audubon in Kentucky
From "The Life of John James Audubon." By His Widow. 1869. That extraordinary woman who bore with such devotion and gallantry the vicissitudes of their early life together published this memoir of her amazing husband, based chiefly on his notebooks. This excerpt appears as Chapter V in the book.

Scenes at Fort Laramie
From "The California and Oregon Trail." 1849. In the first list of "G. P. Putnam, Broadway," issued in 1848, this forthcoming book was announced under the title of "The Oregon Trail," as it first appeared in *The Knickerbocker Magazine*. One suspects that it became "The California and Oregon Trail" because an astute publisher could not but see, in that year of 1849, the commercial value of including California in the title. When the book was subsequently reissued, in 1872, the author went back to the original form. This was the first published work of Parkman, who wrote it when he was twenty-five years old.

Old Ironsides
From *Putnam's Magazine,* May and June, 1853. One of the early ventures of George Palmer Putnam was the republication of several of James Fenimore Cooper's novels, and the edition of his complete novels later issued by Putnam was considered authoritative and was authorized by Cooper's heirs. The novelist died in 1851, and this history of a famous ship, designed as an addition to his "History of the Navy of the United States," was first published, posthumously, in two issues of the new monthly, the first issue of which had appeared in January of the same year.

Colonies and Communities
From "A Yankee Saint: John Humphrey Noyes and the Oneida Community." Copyright by Robert Allerton Parker, 1935. Mr. Parker's book, from which this chapter is taken, is a comprehensive and penetrating study of an extraordinary social, religious, and economic experiment.

Riders All
From "The Pony Express." Copyright by Arthur Chapman, 1932. The late Mr. Chapman, author of this book, was a Westerner and an authority on pioneer days. In gathering his material he interviewed many of the original Pony Express riders.

A South Carolina Rice Plantation in the Fifties
From "A Journey in the Seaboard Slave States." 1904. This account, first published in 1856, together with "A Journey in the Back Country" and other books on his travels in the pre-war South, brought Frederick Law Olmsted considerable fame. He was a versatile man, having made an enduring name for himself as a landscape architect. He laid out Central Park in New York, Prospect Park in Brooklyn, and, for the World's Fair in 1893, Jackson Park in Chicago.

The Background of the Civil War
From "The Secession of the Southern States." Copyright by Gerald W. Johnson, 1933. Mr. Johnson is perhaps best known for his biographies of Andrew Jackson and Randolph of Roanoke; he is also an essayist and novelist of distinction.

Life in Libby Prison
From "A Prisoner of War in Virginia, 1864-65." In 1872 Major George Haven Putnam succeeded his father, George Palmer Putnam, as head of the publishing firm, and he was active in this capacity until his death in 1930. This memoir of his Civil War experience was one of many books by him, among them "The Question of Copyright," "Books and Their Makers in the Middle Ages," a biography of his father, and two volumes of reminiscences.

The Purchase of New York
From *Putnam's Monthly,* October, 1909. Ruth Putnam, a distinguished historian who specialized in Dutch history, was a sister of Major George Haven Putnam.

Ancient Rome and Modern America
From "Aspects of the Study of Roman History." Copyright, 1923. Thomas Spencer Jerome, an able and modest scholar, who thought much and published little, died in 1914. This volume was prepared by his friends and published posthumously.

The Flight to Paris
From "We." Copyright by Charles A. Lindbergh, 1927. A record-making book about an epoch-making achievement.

PERIOD PIECES

The People of Connecticut
From "A History of New York" by "Diedrich Knickerbocker." 1848. The Knickerbocker History was one of the early books (first published in 1809) that George Palmer Putnam took over in 1848. When Irving returned from Spain in 1846, his reputation was in temporary eclipse. His Philadelphia publishers refused to go on with his work, the widespread "piracy" of the day, due to the copyright situation, had cut down his English royalties, and he was seriously considering the necessity of taking—in his middle sixties—a minor position in his brother's law office. A letter from Putnam solved the difficulty, for it offered assured royalties of $2,000 a year, provided that Putnam might take over the publication of all his books and publish any new ones he might write. The arrangement enabled Irving to produce, among other books, his great life of Washington. Nor did the publisher have reason to rue his bargain, for Irving's popularity came back with a rush when his biography of Goldsmith appeared in 1849, and in each year the guaranteed amount was generously exceeded.

Literature in America
American Culture
   From "American Facts." Wiley and Putnam, 1845. Soon after Putnam became a partner of John Wiley (1838) he went to London to open an English branch of the business. In time the misconceptions of the English about his own country so irritated him that he prepared this book as refutation. He little knew how valuable historically it would be to American readers of the twentieth century.

"Our Best Society"
A Meditation by Paul Potiphar, Esq.
   From "The Potiphar Papers." 1853. George William Curtis, then still in his twenties, was one of the editorial staff of *Putnam's Magazine,* and the papers, later collected in book form, first appeared in its pages.

A Fable for Critics
   Published in 1848, this amusing book carried an introduction in rhyme, and the title page, arranged in imitation of old-fashioned books (see page 332), was also in couplets, ending with /SET FORTH IN/ *October, the 21st day, in the year '48,/* G. P. PUTNAM, BROADWAY. A year or two later, when the publisher had changed his place of business, a zealous compositor gave a new edition collector's value and caused a hearty laugh in the town by setting the final line: G. P. PUTNAM, PARK PLACE.

Uncle Tomitudes
   From *Putnam's Magazine,* January, 1853. This essay, in the first issue of the new literary monthly, was by its editorial chairman, Charles F. Briggs, who was also a writer on Greeley's *Tribune* and widely known to his contemporaries under his pseudonym of "Harry Franko."

Christmas with the Chaunceys
   From "The Wide, Wide World." 1851. Susan Warner, who wrote under the nom-de-plume of "Elizabeth Wetherell," achieved national success with this two-volume story for girls. It was widely read for many years.

Living in the Country
   From *Putnam's Magazine,* August, 1855. First published serially under the title given to the individual essay in this present volume, the essays were later issued in book form under the title of "The Sparrowgrass Papers." Frederick S. Cozzens was a delightful and popular writer of the period.

The Roses and the Song
   From "The White Shield." 1912. The collection of short pieces from which this story is taken was published after Myrtle Reed's death. Perhaps no other popular writer so indicates the taste and the point of view of her period. Among her best known books were "Lavender and Old Lace," "A Spinner in the Sun," and "Old Rose and Silver."

BIBLIOGRAPHICAL NOTES 1019

A Stranger in New York
From *Putnam's Monthly,* May, 1909. In the revived *Putnam's* the name of Elliott Flower appears frequently, as the author of both articles and short stories.

Notes from "The Lounger"
These pieces are taken from several issues of *Putnam's Monthly* and were presumably by the editors, Jeannette Gilder and Joseph B. Gilder.

The Fatu-Liva Bird
From "The Cruise of the Kawa" by "Walter E. Traprock." Copyright, 1921. A chronicle of bizarre South Sea adventure calculated to end all books on the South Seas. George S. Chappell is widely suspected of having masqueraded as the redoubtable Dr. Traprock.

Science in Rhyme without Reason
These four poems, enlightening science for the layman, appeared in the book of the same title in 1924. The author, Ralph Barton, was an artist and illustrator of great talent.

Farewell to Model T
A gently reminiscent elegy on a universal friend, published in book form (copyright, 1936) after it had first appeared in *The New Yorker.* The piece is a collaboration of two authors, one of them, it seems judicious to guess, that unique and graceful writer E. B. White.

ESSAYS

An Excursion to Canada
This long essay by Thoreau appeared serially in the first three issues of *Putnam's Magazine,* January, February, and March, 1853.

A Hermit's Notes on Thoreau
From "Shelburne Essays." First series. Copyright, 1904, by Paul Elmer More. This was the first essay in the first book of Shelburne Essays, which eventually reached a total of eleven volumes. Paul Elmer More taught at Bryn Mawr College and was successively literary editor of *The Independent* and the *New York Evening Post* and editor of *The Nation.*

The Literary Strivings of Mr. Joel Barlow
From "Three Men of Letters." 1895. Moses Coit Tyler was also the author of one of the most learned and delightful histories of American literature.

Connecticut Georgics
From *Putnam's Magazine,* April, 1854. Frederick Beecher Perkins was a constant contributor to *Putnam's,* at his best in the essay style and somewhat less successful in the short story form.

Walt Whitman
From "Little Journeys to the Homes of American Authors." 1896. Elbert Hubbard's informal essays, usually biographical, found an amazingly wide public in their day. Seven volumes were published by Putnam. The one in which the Whitman essay appears was, with this exception, a reprint of an earlier book, "Homes of American Authors," published by G. P. Putnam in 1853, in which the essays on Emerson, Audubon, Irving, Hawthorne, Lowell, and six others were by such men as G. W. Curtis, W. C. Bryant, Parke Godwin, C. F. Briggs, and H. T. Tuckerman.

The Ruskin Affair
Altercation with Oscar
Oscar Again
From "The Gentle Art of Making Enemies." 1903. The Ruskin trial is probably the most famous of Whistler's imbroglios; it makes lively reading, and so do his encounters with Wilde.

The Man with the Muck-Rake
From *Putnam's Monthly,* October, 1906. Address delivered by President Roosevelt on April 14, 1906, at the laying of the corner-stone of the Office Building of the House of Representatives. In its printed form T. R. made a few minor alterations and additions.

Provincialism
From *Putnam's Monthly,* October, 1909.

Man and Art
From "Art as Experience." Copyright, 1934, by John Dewey. This essay appears as Chapter I, "The Live Creature," in the book. America's greatest living philosopher was over seventy-five when this book was written, but it shows no evidence of waning power—nor would there be evidence today, in his seventy-ninth year. Dr. Dewey's many-sided contribution to American thought is one of the marvels of our age.

The Credibility of Testimony
From "Aspects of the Study of Roman History." Copyright, 1923.

Apology for Man
From "Apes, Men and Morons." Copyright by Earnest Albert Hooton, 1937. Not often is a distinguished scientist detached enough to make his specialty palatable to the lay reader. Mr. Hooton of Harvard goes further. His spicy humor makes an intellectual holiday of his rather pessimistic summary of man's progress through the ages.

The Eighteenth Century Attitude
From "An Eighteenth Century Miscellany." Copyright, 1936. Louis Kronenberger chose the classics to be included in this omnibus anthology and contributed the distinguished preface that is here reprinted.

BIBLIOGRAPHICAL NOTES

Aries

From "An Almanac for Moderns." Copyright by Donald Culross Peattie, 1934. It is doubtful if any other book in recent years has been given the chorus of discerning praise that welcomed this unique performance by Mr. Peattie. In it a great poet-naturalist came into his own. The Almanac was given the first award of the Gold Medal of the Limited Editions Club as the book of its year most likely to become a classic.

POEMS

The Raven
Lenore
Israfel

From "The Raven and Other Poems." Wiley and Putnam. 1845. "The Raven" was first published in two or three New York periodicals early in the year 1845 before its appearance in book form, bound in paper and priced at thirty-one cents. Poe dedicated the volume, in extravagant terms, to "Miss Elizabeth Barrett of England" and contributed a brief preface to the effect that they were published principally "with a view to their redemption from the many improvements to which they have been subjected while going at random 'the rounds of the press.'" He explains: "I think nothing in this volume of much value to the public, or very creditable to myself."

The Two Angels
My Lost Youth

From *Putnam's Magazine*, April and August, 1855. In the first issue of *Putnam's*, Longfellow's "The Warden of the Cinque Ports" was published; he was thereafter a constant contributor. "My Lost Youth" has been called his most memorable lyric.

Without and Within

From *Putnam's Magazine*, April, 1854. In his many contributions to *Putnam's*, Lowell's mood was prevailingly light and humorous.

Spring or Summer?
Gondola Songs

From *Putnam's Magazine*, January, 1853. Young George William Curtis evidently jumped into the breach in the first issue of the new literary monthly, and was not even averse to having his stuff used as space fillers. No contributions were signed, so, except to those who worked with him, it was perhaps not apparent that he was responsible for four articles and three poems.

Robert of Lincoln

From *Putnam's Magazine*, June, 1855. One of the best known of all Bryant's poems.

1022   AN AMERICAN READER

Sehnsucht
From *Putnam's Magazine*, April, 1854. William Henry Hurlbert was editorial writer of the *New York Times*, famous for his amazing facility and knowledge. His memory was such that he is said to have written at one sitting a detailed and accurate four-column obituary of Lord Palmerston, without looking up a reference.

Song of the Open Road
From "The Complete Works of Walt Whitman." Camden Edition. 1902. The changes of literary taste are nowhere better exemplified than in the altered reputation of the Good Gray Poet, from the execration he received for years after the first publication of "Leaves of Grass" in 1855 to the pinnacle of veneration he finally achieved.

Amavi
From *Putnam's Magazine*, October, 1854. Long considered the dean of American writers, Edmund Clarence Stedman recalled in his old age the daring with which, as a boy in Winsted, Conn., he stuffed his poem into an envelope and mailed it to *Putnam's Magazine*—and the surprise he felt when he saw it actually in type. The poem was "Amavi."

Threnody
From *Putnam's Monthly*, October, 1906. Richard Henry Stoddard was one of the most highly regarded American poets of the latter half of the nineteenth century, and in *Putnam's Magazine* of the 'fifties was probably the most frequent contributor of verse. In the first issue of the revived *Putnam's* in 1906, he was the subject of a eulogistic article by Stedman in which "Threnody," his last poem, written shortly before his death, was first published.

Milton
From *Putnam's Monthly*, February, 1909. One of the notable literary figures of his time, as poet, as the long-time editor of the *Century*, and as a well-loved friend to writers, Richard Watson Gilder was the brother of Jeannette and Joseph B. Gilder, editors of *Putnam's Monthly*.

The Rubicon
From *Putnam's Monthly*, October, 1908. William Winter, for over forty years dramatic critic of the *New York Tribune*, made his first literary reputation as a poet. His first volume was published in 1855, and his output was prolific for many years.

His Submission
From *Putnam's Monthly*, September, 1907. Richard Hovey's brilliant career as a poet was cut short by his death at the age of thirty-six. This poem was published posthumously.

BIBLIOGRAPHICAL NOTES

Rose Song
From *Putnam's Monthly,* August, 1908. Robert Loveman was a Southern poet, of Dalton, Georgia, who published two or three volumes of poetry. He was the author of the well-known lyric, "It is not raining rain to me; it's raining daffodils."

My Romance
A Niello
The Idyl of The Standing-Stone
"My Romance" is from "Days and Dreams," 1891, the other two poems from "Red Leaves and Roses," 1893. Madison Cawein, the Kentucky poet, often attained real heights in his poetry of nature, especially in his sympathetic rendering of scenes in his native state.

When the Great Gray Ships Come In
"The Winds and the Sea Obey Him"
The Débutante
The Fog
From "The Garden of Years and Other Poems." 1904. Guy Wetmore Carryl delighted readers in the 'nineties with his graceful light verse. He was the author of three novels, and "The Garden of Years," published after his untimely death in 1904 at the age of thirty-one, was his one book of serious poetry.

At Twilight
From *Putnam's Monthly,* January, 1908. James Oppenheim was a well-known poet of the early twentieth century who wrote often and eloquently of New York City.

Song
Less than the Cloud to the Wind
The Wayfarer
The Song for Colin
From "Helen of Troy and Other Poems." Copyright, 1911. Sara Teasdale was a delightful lyric poet, who published many volumes of verse, and won the Pulitzer Prize for poetry in 1917.

October
From *Putnam's Monthly,* January, 1908. Don Marquis contributed much verse and many short stories to *Putnam's Monthly*. Little of the material indicates the direction his genius finally took or the rich humanity that made him best-loved of American writers of his time.

At the Road's End
The House in Trouble
Cophetua's Queen
From "As the Larks Rise." Copyright, 1921. A lyric poet of charming, feminine quality, Theodosia Garrison is the author of several collected volumes.

The Winter Is Long
On Farms
Katharsis
   From "High Perils." Copyright, 1933, by Cale Young Rice. The distinguished poet, with many volumes to his credit, is also well known as novelist and dramatist.

Mid Winter
Roads
One Lack I Have
On the Arrogance of Lovers
   From "Fir Trees and Fireflies." Copyright, 1920, by Carolyn Crosby Wilson. This sole volume possesses a fresh and singing quality, but Miss Wilson (Mrs. Henry C. Link) has not followed it as yet with the high accomplishment it promised.

Wooden Ships
Revelation
Moonflowers
Noon of Summer
Prescience
   The first three poems are from "Ships in Harbour," 1921, David Morton's first collection of poems; the other two from "Spell against Time," 1936, his latest book (both copyrighted by the author). In between he has published several volumes, among them "Harvest," "Nocturnes and Autumnals," and "Earth's Processional," of the same high quality, which have established him as one of our foremost writers of sonnets and lyrics.

Close to the Earth
Requiem
Encounter
White Christmas
   From "White Christmas." Copyright, 1931, by Margaret Emerson Bailey. A strongly individual and authentically American note is struck in these poems by Miss Bailey, who is also the author of a collection of short stories, "The Wild Streak."

Beautiful Sunday
The Elfin Wife
Valedictory
   From "The Bulls of Spring." Copyright, 1937. "Jake Falstaff" (Herman Fetzer), was born in 1899 and died in 1935. He was a popular columnist in Cleveland and Akron, Ohio, and acted as guest columnist for "F. P. A." on the *New York World*. "Valedictory" was written at the close of his New York stay. In his introduction to this posthumous volume, William Lyon Phelps wrote: "Jake Falstaff was an affirmer of life, like Whitman; never one who refused or denied it.... An immense geniality glows in all his verses; and while we admire his music, we also love the man."

FICTION

Benito Cereno
From *Putnam's Magazine,* October, November, December, 1856. Herman Melville was perhaps the chief contributor of shorter fiction to the early *Putnam's*. With the exception of "Benito Cereno," it was not in his best vein, though "The Enchanted Isles" also has its advocates. Many of the pieces were later collected in book form under the title of "Piazza Tales."

William Wilson
From "Poe's Tales." Wiley & Putnam, 1845.

Young Goodman Brown
The Celestial Railroad
From "Mosses from an Old Manse." 1851. Nathaniel Hawthorne was a connection by marriage of George Palmer Putnam; so it was natural that this early volume should appear under the Putnam imprint. But the public was slow to appreciate "Mosses from an Old Manse" and Putnam later had occasion to grieve that he did not encourage the author to go on. The later books were published by Ticknor & Fields.

Guests from Gibbet Island
From "Wolfert's Roost." 1855. Washington Irving, in between his "Life of Goldsmith" and the monumental "Life of Washington" relaxed in his old age to write a volume reminiscent of "The Sketch Book." This story, set in the Hudson River background he loved so well, has something of the early "Rip van Winkle" flavor.

Chickamauga
From "In the Midst of Life." 1898. Ambrose Bierce, most mysterious of American literary figures, was at his best in this early collection of short fiction.

The Men of the Jimmy
From "The Strange Schemes of Randolph Mason." Copyright, 1896, by Melville Davisson Post. In Randolph Mason, the skillful manipulator of legal intricacies, Mr. Post created a real character, which he followed through two further volumes, "Corrector of Destinies," and "The Clients."

Helen in Egypt
From "Candaules' Wife and Other Old Stories." Copyright, 1926, by Emily James Putnam. The author of that scholarly and memorable book, "The Lady," hit upon the happy idea of retelling in the modern manner certain of the tales of Herodotus. They appeared first in *The Atlantic Monthly*.

The Bench of Desolation
From *Putnam's Monthly,* 1909-10. Reprinted through the courtesy of Charles Scribner's Sons. It was Philip Guedalla who divided the work of Henry

James into three periods: "James the First, James the Second, and the Old Pretender." This is a good example of James the Second.

ADVENTURE

The Climbing of Mount McKinley
From "The Conquest of Mount McKinley." Copyright, 1913, by Belmore Browne. Mr. Browne proved in this book that, in addition to being an excellent artist and a mountain climber *par excellence,* he was a first-rate writer as well.

April Twenty-sixth, Nineteen Hundred and Twenty-three
From "Galapagos: World's End." Copyright, 1927, by William Beebe. Not often are scientists born writers, but William Beebe is constantly proving himself an exception to the rule. This chapter, telling of the day of a scientist in the field, not only satisfies the curiosity of the layman as to how an investigator actually proceeds, but demonstrates how he is aided by the writer's perceptive eye.

Finding the Baluchitherium
From "On the Trail of Ancient Man." Copyright, 1926, by Roy Chapman Andrews. Dr. Andrews, who has run the gamut of exploration from whales to dinosaur's eggs, is now Director of the American Museum of Natural History. This story of discovering the remains of a prehistoric animal gives an inkling of the excitement there is in his profession. Among his other books are "Ends of the Earth," 1929, and "This Business of Exploring," 1935.

"Roll On"
From "Voyaging: Southward from the Strait of Magellan." Copyright, 1924, by Rockwell Kent. "Wilderness," published in 1920, was Rockwell Kent's first book, telling of a winter in Alaska. "Voyaging," his second, told of his experiences at the southern tip of South America. Both books were fully illustrated by his superb line drawings; he is one of America's best lithographers, and his paintings are represented in the Metropolitan Museum.

Flight to the South Pole
From "Little America." Copyright, 1930, by R. E. Byrd. This version, somewhat condensed from the original chapter in "Little America," appears in this form in "Exploring with Byrd," 1937. Admiral Byrd's other books are "Skyward," 1928, and "Alone," 1938. No other explorer of his time has so captured the imagination and affection of the American people. His expeditions, scientifically planned and equipped and magnificently carried through, are landmarks in the history of exploration.

THIS BOOK HAS BEEN DESIGNED BY ROBERT JOSEPHY, AND MANUFACTURED IN NEW YORK IN SEPTEMBER, 1938, BY THE VAN REES PRESS. IT IS SET IN LINOTYPE GRANJON, PRINTED ON WARREN'S NO. 1854 LAID PAPER, AND BOUND IN HOLLISTON RECORD BUCKRAM.